LES MISERABLES

FIVE VOLUMES IN ONE

LES MISERABLES

A NOVEL BY VICTOR HUGO

In the translation by Lascelles Wraxall authorized

by the Author. Printed with a new Introduction by

André Maurois and with illustrations by Lynd Ward

All Five Volumes in One Volume

NEW YORK, THE HERITAGE PRESS

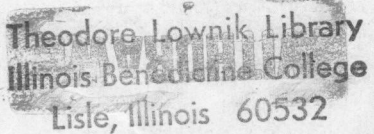

PREFACE

As long as there shall exist, as a consequence of laws and customs, a social damnation artificially creating hells in the midst of civilization, and complicating the destiny which is divine with a fatality which is human; as long as the three problems of the age—the degradation of man by the proletariat, the ruin of woman by hunger, the atrophy of the child by the night—are not solved; as long as in certain regions social asphyxia shall be possible; in other terms, and from a still more extended point of view, as long as there shall be on the earth ignorance and wretchedness, books of the nature of this one cannot be useless.

VICTOR HUGO

HAUTEVILLE HOUSE

1. M. MYRIEL

IN 1815, M. Charles François Bienvenu Myriel was bishop of D. . . . . He was a man about seventy-five years of age, and had held the see of D. . . . since 1806. Although the following details in no way affect our narrative, it may not be useless to quote the rumors that were current about him at the moment when he came to the diocese, for what is said of men, whether it be true or false, often occupies as much space in their life, and especially in their destiny, as what they do. M. Myriel was the son of a councilor of the Parliament of Aix. It was said that his father, who intended that he should be his successor, married him at a very early age, eighteen or twenty, according to a not uncommon custom in parliamentary families. Charles Myriel, in spite of this marriage (so people said), had been the cause of much tattle. He was well built, though of short stature, elegant, graceful, and witty; and the earlier part of his life was devoted to the world and to gallantry. The Revolution came, events hurried on, and the parliamentary families, decimated and hunted down, became dispersed. M. Charles Myriel emigrated to Italy in the early part of the Revolution, and his wife, who had been long suffering from a chest complaint, died there, leaving no children. What next took place in M. Myriel's destiny? Did the overthrow of the old French society, the fall of his own family and the tragic spectacles of '93, more frightful, perhaps, to the emigrés, who saw them from a distance with the magnifying power of terror, cause ideas of renunciation and solitude to germinate in him? Was he, in the midst of one of the distractions and affections which occupied his life, suddenly assailed by one of those mysterious and terrible blows which often prostrate, by striking at his heart, a man whom public catastrophes could not overthrow by attacking him in his existence and his fortune? No one could

3

have answered these questions; all that was known was that when he returned from Italy he was a priest.

In 1804 M. Myriel was curé of B. . . . (Brignolles). He was already aged, and lived in great retirement. Toward the period of the coronation a small matter connected with his curacy, no one remembers what, took him to Paris. Among other powerful persons he applied to Cardinal Fesch on behalf of his parishioners. One day, when the emperor was paying a visit to his uncle, the worthy curé, who was waiting in the anteroom, saw his majesty pass. Napoleon, noticing this old man regard him with some degree of curiosity, turned and asked sharply:

"Who is this goodman who is staring at me?"

"Sire," M. Myriel said, "you are looking at a good man and I at a great man. We may both profit by it."

The emperor, on the same evening, asked the cardinal the curé's name, and some time after M. Myriel, to his great surprise, learned that he was nominated Bishop of D. . . . . What truth, by the way, was there in the stories about M. Myriel's early life? No one knew, for few persons had been acquainted with his family before the Revolution. M. Myriel was fated to undergo the lot of every new-comer to a little town, where there are many mouths that speak, and but few heads that think. He was obliged to undergo it, though he was bishop, and because he was bishop. But, after all, the stories in which his name was mingled were only stories, rumors, words, remarks, less than words, mere *palabres,* to use a term borrowed from the energetic language of the South. Whatever they might be, after ten years of episcopacy and residence at D. . . . , all this gossip, which at the outset affords matter of conversation for little towns and little people, had fallen into deep oblivion. No one would have dared to speak of it, no one have dared to remember it.

M. Myriel had arrived at D. . . . , accompanied by an old maid, Mlle. Baptistine, who was his sister, and ten years younger than himself. Their only servant was a female of the same age as mademoiselle, of the name of Madame Magloire, who, after having been the servant of M. le Curé, now assumed the double title of waiting-woman to mademoiselle, and housekeeper to monseigneur. Mlle. Baptistine was a tall, pale, slim, gentle person; she realized the ideal of what the word "respectable" expresses, for it seems necessary for a woman to be a mother in order to be venerable. She had never been pretty, but her whole life, which had been but a succession of pious works, had eventually cast over her a species of whiteness and clearness, and in growing older she had acquired what may be called the beauty of goodness. What had been thinness in her youth had become in her maturity transparency, and through this diaphanous veil the angel could be seen. She seemed to be a shadow: there was hardly enough body for a sex to exist; she was a little quantity of matter containing a spark of light—an excuse for a soul to remain upon the earth. Madame Magloire was a fair, plump, busy little body, always short of breath,—in the first place, through her activity, and, secondly, in consequence of an asthma.

On his arrival, M. Myriel was installed in his episcopal palace with all the honors allotted by the imperial decrees, which classify the bishop immediately after a major-general. The mayor and the president paid him the first visit, and he on his side paid the first visit to the general and the prefect. When the installation was ended, the town waited to see its bishop at work.

2. M. MYRIEL BECOMES MONSEIGNEUR WELCOME

THE episcopal palace of D. . . . adjoined the hospital. It was a spacious, handsome mansion, built at the beginning of the last century by Monseigneur Henri Puget, Doctor in Theology of the Faculty of Paris, and abbé of Simore, who was bishop of D. . . . in 1712. This palace was a true seigneurial residence: everything had a noble air in it,—the episcopal apartments, the reception-rooms, the bedrooms, the court of honor, which was very wide, with arcades after the old Florentine fashion, and the gardens planted with magnificent trees. In the dining-room, a long and superb gallery on the ground-floor, Monseigneur Henri Puget had given a state dinner on July 29, 1714, to Messeigneurs Charles Brulart de Genlis, prince-archbishop of Embrun,

Antoine de Mesgrigny, Capuchin and bishop of Grasse, Philip de Vendôme, grand prior of France and abbé of St. Honoré de Lérins, François
de Berton de Grillon, baron and bishop of Vence, Cæsar de Sabran de
Forcalquier, bishop, seigneur of Glandève, and Jean Soanen, priest of the
oratory, preacher in ordinary to the king, and lord bishop of Senez. The
portraits of these seven reverend personages decorated the dining-room,
and the memorable date, July 29, 1714, was engraved in golden letters on
a white marble tablet.

The hospital was a small, two-storied house with a little garden.
Three days after his arrival the bishop visited it, and when his visit was
over asked the director to be kind enough to come to his house.

"How many patients have you at this moment?" he asked.

"Twenty-six, monseigneur."

"The number I counted," said the bishop.

"The beds are very close together," the director continued.

"I noticed it."

"The wards are only bedrooms, and difficult to ventilate."

"I thought so."

"And then, when the sun shines, the garden is very small for the
convalescents."

"I said so to myself."

"During epidemics, and we have had the typhus this year, and had
miliary fever two years ago, we have as many as one hundred patients
and do not know what to do with them."

"That thought occurred to me."

"What would you have, monseigneur!" the director said, "we must
put up with it."

This conversation had taken place in the gallery of the dining-hall on
the ground-floor. The bishop was silent for a moment, and then turned
smartly to the director.

"How many beds," he asked him, "do you think that this room alone
would hold?"

"Monseigneur's dining-room?" the stupefied director asked.

The bishop looked round the room, and seemed to be measuring it
with his eye and judging its capacity.

"It would hold twenty beds," he said, as if speaking to himself; and
then, raising his voice, he added:

"Come, director, I will tell you what it is. There is evidently a mistake.
You have twenty-six persons in five or six small rooms. Here there are

only three of us, and we have room for fifty. There is a mistake, I repeat; you have my house and I have yours. Restore me mine; this is yours."

The next day the twenty-six poor patients were installed in the bishop's palace and the bishop was in the hospital. M. Myriel had no property, as his family had been ruined by the Revolution. His sister had an annuity of 500 francs, which had sufficed at the curacy for personal expenses. M. Myriel, as bishop, received from the State 15,000 francs a year. On the same day that he removed to the hospital, M. Myriel settled the employment of the sum, once for all, in the following way. We copy here a note in his own hand-writing.

THE REGULATION OF MY HOUSEHOLD EXPENSES

For the little Seminary	1500	frcs.
Congregation of the Mission	100	"
The Lazarists of Montdidier	100	"
Seminary of Foreign Missions at Paris	200	"
Congregation of the Holy Ghost	150	"
Religious Establishments in the Holy Land	100	"
Societies of Maternal Charity	300	"
Additional for the one at Arles	50	"
Works for improvement of prisons	400	"
Relief and deliverance of prisoners	500	"
For liberation of fathers imprisoned for debt	1000	"
Addition to the salary of poor school-masters in the diocese	2000	"
Distribution of grain in the Upper Alps	100	"
Ladies' Society for gratuitous instruction of poor girls at D...., Manosque, and Sisteron	1500	"
For the poor	6000	"
Personal expenses	1000	"
Total	15,000	"

During the whole time he held the see of D...., M. Myriel made no change in this arrangement. He called this, as we see, regulating his household expenses. The arrangement was accepted with a smile by Mlle. Baptistine, for that sainted woman regarded M. Myriel at once as her brother and her bishop; her friend according to nature, her superior according to the Church. She loved and venerated him in the simplest way. When he spoke she bowed, when he acted she assented. The servant alone, Madame Magloire, murmured a little. The bishop, it will have been noticed, only reserved 1000 francs, and on this sum, with Mlle. Baptistine's pension, these two old women and old man lived. And when a village curé came to D...., the bishop managed to regale him, thanks to the strict economy of Madame Magloire and the sensible management of Mlle. Baptistine. One day, when he had been at D.... about three months, the bishop said:

"For all that, I am dreadfully pressed."

"I should think so," exclaimed Madame Magloire. "Monseigneur has not even claimed the annual sum which the department is bound to pay for keeping up his carriage in town and for his visitations. That was the custom with bishops in other times."

"True," said the bishop, "you are right, Madame Magloire." He made his claim, and shortly after the council-general, taking the demand into consideration, voted him the annual sum of 3000 francs, under the heading, "Allowance to the bishop for maintenance of carriage, posting charges, and outlay in visitations."

This caused an uproar among the cits of the town, and on this occasion a senator of the empire, ex-member of the Council of the Five Hundred, favorable to the 18th Brumaire, and holding a magnificent appointment near D...., wrote to the minister of worship, M. Bigot de Préameneu, a short, angry, and confidential letter, from which we extract these authentic lines:

".... Maintenance of carriage! what can he want one for in a town of less than 4000 inhabitants? Visitation charges! in the first place, what is the good of visitations at all? and, secondly, how can he travel post in this mountainous country, where there are no roads, and people must travel on horseback? The very bridge over the Durance at Château Arnoux can hardly bear the weight of a cart drawn by oxen. These priests are all the same, greedy and avaricious! This one played the good apostle when he arrived, but now he is like the rest, and must have his carriage and post-chaise. He wishes to be as luxurious as the old bishops. Oh this priesthood! My lord, matters will never go on well till the emperor has delivered us from the skullcaps. Down with the pope! [There was a quarrel at the time with Rome.] As for me, I am for Cæsar and Cæsar alone, etc., etc., etc."

The affair, on the other hand, greatly gladdened Madame Magloire. "Come," she said to Mlle. Baptistine, "monseigneur began with others, but he was obliged to finish with himself. He has regulated all his charities, and here are 3000 francs for us at last!"

The same evening the bishop wrote, and gave his sister, a note conceived thus:

CARRIAGE AND TRAVELING EXPENSES

To provide the hospital patients with broth	1500	*frcs.*
The Society of Maternal Charity at Aix	250	"
Ditto, at Draguignan	250	"
For foundlings	500	"
For orphans	500	"
Total	3000	"

Such was M. Myriel's budget. As for the accidental receipts, such as fees for bans, dispensations, consecrating churches or chapels, marriages, etc., the bishop collected them from the rich with so much the more eagerness because he distributed them to the poor. In a short time the monetary offerings became augmented. Those who have and those who want tapped at M. Myriel's door, the latter coming to seek the alms which the former had just deposited. The bishop in less than a year became the treasurer of all charity and the cashier of all distress. Considerable sums passed through his hand, but nothing could induce him to make any change in his mode of life, or add the slightest superfluity to his expenditure.

Far from it, as there is always more wretchedness at the bottom than fraternity above, all was given, so to speak, before being received; it was like water on dry ground: however much he might receive, he had never a farthing. At such times he stripped himself. It being the custom for the bishops to place their Christian names at the head of their mandates and pastoral letters, the poor people of the country had, with a kind of instinctive affection, selected the one among them which conveyed a meaning, and called him Monseigneur Welcome (Bienvenu). We will do like them, and call him so when occasion serves. Moreover, the name pleased him. "I like that name," he would say. "The Welcome corrects the Monseigneur."

We do not assert that the portrait we are here drawing is probable; we confine ourselves to saying that it is a likeness.

3. *A GOOD BISHOP, A HARD BISHOPRIC*

THE bishop, though he had converted his coach into alms, did not the less make his visitations. The diocese of D. . . . is fatiguing; there are few plains and many mountains, and hardly any roads, as we saw just now: twenty-two curacies, forty-one vicarages, and two hundred and eighty-five chapels of ease. It was a task to visit all these, but the bishop managed it. He went on foot when the place was near, in a carriage when it was in the plain, and on muleback when it was in the mountains. The two old females generally accompanied him, but when the journey was too wearing for them he went alone.

One day he arrived at Senez, which is an old episcopal town, mounted on a donkey; his purse, which was very light at the time, had not allowed him any other equipage. The mayor of the city came to receive him at the door of the bishop's palace, and saw him dismount with scandalized eyes. A few cits were laughing round him. "M. Mayor and gentlemen," the bishop said, "I see what it is that scandalizes you. You consider it great pride for a poor priest to ride an animal which our Saviour once rode. I did so through necessity, I assure you, and not through vanity."

On his tours the bishop was indulgent and gentle, and preached less than he conversed. His reasonings and models were never far-fetched, and to the inhabitants of one country he quoted the example of an adjacent country. In those cantons where people were harsh to the needy, he would say, "Look at the people of Briançon. They have given the indigent, the widows, and the orphans the right of mowing their fields three days before all the rest. They rebuild their houses gratuitously when they are in ruins. Hence it is a country blessed of God. For one hundred years not a single murder has been committed there." To those eager for gain and good crops, he said, "Look at the people of Embrun.

If a father of a family at harvest-time has his sons in the army, his daughters serving in town, or if he be ill or prevented from toil, the curé recommends him in his sermon; and on Sunday, after mass, all the villagers, men, women and children, go into his field, and cut and carry home his crop." To families divided by questions of money or inheritance, he said, "Look at the mountaineers of Devolny, a country so wild that the nightingale is not heard there once in fifty years. Well, when the father of a family dies there, the boys go off to seek their fortune, and leave the property to the girls, so that they may obtain husbands." In those parts where the farmers are fond of lawsuits, and ruin themselves in writ, he would say, "Look at those good peasants of the valley of Queyras. There are three thousand souls there. Why, it is like a little republic. Neither judge nor bailiff is known there, and the mayor does everything. He divides the imposts, taxes everybody conscientiously, settles quarrels gratis, allots patrimonies without fees, gives sentences without costs, and is obeyed because he is a just man among simple men." In villages where there was no schoolmaster, he again quoted the people of Queyras. "Do you know what they do? As a small place containing only twelve or fifteen hearths cannot always support a master, they have school-masters paid by the whole valley, who go from village to village, spending a week in one, ten days in another, and teaching. These masters go to the fairs, where I have seen them. They can be recognized by the pens they carry in their hat-bands. Those who only teach reading have but one pen; those who teach reading and arithmetic have two; those who teach reading, arithmetic, and Latin have three. But what a disgrace it is to be ignorant! Do like the people of Queyras."

He spoke thus, gravely and paternally. When examples failed him he invented parables, going straight to the point, with few phrases and a good deal of imagery. His was the eloquence of the Apostles, convincing and persuading.

4. WORKS RESEMBLING WORDS

The bishop's conversation was affable and lively. He condescended to the level of the two old females who spent their life near him, and when he laughed it was a school-boy's laugh. Madame Magloire was fond of calling him "Your Grandeur." One day he rose from his easy-chair and went to fetch a book from his library. As it was on one of the top shelves, and as the bishop was short, he could not reach it. "Madame Magloire," he said, "bring me a chair, for my Grandeur does not rise to that shelf."

One of his distant relatives, the Countess de Lô, rarely let an opportunity slip to enumerate in his presence what she called the "hopes" of her three sons. She had several very old relatives close to death's door, of whom her sons were the natural heirs. The youngest of the three would inherit from a great-aunt 100,000 francs a year; the second would succeed to his uncle's dukedom, the third to his grandfather's peerage. The bishop generally listened in silence to this innocent and pardonable maternal display. Once, however, he seemed more dreamy than usual, while Madame de Lô was repeating all the details of their successions and "hopes." She broke off somewhat impatiently. "Good gracious, cousin," she said, "what are you thinking about?" "I am thinking," said the bishop, "of something singular, which, if my memory is right, is in St. Augustine. 'Place your hopes in him whom no one succeeds'."

On another occasion, receiving a letter announcing the death of a country gentleman, in which, in addition to the dignities of the defunct, all the feudal and noble titles of all his relatives were recorded,—"What a pair of shoulders death has! What a fine load of titles he is made lightly to bear," he exclaimed, "and what sense men must possess thus to employ the tomb in satisfying their vanity." He displayed at times a gentle raillery, which nearly always contained a serious meaning. During one Lent a young vicar came to D. . . . and preached at the cathedral. He was rather eloquent, and the subject of his sermon was charity. He invited the rich to give to the needy in order to escape hell, which he painted in the most frightful way he could, and reach paradise, which he made desirable and charming. There was among the congregation a rich retired merchant, somewhat of an usurer, who had acquired $400,000 by manufacturing coarse cloths, serges, and caddis. In his whole lifetime M. Géborand had never given alms to a beggar, but after this sermon it was remarked that he gave every Sunday a cent to the old beggars at the cathedral gate. There were six women to share it. One day the bishop saw him bestowing his charity, and said to his sister, with a smile, "Look at M. Géborand buying a bit of paradise for a cent."

When it was a question of charity, he would not let himself be rebuffed even by a refusal, and at such times made remarks which caused people to reflect. Once he was collecting for the poor in a drawing-room of the town. The Marquis de Champtercier was present, an old, rich, avaricious man, who contrived to be at once ultra-Royalist and ultra-Voltairian. This variety has existed. The bishop on reaching him touched his arm, "Monsieur le Marquis, you must give me something." The marquis turned and answered dryly: "I have my own poor, monseigneur." "Give them to me," said the bishop. One day he delivered the following sermon at the cathedral:

"My very dear brethren, my good friends, there are in France thirteen hundred and twenty thousand peasants' houses which have only three openings; eighteen hundred and seventeen thousand which have only two openings, the door and the window; and, lastly, three hundred and forty-six thousand cabins which have only one opening, the door. All this comes from a thing called the door and window tax. Just place poor families, aged women and little children, in these houses, and then see the fevers and maladies! Alas. God gives men fresh air and the law sells it to them. I do not accuse the law, but I bless God. In the Isère, in the Var, in the two Alps, Upper and Lower, the peasants have not even trucks, but carry manure on their backs; they have no candles, and burn resinous logs and pieces of rope steeped in pitch. It is the same through all the high parts of Dauphiny. They make bread for six months, and bake it with dried cow-dung. In winter they break this bread with axes and steep it in water for four and twenty hours before they can eat it. Brethren, have pity; see how people suffer around you!"

A Provençal by birth, he easily accustomed himself to all the dialects of the South: *Eh bé! moussu, sès sagé?* as in Lower Languedoc; *Onté anaras passa* as in the Lower Alps; *Puerte un bouen moutou embe un bouen froumage grase,* as in Upper Dauphiny. This greatly pleased the people, and had done no little in securing him admission to all minds. He was, as it were, at home in the hut and on the mountain. He could say the grandest things in the most vulgar idiom, and as he spoke all languages he entered all hearts. However, he was the same to people of fashion as to the lower classes.

He never condemned anything hastily or without taking the circumstances into calculation. He would say, "Let us look at the road by which the fault has come." Being, as he called himself with a smile, an ex-sinner, he had none of the intrenchments of rigorism, and careless of the frowns of the unco' good, he professed loudly a doctrine which might be summed up nearly as follows:

"Man has upon him the flesh which is at once his burden and his temptation. He carries it with him and yields to it. He must watch, restrain, and repress it, and only obey it in the last extremity. In this obedience there may still be a fault; but the fault there committed is venial. It is a fall, but a fall on the knees, which may end in prayer. To be a saint is the exception, to be a just man is the rule. Err, fail, sin, but be just. The least possible amount of sin is the law of man: no sin at all is the dream of angels. All that is earthly is subject to sin, for sin is a gravitation."

When he saw everybody cry out and grow indignant, all of a sudden, he would say with a smile, "Oh! oh, it seems as if this is a great crime which all the world is committing. Look at the startled hypocrites, hastening to protest and place themselves under cover."

He was indulgent to the women and the poor, on whom the weight of human society presses. He would say, "The faults of women, children, servants, the weak, the indigent, and the ignorant are the fault of husbands, fathers, masters, the strong, the rich, and the learned." He also said, "Teach the ignorant as much as you possibly can; society is culpable for not giving instruction gratis, and is responsible for the night it produces. This soul is full of darkness, and sin is committed, but the guilty person is not the man who commits the sin, but he who produces the darkness."

As we see, he had a strange manner, peculiarly his own, of judging things. I suspect that he obtained it from the Gospels. He one day heard in a drawing-room the story of a trial which was shortly to take place. A wretched man, through love of a woman and child he had by her, having exhausted his resources, coined false money, which at that period was an offense punished by death. The woman was arrested while issuing the first false piece manufactured by the man. She was detained, but there was no proof against her. She alone could establish the charge against her lover and ruin him by confessing. She denied. They pressed her, but she adhered to her denial. Upon this, the prosecuting lawyer had an idea: he feigned infidelity on the lover's part, and contrived, by cleverly presenting the woman with fragments of letters, to persuade her that she had a rival, and that the man was deceiving her. Then, exasperated by jealousy, she denounced her lover, confessed everything, proved everything. The man was ruined, and would shortly be tried with his accomplice at Aix. The story was told, and everybody was delighted with the lawyer's cleverness. By bringing jealousy into play, he brought out the truth through passion, and obtained justice through revenge. The bishop listened to all this in silence, and when it was ended he asked: "Where will this man and woman be tried?" "At the assizes." Then he continued, "And where will the prosecuting attorney be tried?"

A tragical event occurred at D. . . . . A man was condemned to death for murder. He was a wretched fellow, not exactly educated, not exactly ignorant, who had been a mountebank at fairs and a public writer. The trial attracted the attention of the towns-people. On the eve of the day of the execution the prison chaplain was taken ill, and a priest was wanted to assist the sufferer in his last moments. The curé was sent for, and it seems that he refused, saying, "It is no business of mine, I have nothing to do with the mountebank, I am ill too; and besides, that is not my place." This answer was carried to the bishop, who said, "The curé is right, it is not his place; it is mine." He went straight to the prison, entered the mountebank's cell, called him by name, took his hand, and spoke to him. He spent the whole day with him, forgetting sleep and food while praying to God for the soul of the condemned man. He told him the best truths, which are the most simple. He was father, brother, friend—bishop only to bless. He taught him everything, while reassuring and consoling him. This man was about to die in desperation; death was to him like an abyss, and he shuddered as he stood on its gloomy brink. He was not ignorant enough to be completely indifferent, and his condemnation, which was a profound shock, had here and there broken through that partition which separates us from the mystery of things, and which we call life. He peered incessantly out of this world through these crevices, and only saw darkness; but the bishop showed him a light.

On the morrow, when they came to fetch the condemned man, the bishop was with him. He followed him, and showed himself to the mob in his purple cassock, and with the episcopal cross round his neck, side by side with this rope-bound wretch. He entered the cart with him, he mounted the scaffold with him. The sufferer, so gloomy and crushed on the previous day, was radiant; he felt that his soul was reconciled, and he hoped for heaven. The bishop embraced him, and at the moment when the knife was about to fall, said: "The man whom his fellow-men kill, God resuscitates. He whom his brothers expel finds the Father again. Pray, believe, enter into life! The Father is there!" When he descended from the scaffold, there was something in his glance which made the people open a path for him; it was impossible to say whether his pallor or his serenity was the more to be admired. On returning to the humble abode, which he called smilingly his palace, he said to his sister: "I have just been officiating pontifically."

As the most sublime things are often those least understood, there were persons in the town who said, in commenting on the bishop's conduct, "It is affectation." This, however, was only the talk of drawing-rooms; the people who do not find evil intents in holy actions were affected, and admired. As for the bishop, the sight of the guillotine was a shock to him, and it was long ere he recovered from it.

The scaffold, in fact, when it stands erect before you has something about it that hallucinates. We may feel a certain amount of indifference about the punishment of death, not express an opinion, and say yes or no, so long as we have never seen a guillotine; but when we have come across one, the shock is violent, and we must decide either for or against. Some admire it, like De Maistre; others execrate it, like Beccaria. The guillotine is the concretion of the law, it calls itself *vindicta;* it is not neutral, and does not allow you to remain neutral. The person who perceives it shudders with the most mysterious of shudders. All the social questions raise their notes of interrogation round this cutter. The scaffold is a vision, it is not a piece of framework, it is not a machine, it is not a lifeless mechanism made of wood, steel, and ropes. It seems to be a species of being possessing a gloomy power of initiative; you might say that the woodwork lives, that the machine hears, that the mechanism understands, that the wood, the steel, and the ropes have a volition. In the frightful reverie into which its presence casts the mind, the scaffold appears terrible, and mixed up with what it does. The scaffold is the accomplice of the executioner; it devours, it eats flesh and drinks blood. The scaffold is a species of monster, manufactured by the judge and the carpenter, a specter that seems to live a sort of horrible life made up of all the death it has produced. Hence the impression was terrible and deep; on the day after the execution, and for many days beyond, the bishop appeared crushed. The almost violent serenity of the mournful moment had departed; the phantom of social justice haunted him. He who usually returned from all his sacred functions with such radiant satisfaction seemed to be reproaching himself. At times he soliloquized, and stammered unconnected sentences in a low voice. Here is one which his sister overheard and treasured up: "I did not believe that it was so monstrous. It is wrong to absorb one's self in the divine law so far as no longer to perceive the human law. Death belongs to God alone. By what right do men touch that unknown thing?"

With time these impressions were attenuated, and perhaps effaced. Still it was noticed that from this period the bishop avoided crossing the execution square.

M. Myriel might be called at any hour to the bedside of the sick and the dying. He was not ignorant that his greatest duty and greatest labor lay there. Widowed or orphaned families had no occasion to send for him, for he came of himself. He had the art of sitting down and holding his tongue for hours by the side of a man who had lost the wife he loved, or of a mother bereaved of her child. As he knew the time to be silent, he also knew the time to speak. What an admirable consoler he was! he did not try to efface grief by oblivion, but to aggrandize and dignify it by hope. He would say: "Take care of the way in which you turn to the dead. Do not think of that which perishes. Look fixedly, and you will perceive the living light of your beloved dead in heaven." He knew that belief is healthy, and he sought to counsel and calm the desperate man by pointing out to him the resigned man, and to transform the grief that gazes at a grave by showing it the grief that looks at a star.

17

M. Myriel's domestic life was full of the same thoughts as his public life. To any one inquiring closely into it, the voluntary poverty in which the bishop lived would have been a solemn and charming spectacle. Like all old men, and like most thinkers, he slept little, but that short sleep was deep. In the morning he remained in contemplation for an hour, and then read mass either at the cathedral or in his house. Mass over, he breakfasted on rye bread dipped in the milk of his own cows. Then he set to work.

A bishop is a very busy man. He must daily receive the secretary to the bishopric, who is generally a canon, and nearly daily his grand vicars. He has congregations to control, permissions to grant, a whole ecclesiastical library to examine, in the shape of diocesan catechisms, books of hours, etc.; mandates to write, sermons to authorize, curés and mayors to reconcile, a clerical correspondence, an administrative correspondence, on one side the State, on the other the Holy See,—in a word, a thousand tasks. The time which these thousand tasks, his offices, and his breviary left him, he gave first to the needy, the sick, and the afflicted; the time which the afflicted, the sick and the needy left him he gave to work. Sometimes he hoed in his garden, at others he read and wrote. He had only one name for both sorts of labor; he called them gardening. "The mind is a garden," he would say.

Toward midday, when the weather was fine, he went out and walked in the country or the town, frequently entering the cottages. He could be seen walking alone in deep thought, looking down, leaning on his long cane, dressed in his violet wadded and warm great-coat, with his violet stockings thrust into clumsy shoes, and wearing his flat hat, through each corner of which were passed three golden acorns as tassels.

It was a festival wherever he appeared; it seemed as if his passing had something warming and luminous about it. Old men and children came to the door to greet the bishop as they did the sun. He blessed them and they blessed him, and his house was pointed out to anybody who was in want of anything. Now and then he stopped, spoke to the little boys and girls, and smiled on their mothers. He visited the poor so long as he had any money; when he had none, he visited the rich. As he made his cassocks last a long time, and he did not wish the fact to be noticed, he never went into town save in his wadded violet coat. This was rather tiresome in summer.

On returning home he dined. The dinner resembled the breakfast. At half-past eight in the evening he supped with his sister, Madame Magloire standing behind them and waiting on them. Nothing could be more frugal than this meal; but if the bishop had a curé to supper, Madame Magloire would take advantage of it to serve monseigneur with some excellent fish from the lake, or famous game from the mountain. Every curé was the excuse for a good meal, and the bishop held his tongue. On other occasions his repast only consisted of vegetables boiled in water and soup made with oil. Hence it was said in the town: "When the bishop does not fare like a curé, he fares like a trappist."

After supper, he conversed for half an hour with Mlle. Baptistine and Madame Magloire; then he returned to his room and began writing again, either on loose leaves or on the margin of some folio. He was well read and a bit of a *savant,* and has left five or six curious Mss. on theological subjects; among others, a dissertation on the verse of Genesis, *The Spirit of God moved on the face of the waters.* He compared this verse with three texts: the Arabic version, *The words of God breathed;* that of Josephus, *A wind from on high fell upon the earth;* and the Chaldee paraphrase of Onkelos, *A wind from God breathed on the face of the waters.* In another of these dissertations he examines the works of Hugo, bishop of Ptolémaïs, great-grand-uncle of him who writes this book, and he proves that to this bishop must be attributed the various opuscules published in the last century under the pseudonym of Barleycourt. At times, in the midst of his reading, no matter the book he held in his hands, he would suddenly fall into a deep meditation, from which he only emerged to write a few lines on the pages of the book. These lines have frequently no connection with the book that contains them. We have before us a note written by him on the margin of a quarto entitled "Correspondence of Lord Germain with Generals Clinton and Cornwallis, and the Admirals of the American Station. Versailles, Poinçot; and Paris, Pissot, Quai des Augustins." Here is the note:

"Oh you who are! Ecclesiastes calls you Omnipotence; the Maccabees call you Creator; the Epistle to the Ephesians calls you Liberty; Baruch calls you Immensity; the Psalms call you Wisdom and Truth; St. John calls you Light; the Book of Kings calls you Lord; Exodus calls you Providence; Leviticus, Holiness; Esdras, Justice; Creation calls you God; man calls you Father; but Solomon calls you Mercy, and that is the fairest of all your names."

About nine o'clock the two females withdrew and went up to their bedrooms on the first-floor, leaving him alone till morning on the ground-floor. Here it is necessary that we should give an exact idea of the bishop's apartments.

6. BY WHOM THE HOUSE WAS GUARDED

THE house he resided in consisted, as we have said, of a ground-floor and one above it, three rooms on the ground, three bedrooms on the first-floor, and above them a store-room. Behind the house was a quarter of an acre of garden. The two women occupied the first-floor, and the bishop lodged below. The first room, which opened on the street, served him as dining-room, the second as bedroom, the third as oratory. You could not get out of the oratory without passing through the bedroom, or out of the bedroom without passing through the sitting-room. At the end of the oratory was a closed alcove with a bed, for any one who staid the night, and the bishop offered this bed to country curés whom business or the calls of their parish brought to D. . . . ..

The hospital surgery, a small building added to the house and built on a part of the garden, had been transformed into kitchen and cellar. There was also in the garden a stable which had been the old hospital kitchen, and in which the bishop kept two cows. Whatever the quantity of milk they yielded, he invariably sent one-half every morning to the hospital patients. "I am paying my tithes," he was wont to say.

His room was rather spacious, and very difficult to heat in the cold weather. As wood is excessively dear at D. . . . , he hit on the idea of partitioning off with planks a portion of the cow-house. Here he spent his evenings during the great frosts, and called it his "winter drawing-room." In this room, as in the dining-room, there was no other furniture but a square deal table and four straw chairs. The dining-room was also adorned with an old buffet stained to imitate rosewood. The bishop had made the altar which decorated his oratory out of a similar buffet, suitably covered with white cloths and imitation lace. His rich penitents and the religious ladies of D. . . . had often subscribed to pay for a handsome new altar for monseigneur's oratory; each time he took the money and gave it to the poor. "The finest of all altars," he would say, "is the soul of an unhappy man who is consoled and thanks God."

There were in his oratory two straw priedieus, and an arm-chair, also of straw, in his bedroom. When he by chance received seven or eight persons at the same time, the prefect, the general, the staff of the regiment quartered in the town, or some pupils of the lower seminary, it was necessary to fetch the chairs from the winter drawing-room, the priedieus from the oratory, and the easy-chair from the bedroom; in this way as many as eleven seats could be collected for the visitors. At each new visit a room was unfurnished. It happened at times that there would be twelve; in such a case, the bishop concealed the embarrassing nature of the situation by standing before the chimney if it were winter, or walking up and down the room were it summer.

There was also another chair in the alcove, but it was half robbed of the straw, and had only three legs to stand on, so that it could only be used when resting against a wall. Mlle. Baptistine also had in her bedroom a very large settee of wood, which had once been gilt and covered with flowered chintz, but it had been necessary to raise this settee to the first-floor through the window, owing to the narrowness of the stairs; and hence it could not be reckoned on in any emergency. It had been Mlle. Baptistine's ambition to buy drawing-room furniture of mahogany and covered with yellow Utrecht velvet; but this would have cost at least 500 francs, and, seeing that she had only succeeded in saving for this object 42 francs 5 sous in five years, she gave up the idea. Besides, who is there that ever attains his ideal?

Nothing more simple can be imagined than the bishop's bedroom,— a long window opening on the garden; opposite the bed, an iron hospital-bed with a canopy of green serge; in the shadow of the bed, behind a curtain, toilet articles, still revealing the old elegant habits of the man of fashion; two doors, one near the chimney leading to the oratory, the other near the library leading to the dining-room. The library was a large glass case full of books; the chimney of wood, painted to imitate marble, was habitually fireless; in the chimney were a pair of iron andirons ornamented with two vases, with garlands and grooves which had once been silvered, a species of episcopal luxury; over the chimney a crucifix of copper, from which the silver had been rubbed off, fastened to threadbare black velvet, in a frame which had lost its gilding; near the window was a large table with an inkstand, loaded with irregularly arranged papers and heavy tomes; before the table the straw arm-chair; in front of the bed a priedieu borrowed from the oratory.

Two portraits, in two oval frames, hung on the wall on either side of the bed. Small gilded inscriptions on the neutral-tinted ground of the canvas by the side of the figures indicated that the portraits represented, one the Abbé de Chaliot, bishop of St. Claude; the other the Abbé Tourteau, vicar-general of Agde and abbé of Grand Champs, belonging to the Cistercian order in the diocese of Chartres. The bishop, on succeeding to the hospital infirmary, found the pictures there and left them. They were priests, probably donors,—two motives for him to respect them. All he knew of the two personages was that they had been nominated by the king, the one to his bishopric, the other to his benefice, on the same day, April 27, 1785. Madame Magloire having unhooked the portraits to remove the dust, the bishop found this circumstance recorded in faded ink, on a small square of paper which time had turned yellow, and fastened by four wafers behind the portrait of the abbé of Grand Champs.

He had at his window an antique curtain of heavy woolen stuff, which had grown so old that Madame Magloire, in order to avoid the expense of a new one, was obliged to make a large patch in the very middle of it. The patch formed a cross, and the bishop often drew attention to it. "How pleasant that is," he would say. All the rooms in the house, ground-floor and first-floor, were whitewashed, which is a barrack and hospital fashion. Still, some years later, Madame Magloire discovered, as we shall see further on, paintings, under the whitewashed paper, in Mlle. Baptistine's bedroom. The rooms were paved with red bricks which were washed every week, and there were straw mats in front of all the beds. This house, moreover, managed by two women, was exquisitely clean from top to bottom: this was the only luxury the bishop allowed himself, for, as he said, "It takes nothing from the poor." We must allow, however, that of the old property there still remained six silver spoons and forks and a soup-ladle, which Madame Magloire daily saw with delight shining splendidly on the coarse white table-cloth. And as we are here depicting the bishop of D. . . . as he was, we must add that he had said, more than once, "I do not think I could give up dining with plate." To this plate must be added two heavy candlesticks of massive silver, which the bishop inherited from a great-aunt. These candlesticks held two wax candles, and usually figured on the bishop's chimney. When he had any one to dinner, Madame Magloire lit the candles and placed the two candlesticks on the table. There was in the bishop's bedroom, at the head of his bed, a small cupboard in the wall, in which Madame Magloire each night placed the plate and the large ladle; I am bound to add that the key was never taken out.

The garden, spoiled to some extent by the ugly buildings to which we have referred, was composed of four walks, radiating round a basin; another walk ran all round the garden close to the surrounding white wall. Between these walks were four box-bordered squares. In three of them Madame Magloire grew vegetables; in the fourth the bishop had placed flowers; here and there were a few fruit trees. Once Madame Magloire had said, with a sort of gentle archness, "Monseigneur, although you turn everything to use, here is an unemployed plot. It would be better to have lettuces there than bouquets." "Madame Magloire," the bishop answered, "you are mistaken; the beautiful is as useful as the useful." He added, after a moment's silence, "More so, perhaps."

This square, composed of three or four borders, occupied the bishop almost as much as his books did. He liked to spend an hour or two there, cutting, raking, and digging holes in which he placed seeds. He was not so hostile to insects as a gardener would have liked. However, he made no pretensions to botany; he was ignorant of groups and solidism; he did not make the slightest attempt to decide between Tournefort and the natural method; he was not a partisan either of Jussieu or Linnæus. He did not study plants, but he loved flowers. He greatly respected the professors, but he respected the ignorant even more; and, without ever failing in these two respects, he watered his borders every summer evening with a green-painted tin pot.

The house had not a single door that locked. The door of the dining-room, which, as we said, opened right on the cathedral square, had formerly been adorned with bolts and locks like a prison gate. The bishop had all this iron removed, and the door was only hasped either night or day; the first passer-by, no matter the hour, had only to push it. At the outset the two women had been greatly alarmed by this never-closed door; but the bishop said to them, "Have bolts placed on the doors of your rooms if you like." In the end they shared his confidence, or at least affected to do so; Madame Magloire alone was from time to time alarmed. As regards the bishop, his idea is explained, or at least indicated, by these three lines, which he wrote on the margin of a Bible: "This is the distinction: the physician's doors must never be closed; the priest's door must always be open." On another book, entitled "Philosophy of Medical Science," he wrote this other note: "Am I not a physician like them? I also have my patients; in the first place, I have theirs, whom they call the sick, and then I have my own, whom I call the unhappy." Elsewhere he also wrote: "Do not ask the name of the man who seeks a bed from you, for it is before all the man whom his name embarrasses that needs an asylum."

It came about that a worthy curé—I forget whether it were he of Couloubroux or he of Pompierry—thought proper to ask him one day, probably at the instigation of Madame Magloire, whether monseigneur was quite certain that he was not acting to some extent imprudently by leaving his door open day and night for any who liked to enter, and if he did not fear lest some misfortune might happen in a house so poorly guarded. The bishop tapped his shoulder with gentle gravity, and said to him, "Nisi Dominus custodierit domum, in vanum vigilant qui custodiunt eam."

Then he spoke of something else. He was fond of saying, too, "There is the priest's bravery as well as that of the colonel of dragoons. The only thing is that ours must be quiet."

7 · CRAVATTE

HERE naturally comes a fact which we must not omit, for it is one of those which will enable us to see what manner of man the bishop of D. . . . was. After the destruction of the band of Gaspard Bès, which had infested the gorges of Ollioules, Cravatte, one of his lieutenants, took refuge in the mountains. He concealed himself for a while with his brigands, the remnant of Bès's band, in the district of Nice, then went to Piedmont, and suddenly re-appeared in France, near Barcelonnette. He was seen first at Jauziers, and next at Tuiles; he concealed himself in the caverns of the Joug de l'Aigle, and descended thence on the hamlets and villages by the ravines of the Ubaye. He pushed on even as far as Embrun, entered the church one night and plundered the sacristy. His brigandage desolated the country, and the gendarmes were in vain placed on his track. He constantly escaped, and at times even offered resistance, for he was a bold scoundrel. In the midst of all this terror, the bishop arrived on his visitation, and the mayor came to him and urged him to turn back. Cravatte held the mountain as far as Arche and beyond, and there was danger, even with an escort. It would be uselessly exposing three or four unhappy gendarmes.

"For that reason," said the bishop, "I intend to go without escort."

"Can you mean it, monseigneur?" the mayor exclaimed.

"I mean it so fully that I absolutely refuse gendarmes, and intend to start in an hour."

"Monseigneur, you will not do that!"

"There is in the mountain," the bishop continued, "a humble little parish, which I have not visited for three years. They are good friends of mine, and quiet and honest shepherds. They are the owners of one goat out of every thirty they guard; they make very pretty woolen ropes of

25

different colors, and they play mountain airs on small six-holed flutes. They want to hear about heaven every now and then, and what would they think of a bishop who was afraid? What would they say if I did not go?"

"But, monseigneur, the brigands!"

"Ah," said the bishop, "you are right; I may meet them. They too must want to hear about heaven."

"Monseigneur, they are a flock of wolves."

"M. Mayor, it may be that this is the very flock of which Christ has made me the pastor. Who knows the ways of Providence?"

"Monseigneur, they will plunder you."

"I have nothing."

"They will kill you."

"A poor old priest who passes by, muttering his mummery? Nonsense, what good would that do them?"

"Oh, good gracious, if you were to meet them!"

"I would ask them for alms for my poor."

"Monseigneur, do not go. In Heaven's name do not, for you expose your life."

"My good sir," said the bishop, "is that all? I am not in this world to save my life, but to save souls."

There was no help for it, and he set out accompanied only by a lad who offered to act as his guide. His obstinacy created a sensation in the country, and caused considerable alarm. He would not take either his sister or Madame Magloire with him. He crossed the mountain on mule-back, met nobody, and reached his good friends, the goatherds, safe and sound. He remained with them a fortnight, preaching, administering the sacraments, teaching, and moralizing. When he was ready to start for home, he resolved to sing a Te Deum pontifically, and spoke about it to the curé. But what was to be done? There were no episcopal ornaments. All that could be placed at his disposal was a poor village sacristy, with a few old faded and pinchbeck-covered chasubles.

"Bah!" said the bishop; "announce the Te Deum in your sermon, for all that. It will come right in the end."

Inquiries were made in the surrounding churches; but all the magnificence of these united humble parishes would not have been sufficient to decently equip a cathedral chorister. While they were in this embarrassment, a large chest was brought and left at the curacy for the bishop by two strange horsemen, who started again at once. The chest was opened and found to contain a cope of cloth of gold, a miter adorned with diamonds, an archiepiscopal cross, a magnificent crozier, and all the pontifical robes stolen a month back from the treasury of Our Lady of Embrun. In the chest was a paper on which were written these words: "Cravatte to Monseigneur Welcome."

"Did I not tell you that it would be all right?" the bishop said; then he added with a smile, "Heaven sends an archbishop's cope to a man who is contented with a curé's surplice."

"Monseigneur," the curé muttered, with a gentle shake of his head, "Heaven or—the devil."

The bishop looked fixedly at the curé and repeated authoritatively, "Heaven!"

When he returned to Chastelar, and all along the road, he was regarded curiously. He found at the presbytery of that town Mlle. Baptistine and Madame Magloire waiting for him, and he said to his sister, "Well, was I right? The poor priest went among these poor mountaineers with empty hands, and returns with his hands full. I started, only taking with me my confidence in Heaven, and I bring back the treasures of a cathedral."

The same evening, before retiring, he said, too, "Never let us fear robbers or murderers. These are external and small dangers; let us fear ourselves; prejudices are the real robbers, vices the true murderers. The great dangers are within ourselves. Let us not trouble about what threatens our head or purse, and only think of what threatens our soul." Then, turning to his sister, he added, "Sister, a priest ought never to take precautions against his neighbor. What his neighbor does God permits, so let us confine ourselves to praying to God when we believe that a danger is impending over us. Let us pray, not for ourselves, but that our brother may not fall into error on our account."

Events, however, were rare in his existence. We relate those we know, but ordinarily he spent his life in always doing the same things at the same moment. A month of his year resembled an hour of his day. As to what became of the treasure of Embrun cathedral, we should be greatly embarrassed if questioned on that head. There were many fine things, very tempting and famous to steal on behalf of the poor. Stolen they were already; one moiety of the adventure was accomplished; the only thing left to do was to change the direction of the robbery, and make it turn slightly toward the poor. Still, we affirm nothing on the subject; we merely mention that among the bishop's papers a rather obscure note was found, which probably refers to this question, and was thus conceived: "The question is to know whether it ought to go to the cathedral or the hospital."

8. *PHILOSOPHY AFTER DRINKING*

THE senator, to whom we have already alluded, was a skillful man, who had made his way with a rectitude that paid no attention to all those things which constitute obstacles, and are called conscience, plighted word, right, and duty; he had gone straight to his object without once swerving from the line of his promotions and his interest. He was an ex-procureur, softened by success, anything but a wicked man, doing all the little services in his power for his sons, his sons-in-law, his relatives, and even his friends; he had selected the best opportunities, and the rest seemed to him something absurd. He was witty, and just sufficiently lettered to believe himself a disciple of Epicurus, while probably only a product of Pigault-Lebrun. He was fond of laughing pleasantly at things infinite and eternal, and at the crotchets "of our worthy bishop." He even laughed at them with amiable authority in M. Myriel's presence. On some semi-official occasion the Count . . . . (this senator) and M. Myriel met at the prefect's table. At the dessert the senator, who was merry but quite sober, said:

"Come, bishop, let us have a chat. A senator and a bishop can hardly meet without winking at each other, for we are two augurs, and I am about to make a confession to you. I have my system of philosophy."

"And you are right," the bishop answered; "as you make your philosophy, so you must lie on it. You are on the bed of purple."

The senator, thus encouraged, continued,—"Let us be candid."

"Decidedly."

"I declare to you," the senator went on, "that the Marquis d'Argens, Pyrrho, Hobbes, and Naigeon are no impostors. I have in my library all my philosophers with gilt backs."

"Like yourself, count," the bishop interrupted him.

The senator proceeded:

"I hate Diderot; he is an ideologist, a declaimer, and a revolutionist, believing in his heart in Deity, and more bigoted than Voltaire. The latter ridiculed Needham, and was wrong, for Needham's eels prove that God is unnecessary. A drop of vinegar in a spoonful of flour supplies the *fiat lux;* suppose the drop larger, and the spoonful bigger, and you have the world. Man is the eel: then, of what use is the Eternal Father? My dear bishop, the Jehovah hypothesis wearies me; it is only fitted to produce thin people who think hollow. Down with the great All which annoys me! Long live Zero, who leaves me at peace! Between ourselves and in order to confess to my pastor, as is right and proper, I confess to you that I possess common sense. I am not wild about your Saviour, who continually preaches abnegation and sacrifice. It is advice offered by a miser to beggars. Abnegation, why? Sacrifice, for what object? I do not see that one wolf sacrifices itself to cause the happiness of another wolf. Let us, therefore, remain in nature. We are at the summit, so let us have the supreme philosophy. What is the use of being at the top, if you cannot see further than the end of other people's noses? Let us live gayly, for life is all in all. As for man having a future elsewhere, up there, down there, somewhere, I do not believe a syllable of it. Oh, yes! recommend sacrifices and abnegation to me. I must take care of all I do. I must rack my brains about good and evil, justice and injustice, *fas et nefas.* Why so? because I shall have to give account for my actions. When? after my death. What a fine dream! after death! He will be a clever fellow who catches me. Just think of a lump of ashes seized by the hand of a shadow. Let us speak the truth, we who are initiated and have raised the skirt of Isis; there is no good, no evil, but there is vegetation. Let us seek reality and go to the bottom; hang it all, we must scent the truth, dig into the ground for it and seize it. Then it offers exquisite delights; then you become strong and laugh. I am square at the base, my dear bishop, and human immortality is a thing which anybody who likes may listen to. Oh! what a charming prospect! What a fine billet Adam has! You are a soul, you will be an angel, and have blue wings on your shoulder-blades. Come, help me; is it not Tertullian who says that the blessed will go from one planet to the other? Very good; they will be the grasshoppers of the planets. And then they will see God. Ta, ta, ta! These paradises are all nonsense, and God is a monstrous fable. I would not say so in the *Moniteur,* of course, but I whisper it between friends, *inter pocula.* Sacrificing the earth for paradise is giving up the substance for the shadow. I am not such an ass as to be the dupe of the Infinite. I am nothing; my name is Count Nothing, Senator. Did I exist before my birth? no; shall I exist after my death? no. What am I? a little dust aggregated by an organism. What have I to do on this earth? I have the choice between suffering and enjoyment. To what will suffering lead me? to nothingness, but I shall have suffered. To what will enjoyment lead me? to nothingness, but I shall have enjoyed. My choice is made; a man must either eat or be eaten, and so I eat, for it is better to be the tooth than the grass. That is my wisdom; after which go on as I impel you; the grave-digger is there; the Pantheon for such as us, and all fall into the large holes. *Finis,* and total liquidation, that is the vanishing point. Death is dead, take my word for it; and I laugh at the idea of any one present affirming the contrary. It is an invention of nurses, old Boguey for children, Jehovah for men. No, our morrow is night; behind the tomb there is nothing but equal nothings. You may have been Sardan-apalus, you may have been St. Vincent de Paul, but it all comes to the same thing. That is the truth, so live above all else; make use of your *me,* so long as you hold it. In truth, I tell you, my dear bishop, I have my philosophy, and I have my philosophers, and I do not let myself be deluded by fables. After all, something must be offered persons who are down in the world,—the barefooted, the strugglers for existence, and the wretched; and so they are offered pure legends—chimeras—the soul —immortality—paradise—the stars—to swallow. They chew that and put it on their dry bread. The man who has nothing has God, and that is something, at any rate. I do not oppose it, but I keep M. Naigeon for myself; God is good for the people."

The bishop clapped his hands.

"That is what I call speaking," he exclaimed. "Ah, what an excellent and truly wonderful thing this materialism is! it is not every man who wishes that can have it. Ah! when a man has reached that point, he is no longer a dupe; he does not let himself be stupidly exiled, like Cato; or stoned, like St. Stephen; or burnt, like Joan of Arc. Those who have succeeded in acquiring this materialism have the joy of feeling them-selves irresponsible, and thinking that they can devour everything with-out anxiety, places, sinecures, power well or badly gained, dignities, lucrative tergiversations, useful treachery, folly, capitulations with their consciences, and that they will go down to the tomb after digesting it all properly. How agreeable this is! I am not referring to you, my dear senator, still I cannot refrain from congratulating you. You great gentlemen have, as you say, a philosophy of your own, and for yourselves, exquisite, refined, accessible to the rich alone, good with any sauce, and admirably seasoning the joys of life. This philosophy is drawn from the profundities, and dug up by special searchers. But you are kind fellows, and think it no harm that belief in God should be the philosophy of the populace, much in the same way as a goose stuffed with chestnuts is the truffled turkey of the poor."

9. THE BROTHER DESCRIBED BY THE SISTER

To give an idea of the domestic life of the bishop of D. . . . , and the manner in which these two saintly women subordinated their actions, their thoughts, even their feminine instincts, which were easily startled, to the habits and intentions of the bishop, before he required to express them in words, we cannot do better than copy here a letter from Mlle. Baptistine to the Viscountess de Boischevron, her friend from childhood. This letter is in our possession.

D. . . . , 16th Dec., 18. .

MY DEAR MADAME: *Not a day passes in which we do not talk about you. That is our general habit, but there is an extra reason at present. Just imagine that, in washing and dusting the ceilings and walls, Madame Magloire has made a discovery, and now our two rooms papered with old whitewashed paper would not disgrace a chateau like yours. Madame Magloire has torn down all the paper, and there are things under it. My*

31

sitting-room, in which there was no furniture, and in which we used to hang up the linen to dry, is fifteen feet in height, eighteen wide, and has a ceiling which was once gilded, and rafters as in your house. It was covered with canvas during the time this mansion was an hospital. But it is my bedroom you should see; Madame Magloire has discovered under at least ten layers of paper paintings which, though not excellent, are endurable. There is Telemachus dubbed a knight by Minerva; and there he is again in the gardens: I forget their names, but where the Roman ladies only went for a single night. What can I tell you? I have Roman ladies (here an illegible word), and so·on. Madame Magloire has got it all straight. This summer she intends to repair a little damage, revarnish it all, and my bedroom will be a real museum. She has also found in a corner of the garret two consoles in the old fashion. They want twelve francs to regild them, but it is better to give that sum to the poor; besides, they are frightfully ugly, and I should prefer a round mahogany table.

I am very happy, for my brother is so good; he gives all he has to the sick and the poor, and we are often greatly pressed. The country is hard in winter, and something must be done for those who are in want. We are almost lighted and warmed, and, as you can see, that is a great comfort. My brother has peculiar habits; when he does talk, he says "that a bishop should be so." Just imagine that the house door is never closed: any one who likes can come in, and is at once in my brother's presence. He fears nothing, not even night; and he says that is his way of showing his bravery. He does not wish me to feel alarmed for him, or for Madame Magloire to do so; he exposes himself to all dangers, and does not wish us to appear as if we even noticed it. We must understand him. He goes out in the rain, he wades through the water, and travels in winter. He is not afraid of the night, suspicious roads, or encounters. Last year he went all alone into a country of robbers, for he would not take us with him. He staid away a whole fortnight, and folks thought him dead, but he came back all right, and said, "Here's the way in which I was robbed," and he opened a chest full of all the treasures of Embrun cathedral, which the robbers had given him. That time I could not refrain from scolding him a little, but was careful only to speak when the wheels made a noise, so that no one could hear me.

At first I said to myself, "There is no danger that checks him, and he is terrible"; but at present I have grown accustomed to it. I make Madame Magloire a sign not to annoy him, and he risks his life as he pleases. I carry off Magloire, go to my bedroom, pray for him, and fall asleep. I am tranquil because I know that if any harm happened to him it would be the death of me. I shall go to heaven with my brother and my bishop. Madame Magloire has had greater difficulty than myself in accustoming herself to what she calls his imprudence, but at present she has learnt to put up with it. We both pray; we are terrified together, and fall asleep. If the Fiend were to enter the house, no one would try to stop him, and after all, what have we to fear in this house? There is always some one with us who is the stronger; the demon may pass by, but our Lord lives in it. That is enough for me, and my brother no longer requires to say a word to me. I understand him without his speaking, and we leave ourselves in the hands of Providence, for that is the way in which you must behave to a man who has grandeur in his soul.

I have questioned my brother about the information you require concerning the De Faux family. You are aware that he knows everything, and what a memory he has, for he is still a good royalist. It is really a very old Norman family belonging to the generality of Caen. Five hundred years ago there were a Raoul, a John, and a Thomas de Faux, who were gentlemen, one of them seigneur of Rochefort. The last was Guy Stephen Alexander; who was major-general, and something in the Brittany Light Horse: his daughter, Maria Louisa, married Adrian Charles de Gramont, son of Duke Louis de Gramont, peer of France, colonel of the French guards, and lieutenant-general in the army. The name is written Faux, Fauq, and Faouq.

My dear madam, recommend us to the prayers of your holy relative, the cardinal. As for your dear Sylvanie, she has done well in not wasting the few moments she passes by your side in writing to me. She is well, works according to your wishes, and loves me still; that is all I desire. Her souvenir sent me through you safely reached me, and I am delighted at it. My health is not bad, and yet I grow thinner every day. Good-bye, my paper is running out and compels me to break off. A thousand kind regards from your

BAPTISTINE.

P. S. Your little nephew is delightful: do you know that he is nearly five years of age? Yesterday he saw a horse pass with knee-caps on, and he said, "What has he got on his knees?" He is such a dear child. His little brother drags an old broom about the room like a coach, and cries, "Hih, hih!"

As may be seen from this letter, the two women managed to yield to the bishop's way, with the genius peculiar to woman who comprehends a man better than he does himself. The bishop of D. . . . , beneath the candid, gentle air which never broke down, at times did grand, bold, and magnificent things, without even appearing to suspect the fact. They trembled, but let him alone. At times Madame Magloire would hazard a remonstrance beforehand, but never during or after the deed. They never troubled him either by word or sign when he had once begun an affair. At certain moments, without his needing to mention the fact, or perhaps when he was not conscious of it, so perfect was his simplicity, they vaguely felt that he was acting episcopally, and at such times they were only two shadows in the house. They served him passively, and if disappearance were obedience, they disappeared. They knew, with an admirable intuitive delicacy, that certain attentions might vex him, and hence, though they might believe him in peril, they understood, I will not say his thoughts, but his nature, and no longer watched over him. They intrusted him to God. Moreover, Baptistine said, as we have just read, that her brother's death would be her death. Madame Magloire did not say so, but she knew it.

10. *THE BISHOP FACES A NEW LIGHT*

At a period rather later than the date of the letter just quoted, he did a thing which the whole town declared to be even more venturesome than his trip in the mountains among the bandits. A man lived alone in the country near D. . . . . This man—let us out with the great word at once!—was an ex-conventionalist, of the name of G. . . . . The people talked about him in the little world of D. . . . with a species of horror. A conventionalist, only think of that! Those men existed at the time

34

when people "thou-ed" one another and were called citizens. This man was almost a monster: he had not voted for the king's death, but had done all but that, and was a quasi-regicide. How was it that this man had not been tried by court-martial, on the return of the legitimate princes? They need not have cut his head off, for clemency is all right and proper, but banishment for life would have been an example, and so on. Moreover, he was an atheist, like all those men. It was the gossip of geese round a vulture.

And was this G. . . . a vulture? Yes, if he might be judged by his ferocious solitude. As he had not voted the king's death, he was not comprised in the decree of exile, and was enabled to remain in France. He lived about three miles from the town, far from every village, every road, in a nook of a very wild valley. He had there, so it was said, a field, a hut, a den. He had no neighbors, not even passers-by; since he had lived in the valley, the path leading to it had become overgrown with grass. People talked of the spot as of the hangman's house. Yet the bishop thought of it, and from time to time gazed at a spot on the horizon where a clump of trees pointed out the old conventionalist's valley, and said, "There is a soul there alone," and he added to himself, "I owe him a visit."

But, let us confess it, this idea, at the first blush quite natural, seemed to him after a moment's reflection strange and impossible, almost repulsive. For, in his heart, he shared the general impression, and the conventionalist inspired him, without his being able to account for it, with that feeling which is the border line of hatred, and which is so well expressed by the word estrangement.

Still the shepherd ought not to keep aloof from a scabby sheep; but, then, what a sheep it was! The good bishop was perplexed; at times he started in that direction, but turned back. One day a rumor spread in the town that a kind of young shepherd who waited on G. . . . in his den had come to fetch a doctor. The old villain was dying; paralysis was overpowering him, and he could not last out the night. Happy release! some added.

The bishop took his stick, put on his overcoat to hide his well-worn cassock, as well as to protect him against the night breeze which would soon rise, and set out. The sun had almost attained the horizon when the bishop reached the excommunicated spot. He perceived with a certain heart-beating that he was close to the wild beast's den. He strode across a ditch, clambered over a hedge, entered a neglected garden, and suddenly perceived the cavern behind some shrubs. It was a low, poor-looking hut, small and clean, with a vine nailed over the front.

In front of the door an old white-haired man, seated in a worn-out wheel-chair, was smiling in the sun. By his side stood the shepherd-boy, who handed him a pot of milk. While the bishop was looking at him the old man uplifted his voice. "Thanks," he said, "I want nothing further," and his smile was turned from the sun to rest on the boy.

The bishop stepped forward, and at the noise of his footsteps the seated man turned his head, and his face expressed all the surprise it is possible to feel after an advanced age.

"Since I have lived here," he said, "you are the first person who has come to me. Who may you be, sir?"

The bishop answered, "My name is Bienvenu Myriel."

"I have heard that name uttered. Are you not he whom the peasants call Monseigneur Welcome?"

"I am."

The old man continued, with a half-smile, "In that case you are my bishop?"

"Yes, a little."

"Come in, sir."

The conventionalist offered his hand to the bishop, but the bishop did not take it; he confined himself to saying:

"I am pleased to see that I was deceived. You certainly do not look ill."

"I am about to be cured, sir," the old man said; then after a pause he added, "I shall be dead in three hours. I am a bit of a physician, and know in what way the last hour comes. Yesterday only my feet were cold; to-day the chill reached my knees, now I can feel it ascending to my waist, and when it reaches the heart I shall stop. The sun is glorious, is it not? I had myself wheeled out in order to take a farewell glance at things. You can talk to me, for it does not weary me. You have done well to come and look at a dying man, for it is proper that there should be witnesses. People have their fancies, and I should have liked to go on till dawn. But I know that I can hardly last three hours. It will be night, but, after all, what matter? Finishing is a simple affair, and daylight is not necessary for it. Be it so, I will die by starlight."

Then he turned to the lad:

"Go to bed. You sat up the other night, and you must be tired."

The boy went into the cabin; the old man looked after him, and added, as if speaking to himself:

"While he is sleeping I shall die; the two slumbers can keep each other company."

The bishop was not so moved as we might imagine he would be. He did not think that he saw God in this way of dying; and—let us out with it, as the small contradictions of great hearts must also be indicated—he, who at times laughed so heartily at his grandeur, was somewhat annoyed at not being called monseigneur, and was almost tempted to reply, citizen. He felt an inclination for coarse familiarity, common enough for doctors and priests, but to which he was not accustomed. This man, after all, this conventionalist, this representative of the people, had been a mighty one of the earth;—for the first time in his life, perhaps, the bishop felt disposed to sternness.

The republican, in the meantime, regarded him with modest cordiality, in which, perhaps, could be traced that humility which is so becoming in a man who is on the point of returning to the dust.

The bishop, on his side, though he generally guarded against curiosity, which according to him was akin to insult, could not refrain from examining the conventionalist with an attention which, as it did not emanate from sympathy, would have pricked his conscience in the case of any other man. The conventionalist produced the effect upon him of being beyond the pale of the law, even the law of charity. G. . . . , almost upright, and possessing a sonorous voice, was one of those grand octogenarians who are the amazement of the physiologist. The revolution possessed many such men, proportioned to the age. The thoroughly tried man could be seen in him, and, though so near his end, he had retained all the signs of health. There was something which would disconcert death in his bright glance, his firm accent, and the robust movement of his shoulders: Azrael, the Mohammedan angel of the sepulchre, would have turned back, fancying that he had mistaken the door.

G. . . . seemed to be dying because he wished to do so; there was liberty in his agony, and his legs alone, by which the shadows clutched him, were motionless. While the feet were dead and cold, the head lived with all the power and life and appeared in full light. G. . . . at this awful moment resembled the king in the Oriental legend, flesh above and marble below. The bishop sat down on a stone and began, rather abruptly:

"I congratulate you," he said, in the tone people employ to reprimand; "*at least* you did not vote the king's death."

The republican did not seem to notice the covert bitterness of this remark, *at least;* he replied, without a smile on his face:

"Do not congratulate me, sir; I voted the death of the tyrant." It was the accent of austerity opposed to that of sternness.

"What do you mean?" the bishop continued.

"I mean that man has a tyrant, Ignorance, and I voted for the end of that tyrant which engendered royalty, which is the false authority, while knowledge is the true authority. Man must only be governed by knowledge."

"And by his conscience," the bishop added.

"That is the same thing. Conscience is the amount of innate knowledge we have in us."

Monseigneur Welcome listened in some surprise to this language, which was very novel to him. The republican continued:

"As for Louis XVI, I said no. I do not believe that I have the right to kill a man, but I feel the duty of exterminating a tyrant, and I voted for the end of the tyrant. That is to say, for the end of prostitution for women; the end of slavery for men; and the end of night for children. In voting for the republic I voted for all this: I voted for fraternity, concord, the Dawn! I aided in the overthrow of errors and prejudices, and such an overthrow produces light; we hurled down the old world, and the old world, that vase of wretchedness, by being poured over the human race, became an urn of joy."

"Mingled joy," said the bishop.

"You might call it troubled joy, and now, after that fatal return of the past, which is called 1814, a departed joy. Alas! the work was incomplete, I grant; we demolished the ancient régime in facts, but were not able to suppress it completely in ideas. It is not sufficient to destroy abuses, but morals must also be modified. Though the mill no longer exists, the wind still blows."

"You demolished; it may be useful, but I distrust a demolition complicated with passion."

"Right has its passion, sir, and that passion is an element of progress. No matter what may be said, the French Revolution is the most powerful step taken by the human race since the advent of Christ. It may be incomplete, but it was sublime. It softened minds, it calmed, appeased, and enlightened, and it spread civilization over the world. The French Revolution was good, for it was the consecration of humanity."

The bishop could not refrain from muttering:

"Yes? '93!"

The republican drew himself up with almost mournful solemnity, and shouted, as well as a dying man could shout:

"Ah! there we have it! I have been waiting for that. A cloud had been collecting for fifteen hundred years, and at the end of that period it burst; you are condemning the thunder-clap."

The bishop, without perhaps confessing it to himself, felt that the blow had gone home; still he kept a good countenance, and answered:

"The judge speaks in the name of justice; the priest speaks in that of pity, which is only a higher form of justice. A thunder-clap must not deceive itself."

And he added as he looked fixedly at the conventionalist:

"And Louis XVII?"

The republican stretched forth his hand and seized the bishop's arm.

"Louis XVII. Let us consider. Whom do you weep for? Is it the innocent child? in that case I weep with you. Is it the royal child? in that case I must ask leave to reflect. For me, the thought of a brother of Cartouche, an innocent lad hung up under the armpits in the Place de Grève until death ensued, for the sole crime of being Cartouche's brother, is not less painful than the grandson of Louis XV, the innocent boy martyrized in the Temple Tower for the sole crime of being the grandson of Louis XV."

"I do not like such an association of names, sir," said the bishop.

"Louis XV? Cartouche? On behalf of which do you protest?"

There was a moment's silence; the bishop almost regretted having come, and yet felt himself vaguely and strangely shaken. The conventionalist continued:

"Ah! sir priest, you do not like the crudities of truth, but Christ loved them; he took a scourge and swept the temple. His lightning lash was a rough discourser of truths. When he exclaimed, 'Suffer little children to come unto me,' he made no distinction among them. He made no difference between the dauphin of Barabbas and the dauphin of Herod. Innocence is its own crown, and does not require to be a highness; it is as august in rags as when crowned with *fleurs de lis*."

"That is true," said the bishop in a low voice.

"You have named Louis XVII," the conventionalist continued; "let us understand each other. Shall we weep for all the innocents, martyrs, and children of the lowest as of the highest rank? I am with you there, but, as I said, in that case we must go back beyond '93, and begin our tears before Louis XVII. I will weep over the children of kings with you, provided that you weep with me over the children of the people."

"I weep for all," said the bishop.

"Equally!" G. . . . exclaimed; "and if the balance must be uneven, let it be on the side of the people, as they have suffered the longest."

There was again a silence, which the republican broke. He rose on his elbow, pinched his cheek with his thumb and forefinger, as a man does mechanically when he is interrogating and judging, and fixed on the bishop a glance full of all the energy of approaching death. It was almost an explosion.

"Yes, sir; the people have suffered for a long time. But let me ask why you have come to question and speak about Louis XVII? I do not know you. Ever since I have been in this country I have lived here alone, never setting my foot across the threshold, and seeing no one but the boy who attends to me. Your name, it is true, has vaguely reached me, and I am bound to say that it was pronounced affectionately, but that means nothing, for clever people have so many ways of making the worthy, simple folk believe in them. By the by, I did not hear the sound of your coach; you doubtless left it down there behind that clump of trees at the cross-roads.

"I do not know you, I tell you; you have informed me that you are the bishop, but that teaches me nothing as to your moral character. In a word I repeat my question, who are you? You are a bishop, that is to say a prince of the church, one of those gilded, escutcheoned annuitants who have fat prebends,—the bishopric of D. . . . , with 15,000 francs income, 10,000 francs in fees, or a total of 25,000 francs,—who have kitchen liveries, keep a good table, and eat water-fowl on Friday; who go about with lackeys before and behind, in a gilded coach, who have palaces and drive your carriage, in the name of the Saviour who walked barefoot! You are a prelate; you have, like all the rest, income, palace, horses, valets, a good table, and like all the rest, you enjoy them: that is all very well, but it says either too much or too little; it does not enlighten me as to your intrinsic and essential value when you come with the probable intention of bringing me wisdom. To whom am I speaking—who are you?"

The bishop bowed his head, and answered, "I am a worm."

"A worm in a carriage!" the republican growled.

It was his turn to be haughty, the bishop's to be humble; the latter continued gently:

"Be it so, sir. But explain to me how my coach, which is a little way off behind the trees, my good table, and the water-fowl I eat on Friday, my palace, my income, and my footmen, prove that pity is not a virtue, that clemency is not a duty, and that '93 was not inexorable."

The republican passed his hand over his forehead, as if to remove a cloud.

"Before answering you," he said, "I must ask you to forgive me. I was in the wrong, sir, for you are in my house and my guest. You discuss my ideas, and I must restrict myself to combating your reasoning. Your wealth and enjoyments are advantages which I have over you in the debate, but courtesy bids me not employ them. I promise not to do so again."

"I thank you," said the bishop.

G. . . . continued: "Let us return to the explanation you asked of me. Where were we? What was it you said, that '93 was inexorable?"

"Yes, inexorable," the bishop said; "what do you think of Marat clapping his hands at the guillotine?"

"What do you think of Bossuet singing a Te Deum over the Dragonnades?"

The response was harsh, but went to its mark with the rigidity of a rapier. The bishop started, and could not parry it, but he was hurt by this way of mentioning Bossuet. The best minds have their fetishes, and at times feel vaguely wounded by any want of respect on the part of logic. The conventionalist was beginning to gasp; that asthma which is mingled with the last breath affected his voice; still he retained perfect lucidity of soul in his eyes. He continued:

"Let us say a few words more upon this head. Beyond the revolution, which, taken in its entirety, is an immense human affirmation, '93, alas, is a reply. You consider it inexorable but what was the whole monarchy? Carrier is a bandit, but what name do you give to Montrevel? Fouquier-Tinville is a scoundrel, but what is your opinion about Lamoignon-Bâville? Maillard is frightful, but what of Saulx-Tavannes, if you please? Father Duchêne is ferocious, but what epithet will you allow me for Père Letellier? Jourdan-Coupe-Tête is a monster, but less so than the Marquis de Louvois. I pity Marie Antoinette, archduchess and queen, but I also pity the poor Huguenot woman who, in 1685, under Louis the Great, while suckling her child, was fastened naked to the waist, to a stake, while her infant was held at a distance. Her breast was swollen with milk, her heart with agony; the babe, hungry and pale, saw that breast and screamed for it, and the hangman said to the wife, mother, and nurse, 'Abjure!' giving her the choice between the death of her infant and the death of her conscience. What do you say of this punishment of Tantalus adapted to a woman? Remember this carefully, sir, the French Revolution had its reasons, and its wrath will be absolved by the future. Its result is a better world; and a caress for the human race issues from its most terrible blows. I must stop, for the game is all in my favor—besides, I am dying."

And ceasing to regard the bishop, the republican finished his thought with the following few calm words:

"Yes, the brutalities of progress are called revolutions, but when they are ended, this fact is recognized: the human race has been chastised, but it has moved onward."

The republican did not suspect that he had carried in turn every one of the bishop's internal intrenchments. One still remained, however, and from this, the last resource of monseigneur's resistance, came this remark, in which all the roughness of the commencement was perceptible.

"Progress must believe in God, and the good cannot have impious servants. A man who is an atheist is a bad guide for the human race."

The ex-representative of the people did not reply. He trembled, looked up to the sky, and a tear slowly collected in his eye. When the lid was full the tear ran down his livid cheek, and he said in a low, shaking voice, as if speaking to himself: "Oh, thou! oh, ideal! thou alone existest!"

The bishop had a sort of inexpressible commotion; after a silence the old man raised a finger to heaven and said:

"The infinite is. It is there. If the infinite had not a me, the I would be its limit; it would not be infinite; in other words, it would not be. But it is. Hence it has a me. This I of the infinite is God."

The dying man uttered these words in a loud voice, and with a shudder of ecstasy, as if he saw some one. When he had spoken, his eyes closed, for the effort had exhausted him. It was evident that he had lived in one minute the few hours left him. The supreme moment was at hand. The bishop understood it; he had come here as a priest, and had gradually passed from extreme coldness to extreme emotion; he looked at these closed eyes, he took this wrinkled and chilly hand and bent down over the dying man.

"This hour is God's. Would you not consider it matter of regret if we had met in vain?"

The republican opened his eyes again; a gravity which suggested the shadow of death was imprinted on his countenance.

"Sir," he said, with a slowness produced perhaps more by the dignity of the soul than by failing of his strength, "I have spent my life in meditation, contemplation, and study. I was sixty years of age when my country summoned me, and ordered me to interfere in its affairs. I obeyed. There were abuses, and I combated them; tyranny, and I destroyed it; rights and principles, and I proclaimed and confessed them; the territory was invaded, and I defended it; France was menaced, and I offered her my breast; I was not rich, and I am poor. I was one of the masters of the State; the bank cellars were so filled with specie that it was necessary to shore the walls up, which were ready to burst through the weight of gold and silver, but I dined in the Rue de l'Arbre Sec, at two-and-twenty sous a head. I succored the oppressed; I relieved the suffering. I tore up the altar-cloth, it is true, but it was to stanch the wounds of the country. I ever supported the onward march of the human race toward light, and I at times resisted pitiless progress. When opportunity served, I protected my adversaries, men of your class. And there is at Peteghem in Flanders, on the same site where the Merovingian kings had their summer palace, a Monastery of Urbanists, the Abbey of St. Claire en Beaulieu, which I saved in 1793. I did my duty according to my strength, and what good I could. After which I was driven out, tracked, pursued, persecuted, maligned, mocked, spat upon, accursed, and proscribed. For many years I have felt that persons believed they had a right to despise me. My face has been held accursed by the poor ignorant mob, and, while hating no one, I accepted the isolation of hatred. Now I am eighty-six years of age and on the point of death; what have you come to ask of me?"

"Your blessing!" said the bishop, and knelt down. When the bishop raised his head again, the conventionalist's countenance had become august: he had just expired. The bishop returned home absorbed in the strangest thoughts, and spent the whole night in prayer. On the morrow, curious worthies tried to make him talk about G. . . . the republican, but he only pointed to heaven. From this moment increased his tenderness and fraternity for the little ones and the suffering.

Any allusion to "that old villain of a G. . . ." made him fall into a singular reverie; no one could say that the passing of that mind before his, and the reflection that great conscience cast upon his, had not something to do with this approach to perfection. This "pastoral visit" nearly created a stir among the small local coteries.

"Was it a bishop's place to visit the death-bed of such a man? It was plain that he had no conversion to hope for, for all these revolutionists are relapsed! Then, why go? What had he to see there? He must have been curious to see the fiend carry off a soul."

One day a dowager, of the impertinent breed which believes itself witty, asked him this question: "Monseigneur, people are asking when your grandeur will have the red cap?" "Oh, oh!" the bishop answered, "that is an ominous color. Fortunately those who despise it in a cap venerate it in a hat."

II. *A RESTRICTION*

WE should run a strong risk of making a mistake were we to conclude from this that Monseigneur Welcome was "a philosophic bishop," or "a patriotic curé." His meeting, which might also be called his conjunction, with the conventionalist G. . . . , produced in him a sort of amazement, which rendered him more gentle than ever. That was all.

Though monseigneur was anything rather than a politician, this is perhaps the place to indicate briefly what was his attitude in the events of that period, supposing that monseigneur ever dreamed of having an attitude. We will, therefore, go back for a few years. A short time after M. Myriel's elevation to the episcopate, the emperor made him a baron, simultaneously with some other bishops. The arrest of the pope took place, as is well known, on the night of July 5, 1809; at which time M. Myriel was called by Napoleon to the synod of French and Italian bishops convened at Paris. This synod was held at Notre-Dame, and assembled for the first time on June 15, 1811, under the presidency of Cardinal Fesch. M. Myriel was one of the ninety-five bishops convened, but he was only present at one session and three or four private conferences. As bishop of a mountain diocese, living so near to nature in rusticity and poverty, it seems that he introduced among these eminent personages ideas which changed the temperature of the assembly. He went back very soon to D. . . . and when questioned about this hurried return he replied, "I was troublesome to them. The fresh air came in with me, and I produced the effect of an open door upon them." Another time he said, "What would you have? these messeigneurs are princes, while I am only a poor peasant bishop."

The fact is, that he had displeased: among other strange things he let the following remarks slip out, one evening when he was visiting one of his most influential colleagues, "What fine clocks! What splendid carpets! What magnificent liveries! You must find all that very troublesome? Oh! I should not like to have such superfluities to yell incessantly in my ears: there are people who are hungry; there are people who are cold; there are poor, there are poor."

Let us remark parenthetically that a hatred of luxury would not be an intelligent hatred, for it would imply a hatred of the arts. Still, in churchmen any luxury beyond that connected with their sacred office is wrong, for it seems to reveal habits which are not truly charitable. An opulent priest is a paradox, for he is bound to live with the poor. Now, can a man incessantly, both night and day, come in contact with distress, misfortune, and want, without having about him a little of that holy wretchedness, like the dust of toil? Can we imagine a man sitting close to a stove and not feeling hot? Can we imagine a workman constantly toiling at a furnace, and have neither a hair burned, a nail blackened, nor a drop of perspiration nor grain of soot on his face? The first proof of charity in a priest, in a bishop especially, is poverty. This was, doubtless, the opinion of the bishop of D. . . . .

We must not believe either that he shared what we might call the "ideas of the age" on certain delicate points; he mingled but slightly in the theological questions of the moment, in which church and state are compromised; but, had he been greatly pressed, we fancy he would have been found to be ultramontane rather than Gallican. As we are drawing a portrait, and do not wish to conceal anything, we are forced to add that he was frigid toward the setting Napoleon. From 1813 he adhered to or applauded all hostile demonstrations; he refused to see him when he passed through on his return from Elba, and abstained from ordering public prayers for the emperor during the hundred days.

Besides his sister, Mlle. Baptistine, he had two brothers, one a general, the other a prefect. He wrote very frequently to both of them. For some time he owed the former a grudge, because the general, who at the time of the landing at Cannes held a command in Provence, put himself at the head of twelve hundred men and pursued the emperor as if he wished to let him escape. His correspondence was more affectionate with the other brother, the ex-prefect, a worthy, honest man, who lived retired at Paris.

Monseigneur Welcome, therefore, also had his hour of partisan spirit, his hour of bitterness, his cloud. The shadow of the passions of the moment fell athwart this gentle and great mind, which was occupied by things eternal. Certainly, such a man would have deserved to have no political opinions. Pray let there be no mistake as to our meaning: we do not confound what are called "political opinions" with the grand aspirations for progress, with that sublime patriotic, democratic and human faith which in our days must be the foundation of all generous intelligence. Without entering into questions which only indirectly affect the subject of this book, we say it would have been better had Monseigneur Welcome not been a royalist, and if his eye had not turned away, even for a moment, from that serene contemplation in which the three pure lights of Truth, Justice, and Charity are seen beaming above the fictions and hatreds of this world, and above the stormy ebb and flow of human affairs.

While allowing that God had not created Monseigneur Welcome for political functions, we could have understood and admired a protest in the name of justice and liberty, a haughty opposition, and a perilous and just resistance offered to the omnipotent Napoleon. But conduct which pleases us toward those who are rising, pleases us less toward those who are falling. We only like the contest so long as there is danger; and, in any case, only the combatants from the beginning have a right to be the exterminators at the end. A man who has not been an obstinate accuser during prosperity must be silent when the crash comes; the denouncer of success is the sole legitimate judge of the fall. For our part, when Providence interferes and strikes we let it do so. 1812 begins to disarm us. In 1813 the cowardly rupture of silence by the taciturn legislative corps, emboldened by catastrophes, could only arouse indignation; it was wrong to applaud it. In 1814, in the presence of the traitor marshals, in the presence of that senate, passing from one atrocity to another, and insulting after deifying, and at the sight of the idolaters deserting and spitting on their idol, it was a duty to turn one's head away. In 1815, as supreme disasters were in the air, as France had a shudder of their sinister approach, as Waterloo, already open before Napoleon, could be vaguely distinguished, the dolorous acclamation offered by the army and the people had nothing laughable about it, and—leaving the despot out of the question—a heart like the bishop of D. . . .'s ought not to have misunderstood how much there was august and affecting in this close embrace between a great nation and a great man on the verge of an abyss.

With this exception, the bishop was in all things just, true, equitable, intelligent, humble, and worthy; beneficent and benevolent, which is another form of beneficence. He was a priest, a sage, and a man. Even in the political opinions with which we have reproached him, and which we are inclined to judge almost severely, we are bound to add that he was tolerant and facile, more so perhaps than the writer of these lines. The porter of the Town Hall had been appointed by the emperor; he was an ex-noncommissioned officer of the old guard, a legionary of Auster-litz, and as Bonapartist as the eagle. This poor fellow now and then made thoughtless remarks, which the law of that day qualified as seditious. From the moment when the Imperial profile disappeared from the Legion of Honor, he never put on his uniform again, that he might not be obliged to bear his cross, as he said. He had himself devotedly removed the Imperial effigy from the cross which Napoleon had given him with his own hands, and, though this made a hole, he would not let anything be put in its place. "Sooner die," he would say, "than wear three frogs on my heart." He was fond of ridiculing Louis XVIII aloud. "The old gouty fellow with his English gaiters, let him be off to Prussia with his salsifis." It delighted him thus to combine in one imprecation the two things he hated most—England and Prussia. He went on thus till he lost his place, and then he was starving in the street with wife and children. The bishop sent for him, gave him a gentle lecturing, and appointed him beadle to the cathedral.

In nine years, through his good deeds and gentle manners, Monseigneur Welcome had filled the town of D. . . . with a sort of tender and filial veneration. Even his conduct to Napoleon had been accepted, and, as it were, tacitly pardoned, by the people, an honest, weak flock of sheep, who adored their emperor but loved their bishop.

1 2. *MONSEIGNEUR'S SOLITUDE*

THERE is nearly always round a bishop a squad of little abbés, as there is a swarm of young officers round a general. They are what that delightful St. Francis de Sales calls somewhere "sucking priests." Every career has its aspirants, who pay their respects to those who have reached the goal; there is not a power without its following, not a fortune without its court,—the seekers for a future buzz round the splendid present. Every metropolitan has his staff; every bishop who is at all influential has his patrol of Seminarist Cherubim, who go the rounds, maintain order in the episcopal palace, and mount guard round monseigneur's smile. Pleasing a bishop is a foot in the stirrup for a sub-deaconry; after all, a man must make his way, and apostles do not despise canonries.

In the same way as there are "gros bonnets," otherwise, there are large miters in the Church. They are bishops who stand well with the court, well endowed, clever, favorites of society, who doubtless know how to pray, but also how to solicit, not scrupulous about having a whole diocese waiting in their anterooms, connecting links between the sacristy and diplomacy, more abbés than priests, rather prelates than bishops. Happy the man who approaches them! As they stand in good credit, they shower around them, on the pressing and the favored, and on all the youth who know the art of pleasing, fat livings, prebendaries, arch-deaconries, chaplaincies, and cathedral appointments while waiting for episcopal dignities. While themselves advancing, they cause their satellites to progress, and it is an entire solar system moving onward. Their beams throw a purple hue over their suite, and their prosperity is showered over the actors behind the scenes in nice little bits of promotions. The larger the patron's diocese, the larger is the cure the favorite obtains. And then there is Rome. A bishop who contrives to become an arch-

48

bishop, an archbishop who manages to become a cardinal, takes you with him as a Conclavist; you enter the rota, you have the pallium, you are an auditor, a chamberlain, a monsignor, and from grandeur to eminence there is but a step, and between eminence and holiness there is only the smoke of the balloting-tickets. Every cassock can dream of the tiara. The priest is in our days the only man who can regularly become a king, and what a king! the supreme king! Hence what a hot-bed of longings is a seminary! How many blushing choristers, how many young abbés, have on their head Perrette's milk jar! how easily ambition calls itself a profession! and perhaps it does so in good faith and in self-deception, for it is so unworldly.

Monseigneur Welcome, humble, poor, and out of the world, was not counted among the large miters. This was visible in the utter absence of young priests around him. We have seen that at Paris "he did not take," and not an aspirant tried to cling to this solitary old man; not the most youthful ambition tried to flourish in his shade. His canons and vicars were good old men, walled up like him in this diocese which had no issue to the cardinal's hat, and who resembled their bishop with this difference, that they had finished while he was completed. The impossibility of growing up near Monseigneur Welcome was so well felt, that young priests whom he ordained at once obtained letters commendatory to the archbishop of Aix, of Auch, and went off at score. For, after all, we repeat, men wished to be pushed upward. A saint who lives in a state of excessive self-denial is a dangerous neighbor; he might possibly communicate to you by contagion an incurable poverty, a stiffening of the joints, useful for advancement, and, in a word, more renunciation than you care for; and such scabby virtue is shunned. Hence came the isolation of Monseigneur Bienvenu. We live in the midst of a gloomy society; success,—such is the teaching which falls drop by drop from the corruption which hangs over our heads.

Success is a very hideous thing, and its resemblance with merit deceives men. For the herd, success has nearly the same profile as supremacy. Success, that Menæchmus of talent, has a dupe in history, and Tacitus and Juvenal alone grumble at it. In our days an almost official philosophy wears the livery of success, and waits in its anteroom. Succeed, that is the theory, for prosperity presupposes capacity. Win in the lottery and you are a clever man, for he who triumphs is revered. All you want is to be born under a fortunate star. Have luck and you will have the rest, be fortunate and you will be thought a great man; leaving out five or six immense exceptions, which form the luster of an age, contemporary admiration is blear-eyed-ness. Gilding is gold, and it does you no harm to be any one so long as you go up. The mob is an old Narcissus, adoring itself and applauding the mob. That enormous faculty by which a man is a Moses, Aeschylus, Dante, Michael Angelo, or Napoleon, the multitude decrees broadcast and by acclamation to any one who attains his object, no matter in what. Let a notary transfigure himself into a deputy; a false Corneille produce Tiridates; an eunuch contrive to possess a harem; a military Prudhomme accidentally gain the decisive battle of an age; an apothecary invent cardboard soles for the army of the Sambre et Meuse, and make out of the cardboard sold for leather an income of 400,000 francs a year; a peddler espouse usury and put it to bed with seven or eight millions, of which he is the father and she the mother; a preacher become a bishop by his nasal twang; let the steward of a good family be so rich on leaving service that he is made chancellor of the exchequer— and men will call it genius, in the same way as they call Mousqueton's face beauty and Claude's muscles majesty. They confound with the constellations of profundity the stars which the duck's feet make in the soft mud of the pond.

13. *WHAT HE BELIEVED*

IT IS not our business to gauge the bishop of D. . . . from an orthodox point of view. In the presence of such a soul we only feel inclined to respect. The conscience of the just man must be believed on its word; besides, certain natures granted, we admit the possibility of the development of all the beauties of human virtue in a creed differing from our own. What did he think of this dogma or that mystery? These heartsecrets are only known to the tomb, which souls enter in a state of nudity.

THE TRANSLATOR'S PREFACE

No other merit is claimed for the following version of "Les Misérables" than the most scrupulous fidelity, and my chief anxiety has been to keep myself out of sight and give the precise meaning of every word as written by the author. This line was enforced on me by the following passage in a letter which I received from Victor Hugo:

"Permit me to ask you to adhere to the utmost fidelity in your task. My book is written to clear up and combat prejudices in France, England, and the whole world. However from the moment when M. Esquiros is your friend, as he is mine, you cannot fail to produce an excellent work, having for guide and counselor that great and noble mind."

INTRODUCTION

HERE is a novel which, immediately upon publication, achieved a prodigious success. "At the present time," Jules Janin wrote in 1862, "M. Victor Hugo and his celebrated book have monopolized the attention of all France. No one mentions anything else but *Les Misérables.*"

Three-quarters of a century have elapsed since this triumph, yet *Les Misérables* has not ceased to arouse lively discussion. The cinema has seized upon these adventures, and, on the screen, they have won the same popular success they enjoyed in book form. And the novel itself still commands a vast public.

It is interesting, therefore, to consider the causes of this enduring good fortune and to decide whether it is justified by the literary and philosophical value of the work.

I.

IT would be irrelevant, in this brief foreword, to relate the life of Victor Hugo; but, to explain the genesis of the novel, it is perhaps necessary to recall at least the essential events in his career.

Victor Hugo was born in 1802, the son of a captain (later a general) in Napoleon's army, and of Sophie Trébuchet, daughter of a bourgeois of Nantes. Through his father's family, he belonged to Lorraine and Bonapartist stock; through his mother's, to Breton and Royalist stock. From earliest childhood, he witnessed serious conflicts between his parents; at the fall of Napoleon, they parted company. The children, entrusted to their mother, were brought up in hatred of their father and of anything connected with Revolution and Empire. The education given Marius in *Les Misérables* obviously recalls that imposed upon his grandson by M. Trébuchet, of Nantes, a *bien pensant,* reactionary old man, filled with hatred for General Hugo and for the Empire. Marius's discovery of his father's heroism and his progressive aversion from his grandfather's royalism describe, with necessary transpositions, actual stages in the evolution of the author's thought.

Hugo's love of the people and his sometimes unjust tendency to hold the ruling minority responsible for all social crimes, are due, in part, to the paternal side of the family, which had known poverty. Further, his hatred of all aristocracy must have developed when, as page to Joseph Bonaparte in Spain, he was educated at Madrid, in the College of Nobles, cheek by jowl with the sons of Spanish grandees, who treated this plebeian upstart with an insulting contempt.

During his childhood, Hugo spent several years in Paris with his mother, at No. 12, Impasse des Feuillantines, a house situated in the middle of a large garden; there he and his brothers had for playmate a girl called Adèle Foucher, whom already he loved, as children love, and whom he was later to marry. Garden and idyll both found their place in *Les Misérables,* in which the couple Cosette and Marius evokes the lovers Victor Hugo and Adèle Foucher. When his mother died in 1821, Victor Hugo, still on hostile terms with his father, was unwilling to ask anything of the latter. He was forced to live, in uttermost poverty, in an attic in the Rue du Dragon. Thus he learned to know the life of the poor student in Paris, which later inspired some of the most delightful chapters in *Les Misérables.*

Official poems first brought him the support of the King and even a royal pension. It was only towards 1825 when, reconciled to his father and married to Adèle Foucher, he broke off with the classical literature favored by the Court. Four years later, he had already become the uncontested leader of the young Romantic school. From 1830 to 1845, he surpassed all the writers of his time, in the drama, in the art of the novel, and even more in poetry. Naturally so brilliant a success created both admirers and opponents. What then was the youthful conqueror's true worth?

He possessed the most amazing verbal genius. Hugo's fecundity, the perfection of his form both in verse and prose, his technical skill, have never been outdone in the whole range of French literature. The very qualities of this abundance involved certain defects. Hugo possessed neither tact nor moderation. His vanity was wondrous. "Ego Hugo," he was often pleased to write. The man considered himself a prophet, a mage "set in the centre of all things as a sonorous echo." Extremely sensual, endowed with an amorous appetite which never flagged until extreme old age, he sometimes compromised himself in rather ridiculous adventures.

But he did, also, possess grandeur and generosity. No one has spoken better than he spoke of the eternal and simple feelings upon which human societies are founded. He savored the joys of family life; he harbored love and respect of childhood; he was open to the sentiment of pity. Even in the remote days when he figured among the official poets of the restored monarchy, he outlined campaigns against certain injustices which shocked him. In the compass of his work, *Les Misérables* does not come as a sudden explosion; the great novel was foreshadowed by short studies such as *Le Dernier Jour d'un Condamné* and *Claude Gueux*. Victor Hugo entertained a deep and sincere pity for the unfortunate, because he himself had been of their number.

2.

As early as 1832, Hugo wrote:

"Civilization is nothing other than a series of successive transformations. What are you about to witness? This: the transformation of our penal system. The merciful rule of Christ shall at long last make its way into the Penal Code; it shall shine, radiant, through it. Crime will be considered a disease. . . . We shall treat in charity an evil we used to treat in anger."

This statement amounted to announcing the rehabilitation of Jean Valjean, the convict, and his salvation by Bishop Myriel.

Already Hugo had in mind a great novel dealing with the misfortunes of the masses; he considered giving it for title *Misères* or *Les Misères*. The popular novel had just come to birth. For the first time, reviews and even newspapers published *feuilletons*—fiction in successive instalments—and invented the formula: *To be continued in our next*. The master of this order of fiction was Eugène Sue; his *Mysteries of Paris,* followed by *The Wandering Jew,* held all France in breathless suspense. Victor Hugo, reading Eugène Sue, felt that he too could create such types which, drawn larger than life, captivated the popular imagination.

From 1830 to 1845, he accumulated notes destined for *Les Misères*. First, he drew up a file about a great bishop: Monseigneur de Miollis, Bishop of Digne, a veritable saint. He planned a volume to be perhaps entitled *The Bishop's Manuscript*. To this file he added notes taken on convicts in general, and, in particular, on a convict who, at Toulon, saved a drowning man's life. Hugo investigated the jade industry of Montreuil-sur-Mer, and wrote a memoir on it; in *Les Misérables,* Jean Valjean, alias Monsieur Madeleine, was to engage in precisely this industry. Finally in 1842, Hugo conceived the character of Fantine thanks to an encounter he has himself related in *Choses Vues*.

The date was January ninth . . . it was snowing . . . snowing . . . Victor Hugo saw a young man, wealthy, judging by his clothing "bend down. . . ." (*Choses Vues,* 52.)

Thus, as he came into his fortieth year and into the full force of his genius, Hugo already owned most of the elements that were to enter into the composition of his great novel. Around 1845, he began to draft it. From 1845 to 1848, *Les Misérables* was his chief task. When the Revolution of 1848 broke out, the book was almost completed. The tempest raged, politics swept off the poet to other things. In the Chamber of Peers his grandiloquent speeches had failed: the bourgeois monarchy was not made for him. He felt more comfortable exposing democratic ideas; he inclined towards a Christian socialism. After the Revolution, he entertained great hopes; he even aspired to the Presidency of the Republic. But he polled few votes. The coup d'état effected by Napoleon III threw Hugo into the opposition, and he trod the road of exile.

About 1856, at Guernsey, he turned again to the manuscript of *Les Misères,* long abandoned for works of satire and of vengeance, like *Les Chatiments* and *Napoléon le Petit.* A journey to Belgium enabled him to write his lengthy description of the Battle of Waterloo, which, in *Les Misérables,* proves to be fine writing, but is nevertheless a digression. At last, on June 30, 1861, *Les Misérables*—to give the novel its definitive title—was completed.

"I have finished *Les Misérables,*" Hugo wrote, "on the battlefield of Waterloo, in the month of Waterloo."

The year 1862 saw the triumph of the book. Before the year was out, the publishers, who had advanced Hugo six hundred thousand francs, had covered their outlay.

3.

THE theme of *Les Misérables* is pity for those to whom society refuses all hope. The convict Jean Valjean, sentenced to hard labor for stealing a loaf of bread, returns from the penitentiary, having served his time. But the horrors of prison life seem to have utterly degraded him. In the towns through which he goes, his convict's passport closes every door to him. All work is refused him. One man, Bishop Myriel, welcomes him. By grace of the love in the bishop's heart, the darkling soul that is Jean Valjean opens out once more to the powers of light.

Jean Valjean assuming a false name, becomes Monsieur Madeleine, a rich and respected industrialist, the mayor of his city. One man alone suspects his identity; Javert of the police, an honest and cruel watchdog. Monsieur Madeleine takes under his protection Fantine, a wretched, unhappy girl who, seduced and abandoned, has had to sell her body (her hair, even, and her teeth) to raise her small daughter Cosette. In saving Fantine, Mayor Madeleine incurs the enmity of Javert, the pitiless champion of social prejudice. The police official unmasks the convict and sends him back to penal servitude.

Once again, Jean Valjean escapes. He sets off in search of Cosette, Fantine's daughter; the child has been left in the care of the Thénardiers, a pair of bandits who call themselves inn-keepers. Valjean snatches her from their hands and, allowing her to believe he is her grandfather, determines to bring her up.

The reader will follow the vicissitudes of the tale across a myriad startling adventures: how Cosette meets handsome Marius . . . how she falls in love with him . . . how Javert persists in hounding Jean Valjean . . . how Jean Valjean, rising to sublimity, saves Javert . . . how the lovers prove their gratitude to the old man . . . and how the convict dies the death of a saint. . . .

The complex events in *Les Misérables,* the various flights and disguises, make of the book, by certain of their aspects, an extraordinarily adroit detective novel. There lies one of the reasons for its enduring success. Victor Hugo proved a worthy disciple of Eugène Sue. But, beyond a mere tale of adventure, Hugo wrote a poem of repentance, of the redemption of the individual, of the power of love. Jean Valjean is materially and spiritually saved by the good works of the bishop, Fantine by those of Jean Valjean. And when even Javert dies, he is touched by some obscure grace.

Christianity, in Hugo's mind, is commingled with Jacobin and revolutionary doctrines. When he shows the agreement *in extremis,* between an old revolutionary and Bishop Myriel, doubtless the give and take of the dialogue resound in Hugo's own soul.

It is easy to understand why most French readers loved a book written in praise of the masses and offering the unfortunate such high hopes of rehabilitation. These simple, gentle ideas moved the crowds of readers for the same reasons as Tolstoy's did later in Russia. But Tolstoy, an aristocrat by birth, and well-acquainted with the élite, gives us a more equitable picture of it than Hugo. It is perhaps valid to find moral greatness in a convict and in a prostitute! it is certainly naïve and quite false to imagine that moral grandeur can be found in them alone.

Lamartine, who witnessed during the Revolution of 1848 what bloody consequences followed a humanitarian optimism, showed, when the book appeared, the dangers of its political romanticism.

"The title of Victor Hugo's book is false," he wrote, "because we have not *Les Misérables,* the Wretched, here, but rather the Guilty and the Lazy, for no one is innocent and no one works in this society of thieves, of debauchees, of whores and of vagabonds. We have here the poem of vices (perhaps too harshly punished) and of the most richly merited chastisements. . . . This book in its arraignment of society should more properly be called the epic of the rabble. . . . I do not understand why Hugo makes the universal suffering of human beings the subject of bitterness, of virulent criticism, of an indictment of society. . . . He has aggravated the condition of the patient instead of con-

soling and curing it. . . . To sow the ideal and the impossible is to sow the
sacred fury of disappointment in the masses."

Lamartine was not wrong. The author of *Les Misérables* clings to a partisan
prejudice which always proves dangerous for the novelist and which was
bound to lead Hugo into obvious improbabilities. One might, at a pinch, admit
the rehabilitation of Jean Valjean; but how does it happen that *nothing whatever* of the primitive Jean Valjean remains in Monsieur Madeleine? How
could a police inspector be so stupidly obstinate as Javert? How can an ex-
convict, in an environment as mistrustful as the French provinces provide,
become mayor of his city? It would be easy to multiply such questions.

Les Misérables is a generous book, and that is a good deal; but it does not
paint, as Balzac and Stendhal do, a faithful picture of human nature. Hugo's
romantic work might, in its epic character, be more readily compared to Zola's.
But even the epic cycle of the Rougon-Macquarts would appear more realistic
than that of *Les Misérables*. There is in Hugo the novelist a theatrical side, a
need to surprise the reader by the violence of contrasts and the glitter of
dialogue. These prove to be serious faults.

4.

Such criticism must inevitably be made. Yet when all is said and done, the
fact remains that the book touches and moves us in a peculiar way.

First of all because of its literary qualities. The moment Hugo avoids prophetic declamation, he writes admirable French. Not only is he a true poet,
but an excellent prose writer as well, brought up on the classics and capable of
creating vast historical frescoes in the most vigorous style. Read in *Les
Misérables* the striking painting Victor Hugo gives of society under the
Restoration in the year 1817; read, too, the celebrated description of Waterloo.
The French language never has been moulded with greater vitality.

But especially because of its moral qualities. It is wholly true that never a
convict on land or sea resembled Jean Valjean, that never a police inspector
resembled Javert, that never a bandit resembled Thénardier, that never students
spoke as Marius and his friends speak. Yet more than one saint has resembled
Monseigneur Myriel; and it is saints rather than average humans that Victor
Hugo attempted to depict in *Les Misérables*. Now the lives of many men, as
Georges Duhamel has so ably shown in Salavin, are but a painful quest of
heroism and of sanctity. Doubtless in this quest almost all men fail; but it is
precisely because of their personal failures that they like to meet, in a noble

book, heroes who, better than they themselves, have conquered their basest passions.

There are some books whose reading debases the reader; he emerges from it the foredoomed victim of every exterior force. There are others, on the contrary, which give him greater confidence in life and in himself. *Les Misérables* belongs to the category of books which speak more to man, as Spinoza said, "of his liberty than of his slavery," and we must congratulate ourselves to-day upon seeing this deservedly illustrious novel take, on the screen and in translation, a new lease on life.

ANDRÉ MAUROIS

LES MISERABLES

VOLUME ONE

CONTENTS · VOLUME I

BOOK I—A JUST MAN

BOOK II—THE FALL

BOOK III—IN THE YEAR 1817

BOOK IV—TO CONFIDE IS SOMETIMES TO ABANDON

BOOK V—THE DESCENT

BOOK VI—JAVERT

BOOK VII—THE CHAMPMATHIEU AFFAIR

BOOK VIII—THE COUNTERSTROKE

FANTINE

BOOK I

A JUST MAN

What we are certain of is, that he never solved difficulties of faith by hypocrisy. It is impossible for the diamond to rot. He believed as much as he possibly could, and would frequently exclaim, "I believe in the Father." He also derived from his good deeds that amount of satisfaction which suffices the conscience, and which whispers to you, "You are with God."

What we think it our duty to note is that, beyond his faith, he had an excess of love. It was through this, "because he loved much," that he was considered vulnerable by "serious men," "grave persons," and "reasonable people," those favorite phrases of our melancholy world in which selfishness is under the guidance of pedantry. What was this excess of love? It was a serene benevolence, spreading over men, as we have already indicated, and on occasion extending even to things. He loved without disdain, and was indulgent to God's creation. Every man, even the best, has in him an unreflecting harshness, which he reserves for animals, but the bishop of D. . . . had not this harshness, which is, however, peculiar to many priests. He did not go so far as the Brahmin, but seemed to have meditated on the words of the ecclesiast—"Who knoweth the spirit of the beast that goeth downward to the earth?" An ugly appearance, a deformity of instinct, did not trouble him or render him indignant; he was moved, almost softened, by them. It seemed as if he thoughtfully sought, beyond apparent life, for the cause, the explanation, or the excuse. He seemed at times to ask for commutation from God. He examined without anger, and with the eye of a linguist deciphering a palimpsest, the amount of chaos which still exists in nature. This reverie at times caused strange remarks to escape from him. One morning he was in his garden and fancied himself alone; but his sister was walking behind, though unseen by him. He stopped and looked at something on the ground. It was a large, black, hairy, horrible spider. His sister heard him mutter, "Poor brute, it is not thy fault." Why should we not repeat this almost divine childishness of goodness? It may be puerile but of such were the puerilities of St. Francis d'Assisi and Marcus Aurelius. One day he sprained himself because he did not wish to crush an ant.

Such was the way in which this just man lived; at times he fell asleep in his garden, and then nothing could be more venerable. Monseigneur Welcome had been formerly, if we may believe the stories about his youth and even his manhood, a passionate, perhaps violent man. His universal mansuetude was less a natural instinct than the result of a grand conviction, which had filtered through life into his heart and slowly dropped into it thought by thought, for in a character, as in a rock, there may be waterholes. Such hollows, however, are ineffaceable, such formations indestructible. In 1815, as we think we have said, he reached his seventy-fifth year, but did not seem sixty. He was not tall, and had a tendency to stoutness, which he strove to combat by long walks; he stood firmly, and was but very slightly bent. But these are details from which we will not attempt to draw any conclusion, for Gregory XVI at the age of eighty was erect and smiling which did not prevent him being a bad bishop. Monseigneur Welcome had what people call "a fine head," which was so amiable that its beauty was forgotten. When he talked with that infantine gayety which was one of his graces, you felt at your ease by his side, and joy seemed to emanate from his whole person. His fresh, ruddy complexion, and all his white teeth, which he had preserved, and displayed when he laughed, gave him that open facile air which makes you say of a man, "He is a good fellow," and of an aged man, "He is a worthy person." That, it will be remembered, was the effect he produced on Napoleon. At the first glance, and when you saw him for the first time, he was in reality only a worthy man, but if you remained some hours in his company, and saw him in thought, he became gradually transfigured and assumed something imposing; his wide and serious brow, already august through the white hair, became also august through meditation; majesty was evolved from the goodness; though the latter did not cease to gleam, you felt the same sort of emotion as you would if you saw a smiling angel slowly unfold his wings without ceasing to smile. An inexpressible respect gradually penetrated you and ascended to your heart, and you felt that you had before you one of those powerful tried, and indulgent souls whose thoughts are so great that they cannot but be gentle.

As we have seen, prayer, celebration of the Mass, almsgiving, consoling the afflicted, tilling a patch of ground, frugality, hospitality, self-denial, confidence, study, and labor filled every day of his life. *Filled* is the exact word, and certainly the bishop's day was full of good thoughts, good words, and good actions. Still, it was not complete if cold or wet weather prevented him from spending an hour or two in the garden before going to bed after the two women had retired. It seemed as if it were a species of rite of his to prepare himself for sleep by meditation, in the presence of the grand spectacle of the heavens by night. At times, even at an advanced hour of night, if the two women were not asleep, they heard him slowly pacing the walks. He was then alone with himself, .contemplative, peaceful, adoring, comparing the serenity of his heart with that of the ether, affected in the darkness by the visible splendor of the constellations, and the invisible splendor of God, and opening his soul to thoughts which fall from the unknown. At such moments, offering up his heart at the hour when the nocturnal flowers offer up their perfumes, he could not have said himself, possibly, what was passing in his mind; but he felt something fly out of him and something descend into him.

He dreamed of the grandeur and presence of God; of future eternity, that strange mystery; of past eternity, that even stranger mystery; of all the infinities which buried themselves before his eyes in all directions: and, without seeking to comprehend the incomprehensible, he gazed at it. He did not study God; he was dazzled by Him. He considered this magnificent concourse of atoms which reveals forces, creates individualities in unity, proportions in space, innumerability in the Infinite, and through light produces beauty. Such a concourse incessantly takes place, and is dissolved again, and hence come life and death.

He would sit down on a wood bench with his back against a rickety trellis, and gaze at the stars through the stunted, sickly profiles of his fruit trees. This quarter of an acre, so poorly planted, and so encumbered with sheds and out-houses, was dear to him, and was sufficient for him. What more was wanting to this aged man, who divided the leisure of his life, which knew so little leisure, between gardening by day and contemplation by night? Was not this limited inclosure with the sky for its roof sufficient for him to be able to adore God by turns in His most delicious and sublime works? Was not this everything in fact? And what could be desired beyond? A small garden to walk about in, and immensity to dream in; at his feet, what can be cultivated and gathered; over his head, what can be studied and meditated; on the earth a few flowers, and all the stars in the heavens.

14. *WHAT HE THOUGHT*

ONE last word.

As these details might, especially at the present day, and to employ an expression which is now fashionable, give the bishop of D. . . . a certain "Pantheistic" physiognomy, and cause it to be believed, either to his praise or blame, that he had in him one of those personal philosophies peculiar to our age, which germinate sometimes in solitary minds, and grow until they take the place of religion, we must lay stress on the fact that not one of the persons who knew Monseigneur Welcome believed himself authorized in thinking anything of the sort. What enlightened this man was his heart, and his wisdom was the product of the light which emanates from it.

He had no systems, but abundance of deeds. Abstruse speculations contain vertigo, and nothing indicates that he ventured his mind amid the Apocalypses. The apostle may be bold, but the bishop must be timid. He probably refrained from going too deep into certain problems reserved to some extent for great and terrible minds. There is a sacred horror beneath the portals of the enigma; the gloomy abyss is gaping before you, but something tells you that you must not enter: woe to the man who does so. Geniuses, in the profundities of abstraction and pure speculation, being situated, so to speak, above dogmas, propose their ideas to God; their prayer audaciously offers a discussion, and their adoration interrogates. This is direct religion, full of anxiety and responsibility for the man who attempts to carry the escarpment by storm.

Human meditation has no limits; at its own risk and peril it analyzes and produces its own bedazzlement; we might almost say that, through a species of splendid reaction, it dazzles nature with it. The mysterious

54

world around us gives back what it receives, and it is probable that the contemplators are contemplated. However this may be, there are in the world men—are they men?—who distinctly perceive on the horizon of dreamland the heights of the Absolute, and have the terrible vision of the mountain of the Infinite. Monseigneur Welcome was not one of these men, for he was not a genius. He would have feared these sublimities, from which even very great men like Swedenborg and Pascal fell into insanity. Assuredly, such powerful reveries have their utility, and by these arduous routes ideal perfection is approached, but he took a short cut—the Gospel. He did not attempt to convert his chasuble into Elijah's cloak; he cast no beam of the future over the gloomy heaving of events; he did not seek to condense into flame the smoldering sparks; there was nothing of the prophet or the Magus about him. This humble soul loved, that was all.

It is probable that he expanded prayer into a superhuman aspiration; but a man can no more pray too much than he can love too much, and if it were a heresy to pray further than the text, St. Theresa and St. Jerome would be heretics. He bent down over all that groaned and all that expiated; the universe appeared to him an immense malady; he felt a fever everywhere; he heard the panting of suffering all around him, and, without trying to solve the enigma, he sought to heal the wound. The formidable spectacle of created things developed tenderness in him; he was solely engaged in finding for himself and arousing in others the best way of pitying and relieving. Existence was to this good and rare priest a permanent subject of sorrow seeking for consolation.

There are some men who toil to extract gold, but he labored to extract pity; the universal wretchedness was his mine. Sorrow all around was only an opportunity for constant kindness. "Love one another," he declared to be complete; he wished for nothing more, and that was his entire doctrine. One day the senator, who believed himself a "philosopher," said to the bishop, "Just look at the spectacle of the world; all are fighting, and the strongest man is the cleverest. Your 'love one another' is nonsense." "Well," Monseigneur Welcome replied, without discussion, "if it be nonsense, the soul must shut itself up in it like the pearl in the oyster." He consequently shut himself up in it, lived in it, was absolutely satisfied with it, leaving on one side those prodigious questions which attract and terrify, the unfathomable perspectives of the abstract, the precipices of Metaphysics, all those depths which for the apostle converge in God, for the atheist in nothingness: destiny, good and evil, the

war of being against being, human consciousness, the pensive somnambulism of the animal, transformation through death, the recapitulation of
existences which the grave contains, the incomprehensible grafting of
successive loves on the enduring Me, essence, substance, the Nil and Ens,
nature, liberty, necessity; in a word, he avoided all the gloomy precipices
over which the gigantic archangels of the human mind bend, the formidable abysses which Lucretius, Manou, St. Paul, and Dante contemplate
with that flashing eye which seems, in regarding Infinity, to make stars
sparkle in it.

Monseigneur Welcome was simply a man who accepted mysterious
questions without scrutinizing, disturbing them, or troubling his own
mind, and who had in his soul a grave respect for the shadow.

BOOK II

THE FALL

1. *THE CLOSE OF A DAY'S MARCH*

A<small>T</small> the beginning of October, 1815, and about an hour before sunset, a man travelling on foot entered the little town of D. . . . . The few inhabitants who were at the moment at their windows or doors, regarded this traveler with a species of uneasiness. It would be difficult to meet a wayfarer of more wretched appearance; he was a man of middle height, muscular and robust, and in the full vigor of life. He might be forty-six to forty-eight years of age. A cap with a leather peak partly concealed his sunburnt face, down which the perspiration streamed. His shirt of coarse yellow calico, fastened at the neck by a small silver anchor, allowed his hairy chest to be seen; he had on a neckcloth twisted like a rope, trousers of blue ticking worn and threadbare, white at one knee and torn at the other; an old gray ragged blouse, patched at one elbow with a rag of green cloth stitched with twine; on his back a large, new, well-buckled, well-filled knapsack, and a large knotty stick in his hand. His stockingless feet were thrust into iron-shod shoes, his hair was cut close, and his beard was long. Perspiration, heat, traveling on foot, and the dust added something sordid to his wretched appearance. His hair was cut close and yet was bristling, for it was beginning to grow a little, and did not seem to have been cut for some time.

No one knew him; he was evidently passing through the town. Where did he come from? The south perhaps, the sea-board, for he made his entrance into D. . . . by the same road Napoleon had driven along seven months previously when going from Cannes to Paris. The man must have been walking all day, for he seemed very tired. Some women in the old suburb at the lower part of the town had seen him halt under the trees on the Gassendi Boulevard, and drink from the fountain at the end of the walk. He must have been very thirsty, for the children that followed him saw him stop and drink again at the fountain on the market-place. On reaching the corner of the Rue Poichevert, he turned to the left and proceeded to the mayor's office. He went in, and came out again a quarter of an hour after. A gendarme was sitting on the stone bench near the door, on which General Drouot had mounted on March 4th, to read to the startled towns-folk of D. . . . the proclamation of the Gulf of Juan. The man doffed his cap and bowed humbly to the gendarme; the latter, without returning his salute, looked at him attentively, and then entered the office.

There was at that time at D. . . . a capital inn, with the sign of the Cross of Colbas. This inn was kept by a certain Jacquin Labarre, a man highly respected in the town for his relationship to another Labarre, who kept the Three Dauphins at Grenoble, and had served in the Guides. When the emperor landed, many rumors were current in the country about the Three Dauphins; it was said that General Bertrand, in the disguise of a wagoner, had stopped there several times in the month of January, and distributed crosses of honor to the soldiers and handfuls of napoleons to the towns-people. The fact was that the emperor, on entering Grenoble, refused to take up his quarters at the prefecture; he thanked the mayor, and said, "I am going to a worthy man whom I know," and he went to the Three Dauphins. The glory of the Grenoble Labarre was reflected for a distance of five-and-twenty leagues on the Labarre of the Cross of Colbas. The towns-people said of him, "He is cousin to the one at Grenoble."

The man proceeded to this inn, which was the best in the town, and entered the kitchen, the door of which opened on the street. All the ranges were lighted, and a large fire blazed cheerily in the chimney. The host, who was at the same time head-cook, went from the hearth to the stew-pans, very busy in attending to a dinner intended for the carriers, who could be heard laughing and talking noisily in an adjoining room. Any one who has traveled knows that no people feed so well as carriers. A fat marmot, flanked by white-legged partridges and grouse, was turning on a long spit before the fire, while two large carp from lake Lauzet and trout from lake Alloz were bubbling on the stove. The landlord, on hearing the door open and a stranger enter, said, without raising his eyes from the stew-pans:

"What do you want, sir?"

"Supper and a bed," the man replied.

"Nothing easier," said mine host. At this moment he looked up, took in the stranger's appearance at a glance, and added, "For payment."

The man drew a heavy leathern purse from the pocket of his blouse, and replied:

"I have money."

"In that case I am at your service," said the host.

The man returned the purse to his pocket, took off his knapsack, placed it on the ground near the door, kept his stick in his hand, and sat down on a low stool near the fire. D. . . . is in the mountains, and the evenings there are cold in October. While going backward and forward, the landlord still inspected his guest.

"Will supper be ready soon?" the man asked.

"Directly."

While the new-comer had his back turned to warm himself, the worthy landlord took a pencil from his pocket, and then tore off the corner of an old newspaper which lay on a small table near the window. On the white margin he wrote a line or two, folded up the paper, and handed it to a lad who seemed to serve both as turnspit and page. The landlord whispered a word in the boy's ear, and he ran off in the direction of the mayor's house. The traveler had seen nothing of this, and he asked again whether supper would be ready soon. The boy came back with the paper in his hand, and the landlord eagerly unfolded it, like a man who is expecting an answer. He read it carefully, then shook his head, and remained thoughtful for a moment. At last he walked up to the traveler, who seemed plunged in anything but a pleasant reverie.

"I cannot make room for you, sir," he said.

The man half turned on his stool.

"What do you mean? Are you afraid I shall not pay? Do you want me to pay in advance? I have money, I tell you."

"It is not that."

"What is it, then?"

"You have money."

"Yes," said the man.

"But I have not a spare bedroom."

The man continued quietly: "Put me in the stables."

"I cannot."

"Why?"

"The horses take up all the room."

"Well," the man continued, "a corner in the loft and a truss of straw; we will see to that after supper."

"I cannot give you any supper."

This declaration, made in a measured but firm tone, seemed to the stranger serious. He rose.

"Nonsense, I am dying of hunger. I have been on my legs since sunrise, and have walked twelve leagues. I can pay, and demand food."

"I have none," said the landlord.

The man burst into a laugh, and turned to the chimney and the range.

"Nothing! why, what is all this?"

"All this is ordered."

"By whom?"

"By the carriers."

"How many are there of them?"

"Twelve."

"There is enough food here for twenty."

The man sat down again, and said, without raising his voice:

"I am at an inn, I am hungry, and so shall remain."

The landlord then stooped down, and whispered with an accent which made him start, "Be off with you."

The stranger at this moment was thrusting some logs into the fire with the ferrule of his stick, but he turned quickly, and as he was opening his mouth to reply, the landlord continued in the same low voice: "Come, enough of this. Do you wish me to tell you your name? It is Jean Valjean. Now, do you wish me to tell you who you are? On seeing you come in, I suspected something; so I sent to the police office, and this is the answer I received. Can you read?"

While saying this, he handed the stranger the paper which had traveled from the inn to the office and back again. The man took a glance at it, and mine host continued, after a moment's silence:

"I am accustomed to be polite with everybody. Be off!"

The man stooped, picked up his knapsack, and went off. He walked along the high street hap-hazard, keeping close to the houses like a sad and humiliated man. He did not look back once; had he done so, he would have seen the landlord of the Cross of Colbas in his doorway, surrounded by all his guests and the passers-by, talking eagerly and pointing to him; and, judging from the looks of suspicion and terror, he might have guessed that ere long his arrival would be the event of the whole town. He saw nothing of all this, for men who are oppressed do not look back, as they know only too well that an evil destiny is following them.

He walked on thus for a long time, turning down streets he did not know, and forgetting his fatigue, as happens in sorrow. All at once he was sharply assailed by hunger; night was approaching, and he looked round to see whether he could not discover a shelter. The best inn was closed against him, and he sought some very humble pot-house, some wretched den. At this moment a lamp was lit at the end of the street, and a fir-branch hanging from an iron bar stood out in the white twilight sky. He went toward it; it was really a pot-house, the pot-house in the Rue Chaffaut. The stranger stopped for a moment and looked through the window into the low tap-room, which was lighted by a small lamp on the table and a large fire on the hearth. Some men were drinking, and the landlord was warming himself; over the flames bubbled a caldron hanging from an iron crane. This pot-house, which is also a sort of inn, has two entrances, one on the street, the other opening on a small yard of manure. The traveler did not dare enter by the street door; he slipped into the yard, stopped once again, and then timidly raised the latch and pushed open the door.

"Who's there?" the landlord asked.

"Some one who wants a supper and bed."

"Very good. They are to be had here."

He went in, and all the topers turned to look at him; they examined him for some time while he was taking off his knapsack. Said the landlord to him, "Here is a fire; supper is boiling in the pot; come and warm yourself, comrade."

He sat down in the ingle and stretched out his feet, which were swollen with fatigue. A pleasant smell issued from the caldron. All that could be distinguished of his face, under his cap-peak, assumed a vague appearance of comfort blended with the other wretched appearance which the habit of suffering produces. It was, moreover, a firm, energetic and sad profile; the face was strangely composed, for it began by appearing humble, and ended by becoming severe. His eyes gleamed under his brows, like a fire through brushwood. One of the men seated at the table was a fishmonger, who, before entering the pot-house, had gone to put up his horse in Labarre's stables. Accident willed it, that on the same morning he had met this ill-looking stranger walking between Bras d'Asse and . . . . (I have forgotten the name, but I fancy it is Escoublon). Now, on meeting him, the man, who appeared very fatigued, had asked him to give him a lift, which had only made the fishmonger go the faster. This fishmonger had been half an hour previously one of the party surrounding Jacquin Labarre, and had told his unpleasant encounter in the morning to the people at the Cross of Colbas. He made an imperceptible sign to the landlord from his seat, and the latter went up to him and they exchanged a few whispered words. The man had fallen back into his reverie.

The landlord went up to the chimney, laid his hand sharply on the man's shoulder and said to him:

"You must be off from here."

The stranger turned and replied gently, "Ah, you know?"

"Yes."

"I was turned out of the other inn."

"And so you will be out of this."

"Where would you have me go?"

"Somewhere else."

The man took his knapsack and stick and went away. As he stepped out, some boys who had followed him from the Cross of Colbas, and seemed to have been waiting for him, threw stones at him. He turned savagely, and threatened them with his stick, and the boys dispersed like a flock of birds. He passed in front of the prison, and pulled the iron bell-handle; a wicket was opened.

"Mr. Turnkey," he said, as he humbly doffed his cap, "would you be kind enough to open the door and give me a night's lodging?"

A voice answered, "A prison is not an inn; get yourself arrested and then I will open the door."

The man entered a small street in which there are numerous gardens; some of them, being merely inclosed with hedges, enliven the street. Among these gardens and hedges he saw a two-storied house, whose window was illuminated, and he looked through the panes as he had done at the pot-house. It was a large whitewashed room, with a bed with printed chintz curtains, and a cradle in a corner, a few chairs, and a double-barreled gun hanging on the wall. A table was laid for supper in the middle of the room; a copper lamp lit up the coarse white cloth, the tin mug glistening like silver and full of wine, and the brown smoking soup-tureen. At this table was seated a man about forty years of age, with a hearty, open face, who was riding a child on his knee. By his side a woman, still young, was suckling another child. The father was laughing, the children were laughing, and the mother was smiling. The stranger stood for a moment pensively before this gentle and calming spectacle. What was going on within him? It would be impossible to say, but it is probable that he thought that this joyous house would prove hospitable, and that where he saw so much happiness he might find a little pity. He tapped very slightly on a window-pane, but was not heard; he tapped a second time, and he heard the woman say, "Husband, I fancy I can hear some one knocking."

"No," the husband answered.

He tapped a third time. The husband rose, took the lamp, and walked to the front door. He was a tall man, half peasant, half artisan; he wore a huge, leathern apron, which came up to his left shoulder, and in it he carried a hammer, a red handkerchief, a powder-flask, and all sorts of things, which his belt held as in a pocket. As he threw back his head, his turned-down shirt-collar displayed his bull neck, white and bare. He had thick eyebrows, enormous black whiskers, eyes flush with his head, a bull-dog lower jaw, and over all this that air of being at home which is inexpressible.

"I beg your pardon," the traveler said, "but would you, for payment, give me a plateful of soup and a corner to sleep in in your garden out-house?"

"Who are you?" the owner of the cottage asked.

The man answered, "I have come from Puy Moisson; I have walked the whole day. Could you do it?—for payment, of course?"

"I would not refuse," the peasant answered, "to lodge any respectable person who paid. But why do you not go to the inn?"

"There is no room there."

"Nonsense! that is impossible; it is neither market nor fair day. Have you been to Labarre's?"

"Yes."

"Well?"

The traveler continued, with some hesitation, "I do not know why, but he refused to take me in."

"Have you been to what is his name in the Rue de Chaffaut?"

The stranger's embarrassment increased; he stammered, "He would not take me either."

The peasant's face assumed a suspicious look, he surveyed the new-comer from head to foot, and all at once exclaimed, with a sort of shudder:

"Can you be the man?"

He took another look at the stranger, placed the lamp on the table, and took down his gun. On hearing the peasant say, "Can you be the man?"

65

his wife had risen, taken her two children in her arms, and hurriedly sought refuge behind her husband, and looked in horror at the stranger as she muttered: *"Tso-maraude!"* (The villain.) All this took place in less time than is needed to imagine it. After examining the man for some minutes as if he had been a viper, the peasant returned to the door and said, "Be off!"

"For mercy's sake," the man continued, "a glass of water."

"A charge of shot!" the peasant said.

Then he violently closed the door, and the stranger heard two bolts fastened. A moment after the window shutters were closed, and the sound of the iron bar being put in reached his ear. Night was coming on apace; the cold wind of the Alps was blowing. By the light of the expiring day the stranger noticed in one of the gardens a sort of hut which seemed to him to be made of sods of turf. He boldly clambered over a railing and found himself in the garden; he approached the hut, which had as entrance a narrow, extremely low door, and resembled the tenements which road-menders construct by the side of the highway. He doubtless thought it was such; he was suffering from cold and hunger, and though he had made up his mind to starve, it was at any rate a shelter against the cold. As this sort of residence is not usually occupied at night, he lay down on his stomach and crawled into the hut; it was warm, and he found a rather good straw litter in it. He lay for a moment motionless on this bed as his fatigue was so great; but as his knapsack hurt his back and was a ready-made pillow, he began unbuckling one of the thongs. At this moment a hoarse growl was audible; he raised his eyes, and the head of an enormous mastiff stood out in the shadow at the opening of the hut, which was its kennel. The dog itself was strong and formidable, hence he raised his stick, employed his knapsack as a shield, and left the kennel as he best could, though not without enlarging the rents in his rags.

He also left the garden, but backward, and compelled to twirl his stick in order to keep the dog at a respectful distance. When he, not without difficulty, had leapt the fence again, and found himself once more in the street alone, without a bed, roof, or shelter, and expelled even from the bed of straw and the kennel, he fell rather than sat on a stone, and a passer-by heard him exclaim, "I am not even a dog." He soon rose and recommenced his walk. He left the town hoping to find some tree or mill in the fields which would afford him shelter. He walked on thus for some time with hanging head; when he found himself far from all human habitations, he raised his eyes and looked around him. He was in a field, and had in front of him one of those low hills, with close-cut stubble, which after harvest resemble cropped heads. The horizon was perfectly black, but it was not solely the gloom of night, but low clouds, which seemed to be resting on the hill itself, rose and filled the whole sky. Still, as the moon was about to rise shortly, and a remnant of twilight still hovered in the zenith, these clouds formed a species of whitish vault whence a gleam of light was thrown on the earth.

The ground was, therefore, more illumined than the sky, which produces a peculiarly sinister effect, and the hill with its poor and weak outlines stood out vaguely and dully on the gloomy horizon. The whole scene was hideous, mean, mournful, and confined; there was nothing in the field or on the hill but a stunted tree, which writhed and trembled a few yards from the traveler. This man was evidently far from possessing those delicate habits of mind which render persons sensible of the mysterious aspects of things, still there was in the sky, this hill, this plain, and this tree, something so profoundly desolate, that after standing motionless and thoughtful for a while he suddenly turned back. There are instants in which nature seems to be hostile.

He went back and found the gates of the town closed. D. . . . , which sustained sieges in the religious wars, was still begirt in 1815 by old walls flanked by square towers, which have since been demolished. He passed through a breach, and re-entered the town. It might be about eight o'clock in the evening, and as he did not know the streets he wandered about without purpose. He thus reached the prefecture and then the seminary; on passing through the Cathedral Square he shook his fist at the church. There is at the corner of this square a printing-office, where the proclamations of the emperor and the imperial guard to the army, brought from Elba, and dictated by Napoleon himself, were first printed. Worn out with fatigue, and hopeless, he lay down on the stone bench at the door of this printing-office. An old woman who was leaving the church at the moment saw the man stretched out in the darkness.

"What are you doing there, my friend?" she said.

He answered harshly and savagely, "You can see, my good woman, that I am going to sleep."

The good woman, who was really worthy of the name, was the Marchioness de R. . . . .

"On that bench?" she continued.

"I have had for nineteen years a wooden mattress," the man said, "and now I have a stone one."

"Have you been a soldier?"

"Yes, my good woman."

"Why do you not go to the inn?"

"Because I have no money."

"Alas!" said Madame de R. . . . , "I have only two-pence in my purse."

"You can give them to me, all the same."

The man took the money, and Madame de R. . . . continued, "You cannot lodge at an inn for so small a sum; still, you should make the attempt, for you cannot possibly spend the night here. Doubtless, you are cold and hungry, and some one might take you in for charity."

"I have knocked at every door."

"Well?"

"And was turned away at all."

The "good woman" touched the man's arm and pointed to a small house next to the bishop's palace.

"You have," she continued, "knocked at every door. Have you done so there?"

"No."

"Then do it."

2. PRUDENCE RECOMMENDED TO WISDOM

ON this evening, the bishop of D. . . . , after his walk in the town, had remained in his bedroom till a late hour. He was engaged on a heavy work on the "duties," which he unfortunately had left incomplete. He carefully analyzed all that the Fathers and Doctors have said on this grave matter. The book was divided into two parts,— first, the duties of all; secondly, the duties of each, according to the classes to which they belonged. The duties of all are the "great duties," four in number. They are indicated by St. Matthew,—duty toward God (Matthew vi.); duty to one's self (Matthew v., 29, 30); duty to one's neighbor, (Matthew vii., 42), and duty to God's creatures (Matthew vi., 20, 25). As regards the other duties, the bishop found them indicated and prescribed elsewhere: to sovereigns and subjects, in the Epistle to the Romans; to magistrates, wives, mothers, and young men, by St. Peter; to husbands, fathers, children, and servants, in the Epistle to the Ephesians; to the faithful, in the Epistle to the Hebrews; to virgins, in the Epistle to the Corinthians. He laboriously made from all these teachings a harmonious whole which he wished to present to souls.

He was still working at eight o'clock, writing rather uncomfortably on small squares of paper, with a large book open on his knees, when Madame Magloire came in as usual to fetch the plate from the wall cupboard near the bed. A moment after, the bishop, feeling that supper was ready and that his sister might be waiting, closed his book, rose from the table, and walked into the dining-room. It was an oblong apartment, as we have said, with a door opening on the street, and a window looking on the garden. Madame Magloire had laid the table, and while attending to her duties was chatting with Mlle. Baptistine. A lamp was on the table, which was close to the fire-place, in which a tolerable fire was lighted.

We can easily figure to ourselves the two women, who had both passed their sixtieth year: Madame Magloire, short, stout, and quick; Mlle. Baptistine, gentle, thin, and frail, somewhat taller than her brother, dressed in a puce-colored silk gown, the fashionable color in 1806, which she had bought in Paris in that year, and which still held out, to borrow common terms which have the merit of saying by a single word an idea which a page would scarcely suffice to express. Madame Magloire had the air of a peasant, Mademoiselle of a lady. Madame Magloire wore a white fluted cap, at her neck a gold *jeannette,* the only piece of feminine jewelry in the house, a very white handkerchief emerging from a black stuff gown with wide and short sleeves, a red and puce checked calico apron, fastened round the waist with a green ribbon, with a stomacher of the same stuff fastened with two pins at the top corners, heavy shoes and yellow stockings, like the Marseilles women. Mlle. Baptistine's gown was cut after the fashion of 1806, short-waisted, with epaulettes on the sleeves, flaps and buttons, and she concealed her gray hair by a curling front called *à l'enfant.* Madame Magloire had an intelligent, quick, and kindly air, though the unevenly raised corners of her mouth and the upper lip, thicker than the lower, gave her a somewhat rough and imperious air. So long as monseigneur was silent, she spoke to him boldly with a mingled respect and liberty, but so soon as he spoke she passively obeyed, like mademoiselle, who no longer replied, but restricted herself to obeying and enduring. Even when she was young the latter was not pretty; she had large blue eyes flush with her face, and a long peaked nose; but all her face, all her person, as we said at the outset, breathed ineffable kindness. She had always been predestined to gentleness, but Faith, Hope, and Charity, those three virtues that softly warm the soul, had gradually elevated that gentleness to sanctity. Nature had only made her a lamb, and religion had made her an angel. Poor holy woman! Sweet vanished reminiscence.

Mademoiselle afterward narrated so many times what took place at the bishopric on this evening that several persons still living remember the slightest details. At the moment when the bishop entered, Madame Magloire was talking with some vivacity; she was conversing with mademoiselle on a subject that was familiar to her, and to which the bishop was accustomed—it was the matter of the front door latch. It appears that while going to purchase something for supper, Madame Magloire had heard things spoken of in certain quarters; people were talking of an ill-looking prowler, that a suspicious vagabond had arrived, who must be somewhere in the town, and that it would possibly be an unpleasant thing, for any one who took a fancy to come home late, to meet him. The police were very badly managed because the prefect and the mayor were not friendly, and tried to injure each other by allowing things to happen. Hence wise people would be their own police, and be careful to close with bolt and bar their houses, *and lock their doors.*

Madame Magloire italicized the last clause, but the bishop had come from his room, where it was rather cold, and was warming himself at the fire while thinking of other matters; in fact, he did not pick up the words which Madame Magloire had just let drop. She repeated them, and then mademoiselle, who wished to satisfy Madame Magloire without displeasing her brother, ventured to say timidly:

"Brother, do you hear what Madame Magloire is saying?"

"I vaguely heard something," the bishop answered; then he half turned his chair, placed his hand on his knees, and looked up at the old servant with his cordial and easily pleased face, which the fire illumined from below: "Well, what is it? what is it? are we in any great danger?"

Then Madame Magloire told her story over again, while exaggerating it slightly, though unsuspicious of the fact. It would seem that a gypsy, a barefooted fellow, a sort of dangerous beggar, was in town at the moment. He had tried to get a lodging at Jacquin Labarre's, who had refused to take him in. He had been seen prowling about the streets at nightfall, and was evidently a gallows-bird, with his frightful face.

"Is he really?" said the bishop.

This cross-questioning encouraged Madame Magloire; it seemed to indicate that the bishop was beginning to grow alarmed, and hence she continued triumphantly:

"Yes, monseigneur, it is so, and some misfortune will occur in the town this night; everybody says so, and then the police are so badly managed [useful repetition]! Fancy living in a mountain town, and not even having lanterns in the streets at night! You go out and find yourself in pitch darkness. I say, monseigneur, and mademoiselle says—"

"I," the sister interrupted, "say nothing; whatever my brother does is right."

Madame Magloire continued, as if no protest had been made:

"We say that this house is not at all safe, and that if monseigneur permits, I will go to Paulin Musebois, the locksmith, and tell him to put the old bolts on the door again; I have them by me, and it will not take a minute; and I say, monseigneur, that we ought to have bolts if it were only for this night, for I say that a door which can be opened from the outside by the first passer-by is most terrible; besides, monseigneur is always accustomed to say 'Come in,' and in the middle of the night, oh my gracious! there is no occasion to ask permission."

At this moment there was a rather loud rap at the front door.

"Come in." said the bishop.

3 · THE HEROISM OF PASSIVE OBEDIENCE

THE door was thrown open wide, as if some one were pushing it energetically and resolutely. A man entered whom we already know; it was the traveler whom we saw just now wandering about in search of a shelter. He entered and stopped, leaving the door open behind him. He had his knapsack on his shoulder, his stick in his hand, and a rough, bold, wearied, and violent expression in his eyes. The firelight fell on him,—he was hideous; it was a sinister apparition.

Madame Magloire had not even the strength to utter a cry; she shivered and stood with widely open mouth. Mlle. Baptistine turned, perceived the man who entered, and half started up in terror; then, gradually turning her head to the chimney, she began looking at her brother, and her face became again calm and serene. The bishop fixed a quiet eye on the man. As he opened his mouth, doubtless to ask the new-comer what he wanted, the man leaned both hands on his stick, looked in turn at the two aged women and the old man, and, not waiting for the bishop to speak, said in a loud voice:

"Look here! my name is Jean Valjean. I am a galley-slave, and have spent nineteen years in the bagne. I was liberated four days ago, and started for Pontarlier, which is my destination. I have been walking for four days since I left Toulon, and to-day I have marched twelve leagues. This evening on coming into the town I went to the inn, but was sent away in consequence of my yellow passport, which I had shown at the police office. I went to another inn, and the landlord said to me, 'Be off.' It was the same everywhere, and no one would have any dealings with me. I went to the prison, but the jailer would not take me in. I got into a dog's kennel, but the dog bit me and drove me off, as if it had been a man; it seemed to know who I was. I went into the fields to sleep in the star-light, but there were no stars. I thought it would rain, and as there was no God to prevent it from raining, I came back to town to find shelter in a doorway. I was lying down on a stone in the square, when a good woman pointed to your house, and said, 'Go and knock there.' What sort of a house is this? do you keep an inn? I have money, one hundred and nine francs fifteen sous, which I earned at the bagne by my nineteen years' toil. I will pay. What do I care? I have money! I am very tired—twelve leagues on foot—and frightfully hungry; will you let me stay here?"

"Madame Magloire," said the bishop, "you will lay another knife and fork."

The man advanced three paces, and approached the lamp which was on the table. "Wait a minute," he continued, as if he had not comprehended, "that will not do. Did you not hear me say that I was a galley-slave, a convict, and have just come from the bagne?" He took from his pocket a large yellow paper, which he unfolded. "Here is my passport, yellow, as you see, which turns me out wherever I go. Will you read it? I can read it, for I learned to do so at the bagne, where there is a school for those who like to attend it. This is what is written in my passport: 'Jean Valjean, a liberated convict, native of'—but that does not concern you—'has remained nineteen years at the galleys. Five years for robbery with house-breaking, fourteen years for having tried to escape four times. The man is very dangerous.' All the world has turned me out, and are you willing to receive me? is this an inn? will you give me some food and a bed? have you a stable?"

"Madame Magloire," said the bishop, "you will put clean sheets on the bed in the alcove."

We have already explained of what nature was the obedience of the two women. Madame Magloire left the room to carry out the orders. The bishop turned to the man.

"Sit down and warm yourself, sir. We shall sup directly, and your bed will be got ready while we are supping."

The man understood this at once. The expression of his face, which had hitherto been gloomy and harsh, was marked with stupefaction, joy, doubt, and became extraordinary. He began stammering like a lunatic.

"Is it true? what? You will let me stay; you will not turn me out, a convict? You call me *Sir;* you do not 'thou' me. 'Get out, dog,' that is what is always said to me; I really believed you would turn me out, and hence told you at once who I am! Oh, what a worthy woman she was who sent me here! I shall have supper, a bed with mattresses and sheets, like everybody else! A bed! For nineteen years I have not slept in a bed! You really mean that I am to stay. You are worthy people; besides, I have money and will pay handsomely. By the way, what is your name, Mr. Landlord? I will pay anything you please, for you are a worthy man. You keep an inn, do you not?"

"I am," said the bishop, "a priest, living in this house."

"A priest!" the man continued. "Oh! what a worthy priest! I suppose you will not ask me for money. The curé, I suppose, the curé of that big church? Oh, yes, what an ass I am; I did not notice your cassock."

While speaking, he deposited his knapsack and stick in a corner, returned his passport to his pocket, and sat down. While Mlle. Baptistine regarded him gently, he went on:

"You are humane, sir, and do not feel contempt. A good priest is very good. Then you do not want me to pay?"

"No," said the bishop, "keep your money. How much have you? Didn't you say a hundred and nine francs?"

"And fifteen sous," added the man.

"A hundred and nine francs fifteen sous. How long did you take in earning them?"

"Nineteen years."

"Nineteen years!" The bishop gave a deep sigh.

The man went on, "I have all my money still; in four days I have only spent twenty-five sous, which I earned by helping to unload carts at Grasse. As you are an abbé I will tell you: we had a chaplain at the bagne, and one day I saw a bishop. They called him Monseigneur. It was the bishop of Majore, at Marseilles. He is the curé over the curés, you know— but pardon me, that's wrong, and, for us, it is so far away, you understand, us convicts. He said mass in the middle of the bagne at an altar, and had a pointed gold thing on his head, which glistened in the bright sunshine; we were drawn up on three sides of a square, with cannons and lighted matches facing us. He spoke, but was too far off, and we did not hear him. That is what a bishop is."

While speaking the bishop had gone to close the door, which had been left open. Madame Magloire came in, bringing a silver spoon and fork, which she placed on the table.

"Madame Magloire," said the bishop, "lay them as near as you can to the fire." And turning to his guest, he said, "The night breeze is sharp on the Alps, and you must be cold, sir."

Each time he said the word *Sir,* with his gentle, grave voice, the man's face was illumined. *Sir* to a convict is the glass of water to the ship-wrecked sailor of the *Medusa.* Ignominy thirsts for respect.

"This lamp gives a very bad light," the bishop continued. Madame Magloire understood, and fetched from the chimney of monseigneur's bedroom the two silver candlesticks, which she placed on the table ready lighted.

"Monsieur le Curé," said the man, "you are good, and do not despise me. You receive me as a friend and light your wax candles for me, and yet I have not hidden from you whence I come, and that I am an unfortunate fellow."

The bishop, who was seated by his side, gently touched his hand. "You need not have told me who you were; this is not my house, but the house of Christ. This door does not ask a man who enters whether he has a name, but if he has sorrow; you are suffering, you are hungry and thirsty, and so be welcome. And do not thank me, or say that I am receiving you in my house, for no one is at home here excepting the man who has need of an asylum. I tell you, who are a passer-by, that you are more at home here than I am myself, and all there is here is yours. Why do I want to know your name? besides, before you told it to me you had one which I knew."

The man opened his eyes in amazement.

"Is it true? you know my name?"

"Yes," the bishop answered, "you are my brother."

"Monsieur le Curé," the man exclaimed, "I was very hungry when I came in, but you are so kind that I do not know at present what ails me; it has passed away."

The bishop looked at him and said:

"You have suffered greatly?"

"Oh! the red jacket, the cannon-ball on your foot, a plank to sleep on, heat, cold, labor, the gang-work, the blows, the double chain for nothing, a dungeon for a word, even when you are ill in bed, and the chain-gang. The very dogs are happier. Nineteen years, and now I am forty-six; and at present the yellow passport! Here it is!"

"Yes," said the bishop, "you have come from a place of sorrow. Listen to me; there will be more joy in heaven over the tearful face of a repentant sinner than over the white robes of one hundred just men. If you leave that mournful place with thoughts of hatred and anger against your fellow-men, you are worthy of pity; if you leave it with thoughts of kindliness, gentleness, and peace, you are worth more than any of us."

In the meanwhile Madame Magloire had served the soup; it was made of water, oil, bread, and salt, and a little bacon, and the rest of the supper consisted of a piece of mutton, figs, a fresh cheese, and a loaf of rye bread. She had herself added a bottle of old Mauves wine. The bishop's face suddenly assumed the expression of gayety peculiar to hospitable natures. "To table," he said eagerly, as he was wont to do when any stranger supped with him; and he bade the man sit down on his right hand, while Mlle. Baptistine, perfectly peaceful and natural, took her seat on his left. The bishop said grace, and then served the soup himself, according to his wont. The man began eating greedily. All at once the bishop said:

"It strikes me that there is something wanting on the table."

Madame Magloire, truth to tell, had only laid the absolutely necessary silver. Now it was the custom in this house, when the bishop had any one to supper, to arrange the whole stock of plate on the table, as an innocent display. This graceful semblance of luxury was a species of childishness full of charm in this gentle and strict house, which elevated poverty to dignity. Madame Magloire took the hint, went out without a word, and a moment after the remaining spoons and forks glittered on the cloth, symmetrically arranged before each of the guests.

4. *DETAILS OF CHEESE-MAKING AT PONTARLIER*

AND now, in order to give an idea of what took place at table we cannot do better than transcribe a passage of a letter written by Mlle. Baptistine to Madame Boischevron, in which the conversation between the convict and the bishop is recorded with simple minuteness:

The man paid no attention to any one; he ate with frightful voracity, but after the soup he said:

"Monsieur le Curé, all this is much too good for me, but I am bound to say that the carriers who would not let me sup with them have better cheer than you."

Between ourselves, this remark slightly offended me, but my brother answered:

"They are harder worked than I am."

"No," the man continued, "they have more money. You are poor, as I can plainly see; perhaps you are not even a curé. Ah, if Heaven were just, you ought to be a curé."

"Heaven is more than just," said my brother. A moment after he added:

"Monsieur Jean Valjean, I think you said you were going to Pontarlier?"

"I am compelled to go there." Then he continued, "I must be off by sunrise to-morrow morning; it is a tough journey, for if the nights are cold, the days are hot."

"You are going to an excellent part of the country," my brother resumed. "When the Revolution ruined my family, I sought shelter first in Franche Comté, and lived there for some time by the labor of my arms. I had a good will, and found plenty to do. One need only choose. There are paper-mills, tanneries, distilleries, oil-mills, wholesale manufactories of clocks, steel-works, copper-works, and at least twenty iron-foundries, of which the four at Lods, Châtillon, Audincourt, and Beure are very large."

I am pretty sure I am not mistaken, and that they are the names my brother mentioned; then he broke off and addressed me:

"My dear sister, have we not some relatives in those parts?"

My answer was, "We used to have some; among others Monsieur de Lucenet, who was captain of the gates at Pontarlier, under the ancient régime."

"Yes," my brother continued, "but in '93 people had no relatives but only their arms, and so I worked. In the country where you are going, Monsieur Valjean, there is a truly patriarchal and pleasing trade. My dear sister, I mean their cheese manufactories, which they call fruitières."

Then my brother, while pressing this man to eat, explained in their fullest details the fruitières of Pontarlier which were divided into two classes— the large farms, which belong to the rich, and where there are *forty or fifty cows, which produce seven to eight thousand cheeses in the summer, and the partnership* fruitières, *which belong to the poor. The peasants of the central mountain district keep their cows in common and divide the produce. They hire a cheesemaker, who is called the* grurin; *he receives the milk from the partners thrice a day, and enters the quantities in a book. The cheese-making begins about the middle of April, and the dairy farmers lead their cows to the mountains toward mid-summer.*

The man grew animated while eating, and my brother made him drink that excellent Mauves wine, which he does not drink himself because he says that it is expensive. My brother gave him all these details with that easy gayety of his which you know, mingling his remarks with graceful appeals to myself. He dwelt a good deal on the comfortable position of the grurin, *as if wishful that this man should understand, without advising him directly and harshly, that it would be a refuge for him. One thing struck me: the man was as I have described him to you; well, my brother, during the whole of supper and, indeed, of the evening, did not, with the exception of some words about the Saviour, when he entered, utter a word which could remind this man of what he was, or tell him who my brother was. It was apparently a good opportunity to give him a little lecture, and let the bishop produce a good effect on the galley-slave. It might have seemed to any one else that, having this wretched man in hand, it would be right to feed his mind at the same time as his body, and address to him some reproaches seasoned with morality and advice, or at any rate a little commiseration, with an exhortation to behave better in the future. My brother did not even ask him where he came from, or his history, for his fault is contained in his history, and my brother appeared to avoid everything which might call it to his mind. This was carried to such a point that at a certain moment, when my brother was talking about the mountaineers of Pontarlier, "who had a pleasant task near heaven," and who, he added, "are happy because they are innocent," he stopped short, fearing lest there might be in the remark something that might unpleasantly affect this man. After considerable reflection, I believe I can understand what was going on in my brother's heart; he doubtless thought that this Jean Valjean had his misery ever present to his mind, that the best thing was to distract his attention, and make him believe, were it only momentarily, that he was a man like the rest, by behaving to him as he would to others. Was not this really charity! Is there not, my dear lady, something truly evangeli-*

cal in this delicacy, which abstains from all lecturing and allusions, and is it not the best pity, when a man has a sore point, not to touch it at all? It seemed to me that this might be my brother's innermost thought; in any case, what I can safely say is that if he had all these ideas, he did not let any of them be visible, even to me; he was from beginning to end the same man he is every night, and he supped with Jean Valjean with the same air and in the same way as if he had been supping with M. Gédéon le Prevôt, or with the parish curé.

Toward the end, when we had come to the figs, there was a knock at the door. It was Mother Gerbaud with her little baby in her arms. My brother kissed the child's forehead and borrowed from me fifteen sous, which I happened to have about me, to give them to the mother. The man, while this was going on, did not seem to pay great attention; he said nothing, and seemed very tired. When poor old Mother Gerbaud left, my brother said grace, and then said to this man, "You must need your bed." Madame Magloire hastily removed the plate. I understood that we must retire in order to let this traveler sleep, and we both went upstairs. I, however, sent Madame Magloire to lay on the man's bed a roebuck's hide, from the Black Forest, which was in my room, for the nights are very cold, and that keeps you warm. It is a pity that this skin is old and the hair is wearing off. My brother bought it when he was in Germany, at Tottlingen, near the source of the Danube, as well as the small ivory-handled knife which I use at meals.

Madame Magloire came up again almost immediately. We said our prayers in the room where the clothes are hung up to dry, and then retired to our bedrooms without saying a word to each other.

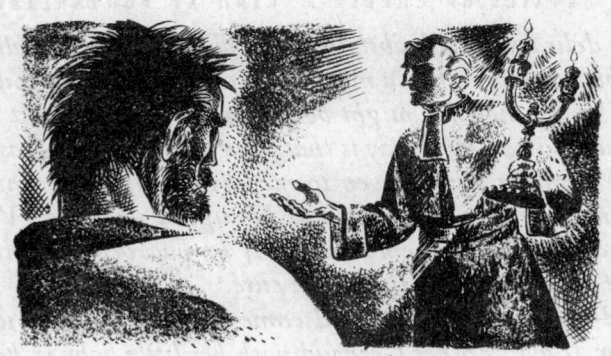

5 . TRANQUILLITY

After bidding his sister good-night, Monseigneur Welcome took up one of the silver candlesticks, handed the other to his guest and said:

"I will lead you to your room, sir."

The man followed him. The reader will remember, from our description, that the rooms were so arranged that in order to reach or leave the oratory where the alcove was, it was necessary to pass through the bishop's bedroom. At the moment when he went through this room, Madame Magloire was putting away the plate in the cupboard over the bed-head; it was the last job she did every night before retiring. The bishop led his guest to the alcove, where a clean bed was prepared for him. The man placed the branched candlestick on a small table.

"I trust you will pass a good night," said the bishop. "To-morrow morning, before starting, you will drink a glass of milk fresh from our cows."

"Thank you, Monsieur l'Abbé," the man said. He had hardly uttered these peaceful words when, suddenly, and without any transition, he had a strange emotion, which would have frightened the two old women to death had they witnessed it. Even at the present day it is difficult to account for what urged him at that moment. Did he wish to warn or to threaten? Was he simply obeying a species of instinctive impulse which was obscure to himself? He suddenly turned to the old man, folded his arms, and, fixing on him a savage glance, he exclaimed hoarsely:

"What! you really lodge me so close to you as that?" He broke off and added with a laugh, in which there was something monstrous: "Have you reflected fully? Who tells you that I have not committed a murder?"

The bishop answered, "That concerns God."

Then gravely moving his lips, like a man who is praying and speaking

80

to himself, he stretched out two fingers of his right hand and blessed the man, who did not bow his head, and returned to his bedroom, without turning his head or looking behind him. When the alcove was occupied, a large serge curtain drawn right across the oratory concealed the altar. The bishop knelt down as he passed before this curtain, and offered up a short prayer; a moment after, he was in his garden, walking, dreaming, contemplating, his soul and thoughts entirely occupied by those grand mysteries which God displays at night to eyes that remain open.

As for the man, he was really so wearied that he did not even take advantage of the nice white sheets. He blew out the candle with his nostrils, after the fashion of convicts, and threw himself in his clothes upon the bed, where he at once fell into a deep sleep. Midnight was striking as the bishop returned from the garden to his room, and a few minutes later everybody was asleep in the small house.

6. JEAN VALJEAN

Toward the middle of the night, Jean Valjean awoke. He belonged to a poor peasant family of la Brie. In his childhood he had not been taught to read, and when he was of man's age he was a pruner at Faverolles. His mother's name was Jeanne Mathieu; his father's, Jean Valjean or Vlajean, probably a sobriquet and a contraction of *Voilà Jean*. Jean Valjean possessed a pensive but not melancholy character, which is peculiar to affectionate natures; but altogether he was a dull, insignificant fellow, at least apparently. He had lost father and mother when still very young; the latter died of a badly managed milk-fever; the former, a pruner, like himself, was killed by a fall from a tree. All that was left Jean Valjean was a sister older than himself, a widow with seven children, boys and girls. This sister brought Jean

Valjean up, and so long as her husband was alive she supported her brother. When the husband died, the oldest of the seven children was eight years of age, the youngest, one, while Jean Valjean had just reached his twenty-fifth year; he took the place of the father, and in his turn supported the sister who had reared him. This was done simply as a duty, and even rather roughly, by Jean Valjean; and his youth was thus expended in hard and ill-paid toil. He was never known to have had a sweetheart, for he had no time for love-making.

At night he came home tired, and ate his soup without saying a word. His sister, mother Jeanne, while he was eating, often took out of his porringer the best part of his meal, the piece of meat, the slice of bacon, or the heart of the cabbage to give to one of her children; he, still eating, bent over the table with his head almost in the soup, and, his long hair falling around his porringer and hiding his eyes, pretended not to see it, and let her do as she pleased. There was at Faverolles, not far from the Valjeans' cottage, on the other side of the lane, a farmer's wife called Marie Claude. The young Valjeans, who were habitually starving, would go at times and borrow in their mother's name a pint of milk from Marie Claude, which they drank behind a hedge or in some corner, tearing the vessel from each other so eagerly that the little girls spilled the milk over their aprons. Their mother, had she been aware of this fraud, would have severely corrected the delinquents, but Jean Valjean, coarse and rough though he was, paid Marie Claude for the milk behind his sister's back, and the children were not punished.

He earned in the pruning season eighteen sous a day, and besides hired himself out as a reaper, laborer, neat-herd, and odd man. He did what he could; his sister worked too, but what could she do with seven children? It was a sad group, which wretchedness gradually enveloped and choked. One winter was hard, and Jean had no work to do, and the family had no bread. No bread, literally none, and seven children.

One Sunday evening, Maubert Isabeau, the baker in the church square at Faverolles, was just going to bed when he heard a violent blow dealt the wired and glazed front of his shop. He arrived in time to see an arm passed through a hole made by a fist through the wires and window-pane; the arm seized a loaf, and carried it off. Isabeau ran out hastily; the thief ran away at his hardest, but the baker caught him up and stopped him. The thief had thrown away the loaf, but his arm was still bleeding; it was Jean Valjean.

This took place in 1795. Jean Valjean was brought before the courts of the day, charged "with burglary committed with violence at night, in an inhabited house." He had a gun, was a splendid shot and a bit of a poacher, and this injured him. There is a legitimate prejudice against poachers, for, like smugglers, they trench very closely on brigandage. Still we must remark that there is an abyss between these classes and the hideous assassins of our cities: the poacher lives in the forest; the smuggler in the mountains and on the sea. Cities produce ferocious men because they produce corrupted men; the forest, the mountain, and the sea produce savage men,—but, while they develop their fierce side, they do not always destroy their human part. Jean Valjean was found guilty, and the terms of the code were formal. There are in our civilization formidable hours; they are those moments in which penal justice pronounces a shipwreck. What a mournful minute is that in which society withdraws and consummates the irreparable abandonment of a thinking being! Jean Valjean was sentenced to five years at the galleys.

On April 22, 1796, men were crying in the streets of Paris the victory of Montenotte, gained by the general-in-chief of the army of Italy, whom the message of the Directory to the Five Hundred of 2 Floréal, year IV, calls Buona-Parte; and on the same day a heavy gang was put in chains at Bicêtre, and Jean Valjean formed a part of the chain. An ex-jailer of the prison, who is now nearly ninety years of age, perfectly remembers the wretched man who was chained at the end of the fourth line, in the north angle of the courtyard. He was seated on the ground like the rest, and seemed not at all to understand his position, except that it was horrible. It is probable that he also saw something excessive through the vague ideas of an utterly ignorant man. While the bolt of his iron collar was being riveted with heavy hammer blows behind his head, he wept, tears choked him, and prevented him from speaking, and he could only manage to say from time to time, "I was a wood-cutter at Faverolles." Then, while still continuing to sob, he raised his right hand, and lowered it gradually seven times, as if touching seven uneven heads in turn, and from this gesture it could be guessed that, whatever the crime he had committed, he had done it to feed and clothe seven little children.

He started for Toulon, and arrived there after a journey of twenty-seven days in a cart, with a chain on his neck. At Toulon he was dressed in the red jacket. All that had hitherto been his life, even to his name, was effaced. He was no longer Jean Valjean, but No. 24,601. What became of his sister, what became of the seven children? Who troubles himself about that? What becomes of the spray of leaves when the stem of the young tree has been cut at the foot? It is always the same story. These poor living beings, these creatures of God, henceforth without support, guide, or shelter, went off hap-hazard, and gradually buried themselves in that cold fog in which solitary destinies are swallowed up, that mournful gloom in which so many unfortunates disappear during the sullen progress of the human race. They left their country; what had once been the steeple of their village church forgot them; what had once been their hedge-row forgot them; and after a few years' stay in the bagne, Jean Valjean himself forgot them. In that heart where there once had been a wound, there was now a scar: that was all. He only heard about his sister once during the whole time he spent at Toulon; it was, I believe, toward the end of the fourth year of his captivity, though I have forgotten in what way the information reached him. She was in Paris, living in the Rue du Geindre, a poor street, near Saint Sulpice, and had only one child with her, the youngest, a boy. Where were the other six? perhaps she did not know herself. Every morning she went to a printing-office, No. 3 Rue du Sabot, where she was a folder and stitcher; she had to be there at six in the morning, long before daylight in winter. In the same house as the printing-office there was a day-school, to which she took the little boy, who was seven years of age, but as she went to work at six and the school did not open till seven o'clock, the boy was compelled to wait in the yard for an hour, in winter,—an hour of night in the open air. The boy was not allowed to enter the printing-office, because it was said that he would be in the way. The workmen as they passed in the morning saw the poor little fellow seated on the pavement, and often sleeping in the darkness, with his head on his satchel. When it rained, an old woman, the portress, took pity on him; she invited him into her den, where there were only a bed, a spinning-wheel, and two chairs, when the little fellow fell asleep in a corner, nestling up to the cat, to keep him warm. At seven o'clock the school opened and the child went in. This is what Jean Valjean was told; it was a momentary flash, as if it were a window suddenly opened in the destiny of the beings he had loved; and then all was closed again; he never heard about them more. Nothing reached him from them; he never saw them again, never met them, and we shall not come across them in the course of this melancholy narrative.

Toward the end of this fourth year, Jean Valjean's turn to escape arrived, and his comrades aided him as they always do in this sorrowful place. He escaped and wandered about the fields at liberty for two days—

if it is liberty to be hunted down; to turn one's head at every moment; to start at the slightest sound; to be afraid of everything, of a chimney that smokes, a man who passes, a barking dog, a galloping horse, the striking of the hour, of day because people see, of night because they do not see, of the highway, the path, the thicket, and even sleep. On the evening of the second day he was recaptured; he had not eaten or slept for six-and-thirty hours. The maritime tribunal added three years to his sentence for his crime, which made it eight years. In the sixth year, it was again his turn to escape; he tried, but could not succeed. He was missing at roll-call, the gun was fired, and at night the watchman found him hidden under the keel of a ship that was building, and he resisted the prison guard who seized him. Escape and rebellion; this fact, foreseen by the special code, was punished by an addition of five years, of which two would be spent in double chains. Thirteen years. In his tenth year his turn came again, and he took advantage of it, but succeeded no better; three years for his new attempt, or sixteen years in all. Finally, I think it was during his thirteenth year that he made a last attempt, and only succeeded so far as to be recaptured in four hours; three years for these four hours, and a total of nineteen years. In October, 1815, he was liberated; he had gone in in 1796 for breaking a window and stealing a loaf.

Let us make room for a short parenthesis. This is the second time that, during his essays on the penal question and condemnation by the law, the author of this book has come across a loaf as the starting-point of the disaster of a destiny. Claude Gueux stole a loaf, and so did Jean Valjean, and English statistics prove that in London four robberies out of five have hunger as their immediate cause. Jean Valjean entered the bagne sobbing and shuddering; he left it stoically. He entered it in despair; he came out of it gloomy. What had taken place in this soul?

7. A DESPERATE MAN'S HEART

LET us try to reveal it.

Society must necessarily look at these things, because they are created by it. He was, as we have said, an ignorant man, but he was not weak-minded. The natural light was kindled within him, and misfortune, which also has its brightness, increased the little daylight there was in this mind. Under the stick and the chain in the dungeon, when at work, beneath the torrid sun of the bagne, or when lying on the convict's plank, he reflected. He constituted himself a court, and began by trying himself. He recognized that he was not an innocent man unjustly punished; he confessed to himself that he had committed an extreme and blamable action; that the loaf would probably not have been refused him had he asked for it; that in any case it would have been better to wait for it, either from pity or from labor; and that it was not a thoroughly un-answerable argument to say, "Can a man wait when he is hungry?" That, in the first place, it is very rare for a man to die literally of hunger; next, that, unhappily or happily, man is so made that he can suffer for a long time, and severely, morally and physically, without dying; that hence he should have been patient; that it would have been better for the poor little children; that it was an act of madness for him, a wretched, weak man, violently to collar society and to imagine that a man can escape from wretchedness by theft; that in any case the door by which a man enters infamy is a bad one by which to escape from wretchedness; and, in short, that he had been in the wrong.

Then he asked himself if he were the only person who had been in the wrong in his fatal history? whether, in the first place, it was not a serious thing that he, a workman, should want for work; that he, laborious as he was, should want for bread? whether, next, when the fault was com-

mitted and confessed, the punishment had not been ferocious and excessive, and whether there were not more abuse on the side of the law in
the penalty than there was on the side of the culprit in the crime?
whether there had not been an excessive weight in one of the scales, that
one in which expiation lies? whether the excess of punishment were not
the effacement of the crime, and led to the result of making a victim
of the culprit, a creditor of the debtor, and definitely placing the right on
the side of the man who had violated it? whether this penalty, complicated by excessive aggravations for attempted escapes, did not eventually
become a sort of attack made by the stronger on the weaker, a crime of
society committed on the individual, a crime which was renewed every
day, and had lasted for nineteen years? He asked himself if human
society could have the right to make its members equally undergo, on
one side, its unreasonable improvidence, on the other its pitiless foresight,
and to hold a man eternally between a want and an excess,—want of
work and excess of punishment? whether it were not exorbitant that
society should treat thus its members who were worst endowed in that
division of property which is made by chance, and consequently the most
worthy of indulgence?

These questions asked and solved, he passed sentence on society and
condemned it—to his hatred. He made it responsible for the fate he
underwent, and said to himself that he would not hesitate to call it to
account some day. He declared that there was no equilibrium between
the damage he had caused and the damage caused him; and he came to
the conclusion that his punishment was not an injustice, but most assuredly an iniquity. Wrath may be wild and absurd; a man may be
wrongly irritated; but he is only indignant when he has some show of
reason somewhere. Jean Valjean felt indignant. And then, again, human
society had never done him aught but harm; he had only seen its wrathful face, which is called its justice, and shows to those whom it strikes.
Men had only laid hands on him to injure him, and any contact with
them had been a blow to him. Never, since his infancy, since his mother
and his sister, had he heard a kind word or met a friendly look. From
suffering after suffering, he gradually attained the conviction that life
was war, and that in this war he was the vanquished. As he had no other
weapon but his hatred, he resolved to sharpen it in the bagne and take it
with him when he left.

There was at Toulon a school for the chain-gang, kept by Ignorantine
Brethren, who imparted elementary instruction to those wretches who

were willing to learn. He was one of the number, and went to school at the age of forty, where he learned reading, writing, and arithmetic; he felt that strengthening his mind was strengthening his hatred. In certain cases, instruction and education may serve to prolong evil. It is sad to say that after trying society, which had caused his misfortunes, he tried Providence, who had made society, and condemned it also. Hence, during these nineteen years of torture and slavery, this soul ascended and descended at the same time; light entered on one side and darkness on the other. As we have seen, Jean Valjean was not naturally bad; he was still good when he arrived at the bagne. He condemned society then, and felt that he was growing wicked; he condemned Providence, and felt that he was growing impious.

Here it is difficult not to meditate for a moment. Is human nature thus utterly transformed? Can man, who is created good by God, be made bad by man? Can the soul be entirely remade by destiny, and become evil if the destiny be evil? Can the heart be deformed, and contract incurable ugliness and infirmity under the pressure of disproportionate misfortune, like the spine beneath too low a vault? Is there not in every human soul, was there not in that of Jean Valjean especially, a primary spark, a divine element, incorruptible in this world, and immortal for the other, which good can develop, illumine, and cause to glisten splendidly, and which evil can never entirely extinguish?

These are grave and obscure questions, the last of which every physiologist would unhesitatingly have answered in the negative, had he seen at Toulon, in those hours of repose which were for Jean Valjean hours of reverie, this gloomy, stern, silent, and pensive galley-slave—the pariah of the law which regarded men passionately—the condemned of civilization, who regarded heaven with severity—seated with folded arms on a capstan bar, with the end of his chain thrust into his pocket to prevent it from dragging. We assuredly do not deny that the physiological observer would have seen there an irremediable misery; he would probably have pitied this patient of the law, but he would not have even attempted a cure; he would have turned away from the caverns he noticed in his soul, and, like Dante at the gates of the Inferno, he would have effaced from this existence that word which God, however, has written on the brow of every man—*hope!*

Was this state of his soul, which we have attempted to analyze, as perfectly clear to Jean Valjean as we have tried to render it to our readers? Did Jean Valjean see after their formation, and had he seen distinctly as they were formed, all the elements of which his moral wretchedness was composed? Had this rude and unlettered man clearly comprehended the succession of ideas by which he had step by step ascended and descended to the gloomy views which had for so many years been the inner horizon of his mind? Was he really conscious of all that had taken place in him, and all that was stirring in him? This we should not like to assert and, indeed, we are not inclined to believe it. There was too much ignorance in Jean Valjean for a considerable amount of vagueness not to remain, even after so much misfortune; at times he did not even know exactly what he experienced. Jean Valjean was in darkness; he suffered in darkness and he hated in darkness. He lived habitually in this shadow, groping like a blind man and a dreamer. At times he was attacked, both internally and externally, by a shock of passion, a surcharge of suffering, a pale and rapid flash which illumined his whole soul, and suddenly made him see all around, both before and behind him, in the glare of a frightful light the hideous precipices and gloomy perspective of his destiny. When the flash had passed, night encompassed him again, and where was he? He no longer knew.

The peculiarity of punishments of this nature, in which naught but what is pitiless, that is to say, brutalizing, prevails, is gradually, and by a species of stupid transfiguration, to transform a man into a wild beast, at times a ferocious beast. Jean Valjean's attempted escapes, successive and obstinate, would be sufficient to prove the strange work carried on by the law upon a human soul; he would have renewed these attempts, so utterly useless and mad, as many times as the opportunity offered itself, without dreaming for a moment of the result, or the experiments already made. He escaped impetuously like the wolf that finds its cage open. Instinct said to him, "Run away"; reasoning would have said to him, "Remain"; but, in the presence of so violent a temptation, reason disappeared and instinct alone was left. The brute alone acted, and when he was recaptured the new severities inflicted on him only served to render him more wild.

One fact we must not omit mentioning is that he possessed a physical strength with which no one in the bagne could compete. In turning a capstan, Jean Valjean was equal to four men; he frequently raised and held on his back enormous weights, and took the place at times of that instrument which is called a jack, and was formerly called *orgueil,* from which by the way, the Rue Montorgueil in Paris derived its name. His comrades surnamed him Jean the Jack. Once, when the balcony of the

Town Hall at Toulon was being repaired, one of those admirable caryatides of Puget's which support the balcony became loose and almost fell. Jean Valjean, who was on the spot, supported the statue with his shoulder, and thus gave the workmen time to come up.

His suppleness even exceeded his vigor. Some convicts, who perpetually dream of escaping, eventually make a real science of combined skill and strength; it is the science of the muscles. A full course of mysterious statics is daily practiced by the prisoners, those eternal enviers of flies and birds. Swarming up a perpendicular, and finding a resting-place where a projection is scarcely visible, was child's play for Jean Valjean. Given a corner of a wall, with the tension of his back and hams, with his elbows and heels clinging to the rough stone, he would hoist himself as if by magic to a third story, and at times would ascend to the very roof of the bagne. He spoke little, and never laughed; it needed some extreme emotion to draw from him, once or twice a year, that mournful convict laugh, which is, as it were, the echo of fiendish laughter. To look at him, he seemed engaged in continually gazing at something terrible. He was, in fact, absorbed. Through the sickly perceptions of an incomplete nature and a crushed intellect, he saw confusedly that a monstrous thing was hanging over him. In this obscure and dull gloom through which he crawled, wherever he turned his head and essayed to raise his eye, he saw, with a terror blended with rage, built up above him, with frightfully scarped sides, a species of terrific pile of things, laws, prejudices, men, and facts, whose outlines escaped him, whose mass terrified him, and which was nothing else but that prodigious pyramid which we call civilization. He distinguished here and there in this heaving and shapeless conglomeration—at one moment close to him, at another on distant and inaccessible plateaux—some highly illumined group—here the jailer and his stick, there the gendarme and his saber, down below the mitered archbishop, and on the summit, in a species of sun, the crowned and dazzling emperor. It seemed to him as if this distant splendor, far from dissipating his night, only rendered it more gloomy and black. All these laws, prejudices, facts, men, and things came and went above him, in accordance with the complicated and mysterious movement which God imprints on civilization, marching over him, and crushing him with something painful in its cruelty, and inexorable in its indifference. Souls which have fallen into the abyss of possible misfortune, hapless men lost in the depths of those limbos into which people no longer look, and the reprobates of the law feel on their heads the whole weight of the human society, so formidable for those outside it, so terrific for those beneath it.

In this situation, Jean Valjean thought, and what could be the nature of his reverie? If the grain of corn had its thoughts when ground by the mill stone, it would doubtless think as Jean Valjean. All these things, realities full of specters, phantasmagorias full of reality, ended by creating for him a sort of internal condition which is almost inexpressible. At times, in the midst of his galley-slave toil, he stopped and began thinking; his reason, at once riper and more troubled than of yore, revolved. All that had happened appeared to him absurd; all that surrounded him seemed to him impossible. He said to himself that it was a dream; he looked at the overseer standing a few yards from him, and he appeared to him a phantom, until the phantom suddenly dealt him a blow with a stick. Visible nature scarce existed for him; we might almost say with truth that for Jean Valjean there was no sun, no glorious summer day, no brilliant sky, no fresh April dawn; we cannot describe the gloomy light which illumined his soul.

In conclusion, to sum up all that can be summed up in what we have indicated, we will confine ourselves to establishing the fact that in nineteen years, Jean Valjean, the inoffensive wood-cutter of Faverolles, and the formidable galley-slave of Toulon, had become, thanks to the manner in which the bagne had fashioned him, capable of two sorts of bad actions: first, a rapid, unreflecting bad deed, entirely instinctive, and a species of reprisal for the evil he had suffered; and, secondly, of a grave, serious, evil deed, discussed conscientiously and meditated with the false ideas which such a misfortune can produce. His premeditations passed through the three successive phases which natures of a certain temperament can alone undergo,—reasoning, will, and obstinacy. He had for his motives habitual indignation, bitterness of soul, the profound feeling of iniquities endured, and reaction even against the good, the innocent, and the just, if such exist. The starting-point, like the goal, of all his thoughts was hatred of human law; that hatred, which, if it be not arrested in its development by some providential incident, becomes within a given time a hatred of society, then a hatred of the human race, next a hatred of creation, and is expressed by a vague, incessant, and brutal desire to injure some one, no matter whom. As we see, it was not unfairly that the passport described Jean Valjean as a highly dangerous man. Year by year this soul had become more and more withered, slowly but fatally. A dry soul must have a dry eye, and, on leaving the bagne, nineteen years had elapsed since he had shed a tear.

8. THE WAVE AND THE SHADOW

Man overboard!

What matter! the vessel does not stop; the wind blows, and that dark ship there has a course she must keep. She sails on. The man disappears, then re-appears; he sinks and rises again to the surface, he calls out, he waves his arms, but no one hears him; the ship, trembling beneath the hurricane, is straining and working in every timber; the sailors and the passengers do not even see the castaway; his wretched head is only a point in the immensity of the billows.

He hurls cries of despair into the depths around him. What a specter is that sail which is moving on! He looks at it, he looks at it with frenzy, as it loses itself in the distance, fades, and diminishes. He was on board just now, he was one of the crew, he went to and fro on the deck like the others, he had air and sunlight, he was a living thing. Now what has happened? He slipped, he fell, and all is over. He is in the monstrous waves, with nothing under his feet but the running and rushing water.

The waves, torn and rent by the wind, are a hideous environment; the swell of the abyss raises him; the ragged spray dashes around his head; a population of waves spits upon him; dark depths half swallow him; every time he sinks he has glimpses of precipices full of night; frightful forms of unknown vegetation seize him, bind his feet, drag him to them; he feels he is becoming part of the abyss, part of the foam; the billows toss him from one to the other, he drinks the bitter brine, the cowardly ocean is furious to drown him, and immensity plays with his agony; it seems as if all this water were so much hate. He struggles, however. He strives to save himself, to keep himself afloat; he makes an effort and swims. This paltry force, just now exhausted, combats the inexhaustible. Where then is the ship? Down there, scarce visible in the pale shadows of the horizon. The storm gusts smite him, the foam of every wave weighs him down; he raises his eyes and sees only the livid masses of the clouds. In the agony of death, he feels and shares the measureless insanity of the sea. He is tortured by this madness, he hears sounds strange to human ears, which seem to come from the other side of the earth, and from some mysterious and terrible beyond. There are birds in the clouds, just as there are angels high above human sorrows, but what can they do for him? The bird flies, sings, and hovers, and he, he has the death-rattle in his throat. He feels himself doubly buried by two infinities: sea and sky,—the one his tomb, the other his shroud. Night descends, he has been swimming for hours, his strength is at an end; that far-away thing where there are men is blotted out, he is alone in the awful twilight-gulf. He sinks, he stiffens himself, he struggles, he feels below him the vague monsters of the invisible. He shouts aloud!

"There are no more men. Where is God?" he shouts aloud. "Some one! Some one!" he shouts incessantly. Nothing is on the horizon, nothing in the sky. He implores the expanse of waters, the sea-weed, the shoals; but they are deaf. He calls on the tempest to succor, but the imperturbable tempest obeys the Infinite alone. Around him are obscurity, sea-fog, solitude, stormy and unconscious tumult, and the ill-defined furrows of fierce waters. In his breast are horror and fatigue, and beneath him the abyss without a foot-hold. He dreams of the darksome adventures of the corpse in the limitless realm of shadow. Cold immeasurable paralyzes him, and his hands shrivel up, close, and grasp nothingness. Winds, clouds, gusts, breezes, stars, all useless! What is to be done? He abandons himself in his despair, and in his weariness takes the part of death, and lets himself drift and drive; he gives up, and is whirled forever in the lugubrious depths that swallow him up.

O implacable progress of human societies! Lost men and lost souls form the path they tread—an ocean where falls all that the law lets fall. Disastrous vanishing of succor. O moral death! The sea is the inexorable night of society into which punishment flings its condemned ones; the sea is infinite wretchedness. The soul drifting in its eddies may become a corpse. Who will reanimate it?

9 · NEW WRONGS

WHEN the hour for quitting the bagne arrived, when Jean Valjean heard in his ear the unfamiliar words, "You are free," the moment seemed improbable and extraordinary, and a ray of bright light, of the light of the living, penetrated to him; but it soon grew pale. Jean Valjean had been dazzled by the idea of liberty and had believed in a new life, but he soon saw that it is a liberty of which a yellow passport is granted. And around this there was much bitterness; he had calculated that his earnings, during his stay at the bagne, should have amounted to 171 francs. We are bound to add that he had omitted to take into his calculations the forced rest of Sundays and holidays, which, during nineteen years, entailed a diminution of about twenty-four francs. However this might be, the sum was reduced, through various local stoppages, to 109 francs fifteen sous, which were paid to him when he left the bagne. He did not understand it all, and fancied that he had been robbed.

On the day after his liberation, he saw at Grasse men in front of a distillery of orange-flower water, men unloading bales; he offered his services, and as the work was of a pressing nature, they were accepted. He set to work, he was intelligent, powerful, and skillful, and his master appeared satisfied. While he was at work a gendarme passed, noticed him, asked for his paper, and he was compelled to show his yellow pass. This done, Jean Valjean resumed his toil. A little while previously, he had asked one of the workmen what he earned for his day's work, and the answer was thirty sous. At night, as he was compelled to start again the next morning, he went to the master of the distillery and asked for payment; the master did not say a word, but gave him fifteen sous, and when he protested, the answer was, "That is enough for you." He became pressing, the man looked him in the face and said, "Mind you don't get into prison."

Here again he regarded himself as robbed; society, the state, by diminishing his earnings, had robbed him wholesale; now it was the turn of the individual to commit retail robbery. Liberation is not deliverance; a man may be freed from the bagne, but not from condemnation. We have seen what happened to him at Grasse, and we know how he was treated at D. . . . .

10. *THE MAN AWAKE*

As two o'clock pealed from the cathedral bell, Jean Valjean awoke. What aroused him was that the bed was too comfortable. For close on twenty years he had not slept in a bed, and, though he had not undressed, the sensation was too novel not to disturb his sleep. He had been asleep for more than four hours, and his weariness had worn off; and he was accustomed not to grant many hours to repose. He opened his eyes and looked into the surrounding darkness, and then he closed them again to go to sleep once more. When many diverse sensations have agitated a day, and when matters preoccupy the mind, a man may sleep, but he cannot go to sleep again. Sleep comes more easily than it returns, and this happened to Jean Valjean. As he could not go to sleep again, he began thinking.

It was one of those moments in which the ideas that occupy the mind are troubled, and there was a species of obscure come-and-go in his brain. His old recollections and his newer recollections crossed each other, and floated confusedly, losing their shape, growing enormously, and then disappearing suddenly, as if in troubled and muddy water. Many thoughts occurred to him, but there was one which constantly reverted and expelled all the rest. This thought we will at once describe; he had noticed the six silver forks and spoons and the great ladle which Madame Magloire put on the table. This plate overwhelmed him—it was there— a few yards from him. When he crossed the adjoining room to reach the one in which he now was, the old servant was putting it in a small cupboard at the bed-head. He had carefully noticed this cupboard—it was on the right as you came in from the dining-room. The plate was heavy and old, the big soup-ladle was worth at least 200 francs, or double what he had earned in nineteen years, though it was true that he would have earned it had not the officials robbed him.

His mind oscillated for a good hour in these fluctuations with which a struggle was most assuredly blended. When three o'clock struck, he opened his eyes, suddenly sat up, stretched out his arms, and felt for his knapsack which he had thrown into a corner of the alcove, then let his legs hang, and felt himself seated on the bedside almost without knowing how. He remained for a while thoughtfully in this attitude, which would have had something sinister about it, for any one who had seen him, the only wakeful person in the house. All at once he stooped, took off his shoes, then resumed his thoughtful posture and remained motionless. In the midst of this hideous meditation, the ideas which we have indicated incessantly crossed his brain, entered, went out, returned, and weighed upon him; and then he thought, without knowing why, and with the mechanical obstinacy of reverie, of a convict he had known at the bagne, of the name of Brevet, whose trousers were only held up by a single knitted brace. The draught-board design of that brace incessantly returned to his mind. He remained in this situation, and would have probably remained so till sunrise, had not the clock struck the quarter or the half hour. It seemed as if this stroke said to him, To work! He rose, hesitated for a moment and listened; all was silent in the house, and he went on tiptoe to the window, through which he peered. The night was not very dark; there was a full moon, across which heavy clouds were chased by the wind. This produced alternations of light and shade, and a species of twilight in the room; this twilight, sufficient to guide him, but intermittent in consequence of the clouds, resembled that livid hue produced by the grating of a cellar over which people are continually passing. On reaching the window, Jean Valjean examined it; it was without bars, looked on the garden, and was only closed, according to the fashion of the country, by a small peg. He opened it, but as a cold, sharp breeze suddenly entered the room, he closed it again directly. He gazed into the garden with that attentive glance which studies rather than looks, and found that it was inclosed by a whitewashed wall, easy to climb over. Beyond it he noticed the tops of the trees standing at regular distances, which proved that this wall separated the garden from a public walk or avenue.

After taking this glance, he walked boldly to the alcove, opened his knapsack, took out something which he laid on the bed, put his shoes in one of the pouches, placed the knapsack on his shoulders, put on his cap, the peak of which he pulled over his eyes, groped for his stick, which he placed in the window nook, and then returned to the bed, and took up the object he had laid on it. It resembled a short iron bar, sharpened, and flattened at one of its ends like a spear. It would have been difficult to distinguish in the darkness for what purpose this piece of iron had been fashioned; perhaps it was a lever, perhaps it was a club. By daylight it could have been seen that it was nothing but a miners' candlestick. The convicts at that day were sometimes employed in extracting rock from the lofty hills that surround Toulon, and it was not infrequent for them to have mining tools at their disposal. The miners' candlesticks are made of massive steel, and have a point at the lower end, by which they are dug into the rock. He took the bar in his right hand, and, holding his breath and deadening his footsteps, he walked toward the door of the adjoining room,—the bishop's, as we know. On reaching this door he found it ajar—the bishop had not shut it.

11. *WHAT HE DID*

JEAN VALJEAN listened, but there was not a sound; he pushed the door with the tip of his finger lightly, and with the furtive, restless gentleness of a cat that wants to get in. The door yielded to the pressure, and made an almost imperceptible and silent movement, which slightly widened the opening. He waited for a moment, and then pushed the door again more boldly. It continued to yield silently, and the opening was soon large enough for him to pass through. But there was near the door a small table which formed an awkward angle with it, and barred the entrance.

Jean Valjean noticed the difficulty; the opening must be increased at all hazards. He made up his mind, and pushed the door a third time, more energetically still. This time there was a badly oiled hinge, which suddenly uttered a hoarse prolonged cry in the darkness. Jean Valjean started; the sound of the hinge smote his ear startlingly and formidably, as if it had been the trumpet of the day of judgment. In the fantastic exaggerations of the first minute, he almost imagined that this hinge had become animated, and suddenly obtained a terrible vitality and barked like a dog to warn and awaken the sleepers. He stopped, shuddering and dismayed, and fell back from tiptoes on his heels. He felt the arteries in his temples beat like two forge-hammers, and it seemed to him that his breath issued from his lungs with the noise of the wind roaring out of a cavern. He fancied that the horrible clamor of this irritated hinge must have startled the whole house like the shock of an earthquake; the door he opened had been alarmed and cried for help; the old man would rise, the two aged women would shriek, and assistance would arrive within a quarter of an hour, the town would be astir, and the gendarmerie turned out. For a moment he believed himself lost.

He remained where he was, petrified like the pillar of salt, and not daring to make a movement. A few minutes passed, during which the door remained wide open. He ventured to look into the room, and found that nothing had stirred. He listened; no one was moving in the house, the creaking of the rusty hinge had not awakened any one. The first danger had passed, but still there was fearful tumult within him. But he did not recoil, he had not done so even when he thought himself lost; he only thought of finishing the job as speedily as possible, and entered the bedroom. The room was in a state of perfect calmness; here and there might be distinguished confused and vague forms, which by day were scattered over the table, open folios, books piled on a sofa, an easy-chair covered with clothes, and a priedieu, all of which at this moment were only dark nooks and patches of white. Jean Valjean advanced cautiously and carefully, and avoided coming into collision with the furniture. He heard from the end of the room the calm and regular breathing of the sleeping bishop. Suddenly he stopped, for he was close to the bed; he had reached it sooner than he anticipated.

Nature at times blends her effects and spectacles with our actions with a species of gloomy and intelligent design, as if wishing to make us reflect. For nearly half an hour a heavy cloud had covered the sky, but at the moment when Jean Valjean stopped at the foot of the bed, this cloud was rent asunder as if expressly, and a moonbeam passing through the tall window suddenly illumined the bishop's pale face. He was sleeping peacefully, and, to protect himself from the cold nights of the Lower Alps, was wrapped up in a long garment of brown wool, which covered his arms down to the wrists. His head was thrown back on the pillow in the easy attitude of repose, and his hand, adorned with the pastoral ring, and which had done so many good deeds, hung out of bed. His entire face was lit up by a vague expression of satisfaction, hope, and beatitude —it was more than a smile and almost a radiance. He had on his forehead the inexpressible reflection of an invisible light, for the soul of a just man contemplates a mysterious heaven during sleep. A reflection of this heaven was cast over the bishop, but it was at the same time a luminous transparency, for the heaven was within him, and was conscience.

At the moment when the moonbeam was cast over this internal light, the sleeping bishop seemed to be surrounded by a glory, which was veiled, however, by an ineffable semi-light. The moon in the heavens, the slumbering landscape, the quiet house, the hour, the silence, the moment, added something solemn and indescribable to this man's venerable repose, and cast a majestic and serene halo round his white hair and closed eyes, his face, in which all was hope and confidence, his aged head, and his infantine slumbers. There was almost a divinity in this unconsciously august man. Jean Valjean was standing in the shadow with his crowbar in his hand, motionless and terrified by this luminous old man. He had never seen anything like this before, and such confidence horrified him. The moral world has no greater spectacle than this, a troubled, restless conscience, which is on the point of committing a bad action, contemplating the sleep of a just man.

This sleep in such isolation, and with a neighbor like himself, possessed a species of sublimity which he felt vaguely, but imperiously. No one could have said what was going on within him, not even himself. In order to form any idea of it, we must imagine what is the most violent in the presence of what is gentlest. Even in his face nothing could have been distinguished with certainty, for it displayed a sort of haggard astonishment. He looked at the bishop, that was all, but what his thoughts were it would be impossible to divine; what was evident was that he was moved and shaken, but of what nature was this emotion? His eye was not once removed from the old man, and the only thing clearly revealed by his attitude and countenance was a strange indecision. It seemed as if he were hesitating betwen two abysses,—the one that saves and the one that destroys; he was ready to dash out the bishop's brains or kiss his hand. At the expiration of a few minutes his left arm slowly rose to his cap, which he took off; then his arm fell again with the same slowness, and Jean Valjean recommenced his contemplation, with his cap in his left hand, his crowbar in his right, and his hair standing erect on his savage head.

The bishop continued to sleep peacefully beneath this terrific glance. A moonbeam rendered the crucifix over the mantel-piece dimly visible, which seemed to open its arms for both, with a blessing for one and a pardon for the other. All at once Jean Valjean put on his cap again, then walked rapidly along the bed, without looking at the bishop, and went straight to the cupboard. He raised his crowbar to force the lock, but, as the key was in it, he opened it, and the first thing he saw was the plate-basket, which he seized. He hurried across the room, not caring for the noise he made, re-entered the oratory, opened the window, seized his stick, put the silver in his pocket, threw away the basket, leaped into the garden, bounded over the wall like a tiger, and fled.

12. *THE BISHOP AT WORK*

THE next morning at sunrise Monseigneur Welcome was walking about the garden, when Madame Magloire came running toward him in a state of great alarm.

"Monseigneur, monseigneur, monseigneur!" she screamed, "does your grandeur know where the plate-basket is?"

"Yes," said the bishop.

"The Lord be praised," she continued; "I did not know what had become of it."

The bishop had just picked up the basket in a flower-bed, and now handed it to Madame Magloire. "Here it is," he said.

"Well!" she said, "there is nothing in it; where is the plate?"

"Ah!" the bishop replied, "it is the plate that troubles your mind. Well, I do not know where that is."

"Good Lord! it is stolen, and that man who came last night is the robber."

In a twinkling Madame Magloire had run to the oratory, entered the alcove, and returned to the bishop. He was stooping down and looking sorrowfully at a cochlearia, whose stem the basket had broken. He raised himself on hearing Madame Magloire scream:

"Monseigneur, the man has gone! the plate is stolen!"

While uttering this exclamation, her eyes fell on a corner of the garden where there were signs of climbing; the coping of the wall had been torn away.

"That is the way he went! he leaped into Cochefilet lane. Ah, what a scoundrel; he has stolen our plate!"

The bishop remained silent for a moment, then raised his earnest eyes, and said gently to Madame Magloire:

"By the way, was that plate ours?"

Madame Magloire was speechless; there was another interval of silence, after which the bishop continued:

"Madame Magloire, I had wrongfully held back this silver, which belonged to the poor. Who was this person? evidently a poor man."

"Good gracious!" Madame Magloire continued; "I do not care for it; nor does mademoiselle, but we feel for monseigneur. With what will monseigneur eat now?"

The bishop looked at her in amazement. "Why, are there not pewter plates to be had?"

Madame Magloire shrugged her shoulders. "Pewter smells!"

"Then iron!"

Madame Magloire made an expressive grimace. "Iron tastes."

"Well, then," said the bishop, "wood!"

A few minutes later, he was breakfasting at the same table at which

Jean Valjean sat on the previous evening. While breakfasting Monseigneur Welcome gayly remarked to his sister, who said nothing, and to Madame Magloire, who growled in a low voice, that spoon and fork, even of wood, are not required to dip a piece of bread in a cup of milk.

"What an idea!" Madame Magloire said, as she went backward and forward, "to receive a man like that, and lodge him by one's side. And what a blessing it is that he only stole! Oh, Lord! the mere thought makes a body shudder."

As the brother and sister were leaving the table there was a knock at the door.

"Come in," said the bishop.

The door opened, and a strange and violent group appeared on the threshold. Three men were holding a fourth by the collar. The three men were gendarmes, the fourth was Jean Valjean. A corporal, who apparently commanded the party, came in and walked up to the bishop with a military salute.

"Monseigneur," he said.

At this word Jean Valjean, who was gloomy and crushed, raised his head with a stupefied air.

"Monseigneur," he muttered, "then he is not the curé."

"Silence!" said a gendarme. "This gentleman is monseigneur the bishop."

In the meanwhile Monseigneur Welcome had advanced as rapidly as his great age permitted.

"Ah! there you are," he said, looking at Jean Valjean. "I am glad to see you. Why, I gave you the candlesticks too, which are also silver, and will fetch you 200 francs. Why did you not take them away with the rest of the plate?"

Jean Valjean opened his eyes and looked at the bishop with an expression which no human language could render.

"Monseigneur," the corporal said, "what this man told us was true then? We met him, and, as he looked as if he were running away, we arrested him. He had this plate—"

"And he told you," the bishop interrupted, with a smile, "that it was given to him by a good old priest at whose house he passed the night? I see it all. And you brought him back here? That is a mistake."

"In that case," the corporal continued, "we can let him go?"

"Of course," the bishop answered.

The gendarmes loosed their hold of Jean Valjean, who tottered back.

"Is it true that I am at liberty?" he said, in an almost inarticulate voice, and as if speaking in his sleep.

"Yes, you are let go; don't you understand?" said a gendarme.

"My friend," the bishop continued, "before you go, take your candlesticks."

He went to the mantel-piece, fetched the two candlesticks, and handed them to Jean Valjean. The two women watched him do so without a word, without a sign, without a look that could disturb the bishop. Jean Valjean was trembling in all his limbs; he took the candlesticks mechanically, and with wandering looks.

"Now," said the bishop, "go in peace. By the bye, when you return, my friend, it is unnecessary to pass through the garden, for you can always enter, day and night, by the front door, which is only latched."

Then, turning to the gendarmes, he said:

"Gentlemen, you can retire."

They did so. Jean Valjean looked as if he were on the point of fainting; the bishop walked up to him and said in a low voice:

"Never forget that you have promised to me to employ this money in becoming an honest man."

Jean Valjean, who had no recollection of having promised anything, stood silent. The bishop, who had laid a stress on these words, continued solemnly:

"Jean Valjean, my brother, you no longer belong to evil, but to good. I have bought your soul of you. I withdraw it from black thoughts and the spirit of perdition, and give it to God."

13. LITTLE GERVAIS

JEAN VALJEAN left the town as if running away; he walked hastily across the fields, taking the roads and paths that offered themselves, without perceiving that he was going round and round. He wandered thus the entire morning, and though he had eaten nothing, he did not feel hungry. He was attacked by a multitude of novel sensations; he felt a sort of passion, but he did not know with whom. He could not have said whether he was affected or humiliated; at times a strange softening came over him, against which he strove, and to which he opposed the hardening of the last twenty years. This condition offended him, and he saw with alarm that the species of frightful calmness, which the injustice of his misfortune had produced, was shaken within him. He asked himself what would take its place; at times he would have preferred being in prison and with the gendarmes, and that things had not happened thus; for that would have agitated him less. Although the season was advanced, there were still here and there in the hedges a few laggard flowers, whose smell recalled childhood's memories as he passed them. These recollections were almost unendurable, for it was so long since they had recurred to him.

Indescribable thoughts were thus congregated within him the whole day through. When the sun was setting and lengthening on the ground the shadow of the smallest pebble, Jean Valjean was sitting behind a bush in a large tawny and utterly deserted plain. There were only the Alps on the horizon; there was not even the steeple of a distant village. Jean Valjean might be about three leagues from D. . . . , and a path that crossed the plain ran a few paces from the bushes. In the midst of this meditation, which would have contributed no little in rendering his rags formidable to any one who saw him, he heard a sound of mirth.

He turned his head and saw a little Savoyard about ten years of age coming along the path, with his hurdy-gurdy at his side and his dormouse-box on his back. He was one of those gentle, merry lads who go about from country to country, displaying their knees through the holes in their trousers.

While singing, the lad stopped every now and then to play at pitch and toss with some coins he held in his hand, which were probably his entire fortune. Among these coins was a two-franc piece. The lad stopped by the side of the bushes without seeing Jean Valjean, and threw up the handful of sous, all of which he had hitherto always caught on the back of his hand. This time the two-franc piece fell, and rolled up to Jean Valjean. Jean Valjean placed his foot upon it. But the boy had looked after the coin, and seen him do it; he did not seem surprised, but walked straight up to the man. It was an utterly deserted spot; as far as eye could extend, there was no one on the plain or the path. Nothing was audible, save the faint cries of a swarm of birds of passage passing through the sky, at an immense height. The boy had his back turned to the sun, which wove golden threads in his hair, and suffused Jean Valjean's face with a purpled, blood-red hue.

"Sir," the little Savoyard said, with that childish confidence which is composed of ignorance and innocence, "my coin?"

"What is your name?" Jean Valjean said.

"Little Gervais, sir."

"Be off," said Jean Valjean.

"Give me my coin, if you please sir."

Jean Valjean hung his head, but said nothing.

The boy began again:

"My two-franc piece, sir."

Jean Valjean's eye remained fixed on the ground.

"My coin," the boy cried, "my silver piece, my money."

It seemed as if Jean Valjean did not hear him, for the boy seized the collar of his blouse and shook him, and at the same time made an effort to remove the iron-shod shoe placed on his coin.

"I want my money, my forty-sous piece."

The boy began crying, and Jean Valjean raised his head. He was still sitting on the ground, and his eyes were misty. He looked at the lad with a sort of amazement, then stretched forth his hand to his stick, and shouted in a terrible voice, "Who is there?"

"I, sir," the boy replied,—"little Gervais. Give me back my two francs, if you please. Take away your foot, sir, if you please." Then he grew irritated, though so little, and almost threatening.

"Come, will you lift up your foot? Lift up your foot, I say!"

"Ah, it is you still," said Jean Valjean; and springing up, with his foot still held on the coin, he added, "Will you be off or not?"

The startled boy looked at him, then began trembling from head to foot, and after a few moments of stupor ran off at full speed, without daring to look back or utter a cry. Still, when he had got a certain distance, want of breath forced him to stop, and Jean Valjean could hear him sobbing. In a few minutes the boy had disappeared. The sun had set, and darkness collected around Jean Valjean. He had eaten nothing all day, and was probably in a fever. He had remained standing and had not changed his attitude since the boy ran off. His breath heaved his chest at long and unequal intervals; his eye, fixed ten or twelve yards ahead, seemed to be studying with profound attention the shape of an old fragment of blue earthenware which had fallen in the grass. Suddenly he started, for he felt the night chill; he pulled his cap over his forehead, mechanically tried to cross and button his blouse, made a step, and stooped to pick up his stick.

At this moment he perceived the two-franc piece, which his foot had half buried in the turf, and which glistened among the pebbles. It had the effect of a galvanic shock upon him. "What is this?" he muttered. He fell back three paces, then stopped, unable to take his eye from the spot his foot had trodden a moment before, as if the thing glistening there in the darkness had an open eye fixed upon him. In a few moments he dashed convulsively at the coin, picked it up, and began looking out into the plain, while shuddering like a straying wild beast which is seeking shelter.

He saw nothing, night was falling, the plain was cold and indistinct, and heavy violet mists rose in the twilight. He set out rapidly in a certain direction, the one in which the lad had gone. After going some thirty yards, he stopped, looked, and saw nothing; then he shouted with all his strength, "Little Gervais, little Gervais!" He was silent, and waited, but there was no response. The country was deserted and gloomy, and he was surrounded by space. There was nothing but a gloom in which his glance was lost, and a silence in which his voice was lost. An icy breeze was blowing, and imparted to things around a sort of mournful life. The bushes shook their little thin arms with incredible fury; they seemed to be threatening and pursuing some one.

He walked onward and then began running, but from time to time he stopped, and shouted in the solitude with a voice the most formidable and agonizing that can be imagined, "Little Gervais, little Gervais!" Assuredly, if the boy had heard him, he would have felt frightened and not have shown himself; but the lad was doubtless a long way off by this time. The convict met a priest on horseback, to whom he went up and said:

"Monsieur le Curé, have you seen a lad pass?"

"No," the priest replied.

"A lad of the name of 'Little Gervais'?"

"I have seen nobody."

The convict took two five-franc pieces from his pouch and handed them to the priest.

"Monsieur le Curé, this is for your poor. He was a boy of about ten years of age, with a dormouse, I think, and a hurdy-gurdy,—a Savoyard, you know."

"I did not see him."

"Can you tell me if there is any one of the name of Little Gervais in the villages about here?"

"If it is as you say, my good fellow, the lad is a stranger. Many of them pass this way."

Jean Valjean violently took out two other five-franc pieces, which he gave the priest. "For your poor," he said, then added wildly, "Monsieur l'Abbé, have me arrested; I am a robber."

The priest urged his horse, and rode away in great alarm, while Jean Valjean set off running in the direction he had first taken. He went on for a long distance, looking, calling, and shouting, but he met no one else. Twice or thrice he ran across the plain to something that appeared to him to be a person lying or sitting down; but he only found heather, or rocks level with the ground. At last he stopped at a spot where three paths met; the moon had risen; he called out for the last time, "Little Gervais, little Gervais, little Gervais!" His shout died away in the mist, without even awakening an echo. He muttered again, "Little Gervais," in a weak and almost inarticulate voice, but it was his last effort. His knees suddenly gave way under him as if an invisible power were crushing him beneath the weight of a bad conscience. He fell exhausted on a large stone, with his hand tearing his hair, his face between his knees, and shrieked, "I am a wretch!" Then his heart melted, and he began to weep; it was the first time for nineteen years.

When Jean Valjean quitted the bishop's house, he was lifted out of his former thoughts, and could not account for what was going on within him. He stiffened himself against the angelic deeds and gentle words of the old man: "You have promised me to become an honest man. I purchase your soul; I withdraw it from the spirit of perverseness, and give it to God." This incessantly recurred to him, and he opposed to this celestial indulgence that pride which is within us as the fortress of evil. He felt instinctively that this priest's forgiveness was the greatest and most formidable assault by which he had yet been shaken; that his hardening would be permanent if he resisted this clemency; that if he yielded he must renounce that hatred with which the actions of other men had filled his soul during so many years, and which pleased him; that this time he must either conquer or be vanquished, and that the struggle, a colossal and final struggle, had begun between his wickedness and that man's goodness.

In the presence of all these gleams, he walked on like a drunken man. While he went on thus with haggard eye, had he any distinct perception of what the result of his adventure at D. . . . might be? Did he hear all that mysterious buzzing which warns or disturbs the mind at certain moments of life? Did a voice whisper in his ear that he had gone through the solemn hour of his destiny, that no middle way was now left him, and that if he were not henceforth the best of men he would be the worst; that he must now ascend higher than the bishop, or sink lower than the galley-slave; that if he wished to be good he must become an angel, and that if he wished to remain wicked he must become a monster?

Here we must ask again the question we previously asked,—did he confusedly receive any shadow of all this into his mind? Assuredly, as we have said, misfortune educates the intellect, still it is doubtful whether Jean Valjean was in a state to draw the conclusions we have formed. If these ideas reached him, he had a glimpse of them rather than saw them, and they only succeeded in throwing him into an indescribable and almost painful trouble. On leaving that shapeless black thing which is called the bagne, the bishop had hurt his soul, in the same way as a too brilliant light would have hurt his eyes on coming out of darkness. The future life, the possible life, which presented itself to him, all pure and radiant, filled him with tremor and anxiety, and he really no longer knew how matters were. Like an owl that suddenly witnessed a sunrise, the convict had been dazzled and, as it were, blinded by virtue.

One thing which he did not suspect is certain, however, that he was

no longer the same man; all was changed in him, and it was no longer
in his power to get rid of the fact that the bishop had spoken to him
and taken his hand. While in this mental condition he met little Gervais,
and robbed him of his two francs. Why did he so; assuredly he could not
explain it. Was it a final and, as it were, supreme effort of the evil thought
he had brought from the bagne, a remainder of impulse, a result of what
is called in statics "acquired momentum"? It was so, and was perhaps
also even less than that. Let us say it simply, it was not he who robbed, it
was not the man, but the brute beast that through habit and instinct
stupidly placed its foot on the coin, while the intellect was struggling
with such novel and extraordinary sensations. When the intellect woke
again and saw this brutish action, Jean Valjean recoiled with agony and
uttered a cry of horror. It was a curious phenomenon, and one only
possible in the situation he was in, that, in robbing the boy of that money,
he committed a deed of which he was no longer capable.

However this may be, this last bad action had a decisive effect upon
him; it suddenly darted through the chaos which filled his mind and
dissipated it, placed on one side the dark mists, on the other the light, and
acted on his soul, in its present condition, like certain chemical re-agents
act upon a troubled mixture, by precipitating one element and clarifying
another. At first, before even examining himself or reflecting, he wildly
strove to find the boy again and return him his money, then, when he
perceived that this was useless and impossible, he stopped in despair. At
the moment when he exclaimed, "I am a wretch!" he had seen himself
as he really was, and was already so separated from himself that he
fancied himself merely a phantom, and that he had there before him, in
flesh and blood, his blouse fastened around his hips, his knapsack full of
stolen objects on his back, with his resolute and gloomy face and his
mind full of hideous schemes, the frightful galley-slave, Jean Valjean.

As we have remarked, excessive misfortune had made him to some
extent a visionary, and this therefore, was a species of vision. He really
saw that Jean Valjean with his sinister face before him, and almost asked
himself who this man who so horrified him was. His brain was in that
violent and yet frightfully calm stage when the reverie is so deep that it
absorbs reality. He contemplated himself, so to speak, face to face, and at
the same time he saw through this hallucination a species of light which
he at first took for a torch. On looking more attentively at this light
which appeared to his conscience, he perceived that it had a human
shape and was the bishop. His conscience examined in turn the two men

standing before him, the bishop and Jean Valjean. By one of those singular effects peculiar to an ecstasy of this nature the more his reverie was prolonged, the taller and more brilliant the bishop appeared, while Jean Valjean grew less and faded out of sight. At length he disappeared and the bishop alone remained, who filled the wretched man's soul with a magnificent radiance.

Jean Valjean wept for a long time, and sobbed with more weakness than a woman, more terror than a child. While he wept, the light grew brighter in his brain, an extraordinary light, at once ravishing and terrible. His past life, his first fault, his long expiation, his external brutalization, his internal hardening, his liberation, accompanied by so many plans of vengeance, that which had happened at the bishop's, the last thing he had done, the robbery of the boy, a crime the more cowardly and monstrous because it took place after the bishop's forgiveness—all this recurred to him, but in a light which he had never seen before. He looked at his life, and it appeared to him horrible; at his soul, and it appeared to him frightful. Still a soft light was shed over both, and he fancied that he saw Satan by the light of paradise.

How many hours did he weep thus? what did he do afterward? whither did he go? No one ever knew. It was stated, however, that on this very night the mail-carrier from Grenoble, who arrived at D. . . . at about three A. M., while passing through the street where the bishop's palace stood, saw a man kneeling on the pavement in the attitude of prayer in front of Monseigneur Welcome's door.

BOOK III

IN THE YEAR 1817

1. THE YEAR 1817

THE year 1817 is the one which Louis XVIII, with a certain royal coolness which was not deficient in pride, entitled the twenty-second of
his reign. It is the year in which M. Bruguière de Sorsum was celebrated.
All the wig-makers' shops, hoping for powder and the return of the
royal bird, were covered with azure and fleurs-de-lis. It was the candid
time when Count Lynch sat every Sunday as church-warden at St.
Germain-des-Prés in the coat of a peer of France, with his red ribbon,
his long nose, and majestic profile peculiar to a man who has done
a brilliant deed. The brilliant deed done by M. Lynch was having, when
mayor of Bordeaux, surrendered the town rather prematurely, on March
12, 1814, to the Duc d'Angoulême; hence his peerage. In 1817 fashion
buried little boys of the age of six and seven beneath vast morocco
leather caps with ear-flaps much resembling Esquimaux fur bonnets.
The French army was dressed in white, like the Austrian; the regiments were called legions, and bore the names of the departments instead
of numbers. Napoleon was at St. Helena, and as England refused him
green cloth, he had his old coats turned. In 1817 Pellegrini sang, and
Mlle. Bigottini danced, Potier reigned, and Odry was not yet known.
Madame Saqui succeeded Florioso. There were still Prussians in France.
M. Delalot was a personage. Legitimacy had just strengthened itself by
cutting off the hand and then the head of Pleignier, Carbonneau and
Tolleron. Prince de Talleyrand, lord high chamberlain, and the Abbé
Louis, minister designate of finance, looked at each other with the laugh
of two augurs. Both had celebrated on July 14, 1790, the mass of the
confederation in the Champ de Mars. Talleyrand had read it as bishop,
Louis had served it as deacon. In 1817, in the sidewalks of the same
Champ de Mars, could be seen large wooden cylinders, lying in the wet

and rotting in the grass, painted blue, with traces of eagles and bees, which had lost their gilding. These were the columns which two years previously supported the emperor's balcony at the Champ de Mai. They were partly blackened by the bivouac fires of the Austrians encamped near Gros Caillou, and two or three of the columns had disappeared in the bivouac fires, and warmed the coarse hands of the Kaiserlichs. The Champ de Mai had this remarkable thing about it, that it was held in the month of June, and on the Champ de Mars. In this year, 1817, two things were popular, the Coltaire-Touquet and the snuff-box *à la Charte*. The latest Parisian sensation was the crime of Dautun, who threw his brother's head into the basin on the Flower Market. People were beginning to grow anxious at the admiralty that no news arrived about that fatal frigate the *Medusa,* which was destined to cover Chaumareix with shame and Géricault with glory. Colonel Selves proceeded to Egypt to become Soliman Pacha there. The palace of the Thermes, in the Rue de la Harpe, served as a shop for a cooper. On the platform of the octagonal tower of the Hôtel de Cluny could still be seen the small wooden hut which had served as an observatory for Messier, astronomer to the admiralty under Louis XVI. The Duchess de Daras was reading to three or four friends, in her boudoir furnished with sky-blue satin X's, her unpublished romance of "Ourika." The N's were scratched off the Louvre, the Austerlitz bridge abdicated, and was called the King's Gardens' bridge—a double enigma which at once disguised the Austerlitz bridge and the Jardin des Plantes. Louis XVIII, while annotating Horace with his nail, was troubled by heroes who made themselves emperors, and cobblers who made themselves dauphins; he had two objects of anxiety— Napoleon and Mathurin Bruneau. The French academy offered as subject for the prize essay "the happiness produced by study." M. Bellart was officially eloquent; and in his shadow could be seen growing up that future Advocate-General de Broë promised to the sarcasms of Paul Louis Courier. There was a false Châteaubriand called Marchangy, while waiting till there should be a false Marchangy called d'Arlincourt. "Claire d'Albe" and "Malek Adel" were masterpieces; and Madame Cottin was declared the first writer of the age. The institute erased from its lists the academician Napoleon Bonaparte. A royal decree constituted Angoulême a naval school, for, as the Duc d'Angoulême was lord high admiral, it was evident that the city from which he derived his title possessed *de jure* all the qualifications of a seaport; if not, the monarchical principle would be encroached on. In the council of ministers the question was discussed whether the wood-cuts representing tumblers, which seasoned Franconi's bills and caused the street scamps to congregate, should be tolerated. M. Paër, author of "Agnese," a square-faced man with a carbuncle on his chin, directed the private concerts of the Marchioness de Sassenaye in the Rue de la Ville d'Evêque. All the young ladies were singing "L'Ermite de Saint Avelle," words by Edmond Géraud. "The Yellow Dwarf" was transformed into "The Mirror." The Café Lemblin stood up for the emperor against the Café Valois, which supported the Bourbons. The Duc de Berry, whom Louvel was already gazing at from the darkness, had just been married to a princess of Sicily. It was a year since Madame de Staël had died. The Life-guards hissed Mlle. Mars. The large papers were all small; their size was limited, but the liberty was great. The *Constitutionnel* was constitutional, and the *Minerva* called Châteaubriand, Châteaubriant; this *t* made the city laugh heartily, at the expense of the great writer. Prostituted journalists insulted in sold journals the proscripts of 1815. David had no longer any talent, Arnault any wit, Carnot any probity. Soult never gained a battle. It was true that Napoleon was no longer a genius. Everybody knows that it is rare for letters sent by post to reach an exile, for the police make it a religious duty to intercept them. The fact is not new, for Descartes, when banished, complained of it. David having displayed some temper in a Belgium paper at not receiving letters written to him, this appeared very amusing to the royalist journals, which ridiculed the proscribed man. The use of the words regicides or voters, enemies or allies, Napoleon or Bonaparte, separated two men more than an abyss. All persons of common sense were agreed that the era of revolutions was eternally closed by Louis XVIII, surnamed "the immortal author of the charter." On the platform of the Pont Neuf the word "Redivivus" was carved on the pedestal which was awaiting the statue of Henri IV. M. Piet was excogitating at No. 4 Rue Thérèse his council to consolidate the monarchy. The leaders of the right said in grave complications, "Bacot must be written to." Messrs. Canuel, O'Mahony, and de Chappedelaine were sketching under the covert approval of Monsieur what was destined to be at a later date "the conspiracy du Bord de l'Eau." The "Black Pin" was plotting on its side. Delaverderie was coming to an understanding with Trogoff. M. Decazes, a rather liberally minded man, was in the ascendant. Châteaubriand, standing each morning at his window, No. 27 Rue Saint Dominique, in trousers and slippers, with his gray hair fastened by a handkerchief, with his eyes fixed on a mirror, and a case of dentist's

instruments open before him, was cleaning his teeth, which were splendid, while dictating "The Monarchy according to the Charter" to M.
Pilorge, his secretary. Authoritative critics preferred Lafon to Talma.
M. de Feletz signed A; M. Hoffman signed Z. Charles Nodier was
writing "Thérèse Aubert." Divorce was abolished. The Lyceums were
called colleges. The collegians, with a gold fleur-de-lis on their collar,
were fighting about the king of Rome. The counter-police of the château
denounced to her Royal Highness Madame, the universally exposed
portrait of the Duc d'Orleans, who looked much handsomer in his uniform of colonel-general of hussars than the Duc de Berry did in his
uniform as colonel-general of dragoons, which was a serious annoyance.
The city of Paris was having the dome of the Invalides regilt at its own
expense. Serious-minded men asked themselves what M. de Trinque-
lague would do in such and such a case. M. Clausel de Montals diverged
on certain points from M. Clausel de Coussergues; M. de Salaberry was
not satisfied. Picard, the comedian, who belonged to the academy of
which Molière was not a member, was playing "The Two Philiberts" at
the Odéon, on the façade of which could still be distinctly read: Théâtre
de l'Imperatrice, although the letters had been torn down. People were
taking sides for or against Cugnet de Montarlot. Fabvier was factious;
Bavoux was revolutionary; Pelicier, the publisher, brought out an edition
of Voltaire with the title, "The Works of Voltaire, Member of the
Academy." "That catches purchasers," the simple publisher said. It was
the general opinion that M. Charles Loyson would be the genius of the
age; envy was beginning to snap at him, which was a sign of glory, and
the following line was written about him:

"Même quand Loyson vole, on sent qu'il a des pattes."

As Cardinal Fesch refused to resign, M. de Pins, archbishop of Amasia,
was administering the diocese of Lyons. The quarrel about the Dappes
valley began between Switzerland and France, through a memorial of
Captain Dufour, who has since become a general. Saint-Simon, utterly
ignored, was building up his sublime dream. There were in the Academy
of Sciences a celebrated Fourier whom posterity has forgotten, and in
some obscure garret a Fourier whom the future will remember. Lord
Byron was beginning to culminate; a note to a poem of Millevoye's
announced him to France in these terms, "un certain Lord Baron."
David d'Angers was trying to mold marble. The Abbé Caron spoke in

terms of praise to a select audience in the Alley of the Feuillantines of an unknown priest called Felicité Robert, who was at a later date Lamennais. A thing that smoked and plashed on the Seine with the noise of a swimming dog, went under the Tuileries windows from the Pont Royal to the Pont Louis XV; it was a mechanism not worth much, a sort of plaything, a reverie of a dreamy inventor, an utopia,—a steamboat. The Parisians looked at this useless thing with indifference. M. de Vaublanc, reformer of the Institute by coup d'état, and distinguished author of several academicians, after making them, could not succeed in becoming one himself. The Faubourg St. Germain and the Pavillon Marsan desired to have M. Delaveau as prefect of police on account of his devoutness. Dupuytren and Récamier quarreled in the theater of the school of medicine, and were going to fight about the divinity of the Saviour. Cuvier, with one eye on Genesis and the other on nature, was striving to please the bigoted reaction by placing fossils in harmony with texts, and letting Moses be flattered by the Mastodons. M. François de Neufchâteau, the praiseworthy cultivator of the memory of Parmentier, was making a thousand efforts to have "pommes de terre" pronounced "parmentière," but did not succeed. The Abbé Grégoire, ex-bishop, ex-conventionalist, and ex-senator, had reached in the royal polemics the state of the "infamous Grégoire." The expression "reached the state" was denounced by M. Royer-Collard as a neologism. In the third arch of Pont de Jena, the new stone could still be distinguished through its whiteness, with which two years previously the mine formed by Blücher to blow up the bridge was stopped up. Justice summoned to her bar a man who, on seeing the Comte d'Artois enter Notre Dame, said aloud, "Sapristi! I regret the days when I saw Napoleon and Talma enter the Bal-Sauvage arm in arm"; seditious remarks punished with six months' imprisonment.

Traitors displayed themselves unblushingly; some, who had passed over to the enemy on the eve of a battle, did not conceal their reward, but walked immodestly in the sunshine with the cynicism of wealth and dignities; the deserters at Ligny and Quatre Bras, well rewarded for their turpitude, openly displayed their monarchical devotion.

Such are a few recollections of the year 1817, which are now forgotten. History neglects nearly all these details, and cannot do otherwise, as the infinity would crush it. Still these details, wrongly called little,—there are no little facts in humanity, or little leaves in vegetation,—are useful, for the face of ages is composed of the physiognomy of years.

In this year 1817 four young Parisians played a capital joke.

2. A DOUBLE QUARTETTE

THESE Parisians came, one from Toulouse, the second from Limoges, the third from Cahors, the fourth from Montauban, but they were students, and thus Parisians; for studying in Paris is being born in Paris. These young men were insignificant, four every-day specimens, neither good nor bad, wise nor ignorant, geniuses nor idiots, and handsome with that charming April which is called twenty years. They were four Oscars, for at that period Arthurs did not yet exist. "Burn for him the perfumes of Araby," the romance said; "Oscar is advancing, I am about to see him." People had just emerged from Ossian; the elegant world was Scandinavian and Caledonian; the English style was not destined to prevail till a later date, and the first of the Arthurs, Wellington, had only just won the battle of Waterloo.

The names of these Oscars were Felix Tholomyès, of Toulouse; Listolier, of Cahors; Fameuil, of Limoges, and Blachevelle, of Montauban. Of course each had a mistress,—Blachevelle loved Favorite, so called because she had been to England; Listolier adored Dahlia, who had taken the name of a flower for her *nom de guerre;* Fameuil idolized Zephine, an abridgement of Josephine; while Tholomyès had Fantine, called the Blonde, owing to her magnificent sun-colored hair. Favorite, Dahlia, Zephine, and Fantine were four exquisitely pretty girls, still to some extent work-women. They had not entirely laid down the needle, and, though deranged by their amourettes, they still had in their faces a remnant of the serenity of toil, and in their souls that flower of honesty which in a woman survives the first fall. One of the four was called the young one, because she was the youngest, and one called the old one, who was only three-and-twenty. To conceal nothing, the three first were more experienced, more reckless, and had flown further into the tumult of life than Fantine the Blonde, who was still occupied with her first illusion.

Dahlia, Zephine, and especially Favorite, could not have said the same. There was already more than one episode in their scarce-begun romance, and the lover who was called Adolphe in the first chapter became Alphonse in the second, and Gustave in the third. Poverty and coquettishness are two fatal counselors: one scolds, the other flatters, and the poor girls of the lower class have them whispering in both ears. Badly guarded souls listen, and hence come the falls they make, and the stones hurled at them. They are crushed with the splendor of all that is immaculate and inaccessible. Alas! if the Jungfrau were to be starving? Favorite, who had been to England, was admired by Zephine and Dahlia. She had a home of her own from an early age. Her father was an old brutal and boasting professor of mathematics, unmarried, and still giving lessons in spite of his age. This professor, when a young man, had one day seen a lady's maid's gown caught in a fender; he fell in love with this accident, and Favorite was the result. She met her father from time to time, and he bowed to her. One morning, an old woman with a hypocritical look came into her room and said, "Do you not know me, miss?" "No." "I am your mother." Then the old woman opened the cupboard, ate and drank, sent for a mattress she had, and installed herself. This mother, who was grumbling and proud, never spoke to Favorite, sat for hours without saying a word, breakfasted, dined, and supped for half a dozen, and spent her evenings in the porter's lodge, where she abused her daughter. What drew Dahlia toward Listolier, toward others perhaps, toward idleness, was having too pretty pink nails. How could she employ such nails in working? a girl who wishes to remain virtuous must not have pity on her hands. As for Zephine, she had conquered Fameuil by her little saucy and coaxing way of saying "Yes, sir." The young men were comrades, the girls friends. Such amours are always doubled by such friendships.

A sage and a philosopher are two persons; and what proves it is that, after making all reservations for these little irregular households, Favorite, Zephine, and Dahlia were philosophic girls, and Fantine a sage girl. Sage, it will be said, and Tholomyès'? Solomon would reply that love forms part of wisdom. We confine ourselves to saying that Fantine's love was a first love, a single love, a faithful love. She was the only one of the four who was thou'd by one man alone.

Fantine was one of those beings who spring up from the dregs of the people; issuing from the lowest depths of the social darkness, she had on her forehead the stamp of the anonymous and the unknown. She was born at M. sur M.; of what parents? who could say? she had never known either father or mother. She called herself Fantine, and why Fantine? she was never known by any other name. At the period of her birth, the Directory was still in existence. She had no family name, as she had no family; and no Christian name, as the church was abolished. She accepted the name given her by the first passer-by, who saw her running bare-footed about the streets. She was called little Fantine, and no one knew any more. This human creature came into the world in that way. At the age of ten, Fantine left the town, and went into service with farmers in the neighborhood. At the age of fifteen she went to Paris, "to seek her fortune." Fantine was pretty and remained pure as long as she could. She was a charming blonde, with handsome teeth; she had gold and pearls for her dower, but the gold was on her head, and the pearls in her mouth.

She worked for a livelihood; and then she loved, still for the sake of living, for the heart is hungry too. She loved Tholomyès; it was a pastime for him, but a passion with her. The streets of the Quartier Latin, which are thronged with students and grisettes, saw the beginning of this dream. Fantine, in the labyrinth of the Pantheon Hill where so many adventures are tied and untied, long shunned Tholomyès, but in such a way as to meet him constantly. There is a manner of avoiding which resembles seeking—in a word, the eclogue was played.

Blachevelle, Listolier, and Fameuil formed a sort of group, of which Tholomyès was the head, for it was he who had the wit. Tholomyès was the antique old student; he was rich, for he had an income of 4000 francs a year, a splendid scandal on the Montagne St. Geneviève. Tholomyès was a man of the world, thirty years of age, and in a bad state of preservation. He was wrinkled and had lost teeth, and he had an incipient baldness, of which he himself said without sorrow: "The skull at thirty, the knee at forty." He had but a poor digestion, and one of his eyes was permanently watery. But in proportion as his youth was extinguished, his gayety became brighter; he substituted jests for his teeth, joy for his hair, irony for his health, and his weeping eye laughed incessantly. He was battered, but still flowering. His youth had beaten an orderly retreat, and only the fire was visible. He had had a piece refused at the Vaudeville theater, and wrote occasional verses now and then. In addition, he doubted everything in a superior way, which is a great strength in the eyes of the weak. Hence, being ironical and bald, he was the leader. We wonder whether irony is derived from the English word "iron"? One day Tholomyès took the other three aside, made an oracular gesture, and said:

"It is nearly a year that Fantine, Dahlia, Zephine, and Favorite have been asking us to give them a surprise, and we promised solemnly to do so. They are always talking about it, especially to me. In the same way as the old women of Naples cry to Saint Januarius, 'Yellow face, perform your miracle!' our beauties incessantly say to me, 'Tholomyès, when will you be delivered of your surprise?' At the same time our parents are writing to us, so let us kill two birds with one stone. The moment appears to me to have arrived, so let us talk it over."

Upon this, Tholomyès lowered his voice, and mysteriously uttered something so amusing that a mighty and enthusiastic laugh burst from four mouths simultaneously, and Blachevelle exclaimed, "That is an idea!" An *estaminet* full of smoke presenting itself, they went in, and the remainder of their conference was lost in the tobacco-clouds. The result of the gloom was a brilliant pleasure excursion that took place on the following Sunday, to which the four young men invited the girls.

3. FOUR TO FOUR

IT is difficult to form an idea at the present day of what a pleasure party of students and grisettes was four-and-forty years ago. Paris has no longer the same environs; the face of what may be termed circum-Parisian life has completely changed during half a century; where there was the coucou, there is a railway carriage; where there was the fly-boat, there is now the steamer; people talk of Fécamp as people did in those days of St. Cloud. Paris of 1862 is a city which has France for its suburbs.

The four couples conscientiously accomplished all the rustic follies possible at that day. It was a bright warm summer day; they rose at five o'clock; then they went to St. Cloud in the stage coach, looked at the dry cascade, and exclaimed, "That must be grand when there is water"; breakfasted at the Tête Noire, where Castaing had not yet put up, ran at the ring in the Quincunx of the great basin, ascended into the Diogenes lantern, gambled for macaroons at the roulette-board by the Sèvres bridge, culled posies at Puteaux, bought reed-pipes at Neuilly, ate apple-tarts everywhere, and were perfectly happy. The girls prattled and chattered like escaped linnets; they were quite wild, and every now and then gave the young men little taps. Oh youthful intoxication of life! adorable years! the wing of the dragon-fly rustles. Oh, whoever you may be, do you remember? have you ever walked in the woods, removing the branches for the sake of the pretty head that comes behind you? have you laughingly stepped on a damp slope, with a beloved woman who holds your hand, and cries, "Oh, my boots, what a state they are in!" Let us say at once that the merry annoyance of a shower was spared the happy party, although Favorite had said on starting, with a magisterial and maternal air, "The slugs are walking about the paths; this is a sign of rain, children."

All four were distractingly pretty. A good old classic poet, then renowned, M. le Chevalier de Labouïsse, a worthy man who had an Eléonore, wandering that day under the chestnut-trees of St. Cloud, saw them pass at about ten in the morning, and exclaimed, "There is one too many"; he was thinking of the Graces. Favorite, the girl who was three-and-twenty and the old one, ran in front under the large green branches, leaped over ditches, strode madly across bushes, and presided over the gayety with the spirit of a young fawn. Zephine and Dahlia, whom accident had created as a couple necessary to enhance each other's beauty by contrast, did not separate, though more through a coquettish instinct than through friendship, and, leaning upon one another, assumed English attitudes. The first Keepsakes had just come out; melancholy was culminating for women, as Byronism did at a later date for men, and the hair of the tender sex was beginning to become disheveled. Zephine and Dahlia had their hair in rolls. Listolier and Fameuil, who were engaged in a discussion about their professors, were explaining to Fantine the difference there was between M. Delvincourt and M. Blondeau. Blachevelle seemed to have been created expressly to carry Favorite's dull-colored, shabby shawl on Sundays.

Tholomyès came last; he was very gay, but there was something dictatorial in his joviality; his principal ornament was nankeen trousers, cut in the shape of elephants' legs, with leathern straps; he had a mighty rattan worth 200 francs in his hand, and, as he was quite reckless, a strange thing called a cigar in his mouth. Nothing being sacred to him, he smoked. "That Tholomyès is astounding," the others were wont to say with veneration. "What trousers! what energy!"

As for Fantine, she was the personification of joy. Her splendid teeth had evidently been made for laughter by nature. She carried in her hand, more willingly than on her head, her little straw bonnet, with its long streamers. Her thick, light hair, inclined to float and which had to be done up continually, seemed made for the flight of Galatea under the willows. Her rosy lips prattled enchantingly; the corners of her mouth voluptuously raised, as in the antique masks of Erigone, seemed to encourage boldness; but her long eye-lashes, full of shade, were discreetly lowered upon the seductiveness of the lower part of the face, as if to command respect. Her whole toilet had something flaming about it; she had on a dress of mauve barège, little buskin slippers, whose strings formed an X on her fine, open-worked stockings, and that sort of muslin spencer, a Marseillaise invention, whose name of canezou, a pronunciation of *quinze août* as corrupted *à la Canebière,* signifies fine weather and heat. The three others, who were less timid, as we said, bravely wore low-necked dresses, which in summer are very graceful and attractive, under bonnets covered with flowers; but, by the side of this bold dress, Fantine's canezou, with its transparency, indiscretion, and reticences, at once concealing and displaying, seemed a provocative invention of decency; and the famous court of Love, presided over by the Vicomtesse de Cette with the sea-green eyes, would have probably bestowed the prize for coquettishness on this canezou, which competed for that of chastity. The simplest things are frequently the cleverest.

Dazzling from a front view, delicate from a side view, with dark-blue eyes, heavy eyelids, arched and small feet, wrists and ankles admirably set on, the white skin displaying here and there the azure arborescences of the veins, with the childish fresh cheek, and robust neck of the Aeginetan Junos, shoulders apparently modeled by Coustou, and having in their center a voluptuous dimple, visible through the muslin; a gayety tempered by reverie; a sculptural and exquisite being,—such was Fantine. You could trace beneath the ribbons and finery a statue, and inside the statue a soul. Fantine was beautiful, without being exactly conscious of it. Those rare dreamers, the mysterious priests of the beautiful, who silently confront everything with perfection, would have seen in this little work-girl the ancient sacred euphony, through the transparency of Parisian grace! This girl had blood in her, and had those two descriptions of beauty which are style and rhythm. Style is the form of the ideal; rhythm is its movement.

We have said that Fantine was joy itself, she was also modesty. Any one who watched her closely would have seen through all this intoxication of youth, the season, and love, an invincible expression of restraint and modesty. She remained slightly astonished, and this chaste astonishment distinguishes Psyche from Venus. Fantine had the long white delicate fingers of the Vestal who stirs up the sacred fire with a golden bodkin. Though she had refused nothing, as we shall soon see, to Tholomyès, her face, when in repose, was supremely virginal; a species of stern and almost austere dignity suddenly invaded it at certain hours, and nothing was so singular and affecting as to see gayety so rapidly extinguished on it, and contemplation succeed cheerfulness without any transition. This sudden gravity, which was at times sternly marked, resembled the disdain of a goddess. Her forehead, nose, and chin offered that equilibrium of outline which is very distinct from the equilibrium of proportion and produces the harmony of the face; in the characteristic space between the base of the nose and the upper lip, she had that imperceptible and charming curve, that mysterious sign of chastity, which made Barbarossa fall in love with a Diana found in the ruins of Iconium. Love is a fault; be it so; but Fantine was innocence floating on the surface of the fault.

4 . *THOLOMYES IS SO MERRY AS TO SING A SPANISH SONG*

THE whole of this day seemed to be composed of dawn; all nature seemed to be having a holiday, and laughing. The pastures of St. Cloud exhaled perfumes; the breeze from the Seine vaguely stirred the leaves; the branches gesticulated in the wind; the bees were plundering the jessamine; a madcap swarm of butterflies settled down on the ragwort, the clover, and the wild oats; there was in the august park of the king of France a pack of vagabonds, the birds. The four happy couples enjoyed the sun, the fields, the flowers, and the trees. And in this community of paradise, three of the girls, while singing, talking, dancing, chasing butterflies, picking bindweed, wetting their stockings in the tall grass, fresh, madcap, but not dissolute, received kisses from all the gentlemen in turn. Fantine alone was shut up in her vague, dreamy resistance, and loved. "You always look strange," Favorite said to her.

Such passings-by of happy couples are a profound appeal to life and nature, and bring caresses and light out of everything. Once upon a time there was a fairy, who made fields and trees expressly for lovers; hence the eternal hedge school of lovers, which incessantly recommences, and will last so long as there are bushes and scholars. Hence the popularity of spring among thinkers; the patrician and the peddler, the duke and the pettifogger, people of the court and people of the city, as they were called formerly, are all subjects of this fairy. People laugh and chase each other. There is the brilliancy of an apotheosis in the air, for what a transfiguration is loving! Notary's clerks are gods. And then the little shrieks, pursuits in the grass, waists caught hold of, that chattering which is so melodious, that adoration which breaks out in the way of uttering a word, cherries torn from lips by neighboring lips, pretty girls sweetly squandering their charms—all this is glorious! People believe that it will

125

never end; philosophers, poets, artists, regard these ecstasies, and know not what to do, as they are so dazzled by them. The departure for Cythera! exclaims Watteau; Lancret, the painter of the middle classes, regards his cits flying away in the blue sky; Diderot stretches out his arms to all these amourettes, and d'Urfé mixes up Druids with them.

After breakfast the four couples went to see, in what was then called the King's Square, a plant newly arrived from the Indies, whose name we have forgotten, but which at that time attracted all Paris to St. Cloud; it was a strange and pretty shrub, whose numerous branches, fine as threads and leafless, were covered with a million of small white flowers, which made it look like a head of hair swarming with flowers; there was always a crowd round it, admiring it. After inspecting the shrub, Tholomyès exclaimed, "I will pay for donkeys!" and, after making a bargain with the donkey man, they returned by Vanves and Issy. At the latter place an incident occurred; the park, a national estate held at this time by Bourguin, the contractor, was accidentally open. They passed through the gates, visited the lay figure hermit in his grotto, and tried the mysterious effect of the famous cabinet of mirrors, a lascivious trap, worthy of a satyr who had become a millionaire, or of Turcaret metamorphosed into Priapus. They bravely pulled the large swing fastened to the two chestnut trees celebrated by the Abbé de Bernis. While swinging the ladies in turn, which produced, amid general laughter, a flying of skirts, by which Greuze would have profited, the Toulousian Tholomyès, who was somewhat of a Spaniard, as Toulouse is the cousin of Tolosa, sang to a melancholy tune the old *gallega,* which was probably inspired by the sight of a pretty girl swinging between two trees:

> *Soy de Badajoz.*
> *Amor me llama.*
> *Toda mi alma*
> *Es en mis ojos*
> *Porque enseñas*
> *A tus pierñas.*

Fantine alone declined to swing.

"I do not like people to be so affected," Favorite muttered rather sharply.

On giving up the donkeys there was fresh pleasure; the Seine was crossed in a boat, and from Passy they walked to the Barrière de l'Etoile.

They had been afoot since five in the morning; but no matter! "There is no such thing as weariness on Sunday," said Favorite; "on Sundays fatigue does not work." At about three o'clock, the four couples, wild with delight, turned into the Montagnes Russes, a singular building, which at that time occupied the heights of Beaujon, and whose winding line could be seen over the trees of the Champs Elysées. From time to time Favorite exclaimed:

"Where is the surprise? I insist on the surprise."

"Have patience," Tholomyès answered.

5. *AT BOMBARDA'S*.

THE Russian mountain exhausted, they thought about dinner, and the radiant eight, at length somewhat weary, put into the Cabaret Bombarda, an off-shoot established in the Champs Elysées by that famous restaurateur Bombarda, whose sign could be seen at that time at the Rue de Rivoli by the side of the Passage Delorme.

A large but ugly room, with an alcove and a bed at the end (owing to the crowded state of the houses on Sundays, they were compelled to put up with it); two windows from which the quay and river could be contemplated through the elm-trees; a magnificent autumn sun illumining the windows; two tables, on one of them a triumphal mountain of bottles, mixed up with hats and bonnets, at the other one, four couples joyously seated round a mass of dishes, plates, bottles, and glasses, pitchers of beer, mingled with wine bottles; but little order on the table, and some amount of disorder under it.

"Ils faisaient sous la table
Un bruit, un trique-trac de pieds épouvantable,"

as Molière says. Such was the state of the pastoral which began at five A. M.; at half-past four P. M. the sun was declining and appetite was satisfied.

The Champs Elysées, full of sunshine and crowd, were all light and dust, two things of which glory is composed. The horses of Marly, those neighing marbles, reared amid a golden cloud. Carriages continually passed along; a squadron of splendid guards, with the trumpeter at their head, rode down the Neuilly avenue; the white flag, tinged with pink by the setting sun, floated above the dome of the Tuileries. The Place de la Concorde, which had again become the Place Louis XV, was crowded with merry promenaders. Many wore a silver fleur-de-lis hanging from a black moiré ribbon, which, in 1817, had not entirely disappeared from the button-holes. Here and there, in the midst of applauding crowds, little girls were singing a royalist *bourrée,* very celebrated at that time, intended to crush the hundred days, and which had a chorus of

> *"Rendez-nous notre père de Gand,*
> *Rendez-nous notre père."*

Heaps of suburbans, dressed in their Sunday clothes, and some wearing fleurs-de-lis like the cits, were scattered over the squares, playing at Quintain, or riding in roundabouts; others were drinking; some who were printers' apprentices wore paper caps, and their laughter was the loudest. All was radiant; it was a time of undeniable peace, and of profound royalist security; it was a period when a private and special report of Anglès, prefect of police to the king, terminated with these lines: "All things duly considered, sire, there is nothing to fear from these people. They are as careless and indolent as cats, and though the lower classes in the provinces are stirring, those in Paris are not so. They are all little men, sire, and it would take two of them to make one of your grenadiers. There is nothing to fear from the populace of the capital. It is remarkable that their height has decreased during the last fifty years, and the people of the suburbs of Paris are shorter than they were before the Revolution. They are not dangerous, and, in a word, are good-tempered *canaille.*"

Prefects of police do not believe it possible that a cat can be changed into a lion; it is so, however, and that is the miracle of the people of Paris. The cat, despised by Count Anglès, possessed the esteem of the old Republics; it was the incarnation of liberty in their eyes, and as if to serve as a pendant to the Minerva Apteros of the Piraeus, there was on the public square of Corinth a colossal bronze statue of a cat. The simple police of the restoration had too favorable an opinion of the people of Paris, and they were not such good-tempered *canaille* as they were supposed to be. The Parisian is to the Frenchman what the Athenian is to the Greek: no one sleeps sounder than he; no one is more frankly frivolous and idle than he; no one can pretend to forget so well as he,—but he must not be trusted; he is suited for every species of nonchalance, but when there is glory as the result, he is wonderful for every sort of fury. Give him a pike, and he will make August 10; give him a musket, and you will have Austerlitz. He is the support of Napoleon, and the resource of Danton. If the country is in danger, he enlists; if liberty is imperiled, he tears up the pavement. His hair, full of wrath, is epical, his blouse assumes the folds of a chlamys. Take care; for of the first Rue Grenéta he comes to, he will make Caudine Forks. If the hour strikes, this suburban grows, the little man looks in a terrible manner, his breath becomes a tempest, and from his weak chest issues a blast strong enough to uproot the Alps. It was through this class of Parisian that the Revolution, joined with armies, conquered Europe. He sings, and that forms his delight; proportion his song to his nature, and you shall see! so long as he has no burden but the Carmagnole, he will merely overthrow Louis XVI; but make him sing the Marseillaise, and he will deliver the world.

After writing this note on the margin of Count Anglès's report, we will return to our four couples. The dinner, as we said, was drawing to a close.

6. MUTUAL ADORATION

LOVE talk and table talk are equally indescribable, for the first is cloud, the second smoke. Fantine and Dahlia were humming a tune, Tholomyès was drinking, Zephine laughing, Fantine smiling, Listolier was blowing a penny trumpet bought at St. Cloud, Favorite was looking tenderly at Blachevelle and saying:

"Blachevelle, I adore you."

This led to Blachevelle asking:

"What would you do, Favorite, if I ceased to love you?"

"I?" Favorite exclaimed. "Oh, do not say that, even in fun! if you ceased to love me, I would run after you, claw you, throw water over you, and have you arrested."

Blachevelle smiled with the voluptuous fatuity of a man whose self-esteem is tickled. Dahlia, while still eating, whispered to Favorite through the noise:

"You seem to be very fond of your Blachevelle?"

"I detest him," Favorite answered in the same key, as she seized her fork again. "He is miserly, and I prefer the little fellow who lives opposite to me. He is a very good-looking young man; do you know him? It is easy to see that he wants to be an actor, and I am fond of actors. So soon as he comes in, his mother says, 'Oh, good heavens, my tranquillity is destroyed; he is going to begin to shout; my dear boy, you give me a headache'; because he goes about the house, into the garrets as high as he can get, and sings and declaims so that he can be heard from the streets. He already earns 20 sous a day in a lawyer's office. He is the son of an ex-chorister at St. Jacques du Haut Pas. Ah! he adores me to such a pitch that one day when he saw me making batter for pancakes, he said to me, 'Mamselle, make fritters of your gloves, and I will eat them.' Only artists are able to say things like that. Ah! he is very good-looking, and I feel as if I am about to fall madly in love with the little fellow. No matter, I tell Blachevelle that I adore him; what a falsehood, eh, what a falsehood?"

After a pause, Favorite continued:

"Dahlia, look you, I am sad. It has done nothing but rain all the summer; the wind annoys me; Blachevelle is excessively mean; there are hardly any green peas in the market,—one does not know what to eat; I have the spleen, as the English say, for butter is so dear, and then it is horrifying that we are dining in a room with a bed in it, and that disgusts me with life."

7. *THE SAGACITY OF THOLOMYÈS*

At length, when all were singing noisily, or talking all together, Tholomyès interfered.

"Let us not talk hap-hazard or too quickly," he exclaimed. "We must meditate if we desire to be striking; too much improvisation stupidly empties the mind. Gentlemen, no haste; let us mingle majesty with our gayety, eat contemplatively, and let *festina lente* be our rule. We must not hurry. Look at the Spring,—if it goes ahead too fast, it is floored; that is to say, nipped by frost. Excessive zeal ruins the peach and apricot trees. Excessive zeal kills the grace and joy of good dinners. No zeal, gentlemen; Grimod de la Reynière is of the same opinion as Talleyrand."

A dull rebellion broke out in the party.

"Tholomyès, leave us at peace," said Blachevelle.

"Down with the tyrant," said Fameuil.

"Sunday exists," Listolier added.

"We are grave," Famueil remarked again.

131

"Tholomyès," said Blachevelle, "regard my calmness *(mon calme)*."

"You are the marquis of the name," Tholomyès replied. This poor pun produced the effect of a stone thrown into a pond. The Marquis de Montcalm was a celebrated Royalist at that day. All the frogs were silent.

"My friends," Tholomyès shouted with the accent of a man who is recapturing his empire, "recover yourselves; too great stupor should not greet this pun which has fallen from the clouds, for everything that falls in such a manner is not necessarily worthy of enthusiasm and respect. Far be it from me to insult puns; I honor them according to their deserts, and no more. All the most august, sublime, and charming members of humanity have made puns; as, for instance, Christ made a pun on St. Peter, Moses on Isaac, Aeschylus on Polynices, and Cleopatra on Octavius. And note the fact that Cleopatra's pun preceded the battle of Actium, and that, were it not for that pun, no one would know the town of Toryne, a Greek word signifying a pot-ladle. This granted, I return to my exhortation. Brethren, I repeat, no zeal, no row, no excess, not even in puns, fun, and playing upon words. Listen to me, for I possess the prudence of Amphiaraüs and the baldness of Cæsar; a limit must even be placed on the rebus, for *est modus in rebus*. There must be a limit even to dinners; you are fond of apple-puffs, ladies, but no abuse; even in the matter of apple-puffs, good sense and art are needed. Gluttony chastises the glutton; *gula* punishes *gulax*. Indigestion was sent into the world to read a lecture to our stomachs; and, bear this in mind, each of our passions, even love, has a stomach which must not be filled too full. In all things, we must write betimes the word *finis,* we must restrain ourselves when it becomes urgent, put a bolt on our appetites, lock up our fancy, and place ourselves under arrest. The wise man is he who knows how, at a given moment, to arrest himself. Place some confidence in me; it does not follow because I know a little law, as my examinations prove; because I have sustained a thesis in Latin as to the mode in which torture was applied at Rome at the time when Munatius Demens was *quæstur parricidæ;* and because I am going to be a Doctor at Law, as it seems; it does not necessarily follow, I say, that I am an ass. I recommend to you moderation in your desires. As truly as my name is Felix Tholomyès, I am speaking the truth. Happy the man who, when the hour has struck, forms an heroic resolve, and abdicates like Sylla or Origen."

Favorite was listening with profound attention. "Felix!" she said, "what a pretty name; I like it. It is Latin, and means prosperous."

Tholymyes continued: "Querites, gentlemen, caballeros, my friends.

Would you feel no sting of passion, dispense with the nuptial couch, and defy love? Nothing more easy. Lemonade, excess in exercise, hard work, tire yourselves, drag logs, do not sleep, keep awake, gorge yourselves with carbonated drinks and ptisanes, take emulsions of poppy and agnus castus, season this with a severe diet, starve yourselves, take cold baths, and wear girdles of herbs."

"I prefer woman," said Listolier.

"Woman!" cried Tholomyès. "Be suspicious of women; woe to the man who surrenders himself to a woman's fickle heart; woman is perfidious and tortuous, and detests the serpent through a professional jealousy. The serpent is the shop over the way."

"Tholomyès," Blachevelle shouted, "you are drunk."

"I hope so!"

"Then be jolly."

"I am agreeable," Tholomyès answered. And filling his glass he rose.

"Glory to wine! *Nunc te, Bacche, canam!* Pardon, ladies, that is Spanish, and the proof, señoras, is this: as the country is, so is the measure. The arroba of Castile contains sixteen quarts, the cantaro of Alicante twelve, the almuda of the Canary Isles twenty-five, the cuartino of the Balearic Isles twenty-six, and Czar Peter's boot thirty. Long live the czar who was great, and his boot which was greater still! Ladies, take a friend's advice; deceive your neighbor, if you think proper. The peculiarity of love is to wander, and it is not made to crouch and stoop like an English servant-girl who has stiff knees from scrubbing. Love is not made for that, but to rove gayly. It is said that error is human, but I say error is amorous. Ladies, I idolize you all. O Zephine, you with your seductive face, you would be charming were you not all askew; your face looks for all the world as if you had been sat upon by mistake. As for Favorite, O ye Nymphs and Muses! one day when Blachevelle was crossing the gutter in the Rue Guérin-Boisseau, he saw a pretty girl with white well-fitting stockings, who displayed her ankles. The prologue was pleasing, and Blachevelle fell in love; the girl he loved was Favorite. O Favorite, you have Ionian lips; there was a Greek painter of the name of Euphorion, who was christened the painter of lips, and this Greek alone would be worthy to paint your mouth. Listen to me: before you there was not a creature deserving of the name; you are made to receive the apple like Venus, or to eat it like Eve. Beauty begins with you. I have just spoken of love; you created her, and you deserve a patent for inventing a pretty woman. You alluded to my name just now; it affected me deeply, but we must be distrustful of names, for they may be deceptive. My name is Felix, and yet I am not happy. Let us not blindly accept the indications they give us; it would be a mistake to write to Liège for corks, or to Pau for gloves.* Miss Dahlia, in your place I would call myself Rose, for a flower ought to smell agreeably, and a woman have spirit. I say nothing of Fantine, for she is a dreamer, pensive and sensitive; she is a phantom, having the form of a nymph and the modesty of a nun, who has strayed into the life of a grisette, but takes shelter in illusions, and who sings, prays, and looks at the blue sky, without exactly knowing what she sees or what she does, and who, with her eyes fixed on heaven, wanders about a garden in which there are more birds than ever existed! O Fantine, be aware of this fact: I, Tholomyès, am an illusion—why, the fair girl of chimeras is not even listening to me! All about her is freshness, suavity, youth, and sweet morning brightness. O Fantine, girl worthy to be called Margaret or Pearl, you are a woman of the fairest East. Ladies, here is a second piece of advice: do not marry, for marriage is a risk, and you had better shun it. But nonsense. I am wasting my words! girls are incurable about wedlock; and all that we sages may say will not prevent waistcoat-makers and shoe-binders from dreaming of husbands loaded with diamonds. Well, beauties, be it so; but bear this in mind, you eat too much sugar. You have only one fault, O women, and that is nibbling sugar. O rodent sex, your pretty little white teeth adore sugar. Now, listen to this: sugar is a salt, and salts are of drying nature, and sugar is the most drying of all salts. It pumps out the fluidity of the blood through the veins; this produces first coagulation and then solidifying of the blood. From this come tubercles in the lungs, and thence death. Hence do not nibble sugar, and you will live. I now turn to my male hearers: Gentlemen, make conquests. Rob one another of your well-beloved ones remorselessly; change partners, for in love there are no friends. Whenever there is a pretty woman, hostilities are opened; there is no quarter, but war to the knife! A pretty woman is a *casus belli* and a flagrant offense. All the invasions of history were produced by petticoats; for woman is the lawful prey of man. Romulus carried off the Sabine women, William the Saxon women, and Cæsar the Roman women. A man who is not loved soars like a vulture over the mistresses of other men; and, for my part, I offer all these unfortunate widowers Bonaparte's sublime proclamation to the army of Italy: 'Soldiers, you want for everything; the enemy possesses it.'"

*An untranslatable pun based on *chène-liège* and *peau*.

Here Tholomyès broke off.

"Take a breather, my boy," said Blachevelle.

At the same time the other three gentlemen struck up to a doleful air one of those studio-songs as devoid of sense as the waving of a twig or the sound of the wind, which are composed extemporaneously, either in rhyme or prose, which spring up from the smoke of pipes, and fly away with it.

> "*Les pères dindons donnèrent*
> *De l'argent à un agent*
> *Pour que Mons. Clermont-Tonnerre*
> *Fut fait pape à la Saint Jean;*
> *Mais Clermont ne put pas être*
> *Fait pape, n'étant pas prêtre;*
> *Alors leur agent rageant*
> *Leur rapporta leur argent.*"

The song was not adapted to calm Tholomyès' inspiration; hence he emptied his glass, filled it again, and began once more.

"Down with wisdom! forget all I have said to you. Be neither prudish, nor prudent, nor *prud'hommes*. I drink the health of jollity; so let us be jolly. Let us complete our legal studies by folly and good food, for indigestion should run in a curricle with digests. Let Justinian be the male and merriment the female! Live, O Creation; the world is one large diamond. I am happy, and the birds are astounding. What a festival all around us; the nightingale is a gratis Elleviou. Summer, I salute thee. O Luxembourg! O ye Georgics of the Rue Madame and the Allée de l'Observatoire! O ye dreaming recruits. O ye delicious nurses, who, while taking care of children, fancy what your own will be like! the pampas of America would please me if I had not the arcades of the Odéon. My soul is flying away to the virgin forests and the savannas. All is glorious; the flies are buzzing in the light; the sun has sneezed forth the humming-bird. Kiss me, Fantine!"

He made a mistake and kissed Favorite.

8. *THE DEATH OF A HORSE*

"IT is a better dinner at Edon's than at Bombarda's," Zephine exclaimed.

"I prefer Bombarda," Blachevelle declared: "there is more luxury; it is more Asiatic. Just look at the dining-room with its mirrors; look at the knives,—they are silver-handled here and bone at Edon's. Now, silver is more precious than bone."

"Excepting for those persons who have a silver chin," Tholomyès observed.

He was looking at this moment at the dome of the Invalides, which was visible from Bombarda's window. There was a pause.

"Tholomyès," exclaimed Fameuil, "Listolier and I have just had a discussion."

"Discussion is good," he replied; "a quarrel is better."

"We were discussing philosophy; which do you prefer, Descartes or Spinoza?"

"Désaugiers," said Tholomyès. Having given this decision he continued: "I consent to live; all is not finished in the world. Since men can still be unreasonable, I return thanks to the immortal gods. Men lie, but they laugh; they affirm, but they doubt; and something unexpected issues from the syllogism. This is grand; there are still in the world human beings who can joyously open and shut the puzzle-box of paradox. This wine, ladies, which you are drinking so calmly is Madeira, you must know, grown at Coural das Freiras, which is three hundred and seventeen *toises* above the sea-level. Attention while drinking! three hundred and seventeen *toises,* and M. Bombarda, the magnificent restaurateur, lets you have these three hundred and seventeen *toises* for four francs, fifty centimes."

Fameuil interrupted again.

"Tholomyès, your opinions are law. Who is your favorite author?"

"Ber . . . ."

"Quin?"

"No; Choux."

Tholomyès drained his glass, and then continued:

"Honor to Bombarda! he would be equal to Munophis of Elephanta if he could ladle me up an Almeh, and to Thygelion of Cheronea if he could procure me an Hetæra! for, ladies, there were Bombardas in Greece and Egypt, as Apuleius teaches us. Alas. Alas! ever the same thing and nothing new; nothing is left unpublished in the creation of the Creator. 'Nothing new under the sun,' says Solomon: *amor omnibus idem,* and Carabine gets into the St. Cloud fly-boat with Carabin, just as Aspasia embarked with Pericles aboard the Samos fleet. One last word: Do you know who Aspasia was, ladies? Although she lived at a time when women had no soul, she was a soul; a soul of a pink and purple hue, hotter than fire, and fresher than the dawn. Aspasia was a woman in whom the two extremes of femininity met; she was a harlot goddess, a Socrates *plus* a Manon Lescaut."

Tholomyès, when started, would hardly have been checked, had not a horse fallen in the street at this very moment. Through the shock, cart and orator stopped short. It was a Beauce mare, old and lean and worthy of the knacker, dragging a very heavy cart. On getting in front of Bombarda's, the beast, exhausted and worn out, refused to go any further, and this incident produced a crowd. The carter, swearing and indignant, had scarce time to utter with the suitable energy the sacramental word, "Cur!" backed up by a pitiless lash, ere the poor beast fell, never again to arise.

Tholomyès' gay hearers turned their heads away on noticing the confusion, while he wound up his speech by the following sad strophe:

> "Elle était de ce monde ou coucous et carrosses,
> Ont le même destin,
> Et, rosse, elle a vécu ce que vivent les rosses,
> L'espace d'un: Matin!"

"Poor horse!" Fantine said with a sigh; and Dahlia shouted:

"Why, here is Fantine beginning to feel pity for horses; how can she be such a fool!"

137

At this moment Favorite crossed her arms and threw her head back; she then looked boldly at Tholomyès, and said:

"Well, how about the surprise?"

"That is true, the hour has arrived," Tholomyès answered. "Gentlemen, it is time to surprise the ladies. Pray, wait for us a moment."

"It begins with a kiss," said Blachevelle.

"On the forehead," Tholomyès added.

Each solemnly kissed the forehead of his mistress; then they proceeded to the door in Indian file, fingers on lips. Favorite clapped her hands as they went out.

"It is amusing already," she said.

"Do not be long," Fantine murmured; "we are waiting for you."

9. *THE JOYOUS END OF JOY*

THE girls, when left alone, leaned out of the windows, two by two, talking, looking out, and wondering. They watched the young men leave the Bombarda cabaret arm in arm; they turned round, made laughing signs, and disappeared in that dusty Sunday mob which once a week invaded the Champs Elysées.

"Do not be long," Fantine cried.

"What will they bring us?" said Zephine.

"I am certain it will be pretty," said Dahlia.

"For my part," Favorite added, "I hope it will be set in gold."

They were soon distracted by the movement on the quay, which they could notice through the branches of the lofty trees, and which greatly amused them. It was the hour for the mail-carts and stages to start, and nearly all those bound for the South and West at that time passed through the Champs Elysées. Most of them went along the quay and out by the Passy gate. Every moment some heavy vehicle, painted yellow and black, heavily loaded and rendered shapeless by trunks and valises, dashed through the crowd with the sparks of a forge, the dust representing the smoke. This confusion amused the girls. Favorite exclaimed, "What a tumult! One might say a heap of chains was flying away."

One of these vehicles, which could hardly be distinguished through the branches, stopped for a moment and then started again at a gallop. This surprised Fantine.

"That is strange," she said, "I fancied that the diligence never stopped."

Favorite shrugged her shoulders.

"This Fantine is really amazing, and is surprised at the simplest things. Let us suppose that I am a traveler and say to the guard of the stage-coach, 'I will walk on and you can pick me up at the quay as you pass.' The coach passes, sees me, stops, and takes me in. That is done every day; you are ignorant of life, my dear."

Some time elapsed; all at once Favorite started as if waking from sleep.

"Well," she said, "where is the surprise?"

"Oh, yes," Dahlia continued, "the famous surprise."

"They are a long time," said Fantine.

Just as Fantine had ended this sigh, the waiter who had served the dinner came in; he held in his hand something that resembled a letter.

"What is that?" Favorite asked.

The waiter answered:

"It is the paper which the gentlemen left for you, ladies."

"Why did you not bring it to us at once?"

"Because the gentlemen," the waiter went on, "ordered that it should not be delivered to you for an hour."

Favorite snatched the paper from the waiter's hands. It was really a letter.

"Stay," she said; "there is no address, but the following words are written upon it, 'THIS IS THE SURPRISE'." She quickly opened the letter and read (she could read):

Well-beloved!

Know that we have relatives; perhaps you are not perfectly cognizant what the word means; it means fathers and mothers in the civil, puerile, and honest code. Well, these relatives are groaning; these old people claim us as their own; these worthy men and women call us prodigal sons. They desire our return home, and offer to kill the fatted calf. We obey them, as we are virtuous; at the hour when you read this, five impetuous steeds will be conveying us back to our papas and mammas. We are making tracks, to quote the language of Bossuet; we are going, gone. We are flying away in the arms of Lafitte and on the wings of Caillard. The Toulouse coach is dragging us away from the abyss, and that abyss is yourselves, pretty dears. We are re-entering society, duty, and order, at a sharp trot, and at the rate of nine miles an hour. It is important for our country that we should become, like everybody else, prefects, fathers of a family, game-keepers, and councilors of state. Revere us, for we are sacrificing ourselves. Dry up your tears for us rapidly, and get a substitute speedily. If this letter lacerates your hearts, treat it in the same fashion. Good-bye. For nearly two years we rendered you happy, so do not owe us any grudge.

(Signed)   BLACHEVELLE.   FAMEUIL.

FELIX THOLOMYÈS.   LISTOLIER.

P. S. The dinner is paid for.

The four girls looked at each other, and Favorite was the first to break the silence.

"I don't care," she said, "it is a capital joke."

"It is very funny," Zephine remarked.

"It must have been Blachevelle who had that idea," Favorite continued; "It makes me in love with him. So soon as he has left me I am beginning to grow fond of him; the old story."

"No," said Dahlia, "that is an idea of Tholomyès. That can be easily seen."

"In that case," Favorite retorted, "down with Blachevelle, and long live Tholomyès!"

And they burst into a laugh, in which Fantine joined; an hour later though, when she returned to her bedroom, she burst into tears. He was, as we have said, her first love; she had yielded to Tholomyès as to a husband, and the poor girl had a child.

BOOK IV

TO CONFIDE IS SOMETIMES TO ABANDON

1. TWO MOTHERS MEET

THERE was in the first quarter of this century a sort of pot-house at Montfermeil, near Paris, which no longer exists. It was kept by a couple of the name of Thénardier, and was situated in the Rue du Boulanger. Over the door a board was nailed to the wall, and on this board was painted something resembling a man carrying on his back another man, who wore large gilt general's epaulettes with silver stars; red dabs represented blood, and the rest of the painting was smoke, probably representing a battle. At the bottom could be read the inscription, "THE SERGEANT OF WATERLOO."

Though nothing is more common than a cart at a pot-house door, the vehicle, or rather fragment of a vehicle, which blocked up the street in front of The Sergeant of Waterloo, one spring evening in 1818, would have certainly attracted the attention of any painter who had passed that way. It was the fore-part of one of those wains used in wood countries for dragging planks and trunks of trees; it was composed of a massive iron axle-tree, in which a heavy pole was imbedded and supported by two enormous wheels. The whole thing was sturdy, crushing, and ugly, and it might have passed for the carriage of a monstrous gun. The ruts had given the wheels, felloes, spokes, axle-tree, and pole a coating of mud, a hideous yellow plaster much like that with which cathedrals are so often adorned. The wood-work was hidden by mud and the iron with rust. Under the axle-tree was festooned a heavy chain, suited for a convict Goliath. This chain made you think, not of the wood it was intended to secure, but of the mastodons and mammoths for which it would have served as harness; it had the air of a cyclopean and superhuman bagne, and seemed removed from some monster. Homer would have bound Polyphemus with it, and Shakespere, Caliban.

Why was this thing at this place in the street? First, to block it up; secondly, to finish the rusting process. There is in the old social order a multitude of institutions which may be found in the same way in the open air, and which have no other reasons for being there. The center of the chain hung rather close to the ground, and on the curve, as on the rope of a swing, two little girls were seated on this evening, in an exquisite embrace, one about two years and a half, the other eighteen months—the younger being in the arms of the elder. An artfully tied handkerchief prevented them from falling, for a mother had seen this frightful chain, and said, "What a famous plaything for my children!" The two children, who were prettily dressed and with some taste, were radiant; they looked like two roses among old iron; their eyes were a triumph, their healthy cheeks laughed; one had auburn hair, the other was a brunette; their innocent faces had a look of surprise; a flowering shrub a little distance off sent to passers-by a perfume which seemed to come from them; and the younger displayed her nudity with the chaste indecency of childhood. Above and around their two delicate heads, molded in happiness and bathed in light, the gigantic pair of wheels, black with rust, almost terrible, and bristling with curves and savage angles, formed the porch of a cavern, as it were. A few yards off, and seated in the inn door, the mother, a woman of no very pleasing appearance, but touching at this moment, was swinging the children by the help of a long cord, and devouring them with her eyes, for fear of an accident, with that animal and heavenly expression peculiar to maternity. At each oscillation the hideous links produced a sharp sound, resembling a cry of anger. The little girls were delighted; the setting sun mingled with the joy, and nothing could be so charming as this caprice of accident which had made of a Titanic chain a cherub's swing. While playing with the little ones the mother sang, terribly out of tune, a romance very celebrated at that day:

"Il le faut, disait un guerrier."

Her song and contemplation of her daughters prevented her hearing and seeing what took place in the street. Some one, however, had approached her, as she began the first couplets of the romance, and suddenly she heard a voice saying close to her ear:

"You have two pretty children, madame."

"—à la belle et tendre Imogine,"

the mother answered, continuing her song, and then turned her head. A woman was standing a few paces from her, who also had a child, which she was carrying in her arms. She also carried a heavy bag. This woman's child was one of the most divine creatures possible to behold; she was a girl between two and three years of age, and could have vied with the two other little ones in the coquettishness of her dress. She had on a hood of fine linen, ribbons at her shoulder and Valenciennes lace in her cap. Her raised petticoats displayed her white, dimpled, fine thigh; it was admirably pink and healthy, and her cheeks made one long to bite them. Nothing could be said of her eyes, except that they were very large, and that she had magnificent lashes, for she was asleep. She was sleeping with the absolute confidence peculiar to her age; a mother's arms are made of tenderness, and children sleep soundly in them. As for the mother, she looked grave and sorrowful, and was dressed like a work-girl who was trying to become a country-woman again. She was young; was she pretty? Perhaps so; but in this dress she did not appear so. Her hair, a light lock of which peeped out, seemed very thick, but was completely hidden beneath a nun's hood, ugly, tight, and fastened under her chin. Laughter displays fine teeth when a person happens to possess them, but she did not laugh. Her eyes looked as if they had not been dry for a long time; she had a fatigued and rather sickly air, and she looked at the child sleeping in her arms in the manner peculiar to a mother who has suckled her babe. A large blue handkerchief, like those served out to the hospital patients, folded like a shawl, clumsily hid her shape. Her hands were rough and covered with red spots, and her fore-finger was hardened and torn by the needle; she had on a brown cloth cloak, a cotton gown, and heavy shoes. It was Fantine.

It was difficult to recognize her, but, after an attentive examination, she still possessed her beauty. A sad wrinkle, which looked like the beginning of a sarcasm, crossed her right cheek. As for her toilette, that aerian toilette of muslin and ribbons which seemed made of gayety, folly, and music, to be full of bells and perfumed with lilacs,—it had faded away like the dazzling hoar-frost which looks like diamonds in the sun; it melts, and leaves the branch quite black.

Ten months had elapsed since the "good joke." What had taken place during these ten months? we can guess. After desertion, want. Fantine at once lost sight of Favorite, Zephine, and Dahlia, for this tie broken on the side of the men separated the women. They would have been greatly surprised, a fortnight after, had they been told that they were friends, for there was no reason for it. Fantine remained alone when the father of her child had gone away—alas! such ruptures are irrevocable. She found herself absolutely isolated; she had lost her habit of working, and had gained a taste for pleasure. Led away by her *liaison* with Tholomyès to despise the little trade she knew, she had neglected her connection, and it was lost. She had no resource. Fantine could hardly read, and could not write; she had been merely taught in childhood to sign her name, and she had sent a letter to Tholomyès, then a second, then a third, through a public writer, but Tholomyès did not answer one of them. One day Fantine heard the gossips say, while looking at her daughter; "Do people ever take children like that to heart? people shrug their shoulders at them." Then she thought of Tholomyès, who shrugged his shoulders at her child, and did not take the innocent creature to heart, and her heart turned away from this man. What was she to do now? She knew not where to turn. She had committed a fault, but the foundation of her nature, we must remember, was modesty and virtue. She felt vaguely that she was on the eve of falling into distress, and gliding into worse. She needed courage, and she had it. The idea occurred to her of returning to her native town, M. sur M. There some one might know her, and give her work; but she must hide her fault. And she vaguely glimpsed at the possible necessity of a separation more painful still than the first; her heart was contracted, but she formed her resolution. Fantine, as we shall see, possessed the stern bravery of life. She had already valiantly given up dress; she dressed in calico, and had put all her silk ribbons and laces upon her daughter, the only vanity left her, and it was a holy one. She sold all she possessed, which brought her in 200 francs; and when she had paid her little debts, she had only about 80 francs left. At the age of two-and-twenty, on a fine spring morning, she left Paris, carrying her child on her back. Any one who had seen them pass would have felt pity for them; the woman had nothing in the world but her child, and the child nothing but her mother in the world. Fantine had suckled her child; this had weakened her chest, and she was coughing a little.

We shall have no further occasion to speak of M. Felix Tholomyès. We will merely say that twenty years later, in the reign of Louis Philippe, he was a stout country lawyer, influential and rich, a sensible elector, and a very strict juror, but always a man of pleasure.

About midday, after resting herself now and then by traveling from time to time, at the expense of three or four sous a league, in what were then called the "little vehicles of the suburbs of Paris," Fantine found herself at Montfermeil, in the Ruelle Boulanger. As she passed The Sergeant of Waterloo, the two little girls in their monster swing had dazzled her, and she stopped before this vision of joy. There are charms in life, and these two little girls were one for this mother. She looked at them with great emotion, for the presence of angels is an announcement of Paradise. She believed she saw above this pot-house the mysterious HERE of Providence. These two little creatures were evidently happy! She looked and admired them with such tenderness that at the moment when the mother was drawing breath between two verses of her song, she could not refrain from saying to her what we have already recorded.

"You have two pretty children, madame."

The most ferocious creatures are disarmed by a caress given to their little ones. The mother raised her head, thanked her, and bade her sit down on the door bench. The two women began talking.

"My name is Madame Thénardier," the mother of the little ones said; "we keep this inn."

Then, returning to her romance, she went on humming—

> *"Il le faut, je suis chevalier,*
> *Et je pars pour la Palestine."*

This Madame Thénardier was a red-headed, thin, angular woman, the soldier's wife in all its ugliness, and, strange to say, with a languishing air, which she owed to reading romances. She was a kind of masculine languisher, for old romances, by working on the imaginations of land-ladies, produce that effect. She was still young, scarce thirty. If this woman, now stooping, had been standing up, perhaps her height and colossal proportions, fitting for a show, would have at once startled the traveler, destroyed her confidence, and prevented what we have to record. A person sitting instead of standing up—destinies hang on this.

The woman told her story with some modification. She was a work-girl; her husband was dead; she could get no work in Paris, and was going to seek it elsewhere, in her native town. She had left Paris that very morning on foot; as she felt tired from carrying her child, she had traveled by the stage-coach to Villemomble; from that place she walked to Montfermeil. The little one had walked a little, but not much, for she was so young, and so she had been obliged to carry her, and the darling had gone to sleep,—and as she said this she gave her daughter a passionate kiss, which awoke her. The babe opened her eyes, large blue eyes like her mother's, and gazed at—what?—nothing, everything, with that serious and at times stern air of infants, which is a mystery of their luminous innocence in the presence of our twilight virtues. We might say that they feel themselves to be angels, and know us to be men. Then the child began laughing, and, though its mother had to check it, slipped down to the ground with the undauntable energy of a little creature wishing to run. All at once she noticed the other two children in their swing, stopped short, and put out her tongue as a sign of admiration. Mother Thénardier unfastened her children, took them out of the swing, and said: "Play about, all three."

Such ages soon grow acquainted, and in a minute the little Thénardiers were playing with the new-comer at making holes in the ground, which was an immense pleasure. The stranger child was very merry; the goodness of the mother is written in the gayety of the baby. She had picked up a piece of wood which she used as a spade, and was energetically digging a grave large enough for a fly. The two went on talking.

"What's the name of your bantling?"

"Cosette."

For Cosette read Euphrasie, for that was the child's real name, but the mother had converted Euphrasie into Cosette, through that gentle, graceful instinct peculiar to mothers and the people, which changes Josefa into Pepita, and Françoise into Silette. It is a species of derivation which deranges and disconcerts the entire science of etymologists. We know a grandmother who contrived to make out of Theodore, Gnon.

"What is her age?"

"Going on for three."

"Just the same age as my eldest."

In the mean time the children were grouped in a posture of profound anxiety and blessedness; an event had occurred. A large worm had crept out of the ground, and they were frightened, and were in ecstasy; their radiant brows touched each other, and they looked like three heads in a halo.

"How soon children get to know one another," Mother Thénardier exclaimed: "why, they might be taken for three sisters."

The word was probably the spark which the other mother had been waiting for; she seized the speaker's hand, looked at her fixedly, and said:

"Will you take charge of my child for me?"

The woman gave one of those starts of surprise which are neither assent nor refusal. Fantine continued:

"Look ye, I cannot take the child with me to my town, for when a woman has a baby, it is hard matter for her to get a situation. People are so foolish in our part. It was Heaven that made me pass in front of your inn; when I saw your little ones so pretty, so clean, so happy, it gave me a turn. I said to myself, 'She is a kind mother.' It is so; they will be three sisters. Then I shall not be long before I come back. Will you take care of my child?"

"We will see," said Mother Thénardier.

"I would pay six francs a month."

Here a man's voice cried from the back of the tap-room:

"Can't be done under seven, and six months paid in advance."

"Six times seven are forty-two," said the landlady.

"I will pay it," said the mother.

"And seventeen francs in addition for first expenses," the man's voice added.

"Total, fifty-nine francs," said Madame Thénardier; and through these figures she sang vaguely:

"*Il le faut, disait un guerrier.*"

"I will pay it," the mother said; "I have eighty francs, and shall have enough left to get home on foot. I shall earn money there, and so soon as I have a little I will come and fetch my darling."

The man's voice continued:

"Has the little one a stock of clothing?"

"It is my husband," said Mother Thénardier.

"Of course she has clothes, poor little treasure. I saw it was your husband; and a fine stock of clothes, too, a wonderful stock, a dozen of everything, and silk frocks like a lady. The things are in my bag."

"They must be handed over," the man's voice remarked.

"Of course they must," said the mother; "it would be funny if I left my child naked."

The master's face appeared.

"All right," he said.

The bargain was concluded, the mother spent the night at the inn, paid her money and left her child, fastened up her bag, which was now light, and started the next morning with the intention of returning soon. Such departures are arranged calmly, but they entail despair. A neighbor's wife saw the mother going away, and went home saying:

"I have just seen a woman crying in the street as if her heart was broken."

When Cosette's mother had gone, the man said to his wife:

"That money will meet my bill for one hundred and ten francs, which falls due to-morrow, and I was fifty francs short. It would have been protested, and I should have had a bailiff put in. You set a famous mouse-trap with your brats."

"Without suspecting it," said the woman.

2. *THE FIRST SKETCH OF TWO UGLY FACES*

THE captured mouse was very small, but the cat is pleased even with a thin mouse. Who were the Thénardiers? We will say one word about them for the present, and complete the sketch hereafter. These beings belonged to the bastard class composed of coarse parvenus and of degraded people of intellect, which stands between the classes called the middle and the lower, and combines some of the faults of the second with nearly all the vices of the first, though without possessing the generous impulse of the working-man or the honest regularity of the tradesman.

Theirs were those dwarf natures which easily become monstrous, when any gloomy fire accidentally warms them. There was in the woman the basis of a brute, in the man the stuff for a beggar. Both were in the highest degree susceptible of that sort of hideous progress which is made in the direction of evil. There are crab-like souls which constantly recoil toward darkness, retrograde in life rather than advance, employ experience to augment their deformity, incessantly grow worse, and grow more and more covered with an increasing blackness. This man and this woman had souls of this sort.

Thénardier was peculiarly troublesome to the physiognomist; there are some men whom you need only look at to distrust them, for they are restless behind and threatening in front. There is something of the unknown in them. We can no more answer for what they have done than for what they will do. The gloom they have in their glance denounces them. Merely by hearing them say a word or seeing them make a gesture, we get a glimpse of dark secrets in their past, dark mysteries in their future. This Thénardier, could he be believed, had been a soldier —sergeant, he said; he had probably gone through the campaign of 1815, and had even behaved rather bravely, as it seems. We shall see presently how the matter really stood. The sign of his inn was an allusion to one of his exploits, and he had painted it himself, for he could do a little of everything—badly. It was the epoch when the old classical romance—which, after being *Clélie,* had now become *Lodoïska,* and, though still noble, was daily growing more vulgar, and had fallen from Mademoiselle de Scudéry to Madame Bournon-Malarme, and from Madame de Lafayette to Madame Barthélemy-Hadot—was inflaming the loving souls of the porters' wives in Paris, and even extended its ravages into the suburbs. Madame Thénardier was just intelligent enough to read books of this nature and lived on them. She thus drowned any brains she possessed, and, so long as she remained young and a little beyond, it gave her a sort of pensive attitude by the side of her husband, who was a scamp of some depth, an almost grammatical ruffian, coarse and delicate at the same time, but who, in matters of sentimentalism, read Pigault-Lebrun, and, "in all that concerned the sex," as he said in his jargon, was a correct and unmixed booby. His wife was some twelve or fifteen years younger than he, and when her romantically flowing locks began to grow gray, when the Megæra was disengaged from the Pamela, she was only a stout, wicked woman who had been pampered with foolish romances. As such absurdities cannot be read with impunity, the result was that her eldest daughter was christened Eponine; as for the younger, the poor girl was all but named Gulnare, and owed it to a fortunate diversion made by a romance of Ducray-Duminil's that she was only christened Azelma.

By the way, all is not ridiculous and superficial in the curious epoch to which we are alluding, and which might be called the anarchy of baptismal names. By the side of the romantic element, which we have just pointed out, there was the social symptom. It is not rare at the present day for a drover's son to be called Arthur, Alfred, or Alphonse, and for the viscount—if there are any viscounts left—to be called Thomas, Pierre, or Jacques. This displacement, which gives the "elegant" name to the plebeian and the rustic name to the aristocrat, is nothing else than an eddy of equality. The irresistible penetration of the new breeze that is blowing is visible in this as in everything else. Beneath this apparent discord, there is a grand and deep thing—the French Revolution.

3 . *THE LARK*

IT is not enough to be bad in order to prosper, and the pot-house was a failure. Thanks to the fifty-nine francs of Fantine, Thénardier had been able to avoid a protest, and honor his signature; but the next month they wanted money again, and his wife took to Paris and pledged Cosette's outfit for sixty francs. So soon as this sum was spent, the Thénardiers grew accustomed to see in the little girl a child they had taken in through charity, and treated her accordingly. As she had no clothes, she was dressed in the left-off chemises and petticoats of the little Thénardiers; that is to say, in rags. She was fed on the leavings of everybody, a little better than the dog, and a little worse than the cat. Dog and cat were her usual company at dinner, for Cosette ate with them under the table off a wooden trencher like theirs.

The mother, who had settled, as we shall see hereafter, at M. sur M., wrote, or, to speak more correctly, had letters written every month to inquire after her child. The Thénardiers invariably replied that Cosette was getting on famously. When the first six months had passed, the mother sent seven francs for the seventh month, and continued to send

the money punctually month by month. The year was not ended before
Thénardier said: "A fine thing that! what does she expect us to do with
seven francs!" and he wrote to demand twelve. The mother, whom they
persuaded that her child was happy and healthy, submitted, and sent the
twelve francs.

Some natures cannot love on one side without hating on the other.
Mother Thénardier passionately loved her own two daughters, which
made her detest the stranger. It is sad to think that a mother's love can
look so ugly. Though Cosette occupied so little room, it seemed to her as
if her children were robbed of it, and that the little one diminished the
air her daughters breathed. This woman, like many women of her class,
had a certain amount of caresses and another of blows and insults to
expend daily. If she had not had Cosette, it is certain that her daughters,
though they were idolized, would have received the entire amount, but
the strange child did the service of diverting the blows on herself, while
the daughters only received the caresses. Cosette did not make a movement that did not bring down on her head a hailstorm of violent and
unmerited chastisement. The poor weak child, unnecessarily punished,
scolded, cuffed, and beaten, saw by her side two little creatures like
herself who lived in radiant happiness.

As Madame Thénardier was unkind to Cosette, Eponine and Azelma
were the same; for children at that age are copies of their mother,—
the form is smaller, that is all. A year passed, then another, and people
said in the village:

"Those Thénardiers are worthy people. They are not well off, and
yet they bring up a poor child left on their hands."

Cosette was supposed to be deserted by her mother; Thénardier, however, having learnt in some obscure way that the child was probably
illegitimate, and that the mother could not confess it, insisted on fifteen
francs a month, saying that the creature was growing and *eating,* and
threatening to send her back. "She must not play the fool with me," he
shouted, "or I'll let her brat fall like a bomb-shell into her hiding-place.
I must have an increase." The mother paid the fifteen francs. Year by
year the child grew, and so did her wretchedness; so long as Cosette was
little she was the scape-goat of the two other children; so soon as she
began to be developed a little,—that is to say, even before she was five
years old,—she became the servant of the house. At five years, the reader
will say, that is improbable, but, alas! it is true. Social suffering begins
at any age. Have we not recently seen the trial of a certain Dumollard,

an orphan, who turned bandit, and who from the age of five, as official documents tell us, was alone in the world and "worked for a living and stole"? Cosette was made to go on messages, sweep the rooms, the yard, the street, wash the dishes, and even carry heavy bundles. The Thénardiers considered themselves the more justified in acting thus, because the mother, who was still at M. sur M., was beginning to pay badly, and was several months in arrear.

If the mother had returned to Monfermeil at the end of three years, she would not have recognized her child. Cosette, so pretty and ruddy on her arrival in this house, was now thin and sickly. She had a timid look about her. "It's cunning!" said the Thénardiers. Injustice had made her sulky and wretchedness had made her ugly. Nothing was left her but her fine eyes, which were painful to look at, because, as they were so large, it seemed as if a greater amount of sadness was visible in them. It was a heart-rending sight to see this poor child, scarce six years of age, shivering in winter under her calico rags, and sweeping the street before daybreak, with an enormous broom in her small red hands and a tear in her large eyes.

The country people called her "the lark"; the lower classes, who are fond of metaphors, had given the name to the poor little creature, who was no larger than a bird, trembling, frightened, and starting, who was always the first awake in the house and the village, and ever in the street or the fields by daybreak.

There was the difference, however,—this poor lark did not sing.

BOOK V

THE DESCENT

1 · PROGRESS IN BLACK BEAD MAKING

WHAT had become of the mother who, according to the people of Montfermeil, appeared to have deserted her child? Where was she, what was she doing? After leaving her little Cosette with the Thénardiers, she had continued her journey and arrived at M. sur M. Fantine had been away from her province for ten years, and while she had been slowly descending from misery to misery, her native town had prospered. About two years before, one of those industrial facts which are the events of small towns had taken place. The details are important, and we think it useful to develop them, we might almost say to understand them.

From time immemorial M. sur M. had as a special trade the imitation of English jet and German black beads. This trade had hitherto only vegetated, owing to the dearness of the material, which reacted on the artisan. At the moment when Fantine returned to M. sur M., an extraordinary transformation had taken place in the production of "black articles." Toward the close of 1815, a man, a stranger, had settled in the town, and had the idea of substituting in this trade gum lac for rosin, and, in bracelets particularly, clasps of bent metal for welded. This slight change was a revolution; it prodigiously reduced the cost of the material, which, in the first place, allowed the wages to be raised, a benefit for the town; secondly, improved the manufacture, an advantage for the consumer; and, thirdly, allowed the goods to be sold cheap, while producing triple the profit, an advantage for the manufacturer.

In less than three years the inventor of the process had become rich, which is a good thing, and had made all rich about him, which is better. He was a stranger in the department; no one knew anything about his origin, and but little about his start. It was said that he had entered the town with but very little money, a few hundred francs at the most; but with this small capital, placed at the service of an ingenious idea, and fertilized by regularity and thought, he made his own fortune and that of the town. On his arrival at M. sur M. he had the dress, manners, and language of a working-man. It appears that on the very December night when he obscurely entered M. sur M. with his knapsack on his back and a knotted stick in his hand, a great fire broke out in the Town Hall. This man rushed into the midst of the flames, and at the risk of his life saved two children who happened to belong to the captain of gendarmes; hence no one dreamed of asking for his passport. On this occasion his name was learned; he called himself Father Madeleine.

2. *MADELEINE*

HE was a man of about fifty, with a preoccupied air, and he was good-hearted. That was all that could be said of him.

Thanks to the rapid progress of this trade which he had so admirably remodeled, M. sur M. had become a place of considerable trade. Spain, which consumes an immense amount of jet, gave large orders for it annually, and in this trade M. sur M. almost rivaled London and Berlin. Father Madeleine's profits were so great that after the second year he was able to build a large factory, in which were two spacious workshops, one for men, the other for women. Any one who was hungry need only to come, and was sure to find there employment and bread. Father Madeleine expected from the men good-will, from the women purity, and from all probity. He had divided the workshops in order to separate the sexes, and enable the women and girls to remain virtuous. On this point he was inflexible, and it was the only one in which he was at all intolerant. This sternness was the more justifiable because M. sur M. was a garrison town, and opportunities for corruption abounded. Altogether his arrival had been a benefit, and his presence was a providence. Before Father Madeleine came everything was languishing, and now all led the healthy life of work. A powerful circulation warmed and penetrated everything; strikes and wretchedness were unknown. There was not a pocket, however obscure, in which there was not a little money, nor a lodging so poor in which there was not a little joy. Father Madeleine, as we have said, employed everybody; he only insisted on one thing,—Be an honest man! Be a good girl.

As we have said, in the midst of this activity, of which he was the cause and the pivot, Father Madeleine made his fortune, but, singularly enough in a plain man of business, this did not appear to be his chief care; he seemed to think a great deal of others and but little of himself. In 1820, he was known to have a sum of 630,000 francs in Lafitte's bank; but before he put that amount on one side he had spent more than a million for the town and the poor. The hospital was badly endowed, and he added ten beds. M. sur M. is divided into an upper and a lower town; the latter, in which he lived, had only one school, a poor tenement falling in ruins, and he built two,—one for boys and one for girls. He paid the two teachers an amount the double of their poor official salary, and to some one who expressed surprise he said, "The two first functionaries of the state are the nurse and the school-master." He had established at his own expense an asylum, a thing at that time almost unknown in France, and a charitable fund for old and infirm workmen. As his factory was a center, a new district, in which there was a large number of indigent families, rapidly sprang up around it, and he opened there a free dispensary.

At the beginning, kind souls said, "He is a man who wants to grow rich"; when it was seen that he enriched the town before enriching himself, the same charitable souls said, "He is ambitious." This seemed the more likely because he was religious, and even practiced it to a certain extent—a thing which was admired in those days. He went regularly to hear low mass on Sundays, and the local deputy, who scented rivalry everywhere, soon became alarmed about this piety. This deputy, who had been a member of the legislative council of the empire, shared the religious ideas of a father of the oratory, known by the name of Fouché, Duc d'Otranto, whose creature and friend he had been. But when he saw the rich manufacturer Madeleine go to seven o'clock low mass, he scented a possible candidate, and resolved to go beyond him; he chose a Jesuit professor, and went to high mass and vespers. Ambition at that time was, in the true sense of the term, a steeple-chase. The poor profited by the alarm, for the honorable deputy founded two beds at the hospital, which made twelve.

In 1819, the report spread one morning through the town that, on the recommendation of the prefect, and in consideration of services rendered the town, Father Madeleine was about to be nominated by the king Mayor of M. . . . . Those who had declared the new-comer an ambitious man, eagerly seized this opportunity to exclaim, "Did we not say so?" All M. . . . was in an uproar; for the rumor was well founded. A few days after, the appointment appeared in the *Moniteur,* and the next day Father Madeleine declined the honor. In the same year, the new processes worked by him were shown at the Industrial Exhibition; and on the report of the jury, the king made the inventor a Chevalier of the Legion of Honor. There was a fresh commotion in the little town; "Well, it was the cross he wanted," but Father Madeleine declined the cross. Decidedly the man was an enigma, but charitable souls got out of the difficulty by saying, "After all, he is a sort of adventurer."

As we have seen, the country owed him much, and the poor owed him everything; he was so useful that he could not help being honored, and so gentle that people could not help loving him. His work-people especially adored him, and he bore this adoration with a sort of melancholy gravity. When he was known to be rich, "people in society" bowed to him, and he was called in the town Monsieur Madeleine, but his workmen and the children continued to call him Father Madeleine, and this caused him his happiest smile. In proportion as he ascended, invitations showered upon him, and society claimed him as its own. The little formal drawing rooms, which had, of course, been at first closed to the artisan, opened their doors wide to the millionaire. A thousand advances were made to him, but he refused. This time again charitable souls were not thrown out, "He is an ignorant man of poor education. No one knows where he comes from. He would not pass muster in society, and it is doubtful whether he can read." When he was seen to be earning money, they said, "He is a tradesman"; when he scattered his money, they said, "He is ambitious"; when he rejected honors, they said, "He is an adventurer," and when he repulsed society, they said, "He is a brute."

In 1820, five years after his arrival at M. . . . , the services he had rendered the town were so brilliant, the will of the whole country was so unanimous, that the king again nominated him mayor of the town. He refused again, but the prefect would not accept his refusal; all the notables came to beg, the people supplicated him on the open streets, and the pressure was so great, that he eventually assented. It was noticed that what appeared specially to determine him was the almost angry remark of an old woman, who cried to him from her door: "A good mayor is useful; a man should not recoil before the good he may be able to do." This was the third phase of his ascent; Father Madeleine had become Monsieur Madeleine, and Monsieur Madeleine became Monsieur le Maire.

3. *SUMS LODGED AT LAFITTE'S*

FATHER MADELEINE remained as simple as he had been on the first day; he had gray hair, a serious eye, the bronzed face of a working-man, and the thoughtful face of a philosopher. He habitually wore a broad-brimmed hat, and a long coat of coarse cloth, buttoned up to the chin. He performed his duties as mayor, but beyond that lived solitary; he spoke to few persons, liked to escape from compliments, smiled to save himself from laughing, and gave to save himself from smiling. The women said of him, "What a good bear!" and his great pleasure was to walk about the fields. He always took his meals with an open book before him, and he had a well-selected library. He was fond of books, for they are cool and sure friends. In proportion as leisure came with fortune, he seemed to employ it in cultivating his mind; it was noticed that with each year he spent in M. . . . his language became more polite, chosen, and gentle.

He was fond of taking a gun with him on his walks, but rarely fired; when by chance he did so, he had an infallible aim, which was almost terrific. He never killed an inoffensive animal or a small bird. Though he was no longer young, he was said to possess prodigious strength; he lent a hand to any one who needed it, raised a fallen horse, put his shoulder to a wheel stuck in the mud, or stopped a runaway bull by the horns. His pockets were always full of halfpence when he went out, and empty when he came home; whenever he passed through a village, the ragged children ran merrily after him, and surrounded him like a swarm of gnats. It was supposed that he must have formerly lived a rustic life, for he had all sorts of useful secrets which he taught the peasants. He showed them how to destroy blight in wheat by sprinkling the granary and pouring into the cracks of the boards a solution of common salt, and to get rid of weevils by hanging up everywhere, on the walls and roofs, flowering orviot. He had recipes to extirpate, from arable land, tares and other parasitic plants which injure wheat, and would defend a rabbit hutch from rats by the mere smell of a little guinea pig, which he placed in it.

One day he saw some countrymen very busy in tearing up nettles; he looked at the pile of uprooted and already withered plants and said; "They are dead, and yet they are good if you know how to use them. When nettles are young, the tops are an excellent vegetable. When they are old, they have threads and fiber like hemp and flax. When chopped up, nettles are good for fowls; when pounded, excellent for horned cattle. The nettle-seed mixed with the food renders the coats of cattle shiny, and the root mixed with salt produces a fine yellow color. The nettle is also excellent hay, which can be mown twice; and what does it require? A little earth, no care, and no cultivation. The only thing is that the seed falls as it ripens, and is difficult to garner. If a little care were taken, the nettle would be useful; but being neglected, it becomes injurious, and is then killed. Here men resemble nettles!" He added after a moment's silence: "My friends, remember this,—there are no bad herbs or bad men; there are only bad cultivators."

The children also loved him, because he could make them pretty little toys of straw and cocoa-nut shells. When he saw a church door hung with black, he went in; he went after a funeral as other persons do after a christening. The misfortunes of others attracted him, owing to his great gentleness; he mingled with friends in mourning, and with the priests round a coffin. He seemed to be fond of hearing those mournful psalms which are full of the vision of another world. With his eyes fixed on heaven, he listened, with a species of aspiration toward all the mysteries of Infinitude, to the sad voice singing on the brink of the obscure abyss of death. He did a number of good actions, while as careful to hide them as if they were bad. He would quietly at night enter houses, and furtively ascend the stairs. A poor fellow, on returning to his garret, would find that his door had been opened, at times forced, during his absence; the man would cry that a robber had been there, but when he entered, the first thing he saw was a gold coin left on the table. The robber who had been there was Father Madeleine.

He was affable and sad; people said, "There is a rich man who does not look proud; a lucky man who does not look happy." Some persons asserted that he was a mysterious character, and declared that no one ever entered his bedroom, which was a real anchorite's cell, furnished with winged hour-glasses and embellished with cross-bones and death's-heads. This was so often repeated that some elegant and spiteful ladies of M. . . . came to him one day, and said, "Monsieur le Maire, *do* show us your bedroom, for people say that it is a grotto." He smiled and led them straightway to the "grotto"; they were terribly punished for their curiosity, as it was a bedroom, merely containing mahogany furniture as ugly as all furniture of that sort, and hung with a paper at six-pence the roll. They could not notice anything but two double-branched candlesticks of an antiquated pattern, standing on the mantel-piece, and seemingly of silver "because they were Hall-marked,"—a remark full of the wit of small towns. People did not the less continue to repeat, however, that no one ever entered this bedroom, and that it was a hermitage, a hole, a tomb. They also whispered that he had immense sums lodged with Lafitte, and with this peculiarity that things were always at his immediate disposal, "so that," they added, "M. Madeleine could go any morning to Lafitte's, sign a receipt, and carry off his two or three millions of francs in ten minutes." In reality, these "two or three millions," were reduced as we have said, to six hundred and thirty or forty thousand francs.

4 · M. MADELEINE GOES INTO MOURNING

At the beginning of 1821, the papers announced the decease of M. Myriel, bishop of D. . . . , "surnamed Monseigneur Welcome," and who died in the odor of sanctity at the age of eighty-two. The bishop of D. . . . , to add here a detail omitted by the papers, had been blind for several years, and was satisfied to be blind, as his sister was by his side.

Let us say parenthetically that to be blind and to be loved is one of the most strangely exquisite forms of happiness upon this earth, where nothing is perfect. To have continually at your side a wife, a sister, a daughter, a charming being, who is there because you have need of her, and because she cannot do without you; to know yourself indispensable to a woman who is necessary to you; to be able constantly to gauge her affection by the amount of her presence which she gives you, and to say to yourself: "She devotes all her time to me because I possess her entire heart"; to see her thoughts in default of her face; to prove the fidelity of a being in the eclipse of the world; to catch the rustling of a dress like the sound of wings; to hear her come and go, leave the room, return, talk, sing, and then to dream that you are the center of those steps, those words, those songs; to manifest at every moment your own attraction, and feel yourself powerful in proportion to your weakness; to become, in darkness and through darkness, the planet round which this angel gravitates—but few felicities equal this. The supreme happiness of life is the conviction of being loved for yourself, or, more correctly speaking, loved in spite of yourself; and this conviction the blind man has. In this distress, to be served is to be caressed. Does he want for anything? No. When you possess love, you have not lost the light. And what a love! a love entirely made of virtues. There is no blindness where there is certainty; the groping soul seeks a soul and finds it, and this fond and tried soul is a woman. A hand supports you,—it is hers; a mouth touches your forehead,—it is hers; you hear a breathing close to you,—it is she.

To have everything of hers, from her worship to her pity, to be never left, to have this gentle weakness to succor you, to lean on this unbending reed, to touch Providence with her hands, and be able to take her in your arms; O God that can be felt, what rapture is this! The heart, that obscure celestial flower, begins to expand mysteriously, and you would not exchange this shadow for all the light! The angel soul is necessarily there. If she go away, it is to return; she disappears like a dream, and reappears like reality. You feel heat approaching you,—it is she. You overflow with serenity, ecstasy, and gayety; you are a sunbeam in the night. And then the thousand little attentions, the nothings which are so enormous in this vacuum! The most ineffable accents of the human voice employed to lull you, and taking the place of the vanished universe. You are caressed with the soul; you see nothing, but you feel yourself adored; it is a paradise of darkness.

It was from this paradise that Monseigneur Welcome had passed to the other. The announcement of his death was copied by the local paper of M. . . . , and on the next day M. Madeleine appeared dressed in black, with crepe on his hat. The mourning was noticed in the town and the people gossiped about it, for it seemed to throw a gleam over M. Madeleine's origin. It was concluded that he was somehow connected with the bishop. "He is mourning for the bishop," was said in drawing-rooms; this added inches to M. Madeleine's stature, and suddenly gave him a certain consideration in the noble world of M. . . . . The microscopic Faubourg St. Germain of the town thought about raising the quarantine of M. Madeleine, the probable relation of a bishop, and M. Madeleine remarked the promotion he had obtained in the increased love of the old ladies, and the greater amount of smiles from the young. One evening a lady belonging to this little great world, curious by right of seniority, ventured to say, "M. le Maire is doubtless a cousin of the late bishop of D. . . . ?"

He answered, "No, Madame."

"But," the dowager went on, "you wear mourning for him."

"In my youth I was a footman in his family," was the answer.

Another thing noticed was, that when a young Savoyard passed through the town looking for chimneys to sweep, the mayor sent for him, asked his name, and gave him money. The Savoyard boys told each other of this, and a great many passed through M. . . . .

5. *VAGUE FLASHES ON THE HORIZON*

By degrees and with time all the opposition died out. At first there had been calumnies against M. Madeleine—a species of law which all rising men undergo; then it was only backbiting; then it was only malice; and eventually all this faded away. The respect felt for him was complete, unanimous, and cordial, and the moment arrived in 1821 when the name of the mayor was uttered at M. . . . with nearly the same accent as "monseigneur the bishop" had been said at D. . . . in 1815. People came for ten leagues round to consult M. Madeleine; he settled disputes, prevented lawsuits, and reconciled enemies. Everybody was willing to accept him as arbiter, and it seemed as if he had the book of natural law for his soul. It was a sort of contagious veneration, which in six or seven years spread all over the countryside.

Only one man in the town and bailiwick resisted this contagion, and, whatever M. Madeleine might do, remained rebellious to it, as if a sort of incorruptible and imperturbable instinct kept him on his guard. It would appear, in fact, as if there is in certain men a veritable bestial instinct, though pure and honest as all instincts are, which creates sympathies and antipathies; which fatally separates one nature from another; which never hesitates; which is not troubled, is never silent, and never contradicts itself; which is clear in its obscurity, infallible, imperious; refractory to all the councils of intelligence and all the solvents of the reason, and which, whatever the way in which destinies are made, surely warns the man-dog of the man-cat, and the man-fox of the presence of the man-lion. It often happened when M. Madeleine passed along the street calmly, kindly, and greeted by the blessings of all, that a tall man, dressed in an iron-gray greatcoat, armed with a thick cane, and wearing a hat with turned-down brim, turned suddenly and looked after him till he disappeared; folding his arms, shaking his head, and raising his upper lip with the lower as·high as his nose, a sort of significant grimace, which may be translated,—"Who is that man? I am certain that I have seen him somewhere. At any rate, I am not his dupe."

This person, who was grave, with an almost menacing gravity, was one of those men who, though only noticed for a moment, preoccupy the observer. His name was Javert, and he belonged to the police, and performed at M. . . . the laborious but useful duties of an inspector. He had not seen M. Madeleine's beginning, for he was indebted for the post he occupied to the secretary of Count Anglés, at that time prefect of police at Paris. When Javert arrived at M. . . . , the great manufacturer's fortune was made, and Father Madeleine had become Monsieur Madeleine. Some police officers have a peculiar face, which is complicated by an air of baseness blended with an air of authority. Javert had this face, less the baseness. In our conviction, if souls were visible we should distinctly see the strange fact that every individual of the human species corresponds to some one of the species of animal creation; and we might easily recognize the truth, which has as yet scarce occurred to the thinker, that, from the oyster to the eagle, from the hog to the tiger, all animals are in man, and that each of them is in a man; at times, several of them at once. Animals are nothing else than the figures of our virtues and our vices wandering before our eyes, the visible phantoms of our souls. God shows these to us in order to make us reflect; but, as animals are only shadows, God has not made them capable of education in the complete sense of the term, for of what use would it be? On the other hand, our souls being realities and having an end of their own, God has endowed them with intelligence; that is to say, possible education. Social education, properly carried out, can always draw out of a soul, no matter its nature, the utility which it contains. Let this be said, it must be well understood, from a narrow point of view of life here on earth, without prejudging the question of the anterior or ulterior personality of the beings which are not man. The visible *me* in no wise justifies the thinker in denying the latent *me*. This qualification being made, let us go on.

Now, if the reader will admit with me for a moment that in every man there is one of the animal species of creation, it will be easy for us to say what Javert the policeman was. The Asturian peasants are convinced that in every litter of wolves there is a dog, which is killed by the mother, for, otherwise, when it grew it would devour the other whelps. Give a human face to this dog-son of a she-wolf, and we shall have Javert. He was born in prison; his mother was a fortune-teller, whose husband was at the galleys. When he grew up he thought that he was beyond the pale of society, and despaired of ever entering it. He noticed that society inexorably keeps at bay two classes of men,—those who attack it, and those who guard it; he had only a choice between these two classes, and at the same time felt within him a rigidness, regularity, and probity, combined with an inexpressible hatred of the race of Bohemians to which he belonged.

He entered the police, got on, and at the age of forty was an inspector. In his youth he was engaged in the southern bagnes.

Before going further, let us explain the words "human face" which we applied just now to Javert. His human face consisted of a stub-nose, with two enormous nostrils, toward which enormous whiskers mounted on his cheeks. You felt uncomfortable the first time that you saw these two forests and these two caverns. When Javert laughed, which was rare and terrible, his thin lips parted, and displayed, not only his teeth, but his gums, and a savage flat curl formed round his nose, such as is seen on the muzzle of a wild beast. Javert when serious was a bull-dog; when he laughed he was a tiger. To sum up, he had but little skull and plenty of jaw; his hair hid his forehead and fell over his brows; he had between his eyes a central and permanent frown, like a star of anger, an obscure glance, a pinched-up and formidable mouth, and an air of ferocious command.

This man was made up of two very simple and relatively excellent feelings, but which he almost rendered bad by exaggerating them,—respect for authority and hatred of rebellion; and in his eyes, robbery, murder, and every crime were only formed of rebellion. He enveloped in a species of blind faith everybody in the service of the state, from the prime minister down to the game-keeper. He covered with contempt, aversion, and disgust every one who had crossed the legal threshold of evil. He was absolute, and admitted of no exceptions; on one side he said: "A functionary cannot be mistaken, a magistrate can do no wrong"; on the other he said: "They are irremediably lost; no good can come of them." He fully shared the opinion of those extreme minds that attribute to the human law some power of making, or, if you like, of proving the existence of demons, and that place a Styx at the bottom of society. He was stoical, stern and austere; a sad dreamer, and humble yet haughty, like all fanatics. His glance was a gimlet, for it was cold and piercing. His whole life was composed in the two words, watching and overlooking.

He had introduced the straight line into what is the most tortuous thing in the world; he was conscious of his usefulness, had religious respect for his duties, and was a spy as well as another is a priest. Woe to the wretch who came into his clutches! he would have arrested his father if escaping from prison, and denounced his mother had she broken her ban. And he would have done it with that sort of inner satisfaction which virtue produces. With all this he spent a life of privation, isolation, self-denial, chastity. He was the implacable duty, the police comprehended as the Spartans comprehended Sparta, a pitiless watchman, a fierce honesty, a marble-hearted spy, a Brutus in a Vidocq.

Javert's entire person expressed the man who spies and hides himself. The mystic school of Joseph de Maistre, which at this epoch was seasoning with high cosmogony what were called the ultra journals, would not have failed to say that Javert was a symbol. His forehead could not be seen for it was hidden by his hat; his eyes could not be seen, because they were lost under his eyebrows; his chin was plunged into his cravat, his hands were covered by his cuffs, and his cane was carried under his coat. But when the opportunity arrived, there could be seen suddenly emerging from all this shadow, as from an ambush, an angular, narrow forehead, a fatal glance, a menacing chin, enormous hands, and a monstrous rattan. In his leisure moments, which were few, he read, though he hated books, and this caused him not to be utterly ignorant, as could be noticed through a certain emphasis in his language. As we have said, he had no vice; when satisfied with himself, he indulged in a pinch of snuff, that was his connecting link with humanity.

Our readers will readily understand that Javert was the terror of all that class whom the yearly statistics of the minister of justice designate under the rubric "Vagabonds." The name of Javert, if uttered, set them to flight; the face of Javert, if seen, petrified them. Such was this formidable man.

Javert was like an eye ever fixed on M. Madeleine, an eye full of suspicion and conjectures. M. Madeleine noticed it in the end; but he considered it a matter of insignificance. He did not even ask Javert his motive; he neither sought nor shunned him, and endured his annoying glance without appearing to notice it. He treated Javert like every one else, easily and kindly. From some remarks that dropped from Javert, it was supposed that he had secretly sought with that curiosity belonging to the breed, and in which there is as much instinct as will, all the previous traces which Father Madeleine might have left. He appeared to know, and sometimes said covertly, that some one had obtained certain information in a certain district about a certain family which had disappeared. Once he happened to say, speaking of himself, "I believe that I have got him"; then he remained thoughtful for three days without saying a word. It seemed that the thread which he fancied he held was broken. However, there cannot be any theory really infallible in a human creature, and it is the peculiarity of instinct that it can be troubled, thrown out, routed. If not, it would be superior to intelligence, and the brute would have a better light than man. Javert was evidently somewhat disconcerted by M. Madeleine's complete naturalness and calmness. One day, however, his strange manner seemed to produce an impression on M. Madeleine. The occasion was as follows:

6. FATHER FAUCHELEVENT

WHEN M. Madeleine was passing one morning through an unpaved lane in the town, he heard a noise and saw a group at some distance, to which he walked up. An old man, known as Father Fauchelevent, had fallen under his cart, and his horse was lying on the ground. This Fauchelevent was one of the few enemies M. Madeleine still had at this time. When M. Madeleine came to these parts, Fauchelevent, a notary and a tolerably well-educated fellow, was doing badly in business, and he saw the simple workman grow rich, while he, a master, was being ruined. This filled him with jealousy, and he had done all in his power, on every possible occasion, to injure M. Madeleine. Then bankruptcy came, and in his old days, having only a horse and cart left, and no family, he turned carter to earn a living.

The horse had both legs broken and could not get up, while the old man was entangled between the wheels. The fall had been so unfortunate that the whole weight of the cart was pressing on his chest, and it was heavily loaded. Fauchelevent uttered lamentable groans, and attempts had been made, though in vain, to draw him out, and any irregular effort, any clumsy help or shock, might kill him. It was impossible to extricate him except by raising the cart from below, and Javert, who came up at the moment of the accident, had sent to fetch a jack. When M. Madeleine came up, the mob made way respectfully.

"Help!" old Fauchelevent cried, "is there no good soul who will save an old man?"

M. Madeleine turned to the spectators.

"Have you a jack?"

"They have gone to fetch one," a peasant answered.

"How soon will it be here?"

"Well, the nearest is at Hachet the blacksmith's, but it cannot be brought here under a good quarter of an hour."

"A quarter of an hour!" Madeleine exclaimed.

It had rained on the previous night, the ground was soft, the cart sunk deeper into it every moment, and more and more pressed the old man's chest. It was evident that his ribs would be broken within five minutes.

"It is impossible to wait a quarter of an hour," said M. Madeleine to the peasants who were looking on.

"We must."

"But do you not see that the cart is sinking into the ground?"

"Hang it, so it is."

"Listen to me," Madeleine continued; "there is still room enough for a man to slip under the cart and raise it with his back. It will only take half a minute, and the poor man can be drawn out. Is there any one here who has strong loins? there are five louis to be earned."

No one stirred.

"Ten louis," Madeleine said.

His hearers looked down, and one of them muttered, "A man would have to be deucedly strong, and, besides, he would run the risk of being smashed."

"Come," Madeleine began again, "twenty louis."

The same silence.

"It is not good-will they are deficient in," a voice cried.

M. Madeleine turned and recognized Javert; he had noticed him when he came up. Javert continued:

"It is the strength. A man would have to be tremendously strong to lift a cart like that with his back."

Then, looking fixedly at M. Madeleine, he continued, laying a marked stress on every word he uttered:

"Monsieur Madeleine, I never knew but *one* man capable of doing what you ask."

M. Madeleine started, but Javert continued carelessly, though without taking his eyes off Madeleine:

"He was a galley-slave."

"Indeed!" said Madeleine.

"At the Toulon bagne."

M. Madeleine turned pale; all this while the cart was slowly settling down, and Father Fauchelevent was screaming:

"I am choking; it is breaking my ribs; a jack! something—oh!"

M. Madeleine looked around him.

"Is there no one here willing to earn twenty louis and save this poor man's life?"

No one stirred, and Javert repeated:

"I never knew but one man capable of acting as a jack, and it was that convict."

"Oh, it is crushing me!" the old man yelled.

M. Madeleine raised his head, met Javert's falcon eye still fixed on him, gazed at the peasants, and sighed sorrowfully. Then, without saying a word, he fell on his knees, and ere the crowd had time to utter a cry, was under the cart. There was a frightful moment of expectation and silence. M. Madeleine, almost lying flat under the tremendous weight, twice tried in vain to bring his elbows up to his knees. The peasants shouted: "Father Madeleine, come out!" and old Fauchelevent himself said: "Monsieur Madeleine, go away! I must die, so leave me; you will be killed too."

M. Madeleine made no answer; the spectators gasped, the wheels had sunk deeper, and it was now almost impossible for him to get out from under the cart. All at once the enormous mass shook, the cart slowly rose, and the wheels half emerged from the rut. A stifled voice could be heard crying, "Make haste, help!" It was M. Madeleine, who had made a last effort. They rushed forward, for the devotion of one man had restored strength and courage to all. The cart was lifted by twenty arms, and old Fauchelevent was saved. M. Madeleine rose; he was livid, although dripping with perspiration; his clothes were torn and covered with mud.

The old man kissed his knees and called him his saviour, while M. Madeleine had on his face a strange expression of happy and celestial suffering, and turned his placid eye on Javert who was still looking at him.

7. FAUCHELEVENT BECOMES A GARDENER AT PARIS

FAUCHELEVENT had put out his knee-cap in his fall, and Father Madeleine had him carried to an infirmary he had established for his workmen in his factory, and which was managed by two sisters of charity. The next morning the old man found a thousand-franc note by his bedside, with a line in M. Madeleine's handwriting: "Payment for your cart and horse, which I have bought." The cart was smashed and the horse dead. Fauchelevent recovered, but his leg remained stiff, and hence M. Madeleine, by the recommendation of the sisters and his curé, procured him a situation as gardener at a convent in the St. Antoine quarter of Paris.

Some time after, M. Madeleine was appointed mayor; the first time Javert saw him wearing the scarf which gave him all authority in the town, he felt that sort of excitement a dog would feel that scented a wolf in its master's clothes. From this moment he avoided him as much as he could, and when duty imperiously compelled him, and he could not do otherwise than appear before the mayor, he addressed him with profound respect.

The prosperity created in M. . . . by Father Madeleine had, in addition to the visible signs we have indicated, another symptom, which, though not visible, was not the less significant, for it is one that never deceives. When the population is suffering, when work is scarce and trade bad, tax-payers exhaust and exceed the time granted them, and the state spends a good deal of money in enforcing payment. When the work abounds, when the country is happy and rich, the taxes are paid cheerfully, and cost the state little. We may say that wretchedness and the public exchequer have an infallible thermometer in the cost of collecting the taxes. In seven years these costs had been reduced three-fourths in the arrondissement of M. . . . , which caused it to be frequently quoted by M. de Villèle, at that time minister of finance.

Such was the state of the town when Fantine returned to it. No one remembered her, but luckily the door of M. Madeleine's factory was like a friendly face; she presented herself at it, and was admitted to the female shop. As the trade was quite new to Fantine, she was awkward at it and earned but small wages; but that was enough, for she had solved the problem,—she was earning her livelihood.

8. *MADAME VICTURNIEN SPENDS THIRTY FRANCS ON MORALITY*

WHEN Fantine saw that she could gain her living, she had a moment of joy. To live honestly by her own toil, what a favor of Heaven! A taste for work really came back to her. She bought a looking-glass, delighted in seeing in it her youth, her fine hair, and fine teeth; forgot many things, only thought of Cosette and her possible future, and was almost happy. She hired a small room and furnished it, on credit, to be paid for out of her future earnings,—this was a relic of her irregular habits.

Not being able to say that she was married, she was very careful not to drop a word about her child. At the outset as we have seen, she punctually paid the Thénardiers, and as she could only sign her name, she was compelled to write to them through the agency of a public writer. It was noticed that she wrote frequently. It was beginning to be whispered in the shop that Fantine "wrote letters," and was "carrying on."

No one spies the actions of persons so much as those whom they do not concern. Why does M. X. never come till nightfall? Why does M. So-and-so never hang up his key on Thursdays? Why does he always take back streets? Why does Madame —— always get out of her hackney coach before reaching her house? Why does she send out to buy a quire of note-paper, when she has a desk full? and so on. There are people who, in order to solve these inquiries, which are matters of utter indifference to them, spend more money, lavish more time, and take more trouble than would be required for ten good deeds; and they do it gratuitously for the pleasure, and they are only paid for their curiosity with curiosity. They will follow a gentleman or a lady for whole days, will stand sentry at the corner of a street or in a gateway at night in the cold and rain, corrupt messengers, intoxicate hackney coachmen and footmen, buy a lady's maid, and make a purchase of a porter—why? For nothing; for a pure desire to see, know, and find out—it is a simple itch for talking. And frequently these secrets, when made known, these mysteries published, these enigmas brought to daylight, entail catastrophes, duels, bankruptcies, ruin of families, to the great delight of those who found it all out, without any personal motives, through pure instinct. It is a sad thing. Some persons are wicked solely through a desire to talk, and this conversation, which is gossip in the drawing-room, scandal in the anteroom, is like those chimneys which consume wood rapidly; they require a great deal of combustible, and this combustible is their neighbor.

Fantine was observed then, and, besides, more than one girl was jealous of her blonde hair and white teeth. It was noticed that she often wiped away a tear in the shop; it was when she was thinking of her child, perhaps of the man she had loved. It is a painful labor to break off all the gloomy connecting links with the past. It was a fact that she wrote, at least twice a month, and always to the same address, and paid the postage. They managed to obtain the address: "Monsieur Thénardier, Publican, Montfermeil." The public writer, who could not fill his stomach with wine without emptying his pocket of secrets, was made to talk at the wine-shop; and, in short, it was known that Fantine had a child. A gossip undertook a journey to Montfermeil, spoke to the Thénardiers, and on her return said, "I do not begrudge my thirty francs, for I have seen the child."

The gossip who did this was a Gorgon of the name of Madame Victurnien, guardian and portress of everybody's virtue. She was fifty-six years of age, and covered the mask of ugliness with the mask of old age. Astounding to say, this old woman had once been young; in her youth, in '93, she had married a monk who escaped from the cloisters in a red cap and passed over from the Bernardines to the Jacobins. She was dry, crabbed, sharp, thorny, and almost venomous, while remembering the monk whose widow she was and who had considerably tamed her. At the Restoration she had turned bigot, and so energetically that the priests forgave her her monk. She had a small estate which she left with considerable ostentation to a religious community, and she was very welcome at the Episcopal Palace of Arras. This Madame Victurnien, then, went to Montfermeil, and when she returned said, "I have seen the child."

All this took time, and Fantine had been more than a year at the factory, when one morning the forewoman handed her fifty francs in the mayor's name, and told her that she was no longer engaged, and had better leave the town, so the mayor said. It was in this very month that the Thénardiers, after asking for twelve francs instead of seven, raised a claim for fifteen instead of twelve. Fantine was startled; she could not leave the town, for she owed her rent and for her furniture, and fifty francs would not pay those debts. She stammered a few words of entreaty, but the forewoman intimated to her that she must leave the shop at once; moreover, Fantine was but an indifferent work-woman. Crushed by shame more than disgrace, she left the factory, and returned to her room; her fault then was now known to all! She did not feel the strength in her to say a word; she was advised to see the mayor, but did not dare do so. The mayor gave her fifty francs because he was kind, and discharged her because he was just; and she bowed her head to the sentence.

9. SUCCESS OF MADAME VICTURNIEN

THE monk's widow, then, was good for something. M. Madeleine, however, knew nothing of all this; and they were combinations of events of
which the world is full. M. Madeleine made it a rule hardly ever to enter
the female workroom; he had placed at its head an old maid whom the
curé had given him, and he had entire confidence in her. She was really
a respectable, firm, equitable, and just person, full of that charity which
consists in giving, but not possessing to the same extent the charity which
comprehends and pardons. M. Madeleine trusted to her in everything,
for the best men are often forced to delegate their authority, and it was
with this full power, and in the conviction that she was acting rightly,
that the forewoman tried, condemned, and executed Fantine. As for
the fifty francs, she had given them out of a sum M. Madeleine had given
her for alms and helping the work-women, and which she did not
account for.

Fantine tried to get a servant's place in the town, and went from
house to house, but no one would have anything to do with her. She
could not leave the town, for the broker to whom she was in debt for her
furniture—what furniture!—said to her, "If you go away, I will have you
arrested as a thief." The landlord, to whom she owed her rent, said to
her, "You are young and pretty, you can pay." She divided the fifty
francs between the landlord and the broker, gave back to the latter three-
fourths of the goods, only retaining what was absolutely necessary, and
found herself without work, without a trade, with only a bed, and still
owing about 100 francs. She set to work making coarse shirts for the
troops, and earned at this sixpence a day, her daughter costing her four-
pence. It was at this moment she began to fall in arrears with the Thénardiers. An old woman, however, who lit her candles for her when she

177

came in at nights, taught her the way to live in wretchedness. Behind living on little, there is living on nothing; there are two chambers,—the first is obscure, the second quite dark.

Fantine learned how she could do entirely without fire in winter, how she must get rid of a bird that cost her a half-penny every two days, how she could make a petticoat of her blanket and a blanket of her petticoat, and how candle can be saved by taking your meals by the light of the window opposite. We do not know all that certain weak beings, who have grown old in want and honesty, can get out of a halfpenny, and in the end it becomes a talent. Fantine acquired this sublime talent, and regained a little courage. At this period she said to a neighbor, "Nonsense, I say to myself; by only sleeping for five hours and working all the others at my needle, I shall always manage to earn bread, at any rate. And then, when you are sad, you eat less. Well! suffering, anxiety, a little bread on one side and sorrow on the other, all will support me."

In this distress, it would have been a strange happiness to have had her daughter with her, and she thought of sending for her. But, what! make her share her destitution? and then she owed money to the Thénardiers! how was she to pay it and the traveling expenses? The old woman who had given her lessons in what may be called indigent life, was a pious creature, poor, and charitable to the poor and even to the rich, who could just write her name, "Marguerite," and believed in God, which is knowledge. There are many such virtues down here, and one day they will be up above, for this life has a morrow.

At the beginning, Fantine had been so ashamed that she did not dare go out. When she was in the streets, she perceived that people turned around to look at her and pointed to her. Every one stared at her, and no one bowed to her; the cold, bitter contempt of the passer-by passed through her flesh and her mind like an east wind. In small towns an unhappy girl seems to be naked beneath the sarcasm and curiosity of all. In Paris, at least, no one knows you, and that obscurity is a garment. Oh! how glad she would have been to be back in Paris. She must grow accustomed to disrespect, as she had done to poverty. Gradually she made up her mind, and after two or three months shook off her shame, and went as if nothing had occurred. "It is no matter to me," she said. She came and went with head erect and with a bitter smile, and felt that she was growing impudent. Madame Victurnien sometimes saw her pass from her window; she noticed the distress of "the creature whom she had made know her place," and congratulated herself. The wicked have a black happiness. Excessive labor fatigued Fantine, and the little dry cough she had grew worse. She sometimes said to her neighbor, "Marguerite, just feel how hot my hands are!" Still, in the morning, when she passed an old broken comb through her glorious hair, which shone like floss silk, she had a minute of happy coquettishness.

10. *RESULT OF HER SUCCESS*

SHE had been discharged toward the end of winter; the next summer passed away, and winter returned. Short days and less work; in winter there is no warmth, no light, no midday, for the evening is joined to the morning; there is fog, twilight, the window is gray, and you cannot see clearly. The sky is like a dark vault, and the sun has the look of a poor man. It is a frightful season; winter changes into stone the water of heaven and the heart of man. Her creditors pressed her, for Fantine was earning too little, and her debt had increased. The Thénardiers, being irregularly paid, constantly wrote her letters, whose contents afflicted her, and postage ruined her. One day they wrote her that little Cosette was quite naked, that she wanted a flannel skirt, and that the mother must send at least ten francs for the purpose. She crumpled the letter in her hands all day, and at nightfall went to a barber's at the corner of the street and removed her comb. Her splendid light hair fell down to her hips.

"What fine hair!" the barber exclaimed.

"What will you give me for it?" she asked.

"Ten francs."

"Cut it off."

She bought a skirt and sent it to the Thénardiers; it made them furious, for they wanted the money. They gave it to Eponine, and the poor lark continued to shiver. Fantine thought, "My child is no longer cold, for I have dressed her in my hair." She wore small round caps which hid her shorn head, and she still looked pretty in them.

A dark change took place in Fantine's heart. When she found that she could no longer dress her hair, she began to hate all around her. She had long shared the universal veneration for Father Madeleine; but, through the constant iteration that he had discharged her and was the cause of her misfortune, she grew to hate him too, and worse than the rest. When she passed the factory she pretended to laugh and sing. An old workman who once saw her doing so, said, "That's a girl who will come to a bad end." She took a lover, the first who offered, a man she did not love, through bravado, and with rage in her heart. He was a scoundrel, a sort of mendicant musician, an idle scamp, who beat her, and left her, as she had chosen him, in disgust. She adored her child. The lower she sank, the darker the gloom became around her, the more did this sweet little angel gleam in her soul. She said: "When I am rich, I shall have my Cosette with me"; and she laughed. She did not get rid of her cough, and she felt a cold perspiration in her back.

One day she received from the Thénardiers a letter to the following effect,—"Cosette is ill with a miliary fever, as they call it, which is very prevalent. She must have expensive drugs, and that ruins us, and we cannot pay for them any longer. If you do not send us forty francs within a week, the little one will be dead." She burst into a loud laugh, and said to her old neighbor, "Oh, what funny people! they want forty francs; where do they expect me to get them? What fools those peasants are!" Still, she went to a staircase window and read the letter again; then she went out into the street, still laughing and singing. Some one who met her said, "What has made you so merry?" and she answered, "It is a piece of stupidity some country folk have written; they want forty francs of me, the asses!"

As she passed across the market-place, she saw a crowd surrounding a vehicle of a strange shape, on the box of which a man dressed in red was haranguing. He was a dentist going his rounds, who offered the public complete sets of teeth, opiates, powders and elixirs. Fantine joined the crowd and began laughing like the rest at this harangue, in which there was slang for the mob and scientific jargon for respectable persons. The extractor of teeth saw the pretty girl laughing, and suddenly exclaimed:

"You have fine teeth, my laughing beauty. If you like to sell me your two top front teeth, I will give you a napoleon apiece for them."

"What a horrible idea!" Fantine exclaimed.

"Two napoleons!" an old toothless woman by her side grumbled; "there's a lucky girl."

Fantine ran away and stopped her ears not to hear the hoarse voice of the man, who shouted: "Think it over, my dear; two napoleons may be useful. If your heart says Yes, come to-night to the *Tillac d'Argent,* where you will find me."

Fantine, when she reached home, was furious, and told her good neighbor Marguerite what had happened. "Can you understand it? is he not an abominable man? How can people like that be allowed to go about the country? Pull out my two front teeth! why, I should look horrible; hair grows again, but teeth! oh, the monster! I would sooner throw myself head first out of a fifth-floor window on to the pavement."

"And what did he offer you?" Marguerite asked.

"Two napoleons."

"That makes forty francs."

"Yes," said Fantine, "that makes forty francs."

She became thoughtful and sat down to her work. At the end of a quarter of an hour, she left the room and read Thénardier's letter again on the staircase. When she returned she said to Marguerite:

"Do you know what a miliary fever is?"

"Yes," said the old woman, "it is an illness."

"Does it require much medicine?"

"Oh, an awful lot."

"Does it attack children?"

"More than anybody."

"Do they die of it?"

"Plenty," said Marguerite.

Fantine went out and read the letter once again on the staircase. At night she went out, and could be seen proceeding in the direction of the Rue de Paris, where the inns are. The next morning, when Marguerite entered Fantine's room before daybreak, for they worked together, and then made one candle do for them both, she found her sitting by her bed, pale and chill. Her cap had fallen on her knees, and the candle had been burning all night, and was nearly consumed. Marguerite stopped in the door-way, horrified by this enormous extravagance, and exclaimed:

"Oh! Lord! the candle nearly burnt out! something must have happened."

Then she looked at Fantine, who turned her close-shaven head toward her, and seemed to have grown ten years older since the previous day.

"Gracious Heaven!" said Marguerite, "what is the matter with you, Fantine?"

"Nothing," the girl answered, "I am all right. My child will not die of that frightful disease for want of assistance, and I am satisfied."

As she said this, she pointed to two napoleons that glistened on the table.

"Oh! Lord!" said Marguerite; "why, 'tis a fortune; wherever did you get them from?"

"I had them by me," Fantine answered.

At the same time she smiled, the candle lit up her face, and it was a fearful smile. A reddish saliva stained the corner of her lips, and she had a black hole in her mouth—the two teeth were pulled out. She sent the forty francs to Monfermeil. It had only been a trick of the Thénardiers to get money, for Cosette was not ill.

Fantine threw her looking-glass out of the window; she had long before left her cell, on the third floor, for a garret under the roof—one of those tenements in which the ceiling forms an angle with the floor, and you knock your head at every step. The poor man can only go to the end of his room, as to the end of his destiny, by stooping more and more. She had no bed left; she had only a rag she called a blanket, a mattress on the ground, and a bottomless chair; a little rose-tree she had had withered away, forgotten, in a corner. In another corner she had a pail to hold water, which froze in winter, and in which the different levels of the water remained marked for a long time by rings of ice. She had lost her shame, and now lost her coquetry; the last sign was, that she went out with dirty caps. Either through want of time or carelessness, she no longer mended her linen, and as the heels of her stockings wore out, she tucked them into her shoes. She mended her worn-out gown with rags of calico, which tore away at the slightest movement. The people to whom she owed money made "scenes," and allowed her no rest; she met them in the street, she met them again on her stairs. Her eyes were very bright, and she felt a settled pain at the top of her left shoulder-blade, while she coughed frequently. She deeply hated Father Madeleine, and sewed for seventeen hours a day; but a speculator hired all the female prisoners, and reduced the prices of the free workmen to nine sous a day. Seventeen hours' work for nine sous! her creditors were more pitiless than ever, and the broker, who had got back nearly all her furniture, incessantly said to her, "When are you going to pay me, you cheat?"

What did they want of her? good Heavens! she felt herself tracked, and something of the wild beast was aroused in her. About the same time Thénardier wrote to her that he had decidedly waited too patiently, and that unless he received one hundred francs at once he would turn poor Cosette, who had scarce recovered, out-of-doors, into the cold, and she must do what she could or die if she liked. "One hundred francs!" Fantine thought, "but where is the trade in which I can earn one hundred sous in a day? Well, I will sell all that is left!"

And the unfortunate girl went on the streets.

11. *CHRISTUS NOS LIBERAVIT*

WHAT, now, is this story of Fantine? It is society buying a slave, buying a slave from misery, from hunger, from cold, from isolation, from abandonment, from destitution. Lamentable bargain, a soul for a morsel of bread! Misery offers and society accepts.

The holy law of Christ governs our civilization, but does not yet penetrate it. Slavery is said to have disappeared from the civilization of Europe. It has not; it still exists, but it weighs down woman alone, and is called prostitution. It weighs down woman, that is to say, grace, weakness, beauty, motherhood. This is not one of the least disgraces of man. At the point at which we have arrived in this lamentable drama, nothing of what she once had been remained in Fantine. In becoming mad, she had become marble; who touches her is chilled; she possesses, she submits, she ignores you, she is the image of dishonor and severity. Life and social order have said their last words to her. All has happened to her that can happen. She has felt all, borne all, experienced all, suffered all, lost all, wept all; she is resigned with that resignation which resembles indifference as death resembles sleep. She shrinks from nothing, she fears nothing. Let all the cloud fall on her, let all the ocean sweep over her; what matter? The sponge is saturated.

She believes so, at least, but it is a mistake to imagine that one has exhausted destiny and touched the bottom of anything.

Alas! what are all these destinies, urged on thus pell-mell? Where go they? Why are they thus?

He who knows this sees the whole shadow. He is one only and is called God.

12. M. BAMATABOIS' AMUSEMENTS

THERE is in all small towns, and there was at M. . . . in particular, a class of young men who squander fifteen hundred francs a year in the provinces with the same air as their congeners in Paris devour two hundred thousand. They are beings of the great neutral species; geldings, parasites, nobodies, who possess a little land, a little folly, and a little wit, who would be rustics in a drawing-room, and believe themselves gentlemen in a pot-house. They talk about my fields, my woods, my peasants, horses, the actresses, to prove themselves men of taste; quarrel with the officers, to prove themselves men of war, shoot, smoke, yawn, drink, smell of tobacco, play at billiards, watch the travelers get out of the stage-coach, live at the café, dine at the inn, have a dog that gnaws bones under the table, and a mistress who places the dishes upon it; haggle over a sou, exaggerate the fashions, admire tragedy, despise women, wear out their old boots, copy London through Paris, and Paris through Pont-à-Mousson; grow stupidly old, do not work, are of no use, and do no great harm. Had M. Felix Tholomyès remained in his province and not seen Paris, he would have been one of them. If they were richer, people would say they are dandies; if poorer, they are good-for-nothings, but they are simply men with nothing to do. Among them there are bores and bored, dreamers, and a few scamps.

At that day, a dandy was composed of a tall collar, a large cravat, a watch and seals, three waistcoats over one another, blue and red inside, a short-waisted olive-colored coat, with a swallow-tail, and a double row of silver buttons, sewn on close together, and ascending to the shoulders, and trousers of a lighter olive, adorned on the seams with an undetermined but always uneven number of ribs, varying from one to eleven, a limit which was never exceeded. Add to this slipper-boots with iron on the heels, a tall, narrow-brimmed hat, hair in a tuft, an enormous cane, and a conversation improved by Potier's puns; over and above all these were spurs and mustaches, for at that period mustaches indicated the civilian, and spurs the pedestrian. The provincial dandy wore longer spurs and more ferocious mustaches. It was the period of the struggle of the South American Republics against the king of Spain, of Bolivar against Morillo. Narrow-brimmed hats were royalist, and called Morillos, while the liberals wore broad brims, which were called Bolivars.

Eight or ten months after the events we have described in the previous chapter, toward the beginning of January, 1823, and on a night when snow had fallen, one of these dandies—a man of "right sentiments," for he wore a Morillo, and was also warmly wrapped up in one of the large Spanish cloaks which at that time completed the fashionable costume in cold weather—was amusing himself by annoying a creature who was prowling about in a low-necked ball-dress and with flowers in her hair, before the window of the officers' café. This dandy was smoking, as that was a decided mark of fashion. Each time this woman passed him, he made some remark to her, which he fancied witty and amusing, as: "How ugly you are!—Why don't you go to kennel?—You have no teeth," etc., etc. This gentleman's name was Monsieur Bamatabois. The woman, a sad-dressed phantom walking backward and forward in the snow, made him no answer, did not even look at him, but still continued silently and with a gloomy regularity her walk, which every few minutes brought her under his sarcasms, like the condemned soldier running the gantlet. The slight effect produced doubtless annoyed the idler, for, taking advantage of her back being turned, he crept up behind her, stooped to pick up a handful of snow, and suddenly plunged it between her bare shoulders. The girl uttered a yell, turned, leapt like a panther on the man, and dug her nails into his face with the most frightful language that could fall from a guardroom into the gutter. These insults, vomited by a voice rendered hoarse by brandy, hideously issued from a mouth in which the two front teeth were really missing. It was Fantine.

At the noise, the officers left the café in a throng, the passers-by stopped, and a laughing, yelling, applauding circle was made round these two beings, in whom it was difficult to recognize a man and a woman,—the man struggling, his hat on the ground, the woman striking with feet and fists, bare-headed, yelling, without teeth or hair, livid with passion, and horrible. All at once a tall man quickly broke through the crowd, seized the woman's satin dress, which was covered with mud, and said: "Follow me." The woman raised her hand, and her passionate voice suddenly died out. Her eyes were glassy, she grew pale instead of being livid, and trembled with fear—she had recognized Javert. The dandy profited by this incident to make his escape.

13. *THE POLICE OFFICE*

JAVERT broke through the circle and began walking with long strides toward the police office, which is at the other end of the market-place, dragging the wretched girl after him. She allowed him to do so mechanically, and neither he nor she said a word. The crowd of spectators, in a paroxysm of delight, followed them with coarse jokes, for supreme misery is an occasion for obscenities. On reaching the police office, which was a low room, heated by a stove, and guarded by a sentry, and having a barred glass door opening on the street, Javert walked in with Fantine, and shut the door after him, to the great disappointment of the curious, who stood on tiptoe, and stretched out their necks in front of the dirty window trying to see. Curiosity is gluttony, and seeing is devouring.

On entering, Fantine crouched down motionless in a corner like a frightened dog. The sergeant on duty brought in a candle. Javert sat down at a table, took a sheet of stamped paper from his pocket, and began writing. Women of this class are by the French laws left entirely to the discretion of the police; they do what they like with them, punish them as they think proper, and confiscate the two sad things which they call their trade and their liberty. Javert was stoical; his grave face displayed no emotion, and yet he was seriously and deeply preoccupied. It was one of those moments in which he exercised without control, but with all the scruples of a strict conscience, his formidable discretionary power. At this instant he felt that his high stool was a tribunal, and himself the judge. He tried and he condemned; he summoned all the ideas he had in his mind round the great thing he was doing. The more he examined the girl's deed, the more outraged he felt; for it was evident that he had just seen a crime committed. He had seen in the street society, represented by a householder and elector, insulted and attacked by a creature beyond the pale of everything. A prostitute had assaulted a citizen, and he, Javert, had witnessed it. He wrote on silently. When he had finished, he affixed his signature, folded up the paper, and said to the sergeant as he handed it to him: "Take three men and lead this girl to prison." Then he turned to Fantine, "You will have six months for it."

The wretched girl started.

"Six months—six months' imprisonment!" she cried; "six months! and only earn seven sous a day! Why, what will become of Cosette, my child, my child! Why, I owe more than one hundred francs to Thénardier, M. Inspector; do you know that?"

She dragged herself across the floor, dirtied by the muddy boots of all these men, without rising, with clasped hands, and taking long strides with her knees.

"Monsieur Javert," she said, "I ask for mercy. I assure you that I was not in the wrong; if you had seen the beginning, you would not say so; I swear by our Saviour that I was not to blame. That gentleman, who was a stranger to me, put snow down my back; had he any right to do that when I was passing gently, and doing nobody a harm? It sent me wild, for you must know I am not very well, and, besides, he had been abusing me—'you are ugly, you have no teeth.' I am well aware that I have lost my teeth. I did nothing, and said to myself, 'This gentleman is amusing himself.' I was civil to him, and said nothing, and it was at this moment he put the snow down my back. My good M. Javert, is there no one who saw it to tell you that this is the truth? I was perhaps wrong to get into a passion, but at the moment, as you are aware, people are not masters of themselves, and I am quick-tempered. And then, something so cold put down your back, at a moment when you are least expecting it! It was wrong to destroy the gentleman's hat, but why has he gone away? I would ask his pardon. Oh! I would willingly do so. Let me off this time. M. Javert, perhaps you do not know that in prison you can only earn seven sous a day; it is not the fault of the government, but you only earn seven sous, and just fancy! I have one hundred francs to pay, or my child will be turned into the street. Oh! I cannot have her with me, for my mode of life is so bad! Oh my Cosette, oh my little angel, whatever will become of you, poor darling! I must tell you that the Thénardiers are inn-keepers, peasants, and unreasonable; they insist on having their money. Oh, do not send me to prison. Look you, the little thing will be turned into the streets in the middle of winter to go where she likes, and you must take pity on that, my kind M. Javert. If she were older she could earn her living, but at her age it is impossible. I am not a bad woman at heart; it is not cowardice and gluttony that have made me what I am. If I drink brandy, it is through wretchedness; I do not like it, but it makes me reckless. In happier times you need only have looked into my chest of drawers, and you would have seen that I was not a disorderly woman, for I had linen, plenty of linen. Take pity of me, M. Javert."

She spoke thus, crushed, shaken by sobs, blinded by tears, wringing her hands, interrupted by a sharp dry cough, and stammering softly, with death imprinted on her voice. Great sorrow is a divine and terrible ray which transfigures the wretched, and at this moment Fantine became lovely again. From time to time she stopped, and tenderly kissed the skirt of the policeman's coat. She would have melted a heart of granite,—but a wooden heart cannot be moved.

"Well," said Javert, "I have listened to you. Have you said all? Be off now; you have six months. The Eternal Father in person could not alter it."

On hearing this solemn phrase, she understood that sentence was passed; she fell all of a heap, murmuring, "Mercy!" But Javert turned his back, and the soldiers seized her arm. Some minutes previously a man had entered unnoticed; he had closed the door, leaned against it, and heard Fantine's entreaties. At the moment when the soldiers laid hold of the unhappy girl, who would not rise, he emerged from the gloom, and said:

"Wait a minute, if you please."

Javert raised his eyes, and recognized M. Madeleine; he took off his hat, and bowed with a sort of vexed awkwardness.

"I beg your pardon, M. le Maire—"

The words "M. le Maire" produced a strange effect on Fantine; she sprang up like a specter emerging from the ground, thrust back the soldiers, walked straight up to M. Madeleine before she could be prevented, and, looking at him wildly, she exclaimed:

"So you are the mayor?"

Then she burst into a laugh, and spat in his face. M. Madeleine wiped his face and said:

"Inspector Javert, set this woman at liberty."

Javert felt for a moment as if he were going mad; he experienced at this instant the most violent emotions he had ever felt in his life, following each other in rapid succession, and almost mingled. To see a girl of the town spit in the mayor's face was so monstrous a thing that he would have regarded it as a sacrilege even to believe it possible. On the other side, he confusedly made a hideous approximation in his mind between what this woman was and what this mayor might be, and then he saw with horror something perfectly simple in this prodigious assault. But when he saw this mayor, this magistrate, calmly wipe his face, and say, "Set this woman at liberty," he had a bedazzlement of stupor, so to speak; thought and language failed him equally, for he had passed the limits of possible amazement. He remained dumb. His sentence had produced an equally strange effect on Fantine; she raised her bare arm, and clung to the chimney-key of the stove like a tottering person. She looked around and began saying in a low voice, as if speaking to herself:

"At liberty! I am to be let go! I shall not be sent to prison for six months! Who said that? it is impossible that any one said it. I must have heard badly; it cannot be that monster of a mayor. Was it you, my kind M. Javert, who said that I was to be set at liberty? Well, I will tell you all about it, and you will let me go. That monster of a mayor, that old villain of a mayor, is the cause of it all. Just imagine, M. Javert, he discharged me on account of a parcel of sluts gossiping in the shop. Was not that horrible! to discharge a poor girl who is doing her work fairly! After that I did not earn enough, and all this misfortune came. In the first place, there is an improvement which the police gentry ought to make, and that is to prevent persons in prison injuring poor people. I will explain this to you; you earn twelve sous for making a shirt, but it falls to nine, and then you can no longer live, and are obliged to do what you can. As I had my little Cosette, I was forced to become a bad woman. You can now understand how it was that beggar of a mayor who did all the mischief. My present offense is that I trampled on the gentleman's hat before the officer's café, but he had ruined my dress with snow; and our sort have only one silk dress for night. Indeed, M. Javert, I never did any harm purposely, and I see everywhere much worse women than myself who are much more fortunate. Oh, Monsieur Javert, you said that I was to be set at liberty, did you not? Make inquiries, speak to my landlord; I pay my rent now, and you will hear that I am honest. Oh, good gracious! I ask your pardon, but I have touched the damper of the stove without noticing it, and made it smoke."

M. Madeleine listened to her with deep attention; while she was talking, he took out his purse, but as he found it empty on opening it he returned it to his pocket. He now said to Fantine:

"How much did you say that you owed?"

Fantine, who was looking at Javert, turned round to him:

"Am I speaking to you?"

Then she said to the soldiers:

"Tell me, men, did you see how I spat in his face? Ah, you old villain of a mayor, you have come here to frighten me, but I am not afraid of you; I am only afraid of Monsieur Javert, my kind Monsieur Javert."

While saying this, she turned again to the inspector: "After all, people should be just. I can understand that you are a just man, M. Javert; in fact, it is quite simple. A man who played at putting snow down a woman's back, made the officers laugh; they must have some amusement, and we girls are sent into the world for them to make fun of. And then you came up; you are compelled to restore order, you remove the woman who was in the wrong, but, on reflection, as you are kind-hearted, you order me to be set at liberty, for the sake of my little girl, for six months' imprisonment would prevent my supporting her. But don't come here again, faggot! Oh, I will not come here again, M. Javert; they can do what they like to me in future, and I will not stir. Still, I cried out to-night because it hurt me; I did not at all expect that gentleman's snow; and then, besides, as I told you, I am not very well; I cough, I have something like a ball in my stomach, that burns, and the doctor says, 'Take care of yourself.' Here, feel, give me your hand; do not be frightened."

She no longer cried, her voice was caressing; she laid M. Javert's large coarse hand on her white, delicate throat, and looked up at him smiling-ly. All at once she hurriedly repaired the disorder in her clothes, let the folds of her dress fall, which had been almost dragged up to her knee, and walked toward the door, saying to the soldiers with a friendly nod:

"My lads, M. Javert says I may go, so I will be off."

She laid her hand on the hasp; one step further, and she would be in the street. Up to this moment Javert had stood motionless, with his eyes fixed on the ground, appearing in the center of this scene like a statue waiting to be put in its proper place. The sound of the hasp aroused him; he raised his head with an expression of sovereign authority—an expression the more frightful, the lower the man in power stands; it is ferocity in the wild beast, atrocity in the nobody.

"Sergeant," he shouted, "do you not see that the wretch is bolting? Who told you to let her go?"

"I did," said M. Madeleine.

Fantine, at the sound of Javert's voice, trembled, and let go the hasp, like a detected thief lets fall the stolen article. At M. Madeleine's voice she turned, and from this moment, without even daring to breathe freely, her eyes wandered from M. Madeleine to Javert, and from Javert to M. Madeleine, according as each spoke. It was evident that Javert must have been lifted "off the hinge," as people say, when he ventured to address the sergeant as he had done, after the mayor's request that Fantine should be set at liberty. Had he gone so far as to forget the mayor's presence? Did he eventually declare to himself that it was impossible for "an authority" to have given such an order, and that the mayor must certainly have said one thing for another without meaning it? Or was it that, in the presence of all the enormities he had witnessed during the last two hours, he said to himself that he must have recourse to a supreme resolution, that the little must become great, the detective be transformed into the magistrate, and that, in this prodigious extremity, order, law, morality, government, and society were personified in him, Javert? However this may be, when M. Madeleine said "I did," the inspector of police could be seen to turn to the mayor, pale, cold, with blue lips, with desperate glance, and an imperceptible tremor all over him, and—extraordinary circumstance!—to say to him, with downcast eyes, but in a fierce voice:

"Monsieur le Maire, that cannot be."

"Why so?"

"This creature has insulted a gentleman."

"Inspector Javert," M. Madeleine replied, with a conciliating and calm accent, "listen to me. You are an honest man, and I shall have no difficulty in coming to an explanation with you. The truth is as follows: I was crossing the market-place at the time you were leading this girl away, a crowd was still assembled, I inquired, and know all; the man was in the wrong, and, in common justice, ought to have been arrested instead of her."

Javert objected:

"The wretched creature has just insulted M. le Maire."

"That concerns myself," M. Madeleine said; "my insult is, perhaps, my own, and I can do what I like with it."

"I ask your pardon, sir; the insult does not belong to you, but to the judicial court."

"Inspector Javert," M. Madeleine replied, "conscience is the highest of all courts. I have heard the woman and know what I am doing."

"And I, Monsieur le Maire, do not know what I am seeing."

"In that case, be content with obeying."

"I obey my duty; my duty orders that this woman should go to prison for six months."

M. Madeleine answered gently:

"Listen to this carefully; she will not go for a single day."

On hearing these decided words, Javert ventured to look fixedly at the mayor, and said to him, though still with a respectful accent:

"I bitterly regret being compelled to resist you. Monsieur le Maire, it is the first time in my life, but you will deign to let me observe that I am within the limits of my authority. As you wish it, sir, I will confine myself to the affair with the gentleman. I was present. This girl attacked M. Bamatabois, who is an elector and owner of that fine four-storied house, built of hewn stone, which forms the corner of the Esplanade. Well, there are things in this world. However this may be, M. le Maire, this is a matter of the street police which concerns me, and I intend to punish the woman Fantine."

M. Madeleine upon this folded his arms, and said in a stern voice, which no one in the town had ever heard before.

"The affair to which you allude belongs to the borough police; and by the terms of articles nine, eleven, fifteen, and sixty-six of the Criminal Code, I try it. I order that this woman be set at liberty."

Javert tried a final effort.

"But, Monsieur le Maire—"

"I call your attention to article eighty-one of the law of December 13th, 1799, upon arbitrary detention."

"Permit me, sir—"

"Not a word!"

"Still—"

"Leave the room!" said M. Madeleine.

Javert received the blow right in his chest, like a Russian soldier; he bowed to the ground to the mayor and went out. Fantine stood up against the door, and watched him pass by her in stupor. She, too, was suffering from a strange perturbation, for she had seen herself, so to speak, contended for by two opposite powers. She had seen two men struggling in her presence, who held in their hands her liberty, her life, her soul, her child. One of these men dragged her toward the gloom, the other restored her to the light. In this struggle, which she gazed at through the exaggeration of terror, the two men seemed to her giants,—one spoke like a demon, the other like her good angel. The angel had vanquished the demon, and the thing which made her shudder from head to foot was that this angel, this liberator, was the very man whom she abhorred, the mayor whom she had so long regarded as the cause of all her woes; and at the very moment when she had insulted him in such a hideous way, he saved her. Could she be mistaken? must she change her whole soul? She did not know, but she trembled; she listened wildly, she looked on with terror, and at every word that M. Madeleine said, she felt the darkness of hatred fade away in her heart, and something glowing and ineffable spring up in its place, which was composed of joy, confidence, and love. When Javert had left the room, M. Madeleine turned to her, and said in a slow voice, like a serious man who is making an effort to restrain his tears:

"I have heard your story. I knew nothing about what you have said, but I believe, I feel, that it is true. I was even ignorant that you had left the factory, but why did you not apply to me? This is what I will do for you: I will pay your debts and send for your child, or you can go for it. You can live here, in Paris, or wherever you please, and I will provide for your child and yourself. I will give you all the money you require, and you will become respectable again in becoming happy, and I will say more than that: if all be as you say, and I do not doubt it, you have never ceased to be virtuous and holy in the sight of God! Poor woman!"

This was more than poor Fantine could endure. To have her Cosette! to leave this infamous life! to live free, rich, happy, and respectable with

Cosette! to see all these realities of Paradise suddenly burst into flower, in the midst of her wretchedness! She looked as if stunned at the person who was speaking, and could only sob two or three times, "Oh, oh, oh!" Her legs gave way, she fell on her knees before M. Madeleine, and, before he could prevent it, he felt her seize his hand and press her lips to it.

Then she fainted.

BOOK VI

JAVERT

1. THE COMMENCEMENT OF REPOSE

M. MADELEINE had Fantine conveyed to the infirmary he had established in his own house, and intrusted her to the sisters, who
put her to bed. A violent fever had broken out; she spent a part of the
night in raving and talking aloud, but at length fell asleep. On the
morrow, at about midday, Fantine woke, and, hearing a breathing close
to her bed, she drew the curtain aside, and noticed M. Madeleine gazing
at something above her head. His glance was full of pity and agony,
and supplicated; she followed its direction and saw that it was fixed
on a crucifix nailed to the wall. M. Madeleine was now transfigured
in Fantine's eyes, and seemed to her surrounded by light. He was absorbed in a species of prayer, and she looked at him for some time without
daring to interrupt him, but at length said, timidly:

"What are you doing there?"

M. Madeleine had been standing at this spot for an hour, waiting till
Fantine should wake. He took her hand, felt her pulse, and answered:

"How are you?"

"Very comfortable; I have slept, and fancy I am better. It will be
nothing."

He continued, answering the question she had asked him first, and as
if he had only just heard it:

"I was praying to the Martyr up there"; and he mentally added, "for
the martyr down here."

M. Madeleine had spent the night and morning in making inquiries,
and had learned everything; he know all the poignant details of Fantine's history. He continued:

"You have suffered deeply, poor mother. Oh! do not complain, for you have at present the dowry of the elect; it is in this way that human beings become angels. It is not their fault; they do not know what to do otherwise. The hell you have now left is the anteroom to heaven, and you were obliged to begin with that." He breathed a deep sigh, but she smiled upon him with the sublime smile in which two teeth were wanting.

Javert had written a letter during the past night, and posted it himself the next morning. It was for Paris, and the address was "Monsieur Chabouillet, secretary to the prefect of police." As a rumor had spread about the affair in the police office, the lady manager of the post, and some other persons who saw the letter before it was sent off and recognized Javert's handwriting, supposed that he was sending in his resignation. M. Madeleine hastened to write to the Thénardiers. Fantine owed them over 120 francs, and he sent them 300, bidding them pay themselves out of the amount, and bring the child at once to M. . . . , where a sick mother was awaiting it. This dazzled Thénardier. "Hang it all," he said to his wife, "we must not let the brat go, for the lark will become a milch cow for us. I see it all; some fellow has fallen in love with the mother." He replied by sending a bill for 500 and odd francs very well drawn up. In this bill two undeniable amounts figured, one from a physician, the other from an apothecary, who had attended Eponine and Azelma in a long illness. Cosette, as we said, had not been ill, and hence it was merely a little substitution of names. At the bottom of the bill Thénardier gave credit for 300 francs received on account. M. Madeleine at once sent 300 francs more, and wrote, "Make haste and bring Cosette."

"Christi!" said Thénardier, "we must not let the child go."

In the meanwhile Fantine did not recover, and still remained in the infirmary. The sisters had at first received and nursed "this girl" with some repugnance. Any one who has seen the bas-relief at Rheims will remember the pouting lower lip of the wise virgins looking at the foolish virgins. This ancient contempt of Vestals for Ambubaïæ is one of the deepest instincts of feminine dignity, and the sisters had experienced it, with the increased dislike which religion adds. But in a few days Fantine disarmed them; she had all sorts of humble and gentle words, and the mother within her was touching. One day the sisters heard her say in the paroxysm of fever, "I have been a sinner, but when I have my child by my side, that will show that God has forgiven me. While I was living badly, I should not have liked to have Cosette with me, for I could not have endured her sad and astonished eyes. And yet it was for her sake that I did wrong, and for that reason God pardons me. I shall feel the blessing of Heaven when Cosette is here; I shall look at her, and it will do me good to see the innocent creature. She knows nothing, as she is an angel. My sisters, at her age the wings have not yet dropped off."

M. Madeleine went to see her twice a day, and every time she asked him, "Shall I see my Cosette soon?"

He would answer:

"To-morrow, perhaps; she can arrive at any moment, for I am expecting her."

And the mother's pale face would grow radiant.

"Oh!" she said, "how happy I shall be!"

We have said that she did not improve; on the contrary, her condition seemed to grow worse week by week. The handful of snow placed between her naked shoulder-blades produced a sudden check of perspiration, which caused the illness that had smoldered in her for years suddenly to break out. Laennec's fine method for studying and treating diseases of the lungs was just beginning to be employed; the physician placed the stethoscope to Fantine's chest, and shook his head. M. Madeleine said to him:

"Well?"

"Has she not a child that she wishes to see?" asked the doctor.

"Yes."

"Well, make haste to send for her."

Madeleine gave a start, and Fantine asked him:

"What did the doctor say to you?"

M. Madeleine forced a smile.

"He said that your child must come at once, for that would cure you."

"Oh," she replied, "he is right; but what do those Thénardiers mean by keeping my Cosette? Oh, she will come, and then I shall see happiness close to me."

Thénardier, however, would not let the child go, and alleged a hundred poor excuses,—Cosette was ailing, and it would be dangerous for her to travel in winter, and then there were some small debts still to pay, which he was collecting, etc.

"I will send some one to fetch Cosette," said Father Madeleine; "if necessary I will go myself."

He wrote to Fantine's dictation the following letter, which she signed:

"M. Thénardier: You will hand over Cosette to the bearer, who will pay up all little matters.

"Yours, FANTINE.*"

About this time, a great incident happened. However cleverly we may have carved the mysterious block of which our life is made, the black vein of destiny ever re-appears in it.

2. *HOW* *"JEAN" MAY BECOME "CHAMP"*

ONE morning M. Madeleine was in his study, engaged in settling some pressing mayoralty matters, in case he decided on the journey to Montfermeil, when he was told that Inspector Javert wished to speak with him. On hearing his name pronounced, M. Madeleine could not refrain from a disagreeable impression. Since the guard-room adventure, Javert had avoided him more than ever, and M. Madeleine had not seen him again.

"Show him in," he said.

Javert entered. M. Madeleine remained at his table near the fireplace, with a pen in his hand and his eyes fixed on a charge book, whose leaves he was turning over and annotating. He did not put himself out of the way for Javert, for he could not refrain from thinking of poor Fantine, and chose to be freezing. Javert bowed respectfully to the mayor, who had his back turned to him; the mayor did not look at him, but continued to make his notes. Javert walked a little way into the study, and then halted without a word. A physiognomist familiar with Javert's nature, and who had studied for any length of time this savage in the service of civilization,—this strange composite of the Roman, the Spartan, the monk, and the corporal, this spy incapable of falsehood, this virgin detective,—a physiognomist aware of his secret and old aversion for M. Madeleine, and his conflict with him about Fantine, and who regarded Javert at this moment, would have asked himself, What has happened? It was evident to any one who knew this upright, clear, sincere, honest, austere, and ferocious conscience, that Javert had just emerged from some great internal struggle. Javert had nothing in his mind which he did not also have in his face, and, like all violent men, he was subject to sudden changes. Never had his face been stranger or more surprising. On entering, he bowed to M. Madeleine with a look in which there was neither rancor, anger, nor suspicion; he had halted a few yards behind the mayor's chair, and was now standing there in an almost military attitude, with the simple cold rudeness of a man who has never been gentle and has ever been patient. He was waiting, without saying a word, without making a movement, in a true humility and tranquil resignation, till the mayor might think proper to turn round— calm, serious, hat in hand, and with an expression which was half-way between the private before his officer and the culprit before the judge. All the feelings as well as all the revolutions he might be supposed to possess had disappeared; there was nothing but a gloomy sadness on this face, which was impenetrable and simple as granite. His whole person displayed humiliation and firmness, and a sort of courageous despondency. At length the mayor laid down his pen and half turned round.

"Well, what is the matter, Javert?"

Javert remained silent for a moment, as if reflecting, and then raised his voice with a sad solemnity, which, however, did not exclude simplicity.

"A culpable deed has been committed, sir."

"What deed?"

"An inferior agent of authority has failed in his respect to a magistrate in the gravest manner. I have come, as is my duty, to bring the fact to your knowledge."

"Who is this agent?" M. Madeleine asked.

"Myself."

"And who is the magistrate who has cause to complain of the agent?"

"You, Monsieur le Maire."

M. Madeleine sat up, and Javert continued, with a stern air and still looking down:

"Monsieur le Maire, I have come to request that you will procure my dismissal from service."

M. Madeleine in his stupefaction opened his mouth, but Javert interrupted him:

"You will say that I could have sent in my resignation, but that is not enough. Such a course is honorable, but I have done wrong, and deserve punishment. I must be dismissed."

And after a pause he added:

"Monsieur le Maire, you were severe to me the other day unjustly, be so to-day justly."

"What is the meaning of all this nonsense?" M. Madeleine exclaimed. "What is the culpable act you have committed? What have you done to me? You accuse yourself; you wish to be removed—"

"Dismissed," said Javert.

"Very good, dismissed. I do not understand it."

"You shall do so, sir."

Javert heaved a deep sigh and continued, still coldly and sadly:

"Six weeks ago, M. le Maire, after the scene about that girl, I was furious, and denounced you."

"Denounced me?"

"To the prefect of police at Paris."

M. Madeleine, who did not laugh much oftener than Javert, burst into a laugh.

"As a mayor who had encroached on the police?"

"As an ex-galley-slave."

The mayor turned livid, but Javert, who had not raised his eyes, continued:

"I thought you were so, and have had these notions for a long time. A resemblance, information you sought at Faverolles, the strength of your loins, the adventure with old Fauchelevent, your skill with fire-arms, your leg which halts a little—and so on. It was very absurd, but I took you for a man of the name of Jean Valjean."

"What name did you say?"

"Jean Valjean; he is a convict I saw twenty years ago when I was assistant keeper at the Toulon bagne. On leaving the galley, this Valjean, as it appears, robbed a bishop, and then committed a highway robbery on a little Savoyard. For eight years he has been out of the way and could not be found, and I imagined—in a word, I did as I said. Passion decided me, and I denounced you to the prefect."

M. Madeleine, who had taken up the charge book again, said with a careless accent:

"And what was the answer you received?"

"That I was mad!"

"Well?"

"They were right."

"It is fortunate that you allow it."

"I must do so, for the real Jean Valjean has been found."

The book M. Madeleine was holding fell from his grasp; he raised his head, looked searchingly at Javert, and said with an indescribable accent: "Oh!"

Javert continued:

"The facts are as follows, M. le Maire. It seems that there was, over at Ailly le Haut Clocher, an old fellow who was called Father Champmathieu. He was very wretched, and no attention was paid to him, for no one knows how such people live. This autumn Father Champmathieu was arrested for stealing cider apples; there was a robbery, a wall climbed over, and branches broken. This Champmathieu was arrested with the branch still in his hand, and was locked up. Up to this point it is only a matter for a police court, but here Providence interposes. As the lock-up was under repair, the magistrates ordered that Champmathieu should be taken to the departmental prison at Arras. In this prison there is an ex-convict of the name of Brevet, under imprisonment for some offense, and he has been made under-turnkey for his good behavior. Champmathieu no sooner arrived than Brevet cries out, 'Why, I know this man; he is an ex-convict. Look at me, old fellow; you are Jean Valjean.' 'Jean Valjean! What do you mean?' says Champmathieu, affecting surprise. 'Don't play the humbug with me,' says Brevet; 'you are Jean Valjean. You were at the Toulon bagne twenty years ago and I was there too.' Champmathieu denied identity, and, as you may suppose, the affair was thoroughly investigated, with the following result. This Champmathieu about thirty years ago was a journeyman wood-cutter at several places, especially at Faverolles, where his trail is lost. A long time after he is found again in Auvergne, and then in Paris, where he says he was a blacksmith, and had a daughter, a washerwoman,—though there is no evidence of this,—and lastly he turned up in these parts. Now, before being sent to the galleys, what was Jean Valjean? a wood-cutter; where? —at Faverolles. And here is another fact: this Valjean's Christian name was Jean, and his mother's Mathieu. What is more natural to suppose than that on leaving the bagne he assumed his mother's name as a disguise, and called himself Jean Mathieu? He went to Auvergne, where

Jean is pronounced Chan, and thus he was transformed into Champ-mathieu. You are following me, I suppose? Inquiries have been made at Faverolles, but Jean Valjean's family is no longer there, and no one knows where it has gone. As you are aware, in those places families frequently disappear in such a way; these people, if they are not mud are dust. And then, again, as the beginning of this story dates back thirty years, there is no one in Faverolles who knew Jean Valjean; and beside Brevet, there are only two convicts who remember him. These two were brought from the bagne and confronted with the pretended Champmathieu, and they did not hesitate for a moment. The same age—fifty-four; the same height, the same look, the same man, in short. It was at this very moment that I sent my denunciation to Paris, and the answer I received was that I had lost my senses, for Jean Valjean was in the hands of justice at Arras. You can conceive that this surprised me, as I fancied that I held my Jean Valjean here. I wrote to the magistrates, who sent for me, and Champmathieu was brought in."

"Well?" M. Madeleine interrupted him.

Javert answered with his incorruptible and sad face:

"Monsieur le Maire, truth is truth. I am sorry, but that man is Jean Valjean; I recognized him too."

M. Madeleine said in a very low voice:

"Are you sure?"

Javert burst into that sorrowful laugh which escapes from a profound conviction:

"Oh! certain."

He stood for a moment pensive, mechanically taking pinches of the blotting powder out of the sprinkler in the inkstand, and added:

"And now that I have seen the real Jean Valjean, I cannot understand how I could have believed anything else. I ask your pardon, M. le Maire."

While addressing these supplicating words to the person who six weeks previously had humiliated him so deeply and bidden him leave the room, this haughty man was unconsciously full of dignity and simplicity. M. Madeleine merely answered his entreaty with the hurried question:

"And what does this man say?"

"Well, Monsieur le Maire, it is ugly business, for if he is Jean Valjean, he is a second offender. Scaling a wall, breaking a branch, and stealing apples is a peccadillo with a child, an offense in a man, but a crime in a convict. It is no longer a matter for the police courts, but the assizes; it is no longer imprisonment for a few days, but the galleys for life. And there is the matter with the Savoyard, which, I trust, will be brought up again. There is enough to settle a man, is there not? but Jean Valjean is artful, and in that I recognize him too. Any other man would find it warm; he would struggle, cry out, refuse to be Jean Valjean, and so on. He pretends, though, not to understand, and says, 'I am Champmathieu, and I shall stick to it.' He has a look of amazement, and plays the brute-beast, which is better. Oh! he is a clever scoundrel! But no matter, the proofs are ready to hand; he has been recognized by four persons, and the old scoundrel will be found guilty. He is to be tried at assizes, and I have been summoned as a witness."

M. Madeleine had turned round to his desk again, taken up his charge book, and was quietly turning over the leaves, and busily reading and writing in turn. He now said to the inspector:

"Enough, Javert; after all, these details interest me but very slightly. We are losing our time, and have a deal of work before us. Javert, you will go at once to Mother Buseaupied, who sells vegetables at the corner of the Rue Saint Saulve, and tell her to take out a summons against Pierre Chesnelong the carter; he is a brutal fellow, who almost drove over this woman and her child, and he must be punished. You will then go to M. Charcellay in the Rue Champigny; he complains that there is a gutter next door which leaks, and is sapping the foundation of his house. But I am giving you a deal to do, and I think you said you were going away. Did you not state you were going to Arras on this matter in a week or ten days?"

"Sooner than that, sir."

"On what day, then?"

"I fancied I told you that the trial comes off to-morrow, and that I should start by to-night's coach."

"And how long will the trial last?"

"A day at the most, and sentence will be passed to-morrow night at the latest. But I shall not wait for that, but return as soon as I have given my evidence."

"Very good," said M. Madeleine, and he dismissed Javert with a wave of his hand, but he did not go.

"I beg your pardon, M. le Maire," he said.

"What's the matter now?" M. Madeleine asked.

"I have one thing to remind you of, sir."

"What is it!"

"That I must be discharged."

M. Madeleine rose.

"Javert, you are a man of honor, and I esteem you; you exaggerate your fault, and besides, it is an offense which concerns only me, Javert; you are worthy of rising, not of sinking, and I insist on you keeping your situation."

Javert looked at M. Madeleine with his bright eyes, in which it seemed as if his unenlightened but rigid and chaste conscience could be seen, and he said quietly:

"M. le Maire, I cannot allow it."

"I repeat," M. Madeleine replied, "that the affair concerns myself."

But Javert, only attending to his own thoughts, continued:

"As for exaggerating, I am not doing so, for this is how I reason. I suspected you unjustly. That is nothing; it is the duty of men like myself to suspect, though there is an abuse in suspecting those above us. But without proofs, in a moment of passion and for the purpose of revenge, I denounced you, a respectable man, a mayor and a magistrate. This is serious, very serious; I, an agent of the authority, insulted that authority in your person. Had any of my subordinates done what I have done, I should have declared him unworthy of the service and discharged him. Stay, M. le Maire, one word more: I have often been severe in my life to others, for it was just, and I was doing my duty, and if I were not severe to myself now, all the justice I have done would become injustice. Ought I to spare myself more than others? No. What! I have been only good to punish others and not myself? Why, I should be a scoundrel, and the people who call me that rogue of a Javert would be in the right! M. le Maire, I do not wish you to treat me with kindness, for your kindness causes me sufficient ill-blood when dealt to others, and I want none for myself. The kindness that consists in defending the street-walker against the gentleman, the police agent against the mayor, the lower classes against the higher, is what I call bad kindness, and it is such kindness that disorganizes Society. Good Lord! it is easy enough to be good, but the difficulty is to be just. Come! if you had been what I believed you, I should not have been kind to you, as you would have seen. M. le Maire, I am bound to treat myself as I would treat another man; when I repressed malefactors, when I was severe with scamps, I often said to myself, 'If you ever catch yourself tripping, look out.' I have tripped, I have committed a fault, and all the worse for me. I have strong arms and will turn laborer. M. le Maire, the good of the service requires an example. I simply demand the discharge of Inspector Javert."

All this was said with a humble, proud, despairing, and convinced accent, which gave a peculiar grandeur to this strangely honest man.

"We will see," said M. Madeleine, and he offered him his hand, but Javert fell back and said sternly:

"Pardon me, sir, but that must not be; a mayor ought not to give his hand to a spy."

He added between his teeth:

"Yes, a spy; from the moment when I misused my authority, I have been only a spy."

Then he bowed deeply and walked to the door. When he reached it he turned round and said, with eyes still bent on the ground:

"M. le Maire, I will continue on duty till my place is filled up."

He went out. M. Madeleine thoughtfully listened to his firm, sure step as he walked along the paved passage.

BOOK VII

THE CHAMPMATHIEU AFFAIR

I. *SISTER SIMPLICE*

THE incidents we are about to record were only partially known at M. . . . , but the few which were known left such a memory in that town that it would be a serious gap in this book if we did not tell them in their smallest details. In these details the reader will notice two or three improbable circumstances, which we retain through respect for truth. In the afternoon that followed Javert's visit, M. Madeleine went to see Fantine as usual; but before going to her, he asked for Sister Simplice. The two nuns who managed the infirmary, who were Lazarists, like all sisters of charity, were known by the names of Sisters Perpetua and Simplice. Sister Perpetua was an ordinary village girl, a clumsy sister of charity, who had entered the service of Heaven just as she would have taken a cook's place. This type is not rare, for the monastic orders gladly accept this clumsy peasant clay, which can be easily fashioned into a Capuchin friar or an Ursuline nun; and these rusticities are employed in the heavy work of devotion. The transition from a drover to a Carmelite is no hard task; the common substratum of village and cloister ignorance is a ready-made preparation, and at once places the countryman on a level with the monk. Widen the blouse a little and you have a gown. Sister Perpetua was a strong nun belonging to Marines, near Pontoise, who talked with a country accent, sang psalms to match, sugared the *tisane* according to the bigotry or hypocrisy of the patient, was rough with the sick, and harsh with the dying, almost throwing God in their faces, and stoning their last moments with angry prayer. Withal she was bold, honest, and red-faced.

Sister Simplice was pale, and looked like a wax taper by the side of Sister Perpetua, who was a tallow candle in comparison. Vincent de Paul has divinely described the sister of charity in those admirable words in which so much liberty is blended with slavery. "They will have no other convent but the hospital, no other cell but a hired room, no chapel but the parish church, no cloister beyond the streets or the hospital wards, no walls but obedience, no grating but the fear of God, and no veil but modesty." Sister Simplice was the living ideal of this; no one could have told her age, for she had never been young and seemed as if she would never grow old. She was a gentle, austere, well-nurtured, cold person— we dare not say a woman—who had never told a falsehood; she was so gentle that she appeared fragile, but she was more solid than granite. She touched the wretched with her delicate and pure fingers. There was, so to speak, silence in her language; she only said what was necessary, and possessed an intonation of voice which would at once have edified a confessional and delighted a drawing-room. This delicacy harmonized with the rough gown, for it formed in this rough contact a continual reminder of heaven. Let us dwell on one detail,—never to have told a falsehood, never to have said, for any advantage, or even indifferently, a thing which was not the truth, the holy truth, was the characteristic feature of Sister Simplice. She was almost celebrated in the congregation for this imperturbable veracity, and the Abbé Suard alludes to Sister Simplice in a letter to the deaf-mute Massieu. However sincere and pure we may be, we have all the brand of a little white lie on our candor, but she had not. Can there be such a thing as a white lie, an innocent lie? Lying is the absolute of evil. Lying a little is not possible; the man who lies tells the whole lie; lying is the face of the fiend, and Satan has two names—he is called Satan and Lying. That is what she thought, and she practiced as she thought. The result was the whiteness to which we have alluded, a whiteness which even covered with its radiance her lips and eyes, for her smile was white, her glance was white. There was not a spider's web nor a grain of dust on the window of this conscience; on entering the obedience of St. Vincent de Paul, she took the name of Simplice through special choice. Simplice of Sicily, our readers will remember, is the saint who sooner let her two breasts be torn off than say she was a native of Segeste, as she was born at Syracuse, though the falsehood would have saved her. Such a patron saint suited this soul.

Simplice on entering the order had two faults, of which she had gradually corrected herself,—she had a taste for dainties and was fond of receiving letters. Now she never read anything but a prayer-book in large type and in Latin; though she did not understand the language she understood the book. This pious woman felt an affection for Fantine, as she probably noticed the latent virtue in her, and nearly entirely devoted herself to nursing her. M. Madeleine took Sister Simplice on one side and recommended Fantine to her with a singular accent, which the sister remembered afterward. On leaving the sister he went to Fantine. The patient daily awaited the appearance of M. Madeleine, as if he brought her warmth and light; she said to the sisters, "I only live when M. le Maire is here." This day she was very feverish, and so soon as she saw M. Madeleine she asked him:

"Where is Cosette?"

He replied with a smile, "She will be here soon."

M. Madeleine behaved to Fantine as usual, except that he remained with her an hour instead of half an hour, to her great delight. He pressed everybody not to allow the patient to want for anything, and it was noticed at one moment that his face became very dark, but this was explained when it was learned that the physician had bent down to his ear and said, "She is rapidly sinking." Then he returned to the mayoralty, and the office clerk saw him attentively examining a roadmap of France, which hung in his room, and write a few figures in pencil on a piece of paper.

2. SCAUFFLAIRE'S PERSPICACITY

FROM the mayoralty M. Madeleine proceeded to the end of the town to a Fleming called Master Scaufflaer, gallicized into Scaufflaire, who let out horses and gigs by the day. To reach his yard the nearest way was through an unfrequented street, in which stood the house of the parish priest. The curé was said to be a worthy and respectable man, who gave good advice. At the moment when M. Madeleine came in front of his house, there was only one person in the street, and he noticed the following circumstances: M. le Maire, after passing the house, stopped for a moment, then turned back and walked up to the curé's door, which had an iron knocker. He quickly seized the knocker and lifted it; then he stopped again as if in deep thought, and after a few seconds, instead of knocking, he softly let the knocker fall back in its place and went on with a spring of haste which he had not displayed previously. M. Madeleine found Master Scaufflaire at home and engaged in mending a set of harness.

"Master Scaufflaire," he asked him, "have you a good horse?"

"M. le Maire," the Fleming replied, "all my horses are good. What do you mean by a good horse?"

I mean a horse that can cover twenty leagues of ground in a day."

"Harnessed in a gig?"

"Yes."

"And how long will it rest after the journey?"

"It must be in a condition to start again the next morning if necessary."

"To go the same distance back?"

"Yes."

"Hang it all, and it is twenty leagues?"

M. Madeleine took from his pocket the paper on which he had penciled the figures; they were 5, 6, 8½.

"You see," he said, "total, nineteen and a half, or call them twenty leagues."

"M. le Maire," the Fleming continued, "I can suit you. My little white horse—you may have seen it pass sometimes—is an animal from the Bas Boulonnais and full of fire. They tried at first to make a saddle-horse of it, but it reared and threw everybody that got on its back. It was supposed to be vicious, and they did not know what to do with it; I bought it and put it in a gig. That was just what it wanted; it is as gentle as a maid and goes like the wind. But you must not try to get on its back, for it has no notion of being a saddle-horse. Everybody has his ambition, and it appears as if the horse had said to itself,—'Draw, yes; carry, no'."

"And it will go the distance?"

"At a trot, and under eight hours, but on certain conditions."

"What are they?"

"In the first place, you will let it blow for an hour half-way; it will feed, and you must be present while it is doing so, to prevent the ostler stealing the oats, for I have noticed that at inns oats are more frequently drunk by the stable-boys than eaten by the horses."

"I will be there."

"In the next place, is the gig for yourself, sir?"

"Yes."

"Do you know how to drive?"

"Yes."

"Well, you must travel alone and without luggage, in order not to overweight the horse."

"Agreed."

"I shall expect thirty francs a day, and the days of rest paid as well. Not a farthing less, and you will pay for the horse's keep."

M. Madeleine took three napoleons from his purse and laid them on the table.

"There are two days in advance."

"In the fourth place, a cabriolet would be too heavy for such a journey and tire the horse. You must oblige me by traveling in a little tilbury I have."

"I consent."

"It is light, but it is open."

"I do not care."

"Have you thought, sir, that it is now winter?"

M. Madeleine made no answer, and the Fleming continued:

"That it is very cold?"

M. Madeleine was still silent.

"That it may rain?"

The mayor raised his head and said:

"The tilbury and the horse will be before my door at half-past four to-morrow morning."

"Very good, sir," Scaufflaire answered; then, scratching with his thumb-nail a stain in the wood of his table, he continued, with that careless air with which the Flemings so cleverly conceal their craft:

"Good gracious, I have not thought of asking where you are going; be kind enough to tell me, sir."

He had thought of nothing else since the beginning of the conversation, but somehow he had not dared to ask the question.

"Has your horse good legs?" said M. Madeleine.

"Yes, M. le Maire, you will hold it up a little in going down-hill. Are there many hills between here and the place you are going to?"

"Do not forget to be at my door at half-past four exactly," M. Madeleine answered, and went away.

215

The Fleming stood "like a fool," as he said himself, a little while after. M. le Maire had been gone some two or three minutes when the door opened again; it was M. le Maire. He still wore the same impassive and preoccupied air.

"M. Scaufflaire," he said, "at how much do you value the tilbury and horse you are going to let me, one with the other?"

"Do you wish to buy them of me, sir?"

"No, but I should like to guarantee them against any accident, and when I come back you can return me the amount. What is the estimated value?"

"Five hundred francs, M. le Maire."

"Here they are."

M. Madeleine laid a bank-note on the table, then went out, and this time did not come back. Master Scaufflaire regretted frightfully that he had not said a thousand francs, though tilbury and horse, at a fair valuation, were worth just three hundred. The Fleming called his wife and told her what had occurred. "Where the deuce can the mayor be going?" They held a council. "He is going to Paris," said the wife. "I don't believe it," said the husband. M. Madeleine had left on the table the paper on which he had written the figures; the Fleming took it up and examined it. "Five, six, eight and half; why that must mean post stations." He turned to his wife: "I have found it out." "How?" "It is five leagues from here to Hesdin, six from there to St. Pol, and eight and a half from St. Pol to Arras. He is going to Arras."

In the meanwhile the mayor had returned home, and had taken the longest road, as if the gate of the priest's house were a temptation to him which he wished to avoid. He went up to his bedroom and locked himself in, which was not unusual, for he was fond of going to bed at an early hour. Still the factory portress, who was at the same time M. Madeleine's only servant, remarked that his candle was extinguished at a quarter-past eight, and mentioned the fact to the cashier when he came in, adding:

"Can master be ill? I thought he looked very strange to-day." The cashier occupied a room exactly under M. Madeleine's. He paid no attention to the remarks of the portress, but went to bed and fell asleep. About midnight he woke with a start, for he heard in his sleep a noise above his head. He listened; it was a footfall coming and going, as if some one were walking about the room above him. He listened more attentively, and recognized M. Madeleine's step; and this seemed to him strange, for usually no sound could be heard from the mayor's room till he rose. A moment later the cashier heard something like a wardrobe open and shut; a piece of furniture was moved, there was a silence, and the walking began again. The cashier sat up in bed, broad awake, looked out, and through his window noticed on a wall opposite the red reflection of a lighted window; from the direction of the rays it could only be the window of M. Madeleine's bedroom. The reflection flickered as if it came from a fire rather than a candle, while the shadow of the framework could not be traced, which proved that the window was wide open, and this was a curious fact, regard being had to the coldness. The cashier fell asleep and woke again some two hours after; the same low and regular footfall was still audible above his head. The reflection was still cast on the wall, but was now pale and quiet, as if it came from a lamp or a candle. The window was still open. This is what was occurring in M. Madeleine's bedroom.

3. *A TEMPEST IN A BRAIN*

The reader has, of course, guessed that M. Madeleine is Jean Valjean. We have already looked into the depths of this conscience, and the moment has arrived to look into them again. We do not do this without emotion or tremor, for there is nothing more terrifying than this species of contemplation. The mental eye can nowhere find greater brilliancy or greater darkness than within man; it cannot dwell on anything which is more formidable, complicated, mysterious, or infinite. There is a spectacle grander than the ocean, and that is the sky; there is a spectacle grander than the sky, and it is the interior of the soul. To write the poem of the human conscience, were the subject only one man, and he the lowest of men, would be reducing all epic poems into one supreme and final epos. Conscience is the chaos of chimeras, envies, and attempts, the furnace of dreams, the lurking-place of ideas we are ashamed of; it is the pandemonium of sophistry, the battle-field of the passions. At certain hours, look through the livid face of a reflecting man, look into his soul, peer into the darkness. Beneath the external silence, combats of giants are going on there, such as we read of in Homer; *mêlées* of dragons and hydras and clouds of phantoms, such as we find in Milton; and visionary spirals, as in Dante. An awful thing in the infinitude which every man bears within him, and by which he desperately measures the volitions of his brain and the actions of his life. Dante one day came to a sinister gate, before which he hesitated; we have one before us, on the threshold of which we also hesitate, but we will enter.

We have but little to add to what the reader already knows as having happened to Jean Valjean since his adventure with Little Gervais. From this moment, as we have seen, he became another man, and he made himself what the bishop wished to make him. It was more than a transformation, it was a transfiguration. He succeeded in disappearing, sold the Bishop's plate, only keeping the candlesticks as a souvenir, passed through France, reached M. . . . , had the idea we have described, accomplished what we have narrated, managed to make himself unseizable and inaccessible, and henceforth settled at M. . . . , happy at feeling his conscience saddened by the past, and the first half of his existence contradicted by the last half; he lived peacefully, reassured and trusting, and having but two thoughts—to hide his name and sanctify his life; escape from men and return to God. These two thoughts were so closely blended in his mind that they only formed one; they were both equally absorbing and imperious, and governed his slightest actions. Usually they agreed to regulate the conduct of his life; they turned him to the shadow; they rendered him beneficent and simple, and they counseled him the same things. At times, however, there was a conflict between them, and in such cases the man whom the whole town of M. . . . called Monsieur Madeleine did not hesitate to sacrifice the first to the second,—his security to his virtue. Hence, despite all his caution and prudence, he had kept the bishop's candlesticks, worn mourning for him, questioned all the little Savoyards who passed through the town, inquired after the family at Faverolles, and saved the life of old Fauchelevent, in spite of the alarming insinuations of Javert. It seemed, as we have already remarked that he thought, after the example of all those who have been wise, holy, and just, that his first duty was not toward himself.

Still we are bound to say, nothing like the present had before occurred; never had the two ideas which governed the unhappy man whose sufferings we are describing entered upon so serious a struggle. He comprehended it confusedly, but deeply, from the first words which Javert uttered on entering his study. At the moment when the name which he had buried so deeply was so strangely pronounced, he was struck with stupor, and, as it were, intoxicated by the sinister peculiarity of his destiny. And through this stupor he felt that quivering which precedes great storms; he bowed like an oak at the approach of a storm, like a soldier before a coming assault. He felt the shadows full of thunder and lightning collecting over his head; while listening to Javert he had a thought of running off, denouncing himself, taking Champmathieu out of prison, and taking his place. This was painful, like an incision in the flesh, but it passed away, and he said to himself, "We will see!" He repressed this first generous movement, and recoiled before his heroism.

It would doubtless be grand if, after the bishop's holy remarks, after so many years of repentance and self-denial, in the midst of a penitence so admirably commenced, this man, even in the presence of such a terrible conjecture, had not failed for a moment, but continued to march at the same pace toward this open abyss, at the bottom of which heaven was; this would be grand, but it did not take place. We are bound to describe all the things that took place in his mind, and cannot say that this was one of them. What carried him away first was the instinct of self-preservation. He hastily collected his ideas, stifled his emotion, adjourned any resolution with the firmness of terror, deadened himself against what he had to do, and resumed his calmness as a gladiator picks up his buckler. For the remainder of the day he was in the same state,—a hurricane within, a deep tranquillity outside,—and he only took what may be called "conservative measures." All was still confused and jumbled in his brain; the trouble in it was so great that he did not see distinctly the outline of any idea, and he could have said nothing about himself, save that he had received a heavy blow. He went as usual to Fantine's bed of pain, and prolonged his visit, with a kindly instinct, saying to himself that he must act thus, and recommend her to the sisters in the event of his being obliged to go away. He felt vaguely that he must perhaps go to Arras; and, though not the least in the world decided about the journey, he said to himself that, safe from suspicion as he was, there would be no harm in being witness of what might take place, and he hired Scaufflaire's tilbury, in order to be ready for any event.

He dined with considerable appetite, and, on returning to his bed-room, reflected. He examined his situation, and found it extraordinary, —so extraordinary that, in the midst of his reverie, through some almost inexplicable impulse of anxiety, he rose from his chair and bolted his door. He was afraid lest something might enter, and he barricaded him-self against the possible. A moment after, he blew out his light, for it annoyed him, and he fancied that he might be overseen. By whom! Alas, what he wanted to keep out had entered; what he wished to blind was looking at him. It was his conscience; that is to say, God. Still, at the first moment, he deceived himself; he had a feeling of security and solitude. When he put in the bolt, he thought himself impregnable; when the candle was out, he felt himself invisible. He then regained his self-possession; and he put his elbows on the table, leaned his head on his hand, and began dreaming in the darkness.

"Where am I? Am I not dreaming? What was I told? Is it really true that I saw that Javert, and that he spoke to me so? Who can this Champ-mathieu be? it seems he resembles me. Is it possible? When I think that I was so tranquil yesterday, and so far from suspecting anything! What was I doing yesterday at this hour? What will be the result of this event? What am I to do?"

Such was the trouble he was in that his brain had not the strength to retain ideas. They passed like waves, and he clutched his forehead with both hands to stop them. From this tumult which overthrew his wits and reason, and from which he sought to draw an evidence and a resolution, nothing issued but agony. His head was burning; and he went by the window and threw it wide open. There were no stars in the heavens, and he went back to the table and sat down by it. The first hour passed away thus, but gradually vague features began to shape themselves and become fixed in his thoughts, and he could observe with the precision of reality some details of the situation, if not its entirety. He began by noticing that, however critical and extraordinary his situation might be, he was utterly the master of it, and his stupor was only augmented.

Independently of the stern and religious object he proposed to him-self in his actions, all that he had done up to this day was only a hole he dug in which to bury his name. What he had always most feared in his hours of reflection, as in his sleepless nights, was ever to hear *that* name pronounced. He said to himself that this would be to him the end of everything; that on the day when that name re-appeared it would cause his new life to fade away, and possibly the new soul he had within. He shuddered at the mere thought that this could happen. Assuredly, if any one had told him at such moments that the hour would arrive in which this name would echo in his ear, when the hideous name of Jean Valjean would suddenly emerge from the night and rise before him, when this formidable light which dissipated the mystery with which he surrounded himself would suddenly shine above his head, and that the name would no longer menace him; that the light would produce only a denser gloom; that this rent veil would increase the mystery; that the earthquake would consolidate his edifice; that this prodigious incident would have no other result, if he thought proper, but to render his existence clearer and yet more impenetrable, and that from his confrontation with the phantom of Jean Valjean, the good and worthy M. Madeleine would come forth more honored, more peaceful, and more respected than ever, —if any one had told him this, he would have shaken his head and considered such remarks insensate. And yet all this had really happened, and this heap of impossibilities was a fact, and Heaven had permitted all these wild things to become real.

His reverie continued to grow clearer, and each moment he comprehended his position better. It seemed to him that he had just awakened from a dream, and that he was descending an incline in the middle of the night, shuddering and recoiling in vain from the brink of an abyss. He distinctly saw in the shadows an unknown man, a stranger, whom destiny took for him and thrust into the gulf in his place. In order that the gulf should close, either he or another must fall in. He had no necessity to do anything, the clearness became complete, and he confessed to himself that his place was vacant at the galleys; that, whatever he might do, it constantly expected him, that the robbery of Little Gervais led him back to it, that this vacant place would wait for him and attract him until he filled it, and that this was inevitable and fatal. And then he said to himself that at this moment he had a substitute; that it seemed a man of the name of Champmathieu had this ill-luck; and that, in future, himself at the bagne in the person of this Champmathieu, and present in society under the name of M. Madeleine, would have nothing more to fear, provided that he did not prevent justice from laying over the head of this Champmathieu the stone of infamy which, like the tombstone, falls once and is never raised again.

All this was so violent and so strange that he suddenly felt within him that species of indescribable movement which no man experiences more than twice or thrice in his life, a sort of convulsion of the conscience, which disturbs everything doubtful in the heart, which is composed of irony, joy, and despair, and what might be called an internal burst of laughter. He suddenly relit his candle.

"Well, what am I afraid of?" he said to himself; "what reason have I to have such thoughts? I am saved, and all is settled. There was only one open door through which my past could burst in upon my life; and that door is now walled up forever. That Javert, who has so long annoyed me, the formidable instinct which seemed to have scented me, and, by Heavens! had scented me, the frightful dog ever making a point at me, is routed, engaged elsewhere, and absolutely thrown out! He is henceforth satisfied, he will leave me at peace, for he has got his Jean Valjean! It is possible that he may wish to leave the town too. And all this has taken place without my interference, and so, what is there so unlucky in it all? On my word, any people who saw me would believe that a catastrophe had befallen me. After all, if some people are rendered unhappy, it is no fault of mine. Providence has done it all, and apparently decrees it. Have I the right to derange what He arranges? What is it that I am going to interfere in? it does not concern me. What! I am not satisfied? Why! what else can I want? I have attained the object to which I have been aspiring for so many years, the dream of my nights, the matter of my prayers—security. It is Heaven that wills it, and I have done nothing contrary to God's desire. And why has Heaven decreed it? that I may continue what I have begun; that I may do good; that I may one day be a grand and encouraging example; that it may be said that there is, after all, a little happiness attaching to the penance I have undergone. I really cannot understand why I was so afraid just now about visiting that worthy curé, telling all to him as to a confessor, and asking his advice, for this is certainly what he would have advised me. It is settled; I will let matters take their own course, and leave the decision to Heaven."

He spoke this in the depths of his conscience, while leaning over what might be called his own abyss. He got up from his chair and walked about the room. "Come," he said, "I will think no more of it; I have made up my mind"; but he felt no joy. It is no more possible to prevent thought from reverting to an idea than the sea from returning to the shore. With the sailor this is called the tide; with the culprit it is called remorse; God heaves the soul like the ocean. After a few moments, whatever he might do, he resumed the dialogue in which it was he who spoke and he who listened, saying what he wished to be silent about, listening to what he did not desire to hear, and yielding to that mysterious power which said to him "think," as it did, two thousand years ago, to another condemned man, "go on."

Before going further, and in order to be fully understood, let us dwell on a necessary observation. It is certain that men talk to themselves; and there is not a thinking being who has not realized the fact. It is only in this sense that the words frequently employed in this chapter, *he said, he exclaimed,* must be understood; men talk to themselves, speak to themselves, cry out within themselves, but the external silence is not interrupted. There is a grand tumult; everything speaks within us, excepting the mouth. The realities of the soul, for all they are not visible and palpable, are not the less realities. He asked himself then what he had arrived at, and cross-questioned himself about the resolution he had formed. He confessed to himself that all he had arranged in his mind was monstrous, and that leaving "God to act" was simply horrible. To allow this mistake of destiny and of men to be accomplished, not to prevent it, to lend himself to it, do nothing, in short, was to do everything; it was the last stage of hypocritical indignity! it was a low, cowardly, cunning, abject, hideous crime. For the first time during eight years this hapless man had the taste of a bad thought and a bad action, and he spat it out in disgust.

He continued to cross-question himself. He asked himself what he had meant by the words, "My object is attained!" He allowed that his life had an object, but what was its nature?—conceal his name! deceive the police. Was it for so paltry a thing that he had done all that he had effected? Had he not another object which was the great and true one, to save not his person, but his soul—to become once again honest and good? To be a just man! was it not that he had solely craved after, and what the bishop had ordered him? Close the door on his past? but, great Heaven, he opened it again by committing an infamous action. He was becoming a robber once more, and the most odious of robbers! he was robbing another man of his existence, his livelihood, his peace, and his place in the sunshine. He was becoming an assassin, he was killing, morally killing, a wretched man; he was inflicting on him the frightful living death, the open-air death, which is called the galleys. On the other hand, if he gave himself up, freed this man who was suffering from so grievous an error, resumed his name, became through duty the convict Jean Valjean,—that would be really completing his resurrection, and eternally closing the hell from which he was emerging! Falling back into it apparently would be leaving it in reality! He must do this; he would have done nothing unless he did this; all his life would be useless; all his reputation thrown away. He felt that the bishop was here, that he was the more present because he was dead, that the bishop was steadfastly looking at him, and that henceforth Madeleine the mayor would be an abomination to him, and Jean Valjean the convict admirable and pure in his sight. Men saw his mask, but the bishop saw his face; men saw his life, but the bishop saw his conscience. He must consequently go to Arras, deliver the false Jean Valjean, and denounce the true one. Alas! this was the greatest of sacrifices, the most poignant of victories, the last step to take; but he must take it. Frightful destiny his! he could not obtain sanctity in the sight of Heaven unless he returned to infamy in the sight of man.

"Well," he said, "I will make up my mind to this—I will do my duty and save this man."

He uttered those words aloud without noticing he had raised his voice. He fetched his books, verified and put them in order. He threw into the fire a number of claims which he held against needy small business men. He wrote a letter, which he sealed, and on the envelope of which a person, had one been in the room that moment, could have read: "To M. Lafitte, banker, Rue d'Artois, Paris." He then took from his desk a pocket-book, which contained a few bank-notes and the passport he had employed just previously to go to the elections. Any one who had seen him while he was accomplishing these various acts, with which such grave meditation was mingled, would not have suspected what was taking place in him. At moments his lips moved; at others he raised his head and looked at a part of the wall, as if there were something there which he desired to clear up or question.

When the letter to M. Lafitte was finished, he put it into his portfolio, and began his walk once more. His reverie had not deviated; he continued to see his duty clearly written in luminous letters which flashed before his eyes and moved about his glance, "Name yourself, denounce yourself!" He could also see the two ideas which had hitherto been the double rule of his life—to hide his name and sanctify his life—moving before him, as it were, in a tangible shape. For the first time they seemed to him absolutely distinct, and he saw the difference that separated them. He recognized that one of these ideas was necessarily good, while the other might become bad; that the former was devotion, the latter selfishness; that one said, "My neighbor," the other "Myself"; that one came from the light, and the other from darkness. They strove with each other, and he could see them doing so. While he was thinking, they had grown before his mental eye, and they had now colossal forms, and he fancied he could see a god and a giant wrestling within him, in the infinitude to which we just now alluded, and in the midst of obscurity and flashes of light. It was a horrible sight, but it seemed to him as if the good thought gained the victory. He felt that he was approaching the second decisive moment of his life; that the bishop marked the first phase of his new life, and that this Champmathieu marked the second. After the great crisis came the great trial.

The fever, appeased for a moment, gradually returned, however. A thousand thoughts crossed his mind, but they continued to strengthen him in his resolution. At one moment he said to himself that he perhaps regarded the matter too seriously; that, after all, this Champmathieu did not concern him, and in any case was a thief. He answered himself: "If this man has really stolen apples, he will have a month's imprisonment, but that is a long way from the galleys. And then, again, is it proved that he has committed a robbery? The name of Jean Valjean is crushing him, and seems to dispense with proofs. Do not public prosecutors habitually act in this way? A man is believed to be a thief because he is known to be a convict." At another moment the idea occurred to him that when he had denounced himself the heroism of his deed might perhaps be taken into consideration, as well as his life of honesty during the last seven years, and the good he had done the town, and that he would be pardoned. But this supposition soon vanished, and he smiled bitterly at the thought that the robbery of the forty sous from Gervais rendered him a relapsed convict, that this affair would certainly be brought forward, and, by the precise terms of the law, sentence him to the galleys for life.

He turned away from all illusions, detached himself more and more from earth, and sought consolation and strength elsewhere. He said to himself that he must do his duty, that perhaps, he would not be more wretched after doing it than he would have been had he eluded it; that, if he let matters take their course and remained at M. . . . , his good name, good deeds, charity, wealth, popularity, and virtue would be tainted by a crime; and what flavor would all these sacred things have, when attached to this hideous thought; while, if he accomplished his sacrifice, he would mingle a heavenly idea with the galleys, the chain, the green cap, the unrelaxing toil, and the pitiless shame. At last he said to himself that it was a necessity, that his destiny was thus shaped, that he had no power to derange the arrangements of Heaven, and that in any case he must choose either external virtue and internal abomination, or holiness within and infamy outside him. His courage did not fail him in revolving so many mournful ideas, but his brain grew weary. He began thinking involuntarily of other and indifferent matters. His arteries beat violently in his temples, and he was still walking up and down; midnight struck, first from the parish church, and then from the Town Hall; he counted the twelve strokes of the two clocks, and compared the sound of the two bells. They reminded him that, a few days before, he had seen an old bell at a marine store, on which was engraved the name Antoine Albin, Romainville.

As he felt cold, he lit a fire, but did not dream of closing the window. Then he fell back into his stupor, obliged to make a mighty effort to remember what he had been thinking of before midnight struck. At last he succeeded.

"Ah, yes," he said to himself, "I had formed the resolution to denounce myself."

And then he suddenly began thinking of Fantine.

"Stay," he said, "and that poor woman!"

Here a fresh crisis broke out; Fantine, suddenly appearing in the midst of his reverie, was like a ray of unexpected light. He fancied that all changed around him, and exclaimed:

"Wait a minute! Hitherto I have thought of myself and consulted my own convenience. Whether it suits me to be silent or denounce myself—hide my person or save my soul—be a contemptible and respected magistrate, or an infamous and venerable convict, it is always self, naught but self. Good heavens! all this is egotism; under different shapes, 'tis true, but still egotism. Suppose I were to think a little about others! It is the first duty of a Christian to think of his neighbor. Well, let me examine; when I am effaced and forgotten, what will become of all this? If I denounce myself, that Champmathieu will be set at liberty. I shall be sent back to the galleys, and what then? What will occur here? Here are a town, factories, a trade, work-people, men, women, old grandfathers, children, and poor people; I have created all this. I keep it all alive; wherever there is a chimney smoking, I placed the brand in the fire and the meat in the saucepan; I have produced easy circumstances, circulation, and credit. Before I came there was nothing of all this; I revived, animated, fertilized, stimulated, and enriched the whole district.

When I am gone the soul will be gone; if I withdraw all will die; and then, this woman, who has suffered so greatly, who has so much merit in her fall, and whose misfortune I unwittingly caused,—and the child which I intended to go and fetch and restore to the mother. Do not I also owe something to this woman, in reparation of the wrong which I have done her? If I disappear, what will happen?—the mother dies, and the child will become what it can. This will happen if I denounce myself. If I do not denounce myself? Come, let me see."

After asking himself this question, he hesitated, and trembled slightly, but this emotion lasted but a short time, and he answered himself calmly:

"Well, this man will go to the galleys, it is true, but he has stolen. Although I may say to myself that he has not stolen, he has done so! I remain here and continue my operations; in ten years I shall have gained ten millions. I spread them over the country; I keep nothing for myself; but what do I care? I am not doing this for myself. The prosperity of all is increased; trades are revived, factories and forges are multiplied, and thousands of families are happy; the district is populated; villages spring up where there are only farms, and farms where there is nothing; wretchedness disappears, and with it debauchery, prostitution, robbery, murder, all the vices, all the crimes—and this poor mother brings up her child. Why, I was mad, absurd, when I talked about denouncing myself, and I must guard against precipitation. What! because it pleases me to play the grand and the generous,—it is pure melodrama, after all, —because I only thought of myself, and in order to save from a perhaps exaggerated though substantially just punishment a stranger, a thief, and an apparent scoundrel—a whole department must perish! a poor woman die in the hospital, and a poor child starve in the streets, like dogs! Why, it is abominable! without the mother seeing her child again, or the child knowing her mother! and all this on behalf of an old scamp of an apple-stealer, who has assuredly deserved the galleys for something else, if not for that. These are fine scruples that save a culprit and sacrifice the innocent, that save an old vagabond who has not many years to live, and will not be more unhappy at the galleys than in his hovel, and destroy an entire population,—mothers, wives, and children. That poor little Cosette, who has only me in the world, and is doubtless at this moment shivering with cold in the den of those Thénardiers. There is another pair of wretches. And I would fail in my duties to all these poor creatures, and commit such a folly as to denounce myself! Let us put things at the worst: suppose that I am committing a bad action in this, and that my conscience reproaches me with it some day,—there will be devotion and virtue in accepting, for the good of my neighbor, these reproaches, which only weigh on me, and this bad action, which only compromises my own soul."

He got up and began walking up and down; this time he seemed to be satisfied with himself. Diamonds are only found in the darkness of the earth; truths are only found in the depths of the thought. It seemed to him that after descending into these depths, after groping for some time in the densest of this darkness, he had found one of these diamonds, one of these truths, which he held in his hand and which dazzled his eyes when he looked at it.

"Yes," he thought, "I am on the right track and hold the solution of the problem. A man must in the end hold on to something, and my mind is made up. I will let matters take their course, so no more vacillation or backsliding. It is for the interest of all, not of myself. I am Madeleine, and remain Madeleine, and woe to the man who is Jean Valjean. I am no longer he. I do not know that man, and if any one happen to be Jean Valjean at this moment, he must look out for himself, for it does not concern me. It is a fatal name that floats in the night, and if it stop and settle on a head, all the worse for that head."

He looked into the small looking-glass over the mantel-piece, and said to himself:

"How greatly has forming a resolution relieved me! I am quite a different man at present."

He walked a little way and then stopped. "Come," he said, "I must not hesitate before any of the consequences of the resolution I have formed. There are threads which still attach me to Jean Valjean which must be broken. There are in this very room objects which would accuse me, dumb things which would serve as witnesses, and they must all disappear."

He took his purse from his pocket, and drew a small key out of it. He put this key in a lock, the hole of which could scarcely be seen, for it was hidden in the darkest corner of the design on the paper that covered the walls. A sort of false cupboard made between the corner of the wall and the mantel-piece was visible. In this hiding place there were only a few rags—a blue blouse, worn trousers, an old knapsack, and a large thorn-stick, shod with iron at both ends. Any one who saw Jean Valjean pass through D. . . . in October, 1815, would easily have recognized all these

wretched articles. He had preserved them, as he had done the candlesticks, that they might constantly remind him of his starting-point; still
he hid what came from the galleys, and displayed the candlesticks which
came from the bishop. He took a furtive glance at the door, as if afraid
that it might open in spite of the bolt; and then with a rapid movement
he made but one armful of the things he had so religiously and perilously
kept for so many years, and threw them all—rags, stick, and knapsack—
into the fire. He closed the cupboard, and redoubling his precautions,
which were now useless, since it was empty, dragged a heavy piece of
furniture in front of it. In a few seconds, the room and opposite wall
were lit up with a large red and flickering glow; all was burning, and
the thorn-stick crackled and threw out sparks into the middle of the
room. From the knapsack, as it burned with all the rags it contained, fell
something that glistened in the ashes. On stooping, it could be easily
recognized as a coin; it was doubtless the little Savoyard's two-franc piece.
He did not look at the fire, and continued his walk backward and forward. All at once his eyes fell on the two candlesticks which the fire-light
caused to shine vaguely on the mantel-piece.

"Stay," he thought, "all Jean Valjean is in them, and they must be
destroyed too."

He seized the candlesticks—there was a fire large enough to destroy
their shape and convert them into unrecognizable ingots. He leaned
over the hearth and warmed his hands for a moment; it was a great
comfort to him.

He stirred up the ashes with one of the candlesticks—a moment more
and both would have been in the fire. All at once he fancied he heard a
voice cry within him, "Jean Valjean! Jean Valjean!" His hair stood erect,
and he became like a man who is listening to a terrible thing.

"Yes, that is right; finish!" the voice said; "complete what you are
about; destroy those candlesticks, annihilate that reminiscence! forget
the bishop! forget everything! ruin that Champmathieu; that is right.
Applaud yourself; come, all is settled and resolved on. This old man,
who does not know what they want with him, who is perhaps innocent,
whose whole misfortune your name causes, on whom your name weighs
like a crime, is going to be taken from you, sentenced, and will end his
days in abjectness and horror. That is excellent! Be an honest man yourself, honorable and honored, enrich the town, assist the indigent, bring
up orphans, live happy, virtuous, and applauded; and during this time
while you are here in joy and light, there will be somebody who wears

your red jacket, bears your name in ignominy, and drags along your chain at the galleys. Yes, that is excellently arranged. Oh! you scoundrel!"

The perspiration beaded on his forehead, and he fixed his haggard eyes upon the candlesticks. The voice within him, however, had not ended yet.

"Jean Valjean! there will be around you many voices making a great noise, speaking very loud and blessing you, and one which no one will hear, and which will curse you in the darkness. Well, listen, infamous man! all these blessings will fall back on the ground before reaching Heaven, and the curse alone will ascend to God!"

This voice, at first very faint, and which spoke from the obscurest nook of his conscience, had gradually become sonorous and formidable, and he now heard it in his ear. He fancied it was not his own voice, and he seemed to hear the last words so distinctly that he looked around the room with a species of terror.

"Is there any one here?" he asked in a loud voice and wildly.

Then he continued, with a laugh which seemed almost idiotic:

"What a fool I am! there can be nobody."

There was somebody; but He was not of those whom the human eye can see. He placed the candlesticks on the mantel-piece, and then resumed that melancholy, mournful walk which aroused the sleeper underneath him. This walking relieved him, and at the same time intoxicated him. It appears sometimes, as if on supreme occasions, people move about to ask advice of everything they pass. At the end of a few moments he no longer knew what result to arrive at. He now recoiled with equal horror from the two resolutions he had formed in turn; the two ideas that counseled him seemed each as desperate as the other. What a fatality that this Champmathieu should be taken for him! He was hurled down precisely by the means which Providence at first seemed to have employed to strengthen his position.

There was a moment during which he regarded his future,—denounce himself! great heavens! give himself up! He thought with immense despair of all that he must give up, of all that he must resume. He would be forced to bid adieu to this good, pure, radiant life,—to the respect of all classes,—to honor, to liberty! He would no longer walk about the fields, he would no longer hear the birds sing in May, or give alms to the little children! He would no longer feel the sweetness of glances of gratitude and love fixed upon him! He would leave this little house, which he had built, and his little bedroom. All appeared charming to him at this moment. He would no longer read those books or write at the little deal table; his old servant would no longer bring up his coffee in the morning. Great God! instead of all this, there would be the gang, the red jacket, the chain on his foot, fatigue, the dungeon, the camp-bed, and all the horrors he knew! At his age, after all he had borne! it would be different were he still young. But to be old, coarsely addressed by anybody, searched by the jailer, and receive blows from the keeper's stick! to thrust his naked feet into iron-shod shoes! to offer his leg morning and night to the man who examines the fetters! to endure the curiosity of strangers who would be told, "That is the famous Jean Valjean, who was mayor of M. . . . ." At night, when pouring with perspiration and crushed by fatigue, with a green cap on his head, to go up two by two, under the sergeant's whip, the side ladder of the hulks! Oh, what misery! Destiny, then, can be as wicked as an intelligent being and prove as monstrous as the human heart.

And, whatever he might do, he ever fell back into this crushing dilemma, which was the basis of his reverie. Remain in paradise, and become a demon there; or re-enter hell, and become an angel? What should he do, great God! what should he do? The trouble, from which he had escaped with such difficulty, was again let loose on him, and his thoughts became confused once more. They assumed something stupefied and mechanical, which is peculiar to despair. The name of Romainville incessantly returned to his mind, with two lines of a song which he had formerly heard. He remembered that Romainville is a little wood, near Paris, where lovers go to pick lilac in April. He tottered both externally and internally; he walked like a little child allowed to go alone. At certain moments, he struggled against his lassitude, and tried to recapture his intelligence; he tried to set himself, for the last time, the problem over which he had fallen in a state of exhaustion,—must he denounce himself, or must he be silent? He could not succeed in seeing anything distinct, the vague outlines of all the reasonings sketched in by his reverie were dissipated in turn like smoke. Still, he felt that, however he resolved, and without any possibility of escape, something belonging to him was about to die; that he entered a sepulcher, whether on his right hand or his left, and that either his happiness or his virtue would be borne to the grave.

Alas! all his irresolution had seized him again, and he was no further advanced than at the beginning. Thus the wretched soul writhed in agony! Eighteen hundred years before this hapless man, the mysterious

Being in whom are resumed all the sanctities and all the suffering of humanity, He, too, while the trees on the Mount of Olives were shuddering before the wild wind of the infinite, long sought to put away the bitter cup which appeared before Him, dripping with shadow and overflowing with darkness in starry depths.

4. THE FORMS THAT SUFFERING TAKES IN SLEEP

THREE A. M. had struck, and he had been walking about in this way for five hours without a break, when he fell into his chair. He fell asleep, and had a dream. This dream, like most dreams, was only connected with his situation by something poignant and mournful, but it made an impression on him. This nightmare struck him so much that he wrote it down at a later date, and we think we are bound to transcribe it verbatim, for, whatever the history of this man may be, it would be incomplete if we omitted it. Here it is then; on the envelope we notice the line—*"The dream I had on that night."*

I was upon a plain, a large, mournful plain, on which no grass grew. It did not seem to me to be day, but it was not night. I was walking with my brother, the brother of my boyish years, of whom I am bound to say I never think, and whom I scarce remember. We were talking, and met travelers. We spoke about a woman, formerly a neighbour of ours, who had always worked with her window open since she had occupied a front room. While talking, we felt cold on account of this open window. There were no trees on the plain. We saw a man pass close by us; he was a perfectly naked man, of the color of ashes, mounted on a horse of an earthen color. The man had no hair, and I could see his skull and the veins on his skull. He held in his hand a wand, which was supple as a vine-twig and heavy as lead. This horseman passed and said nothing to us.

My brother said to me: "Let us turn into the hollow way."

It was a hollow way in which not a bramble or even a patch of moss could be seen; all was earth-colored, even the sky. After going a few yards, I received no answer when I spoke, and I noticed that my brother was no longer with me. I entered a village that I saw, and I fancied that it must be Romainville. (Why Romainville?)* The first street I entered was deserted; I entered a second street, and behind the angle formed by the two streets a man was standing against the wall. I asked this man, "What is this place? where am I?" but he gave me no answer. I saw the door of a house open, and walked in.

The first room was deserted, and I entered a second. Behind the door of this room there was a man leaning against the wall. I asked him, "To whom does this house belong? Where am I?" but the man gave me no answer. I went out into the garden of the house, and it was deserted. Behind the first tree I found a man standing. I said to the man, "Whose is this garden? Where am I?" but he made me no answer.

I wandered about this village and perceived that it was a town. All the streets were deserted, all the doors open. Not a living soul passed along the street, moved in the rooms, or walked in the gardens. But there was behind every corner, every door, and every tree, a man standing silently. I never saw more than one at a time, and these men looked at me as I passed.

I left the village and began walking about the fields. At the end of some time I turned back and saw a great crowd coming after me. I recognized all the men whom I had seen in the town, and they had strange heads. They did not appear to be in a hurry, and yet they walked faster than I and made no noise in walking. In an instant this crowd joined me and surrounded me. The faces of these men were earth-colored. Then the man I had seen first and questioned when I entered the town, said to me, "Where are you going? Do you know that you have been dead for a long time?" I opened my mouth to answer, and I perceived that there was no one near me.

He woke up, chilled to the marrow, for a wind, cold as the morning breeze, was shaking the open window. The fire had died away, the candle was nearly burned out, and it was still black night. He rose and

---

* This parenthesis is by Jean Valjean.

went to the window: there were still no stars in the sky. From this window he could see the yard and his street, and a dry, sharp sound on the ground below him induced him to look out. He saw two red stars whose rays lengthened and shortened curiously in the gloom. As his mind was half submerged in the mist of dreams, he thought, "There are no stars in the sky; they are on earth now." A second sound like the first completely woke him, and he perceived that those two stars were carriage-lamps, and by the light which they projected he could distinguish the shape of the vehicle—it was a tilbury, in which a small white horse was harnessed. The sound he had heard was the pawing of the horse's hoof on the ground.

"What's the meaning of this conveyance?" he said to himself; "who can have come at so early an hour?"

At this moment there was a gentle tap at his bedroom door. He shuddered from head to foot, and shouted in a terrible voice, "Who's there?"

Some one replied, "I, sir," and he recognized his old servant's voice.

"Well," he continued, "what is it?"

"It is getting on for four o'clock, sir."

"What has that to do with me?"

"The tilbury has come, sir."

"What tilbury?"

"Did you not order one?"

"No," he said.

"The ostler says that he has come to fetch M. le Maire."

"What ostler?"

"M. Scaufflaire's."

This name made him start as if a flash of lightning had passed before his eyes.

"Ah, yes," he repeated, "M. Scaufflaire."

Could the old woman have seen him at this moment, she would have been horrified. There was a lengthened silence, during which he stupidly examined the candle flame, and rolled up some of the wax in his fingers. The old woman, who was waiting, at length mustered up courage to raise her voice again.

"M. le Maire, what answer am I to give?"

"Say it is quite right, and that I shall be down directly."

THE postal service between Arras and M. . . . was still conducted by small mail-carts, dating from the empire. They were two-wheeled vehicles, lined with tawny leather, hung on springs, and having only two seats, one for the driver and another for a passenger. The wheels were armed with those long offensive axle-trees which kept other carriages at a distance, and may still be seen on German roads. The compartment for the bags was an immense oblong box at the back; it was painted black, and the carriage yellow. These vehicles, like which we have nothing at the present day, had something ugly and hump-backed about them, and when you saw them pass at a distance, or creeping up a hill on the horizon, they resembled those insects called, we think, termites, and which with a small body drag a heavy load after them. They went very fast, however, and the mail which left Arras at one in the morning, after the Paris mail had arrived, reached M. . . . a little before five A. M.

On this morning, the mail-cart, just as it entered M. . . . , and while turning a corner, ran into a tilbury drawn by a white horse, coming in the opposite direction, and in which there was only one sitter, a man wrapped in a cloak. The wheels of the tilbury received a rather heavy blow, and though the driver of the mail-cart shouted to the man to stop, he did not listen, but went on at a smart trot.

"That man is in a deuce of a hurry," said the courier.

The man in this hurry was he whom we have just seen struggling in convulsions, assuredly deserving of pity. Where was he going? he could not have told. Why was he hurrying? he did not know. He was going onward unthinkingly. Where to? Doubtless to Arras; but he might also be going elsewhere. He buried himself in the darkness as in a gulf. Something urged him on; something attracted him. What was going on in him no one could tell, but all will understand it,—for what man has not entered, at least once in his life, this obscure cavern of the unknown? However, he had settled, decided, and done nothing; not one of the acts of his conscience had been definite, and he was still as unsettled as at the beginning.

Why was he going to Arras? He repeated what he had already said on hiring the gig of Scaufflaire—that, whatever the result might be, there would be no harm in seeing with his own eyes, and judging matters for himself; that this was prudent, and he was bound to know what was going on; that he could not decide anything till he had observed and examined; that, at a distance, a man made mountains of mole-hills; that after all, when he had seen this Champmathieu, his conscience would probably be quietly relieved, and he could let the scoundrel go to the galleys in his place; that Javert would be there and the three convicts who had known him,—but, nonsense! they would not recognize him, for all conjectures and suppositions were fixed on this Champmathieu, and there is nothing so obstinate as conjectures and suppositions,—and that hence he incurred no danger. It was doubtless a black moment, but he would emerge from it. After all, he held his destiny, however adverse it might try to be, in his own hands, and was master of it. He clung wildly to the latter thought.

Although, to tell the whole truth, he would have preferred not to go to Arras, yet he went. While reflecting he lashed the horse, which was going at that regular and certain trot which covers two leagues and a half in an hour; and, as the gig advanced, he felt something within him recoil. At daybreak he was in the open country, and the town of M. . . . was far behind him. He watched the horizon grow white; he looked, without seeing them, at all the cold figures of a winter dawn. Morning has its specters like night. He did not see them, but unconsciously, and through a sort of almost physical penetration, these black outlines of trees and hills added something gloomy and sinister to the violent state of his soul. Each time that he passed one of those isolated houses which skirt high-roads, he said to himself: "And yet there are people asleep in them." The trot of the horse, the bells on the harness, the wheels on the stones, produced a gentle and monotonous sound, which is delightful when you are merry, and mournful when you are sad.

It was broad daylight when he reached Hesdin, and he stopped at the inn to let the horse breathe and give it a feed. This horse, as Scaufflaire had said, belonged to that small Boulonnais breed which has too large a head, too much stomach, and too weak loins, but which also has an open chest, a wide croup, dry, fine legs, and a solid hoof; it is an ugly but strong and healthy breed. The capital little beast had done five leagues in two hours, and had not turned a hair.

He did not get out of the tilbury; the ostler who brought the oats suddenly stooped down and examined the left wheel.

"Are you going far in this state?" the man said.

He answered, almost without emerging from his reverie:

"Why do you ask?"

"Have you come any distance?" the ostler continued.

"Five leagues."

"Ah!"

"Why do you say ah?"

The ostler bent down again, remained silent for a moment, with his eye fixed on the wheel, and then said, as he drew himself up:

"Because this wheel, which may have gone five leagues, cannot possibly go another mile."

He jumped out of the tilbury.

"What are you saying, my friend?"

"I say that it is a miracle you and your horse did not roll into a ditch by the roadside. Just look."

The wheel was, in fact, seriously damaged. The blow dealt it by the mail-cart had broken two spokes, and almost carried away the axle-tree.

"My good fellow," he said to the ostler, "is there a wheelwright here?"

"Of course, sir."

"Be good enough to go and fetch him."

"He lives close by. Hilloh, Master Bourgaillard!"

Master Bourgaillard was standing in his door-way; he examined the wheel, and made a face like a surgeon regarding a broken leg.

"Can you mend this wheel?"

"Yes, sir."

"When can I start again?"

"To-morrow; there is a good day's work. Are you in a hurry, sir?"

"In a great hurry; I must set out again in an hour at the latest."

"It is impossible, sir."

"I will pay anything you ask."

"Impossible."

"Well, in two hours?"

237

"It is impossible for to-day; you will not be able to go on till to-morrow."

"My business cannot wait till to-morrow. Suppose, instead of mending this wheel, you were to put another on?"

"How so?"

"You are a wheelwright and have probably a wheel you can sell me, and then I could set out again directly."

"I have no ready-made wheel to suit your gig, for wheels are sold in pairs, and it is not easy to match one."

"In that case, sell me a pair of wheels."

"All wheels, sir, do not fit all axle-trees."

"At any rate, try."

"It is useless, sir; I have only cart-wheels for sale, for ours is a small place."

"Have you a gig I can hire?"

The wheelwright had noticed at a glance that the tilbury was a hired vehicle; he shrugged his shoulders.

"You take such good care of gigs you hire, that if I had one I would not let it to you."

"Well, one to sell me?"

"I have not one."

"What, not a tax-cart? I am not particular, as you see."

"This is a small place. I have certainly," the wheelwright added, "an old calèche in my stable which belongs to a person in the town, and who uses it on the thirty-sixth of every month. I could certainly let it out to you, for it is no concern of mine, but the owner must not see it pass; and, besides, it is a calèche, and will want two horses."

"I will hire post-horses."

"Where are you going to, sir?"

"To Arras."

"And you wish to arrive to-day?"

"Certainly."

"By taking post-horses?"

"Why not?"

"Does it make any difference to you if you reach Arras at four o'clock to-morrow morning?"

"Of course it does."

"There is one thing to be said about hiring post-horses—have you your passport, sir?"

"Yes."

"Well, if you take post-horses, you will not reach Arras before to-morrow. We are on the cross-country road. The relays are badly served, and the horses are out at work. This is the plowing season, and as strong teams are required, horses are taken anywhere, from the post-houses like the rest. You will have to wait three or four hours, sir, at each station, and only go at a foot-pace, for there are many hills to ascend."

"Well, I will ride. Take the horse out—I suppose I can purchase a saddle here?"

"Of course, but will this horse carry a saddle?"

"No, I remember now that it will not."

"In that case—?"

"But surely I can hire a saddle-horse in the village?"

"What, to go to Arras without a break?"

"Yes."

"You would want a horse such as is not to be found in these parts. In the first place, you would have to buy it, as you are a stranger, but you would not find one to buy or hire for five hundred francs,—not for a thousand."

"What is to be done?"

"The best thing is to let me mend the wheel and put off your journey till to-morrow."

"To-morrow will be too late."

"Confound it."

"Is there not the Arras mail-cart? When does that pass?"

"Not till to-night."

"What! you will take a whole day in mending that wheel?"

"An honest day."

"Suppose you employed two workmen?"

"Ay, if I had ten."

"Suppose the spokes were tied with cords?"

"What is to be done with the axle? besides, the felloe is in a bad state."

"Is there any one who lets out vehicles in the town?"

"No."

"Is there another wheelwright?"

The ostler and the wheelwright replied simultaneously:

"No."

He felt an immense joy, for it was evident that Providence was interfering. It was He who had broken the tilbury wheel and stopped his journey. He had not yielded to this species of first summons; he had

239

made every possible effort to continue his journey; he had loyally and scrupulously exhausted all resources; he had not recoiled before the season, fatigue, or expense; and he had nothing to reproach himself with. If he did not go further, it did not concern him; it was not his fault, it was not the doing of his conscience, but of Providence. He breathed freely and fully for the first time since Javert's visit. He felt as if the iron hand which had been squeezing his heart for twenty hours had relaxed its grasp; God now appeared to be on his side, and declared Himself openly. He said to himself that he had done all in his power, and at present need only return home quietly .

Had the conversation with the wheelwright taken place in an inn-room, it would probably have not been heard by any one,—matters would have remained in this state, and we should probably not have had to record any of the following events, but the conversation took place in the street. Any colloquy in the street inevitably produces a crowd for there are always people who only ask to be spectators. While he was questioning the wheelwright, some passers-by stopped around, and a lad to whom no one paid any attention, after listening for some moments, ran off. At the instant when the traveler made up his mind to turn back, this boy returned, accompanied by an old woman.

"Sir," the woman said, "my boy tells me that you wish to hire a conveyance?"

This simple remark, made by an old woman led by a child, made the perspiration pour down his back. He fancied he saw the hand which had let him loose re-appear in the shadow behind him, ready to clutch him again. He replied:

"Yes, my good woman, I want to hire a gig."

And he hastily added, "But there is not one in the town."

"Yes there is," said the old woman.

"Where?" the wheelwright remarked.

"At my house," the old crone answered.

He gave a start, for the fatal hand had seized him again. The poor woman really had a sort of wicker-cart under a shed. The wheelwright and the ostler, sorry to see the traveler escape them, interfered:

"It was a frightful rattle-trap, and had no springs,—it is true that the inside seats were hung with leathern straps,—the rain got into it—the wheels were rusty, and ready to fall to pieces—it would not go much further than the tilbury—the gentleman had better not get into it,"—and so on.

All this was true, but the rattle-trap, whatever it might be, rolled on two wheels, and could go to Arras. He paid what was asked, left the tilbury to be repaired against his return, had the horse put into the cart, got in and went his way. At the moment when the cart moved ahead, he confessed to himself that a moment previously he had felt a sort of joy at the thought that he could not go where he was going. He examined this joy with a sort of passion, and found it absurd. Why did he feel joy at turning back? After all, he was making this journey of his free will, and no one forced him to do so. And assuredly nothing could happen, except what he liked.

As he was leaving Hesdin, he heard a voice shouting to him, "Stop, stop!" He stopped the cart with a hurried movement in which there was something feverish and convulsive that resembled joy. It was the old woman's boy.

"Sir," he said, "it was I who got you the cart."

"Well?"

"You have given me nothing."

He who gave to all, and so easily, considered this demand exorbitant, and almost odious.

"Oh, it's you, scamp," he said; "well, you will not have anything."

He flogged his horse, which started again at a smart trot. He had lost much time at Hesdin, and would have liked to recover it. The little horse was courageous, and worked for two; but it was February, it had been raining, the roads were bad. The cart, too, ran much more heavily than the tilbury, and there were numerous ascents. He took nearly four hours in going from Hesdin to St. Pol; four hours for five leagues! At St. Pol he pulled up at the first inn he came to, and had the horse put in a stable. As he had promised Scaufflaire, he stood near the crib while it was eating, and had troubled and confused thoughts. The landlady entered the stable.

"Do you not wish to breakfast, sir?"

"Eh! yes, of course!" he said, "I am even very hungry."

He followed the woman, who had a healthy, ruddy face; she led him to a ground-floor room, in which were tables covered with oil-cloth.

"Make haste," he remarked, "for I am in a great hurry."

A plump Flemish servant girl hastened to lay the cloth, and he looked at her with a feeling of comfort.

"That is what ailed me," he thought, "I had not breakfasted."

He seized the bread, bit a mouthful, and then slowly laid it back on the table and did not touch it again. A wagoner was sitting at another table, and he said to him:

"Why is this bread so bitter?"

The wagoner was a German, and did not understand him; he returned to his horse. An hour later he had left St. Pol, and was proceeding toward Tinques, which is only five leagues from Arras. What did he do during the drive? what was he thinking of? As in the morning, he looked at the trees, the roofs, the plowed fields, and the diversities of a landscape which every turn in the road changed as he passed them. To see a thousand different objects for the first and last time is most melancholy! traveling is birth and death at every moment. Perhaps, in the vaguest region of his mind he made a comparison between the changing horizon and human existence, for everything in this life is continually flying before us. Shadow and light are blended; after a bedazzlement comes an eclipse; every event is a turn in the road, and all at once you are old. You feel something like a shock, all is black, you distinguish an obscure door, and the gloomy horse of life which dragged you, stops, and you see a veiled, unknown form unharnessing it. Twilight was setting in at the moment when the school-boys, leaving school, saw this traveler enter Tinques. He did not halt there, but as he left the village, a road-mender, who was laying stones, raised his head, and said to him:

"Your horse is very tired."

The poor brute, in fact, could not get beyond a walk.

"Are you going to Arras?" the road-mender continued.

"Yes."

"If you go at that pace, you will not reach it very soon."

He stopped his horse, and asked the road-mender:

"How far is it from here to Arras?"

"Nearly seven long leagues."

"How so? the post-book says only five and a quarter leagues."

"Ah," the road-mender continued, "you do not know that the road is under repair; you will find it cut up about a mile further on, and it is impossible to pass."

"Indeed?"

"You must take the road on the left, that runs to Carency, and cross the river; when you reach Camblin you will turn to the right, for it is the Mont Saint Eloy road that runs to Arras."

"But I shall lose my way in the dark."

"You do not belong to these parts?"

"No."

"And it is a cross-road; stay, sir," the road-mender continued, "will you let me give you a piece of advice? Your horse is tired, so return to Tinques, where there is a good inn; sleep there, and go to Arras to-morrow."

"I must be there to-night."

"That is different. In that case, go back to the inn all the same, and hire a second horse. The stable boy will act as your guide across the country."

He took the road-mender's advice, turned back, and half an hour after passed the same spot at a sharp trot with a strong second horse. A stable lad, who called himself a postilion, was sitting on the shafts of the cart. Still he felt that he had lost time, for it was now dark. They entered the cross-road, and it soon became frightful; the cart fell out of one rut into another, but he said to the postilion:

"Keep on at a trot, and I will give you a double fee."

In one of the jolts the splinter-bar broke

"The bar is broken, sir," said the postilion, "and I do not know how to fasten my horse, and the road is very bad by night. If you will go back and sleep at Tinques, we can get to Arras at an early hour to-morrow."

He answered, "Have you a piece of rope and a knife?"

"Yes, sir."

He cut a branch and made a bar; it was a further loss of twenty minutes, but they started at a gallop. The plain was dark, and a low, black fog was creeping over the hills. A heavy wind, which came from the sea, made in all the corners of the horizon a noise like that of furniture being moved. All that he could see had an attitude of terror, for how many things shudder beneath the mighty breath of night! The cold pierced him, for he had eaten nothing since the previous morning. He vaguely recalled his other night-excursion on the great plain of D. . . . eight years before, and it seemed to him to be yesterday. A clock struck from a distant steeple and he asked the lad:

"What o'clock is that?"

"Seven, sir, and we shall be at Arras by eight, for we have only three leagues to go."

At this moment he made for the first time this reflection, and considered it strange that it had not occurred to him before, that all the trouble he was taking was perhaps thrown away; he did not even know the hour for the trial, and he might at least have asked about that; it was extravagant to go on thus, without knowing if it would be of any service. Then he made some mental calculations: usually the sittings of assize courts began at nine o'clock, this matter would not occupy much time, the theft of the apples would be easily proved, and then there would be merely the identification, four or five witnesses to hear, and little for counsel to say. He would arrive when it was all over.

The postilion flogged the horses; they had crossed the river and left Mont Saint Eloy behind them; the night was growing more and more dark.

6. SISTER SIMPLICE IS SORELY TRIED

AT this very moment Fantine was joyful. She had passed a very bad night, she had coughed fearfully, and her fever had become worse. In the morning, when the physician paid his visit, she was raving; he felt alarmed, and begged to be sent for so soon as M. Madeleine arrived. All the morning she was gloomy, said little, and made folds in her sheet, while murmuring in a low voice and calculating what seemed to be distances. Her eyes were hollow and fixed; they seemed almost extinct, and then, at moments, they were relit and flashed like stars. It seems as if, on the approach of a certain dark hour, the brightness of Heaven fills those whom the brightness of earth is quitting. Each time that Sister Simplice asked her how she was, she invariably answered, "Well, but I should like to see M. Madeleine."

A few months previously, at the time when Fantine lost her last modesty, her last shame, and her last joy, she was the shadow of herself; now she was the ghost. Physical suffering had completed the work of moral suffering. This creature five-and-twenty years of age had a wrinkled forehead, sunken cheeks, a pinched nose, a leaden complexion, a bony neck, projecting shoulder-blades, thin limbs, an earthy skin, and white hairs were mingled with the auburn. Alas! how illness improvises old age! At midday, the physician returned, wrote a prescription, inquired whether M. Madeleine had been to the infirmary, and shook his head. M. Madeleine usually came at three o'clock, and as punctuality was kindness, he was punctual. At about half-past two Fantine began to grow agitated, and in the next twenty minutes asked the nun more than ten times, "What o'clock is it?"

Three o'clock struck; at the third stroke Fantine, who usually could scarce move in her bed, sat up; clasped her thin yellow hands in a sort of convulsive grasp, and the nun heard one of those deep sighs, which seem to remove a crushing weight, burst from her chest. Then Fantine turned and looked at the door; but no one entered, and the door was not opened. She remained thus for a quarter of an hour, with her eyes fixed on the door, motionless, and holding her breath. The nun did not dare to speak to her and as the clock struck the quarter, Fantine fell back on her pillow. She said nothing and began again making folds in her sheet. The half-hour passed, then the hour, and no one came. Each time the clock struck Fantine sat up, looked at the door, and then fell back again. Her thoughts could be clearly read, but she did not say a word, complain, or make any accusation, she merely coughed in a sad way. It seemed as if something dark was settling down on her, for she was livid and her lips were blue. She smiled every now and then.

When five o'clock struck, the nun heard her say very softly and sweetly, "As I am going away to-morrow, it was wrong of him not to come to-day." Sister Simplice herself was surprised at M. Madeleine's delay. In the meanwhile Fantine looked up at the top of her bed, and seemed to be trying to remember something; all at once she began singing in a voice faint as a sigh. The nun listened; this was Fantine's song:

Nous achèterons de bien belles choses
En nous promenant le long des faubourgs.
Les bleuets sont bleus, les roses sont roses,
Les bleuets sont bleus, j'aime mes amours.

La vierge Marie auprès de mon poêle
Est venue hier en manteau brodé,
Et m'a dit:—Voici, caché sous mon voile,
Le petit qu'un jour tu m'as demandé.—
Courez à la ville, ayez de la toile,
Achetez du fil, achetez un dé.

Nous achèterons de bien belles choses
En nous promenant le long des faubourgs.

Bonne sainte Vierge, auprès de mon poêle
J'ai mis un berceau de rubans orné.
Dieu me donnerait sa plus belle étoile,
J'aime mieux l'enfant que tu m'as donné.
—Madame, que faire avec cette toile?
—Faites un trousseau pour mon nouveau-né.

Les bleuets sont bleus, les roses sont roses,
Les bleuets sont bleus, j'aime mes amours.

Lavez cette toile.—Ou?—Dans la rivière.
Faites-en, sans rien gâter ni salir,
Une belle jupe avec sa brassière
Que je veux broder et de fleurs emplir.
—L'enfant n'est plus là, madame, qu'en faire?
—Faites-en un drap pour m'ensevelir.

Nous achèterons de bien belles choses
En nous promenant le long des faubourgs.
Les bleuets sont bleus, les roses sont roses,
Les bleuets sont bleus, j'aime mes amours.

It was an old cradle-song with which she had in former times lulled her little Cosette to sleep, and which had not once recurred to her during the five years she had been parted from her child. She sang with so sad a voice and to so soft an air, that it was enough to make any one weep, even a nun. The sister, who was accustomed to austere things, felt a tear in her eye. The clock struck six and Fantine did not seem to hear it; she appeared not to pay any attention to things around her. Sister Simplice sent a servant-girl to inquire of the portress of the factory whether M. Madeleine had returned and would be at the infirmary soon; the girl came back in a few moments. Fantine was still motionless and apparently engaged with her own thoughts. The servant told Sister Simplice in a very low voice that the mayor had set off before six o'clock that morning in a small tilbury; that he had gone alone, without a driver; that no one knew what direction he had taken, for while some said they had seen him going along the Arras road, others declared they had met him on the Paris road. He was, as usual, very gentle and he had merely told his servant she need not expect him that night.

While the two women were whispering with their backs turned to Fantine, the sister questioning and the servant conjecturing, Fantine, with the feverish vivacity of certain organic maladies which blend the free movements of health with the frightful emaciation of death, had knelt up in bed, with her two clenched hands supported by the pillow, and listened with·her head thrust between the curtains. All at once she cried:

"You are talking about M. Madeleine; why do you whisper? What is he doing, and why does he not come?"

Her voice was so loud and hoarse that the two women fancied it a man's voice, and they turned round in alarm.

"Answer!" Fantine cried.

The servant stammered:

"The portress told me that he could not come to-day."

"My child," the sister said, "be calm and lie down again."

Fantine, without changing her attitude, went on in a loud voice and with an accent at once imperious and heart-rending:

"He cannot come; why not? You know the reason. You were whispering it to one another, and I insist on knowing."

The servant hastily whispered in the nun's ear, "Tell her that he is engaged at the municipal council."

Sister Simplice blushed slightly, for it was a falsehood that the servant proposed to her. On the other hand, it seemed to her that telling the truth would doubtless deal her a terrible blow, and this was serious in Fantine's present condition. The blush lasted but a little while; the sister fixed her calm, sad eyes on Fantine, and said:

"The mayor is gone on a journey."

Fantine rose and sat up on her heels, her eyes sparkled, and an ineffable joy shone on her sad face.

"He has gone to fetch Cosette," she exclaimed.

Then she raised her hands to Heaven, and her lips moved; she was praying. When she had finished she said, "My sister, I am willing to lie down again and do everything you wish; I was naughty just now. I ask your pardon for having spoken so loud, for I know that is wrong, good sister; but look you, I am so happy. God is good, and M. Madeleine is good; only think, he has gone to Montfermeil to fetch my little Cosette."

She lay down again, helped the nun to smooth her pillow, and kissed a little silver cross she wore on her neck, and which Sister Simplice had given her.

"My child," the sister said, "try to go to sleep now, and do not speak any more."

"He started this morning for Paris, and indeed had no occasion to go there; for Montfermeil is a little to the left before you get there. You remember how he said to me yesterday when I asked him about Cosette, 'Soon, soon'? He wishes to offer me a surprise, for, do you know, he made me sign a letter to get her back from the Thénardiers. They cannot refuse to give up Cosette, can they? for they are paid; the authorities would not allow a child to be kept, for now there is nothing owing. Sister, do not make me signs that I must not speak, for I am extremely happy. I am going on very well; I feel no pain at all; I am going to see Cosette again, and I even feel very hungry. It is nearly five years since I saw her; you cannot imagine how a mother clings to her child,—and then she must be so pretty. She has such pretty pink fingers, and she will have beautiful hands. She must be a great girl now, for she is going on for seven. I call her Cosette but her real name is Euphrasie. This morning I was looking at the dust on the mantel-piece, and I had a notion that I should soon see Cosette again. Good Lord! how wrong it is for a mother to be so many years without seeing her child! she ought to reflect that life is not eternal. Oh! how kind it is of the mayor to go! Is it true that it is so cold? I hope he took his cloak. He will be here again to-morrow, will he not? and we will make a holiday of it. To-morrow morning, sister, you will remind me to put on my little cap with the lace border. Montfermeil is a great distance, and I came from there to this town on foot, and it took me a long time; but the stage-coaches travel so quickly! He will be here to-morrow with Cosette. How far is it to Montfermeil?"

The sister, who had no notion of distances, answered, "Oh, I believe he can be here to-morrow."

"To-morrow! to-morrow!" said Fantine; "I shall see Cosette to-morrow! my good sister. I am not ill now; I feel wild, and would dance if you permitted me."

Any one who had seen her a quarter of an hour before would not have understood it; she was now quite flushed, she spoke with an eager, natural voice, and her whole face was a smile. At times she laughed while speaking to herself in a low voice. A mother's joy is almost a childish joy.

"Well!" the nun said, "you are now happy. So obey me and do not speak any more."

Fantine laid her head on the pillow, and said in a low voice, "Yes, lie down, behave yourself, as you are going to have your child. Sister Simplice is right; all in this place are right."

And then without stirring, without moving her head, she began looking around with widely opened eyes and a joyous air, and said nothing more. The sister closed the curtains, hoping she would fall off to sleep. The physician arrived between seven and eight o'clock. Hearing no sound, he fancied Fantine asleep. He entered softly and walked up to the bed on tiptoe. He opened the curtains, and by the light of the lamp saw Fantine's large, calm eyes fixed on him. She said to him:

"Oh, sir, my child will be allowed to sleep in a little cot by my bedside?"

The physician fancied she was delirious. She added:

"Only look; there is exactly room."

The physician took Sister Simplice on one side, who explained the matter to him; that M. Madeleine was absent for a day or two, and being in doubt, they had not thought it right to undeceive the patient, who fancied that he had gone to Montfermeil, and she might possibly be in the right. The physician approved, and returned to Fantine's bed who said to him:

"In the morning, when the little puss wakes up, I will say good-day to her, and at night I, who do not sleep, will listen to her sleeping. Her gentle little breathing will do me good."

"Give me your hand," said the physician.

"Oh, yes, you do not know that I am cured. Cosette arrives to-morrow."

The physician was surprised to find her better; the oppression was slighter, her pulse had regained strength, and a sort of recovered life was animating the poor exhausted girl.

"Doctor," she continued, "has the sister told you that M. Madeleine has gone to fetch my darling?"

The physician recommended silence, and that any painful emotion should be avoided. He prescribed a dose of quinine, and if the fever returned in the night, a sedative; and as he went away he said to the sister: "She is better. If the mayor were to arrive with the child to-morrow, I do not know what would happen; there are such astounding crises. Great joy has been known to check diseases, and though hers is an organic malady, and in an advanced stage, it is all a mystery, we might perchance save her."

7. THE TRAVELER TAKES PRECAUTIONS FOR HIS RETURN

IT was nearly eight in the evening when the cart we left on the road drove under the archway of the post-house at Arras. The man whom we have followed up to this moment got out, discharged the second horse, and himself led the white pony to the stables; then he pushed open the door of a billiard-room on the ground-floor, sat down, and rested his elbows on the table. He had taken fourteen hours in a journey for which he had allowed himself six. He did himself the justice that it was no fault of his, but in his heart he was not sorry at it. The landlady came in.

"Will you sleep here, sir?"

He nodded in the negative.

"The ostler says that your horse is extremely tired."

"Will it not be able to start again to-morrow morning?"

"Oh, dear, no, sir; it requires at least two days' rest."

"Is not the post-office in this house?"

"Yes, sir."

The landlady led him to the office, where he showed his passport, and inquired whether he could return to M. . . . the same night by the mail-cart. Only one seat was vacant and he took it and paid for it. "Do not fail, sir," said the clerk, "to be here at one o'clock precisely."

This done, he left the hotel, and began walking about the streets. He was not acquainted with Arras, the streets were dark, and he walked about hap-hazard, but he seemed obstinately determined not to ask his way of passers-by. He crossed the little river Crinchon, and found himself in a labyrinth of narrow lanes, in which he lost his way. A citizen came toward him with a lantern, whom, after some hesitation, he resolved to address, though not till he had looked before and behind him, as if afraid lest anybody should overhear the question he was about to ask.

"Will you be kind enough to tell me the way to the courts of justice, sir?" he said.

"You do not belong to the town, sir?" replied the man, who was rather old; "well, follow me. I am going in the direction of the courts, that is to say of the prefecture, for the courts are under repair at present, and the sittings take place temporarily at the prefecture."

"Are the assizes held there?" he asked.

"Of course, sir; you must know that what is now the prefecture was the bishop's palace before the Revolution. Monsieur de Conzlé, who was bishop in '92, had a large hall there, and the trials take place in this hall."

On the road, the citizen said to him:

"If you wish to witness a trial, you are rather late, for the court usually closes at six o'clock."

However, when they arrived in the great square the old man showed him four lofty lighted windows in a vast, gloomy building.

"On my word, sir," he said, "you have arrived in time, and are in luck's way. Do you see those four windows? they belong to the assize courts. As there are lights, it is not closed yet; there must have been a long trial, and they are having an evening session. Are you interested in the trial? is it a criminal offense, or are you a witness?"

He answered:

"I have not come for any trial; I only wish to speak to a solicitor."

"That is different. That is the door, sir, where the sentry is standing, and you have only to go up the large staircase."

He followed the old man's instructions, and a few minutes later was in a large hall, in which there were a good many people, and groups of robed barristers were gossiping together. It is always a thing that contracts the heart, to see these assemblies of men dressed in black, conversing in a low voice on the threshold of a court of justice. It is rare for charity and pity to be noticed in their remarks, for they generally express condemnations settled before trial. All such groups appear to the thoughtful observer so many gloomy hives, in which buzzing minds build in community all sorts of dark edifices. This hall, which was large and only lighted by one lamp, served as a waiting-room, and folding doors, at this moment closed, separated it from the grand chamber in which the assizes were being held. The obscurity was so great that he was not afraid of addressing the first barrister he came across.

"How is it going, sir?" he said.

"It is finished."

"Finished!" This word was repeated with such an accent that the barrister turned round.

"I beg your pardon, sir, but perhaps you are a relative?"

"No, I know no one here. Was a verdict of guilty brought in?"

"Of course; it could not possibly be otherwise."

"The galleys?"

"For life."

He continued in a voice so faint that it was scarcely audible:

"Then the identity was proved?"

"What identity?" the barrister retorted. "Nothing of the sort was required; the affair was simple,—the woman had killed her child, the infanticide was proved, the jury recommended her to mercy, and she was sentenced to imprisonment for life."

"You are alluding to a woman, then?"

"Why, of course; a girl of the name of Limosin. To whom were you referring, pray?"

"To nobody; but as the trial is over, how is it that the court is still lighted?"

"It is for the other trial which began about two hours back."

"What other trial?"

"Oh, it is clear too; he is a sort of beggar, a galley-slave, who has been robbing. I forget his name, but he has a regular bandit face, on the strength of which I would send him to the galleys if for nothing else."

"Is there any way of entering the court, sir?"

"I do not think so, for it is very full. Still, the trial is suspended, and some persons have gone out. When the court resumes, you can try."

"Which is the way in?"

"By that large door."

The barrister left him; in a few minutes he had experienced almost simultaneously, and confusedly blended, every emotion possible. The words of this indifferent person had by turns pierced his heart like needles of ice and like red-hot sword-blades. When he found that the trial was not over, he breathed again; but he could not have said whether what he felt were satisfaction or pain. He walked up to several groups and listened to what they were saying; as the trial list was very heavy, the president had selected for this day two simple and short affairs. They had begun with the infanticide, and were now engaged with the relapsed convict, the "return horse." This man had stolen apples. This did not seem clearly proved, but it was proved that he had already been at the

Toulon galleys. It was this that made his affair bad. His examination and the depositions of the witnesses were over; but there were still the speech for the defense and the summing up, and hence it would not be over till midnight. The man would probably be condemned, for the public prosecutor was sharp, and did not "miss" his man; he was a witty fellow who wrote verses. An usher was standing near the door communicating with the court, and he asked him:

"Will this door be opened soon?"

"It will not be opened," said the usher.

"Will it not be opened when the court resumes its sitting?"

"It has resumed," the usher replied, "but the door will not be opened."

"Why not?"

"Because the hall is full."

"What! is there no room?"

"Not for a soul more. The door is closed, and no one can go in."

The usher added after a pause: "There are certainly two or three seats, behind the president, but he only admits public officials to them."

After saying this, the usher turned his back on him. He withdrew with hanging head, crossed the waiting-room, and slowly went down the stairs, hesitating at every step. He was probably holding counsel with himself; the violent combat which had been going on in him since the previous day was not finished, and every moment he entered some new phase. On reaching the landing, he leaned against the balusters and folded his arms; but all at once he took his pocket-book, tore a leaf from it, wrote in pencil upon it, "M. Madeleine, Mayor of M. sur M."; then he hurried up the stairs, cleft the crowd, walked up to the usher, handed him the paper, and said to him with an air of authority, "Hand this to the president." The usher took the paper, glanced at it, and obeyed.

8. *INSIDE THE COURT*

WITHOUT suspecting the fact, the mayor of M. . . . enjoyed a species of celebrity. During the seven years that his reputation for virtue had filled the whole of the Bas Boulonnais, it had gradually crossed the border line into two or three adjoining departments. In addition to the considerable service he had done the chief town, by restoring the glass bead trade, there was not one of the hundred and forty parishes in the bailiwick of M. . . . which was not indebted to him for some kindness. He had ever assisted and promoted, when necessary, the trades of other departments; thus he had supported, with his credit and funds, the tulle factory at Boulogne, the flax-spinning machine at Nivers, and the hydraulic manufacture of canvas at Bourbus sur Cauche. The name of M. Madeleine was everywhere pronounced with veneration. And Arras and Douai envied the fortunate little town of M. . . . its mayor. The councilor of the royal court of Douai, who presided at the present Arras assizes, like every one else, was acquainted with this deeply and universally honored name. When the usher discreetly opened the door of the judges' robing-room, leaned over the president's chair, and handed him the paper, adding, "This gentleman wishes to hear the trial," the president made a deferential movement, took up a pen, wrote a few words at the foot of the paper, and returned it to the usher, saying, "Show him in."

The unhappy man whose history we are recording had remained near the door of the court at the same spot and in the same attitude as when the usher left him. He heard through his reverie some one say to him, "Will you do me the honor of following me, sir?" It was the same usher who had turned his back on him just before and was now bowing to the ground. At the same time the usher handed him the paper; he unfolded it, and as he happened to be near the lamps he was able to read, "The President of the assize court presents his respects to M. Madeleine." He crumpled the paper in his hands, as if the words had a strange and bitter after-taste for him. He followed the usher, and a few minutes later found himself alone in a stern-looking room, lighted by two wax candles standing on a green-baize-covered table. He still had in his ears the last words of the usher, who had just left him,—"You are in the council chamber; you have only to turn the handle of that door, and you will find yourself in court behind the president's chair." These words were mingled in his thoughts with a confused recollection of narrow passages and black staircases which he had just passed through. The usher had left him alone—the supreme moment had arrived. He tried to collect himself, but could not succeed; for it is especially in the hours when men have the most need of thought that all the threads are broken in the brain. He was at the actual spot where the judges deliberate and pass sentence. He gazed with stupid tranquility at this peaceful and yet formidable room, in which so many existences had been broken, where his name would be echoed ere long, and which his destiny was traversing at this moment. He looked at the walls and then at himself, astonished that it was this room and that it was he. He had not eaten for more than twenty-four hours, he was tired by the shaking of the cart, but he did not feel it; it seemed to him that he did not feel anything. He walked up to a black frame hanging on the wall, and which contained under glass an autograph letter of Jean Nicolas Pache, mayor of Paris, and minister, dated, doubtless in error, Juin 9 an II., and in which Pache sent to the commune a list of the ministers and deputies under arrest at their own houses. Any who saw him at this moment would doubtless have imagined that this letter appeared to him very curious, for he did not remove his eyes from it, and read it two or three times. But he read it without paying attention, and unconsciously he was thinking of Fantine and Cosette.

While thinking, he turned, and his eyes met the brass handle of the door that separated him from the assize court. He had almost forgotten this door, but his eye, at first calm, rested on it, then became wild and fixed, and was gradually filled with terror. Drops of perspiration stood out between his hair and poured down his temples. At one moment he made, with a species of authority blended with rebellion, that indescribable gesture which means and says so well,—"By heaven, who forces me?" Then he turned hurriedly, saw before him the door by which he had come in, walked up, opened it, and went out. He was no longer in that room, but in a passage, a long, narrow passage, cut up by steps and wickets, making all sorts of turns, lit up here and there by lamps resembling sick persons' night-lights—the passage by which he had come. He breathed, he listened, not a sound behind him, not a sound before him, and he began to fly as if he were pursued. When he had passed several turnings, he listened again,—there were still the same silence and gloom around him. He panted, tottered, and leaned against the wall; the stone was cold, the perspiration was frozen on his forehead, and he drew himself up with a shudder. Then, standing there alone, trembling from cold, and perhaps from something else, he thought. He had thought all night, he had thought all day; but he only heard within him a voice that said, Alas!

A quarter of an hour passed thus; at length he inclined his head, sighed with agony, let his arms droop, and turned back. He walked slowly, and as if stunned; it looked as if he had been caught up in his flight and was being brought back. He entered the board's room, and the first thing he saw was the handle of the door. This handle, which was round and made of polished brass, shone for him like a terrific star; he looked at it as a sheep would look at the eye of a tiger. His eyes would not leave it, and from time to time he took a step which brought him nearer to the door. Had he listened he would have heard, like a species of confused murmur, the noise in the adjoining court, but he did not listen and did not hear. All at once, and without knowing how, he found himself close to the door; he convulsively seized the handle, and the door opened. He was in the assize court.

9 . THE TRIAL

HE advanced a step, closed the door mechanically after him, and gazed at the scene before him. It was a dimly lighted large hall, at one moment full of sounds and at another of silence, in which all the machinery of a criminal trial was displayed, with its paltry and lugubrious gravity, in the midst of a crowd. At one of the ends of the hall, the one where he was, judges with a vacant look, in shabby gowns, biting their nails or shutting their eyelids; barristers in all sorts of attitudes; soldiers with honest, harsh faces; old stained wainscoting, a dirty ceiling; tables covered with baize, which was rather yellow than green; doors blackened by hands; pot-house sconces, that produce more smoke than light, hanging from nails driven into the wall; upon the tables brass candlesticks,—all was obscurity, ugliness, and sadness. But all this yet produced an austere and august impression, for the grand human thing called law and the great divine thing called justice could be felt in it.

No one in this crowd paid any attention to him, for all eyes converged on a single point—a wooden bench placed against a little door, along the wall on the left of the president. On this bench, which was illumined by several candles, sat a man between two gendarmes. This man was the man; he did not seek him, he saw him; his eyes went there naturally, as if they had known beforehand where that face was. He fancied he saw himself aged, not absolutely alike in face, but exactly similar in attitude and appearance, with his bristling hair, with his savage, restless eyeballs, and the blouse, just as he was on the day when he entered D. . . . , full of hatred, and concealing in his mind that hideous treasure of frightful thoughts which he had spent nineteen years in collecting on the pavement of the bagne. He said to himself with a shudder, "Great God, shall

I become again like that?" This being appeared to be at least sixty years of age; he had something about him rough, stupid, and startled. On hearing the sound of the door, persons made way for the new-comer; the president had turned his head, and guessing that the gentleman who had just entered was the mayor of M. . . . , he bowed to him. The public prosecutor, who had seen M. Madeleine at M. . . . , whither his duties had more than once called him, recognized him and also bowed. He scarce noticed it, for he was under a species of hallucination; he was looking at a judge, a clerk, gendarmes, a number of cruelly curious faces, —he had seen all this once, formerly, seven-and-twenty years ago. These mournful things he found again,—they were there, stirring, existing; it was no longer an effort of his memory, a mirage of his mind; they were real gendarmes, real judges, a real crowd, and real men in flesh and bone. He saw all the monstrous aspects of his past re-appear and live again around him, with all the terror that reality possesses. All this was yawning before him; he felt terrified, closed his eyes, and exclaimed in the depths of his mind, "Never!" And by a tragic sport of fate which made all his ideas terrible and rendered him nearly mad, it was another himself who was there. This man who was being tried, everybody called Jean Valjean. He had before him an unheard-of vision, a species of representation of the most horrible moment of his life played by his phantom. All was there,—it was the same machinery, the same hour of the night, almost the same faces of judges, soldiers, and spectators. The only difference was that there was a crucifix over the president's head, which had been removed from the courts at the time of his condemnation. When he was tried, God was absent. There was a chair behind him, into which he fell, terrified by the idea that people could see him. When he was seated, he took advantage of a pile of pasteboard cases on the judges' desk to hide his face from the spectators. He could now see without being seen; he fully regained the feeling of the real, and gradually recovered. He attained that phase of calmness in which a man can listen. Monsieur Bamatabois was serving on the jury. He looked for Javert, but could not see him, for the witnesses' bench was hidden by the clerk's table, and then, as we have said, the court was hardly lighted.

At the moment when he came in, the counsel for the defense was ending his speech. The attention of all was excited to the highest pitch; for three hours they had seen a man, a stranger, a species of miserable being, deeply stupid, or deeply clever, being gradually crushed by the weight of a terrible resemblance. This man, as we know already, was a vagabond who was found in a field, carrying a branch covered with ripe apples, which had been broken off a tree in a neighboring orchard. Who was this man? Inquiries had been made, and witnesses heard; they were unanimous, and light had been thrown by every incident of the trial. The prosecutor said "We have got hold not only of a fruit-stealer, a marauder, but we have under our hand a bandit, a man who has broken his ban, an ex-convict, a most dangerous villain, a malefactor of the name of Jean Valjean, whom justice has been seeking for a long time, and who, eight years ago, on leaving Toulon, committed a highway robbery with violence on a Savoyard lad, called Little Gervais, a crime provided for by Article 383 of the penal code, for which we intend to prosecute him hereafter, when the identity has been judicially proved. He has just committed a fresh robbery, and that is a case of relapse. Find him guilty of the new offense, and he will be tried at a later date for the old one." The prisoner seemed highly amazed at this accusation and the unanimity of the witnesses; he made gestures and signs, intended to deny, or else looked at the ceiling. He spoke with difficulty, answered with embarrassment, but from head to foot his whole person denied. He was like an idiot in the presence of all these intellects ranged in battle-array round him, and like a stranger in the midst of this society which seized him. Still, a most menacing future was hanging over him, the probability of his being Jean Valjean increased with each moment, and the entire crowd regarded with greater anxiety than himself the sentence of calamity which was gradually settling down on him. An eventuality even offered a glimpse of a death-penalty should the identity be proved, and he was hereafter found guilty of the attack on Little Gervais. Who was this man? Of what nature was his apathy? Was it imbecility or cunning? Did he understand too much, or did he understand nothing at all? These questions divided the crowd, and the jury seemed to share their opinion. There was in this trial something terrific and something puzzling; the drama was not only gloomy, but it was obscure.

The counsel for the defense had argued rather cleverly, in the provincial language which for a long time constituted the eloquence of the bar, and which all barristers formerly employed, not only at Paris, but at Romorantin or Montbrison, and which at the present day, having become classical, is only spoken by public prosecutors, whom it suits through its serious sonorousness and majestic movements. It is the language in which a husband is called a "consort"; a wife, a "spouse"; Paris, "the center of the arts and of civilization"; the king, the "monarch"; the bishop, a "holy pontiff"; the public prosecutor, the "eloquent interpreter of the majesty of the law"; the pleadings, the "accents which we have heard"; the age of Louis XIV, "the great age"; a theater, the "temple of Melpomene"; the reigning family, the "august blood of our kings"; a concert, "a musical solemnity"; the general commanding in the department, the "illustrious warrior who, etc."; the pupils of the seminary, "those tender Levites"; the mistakes imputed to the newspapers, "the imposture which distills its venom in the columns of these organs," etc., etc. The barrister had, consequently, begun by explaining away the robbery of the apples—rather a difficult thing in this grand style; but Bénigne Bossuet himself was obliged to allude to a fowl in the midst of a formal speech and got out of the difficulty with glory. The barrister had established the fact that the apple robbery was not materially proved. His client, whom, in his quality as defender, he persistently called Champmathieu, had not been seen by any one scaling a wall or breaking the branch; he had been arrested with the branch in his possession, but he declared that he found it on the ground and picked it up. Where was the proof of the contrary? This branch had been broken off and then thrown away by the frightened robber, for doubtless there was one. But where was the evidence that this Champmathieu was a robber? Only one thing—his being an ex-convict. The counsel did not deny that this fact seemed unluckily proved. The prisoner had lived at Faverolles; he had been a wood-cutter; the name Champmathieu might possibly be derived from Jean Mathieu; lastly, four witnesses unhesitatingly recognized Champmathieu as the galley-slave Jean Valjean. To these indications, to this testimony, the counsel could only oppose his client's denial, which was certainly interesting, but, even supposing that he was the convict Jean Mathieu, did that prove that he was the apple-stealer? it was a presumption at the most, but not a proof. The accused, it was true, —and his counsel was obliged "in his good faith" to allow it,—had adopted a bad system of defense; he insisted on denying everything,—not merely the robbery, but his quality as convict. A confession on the latter point would have doubtless been better, and gained him the indulgence of his judges; the counsel had advised him to do so, but the prisoner had obstinately refused, probably in the belief that he would save everything by confessing nothing. This was wrong, but should not his scanty intellect be taken into consideration? This man was visibly stupid; a long misery at the galleys, a long wretchedness out of them, had brutalized him, etc., etc.; his defense was bad, but was that a reason to find him guilty? As for the offense on Little Gervais, the counsel need not argue that, as it was not included in the indictment. The counsel wound up by imploring the jury and the court, if the identity of Jean Valjean appeared to them proved, to punish him as a criminal who had broken his ban, and not apply the fearful chastisement which falls on the relapsed convict.

The public prosecutor replied. He was violent and flowery, as public prosecutors usually are. He congratulated the counsel for the defense on his "fairness," and cleverly took advantage of it; he attacked the prisoner with all the concessions which his counsel had made. He appeared to allow that the prisoner was Jean Valjean, and he therefore was so. This was so much gained for the prosecution, and could not be contested; and here, reverting cleverly to the sources and causes of criminality, the public prosecutor thundered against the immorality of the romantic school, at that time in its dawn under the name of the "Satanic school," which the critics of the *Quotidienne* and the *Oriflamme* had given it; and he attributed, not without some show of reason, the crime of Champmathieu, or, to speak more correctly, of Jean Valjean, to this perverse literature. These reflections exhausted, he passed to Jean Valjean himself. Who was this Jean Valjean? Here came a description of Jean Valjean, a monster in human form, etc. The model of this sort of description will be found in the story of Théramène, which is not only useful to tragedy but daily renders great services to judicial eloquence. The audience and the jury "quivered," and when the description was ended, the public prosecutor went on with an oratorical outburst intended to excite to the highest pitch the enthusiasm of the country papers which would appear the next morning. "And it is such a man, etc., etc., etc., a vagabond, a beggar, having no means of existence, etc., etc., etc., accustomed through his past life to culpable action, and but little corrected by confinement in the bagne as is proved by the crime committed on Little Gervais, etc., etc., etc.,—it is such a man, who, found on the high-road with the proof of robbery in his hand, and a few paces from the wall he had climbed over, denies the fact, the robbery, denies everything, even to his name and his identity. In addition to a hundred proofs to which we will not revert, four witnesses recognize him,—Javert, the upright inspector of police, and three of his old comrades in ignominy, the convicts Brevet, Chenildieu, and Cochepaille. And what does he oppose to this crushing unanimity? he denies. What hardness of heart! But you will do justice, gentlemen of the jury, etc., etc., etc."

While the public prosecutor was speaking, the prisoner listened with open mouth, and with a sort of amazement in which there was certainly some admiration. He was evidently surprised that a man could speak like this. From time to time, at the most energetic apostrophes, when eloquence, unable to restrain itself, overflows in a flux of branding epithets, and envelopes the prisoner in a tempest, he slowly moved his head from right to left, and from left to right, in a sort of dumb and melancholy protest, with which he had contented himself ever since the beginning of the trial. Twice or thrice the spectators standing nearest to him heard him say in a low voice: "All this comes from not asking Monsieur Baloup." The public prosecutor drew the attention of the jury to this dull attitude, which was evidently calculated, and which denoted, not imbecility, but skill, cunning, and the habit of deceiving justice, and which brought out in full light the "profound perverseness" of this man. He concluded by reserving the affair of Little Gervais, and by demanding a severe sentence. The counsel for the defense rose, began by complimenting the public prosecutor on his "admirable speech," and then replied as well as he could, but feebly; it was plain that the ground was giving way under him.

10. *THE SYSTEM OF DENIALS*

THE moment for closing the trial had arrived; the president ordered the prisoner to stand up, and asked him the usual question: "Have you anything to add to your defense?" The man, who was rolling in his hands the hideous cap he had, made no reply, and the president repeated his question. This time the man heard, and seemed to understand; he moved like a person who is waking up, looked around him at the public, the gendarmes, his counsel, the jury, and the court, laid his monstrous fist on the wood-work in front of his bench, and, suddenly fixing his eyes on the public prosecutor, began to speak. It was an eruption; from the way in which the words escaped from his lips, incoherent, impetuous, and pell-mell, it seemed as if they were all striving to get out before each other. He said:

"I have this to say. That I was a wheelwright in Paris, and worked for Master Baloup. It is a hard trade is a wheelwright's; you always work in the open air, in yards, under sheds when you have a good master, but never in a room, because you want space, look you. In winter you are so cold that you swing your arms to warm you, but the masters don't like that, for they say it wastes time. Handling iron when there is ice between the stones, is rough work; it soon uses a man up. You are old when quite young in that trade. At forty a man is finished. I was fifty-three, and had hard lines of it. And then the workmen are so unkind. When a man is not so young as he was, they call him an old canary, an old brute! I only earned thirty sous a day, for the masters took advantage of my age, and paid me as little as they could. With that I had my daughter who was a washerwoman in the river. She earned a little for her part, and the pair of us managed to live. She was bothered, too. All day in a tub up to your waist, in the snow and rain, and with the wind that cuts your face. When it freezes, it is all the same, for you must wash; there are persons who have not much linen, and expect it home; if a woman did not wash, she would lose her customers. The planks are badly joined, and drops of water fall on you everywhere. Her petticoats were wet through, over and under. That penetrates. She also worked at the wash-house of the Enfants Rouges, where the water is got from taps. You are no longer in the tub; you wash at the tap before you, and rinse in the basin behind you. As it is shut up, you don't feel so cold. But there is a stream of hot water which ruins your sight. She came home at seven in the evening, and went to bed directly, for she was so tired. Her husband used to beat her. He is dead. We were not very happy. She was a good girl, who did not go to balls, and was very quiet. I remember a Mardi-gras on which she went to bed on eight o'clock. I am telling the truth. You need only inquire. Oh, yes, inquire! what an ass I am. Paris is a gulf. Who is there that knows Father Champmathieu? and yet, I tell you, Monsieur Baloup. Ask him. After all, I do not know what you want of me."

The man ceased speaking, and remained standing; he had said all this in a loud, quick, hoarse, hard voice, with a sort of wretched and savage energy. Once he broke off to bow to somebody in the crowd. The affirmations which he seemed to throw out hap-hazard came from him in gasps, and he accompanied each by the gesture of a man who is chopping wood. When he had finished, his hearers burst into a laugh; he looked at the public, seeing they were laughing, and understanding nothing, he began to laugh himself. That did him mischief. The president, a grave and kind man, began speaking. He reminded the "gentlemen of the jury" that "Monsieur Baloup, formerly a wheelwright in whose service the accused declared that he had been, was a bankrupt, and had not been found when an attempt was made to serve him with a subpœna." Then, turning to the prisoner, he requested him to listen to what he was about to say, and added: "You are in a situation which should cause you to reflect. The heaviest presumptions are weighing upon you, and may entail capital punishment. Prisoner, I ask you for the last time to explain yourself clearly on the two following facts: In the first place, did you—yes or no—climb over the wall, break a branch, and steal apples; that is to say, commit a robbery with escalade? secondly,—yes or no,—are you the liberated convict, Jean Valjean?"

The prisoner shook his head with a confident air, like a man who understands and knows what answer he is going to make. He opened his mouth, turned to the president, and said:

"In the first place—"

Then he looked at his cap, looked at the ceiling, and held his tongue.

"Prisoner," the public prosecutor said in a stern voice, "pay attention. You make no answer to the questions that are asked you, and your confusion condemns you. It is evident that your name is not Champmathieu, but Jean Valjean, at first concealed under the name of Jean Mathieu, your mother's name; that you went to Auvergne; that your birthplace is Faverolles, where you were a wood-cutter. It is evident that you stole ripe apples by clambering over a wall, and the gentlemen of the jury will appreciate the fact."

The prisoner had sat down again, but he hurriedly rose when the public prosecutor had finished, and exclaimed:

"You are a wicked man. This is what I wanted to say, but I could not think of it at first. I have stolen nothing, for I am a man who does not eat every day. I was coming from Ailly, and walking after a flood, which had made the whole country yellow; the very ponds had overflowed, and nothing grew in the sand except a few little blades of grass by the roadside. I found a branch with apples lying on the ground, and picked it up, little thinking it would bring me into trouble. I have been in prison and bullied for three months, and after that people talk against me, I don't know why, and say to me, 'Answer.' The gendarme, who is a good-hearted fellow, nudges me with his elbow, and says, 'Why don't you answer?' I cannot explain myself, for I am no scholar, but only a poor man, and you are wrong not to see it. I have not stolen, I have only picked up things lying on the ground. You talk about Jean Valjean and Jean Mathieu. I do not know these persons, they are country folk. I used to work for Monsieur Baloup, Boulevard de l'Hôpital, and my name is Champmathieu. You are a very clever fellow to tell me where I was born, for I don't know. It is not everybody who has a house to come into the world in. That would be too comfortable. I believe that my father and mother were persons who went about the roads, but I do not know it, after all. When I was a boy I was called little, and now I am called old. Those are my Christian names, and you can take them as you please. I have been in Auvergne, I have been at Faverolles. Well, may not a man have been at those two places without having been to the galleys? I tell you that I have not stolen, and that my name is Champmathieu. I worked for M. Baloup, and was a housekeeper. You vex me with your nonsense. Why is everybody so spiteful against me?"

The public prosecutor, who had not sat down, here addressed the president:

"In the presence of these confused but very clear denials on the part of the prisoner, who would like to pass for an idiot, but will not succeed, we warn him,—we request that it may please you, sir, and the court to recall the prisoners Brevet, Cochepaille, and Chenildieu, and Police Inspector Javert, and examine them again as to the identity of the prisoner with Jean Valjean."

"I must remark," said the president, "that Inspector Javert, having been recalled to his duties at a neighboring town, left the hall and the town immediately after giving his evidence; we authorized him to do so, with the consent of the public prosecutor and the counsel for the defense."

"Perfectly correct, sir," the public prosecutor continued. "In the absence of Inspector Javert, I believe it my duty to remind the gentlemen of the jury of the statement he made here a few hours ago. Javert is a worthy man, who honors by his rigorous and strict probity inferior but important functions. His evidence is as follows: 'I do not require moral presumptions and material proof to contradict the prisoner's assertions, for I recognize him perfectly. This man's name is not Champmathieu; he is Jean Valjean, an ex-convict of a very violent and formidable character.

It was with great reluctance that he was liberated when he completed his time. He had nineteen years' hard labor for qualified robbery, and made five or six attempts to escape. In addition to the Little Gervais robbery and the larceny of the apples, I also suspect him of a robbery committed in the house of his grandeur the late bishop of D. . . . . I frequently saw him when I was assistant jailer at Toulon, and I repeat that I recognize him perfectly'."

Such a precise declaration seemed to produce a lively effect on the audience and the jury, and the public prosecutor wound up by requesting that the other three witnesses should be brought in and reexamined. The president gave an order to an usher, and a moment after the door of the witness-room opened. The usher, accompanied by a gendarme, brought in the prisoner Brevet. The audience were all in suspense, and their chests heaved as if they had but one soul among them. The ex-convict Brevet wore the black and gray jacket of the central prisons; he was a man about sixty years of age, who had the face of a business man and the look of a rogue—these are sometimes seen together. He had become a sort of jailer in the prison to which new offenses had brought him, and was a man of whom the officials said, "He tries to make himself useful." The chaplains bore good testimony to his religious habits, and it must not be forgotten that this trial took place under the Restoration.

"Brevet," said the president, "as you have undergone a degrading punishment, you cannot be sworn."

Brevet looked down humbly.

"Still," the president continued, "there may remain, by the permission of Heaven, a feeling of honor and equity even in the man whom the law has degraded, and it is to that feeling I appeal in this decisive hour. If it still exist in you, as I hope, reflect before answering me. Consider, on one hand, this man whom a word from you may ruin; on the other, the justice which a word from you may enlighten. The moment is a solemn one, and there is still time for you to retract, if you believe you are mistaken. Prisoner, stand up. Brevet, look at the prisoner. Think over your past recollections and tell us on your soul and conscience whether you still persist in recognizing this man as your old mate at the galleys, Jean Valjean."

Brevet looked at the prisoner, and then turned to the court.

"Yes, sir, I was the first who recognized him, and I adhere to it. This man is Jean Valjean, who came to Toulon in 1796 and left in 1815. I came out a year later. He looks like a brute now, but in that case age has brutalized him, for he was cunning at the hulks. I recognize him positively."

"Go and sit down," said the president. "Prisoner, remain standing."

Chenildieu was next brought in, a convict for life, as was shown by his red jacket and green cap. He was serving his time at Toulon, whence he had been fetched for this trial. He was a little man about fifty years of age, quick, wrinkled, thin, yellow, bold, and feverish, who had in all his limbs and his whole person a sort of sickly weakness, and immense force in his look. His mates at the galleys had surnamed him Je-nie-Dieu. The president addressed him much as he had done Brevet. At the moment when he reminded him that his degradation robbed him of the right of taking an oath, Chenildieu raised his head and looked boldly at the crowd. The president begged him to reflect, and asked him if he still persisted in recognizing the prisoner. Chenildieu burst into a laugh:

"I should think I do! why, we were fastened to the same chain for five years. So you are sulky, old fellow?"

"Go and sit down," said the president.

The usher brought in Cochepaille. This second convict for life who had been fetched from the galleys and was dressed in red like Chenildieu, was a peasant of Lourdes and a semi-bear of the Pyrenees. He had been a shepherd in the mountains, and had gradually slipped into brigandage. Cochepaille was no less savage, and appeared even more stupid than the prisoner; he was one of those wretched men whom nature has sketched as wild beasts and whom society finishes as galley-slaves. The president tried to move him by a few grave and pathetic words, and asked him, like the two others, whether he still persisted, without any hesitation or trouble, in recognizing the man standing before him.

"It is Jean Valjean," said Cochepaille. "He was nicknamed Jean the Jack, because he was so strong."

Each of the affirmations of these three men, evidently sincere and made in good faith, had aroused in the audience a murmur of evil omen for the prisoner—a murmur which grew louder and more prolonged each time that a new declaration was added to the preceding one. The prisoner himself listened to them with that amazed face which, according to the indictment, was his principal means of defense. At the first the gendarmes heard him grind between his teeth, "Well, there's one," after the second he said rather louder, and with an air of satisfaction, "Good!" at the third he exclaimed, "Famous!" The president addressed him:

"You have heard the evidence, prisoner; have you any answer to make?"

He answered:

"I say—famous!"

A laugh broke out in the audience and almost affected the jury. It was plain that the man was lost.

"Ushers," said the president, "produce silence in the court; I am about to sum up."

At this moment there was a movement by the president's side, and a voice could be heard exclaiming:

"Brevet, Chenildieu, and Cochepaille, look this way." All those who heard the voice felt chilled to the heart, for it was so lamentable and terrible. All eyes were turned in the direction whence it came; a man seated among the privileged audience behind the court had risen, pushed open the gate that separated the judges' bench from the public court, and stepped down. The president, the public prosecutor, M. Bamatabois, twenty persons, recognized him, and exclaimed simultaneously, "Monsieur Madeleine!"

11. CHAMPMATHIEU MORE AND MORE ASTOUNDED

It was he, in truth; the clerk's lamp lit up his face; he held his hat in his hand, there was no disorder in his attire, and his coat was carefully buttoned. He was very pale and trembled slightly, and his hair, which had been gray when he arrived at Arras, was now perfectly white—it had turned so during the hour he had passed in the court. Every head was raised, the sensation was indescribable, and there was a momentary hesitation among the spectators. The voice had been so poignant, the man standing there seemed so calm, that at first they did not understand, and asked each other who it was that had spoken. They could not believe that this tranquil man could have uttered that terrific cry. This indecision lasted but a few moments. Before the president and the public prosecutor could say a word, before the gendarmes and ushers could make a move, the man, whom all still called at this moment M. Madeleine, had walked up to the witnesses, Brevet, Chenildieu, and Cochepaille.

"Do you not recognize me?" he asked them.

All three stood amazed, and gave a nod to show that they did not know him, and Cochepaille, who was intimidated, gave a military salute. M. Madeleine turned to the jury and the court, and said in a gentle voice:

"Gentlemen of the jury, acquit the prisoner. Monsieur le President, have me arrested. The man you are seeking is not he, for—I am Jean Valjean."

Not a breath was drawn,—the first commotion of astonishment had been succeeded by a sepulchral silence; all felt that species of religious terror which seizes on a crowd when something grand is being accomplished. The president's face, however, displayed sympathy and sorrow; he exchanged a rapid look with the public prosecutor, and a few words in a low voice with the assessors. He then turned to the spectators, and asked with an accent which all understood:

"Is there a medical man present?"

The public prosecutor then said:

"Gentlemen of the jury, the strange and unexpected incident which has disturbed the trial inspires us, as it does yourselves, with a feeling which we need not express. You all know, at least by reputation, the worthy M. Madeleine, Mayor of M. . . . ; if there be a medical man here, we join with the president in begging him to attend M. Madeleine and remove him to his house."

M. Madeleine did not allow the public prosecutor to conclude, but interrupted him with an accent full of gentleness and authority. These are the words he spoke; we produce them literally as they were written down by one of the witnesses of this scene, and as they still live in the ears of those who heard them just forty years ago:

"I thank you, sir, but I am not mad, as you will soon see. You were on the point of committing a great error. Set that man at liberty; I am accomplishing a duty, for I am the hapless convict. I am the only man who sees clearly here, and I am telling you the truth. What I am doing at this moment, God above is looking at, and that is sufficient for me. You can seize me, for here I am; and yet I did my best. I hid myself under a name, I became rich, I became mayor, and I wished to get back among honest men, but it seems that this is impossible. There are many things I cannot tell you, as I am not going to describe my life to you, for one day it will be known. It is true that I robbed the bishop; also that I robbed Little Gervais, and they were right in telling you that Jean Valjean was a dangerous villain—though perhaps all the fault did not lie with him. Listen, gentlemen of the court. A man so debased as myself cannot remonstrate with Providence, or give advice to society; but I will say that the infamy from which I sought to emerge is an injurious thing, and the galleys make the convict. Be good enough to bear that fact in mind. Before I went to Toulon I was a poor peasant, with but little intelligence and almost an idiot; but the galleys changed me. I was stupid, and became wicked; I was a log, and I became a brand. At a later date indulgence and goodness saved me, in the same way as severity had destroyed me. But, forgive me, you cannot understand what I am saying. At my house the two-franc piece I stole seven years ago from Little Gervais will be found among the ashes in the fire-place. I have nothing more to add, so seize me. Good Heavens! the public prosecutor shakes his head. You say M. Madeleine has gone mad, and do not believe me. This is afflicting; at least, do not condemn this man. What! these three do not recognize me! Oh, I wish that Javert were here, for he would recognize me!"

No pen could render the benevolent and sombre melancholy of the accent which accompanied these words. He then turned to the three convicts:

"Well, I recognize you. Brevet, do you not remember me?" He broke off, hesitated for a moment, and said:

"Can you call to mind the chequered braces you used to wear at the galleys?"

Brevet gave a start of surprise and looked at him from head to foot in terror. He continued:

"Chenildieu,—who called yourself Je-nie-Dieu,—you have a deep burn in your right shoulder, because you placed it one day on a pan of charcoal in order to efface the three letters, T. F. P., which, however, are still visible. Answer me—is it so?"

"It is true," said Chenildieu.

"Cochepaille, you have near the hollow of your left arm a date made in blue letters with burnt gunpowder; the date is that of the emperor's landing at Cannes, March 1, 1815. Turn up your sleeve."

Cochepaille did so, and every eye was turned to his bare arm; a gendarme brought up a lamp, and the date was there. The unhappy man turned to the audience and the judges, with a smile, which to this day affects those who saw it. It was the smile of triumph, but it was also the smile of despair.

"You see plainly," he said, "that I am Jean Valjean."

In the hall there were now neither judges, accusers, nor gendarmes; there were only fixed eyes and heaving hearts. No one thought of the part he might be called on to perform—the public prosecutor that he was there to prove a charge, the president to pass sentence, and the prisoner's counsel to defend. It was a striking thing that no question was asked, no authority interfered. It is the property of sublime spectacles to seize on all minds and make spectators of all the witnesses. No one perhaps accounted for his feelings, no one said to himself that he saw a great light shining, but all felt dazzled in their hearts. It was evident that they had Jean Valjean before them. The appearance of this man had been sufficient to throw a bright light on the affair which was so obscure a moment previously; without needing any explanation, the entire crowd understood, as if through a sort of electric revelation, at once and at a glance, the simple and magnificent story of a man who denounced himself in order that another man might not be condemned in his place. Details, hesitation, any possible resistance, were lost in this vast, luminous fact. It was an impression which quickly passed away, but at the moment was irresistible.

"I will not occupy the time of the court longer," Jean Valjean continued; "I shall go away, as I am not arrested, for I have several things to do. The public prosecutor knows who I am, he knows where I am going, and he will order me to be arrested when he thinks proper."

He walked toward the door, and not a voice was raised, not an arm stretched forth to prevent him. All fell back, for there was something divine in this incident, which causes the multitude to recoil and make way for a single man. He walked on; it was never known who opened the door, but it is certain that he found it opened when he reached it. When there, he turned and said:

"I am at your orders, sir."

Then he addressed the audience:

"I presume that all of you consider me worthy of pity? Great God, when I think of what I was on the point of doing, I consider myself worthy of envy. Still I should have preferred that all this had not taken place."

He went out, and the door was closed as it had been opened, for men
who do certain superior deeds are always sure of being served by some
one in the crowd. Less than an hour after, the verdict of the jury acquitted
Champmathieu, and Champmathieu, who was at once set at liberty,
went away in stupefaction, believing all the men mad, and not at all
comprehending this vision.

BOOK VIII

THE COUNTERSTROKE

1 . M. MADELEINE LOOKS AT HIS HAIR

DAY was beginning to dawn. Fantine had passed a sleepless and feverish night, though full of bright visions, and toward morning fell asleep. Sister Simplice, who was watching, took advantage of this slumber to go and prepare a fresh dose of bark. The worthy sister had been for some time in the surgery, stooping over her drugs and bottles, and looking carefully at them on account of the mist which dawn spreads over objects. All at once she turned her head and gave a slight shriek. M. Madeleine had entered silently, and was standing before her.

"Is it you, sir?" she exclaimed.

He answered in a low voice:

"How is the poor creature?"

"Not so bad just at present, but she has frightened us terribly."

She explained to him what had occurred, how Fantine had been very ill the previous day, but was now better, because she believed that he had gone to Montfermeil to fetch her child. The sister did not dare question him, but she could see from his looks that he had not been there at all.

"All that is well," he said. "You did right in not undeceiving her."

"Yes," the sister continued, "but now that she is going to see you, sir, and does not see her child, what are we to tell her?"

He remained thoughtful for a moment.

"God will inspire us," he said.

"Still, it is impossible to tell a falsehood," the sister murmured in a low voice.

It was now bright day in the room, and it lit up M. Madeleine's face. The sister raised her eyes by chance.

275

"Good gracious, sir," she exclaimed, "what can have happened to you? Your hair is quite white."

"What!" he said.

Sister Simplice had no mirror, but she took from a drawer a small looking-glass which the infirmary doctor employed to make sure that a patient was dead. M. Madeleine took this glass, looked at his hair, and said, "So it is." He said it carelessly and as if thinking of something else, and the sister felt chilled by some unknown terror of which she caught a glimpse in all this. He asked:

"Can I see her?"

"Will you not procure her child for her, sir?" the sister said, hardly daring to ask the question.

"Of course; but it will take at least two or three days."

"If she were not to see you till then, sir," the sister continued timidly, "she would not know that you had returned; it would be easy to keep her quiet, and when her child arrived she would naturally think that you had returned with it. That would not be telling a falsehood."

M. Madeleine appeared to reflect for a few moments, and then said with his calm gravity:

"No, sister, I must see her, for I am possibly pressed for time."

The nun did not seem to notice the word "possibly," which gave an obscure and singular meaning to the mayor's remark. She answered in a low voice:

"In that case you can go in, sir, though she is asleep."

He made a few remarks about a door that closed badly and whose creaking might awake the patient, then entered Fantine's room, went up to the bed, and opened the curtains. She was asleep; her breath issued from her chest with that tragic sound, peculiar to these diseases, which crushes poor mothers who sit up at nights by the side of their sleeping child for whom there is no hope. But this painful breathing scarce disturbed an ineffable serenity spread over her face, which transfigured her in her sleep. Her pallor had become whiteness; her cheeks were carnations. Her long, fair eye-lashes, the sole beauty that remained of her virginity and youth, quivered, though remaining closed. Her whole person trembled as if she had wings which were on the point of expanding and bearing her away. To see her thus, no one could have believed that she was in an almost hopeless state, for she resembled rather a woman who is about to fly away than one who is going to die. The branch, when the hand approaches to pluck the flowers, quivers and seems at once to retire and advance. The human body undergoes something like this quiver when the moment arrives for the mysterious fingers of death to pluck the soul.

M. Madeleine stood for some time motionless near this bed, looking first at the patient and then at the crucifix, as he had done two months previously, on the day when he came the first time to see her in this asylum. They were both in the same attitude—she sleeping, he praying; but in those two months her hair had turned gray, and his white. The sister had not come in with him; he was standing by the bedside, finger on lip, as if there were some one in the room whom he was bidding to be silent. She opened her eyes, saw him, and said calmly and with a smile.

"And Cosette?"

2. *FANTINE IS HAPPY*

SHE gave no start of surprise, no start of joy, for she was joy itself. The simple question, "And Cosette?" was asked in such profound faith, with so much certainty, with such an utter absence of anxiety and doubt, that he could not find a word to say. She continued:

"I knew you were there, for though I was asleep, I saw. I have seen you for a long time, and have been looking after you all night; you were in a glory, and had around you all sorts of heavenly faces."

She looked up to the crucifix.

"But," she continued, "tell me where Cosette is? why was she not laid in my bed so that I could see her directly I woke?"

He answered something mechanically which he could never remember. Luckily the physician, who had been sent for, came to M. Madeleine's assistance.

"My dear girl," said the physician, "calm yourself; your child is here."

Fantine's eyes sparkled and covered her whole face with brightness;

she clasped her hands with an expression which contained all the violence and all the gentleness a prayer can have simultaneously.

"Oh," she exclaimed, "bring her to me!"

Touching maternal illusion! Cosette was still to her the little child who must be carried.

"Not yet," the physician continued, "not at this moment; you have a little fever hanging about you; the sight of your child would agitate you and do you harm. You must get well first."

She impetuously interrupted him:

"But I am well! I tell you I am well. What a donkey this doctor is. I insist on seeing my child."

"There, you see," the physician said, "how violent you are! So long as you are like that, I will prevent your having your child. It is not enough to see her, but you must live for her. When you grow reasonable, I will bring her myself."

The poor mother hung her head.

"Doctor, I ask your pardon; I sincerely ask your pardon. In former times I should not have spoken as I did just now, but I have gone through so much unhappiness that I do not know at times what I am saying. I understand; you are afraid of the excitement; I will wait as long as you like, but I swear to you that it would not do me any harm to see my child. Is it not very natural that I should want to see my child, who has been fetched from Montfermeil expressly for me? I am not angry, for I know very well that I am going to be happy. The whole night I have seen white things and smiling faces. The doctor will bring me Cosette when he likes; I have no fever now, because I am cured; I feel that there is nothing the matter with me, but I will behave as if I were ill, and not stir, so as to please these ladies. When you see that I am quite calm, you will say, we must give her her child."

M. Madeleine had seated himself in a chair by the bedside; she turned to him, visibly making an effort to appear calm and "very good," as she said in that weakness of illness which resembles childhood, in order that, on seeing her so peaceful, there might be no difficulty in bringing Cosette to her. Still, while checking herself, she could not refrain from asking M. Madeleine a thousand questions.

"Have you had a pleasant journey, sir? Oh, how kind it was of you to go and fetch her for me! Only tell me how she is. Did she stand the journey well? Alas! she will not recognize, she will have forgotten me in all this time, poor darling. Children have no memory. They are like the birds; to-day they see one thing and another to-morrow, and do not think about anything. Had she got clean underclothing? did those Thénardiers keep her clean? What food did they give her? Oh, if you only knew how I suffered when I asked myself all these questions during the period of my wretchedness! but now it is all passed away and I am happy. Oh! how I should like to see her! Did you not find her very pretty, sir? You must have been very cold in the stage-coach? Can she not be brought here if only for a moment? she could be taken away again directly afterward. You could do it if you liked, as you are the mayor."

He took her hand and said: "Cosette is lovely, she is well, you will see her soon, but calm yourself. You speak too eagerly, and put your arms out of bed, which will make you cough."

In fact, a fit of coughing interrupted Fantine at nearly every word. She did not object, she feared lest she had injured the confidence she had wished to inspire, by some too impassioned entreaties, and she began talking of indifferent matters.

"Montfermeil is rather a pretty place, is it not? In summer, pleasure parties go there. Have those Thénardiers a good trade? not many people pass through the village, and theirs is a sort of pot-house."

M. Madeleine still held her hand, and was looking at her anxiously; it was evident that he had come to tell her something at which he now hesitated. The physician had left and Sister Simplice alone remained near them. "I can hear her, I can hear her!" She held out her arms to command silence, held her breath, and began listening with ravishment. A child was playing in the yard, and probably belonged to one of the workmen. It was one of those accidents which constantly occur and seem to form part of the mysterious *mise-en-scene* of mournful events. The child, a little girl, was running about to warm herself, laughing and singing loudly. Alas! what is there in which children's games are not mingled?

"Oh!" Fantine continued, " 'tis my Cosette! I recognize her voice."

The child went away again. Her voice died away. Fantine listened for some time, and then her face was clouded and M. Madeleine could hear her murmuring, "How unkind that doctor is not to let me see my child! That man has a bad face."

Still, her merry ideas returned to her, and she continued to talk to herself, with her head on the pillow. "How happy we are going to be! We will have a small garden, for M. Madeleine has promised me that. My child will play in the garden. She must know her alphabet by this time, and I will teach her to spell. She will chase butterflies, and I shall look at her. Then she will take her first communion; let me see when that will be."

She began counting on her fingers:

"One, two, three, four—she is now seven years old; in five years, then, she will wear a white open-work veil, and look like a little lady. Oh, my good sister, you cannot think how foolish I am, for I am thinking of my daughter's first communion."

And she began laughing. He had let go Fantine's hand, and listened to these words as one listened to the soughing breeze, with his eyes fixed on the ground, and his mind plunged into unfathomable reflections. All at once she ceased speaking; and this made him raise his head mechanically. Fantine had become frightful to look at. She no longer spoke, she no longer breathed; she was half sitting up, and her thin shoulder projected from her night-gown; her face, radiant a moment previously, was hard, and she seemed to be fixing her eyes, dilated by terror, upon something formidable that stood at the other end of the room.

"Great Heaven!" he exclaimed, "What is the matter with you, Fantine?"

She did not answer, she did not remove her eyes from the object—whatever it might be—which she fancied she saw; but she touched his arm with one hand, and with the other made him a sign to look behind him. He turned back and saw Javert.

3. *JAVERT IS SATISFIED*

THIS is what had occurred. Half-past twelve was striking when M. Madeleine left the assize court of Arras; and he returned to the hotel just in time to start by the mail-cart in which he had booked his place. A little before six A. M. he reached M. . . . , and his first care was to post the letter for M. Lafitte, and then proceed to the infirmary and see Fantine. Still, he had scarce quitted the court ere the public prosecutor, recovering from his stupor, rose on his legs, deplored the act of mania on the part of the honorable mayor of M. . . . , declared that his convictions were in no way modified by this strange incident, which would be cleared up at a later date, and demanded in the interim the conviction of this Champmathieu, evidently the true Jean Valjean. The persistency of the public prosecutor was visibly in contradiction with the feelings of all,—the public, the court, and the jury. The counsel for the defense had little difficulty in refuting his arguments and establishing that through the revelations of M. Madeleine, that is to say, the real Jean Valjean, circumstances were entirely altered, and the jury had an innocent man before them. The barrister deduced a few unluckily rather stale arguments about judicial errors, etc.; the president, in his summing-up, supported the defense, and the jury in a few moments acquitted Champmathieu. Still, the public prosecutor wanted a Jean Valjean; and, as he no longer had Champmathieu, he took Madeleine. Immediately after Champmathieu was acquitted, he had a conference with the president as to the necessity of seizing the person of the mayor of M. . . . , and after the first emotion had passed, the president raised but few objections. Justice must take its course, and then, to tell the whole truth, although the president was a kind and rather sensible man, he was at the same time a very ardent Royalist, and had been offended by the way in which the mayor of M. . . . , in alluding to the landing at Cannes, employed the words "the emperor," and not "Bonaparte." The order of arrest was consequently made out, and the prosecutor at once sent it off by express to M. . . . , addressed to Inspector Javert, who, as we know, returned home immediately after he had given his evidence.

Javert was getting up at the moment when the messenger handed him the order of arrest and the warrant. This messenger was himself a very skillful policeman, who informed Javert in two words of what had occurred at Arras. The order of arrest, signed by the public prosecutor, was thus conceived: "Inspector Javert will apprehend Monsieur Madeleine, mayor of M. . . . , who in this day's session was recognized as the liberated convict, Jean Valjean." Any one who did not know Javert and had seen him at the moment when he entered the infirmary anteroom, could not have guessed what was taking place, but would have considered him to be as usual. He was cold, calm, serious, his gray hair was smoothed down on his temples, and he went up the stairs with his usual slowness. But any one who was acquainted with him, and examined him closely, would have shuddered; the buckle of his leather stock, instead of sitting in the nape of his neck, was under his left ear. This revealed an extraordinary agitation. Javert was a complete character, without a crease in his duty or in his uniform; methodical with criminals, and rigid with his coat-buttons. For him to have his stock out of order, it was necessary for him to be suffering from one of those emotions which might be called internal earthquakes. He had merely fetched a corporal and four men from the guard-house close by, left them in the yard, and had Fantine's room pointed out to him by the unsuspecting portress, who was accustomed to see policemen ask for the mayor.

On reaching Fantine's door, Javert turned the key, pushed the door with the gentleness either of a sick nurse or a spy, and entered. Correctly speaking, he did not enter; he stood in the half-opened door with his hat on his head, and his left hand thrust into the breast of his great-coat, which was buttoned to the chin. Under his elbow could be seen the leaden knob of his enormous cane, which was concealed behind his back. He remained thus for nearly a minute, no one perceiving his presence. All at once Fantine raised her eyes, saw him, and made M. Madeleine turn. At the moment when Madeleine's glance met Javert's, the latter, without stirring or drawing near, became fearful. No human feeling can succeed in being so horrible as joy. It was the face of a fiend who has just found a condemned soul again. The certainty of at length holding Jean Valjean caused all he had in his soul to appear on his countenance, and the stirred-up sediment rose to the surface. The humiliation of having lost the trail for a while and having been mistaken with regard to Champmathieu was effaced by his pride at having guessed so correctly at the beginning, and having a right instinct for such a length of time. Javert's satisfaction was displayed in his sovereign attitude, and the deformity of triumph was spread over his narrow forehead.

Javert at this moment was in Heaven; without distinctly comprehending the fact, but still with a confused intuition of his necessity and his success, he, Javert, personified justice, light, and truth in their celestial function of crushing evil. He had behind him, around him, at an infinite depth, authority, reason, the legal conscience, the public vindication, all the stars; he protected order, he drew the lightning from the law, he avenged society, he rendered assistance to the absolute. There was in his victory a remnant of defiance and contest; upright, haughty, and dazzling, he displayed the superhuman bestiality of a ferocious archangel in the bright azure of Heaven. The formidable shadow of the deed he was doing rendered visible to his clutching fist the flashing social sword. Happy and indignant, he held beneath his heel crime, vice, perdition, rebellion, and hell; he was radiant, he exterminated, he smiled, and there was an incontestable grandeur in this monstrous St. Michael. Javert, though terrifying, was not ignoble. Probity, sincerity, candor, conviction, and the idea of duty are things which, by deceiving themselves, may become hideous, but which, even if hideous, remain grand; their majesty, peculiar to the human conscience, persists in horror; they are virtues which have but one vice, error. The pitiless joy of a fanatic, in the midst of his atrocity, retains a mournfully venerable radiance. Without suspecting it, Javert, in his formidable happiness, was worthy of pity, like every ignorant man who triumphs; nothing could be so poignant and terrible as this face, in which was displayed all that may be called the **wickedness of good.**

4. AUTHORITY RESUMES ITS RIGHTS

FANTINE had not seen Javert since the day when the mayor tore her out of his clutches, and her sickly brain could form no other thought but that he had come to fetch her. She could not endure his frightful face; she felt herself dying. She buried her face in her hands, and cried with agony:

"Monsieur Madeleine, save me!"

Jean Valjean—we will not call him otherwise in future—had risen, and said to Fantine in his gentlest, calmest voice:

"Do not be alarmed; he has not come for you."

Then he turned to Javert and said:

"I know what you want."

And Javert answered:

"Come, make haste—"

There was something savage and frenzied in the accent that accompanied these words; no orthographer could write it down, for it was no longer human speech, but a roar. He did not behave as usual, he did not enter into the matter or display his warrant. To him Jean Valjean was a sort of mysterious combatant, a dark wrestler with whom he had been struggling for five years, and had been unable to throw him. This arrest was not a beginning but an end, and he confined himself to saying, "Come, make haste." While speaking thus, he did not advance; he merely darted at Jean Valjean the look which he threw out as a grapple, and with which he violently drew wretches to him. It was this hook which Fantine had felt pierce to her marrow two months before. On hearing Javert's roar, Fantine opened her eyes again; but the mayor was present, so what had she to fear? Javert walked into the middle of the room and cried:

"Well, are you coming?"

The unhappy girl looked around her. No one was present but the nun and the mayor; to whom, then, could this humiliating remark be addressed? only to herself. She shuddered. Then she saw an extraordinary thing, so extraordinary that nothing like it had ever appeared in the darkest delirium of fever. She saw the policeman Javert seize the mayor by the collar, and she saw the mayor bow his head. It seemed to her as if the end of the world had arrived.

"Monsieur le Maire!" Fantine screamed.

Javert burst into a laugh, that frightful laugh which showed all his teeth.

"There is no Monsieur le Maire here."

Jean Valjean did not attempt to remove the hand that grasped his collar; he said:

"Javert—"

Javert interrupted him: "Call me Monsieur the Inspector."

"I should like to say a word to you in private, sir," Jean Valjean continued.

"Speak up," Javert answered, "people talk aloud to me."

Jean Valjean went on in a low voice:

"It is a request I have to make of you."

"I tell you to speak up."

"But it must only be heard by yourself—"

"What do I care for that? I am not listening!"

Jean Valjean turned to him and said rapidly, and in a very low voice:

"Grant me three days! three days to go and fetch this unhappy wo-man's child! I will pay whatever you ask, and you can accompany me if you like."

"You must be joking," Javert cried. "Why, I did not think you such a fool! You ask three days of me that you may bolt! You say that it is to fetch this girl's brat! ah, ah, that is fine, very fine."

Fantine had a tremor.

"My child," she exclaimed, "to go and fetch my child? Then she is not here! Sister, answer me,—where is Cosette? I want my child! Mon-sieur Madeleine, M. le Maire!"

Javert stamped his foot.

"There is the other beginning now; will you be quiet, wench? A devil's own country, where galley-slaves are magistrates, and street-walkers are nursed like countesses. Well, well, it will be altered now, and it's time for it."

He looked fixedly at Fantine, and added, as he took a fresh hold of Jean Valjean's cravat, shirt, and coat-collar:

"I tell you there is no M. Madeleine and no Monsieur le Maire, but there is a robber, a brigand, a convict of the name of Jean Valjean, and I've got him,—that's what there is."

Fantine rose, supporting herself on her stiffened arms and hands; she looked at Jean Valjean; she looked at Javert; she looked at the nun; she opened her mouth as if to speak, but there was a rattle in her throat, her teeth chattered, she stretched out her arms, convulsively opening her hands, clutching like a drowning man, and then suddenly fell back on the pillow. Her head struck against the bed-head, and fell back on her breast with gaping mouth and open eyes;—she was dead. Jean Valjean laid his hand on that one of Javert's which held him, opened it as if it had been a child's hand, and then said to Javert:

"You have killed this woman."

"Enough of this," Javert shouted furiously. "I am not here to listen to abuse, so you can save your breath. There is a guard below, so come quickly, or I shall handcuff you."

There was in a corner of the room an old iron bedstead in a bad condition, which the sisters used as a sofa when they were sitting up at night. Jean Valjean went to this bed, tore off in a twinkling the head-piece, an easy thing for muscles like his, seized the supporting bar, and looked at Javert. Javert recoiled to the door. Jean Valjean, with the iron bar in his hand, walked slowly up to Fantine's bed; when he reached it, he turned and said to Javert in a scarcely audible voice:

"I would advise you not to disturb me just at present."

One thing is certain,—Javert trembled. He thought of going to fetch the guard, but Jean Valjean might take advantage of the moment to escape. He, therefore, remained, clutched his stick by the small end and leaned against the door-post, without taking his eyes off Jean Valjean. The latter rested his elbow on the bedstead, and his forehead on his hand, and began contemplating Fantine, who lay motionless before him. He remained thus, absorbed and silent, and evidently not thinking of anything else in the world. On his face and in his attitude there was only an indescribable pity. After a few minutes passed in this reverie, he stooped over Fantine and spoke to her in a low voice. What did he say to her? what could this outcast man say to this dead woman? No one on earth heard the words, but did that dead woman hear them? There are touching illusions, which are perhaps sublime realities. One thing is indubitable, that Sister Simplice, the sole witness of what took place, has frequently declared, that, at the moment when Jean Valjean whispered in Fantine's ear, she distinctly saw an ineffable smile playing round her pale lips and in her vague eyeballs, which were full of the amazement of the tomb. Jean Valjean took Fantine's head in his hands, and laid it on the pillow, as a mother might have done to a child. Then he tied the strings of her night-gown, and thrust her hair under her cap. When this was done, he closed her eyes. Fantine's face at this moment seemed strangely illumined, for death is the entrance into brilliant light. Fantine's hand was hanging out of bed; Jean Valjean knelt down by this hand, gently raised and kissed it. Then he rose and returned to Javert:

"Now I am at your service."

5. *A FITTING TOMB*

JAVERT placed Jean Valjean in the town jail. The arrest of M. Madeleine
produced an extraordinary commotion in M. . . . , but it is sad to have
to say that nearly everybody abandoned him on hearing that he was a
galley-slave. In less than two hours all the good he had done was forgotten, and he was only a galley-slave. It is fair to say though, that they
did not yet know the details of the affair at Arras. The whole day
through, conversations like the following could be heard in all parts
of the town;

"Don't you know? he is a liberated convict.—Who is?—The mayor.—
Nonsense. M. Madeleine?—Yes.—Really?—His name is not Madeleine,
but some hideous thing like Bejean, Bojean, Boujean.—Oh, my goodness
—he has been arrested, and will remain in the town jail till he is removed.
—Removed? where to?—He will be tried at the assizes for a highway
robbery which he formerly committed.—Well, do you know I always
suspected that man, for he was too kind, too perfect, too devout. He
refused the cross, and gave half-pence to all the little scamps he met. I
always thought that there was some black story behind."

The "drawing-rooms" greatly improved the occasion. An old lady,
who subscribed to the *Drapeau blanc,* made this remark, whose depth it
is almost impossible to fathom:

"Well, I do not feel sorry at it, for it will be a lesson to the Bonapartists."

It is thus that the phantom which called itself M. Madeleine faded
away at M. . . . . Only three or four persons in the whole town remained
faithful to his memory, and his old servant was one of them. On the
evening of the same day this worthy old woman was sitting in her lodge,
still greatly startled and indulging in sad thoughts. The factory had been
closed all day, gates were bolted, and the street was deserted. There was

no one in the house but the two nuns, who were watching by Fantine's body. Toward the hour when M. Madeleine was wont to come in, the worthy portress rose mechanically, took the key of M. Madeleine's bedroom from a drawer, and the candlestick which he used at night to go upstairs; then she hung the key on the nail from which he usually took it, and placed the candlestick by its side, as if she expected him. Then she sat down again and began thinking. The poor old woman had done all this unconsciously. She did not break off her reverie for two or three hours, and then exclaimed: "Only think of that! I have hung his key on the nail!"

At this moment the window of the lodge was opened, a hand was passed through the opening, which seized the key and lit the candle by hers. The portress raised her eyes and stood with gaping mouth, but she repressed the cry which was in her throat; for she recognized this hand, this arm, this coat-sleeve, as belonging to M. Madeleine. It was some minutes ere she could speak, for she "was struck," as she said afterward when describing the adventure.

"Good gracious, M. le Maire," she at length exclaimed, "I fancied—"

She stopped, for the end of the sentence would have been disrespectful to the first part. Jean Valjean was still Monsieur le Maire with her. He completed her thought.

"That I was in prison?" he said. "I was so, but I pulled out a bar, leaped out, and here I am. I am going up to my room; go and fetch Sister Simplice, who doubtless is by the side of that poor woman."

The old servant hastened to obey, he said nothing further to her, for he was quite sure that she would guard him better than he could himself. It was never known how he managed to get into the yard without having the gate opened. He always carried about him a master-key which opened a little side door, but he must have been searched and this key taken from him. This point was not cleared up. He went up the stairs that led to his room, and, on reaching the landing, left the candle on the top stair, closed his window and shutters, and then entered the room with the candle. This precaution was useful, for it will be remembered that his window could be noticed from the street. He took a glance around him, at his table, his chair, his bed, which had not been slept in for three nights. No trace of that night's disorder remained, for the portress "had done his room"; but she had picked out of the ashes and laid neatly on the table the two iron ends of the stick and the forty-sous piece, which was blackened by the fire. He took a sheet of paper, on which he wrote, "This is the two-franc piece stolen from Little Gervais, to which I alluded in court," and he laid the coin on the paper, so that it should be the first thing seen on entering the room. He took from a drawer an old shirt, which he tore up, and wrapped the two candlesticks in the rags. Still, he displayed no haste or agitation, and while wrapping up the candlesticks he ate a piece of black bread—probably the prison bread which he took with him on his escape. This fact was proved by the crumbs found on the boards when the authorities made an investigation at a later date. There were two gentle taps at the door.

"Come in," he said.

It was Sister Simplice; she was pale, her eyes were red, and the candle she held shook in her hand. Violent events of destiny have this peculiarity, that however perfect or cold we may be, they draw human nature out of our entrails and compel it to re-appear on the surface. In the emotions of this day the nun had become a woman again; she had wept and was trembling. Jean Valjean had just finished writing some lines on a piece of paper, which he handed to the sister, "Sister, you will deliver this to the curé?"

As the paper was open, she turned her eyes on it. "You may read it," he said.

She read, "I request the curé to take charge of all that I leave here. He will be good enough to defray out of it the costs of my trial and the interment of the woman who died this morning. The rest will be for the poor."

The sister attempted to speak, but could only produce a few inarticulate sounds; at length she managed to say:

"Do you not wish to see the poor unhappy girl for the last time, sir?"

"No," he said, "I am pursued, and if I were to be arrested in her room it would disturb her."

He had scarce said this ere a great noise broke out on the staircase; they heard a tumult of ascending steps, and the old servant cry in her loudest and most piercing voice:

"My good sir, I can take my oath that no one has come in here all day or all the evening, and I have not left my lodge once."

A man answered:

"But there is a light in that room?"

They recognized Javert's voice. The room was so built that the door, on being thrown open, concealed a nook in the right-hand wall; Jean Valjean blew out the light and crept into the nook. Sister Simplice fell on her knees by the table as the door opened and Javert entered. The voices of several men and the protestations of the old portress could be heard. The nun did not raise her eyes; she was praying. Her candle was on the chimney and gave but little light, and on noticing the nun Javert halted in great confusion. It will be remembered that the very basis of Javert, his element, the air he breathed, was reverence for all authority; he was all of one piece and allowed no objection or limitation. With him, of course, ecclesiastical authority was the highest of all; he was religious, superficial, and correct on this point as on all. In his eyes, a priest was a spirit who does not deceive; a nun, a creature who does not sin. Theirs were souls walled up against the world with only one door, which never opened except to let truth pass out. On noticing the sister, his first movement was to withdraw, but he had another duty, too, which imperiously urged him in an opposite direction. His second impulse was to remain and at least venture one question. Sister Simplice had never told a falsehood in her life; Javert was aware of this, and especially revered her for it.

"Sister," he asked, "are you alone in the room?"

There was a terrible moment, during which the old servant felt as if she were going to faint; the sister raised her eyes and said, "Yes."

"In that case," Javert continued, "I beg your pardon for pressing you, but it is my duty,—you have not seen this evening a person, a man who has escaped and whom we are seeking—that fellow of the name of Jean Valjean. Have you seen him?"

The sister answered, "No."

She had told two falsehoods, one upon the other, without hesitation, rapidly, as if devoting herself.

"I beg your pardon," said Javert; and he withdrew with a deep bow.

Oh, holy woman, it is many years since you were on this earth; you have rejoined in the light your sisters the virgins and your brothers the angels; may this falsehood be placed to your credit in Paradise!

The sister's assertion was so decisive for Javert that he did not notice the singular fact of the candle just blown out and which was still smoking on the table.

An hour later a man, making his way through the fog, was hurrying away from M. . . . in the direction of Paris. This man was Jean Valjean; and it was proved by the testimony of two or three carriers who met him, that he was carrying a bundle and was dressed in a blouse. Where did he procure this blouse from? It was never known; but, a few days before, an old workman had died in the infirmary of the factory, only leaving a blouse. It might have been that one.

One last word about Fantine. We have all one mother, the earth, and Fantine was given back to that mother. The curé thought he was doing his duty, and perhaps did it, in keeping as much money as he possibly could out of what Jean Valjean left him for the poor. After all, who were the people interested?—a convict and a street-walker; hence he simplified Fantine's interment, and reduced it to what is called the "public grave." Fantine was therefore interred in the gratis corner of the cemetery, which belongs to everybody and to nobody, and where the poor are lost. Fortunately God knows where to look for a soul. Fantine was laid in the darkness among a pile of promiscuous bones in the public grave. Her tomb resembled her bed.

VOLUME TWO
Cosette

CONTENTS · VOLUME II

BOOK IV—THE GORBEAU TENEMENT

BOOK V—FOR A STILL HUNT— DUMB DOGS

BOOK VI—PETIT-PICPUS

COSETTE

BOOK I

WATERLOO

1. ON THE NIVELLES ROAD

ON a fine May morning last year (1861) a wayfarer, the person who is telling this story, was coming from Nivelles and was proceeding toward La Hulpe. He was on foot and following, between two rows of trees, a wide paved road which undulates over a constant succession of hills that raise the road and let it fall again, and form, as it were, enormous waves. He had passed Lillois and Bois-Seigneur Isaac, and noticed in the west the slate-covered steeple of Braine l'Alleud, which looks like an overturned vase. He had just left behind him a wood upon a hill, and at the angle of a cross-road by the side of a sort of worm-eaten gallows, which bore the inscription, "Old barrier, No. 4," a wine-shop, having on its front the following notice: "The four winds, Echabeau, private coffee-house."

About half a mile beyond this pot-house he reached a small valley, in which there is a stream that runs through an arch formed in the causeway. The clump of trees, wide-spread, but very green, which fills the valley on one side of the road, is scattered on the other over the fields, and runs gracefully and capriciously toward Braine l'Alleud.

On the right, and skirting the road, were an inn, a four-wheeled cart in front of the door, a large bundle of hop-poles, a plow, a pile of dry brushwood near a quickset hedge, lime smoking in a square hole, and a ladder lying along an old shed with bins for straw. A girl was hoeing in a field, where a large yellow bill—probably of a show at some Kermesse—was flying in the wind. At the corner of the inn, a badly paved path ran into the bushes by the side of a pond, on which a flotilla of ducks was navigating. The wayfarer turned into this path.

After proceeding about one hundred yards along a wall of the fifteenth century, surmounted by a coping of crossed bricks, he found himself in front of a large arched stone gate, with a rectangular molding, in the

3

stern style of Louis XIV, supported by two flat medallions. A severe
facade was over this gate; a wall perpendicular to the façade almost
joined the gate and flanked it at a right angle. On the grass-plot in front
of the gate lay three harrows, through which the May flowers were
growing pell-mell. The gate was closed by means of two decrepit folding-
doors ornamented by an old rusty knocker.

The sun was delightful, and the branches made that gentle May
rustling which seems to come from nests even more than from the wind.
A gay little bird, probably in love, was singing with all its might in a
high tree.

The wayfarer stooped and looked at a rather large circular excavation
in the stone to the right of the gate, which resembled the hollow of a
sphere. At this moment the gates opened and a peasant woman came out.

She saw the wayfarer and noticed what he was looking at.

"It was a French cannon-ball that made it," she said.

And she added: "What you see higher up there, on the gate near a
nail, is the hole of a large grape-shot, which did not penetrate the wood."

"What is the name of this place?" the wayfarer asked.

"Hougomont," said the woman.

The wayfarer drew himself up, he walked a few steps, and then
looked over the hedge. He could see on the horizon through the trees
a species of mound, and on this mound something which, at a distance,
resembled a lion.

He was on the battle-field of Waterloo.

2 . *HOUGOMONT*

HOUGOMONT was a mournful spot, the beginning of the obstacle, the
first resistance which that great woodman of Europe, called Napoleon,
encountered at Waterloo; the first knot under the axe-blade.

It was a château, and is now but a farm. For the antiquarian Hougomont is Hugo-mons; it was built by Hugo, Sire de Somerel, the same who endowed the sixth chapelry of the abbey of Villers.

The wayfarer pushed open the door, elbowed an old calèche under a porch, and entered a yard.

The first thing that struck him in this inclosure was a gate of the sixteenth century, which now resembles an arcade, as all has fallen around it. A monumental aspect frequently springs up from ruins. Near the arcade there is another gate-way in the wall, with key-stones in the style of Henri IV, through which can be seen the trees of an orchard. By the side of this gate-way a dunghill, mattocks, and shovels, a few carts, an old well with its stone slab and iron windlass, a frisking colt, a turkey displaying its tail, a chapel surmounted by a little belfry, and a blossoming pear-tree growing in *espalier* along the chapel wall,—such is this yard, the conquest of which was a dream of Napoleon's. This nook of earth, had he been able to take it, would probably have given him the world. Chickens are scattering the dust there with their beaks, and you hear a growl,—it is a large dog, which shows its teeth and fills the place of the English.

The English were admirable here; Cooke's four companies of guards resisted at this spot for seven hours the furious attack of an army.

Hougomont, seen on a map, buildings and inclosures included, presents an irregular quadrangle, of which one angle has been broken off. In this angle is the southern gate, within point-blank range of this wall. Hougomont has two gates,—the southern one, which belongs to the château, and the northern, which belongs to the farm. Napoleon sent against Hougomont his brother Jerome; Guilleminot's, Foy's, and Bachelu's divisions were hurled at it; nearly the whole of Reille's corps was employed there and failed; and Kellermann's cannon-balls rebounded from this heroic wall. Bauduin's brigade was not strong enough to force Hougomont on the north, and Soye's brigade could only attack it on the south without carrying it.

The farm-buildings border the court-yard on the south, and a piece of the northern gate, broken by the French, hangs from the wall. It consists of four planks nailed on two cross-beams, and the scars of the attack may still be distinguished upon it.

The northern gate, which was broken down by the French, and in which a piece has been let in to replace the panel hanging to the wall, stands, half open, at the extremity of the yard; it is cut square in a wall which is stone at the bottom, brick at the top, which closes the yard on the north side. It is a simple gate, such as may be seen in all farm-yards, with two large folding-doors made of rustic planks; beyond it are fields. The dispute for this entrance was furious; for a long time all sorts of marks of bloody hands could be seen on the side-post of the gate, and it was here that Bauduin fell.

The storm of the fight still lurks in the court-yard; horror is visible there; the incidents of the fearful struggle are petrified in it; people are living and dying in it,—it was only yesterday. The walls are in the pangs of death, the stones fall, the breaches cry out, the holes are wounds, the bent and quivering trees seem making an effort to fly.

This yard was more built upon in 1815 than it is now; buildings, which have since been removed, formed in it redans and angles and corners.

The English barricaded themselves in it; the French penetrated but could not hold their ground there. By the side of the chapel stands a wing of the château, the sole relic left of the manor of Hougomont, in ruins, we might almost say gutted. The château was employed as a keep, the chapel served as a block-house. Men exterminated each other there. The French, fired upon from all sides, from behind walls, from granaries, from cellars, from every window, from every air-hole, from every crack in the stone, brought up fascines, and set fire to the walls and men; the musketry was replied to by conflagration.

In the ruined wing you can look through windows, defended by iron bars, into the dismantled rooms of a brick building; the English guards were ambuscaded in these rooms, and the spiral staircase, cracked from ground-floor to roof, appears like the interior of a broken shell. The staircase has two landings; the English, besieged on this landing and massed on the upper stairs, broke away the lowest. They are large slabs of blue stone which form a pile among the nettles. A dozen steps still hold to the wall; on the first the image of a trident is carved, and these inaccessible steps are solidly set in their bed. All the rest resemble a toothless jaw. There are two trees here, one of them dead, and the other, which was wounded on the foot, grows green again in April. Since 1815 it has taken to growing across the staircase.

Men massacred each other in the chapel, and the interior, which is grown quiet again, is strange. Mass has not been said in it since the carnage, but the altar has been left—an altar of coarse wood supported by a foundation of rough stone. Four whitewashed walls, a door opposite the altar, two small arched windows, a large wooden crucifix over the

6

door, above the crucifix a square air-hole stopped up with hay; in a corner, on the ground, an old window-sash, with the panes all broken,— such is the chapel. Nailed up near the altar is a wooden statue of St. Anne, belonging to the fifteenth century; the head of the infant Jesus has been carried away by a shot. The French, masters for a moment of the chapel and then dislodged, set fire to it. The flames filled the building, and it became a furnace; the door burnt, the flooring burnt, but the wooden crucifix was not burnt; the fire nibbled away the feet, of which only the blackened stumps can now be seen, and then stopped. It was a miracle, say the country people.

The walls are covered with inscriptions. Near the feet of Christ you read the name Henquinez; then these others, Conde de Rio Maïor, Marquis y Marquisa de Almagro (Habana). There are French names with marks of admission, signs of anger. The wall was whitewashed again in 1849, for the nations insulted each other upon it.

It was at the door of this chapel that a body was picked up, holding an axe in its hand; it was the body of sub-lieutenant Legros.

On leaving the chapel you see a well on your left hand. As there are two wells in this yard, you ask yourself why this one has no bucket and windlass? Because water is no longer drawn from it. Why is it not drawn? Because it is full of skeletons.

The last man who drew water from this well was a man called Willem van Kylsom; he was a peasant who lived at Hougomont, and was gardener there. On June 18, 1815, his family took to flight and concealed themselves in the woods.

The forest round the abbey of Villers sheltered for several days and nights the dispersed luckless country people. Even at the present day certain vestiges, such as old burnt trunks of trees, mark the spot of these poor encampments among the thickets.

Willem van Kylsom remained at Hougomont "to take care of the château," and concealed himself in a cellar. The English discovered him there; he was dragged from his lurking-place, and the frightened man was forced by blows with the flat of a saber to wait on the combatants. They were thirsty, and this Willem brought them drink, and it was from this well he drew the water. Many drank there for the last time, and this well, from which so many dead men drank, was destined to die too.

After the action, the corpses were hastily interred; death has a way of its own of harassing victory, and it causes pestilence to follow glory. Typhus is an annex of triumph. This well was deep and was converted

7

into a tomb. Three hundred dead were thrown into it, perhaps with too much haste. Were they all dead? the legend says no. And it seems that, on the night following the burial, weak voices were heard calling from the well.

This well is isolated, in the center of the yard; three walls, half of brick, half of stone, folded like the leaves of a screen, and resembling a square tower, surround it on three sides, while the fourth, where the water was drawn, is open. The back wall has a sort of shapeless bull's-eye, probably made by a shell. This tower once had a roof of which only the beams remain, and the iron braces of the right-hand wall form a cross. You bend over and look down into a deep black cylinder full of gloom. All round the well the lower part of the wall is hidden by nettles.

This well has not in front of it the large blue slab usually seen at all Belgian wells. Instead of it, there is a frame-work supporting five or six shapeless logs of knotted wood which resemble large bones. There is no bucket, chain, or windlass remaining; but there is still the stone trough which carried off the waste water. The rain-water collects in it, and from time to time a bird comes from the neighboring forest to drink from it and then fly away.

One house in this ruin, the farm-house, is still inhabited, and the door of this house opens on the yard. By the side of a pretty Gothic lock-plate on this gate there is a trefoiled iron handle. At the moment when the Hanoverian lieutenant Wilda seized this handle in order to take shelter in the farm, a French sapper cut off his hand with a blow of his axe.

The old gardener, Van Kylsom, who has long been dead, was grand-father of the family which now occupies the house. A gray-headed woman said to me: "I was here, I was three years old, and my sister, who was older, felt frightened and cried. I was carried away to the woods in my mother's arms, and people put their ears to the ground to listen. I imitated the cannon and said, 'boom, boom'."

A door on the left-hand of the yard, as we said, leads into the orchard. The orchard is terrible.

It is in three parts; we might almost say in three acts. The first part is a garden, the second the orchard, the third a wood. These three parts have one common *enceinte;* near the entrance, the buildings of the château and the farm, on the left a hedge, on the right a wall, and at the end a wall. The right-hand wall is of brick, the bottom one of stone. You enter the garden first; it slopes, is planted with gooseberry-bushes, is covered with wild vegetation, and is closed by a monumental terrace of cut stones with balusters. It was a seigneurial garden in the first French style that preceded Le Notre; now it is ruins and briars. The pilasters are surmounted by globes that resemble stone cannon-balls. Forty-three balusters are still erect; the others are lying in the grass, and nearly all have marks of musket-balls. One fractured baluster stood upon the stem like a broken leg.

It was in this garden, which is lower than the orchard, that six voltigeurs of the first light regiment, having got in and unable to get out, and caught like bears in a trap, accepted combat with two Hanoverian companies, one of which was armed with rifles. The Hanoverians lined the balustrade and fired down; the voltigeurs, firing up, six intrepid men against two hundred, and having no shelter but the gooseberry-bushes, took a quarter of an hour in dying.

You climb up a few steps and reach the orchard, properly so called. Here, on these few square yards, fifteen hundred men fell in less than an hour. The wall seems ready to recommence the fight, for the thirty-eight loop-holes pierced by the English at irregular heights may still be seen. In front of the sixteenth are two English tombs made of granite. There are only loop-holes in the south wall, for the principal attack was on that side. This wall is concealed on the outside by a quickset hedge. The French came up under the impression that they had only to carry this hedge, and found the wall an obstacle and an ambuscade; the English Guards behind the thirty-eight loop-holes firing at once a storm of grape and bullets; and Soye's brigade was dashed to pieces against it. Waterloo began thus.

The orchard, however, was taken; as the French had no ladders, they climbed up with their nails. A hand-to-hand fight took place under the trees, and all the grass was soaked with blood, and a battalion of Nassau, seven hundred strong, was cut to pieces here. On the outside, the wall, against which Kellermann's two batteries were pointed, is pock-marked with grape.

This orchard is sensitive like any other to the month of May; it has its buttercups and its daisies, the grass is tall in it, the plow-horses browse in it, hair ropes on which linen is hung to dry occupy the space between the trees and make the visitor bow his head, and as you walk along your foot sinks in mole-holes. In the middle of the grass you notice an uprooted, outstretched, but still flourishing tree. Major Blackman leaned against it to die. Under another large tree close by fell the German General Duplat, a French refugee belonging to a family that fled upon the revocation of the edict of Nantes. Close at hand an old sickly apple-tree, poulticed with a bandage of straw and clay, hangs its head. Nearly all the apple-trees are dying of old age, and there is not one without its cannon-ball or bullet. Skeletons of dead trees abound in this orchard, crows fly about in the branches, and at the end is a wood full of violets.

Bauduin killed; Foy wounded; fire, slaughter, carnage, a stream composed of English, French, and German blood furiously mingled; a well filled with corpses; the Nassau regiment and the Brunswick regiment destroyed; Duplat killed; Blackman killed; the English Guards mutilated; twenty French battalions of the forty composing Reille's corps decimated; three thousand men in this château of Hougomont alone, sabered, gashed, butchered, shot, and burned,—all this that a peasant may say to a traveler at the present day, "If you like to give me three francs, sir, I will tell you all about the battle of Waterloo."

3. JUNE 18, 1815

LET us go back, for that is one of the privileges of the narrator, and place ourselves once again in the year 1815, a little prior to the period when the matters related in the first part of this book begin.

If it had not rained on the night of the 17th and 18th June, 1815, the future of Europe would have been changed; a few drops of rain more or less made Napoleon oscillate. In order to make Waterloo the end of Austerlitz, Providence only required a little rain, and a cloud crossing the sky at a season when rain was not expected was sufficient to overthrow an empire.

The battle of Waterloo could not begin till half-past eleven, and that gave Blücher time to come up. Why? because the ground was moist, and it was necessary for it to become firmer, that the artillery might maneuver.

Napoleon was an artillery officer, and always showed himself one; all his battle plans are made for the cannon-ball. Making artillery converge at a given point was his key to victory. He treated the strategy of the opposing general as a citadel, and breached it; he crushed the weak point under grape-shot, and he began and ended his battles with artillery. Driving in squares, pulverizing regiments, breaking lines, destroying and dispersing masses,—all this must be done by striking, striking, striking incessantly, and he confided the task to artillery. It was a formidable method, and, allied to genius, rendered this gloomy pugilist of war invincible for fifteen years.

On June 18, 1815, he counted the more on his artillery, because he held the numerical superiority. Wellington had only one hundred and fifty-nine guns, while Napoleon had two hundred and forty.

Had the earth been dry and the artillery able to move, the action would have begun at six A. M. It would have been won and over at two P. M., three hours before the Prussian denouement.

How much blame was there on Napoleon's side for the loss of this battle? Is the shipwreck imputable to the pilot?

Was the evident physical decline of Napoleon at that period complicated by a certain mental decline? Had twenty years of war worn out the blade as well as the scabbard, the soul as well as the body? Was the veteran being awkwardly displayed in the captain? In a word, was the genius, as many historians of reputation have believed, eclipsed? In order to conceal his own weakening from himself, was he beginning to oscillate with the veering of every chance wind? Was he, a serious thing in a general, becoming conscious of danger? In that class of great material men who may be called the giants of action, is there an age when genius becomes short-sighted? Old age has no power over ideal genius; with the Dantes and Michael Angelos old age is increase, but is it decrease for the Hannibals and the Bonapartes? Had Napoleon lost the direct sense of victory? Had he reached a point where he no longer saw the shoal, guessed the snare, and could not discern the crumbling edge of the abyss? Could he not scent catastrophes? Had the man who formerly knew all the roads to victory and pointed to them with a sovereign finger, from his flashing car, now a mania for leading his tumultuous team of legions to the precipices? Was he attacked at the age of forty-six by a supreme madness? Was the Titanic charioteer of destiny now only a Phaëton?

We do not believe it.

His plan of action, it is allowed by all, was a masterpiece. Go straight at the center of the allied line, make a hole through the enemy, cut him in two, drive the British half over Hall and the Prussians over Tongres, carry Mont St. Jean, seize Brussels, drive the Germans into the Rhine and the Englishman into the sea—all this was contained for Napoleon in this battle; afterward he would see.

We need hardly say that we do not pretend to tell the story of Waterloo here; one of the generating scenes of the drama we are recounting is attached to this battle, but the story of Waterloo has been already told and magisterially discussed from one point of view by Napoleon, from another by a Pleiad of historians. For our part, we leave the historians to contend; we are only a distant witness, a passer-by along the plain, a seeker bending over the earth molded of human flesh, and perhaps taking appearances for realities; we possess neither the military practice nor the strategic competency that authorizes a system; in our opinion, a chain of accidents governed both captains at Waterloo; and when destiny, that mysterious accused, enters on the scene, we judge, like the people, that simple-minded judge.

4 . A

THOSE who wish to form a distinct idea of the battle of Waterloo need only imagine a capital A laid on the ground. The left leg of the A is the Nivelles road, the right one the Genappe road, while the string of the A is the broken way running from Ohain to Braine l'Alleud. The top of the A is Mont St. Jean, where Wellington is; the left lower point is Hougomont, where Reille is with Jerome Bonaparte; the right lower point is la Belle Alliance, where Napoleon is. A little below the point where the string of the A meets and cuts the right leg, is La Haye Sainte; and in the center of this string is the exact spot where the battle was concluded. It is here that the lion is placed, the involuntary symbol of the heroism of the Imperial Guard.

The triangle comprised at the top of the A, between the two legs and the string, is the plateau of Mont St. Jean; the dispute for this plateau was the whole battle.

The wings of the two armies extend to the right and left of the Genappe and Nivelles roads, d'Erlon facing Picton, Reille facing Hill.

Behind the point of the A, behind the plateau of St. Jean, is the forest of Soignies.

As for the plain itself, imagine a vast undulating ground; each ascent commands the next ascent, and all the undulations ascend to Mont St. Jean, where they end at the forest.

Two hostile armies on a battle-field are two wrestlers,—one tries to throw the other; they cling to everything,—a thicket is a basis; for want of a hut or two to support it, a regiment gives away; a fall in the plain, a transverse hedge in a good position, a wood, a ravine may arrest the heel of that colossus which is called an army and prevent it slipping. The one who leaves the field is beaten; and hence the necessity for the responsible chief to examine the smallest clump of trees and investigate the slightest rise in the ground.

The two generals had attentively studied the plain of Mont St. Jean, which is called at the present day the field of Waterloo. In the previous year, Wellington, with prescient sagacity, had examined it as suitable for a great battle. On this ground and for this duel of June 18, Wellington had the good side and Napoleon the bad, for the English army was above, the French below.

It is almost superfluous to sketch here the appearance of Napoleon, mounted, and with his telescope in his hand, as he appeared on the heights of Rossomme at the dawn of June 18. Before we show him, all the world has seen him. The calm profile under the little hat of the Brienne school, the green uniform, the white facings concealing the decorations, the great-coat concealing the epaulettes, the edge of red ribbon under the waistcoat, the leather breeches, the white horse with its housings of purple velvet, having in the corners crowned N's and eagles, the riding-boots drawn over silk stockings, the silver spurs, the sword of Marengo,—the whole appearance of the last of the Cæsars rises before every mind, applauded by some and regarded sternly by others.

This figure has for a long time stood out all light; this was owing to a certain legendary obscuration which most heroes evolve, and which always conceals the truth for a longer or shorter period, but at the present day we have history and light.

That brilliancy called history is pitiless; it has this strange and divine thing about it, that, all light as it is, and because it is light, it often throws shadows over spots before luminous, it makes of the same man two different phantoms, and one attacks the other, and the darkness of the despot struggles with the lustre of the captain. Hence comes a truer proportion in the definitive appreciation of nations; Babylon violated, diminishes Alexander; Rome enchained, diminishes Cæsar; Jerusalem killed, diminishes Titus. Tyranny follows the tyrant, and it is a misfortune for a man to leave behind him a night which has his form.

5. THE QUID OBSCURUM OF BATTLES

ALL the world knows the first phase of this battle—a troubled, uncertain, hesitating opening, dangerous for both armies, but more so for the English than the French.

It had rained all night; the ground was saturated; the rain had collected in hollows of the plain as in tubs; at certain points the ammunition wagons had sunk in up to the axle-trees and the girths of the horses; if the wheat and barley laid low by this mass of moving vehicles had not filled the ruts and made a litter under the wheels, any movement, especially in the valleys, in the direction of Papelotte would have been impossible.

The battle began late, for Napoleon, as we have explained, was accustomed to hold all his artillery in hand like a pistol, aiming first at one point, then at another of the battle, and he resolved to wait until the field batteries could gallop freely, and for this purpose it was necessary that the sun should appear and dry the ground. But the sun did not come out;

it was no longer the rendezvous of Austerlitz. When the first cannon-shot was fired, the English General Colville drew out his watch, and saw that it was twenty-five minutes to twelve.

The action was commenced furiously, more furiously, perhaps, than the emperor desired, by the French left wing on Hougomont. At the same time Napoleon attacked the center by hurling Quiot's brigade on La Haye Sainte, and Ney pushed the French right wing against the English left, which was leaning upon Papelotte.

The attack on Hougomont was to a certain extent a feint, for the plan was to attract Wellington there, and make him strengthen his left. This plan would have succeeded had not the four companies of Guards and Perponcher's Belgian division firmly held the position, and Wellington, instead of massing his troops, found it only necessary to send as a reënforcement four more companies of Guards and a battalion of Brunswickers.

The attack of the French right on Papelotte was serious; to destroy the English left, cut the Brussels road, bar the passage for any possible Prussians, force Mont St. Jean, drive back Wellington on Hougomont, then on Braine l'Alleud, and then on Hall,—nothing was more distinct. Had not a few incidents supervened, this attack would have succeeded, for Papelotte was taken and La Haye Sainte carried.

There is a detail to be noticed here. In the English infantry, especially in Kempt's brigade, there were many recruits, and these young soldiers valiantly withstood our formidable foot, and they behaved excellently as sharp-shooters. The soldier when thrown out *en tirailleur,* being left to some extent to his own resources, becomes, as it were, his own general; and these recruits displayed something of the French invention and fury. These novices displayed an impulse, and it displeased Wellington.

After the taking of La Haye Sainte, the battle vacillated.

There is an obscure interval in this day, between twelve and four; the middle of this battle is almost indistinct and participates in the gloom of the *mêlée.* A twilight sets in, and we perceive vast fluctuations in this mist, a dizzying mirage, the panoply of war at that day, unknown in our times; flaming colbacks; flying sabretaches; cross-belts; pouches for grenades; Hussar dolmans; red boots with a thousand wrinkles; heavy shakos enwreathed with gold twist; the nearly black Brunswick infantry mingled with the scarlet infantry of England; the English soldiers wearing clumsy white cushions for epaulettes; the Hanoverian light horse with their leathern helmets, brass bands, and red horse-tails; the Highlanders with their bare knees and chequered plaids, and the long white gaiters of our Grenadiers,—pictures, but not strategic lines; what a Salvator Rosa, but not a Gribeauyal, would have reveled in.

A certain amount of tempest is always mingled with a battle, *quid obscurum, quid divinum.* Every historian traces to some extent the lineament that pleases him in the hurly-burly. Whatever the combination of the generals may be, the collision of armed masses has incalculable ebbs and flows; in action the two plans of the leaders enter into each other and destroy their shape. The line of battle floats and winds like a thread, the streams of blood flow illogically, the fronts of armies undulate, the regiments in advancing or retiring form capes or gulfs, and all these shoals are continually shifting their position; where infantry was, artillery arrives; where artillery was, cavalry dash in; the battalions are smoke. There was something there, but when you look for it, it has disappeared; the gloomy masses advance and retreat; a species of breath from the tomb impels, drives back, swells, and disperses these tragic multitudes. What is a battle? an oscillation. The immobility of a mathematical plan expresses a minute, and not a day. To paint a battle, those powerful painters who have chaos in their pencils are needed. Rembrandt is worth more than Vandermeulin, for Vandermeulin, exact at midday, is incorrect at three o'clock. Geometry is deceived, and the hurricane alone is true, and it is this that gives Follard the right to contradict Polybius. Let us add that there is always a certain moment in which the battle degenerates into a combat, is particularized and broken up into countless detail facts which, to borrow the expression of Napoleon himself, "belong rather to the biography of regiments than to the history of the army." The historian, in such a case, has the evident right to sum up; he can only catch the principal outlines of the struggle, and it is not given to any narrator, however conscientious he may be, to absolutely fix the form of that horrible cloud which is called a battle.

This, which is true of all great armed collisions, is peculiarly applicable to Waterloo. Still, at a certain moment in the afternoon, the battle began to assume a settled shape.

6. FOUR O'CLOCK IN THE AFTERNOON

At about four o'clock P. M. the situation of the English army was serious. The Prince of Orange commanded the center, Hill the right, and Picton the left. The Prince of Orange, wild and intrepid, shouted to the Dutch Belgians: "Nassau, Brunswick, never yield an inch." Hill, fearfully weakened, had just fallen back on Wellington, while Picton was dead. At the very moment when the English took from the French the flag of the 105th line regiment, the French killed General Picton with a bullet through his head. The battle had two bases for Wellington—Hougomont and La Haye Sainte. Hougomont still held out, though on fire, while La Haye Sainte was lost. Of the German battalion that defended it, forty-two men only survived; all the officers but five were killed or taken prisoners. Three thousand combatants had been massacred in that focus; a sergeant of the English Guards, the first boxer of England and reputed invulnerable by his comrades, had been killed there by a little French drummer. Baring was dislodged, and Alten was sabered; several flags had been lost, one belonging to Alten's division and one to the Lunebourg battalion, which was born by a prince of the Deux-ponts family. The Scotch Greys no longer existed; Ponsonby's heavy dragoons were cut to pieces,—this brave cavalry had given way before the Lancers of Bro and the cuirassiers of Travers. Of twelve hundred sabers, only six hundred remained; of three lieutenant-colonels, two were kissing the ground, Hamilton wounded, and Mather killed. Ponsonby had fallen, pierced by seven lance-wounds; Gordon was dead, March was dead, and two divisions, the fifth and the sixth, were destroyed.

Hougomont attacked, La Haye Sainte taken; there was only one knot left, the center, which still held out. Wellington reënforced it; he called in Hill from Merle-Braine and Chassé from Braine l'Alleud.

17

The center of the English army, which was slightly concave, very dense and compact, was strongly situated; it occupied the plateau of Mont St. Jean, having the village behind it, and before it the slope, which at that time was rather steep. It was supported by that strong stone house, which at that period was a domanial property of Nivelles, standing at the cross-road, and an edifice dating from the sixteenth century, so robust that the cannon-balls rebounded without doing it any injury. All round the plateau the English had cut through the hedges at certain spots, formed embrasures in the hawthorns, thrust guns between branches, and loop-holed the shrubs,—their artillery was ambuscaded under the brambles. This Punic task, incontestably authorized by the rules of war which permit snares, had been so well effected that Haxo, who had been sent by the emperor at eight o'clock to reconnoiter the enemy's batteries, returned to tell Napoleon that there was no obstacle, with exception of the barricades blocking the Nivelles and Genappe roads. It was the season when the wheat is still standing, and along the edge of the plateau a battalion of Kempt's brigade, the 95th, was lying in the tall corn.

Thus assured and supported, the center of the Anglo-Dutch army was in a good position.

The peril of this position was the forest of Soignies, at that time contiguous to the battle-field and intersected by the ponds of Groenendael and Boitsford. An army could not have fallen back into it without being dissolved, regiments would have been broken up at once, and the artillery lost in the marshes. The retreat, according to the opinion of several professional men, contradicted, it is true, by others, would have been a flight.

Wellington added to this center a brigade of Chassé's removed from the right wing, one of Wicke's from the left wing, and Clinton's division. He gave to his English—Halkett's regiments, Mitchell's brigade, and Maitland's guards—as epaulments and counterforts, the Brunswick infantry, the Nassau contingent, Kielmansegge's Hanoverians, and Ompteda's Germans. He had thus twenty-six battalions under his hand; as Charras says, "the right wing deployed earth-bags, at the very spot where what was called "the Museum of Waterloo" now stands, and Wellington also had in a little hollow Somerset's Dragoon Guards, counting one thousand four hundred sabers. They were the other moiety of the so justly celebrated English cavalry; though Ponsonby was destroyed, Somerset remained.

The battery which, had it been completed, would have been almost a redoubt, was arranged behind a very low wall, hastily lined with sandbags and a wide slope of earth. This work was not finished, as there was not time to palisade it.

Wellington, restless but impassive, was mounted, and remained for the whole day in the same attitude, a little in front of the old mill of Mont St. Jean, which still exists, and under an elm-tree, which an Englishman, an enthusiastic Vandal, afterward bought for two hundred francs, cut down and carried away. Wellington was coldly heroic; there was a shower of cannon-balls, and his aide-de-camp Gordon was killed by his side. Lord Hill, pointing to a bursting shell, said to him, "My Lord, what are your instructions, and what orders do you leave us, if you are killed?" "Do as I am doing," Wellington answered. To Clinton he said, laconically, "Hold out here to the last man." The day was evidently turning badly, and Wellington cried to his old comrades of Vittoria, Talavera, and Salamanca, "Boys, can you think of giving way? Remember old England."

About four o'clock, the English line fell back all at once; nothing was visible on the crest of the plateau but artillery and sharp-shooters; the rest had disappeared. The regiments, expelled by the French shell and cannon-balls, fell back into the hollow, which at the present day is intersected by the lane that runs to the farm of Mont St. Jean. A retrograde movement began, the English front withdrew. Wellington was recoiling. "It is the beginning of the retreat," Napoleon cried.

7. *NAPOLEON IN GOOD HUMOR*

THE emperor, though ill and suffering on horseback from a local injury, had never been so good-tempered as on this day. From the morning his impenetrability had been smiling, and on June 18, 1815, this profound soul, coated with granite, was radiant. The man who had been somber at Austerlitz was gay at Waterloo. The greatest predestined men offer these contradictions, for our joys are a shadow and the smile belongs to God.

Ridet Cæsar, Pompeius flebit, the legionaries of the Fulminatrix legion used to say. On this occasion Pompey was not destined to weep, but it is certain that Cæsar laughed. At one o'clock in the morning, amid the rain and storm, he had explored with Bertrand the hills near Rossomme, and was pleased to see the long lines of English fires illumining the horizon from Frischemont to Braine l'Alleud. It seemed to him as if destiny had made an appointment with him on a fixed day and was punctual. He stopped his horse, and remained for some time motionless, looking at the lightning and listening to the thunder. The fatalist was heard to cast into the night the mysterious words, "We are agreed." Napoleon was mistaken; they were no longer agreed.

He had not slept for a moment; all the instants of the past night had been marked with joy for him. He rode through the entire line of main guards, stopping every now and then to speak to the videttes. At half-past two he heard the sound of a marching column near Hougomont, and believed for a moment in a retreat on the side of Wellington. He said to Bertrand, "The English rear-guard is preparing to decamp. I shall take prisoners the six thousand English who have just landed at Ostende." He talked cheerfully, and had regained the spirits he had displayed during the landing of March 1, when he showed to the grand marshal the enthusiastic peasant of the Juan Gulf and said, "Well, Bertrand, here is a reënforcement already." On the night between June 17 and 18 he made fun of Wellington. "This little Englishman requires a lesson," said Napoleon. The rain became twice as violent. And it thundered while the emperor was speaking.

At half-past three A. M. he lost one illusion; officers sent to reconnoiter informed him that the enemy was making no movement. Nothing was stirring, not a single bivouac fire was extinguished, and the English army was sleeping. The silence was profound on earth, and there was only noise in the heavens. At four o'clock a peasant was brought to him by the scouts; this peasant had served as guide to a brigade of English cavalry, probably Vivian's, which had taken up a position on the extreme left in the village of Ohain. At five o'clock two Belgian deserters informed him that they had just left their regiments, and the English army meant fighting. "All the better," cried Napoleon, "I would sooner crush them than drive them back."

At daybreak he dismounted on the slope which forms the angle of the Plancenoit road, had a kitchen table and a peasant chair brought from the farm of Rossomme, sat down with a truss of straw for a carpet, and laid on the table the map of the battle-field, saying to Soult, "It is a pretty chess-board."

Owing to the night rain, the commissariat wagons, which stuck in the muddy roads, did not arrive by daybreak. The troops had not slept, were wet through and fasting, but this did not prevent Napoleon from exclaiming cheerfully to Soult, "We have ninety chances out of a hundred in our favor." At eight o'clock the emperor's breakfast was brought and he invited several generals to share it with him. While breakfasting, somebody said that Wellington had been the last evening but one at a ball in Brussels, and Soult, the rough soldier with his arch-bishop's face, remarked, "The ball will be to-day." The emperor teased Ney for saying, "Wellington will not be so simple as to wait for your majesty." This was his usual manner. "He was fond of a joke," says Fleury de Chaboulon; "The basis of his character was a pleasant humor," says Gourgaud; "He abounded with jests more peculiar than witty," says Benjamin Constant. This gayety of the giant is worth dwelling on; it was he who called his Grenadiers "Growlers"; he pinched their ears and pulled their mustaches. "The emperor was always playing tricks with us," was the remark made by one of them. During the mysterious passage from Elba to France, on February 27, the French brig of war, the Zephyr, met the Inconstant, on board which Napoleon was concealed, and inquiring after Napoleon, the emperor, who still had in his hat the white and violet cockade studded with bees, which he had adopted at Elba, himself laughingly took up the speaking-trumpet, and answered, "The emperor is quite well." A man who jests in this way is on familiar terms with events. Napoleon had several outbursts of this laughter during the breakfast at Waterloo; after breakfast he reflected for a quarter of an hour; then two generals sat down on the truss of straw, each with a pen in his hand and a sheet of paper on his knee, and the emperor dictated to them the plan of the battle.

At nine o'clock, the moment when the French army, échelonned and moving in five columns, began to deploy, the divisions in two lines, the artillery between, the bands in front, drums rattling and bugles braying, —a powerful, mighty, joyous army, a sea of bayonets and helmets on the horizon,—the emperor, much affected, twice exclaimed, "Magnificent! magnificent!"

Between nine and half-past ten, although it seems incredible, the whole army took up position, and was drawn up in six lines, forming, to repeat the emperor's expression, "the figure of six V's." A few minutes after the formation of the line, and in the midst of that profound silence which precedes the storm of the battle, the emperor, seeing three twelve-pounder batteries defile, which had been detached by his orders from Erlon, Reille, and Lobau's brigade, and which were intended to begin the action at the spot where the Nivelles and Genappe roads crossed, tapped Haxo on the shoulder, and said, "There are twenty-four pretty girls, general."

Sure of the result, he encouraged with a smile the company of sappers of the first corps as it passed him, which he had selected to barricade itself in Mont St. Jean so soon as the village was carried. All this security was only crossed by one word of human pity; on seeing at his left, at the spot where there is now a large tomb, the admirable Scotch Greys massed with their superb horses, he said, "It is a pity."

Then he mounted his horse, rode toward Rossomme, and selected as his observatory a narrow strip of grass on the right of the road running from Genappe to Brussels, and this was his second station. The third station, the one he took at seven in the evening, is formidable,—it is a rather lofty mound which still exists, and behind which the guard was massed in a hollow. Around this mound the balls ricochetted on the pavement of the road and reached Napoleon. As at Brienne, he had round his head the whistle of bullets and canister. Almost at the spot where his horse's hoofs stood, cannon-balls, old saber-blades, and shapeless rust-eaten projectiles, *scabra rubigine,* have been picked up; a few years ago a live shell was dug up, the fuse of which had broken off: It was at this station that the emperor said to his guide, Lacoste, a hostile timid peasant, who was fastened to a hussar's saddle, and tried at each volley of canister to hide himself behind Napoleon, "You ass, it is shameful; you will be killed in the back." The person who is writing these lines himself found, while digging up the sand in the friable slope of this mound, the remains of a shell rotted by the oxide of forty-six years, and pieces of iron which broke like sticks of barley-sugar between his fingers.

Everybody is aware that the undulations of the plains on which the encounter between Napoleon and Wellington took place, are no longer as they were on June 18, 1815. On taking from this mournful plain the material to make a monument, it was deprived of its real relics, and history, disconcerted, no longer recognizes itself; in order to glorify, they disfigured. Wellington, on seeing Waterloo two years after, exclaimed, "My battle-field has been altered." Where the huge pyramid of earth surmounted by a lion now stands, there was a crest which on the side of the Nivelles road had a practicable ascent but which on the side of the Genappe road was almost an escarpment. The elevation of this escarpment may still be imagined by the height of the two great tombs which skirt the road from Genappe to Brussels; the English tomb on the left, the German tomb on the right. There is no French tomb,—for France, the whole plain is a sepulcher. Through the thousands of cart-loads of earth employed in erecting the mound, which is one hundred and fifty feet high and half a mile in circumference, the plateau of Mont St. Jean is now accessible by a gentle incline, but on the day of the battle, and especially on the side of La Haye Sainte, it was steep and abrupt. The incline was so sharp that the English gunners could not see beneath them the farm situated in the bottom of the valley, which was the center of the fight. On June 18, 1815, the rain had rendered the steep road more difficult, and the troops not only had to climb up, but slipped in the mud. Along the center of the crest of the plateau ran a species of ditch, which it was impossible for a distant observer to guess.

We will state what this ditch was. Braine l'Alleud is a Belgian village and Ohain is another; these villages, both concealed in hollows, are connected by a road about a league and a half in length, which traverses an undulating plain, and frequently buries itself between hills, so as to become at certain spots a ravine. In 1815, as to-day, this road crossed the crest of the plateau of Mont St. Jean, but at the present day it is level with the ground, while at that time it was a hollow way. The two slopes have been carried away to form the monumental mound. This road was, and still is, a trench for the greater part of the distance; a hollow trench, in some places twelve feet deep, whose scarped sides were washed down here and there by the winter rains. Accidents occurred there; the road was so narrow where it entered Braine l'Alleud, that a wayfarer was crushed there by a wagon, as is proved by a stone cross standing near the graveyard, which gives the name of the dead man as "Monsieur Bernard Debrye, trader of Brussels," and the date, "February, 1637." It was so deep on the plateau of Mont St. Jean, that a peasant, one Mathieu Nicaise, was crushed there in 1783 by a fall of earth, as is proved by another stone cross, the top of which disappeared in the excavation, but whose overthrown pedestal is still visible on the grass slope to the left of the road between La Haye Sainte and the farm of Mont St. Jean.

On the day of the battle, this hollow way, whose existence nothing revealed, a trench on the top of the escarpment, a rut hidden in the earth, was invisible, that is to say, terrible.

This is the inscription:

D. O. M.

CY A ETE ECRASE
PAR MALHEUR
SOUS UN CHARIOT
MONSIEUR BERNARD
DE BRYE MARCHAND
A BRUXELLE LE *(illegible)*
FEBVRIER 1637.

8. *THE EMPEROR ASKS THE GUIDE A QUESTION*

ON the morning of Waterloo, then, Napoleon was cheerful. He had reason to be so,—for the plan he had drawn up was admirable.

Once the battle had begun, its various incidents—the resistance of Hougomont; the tenacity of La Haye Sainte; Bauduin killed and Foy placed *hors de combat;* the unexpected wall against which Soye's brigade was broken; the fatal stupidity of Guilleminot, who had no petards or powder-bags to destroy the farm gates; the sticking of the artillery in the mud; the fifteen guns without escort captured by Uxbridge in a hollow way; the slight effect of the shells falling in the English lines, which buried themselves in the moistened ground, and only produced a volcano of mud, so that the troops were merely plastered with mud; the inutility of Piret's demonstration on Braine l'Alleud, and the whole of his cavalry, fifteen squadrons, almost annihilated; the English right but slightly disquieted and the left poorly attacked; Ney's strange mistake in massing instead of échelonning the four divisions of the first corps; a depth of twenty-seven ranks and a line of two hundred men given up in this way to the canister; the frightful gaps made by the cannon-balls in these masses; the attacking columns disunited; the oblique battery suddenly unmasked on their flank; Bourgeois, Donzelot, and Durette in danger; Quiot repulsed; Lieutenant Viot, that Hercules who came from the polytechnic school, wounded at the moment when he was beating in with an axe the gates of La Haye Sainte, under the plunging fires of the English barricade on the Genappe road; Marcognet's division caught between infantry and cavalry, shot down from the wheat by Best and Pack, and sabered by Ponsonby; its battery of seven guns spiked; the Prince of Saxe Weimar holding and keeping in defiance of Count d'Erlon, Frischemont and Smohain; the flags of the 105th and 45th regiments captured; the Prussian black Hussar arrested by the scouts of the flying column of three hundred chasseurs, who were beating the country between Wavre and Plancenoit; the alarming things which this man said; Grouchy's delay; the fifteen hundred men killed in less than an hour in the orchard of Hougomont; the eighteen hundred laid low even in a shorter space of time round La Haye Sainte,—all these stormy incidents, passing like battle-clouds before Napoleon, had scarce disturbed his glance or cast a gloom over this imperial face. Napoleon was accustomed to look steadily at war; he never reckoned up the poignant details; he cared little for figures, provided that they gave the total— victory. If the commencement went wrong, he did not alarm himself, as he believed himself master and owner of the end; he knew how to wait, and treated destiny as an equal. He seemed to say to fate, "You would not dare!"

One-half light, one-half shade, Napoleon felt himself protected in good and tolerated in evil. There was, or he fancied there was, for him a connivance, we might say, almost a complicity on the part of events, equivalent to the ancient invulnerability.

Yet, when a man has behind him the Beresina, Leipzig, and Fontainebleau, it seems as if he could be distrustful of Waterloo. A mysterious frown becomes visible on the face of Heaven.

At the moment when Wellington retrograded, Napoleon quivered. He suddenly saw the plateau of Mont St. Jean deserted, and the front of the English army disappear. It was rallying, but was out of sight.

The emperor half raised himself in his stirrups, and the flash of victory passed into his eyes. If Wellington were driven back into the forest of Soignies and destroyed, it would be the definitive overthrow of England by France. It would be Cressy, Poictiers, Malplaquet, and Ramilies avenged; the man of Marengo would erase Agincourt.

The emperor, while meditating on this tremendous denouement, turned his telescope to all parts of the battle-field. His Guards, standing at ease behind him, gazed at him with a sort of religious awe. He was reflecting, he examined the slopes, noted the inclines, scrutinized the clumps of trees, the patches of barley, and the paths; he seemed to be counting every tuft of gorse. He looked with some fixity at the English barricades, two large masses of felled trees, the one on the Genappe road defended by two guns, the only ones of all the English artillery which commanded the battle-field, and the one on the Nivelles road, behind which flashed the Dutch bayonets of Chassé's brigade. He remarked near this barricade the old chapel of St. Nicholas, which is at the corner of the cross-road leading to Braine l'Alleud. He bent down and spoke in a low voice to the guide Lacoste. The guide shook his head with a probably perfidious negative.

The emperor drew himself up and reflected.

Wellington was retiring.

All that was needed now was to complete this retreat by an overthrow.

Napoleon hurriedly turned and sent off a messenger at full speed to Paris to announce that the battle was gained.

Napoleon was one of those geniuses from whom thunder issues.

He had just found his thunder-stroke.

He gave Milhaud's cuirassiers orders to carry the plateau of Mont St. Jean.

9. A SURPRISE

THEY were three thousand five hundred in number, and formed a front a quarter of a league in length; they were gigantic men mounted on colossal horses. They formed twenty-six squadrons, and had behind them, as a support, Lefebvre Desnouette's division, composed of the one hundred and sixty gendarmes, the chasseurs of the Guard, eleven hundred and ninety-seven sabers, and the lancers of the Guard, eight hundred and eighty lances. They wore a helmet without a plume, and a cuirass of wrought steel, and were armed with pistols and a straight saber. In the morning the whole army had admired them when they came up at nine o'clock, with bugles sounding, while all the bands played "Veillons au salut de l'Empire," in close column with one battery on their flank, the others in their center, and deployed in two ranks, and took their place in that powerful second line, so skillfully formed by Napoleon, which, having at its extreme left Kellermann's cuirassiers, and on its extreme right Milhaud's cuirassiers, seemed to be endowed with two wings of steel.

The aide-de-camp Bernard carried to them the emperor's order. Ney drew his saber and placed himself at their head, and the mighty squadrons started.

Then a formidable spectacle was seen.

The whole of this cavalry, with raised sabers, with standards flying, and formed in columns of division, descended, with one movement and as one man, with the precision of a bronze battering-ram opening a breech, the hill of the Belle Alliance. They entered the formidable valley in which so many men had already fallen, disappeared in the smoke, and then, emerging from the gloom, re-appeared on the other side of the valley, still in a close, compact column, mounting at a trot, under a tremendous canister fire, the frightful muddy incline of the plateau of Mont St. Jean. They ascended it, stern, threatening, and imperturbable; between the breaks in the artillery and musketry fire, the colossal tramp could be heard. As they formed two divisions, they were in two columns: Wathier's division was on the right, Delord's on the left. One seemed to see from a distance two immense steel snakes crawling toward the crest of the plateau; they traversed the battle-field like a flash.

Nothing like it had been seen since the capture of the great redoubt of the Moskova by the heavy cavalry; Murat was missing, but Ney was there. It seemed as if this mass had become a monster, and had but one soul; each squadron undulated and swelled like the rings of a polyp. This could be seen through a vast smoke which was rent asunder at intervals; it was a pell-mell of helmets, shouts, and sabers, a stormy bounding of horses among cannon, and a disciplined and terrible array; while above it all flashed the cuirasses like the scales of the dragon.

Such narratives seemed to belong to another age; something like this vision was doubtless traceable in the old Orphean epics describing the men-horses, the ancient hippanthropists, those Titans with human faces and equestrian chest, whose gallop escaladed Olympus,—horrible, invulnerable, sublime gods and brutes.

It was a curious numerical coincidence that twenty-six battalions were preparing to receive the charge of these twenty-six squadrons. Behind the crest of the plateau, in the shadow of the masked battery, thirteen English squares, each of two battalions and formed two deep, with seven men in the first lines and six in the second, were waiting, calm, dumb, and motionless, with their muskets, for what was coming. They did not see the cuirassiers, and the cuirassiers did not see them; they merely heard this tide of men ascending. They heard the swelling sound of three thousand horses, the alternating and symmetrical sound of the hoofs, the clang of the cuirasses, the clash of the sabers, and a species of great and formidable breathing. There was a long and terrible silence, and then a long file of raised arms, brandishing sabers and helmets, and bugles and standards, and three thousand heads with great mustaches, shouting, "Long live the emperor!" appeared above the crest. The whole of this cavalry debouched on the plateau, and it was like the commencement of an earthquake.

All at once, terrible to relate, the head of the column of cuirassiers facing the English left reared with a fearful clamor. On reaching the culminating point of the crest, furious and eager to make their exterminating dash on the English squares and guns, the cuirassiers noticed between them and the English a trench, a grave. It was the hollow road of Ohain.

It was a frightful moment,—the ravine was there, unexpected, yawning, almost precipitous, beneath the horses' feet, and with a depth of twelve feet between its two sides. The second rank thrust the first into the abyss; the horses reared, fell back, slipped with all four feet in the air, crushing and throwing their riders. There was no means of escaping; the entire column was one huge projectile. The force acquired to crush the English, crushed the French, and the inexorable ravine would not yield till it was filled up. Men and horses rolled into it pell-mell, crushing each other, and making one large charnel-house of the gulf, and when this grave was full of living men the rest passed over them. Nearly one-third of Dubois's men rolled into the abyss.

This commenced the loss of the battle.

A local tradition, which evidently exaggerates, says that two thousand horses and fifteen hundred men were buried in the hollow way of Ohain. These figures probably comprise the other corpses cast into the ravine on the day after the battle.

Let us note in passing that in this brigade Dubois was the one who, charging alone, an hour before, had taken the Hanoverian standard.

Napoleon, before ordering this charge, had surveyed the ground, but had been unable to see this hollow way, which did not form even a ripple on the crest of the plateau. Warned, however, by the little white chapel which marks its juncture with the Nivelles road, he had asked Lacoste a question, probably as to whether there was any obstacle. The guide answered no, and we might almost say that Napoleon's catastrophe was brought about by a peasant's shake of the head.

Other fatalities were yet to arise.

Was it possible for Napoleon to win the battle? We answer in the negative. Why? On account of Wellington, on account of Blücher? No; on account of God.

Bonaparte, victor at Waterloo, did not harmonize with the law of the nineteenth century. Another series of facts was preparing, in which Napoleon no longer had a place; the ill-will of events had been displayed long previously.

It was time for this vast man to fall.

His excessive weight in human destiny disturbed the balance. This individual alone was of more account than the universal group; such plethoras of human vitality concentrated in a single head—the world mounting to one man's brain—would be mortal to civilization if they endured. The moment had arrived for the incorruptible supreme equity to reflect, and it is probable that the principles and elements on which the regular gravitations of the moral order as of the material order depend, complained. Streaming blood, overcrowded grave-yards, mothers in tears, are formidable pleaders. When the earth is suffering from an excessive burden, there are mysterious groans from the shadow, which the abyss hears.

Napoleon had been denounced in infinitude, and his fall was decided. He annoyed God.

Waterloo is not a battle, but a transformation of the universe.

10. *THE PLATEAU OF MONT ST. JEAN*

THE battery was unmasked simultaneously with the ravine.

Sixty guns and the thirteen squares thundered at the cuirassiers at point-blank range. The intrepid General Delord gave a military salute to the English battery.

The whole of the English field artillery had entered the squares at a gallop; the cuirassiers had not even a moment for reflection. The disaster of the hollow way had decimated but not discouraged them; they were of that nature of men whose hearts grow large when their number is diminished.

Wathier's column alone suffered in the disaster; but Delord's column, which he had ordered to wheel to the left, as if he suspected the trap, arrived entire.

The cuirassiers rushed at the English squares at full gallop, with hanging bridles, sabers in their mouths, and pistols in their hands.

There are moments in a battle when the soul hardens a man, so that it changes the soldier into a statue, and all flesh becomes granite. The English battalions, though fiercely assailed, did not move.

Then there was a frightful scene.

All the faces of the English squares were attacked simultaneously, and a frenzied whirl surrounded them. But the cold infantry remained impassive; the front rank, kneeling, received the cuirassiers on their bayonets, while the second fired at them; behind the second rank the artillerymen loaded their guns, the front of the square opened to let an eruption of canister pass, and then closed again. The cuirassiers responded by attempts to crush their foe; their great horses reared, leaped over the bayonets, and landed in the center of the four living walls. The cannonballs made gaps in the cuirassiers, and the cuirassiers made breaches in the squares. Files of men disappeared, trampled down by the horses, and bayonets were buried in the entrails of these centaurs. Hence arose horrible wounds, such as were probably never seen elsewhere. The squares, where broken by the impetuous cavalry, contracted without yielding an inch of ground; inexhaustible in canister, they produced an explosion in the midst of the assailants. The aspect of this combat was monstrous; these squares were no longer battalions, but craters; these cuirassiers were no longer cavalry, but a tempest,—each square was a volcano attacked by a storm; the lava combated the lightning.

The extreme right square, the most exposed of all, as it was in the air, was nearly annihilated in the first attack. It was formed of the 75th Highlanders; the piper in the center, while his comrades were being exterminated around him, was seated on a drum, with his bagpipe under his arm, and playing mountain airs. These Scotchmen died, thinking of Ben Lothian, as the Greeks did, remembering Argos. A cuirassier's saber, by cutting through the pipe and the arm that held it, stopped the tune by killing the player.

The cuirassiers, relatively few in number, and reduced by the catastrophe of the ravine, had against them nearly the whole English army; but they multiplied themselves, and each man was worth ten. Some Hanoverian battalions, however, gave way; Wellington saw it, and thought of his cavalry. Had Napoleon at this minute thought of his infantry, the battle would have been won, and this forgetfulness was his great and fatal fault.

All at once the assailers found themselves assailed; the English cavalry were on their backs, before them the squares, behind them Somerset with the one thousand four hundred dragoon guards. Somerset had on his right Dornberg with the German chevau-legers, and on his left Trip with the Belgian carbineers; the cuirassiers, attacked on the flank and in front, before and behind, by infantry and cavalry, were compelled to make a front on all sides. But what did they care? They were a whirl-wind, their bravery became indescribable.

In addition they had behind them the still thundering battery, and it was only in such a way that these men could be wounded in the back. One of these cuirasses, with a hole through the left scapula, is in the Waterloo Museum.

For such Frenchmen, nothing less than such Englishmen was required.

It was no longer a mêlée, it was a headlong fury, a hurricane of flashing swords. In an instant the one thousand four hundred dragoons were only eight hundred, and Fuller, their lieutenant-colonel, was dead. Ney dashed up with Lefebvre Desnouette's lancers and chasseurs; the plateau of Mont St. Jean was taken and retaken, and taken again. The cuirassiers left the cavalry to attack the infantry, or, to speak more correctly, all these men collared each other and did not loose their hold.

The squares still held out after twelve assaults. Ney had four horses killed under him, and one-half of the cuirassiers remained on the plateau. This struggle lasted two hours.

The English army was profoundly shaken; and there is no doubt that, had not the cuirassiers been weakened in their attack by the disaster of the hollow way, they would have broken through the center and decided the victory. This extraordinary cavalry petrified Clinton, who had seen Talavera and Badajoz. Wellington, three parts vanquished, admired heroically; he said in a low voice, "Splendid!"

The cuirassiers annihilated seven squares out of thirteen, captured or spiked sixty guns, and took six English regimental flags, which three cuirassiers and three chasseurs of the guard carried to the emperor before the farm of la Belle Alliance.

Wellington's situation had grown worse. This strange battle resembled a fight between two savage wounded men, who constantly lose their blood while continuing the struggle. Which would be the first to fall?

The combat for the plateau continued.

How far did the cuirassiers get? no one could say; but it is certain that on the day after the battle a cuirassier and his horse were found dead on the weighing-machine of Mont St. Jean, at the very spot where the

Nivelles, Genappe, La Hulpe, and Brussels roads intersect each other. This horseman had pierced the English lines. One of the men who picked up this corpse still lives at Mont St. Jean; his name is Dehaze, and he was eighteen years of age at the time. Wellington felt himself giving way, and the crisis was close at hand.

The cuirassiers had not succeeded, in the sense that the English center had not been broken. Everybody held the plateau, and nobody held it; but in the end the greater portion remained in the hands of the English. Wellington had the village and the plain; Ney, only the crest and the slope. Both sides seemed to have taken root in this mournful soil.

But the weakness of the English seemed irremediable, for the hemorrhage of this army was horrible. Kempt on the left wing asked for re-enforcements. "There are none," Wellington replied. Almost at the same moment, by a strange coincidence which depicts the exhaustion of both armies, Ney asked Napoleon for infantry, and Napoleon answered, "Infantry? where does he expect me to get them? Does he think I can make them?"

Still the English army was the worse off of the two; the furious attacks of these great squadrons with their iron cuirasses and steel chests had crushed their infantry. A few men round the colors marked the place of a regiment, and some battalions were only commanded by a captain or a lieutenant. Alten's division, already so maltreated at La Haye Sainte, was nearly destroyed; the intrepid Belgians of Van Kluze's brigade lay among the wheat along the Nivelles road; hardly any were left of those Dutch Grenadiers, who, in 1811, fought Wellington in Spain, on the French side, and who, in 1815, joined the English and fought Napoleon. The loss in officers was considérable. Lord Uxbridge, who had his leg interred the next day, had a fractured knee. If on the side of the French in this contest of the cuirassiers Delord, l'Heretier, Colbert, Dnop, Travers, and Blancard were *hors de combat,* on the side of the English, Alten was wounded, Barnes was wounded, Delancy killed, Van Meeren killed, Ompteda killed, Wellington's staff decimated,—and England had the heaviest scale in this balance of blood. The second regiment of foot-guards had lost five lieutenant-colonels, four captains, and three ensigns; the first battalion of the 30th had lost twenty-four officers and one hundred and twelve men; the 79th Highlanders had twenty-four officers wounded and eighteen officers and four hundred and fifty men killed. Cumberland's Hanoverian Hussars, an entire regiment, having their Colonel Hacke at their head, who, at a later date was tried and cashiered, turned bridle during the fight and fled into the forest of Soignies, spreading the rout as far as Brussels. The wagons, ammunition trains, baggage trains, and ambulance carts full of wounded, on seeing the French, gave ground, and, approaching the forest rushed into it; the Dutch, sabered by the French cavalry, broke in confusion. From Vert Coucou to Groenendael, a distance of two leagues on the Brussels roads, there was, according to the testimony of living witnesses, a dense crowd of fugitives, and the panic was so great that it assailed the Prince de Condé at Mechlin and Louis XVIII at Ghent. With the exception of the weak reserve échelonned behind the field hospital established at the farm of Mont St. Jean, and Vivian's and Vandeleur's brigades, which flanked the left wing, Wellington had no cavalry left, and many of the guns lay dismounted. These facts are confessed by Siborne, and Pringle, exaggerating the danger, goes so far as to state that the Anglo-Dutch army was reduced to thirty-four thousand men. The Iron Duke remained firm, but his lips blanched. The Austrian commissioner Vincent, and the Spanish commissioner Alava, who were present at the battle, thought the Duke lost; at five o'clock Wellington looked at his watch, and could be heard muttering, "Blücher or night."

It was at this moment that a distant line of bayonets glistened on the heights on the side of Frischemont.

This was the climax of the gigantic drama.

11. *BÜLOW TO THE RESCUE*

EVERYBODY knows Napoleon's awful mistake; Grouchy expected, Blücher coming up, death instead of life.

Destiny has such turnings as this; men expect the throne of the world, and perceive St. Helena.

If the little shepherd who served as guide to Bülow, Blücher's lieutenant, had advised him to debouch from the forest above Frischemont, instead of below Plancenoit, the form of the nineteenth century would have been different, for Napoleon would have won the battle of Waterloo. By any other road than that below Plancenoit the Prussian army would have come upon a ravine impassable by artillery, and Bülow would not have arrived.

Now one hour's delay—the Prussian general Muffling declares it—and Blücher would not have found Wellington erect,—"the battle was lost."

It was high time, as we see, for Bülow to arrive, and as it was he had been greatly delayed. He had bivouacked at Dion-le-Mont and started at daybreak, but the roads were impracticable, and his division stuck in the mud. The ruts came up to the axle-tree of the guns; moreover, he was compelled to cross the Dyle by the narrow bridge of Wavre; the street leading to the bridge had been burned by the French, and artillery train and limbers, which could not pass between the two rows of blazing houses, were compelled to wait till the fire was extinguished. By midday Bülow's vanguard had scarce reached Chapelle Saint Lambert.

Had the action begun two hours sooner, it would have been over at four o'clock, and Blücher would have fallen upon the battle gained by Napoleon.

At midday, the emperor had been the first to notice, through his telescope, on the extreme horizon, something which fixed his attention, and he said, "I see over there a cloud which appears to me to be troops." Then he asked the Duke of Dalmatia, "Soult, what do you see in the direction of Chapelle Saint Lambert?" The marshal, after looking through his telescope, replied, "Four or five thousand men, sir." It was evidently Grouchy, still they remained motionless in the mist. All the staff examined the cloud pointed out by the emperor, and some said, "They are columns halting," but the majority were of opinion that they were trees. The truth is that the cloud did not move, and the emperor detached Domon's division of light cavalry to reconnoiter in the direction of this dark point.

Bülow, in fact, had not stirred, for his vanguard was very weak and could effect nothing. He was obliged to wait for the main body of the army, and had orders to concentrate his troops before forming line; but at five o'clock, Blücher, seeing Wellington's danger, ordered Bülow to attack, and employed the remarkable phrase, "We must let the English army breathe."

A short time after, Losthin's, Hiller's, Hacke's and Ryssel's brigades deployed in front of Lobau's corps, the cavalry of Prince William of Prussia debouched from the Bois de Paris, Plancenoit was in flames, and the Prussian cannon-balls began pouring even upon the ranks of the guard held in reserve behind Napoleon.

12. *THE GUARD*

THE rest is known,—the irruption of a third army; the battle dislocated; eighty-six cannon thundering simultaneously; Pirch I. coming up with Bülow; Ziethen's cavalry led by Blücher in person; the French driven back; Marcognet swept from the plateau of Ohain; Durutte dislodged from Papelotte; Donzelot and Quiot falling back; Lobau attacked on the flank; a new battle rushing at nightfall on the weakened French regiments; the whole English line resuming the offensive and pushed forward; the gigantic gap made in the French army by the combined English and Prussian batteries; the extermination, the disaster in front, the disaster on the flank, and the guard forming line amid this fearful convulsion.

As they felt they were going to death, they shouted, "Long live the emperor!" History has nothing more striking than this death-rattle breaking out into acclamations.

The sky had been covered the whole day, but at this very moment, eight o'clock in the evening, the clouds parted in the horizon, and the sinister red glow of the setting sun was visible through the elms on the Nivelles road. It had been seen to rise at Austerlitz.

Each battalion of the guard, for this *dénouement,* was commanded by a general: Friant, Michel, Roguet, Harlot, Mallet, and Poret de Morvan were there. When the tall bear-skins of the Grenadiers of the guard with the large eagle device appeared, symmetrical in line and calm, in the twilight of this fight, the enemy felt a respect for France; they fancied they saw twenty victories entering the battle-field with outstretched wings, and the men who were the victors, esteeming themselves vanquished, fell back; but Wellington shouted, "Up, guards, and take steady aim." The red regiment of English guards, which had been lying down behind the hedges, rose; a storm of canister rent the tricolor flag waving above the heads of the French; all rushed forward, and the supreme carnage commenced. The imperial guard felt in the darkness the army giving way around them, and the vast staggering of the rout; they heard the cry of "Sauve qui peut!" substituted for the "Vive l'empereur!" and with flight behind them they continued to advance, hundreds falling at every step they took. None hesitated or evinced timidity; the privates were as heroic as the generals, and not one attempted to escape suicide.

Ney, wild, and grand in the consciousness of accepted death, offered himself to every blow in this combat. He had his fifth horse killed under him here. Bathed in perspiration, with a flame in his eye and foam on his lips, his uniform unbuttoned, one of his epaulettes half cut through by the saber-cut of a horse-guard, and his decoration of the great eagle dinted by a bullet,—bleeding, muddy, magnificent, and holding a broken sword in his hand, he shouted, "Come and see how a marshal of France dies on the battle-field!" But it was in vain—he did not die. He was haggard and indignant, and hurled at Drouet d'Erlon the question, "Are you not going to get yourself killed?" He yelled amid the roar of all this artillery, crushing a handful of men, "Oh! there is nothing for me! I should like all these English cannon-balls to enter my chest!" You were reserved for French bullets, unfortunate man.

1 3 . *THE CATASTROPHE*

THE rout in the rear of the guard was mournful.

The army suddenly gave way on all sides simultaneously at Hougomont, La Haye Sainte, Papelotte, and Plancenoit. The cry of "treachery" was followed by that of "Sauve qui peut!" An army which disbands is like a thaw,—all gives way, cracks, floats, rolls, falls, comes into collision, and dashes forward. Ney borrows a horse, leaps on it, and without hat, stock, or sword dashes across the Brussels road, stopping at once English and French. He tries to hold back the army, he recalls it, he insults it, he clings wildly to the rout to hold it back. The soldiers fly from him, shouting "Long live Marshal Ney!" Two regiments of Durutte's move backward and forward in terror, and, as it were, tossed between the sabers of the Hussars and the musketry fire of Kempt's, Best's, and Pack's brigades. A rout is the highest of all confusions, for friends kill each other in order to escape, and squadrons and battalions dash against and destroy each other. Lobau at one extremity and Reille at the other are carried away by the torrent. In vain does Napoleon build a wall of what is left of the guard; in vain does he expend the squadrons of his body-guard in a final effort. Quiot retires before Vivian, Kellermann before Vandeleur, Lobau before Bülow, Moraud before Pirch, and Domon and Subervic before Prince William of Prussia. Guyot, who led the emperor's squadrons to the charge, falls beneath the horses of English dragoons. Napoleon gallops along the line of fugitives, harangues, urges, threatens, and implores them; all the mouths that shouted "Long live the emperor" in the morning, remained wide open; they hardly knew him. The Prussian cavalry, who had come up fresh, dash forward, cut down, kill, and exterminate. The artillery horses dash forward with the guns; the train soldiers unharness the horses from the caissons and escape on them; wagons overthrown and with their four wheels in the air block up the road and supply opportunities for massacre. Men crush each other, and trample over the dead and over the living. A multitude, wild with terror, fill the roads, the paths, the bridges, the plains, the hills, the valleys, and the woods, which are thronged by this flight of forty thousand men. Cries, desperation; knapsacks and muskets cast into the wheat; passages cut with the edge of the sabers; no comrades, no officers, no generals recognized—an indescribable terror. Ziethen sabering France at his ease. The lions become kids. Such was this fight.

At Genappe, an effort was made to turn and rally; Lobau collected three hundred men; the entrance of the village was barricaded, but at the first round of Prussian canister all began flying again, and Lobau was made prisoner. This volley may still be seen, buried in the gable of an old brick house on the right of the road, just before you reach Genappe. The Prussians dashed into Genappe, doubtless furious at being such small victors, and the pursuit was monstrous, for Blücher commanded extermination. Roguet had given the mournful example of threatening with death any French Grenadier who brought in a Prussian prisoner, and Blücher surpassed Roguet. Duchesme, general of the young guard, who was pursued into the door-way of an inn in Genappe, surrendered his sword to an Hussar of death, who took the sword and killed the prisoner. The victory was completed by the assassination of the vanquished. Let us punish, as we are writing history,—old Blücher dishonored himself. This ferocity set the seal on the disaster; the desperate rout passed through Genappe, passed through Quatre Bras, passed through Sombreffe, passed through Frasnes, passed through Thuin, passed through Charleroi, and only stopped at the frontier. Alas! and who was it flying in this way? The grand army.

Did this vertigo, this terror, this overthrow of the greatest bravery that ever astonished history, take place without a cause? No. The shadow of a mighty right hand is cast over Waterloo; it is the day of destiny, and the force which is above man produced that day. Hence the terror, hence all those great souls laying down their swords. Those who had conquered Europe fell crushed, having nothing more to say or do, and feeling a terrible presence in the shadow. *Hoc erat in fatis.* On that day the perspective of the human race was changed, and Waterloo is the hinge of the nineteenth century. The disappearance of the great man was necessary for the advent of the great age, and He who cannot be answered undertook the task. The panic of the heroes admits of explanation; in the battle of Waterloo, there is more than a storm—there is a meteor.

At nightfall, Bernard and Bertrand seized by the skirt of his coat, in a field near Genappe, a haggard, thoughtful, gloomy man, who, carried so far by the current of the rout, had just dismounted, passed the bridle over his arm and was now, with wandering eye, returning alone to Waterloo. It was Napoleon, the immense somnambulist of the shattered dream still striving to advance.

14. *THE LAST SQUARE*

A FEW squares of the guard, standing motionless in the swash of the rout, like rocks in running water, held out till night. They awaited the double shadow of night and death, and let them surround them. Each regiment, isolated from the others, and no longer connected with the army which was broken on all sides, died where it stood. In order to perform this last exploit, they had taken up a position, some on the heights of Rossomme, others on the plain of Mont St. Jean. The gloomy squares, deserted, conquered, and terrible, struggled formidably with death, for Ulm, Wagram, Jena, and Friedland were dying in it.

When twilight set in at nine in the evening, one square still remained at the foot of the plateau of Mont St. Jean. In this mournful valley, at the foot of the slope scaled by the cuirassiers, now inundated by the English masses, beneath the converging fire of the hostile and victorious artillery, under fearful hailstorm of projectiles, this square still resisted. It was commanded by an obscure officer of the name of Cambronne. At each volley the square diminished, but continued to reply to the canister with musketry fire, and each moment contracted its four walls. Fugitives in the distance, stopping at moments to draw breath, listened in the darkness to this gloomy diminishing thunder.

When this legion had become only a handful, when their colors were but a rag, when their ammunition was exhausted and muskets were clubbed, and when the pile of corpses was greater than the living group, the victors felt a species of sacred awe, and the English artillery ceased firing. It was a sort of respite; these combatants had around them an army of specters, outlines of mounted men, the black profile of guns, and the white sky visible through the wheels; the colossal death's-head, which heroes ever glimpse in the smoke of a battle, advanced and looked at

40

them. They could hear in the twilight gloom that the guns were being loaded; the lighted matches, resembling the eyes of a tiger in the night, formed a circle round their heads. The linstocks of the English batteries approached the guns, and at this moment an English general, Colville according to some, Maitland according to others, holding the supreme moment suspended over the heads of these men, shouted to them, "Brave Frenchmen, surrender!"

Cambronne answered: "Merde."

15. *CAMBRONNE*

AS THE French reader desires to be respected, the most sublime word ever uttered by any Frenchman cannot be repeated. "Post no sublimity on history."

At our own risk and peril we will defy this notice.

Among these giants, then, there was a Titan, Cambronne.

To utter this word and then die, what could be more grand! To die is to be willing to die, and it is not the fault of this man, if, mowed down by grape-shot, he survived.

The man who gained the battle of Waterloo was not Napoleon with his routed army; it was not Wellington, giving way at four o'clock, and desperate at five; it was not Blücher, for he had not fought,—the man who won the battle of Waterloo is Cambronne.

To smite with the lightning of such a word the thunderbolt which kills you is to be victorious.

To make such a reply to disaster, to say this to destiny, to lay such a base for the future lion, to hurl this answer to the rain of the night, to the treacherous wall of Hougomont, to the Hollow Road of Ohain, to the delay of Grouchy, to the arrival of Blücher, to be irony in the tomb, to stand erect, as it were, after one shall have fallen to submerge in two syllables the European coalition, to present to kings the latrines already known by the Cæsars, to make the last words the first, by imparting to it the brilliancy of France, to insultingly close Waterloo by Shrove Tuesday repartee, to complete Leonidas by Rabelais, to sum up this victory in one supreme word, impossible to pronounce, to lose ground and preserve history, after such a carnage to have the laughers on your side,—this is immense.

It is to defy the lightning with Æschylean grandeur.

The utterance of Cambronne has the effect of a breakage. It is the breaking of the bosom by disdain, it is the excess of the agony which makes the explosion. Who conquered? Wellington? No. Without Blücher he had been lost. Is it Blücher? No. If Wellington had not begun, Blücher could not have finished. This Cambronne, this passer-by at the last hour, this unknown soldier, this infinitely little bit of the war, feels that there is a lie beneath the catastrophe doubly bitter; and at the instant when he is bursting with rage they offer him that absurdity—life! How could he refrain from breaking out? There they are, all the kings of Europe, the lucky generals, the thundering Joves; they have one hundred thousand victorious soldiers; behind them, a hundred thousand, a million; their cannon, with matches lighted, are gaping; they have under their heels the Imperial guard and the Grand army; they have crushed Napoleon, Cambronne only remains,—only this earth-worm is left to protest, and he will protest. He looked for a word as he would for a sword. Foam is on his lips, and this foam is the word. In presence of this victory, prodigious yet commonplace, of this victory without victors, the desperate man erects himself; he submits to its magnitude, but he demonstrates its nothingness; he does more than spit on it, and under the crushing load of numbers, force, and material he finds for his soul one sole term—*excrement*. We repeat it, to say this, to do this, to invent this, is to be the victor.

At this fated moment the spirit of the great days entered this unknown man. Cambronne found the word of Waterloo as Rouget de l'Isle found the *Marseillaise* by an inspiration from on high. A breath of the divine hurricane passed over these men, and they shuddered; one sings the supreme song, the other utters the fearful cry. This word, full of Titanic scorn, was hurled by Cambronne not only at Europe in the name of the Empire,—that would have been little,—but at the past in the name of the Revolution. We hear and see in Cambronne the old soul of the giants; it seems as if Danton were speaking or Kleber roaring.

To Cambronne's exclamation, an English voice replied, "Fire!" The batteries flashed, the hillside trembled, from all these throats of brass came a last eruption of grape, a vast cloud of smoke vaguely whitened by the rising moon rolled up, and when the smoke had been dissipated there was nothing. The dreaded remnant was annihilated, the guard was dead. The four walls of the living redoubt lay low, with here and there a scarcely perceptible quiver among the corpses. Thus the French legions, grander than those of Rome, expired at Mont St. Jean, on the earth sodden with rain and blood, in the gloomy corn-fields at the spot where now at four o'clock in the morning Joseph, the driver of the mail-cart from Nivelles, passes, whistling and gayly whipping up his horse.

16. *QUOT LIBRAS IN DUCE?*

THE battle of Waterloo is an enigma as obscure for those who gained it as for him who lost it. To Napoleon it is a panic;* Blücher sees nothing in it but fire; Wellington does not understand it at all. Look at the reports; the bulletins are confused; the commentaries are entangled; the latter stammer, the former stutter. Jomini divides the battle of Waterloo into four moments; Muffling cuts it into three acts; Charras, although we do not entirely agree with him in all his appreciations, has alone caught with his haughty eye the characteristic lineaments of this catastrophe of human genius contending with divine chance. All the other historians suffer from a certain bedazzlement in which they grope about. It was a flashing day; in truth, the overthrow of the military monarchy which, to the great stupor of the kings, has dragged down all kingdoms, the downfall of strength and the rout of war.

* Une bataille terminée, une journée finie, de fausses mésures reparées, de plus grands succès assurés pour le lendemain, tout fut perdu par un moment de terreur panique.

(Napoleon at St. Helena.)

In this event, which bears the stamp of superhuman necessity, men play but a small part.

If we take Waterloo from Wellington and Blücher, does that deprive England and Germany of anything? No. Neither illustrious England nor august Germany is in question in the problem of Waterloo, for, thank heaven! nations are great without the mournful achievements of the sword. Neither Germany nor England nor France is held in a scabbard; at this day, when Waterloo is only a clash of sabers, Germany has Goethe above Blücher, and England Byron above Wellington. A mighty dawn of ideas is peculiar to our age, and in this dawn England and Germany have their own magnificent flash. They are majestic because they think; the high level they bring to civilization is intrinsic to them; it comes from themselves, and not from an accident. Any aggrandizement the nineteenth century may have cannot boast of Waterloo as its fountain-head; for only barbarous nations grow suddenly after a victory—it is the transient vanity of torrents swollen by a storm. Civilized nations, especially at the present day, are not elevated or debased by the good or evil fortune of a captain, and their specific weight in the human family results from something more than a battle. Their honor, dignity, enlightenment, and genius are not numbers which those gamblers, heroes and conquerors, can stake in the lottery of battles. Very often a battle lost is progress gained, and less of glory more of liberty. The drummer is silent and reason speaks; it is the game of who loses wins. Let us, then, speak of Waterloo coldly from both sides, and render to chance the things that belong to chance, and to God what is God's. What is Waterloo,—a victory? No; a prize in the lottery.

A prize won by Europe and paid by France.

It was hardly worth while erecting a lion for it.

Waterloo, by the way, is the strangest encounter recorded in history; Napoleon and Wellington are not enemies, but contraries. Never did God, who delights in antitheses, produce a more striking contrast or a more extraordinary confrontation. On one side precision, foresight, geometry, prudence, a retreat assured, reserves prepared, an obstinate coolness, an imperturbable method, strategy profiting by the ground, tactics balancing battalions, carnage measured by a plumb-line, war regulated watch in hand, nothing left voluntarily to accident, old classic courage and absolute correctness. On the other side we have intuition, divination, military strangeness, superhuman instinct, a flashing glance; something that gazes like the eagle and strikes like lightning, all the mysteries of a profound mind, association with destiny; the river the plain, the forest and the hill summoned, and to some extent compelled, to obey, the despot going so far as even to tyrannize over the battle-field; faith in a star blended with strategic science, heightening but troubling it. Wellington was the Bareme of war, Napoleon was its Michael Angelo, and this true genius was conquered by calculation.

On both sides somebody was expected; and it was the exact-calculator who succeeded. Napoleon waited for Grouchy, who did not come; Wellington waited for Blücher, and he came.

Wellington is the classical war taking its revenge; Bonaparte, in his dawn, had met it in Italy and superbly defeated it,—the old owl fled before the young vulture. The old tactics had been not only overthrown, but scandalized. Who was this Corsican of six-and-twenty years of age? what meant this splendid ignoramus who, having everything against him, nothing for him, without provisions, ammunition, guns, shoes, almost without an army, with a handful of men against masses, dashed at allied Europe, and absurdly gained impossible victories? Who was this new-comer of war who possessed the effrontery of a planet? The academic military school excommunicated him, while bolting, and hence arose an implacable rancor of the old Cæsarism against the new, of the old saber against the flashing sword, and of the chess-board against genius. On June 18, 1815, this rancor got the best; and beneath Lodi, Montebello, Montenotte, Mantua, Marengo, and Arcola, it wrote,—Waterloo. It was a triumph of mediocrity, sweet to majorities, and destiny consented to this irony. In his decline, Napoleon found a young Wurmser before him.

In fact, it is only necessary to blanch Wellington's hair in order to have a Wurmser.

Waterloo is a battle of the first class, gained by a captain of the second.

What must be admired in the battle of Waterloo is England, the English firmness, the English resolution, the English blood, and what England had really superb in it is (without offense) herself; it is not her captain, but her army.

Wellington, strangely ungrateful, declares in his dispatch to Lord Bathurst, that his army, the one which fought on June 18, 1815, was a "detestable army." What does the gloomy pile of bones buried in the trenches of Waterloo think of this?

England has been too modest to herself in her treatment of Wellington, for making him so great in making herself small. Wellington is merely a hero like any other man. The Scotch Greys, the Life Guards, Maitland and Mitchell's regiments, Pack and Kempt's infantry, Ponsonby and Somerset's cavalry, the Highlanders playing the bagpipes under the shower of canister, Ryland's battalions, the fresh recruits who could hardly manage a musket, and yet held their ground against the old bands of Essling and Rivoli—all this is grand. Wellington was tenacious; that was his merit, and we do not deny it to him, but the lowest of his privates and his troopers was quite as solid as he, and the iron soldier is as good as the iron duke. For our part, all our glorification is offered to the English soldier, the English army, the English nation; and if there must be a trophy, it is to England that this trophy is owing. The Waterloo column would be more just, if, instead of the figure of a man, it raised to the clouds the statue of a people.

But this great England will be irritated by what we are writing here; for she still has feudal illusions, after her 1688 and the French 1789. This people believes in inheritance and hierarchy, and while no other excels it in power and glory, it esteems itself as a nation and not as a people. As a people, it readily subordinates itself, and takes a lord as its head; the workman lets himself be despised; the soldier puts up with flogging.

It will be remembered that, at the battle of Inkermann, a sergeant, who, it appears, saved the British army, could not be mentioned by Lord Raglan, because the military hierarchy does not allow any hero below the rank of officer to be mentioned in dispatches.

What we admire before all, in an encounter like Waterloo, is the prodigious skill of chance. The night rain, the wall of Hougomont, the hollow way of Ohain, Grouchy deaf to the cannon, Napoleon's guide deceiving him, Bulow's guide enlightening him—all this cataclysm is marvelously managed.

Altogether, we will assert, there is more of a massacre than of a battle in Waterloo.

Waterloo, of all pitched battles, is the one which had the smallest front for such a number of combatants. Napoleon's, three-quarters of a league, Wellington's, half a league, and seventy-two thousand combatants on either side. From this density came the carnage.

The following calculation has been made and proportion established: loss of men, at Austerlitz, French, fourteen per cent; Russian, thirty per cent; Austrian, forty-four per cent; at Wagram, French, thirteen per cent; Austrian, fourteen per cent; at Moskova, French, thirty-seven per cent; Russian, forty-four per cent; at Bautzen, French, thirteen per cent; Russian and Prussian, fourteen per cent; at Waterloo, French, fifty-six per cent; Allies, thirty-one per cent—total for Waterloo, forty-one per cent; or out of one hundred and forty-four thousand fighting men, sixty thousand killed.

The field of Waterloo has at the present day that calmness which belongs to the earth, and resembles all plains.

At night a sort of visionary mist rises from it, and if any traveler walk about it, and listen and dream like Virgil on the mournful plain of Philippi, the hallucination of the catastrophe seizes upon him. The frightful June 18 lives again, the false monumental hill is leveled, the wondrous lion is dissipated, the battle-field resumes its reality, lines of infantry undulate on the plain, furious galloping crosses the horizon; the startled dreamer sees the flash of sabers, the sparkle of bayonets, the red light of shells, the monstrous collision of thunderbolts; he hears, like a death-groan from the tomb, the vague clamor of the phantom battle. These shadows are grenadiers; these flashes are cuirassiers; this skeleton is Napoleon; this skeleton is Wellington; all this is non-existent, and yet still combats, and the ravines are stained purple, and the trees rustle, and there is fury even in the clouds and in the darkness, while all the stern heights, Mont St. Jean, Hougomont, Frischemont, Papelotte, and Plancenoit, seem confusedly crowned by hosts of specters exterminating one another.

17. OUGHT WATERLOO TO BE APPROVED?

THERE exists a highly respectable liberal school which does not detest Waterloo, but we do not belong to it. For us Waterloo is only the stupefied date of liberty; for such an eagle to issue from such a shell is assuredly unexpected.

Waterloo, if we place ourselves at the culminating point of the question, is intentionally a counter-revolutionary victory,—it is Europe against France; it is Petersburg, Berlin, and Vienna against Paris; it is the *statu quo* opposed to the initiative; it is the 14th July, 1789, attacked through March 20, 1815; it is all the monarchies clearing the decks to conquer the indomitable French spirit of revolt. The dream was to extinguish this vast people which had been in a state of eruption for six-and-twenty years, and for this purpose, Brunswick, Nassau, the Romanoffs, Hohenzollern and the Hapsburger coalesced with the Bourbons, and Waterloo carries divine right on its pillion. It is true that as the empire was despotic, royalty, by the natural reaction of things, was compelled to be liberal, and a constitutional order issued from Waterloo, much to the regret of the conquerors. The fact is, that the Revolution can never be really conquered, and being providential and absolutely fatal, it constantly reappears,—before Waterloo in Napoleon overthrowing the old thrones, after Waterloo in Louis XVIII granting and enduring the charter. Bonaparte places a postilion on the throne of Naples and a sergeant on the throne of Sweden, employing inequality to demonstrate equality; Louis XVIII at St. Ouen countersigns the declaration of the rights of man. If you wish to understand what revolution is, call it progress; and if you wish to understand what progress is, call it to-morrow. To-morrow ever does its work irresistibly and does it to-day, and it ever strangely attains its object. It employs Wellington to make an orator of Foy, who was only a soldier. Foy falls at Hougomont and raises himself in the tribune. Such is the process of progress, and that workman has no bad tools; it fits to its divine work the man who bestrode the Alps and the old tottering patient of Père Elysée, and it employs both the gouty man and the conqueror—the conqueror externally, the gouty man at home. Waterloo, by cutting short the demolition of thrones by the sword, had no other effect than to continue the revolutionary work on another side. The sabers have finished, and the turn of the thinkers arrives; the age which Waterloo wished to arrest marched over it, and continued its route, and this sinister victory was vanquished by liberty.

Still it is incontestable that what triumphed at Waterloo; what smiled behind Wellington; what procured him all the marshals' staffs of Europe, including, by the way, that of Marshal of France; what rolled along joyously the wheel-barrows of earth mingled with bones, to erect the foundation for the lion, on whose pedestal is inscribed the date June 18, 1815; what encouraged Blücher in cutting down the routed army; and what from the plateau of Mont St. Jean hovered over France like a prey, was the counter-revolution. It is counter-revolution that muttered the hideous word, "dismemberment"; but on reaching Paris it had a close view of the crater,—it felt that the ashes burned its feet, and it reflected. It went back to the job of stammering a charter.

Let us only see in Waterloo what there really is in it. There is no intentional liberty, for the counter-revolution was involuntarily liberal in the same way as Napoleon, through a corresponding phenomenon, was involuntarily a Revolutionist. On June 18, 1815, Robespierre on horseback was thrown.

18. RESTORATION OF DIVINE RIGHT

WITH the fall of the dictatorship, an entire European system crumbled away.

The Empire vanished in a shadow which resembled that of the expiring Roman world. Nations escaped from the abyss as in the time of the barbarians, but the barbarism of 1815, which could be called by its familiar name, the counter-revolution, had but little breath, soon began to pant, and stopped. The empire, we confess, was lamented and by heroic eyes, and its glory consists in the sword-made scepter,—the empire was glory itself. It had spread over the whole earth all the light that tyranny can give—a dim light, we will say, an obscure light, for, when compared with real day, it is night.

This disappearance of the night produced the effect of an eclipse.

Louis XVIII reëntered Paris, and the dances of July 8 effaced the enthusiasm of March 20. The Corsican became the antithesis of the Béarnais, and the flag on the dome of the Tuileries was white. The exile was enthroned, and the deal table of Hartwell was placed before the fleur-de-lised easy-chair of Louis XIV. People talked of Bouvines and Fontenoy as if they had occurred yesterday, while Austerlitz was antiquated. The throne and the altar fraternized majestically, and one of the most indubitable forms of the welfare of society in the nineteenth century was established in France and on the Continent—Europe took the white cockade. Trestaillon was celebrated, and the motto *nec pluribus impar* re-appeared in the stone beams representing a sun on the front of the barracks, on the Quai d'Orsay. Where there had been an imperial guard, there was a "red household"; and the arch of the Carrousel, if loaded with badly endured victories, feeling not at home in these novelties, and perhaps slightly ashamed of Marengo and Arcola, got out of the difficulty by accepting the statue of the Duc d'Angoulême. The cemetery of the Madeleine, a formidable public grave in '93, was covered with marble and jasper, because the bones of Louis XVI and Marie Antoinette were mingled with that dust. In the moat of Vincennes a tomb emerged from the ground, as a reminder that the Duc d'Enghien died there in the same month in which Napoleon was crowned. Pope Pius VII, who had performed the ceremony very close upon that death, tranquilly blessed the downfall, as he had blessed the elevation. There was at Schönbrunn a shadow four years of age, whom it was seditious to call the king of Rome. And these things took place, and these kings regained their thrones, and the master of Europe was put in a cage, and the old régime became the new, and the light and the shadow of the earth changed places, because on the afternoon of a summer day a peasant boy said to a Prussian in a wood, "Go this way and not that!"

That 1815 was a sort of melancholy April; the old unhealthy and venomous realities assumed a new aspect. Falsehood espoused 1789; divine right put on the mask of a charter; fictions became constitutional; prejudices, superstitions, and after-thoughts, having article fourteen in their hearts, varnished themselves with liberalism. The snakes cast their slough.

Man had been at once aggrandized and lessened by Napoleon; idealism, in this reign of splendid materialism, received the strange name of ideology. It was a grave imprudence of a man to ridicule the future, but the people, that food for powder, so fond of the gunners, sought him. "Where is he? What is he doing?" "Napoleon is dead," said a passer-by to an invalid of Marengo and Waterloo. "He dead!" the soldier exclaimed; "much you know about him!" Imaginations deified this man overthrown. Europe after Waterloo was dark, for some enormous gap was long left unfilled after the disappearance of Napoleon.

The kings placed themselves in this gap, and old Europe took advantage of it to effect a reformation. There was a holy alliance—Belle Alliance, the fatal field of Waterloo had said beforehand.

In the presence of the old Europe reconstituted, the lineaments of a new France were sketched in. The future, derided by the emperor, made its entry and wore on its brow the star—Liberty. The ardent eyes of the youthful generation were turned toward it, but, singular to say, they simultaneously felt equally attached to this future liberty and to the past Napoleon. Defeat had made the conquered man greater; Napoleon fallen seemed better than Napoleon standing on his feet. Those who had triumphed were alarmed. England had him guarded by Hudson Lowe, and France had him watched by Montchenu. His folded arms became the anxiety of thrones, and Alexander christened him his insomnia. This terror resulted from the immense amount of revolution he had in him, and it is this which explains and excuses Bonapartistic liberalism. This phantom caused the old world to tremble, and kings sat uneasily on their thrones, with the rock of St. Helena on the horizon.

While Napoleon was dying at Longwood, the sixty thousand men who fell at Waterloo rotted calmly, and something of their peace spread over the world. The congress of Vienna converted it into the treaties of 1815, and Europe called that the Restoration.

Such is Waterloo.

But what does the infinite care? all this tempest, all this cloud, this war, and then this peace; all this shadow did not for a moment disturb the flash of that mighty eye before which a grub, leaping from one blade of grass to another, equals the eagle flying from tower to tower at Notre Dame.

19. *THE BATTLE-FIELD BY NIGHT*

WE must return, for it is a necessity of the story, to the fatal battle-field of June 18, 1815.

The moon shone brightly, and this favored Blücher's ferocious pursuit, revealed the trail of the fugitives, surrendered this ill-starred crowd to the Prussian cavalry, and assisted the massacre. Such tragical complacency of the night is witnessed at times in catastrophes.

After the last cannon was fired, the plain of Mont St. Jean remained deserted.

The English occupied the French encampment, for the usual confirmation of victory is to sleep in the beds of the conquered. They established their bivouac a little beyond Rossomme, and while the Prussians followed up the fugitives, Wellington proceeded to the village of Waterloo to draw up his report for Lord Bathurst.

Were ever the *Sic vos non vobis* applicable, it is most certainly to this village of Waterloo, which did nothing, and was half a league away from the action. Mont St. Jean was cannonaded, Hougomont burned, Papelotte burned, Plancenoit burned, La Haye Sainte carried by storm, and La Belle Alliance witnessed the embrace of the two victors; but these names are scarce known, and Waterloo, which did nothing during the battle, has all the honor of it.

We are not of those who flatter war, and when the opportunity offers we tell it the truth. War has frightful beauties which we have not concealed; but it has also, we must allow, some ugly features. One of the most surprising is the rapid stripping of the dead after victory; the dawn that follows a battle always rises on naked corpses.

Who does this? Who sullies the triumph in this way? Whose is the hideous, furtive hand which slips into the pocket of victory? Who are the villains dealing their stroke behind the glory? Some philosophers, Voltaire among them, assert that they are the very men who have made the glory; they say that those who keep their feet plunder those lying on the ground, and the hero of the day is the vampire of the night. After all a man has the right to strip a corpse of which he is the author. We do not believe it, however; reaping a crop of laurels and stealing the shoes of a dead man do not seem to us possible from the same hand.

One thing is certain, that, as a usual rule, robbers come after the conquerors, but we must leave the soldier, especially him of to-day, out of the question.

Every army has a tail; and it is that which must be accused. Batlike beings, half servants, half brigands, all the species of the vespertilio which the twilight called war engenders, wearers of uniform who do not fight, malingerers, formidable invalids, interloping sutlers, trotting with their wives in small carts and stealing things which they sell again, beggars offering themselves as guides to officers, villains, marauders,—all these, armies marching in former times (we are not alluding to the present day) had with them, so that in the special language they were called "the stragglers." No army and no nation were responsible for these beings,—they spoke Italian and followed the Germans; they spoke French and followed the English. It was by one of these scoundrels, a Spanish camp-follower who spoke French, that the Marquis de Fervacques, deceived by his Picardy accent, and taking him for a Frenchman, was killed and robbed on the battle-field during the night that followed the victory of Cerisolles. The detestable maxim, "Live on the enemy," produced this leprosy, which strict discipline could alone cure. There are some reputations which deceive, and we do not always know why certain generals, in other respects great, became so popular. Turenne was adored by his troops, because he tolerated plunder; evil permitted is kindness, and Turenne was so kind that he allowed the Palatinate to be destroyed by sword and fire. A larger or smaller amount of marauders followed an army, according as the chief was more or less severe. Hoche and Morceau had no camp-followers, and Wellington, we willingly do him the justice of stating, had but few.

Still on the night of June 18 the dead were stripped. Wellington was strict; he ordered that everybody caught in the act should be shot; but rapine is tenacious, and marauders plundered in one corner of the field while they were being shot in the other.

The moon shot sinister gleams over the plain.

About midnight a man was prowling, or rather crawling, about the hollow road of Ohain; he was, according to all appearances, one of those whom we have just described,—neither English nor French, nor peasant nor soldier, less a man than a ghoul, attracted by the smell of the dead, whose victory was robbery, and who had come to plunder Waterloo. He was dressed in a blouse, which looked something like a gown, was anxious and daring, and looked behind him while he went onward. Who was this man? Night knew probably more about him than did day. He had no bag, but evidently capacious pockets under his blouse. From time to time he stopped, examined the plain around him as if to see whether he was watched, bent down quickly, disturbed something lying silent and motionless on the ground, and then drew himself up and again stepped away. His attitude and his rapid, mysterious movements made him resemble those twilight *larvæ* which haunt ruins, and which the old Norman legends call "les alleurs."

Certain nocturnal fowlers display the same outline on the marshes.

Any one who had attentively examined would have seen behind the house which stands at the intersection of the Nivelles and Mont St. Jean roads, a sort of small vivandière's cart with a tilt of tarpaulin stretched over wicker-work, drawn by a hungry-looking, staggering horse, which was nibbling the nettles. In this cart a woman was seated on chests and bundles, and there was probably some connection between this cart and the prowler.

There was not a cloud in the sky, and though the ground may be blood-red, the moon remains white; that is the indifference of nature. In the fields branches of trees broken by cannon-balls, but still holding on by the bark, waved softly in the night breeze. A breath shook the brambles, and there was a quiver in the grass that resembled the departure of souls.

In the distance could be confusedly heard the march of the English patrols and rounds.

Hougomont and La Haye Sainte continued to burn, making one in the west, the other in the east—two large bodies of flames, to which were joined the English bivouac fires, stretching along the hills on the horizon, in an immense semicircle. The scene produced the effect of an unfastened ruby necklace, with a carbuncle at either end.

We have described the catastrophe of the Ohain road,—the heart is chilled by the thought of what this death had been for so many brave men.

If there be anything frightful, if there exist a reality which surpasses dreaming, it is this,—to live, to see the sun; to be in full possession of manly vigor; to have health and joy; to laugh valiantly; to run toward a glory glittering before you: to feel in your chest lungs that breathe, a heart that beats, and a will that reasons; to speak, to think, to hope, to love; to have a mother, a wife, and children; to have light,—and then suddenly, before there is time for a cry, to be hurled into an abyss; to fall, roll, crush, and be crushed; to see cornstalks, flowers, leaves, and branches, and to be unable to hold on to anything; to feel your saber useless, men under you and horses over you; to struggle in vain; to have your ribs fractured by some kick in the gloom; to feel a heel on your eyes; to bite with rage the horses' shoes; to stifle, to yell, to writhe; to be underneath, and say to yourself, "A moment ago I was a living man!"

At the spot where this lamentable disaster occurred, all was now silence. The hollow way was filled with an inextricable pile of horses and their riders. There was no slope now, for the corpses leveled the road with the plain, and came up flush to the top, like a fairly measured bushel of barley. A pile of dead atop, a stream of blood at bottom,—such was the road on the night of June 18, 1815. The blood ran as far as the Nivelles road, and extravasated there in a wide pool in front of the barricade, at a spot which is still pointed out.

It will be remembered that the destruction of the cuirassiers took place at the opposite point, near the Genappe road. The depth of the corpses was proportionate to that of the hollow way; toward the middle, at the spot where Delord's division passed, the layer of dead was thinner.

The nocturnal prowler, at whom we have allowed the reader a glance, proceeded in that direction, searching this immense tomb. He looked around and held a hideous review of the dead; he walked with his feet in the blood.

All at once he stooped.

A few paces before him in the hollow way, at the point where the pile of dead ended, an open hand illumined by the moon, emerged from the heap of men and horses.

This hand had on one finger something that glittered, and was a gold ring.

The man bent down, and when he rose again there was no longer a ring on this finger.

He did not exactly rise; he remained in a savage and shy attitude, turning his back to the pile of dead, investigating the horizon, supporting

55

himself on his two forefingers, and his head spying over the edge of the hollow way. The four paws of the jackal are suited for certain actions.

Then, making up his mind, he rose.

At the same moment he started, for he felt that some one was holding him behind.

He turned and found that it was the open hand which had closed and seized the skirt of his coat.

An honest man would have been frightened, but this one began laughing.

"Hilloh!" he said, "It is only the dead man. I prefer a ghost to a gendarme."

The hand, however, soon relaxed its hold, for efforts are quickly exhausted in the tomb.

"Can this dead man be alive?" the marauder continued. "Let me have a look."

He bent down again, removed all the obstacles, seized the hand, liberated the head, pulled out the body, and a few moments later dragged an inanimate, or at least fainting, man into the shadow of the hollow way. He was an officer of cuirassiers of a certain rank, for a heavy gold epaulette peeped out from under his cuirass. This officer had lost his helmet, and a furious saber-cut crossed his face, which was covered with blood.

He did not appear, however, to have any bones broken, and through some fortunate accident, if such a word be possible here, the dead had formed an arch over him so as to save him from being crushed. His eyes were closed.

He had on his cuirass the silver cross of the Legion of Honor.

The prowler tore away this cross, which disappeared in one of the gulfs he had under his blouse.

After this he felt the officer's fob, found a watch and took it; then he felt in his pockets and drew from them a purse.

When he was at this stage of the assistance he was rendering the dying man, the officer opened his eyes.

"Thanks," he said feebly.

The roughness of the man's movements, the freshness of the night, and the freely inhaled air, had aroused him from his lethargy.

The prowler did not answer, but raised his head. A sound of footsteps could be heard on the plain; it was probably some patrol approaching.

The officer murmured, for there was still the agony of death in his voice:

"Who won the battle?"

"The English," the marauder answered.

The officer continued:

"Feel in my pockets; you will find a purse and a watch which you can take."

Though this was already done, the prowler did what was requested, and said:

"There is nothing in them."

"I have been robbed," the officer continued; "I am sorry for it, as I meant the things for you."

The footsteps of the patrol became more and more distinct.

"Some one is coming," the marauder said, preparing to go away.

The officer, raising his arm with difficulty, stopped him.

"You have saved my life; who are you?"

The prowler answered rapidly, and in a low voice: "I belong, like yourself, to the French army, but I must leave you; for if I were caught I should be shot,—I have saved your life, so now get out of the scrape as you can."

"What is your rank?"

"Sergeant."

"Your name?"

"Thénardier."

"I shall not forget that name," the officer said; "and do you remember mine—it is Pontmercy."

BOOK II

THE SHIP ORION

1. *No. 24,601* BECOMES *No. 9430*

J EAN VALJEAN was recaptured.

As our readers will probably thank us for passing rapidly over painful details, we confine ourselves to the quotation of two paragraphs published by the newspapers of the day, a few months after the occurrence of the surprising events at M. . . . .

These articles are rather summary, but it must be remembered that no *Gazette des Tribunaux* existed at that period.

The first we take from the *Drapeau Blanc,* dated July 25, 1823:

"A bailiwick of the Pas de Calais has just been the scene of an uncommon event. A man, who was a stranger to the department and called M. Madeleine, had some years previously revived by a new process an old local trade, the manufacture of jet and black beads. He made his own fortune, and, let us add, that of the bailiwick, and in acknowledgment of his services he was appointed mayor. The police discovered that M. Madeleine was no other man than an ex-convict, who had broken his ban, condemned in 1796 for robbery, of the name of Jean Valjean. He had been sent back to the bagne. It appears that prior to his arrest he succeeded in withdrawing from M. Lafitte's a sum of more than half a million, which he had banked there, and which, it is said, he had honestly acquired by his trade. Since his return to Toulon, futile efforts have been made to discover where this amount is concealed."

The second article, which is rather more detailed, is extracted from the *Journal de Paris* of the same date:

"An ex-convict of the name of Jean Valjean has just been tried at the Var assizes, under circumstances which attract attention. This villain had

61

succeeded in deceiving the vigilance of the police, and had behaved so cleverly as to be made mayor of one of our small towns in the north, where he established a rather considerable trade. He was at length unmasked and arrested through the indefatigable zeal of the public authorities. He had, as his concubine, a girl of the town, who died of a fit at the moment of his arrest. This scoundrel, who is endowed with Herculean strength, managed to escape, but three or four days later the police again captured him in Paris, at the moment when he was entering one of those small coaches which run from the capital to the village of Montfermeil (Seine et Oise). It is said that he took advantage of these three or four days of liberty to withdraw from one of our chief bankers an amount estimated at six or seven hundred thousand francs. According to the indictment he buried it at some spot only known to himself, and it has not been found; but, however this may be, this Jean Valjean has just been tried at Var assizes for a highway robbery, committed with violence some eight years ago upon one of those honest lads, who, as the patriarch of Ferney has said in immortal verse:

> *'—De Savoie arrivent tous les ans*
> *Et dont la main légèrement essuie*
> *Ces longs canaux engorgés par la suie.'*

This bandit made no defense, but it was proved by the skillful and eloquent organ of public justice that Jean Valjean was a member of a band of robbers in the south. Consequently Valjean was found guilty and sentenced to death. The criminal refused to appeal to the court of cassation, but the king, in his inexhaustible mercy, deigned to commute his sentence into penal servitude for life. Jean Valjean was immediately removed to the galleys at Toulon."

It will not be forgotten that Jean Valjean had displayed religious tendencies at M. . . . , and some of the papers, among them the *Constitutionnel,* regarded this commutation as a triumph of the priest party.

Jean Valjean changed his number at Toulon, and was known at 9430.

Let us state here, once and for all, that with M. Madeleine the prosperity of M. . . . disappeared; all he had foreseen in his night of hesitation and fever was realized; his absence was in truth the absence of the soul. After his fall there took place at M. . . . that selfish division of great fallen existences, that fatal break-up of flourishing things, which is daily accomplished obscurely in the human community and which history has only noticed once because it occurred after the death of Alexander. Lieutenants crown themselves kings; overseers suddenly became manufacturers, and envious rivalries sprang up. M. Madeleine's large workshops were shut up; the buildings fell into a ruinous condition, and the artisans dispersed, some leaving the town, others the trade. All was henceforth done on a small scale instead of a large one, for lucre instead of the public welfare. There was no center, but on all sides violent competition. M. Madeleine had commanded and directed everything. When he fell, a spirit of contest succeeded that of organization, bitterness succeeded cordiality, and mutual hatred the good-will of the common founder. The threads tied by M. Madeleine became knotted and broken; the process was falsified, the articles became worse, and confidence was destroyed; the outlets diminished and there were fewer orders; wages fell, there were stoppages, and lastly came bankruptcy.

The state itself perceived that some one had been crushed somewhere, for less than four years after the sentence of the court identifying M. Madeleine and Jean Valjean to the profit of the galleys, the cost of collecting the taxes was doubled in the bailiwick of M. . . . . M. de Villèle made a remark to that effect in the House in February, 1827.

2. *TWO LINES OF A DOUBTFUL ORIGIN*

BEFORE going further, we will enter into some details about a strange fact that occurred at about the same period at Montfermeil, and which may possibly possess some coincidence with certain police conjectures.

There is at Montfermeil a very old superstition, which is the more curious and valuable because a popular superstition in the neighborhood of Paris is like an aloe-tree in Siberia. We are of those who respect everything which is in the condition of a rare plant. This, then, is the Montfermeil superstition: it is believed that from time immemorial the fiend has selected the forest as the spot where he buries his treasure. Old women declare that it is not rare to meet at nightfall, and in remote parts of the forest, a black man resembling a wagoner or wood-cutter, dressed in wooden shoes and canvas trousers and blouse, and recognizable from the fact that he has on his head two enormous horns in place of cap or hat. This man is usually engaged in digging a hole, and there are three modes of action in the event of meeting him. The first is to go up to the man and address him; in that case you perceive that he is simply a peasant, that he appears black because it is twilight, and that he is not digging a hole, but cutting grass for his kine, and that what you had taken for horns is nothing but a dung-fork he carries on his back, whose prongs seem to grow out of his head. You go home and die within the week. The second plan is to watch him, wait till he has dug his hole and filled it up and gone away; then you run up to the hole and take out the treasure which the black man had necessarily deposited in it. In this case you die within the month. The last way is not to speak to the black man at all, not to look at him, but run away at full speed, and you die within the year.

All three modes have their inconveniences, but the second, which offers at any rate some advantages, among others that of possessing a treasure, if only for a month, is the one most generally adopted. Bold men whom chances tempt have consequently, so it is declared, frequently re-opened the hole dug by the black man, and robbed the demon. It seems, however, as if the profits are small; at any rate, if we may believe tradition, and particularly and especially two enigmatical lines in dog Latin, which a wicked Norman monk, a bit of a sorcerer, and of the name of Tryphon, left on the subject. This Tryphon lies at St. George's abbey at Bocherville, near Rouen, and frogs are born on his tomb.

A man makes enormous exertions, then, for the holes are generally very deep; he perspires, works the whole night through (for the operation must be carried out at night), gets a wet shirt, burns out his candle, breaks his pick, and when he at last reaches the bottom of the hole and lays his hand on the treasure, what does he find? What is the fiend's treasure?—a sou, at times a crown-piece, a stone, a skeleton, a bleeding corpse, or a specter folded up like a sheet of paper in a pocket-book, and sometimes nothing at all! This appears to be revealed to the searchers by Tryhon's lines,

"Fodit, et in fossâ thesauros condit opacâ,
As, nummos, lapides, cadaver, simulacra, nihilque."

It seems that in our days there are also found sometimes a gunpowder-flask and balls, or an odd pack of greasy, dirty cards which have evidently been used by the fiends. Tryphon does not record these two facts, because he lived in the twelfth century, and it does not appear that the fiend had the sense to invent gunpowder before Roger Bacon, or playing-cards before Charles VI.

If you play with the cards, you are safe to lose all you possess, while the gunpowder displays the peculiarity of making your gun burst in your face.

A very short time after the period when it occurred to the police that Jean Valjean during his four days of liberty had been prowling round Montfermeil, it was noticed in the same village that a certain old road-mender of the name of Boulatruelle was "up to his tricks" in the forest. It was believed generally that this Boulatruelle had been to the galleys; he was to some extent under police inspection, and as he could not find work anywhere, the administration employed him at a low wage as mender of the cross-road from Gagny to Lagny.

This Boulatruelle was a man looked on askance by the villagers, as he was too respectful, too humble, ready to doff his cap to everybody, trembling and fawning before the gendarmes, and probably allied with the robbers, so it was said, and suspected of lurking about the roads after dark. The only thing in his favor was that he was a drunkard.

This is what people fancied that they noticed.

For some time past Boulatruelle had left work at an early hour, and gone into the forest with his pick-axe. He was met toward evening in the most desolate clearings, in the wildest thickets, apparently seeking something and at times digging holes. The old women who passed at first took him for Beelzebub, and when they recognized Boulatruelle did not feel at all more easy in mind. Such meetings greatly annoyed Boulatruelle, and hence it was plain that he tried to hide himself, and that there was a mystery in what he was doing.

It was said in the village, "It is clear that the fiend has made its appearance. Boulatruelle saw him, and is seeking; well, he is cunning enough to pocket Lucifer's treasure." The Voltairians added, "Will Boulatruelle cheat the demon or the demon cheat Boulatruelle?" while the old women crossed themselves repeatedly.

Boulatruelle, however, discontinued his forest rambles, and regularly resumed his work, whereupon something else was talked about.

Some persons, however, remained curious, thinking that there was probably in the affair, not the fabulous treasure of the legend, but something more palpable and tangible than the fiend's bank-notes, and that the road-mender had doubtless found out half the secret. The most puzzled were the school-master and Thénardier, the publican, who was everybody's friend, and had not disdained an intimacy with Boulatruelle.

"He has been to the galleys," Thénardier would say. "Well, good gracious, we do not know who is there, or who may go there."

One evening the school-master declared that in other times the authorities would have inquired what Boulatruelle was about in the wood, and that he would have been obliged to speak; they would have employed torture if necessary, and Boulatruelle would not have resisted the ordeal of water, for instance. "Let us give him the ordeal of wine," said Thénardier.

They set to work, and Boulatruelle drank enormously, but held his tongue. He combined, with admirable tact and in magisterial proportions, the thirst of a sponge with the discretion of a judge. Still, by returning to the charge, and by putting together the few obscure words that escaped him, this is what Thénardier and the school-master fancied that they could make out.

Boulatruelle, on going to work at daybreak one morning, was surprised at seeing under a bush a spade and a pick, which "looked as if they were hidden"; still he thought that they belonged to Father Six-fours, the water-carrier, and did not think any more of the matter. On the evening of the same day, however, he saw, without being himself seen, as he was hidden behind a tree, "an individual who did not belong to these parts, and whom he, Boulatruelle, knew," proceeding toward the most retired part of the wood. This Thénardier translated as "a comrade at the galleys," but Boulatruelle obstinately refused to mention his name. This individual was carrying a bundle, something square, like a box or small chest. Boulatruelle was surprised, but it was not till some ten minutes later that the idea of following the "individual" occurred to him. But it was too late, the individual was already among the trees, night had fallen, and Boulatruelle was unable to catch him up. Then he resolved to watch the skirt of the wood, and the moon was shining. Boulatruelle, some two or three hours after, saw his individual come out of the wood, not carrying the box, however, but a spade and pick. Boulatruelle allowed him to pass, and did not address him, for he said to himself that the other man was thrice as strong as he, and, being armed with a pick, would probably smash him on recognizing him and finding himself recognized,—a touching effusion on the part of two old comrades who suddenly meet. But the spade and pick were a ray of light for Boulatruelle; he hurried to the bush at daybreak, and no longer found them there. From this he concluded that his individual, on entering the wood, had dug a hole with his pick, buried his box in it, and then covered it up with the spade. Now, as the box was too small to contain a corpse, it must contain money, and hence his researches. Boulatruelle explored the forest in all directions, and especially at spots where the ground seemed to have been recently turned up, but it was all of no use.

He discovered nothing. Nobody in Montfermeil thought any more of the matter, except some worthy gossips, who said, "You may be sure that the road-mender did not take all that trouble for nothing; it is certain that the fiend has been here."

3. ON BOARD THE ORION

TOWARD the close of October, in the same year, 1823, the inhabitants of Toulon saw a vessel enter their port which had sustained some damage in a heavy storm. It was the Orion, which at a later date was employed at Brest as a training school, but now formed part of the Mediterranean fleet.

This vessel, battered as it was, for the sea had ill-treated it, produced an effect on entering the roads. It displayed some flag which obtained it the regulation salute of eleven guns, to which it replied round for round—a total of two-and-twenty rounds. It has been calculated that in salvos, royal and military politeness, exchanges of courtesy signals, formalities of roads and citadels, sunrise and sunset saluted every day by all the fortresses and vessels of war, opening and closing gates, etc., the civilized world fired every twenty-four hours, and in all parts of the globe, one hundred and fifty thousand useless rounds. At six francs the round, this makes 900,000 francs a day. Three hundred millions a year expended in smoke. During this time poor people are dying of starvation.

The year 1823 was what the Restoration called "the epoch of the Spanish war."

This war contained many events in one, and many singularities. It was a great family affair for the House of Bourbon, the French branch succoring and protecting the Madrid branch; that is to say, proving its majority,—an apparent return to national traditions, complicated by servitude and subjection to the northern cabinets. The Duc d'Angoulême, surnamed by the liberal papers the "hero of Andujar," repressing in a triumphal attitude, which was somewhat spoiled by his peaceful looks, the old and very real terrorism of the holy office, which was contending with the chimerical terrorism of the liberals; the sans-culottes, resuscitated to the great alarm of dowagers, under the name of *Descamisados;* monarchy offering an obstacle to the progress which it termed anarchy; the theories of '89 suddenly interrupted in their sap; a European check suddenly given to the French idea which was making its voyage round the world; by the side of the generalissimo son of France, the Prince de Carignan, afterward Charles Albert, enrolling himself as a volunteer with the red wool epaulettes of a grenadier in this crusade of the kings against the peoples; the soldiers of the empire taking the field again after eight years' rest, aged, sad, and wearing the white cockade; the tricolor waved in a foreign country by an heroic handful of Frenchmen, as the white flag had been at Coblenz thirty years previously; monks mingled with the French troopers; the spirit of liberty and novelty set right by bayonets; principles checkmated by artillery; France undoing by her arms what she had done by her mind; the enemy's leaders sold; the soldiers hesitating; towns besieged by millions; no military perils, and yet possible explosions, as in every mine which is surprised and invaded; disgrace for a few persons, and glory for none,—such was this war, brought about by princes who descended from Louis XIV, and conducted by generals who issued from Napoleon. It had the sad fate of recalling neither the great war nor the great policy.

Some engagements were serious; the passage of the Trocadero, for instance, was a brilliant military achievement; but on the whole, we repeat, the trumpets of that war have a cracked sound, the whole affair was suspicious, and history agrees with France in the difficulty of accepting this false triumph. It seemed certain that certain Spanish officers, ordered to resist, yielded too easily, and the idea of corruption was evolved from the victory; it seemed as if generals rather than battles had been gained, and the victorious soldier returned home humiliated. It was, in truth, a diminishing war, and the words "Bank of France" could be read in the folds of the flag.

The soldiers of the war of 1808, on whom the ruins of Saragossa fell so formidably, frowned in 1823 at the easy opening of citadel gates, and began regretting Palafox. It is the humor of France to prefer a Rostopchin before her rather than a Ballesteros.

From a more serious point of view, on which it is right to dwell here, this war, which offended the military spirit in France, humiliated the democratic spirit. It was undertaken on behalf of serfdom; in this campaign the object of the French soldier, who was the son of democracy, was to bow others under the yoke. This was a hideous mistake, for France has the mission of arousing the soul of nations, and not stifling it. Since 1792 all the revolutions of Europe have been the French Revolution, and liberty radiates from France. He must be a blind man who does not recognize this, and it was Bonaparte who said so.

The war of 1823, an attempt upon the generous Spanish nation, was therefore at the same time an attack on the French Revolution. It was France that committed this monstrous act of violence; for, with the exception of wars of liberation, all that armies do they do by force, as the words "passive obedience" indicate. An army is a strange masterpiece of combination, in which strength results from an enormous amount of impotence. In this way we can explain war carried on by humanity against humanity, in spite of humanity.

The war of 1823 was fatal to the Bourbons; they regarded it as a triumph, for they did not see what danger there is in killing an idea by a countersign. In their simplicity they committed the mistake of introducing into this establishment the immense weakness of a crime as an element of strength; the spirit of ambuscading entered into their policy, and 1830 germinated in 1823. The Spanish campaign became in their councils an argument for oppression, and the government by right divine. France, having reestablished *el rey neto* in Spain, could establish the absolute king at home. They fell into the formidable error of taking the obedience of the soldier for the consent of the nation, and such a confidence is the destruction of thrones. Men must neither go to sleep in the shadow of a manchineal tree nor in that of an army.

Let us now return to the Orion.

During the operations of the army commanded by the prince generalissimo, a squadron cruised in the Mediterranean, to which, as we said, the Orion belonged, and was driven into Toulon roads to repair damages.

The presence of a man-of-war in a port has something about it which attracts and occupies the mob. It is grand, and the multitude love anything that is grand.

A vessel of the line is one of the most magnificent encounters which the genius of man has with the might of nature.

It is composed simultaneously of what is the heaviest and lightest of things, because it has to deal with three forms of substance at once, the solid, the liquid, and the fluid, and must contend against all three. It has cloven iron claws to seize the granite of the sea-bed, and more wings and antennæ than the two-winged insect to hold the wind. Its breath issues from its one hundred and twenty guns as through enormous bugles, and haughtily replies to the thunder. Ocean tries to lead it astray in the frightful similitude of its waves, but the vessel has its soul in its compass, which advises it and always shows it the north, and on dark nights its lanterns take the place of the stars. Hence it has tackle and canvas to oppose the wind; wood to oppose water; iron, copper, and lead to oppose the rocks; light to oppose darkness, and a needle to oppose immensity.

If we wish to form an idea of all the gigantic proportions whose *ensemble* constitute a vessel of the line, we need only enter one of the covered building docks at Toulon or Brest, where the vessels in course of construction are under glass, if we may venture the expression. That colossal beam is a yard; that huge column of wood of enormous length lying on the ground is the mainmast. Measuring from its root in the keel to its truck in the clouds, it is three hundred and sixty feet in length, and is three feet in diameter at its base. The navy of our fathers employed hemp cables, but ours has chains; the simple pile of chain cable for a hundred-gun vessel is four feet high and twenty feet in width. And then, again, in building such a vessel three thousand loads of wood are used— it is a floating forest.

And it must not be left out of sight that we are here describing a man-of-war of forty years ago, a simple sailing vessel; steam, then in its infancy, has since added new miracles to the prodigy which is called a vessel of war. At the present day, for instance, the screw man-of-war is a surprising machine, impelled by a surface of canvas containing three thousand square yards, and a boiler of two thousand five hundred horse-power.

Without alluding to these new marvels, the old vessel of Christopher Columbus and de Ruyter is one of the great master-pieces of man; it is inexhaustible in strength as infinity is in width; it garners the wind in its sails; it is exact in the immense diffusion of the waves; it floats and it reigns.

And yet the hour arrives when a gust breaks like a straw this yard, fifty feet in length; when the wind bends like a reed this mast, four hundred feet in height; when this anchor, weighing thousands of pounds, twists in the throat of the waves like a fisherman's hook in the mouth of a pike; when these monstrous cannon utter plaintive and use-less groans, which the wind carries away into emptiness and night, and when all this power and majesty are swollen up by a superior power and majesty.

Whenever an immense force is displayed in attacking immense weak-ness, it causes men to reflect. Hence at seaports curious persons throng around these marvelous machines of war and navigation, without exactly explaining the reason to themselves.

Every day, then, from morning till night the quays and piers of Toulon were covered with numbers of idlers, whose business it was to look at the Orion.

This vessel had long been in a sickly state. During previous voyages, barnacles had collected on her hull to such an extent that she lost half her speed; she had been taken into dry dock the year previous to scrape off these barnacles, and then put to sea again. But this scraping had injured the bolts, and when off the Balearic Isles she sprang a leak and took in water, as vessels were not coppered in those days. A violent equi-noctial gale supervened, which injured her larboard bows and destroyed the fore-chains. In consequence of this damage the Orion put into Toulon.

She anchored near the arsenal for repairs. The hull was uninjured, but a few planks had been unnailed here and there to let air in, as is usually the case.

One morning the crowd witnessed an accident.

The crew were engaged in bending the sails, and the top-man, who was out at the starboard earing of the main-topsail, lost his balance. He was seen to totter, the crowd on the arsenal quay uttered a cry, his head dragged him downward, and he turned round the yard, with his hands stretched down to the water; but he caught hold of the foot-rope as he passed it, first with one hand, then with the other, and remained hanging from it. The sea was below him at a dizzy depth, and the shock of his fall had given the foot-rope a violent swinging movement. The man swung at the end of the rope like a stone in a sling.

To go to his assistance would be running a frightful risk, and not one of the sailors, all coast fishermen lately called in for duty, dared to venture it. Still the unhappy top-man was growing tired; his agony could not be seen in his face, but his exhaustion could be distinguished in all his limbs, and his arms were awfully dragged. Any effort he made to raise himself only caused the foot-rope to oscillate the more, and he did not cry out, for fear of exhausting his strength. The minute was close at hand when he must leave go the rope, and every now and then all heads were turned away not to see it happen. There are moments in which a rope, a pole, the branch of a tree, is life itself, and it is a fearful thing to see a living being leave go of it and fall like ripe fruit.

All at once a man could be seen climbing up the shrouds with the agility of a tiger-cat. As he was dressed in red, this man was a convict; as he wore a green cap, he was a convict for life. On reaching the top a puff of wind blew away his cap and displayed a white head; hence he was not a young man.

A convict, employed on board with the gang, had, in fact, at once run up to the officer of the watch, and in the midst of the trouble and confusion, while all the sailors trembled and recoiled, asked permission to risk his life in saving the top-man. At a nod of assent from the officer he broke with one blow of the hammer the chain riveted to his ankle, took up a rope, and darted up the shrouds. No one noticed at the moment with what ease the chain was broken; and the fact was not remembered till afterward.

In a second he was upon the yard, where he stood for a little while as if looking round him. These seconds, during which the wind swung the top-man at the end of a thread, seemed ages to the persons who were looking at him. At length the convict raised his eyes to Heaven and advanced a step. The crowd breathed again as they saw him run along the yard. On reaching the end, he fastened to it the rope he had brought with him, let it hang down, and then began going down it hand over hand. This produced a feeling of indescribable agony, for, instead of one man hanging over the gulf, there were now two.

He resembled a spider going to seize a fly; but, in this case, the spider brought life and not death. Ten thousand eyes were fixed on the group; not a cry, not a word could be heard; every mouth held its breath, as if afraid of increasing in the slightest degree the wind that shook the two wretched men. The convict in the interim had managed to get close to the sailor, and it was high time, for a minute later the man, exhausted and desperate, would have let himself drop into the sea. The convict fastened him securely with the rope to which he clung with one hand, while he worked with the other. At length he was seen to climb back to the yard and haul the sailor up; he supported him there for a moment to let him regain his strength, then took him in his arms and carried him along the yard to the cap, and thence to the top, where he left him with his comrades.

The crowd applauded him, and several old sergeants of the chain-gang had tears in their eyes; women embraced each other on the quay, and every voice could be heard shouting with a species of frenzy: "Pardon for that man!"

The convict, however, began going down again immediately to rejoin his gang. In order to do so more rapidly he slid down a rope and ran along a lower yard. All eyes followed him, and at one moment the spectators felt afraid, for they fancied they could see him hesitate and totter, either through fatigue or dizziness; all at once the crowd uttered a terrible cry,—the convict had fallen into the sea.

The fall was a dangerous one, for the Algésiras frigate was anchored near the Orion, and the poor galley-slave had fallen between the two ships, and might be sucked under one of them. Four men hastily got into a boat, and the crowd encouraged them, for all felt anxious again. The man did not come to the surface again, and disappeared in the sea without making a ripple, just as if he had fallen into a barrel of oil. They dragged for him, but in vain; they continued the search till nightfall, but his body was not even found.

The next day the Toulon paper printed the following lines: "Nov. 17, 1823.—Yesterday a convict, one of a gang on board the Orion, fell into the sea and was drowned, as he was returning from assisting a sailor. His body has not been found, and is supposed to be entangled among the piles at Arsenal point. The man was imprisoned under the No. 9430, and his name was Jean Valjean."

BOOK III

FULFILLMENT OF THE PROMISE
MADE TO THE DEAD

1. THE WATER QUESTION AT MONTFERMEIL

MONTFERMEIL is situated between Livry and Chelles, on the southern slope of the lofty plateau which separates the Ourque from the Marne. At the present day it is a rather large place, adorned with stucco villas all the year round, and with holiday-making cits on Sunday. In 1823 there were neither so many white houses nor so many happy cits as there are now, and it was merely a village in the woods. A visitor certainly came across here and there a few country houses of the last century, recognizable by their air of pretension, their balconies of twisted iron, and the tall windows in which the little squares produce all sorts of green hues on the white of the closed shutters. But Montfermeil was not the less a village; retired cloth-dealers and persons fond of country life had not yet discovered it. It was a quiet, pleasant spot which was not on a road to anywhere. Persons lived there cheaply that peasant life which is so tranquil and abundant. The only thing was that water was scarce, owing to the elevation of the plateau.

It had to be fetched from some distance. That end of the village which was on the Gagny side obtained its water from the splendid ponds in the forest there; but the other end, which surrounds the church and is on the Chelles side, could only obtain drinking-water from a little spring about a quarter of an hour's walk from Montfermeil, near the road to Chelles.

Laying in water was, therefore, a hard task for every family. The large houses and the aristocracy, among which Thénardier's pot-house may be reckoned, paid a liard a bucket to a man whose trade it was, and who earned by it about eight sous a day. But this man only worked till seven P. M. in summer, and till five in winter; and once night had set in and the ground-floor shutters were closed, any person who had no water to drink must either fetch it or go without.

77

This was the terror of the poor creature whom the reader will not have forgotten—little Cosette. It will be remembered that Cosette was useful to the Thénardiers in two ways,—they made the mother pay and the child act as servant. Hence when the mother ceased payment, for the reason which we know, the Thénardiers kept Cosette, who took the place of a servant. In this quality she had to fetch water when it was wanted, and the child, terrified at the idea of going to the spring at night, was very careful that the house should never be without water. Christmas of 1823 was peculiarly brilliant at Montfermeil; the beginning of the winter was mild, and there had been neither snow nor frost. Some mountebanks, who came from Paris, had obtained leave from the mayor to erect their booth in the village high-street, and a party of traveling hawkers had put their stalls in the church square, and even in the lane in which Thénardier's pot-house was situated. This filled the inns and pot-houses, and produced a noisy, joyous life in this quiet little place. As a faithful historian, we are bound to add that among the curiosities displayed in the market-place was a menagerie, in which some ragged fellows showed the peasants of Montfermeil one of those terrific Brazil vultures of which the Paris Museum did not possess a specimen till 1845, and which had a tricolor cockade for an eye. Naturalists, I believe, call the bird Caracara Polyborus; it belongs to the Apicide order and the vulture family. A few old Bonapartist soldiers living in the village went to see this bird with devotion, and the owners declared that the tricolor cockade was an unique phenomenon, and expressly produced by nature for their menagerie.

On the Christmas evening several carters and hawkers were sitting to drink, round four or five candles, in Thénardier's tap-room. This room was like those usually found in pot-houses; there were tables, pewter pots, bottles, drinkers, and smokers, but little light and a good deal of uproar. The date of the year was, however, indicated by the two objects, fashionable at that time among tradespeople, and which were on a table—a kaleidoscope and a lamp of clouded tin. Madame Thénardier was watching the supper, which was roasting before a bright clear fire, while her husband was drinking with his guests and talking politics.

In addition to the political remarks, which mainly referred to the Spanish war and the Duc d'Angoulême, local parentheses like the following could be heard through the babel:

"Over at Nanterre and Suresne the vintage has been very productive, and where people expected ten barrels they have twelve. The grapes were very juicy when put under the press."—"But the grapes could not have

78

been ripe?"—"In these parts, they need not be ripe, for the wine becomes oily in spring."—"Then it must be a very poor wine?"—"There are poorer wines than those about here," etc.

Or else a miller exclaimed:

"Are we responsible for what there is in the sack? we find a lot of small seeds which we can't waste time in sifting, and which must pass under the mill-stones; such as tares, lucern, cockles, vetches, amaranths, hemp-seed, and a number of other weeds, without counting the pebbles which are so frequent in some sorts of wheat, especially Breton wheat. I don't like grinding Breton wheat, any more than sawyers like sawing beams in which there are nails. You can fancy the bad dust all this makes in the hopper, and then people complain unfairly of the flour, for it is no fault of ours."

Between two windows a mower seated at a table with a farmer, who was making a bargain to have a field mown in spring, said:

"There is no harm in the grass being damp, for it cuts better. But your grass is tender, and hard to cut, sir, for it is so young, and bends before the scythe," etc., etc.

Cosette was seated at her usual place, the cross-bar of the table, near the chimney; she was in rags, her bare feet were thrust into wooden shoes, and she was knitting, by the fire-light, stockings intended for the young Thénardiers. Two merry children could be heard laughing and prattling in an adjoining room; they were Eponine and Azelma.

A cat-o'-nine-tails hung from a nail by the side of the chimney.

At times, the cry of a baby somewhere in the house was audible through the noise of the tap-room; it was a little boy Madame Thénardier had given birth to one winter, "without knowing how," she used to say, "it was the effect of the cold," and who was a little over three years of age. The mother suckled him, but did not love him; when his cries became too troublesome, Thénardier would say, "There's your brat squalling; go and see what he wants." "Bah!" the mother would answer, "he's a nuisance"; and the poor deserted little wretch would continue to cry in the darkness.

2. *TWO FULL-LENGTH PORTRAITS*

Up to the present, only a side view of the Thénardiers has been offered the reader of this book, but the moment has now arrived to walk round the couple and regard them on all sides.

Thénardier had passed his fiftieth year; Madame Thénardier was just on her fortieth, which is fifty in a woman; and in this way there was a balance of age between husband and wife.

Our readers may probably have retained, from the first meeting, some recollection of this tall, light-haired, red, fat, square, enormous, and active woman. She belonged, as we said, to the race of giantesses who show themselves at fairs, with paving-stones hanging from their hair. She did everything in the house,—made the beds, cleaned the rooms, was cook and laundress, produced rain and fine weather, and played the devil. Her only assistant was Cosette, a mouse in the service of an elephant. All trembled at the sound of her voice,—windows, furniture, and people; and her large face, dotted with freckles, looked like a skimmer. She had a beard, and was the ideal of a Billingsgate porter dressed in female attire. She swore splendidly, and boasted of being able to crack a walnut with a blow of her fist. Had it not been for the romances she had read and which at times made the finnikin woman appear under the ogress, no one would ever have dreamed of thinking that she was feminine. She seemed to be the product of a cross between a young damsel and a fish-hag. When people heard her speak, they said, "'Tis a gendarme"; when they saw her drink, they said, "'Tis a carter"; and when they saw her treatment of Cosette, they said, "'Tis the hangman"; when she was quiet, a tooth projected from her mouth.

Thénardier was a short, thin, sallow, angular, bony, weak man, who looked ill and was perfectly well—his cunning began with this. He smiled habitually through caution and was polite to nearly everybody, even to the beggar whom he refused a halfpenny. He had the eye of a ferret and the face of a man of letters, and greatly resembled the portraits of Abbé Delille. His coquetry consisted in drinking with carriers, and no one had ever been able to intoxicate him. He wore a blouse and under it an old black coat, and had pretensions to literature and materialism. There were some names he frequently uttered in order to support an argument, such as Voltaire, Raynal, Parny, and, strangely enough, St. Augustine. He declared that he had "a system." He was a thorough scamp, however. It will be remembered that he asserted he had been a soldier, and told people with some pomp how, at Waterloo, where he was sergeant in the 6th or 9th light something, he alone, against a squadron of Hussars of death, had covered with his body and saved "a severely wounded general." Hence came his flaming sign, and the name by which his house was generally known, "The Sergeant of Waterloo." He was liberal, classical, and Bonapartist; he had subscribed to the Champ d'Asile, and it was said in the village that he had studied for the priesthood.

We believe that he had simply studied in Holland to be an inn-keeper. This scoundrel of a composite order was in all probability some Fleming of Lille, a Frenchman at Paris, a Belgian at Brussels, conveniently striding over the two frontiers. We know his prowess at Waterloo, and, as we see, he exaggerated slightly. Ebb and flow and wandering adventures were the elements of his existence. A tattered conscience entails an irregular life, and probably at the stormy period of June 18, 1815, Thénardier belonged to that variety of marauding sutlers to whom we have alluded, who go about the country selling to some and robbing others, and moving about in a halting cart after marching troops, with the instinct of always joining the victorious army. When the campaign was over, having, as he said, "some brads," he opened a pot-house at Montfermeil.

These "brads," consisting of purses and watches, gold rings and silver crosses, collected in ditches filled with corpses, did not make a heavy total, and did not carry very far this sutler turned inn-keeper.

Thénardier had something rectangular in his movements, which, when joined to an oath, recalls the barrack, to the sign of the cross, the seminary. He was a clever speaker, and liked to be thought educated, but the school-master noticed that he made mistakes. He drew up a traveler's bill in a masterly way, but practiced eyes sometimes found orthographical errors in it. Thénardier was cunning, greedy, indolent, and skillful; he did not despise his servant girls, and for that reason his wife no longer kept any. This giantess was jealous, and fancied that this little yellow man must be an object of universal covetousness.

Thénardier above all, as a crafty and well-balanced man, was a villain of the temperate genius, and this breed is the worst, as hypocrisy is mixed up in them.

It was not that Thénardier was not at times capable of passion, at least quite as much as his wife, but it was very rare, and at such moments—as he owed a grudge to the whole human race, as he had within him a profound furnace of hatred, as he was one of those persons who avenge themselves perpetually, who accuse everybody who passes before them for what falls upon them, and who are ever ready to cast on the first-comer, as a legitimate charge, the whole of the annoyances, bankruptcies, and deceptions of their life—when all this leaven was working in him and boiling in his mouth and eyes, he was fearful. Woe to the person who came under his fury at such times.

In addition to his other qualities, Thénardier was attentive and penetrating, silent or chattering according to occasion and always with great intelligence. He had the glance of sailors who are accustomed to wink when looking through a telescope. Thénardier was a statesman.

Any new-comer, on entering the pot-house, said upon seeing the woman, "That is the master of the house"; but it was an error,—she was not even mistress. Her husband was both master and mistress. She did and he created; he directed everything by a species of invisible and continuous magnetic action; a word, sometimes a sign, from him, was sufficient, and the mastodon obeyed. The husband was to his wife, though she did not know it, a species of peculiar and sovereign being. However much she might dissent from "Monsieur Thénardier,"—an inadmissible hypothesis,—she would never prove him publicly in the wrong for any consideration. She would never have committed "in the presence of strangers" that fault which wives so often commit, and which is called, in parliamentary language, "exposing the crown." Although their agreement only resulted in evil, there was contemplation in Madame Thénardier's submission to her husband. This mountain of noise and flesh moved under the little finger of this frail despot; seen from its dwarfish and grotesque aspect, it was the great universal thing—adoration of matter for the mind. There was something strange in Thénardier, and hence came the absolute dominion of this man over this woman. At certain moments she saw him as a lighted candle, at others she felt him as a claw.

This woman was a formidable creature, who loved only her children, and feared only her husband. She was a mother because she was mammiferous; her maternity ceased, however, with her girls, and, as we shall see, did not extend to boys. Thénardier, himself, had only one thought—to enrich himself.

He did not succeed, for a suitable stage was wanting for this great talent. Thénardier ruined himself at Montfermeil, if ruin is possible at zero; in Switzerland or the Pyrenees he would have become a millionaire. But where fate fastens a landlord he must browse.

In this year, 1823, Thénardier was in debt to the amount of 1500 francs, which rendered him anxious.

Whatever might be the obstinate injustice of destiny against him, Thénardier was one of those men who thoroughly understand, and in the most modern fashion, the theory which is a virtue in barbarous nations, and an article of sale among civilized nations—hospitality. He was also an admirable poacher, and renowned for the correctness of his aim, and he had a certain, cold, and peaceful laugh, which was peculiarly dangerous.

His landlord theories burst forth from him at times in flashes, and he had professional aphorisms which he drove into his wife's mind. "The duty of a landlord," he said one day savagely, and in a low voice, "is to sell to the first-comer ragouts, rest, light, fire, dirty sheets, chambermaids, fleas, and smiles; to arrest passers-by, empty small purses, and honestly lighten heavy ones; to shelter respectfully traveling families, rasp the husband, pick the wife, and pluck the children; to set a price on the open window, the shut window, the chimney-corner, the easy-chair, the sofa, the stool, the feather bed, the mattress, and the palliasse; to know how much the reflection wears off the looking-glass, and charge for it, and by the five hundred thousand fiends to make the traveler pay for everything, even to the flies his dog eats!"

This husband and this wife were craft and rage married, and formed a hideous and terrible pair.

While the husband ruminated and combined, the she Thénardier did not think about absent creditors, had not thought of yesterday or to-morrow, and lived violently only for the moment.

Such were these two beings between whom Cosette stood, enduring their double pressure, like a creature who was being at once crushed by a mill-stone and torn with a pair of pincers. Man and wife had each a different way. Cosette was beaten,—that came from the wife; she went about barefoot in winter,—that came from the husband.

Cosette went up and down stairs, washed, brushed, scrubbed, swept, ran about, panted for breath, moved heavy weights, and, little though she was, did all the hard work. She could expect no pity from a ferocious mistress and a venomous master, and "The Sergeant of Waterloo" was, as it were, a web in which Cosette was caught and trembled. The ideal of oppression was realized by this gloomy household, and it was something like a fly serving spiders.

The poor child was passively silent.

What takes place in these souls, which have just left the presence of God, when they find themselves thus, in their dawn, all little and naked **among** human beings?

3. MEN WANT WINE AND HORSES WATER

FOUR new travelers arrived.

Cosette was sorrowfully reflecting, for, though only eight years of age, she had already suffered so much that she thought with the mournful air of an old woman.

Her eyelid was blackened by a blow which the woman had given her, which made madame say now and then, "How ugly she is with her black eye!"

Cosette was thinking then that it was late, very late; that she had been suddenly obliged to fill the jugs and bottles in the rooms of the travelers who had just arrived, and that there was no water in the cistern.

What reassured her most was the fact that but little water was drunk at "The Sergeant of Waterloo." There was no lack of thirsty souls, but it was that sort of thirst which applies more readily to the wine-jar than to the water-bottle. Any one who asked for a glass of water among the glasses of wine would have appeared a savage to all these men. At one moment, however, the child trembled; her mistress raised the cover of a stew-pan, bubbling on a stove, then took a glass and hurried to the cistern. The child had turned, and was watching all the movements. A thin stream of water ran from the tap and filled the glass. "Hilloh," she said, "there is no water"; then she was silent for a moment, during which the child did not breathe.

"Well," Madame Thénardier continued, as she examined the half-filled glass, "this will be enough."

Cosette returned to her work, but for more than a quarter of an hour she felt her heart beating in her chest.

She counted the minutes that passed thus, and wished that it were next morning.

From time to time one of the topers looked out into the street and said, "It's as black as pitch," or "A man would have to be a cat to go into the street at this hour without a lantern," and Cosette shivered.

All at once, one of the peddlers lodging at the inn came in and said in a harsh voice:

"My horse has had no water."

"Oh, yes, it has," said Madame Thénardier.

"I tell you it has not, mother," the peddler went on.

Cosette had crept out from under the table.

"Oh, yes, sir," she said, "your horse drank a bucketful, and I gave it the water and talked to it."

This was not true.

"There's a girl no bigger than one's fist who tells a lie as big as a house," the dealer exclaimed. "I tell you it has not had any water, you little devil; it has a way of breathing which I know well when it has not drunk."

Cosette persisted, and added in a voice rendered hoarse by agony, and which was scarce audible:

"Oh, indeed, the horse drank a lot."

"Enough of this," the dealer said savagely, "give my horse water."

Cosette went back under the table.

"Well, that is but fair," said madame, "if the brute has not drunk it ought to drink."

Then she looked around her.

"Why, where is the little devil?"

She stooped down and discovered Cosette hidden at the other end of the table, almost under the feet of the topers.

"Come out of that," her mistress shouted.

Cosette came out of the hole in which she had hidden herself, and the landlady continued:

"Miss what's your name, give the horse water."

"There is no water, madame," Cosette said, faintly.

Her mistress threw the street door wide open.

"Well, go and fetch some."

Cosette hung her head and fetched an empty bucket standing in a corner near the chimney.

The bucket was larger than herself, and she could have sat down in it comfortably.

Madame Thénardier returned to her stove and tasted the contents of a stew-pan with a wooden spoon, while growling: "There's plenty at the spring. I believe it would have been better to sift the onions."

Then she rummaged in a drawer which contained half-pence, pepper, and shallots.

"Here, Miss Toad," she added, "as you come back, you will fetch a loaf from the baker's. Here's a fifteen-sous piece."

Cosette had a small pocket in her apron, in which she placed the coin.

Then she stood motionless, bucket in hand, and with the door open before her. She seemed to be waiting for some one to come to her help.

"Be off," her mistress shouted.

Cosette went out and shut the door after her.

4. *A DOLL COMES ON THE STAGE*

THE file of open-air shops, it will be remembered, ran as far as Thénardier's inn. These stalls, owing to the approaching passing of persons going to midnight mass, were all lit up with candles in paper shades, which, as the school-master, who was seated at this moment in Thénardier's tap-room, declared, produced a "magical effect." To make up for this, not a star glittered in the sky.

The last of these shops, right facing Thénardier's door, was a child's toy establishment, all flashing with tinsel, glass beads, and magnificent things in block-tin. Right in front, the dealer had placed, on a white napkin, an enormous doll, nearly two feet high, which was dressed in a pink crêpe gown, with golden wheat-cars in her hair, which was real hair, and had enamel eyes. The whole day had this marvel been displayed, to the amazement of all passers-by under ten years of age, but not a mother in Montfermeil had been rich enough or extravagant enough to give it to her child. Eponine and Azelma had spent hours in contemplating it, and even Cosette had ventured to take a furtive look at it.

At the moment when Cosette went out, bucket in hand, though she felt so sad and desolate, she could not refrain from raising her eyes to the prodigious doll, the "lady," as she called it. The poor child stopped, petrified, for she had not seen this doll so close before. The whole stall seemed to her a palace, and this doll was not a doll, but a vision. Joy, splendor, wealth, and happiness appeared in a sort of chimerical radiance to the unhappy little creature, who was deeply buried in mournful and cold wretchedness. Cosette measured with the simple and sad sagacity of childhood the abyss which separated her from this doll. She said to herself that a person must be a queen or a princess to have a "thing" like that. She looked at the fine dress, the long smooth hair, and thought, "How happy that doll must be!" She could not take her eyes off this fantastic shop, and the more she looked the more dazzled she became, and she fancied she saw Paradise. There were other dolls behind the large one, which appeared to her fairies and genii. The tradesman, who walked about at the back of the shop, seemed to her something more than mortal.

In this adoration she forgot everything, even the task on which she was sent, but suddenly the rough voice of her mistress recalled her to the reality. "What, you little devil, you have not gone! just wait till I come to you, you little toad."

Madame Thénardier had taken a look out into the street, and noticed Cosette in ecstasy.

The child ran off with her bucket, making enormous strides.

5. COSETTE ALONE

As Thénardier's inn was in that part of the village near the church, Cosette had to fetch the water from the spring in the forest on the Chelles side.

She did not look at another stall; so long as she was in the lane and the vicinity of the church, the illuminated booths lit up the road, but the last gleam of the last stall soon disappeared, and the poor child found herself in darkness. She went further into it, but, as she felt some emotion while walking, she shook the handle of her bucket as much as she could, which produced a noise that gave her company.

The further she went, the more dense the gloom became; there was no one in the streets except a woman, who turned on seeing her pass, and muttered between her teeth, "Wherever can the child be going? can she be a goblin?" Then she recognized Cosette. "Why," she said, "It is the Lark."

Cosette, in this way, went through the labyrinth of winding, deserted streets which end the village of Montfermeil on the side of Chelles; and so long as she had houses, or even walls, on both sides of the way, she walked rather boldly. From time to time she saw a candle glimmering through the crack of a shutter; it was light and life, people were there, and this reassured her. Still, in proportion as she advanced, her step became slower, as if mechanically, and when she had passed the corner of the last house, Cosette stopped. Going beyond the last stall had been difficult, but going further than the last house became an impossibility. She put her bucket on the ground, plunged her hand into her hair, and began scratching her head slowly—a gesture peculiar to terrified and undecided children. It was no longer Montfermeil, but the fields, and black deserted space was before her. She looked despairingly at this space in which there was nobody, but where there were beasts, and there might be ghosts. She looked out, and heard the beasts walking in the grass, and distinctly saw the ghosts moving among the trees. Then she took her bucket again, and fear gave her boldness. "Well," she said, "I will tell her that there was no water"; and she boldly reëntered Montfermeil.

She had scarce gone one hundred yards when she stopped and began scratching her head again. Now it was her mistress who appeared to her—her hideous mistress with her hyæna mouth, and her eyes flashing with passion. The child took a lamentable glance before and behind her. What should she do? what would become of her? where should she go? It was from her mistress she recoiled; she turned back in the direction of the spring, and began running. She left the village running, she entered the wood running, looking at nothing, hearing nothing. She did not stop till breath failed her, but she still went on ahead, wildly.

While running she felt inclined to cry, for the nocturnal rustling of the forest completely surrounded her.

She did not think, she did not see; the immensity of night was opposed to this little creature; on one side was darkness, on the other an atom.

It was only seven or eight minutes' walk from the skirt of the wood to the spring, and Cosette knew the road from having gone there several times by day. Strange to say, she did not lose her way, for a remnant of instinct vaguely guided her; still she did not look either to the right or left, for fear of seeing things in the branches and shrubs. In this way she reached the spring.

It was a narrow natural basin hollowed by the water in the dry soil, about two feet in depth, surrounded by moss and that gauffered grass which is called Henri IV's ruff, and paved with a few heavy stones. A rivulet escaped from it with a gentle murmur.

Cosette did not take the time to breathe; it was very dark, but she was accustomed to come to this fountain. She felt in the obscurity for a young oak that leaned over the spring, and usually served her as a support, caught a branch, stooped down, and plunged the bucket into the water. She was in such a violent state that her strength was tripled. While thus bent, she did not notice that the pocket of her apron emptied itself into the stream, and that the fifteen-sous piece fell into the water. Cosette neither saw nor heard it fall; she drew up the bucket nearly full, and placed it on the grass.

This done, she felt that she was exhausted with fatigue; she would have liked to start again at once, but the effect of filling the bucket had been so great that she found it impossible to move a step. She fell on the grass, and lay there, utterly exhausted.

She shut her eyes, then opened them again, not knowing why, but unable to do otherwise. By her side the water stirring in the bucket made circles that resembled snakes of white fire.

Over her head the sky was covered with large black clouds which seemed like smoke; the tragic mask of the gloom seemed to bend vaguely over this child.

Jupiter was setting in the profundity.

The child gazed with a wondering eye at this large star, which she did not know, and which terrified her. The planet, in fact, was at this moment very near the horizon, and was passing through a dense fog, which gave it a horrible redness. The fog, which was of a gloomy purple hue, enlarged the planet, and it looked like a luminous wound. A cold wind blew from the plain; the wood was dark, but there was no rustling of leaves, and none of the vague and fresh gleams of summer. Large branches stood out frightfully, and shapeless, stunted bushes soughed in the glades. The tall grass twined under the breeze like eels, and the brambles writhed like long arms provided with claws seeking to clutch their prey. A few withered patches of fern, impelled by the breeze, passed rapidly, and seemed to be flying before something that was coming up.

Darkness produces a dizziness; man requires light, and any one who enters the opposite of light feels his heart contracted. When the eye sees darkness, the soul sees trouble, in an eclipse, in night, in sooty opaqueness, there is anxiety even for the strongest men. No one walks alone at night in a forest without a tremor, for shadows and trees are formidable densities. A chimerical reality appears in the indistinct profundity; the inconceivable is visible a few paces from you with spectral clearness. You see floating in space, or in your own brain, something vague and intangible, like the dreams of sleeping flowers. There are stern attitudes on the horizon, and you breathe the effluvia of the great black vacuum. You feel frightened and inclined to look behind you. The cavities of night, the silent outlines which disperse as you advance, the irritated tufts, the lurid pools, the lugubrious reflected in the mournful, the sepulchral immensity of silence, the possible strange beings, the bending of mysterious branches, the frightful torsos of trees, the long waves of quivering grass;—you are defenseless against this. There is no man, however bold, who does not shudder and feel this proximity of agony; something hideous is experienced, as if the soul were amalga-mated with the shades. This penetration of darkness is indescribably sinister in a child.

Forests are apocalypses, and the beating of the wings of a little soul produces a sound of death beneath their monstrous dome.

Without understanding what she experienced, Cosette felt herself affected by this black enormity of nature; it was no longer terror alone that overpowered her, but something even more terrible than terror. She shuddered, and words fail us to describe the strange nature of this shud-der which chilled her to the heart. Her eye had become stern, and she felt as if she could not prevent herself from returning to the same spot on the morrow.

Then, by a species of instinct, and in order to emerge from this singular state which she did not understand, but which terrified her, she began counting aloud, one, two, three, four, up to ten, and when she finished she began again. This restored her a true perception of the things that surrounded her; she felt the coldness of her hands, which she had wetted in drawing the water. She rose, for fear had seized upon her again, a natural and insurmountable fear. She had only one thought left, to fly, fly at full speed through the wood, and across the fields, as far as the houses, the windows, and the lighted candles. Her eye fell on the bucket before her; and such was the terror with which her mistress inspired her that she did not dare fly without the bucket. She seized the handle with both hands and found it difficult to lift.

She proceeded thus for about a dozen yards, but the bucket was full and heavy, and she was compelled to set it on the ground. She breathed for a moment, and then lifted the bucket and started again, this time going a little further. But she was still obliged to stop once more, and after a few moments' rest set out again. She walked with body bent forward and drooping head, like an old woman; and the weight of the bucket stiffened her thin arms. The iron handle swelled and froze her small white hands. From time to time she was forced to stop, and each time she did so the cold water from the bucket splashed her bare legs. This occurred in the heart of a wood, at night in winter, far from any human eye. She was a child eight years of age, and God alone at this moment saw this sorrowful sight.

And her mother too, doubtless!

For there are things which open the eyes of the dead in their graves.

She breathed with a sort of dolorous rattle; sobs contracted her throat, but she did not dare cry, for she was so afraid of her mistress, even at a distance. It was her habit always to imagine Madame Thénardier present.

Still, she did not make much progress in this way, and she walked very slowly, although she strove to lessen the length of her halts and walk as long as she possibly could between them. She thought with agony that it would take her more than an hour to get back to Montfermeil in this way, and that her mistress would beat her. This agony was mingled with her terror at being alone in the wood at night; she was worn out with fatigue, and had not yet left the forest. On reaching an old chestnut-tree which she knew, she made a longer halt than the others to rest herself thoroughly; then she collected all her strength, took up the bucket again, and began walking courageously. Still the poor little creature in her despair could not refrain from exclaiming, "O God! O God!"

Suddenly she felt that the bucket no longer weighed anything; a hand, which seemed to her enormous, had seized it, and was vigorously lifting it. She raised her head, and saw a tall black form walking by her side; it was a man who had come up behind her, and whom she had not heard. This man, without saying a word, had seized the handle of the bucket which she was carrying.

There is an instinct in every meeting of this life.

The child felt no fear.

6. BOULATRUELLE MAY HAVE BEEN RIGHT

On the afternoon of this same Christmas day, 1823, a man walked for a long time about the most desolate part of the Boulevard de l'Hôpital, at Paris. He seemed to be looking for a lodging, and to stop for choice at the most shabby houses in this skirt of Faubourg St. Marceau.

As we shall see presently, this man had really hired a bedroom in this isolated district.

Both in dress and person he realized the type of what might be called the respectable mendicant, or extreme misery combined with extreme cleanliness. This is a very rare blending, which inspires intelligent minds with the twofold respect which is felt for the very poor and the very worthy man. He wore a very old and carefully brushed round hat, a threadbare coat of coarse yellow-ochre-colored cloth, a color which was not absolutely odd at that day, a long waist-coat with enormous pockets, black breeches which had turned gray at the knees, black worsted stockings, and stout shoes with brass buckles. He looked like the ex-tutor of a good family returned from emigration. From his white hair, wrinkled forehead, livid lips, and his face in which everything revealed weariness of life, he might have been supposed much beyond sixty years of age; but his firm though slow step, and the singular vigor imprinted on all his movements, made him look scarce fifty. The wrinkles on his forehead were well placed, and would have favorably disposed any one who observed him closely; his lip was contracted by a strange curve, which seemed stern but was humble, and there was a lugubrious serenity in his look. He carried in his left hand a small parcel tied up in a handkerchief, and in his right he had a stick cut from a hedge. This stick had been carved with some care, and was not too bad-looking; advantage had been taken of the knots, and a coral knob had been made with red sealing-wax,—it was a cudgel and seemed a cane.

Few people pass along this boulevard, especially in winter; this man, however, seemed to avoid rather than seek them, though without affectation.

At this period, Louis XVIII went almost daily to Choisy le Roi, which was one of his favorite drives. At two o'clock the royal carriage and escort could almost invariably be seen passing at full gallop along the Boulevard de l'Hôpital.

This did as well as a clock or watch for the poor women of the district, who said, "It is two o'clock, for he is returning to the Tuileries."

And some ran up and others drew up, for a king who passes always produces a tumult. Moreover the appearance and disappearance of Louis XVIII produced a certain effect in the streets of Paris, for it was rapid but majestic. This impotent king had a taste for galloping; unable to walk, he wished to run; and this cripple would have liked to be drawn by lightning. He passed, peaceful and stern, amid drawn sabers; his heavy gilded berline, with large branches of lilies painted on the panels, rolled noisily along. There was scarce time to take a glance at him; you saw in the right-hand corner a broad, firm, red face, a healthy forehead powdered *à l'oiseau royal,* a proud, harsh, artful eye, an intelligent smile, two heavy epaulettes with hanging fringe upon a civilian coat; the golden fleece, the cross of St. Louis, the cross of the Legion of Honor, the silver plate of the Holy Ghost, a large stomach and a wide blue ribbon,—it was the king. When out of Paris he carried his white feathered hat on his knees, up to which came tall English gaiters; when he returned to the city he put his hat on his head, and bowed rarely. He looked at the people coldly, and they returned the compliment. When he appeared for the first time in the Faubourg St. Marceau, his entire success consisted in a remark made by a workman to his chum,—"That fat man is the government."

The infallible passage of the king at the same hour was hence the daily event of the Boulevard de l'Hôpital.

The promenader in the yellow coat plainly did not belong to that quarter, and probably not to Paris, for he was ignorant of the fact. When at two o'clock, the royal carriage, surrounded by Life Guards with their silver aiguillettes, turned into the boulevard, after coming round the Salpetrière, he seemed surprised and almost terrified. As he was alone in the walk, he quickly concealed himself behind an angle of the wall; but this did not prevent the Duc d'Havré from noticing him. The duc, as captain of the guards on duty that day, was seated in the carriage opposite to the king, and said to His Majesty, "There is an ill-looking fellow." The policemen who cleared the way for the king also noticed him, and one of them received orders to follow him. But the man turned into the solitary streets of the Faubourg, and, as night was setting in, the agent lost his trail, as is proved by a report addressed the same evening to Count Anglès, minister of state and prefect of police.

When the man in the yellow coat had thrown out the police agent, he doubled his pace, though not without looking back many times to make sure that he was not followed. At a quarter-past four, that is to say, at nightfall, he passed in front of the Porte St. Martin theater, where the "Two Convicts" would be performed that evening. This bill, lit up by theater lamps, struck him, for, though he was walking rapidly, he stopped to read it. A moment later he entered "The Pewter Platter," which was at that time the office of the Lagny coach, which started at half-past four. The horses were put in, the passengers, summoned by the driver, were hastily clambering up the iron steps of the vehicle.

The man asked: "Have you a seat left?"

"Only one, by my side, on the box," the driver said.

"I will take it."

"Get up," the driver said.

Before starting, however, he took a glance at the passenger's poor dress, and the smallness of his bundle, and asked for the fare.

"Are you going all the way to Lagny?" he said.

"Yes," the man answered.

The traveler paid his fare to Lagny and the coach started. After passing the city gate, the driver tried to get up a conversation, but the traveler only answered in monosyllables, so the driver began whistling and swearing at his horses.

As the night was cold, the driver wrapped himself in his cloak, but the passenger did not seem to notice it. At about six o'clock they reached Chelles, where the driver stopped for a moment to let his horses breathe, at an inn opened in the old buildings of the Royal Abbey.

"I shall get down here," the man said

He took his bundle and stick and jumped off the coach.

A moment after he had disappeared.

He did not enter the inn.

When the coachman started again a few moments after, he did not meet him in the high-street of Lagny, and he turned round to his inside passengers.

"That man," he said, "does not belong to these parts, for I do not know him. He looks as if he had not a penny, and yet he don't care for money, as he paid his fare to Lagny and only came as far as Chelles. It is night, all the houses are closed, he has not gone into the inn, and yet I can't see him, so he must have sunk into the ground."

The man had not sunk into the ground, but walked hastily along the main street of Chelles, in the darkness; then he turned to his left before reaching the church, into a crossroad that runs to Montfermeil, like a man who knows the country and had been there before.

He followed this road rapidly, and at the spot where it is intersected by the old road that runs from Lagny to Gagny he heard wayfarers coming. He hurriedly concealed himself in a ditch and waited till they had passed; the precaution, however, was almost superfluous, for, as we have said, it was a very dark December night, and only two or three stars were visible in the sky.

The man did not return to the Montfermeil road, but went to his right across the fields, and hurried in the direction of the wood.

95

When he was in the wood, he slackened his pace and began looking carefully at all the trees, walking step by step, as if seeking and following a mysterious road known to himself alone. There was a moment at which he seemed to lose himself and appeared undecided, but at last, by repeated groping, he reached a glade in which there was a pile of large white stones. He walked hurriedly toward these stones and attentively examined them, as if passing them in review. A large tree, covered with those excrescences which are the warts of vegetation, was a few paces from the heap; he went up to it and passed his hand over the back, as if trying to recognize and count all the warts.

Opposite this tree, which was an ash, there was a sickly chestnut shedding its bark, upon which a ring of zinc had been placed as a poultice; he stood on tiptoe and felt this ring.

Then he examined for some time the ground in the space contained between the tree and the stones, as if assuring himself that the ground had not been freshly turned up.

This done, he looked about him and resumed his walk through the wood.

It was this man who came across Cosette.

While proceeding in the direction of Montfermeil, he perceived this little shadow depositing a load on the ground, and then taking it up again and continuing her journey. He went up and saw that it was a young child carrying an enormous bucket. Then he drew to her side and silently took the bucket-handle.

7. *COSETTE IN THE DARK WITH A STRANGER*

Cosette, as we stated, was not frightened.

The man spoke to her in a serious, almost low voice:

"My child, what you are carrying is very heavy."

Cosette raised her head and replied:

"Yes, sir."

"Give it to me," the man continued; "I will carry it."

Cosette let go the bucket and the man walked on by her side.

"It is really very heavy," he muttered; then added:

"What is your age, little one?"

"Eight years, sir."

"And have you come far with this?"

"From the spring in the wood."

"And how far have you to go?"

"About a quarter of an hour's walk."

The man stopped for a moment, and then suddenly said:

"Then you have not a mother?"

"I do not know," the child answered.

Before the man had time to speak, she continued:

"I do not think so; other girls have one, but I have not."

And after a silence she added:

"I believe that I never had one."

The man stopped, put the bucket on the ground, and laid his two hands on her shoulders, making an effort to see her face in the darkness. Cosette's thin, sallow countenance was vaguely discerned in the vivid gleam of the sky.

"What is your name?" the man asked her.

"Cosette."

The man seemed to have an electric shock; he looked at her again, then removed his hands, took the bucket up again, and continued his walk.

A moment after he asked:

"Where do you live, little one?"

"At Montfermeil, if you know the place."

"Are we going there?"

"Yes, sir."

There was another pause, and then he began again:

"Who was it that sent you to fetch water from the wood at this hour?"

"Madame Thénardier."

The man continued with an accent which he strove to render careless, but in which there was, for all that, a singular tremor:

"What is this Madame Thénardier?"

"She is mistress," the child said, "and keeps the inn."

97

"The inn?" remarked the man; "well, I am going to lodge there to-night. Show me the way."

"We are going to it."

Though the man walked rather quickly, Cosette had no difficulty in keeping up with him; she no longer felt fatigue, and from time to time raised her eyes to this man with a sort of indescribable calmness and confidence. She had never been taught to turn her eyes toward Providence, and yet she felt within her something that resembled hope and joy, and which rose to Heaven.

After the lapse of a few minutes the man continued:

"Does Madame Thénardier keep no servant?"

"No, sir."

"Is there no one but you?"

"No, sir."

There was another interruption, and then Cosette raised her voice:

"That is to say, there are two little girls."

"What little girls?"

"'Ponine and 'Zelma."

The child simplified in this way the romantic names dear to Madame Thénardier.

"Who are they?"

"They are Madame Thénardier's young ladies, as you may say,—her daughters."

"And what do they do?"

"Oh!" said the child, "they have handsome dolls, and things all covered with gold. They play about and amuse themselves."

"All day?"

"Yes, sir."

"And you?"

"Oh, I work."

"All day?"

The child raised her large eyes, in which stood a tear, invisible in the darkness, and replied softly:

"Yes, sir." After a silence she continued, "Sometimes, when I have finished my work, and they allow me, I amuse myself."

"In what way?"

"As I can; they let me be, but I have not many toys. 'Ponine and 'Zelma do not like me to play with their dolls, and I have only a little leaden sword, no longer than that."

The child held out her little finger.

"And which does not cut?"

"Oh, yes, sir," said the child, "it cuts salad and chops flies' heads off."

They reached the village, and Cosette guided the stranger through the streets. When they passed the baker's, Cosette did not think of the loaf which she was to bring in. The man had ceased questioning her, and preserved a gloomy silence, but when they had left the church behind them, on seeing all the open-air shops, he asked Cosette:

"Is it the fair-time?"

"No, sir, it is Christmas."

When they approached the inn, Cosette touched his arm timidly.

"Sir."

"What is it, my child?"

"We are close to the house."

"Well?"

"Will you let me carry my bucket now?"

"Why?"

"Because madame will be at me if she sees that it has been carried for me."

The man gave her the bucket, and a moment later they were at the door of the pot-house.

8. *IS HE RICH OR POOR?*

COSETTE could not refrain from taking a side glance at the large doll which was still displayed at the toy-shop, and then tapped at the door; it opened and Madame Thénardier appeared, candle in hand.

"Oh, it's you, you little devil; well, I'll be hanged if you have not taken time enough; you've been playing, I expect."

"Madame," said Cosette with a violent tremor, "this gentleman wants a bedroom."

Madame Thénardier exchanged her coarse look for an amiable grimace, a change peculiar to landladies, and greedily turned her eyes on the new-comer.

"Is this the gentleman?" she said.

"Yes, madame," the man answered, touching his hat.

Rich travelers are not so polite. This gesture and the inspection of the stranger's clothes and luggage, which the landlady took in at a glance, caused the amiable grimace to disappear and the rough look to return. She continued dryly:

"Come in, my good man."

The "good man" entered; the landlady gave him a second look, carefully examined his threadbare coat and broken-brimmed hat, and consulted her husband, who was still drinking with the carter, by a toss of the head, a curl of her nose, and a wink. The husband answered with that imperceptible movement of the forefinger which, laid on the puffed-out lips, signifies, "No go." Upon this the landlady exclaimed:

"My good man, I am very sorry, but I haven't a bedroom disengaged."

"Put me where you like," the man said, "in the loft or the stable. I will pay as if it were a bedroom."

"Forty sous."

"Be it so."

"Forty sous!" a carrier whispered to the landlady; "why, it is only twenty sous."

"It's forty for a man like him," Madame Thénardier replied in the same tone. "I do not lodge poor people under."

"That is true," the husband added gently; "it injures a house to have customers of that sort."

In the mean while the man, after leaving his bundle and stick on a form, sat down at a table on which Cosette had hastened to place a bottle of wine and a glass. The peddler who had asked for the bucket of water himself carried it to his horse, while Cosette returned to her place under the kitchen table and her knitting.

The man, who had scarce moistened his lips with the glass of wine he poured out, gazed at the child with strange attention.

Cosette was ugly, but had she been happy she might possibly have been pretty. We have already sketched her little overclouded face; Cosette was thin and sickly, and, though eight years of age, looked hardly six. Her large eyes, buried in a species of shadow, were almost extinguished by constant crying, while the corners of her mouth had the curve of habitual agony, which may be observed in condemned prisoners and in patients who are given over. "Her hands were," as her mother had foretold, "ruined with chilblains." The fire-light, which shone upon her at this moment, brought out the angles of her bones and rendered her thinness frightfully visible; as she constantly shivered, she had grown into the habit of always keeping her knees pressed against each other. Her entire clothing was one rag, which would have aroused pity in summer and caused horror in winter. She had only torn calico upon her person, and not a morsel of woolen stuff; her skin was here and there visible, and everywhere could be distinguished blue or black marks, indicating the spots where her mistress had beaten her. Her bare legs were red and rough, and the hollow between her shoulder-blades would have moved you to tears. The whole person of this child, her attitude, the sound of her voice, the interval between one word and the next, her look, her silence, her slightest movement, expressed and translated but one idea—fear.

Fear was spread over her; she was, so to speak, clothed in it; fear drew up her elbows against her hips, withdrew her heels under her petticoats, made her occupy as little room as possible, breathe when only absolutely necessary, and had become what might be called the habit of her body, without any possible variation save that of increasing. There was a corner in her eye in which terror lurked.

This fear was so great that Cosette on returning wet through did not dare go to the fire, but silently began her work again.

The expression of this child's eye was habitually so gloomy and at times so tragical, that it seemed at certain moments as if she were on the point of becoming either an idiot or a demon.

Never, as we said, had she known what prayer was, never had she set foot in a church. "Can I spare the time for it?" Madame Thénardier used to say.

The man in the yellow coat did not take his eyes off Cosette.

All at once her mistress cried:

"Hilloh! where's the loaf?"

Cosette, according to her custom whenever Madame Thénardier raised her voice, quickly came from under the table.

She had completely forgotten the loaf, and had recourse to the expedient of terrified children,—she told a falsehood.

"Madame, the baker's was shut up."

"You ought to have knocked."

"I did so, but he would not open."

"I shall know to-morrow whether that is the truth," said her mistress, "and if it is not, look out, that's all. In the mean while give me back my fifteen-sous piece."

Cosette plunged her hand into the pocket of her apron and turned green; the coin was no longer in it.

"Well," her mistress said, "did you not hear me?"

Cosette turned her pocket out, but there was nothing in it; what could have become of the money? The wretched little creature could not find a word to say; she was petrified.

"Have you lost it?" her mistress asked, "or are you trying to rob me?"

At the same time she stretched out her hand to the cat-o'-nine-tails.

This formidable gesture restored Cosette the strength to cry:

"Mercy, madame; I will never do it again."

Madame Thénardier took down the whip.

The man in the yellow coat had been feeling in his waist-coat pocket, though no one noticed it. Moreover, the other guests were drinking or card-playing, and paid no attention to him.

Cosette had retreated in agony to the chimney-corner, shivering to make herself as little as she could, and protect her poor half-naked limbs. Her mistress raised her arm.

"I beg your pardon, madame," said the man, "but just now I saw something fall out of the little girl's pocket, rolling away. It may be that."

At the same time he stooped and appeared to be searching, for a moment.

"Yes, here it is," he continued, as he rose and held out a coin to the landlady.

"Yes, that's it," she said.

It was not the real coin, it was a twenty-sous piece, but madame made a profit by the transaction. She put it in her pocket, and confined herself to giving the child a stern glance, saying, "That had better not happen again."

Cosette returned to what her mistress called her niche, and her large eyes, fixed on the strange traveler, began to assume an expression they had never had before. It was no longer a simple astonishment, but a sort of stupefied confidence was mingled with it.

"Do you want any supper?" the landlady asked the traveler.

He did not reply, but seemed to be lost in thought.

"What can this man be?" she muttered to herself; "he is some wretched beggar who has not a penny to pay for his supper. Will he be able to pay for his bedroom? It is lucky, after all, that he did not think of stealing the silver coin that was on the ground."

At this moment a door opened, and Eponine and Azelma came in.

They were really two pretty little girls, rather tradesmen's daughters than peasants, and very charming, one with her auburn well-smoothed tresses, the other with long black plaits hanging down her back; both were quick, clean, plump, fresh, and pleasant to look on through their beaming health. They were warmly clothed, but with such maternal art that the thickness of the stuff did not remove anything of the coquetry of the style; winter was foreseen, but spring was not effaced. In their dress, their gayety and the noise which they made, there was a certain queenliness. When they came in, their mother said to them in a scolding voice, which was full of adoration, "There you are, then."

Then, drawing them on to her knees in turn, smoothing their hair, retying their ribbons, and letting them go with that gentle shake which is peculiar to mothers, she exclaimed, "How smart they are!"

They sat down by the fire-side, with a doll which they turned over on their knees with all sorts of joyous prattle. At times Cosette raised her eyes from her knitting and mournfully watched their playing.

Eponine and Azelma did not look at Cosette, for to them she was like the dog. These three little girls did not count four-and-twenty years between them, and already represented human society,—on one side, envy; on the other, disdain.

The doll was very old and broken, but it did not appear the less wonderful to Cosette, who never in her life possessed a doll, a "real doll," to employ an expression which all children will understand.

All at once the landlady, who was going about the room, noticed that Cosette was idling, and watching the children instead of working.

"Ah, I have caught you," she exclaimed; "that's the way you work, is it? I'll make you work with the cat-o'-nine-tails."

The stranger, without leaving his chair, turned to Madame Thénardier.

"Oh, madame," he said with an almost timid smile, "let her play."

Such a wish would have been a command from any traveler who had ordered a good supper and drunk a couple of bottles of wine, and who did not look like a beggar. But the landlady did not tolerate a man who had such a hat, having a desire! and one who wore such a coat daring to have a will of his own! Hence she answered sharply:

"She must work, since she eats; I do not keep her to do nothing."

"What is she doing, pray?" the stranger continued, in that gentle voice which formed such a strange contrast with his beggar clothes and porter shoulders.

The landlady deigned to reply:

"She is knitting stockings, if you please, for my little girls, who have none, so to speak, and are forced to go about barefooted."

The man looked at Cosette's poor red feet, and said:

"When will she have finished that pair of stockings?"

"She has three or four good days' work, the idle slut."

"And how much may such a pair be worth when finished?"

The landlady gave him a contemptuous glance.

"At least thirty sous."

"Will you sell them to me for five francs?" the man continued.

"By Jove," a carrier who was listening exclaimed, with a coarse laugh, "I should think so,—five balls!"

M. Thénardier thought it his duty to speak.

"Yes, sir, if such be your fancy, you can have the pair of stockings for five francs; we cannot refuse travelers anything."

"Cash payment," the landlady said in her peremptory voice.

"I buy the pair of stockings," the man said, and added, as he drew a five-franc piece from his pocket and laid it on the table, "I pay for them."

Then he turned to Cosette: "Your labor is now mine, so play, my child."

The carrier was so affected by the five-franc piece that he left his glass and hurried up.

"It is real!" he exclaimed, after examining it, "a true hind-wheel and no mistake."

Thénardier came up and silently put the coin in his pocket.

The landlady could make no answer, but she bit her lips, and her face assumed an expression of hatred.

Cosette was trembling, but still ventured to ask:

"Is it true, madame? May I play?"

"Play," her mistress said in a terrible voice.

And while her lips thanked the landlady, all her little soul thanked the traveler.

Thénardier had returned to his glass, and his wife whispered in his ear:

"What can this yellow man be?"

"I have seen," Thénardier replied, with a sovereign air, "millionaires who wore a coat like his."

Cosette had laid down her needle, but did not dare leave her place, for, as a rule, she moved as little as possible. She took from a box behind her a few old rags and her little leaden sword.

Eponine and Azelma paid no attention to what was going on, for they were carrying out a very important operation. They had seized the cat, thrown the doll on the ground, and Eponine, who was the elder, was wrapping up the kitten, in spite of its miaulings and writhings, in a quantity of red and blue rags. While performing this serious and difficult task, she was saying to her sister in the sweet and adorable language of children, the grace of which, like the glistening of butterflies' wings, disappears when you try to fix it:

"This doll, sister, is more amusing than the other, you see, for it moves, cries, and is warm; so we will play with it. It is my little daughter, and I am a lady; you will call upon me and look at it. By degrees you will see its whiskers, and that will surprise you, and then you will see its ears and its tail, and that will surprise you too, and you will say to me, 'Oh, my goodness!' and I shall answer, 'Yes, madame, it is a little child I have like that; little children are so at present'."

Azelma listened to Eponine in admiration.

In the mean while the topers had begun singing an obscene song at which they laughed till the ceiling shook, Thénardier encouraging and accompanying them.

In the same way as birds make a nest of everything, children make a doll of no matter what. While Eponine and Azelma were wrapping up the kitten, Cosette on her side was performing the same operation on her sword. This done, she laid it on her arm, and sang softly to lull it to sleep.

A doll is one of the most imperious wants, and at the same time one of the most delicious instincts, of feminine childhood. To clean, clothe, adorn, dress, undress, dress again, teach, scold a little, nurse, lull, send to sleep, and imagine that something is somebody—the whole future of a woman is contained in this. While dreaming and prattling, making little trousseaux and cradles, while sewing little frocks and aprons, the child becomes a girl, the girl becomes a maiden, and the maiden a woman. The first child is a continuation of the last doll.

A little girl without a doll is nearly as unhappy and quite as impossible as a wife without children.

Cosette, therefore, made a doll of her sword.

The landlady, in the mean while, walked up to the "yellow man." "My husband is right," she thought, "it is perhaps M. Lafitte. Some rich men are so whimsical."

She leaned her elbow on the table, and said, "Sir—"

At the word "Sir" the man turned round, for the female Thénardier had up to the present only addressed him as "My good man."

"You see, sir," she continued, assuming her gentle air, which was still more dreadful to see than her fierce look, "I am glad to see the child play, and do not oppose it, and it is all right for once, as you are generous. But, you see, she has nothing, and must work."

"Then, she is not a child of yours?" the man asked.

"Oh! Lord, no, sir; she is a poor little girl we took in out of charity. She is a sort of imbecile, and I think has water on the brain, for she has a big head. We do all we can for her, but we are not rich, and though we write to her people we have not had an answer for six months. It looks as if the mother were dead."

"Ah!" said the man, and fell back into his reverie.

"The mother couldn't have been much," the landlady added, "for she deserted her child."

During the whole conversation, Cosette, as if an instinct warned her that she was being talked about, did not take her eyes off her mistress. She listened and heard two or three indistinct words here and there.

In the mean while, the drinkers, who were three parts intoxicated, struck up their unclean song again with redoubled gayety, and Madame Thénardier went to take part in the bursts of laughter. Cosette, under her table, looked at the fire, which was reflected in her fixed eyes; she had begun rocking her doll again, and, while lulling it to sleep, sang in a low voice, "My mother is dead, my mother is dead, my mother is dead."

On being pressed again by the landlady, the yellow man, the "millionaire," consented to take some supper.

"What will you have, sir?"

"Bread and cheese."

"He is certainly a beggar," the landlady thought.

The drunkards were still singing their song, and the child under the table still sang hers.

All at once Cosette broke off, she turned and perceived the doll lying on the ground a few paces from the kitchen table, which the children had thrown down on taking up the kitten.

She let the wrapped-up sword, which only half satisfied her, fall, and

then slowly looked round the room. The landlady was whispering to her
husband and reckoning some change. Eponine and Azelma were playing
with the kitten, the guests were eating, drinking, or singing, and no one
noticed her. She had not a moment to lose, so she crept on her hands and
knees from under the table, assured herself once again that she was not
watched, and seized the doll. A moment after she was back in her seat,
and turned so that the doll which she held in her arms should be in the
shadow. The happiness of playing with this doll was almost too much
for her.

No one had seen her excepting the traveler, who was slowly eating his
poor supper.

This joy lasted nearly a quarter of an hour.

But, in spite of the caution which Cosette took, she did not notice that
one of the doll's feet was peeping out, and that the fire lit it up very
distinctly. This pink luminous foot emerging from the glow suddenly
caught the eye of Azelma, who said to Eponine, "Look, sister."

The two little girls were stupefied. Cosette had dared to take their
doll!

Eponine rose, and, without letting the cat go, ran to her mother and
plucked the skirt of her dress.

"Let me be," said the mother, "what do you want now?"

"Mother," said the girl, "just look!"

And she pointed to Cosette.

Cosette, yielding entirely to the ecstasy of possession, saw and heard
nothing more.

The landlady's face assumed that peculiar expression which is composed of the terrible, blended with the trifles of life, and which has caused
such women to be christened Megæras.

This time wounded pride exasperated her wrath; Cosette had leaped
over all bounds, and had made an assault on the young ladies' doll. A
czarina who saw a moujik trying on her imperial son's blue ribbon would
not have a different face.

She cried, in a voice which indignation rendered hoarse:

"Cosette!"

Cosette started as if the earth had trembled beneath her, and turned
round.

"Cosette!" her mistress repeated.

Cosette gently laid the doll on the ground with a species of veneration
mingled with despair; then, without taking her eyes off it, she clasped

her hands, and, frightful to say of a child of her age, wrung them, and then burst into tears, a thing which none of the emotions of the day had caused,—neither the walk in the wood, the weight of the bucket, the loss of the coin, the sight of the lash, nor the harsh remarks of her mistress.

The traveler had risen from his chair. "What is the matter?" he asked the landlady.

"Don't you see?" she replied, pointing to the *corpus delicti* which lay at Cosette's feet.

"Well, what?" the man continued.

"That wretch," the landlady answered, "has had the audacity to touch my children's doll."

"So much noise about that!" the man said; "well, suppose that she play with the doll!"

"She has touched it with her dirty hands," the landlady continued, "her frightful hands."

Here Cosette redoubled her sobs.

"Will you be quiet?" her mistress yelled.

The man went straight to the street door, opened it, and walked out.

The landlady took advantage of his absence to give Cosette a kick under the table, which made her scream.

The door opened again, and the man re-appeared, carrying in his hands the fabulous doll to which we have alluded, and which all the village children had been contemplating since the morning. He placed it on its legs before Cosette, saying:

"Here, this is for you."

We must suppose that, during the hour he had been sitting in a reverie, he had confusedly noticed the toyman's shop, which was so brilliantly illumined with lamps and candle that it could be seen through the tap-room window like an illumination.

Cosette raised her eyes; she had looked at the man coming toward her with the doll, as if he were the sun; she heard the extraordinary words "this is for you"; she looked at him, looked at the doll, then drew back slowly and concealed herself entirely in a corner under the table.

She did not cry, she did not speak, but looked as if she dared hardly breathe.

The landlady, Eponine, and Azelma were so many statues; the topers themselves had stopped drinking, and there was a solemn silence in the tap-room.

The mother, petrified and dumb, began her conjectures again. "Who is this man? is he poor or a millionaire? He is, perhaps, both; that is to say, a thief."

The husband's face offered that expressive wrinkle which marks the human face each time that the ruling instinct appears on it with all its bestial power. The landlord looked in turn at the doll and the traveler; he seemed to be sniffing round the man, as he would have done round a money-bag. This only lasted for a second; then he went up to his wife and whispered:

"That machine costs at least thirty francs. No nonsense, crawl in the dust before the man."

Coarse natures have this in common with simple natures, that they have no transitions.

"Well, Cosette," the landlady said, in a voice which strove to be gentle, and which was composed of the bitter honey of wicked women, "Why don't you take your doll?"

Cosette ventured to crawl out of her hole.

"My little Cosette," her mistress continued fawningly, "this gentleman gives you the doll, so take it, for it is yours."

Cosette gazed at the wonderful doll with a sort of terror; her face was still bathed in tears, but her eyes were beginning to fill, like the sky at dawn, with strange rays of joy. What she felt at this moment was something like what she would have felt had some one suddenly said to her, "Little girl, you are Queen of France."

It seemed to her that if she touched this doll thunder would issue from it.

This was true to a certain point, for she said to herself that her mistress would scold and beat her.

Still, the attraction gained the victory; she at length crawled up to the doll and murmured timidly, as she turned to the landlady:

"May I, madame?"

No expression could render this air, which was at once despairing, terrified, and ravished.

"Of course," said her mistress, "since this gentleman gives it to you."

"Is it true, sir?" Cosette continued, "is the lady really mine?"

The stranger's eyes were full of tears, and he seemed to have reached that point of emotion when a man does not speak in order that he may not weep. He nodded to Cosette, and placed the "lady's" little hand in hers. Cosette quickly drew back her hand as if the lady's burned her, and looked down at the brick floor. We are compelled to add that at this moment she put her tongue out to an enormous length; all at once she turned and passionately seized the doll.

"I will call her Catherine," she said.

It was a strange sight when Cosette's rags met and held the doll's rosy ribbons and fresh muslins.

"May I put her in a chair, madame?" she continued.

"Yes, my child," her mistress answered.

It was now the turn of Eponine and Azelma to look enviously at Cosette.

She placed Catherine in a chair, and then sat down on the ground before her, motionless, without saying a word, and in a contemplative attitude.

"Play, Cosette," the stranger said.

"Oh! I am playing," the child answered.

This unknown man, this stranger, who had the air of a visitor sent by Providence to Cosette, was at the moment the person whom Madame Thénardier hated most in the world; still she must put a constraint on herself. This emotion was more than she could endure, accustomed to dissimulation though she was by the copy which she had to take of her husband in all his actions.

She hastened to send her children to bed, and then asked the yellow man's leave to send off Cosette, "who had been very tired during the day," she added with a maternal air. Cosette went off to bed, carrying Catherine in her arms.

The landlady went from time to time to the other end of the room, where her husband was, to relieve her mind, she said. She exchanged with him a few sentences, which were the more furious because she dared not utter them aloud.

"Old ass! what has he got in his noddle to come and disturb us in this way! to wish that little monster to play! to give her dolls worth forty francs, to a wretch whom I would gladly sell for forty sous! a little more, and he would call her Your Majesty, like the Duchesse de Berry. Can he be in his senses? The mysterious old fellow must be cracked."

"Why so? it is very simple," Thénardier replied. "Suppose it amuses him? It amuses you that the little one should work—it amuses him to see her play. He has a right, for a traveler can do as he likes so long as he pays. If this old man is a philanthropist, how does it concern you? If he is an ass, it is no business of yours. Why do you interfere, so long as he has money?"

This was the language of a master, and the reasoning of a landlord, neither of which admitted a reply.

The man was resting his elbow on the table, and had resumed his thoughtful attitude; the other travelers, peddlers, and carriers had gone away or left off singing. They regarded him from a distance with a sort of respectful fear; this poorly clad individual, who drew hind-wheels from his pockets with such ease, and lavished gigantic dolls on ragged girls, was assuredly a magnificent and formidable man.

Several hours passed, midnight mass was finished, the matin bell had been rung, the drinkers had gone away, the pot-house was closed, the fire was out in the tap-room, but the stranger still remained at the same spot and in the same posture. From time to time he changed the elbow on which he was leaning, that was all; but he had not uttered a syllable since Cosette went off to bed.

The Thénardiers alone remained in the room, through politeness and curiosity.

"Is he going to pass the night like that?" the landlady pouted. When it struck two, she declared herself conquered, and said to her husband, "I am off to bed; you can do as you like." The husband sat down at a table in a corner, lit a candle, and began reading the *Courrier Francais*.

A good hour passed, during which the worthy host read the paper through thrice from the date of the number to the imprint, but the stranger did not stir.

Thénardier moved, coughed, spat, and made his chair creak, but the man made no movement. "Can he be asleep?" Thénardier thought; the man was not asleep, but no movement aroused him.

At length the landlord doffed his cap, walked up gently, and ventured to say:

"Do you not wish for repose, sir?"

"To sleep" would have appeared to him excessive and familiar, while "repose" hinted at luxury, and was respectful. Such words have the mysterious and admirable quality of swelling the bill on the next morning; a room in which you sleep costs twenty sous; one in which you repose costs twenty francs.

"Why, you are right," said the stranger, "where is your stable?"

"I will show you the way, sir," Thénardier replied, with a smile.

He took the candle; the man fetched his stick and bundle, and Thénardier led him to a room on the second-floor, which was most luxurious, with its mahogany furniture, and the bed with its red cotton curtains.

"What is this?" the traveler asked.

"Our own wedding bedroom," the landlord replied; "my wife and I occupy another, and this room is only entered three or four times a year."

"I should have preferred the stable," the man said roughly.

Thénardier pretended not to hear this disagreeable reflection.

He lit two new wax candles standing on the mantel-piece. A rather large fire was flashing in the grate.

Upon the mantel-piece was also a woman's head-dress, made of silver tissue and orange flowers, under a glass shade.

"And what is this?" the stranger continued.

"That, sir," Thénardier said, "is my wife's wedding bonnet."

The traveler looked at the object in a way that seemed to say, "Then there was a moment when this monster was a virgin."

This was a falsehood of Thénardier's; when he hired the house to convert it into a public, he found this room thus furnished, and bought the lot, thinking that it would cast a graceful shadow over his "spouse," and that his house would derive from it what the English call respectability.

When the traveler turned round, Thénardier had disappeared, without saying good evening, as he did not wish to treat with disrespectful cordiality a man whom he intended to flay royally the next morning.

The landlord went to his room, where his wife was in bed, but not asleep. So soon as she heard her husband's footstep, she said to him: "You know that I mean to turn Cosette out to-morrow?"

Thénardier coldly answered: "How you go on."

They exchanged no more words, and a few minutes after the candle was extinguished.

For his part, the stranger had placed his stick and bundle in a corner. When the landlord had withdrawn, he sat down in an easy-chair and remained pensive for a time; then he took off his shoes, seized one of the candlesticks, and left the room, looking about him as if in search of something. He went along a passage and reached the staircase; here he heard a very gentle sound, like the breathing of a child. He followed the sound, and reached a triangular closet under the stairs, or, to speak more correctly, formed by the stairs themselves. Here, among old hampers and potsherds, in dust and cobwebs, there was a bed, if we may apply the term to a palliasse so rotten as to show the straw, and a blanket so torn as to show the mattress. There were no sheets, and all this lay on the ground.

In this bed Cosette was sleeping.

The man walked up and gazed at her.

Cosette was fast asleep and fully dressed; in winter she did not take off her clothes, that she might be a little warmer.

She was holding to her bosom the doll, whose large open eyes glistened in the darkness; from time to time she gave a heavy sigh, as if about to awake, and pressed the doll almost convulsively in her arms. There was nothing by her bedside but one of her wooden shoes.

Through an open door close by, a large room could be seen, through which the stranger entered. At the end two little white beds were visible through a glass door, and which belonged to Eponine and Azelma. Behind this a wicker curtainless cradle was half hidden, in which slept the little boy who had been crying all the evening.

The stranger conjectured that this room communicated with that of the Thénardiers. He was about to return, when his eye fell on the chimney, one of those vast inn chimneys in which there is always so little fire when there is a frost, and which are so cold to look at. In this chimney there was no fire, not even ashes; but what there was in it attracted the traveler's attention. He saw two little children's shoes of coquettish shape and unequal size; and the traveler recollected the graceful and immemorial custom of children who place their shoes in the chimney on Christmas night, in order to obtain some glittering present from their good fairy in the darkness. Eponine and Azelma had not failed in this observance.

The traveler bent down.

The fairy, that is, the mother, had already paid her visit, and in each shoe a handsome ten-sous piece could be seen shining.

The man rose and was going away, when he observed another object in the darkest corner of the hearth; he looked at it, and recognized a hideous wooden shoe, half broken and covered with ashes and dried mud. It was Cosette's; with the touching confidence of children who may be disappointed, but are never discouraged, she had also placed her shoe in the chimney.

Hope in a child that has never known aught but despair is a sublime and affecting thing.

There was nothing in this shoe.

The stranger felt in his pocket and laid a louis d'or in it.

Then he crept noiselessly back to his bedroom.

9 . THENARDIER AT WORK

THE next morning almost two hours before daybreak, Thénardier was seated, pen in hand, at a table in the tap-room, and making out the bill of the yellow-coated traveler.

His wife, standing behind him, was watching him; they did not exchange a syllable: on one side there was a profound meditation, on the other that profound admiration with which people watch a marvel of the human mind expanding. A noise could be heard in the house; it was the Lark sweeping the stairs.

At the end of a quarter of an hour and some erasures, Thénardier produced this master-piece:

THE GENT. IN NO. I.

Supper	3 *frcs.*
Bed	10 "
Candles	5 "
Fire	4 "
Atendence	I "
Total	23 *frcs.*

"Twenty-three francs!" the wife exclaimed, with an admiration mingled with some hesitation.

Like all great artists, Thénardier was not satisfied, and said, "Pooh!"

It was the accent of Castlereagh drawing up the little bill for France to pay at the Congress of Vienna.

"Monsieur Thénardier, you are right, he certainly owes it," the wife muttered, thinking of the doll given to Cosette in the presence of her children; "it is fair, but it is too much; he will not pay it."

Thénardier gave his cold laugh, and said, "He will pay it."

This laugh was the supreme signification of certainty and authority; what was said in this way must be. The wife made no objection, but began arranging the tables, while her husband walked up and down the room; a moment after, he added:

"Why, I owe fifteen hundred francs."

He sat down in the ingle-nook, meditating, with his feet in the warm ashes.

"By the bye," the wife continued, "you don't forget that I mean to fling Cosette out to-day? The monster! she eats my heart with her doll; I would sooner marry Louis XVIII than keep her a day longer in the house."

Thénardier lit his pipe, and said between two puffs:

"You will hand the man the bill."

Then he went out.

He had scarce left the room ere the traveler entered.

Thénardier at once appeared behind and stood in the half-open door, only visible to his wife.

The yellow man carried his stick and bundle in his hand.

"Up so soon?" the landlady said. "Are you going to leave us already, sir?"

While speaking this, she turned the bill in her hands with an embarrassed air, and made folds in it with her nails; her harsh face had an unusual look of timidity and scruple.

It seemed to her difficult to present such a bill to a man who looked so thoroughly poor.

The traveler seemed absent and preoccupied, as he replied:

"Yes, madame, I am going."

"Then you had no business to transact in Montfermeil, sir?" she continued.

"No, I am merely passing through, that is all. What do I owe you, madame?"

The landlady, without replying, handed him the folded paper; he opened and looked at it, but his attention was visibly elsewhere.

"Do you do a good business here?" he asked.

"Tolerably well, sir," the landlady answered, stupefied at not seeing any other explosion; then she went on with an elegiac and lamentable accent:

"Oh, sir, times are very bad! and then there are so few respectable people in these parts. It is lucky we have now and then generous and rich travelers like yourself, sir, for the expenses are so high. Why, that little girl costs us our eyes out of our head."

"What little girl?"

"Why, you know, Cosette; the Lark, as they call her hereabout."

"Oh!" said the man.

She continued:

"What asses these peasants are with these nicknames! she looks more like a bat than a lark. You see, sir, we don't ask for charity, but we can't give it; our earnings are small and our expenses great,—the license, the door and window-tax, and so on! You know, sir, that the government claims a terrible deal of money. And then I have my own daughters, and do not care to support another person's child."

The man replied, in a voice which he strove to render careless, and in which there was a tremor:

"And suppose you were freed of her?"

"Of whom?—Cosette?"

The landlady's red and violent face was illumined by a hideous grin.

"Ah, sir, my good sir, take her, keep her, carry her off, sugar her, stuff her with truffles, eat her, drink her, and may all the saints in Paradise bless you."

"It is settled."

"You really will take her away at once?"

"At once; call her."

"Cosette," the landlady shouted.

"In the mean while," the man continued, "I will pay my score; how much is it?"

He took a glance at the bill, and could not restrain a start of surprise.

"Twenty-three francs!"

He looked at the landlady and said again slowly, "Twenty-three francs?"

There was in his pronunciation of the two words the accent which separates the point of exclamation from the point of interrogation.

Madame Thénardier had had time to prepare for the collision, and hence answered with assurance:

"Yes, sir, twenty-three francs."

The stranger laid five five-franc pieces on the table.

"Go and fetch the girl," he said.

At this moment Thénardier walked into the middle of the room, and said:

"The gentleman owes twenty-six sous."

"Twenty-six sous!" the wife exclaimed.

"Twenty sous for the bedroom," Thénardier continued coldly, "and six for the supper. As for the girl, I must talk a little with the gentleman first. Leave us, wife."

The landlady had one of those bedazzlements which unforeseen flashes of talent produce; she felt that the great actor had come on the stage, made no answer, and went out.

So soon as they were alone, Thénardier offered the traveler a chair; he sat down. Thénardier remained standing, and his face assumed a singular expression of kindliness and simplicity.

"I must tell you," he said, "sir, that I adore the child."

The stranger looked at him fixedly.

"What child?"

Thénardier continued:

"How strange it is, but you grow attached to them. What is the meaning of all that money? put it back in your pocket; I adore the child."

"What child?" the stranger asked.

"Why, our little Cosette! don't you wish to take her from us? Well, I speak frankly, and as true as you are an honest man, I cannot consent. I should miss the child, for I have known her since she was a baby; it is true that she costs us money, that she has her faults, that we are not rich, and that I paid more than upward of four hundred francs for medicines alone in one of her illnesses. She has neither father nor mother, and I brought her up; and I have bread both for her and for me. Look you, I am fond of the child; affection grows on you; I am a good foolish fellow, and don't reason; I love the girl, and though my wife is quick, she loves her too. She is like our own child, and I want to hear her prattle in the house."

The stranger still looked at him fixedly, as he continued:

"Excuse me, sir, but a child can't be given like that to the first passer-by. You will allow that I am right. I don't say that you are not rich and look like a very worthy man, and that it may be for her welfare! but I am bound to know. You understand? Supposing that I let her go and sacrificed myself, I should like to know where she is going, and not lose her out of sight; I should wish to know where she is, and go and see her now and then, to convince the child that her foster-father is watching over her. In short, there are some things which are not possible; I don't even know your name. I ought at least to see some scrap of paper, a passport, and so on."

The stranger, without ceasing to fix on him that look which pierces to the bottom of the conscience, said in a grave, firm voice:

"Monsieur Thénardier, a man does not require a passport to go four leagues from Paris; and if I take Cosette away, I take her away, that is all. You will not know my name, my residence, or where she is, and it is my intention that she shall never see you again. I break the string which she has round her foot, and away she flies; does that suit you? yes or no?"

In the same way as demons and genii recognize by certain signs the presence of a superior deity, Thénardier understood that he had to do with a very strong man. It was a sort of intuition, and he comprehended with his distinct and sagacious promptitude. On the previous evening, while drinking, smoking, and singing, he had constantly looked at the stranger, watching him like a cat and studying him like a mathematician. He had both watched him on his own account, through pleasure and instinct, and played the spy on him as if paid to do so. Not a gesture or movement of the yellow-coated man escaped him, and even before the stranger so clearly manifested his interest in Cosette, Thénardier divined it. He surprised the profound glances of this old man which constantly reverted to the child. Why this interest? who was this man? why was his attire so wretched when his purse was so full? These questions he asked himself and could not answer them, and they irritated him; he reflected on them the whole night. He could not be Cosette's father; was he her grandfather? then, why did he not make himself known at once? When a man has a claim, he proves it, and this man evidently had no claim on Cosette. In that case, what was it? Thénardier lost himself in suppositions; he caught a gleam of everything and saw nothing. However this might be, on beginning the conversation, feeling sure that there was a secret in all this, and that the man was interested in remaining in the shadow, he felt himself strong; but on hearing the stranger's firm and distinct answer, when he saw that this mysterious person was simply mysterious, he felt himself weak. He had not expected anything of this sort, and it routed his conjectures. He rallied his ideas, and weighed all this in a second. Thénardier was one of those men who judge of a situation at a glance, and considered that it was the moment to advance straight and rapidly. He behaved like great captains at that decisive instant which they alone can recognize, and suddenly unmasked his battery.

"Sir," he said, "I want one thousand five hundred francs."

The stranger drew from his pocket an old black leathern portfolio, and took from it three bank-notes, which he laid on the table; then he placed his large thumb on the notes, and said to the landlord:

"Bring Cosette here."

While this was taking place, what was Cosette about?

On waking, she ran to her sabot and found the gold coin in it; it was not a napoleon, but one of those new twenty-franc pieces of the Restoration, on which the Prussian queue was substituted for the crown of laurels. Cosette was dazzled, and her destiny was beginning to intoxicate her; she knew not what a gold piece was, she had never seen one, and she hurriedly hid it in her pocket, as if she had stolen it. She felt it was really hers, she guessed whence the gift came, but she experienced a feeling of joy full of fear. She was happy, but she was more stupefied; the magnificent things did not seem to her real,—the doll frightened her, the gold coin frightened her, and she trembled vaguely at this magnificence. The stranger alone did not frighten her; on the contrary, he reassured her since the previous evening. Through her amazement and her sleep, she thought in her little childish mind of this man, who looked so old, and poor, and sad, and who was so rich and good. Ever since she met him in the wood, all had changed for her, as it were. Cosette, less happy than the meanest swallow, had never yet known what it is to take refuge in the shadow and beneath the wing of her mother; for five years, that is to say, so far back as her thoughts went, the poor child had trembled and shuddered. She had ever been exposed in her nudity to the bleak blast of misfortune, and she felt as if she were clothed; formerly her soul was cold, now it was warm. Cosette no longer felt afraid of her mistress, for she was no longer alone; she had some one by her side.

She had set about her daily work very quickly, and the louis, which she had in the same pocket from which the fifteen-sous piece fell on the previous night, caused her thoughts to stray. She did not dare touch it, but she looked at it for five minutes at a time. While sweeping the stairs, she stood motionless, forgetting her broom and the whole world, engaged in watching this star sparkle in her pocket. It was during one of these contemplations that her mistress came to her.

By her husband's order she had come to fetch the child, and, extraordinary to say, did not strike her, or even abuse her.

"Cosette," she said, almost gently, "come directly."

A moment after, Cosette entered the tap-room.

The stranger took his bundle and untied it; it contained a complete morning dress for a child of seven years of age.

"My dear," the man said, "take these and go and dress yourself quickly."

Day was breaking, when those inhabitants of Montfermeil who were beginning to open their doors saw a poorly clad man, and a girl holding a large doll, going along the Paris road toward Livry.

It was the man of our story and Cosette.

No one knew the man, and few recognized Cosette in her new dress. Cosette was going away. With whom? she was ignorant. Where to? she did not know. All she understood was that she was leaving Thénardier's pot-house behind her; no one thought of saying good-bye to her, or she to any one. She left the house, hated and hating.

Poor gentle being, whose heart up to this hour had only been compressed!

Cosette walked gravely, opening her large eyes and looking at the sky; she had placed her louis in the pocket of her new apron, and from time to time stooped down and looked at it, and then at her companion.

10. *THÉNARDIER HAS ONE REGRET*

MADAME THÉNARDIER, according to her habit, had left her husband to act, and anticipated grand results. When the man and Cosette had left, Thénardier let a good quarter of an hour elapse, then took her on one side, and showed her the fifteen hundred francs.

"Is that all?" she said.

It was the first time since her marriage that she ventured to criticise an act of her master.

The blow went home.

"You are right," he said, "and I am an ass. Give me my hat."

He thrust the three notes into his pocket and went out, but he made a mistake and first turned to the right. Some neighbors of whom he inquired put him on the right track, and he walked along at a great rate, and soliloquizing:

"The man is evidently a millionaire dressed in yellow, and I am an animal. He gave first twenty sous, then five francs, then fifty francs, then fifteen hundred francs, and all with the same facility. He would have given fifteen thousand francs! but I shall catch him up."

And then, the bundle of clothes prepared beforehand was singular, and there was a mystery behind it. Now, mysteries must not be let go when you hold them, for the secrets of the rich are sponges full of gold if you know how to squeeze them. All these thoughts whirled about his brain. "I am an animal," he said.

On leaving Montfermeil and reaching the angle formed by the Lagny road, you can see it running a long distance before you upon the plateau. On getting to this point he calculated that he should see the man and child, and looked as far as he could, but saw nothing. He inquired again, and passers-by told him that the people he was looking for had gone in the direction of Gagny wood.

He followed them, for, though they had the start of him, a child walks slowly. He went fast, and then, again, the country was familiar to him.

All at once he stopped and smote his forehead, like a man who has forgotten the essential thing, and is ready to retrace his steps.

"I ought to have brought my gun," he said to himself.

Thénardier was one of those double natures that pass at times among us without our knowledge, and disappear unknown, because destiny has only shown us one side of them; it is the fate of many men to live thus half submerged. In an ordinary situation Thénardier had everything necessary to make him—we do not say to be—what is conventionally termed an honest tradesman, or a worthy citizen. At the same time, certain circumstances being given, certain shocks stirring up his nature from the bottom, he had everything required to make him a villain. He was a shop-keeper in whom there was a monster. Satan must at times crouch in a corner of the lair in which Thénardier lived, and dream before this hideous master-piece.

After a moment's hesitation he thought:

"Nonsense, they would have time to escape."

And he continued his walk, going rapidly ahead and almost with an air of certainty, displaying the sagacity of a fox that scents a hare in its form.

In fact, when he had passed the ponds and cut across the great clearing to the right of the Avenue de Bellevue till he reached the wide turfed glade which covers the old water-way of the Abbey de Chelles, he noticed under a shrub a hat, on which he built up many conjectures. The shrub was low, and Thénardier saw that the man and Cosette were sitting under it. The child could not be seen, but the doll's head was visible.

Thénardier was not mistaken; the man had sat down there to let the child rest a little, and the tavern-keeper dodged round the shrub and suddenly appeared before those whom he was seeking.

"Excuse me, sir," he said, panting, "but there are your fifteen hundred francs."

The man raised his eyes.

"What is the meaning of this?"

Thénardier answered respectfully:

"It means, sir, that I am going to take Cosette back."

The child started, and clung to the man.

The latter answered, looking fixedly at Thénardier, and leaving a space between each word:

"You—take—Cosette—back?"

"Yes, sir, I do; and I must tell you that I have reflected. The truth is, that I have no right to give her to you. Look you, I am an honest man; the little one does not belong to me, but to her mother, who entrusted her to me, and I can only give her back to her mother. You will say to me, 'Her mother is dead.' Good. In that case I can only surrender Cosette to a person who brings me a written authority from her mother. That is clear enough."

The man, without answering, felt in his pocket, and Thénardier saw the portfolio with the bank-notes re-appear.

He gave a start of joy.

"Good," he thought, "I have him, he is going to bribe me."

Before opening the portfolio the traveler looked around him; the place was utterly deserted, and there was not a soul in the valley. The man opened his pocketbook and took out, not the handful of bank-notes which Thénardier anticipated, but a simple sheet of paper, which he opened and handed to the landlord, saying:

"You are right; read."

Thénardier took the paper and read:

"M. sur M., March 25, 1823.

"Monsieur Thénardier,—You will hand over Cosette to the bearer, who will pay up all little matters.

I have the honor to remain,

Yours, FANTINE."

"Do you know the signature?" the man continued.

It was really Fantine's, and Thénardier recognized it and had no reply. He felt a double annoyance, first at having to renounce the bribery which he expected, and, secondly, that of being beaten. The man added:

"You can keep that paper as your discharge."

Thénardier folded it up neatly, and growled:

"The signature is tolerably well imitated. Well, be it so." Then he attempted a desperate effort.

"So far so good, sir, since you are the bearer; but the expenses must be paid, and there is a heavy sum owing me."

The man rose, and said as he dusted his threadbare cuff:

"Monsieur Thénardier, in January the mother calculated that she owed you one hundred and twenty francs; in February you sent in an account of five hundred francs; you received three hundred at the end of that month, and three hundred more early in March. Since then nine months have elapsed at the agreed on price of fifteen francs, which makes one hundred and thirty-five francs. You had received one hundred francs too much, so this leaves thirty-five francs owing you, and I have just given you fifteen hundred."

Thénardier felt just like the wolf when it is caught by the leg in a steel trap.

"Who in the fiend's name is this man?" he thought.

He behaved like the wolf; he shook himself; impudence had carried him through before now.

"Monsieur, I don't know your name," he said boldly, and putting off his respectful manner; "if you do not give me three thousand francs, I shall take Cosette back."

The stranger said quietly:

"Come, Cosette."

He took the child by his left hand, and with the right picked up his stick.

Thénardier noticed the enormous size of the stick and the solitude of the spot; the man buried himself in the wood, leaving the landlord motionless and confounded.

As he walked away Thénardier regarded his broad shoulders and enormous fists, then his eye fell on his own thin arms.

"I must have been a fool," he said, "not to bring my gun, as I was going to the chase."

Still the tavern-keeper did not give in.

"I will know where he goes," he said, and began following them at a distance. Two things remained in his hands,—irony, in the shape of the scrap of paper signed *Fantine,* and a consolation in the fifteen hundred francs.

The man led Cosette in the direction of Bondy; he walked slowly, with drooping head in a pensive attitude. Winter had rendered the wood transparent, and hence Thénardier did not lose them out of sight, while keeping some distance off. From time to time the man turned round and looked to see whether he was followed, and suddenly perceived Thénardier. He drew Cosette into a clump of trees, in which they both disappeared. "Confusion!" said Thénardier, as he doubled his pace.

The closeness of the trees compelled him to draw nearer to them, and when the man was at the thickest part he turned round and saw Thénardier, although the latter tried to conceal himself behind a trunk. The man gave him a restless glance, then tossed his head and continued his walk. Thénardier followed him, but, after going some two hundred yards, the man turned and looked at him so menacingly that the landlord thought it "useless" to go any further, and turned back.

11. *NO.* 9430 *RE-APPEARS AND COSETTE*
WINS IT IN THE LOTTERY

JEAN VALJEAN was not dead, when he fell, or, rather, threw himself into the sea. He was, as we have seen, without irons. He swam between the waves to a ship at anchor, to which a boat was moored. Here he found means to conceal himself till night, when he again took to swimming and reached the shore not far from Cape Brun. There, as he had money, he could change his dress; a pot-house near Balaguier then served as dressing-room to escaped convicts,—a lucrative trade. Next, Jean Valjean, like all these sad fugitives who seek to throw the law and social fatality off the scent, followed an obscure and winding road. He first found an asylum at Pradeaux, near Beausset, then he turned toward Grand Villard near Briançon, in the Upper Alps,—an uneasy, groping flight; the path of a mole with unknown branches. Later on, some traces of his passing could be found in Ain, in the ditsrict of Cevrieux, in the Pyrenees at Acon, at a spot called Grange-le-Doumecq, near Chavailles, and in the vicinity of Perigueux at Brunies, in the canton of Chapelle Gonaguet. He reached Paris; we have just seen him at Montfermeil.

It may be remembered that after his preceding escape, or about that time, he had made a mysterious journey, of which justice had caught a glimpse.

For the rest, it was thought he was dead, and this deepened the darkness around him. He came across a newspaper announcing the fact, and felt reassured and almost as much at peace as if he were really dead.

On the evening of the day when Jean Valjean had rescued Cosette from the claws of the Thénardiers, he reëntered Paris. It was nightfall as he passed the barrier Monceaux. There he took a cab to the esplanade of the observatory. He left it there, paid the driver, took Cosette by the hand,

and together they walked toward the Boulevard de l'Hôpital, through the black night and the deserted streets adjacent to the Ourcine and the Glacière.

The day had been strange and full of emotions for Cosette; they had eaten behind hedges bread and cheese bought at isolated taverns; they had changed carriages often, and walked parts of the road on foot; she did not complain, but felt tired, and Jean Valjean felt by his hand that she was hanging back more and more as she walked. He took her on his back, and Cosette, without letting go of Catherine, dropped her head on his shoulder and fell asleep.

BOOK IV

THE GORBEAU TENEMENT

1. MASTER GORBEAU

FORTY years ago the solitary walker who ventured into the lost districts of the Salpetrière, and went up the Boulevard as far as the Barrière d'Italie, reached a quarter where it might be said that Paris disappeared. It was not solitude, for there were passers-by; it was not the country, for there were houses and streets; it was not a town, for the streets had ruts as large as those in the high-roads, and grass grew in them; and it was not a village, for the houses were too lofty. What was it, then? It was an inhabited place where there was nobody, a deserted spot where there was somebody; it was a boulevard of the great city, a street of Paris, more ferocious at night than a forest, more gloomy by day than a cemetery.

It was the old quarter of the Marché-aux-Chevaux.

The rambler, if he risked himself beyond the tottering walls of the market, if he even consented to pass the Rue du Petit-banquier, reached the corner of the Rue des Vignes St. Marcel, a but little known latitude, after leaving on his right a garden protected by high walls, next a field in which stood tan mills, resembling gigantic beaver dams, next an inclosure encumbered with planks, tree-stumps, saw-dust, and chips, on the top of which a large dog barked; then a long low wall, all in ruins, with a small, decrepit back gate, covered with moss, which burst into flower in spring, and lastly, in the most desolate spot, a hideous and decrepit building, on which could be read in large letters, POST NO BILLS. Here, close to a foundry, and between two garden walls, could be seen, at the time of which we write, a poor house, which, at the first glance, seemed small as a cottage, but was in reality large as a cathedral. It turned its gable end to the public thoroughfare, and hence came its apparent smallness; nearly the whole house was concealed, and only a door and a window could be perceived. This house was only two stories high.

On examining it, the first fact that struck you was that the door could never have been other than that of a low lodging-house, while the window, had it been carved in stone instead of made of stucco, might have belonged to a mansion.

The door was nothing but a collection of worm-eaten planks, clumsily held together by roughly planed cross-beams. It opened immediately on a steep staircase, muddy, dirty, and dusty, of the same width as itself, which could be seen from the street, mounting steep as a ladder, and disappearing in the gloom between two walls. The top of the clumsy opening in which the door stood was masked by a thin deal plank, in which a triangular hole had been cut. On the inside of the door, a brush dipped in ink had clumsily traced No. 52, while over the skylight the same brush had painted No. 50, so people hesitated. Dust-colored rags hung like a drapery over the triangular skylight.

The window was wide, tolerably lofty, filled with large panes of glass, and protected by Venetian shutters; but these panes had various wounds, at once concealed and betrayed by an ingenious bandage of paper, and the Venetian shutters, broken and hanging from their hinges, threatened passers-by more than they protected the inhabitants. The horizontal screen-boards were wanting here and there, and these places had been filled up with boards nailed on perpendicularly; so that the affair began by being a Venetian screen, and ended by being a shutter.

This door, which had an unclean look, and this window, which looked honest, though fallen in the world, produced the effect of two beggars, walking side by side, with two different faces under the same rags, the one having always been a mendicant, while the other had once been a gentleman.

The staircase led to a very large building, which resembled a shed which had been converted into a house. This building had as its intestinal tube, a long passage, upon which opened, right and left, compartments of various dimensions, habitable at a pinch, and more like booths than cells. These rooms looked out on the dreary landscape around.

The whole was dark, wearisome, dull, melancholy and sepulchral, and traversed, according as the cracks were in the roof or the door, by cold sunbeams or sharp draughts. An interesting and picturesque peculiarity of houses of this description is the enormous size of the cobwebs.

To the left of the door, on the boulevard, and at about six feet from the ground, a bricked-up window formed a square hole filled by passing lads with stones.

A portion of this building has been recently demolished, but what still remains will allow an idea to be formed of what it was. The whole affair is not more than a century old; one hundred years are the youth of a church and the old age of a human abode. It seems as if the house of man shares his brief tenure, and the house of God His eternity.

The postman called this house No. 50-52, but it was known in the quarter by the name of Maison Gorbeau.

Let us state whence this title came.

The collectors of things not generally known, who make anecdotal herbals and prick fugacious dates into their memory with a pin, know that there were in Paris, about the year 1770, two advocates at the Châtelet of the names of Corbeau and Renard—two names foreseen by Lafontaine. The opportunity was too good to be neglected, and ere long the following parody, in rather halting verse, was in everybody's mouth:

> *Mâitre Corbeau, sur un dossier perché,*
> *Tenait dans son bec une saisie exécutoire;*
> *Mâitre Renard, par l'odeur alléché,*
> *Lui fit à peu près cette histoire:*
> *Eh, bonjour, &c.*

Two honest lawyers, who were unable to hold their heads up under the outbursts of laughter that followed them, resolved to get rid of their names, and for that purpose appealed to the king. The petition was handed to Louis XV on the very day when the Papal Nuncio kneeling on one side, and Cardinal de la Roche Aymon on the other, were drawing the slippers on to the bare feet of Madame Du Barry, who had just left her couch. The king, who was laughing, continued to laugh, gayly passed from the two bishops to the two lawyers, and forgave them their names, or nearly so. By royal authority Master Corbeau was allowed to add a tail to his initial letter and become Gorbeau; but Master Renard was less fortunate,—he could only obtain leave to place a P before his R, and call himself Prenard, so that the latter name was nearly as significant as the first.

Now, according to local tradition, Master Gorbeau had been owner of the building numbered 50-52 on the Boulevard de l'Hôpital, and was even author of the grand window.

Hence the tenement was called the Gorbeau house.

Opposite the house there stands, amid the boulevard trees, an elm which is nearly three parts dead; a little further on is the Rue de la

Barrière des Gobelins, a street at that time without houses, unpaved, planted with badly growing trees, and which ran straight down to the city walls. A copperas smell issues in puffs from the roof of an adjacent manufactory. The barrier was close by, and in 1823, the city walls were still in existence.

The barrier itself cast a gloom over the mind, for it was on the road to Bicêtre. Under the empire and the Restoration, men condemned to death returned to Paris through it on the day of their execution. Here was committed, about the year 1829, that mysterious assassination called "the murder of the Barrière de Fontainebleau," a frightful problem which has never been elucidated, a mournful enigma which has never been solved. A few steps further on you come to the fatal Rue Croulebarbe, in which Ulbach stabbed the woman who looked after the goats at Ivry to the sound of thunder, as in a melodrama. A few more steps and you reach the abominable pollard-elms of the Barrière Saint Jacques, that philanthropic expedient concealing the scaffold, the paltry disgraceful Place de Greve of a shop-keeping society, which has recoiled before the penalty of death, though not daring to abolish it with grandeur or keep it up with authority.

Thirty-seven years ago, and leaving aside this Place St. Jacques, which was, as it were, predestined, and has always been horrible, the gloomiest point perhaps of all this gloomy boulevard was that where No. 50-52 stood.

Tradespeople did not begin to brood there till five-and-twenty years later. The place was morose, for you felt yourself between La Salpetrière, whose dome was just visible, and Bicêtre, whose barrier you could touch; that is to say, between male and female mania. As far as the eye could reach nothing was visible save the slaughter-houses, the city wall, and a few rare frontages of foundries, resembling barracks, or monasteries. Everywhere were sheds and rubbish, old walls black as coffins, new walls white as winding-sheets; everywhere parallel rows of trees, buildings standing in rows, long odd lines, and the gloomy sadness of right angles. There was not a diversity of the soil, not a single architectural whim; the *ensemble* was freezing, regular, and hideous. Nothing contracts the heart like symmetry, because symmetry is ennui, and ennui is the basis of mourning, a yawning despair. It is possible to imagine something more horrible than an Inferno in which people suffer; it is one in which they are bored. If such an Inferno existed, this section of the Boulevard de l'Hôpital might be its avenue.

At nightfall, at the moment when night disappears, and before all in winter, at the hour when the evening breeze is tearing from the elms their last rusty leaves, when the darkness is profound and starless, and when the moon and the wind make rents in the clouds, this boulevard became really terrifying. The black outlines were lost in the gloom, and the passer-by could not refrain from thinking of the countless gallows traditions of the spot. This solitude, in which so many crimes had been committed, had something awful about it; traps could almost be foreseen in the darkness, all the confused shapes of the darkness appeared suspicious, and the long, hollow squares noticed between the trees seemed graves. By day it was ugly, in the evening lugubrious, and at night, sinister.

In the summer twilight, a few old women might be seen sitting under the elms upon raw, rotten benches; those worthy old ladies had a partiality for begging.

Even at the time of which we write, however, this quarter, which looked more superannuated than ancient, was striving to transform itself, and any one who wished to see it was obliged to make haste, for each day some detail disappeared from the *ensemble*. For the last twenty years the Orleans railway station has been by the side of the old faubourg, and has worked it up; for wherever a station is built on the skirts of a capital, it is the death of a suburb and the birth of a town. Round these centers of popular movement, at the rolling of these mighty machines, under the breath of these monstrous horses of civilization which devour coal and snort fire, the earth trembles and opens to swallow up the old abodes of men and bring forth new ones; the old houses crumble away, and new ones rise in their place.

From the day when the Orleans railway station invaded the territory of the Salpetrière, the old narrow streets that border the Jardin des Plantes have been shaken down, traversed as they are three or four times a day by those currents of diligences, hackney coaches, and omnibuses, which, within a given time, drive back the houses on both sides; for it is a curious though perfectly true fact that, just as in large capitals the sun makes the fronts of houses grow and expand to the south, the frequent passing of vehicles widens streets. The symptoms of a new life are visible in the remotest corners of this old provincial district; pavement is being laid down and is beginning to extend to spots where there are as yet no wayfarers.

One memorable morning in July, 1845, the bitumen caldrons were suddenly seen smoking there, and on that day it may be said that civilization reached the Rue de l'Oursine, and that Paris entered the Faubourg St. Marceau.

2. THE NEST OF AN OWL AND A LINNET

JEAN VALJEAN stopped before No. 50-52. Like the dull bird, he had selected this deserted spot in which to build his nest.

He felt in his pocket, took out a latch-key, opened and carefully shut the door again, and went upstairs, still carrying Cosette on his back.

When he reached the landing, he took from his pocket a key, with which he opened another door. The room he entered was a sort of spacious garret, furnished with a mattress laid on the ground, a table, and a few chairs. There was a burning stove in the corner, and the boulevard lamp faintly illumined this poor interior. At the end of the room was a closet with a poor bedstead, to which Jean Valjean carried the child and laid her on it, without awaking her.

He struck a light and lit a candle,—all this had been prepared on the previous day,—and he then began gazing at Cosette with a look full of ecstasy, in which the expression of kindness and tenderness almost attained delirium. The little girl, with that calm confidence which only appertains to extreme strength and extreme weakness, had fallen asleep without knowing with whom she was, and continued to sleep without knowing where she was.

Jean Valjean bent down and kissed the child's hand.

Nine months previously he had kissed her mother's hand, who had also just fallen asleep.

The same painful, religious, poignant feeling filled his heart.

He knelt down by the side of Cosette's bed.

Long after daybreak the child was still asleep. A pale beam of the

December sun filtered through the window and made large strips of light and shadow on the ceiling. Suddenly a heavily laden wagon, passing along the boulevard, shook the house like a blast of wind, and made it tremble from top to bottom.

"Yes, madame," Cosette cried, waking with a start, "I am coming directly."

And she jumped out of bed, her eyelids still half closed by the weight of sleep, and stretched out her arms to a corner of the wall.

"Oh, goodness, my broom!" she said.

She opened her eyes thoroughly, and saw Jean Valjean's smiling face.

"Ah, it is true," the child said. "Good-morning, sir."

Children accept at once and familiarly joy and happiness, for they are themselves by nature happiness and joy.

Cosette saw Catherine at the foot of her bed, caught her up and, while playing, asked Jean Valjean a hundred questions: "Where was she? was Paris large? was Madame Thénardier a long way off? and would she never return?" etc., etc., etc. All at once she exclaimed, "How pretty it is here!"

It was a frightful hole, but she felt herself free.

"Must I sweep?" she at length continued.

"Play," said Jean Valjean.

The day passed in this way, and Cosette, not feeling any anxiety at understanding nothing, was inexpressibly happy between her doll and this good man.

THE next morning at daybreak Jean Valjean was again standing by Cosette's bed-side; he was motionless and waiting for her to awake.

Something new was entering his soul.

Jean Valjean had never loved anything. For twenty-five years he had been alone in the world and had never been father, lover, husband, or friend. At the galleys he was wicked, gloomy, chaste, ignorant, and ferocious—the heart of the old convict was full of virginities. His sister and his sister's children had only left in him a vague and distant reminiscence, which in the end entirely faded away; he had made every effort to find them again, and, not being able to do so, forgot them—human nature is thus constituted. The other tender emotions of his youth, if he had any, had fallen into an abyss.

When he saw Cosette, when he carried her off, he felt his entrails stirred up; all the passion and affection there was in him was aroused and rushed toward this child. He went up to the bed on which she slept, and he trembled with joy; he felt pangs like a mother, and knew not what it was, for the great and strange emotion of a heart which is preparing to love is a very obscure and sweet thing.

Poor old heart still fresh!

Still, as he was fifty-five years of age, and Cosette eight, all the love he might have felt during life was melted into a species of ineffable glow.

This was the second white apparition he met; the bishop had caused the dawn of virtue to rise on his horizon, and Cosette now produced that of love.

The first days passed in this bedazzlement.

On her side Cosette became unconsciously different, poor little creature! She was so little when her mother left her that she did not remember; and like all children, who resemble the young vine-twigs that cling to everything, she tried to love, and had not succeeded. All had repulsed her—the Thénardiers, their children, and other children; she had loved the dog which died, and after that nothing and nobody would have anything to do with her. It is a sad thing to say, but at the age of eight she had a cold heart; it was not her fault, it was not that she lacked the faculty of loving, but it was, alas! the possibility. Hence, from the first day, all that felt and thought within her began to love the good man and she experienced what she had never known before—a feeling of expansion.

The man no longer even produced the effect upon her of being old or poor; she found Jean Valjean handsome, in the same way as she found the garret pretty.

Such are the effects of dawn, childhood, youth, and joy. The novelty of earth and life has something to do in it, and nothing is so charming as the coloring reflection of happiness upon an attic; in this way we have all a blue garret in our past.

Nature had placed a profound interval of fifty years between Jean Valjean and Cosette; but destiny filled up this separation. Destiny suddenly united and affianced with its irresistible power these two uprooted existences, so different in age, so similar in sorrow, and the one, in fact, was the complement of the other. Cosette's instinct sought a father, in the same way as Jean Valjean's sought a child, and to meet was to find each other. At the mysterious moment when their two hands clasped, they were welded together, and when their two souls saw each other, they recognized that each was necessary to the other, and joined in a close embrace.

Taking the words in their most comprehensive and absolute meaning, we may say that, separated from everything by the walls of the tombs, Jean Valjean was the widower as Cosette was the orphan, and this situation caused Jean Valjean to become in a celestial manner Cosette's father.

And, in truth, the mysterious impression produced upon Cosette in the Chelles wood by Jean Valjean's hand grasping hers in the darkness was not an illusion, but a reality. His entrance into her destiny was the entrance of God.

Jean Valjean had selected his asylum well, and in a security which might appear perfect.

The room he occupied with Cosette was the one whose window looked out on the boulevard, and as it was the only one of the sort in the house, he had not to fear the curiosity of neighbors, either in front or on his side.

The ground-floor of 50-52, a sort of rickety pentice, was employed as a tool-house by nursery gardeners, and had no communication with the upper floor. The latter, as we have said, contained several rooms and a few garrets, one of which alone was occupied by the old woman who looked after Jean Valjean.

It was this old woman who was known as the "chief lodger," and who in reality performed the duties of porter, that let him the room on Christmas day. He had represented himself as an annuitant ruined by the Spanish bonds, who meant to live there with his little daughter. He paid six months' rent in advance, and requested the old woman to furnish the room in the way we have seen, and it was this woman who lit the stove and prepared everything on the evening of their arrival.

Weeks passed away, and these two beings led a happy life in this wretched garret.

With the dawn Cosette began laughing, chattering, and singing, for children, like the birds, have their matin song.

At times it happened that Jean Valjean took her little red chilblained hand and kissed it; the poor child. accustomed to be beaten, did not know what this meant, and went away quite ashamed.

At times she became serious and looked at her little black frock. Cosette was no longer dressed in rags, but in mourning; she had left wretchedness and was entering life.

Jean Valjean set to work teaching her to read. At times he thought that it was with the idea of doing evil that he learned to read at the galleys, and this idea had turned to teaching a child to read. Then the old galley-slave smiled the pensive smile of the angels.

He felt in it a premeditation of Heaven, and he lost himself in a reverie, for good thoughts have their depths as well as the wicked.

Teaching Cosette to read and letting her play almost constituted Jean Valjean's entire life; and then he spoke to her about her mother, and made her play. She called him "father," and knew him by no other name.

He spent hours in watching her dress and undress her doll and listening to her prattle. From this moment life appeared to him full of interest; men seemed to him good and just; he no longer reproached any one in his thoughts, and perceived no reason why he should not live to a great age, now that this child loved him. He saw a future illumined by Cosette, as by a delicious light; and as the best men are not exempt from a selfish thought, he said to himself at times joyfully that she would be ugly.

Although it is only a personal opinion, we fancy that at the point which Jean Valjean had reached when he began to love Cosette he required this fresh impulse to continue in the right path. He had just seen, under new aspects, the wickedness of men and the wretchedness of society, but the aspects were incomplete, and only fatally showed him one side of the truth,—the fate of woman comprised in Fantine, and public authority personified in Javert; he had returned to the galleys, but this time for acting justly; he had drunk the new cup of bitterness to the dregs; disgust and weariness seized upon him; the very recollection of the bishop was approaching an eclipse, and though it would have perhaps re-appeared afterward luminous and triumphant, still this holy recollection was beginning to fade. Who knows whether Jean Valjean was not on the eve of growing discouraged and relapsing? but he loved and became strong again. Alas! he was no less tottering than Cosette; he protected her and she strengthened him; through him, she was able to advance in her life; through her, he could continue in the path of virtue. Oh, unfathomable and divine mystery of the equilibrium of destiny!

4. THE REMARKS OF THE CHIEF LODGER

JEAN VALJEAN was so prudent as never to go out by day; every evening he walked out for an hour or two, sometimes alone, but generally with Cosette, in the most retired streets, and entering the churches at nightfall. When he did not take Cosette with him, she remained with the old woman, but it was her delight to go out with him. She preferred an hour with him to the ravishing *têtes-à-têtes* with Catherine. He walked along, holding her by the hand and talking pleasantly with her, for Cosette's temper turned to be extremely gay.

The old woman cleaned, cooked, and bought food for them.

They lived quietly, always having a little fire, but as if they were very poor. Jean Valjean had made no change in the furniture since the first day, except that he had a wooden door put up in place of the glass door in Cosette's sleeping-closet.

He still wore his yellow coat, black breeches, and old hat, and in the streets he was taken for a poor man. It happened at times that charitable women turned and gave him a sou, which Jean Valjean accepted with a deep bow. It happened at times also that he met some wretch asking for charity; in such a case he looked behind to see that no one was watching, furtively approached the beggar, gave him money, now and then silver, and hurried away. This entailed inconveniences, for people began to know him in the district under the name of the alms giving beggar.

The old *chief lodger,* a spiteful creature, full of envy and uncharitableness toward her neighbors, watched him closely, though he did not suspect it. She was rather deaf, which rendered her prone to gossip, and there remained to her from the past two teeth, one at top and one at bottom, which she constantly rattled against each other. She questioned Cosette, who, knowing nothing, could say nothing, except that she came from Montfermeil. One day this spy saw Jean Valjean go into one of the uninhabited rooms in a way that seemed to her peculiar. She followed him with the stealthy step of an old cat, and was able to watch him, herself unseen, through the crack of the door, to which Jean Valjean turned his back, doubtless as a greater precaution. She saw him take out of his pocket a pair of scissors, needle and thread, and then begin ripping up the lining of his coat, and pull out a piece of yellow paper, which he unfolded. The old woman recognized with horror that it was a thousand-franc note, the second or third she had seen in her life, and she fled in terror.

A moment after Jean Valjean addressed her, and requested her to change the note for him, adding that it was his half year's dividend, which he had received on the previous day. "When?" the old woman thought; "he did not go out till six in the evening, and the bank is certainly not open at that hour." The old woman went to change the note and made her conjectures; the amount of money, being considerably multiplied, afforded a grand topic of conversation for the gossips of the Rue des Vignes Saint Marcel.

A few days later, it happened that Jean Valjean, in his shirt-sleeves, was chopping wood in the passage, and the old woman was in his room cleaning up. She was alone, for Cosette was admiring the wood-chopping. She saw the coat hanging on a nail, and investigated it. The lining had been sewn up again, but the good woman felt it carefully, and fancied she could notice folds of paper between the cloth and the lining. More bank-notes, of course!

She also noticed that there were all sorts of things in the pockets; not only the needles, scissors, and thread she had seen, but a large portfolio, a big clasp-knife, and, most suspicious fact of all, several different-colored wigs. Each pocket of this coat seemed to be a species of safeguard against unexpected events.

The inhabitants of the house thus reached the last days of winter.

5. A NEW TENANT

THERE was near St. Medard's church a poor man who usually sat on the edge of a disused well, to whom Jean Valjean liked to give alms. He never passed him without giving him a trifle, and at times spoke to him. The persons who envied this beggar said that he belonged to the police, and he was an ex-beadle seventy-five years of age, who was constantly telling his beads.

One evening, when Jean Valjean passed alone, he perceived the beggar at his usual place under the lamp, which had just been lit. The man, according to his habit, seemed to be praying and was crouched. Jean Valjean went up to him and placed his usual charity in his hand, and the beggar suddenly raised his eyes, looked fixedly at Jean Valjean, and then let his head hang again. This movement was like a flash, but Jean Valjean gave a start; he fancied he had seen by the flickering light of the lamp, not the placid and devout face of the old beadle, but a terrifying and familiar face. He had such a feeling as he would have had had he suddenly found himself face to face with a tiger in the darkness. He recoiled, terrified and petrified, not daring to breathe, remain, or fly, staring at the beggar, who had let his head fall, and did not appear to know that he was there. At this strange moment an instinct, perhaps that of self-preservation, urged Valjean not to utter a syllable. The beggar was of the same height, wore the same rags, and looked as he did every day. "Stuff," said Valjean, "I am mad, dreaming; it is impossible!" And he went home sorely troubled in mind.

He hardly dared to confess to himself that the face which he fancied he had seen was Javert's.

At night, on reflecting, he regretted that he had not spoken to the man and made him raise his head a second time.

141

The next evening he returned and found the beggar at his seat. "Good-day, my man," Jean Valjean said resolutely, as he gave him a sou. The beggar raised his head, and replied in a complaining voice, "Thank you, my good gentleman." It was certainly the old beadle.

Jean Valjean felt fully reassured, and began laughing. "How on earth could I have thought that it was Javert? why, am I now to grow wool-gathering?" and he thought no more of it.

A few days later, at about eight in the evening, he was giving Cosette a spelling lesson, when he heard the house door open and then close again. This appeared to him singular, for the old woman, who alone lived in the house beside himself, always went to bed at nightfall to save candle. Jean Valjean made Cosette a sign to be silent, for he heard some one coming upstairs. After all it might be the old woman, who felt unwell, and had been to the chemist's. Jean Valjean listened.

The footstep was heavy and sounded like a man's, but the old woman wore thick shoes, and nothing so closely resembles a man's footstep as an old woman's. For all that, though, Jean Valjean blew out his candle.

He had sent Cosette to bed, saying in a whisper, "Make no noise," and while he was kissing her forehead the footsteps stopped.

Jean Valjean remained silently in his chair, with his back turned to the door, and holding his breath in the darkness.

After a long interval, hearing nothing more, he turned noiselessly, and, on looking at his door, saw a light through the keyhole, which formed a sort of sinister star in the blackness of the door and the wall. There was evidently some one there holding a candle in his hand and listening.

A few minutes passed, and then the light went away; still he did not hear the sound of footsteps, which seemed to indicate that the man who came to listen had taken off his shoes.

Jean Valjean threw himself fully dressed on his bed, and could not close his eyes all night.

At daybreak, when he was just yielding to fatigue, he was aroused by the creaking of a door which opened into a room at the end of the passage, and then heard the same footstep which had ascended the stairs the previous evening drawing nearer. He put his eye to the keyhole, which was rather large, in the hope of seeing the man who had listened at his door overnight. It was really a man, who this time passed Jean Val-jean's door without stopping. The passage was still too dark for him to distinguish his face; but when the man reached the staircase a ray of light from outside fell upon him, and Jean Valjean saw his back perfectly. He was a tall man, dressed in a long coat, with a cudgel under his arm; and he was very like Javert.

Valjean might have tried to see him on the boulevard through his window, but for that purpose he must have opened it, and that he dared not do.

It was plain that this man came in with a key and was quite at home. Who gave him this key? what did it mean?

At seven o'clock, when the old woman came to clean up, Jean Valjean gave her a piercing glance, but did not question her. The good woman was as calm as usual, and while sweeping she said to him;

"I suppose you heard some one come in last night, sir?"

At that age, and on that boulevard, eight in the evening is the blackest night.

"Yes, I remember," he said, with the most natural accent; "who was it?"

"A new lodger in the house."

"What is his name?"

"I forget—Dumont or Daumont, something like that."

"And what may he be?"

The old woman looked at him with her little ferret eyes and answered: "He lives on his property, like yourself."

Perhaps she meant nothing, but Jean Valjean fancied that he could detect a meaning.

When the old woman had gone off, he made a rouleau of some hundred francs which he had in a chest of drawers, and put it in his pocket. Whatever precautions he took to keep the money from rattling, a five-franc piece fell from his hand and rolled noisily on the floor.

At nightfall he went down and looked attentively all along the boulevard; he saw nobody, and it seemed utterly deserted. It is true that some one might have been concealed behind the trees.

He went up again and said to Cosette, "Come!"

He took her hand and both left the house together.

BOOK V

FOR A STILL HUNT—DUMB DOGS

1 . *STRATEGIC ZIGZAGS*

An observation is necessary here about the present pages and others which will follow.

It is now many years that the author of this work, forced, he regrets to say, to allude to himself, has been absent from Paris, and since he left that city it has been transformed, and a new city has sprung up, which is, to some extent, unknown to him. He need not say that he is fond of Paris, for it is his mental birthplace. Owing to demolitions and rebuilding, the Paris of his youth, the Paris which he religiously carried away in his memory, is at this hour a Paris of the past. Permit him, then, to speak of that Paris as if it still existed. It is possible that at the present day there is neither street nor house at the spot where the author purposes to lead the reader, saying, "In such a street there is such a house." If the readers like to take the trouble they can verify. As for him, he does not know new Paris, and writes with old Paris before his eyes in an illusion which is precious to him. It is sweet to him to fancy that something still remains of what he saw when he was in his own country, and that all has not faded away. So long as you move about in your native land, you imagine that these streets are matters of indifference to you, that these roofs and doors are as nothing, that these walls are strange to you, that these trees are no better than the first tree you come across, that these houses which you do not enter are useless to you, and that the pavement on which you walk is made of stones and nothing more. At a later date, when you are no longer there, you perceive that these streets are dear to you, that you miss these roofs, windows, and doors, that the walls are necessary to you, that you love the trees, that these houses which you did not enter you entered daily, and that you left some of your entrails, your blood and your heart, on these paving-stones. All these spots which you no longer see, which perhaps you may never see again, and of which you have retained the image, assume a melancholy charm, return to you with the sadness of an apparition, make the sacred land visible to you, and are, so to speak, the very form of France; and you love and evoke them such as they are, such as they were, obstinately refusing to make any change in them, for you cling to the face of your country as to the countenance of your mother.

Let us be permitted, then, to speak of the past as present; we will beg our readers to bear this in mind, and will continue our narrative.

Jean Valjean at once left the boulevard and entered the streets, making as many turnings as he could, and at times retracing his steps to make sure that he was not followed.

This maneuver is peculiar to the tracked deer, and on ground where traces are left it possesses the advantage of deceiving huntsmen and dogs;—in venery it is called a "false reimbushment."

The moon was at its full, and Jean Valjean was not sorry for it, for as the luminary was still close to the horizon, it formed large patches of light and shade in the streets. Valjean was able to slip along the houses and walls on the dark side and watch the bright side; perhaps he did not reflect sufficiently that the dark side escaped his notice. Still, in all the deserted lanes which border the Rue de Poliveau he felt certain that no one was following him.

Cosette walked on without asking questions; the sufferings of the first six years of her life had introduced something passive into her nature. Moreover,—and this is a remark to which we shall have to revert more than once,—she was accustomed to the singularities of her companion and the strange mutations of fate; and then she felt in safety, as she was with him. Jean Valjean did not know any more than Cosette whither he was going; he trusted to God as she trusted to him. He fancied that he also held some one greater than himself by the hand and felt an invincible being guiding him. However, he had no settled idea, plan, or scheme; he was not absolutely certain that it was Javert; and then again it might be Javert, ignorant that he was Jean Valjean. Was he not disguised? Was he not supposed to be dead? Still, during the last few days several things had occurred which were becoming singular, and he wanted nothing more. He was resolved not to return to No. 50-52, and, like the animal driven from its lair, he sought a hole in which to hide himself until he could find a lodging.

Jean Valjean described several labyrinths in the Quartier Mouffetard, which was as fast asleep as if it were still under mediæval discipline and the yoke of the Curfew, and combined several streets into a clever strategic system. There were lodging-houses where he now was, but he did not enter them, as he did not find anything to suit him, and he did not suppose for a moment that if persons were on his trail they had lost it again.

As the clock of St. Etienne du Mont struck eleven, he passed the police office at No. 14, in the Rue de Pontoise. A few minutes after, the instinct to which we have referred made him look round, and he distinctly saw, by the office lamp which betrayed them, three men, who were following him rather closely, pass in turn under this lamp on the dark side of the street. One of these men turned into the office, and another, who was in front, appeared to him decidedly suspicious.

"Come, child," he said to Cosette, and he hastened out of the Rue de Pontoise.

He made a circuit, skirted the Passage des Patriarches, which was closed at that hour, and eventually turned into the Rue des Postes.

There is an open space here, where the Rollin college now stands, and into which the Rue Neuve St. Geneviève runs.

(We need hardly say that the Rue Neuve St. Geneviève is an old street and that a post-chaise does not pass along the Rue des Postes once in ten years. This street was inhabited by potters in the 13th century, and its real name is Rue des Pots.)

The moon threw a bright light upon this open space, and Jean Valjean hid himself in the door-way, calculating that if the men were still following him he could not fail to have a good look at them as they crossed the open space.

In fact, three minutes had not elapsed when the men appeared. There were now four of them, all tall, dressed in long brown coats and round hats, and holding large sticks in their hands. They were no less alarming through their stature and huge fists than through their sinister movements in the darkness; they looked like four specters disguised as citizens.

They stopped in the center of the square, and formed a group as if consulting, and apparently undecided. The leader turned and pointed with his right hand in the direction Jean Valjean had taken, while another seemed to be pointing with some degree of obstinacy in the opposite direction. At the moment when the first man turned the moon lit up his face brilliantly, and Jean Valjean recognized Javert perfectly.

2. *THE BRIDGE OF AUSTERLITZ*

UNCERTAINTY ceased for Jean Valjean; but fortunately it still lasted with the men. He took advantage of their hesitation, for it was time lost by them and gained by him. He left the gate-way in which he was concealed, and pushed on along the Rue des Postes toward the region of the Jardin des Plantes. As Cosette was beginning to feel tired, he took her in his arms and carried her. No one was passing, and the lamps had not been lit on account of the moon.

He doubled his pace.

In a few strides he reached the Goblet pottery, on the front of which the moonshine made the old inscription distinctly visible:

> *Du Goblet fils c'est içi la fabrique:*
> *Venez choisir des cruches et des brocs:*
> *Des pots à fleurs, des tuyaux, de la brique,*
> *A tout venant le Cœur vend des carreaux.*

He left behind him the Rue de la Clef, skirted the Jardin des Plantes, and reached the quay. Here he turned: the quay was deserted; the streets were deserted. There was no one behind him, and he breathed again.

He reached the Austerlitz bridge, where a toll still existed at the time, and he handed the tollman a sou.

"It is two sous," said the man; "you are carrying a child who can walk, so you must pay for two."

He paid, though greatly vexed that his passing had given rise to any remark.

A heavy wain was passing the river at the same time as himself, and also proceeding to the right bank. This was useful for him, as he could cross the whole of the bridge in its shadow.

On reaching the arches of the bridge, Cosette, whose feet were numbed, asked to be put down; he did so, and took her by the hand again.

After crossing the bridge, he saw a little to his right building-yards toward which he proceeded. In order to reach them he must cross an open brilliantly lighted space, but he did not hesitate. His pursuers were evidently thrown out, and Jean Valjean believed himself out of danger; he might be looked for, but he was not followed.

A little street, the Rue du Chemin Vert St. Antoine, ran between two timber-yards; it was narrow, dark, and seemed expressly made for him, but before entering it he looked back.

From the spot where he was he could see the whole length of the bridge of Austerlitz.

Four shadows had just come upon it, and were walking toward the right bank.

They were the four men.

Jean Valjean gave a start like a recaptured animal.

One hope was left him; it was that the four men had not been upon the bridge at the moment when he crossed the large illumined space with Cosette.

In that case, by entering the little street before him, he might escape, if he could reach the timber-yards, kitchen-gardens, fields, and land not yet built on.

He fancied that he could trust to this little silent street, and entered it.

3. *CONSULT THE PLAN OF PARIS IN 1727*

AFTER going three hundred yards he came to a spot where the road formed two forks, and Jean Valjean had before him, as it were, the two branches of a Y. Which should he choose?

He did not hesitate, but took the right one, because the other ran toward the faubourg, that is to say, inhabited parts, while the right branch went in the direction of the country, or deserted parts.

Still they did not walk very rapidly, for Cosette checked Jean Valjean's pace, and hence he began carrying her again, and Cosette laid her head on his shoulder and did not say a word.

At times he looked back, while careful to keep on the dark side of the street.

The first twice or thrice that he turned he saw nothing, the silence was profound, and he continued his walk with a little more confidence.

All at once, on turning suddenly, he fancied that he saw something moving on the dark part of the street which he had just passed.

He rushed forward rather than walked, hoping to find some side lane by which he could escape, and once again break his trail.

He reached a wall, which, however, did not render further progress impossible, for it was a wall skirting a cross-lane, into which the street Jean Valjean had entered ran. Here he must make his mind up again whether to turn to the right or left. He looked to the right; the lane ran for some distance between buildings, which were barns or sheds, and then stopped.

The end of the blind alley, a tall white wall, was distinctly visible. He looked to the left; on this side the lane was open, and at a distance of about two hundred yards fell into a street, of which it was an affluent.

On that side safety lay.

At the moment when Jean Valjean turned to his left in order to reach this street he saw at the angle formed by the street and the lane a species of black and motionless statue; it was evidently a man posted there to prevent him passing.

Jean Valjean fell back.

The part of Paris where Jean Valjean now was, situated between the Faubourg St. Antoine and la Rapée, was one of those which have been utterly transformed by those recent works which some call disfigurements, others beautifying. The fields, the timber-yards, and old buildings have been removed, and there are now brand-new wide streets, arenas, circuses, hippodromes, railway stations, and a prison, Mazas,—progress, as we see, with its corrective.

Half a century back, in that popular language all made up of traditions, which insists on calling the Institute "les Quatre Nations," and the Opera Comique "Feydeau," the precise spot where Jean Valjean now stood was

called "le Petit Picpus." The Porte St. Jacques, the Porte Paris, the Barrière des Sergents, the Porcherons, the Galiote, the Celestins, the Capu-
cins, the Mail, the Bourbe, the tree of Cracow, little Poland, and little
Picpus are names of old Paris, swimming on the surface of the new. The
memory of the people floats on the flotsam of the past.

Little Picpus, which, by the way, scarce existed, and was never more
than the outlines of a quarter, had almost the monastic look of a Spanish
town. The streets were scarce paved, and hardly any houses lined them;
excepting two or three streets, to which we are about to refer, all was
wall and solitude. There was not a shop or a vehicle, scarce a candle
lighted in the windows, and every light was put out by ten o'clock.
The quarter consisted of gardens, convents, timber-yards, and kitchen-
grounds, and there were a few low houses with walls as lofty as themselves.

Such was the quarter in the last century; the Revolution fiercely assailed it, and the Republican board of works demolished and made gaps
in it; rubbish was allowed to be shot there. Thirty years ago this quarter
was disappearing under the erasure of new buildings, and now it is
entirely obliterated. Little Picpus, of which no modern map retains a
trace, is very clearly indicated in the plan of 1727, published at Paris by
Denis Thierry, Rue St. Jacques, opposite the Rue du Plâtre; and at Lyons
by Jean Girin, Rue Mercière. Little Picpus had what we have just called
a Y of streets formed by the Rue du Chemin Vert St. Antoine dividing
into two branches, the left-hand one taking the name of the Petite Rue
Picpus, and the right-hand that of Rue Polonceau. The two branches of
the Y were joined at their summit by a sort of cross-bar called Rue Droit-
mur. Any one, who, coming from the Seine, reached the end of Rue
Polonceau, had on his left Rue Droit-mur, turning sharply at a right
angle, in front of him the wall of that street, and on his right a truncated
prolongation of the Rue Droit-mur called the Cul de sac Genrot.

It was here that Jean Valjean was.

As we said, on perceiving the black shadow, standing on watch at the
corner of the Rue Droit-mur and the Petite Rue Picpus, he fell back, for
he was doubtless shadowed by this phantom.

What was to be done?

He had no time to retrograde, for what he had seen moving in the
shadow a few moments previously in his rear was, of course, Javert and
his squad. Javert was probably already at the beginning of the street at
the end of which Jean Valjean was. Javert, according to appearances,

was acquainted with this labyrinth, and had taken his precautions by sending one of his men to guard the outlet. These conjectures, which so closely resembled certainty, whirled suddenly in Jean Valjean's troubled brain like a handful of dust raised by an unexpected puff of wind. He examined the blind alley, that was barred; he examined the Rue Picpus, a sentry was there, and he saw his black shadow distinctly thrown on the white moon-lit pavement. To advance was falling into this man's clutches; to fall back was throwing himself into Javert's arms. Jean Valjean felt himself caught in a net which was being slowly hauled in, and looked up to Heaven in despair.

4. *ATTEMPTS TO ESCAPE*

In order to understand the following the reader must form an exact idea of the Droit-mur lane, and in particular of the angle which the visitor left on his left when he turned out of the Rue Polonceau into this lane. The lane was almost entirely bordered on the right by poor-looking houses, on the left by single slim-looking edifices, composed of several *corps de logis,* which gradually rose from two floors to three as they approached Little Rue Picpus, so that this building, which was very lofty on that side, was very low on the side of Rue Polonceau, where, at the corner to which we have alluded, it sank so low as to be only a wall. This wall did not run parallel with the lane, but formed a very deep cant, concealed by its corners from any observers in Rue Polonceau and Rue Droit-mur.

From this cant the wall extended along Rue Polonceau up to a house bearing the number 49, and in Rue Droit-mur, where it was much shorter, up to the frowning building to which we have referred, whose gable it intersected, thus forming a new reëntering angle in the street.

This gable had a gloomy appearance, for only one window was visible, or, to speak more correctly, two shutters covered with sheet zinc and always closed.

The description of the locality which we are now giving is strictly correct, and will doubtless arouse a very precise souvenir in the mind of the old inhabitants of the quarter.

The cant in the wall was entirely occupied by a thing that resembled a colossal and wretched gate-way; it was a vast collection of perpendicular planks, the top ones wider than those below, and fastened together by long cross-strips of iron. By the side of this gate was a porte cochère of ordinary dimensions, which had apparently been made in the wall about fifty years previously.

A linden-tree displayed its branches above the cant, and the wall was covered with ivy on the side of the Rue Polonceau.

In Jean Valjean's desperate situation, this gloomy building had an uninhabited and solitary look about it which tempted him. He hurriedly examined it, and said to himself that if he could only enter it he might perhaps be saved.

In the center of the frontage of this building, turned to the Rue Droit-mur, there were old leaden drain-pipes at all the windows of the different floors. The various branches which led to a central pipe formed a species of tree on the façade; these ramifications with their hundred elbows imitated those old vine branches which cling to the front of old farm-houses.

This strange espalier of lead and iron branches was the first thing that caught Jean Valjean's attention. He put Cosette down with her back against a post, bidding her be silent, and hurried to the spot where the main pipe reached the ground. Perhaps there might be a way to scale it and enter the house, but the pipe was worn out and scarce held in its cramps; besides, all the windows of this silent house were defended by thick iron bars, even the garrets. And then the moon shone full on this front, and the man watching at the end of the street would see Jean Valjean climb up; and then, what was he to do with Cosette? how was he to hoist her up a three-storied house?

He gave up all idea of climbing by the pipe and crawled along the wall to reënter Rue Polonceau.

When he reached the cant where he had left Cosette, he noticed that no one could see him there. As we stated, he was safe from all eyes, no matter on what side; moreover, he was in the shadow, and then lastly, there were two gates, which might perhaps be forced. The wall over which he saw the linden-tree and the ivy evidently belonged to a garden in which he could at least conceal himself, though there was no foliage on the trees, and pass the rest of the night.

Time was slipping away, and he must set to work at once. He felt the porte cochère, and at once perceived that it was fastened up inside and out; and then went to the other great gate with more hope.

It was frightfully decrepit, its very size rendered it less solid, the planks were rotten, and the iron bands, of which there were only three, were rusty. It seemed possible to break through this affair.

On examining this gate, however, he saw that it was not a gate; it had no hinges, lock, or partition in the center; the iron bands crossed it from side to side without any solution of continuity. Through the cracks of the planks he caught a glimpse of coarsely mortared rag stone, which passers-by might have seen ten years back. He was forced to confess to himself with consternation that this fancied gate was simply a make-believe; it was easy to pull down a plank, but he would find himself face to face with a wall.

5. *A THING IMPOSSIBLE IN GAS-LIGHT*

At this moment a hollow, cadenced sound began to grow audible a short distance off, and Jean Valjean ventured to take a peep round the corner of the street. Seven or eight soldiers were entering the street; he could see their bayonets gleaming, and they were coming toward him.

These soldiers, at the head of whom he distinguished Javert's tall form, advanced slowly and cautiously, and frequently halted; it was plain that they were exploring all the corners and all the doors and lanes.

It was—and here conjecture could not be wrong—some patrol which Javert had met and requested to assist him.

Judging from the pace at which they marched, and the halts they made, they would require about a quarter of an hour to reach the spot where Jean Valjean was. It was a frightful thought; a few moments separated Jean Valjean from the awful precipice which yawned before him for the third time. And the galleys were now not merely the galleys, but Cosette lost forever; that is to say, a life resembling the interior of a tomb.

There was only one thing possible.

Jean Valjean had one peculiarity, that he might be said to carry two wallets: in one he had the thoughts of a saint; in the other the formidable talents of a convict, and he felt in one or the other as opportunity offered.

Among other resources, owing to his numerous escapes from the Toulon galleys, he had become a perfect master in the incredible art of raising himself without ladder, cramping-irons, and by his mere muscular strength, and holding on by his shoulders and knees, in the right angle of a wall, to the sixth floor if necessary, an art which rendered so terrible and so celebrated that corner of the yard in the Paris conciergerie by which the condemned convict Battemolle escaped twenty years ago.

Jean Valjean measured the height of the wall above which he saw the linden-tree, and found that it was about eighteen feet. The lower part of the angle, which it made with the gable end of the large building, was filled up with a triangular mass of masonry, very common in Parisian corners.

This mass was about five feet high, and the space to be cleared from the top of it was not more than fourteen; but the difficulty was Cosette, for she could not climb a wall. Abandon her? Jean Valjean did not think of it, but carrying her was impossible; a man requires his whole strength to carry out such an ascent, and the slightest burden would displace his center of gravity and hurl him down.

He required a rope, but he had none. Where was he to find a rope at midnight in the Rue Polonceau? Assuredly at this moment, if Jean Valjean had possessed a kingdom, he would have given it for a rope.

All extreme situations have their flashes, which at one moment blind, at another illumine us.

Jean Valjean's desperate glance fell on the lamp-post in the blind alley.

In those days there were no gas-lights in the streets of Paris; at nightfall lamps were lit at regular distances, which were pulled up and down by a rope that crossed the street, and fitted into a groove in a post. The end of the rope was kept in an iron box under the lantern, of which the lamp-lighter had the key, and the rope itself was protected by a metal case.

Jean Valjean leaped across the street, burst the lock of the box with the point of his knife, and a moment later was again by Cosette's side, holding a rope. Such gloomy finders of expedients, when struggling with fatality, set rapidly to work.

We have mentioned that the lamps were not lit on this night; the one in the blind alley, therefore, was naturally extinguished, and any one might have passed close without noticing that it was no longer in its place.

The hour, the place, the darkness, Jean Valjean's pre-occupation, his singular gestures, his coming and going, were all beginning to alarm Cosette. Any other child would have begun crying loudly long before, but she confined herself to pulling the skirt of his coat. The noise of the approaching patrol constantly became more distinct.

"Father," she whispered, "I am frightened; who is coming?"

"Silence," the unhappy man replied; "it is Madame Thénardier."

The child trembled, and he added:

"Do not say a word, but leave me to act; if you cry out or sob, she will catch you and take you back again."

Then, without hurry, but without doing anything twice over, with a firm and sharp precision, which was the more remarkable at such a moment, when the patrol and Javert might be instantly expected, he undid his cravat, fastened it under Cosette's armpits, while careful not to hurt her, fastened the rope to the cravat, took the other end in his teeth, took off his shoes and stockings, which he threw over the wall, and began raising himself in the corner of the wall with as much certainty as if he had cramping-irons under his heels and elbows. Half a minute had not elapsed ere he was astride the coping.

Cosette looked at him in stupor, without saying a word; for Jean Valjean's mention of the landlady's name had frozen her. All at once she heard Jean Valjean say to her, in a very low voice:

"Lean against the wall."

She obeyed.

"You must not say a word, or feel frightened," he continued.

And she felt herself lifted from the ground, but before she had time to look around she found herself on the top of the wall.

Jean Valjean placed her on his back, took her two little hands in his

158

left hand, and crawled along the wall until he reached the cant. As he had suspected, there was a building here, whose roof began at the top of the bastard gate and descended in a gentle slope nearly to the ground, grazing the linden-tree. This was a fortunate circumstance, for the wall was much higher on this side than on that of the street, and Jean Valjean could scarce see the ground, so far was it beneath him.

He had just reached the sloping roof, and had not yet loosed his hold of the coping, when a violent uproar announced the arrival of the patrol, and he heard Javert's thundering voice:

"Search the blind alley; all the streets are guarded, and I will wager that he is in it."

The soldiers rushed forward into the alley Genrot.

Jean Valjean slipped down the roof, still supporting Cosette, reached the linden-tree and leaped on the ground. Either through terror or courage, the child had not said a word; her hands were only slightly grazed.

6. THE BEGINNING OF AN ENIGMA

JEAN VALJEAN found himself in a large garden of most singular appearance, one of those gloomy gardens that appear made to be looked at in winter and by night. This garden was of an oblong shape, with a walk of tall poplars at the end, tall shrubs in the corner, and an un-shadowed space in the center of which an isolated tree could be distinguished. There were also a few stunted fruit-trees bristling like brambles, vegetable plots, a melon bed, whose frames glistened in the moonlight, and an old well. Here and there were stone benches that seemed black with moss; the walks were bordered with small gloomy-looking and upright shrubs; grass covered one half of the walks, and a green mold the other half.

Jean Valjean had by his side the building by help of whose roof he had descended, a pile of faggots, and behind the latter, close to the wall, a stone statue, whose mutilated face was merely a shapeless mass, appearing indistinctly in the darkness.

The building was a species of ruin, containing several dismantled rooms, of which one was apparently employed as a shed.

The large edifice of the Rue Droit-mur had two façades looking into this garden at right angles, and these façades were even more melancholy than those outside. All the windows were barred, and not a single light could be seen, while at the upper window there were scuttles as in prisons. One of these frontages threw its shadow upon the other which fell back on the garden like an immense black cloth.

No other house could be noticed, and the end of the garden was lost in mist and night. Still, walls could be indistinctly noticed intersecting each other, as if there were other gardens beyond, and the low roofs in the Rue Polonceau.

Nothing more stern and solitary than this garden could well be imagined; there was no one in it, as was natural at such an hour, but it did not look as if the spot were made for any one to walk in, even in bright daylight.

Jean Valjean's first care was to put on his shoes and stockings again, and then enter the shed with Cosette. A man who is escaping never considers himself sufficiently concealed, and the child, who was still thinking of Madame Thénardier, shared his instinct for concealment.

Cosette trembled and clung close to him; for she could hear the tumultuous noise of the patrol searching the street and lane, the blows of the musket-butts against the stones, Javert's appeals to the men whom he had posted, and his oaths, mingled with words which could not be distinguished.

At the expiration of a quarter of an hour this species of stormy grumbling appeared to be retiring, and Jean Valjean could scarce breathe.

He gently laid his hand on Cosette's mouth.

The solitude in which he found himself was so strangely calm, however, that the furious uproar so close at hand did not even cast the shadow of a trouble over it. All at once, in the midst of this profound calm, a new sound burst forth,—a heavenly, divine, ineffable sound, as ravishing as the other had been horrible. It was a hymn that issued from the darkness, a dazzling blending of prayer and harmony in the dark and fearful silence of the night; female voices, but composed at once of the pure accent of virgins and the simple voices of children, such voices as do not belong to earth, and resemble those which the new-born still hear and the dying begin to hear. This chant came from the gloomy building that commanded the garden, and at the moment when the noise of the demons was retiring it seemed like a choir of angels approaching in the dark.

Cosette and Jean Valjean fell on their knees.

They knew not what it was, they knew not where they were, but both man and child, the penitent and the innocent, felt that they must fall on their knees.

The voices had this strangeness about them, that they did not prevent the edifice from appearing deserted; it seemed like a supernatural chant in an uninhabited house.

While the voices sang, Jean Valjean thought of nothing else; he no longer saw the night, but an azure sky. He fancied that the wings which we all of us have within us were expanding within him.

The singing ceased; it had probably lasted some time, but Jean Valjean could not have said how long, for hours of ecstasy never occupy more than a minute.

All had become silent again; there was no sound in the garden, no sound in the street; all that that threatened, all that that reassured, had faded away. The wind shook on the coping of the wall some dry grass, which produced a soft and melancholy sound.

7. CONTINUATION OF THE ENIGMA

THE night breeze had risen, which proved that it must be between one and two in the morning. Cosette said nothing, and as she was leaning her head against him, Jean Valjean fancied that she was asleep. He bent down and looked at her; her eyes were wide open, and she had a pensive look which hurt Jean Valjean.

She was still trembling.

"Do you feel inclined to sleep?" he asked her.

"I am very cold," she answered.

A moment after she continued:

"Is she still there?"

"Who?" Jean Valjean asked.

"Madame Thénardier."

Jean Valjean had forgotten the way he had employed to keep Cosette silent.

"Ah," he said, "she is gone, and you have nothing to fear."

The child sighed, as if a weight had been taken off her chest.

The ground was damp, the shed open on all sides, and the wind grew more cutting every moment. He took off his coat and wrapped Cosette up in it.

"Are you less cold now?" he said.

"Oh! yes, father."

"Well, wait for me a minute."

He left the ruin, and began walking along the large building in search of some better shelter. He came to doors, but they were closed, and there were bars on all the ground-floor windows.

After passing the inner angle of the edifice he noticed that he had come to some arched windows, and perceived a faint light. He raised

162

himself on tiptoe and looked through one of the windows; they all belonged to a large hall, paved with stones, in which nothing could be distinguished but a little light and great shadows. The light came from a night-lamp burning in the corner. This hall was deserted and nothing was stirring in it, and yet, after a long look, he fancied that he could see on the ground something that seemed to be covered with a pall and resembled a human form. It was stretched out flat, with its face against the stones, its arms forming a cross, and motionless as death. From a species of snake which dragged along the pavement, it looked as if this sinister form had a rope round its neck.

The whole hall was bathed in that mist of badly lighted places which intensifies the horror.

Jean Valjean often said afterward that, although he had witnessed many mournful sights in his life, he had never seen one more chilling or terrifying than this enigmatical figure performing some strange mystery at this gloomy spot, and thus caught sight of through the darkness. It was frightful to suppose that it might be dead, and more frightful still to think that it might possibly be still alive.

He had the courage to place his face to the pane, and watch whether the figure would stir; but though he remained for a time, which appeared to him very long, the outstretched form made no movement. All at once he felt himself assailed by an indescribable horror, and he ran off toward the shed without daring to look back; he fancied that if he turned his head he should see the figure walking after him and waving its arms.

When he reached the ruin he was panting, his knees gave way, and the perspiration was running down his back.

Where was he? who could have imagined anything like this species of sepulcher in the heart of Paris? What was the strange house? An edifice full of nocturnal mystery, calling souls in the darkness, the voice of angels, and when they arrive, suddenly offering them this frightful vision; promising to open the bright gate of Heaven, and, instead, opening the horrible gate of the tomb! and it was really a mansion, a house which had its number in a street. It was not a dream; but he was obliged to touch the stones in order to believe it.

Cold, anxiety, apprehension, and the emotion of the night brought on him a real fever, and all his ideas were confused in his brain.

8. *THE ENIGMA DEEPENS*

THE child had laid her head on a stone and fallen asleep.

Jean Valjean sat down by her side and began gazing at her; gradually, as he looked, he grew calm and regained possession of his freedom of mind.

He clearly perceived this truth, the basis of his future life, that, so long as she was there, so long as he had her by his side, he would require nothing except for her, nor fear anything save on her account. He did not even feel the cold particularly, for, though he had taken off his coat, it was to cover her.

Still, through the reverie into which he had fallen, he had heard for some time past a singular noise, like a bell being rung, and it was in the garden. It could be heard distinctly, though faintly, and resembled those cattle-bells which produce a gentle melody at night in the grazing fields.

This noise made Jean Valjean turn, and he saw that there was some one in the garden.

A being looking like a man was walking among the melon frames, rising, stooping, and stopping with regular movements, as if he were dragging or stretching out something on the ground. This man was apparently lame.

Jean Valjean gave the continual, trembling start of the unhappy; everything is hostile and suspicious to them; they distrust the day because it allows them to be seen, and night because it helps in surprising them. Just now he shuddered because the garden was deserted, and now he shuddered because there was some one in it.

He fell back from chimerical into real terror; he said to himself that Javert and the police had probably not gone away, that they had, in any case, left watchmen in the street; and that if this man discovered him he would give an alarm and hand him over to the police. He gently raised the still sleeping Cosette in his arms, and carried her behind a mass of old furniture in the most remote part of the shed; Cosette did not stir.

From this spot he observed the movements of the being in the melon ground; the strange thing was that the noise of the bell followed this man's every movement. When he approached, the sound approached; when he went away, the sound went away. If he made a sudden movement, a little peal followed the movement, and when he stopped, the noise ceased. It appeared evident that the bell was fastened to this man; but in that case what could be the meaning of it? Who was the man to whom a bell was fastened, as if he were a ram or an ox?

While asking himself these questions, he touched Cosette's hands; they were chilled.

"O Heaven!" he said.

And he asked in a whisper, "Cosette!"

She did not open her eyes. He shook her sharply, but she did not awake.

"Can she be dead?" he said to himself, and he rose, shivering from head to foot.

The most frightful thoughts crossed his mind pell-mell. There are moments when hideous suppositions assail us like a band of furies, and violently force the bolts of our brain. When it is a question about people whom we love, our prudence invents all sorts of follies. He remembered that sleep in the open air on a cold night might be mortal.

Cosette was lying stretched out motionless at his feet.

He listened for her breath; she was breathing, but so faintly that it seemed as if the respiration would cease at any moment.

How was he to warm her? how was he to wake her? All that did not refer to this slipped from his mind, and he rushed wildly from the shed.

It was absolutely necessary that Cosette should be in bed before a fire within a quarter of an hour.

9. THE MAN WITH THE BELL

JEAN VALJEAN walked straight up to the man whom he saw in the garden, and while doing so took from his pocket the rouleau of silver.

This man was looking down, and did not see him coming, and in a few strides Jean Valjean was by his side, and addressed him with the cry, "One hundred francs."

The man started and raised his eyes.

"One hundred francs to be gained," Jean Valjean continued, "if you will find me a shelter for this night."

The moon fully lit up Jean Valjean's alarmed face.

"Why, is it you, Father Madeleine!" the man said.

The name uttered thus in the darkness at this strange spot, by this strange man, made Jean Valjean recoil.

He expected everything save that. The man who addressed him was a stooping, lame old man, dressed nearly like a peasant, and wearing on his left leg a leathern knee-cap, from which hung a rather large bell.

It was impossible to distinguish his face, which was in the shadow; still the man had doffed his bonnet, and said all in a tremor:

"O Lord, how did you get here, Father Madeleine? Which way did you come in? Why, you must have fallen from Heaven. Well, if ever you do fall, it will be from there. And then, what a state you are in! you have no cravat, no hat, and no coat! do you know that you would have frightened anybody who did not know you? No coat! oh, my goodness, are the saints going mad at present? But how *did* you get in here?"

One word did not wait for the next, the old man spoke with a rustic volubility, in which there was nothing alarming; and it was all said with a mixture of stupefaction and simple kindness.

"Who are you? and what is this house?" Jean Valjean asked.

"O Lord, that is too strong," the old man exclaimed. "Why, did you not get me the situation, and in this house too? What, don't you recognize me?"

"No," said Jean Valjean, "and how is it that you know me?"

"You saved my life," the man said.

He turned, a moonbeam played on his face, and Jean Valjean recognized old Fauchelevent.

"Ah!" he said, "it is you? oh, now I recognize you."

"That is lucky," the old man said, reproachfully.

"And what are you doing here?" Jean Valjean asked.

"Why! I am covering my melons."

Old Fauchelevent really held in his hand at the moment when Jean Valjean accosted him a piece of matting, which he was engaged in spreading over the melon frame. He had laid a good many pieces during the hour he had been in the garden, and it was this operation that produced the peculiar movements Jean Valjean had noticed from the shed.

He continued:

"I said to myself, there is a bright moon and it is going to freeze, so I had better put these great coats on my melons." And he added, as he looked at Jean Valjean, with a grin, "You should have done the same. But how have you got here?"

Jean Valjean, feeling himself known by this man, at least under the name of Madeleine, only advanced cautiously. He multiplied his questions, and, curiously enough, they changed parts,—he, the intruder, became the questioner.

"And what is that bell you have on your knee?"

"That?" Fauchelevent said; "it is, that they may avoid me."

"What on earth do you mean?"

Old Fauchelevent gave an inimitable wink.

"O Lord, they are only women in this house, and lots of girls. It seems that I should be dangerous to meet, and so the bell warns them; when I come, they go."

"What is this house?"

"Oh, nonsense, you know."

"Indeed I do not."

"Why, you got me the gardener's place here."

"Answer me as if I knew nothing."

"Well, it is the convent of the Little Picpus, then."

Jean Valjean's recollections returned to him. Chance, that is to say,

Providence, had brought him to the very convent in the Quartier St. Antoine, where Fauchelevent, after his accident, had been engaged on his recommendation two years back.

He repeated, as if speaking to himself:

"Little Picpus!"

"But come, tell me," Fauchelevent continued, "how the deuce did you get in here, Father Madeleine? for though you are a saint, you are a man, and no men are admitted here."

"Why, you are."

"Well, only I."

"And yet," Jean Valjean continued, "I must remain."

"O Lord!" Fauchelevent exclaimed.

Jean Valjean walked up to the gardener and said in a grave voice:

"Fauchelevent, I saved your life."

"I was the first to remember it," Fauchelevent answered.

"Well, you can do for me to-day what I did for you formerly."

Fauchelevent took Jean Valjean's muscular hands in his old wrinkled and trembling hands, and for some seconds seemed as if unable to speak; at length he exclaimed:

"Oh! it would be a blessing from Heaven if I could repay you a slight portion! Save your life! M. Madeleine, you can dispose of an old man as you please."

An admirable joy had transfigured the aged gardener, and his face seemed radiant.

"What do you wish me to do?" he continued.

"I will explain; have you a room?"

"I have a cottage behind the ruins of the old convent, in a corner which no one visits, with three rooms."

"Good," said Jean Valjean; "now, I will ask two things of you."

"What are they, M. le Maire?"

"First, that you will tell nobody what you know about me; and, secondly, that you will not try to learn anything further."

"As you please. I know that you can do nothing but what is honest, and that you have ever been a man after God's heart. And then, again, it was you who got me this situation, and I am at your service."

"Enough; now come with me, and we will go and fetch the child."

"Ah," said Fauchelevent, "there is a child."

He did not add a word, but followed Jean Valjean as a dog follows its master.

In less than half an hour, Cosette, who had become rosy again by the heat of a good fire, was asleep in the old gardener's bed. Jean Valjean had put on his cravat and coat again; the hat thrown over the wall had been found and picked up, and Fauchelevent took off his knee-cap and bell, which now adorned the wall by the side of a door. The two men were seated near the fire at a table on which Fauchelevent had placed a lump of cheese, biscuits, a bottle of wine, and two glasses, and the old man said to Jean Valjean as he laid his hand on his knee:

"Ah, Father Madeleine! you did not recognize me at once; you save people's lives and forget them afterward! Oh, that is wrong, for they remember you; you are an ungrateful man."

10. HOW JAVERT ONLY FOUND THE NEST

THE events of which we have just seen the back, so to speak, had occurred under the simplest conditions.

When Jean Valjean, on the night of the day on which Javert arrested him by Fantine's death-bed, broke out of M. . . . jail, the police supposed that the escaped convict would proceed to Paris. Paris is a maelstrom in which everything is lost and disappears in the whirlpool of the streets; no forest can conceal a man so well as that crowd, and fugitives of every description are aware of the fact. They go to Paris to be swallowed up, for that is at times a mode of safety. The police are aware of this too, and it is at Paris that they seek what they have lost elsewhere. They sought there the ex-mayor of M. . . . , and Javert was summoned to assist in the search, and in truth powerfully assisted in recapturing Jean Valjean. The zeal and intelligence he displayed in this office were noticed by M. Chabouillet, secretary of the prefecture under Count Anglès, and this gentleman, who had before been a friend to Javert, had the police inspector of M. . . . appointed to the Paris district. Here Javert proved himself variously and—let us say it, though the word seems inappropriate when applied to such services—honorably useful.

He thought no more of Jean Valjean—with these dogs ever on the hunt, the wolf of to-day causes the wolf of yesterday to be forgotten—until in December, 1823, he, who never read newspapers, read one. But Javert, who was a legitimist, was anxious to learn the details of the triumphal entry of the "Prince Generalissimo" into Bayonne. When he had finished the article that interested him, a name, the name of Jean Valjean, at the foot of a column, attracted him. The newspaper announced that the convict Jean Valjean was dead, and published the fact in such formal terms that Javert did not doubt it. He musingly said, "That is the best bolt," then threw away the paper, and thought no more on the subject.

Some time after, it happened that a report was sent by the prefecture of the Seine et Oise to that of Paris, about the abduction of a child, which took place, it was said, under peculiar circumstances, in the parish of Montfermeil. A little girl seven or eight years of age, who had been entrusted by her mother to a publican in the town, had been stolen by a stranger. The child answered to the name of Cosette, and her mother was a certain Fantine, who had died in an hospital, it was not known when or where. This report passed under Javert's eyes, and rendered him thoughtful.

The name of Fantine was familiar to him; he remembered that Jean Valjean had made him laugh by asking him for a respite of three days to go and fetch this creature's child. He remembered that Jean Valjean was arrested at Paris at the very moment when he was getting into the Montfermeil coach, and some facts had led to the supposition at the time that he had taken a trip to the vicinity of the village on the previous day, for he had not been seen in the village itself. What was his business at Montfermeil? no one was able to guess; but Javert now understood it—Fantine's daughter was there, and Jean Valjean had gone to fetch her. Now this child had just been stolen by a stranger; who could the stranger be? could it be Jean Valjean?—but he was dead. Javert, without saying a word to anybody, took the coach at the "Pewter Platter," and went off to Montfermeil.

He expected to find here a great clearing up, but only found a great obscurity.

At the beginning, the Thénardiers, in their vexation, had chattered, and the disappearance of the Lark produced a sensation in the village.

There were at once several versions of the story, which finally settled down into abduction, and hence the police report. Still, after he had got over his first outburst of temper, Thénardier, with his admirable instinct, very speedily comprehended that it is never useful to set the authorities at work, and that his complaint about the abduction of Cosette would have the primary result of fixing the flashing gaze of justice upon himself and many dark matters he was mixed up in. The thing that owls least like is to have a candle brought to them. And then, again, how would he get out of the fifteen hundred francs which he had received? He stopped short, put a gag in his wife's mouth, and affected amazement when people spoke about "the stolen child." He did not at all understand; he had certainly complained at the first moment about his little darling being taken from him so suddenly; he should have liked to keep her for two or three days longer through affection; but it was her grandfather who had come to fetch her in the most natural way in the world. He added the "grandfather," which produced a good effect, and it was on this story that Javert fell upon reaching Montfermeil. The grandfather caused Jean Valjean to fade out of memory.

Javert, however, drove a few questions like probes into Thénardier's story. "Who was this grandfather, and what was his name?" Thénardier answered simply, "He is a rich farmer; I saw his passport, and I fancy his name was M. Guillaume Lambert."

Lambert is a respectable and most reassuring name, and so Javert returned to Paris.

"Jean Valjean is really dead," he said to himself, "and I am an ass."

He was beginning to forget the whole affair again, when in the course of March, 1824, he heard talk of a peculiar character who lived in the parish of St. Medard, and was surnamed the "beggar who gives alms." This man was said to be an annuitant, whose name no one exactly knew, and who lived alone with a little girl eight years of age, who knew nothing about herself, except that she came from Montfermeil. Montfermeil! that name constantly returned, and made Javert prick up his ears. An old begging spy, an ex-beadle, to whom this person was very charitable, added a few more details. "He was a very stern person; he never went out till night; he spoke to nobody, except to the poor now and then, and let no one approach him. He wore a horrible old yellow coat, which was worth several millions, as it was all lined through with bank-notes." This decidedly piqued Javert's curiosity. In order to see this annuitant closer, without startling him, he one day borrowed the beadle's rags and the place where the old spy crouched every evening, snuffling his orisons through his nose, and spying between his prayers.

"The suspicious individual" really came up to Javert, thus travestied, and gave him alms. At this moment Javert raised his head, and the shock which Jean Valjean received on fancying that he recognized Javert, Javert received on fancying that he recognized Jean Valjean.

Still the darkness might have deceived him; and Jean Valjean's death was official. Javert felt serious doubts, and when in doubt, Javert, a scrupulous man, never collared anybody.

He followed this man to No. 50-52, and made the old woman talk, which was no difficult task. She confirmed the fact of the great-coat lined with millions, and told the story about the thousand-franc note; she had seen it! she had felt it! Javert hired a room, and took possession of it that same night. He listened at the door of the mysterious lodger, in the hope of hearing his voice, but Jean Valjean saw his candle through the keyhole, and foiled the spy by holding his tongue.

On the next day, Jean Valjean decamped, but the noise of the five-franc piece which he let drop was noticed by the old woman, who supposed that he was about to leave, and hastened to warn Javert. Hence, when Jean Valjean left the house at night, Javert was waiting for him behind the trees with two men.

Javert had requested assistance at the prefecture, but had not mentioned the name of the individual whom he hoped to seize. That was his secret, and he kept it for three reasons: first, because the slightest indiscretion might give Jean Valjean the alarm; secondly, because laying hands on an old escaped convict, supposed to be dead, on a condemned man, whom Justice had already classified forever among "the malefactors of the most dangerous class," was a magnificent success, which the older policemen of Paris would certainly not leave to a new-comer, like Javert, —and he was afraid lest he might be robbed of his galley-slave; lastly, because Javert, having artistic tastes, was fond of anything unexpected. He hated those successes which are deflowered by being talked of a long time beforehand, and he liked to elaborate his master-pieces in the darkness and suddenly unveil them.

Javert followed Jean Valjean from tree to tree, and then from street-corner to street-corner, and had not once taken his eye off him; even at the moment when Jean Valjean fancied himself the safest, Javert's eye was upon him. Why did Javert not arrest him, though? Because he was still in doubt.

It must be borne in mind, that at this period, the police were not exactly at their ease, and the free press annoyed them. A few arbitrary arrests, denounced by the newspapers, had found an echo in the chambers, and rendered the prefecture timid. Attacking individual liberty was a serious matter; the agents were afraid of being deceived, for the prefect made them answerable, and a mistake was dismissal. Just imagine the effect which would have been produced in Paris by the following short paragraph reproduced by twenty papers: "Yesterday, an old, white-haired grandfather, a respectable fund-holder, who was taking a walk with his granddaughter, eight years of age, was arrested and taken to the house of detention as an escaped convict."

Let us repeat also that Javert had scruples of his own; the warnings of his conscience were added to those of the prefect, and he really doubted.

Jean Valjean had his back turned to him, and was walking in the dark; sorrow, anxiety, despondency, the fresh misfortune of being compelled to fly by night and seek a chance refuge for Cosette and himself in Paris, the necessity of regulating his pace by that of a child—all this had unconsciously changed Jean Valjean's demeanor, and imparted to him such a senility, that the very police incarnated in Javert might be deceived, and were deceived. The impossibility of approaching close, his attire as an old emigré tutor, Thénardier's statement which made him out a grandpapa, and, lastly, the belief in his death at the galleys, added to the uncertainty that clouded Javert's mind.

For a moment he had the idea of suddenly asking for his papers; but if the man was not Jean Valjean, and if he were not a respectable fund-holder, he was, in all probability, some fellow deeply entangled in the meshes of Parisian crime; some leader of a band, who gave alms to hide his other talents, and who had his "pals," his accomplices, and his lurking-places, where he could conceal himself. All the turnings this man made in the streets seemed to indicate that all was not quite right with him, and arresting him too quickly would be "killing the goose with the golden eggs?" Where was the harm of waiting! Javert felt quite certain that he could not escape.

He walked along, therefore, in great perplexity, asking himself a hundred questions about this enigmatical personage.

It was not till some time after that he decidedly recognized Jean Valjean in the Rue Pontoise, by the brilliant light that poured from a wine shop.

There are only two beings in the world that quiver profoundly,—the mother who recovers her child and the tiger that finds its prey again, but Javert suffered the same quiver.

So soon as he had positively recognized Jean Valjean, the formidable convict, he noticed that he had only two companions, and asked for support at the police office in the Rue Pontoise. Before catching hold of a thorn-bush, people put on gloves.

This delay and the halt at the Rollin square to arrange with his agents, all but made him lose the trail, but he quickly guessed that Jean Valjean wished to place the river between himself and his hunters. He hung his head and reflected, like a blood-hound putting its nose to the ground to lift the scent, and then, with the powerful correctness of his instinct walked to the Austerlitz bridge. One remark of the toll collector's put him on his track. "Have you seen a man with a little girl?" "I made him pay two sous," the collector answered. Javert reached the bridge just in time to see Jean Valjean leading Cosette across the moonlit square; he saw him enter the Rue du Chemin Vert St. Antoine; he thought of the blind alley arranged there like a trap, and the sole issue from it by the little Rue Picpus; and in order to stop the earth, as sportsmen say, he sent off a policeman by a detour to guard the issue. A patrol, which was returning to the arsenal, happening to pass, he requested its assistance, for in such games as this soldiers are trumps, and, moreover, it is a principle that, in forcing a boar from its lair, the hunter must be scientific, and there must be a strong pack of hounds. These arrangements made, Javert, feeling that Jean Valjean was caught between the blind alley on the right, his own agent on the left, and himself behind, took a pinch of snuff.

Then he began playing and enjoying a delicious and infernal moment; he let his man go before him, knowing that he held him, but desiring to defer as long as possible the moment of arresting him; delighted at feeling him caught, and at seeing him free, and watching him with the pleasure of the spider that lets the fly flutter for a while, and the cat that lets the mouse run. The claw and the talon have a monstrous sensuality in the fluttering movements of the animal imprisoned in their prisons; what a delight such a strangling must be!

Javert was playing; the meshes of his net were so solidly made, he was certain of success, and now he only needed to close his hand.

Accompanied as he was, the idea of resistance was impossible, however energetic, vigorous, and desperate Jean Valjean might be.

Javert advanced slowly, examining and searching as he passed every corner of the street, like the pockets of a thief; but when he reached the center of the web he did not find his fly.

We can imagine his exasperation.

He questioned his watchmen, but they quietly declared that they had not seen the man pass.

It happens at times that a stag will escape with the pack at its heels, and in such cases the oldest huntsmen know not what to say. In a disappointment of this nature, Artonge exclaimed: "It is not a stag, but a sorcerer."

Javert would have gladly uttered the same cry, for his disappointment was midway between despair and fury.

It is certain that errors were committed by Napoleon in the Russian war, by Alexander in the Indian war, by Cæsar in his African war, by Cyrus in the Scythian war,—and by Javert in his campaign against Jean Valjean. He was probably wrong in hesitating to recognize the ex-galley-slave, for a glance ought to have been sufficient for him. He was wrong in not apprehending him purely and simply at No. 50-52. He was wrong in not arresting him, upon recognition, in the Rue Pontoise. He was wrong to arrange with his colleagues in the bright moonlight, although certainly advice is useful, and it is as well to interrogate those dogs which deserve credence. But the hunter cannot take too many precautions when he is following restless animals, like the wolf and the convict, and Javert, by displaying too much anxiety in setting the bloodhounds on the track, alarmed his game and started it off. Above all, he was wrong, on finding the trail again at Austerlitz bridge, in playing the dangerous and foolish trick of holding such a man by a string. He fancied himself stronger than he really was, and that he could play with the lion as if it were a mouse. At the same time he imagined himself too weak when he fancied that he must procure help; it was a fatal precaution, and the loss of precious time.

Javert committed all these faults, but for all that was not the less one of the cleverest and most certain spies that ever existed. He was, in the full acceptation of the term, a dog that runs cunning; but where is the man who is perfect?

Great strategicians have their eclipses.

Great follies are often made, like stout ropes, of a multitude of fibers. Take the cable, thread by thread, catch hold of the small determining motives separately, and you break them one after the other, and say to yourself, "It is only that"; but twist them together and you have an enormity. It is Attila hesitating between Marcianus in the East and

Valentinianus in the West; it is Hannibal delaying at Capua; it is Danton falling asleep at Arcis-sur-Aube.

However this may be, even at the moment when Javert perceived that Jean Valjean had slipped from his clutches he did not lose his head. Certain that the convict could not be very far off, he established watches, organized mouse-traps and ambuscades, and beat up the quarter the whole night through. The first thing he saw was the cut cord of the lantern. This was a valuable sign, which, however, led him astray so far that it made him turn all his attention to the Genrot blind alley. There are in this alley, low walls, surrounding gardens which skirt open fields, and Jean Valjean had evidently fled in that direction. The truth is, that if he had gone a little further down the blind alley he would, in all probability, have done so, and been a lost man.

Javert explored the gardens and fields as if looking for a needle, and at daybreak he left two intelligent men on duty, and returned to the prefecture of police, looking as hang-dog as a spy captured by a robber.

BOOK VI

PETIT-PICPUS

1. *NO. 62, RUE PICPUS*

HALF a century ago nothing more resembled any ordinary porte
cochère than that of No. 62, Petit Rue Picpus. This door, generally
half-open in the most inviting manner, allowed you to see two things
which are not of a very mournful nature—a courtyard with walls covered
with vines, and the face of a lounging porter. Above the bottom wall tall
trees could be seen, and when a sunbeam enlivened the yard, and a glass
of wine had enlivened the porter, it was difficult to pass before No. 62 and
not carry away a laughing idea. And yet you had had a glimpse of a very
gloomy place.

The threshold smiled, but the house prayed and wept.

If you succeeded, which was not easy, in passing the porter,—as was,
indeed, impossible for nearly all, for there was an "Open, Sesame,"
which it was necessary to know,—you entered at the right a small hall
from which ran a staircase inclosed between two walls, and so narrow
that only one person could go up at a time; if you were not frightened
by the canary-colored plaster and chocolate wainscot of this staircase, and
still boldly ascended, you crossed two landings and found yourself in a
passage on the first-floor, where the yellow distemper and chocolate
board-skirting followed you with a quiet pertinacity. The staircase and
passage were lighted by two fine windows, but the latter soon made a
bend and became dark. When you had doubled this cape, you found
yourself before a door, which was the more mysterious because it was
not closed. You pushed it open, and found yourself in a small room about
six feet square, well scrubbed, clean, and frigid, and hung with a yellow-
green sprigged paper, at fifteen sous the piece. A white pale light came
through a large window with small panes, which was on the left and
occupied the whole width of the room; you looked about you but saw

nobody; you listened, but heard neither a footstep nor a human sound; the walls were bare and the room unfurnished—there was not even a chair.

You looked again, and saw in the wall facing the door a square hole, covered with a black, knotty, substantial cross-barred grating, which formed diamonds—I had almost written meshes—at least an inch and a half across. The little green sprigs on the yellow paper came right up to these bars, calmly and orderly, and the funereal contact did not make them start or wither. Even supposing that any human being had been so wondrously thin as to attempt to go in or out by the square hole, the bars would have prevented him; but, though they did not let the body pass, the eyes, that is to say, the mind could. It seemed as if this had been thought of, for it had been lined with a tin plate in which were bored thousands of holes more microscopic than those of a strainer. Beneath this plate was an opening exactly like the mouth of a letter-box, and a bell-wire hung by the side of this hole.

If you pulled this wire, a bell tinkled, and you heard a voice close to you which made you start.

"Who is there?" the voice asked.

It was a female voice, a gentle voice, so gentle that it was melancholy.

Here, again, there is a magic word which it was necessary to know; if you did not know it, the voice ceased, and the wall became silent again, as if the terrifying darkness of the tomb were on the other side.

If you knew the word, the voice continued,—"Turn to the right."

You then noticed, facing the window, a door, the upper part of which was of gray painted glass. You raised the latch, walked in, and experienced precisely the same expression as when you enter a box at the theater, before the gilt grating has been lowered and the chandelier lighted. You were, in fact, in a species of box, scarce lighted by the faint light that came through the glass door, narrow, furnished with two old chairs and a ragged sofa—a real box with a black entablature to represent the front. This box had a grating, but it was not made of gilt wood as at the opera, but was a monstrous trellis-work of frightfully inter-laced iron bars, fastened to the wall by enormous clamps that resembled clenched fists.

When the first few moments were past, and your eye began to grow accustomed to this cellar-like gloom, you tried to look through the grating, but could not see more than six inches beyond it; there it met a barrier of black shutters, connected and strengthened by cross-beams, and painted a ginger-bread yellow. These shutters were jointed, divided into long thin planks, and covered the whole width of the grating; they were always closed.

At the expiration of a few minutes, you heard a voice calling to you from behind the shutters, and saying to you:

"I am here, what do you want with me?"

It was a loved voice, sometimes an adored voice, but you saw nobody, and could scarce hear the sound of breathing. It seemed, as it were, an evocation addressing you through the wall of a tomb.

If you fulfilled certain required and very rare conditions, the narrow plank of one of the shutters opened opposite to you, and the evocation became an apparition. Behind the grating, behind the shutter, you perceived, as far as the grating would allow, a head, of which you only saw the mouth and chin, for the rest was covered by a black veil. You caught a glimpse of a black wimple and of a scarce distinct form, covered by a black pall. This head spoke to you, but did not look at you, and never smiled.

The light that came from behind you was so arranged that you saw her in brightness and she saw you in darkness; this light was a symbol.

Still your eyes plunged eagerly through the opening into this place, closed against all looks,—a profound vacuum surrounded this form clothed in mourning. Your eyes investigated this vacuum and tried to distinguish what there was around the apparition, but in a very little time you perceived that you could see nothing. What you saw was night, emptiness, gloom, a winter fog mingled with the vapor from a tomb; a sort of terrifying peace; a silence in which nothing could be heard, not even sighs; a shadow in which nothing could be distinguished, not even phantoms.

What you saw was the interior of a nunnery.

It was the interior of that gloomy and stern house which was called the convent of the Perpetual Adoration. The box in which you found yourself was the parlor, and the first voice that addressed you was that of a lay sister, who always sat silent and motionless, on the other side of the wall, near the square opening which was defended by the iron grating and tin plate with the thousand holes like a double visor.

The obscurity in which the grated box was plunged resulted from the fact that the parlor, which had a window on the side of the world, had none on the side of the convent; profane eyes must not see any portion of this sacred spot.

Still there was something beyond the shadow; there was a light and life amid this death. Although this convent was the most strictly immured of all, we will try to enter it and take the reader in with us, and describe, with due regard to decorum, things which novelists have never seen, and consequently never recorded.

2. *THE OBEDIENCE OF MARTIN VERGA*

THIS convent, which had existed for many years prior to 1824 in the Rue Picpus, was a community of Bernardines belonging to the obedience of Martin Verga.

These Bernardines, consequently, were not attached to Clairvaux, like the Bernardine brothers, but to Citeaux, like the Benedictines. In other words, they were subjects, not of St. Bernard, but of St. Benedict.

Anyone who has at all turned over folios knows that Martin Verga founded, in 1425, a congregation of Bernardo-Benedictines, whose headquarters were Salamanca, and which had Alcala as an offshoot.

Such a grafting of one order upon another is not at all unusual in the Latin Church. If we confine our attention merely to the Order of St. Benedict, we find four congregations attached to it, besides the obedience of Martin Verga; in Italy two, Monte Cassino and Saint Justina of Padua; two in France, Cluny and St. Maur, and nine orders,—Valombrosa, Grammont, the Celestins, the Calmalduli, the Chartreux, the Humiliated, the Olivateurs, and the Silvestrines, and, lastly Citeaux; for Citeaux itself, while a trunk for others, is only a branch for St. Benedict. Citeaux dates from St. Robert, abbot of Molesmes, in the diocese of Langres, in 1098. Now it was in 529 that the Devil who had retired to the desert of Subiaco (he was old—did he turn hermit?), was expelled from the temple of Apollo, in which he resided, by St. Benedict, a youth seventeen years of age.

Next to the rule of the Carmelites, who walk barefoot, wear a piece of wicker-work on their throat, and never sit down, the hardest rule is that of the Bernardo-Benedictines of Martin Verga. They are dressed in black with a wimple, which, by the express order of St. Benedict, comes up to the chin; a serge gown with wide sleeves, a large woolen veil, the wimple cut square on the chest, and the coif which comes down to their eyes,—such is their dress. All is black, excepting the coif, which is white. Novices wear the same garb, but all white, while the professed nuns also wear a rosary by their side.

The Bernardo-Benedictines of Martin Verga practise the Perpetual Adoration, in the same way as those Benedictines called the ladies of the Holy Sacrament, who, at the beginning of this century, had two houses in Paris, one in the Temple, the other in the Rue Neuve Ste. Geneviève. In other respects, the nuns of the Little Picpus to whom we are referring entirely differ from the ladies of the Holy Sacrament; there were several distinctions in the rule as well as in the dress. The nuns of Little Picpus wore a black wimple, the former a white one, and had also on their chest a Holy Sacrament, about three inches in length, of plate or gilt brass. The nuns of the Little Picpus did not wear this decoration. The Perpetual Adoration, while common in Little Picpus and the Temple house, leaves the two orders perfectly distinct. This practise is the only resemblance between the ladies of the Holy Sacrament and the Bernardines of Martin Verga, in the same way as there was a similitude, for the study and glorification of all the mysteries attaching to the infancy, life, and death of the Saviour, between two orders which were greatly separated and at times hostile,—the oratory of Italy, established at Florence by Philippe de Neri, and the oratory of France, established in Paris by Pierre de Bérulle. The Paris oratory claimed precedence because Philippe de Neri was only a saint, while Bérulle was a cardinal.

But to return to the Spanish rule of Martin Verga.

The Bernardo-Benedictines of this obedience abstain from meat the whole year; fast all Lent, and on many other days, special to themselves; get up in their first sleep, from one to three A. M., in order to read their breviary and chant matins; sleep in serge sheets at all seasons, and on straw; never bathe or light fires; chastise themselves every Friday; observe the rule of silence; only speak during recreation, which is very short; and wear coarse flannel chemises for six months, from September

14th, which is the Exaltation of the Holy Cross, up to Easter. These six months are a moderation—the rule says all the year, but the flannel chemise, insupportable in the heat of summer, produced fevers and nervous spasms. Even with this relief, when the nuns put on the flannel chemise on September 14th, they suffer from fever for three or four days. Obedience, poverty, chastity, perseverance—such are their vows, which are greatly aggravated by the rule.

The prioress is elected for three years by mothers, called "Mères Vocales," because they have a voice in the chapter. She can be only reëlected twice, which fixes the longest possible reign of a prioress at nine years.

They never see the officiating priest, who is hidden from them by a green baize curtain nine feet high. At the sermon, when the preacher is in the chapel, they draw their veils over their faces; they must always speak low, and walk with their eyes fixed on the ground. Only one man is allowed to enter the convent, and he is the diocesan archbishop.

There is certainly another, who is the gardener; but he is always an aged man, and in order that he may be constantly alone in the garden, and that the nuns may avoid him, a bell is fastened to his knee. The nuns must display absolute and passive submission to the prioress, and it is canonical subjection in all its self-denial. They must obey as if it were the voice of Christ, *ut voci Christi,* at a nod, at the first signal, *ad nutum, ad primum signum;* at once, cheerfully, perseveringly, and with a certain bland obedience, *promptè, hilariter, perseveranter, et cæcâ quâdam obedientiâ;* like the file in the workman's hand, *quasi limam in manibus fabri,* and are not allowed to read or write anything without express permission, *legere vel scribere non ediscerit sine expressâ superioris licentiâ.*

Each of them performs in turn what they call the "reparation." This reparation is a prayer for all the sins, faults, irregularities, violations, iniquities, and crimes performed upon earth. For twelve consecutive hours, from four in the evening till four the next morning, the sister who performs the reparation remains on her knees, on the stone before the Holy Sacrament, with her hands clasped and a rope round her neck. When the fatigue becomes insupportable, she prostrates herself with her face on the ground, and her arms forming a cross,—that is her sole relief. In this attitude, she prays for all the guilty in the world; it is a grand, almost a sublime idea.

As this act is accomplished in front of a post on the top of which a wax candle is burning, it is called either "making reparation," or "being at the post." The nuns through humility, indeed, prefer the latter expression, which contains an idea of punishment and abasement.

Making reparation is a function in which the whole soul is absorbed; the sister at the post would not turn round were a thunder-bolt to fall behind her.

Moreover, there is always a nun on her knees before the Holy Sacrament; this station lasts an hour, and they relieve each other like sentries. That is the Perpetual Adoration.

The prioress and mothers nearly all have names imprinted with peculiar gravity, recalling, not saints and martyrs, but the incidents in the life of the Saviour,—such as Mother Nativity, Mother Conception, Mother Presentation, and Mother Passion; still the names of saints are not interdicted.

When you see them, you never see more of them than their mouth.

They all have yellow teeth, for a tooth-brush never entered the convent. Cleaning the teeth is the first rung of the ladder, at the foot of which is "losing the soul."

They do not call anything "mine"; they have nothing of their own, and must not be attached to anything. They say of everything "ours," thus, our veil, our beads; if they were to allude to their chemise they would say "our chemise." Sometimes they become attached to some trifling object, a book of hours, a relic, or consecrated medal, but so soon as they perceive that they are beginning to grow fond of it, they are obliged to give it away. They remember the remark of Saint Theresa, to whom a great lady said, at the moment of entering her order, "Allow me, holy mother, to send for a Bible to which I am greatly attached." "Ah, you are still attached to something! in that case do not come among us."

No one must lock herself in under any pretense, or have a room of her own, and they live with open doors. When they pass each other, one says, "The most Holy Sacrament of the Altar be blessed and adored," and others answer, "Forever." There is the same ceremony when one sister raps at another sister's door; the door has scarce been touched ere a gentle voice is heard saying hurriedly from within, "Forever." Like all practices, this one becomes mechanical through habit; and a sister will sometimes say "Forever," before the other has had time to utter the long sentence, "The most Holy Sacrament of the Altar be blessed and adored!"

Among the Visitandines, the one who enters says, "Ave Maria," to which the other replies, "Gratia plena"; this is their greeting, which is truly full of grace.

At each hour of the day, three supplementary strokes are struck on the chapel bell, and at this signal, prioress, vocal mothers, professed nuns, lay sisters, novices, and postulants break off what they are saying, doing, or thinking, and all repeat together,—if it be five o'clock, for instance,— "At five o'clock, and at every hour, may the most Holy Sacrament of the Altar be blessed and adored," and so on, according to the hour.

This custom which is intended to break off thoughts and ever lead them back to God, exists in many communities, the form alone varying. Thus, at the Infant Jesus, they say, "At the present hour, and at every hour, may the love of Jesus inflame my heart!"

The Bernardo-Benedictines of Martin Verga sing the offices to a grave, full chant, and always in a loud voice, during the whole of the service. Whenever there is an asterisk in the missal, they pause, and say in a loud voice, "Jesus, Maria, Joseph." In the service for the dead they employ such a deep note that female voices can scarce descend to it, and there results from it a striking and tragical effect.

The sisters of Little Picpus had a vault under their high altar for the burial of their community, but the government, as they call it, would not allow coffins to be placed in this vault, and they therefore left the convent when they were dead; this afflicted and consternated them like an infraction.

They had obtained the slight consolation of being buried at a special hour and in a special corner of the old Vaugirard cemetery, which was established in a field that had once belonged to the community.

On Thursday these nuns attend high mass, vespers, and all the services as on Sunday; and they also scrupulously observe all the little festivals unknown to people of the world, of which the church was formerly so prodigal in France, and still remains so in Spain and Italy. Their stations in the chapels are innumerable, and as for the number and length of their prayers, we cannot give a better idea than by quoting the simple remark of one of them,—"The prayers of the postulants are frightful, those of the novices worse and those of the professed nuns worse still."

Once a week the chapter meets, the prioress presiding and the vocal mothers assisting. Each sister comes in her turn to kneel on the stone, and confesses aloud, in the presence of all, the faults and sins which she has committed during the week. The vocal mothers consult after each confession and inflict the penances aloud.

In addition to the loud confession, for which all faults at all serious are reserved, they have for venial faults what they call "la coulpe." The penitent prostrates herself on her face during service in front of the prioress, who is never addressed otherwise than "Our Mother"; until the latter warns the sufferer, by a slight tap on the arm of her stall, that she can get up. The nuns perform this penance for very trivial things; breaking a glass, tearing a veil, an involuntary delay of a few seconds in attending service, false note in the chapel, that is enough. This penance is quite voluntary, and the culprit (this word is etymologically in its place here) tries and punishes herself. On festivals and Sundays there are four singing mothers, who chant at a large lectern with four desks. One day a singing mother was striking up a psalm, which began with the word *Ecce,* and said instead, quite loud, *ut, si, sol;* and for this absence of mind she underwent a penance which lasted the whole service. What rendered the fault enormous was that the chapter laughed.

When a nun is summoned to the parlor, even if she be the prioress, she pulls down her veil in such a way as only to show her mouth.

The prioress alone can communicate with strangers; the others can only see their nearest relations, and that very rarely. If by chance a person from the outer world requests to see a nun whom she had formerly known or loved, a lengthened negotiation is required. If it be a woman, the permission may possibly be granted. The nun comes and is spoken to through the shutters, which are only opened for a mother or a sister. We need hardly say that permission is never granted to men.

Such is the rule of St. Benedict, aggravated by Martin Verga.

These nuns are not gay, rosy, and fresh, as we find sometimes in other orders,—they are pale and serious, and between 1825 and 1830 three of them went mad.

ANY one desirous of joining the community of Martin Verga must be at least two years a postulant, sometimes four, and four years a novice. It is rare for the final vows to be taken before the age of twenty-three or twenty-four years. The Bernardo-Benedictines of Martin Verga admit no widows into their order.

In their cells they undergo many strange macerations, of which they are not allowed to speak.

On the day when a novice professes, she is dressed in her best clothes, wears a wreath of white roses, has her hair curled, and then prostrates herself; a large black veil is spread over her, and the service for the dead is performed. Then the nuns divide into two files, one of which passes her, saying in a plaintive voice, "Our sister is dead," and the other answers triumphantly, "Living in Jesus Christ."

At the period when this story is laid, there was a boarding-school attached to the convent, the pupils being young ladies of noble birth, and generally rich. Among them could be noticed Mlles. de Ste. Aulaire and de Bélisseu, and an English girl, bearing the illustrious Catholic name of Talbot. These young ladies, educated by the nuns between four walls, grew up with a horror of the world and of the century; one of them said to us one day, "Seeing the street pavement made me shudder from head to foot." They were dressed in blue with a white cap, and a plated or gilt Holy Ghost on the chest. On certain high festivals, especially Saint Martha, they were allowed, as a high favor and supreme happiness, to dress themselves like nuns and perform the offices and practices of St. Benedict for the whole day. At first the nuns lent them their black robes, but this was deemed a profanity, and the prioress forbade it so the novices alone were permitted to make such loans. It is remarkable that these represen-

188

tations, doubtless tolerated in the convent through a secret spirit of proselytism, and in order to give their children some foretaste of the sacred dress, were a real happiness and a true recreation for the boarders; they were amused by them, for "it was a novelty and changed them,"—candid reasons of children, which do not succeed, however, in making us worldly-minded people understand the felicity of holding a holy-water brush in one's hand, and standing for hours before a lectern and singing quartettes.

The pupils conformed to all the practices of the convent, though not to all the austerities. We know a young lady who, after returning to the world and being married for some years, could not break herself of hastily saying, each time that there was a rap at the door, "Forever!" like the nuns. The boarders only saw their parents in the parlor,—their mothers themselves were not even allowed to kiss them. To show how far this severity was carried, a young lady was visited one day by her mother, accompanied by a little sister three years of age. The young lady cried, because she would have liked to kiss her sister, but it was impossible. She implored at least permission for the child to pass her hand through the bars, so that she might kiss it, but it was refused almost as a scandal.

4. GAYETIES

For all this, though, the young ladies filled this grave house with delightful reminiscences.

At certain hours childhood sparkled in this cloister. The bell for recreation was rung, the gate creaked on its hinges, and the birds whispered to each other, "Here are the children." An irruption of youth inundated this garden, which, with its cross-walks, resembled a pall. Radiant faces, white foreheads, ingenuous eyes, full of gay light—all sorts of dawn—spread through the gloom. After the psalm-singing, the bell-ringing, and the services, the noise of girls, softer than the buzzing of bees, suddenly burst out. The hive of joy opened, and each brought her honey; they played, they called each other, they formed groups, and ran about; pretty little white teeth chattered at corners; in the distance, veils watch the laughter, shadows guarded the beams,—but what matter; they were radiant, and laughed. These four mournful walls had their moment of bedazzlement; vaguely whitened by the reflection of so much joy, they watched this gentle buzzing of the swarm. It was like a shower of roses falling on this morning. The girls sported beneath the eye of the nuns, for the glance of impeccability does not disturb innocence; and, thanks to these children, there was a simple hour among so many austere hours. The little girls jumped about and the elder danced, and nothing could be so ravishing and august as all the fresh, innocent expansion of these childish souls. Homer would have come here to dance with Perrault, and there were in this black garden youth, health, noise, cries, pleasure, and happiness enough to unwrinkle the brows of all the ancestry, both of the epic poem and the fairy tale, of the throne and the cottage, from Hecuba down to la Mère Grand.

In this house, more perhaps than elsewhere, those childish remarks were made which possess so much grace, and which make the hearer laugh thoughtfully. It was within these four gloomy walls that a child four years of age one day exclaimed, "Mother, a grown-up girl has just told me that I have only nine years and ten months longer to remain here. What happiness!"

Here, too, it was that the memorable dialogue took place.

A vocal mother: "Why are you crying, my child?"

The child (six years old), sobbing: "I said to Alix that I knew my French history. She says that I don't know it, but I do know it."

Alix, the grown-up girl (just nine): "No. She does not know it."

The mother: "How so, my child?"

Alix: "She told me to open the book hap-hazard, and ask her a question out of the book, which she would answer."

"Well?"

"She did not answer it."

"What was it you asked her?"

"I opened the book as she said, and I asked her the first question that I came across."

"And pray what was the question?"

"It was '*And what happened next?*'"

It was here that the profound observation was made about a rather dainty parrot which belonged to a lady boarder. "How well bred it is! it eats the top of the slice of bread and butter, just like a lady."

In one of these cloisters was also picked up the following confession, written beforehand, so as not to forget it, by a little sinner seven years of age.

"My father, I accuse myself of having been avaricious.

"My father, I accuse myself of having committed adultery.

"My father, I accuse myself of having raised my eyes to gentlemen."

It was on one of the benches in the garden that the following fable was improvised by rosy lips six years of age, and listened to by blue eyes of four and five years.

"There were three little cocks, which lived in a place where there were many flowers. They picked the flowers and put them in their pockets; after that they plucked the leaves and put them in their playthings. There was a wolf in those parts, and there was a great deal of wood; and the wolf was in the wood, and he ate all the little cocks."

It was here, too, that the following sweet and affecting remark was made by a foundling child whom the convent brought up through charity. She heard the others speaking of their mothers, and she murmured in her corner, "My mother was not there when I was born."

There was a fat portress who could continually be seen hurrying along the passage, with her bunch of keys, and whose name was Sister Agatha. The grown-up girls—those above ten years of age—called her Agathoclès (Agathe aux clefs.)

The refectory, a large, rectangular room, which only received light through an arched window, looking on the garden, was gloomy and damp, and, as children say, full of animals. All the surrounding places furnished their contingent of insects.

Each of the four corners had received a private and expressive name, in the language of the boarders. There were Spider corner, Caterpillar corner, Wood-louse corner, and Cricket corner; the latter was near the kitchen, and highly esteemed, for it was warmer there. The names had passed from the refectory to the school-room, and served to distinguish four nations, as in the old Mazarin College. Every boarder belonged to one or other of these nations, according to the corner of the refectory in which they sat at meals. One day the archbishop, while paying a pastoral visit, noticed a charming little rosy-faced girl, with glorious light hair, pass, and he asked another boarder, a pretty brunette with pink cheeks, who was near him:

"Who is that?"

"She is a spider, sir."

"Nonsense; and this other?"

"Is a cricket."

"And this one?"

"A caterpillar."

"Indeed! and what may you be?"

"I am a wood-louse, monseigneur."

Each house of this nature has its peculiarities; at the beginning of this century, Ecouen was one of those places in which the childhood of children is passed in an almost august gloom. At Ecouen a distinction was made between the virgins and flower-girls, in taking rank in the procession of the Holy Sacrament. There were also the "canopies" and the "censers," the former holding the cords of the canopy, the latter swinging the censers in front of the Holy Sacrament, while four virgins walked in front. On the morning of the great day it was not rare to have people say in the dormitory, "Who is a virgin?"

Madame Campan mentions a remark made by a little girl of seven to a grown-up girl of sixteen, who walked at the head of the procession, while she, the little one, remained behind: "You are a virgin, you, but I am not one."

5. *AMUSEMENTS*

ABOVE the refectory door was painted in large black letters the following prayer, which was called the "White Paternoster," and which had the virtue of leading persons straight to Paradise.

"Little white Paternoster, which God made, which God said, which God placed in Paradise. At night, when I went to bed, I found three angels at my bed,—one at the foot, two at the head, and the good Virgin Mary in the middle,—who told me to go to bed and fear nothing. The Lord God is my father, the good Virgin is my mother, the three apostles are my brothers, the three virgins are my sisters. My body is wrapped up in the skirt in which God was born: the cross of St. Marguerite is written on my breast. Madame the Virgin weeping for the Lord went into the fields and met there M. St. John. 'Monsieur St. John, where do you come from?' 'I have come from the *Ave Salus*.' 'You have not seen the Lord, have you?' 'He is on the tree of the cross with hanging feet, nailed-up hands, and a little hat of white thorn on his head.' Whosoever repeats this, thrice at night and thrice in the morning, will gain Paradise in the end."*

In 1827, this characteristic orison had disappeared beneath a triple coat of whitewash, and at the present day it is almost effaced from the memory of those who were young girls then, and old women now.

A large crucifix fastened to the wall completed the decoration of this refectory, whose only door opened on the garden. Two narrow tables, with wooden benches on each side, formed two long parallel lines from one end to the other of the refectory. The walls were white, the tables black; for these two mourning colors are the sole variations in convents. The meals were poor, and the food of even the children scanty; a single plate of meat and vegetables or salt-fish was the height of luxury. This ordinary, reserved for the boarders alone, was, however, an exception. The children ate and held their tongues under the guardianship of the mother of the week, who, from time to time, if a fly dared to move or buzz contrary to regulation, noisily opened and closed a wooden book. This silence was seasoned with the "Lives of the Saints," read aloud from a little desk standing at the foot of the crucifix, the reader being a grown-up pupil, appointed for the week. At regular distances on the bare table there were earthenware bowls, in which the pupils themselves washed

---

* This Paternoster is so curious that I have thought it better to quote the original:

"Petite Patenôtre blanche, que Dieu dit, que Dieu fit, que Dieu mit en Paradis. Au soir, m'allant coucher, je trouvis (sic) trois anges à mon lit couchis, un aux pieds, deux au chevet, la bonne Vierge Marie au millieu, qui me dit que je m'y couchis, qui rien ne doutis. Le bon Dieu est mon père, la bonne Vierge est ma mère, les trois apôtres sont mès frères, les trois vierges sont mes soeurs. La chemise où Dieu fut né, mon corps en est enveloppé; la Croix Sainte Marguerite à ma poitrine est écrite. Madame la Vierge s'en va sur les champs, Dieu pleurant, rencontrit M. St. Jean. 'Monsieur St. Jean, d'où venez-vous?' 'Je viens d' *Ave Salus*.' 'Vous n'avez pas vu le bon Dieu, si est?' 'Il est dans l'arbre de la Croix, les pieds pendants, les mains clouants, un petit chapeau d'épine blanche sur la tête.' Qui la dira trois fois au soir, trois fois au matin, gagnera le Paradis à la fin."

their cups and forks and spoons, and sometimes threw in a piece of hard meat or spoiled fish, but this was severely punished.

Any child who broke the silence made a cross with her tongue. Where? On the ground: she licked the stones. Dust, that finale of all joys, was ordered to chastise these poor little roseleaves that were guilty of prattling.

There was in the convent a book of which only one copy was printed, and which no one was allowed to read. It is the "Rule of St. Benedict," a mystery which no profane eye must penetrate. *Nemo regulas seu constitutiones nostras externas communicabit.*

The boarders succeeded one day in getting hold of this book and began perusing it eagerly, though frequently interrupted by a fear of being surprised, which made them close the book hurriedly. They only derived a slight pleasure from the danger they incurred; for the most interesting portion was a few unintelligible pages about the sins of lads.

They played in a garden walk, bordered by a few stunted fruit-trees. In spite of the extreme watch and the severity of the punishment, when the wind shook the trees they at times succeeded in picking up furtively a green apple, or a spoiled apricot, or a wasp-inhabited pear. I will here let a letter speak which I have before me, a letter written by an ex-boarder five-and-twenty years ago, who is now the Duchesse de ——, and one of our most elegant women in Paris. I quote exactly: "We hide our pear, or our apple, as we can. When we go up to lay our veil on the bed before supper, we thrust it under a pillow, and eat it at night in bed, and when that is not possible we eat it in the closet." This was one of their liveliest pleasures.

On one occasion, at a period when the archbishop was paying a visit at the convent, one of the young ladies, Mademoiselle Bouchard, who was related to the Montmorencys, laid a wager that she would ask him for a holiday, an enormity in such an austere community. The wager was taken, but not one of those who took it believed in it. When the moment arrived for the archbishop to pass before the boarders, Mademoiselle Bouchard, to the indescribable horror of her companions, stepped out of the ranks and said, "Monseigneur, a holiday." Mademoiselle Bouchard was fresh and tall, and had the prettiest pink-and-white face in the world. M. de Quélen smiled, and said, "What, my dear child, a day's holiday! three, if you like; I grant three days." The prioress could do nothing, as the archbishop had said it. It was a scandal for the convent, but a joy for the boarding-school. Just imagine the effect.

This harsh convent, however, was not so well walled in but that the passions of the outer world, the dramas, and even the romance of life, entered it. To prove this, we will briefly describe a real and incontestable fact, though it is in no way connected with the story which we are narrating. We mention the fact in order to complete the physiognomy of the convent in the reader's mind.

About this period, then, there was in the convent a mysterious personage, who was not a nun, but was treated with great respect, and called Madame Albertine. Nothing was known about her except that she was dead,—and that in the world she was supposed to be dead. It was said that behind the story were certain monetary arrangements necessary for a grand marriage.

This woman, who was scarce thirty years of age and a rather pretty brunette, looked vacantly around with her large black eyes. Did she see? it was doubted. She glided along rather than walked; she never spoke, and people were not quite sure whether she breathed. Her nostrils were pinched up and livid, as if she had drawn her last sigh; touching her hand was like touching snow, and she had a strange spectral pace. Wherever she entered she produced a chill; and one day, a sister, seeing her pass, said to another, "She is supposed to be dead." "Perhaps she is so," the other replied.

A hundred stories were current about Madame Albertine, and she was the eternal object of curiosity with the boarders. There was in this chapel a gallery called "L'œil de Bœuf," and it was in this place that Madame Albertine attended service. She was usually alone there, because, as the gallery was high, the preacher could be seen from it, which was prohibited to the nuns. One day the pulpit was occupied by a young priest of high rank, le Duc de Rohan, peer of France, officer in the Red Mousquetaires, in 1815, when he was Prince de Leon, and who died after 1830, a cardinal, and archbishop of Besançon. It was the first time this M. de Rohan preached at the Little Picpus. Madame Albertine usually sat in perfect calmness through the service, but on this day, so soon as she perceived M. de Rohan, she half rose, and cried aloud, "Why, it is Auguste!" The whole community looked round in stupefaction, the preacher raised his eyes, but Madame Albertine had fallen back into her apathy; a breath from the outer world, a flash of light, had momentarily passed over this set face, then faded away, and the maniac became once again a corpse.

This remark, however, made everybody in the convent who could speak, talk incessantly. What revelations were contained in this "Why, it is Auguste!" It was evident that Madame Albertine had moved in the highest society, since she knew M. de Rohan, spoke about so great a nobleman in such a familiar way, and was at least a near relation of his, since she knew his Christian name.

Two very strict duchesses, Mesdames de Choiseul and de Serent, frequently visited the community, doubtless by virtue of their privilege as *Magnates Mulieres,* and terribly frightened the boarders. When the two old ladies passed, all the poor girls trembled and let their eyes fall.

M. de Rohan was, besides, unwittingly the object of attention among the boarders. He had just been appointed, while waiting for a bishopric, grand vicar of the archbishop of Paris, and it was one of his habits to serve mass in the chapel of the Little Picpus convent. Not one of the young recluses could see him, on account of the baize curtain, but he had a soft and rather shrill voice, which they had managed to recognize and distinguish. He had been a Mousquetaire, and, besides, he was said to be somewhat of a dandy, with fine chestnut hair curled round his head, and that he wore a wide scarf of magnificent moiré, and his black cassock was cut in the most elegant style. He greatly occupied all their youthful imaginations.

No external sound penetrated the convent, and yet one year the sound of a flute reached it. It was an event, and the boarders of that day still remember it.

It was a flute which some one was playing in the neighborhood. It was the same tune, one now very aged, "Ma Zétulbé, viens regner sur mon âme," and it was heard two or three times a day. The girls spent hours in listening, the vocal mothers were upset, brains were at work, and punishments were constant. This lasted several months; the boarders were more or less enamored of the unknown musician, and each fancied herself Zétulbé. The sound of the flute came from the direction of the Rue Droitmur. They would have given anything, risked anything, attempted anything, in order to see, if only for a moment, the young man who played the flute so exquisitely, and at the same time played on all their minds. Some of them slipped out through a back door, and ascended to the third story looking out on the street, in order to try and see him through the grating, but it was impossible; one went so far as to pass her arm between the bars and wave her handkerchief. Two others were even bolder; they managed to climb on to the roof, and at length succeeded in seeing the "young man." It was an old emigré gentleman, blind and ruined, who played the flute in his garret in order to kill time.

6. *THE LITTLE CONVENT*

THERE were within the walls of Little Picpus three perfectly distinct buildings,—the great convent inhabited by the nuns, the school-house in which the boarders were lodged, and lastly, what was called the little convent. The latter was a house with a garden, in which all sorts of old nuns of various orders, the remains of convents broken up in the Revolution, dwelt in common,—a reunion of all black, white, and gray gowns of all the communities, and all the varieties possible; what might be called, were such a conjunction of words permissible, a harlequin-convent.

Under the empire all these dispersed and homeless women were allowed to shelter themselves under the wings of the Bernardo-Benedictines; the Government paid them a small pension, and the ladies of Little Picpus eagerly received them. It was a strange pell-mell, in which each followed her rule. At times boarders were allowed, as a great recreation, to pay them a visit, and it is from this that these young minds have retained a recollection of Holy Mother Bazile, Holy Mother Scholastica, and Mother Jacob.

One of these refugees was almost at home here; she was a nun of Saint Aure, the only one of her order who survived. The old convent of the ladies of Saint Aure occupied at the beginning of the eighteenth century the same house which at a later date belonged to the Benedictines of Martin Verga. This holy woman, who was too poor to wear the magnificent dress of her order, which was a white robe with a scarlet scapulary, had piously dressed up in it a small doll, which she was fond of showing, and left at her death to the house. In 1824 only one nun of this order remained; at the present day only a doll is left.

In addition to these worthy mothers, a few old ladies of the world, like

197

Madame Albertine, had gained permission from the prioress to retire into the little convent. Among them were Madame de Beaufort d'Hautpoul and the Marquise Dufresne; another was only known in the convent by the formidable noise she made in using her handkerchief, and hence the boarders called her Madame Vacarmini.

About the year 1820, Madame de Genlis, who edited at that period a small periodical called *L'Intrépide,* asked leave to board at the Little Picpus, and the Duc d'Orleans recommended her. There was a commotion in the hive, and the vocal mothers were all of a tremor, for Madame de Genlis had written romances; but she declared that she was the first to detest them, and, moreover, she had reached her phase of savage devotion. By the help of Heaven and the prince, she entered, and went away again at the end of six or eight months, alleging as a reason that the garden had no shade. The nuns were delighted at it. Although very old, she still played the harp, and remarkably well too.

When she went away she left her mark on her cell. Madame de Genlis was superstitious and a Latin scholar, and these two terms give a very fair idea of her. A few years ago there might still be seen, fixed in the inside of a small cupboard of her cell, in which she kept her money and jewelry, the following five Latin verses, written in her own hand with red ink on yellow paper, and which, in her opinion, had the virtue of frightening away robbers:

Imparibus meritis pendent tria corpora ramis:
Dismas et Gesmas, media est divina potestas;
Alta petit Dismas, infelix, infima, Gesmas;
Nos et res nostras conservet summa potestas.
Hos versus dicas, ne tu furto tua perdas.

These verses in sixteenth-century Latin raise the question whether the two thieves of Calvary were called, as is commonly believed, Demas and Gestas, or Dismas and Gesmas. The latter orthography would thwart the claims made in the last century by the Viscomte de Gestas, to be descended from the wicked thief. However, the useful virtue attached to these verses is an article of faith in the order of the Hospitaler nuns.

The church, so built as to separate the great convent from the boarding-school, was common to the school and the great and little convents. The public were even admitted by a sort of quarantine entrance from the street; but everything was so arranged that not one of the inhabitants of the convent could see a single face from the outer world. Imagine a church whose choir was seized by a gigantic hand, and crushed so as no longer to form, as in ordinary chapels, a prolongation behind the altar, but a sort of obscure cavern on the side of the officiating priest; imagine this hall closed by the green baize curtain to which we have referred; pile up in the shadow of this curtain upon wooden seats the nuns on the left, the boarders on the right, and the lay sisters and novices at the end,—and you will have some idea of the Little Picpus nuns attending divine service. This cavern, which was called the choir, communicated with the convent by a covered way, and the church obtained its light from the garden. When the nuns were present at those services at which their rule commanded silence, the public were only warned of their presence by the sound of the seats being noisily raised and dropped.

7. A FEW PROFILES FROM THE SHADOW

DURING the six years between 1819 and 1825 the prioress of Little Picpus was Mlle. de Blémeur, called in religion Mother Innocent. She belonged to the family of that Marguerite de Blémeur who was authoress of the "Lives of the Saints of the Order of St. Benedict." She was a lady of about sixty years, short, stout, and with a voice "like a cracked pot," says the letter from which we have already quoted; but she was an excellent creature, the only merry soul in the convent, and on that account adored.

She followed in the footsteps of her ancestress Marguerite, the Dacier of the order; she was lettered, learned, competent, versed in the curiosities of history, stuffed with Latin, Greek, and Hebrew, and more a monk than a nun.

The sub-prioress was an old Spanish nun, almost blind, Mother Cineres.

The most estimated among the "vocals" were Mother Ste. Honorine, the treasurer; Mother Ste. Gertrude, first mistress of the novices; Mother Ste. Ange, second mistress; Mother Annunciation, Sacristan; Mother Ste. Augustine, head of the infirmary, the only unkind person in the convent; then Mother Ste. Mechtilde (Mlle. Gauvain), who was young, and had an admirable voice; Mother des Anges (Mlle. Drouet), who had been in the convent of the Filles Dieu, and that of the Treasury near Gisors; Mother Ste. Joseph (Mlle. de Cogolludo); Mother Ste. Adelaide (Mlle. D'Auverney); Mother Miséricorde (Mlle. de Cifuentes, who could not endure the privations); Mother Compassion (Mlle. de La Miltière, received at the age of sixty, contrary to the rule, but very rich); Mother Providence (Mlle. de Laudinière); Mother Presentation (Mlle. de Siguenza), who was prioress in 1847; and lastly, Mother Ste. Celigne (sister of Ceracchi the sculptor), who went mad; and mother Ste. Chantal (Mlle. de Suzon), who also went mad.

Among the prettiest was a charming girl of three-and-twenty, who belonged to the Bourbonnais, and was descended from the Chevalier Roze, who was called in the world Mlle. Roze, and in religion Mother Assumption.

Mother Ste. Mechtilde, who had charge of the singing arrangements, was glad to make use of the boarders for this purpose; she generally selected a complete musical scale, that is to say, seven assorted voices, from ten to sixteen years inclusive, whom she drew up in a line, ranging from the shortest to the tallest. In this way she produced a species of living Pandean pipes, composed of angels.

The lay sisters, whom the boarders liked most, were Sister Ste. Euphrasie, Sister Ste. Marguerite, Sister Ste. Marthe, who was childish, and Sister Ste. Michel, at whose long nose they laughed.

All these nuns were kind to the children, and only stern to themselves; there were no fires lit except in the school-house, and the food there was luxurious when compared with that of the convent. The only thing was that when a child passed a nun and spoke to her, the latter did not answer.

This rule of silence produced the result, that in the whole convent language was withdrawn from human creatures and given to inanimate objects. At one moment it was the church bell that spoke, at another the gardener's; and a very sonorous gong, placed by the side of the sister porter, and which could be heard all through the house, indicated by various raps, which were a sort of acoustic telegraphy, all the actions of natural life which had to be accomplished, and summoned a nun, if required, to the parlor. Each person and each thing had its raps: the

prioress had one and one; the sub-prioress one and two; six-five announced school-hour, so that the pupils talked of going to six-five; four-
four was Madame Genlis's signal, and, as it was heard very often,
uncharitable persons said she was the "diable à quatre." Nineteen strokes
announced a great event,—it was the opening of the cloister door, a
terrible iron plate all bristling with bolts, which only turned on its hinges
before the archbishop. With the exception of that dignitary and the
gardener, no other man entered the convent, but the boarders saw two
others,—one was the chaplain, Abbé Banès, an old ugly man, whom they
were allowed to contemplate through the grating; while the other was
M. Ansiaux, the drawing-master, whom the letter, which we have
already quoted, called "M. Anciot," and described as an odious old hunch-
back.

So we see that all the men were picked.

Such was this curious house.

8. *POST CORDA LAPIDES*

AFTER sketching the moral figure, it may not be time lost to indicate in
a few words the material configuration, of which the reader already possesses some idea.

The convent of the Little Picpus occupied a large trapeze, formed by
the four streets to which we have so frequently alluded, and which surrounded it like a moat. The convent was composed of several buildings
and a garden. The main building, regarded in its entirety, was a juxtaposition of hybrid constructions, which, looked at from a balloon, would
very exactly form a gallows laid on the ground. The long arm of the
gallows occupied the whole of the Rue Droit-mur, comprised between
the Little Rue Picpus and the Rue Polonceau, while the shorter arm was

a tall, gray, stern, grated façade, looking on the Little Rue Picpus, of which the porte cochère, No. 62, was the extremity. Toward the center of the façade dust and ashes whitened an old, low-arched gate, where the spiders made their webs, and which was only opened for an hour or two on Sundays, and on the rare occasions when the coffin of a nun left the convent; this was the public entrance to the church. The elbow of the gallows was a square room, used as an office, and which the nuns called the "buttery." In the long arm were the cells of the mothers, sisters, and novices; in the short one the kitchens, the refectory, along which a cloister ran, and the church. Between No. 62 and the corner of Aumarais lane was the school, which could not be seen from the exterior. The rest of the trapeze formed the garden, which was much lower than the level of the Rue Polonceau, and this caused the walls to be much loftier inside than out. The garden, which was slightly arched, had at its center on the top of a mound a fine-pointed and conical fir-tree, from which ran, as from the boss of a shield, four large walks, with eight smaller ones arranged two and two, so that, had the inclosure been circular, the geometrical plan of the walks would have resembled a cross laid upon a wheel. The walks, which all ran to the extremely irregular walls of the garden, were of unequal length, and were bordered by gooseberry bushes. At the end a poplar walk ran from the ruins of the old convent which was at the angle of the Rue Droit-mur, to the little convent, which was at the corner of Aumarais lane. In front of the little convent was what was called the small garden. If we add to this *ensemble* a court-yard, all sorts of varying angles formed by the inside buildings, prison walls, and the long black line of roofs that ran along the other side of the Rue Polonceau, as the sole prospect, we can form an exact idea of what the house of the Bernardines of Little Picpus was five-and-forty years ago. This sacred house was built on the site of a famous racket court in the sixteenth century, which was called the "Tripot des onze mille diables."

All these streets, indeed, were the oldest in Paris; the names Droit-mur and Aumarais are very old, but the streets that bear them are far older. Aumarais lane was before called Maugout lane; the Rue Droit-mur was called the Rue des Eglantines, for God opened the flowers before man cut building-stones.

9. A CENTURY UNDER A WIMPLE

As we are giving details of what was formerly the Little Picpus convent, and have ventured to let in light upon this discreet asylum, the reader will perhaps permit us another slight digression, which has nothing to do with the story, but is characteristic and useful in so far as it proves that a convent can have its original people.

There was in the little convent a centenarian, who came from the abbey of Fontevrault, and before the Revolution she had even been in the world. She talked a good deal about M. de Miromesnil, keeper of the seals under Louis XVI, and the wife of a President Duplat, who had been a great friend of hers. It was her pleasure and vanity to drag in these two names on every possible occasion. She told marvels about the abbey of Fontevrault, which was like a town, and there were streets in the convent.

She spoke with a Picard accent which amused the boarders; every year she renewed her vows, and at the moment of taking the oath would say to the priest: "Monseigneur St. Francis took it to Monseigneur St. Julien, Monseigneur St. Julien took it to Monseigneur St. Eusebius, Monseigneur St. Eusebius took it to Monseigneur St. Procopius, etc., etc., and thus I take it to you, father." And the boarders would laugh, not in their sleeves, but under their veils,—a charming little suppressed laugh, which made the vocal mothers frown.

At other times the Centenarian told anecdotes. She said that in her youth the Bernardines took precedence of the Mousquetaires; it was a century that spoke, but it was the eighteenth century. She described the Champenois and Burgundian custom of the four wines before the Revolution. When a great personage, a marshal of France, a prince, a duke and peer, passed through a town of Champagne or Burgundy, the authorities addressed and presented him with four silver cups filled with four different sorts of wine. On the the first cup was the inscription "ape-wine," on the second, "lion-wine," on the third, "sheep-wine," and on the fourth, "hog-wine." These four mottoes expressed the four stages of intoxication—the first that enlightens, the second that irritates, the third that dulls, and the fourth that brutalizes.

She had a mysterious object, to which she was greatly attached, locked up in a cupboard, and the rule of Fontevrault did not prohibit this. She would not show it to anybody; she locked herself in, which her rule also permitted, and hid herself each time that a desire was expressed to see it. If she heard footsteps in the passage, she closed the cupboard as hastily as she could with her aged hands. So soon as it was alluded to, she, who was so fond of talking, held her tongue; the most curious persons were foiled by her silence, and the most tenacious by her obstinacy. This was a subject of comment for all the idlers and gossips in the convent. What could this precious and hidden thing be which was the centenarian's treasure? of course some pious book or unique rosary, or well-tried relic. On the poor woman's death they ran to the cupboard, more quickly than was befitting, and opened it. They found the object under three folds of linen. It was a Faenza plate representing Cupids flying away, and pursued by apothecaries' apprentices armed with enormous squirts. The pursuit is full of comical grimaces and postures; one of the charming little Cupids is already impaled. He writhes, flutters his wings, and strives to fly away, but the assassin laughs a satanic laugh. Moral—love conquered by a colic. This plate, which is very curious and perhaps had the honor of furnishing Molière with an idea, still existed in September, 1845; it was for sale at a curiosity shop on the Boulevard Beaumarchais.

This good old woman would not receive any visitors, "because," as she said, "the parlor is too melancholy."

10. ORIGIN OF THE PERPETUAL ADORATION

THIS almost sepulchral parlor which we have described is a thoroughly local fact, which is not reproduced with the same severity in other convents. In the convent of the Rue du Temple, which, it is true, belonged to another order, brown curtains were substituted for the black shutters, and the parlor itself was a boarded room with white muslin curtains at the windows, while the walls admitted all sorts of pictures—the portrait of a Benedictine nun with uncovered face, painted bouquets, and even a Turk's-head.

It was in the garden of this convent that the chestnut-tree grew, which was considered the handsomest and largest in France, and which had the reputation among the worthy eighteenth-century folk of being "the father of all the chestnut-trees in the kingdom."

As we said, this convent of the Temple was occupied by Benedictines of the Perpetual Adoration, who greatly differed from those Benedictines who descended from Citeaux. This order of the Perpetual Adoration is not the oldest, and does not date back beyond two hundred years.

In 1640 the Holy Sacrament was twice profaned at an interval of a few days, in two parish churches, St. Sulpice and St. Jean en Grève, a frightful and rare sacrilege, which stirred up the whole city. The prior grand-vicar of St. Germain-des-Prés ordered a solemn procession of all his clergy in which the Papal Nuncio officiated, but this expiation was not sufficient for two worthy ladies, Madame Courtin, Marquise de Boucs, and the Countess de Châteauvieux. This outrage done to the "most august Sacrament of the Altar," though transient, would not leave their pious minds, and it seemed to them that it could alone be repaired by a "perpetual adoration" in some nunnery. In 1662 and 1663 both gave considerable sums of money to Mother Catherine de Bar, called of the Holy Sacrament and a Benedictine nun, for the purpose of founding for this pious object a convent of the order of St. Benedict. The first permission for this foundation was given to Mother Catharine de Bar by M. de Metz, abbé of St. Germain, "on condition that no person should be received unless she brought a pension of three hundred livres, or a capital sum of six thousand livres." After this the king granted letters patent, which were countersigned in 1654 by the chamber of accounts and the parliament.

Such are the origin and legal consecration of the establishment of the Benedictines of the Perpetual Adoration of the Holy Sacrament at Paris. The first convent was built for them in the Rue Cassette, with the funds of Mesdames de Boucs and Châteauvieux.

This order as we see, must not be confounded with the Benedictines of Citeaux. It was a dependency of the abbé of St. Germain-des-Près, in the same manner as the ladies of the Sacred Heart are subjects of the Jesuits, and the Sisters of Charity of the general of the Lazarists.

It was also entirely different from the order of the Bernardines of Little Picpus, whose interior we have just shown. In 1657 Pope Alexander VII authorized, by special brief, the Bernardines of Little Picpus to practise the Perpetual Adoration like the Benedictines of the Holy Sacrament, but the two orders did not remain the less distinct.

11. *END OF LITTLE PICPUS*

Toward the beginning of the Restoration, Little Picpus began to pine away; it shared in the general death of the order, which, after the eighteenth century, began to decay, like all religious orders. Contemplation, like prayer, is a want of humanity; but, like all that the Revolution has touched, it will be transformed, and will become favorable to human progress, instead of being hostile to it.

The house of Little Picpus became rapidly depopulated; in 1840 the little convent and the school had disappeared; there were no old women or young girls left; the former were dead, the latter had fled away. *Volaverunt.*

The rule of the Perpetual Adoration is so strict that it horrifies; novices hold back, and the order is not recruited. In 1845 a few lay sisters were still found here and there, but no professed nuns. Forty years ago there were nearly one hundred nuns; fifteen years ago there were only twenty-eight; how many are there now? In 1847 the prioress was young, a sign that the choice was becoming restricted. In proportion as the number diminishes, the fatigue is augmented; the service of each becomes more painful; and the moment may be seen approaching at which there will be only a dozen sore and bent shoulders to bear the heavy rule of St. Benedict. The burden is implacable, and remains the same for the few as for the many; it used to press, but now it crushes. Hence they die out. At the time when the author of this book still resided in Paris, two died,—one twenty-five, the other twenty-three, years of age. The latter can say, like Julia Alpinula, *Hic jaceo. Vixi annos viginti et tres.* It was owing to this decadence that the convent has given up the education of girls.

We were unable to pass by this extraordinary, unknown, and obscure house without entering it, and taking with us those who are reading—we trust with some advantage to themselves—the melancholy story of Jean Valjean. We have penetrated into this community so full of those old practices which seem so novel at the present day. It is the closed garden, *Hortus Conclusus.* We have spoken of this singular place in detail, but with respect, as far, at least, as they can be reconciled. We do not understand all, but we insult nothing. We are equally removed from the Hosanna of Joseph de Maistre consecrating the executioner, and from the grins of Voltaire sneering at the crucifix.

Illogical is Voltaire, be it said in passing; Voltaire would have defended Christ as he defended Calas. Even for those who deny superhuman incarnations, what does the crucifix represent? The wise man murdered.

In the nineteenth century the religious idea passed through a crisis. Some things were unlearned; excellent theory provided that in unlearning one thing we learn another. There can be no vacuum in the human heart. Certain demolitions take place, and it is right they should, on condition that they are followed by reconstructions.

Meanwhile, let us study things that have passed away. It is necessary to know them, if only to avoid them. The counterfeits of the past assume false names and like to call themselves the future. The past can falsify its passport. Let us distrust the trick. The past has a countenance, superstition, and a mask,—hypocrisy. Let us display the countenance and tear off the mask.

The question of convents is complex; it touches civilization which condemns them, and liberty which protects them.

BOOK VII

A PARENTHESIS

1. THE CONVENT AS AN ABSTRACT IDEA

THIS book is a drama in which the first personage is the Infinite. Man is the second.

This being the case, as a convent is found on our road, we have felt it our duty to enter it. Why? Because the convent is an institution of the East as well as of the West, of antiquity and modern days, of paganism, Buddhism, and Mohammedanism as well as of Christianity, is one of optical instruments directed by man on the Infinite.

This is not the place to develop, without qualification, certain ideas; nevertheless, while strictly maintaining our reservations, restrictions, and even indignation, we are bound to say that as often as we find the Infinite, ill or well understood, in man we feel the deepest respect. In the synagogue, the mosque, the pagoda, the wigwam, there is a hideous side which we execrate, and a sublime side which we adore. What a subject of contemplation for the soul, but an unfathomable reverie, the reverberation of God on the human wall!

2. THE CONVENT AS AN HISTORICAL FACT

FROM the point of view of history, reason, and truth, monachism is condemned.

Monasteries, when numerous in a nation, are tourniquets on the circulation, embarrassing establishments, centers of idleness where there ought to be centers of labor. Monastic communities are to the great social community what the gall-nut is to the oak, or the wart to the body. Their prosperity and their development are the impoverishment of the country. The monastic rule, excellent at the start of civilization, useful in subjugating the corporeal by the spiritual, is injurious to the manhood of nations. Moreover, when it relaxes and enters on its period of disorder, as it continues to be the example, it is evil for all the reasons which make it salutary in its period of purity.

The claustral system has had its time. The cloister, useful in the early education of modern civilization, has been hurtful to its growth and injurious to its development. As an institution and a method of training men, the monastery, good in the tenth century, doubtful in the fifteenth, is detestable in the nineteenth. The leprosy of monasticism has eaten almost to a skeleton two great nations,—Italy and Spain, one the light, the other the splendor of Europe for centuries; and at the present time these two illustrious nations are only beginning to recover, thanks to the sound, vigorous hygiene of 1789.

The convent, especially the old convent for women, such as it still existed, on the threshold of this century, in Italy, Austria, and Spain, is one of the most gloomy products of the middle ages. It is the point where terrors intersect. The Catholic convent, properly so called, is filled with the black radiations of death.

The Spanish convent, especially, is funereal. There, in the obscurity, under vaults full of misty gloom, under domes which the shadows render vague, rise massive Babel-like altars, high as cathedrals; there are suspended by chains in the darkness immense white crucifixes; there huge Christs of ivory are displayed, naked, against a background of ebony, more than bloody, bleeding, hideous, and magnificent. The elbows display the bones, the knees display the integuments, the wounds display the flesh, crowned with thorns of silver, pierced with nails of gold, with blood-drops of rubies on the brow, and tears of diamonds in the eyes. The diamonds and rubies seem dripping, and draw tears, down below in the shadows, from veiled figures which have their loins tortured by the shirt of hair, or by the scourge with its points of iron, and their breasts crushed by woven wicker-work, and their knees flayed by prayer: women who believe themselves spouses, ghosts who believe themselves seraphim. Do these women think? No! Do they have a will? No! Do they love? No! Their nerves have become bone, their bones stone; their veil is woven night, and beneath it their breathing comes like some—we know not what—tragic respiration of death. The Abbess, a specter, consecrates and terrifies them. The Immaculate is there, in stern fierceness. Such are the old monasteries of Spain, haunts of terrible devotion, dens of virgins, savage lairs.

Catholic Spain was more Roman than Rome herself, and the Spanish convent was preëminently the Catholic convent. There was an air of the Orient in it; the archbishop, the *Kislar-agar of heaven,* kept watch and ward over this seraglio of souls reserved for God. The nun was the odalisque, the priest the eunuch. The fervent became in dreams the chosen ones who possessed Christ; at night, the beautiful naked youth came down from the cross and became the ecstasy of the cell. Lofty walls guarded from all living distractions the mystic sultana who had the crucified one for the sultan; a glance outside was an infidelity. The *in pace* took the place of the sack, and was hurled into the sea in the East, was flung into the earth in the West. In both, women were writhing their arms; the wave for these, the grave for the others; here the drowned, there the buried. Hideous parallel!

To-day defenders of the past, as they cannot deny these things, have assumed to smile at them. There is a strange and convenient fashion in vogue for suppressing the revelations of history, for weakening the deductions of philosophy, and getting rid of all troublesome facts and disagreeable questions. "Mere declamation," say the clever ones. "Declamation," repeat the silly. Rousseau, Diderot, both declaimers; Voltaire speaking of Calas, Labarre, and Sirven, a mere declaimer; some one or other has lately discovered that Tacitus was a declaimer, Nero a victim, and that decidedly one ought to pity "poor Holofernes."

Facts, however, are hard to refute, and are inflexible. The writer of this has seen with his own eyes, within eight leagues of Brussels, where all the world can find a piece of the middle ages, at the Abbey of Villers, the hole of the dungeons in the middle of what was the yard of the convent, and, on the banks of the Thil, four stone cells, half under ground, half under water. These were the *in pace*. Each of these dungeon cells has the remains of an iron gate, a privy, and a grated aperture,— outside, two feet above the river; inside, six feet below the soil. Four feet depth of water runs above the exterior of the wall. The soil is always damp, and on this damp soil the inhabitants of the *in pace* had their beds. In one of the cells is the fragment of a collar fastened to the wall; in another is a kind of square box made of four slabs of granite, too short to lie in, too low to stand in. A living being was placed within it, with a stone covering over all. It is there, you can see it, you can touch it. These *in pace,* these cells, these iron hinges, these collars, this light-hole on a level with the river, this stone box closed with a granite covering like a tomb, with this difference, that here the dead was a living creature, this soil of mud, this hole of sewage, these dripping walls, what "declaimers" they are!

3. ON WHAT CONDITIONS THE PAST IS TO BE RESPECTED

MONACHISM, as it existed in Spain, and as it exists in Thibet, is the phthisis of civilization. It stops life short; it simply depopulates. Claustration is castration. It has been the curse of Europe. Add to all this violated consciences, forced vocations, feudalism relying on the cloister, primogeniture turning over to monastic life the overplus of the family, the cruelties just mentioned, the *in pace,* the closed lips, the walled-up brains, so many hapless intellects imprisoned in eternal vows, the assumption of the habit, the interment of souls alive. Add individual sufferings to national degradation and, whoever you may be, you will tremble before the frock and the veil, these two shrouds of human invention.

Still, in certain places, in spite of philosophy and progress, the monastic spirit survives in the full nineteenth century, and a strange ascetic revival astonishes, at this moment, the civilized world. The persistence of antiquated institutions in perpetuating themselves resembles the determination of rancid perfume to cling to our hair, the claim of spoiled fish to be eaten, the struggle of a child's garment to clothe a man, and the tenderness of corpses returning to embrace the living.

Ingrates! cries the garment. I protected you in bad weather; why are you tired of me? I come from the open sea, says the fish; I have been the rose, says the perfume; I have loved you, says the corpse; I have civilized you, says the convent.

To this there is only one reply,—Once upon a time.

To dream of the indefinite prolongation of dead things, and the government of man by mummies, to revive decayed dogmas, regild the shrines, repaint the cloisters, revarnish the reliquaries, repair the superstitions, renew the holy-water brushes and the swords, reconstitute monachism and militarism, to believe in the saving of society by the multiplication of parasites, to impose the past on the present, seems indeed strange. But the theorists who support such theories, men of talent in other respects, have a simple method of procedure; they give to the past a coating which they call social order, divine right, morality, family, respect to ancestry, ancient authority, holy tradition, legitimacy, religion, and they rush about crying, "Here, good people, here is the thing for you." This logical process was known to the ancients and the aruspices practised it. They chalked a black heifer and said, She is white. *Bos cretatus.*

As for us, we respect here and there, and spare everywhere the past, provided it consents to be dead. If it resolves to be alive, we attack it and make haste to kill it.

Superstitions, bigotry, idiocy, prejudice,—these specters are, specters though they be, tenacious of life; they have teeth and claws in their smoke; we must grasp them and assail them at close quarters, and wage a war without truce; for it is one of the fatalities of humanity to be condemned to an eternal war with phantoms, and a phantom is difficult to take by the throat and hurl to earth.

A convent in France, in the noon of this century, is a college of owls in daylight. A convent, in the overt act of asceticism in the society of '89, of 1830 and of 1848, is an anachronism. In ordinary times, to dissipate an anachronism and make it vanish, one needs only to spell the year in the calendar. But we are not in ordinary times.

Let us fight.

Let us fight then, but distinguish. Truth never goes to excess, why need she exaggerate? Something has to be destroyed, and something has simply to be looked at and cleared up. What force is in kindly and grave examination? Let us not take fire where light suffices.

Given, then, this nineteenth century, we are against ascetic monasticism, on general principles, in every nation, in Asia and Europe, in India and in Turkey. The word convent means a swamp; their putrescence is evident, their stagnation unhealthy, their fermentation breeds fever and wasting sickness, their multiplication is a plague of Egypt. We cannot think without a shudder of those countries where fakirs, bonzes, santons, caloyers, marabouts, talapoins, and dervishes sprout till they are swarms of vermin.

But the religious question remains. This question has certain sides which are mysterious and almost appalling. Let us look at it steadily.

4. *THE CONVENT FROM THE POINT OF VIEW*
OF PRINCIPLE

MEN write and live in common, in virtue of the right of association.

They shut themselves up, in virtue of the right which every one has of closing his door.

They do not go out, in virtue of the right of free movement which implies the right of staying at home.

What do they do at home?

They speak low, lower their eyes, labor, renounce the world, the city, joys of the senses, pleasures, vanities, pride, interest. They are clad in coarse wool or coarse linen. Not one of them possesses as property anything whatever; on entering, the rich become poor, for what he has, he gives to all. He that is called noble or greatly born is the equal of him that was a peasant. The cell is the same for all; all undergo the same torture, wear the same robe, eat the same black bread, sleep on the same straw, and die on the same ashes. The same sackcloth is on every back, the same cord round every waist. If the rule is to go barefoot, all go barefoot. There may be a prince there; he is the same shadow as the others. No more titles; even family names have disappeared; they only bear first names, and all bend beneath the equality of baptismal names. They have abolished the carnal family and constituted in their community the spiritual family; they have no kindred except all men; they succor the poor, nurse the sick, elect those they obey, and call each other "Brother."

You stop me with the exclamation: Why thus is the ideal convent!

That it is the possible convent is sufficient to induce me to examine it.

Hence it is that in the preceding book I have spoken of a convent in a respectful tone. Setting aside the middle ages and Asia, reserving the historical and political question, from a fairly philosophic point of view, apart from the necessities of aggressive politics, I shall always, on condition that the monastery be voluntary and contain only willing members, regard monastic communities with a certain attentive gravity, and in certain points with respect. Where there is a community there is a commune, and in the commune is the Right. The monastery is the result of the formulas, Equality, Fraternity. Ah, Liberty is great; how splendid is the transfiguration! Liberty can transform the monastery into the Republic!

Let us continue. These men or women behind these four walls dress coarsely, are equal, and call each other brothers or sisters. It is well. Do they do anything else?

Yes.

What?

They gaze into the shadows beyond this world, they kneel and join their hands.

What means that?

5 · PRAYER

THEY are praying.

To whom?

God.

What means praying to God?

Is there an infinite without us? Is this infinite one, immanent and permanent, necessarily substantial because it is infinite, and because if it were devoid of matter it would on that side be limited; necessarily intelligent because it is infinite, and because if it were devoid of intelligence it would be finite on that side? Does this infinite awake in us the idea of being, while we can only attribute to ourselves the idea of existence? In other terms, is it not the absolute and we the relative?

At the same time that there is an infinite without us, is there not an infinity within us? These two infinities (terrible plural), are they superimposed one on the other? Is not the second infinity, so to speak, subjacent to the first? Is it not the mirror, the reflection, the echo thereof, an abyss concentric to another abyss? Is this second infinite also intelligent? Does it think? Does it love? Does it will? If these two infinites are intelligent, each of them has a principle that wills, and there is an I to the infinite on high as there is an I to the infinite below. The I below is the soul; the I above is God.

To bring, by means of thought, the infinite above in contact with the infinite below, is prayer.

We take nothing from the human soul, for all suppression is evil; it must be reformed and transformed. Certain of our faculties are directed toward the Infinite; such are thought, reverie, and prayer. The Infinite is an ocean, our conscience is our compass. Thought, reverie, prayer, are great mysterious radiations; let us respect them. Whither go these majestic radiations of the soul? To the shadow, that is to say, to the light.

The greatness of democracy is to deny nothing and renounce nothing of humanity. Beside the Rights of Man are the Rights of the soul.

To crush fanaticism and venerate the infinite is the law. Let us not confine ourselves to prostration before the tree of creation, and to contemplation of its immense branchings filled with stars; we have a duty, to work for the human soul, to defend mystery against miracle, to adore the incomprehensible and reject the absurd, to admit as inexplicable only what is necessary, to heal faith, to remove superstition from religion, to brush the canker-worm from God.

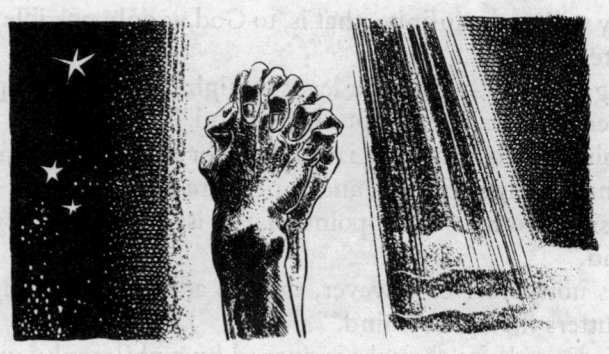

6. *ABSOLUTE GOODNESS OF PRAYER*

As regards modes of prayer, all are good provided they are sincere.

Turn over your book and be in the infinite.

There is a philosophy, we know, that denies the infinite, and also a philosophy, classed in pathology, that denies the sun, and is called Blindness.

To make the absence of a sense the source of truth, is the cool audacity of a blind man.

It is curious to note the haughty air of superiority and pity which this philosophy that gropes its way assumes toward the philosophy that sees; it is like a mole crying, "I am sorry for them and their sun!"

There are, we know, illustrious atheists with great intellectual powers. At bottom, these men, brought back to truth by these very powers, are not quite sure of being atheists; it is with them merely a question of depositions, and, in all cases, if they do not believe in God, they, as they are great men, prove the existence of God.

We salute them as philosophers, but reject their philosophy.

It is curious, too, to see with what facility men juggle with words. A northern school of metaphysics, somewhat impregnated with fog, thinks it has made a revolution in the human understanding by replacing the word "Force" by the word "Will."

To say "the plant wills," instead of "the plant grows," would be fertile enough if it is added, "the universe wills," because the inference could be drawn, the plant wills, therefore it has an I; the universe wills, therefore there is a God.

To us who reject nothing *a priori,* the will in a plant accepted by this school, seems more difficult to admit than a will in the universe which it denies.

To deny will to the infinite, that is, to God, is only possible by denying the infinite.

The negation of the infinite leads straight to Nihilism, properly so-called; everything is a "concept of the mind."

With nihilism no discussion is possible, for the nihilist logician doubts the existence of his opponent, and is not sure of his own.

It is possible, from his stand-point, that he is for himself only a "concept of his mind."

He does not perceive, however, that he admits everything he denies when he utters the word "mind."

In brief, no path for thought is opened by a philosophy which makes everything end in No.

To No there is only one answer,—Yes.

Nihilism carries no distance.

There is not nothingness, zero does not exist, everything is something, nothing is nothing.

Man lives by affirmation more than by bread.

To see and show is not enough, Philosophy must be an energy, and have for aim and result the amelioration of man. Socrates must enter into Adam and produce Marcus Aurelius; that is, produce from the man of happiness the man of wisdom, and change Eden into the Lyceum. Knowledge ought to be a tonic. Enjoyment—a sad, mean, paltry ambition—felt by the brute; thought is the triumph of the soul. To offer thought to the thirst of men, to give them all the idea of God, to make science and conscience fraternize, to make men just by this mysterious juxtaposition is the function of real philosophy. Morality is truth in bloom; to contemplate leads to action, the absolute ought to be practical, the ideal must be what the soul can eat, drink, and breathe. The ideal has the right to say, "This is my flesh, this is my blood," and wisdom is a holy communion. In this condition it ceases to be a sterile love of science to become the one sovereign mode of human restoration, and becomes a religion in place of a philosophy.

Philosophy must not be a tower built over mystery to look down on it with ease, and only convenient for curiosity.

In adjourning to another occasion the development of one thought, we confine ourselves here to saying that we cannot understand man as the starting-point, nor progress as the goal, without these two motive powers, faith and love.

Progress is the goal; the ideal, the type.

What is this ideal? God.

Ideal, Absolute, Perfection, Infinite, synonymous terms.

7. *CAUTIONS IN CENSURE*

HISTORY and philosophy have eternal duties which are also simple duties. To combat Caiphas as High Priest, Draco as judge, Trimalcion as a law-giver, Tiberius as emperor, is clear and direct and presents no difficulty; but the right to live apart from the world must be proved and carefully dealt with. Cœnobitic life is a human problem.

In speaking of convents, those abodes of error and innocence, of lost paths and good intentions, of ignorance and piety, of torture and martyrdom, we must nearly always say yes and no.

A convent is a contradiction, the aim is salvation, the means sacrifice, supreme egotism resulting in supreme self-denial.

The motto of monachism seems to be "Abdicate in order to reign."

In the cloister men suffer in order to enjoy, draw bills of exchange on death, and discount the light of heaven in the night of earth; in the cloister hell is accepted as an advance on paradise.

Taking the veil or frock is a suicide paid by eternity.

On such a subject mockery is out of place; everything here is serious, whether it be good or evil.

The just man contracts his brow, but never smiles a malicious smile. We understand wrath, not malignity.

8. *FAITH—LAW*

A FEW words more.

We blame the church when it is saturated with intrigue; we censure the spiritual when it is austere to the temporal, but we honor always the thinking man.

We reverence the man who kneels.

A faith is a necessity for man. Woe to him who believes nothing.

To be absorbed is not to be unoccupied, there is an invisible as well as a visible labor.

To contemplate is to labor, to think is to act.

Crossed arms toil and folded hands perform, a glance at heaven is a work done.

Thales remained four years motionless, and created philosophy.

Monks are not idlers, nor hermits sluggards.

To think of the shadow-world is a serious thing.

Without retracting a word of what we have said, we believe that a perpetual reminder of the tomb is good for the living. Poet and philosopher here agree. "We must die" is the response of La Trappe to Horace.

To mix with life a certain presence of the sepulcher is the law of the sage and of the ascetic, who, in this respect, converge.

There is a material increase which we desire and a moral grandeur we cling to.

Certain irreflective and precipitate souls ask:

"To what use these figures motionless by the side of mystery? What good are they? What do they do?"

Alas! in the presence of the obscurity which surrounds and awaits us, ignorant of what the dispersion of all things shall make of us, we reply: "No work, perhaps, is more sublime than what these souls do." And we add: "Perhaps no labor is more useful."

There is need of those who pray always for those who pray never.

All the question is the quantity of thought put into the prayer.

Leibnitz praying is great, Voltaire worshipping is beautiful. *Deo erexit Voltaire*.

We are for religion against religions.

We believe in the pity of orisons and the sublimity of prayer.

At this period, a period which, happily, will leave no impress on the century, when so many men have the forehead low, and the soul not high, among so many living creatures whose moral code is enjoyment, and who are busied with brief, deformed, material things, the self-exile is venerable.

The convent is abnegation; sacrifice, wrong it may be, is still sacrifice. There is grandeur in taking a stern error for duty.

By itself, ideally, examining truth under every possible aspect, the convent, the nunnery especially, for in our society it is the woman who suffers most, and in this self-exile she makes her protest, the nunnery possesses a certain majesty.

This cloistered existence, so austere and dark, some lineaments of which we have indicated, is not life, for it is not liberty; it is not the tomb, for it is completion. It is the strange spot where, as it were, from some mountain crest is seen, on one side the abyss in which we are, on the other, the abyss in which we shall be; a narrow, misty frontier between two worlds, illumined and obscured by both at once, where the enfeebled ray of life mingles with the vague ray of death, the penumbra of the tomb.

We, who do not believe what these women believe, but who, like them, live by faith, have never been able to contemplate without a holy and tender terror, and a kind of pity full of envy, these devoted creatures, trembling and confident, their humble and august souls which dare live on the very edge of mystery, expectant between the world which is closed and the heaven which is not open, turned to the brightness they see not with only the happiness of thinking they know where it is, aspiring to the gulf and the unknown with eyes fixed on motionless obscurity, kneeling, broken-hearted, stupefied, shuddering, half lifted on high at certain hours by the profound respirations of eternity.

BOOK VIII

CEMETERIES TAKE WHAT IS GIVEN THEM

1. HOW TO GET INTO A CONVENT

IT was into this house that Jean Valjean had fallen from Heaven, as Fauchelevent said.

He climbed the garden-wall which formed the angle of the Rue Polonceau; the hymn of angels which he heard in the middle of the night was the nuns chanting matins; the hall which he had caught a glimpse of in the darkness was the chapel; the phantom he had seen stretched out on the ground was the phantom making reparation; and the bell which had so strangely surprised him was the gardener's bell fastened to Fauchelevent's knee.

So soon as Cosette was in bed, Jean Valjean and Fauchelevent supped on a glass of wine and a lump of cheese before a good blazing log; then, as the only bed in the cottage was occupied by Cosette, each threw himself on a truss of straw.

Before closing his eyes Jean Valjean said, "I must stop here henceforth," and this remark trotted about Fauchelevent's head all night.

In fact, neither of them slept.

Jean Valjean, feeling himself discovered and Javert on his track, understood that he and Cosette were lost if they entered Paris. Since the new blast of wind had blown him into this convent, Jean Valjean had but one thought, that of remaining in it. Now, for a wretch in his position, this convent was at once the most dangerous and the safest place,—the most dangerous, because as no man was allowed to enter it, if he were discovered it would be a crime, and Jean Valjean would only take one step from the convent to the prison,—the safest, because if he succeeded in remaining in it, who would come to seek him there? Inhabiting an impossible spot was salvation.

On his side, Fauchelevent racked his brains. He began by declaring to himself that he understood nothing. How was M. Madeleine, in spite of all the surrounding walls, here?—and convent walls cannot be passed at a stride. How was he here with a child? people do not scale a perpendicular wall with a child in their arms. Who was this child? Where did they both come from? Since Fauchelevent had been in the convent he had received no news from M. . . . , and did not know what had occurred there. Father Madeleine had that look which discourages questioning, and, moreover, Fauchelevent said to himself, "A saint is not to be cross-questioned." It was only from a few words which escaped Jean Valjean that the gardener fancied he could come to the conclusion that M. Madeleine had probably been made bankrupt by the hard times, and was pursued by his creditors; or else he was compromised in a political affair and was in hiding, which idea did not displease Fauchelevent, because, like most of the peasants in the north of France, he was a stanch Bonapartist. M. Madeleine had chosen the convent as his asylum, and it was simple that he should wish to remain there. But the inexplicable thing, to which Fauchelevent constantly recurred and which addled his brains, was that M. Madeleine was here, and here with this child. Fauchelevent saw them, touched them, spoke to them, and did not believe it. The gardener was stumbling among conjectures and saw nothing clear but this,—"M. Madeleine saved my life." This sole certainty was sufficient, and decided him; he said to himself, "it is my turn now." He added in his conscience, "M. Madeleine did not deliberate long when he had to get under the cart to save me," and he decided upon saving M. Madeleine.

He, however, asked himself several questions, to which he gave divers answers. "After what he did for me, should I save him, if he were a robber? all the same. If he were an assassin, would I save him? all the same. Since he is a saint, shall I save him? all the same."

What a problem it was, though, to enable him to remain in the convent! Still, Fauchelevent did not recoil before this almost chimerical attempt; this poor Picard peasant, who had no other ladder but his devotion, his good-will, and a small stock of old rustic craft, his time turned to a generous purpose, undertook to scale the impossibilities of the convent and the rough escarpments of the rule of St. Benedict. Fauchelevent was an old man, who had been during life selfish, and who, at the end of his days, limping, infirm, and taking no interest in the world, found it pleasant to be grateful, and seeing a virtuous action to be done, flung himself upon it like a man who, on the point of death, lays his hand on a glass of good wine which he had never tasted, and eagerly drinks it off.

We may add, that the air which he had been breathing for some years in this convent had destroyed his personality, and had eventually rendered some good deed a necessity for him. He, therefore, formed the resolution of devoting himself for M. Madeleine.

We have just called him a "poor Picard peasant"; the qualification is correct, but incomplete. At the present stage of our story a little physiological examination of Father Fauchelevent becomes useful. He was a peasant, but he had been a notary, which added chicanery to his cunning and penetration to his simplicity. Having, through various reasons, failed in his business, he descended from a notary to be a carter and day-laborer; but, in spite of the oaths and lashes necessary for horses, as it seems, something of the notary had clung to him. He had some natural wit; he did not say "I are" or "I has"; he could converse, which was a rare thing in a village, and the other peasants used to say of him, "He talks exactly like a gentleman in a hat." Fauchelevent, in fact, belonged to that species which the impertinent and light vocabulary of the last century qualified as "a bit of rustic and a bit of a townsman, pepper and salt." Fauchelevent, though sorely tried and much worn by fate, a sort of poor old threadbare soul, was still a man to act on the first impulse, and spontaneously,—a precious quality which prevents a man from ever being wicked. His defects and vices, for he had such, were on the surface, and altogether his physiognomy was one of those which please the observer. His old face had none of those ugly wrinkles on the top of the forehead which signify wickedness or stupidity.

At daybreak, after thinking enormously, Father Fauchelevent opened his eyes and saw M. Madeleine sitting on his truss of straw and looking at the sleeping Cosette; Fauchelevent sat up too, and said:

"Now that you are here, how will you manage to get in?"

This remark summed up the situation, and aroused Jean Valjean from his reverie.

The two men held counsel.

"In the first place," said Fauchelevent, "you must begin by not setting food outside this cottage, neither you nor the little one. One step in the garden, and we are done."

"That is true."

"Monsieur Madeleine," Fauchelevent continued, "you have arrived at a very lucky moment,—I ought to say a very unhappy one,—for one of our ladies is dangerously ill. In consequence of this, folk will not look much this way. It seems that she is dying, and the forty hours' prayers are being said. The whole community is aroused, and that occupies them. The person who is on the point of going off is a saint. In fact, though, we are all saints here; the only difference between them and me is that they say 'our cell,' and I say 'my cottage.' There will be a service for the dying, and then the service for the dead. For to-day we shall all be quiet here; but I do not answer for to-morrow."

"Still," Jean Valjean observed, "this cottage is retired, it is hidden by a sort of ruin; there are trees, and it cannot be seen from the convent."

."And I may add that the nuns never approach it."

"Well?" Jean Valjean asked.

The interrogation that marked this "well" signified, "I fancy that we can remain concealed here," and it was to this interrogation that Fauchelevent replied:

"There are the little ones."

"What little ones?" Jean Valjean asked.

As Fauchelevent opened his mouth to answer, a stroke rang out from a bell.

"The nun is dead," he said, "that is the knell."

And he made Jean Valjean a sign to listen.

A second stroke rang out.

"It is the passing bell, Monsieur Madeleine. The bell will go on so minute after minute for twenty-four hours, till the body leaves the church. You see they play about; at recreations they need only lose a ball, and, in spite of the prohibition, they will come and look for it here and ransack everything. Those cherubs are little devils."

"Who?" Jean Valjean asked.

"The little ones; I can tell you that you would soon be discovered. They would cry out, 'Why, it's a man!' But there is no danger to-day, for there will be no recreation. The day will be spent in prayer. You hear the bell, as I told you, one stroke a minute,—it is the knell."

"I understand, Father Fauchelevent, they are boarders."

And Jean Valjean thought to himself:

"It is a chance for educating Cosette."

Fauchelevent exclaimed:

"By Jove, I should think they are boarders! they would sniff round you and then run away. To be a man here is to have the plague, as you can see; a bell is fastened to my paw as if I were a wild beast."

Jean Valjean reflected more and more deeply. "This convent would save us," he muttered.

Then he added aloud: "Yes, the difficulty is to remain."

"No," said Fauchelevent, "it is to go out."

Jean Valjean felt the blood rush back to his heart.

"Go out?"

"Yes, M. Madeleine, in order to come in, you must go out."

And, after waiting till a knell had died out in air, Fauchelevent continued:

"You must not be found here like that. Where do you come from? for me, you fall from Heaven, because I know you, but the nuns require that people should come in by the front door."

All at once a complicated ringing of another bell could be heard.

"Ah!" said Fauchelevent, "the vocal mothers are being summoned to a chapter,—a chapter is always held when any one dies. She died at daybreak, and they generally die at daybreak. But can't you go out by the way you came in? Come, I don't want to ask you a question,—but where did you come in?"

Jean Valjean turned pale. The mere idea of going back to that formidable street made him tremble. Come out of a forest full of tigers, and once out of it, just imagine a friend advising you to go in again. Jean Valjean figured to himself the police still searching in the quarter, the agents watching, vedettes everywhere, frightful fists stretched out toward his collar, and Javert perhaps in a corner lurking for his prey.

"Impossible!" he said. "Suppose, Father Fauchelevent, that I really fell from above."

"Why, I believe so," Fauchelevent continued, "you need not tell me so. Well, there is another peal; it is to tell the porter to go and warn the municipal authorities that they should send and inform the physician of the dead, so that he may come and see there is a dead woman here. All that is the ceremony of dying. The good ladies are not very fond of such visits, for a doctor believes in nothing; he raises the veil, and sometimes raises something else. What a hurry they have been in to warn the doctor this time! What is up, I wonder? Your little girl is still asleep; what is her name?"

"Cosette."

"Is she your daughter? I mean, are you her grandfather?"

"Yes."

"To get her out will be easy, I have my special door, which opens into the yard, I knock, the porter opens. I have my pannier on my back, with the little girl in it, and go out. You will tell her to be very quiet, and she will be under the lid. I will leave her for the necessary time with an old friend of mine, a fruiteress in the Rue du Chemin Vert, who is deaf and where there is a little bed. I will shout in her ear that it is my niece, and bid her keep her for me till to-morrow; then the little one will come in with you, for I mean to bring you in again. But how will you manage to get out?"

Jean Valjean shook his head.

"The great point is that no one sees me, Father Fauchelevent. Find means to get me out in the same way as Cosette."

Fauchelevent scratched the tip of his ear with the middle finger of his left hand, which was a sign of serious embarrassment.

A third peal caused a diversion.

"That is the doctor going away," said Fauchelevent. "He has had a look and said, 'She is dead, all right.' When the doctor has countersigned the Passport for Paradise, the undertakers send a coffin. If it is a mother, the mothers put her in it; if a sister, the sisters; and after that I nail it up. That is part of my gardening, for a gardener is a bit of a grave-digger. The coffin is placed in the vestry-room which communicates with the street, and which no man is allowed to enter but the doctor, for I don't count the undertakers and myself as men. It is in this room that I nail up the coffin, the undertakers fetch it, and then—Gee-up, driver—that's the way people go to heaven. A box is brought, in which there is nothing, and it is carried off with something in it; and that's what a burial is. *De Profundis.*"

A horizontal sunbeam illumined the face of the sleeping Cosette, who opened her lips and looked like an angel imbibing light. Jean Valjean was gazing at her again, and no longer listened to Fauchelevent.

Not to be heard is no reason why a man should hold his tongue, so the worthy old gardener quickly continued his chatter:

"The grave is dug in the Vaugirard cemetery; people say that it is going to be shut up. It is an old cemetery, which has no uniform, and is going on half-pay; it is a pity, for it is convenient. I have a friend there, Father Mestienne, the grave-digger. The nuns of this house possess the privilege of being carried to that cemetery at nightfall; they have a decree of the prefecture expressly for them. But what events since yesterday! Mother Crucifixion is dead, and Father Madeleine—"

"Is buried," Jean Valjean said, with a sad smile.

Fauchelevent returned the word.

"Well, if you were here altogether, it would be a real burial."

A fourth peal rang out. Fauchelevent quickly took down his kneecap and put it on.

"This time it is for me. The mother prioress wants me. There, I have pricked myself with the tongue of my buckle. M. Madeleine, don't stir, but wait for me. There is something up; if you are hungry, there is bread, wine, and cheese."

And he left the cottage, saying, "Coming, coming."

Jean Valjean watched him hurrying across the garden as rapidly as his leg would allow, while taking a side glance at his melon frames.

Less than ten minutes after, Father Fauchelevent, whose bell routed all the nuns as he passed, tapped gently at a door, and a soft voice answered, "Forever, forever," that is to say, "Come in."

It was the door of the parlor reserved expressly for the gardener, and adjoining the chapter room. The prioress, seated on the only chair in the room, was waiting for Fauchelevent.

2. *FAUCHELEVENT FACES THE DIFFICULTY*

To have an agitated and serious air is peculiar, on critical occasions, to certain characters and professions, and notably to priests and monks. At the moment when Fauchelevent entered, this double form of preoccupation was imprinted on the face of the prioress, who was that charming and learned Mademoiselle de Blémeur, or Mother Innocent, who was usually so cheerful.

The gardener gave a timid bow, and remained in the doorway of the cell; the prioress, who was telling her beads, raised her eyes, and said:

"Oh, it is you, Father Fauvent?"

This abbreviation had been adopted at the convent.

Fauchelevent began his bows again.

233

"Father Fauvent, I summoned you."

"Here I am, reverend mother."

"I wish to speak with you."

"And I, on my side," said Fauchelevent, with a boldness which made him tremble inwards, "have something to say to the most reverend mother."

The prioress looked at him.

"Ah, you have a communication to make to me?"

"A request."

"Well, speak."

Fauchelevent, the ex-notary, belonged to that class of peasants who possess coolness. A certain skillful ignorance is a strength; people do not suspect it, and you have them. During the two years Fauchelevent had lived in the convent, he had made a success in the community, and while alone and attending to his gardening, he had nothing else to do than be curious. Remote as he was from all these veiled women, he saw nothing before him but an agitation of shadows, but, by constant attention and penetration, he had succeeded in putting flesh on these phantoms, and these dead lived for him. He was like a deaf man whose sight is improved, and a blind man whose hearing is sharpened. He had turned his mind to discover the meaning of the various peals, and had succeeded, so that his enigmatical and mysterious convent had nothing hidden from him; and this sphinx whispered all its secrets in his ear. Fauchelevent, while know-ing everything, concealed everything, and that was his art; the whole convent believed him to be stupid, and that is a great merit in religion. The vocal mother set value on Fauchelevent, for he was a curious dumb man and inspired confidence. Moreover, he was regular, and only went out when absolutely compelled by the claims of his orchard or kitchen garden, and this discretion was placed to his credit. But, for all that, he had made two men talk: in the convent, the porter, and he thus knew all the peculiarities of the parlor; and at the cemetery, the grave-digger and he knew the regular forms of burial; so that he possessed a double light about these nuns—the light of life and the light of death. But he made no abuse of his knowledge, and the congregation were attached to him. Old, lame, seeing nothing, and probably rather deaf; what qualifications! It would be difficult to fill up his place.

The good man, with the assurance of a servant who knows his value, began a rustic address to the prioress, which was rather diffuse and very artful. He talked a good deal about his age, his infirmities, years henceforward, reckoning double for him, the growing demands of his work, nights to pass, as for instance, the last, in which he was obliged to draw matting over the melon frames owing to the moon; and he ended with this, that he had a brother (the prioress gave a start)—a brother who was not young (a second start, but not so alarmed)—that if leave were granted, this brother would come and live with him and help him; that he was an excellent gardener, and would be of more use to the community than himself was; and that, on the other hand, if his brother's services were not accepted, as he, the elder, felt worn out and unequal to his work, he would be compelled, to his great regret, to give up his situation; and that his brother had a little girl whom he would bring with him, and who would be brought up in the house, and might—who knew?—become a nun some day.

When he had finished speaking, the prioress broke off her occupation of letting the beads of her rosary slip through her fingers, and said:

"Could you procure a strong iron bar between this and to-night?"

"What to do?"

"To act as a lever."

"Yes, reverend mother," Father Fauchelevent replied.

The prioress, without adding a syllable, rose and walked into the adjoining room where the chapter was assembled. Fauchelevent was left alone.

3. *MOTHER INNOCENT*

About a quarter of an hour passed ere the prioress came in again and sat down on a chair.

The two speakers appeared preoccupied. We will do the best to record their conversation accurately.

"Father Fauvent?"

"Reverend mother?"

"Do you know the chapel?"

"I have a little cage in it where I hear mass and the offices."

"And have you gone into the choir for your work?"

"Two or three times."

"A stone will have to be lifted."

"A heavy one?"

"The one at the side of the altar."

"The stone that closes the vault?"

"Yes."

"That is a job where two men would be useful."

"Mother Ascension, who is as strong as a man, will help you."

"A woman is never a man."

"We have only a woman to help you, and everybody does the best. Although Dom. Mabillon gives four hundred and seventeen epistles of St. Bernard, and Merlonus Horstius only gives three hundred and sixty-seven, I do not despise Merlonus Horstius."

"Nor I."

"The merit is to work according to your strength. A convent is not a work-yard."

"And a woman is not a man. My brother is a strong fellow."

"And, then, you will have a crowbar."

"It is the only sort of key that fits such locks."

"There is a ring in the stone."

"I will put the crowbar through it."

"And the stone works on hinges."

"All right, reverend mother; I will open the vault."

"And the four chanting mothers will help you."

"And when the vault is open?"

"You must shut it again."

"Is that all?"

"No."

"Give me your orders, most reverend mother."

"Fauvent, we place confidence in you."

"I am here to do everything."

"And to hold your tongue about everything."

"Yes, reverend mother."

"When the vault is opened—"

"I will shut it again."

"But, first—"

"What, reverend mother?"

"You must let down something into it."

There was a silence, and the prioress, after a pout of the lower lip, which looked like hesitation, continued:

"Father Fauvent?"

"Reverend mother?"

"You are aware that a mother died this morning?"

"No."

"Did you not hear the bell?"

"Nothing can be heard at the end of the garden."

"Really, now?"

"I can hardly distinguish my own ring."

"She died at daybreak."

"And besides, this morning the wind did not blow in my direction."

"It is Mother Crucifixion, a blessed saint."

The prioress was silent, moved her lips for a moment, as if in mental prayer, and went on:

"Three years ago, through merely seeing Mother Crucifixion pray, a Jansenist, Madame de Bethune, became orthodox."

"Oh, yes, I hear the passing bell now, reverend mother."

"The mothers have carried her into the dead-room adjoining the church."

"I know."

"No other man than you can, or ought, to enter that room, so keep careful watch. It would be a fine thing to see another man enter the house of the dead!"

"More often."

"Eh?"

"More often."

"What do you mean?"

"I say more often."

"More often than what?"

"Reverend mother, I did not say more often than what, but more often."

"I do not understand you; why do you say more often?"

"To say the same as yourself, reverend mother."

"But I did not say more often."

"You did not say it, but I said it to say the same as you."

At this moment nine o'clock struck.

"At nine in the morning and every hour be the most Holy Sacrament of the altar blessed and adored," said the prioress.

"Amen," said Fauchelevent.

The hour struck opportunely, for it cut short the "more often." It is probable that, without it, the prioress and Fauchelevent would never have got out of this tangle.

Fauchelevent wiped his forehead, and the prioress gave another internal murmur, and then raised her voice.

"In her lifetime, Mother Crucifixion performed conversions; after her death, she will perform miracles."

"She will do them," Fauchelevent said, determined not to give ground again.

"Father Fauvent, the community was blessed in Mother Crucifixion. Of course it is not granted to every one to die, like Cardinal de Berulle, while reading the holy mass, and exhale his soul to God while uttering the words *Hanc igitur oblationem.* But, though she did not attain such happiness, Mother Crucifixion had a very blessed death. She retained her senses up to the last moment; she spoke to us, and then conversed with the angels. She gave us her last commands; if you had more faith, and if you had been in her cell, she would have cured your leg by touching it. She smiled, and we all felt that she was living again in God,— there was Paradise in such a death."

Fauchelevent fancied that it was the end of a prayer.

"Amen," he said.

"Father Fauvent, what the dead wish must be carried out."

The prioress told a few beads. Fauchelevent held his tongue.

Then the lady continued:

"I have consulted on this point several ecclesiastics, who labor in our Lord, who turn their attention to the exercise of clerical life, and reap an admirable harvest."

"Reverend mother, the knell is heard better here than in the garden."

"Moreover, she is more than a dead woman; she is a saint."

"Like yourself, reverend mother."

"She slept in her coffin for more than twenty years, by express permission of our Holy Father Pius VII."

"The same who crowned the emp—Bonaparte."

For a clever man like Fauchelevent, the recollection was ill-timed.

Luckily the prioress, who was deep in thought, did not hear him, and went on:

"Father Fauvent?"

"Reverend mother?"

"Saint Diodorus, archbishop of Cappadocia, requested that only one word should be inscribed on his tombstone, *Acarus,* which means a worm, and it was done. Is that true?"

"Yes, reverend mother."

"The blessed Mezzocane, abbot of Aquila, wished to be buried under the gallows, and it was done."

"That is true."

"Saint Terentius, bishop of Porto, at the mouth of the Tiber on the sea, ordered that there should be engraved on his tombstone the symbol which was placed on the graves of parricides, in the hope that passers-by would spit on his tomb, and it was done, for the dead ought to be obeyed."

"So be it."

"The body of Bernard Guidonis, who was born in France, near Roche Abeille, was, as he ordered, and in defiance of the king of Castile, conveyed to the church of the Dominicans of Limoges, although Bernard Guidonis was bishop of Tuy in Spain. Can you say the contrary?"

"Certainly not, reverend mother."

"The fact is attested by Plantavit de la Fosse."

A few beads were told in silence, and then the prioress resumed:

"Father Fauvent, Mother Crucifixion will be buried in the coffin in which she has slept for twenty years."

"That is but fair."

"It is a continuation of sleep."

"Then I shall have to nail her up in that coffin?"

"Yes."

"And we shall not employ the undertaker's coffin?"

"Exactly."

"I am at the orders of the most reverend community."

"The four singing mothers will help you."

"To nail up the coffin? I do not want them."

"No, to let it down."

"Where?"

"Into the vault."

"What vault?"

"Under the altar."

239

Fauchelevent started.

"The vault under the altar?"

"Yes."

"But—"

"You have an iron bar."

"Yes, still—"

"You will lift the stone by passing the bar through the ring."

"But—"

"We must obey the dead. It was the last wish of Mother Crucifixion to be buried in the vault under the chapel altar, not to be placed in profane soil, and to remain when dead at the place where she had prayed when alive. She asked this of us; indeed, ordered it."

"But it is forbidden."

"Forbidden by man, ordered by God."

"Suppose it oozed out?"

"We have confidence in you."

"Oh, I am a stone of your wall."

"The chapter is assembled; the vocal mothers whom I have just consulted once again, and who are deliberating, have decided that Mother Crucifixion should be interred, according to her wish, under our altar. Only think, Father Fauvent, if miracles were to take place here! What a glory in God for the community! miracles issue from tombs."

"But, reverend mother, supposing the sanitary commissioner—"

"St. Benedict II, in a matter of burial, resisted Constantine Pogonatus."

"Still, the inspector—"

"Chonodemairus, one of the seven German kings who entered Gaul during the empire of Constantius, expressly recognized the right of monks to be buried in religion; that is to say, beneath the altar."

"But the inspector of the prefecture—"

"The world is as nothing in presence of the cross. Martin, eleventh general of the Carthusians, gave his order this device, *Stat crux dum volvitur orbis.*"

"Amen!" Fauchelevent said, who imperturbably got out of the scrape in that way whenever he heard Latin.

Anybody answers as audience for a person who has been a long time silent. On the day when Gymnastoras, the rhetorician, left prison, with a great many dilemmas and syllogisms in his inside, he stopped before the first tree he came to, harangued it, and made mighty efforts to convince it. The prioress, whose tongue was usually stopped by the dam of silence, and whose reservoir was overfull, rose and exclaimed with the loquacity of a raised sluice:

"I have on my right hand Benedict, and on my left Bernard. Who is Bernard? the first abbot of Clairvaux. Fontaines in Burgundy is a blessed spot for having witnessed his birth. His father's name was Técelin, his mother's Aleth; he began with Citeaux to end with Clairvaux; he was ordained abbot by William de Champeaux, bishop of Chalons sur Saône; he had seven hundred novices, and founded one hundred and sixty monasteries; he overthrew Abeilard at the council of Sens in 1140, and Pierre de Bruys and Henry his disciple, as well as an errant sect called the Apostolicals; he confounded Arnold of Brescia, crushed the Monk Raoul, the Jew-killer; led the Council of Rheims in 1148, condemned Gilbert de la Porée, bishop of Poictiers, and Eon de l'Etoile; settled the disputes of the princes, enlightened King Louis the young, advised Pope Eugene III, regulated the templars, preached the Crusade, and performed two hundred and fifty miracles in his life, and as many as thirty-seven in one day. Who is Benedict? he is the patriarch of Monte Cassino; he is the second founder of claustral holiness, the Basil of the West. His order has produced fourteen popes, two hundred cardinals, fifty patriarchs, one thousand six hundred archbishops, four thousand six hundred bishops, four emperors, twelve empresses, forty-six kings, forty-one queens, three thousand six hundred canonized saints, and still exists after one thousand four hundred years. On one side Saint Bernard, on the other the sanitary inspector! On one side St. Benedict, on the other the inspector of the streets! What do we know about the state, the regulations, the administration, and the public undertaker? Any witnesses would be indignant at the way in which we are treated; we have not even the right to give our dust to Christ! your salubrity is a revolutionary invention. God subordinate to a police inspector; such is the age! Silence, Fauvent!"

Fauchelevent did not feel very comfortable under this douche, but the prioress continued:

"The right of the monasteries to sepulture is indubitable, and it can only be denied by fanatics, and schismatics. We live in times of terrible confusion; people do not know what they should, and know what they should not. Men are crass and impious, and there are people at the present day who cannot distinguish between the most mighty St. Bernard and that Bernard called of the poor Catholics, a certain worthy ecclesiastic who lived in the thirteenth century. Others are so blasphemous as to compare the scaffold of Louis XVI with the cross of our Saviour. Louis

XVI was only a king. There are no just or unjust persons left, the name of Voltaire is known and that of Cæsar de Bus unknown, but Cæsar de Bus is blessed, while Voltaire is damned. The last archbishop, Cardinal de Perigord, did not even know that Charles de Gondren succeeded to Berullus, and François Bourgoin Gondren, and Jean François Senault to Bourgoin, and Father de Sainte Marthe Jean to François Senault. The name of Father Coton is known not because he was one of the three who urged the foundation of the oratory, but because he supplied the Huguenot King Henry IV with material for an oath. What makes people of the world like St. Francis de Sales is that he cheated at play. And, then, religion is attacked, and why? because there have been bad priests, because Sagittarius, bishop of Gap, was brother of Salone, bishop of Embrun, and both followed Mommolus. Of what consequence is all this? Does it prevent Martin of Tours from being a saint, and having given one-half of his cloak to a poor man? The saints are persecuted, and people close their eyes against the truth. They are accustomed to the darkness, and the most ferocious beasts are blind beasts. No one thinks of hell seriously; oh! the wicked people. 'By the king's order,' means at the present day by order of the Revolution. People forget what they owe, either to the living or the dead. We are forbidden to die in holiness, burial is a civil affair, and this is horrible. St. Leon II wrote two letters expressly —one to Peter Notarius, the other to the king of the Visigoths—to combat and reject, in questions that affect the dead, the authority of the exarchus and the supremacy of the emperor. Gauthier, bishop of Chalons, opposed Otho, duke of Burgundy, in this matter. The old magistrates coincided, and we formerly had a voice in the chapter itself upon temporal affairs. The abbot of Citeaux, general of the order, was councilor *ex officio* in the parliament of Burgundy. We do what we like with our dead. Is not the body of Saint Benedict himself in France, at the abbey of Fleury, called St. Benedict, in the Loire, although he died at Monte Cassino in Italy, on Saturday, March 21, 543? All this is incontestable. I abhor the psalm-singers, I hate the prayer-makers, I execrate heretics, but I should detest even worse any one who opposed my views in this matter. It is only necessary to read Arnoul Wion, Gabriel Bucelinus, Trithemius, Maurolius, and Dom. Luc d'Achery."

The prioress breathed, and then turned to Fauchelevent.

"Father Fauvent, is it settled?"

"It is, reverend mother."

"Can we reckon on you?"

"I will obey."

"Very good."

"I am entirely devoted to the convent."

"You close the coffin, and the sisters will carry it into the chapel. The office for the dead will be read, and then we shall return to the cloisters. Between eleven and twelve you will come with your iron bar, and everything will be performed with the utmost secrecy; there will be no one in the chapel but the four singing mothers, Mother Ascension, and yourself."

"And the sister at the post?"

"She will not turn round."

"But she will hear."

"She will not listen. Moreover, what the convent knows the world is ignorant of."

There was another pause, after which the prioress continued:

"You will remove your bell, for it is unnecessary for the sister at the post to notice your presence."

"Reverend mother?"

"What is it, Father Fauvent?"

"Has the physician of the dead paid his visit?"

"He will do so at four o'clock to-day; the bell has been rung to give him notice. But do you not hear any ringing?"

"I only pay attention to my own summons."

"Very good, Father Fauvent."

"Reverend mother, I shall require a lever at least six feet long."

"Where will you get it?"

"Where there are plenty of gratings there are plenty of iron bars; I have a pile of old iron at the end of the garden."

"About three-quarters of an hour before midnight, do not forget."

"Reverend mother?"

"What is it?"

"If you have other jobs like this, my brother is a strong fellow for you, a Turk."

"You will be as quick as possible."

"I cannot do things quickly, for I am infirm, and for that reason require an assistant. I halt."

"Halting is not a crime, and may be a blessing. The Emperor Henry II, who combated the Antipope Gregory and reëstablished Benedict VIII, has two surnames—the saint and the cripple."

"Two excellent surtouts," muttered Fauchelevent, who was rather hard of hearing.

"Father Fauvent, now I think of it, take a whole hour, for it will not be too much. Be at the high altar with your crowbar at eleven o'clock, for the service begins at midnight and all must be finished a good quarter of an hour previously."

"I will do everything to prove my zeal to the community. I will nail up the coffin, and be in the chapel at eleven o'clock precisely; the singing mothers and Mother Ascension will be there. Two men would be better, but no matter, I shall have my crowbar, we will open the vault, let down the coffin, and close it again. After that there will not be a trace, and the government will have no suspicion. Reverend mother, is all arranged thus?"

"No."

"What is there still?"

"There is the empty coffin."

This was a difficulty; Fauchelevent thought of and on it, and so did the prioress.

"Father Fauvent, what must be done with the other coffin?"

"It must be buried."

"Empty?"

Another silence. Fauchelevent made with his left hand that sort of gesture which dismisses a disagreeable question.

"Reverend mother, I will nail up the coffin and cover it with the pall."

"Yes, but the bearers, while placing it in the hearse and lowering it into the grave, will soon perceive that there is nothing in it."

"Oh, the de—!" Fauchelevent exclaimed.

The prioress began a cross and looked intently at the gardener; the *evil* stuck in his throat.

He hastily improvised an expedient to cause the oath to be forgotten.

"Reverend mother, I will put earth in the coffin, which will produce the effect of a body."

"You are right, for earth is the same as a human being. So you will manage the empty coffin?"

"I take it on myself."

The face of the prioress, which had hitherto been troubled and clouded, now grew serene. She made the sign of a superior dismissing an inferior, and Fauchelevent walked toward the door. As he was going out, the prioress gently raised her voice.

"Father Fauvent, I am satisfied with you; to-morrow, after the interment, bring me your brother, and tell him to bring me his daughter."

4. *A PLAN OF ESCAPE*

THE strides of halting men are like the glances of squinters, they do not reach their point very rapidly. Monsieur Fauchelevent was perplexed, and he spent upward of a quarter of an hour in returning to the garden cottage. Cosette was awake, and Jean Valjean had seated her by the fireside. At the moment when Fauchelevent entered, Jean Valjean was pointing to the gardener's basket leaning in a corner, and saying to her:

"Listen to me carefully, little Cosette. We are obliged to leave this house, but shall return to it, and be very happy. The good man will carry you out in that thing upon his back, and you will wait for me with a lady till I come to fetch you. If you do not wish Madame Thénardier to catch you again, obey and say not a word."

Cosette nodded her head gravely.

At the sound Fauchelevent made in opening the door, Valjean turned round.

"Well?"

"All is arranged, and nothing is so," said Fauchelevent. "I have leave to bring you in, but to bring you in you must go out. That is the difficulty; it is easy enough with the little one."

"You will carry her out?"

"Will she be quiet?"

"I answer for that."

"But you, Father Madeleine?"

And after an anxious silence Fauchelevent cried:

"Why, go out in the same way as you came in."

245

Jean Valjean, as on the first occasion, confined himself to saying, "Impossible!"

Fauchelevent, speaking to himself rather than to Jean Valjean, growled:

"There is another thing that troubles me. I said that I would put earth in it, but now I come to think of it, earth instead of a body will not do, for it will move about and the men will notice it. You understand, Father Madeleine, the government will perceive the trick?"

Jean Valjean looked at him, and fancied that he must be raving.

Fauchelevent continued:

"How the deuce are you going to get out? for everything must be settled to-morrow, as the prioress expects you then."

Then he explained to Valjean that it was a reward for a service which he, Fauchelevent, was rendering the community. It was part of his duty to attend to the funerals, nail up the coffin, and assist the grave-digger at the cemetery. The nun who had died that morning requested to be buried in the coffin which served her as bed in the vault under the altar of the chapel. This was forbidden by the police regulations, but she was one of those women to whom nothing could be refused. The prioress and the vocal mothers intended to carry out the wishes of the deceased, and so, all the worse for the government. He, Fauchelevent, would nail up the coffin in the cell, lift the stone in the chapel, and let down the body into the vault. As a reward for this, the prioress would admit into the house his brother as gardener, and his niece as boarder. The prioress had told him to bring his brother the next day, after the pretended funeral, but he could not bring M. Madeleine in from outside if he were not there. This was his first embarrassment, and then he had a second in the empty coffin.

"What do you mean by the empty coffin?" Valjean asked.

Fauchelevent replied: "Why, the government coffin."

"I do not understand you."

"A nun dies, and the physician of the municipality comes and says: 'There is a nun dead.' Government sends a coffin, the next day it sends a hearse and undertaker's men to fetch the coffin and carry it to the cemetery. They will come and lift the coffin, and there's nothing in it."

"Put something in it."

"A dead person? I haven't such a thing."

"Well, then, a living one."

"Who?"

"Myself," said Jean Valjean.

Fauchelevent, who was seated, sprang up as if a shell had exploded under his chair.

"You?"

"Why not?"

Jean Valjean had one of those rare smiles which resemble a sunbeam in a wintry sky.

"You know that you said, Fauchelevent, Mother Crucifixion is dead, and I added, 'And Father Madeleine is buried.' It will be so."

"Oh, you are joking, not speaking seriously."

"Most seriously. Must I not get out of here?"

"Of course."

"I told you I would find a basket and a cover too."

"Well?"

"The basket will be of deal, and the cover of black cloth."

"No, white cloth. Nuns are buried in white."

"All right, then, white cloth."

"You are not like other men, Father Madeleine."

To see such ideas, which are naught but the wild and daring inventions of the hulks, issue from his peaceful surroundings and mingle with what he called "the slow pace of the convent," produced in Fauchelevent a stupor comparable to that which a passer-by would feel on seeing a whaler fishing in the gutter of the Rue St. Denis.

Jean Valjean went on:

"The point is to get out of here unseen, and that is a way. But just tell me, how does it all take place? where is the coffin?"

"The empty one?"

"Yes."

"In what is called the dead-house. It is upon two trestles, and covered with the pall."

"What is the length of the coffin?"

"Six feet."

"What is this dead-house?"

"A ground-floor room with a grated window looking on the garden, and two doors, one leading to the church, the other to the convent."

"What church?"

"The street church, the one open to everybody."

"Have you the keys of these doors?"

"No; I have the key of the one communicating with the convent, but the porter has the other."

247

"When does he open it?"

"Only to let the men pass who come to fetch the body. When the coffin has gone out the door is locked again."

"Who nails up the coffin?"

"I do."

"Who places the pall over it?"

"I do."

"Are you alone?"

"No other man, excepting the doctor, is allowed to enter the dead-house. It is written on the wall."

"Could you hide me in that house to-night when all are asleep in the convent?"

"No, but I can hide you in a dark hole opening out of the dead-house, in which I put the burial tools, of which I have the key."

"At what hour to-morrow will the hearse come to fetch the body?"

"At three in the afternoon. The interment takes place at the Vaugirard cemetery a little before nightfall, for the ground is not very near here."

"I will remain concealed in your tool-house during the night and morning. How about food? for I shall be hungry."

"I will bring you some."

"You can nail me up in the coffin at two o'clock."

Fauchelevent recoiled and cracked his finger-bones.

"Oh, it is impossible."

"Nonsense! to take a hammer and drive nails into a board?"

What seemed to Fauchelevent extraordinary, was, we repeat, quite simple to Jean Valjean, for he had gone through worse straits, and any man who has been a prisoner knows how to reduce himself to the diameter of the mode of escape. A prisoner is affected by flight just as a sick man is by the crisis which saves or destroys him, and an escape is a cure. What will not a man undergo for the sake of being cured? To be nailed up and carried in a box, to live for a long time in a packing-case, to find air where there is none, to economize one's breath for hours, to manage to choke without dying, was one of Jean Valjean's melancholy talents.

Besides, a coffin in which there is a living body! this convict's expedient is also an imperial expedient. If we may believe the monk Austin Castillejo, it was the way employed by Charles V, who, wishing to see La Plombes for the last time after his abdication, contrived to get her in and out of the monastery of Saint Yuste.

Fauchelevent, when he had slightly recovered, exclaimed:

"But how will you manage to breathe?"

"I will manage it."

"In that box? why, the mere idea of it chokes me."

"You have a gimlet. You will make a few holes round the mouth and nail down the lid, without closing it tightly."

"Good! and suppose you cough or sneeze?"

"A man who is escaping does not do such a thing."

And Jean Valjean added:

"Father Fauchelevent, we must make up our mind; I must either be captured here or go out in the hearse."

Everybody must have noticed the fancy which cats have of stopping and sniffing in a half-open door, and most of us have said to it, "Pray come in." There are men who, when an incident stands half-open before them, have also a tendency to remain undecided between two resolutions, at the risk of being crushed by destiny as it hurriedly closes the adventure. The more prudent, cats though they are, and because they are cats, often incur greater danger than the more daring. Fauchelevent was of this hesitating nature; still, Jean Valjean's coolness involuntarily mastered him, and he growled:

"After all, there is no other way."

Jean Valjean continued:

"The only thing I am anxious about is what will take place at the cemetery."

"There is the very thing I am not anxious about," said Fauchelevent. "If you feel sure of getting out of the coffin I feel sure of getting you out of the grave. The grave-digger is a friend of mine, and a drunkard, of the name of Father Mestienne; he puts the dead in the grave, and I put the grave-digger in my pocket. I will tell you what will occur. We shall arrive a little before twilight, three-quarters of an hour before the cemetery gates are closed. The hearse will drive up to the grave, and I shall follow, for that is my business. I shall have a hammer, a chisel, and pincers in my pocket; the hearse stops, the undertaker knots a cord round your coffin and lets you down; the priest says the prayers, makes the sign of the cross, sprinkles the holy water, and bolts; I remain alone with Father Mestienne, and he is a friend of mine, I tell you. One of two things is certain; he will either be drunk or not be drunk. If he is not drunk, I shall say to him, 'Come and have a drain before the *Bon Coing* closes.' I take him away, make him drunk, which does not take long, as he has always made a beginning; I lay him under the table, take his card, and return to the cemetery without him. You will have only to deal with me. If he is drunk, I shall say to him, 'Be off, I will do your work for you.' He will go, and I get you out of the hole."

Jean Valjean held out his hand, which Father Fauchelevent seized with a touching peasant devotion.

"It is settled, Father Fauchelevent. All will go well."

"Providing that nothing is deranged," Fauchelevent thought; "suppose the affair was to have a terrible ending!"

5 . *A DRUNKARD IS NOT IMMORTAL*

THE next day, as the sun was setting, the few passers-by on the Boulevard du Maine took off their hats to an old-fashioned hearse, ornamented with death's-head, thigh-bones, and tears. In this hearse was a coffin covered with a white pall, on which lay an enormous black cross, like a tall dead woman with hanging arms. A draped carriage, in which could be noticed a priest in his surplice, and a chorister in his red skull-cap, followed. Two mutes in a gray uniform with black facings walked on the right and left of the hearse, while behind them came an old man in workman's garb, who halted. The procession proceeded toward the Vaugirard cemetery.

You could see, projecting from his pocket, the handle of a hammer, a chisel, and a pair of pincers.

This cemetery formed an exception to the others in Paris. It had its peculiar usages, just as it had a large gate and a side gate, which old people in the quarters, tenacious to old names, called the horseman's gate and the footman's gate. The Bernardo-Benedictines of the Little Picpus had obtained, as we have stated, permission to be buried there in a separate corner, and by night, because the cemetery had formerly belonged to their community. The grave-diggers, having thus an evening duty in summer and a night duty in winter, were subject to special rules. The gates of Parisian cemeteries were closed at that period at sunset, and as this was a police measure the Vaugirard cemetery was subjected to it like the rest. The two gates adjoined a pavilion built by the architect Perronet, in which the porter lived, and they were inexorably closed at the moment when the sun disappeared behind the dome of the Invalides. If any grave-digger were detained at that moment in the cemetery, he had only one way to get out,—his card, with which the undertaker's department supplied him. There was a species of letterbox in the shutter of the porter's window; the grave-digger threw his card into this box, the porter heard it fall, pulled the string, and the small gate opened. If the grave-digger had not his card, he gave his name; the porter got up, recognized him, and opened the gate with his key; but in that case the grave-digger paid a fine of fifteen francs.

This cemetery, with its own regulations, was a flaw on the administrative symmetry, and it was put down shortly after 1830. The cemetery of Mont Parnasse succeeded it, and inherited the famous cabaret attached to the Vaugirard cemetery, which was known by the sign, *au bon Coing,* one side of which looked out on the drinking-tables, the other on the tombs.

It was what might be called a faded cemetery, and it was falling into decay; green mold was invading it, and the flowers deserted it. Respectable tradesmen did not care to be buried at Vaugirard, for it had a poverty-stricken smell. Le père Lachaise, if you like! to be buried there was like having a mahogany suit of furniture. The Vaugirard cemetery was a venerable inclosure, laid out like an old French garden; in it were straight walks, box-trees, holly-trees, old tombs under old yew-trees, and very tall grass. At night it was a tragical-looking spot.

The sun had not yet set when the hearse with the white pall and black cross entered the avenue of this cemetery, and the halting man who followed it was no other than Fauchelevent.

The interment of Mother Crucifixion in the vault under the altar, getting Cosette out, and introducing Jean Valjean into the dead-house, had been effected without the slightest hitch.

Let us say, in passing, that the burial of Mother Crucifixion beneath the altar is to us a very venial thing, and one of those faults which resemble a duty. The nuns had accomplished it, not only without feeling troubled, but with the applause of their conscience. In a convent, what is called "the government" is only an interference with the authorities, which admits of discussion. First comes the rule—as for the code, time enough for that. Men, make as many laws as you please, but keep them for yourselves. Rendering unto Cæsar only comes after rendering unto God, and a prince is nothing by the side of a principle.

Fauchelevent limped after the hearse with great satisfaction; his twin plots, the one with the nuns, the other with M. Madeleine, one for, the other against, the convent, were getting on famously. The calmness of Jean Valjean was one of those powerful tranquilities which are contagious, and Fauchelevent no longer doubted of success.

What he still had to do was nothing; during the last two years he had made the grave-digger drunk a dozen times, and he played with him.

He could do what he liked with Father Mestienne, and his head exactly fitted Fauchelevent's cap. The gardener's security was complete.

At the moment when the procession entered the avenue leading to the cemetery, Fauchelevent looked at the hearse with delight, and rubbed his huge hands as he said in a low voice:

"What a lark!"

All at once the hearse stopped; it had reached the gates, and the permission for burying must be shown. The undertaker conversed with the porter, and during this colloquy, which occupied two or three minutes, a stranger stationed himself behind the hearse by Fauchelevent's side. He was a sort of workman, wearing a jacket with wide pockets, and holding a spade under his arm.

Fauchelevent looked at the stranger, and asked him:

"Who are you?"

The man replied: "The grave-digger."

If any man could survive a cannon-ball right in the middle of his chest, he would cut such a face as Fauchelevent did.

"The grave-digger?"

"Yes."

"You?"

"Me!"

"Why, Father Mestienne is the grave-digger."

"Was."

"How, was?"

"He is dead."

Fauchelevent was prepared for anything except this, that a grave-digger could die; and yet it is true that grave-diggers themselves die; while digging holes for others, they prepare one for themselves.

Fauchelevent stood with widely opened mouth, and had scarce strength to stammer:

"Why, it is impossible."

"It is the case."

"But the grave-digger," he went on feebly, "is Father Mestienne."

"After Napoleon, Louis XVIII. After Mestienne, Gribier. Rustic, my name is Gribier."

Fauchelevent, who was very pale, stared at Gribier.

He was a tall, thin, livid, thoroughly funereal man. He looked like a broken-down doctor who had turned grave-digger.

Fauchelevent burst into a laugh.

"Ah, what funny things do happen! Father Mestienne is dead; little Father Mestienne is dead, but long live little Father Lenoir! Do you know who he is? a bottle of Surêne, morbigou! real Paris Surêne. And so Father Mestienne is dead; I feel sorry for him, as he was a jolly fellow. But you are a jolly fellow too, are you not, comrade? We will drink a glass together, eh?"

The man answered, "I have been at college, and I never drink."

The hearse had set out again, and was now going along the main avenue.

Fauchelevent had decreased his pace, and limped more through anxiety than infirmity.

The grave-digger walked in front of him, and Fauchelevent once again surveyed this unknown Gribier.

He was one of those men who, when young, look old, and who, though thin, are very strong.

"Comrade!" Fauchelevent cried. The man turned round. "I am the convent grave-digger."

"My colleague," the man said.

Fauchelevent, uneducated though very sharp, understood that he had to deal with a formidable species, a fine speaker; he growled:

"So, then, Father Mestienne is dead."

The man answered, "Completely. Le bon Dieu consulted his bill-book. Father Mestienne was due, and so Father Mestienne is dead."

Fauchelevent repeated mechanically, "Le bon Dieu."

"Le bon Dieu," the man said authoritatively, "with philosophers the Eternal Father, with Jacobins the Supreme Being."

"Are we not going to form an acquaintance?" Fauchelevent stammered.

"It is formed. You are a rustic, I am a Parisian."

"People never know one another thoroughly till they have drunk together, for when a man empties his glass he empties his heart. You will come and drink with me; such an offer cannot be refused."

"Work first."

Fauchelevent thought, "It's all over with me."

They had only a few more yards to go before reaching the nuns' corner. The grave-digger added:

"Peasant, I have seven children to feed, and as they must eat I must not drink."

And he added, with the satisfaction of a serious man who is laying down an axiom:

"Their hunger is the enemy of my thirst."

The hearse left the main avenue, and turned down a smaller one, which indicated the immediate proximity of the grave. Fauchelevent reduced his pace, but could not reduce that of the hearse. Fortunately, the ground was saturated with winter rains, and rendered their progress slower. He drew closer to the grave-digger.

"There is such a capital Argenteuil wine," he muttered.

"Villager," the man replied, "I was not meant to be a grave-digger. My father was porter at the Prytanæum, and destined me for literature, but he was unfortunate in his speculations on the Exchange. Hence I was compelled to relinquish the profession of author, but I am still a public writer."

"Then you are not a grave-digger?" Fauchelevent retorted, clinging to this very weak branch.

"One does not prevent the other, so I double the parts—"

Fauchelevent did not understand the last word.

"Let us go to drink," he said.

Here a remark is necessary. Fauchelevent, however great his agony might be, proposed drinking, but did not explain himself on one point. Who was to pay? As a general rule, Fauchelevent proposed and Father Mestienne paid. A proposal to drink evidently resulted from the new situation created by the new grave-digger, and that proposal the gardener must make, but he left, not undesignedly, the proverbial quarter of an hour called Rabelais' in obscurity. However affected Fauchelevent might be, he did not feel anxious to pay.

The grave-digger continued with a grand smile:

"As a man must live, I accept Father Mestienne's inheritance. When a man has nearly completed his course of studies, he is a philosopher, and I have added the work of my arms to that of my hand. I have my writers' stall at the market in the Rue de Sèvres—you know, the umbrella market? all the cooks of the Croix Rouge apply to me, and I compose their declarations to the soldiers. In the morning I write billets-doux, in the evening I dig graves; such is life, Rustic."

The hearse went on, and Fauchelevent looked all about him with the greatest anxiety; heavy drops of perspiration fell from his forehead.

"Still," the grave-digger continued, "a man cannot serve two mistresses, and I must choose between the pick and the pen. The pick ruins my hand."

The hearse stopped.

The chorister got out of the coach, and then the priest; one of the small front wheels of the hearse was slightly raised by a heap of earth, beyond which an open grave was visible.

"Here's a joke!" Fauchelevent said in consternation.

6. BETWEEN FOUR PLANKS

Who was in the coffin? It was, as we know, Jean Valjean.

He had so contrived as to be able to live in it, and could almost breathe.

It is a strange thing to what an extent security of conscience produces other security; the whole combination premeditated by Valjean had been going on since the previous evening, and was still going on excellently. He calculated, like Fauchelevent upon Father Mestienne, and did not suspect the end. Never was a situation more critical or a calm more perfect.

The four planks of a coffin exhale a species of terrible peace, and it seemed as if some of the repose of the dead were blended with Valjean's tranquillity.

From the bottom of this coffin he had been able to follow, and did follow, all the phases of the formidable drama which he performed with death.

A short while after Fauchelevent had finished nailing down the coffin lid, Valjean felt himself raised and then carried along. Through the cessation of the jolting, he felt that they had passed from the pavement to the stamped earth; that is to say, the hearse had left the streets, and turned into the boulevards. From the hollow sound he guessed that he was crossing the bridge of Austerlitz; at the first halt he understood that he was entering the cemetery, and at the sound he said to himself, "Here is the grave."

He suddenly felt hands seize the coffin, and then noticed a rumbling grating on the planks; he guessed that a rope was was being fastened round the coffin in order to let it down into the grave.

After this, he felt dizzy for a while.

In all probability the men had made the coffin oscillate and let the head down before the feet. He perfectly recovered when he found himself horizontal and motionless. He felt a certain amount of cold.

A chill and solemn voice was raised above him, and he heard Latin words, which he did not understand, pass away so slowly that he could distinguish each in turn.

Qui dormiunt in terræ pulvere, evigilabunt; alii in vitam æternam, et alii in opprobrium, ut videant semper.

A boyish voice said:

"De profundis."

The grave voice began again:

"Requiem æternam dona ei, Domine."

The boyish voice replied:

"Et lux perpetua luceat ei!"

He heard something like the gentle plash of rain upon the coffin lid; it was, probably, the holy water.

He thought, "It is finished, and I only need a little patience. The priest will go away, and Fauchelevent take Mestienne off to drink. I shall be left here till Fauchelevent returns alone, and I shall get out. It will take about an hour."

The great voice continued:

"Requiescat in pace."

And the boyish voice said:

"*Amen.*"

Jean Valjean, who was listening attentively, heard something like the sound of retreating footsteps.

"They are going away," he thought. "I am alone."

All at once he heard over his head a noise which appeared to him like a thunder-clap.

It was a spadeful of earth falling on the coffin. A second spadeful fell, and one of the holes by which he breathed was stopped.

A third shovelful fell and then a fourth.

There are some things stronger than the strongest man, and Jean Valjean lost his senses.

7. FAUCHELEVENT HAS AN IDEA

THIS is what took place above the coffin which contained Jean Valjean.

When the hearse had gone away, when the priest and the chorister had driven off in the coach, Fauchelevent, who did not once take his eyes off the grave-digger, saw him stoop down and seize the spade, which was standing upright in the heap of earth.

Fauchelevent formed a supreme resolution; he placed himself between the grave and the digger, folded his arms, and said: "I'll pay."

The grave-digger looked at him in amazement, and replied:

"What, peasant?"

Fauchelevent repeated:

"I'll pay for the wine."

"What wine?"

"The Argenteuil."

"Where is it?"

"At the Bon Coing!"

"Go to the deuce," said the grave-digger.

And he threw a spadeful of earth on the coffin.

The coffin uttered a hollow sound, Fauchelevent tottered, and was himself ready to fall into the grave. He cried, in a voice with which a death-rattle was beginning to be mingled.

"Come along, mate, before the Bon Coing closes."

The grave-digger filled his spade again, and Fauchelevent continued, "I'll pay."

And he seized the grave-digger's arm.

"Listen to me, mate; I am the convent grave-digger, and have come to help you. It is a job which can be done by night, so let us begin by going to have a drain."

And while speaking, while clinging to this desperate pressing, he made the melancholy reflection, "And suppose he does drink, will he get drunk?"

"Provincial," said the grave-digger, "since you are so pressing, I consent. We will drink, but after work, not before."

And he raised his spade, but Fauchelevent restrained him.

"It is Argenteuil wine."

"Why," said the grave-digger, "you must be a bell-ringer; ding, dong, ding, dong. You can only say that. Go and have yourself pulled."

And he threw the second shovelful.

Fauchelevent had reached that moment when a man is no longer aware of what he says.

"But come and drink," he cried, "since I offer to pay."

"When we have put the child to bed," said Gribier.

He threw the third spadeful.

Then he added, as he dug the shovel into the ground:

"It will be very cold to-night! and the dead woman would halloo after us if we were to leave her here without a blanket."

At this moment the grave-digger stooped to fill his spade, and his jacket-pocket gaped.

Fauchelevent's wandering glance fell mechanically into his pocket and remained there.

The sun was not yet hidden by the horizon, and there was still sufficient light to distinguish something white at the bottom of this gaping pocket.

All the brightness of which the Picard peasant's eye is capable glistened in Fauchelevent's; an idea had struck him.

Unnoticed by the grave-digger, he thrust his hand into his pocket from behind, and drew out the white thing at the bottom.

The grave-digger threw the fourth shovelful into the grave, and as he hurried to raise a fifth, Fauchelevent looked at him with profound calmness, and said:

"By the way, my novice, have you your card?"

The grave-digger paused.

"What card?"

"The sun is just going to set."

"Very good, it can put on its night-cap."

"The cemetery gates will be shut."

"Well, and what then?"

"Have you your card?"

"Ah! my card," the grave-digger said; and he felt in one pocket and then in another, he passed to his fobs and turned them inside out.

"No," he said, "I have not got my card; I must have forgotten it."

"Fifteen francs fine," said Fauchelevent.

The grave-digger turned green, for the pallor of livid men is green.

"O Lord, have mercy upon me," he exclaimed; "fifteen francs fine!"

"Three one hundred-sous pieces," said Fauchelevent.

The grave-digger let his shovel fall.

Fauchelevent's turn had arrived.

"Come, conscript," said the old gardener, "no despair; you need not take advantage of the grave to commit suicide. Fifteen francs are fifteen francs, and, besides, you can avoid paying them. I am old and you a new-comer, and I am up to all the tricks and dodges. I will give you a piece of friendly advice. One thing is clear, the sun is setting, it is touching the dome, and the cemetery will shut in five minutes."

"That is true."

"Five minutes will not be enough for you to fill up this grave, which is deuced deep, and reach the gates in time to get out before they close."

"Perfectly correct."

"In that case, fifteen francs fine. But you have time,—where do you live?"

"Hardly a quarter of an hour's walk from here, at No. 87, Rue de Vaugirard."

"You have just time enough to get out, if you look sharp."

"So I have."

"Once outside the gates, you will gallop home and fetch your card, and when you return, the porter will open the gate for you gratis. And you will bury your dead woman, whom I will stop from running away during your absence."

"I owe you my life, peasant."

"Be off at once," said Fauchelevent.

The grave-digger, who was beside himself with gratitude, shook his hand and ran off.

When he had disappeared behind a clump of trees, Fauchelevent listened till his footsteps died away, then bent over the grave, and said in a low voice:

"Father Madeleine!"

There was no reply.

Fauchelevent trembled; he tumbled all of a heap into the grave, threw himself on the coffin-lid, and cried:

"Are you there?"

There was silence in the coffin, and Fauchelevent, who could not breathe for trembling, took out his chisel and hammer and pried off the coffin-lid.

He could see Jean Valjean's face in the gloom, pale, and with the eyes closed.

The gardener's hair stood on an end; he got up, and then fell against the side of the grave. He gazed at Jean Valjean, who lay livid and motionless.

Fauchelevent murmured in a voice faint as a breath:

"He is dead!"

And drawing himself up, he folded his arms so violently that his clenched fists struck his shoulders, and cried:

"That is the way in which I save him!"

Then the poor old man began sobbing and soliloquizing, for it is a mistake to suppose that there is no soliloquy in nature. Powerful agitations often talk aloud.

"It is Father Mestienne's fault. Why did that ass die? Had he any occasion to go off the hooks so unexpectedly? It is he who has killed Monsieur Madeleine. Father Madeleine! he is in his coffin, and it is all over with him. Has such a thing as this any common sense? oh, my goodness, he is dead! Well, and what shall I do with his little girl? What will the greengrocer say? Is it possible that such a man can die in such a way? When I think how he got under my cart! Father Madeleine! Father Madeleine! By Heavens, he is suffocated, as I said he would be, and he would not believe me. Well, this is a pretty trick of my performance. The worthy man is dead, the best man among all God's good people; and his little one? Well, I sha'n't go back to the convent, but stop here. To have done such a thing as this! it is not worth while being two old men to be two old fools. But how did he manage to get into the convent? that was the beginning, and a man ought not to do things like that. Father Madeleine, Madeleine, Monsieur Madeleine, Monsieur le Maire! He does not hear me. Get out of it now as best you can."

And he tore his hair.

A shrill grating sound was audible at a distance through the trees: it was the closing of the cemetery gate. Fauchelevent bent over Jean Valjean, and all at once bounded back to the further end of the grave—Jean Valjean's eyes were open and staring at him.

If seeing a death is fearful, seeing a resurrection is nearly as frightful. Fauchelevent became like stone. He was pale, haggard, confounded by such excessive emotion, not knowing if he had to do with a dead man or a living man, and looking at Jean Valjean, who looked at him.

"I was falling asleep," said Valjean.

And he sat up. Fauchelevent fell on his knees.

"Holy Virgin! how you frightened me!"

Then he rose and cried:

"Thank you, Father Madeleine!"

Jean Valjean had only fainted, and the fresh air aroused him again.

Joy is the reflux of terror, and Fauchelevent had almost as much difficulty in recovering himself as had Jean Valjean.

"Then you are not dead! oh, what a clever fellow you are! I called to you so repeatedly that you came back. When I saw your eyes closed, I said, 'There, he is suffocated!' I should have gone stark mad, fit for a strait-waistcoat, and they would have put me in Bicêtre. What would you have me do if you were dead? and your little girl? the greengrocer's wife would not have understood it at all. A child is left upon her hands, and the grandfather is dead! What a story! oh, my good saints in Paradise, what a story! Well, you are alive, that's the great thing."

"I am cold," said Valjean.

This remark completely recalled Fauchelevent to the reality, which was urgent. These two men, who had scarce recovered, had a troubled mind, they knew not why, which emanated from the gloomy place where they were.

"Let us get out of this at once," said Fauchelevent.

He felt in his pocket and produced a flask.

"But a dram first," he said.

The flask completed what the fresh air had begun. Valjean drank a mouthful of spirits and regained perfect possession of himself.

He got out of the coffin, and helped Fauchelevent to nail on the lid again.

Three minutes later they were out of the grave.

Fauchelevent was calm, and took his time. The cemetery was closed, and there was no fear of Gribier returning. That "conscript" was at home busily seeking his card, and prevented from finding it because it was in Fauchelevent's pocket. Without it he could not return to the cemetery.

Fauchelevent took the spade, and Jean Valjean the pick, and they together buried the empty coffin. When the grave was filled up Fauchelevent said:

"Come along; you may carry the pick and I will carry the spade." The night was descending.

Jean Valjean felt some difficulty in moving and walking, for in the coffin he had grown stiff, and become to some extent a corpse. The rigidity of death had seized upon him between these four planks, and he must, so to speak, become thawed.

"You are stiff," said Fauchelevent; "it is a pity that I am a cripple, or we might have a run."

"Nonsense," said Valjean, "half a dozen strides will make my legs all right again."

They went along the avenues by which the hearse had passed, and, on reaching the gate, Fauchelevent threw the grave-digger's card into the box; the porter pulled the string, and they went out.

"How famously it has all gone," said Fauchelevent; "it was an excellent idea you had, Father Madeleine!"

They passed through the Vaugirard barrier in the simplest way in the world, for, in the vicinity of a cemetery, a spade and a pick are two passports.

The Rue de Vaugirard was deserted.

"Father Madeleine," Fauchelevent said, as they walked along, "you have better eyes than I have, so show me No. 87."

"Here it is," said Valjean.

"There is no one in the street," Fauchelevent continued, "give me the pick, and wait for me a couple of minutes."

Fauchelevent entered No. 87, went right to the top, guided by that instinct which ever leads the poor man to the garret, and rapped at the door in the darkness.

A voice replied, "Come in." It was Gribier's voice.

Fauchelevent pushed the door. The grave-digger's room was like all these wretched abodes, an impoverished and crowded garret. A packing-case—possibly a coffin—occupied the place of a chest of drawers, a butter-jar was the water-cistern, a palliasse represented the bed, while the floor filled the place of chairs and table. In one corner, on an old ragged piece of carpet, were a thin woman and a heap of children.

The whole of this poor interior displayed signs of a convulsion, and it seemed as if an earthquake "for one" had taken place there. The blankets were torn away, the rags scattered about, the jug was broken, the mother had been crying, and the children probably beaten,—there were evident signs of an obstinate and savage search. It was plain that the grave-digger had been wildly looking for his card, and made everything in the garret responsible for it, from his jug to his wife.

He looked desperate, but Fauchelevent was too eager to notice this sad side of his success; he went in, and said:

"I have brought you your spade and pick."

Gribier looked at him in stupefaction.

"Is it you, peasant?"

"And to-morrow morning you will find your card with the porter of the cemetery."

And he placed the shovel and pick on the ground.

"What does this mean?" Gribier asked.

"It means that you let your card fall out of your pocket, that I found it on the ground when you had left, that I have buried the dead woman, filled up the grave, done your work, the porter will give you your card, and you will not pay fifteen francs. That's what it is, conscript!"

"Thanks, villager," said Gribier, quite dazzled, "next time I will pay for a bottle."

8. A SUCCESSFUL EXAMINATION

An hour later two men and a child presented themselves in the darkness of night at No. 69, Little Rue Picpus. The elder of the two men raised the knocker and rapped.

They were Fauchelevent, Jean Valjean, and Cosette.

The two men had fetched Cosette from the greengrocer's where Fauchelevent had left her on the previous evening. Cosette had spent the four-and-twenty hours in understanding nothing, and silently trembling; she trembled so greatly that she had not cried, nor had she eaten or slept. The worthy greengrocer had asked her a hundred questions, but had only obtained as answer a gloomy look, ever the same. Cosette did not breathe a syllable of what she had seen or heard during the last two days, for she guessed that she was passing through a crisis, and felt deeply that she must be "good." Who has not experienced the sovereign power of the words, "say nothing," uttered with a certain accent in the ear of a little startled being? Fear is dumb; besides, no one can keep a secret like a child.

The only thing was, that when she saw Jean Valjean again after these mournful four-and-twenty hours, she uttered such a cry of joy that any thoughtful person who had heard it would have divined in this cry an escape from a gulf.

Fauchelevent belonged to the convent, and knew all the pass-words; hence doors readily opened to him, and thus solved the double and startling problem, "how to get in, and how to get out."

The porter, who had his instructions, opened the little gate which communicated between the court-yard and the garden in the wall of the former facing the gate-way, which might be seen from the street twenty years ago.

The porter showed them all three through this gate, and thence they reached the inner private parlor where Fauchelevent had received the orders of the prioress on the previous day.

The prioress was waiting for them, rosary in hand, and a vocal mother, with her veil down, was standing near her.

A discreet candle lit up, or, to speak more correctly, pretended to light up, the parlor.

The prioress took a thorough look at Jean Valjean, for no eye examines like a drooping one.

Then she questioned him.

"Are you the brother?"

"Yes, reverend mother," Fauchelevent answered.

"What is your name?"

Fauchelevent answered: "Ultime Fauchelevent."

He had really had a brother of that name, who was dead.

"Where do you come from?"

Fauchelevent: "From Picquigny, near Amiens."

"What is your age?"

Fauchelevent: "Fifty."

"What is your trade?"

Fauchelevent: "Gardener."

"Are you a good Christian?"

Fauchelevent: "All the members of our family are so."

"Is this little girl yours?"

Fauchelevent: "Yes, reverend mother."

"Are you her father?"

Fauchelevent: "Her grandfather."

The vocal mother said to the prioress in a whisper:

"He answers well."

Jean Valjean had not said a word.

The prioress looked attentively at Cosette, and whispered to the vocal mother:

"She will be ugly."

The two mothers consulted for a few minutes in a very low voice in a corner of the parlor, and then the prioress turned and said:

"Father Fauvent, you will get another knee-cap and bell, for we shall require two in future."

On the morrow two bells were really heard in the garden and the nuns could not resist the temptation of raising a corner of their veils. They could see, under the shade of the trees, two men digging side by side, Fauvent and another. It was an enormous event, and silence was so far broken that they whispered: "It is an assistant gardener," while the vocal mothers added: "It is a brother of Father Fauvent's."

Jean Valjean was, in fact, permanently installed; he had the leathern knee-cap and bell, and was henceforth official. He called himself Ultime Fauchelevent.

The most powerful determining cause of his admission was the remark of the prioress with reference to Cosette,—*she will be ugly*.

The prioress, once she had prognosticated this, felt an affection for Cosette, and gave her a place in the boarding-school.

This is very logical, after all; for, although there may be no looking-glasses in a convent, women are conscious of their face. Now, girls who feel themselves pretty have a disinclination to take the veil, and as inclination is generally in an inverse ratio to the beauty, more is hoped from ugly than from pretty girls.

All this adventure aggrandized Fauchelevent, for he had a threefold success,—with Jean Valjean, whom he saved and sheltered; with Gribier, who said to himself, he saved me fifteen francs; and with the convent, which, thanks to him, while keeping the coffin of Mother Crucifixion under the altar, eluded Cæsar and sanctified God. There was a coffin with a body at the Little Picpus, and a coffin without a body in the Vaugirard cemetery; public order was doubtless deeply affected by this, but did not perceive the fact.

As for the convent, its gratitude to Fauchelevent was great; he became the best of servants and most precious of gardeners. On the archbishop's very next visit the prioress told the whole affair to the Grandeur, partly in confusion and partly in a boastful spirit. The archbishop, on leaving the convent, spoke about it, applaudingly and in a whisper, to M. de Latil, confessor to monseigneur, and afterward archbishop of Rheims and cardinal. The admiration felt for Fauchelevent traveled all the way to Rome, and we have seen a letter addressed by the then reigning pope, Leo XII, to one of his relatives, Monsignore, in the Paris Nunciature, and called, like himself, Della Genga, in which were the following lines: "It appears that there is at a convent in Paris an excellent gardener, who is a holy man, of the name of Fauvent."

Nothing of all this triumph reached Fauchelevent in his hut; he went on grafting, hoeing, and covering his melon beds, quite unaware of his excellence and sanctity. He no more suspected his glory than does a Durham or Surrey steer whose portrait is published in the *Illustrated London News,* with the inscription, "The ox that won the short-horn prize."

9. *IN THE CONVENT*

COSETTE in the convent continued to be silent.

She naturally thought herself Valjean's daughter, but as she knew nothing, she could say nothing, and in any case would have said nothing, as we have remarked; for nothing trains children to silence like misfortune. Cosette had suffered so greatly that she feared everything, even to speak, even to breathe, for a word had so often brought down an avalanche upon her! She had scarce begun to grow reassured since she had belonged to Jean Valjean, but she grew very soon accustomed to the convent. The only thing she regretted was Catherine, but she did not dare say so; one day, however, she remarked to Valjean, "If I had known, I would have brought her with me."

Cosette, on becoming a boarder at the convent, was obliged to assume the garb of the pupils of the house. Jean Valjean begged and obtained the old clothes she left off,—the same mourning clothes he made her put on when he removed her from the Thénardiers, and they were not much worn. Jean Valjean placed these clothes and her shoes and stockings, with a quantity of camphor and other odorous drugs with which convents abound, in a small valise which he managed to procure. He placed this valise on a chair by his bed-side, and always had the key about him.

"Father," Cosette asked him one day, "what is that box which smells so nice?"

Father Fauchelevent, in addition to the glory we have described and of which he was ignorant, was rewarded for his good deed; in the first place, he was happy, and, in the second place, he had much less to do, owing to the division of labor. Lastly, as he was very fond of snuff, he had from M. Madeleine's presence the advantage that he took thrice as much as before, and in a far more voluptuous manner, because M. Madeleine paid for it.

The nuns did not adopt the name of Ultime; they called Jean Valjean "the other Fauvent."

Had these holy women had any of Javert's temper about them, they must have noticed that when anything had to be procured from outside for the garden, it was always the elder Fauvent, the cripple, who went out, and never the other; but either because eyes constantly fixed on God know not how to spy, or because they preferred to watch one another, they paid no attention to the fact.

However, Jean Valjean did quite right in keeping shy and not stirring, for Javert watched the quarter for a whole month.

This convent was to Jean Valjean like an island surrounded by gulfs, and these four walls were henceforth the world for him; he saw enough of the sky there to be secure, and enough of Cosette to be happy.

He lived with old Fauchelevent in the hovel at the end of the garden. This lath and plaster tenement, which still existed in 1845, was composed of three rooms which had only the bare walls. The largest room was surrendered by force, for Jean Valjean resisted in vain, by Father Fauchelevent to M. Madeleine. The wall of this room had for ornament, in addition to the two nails for hanging up the knee-cap and the basket, a Royalist note for ten livres, date '93, fastened above the mantel-piece. This Vendean assignat had been nailed to the wall by the previous gardener, an ex-chouan, who died in the convent, and was succeeded by Fauchelevent.

Jean Valjean worked daily in the garden, and was very useful. As he had once been a pruner, he was glad to become a gardener. It will be remembered that he had a great number of receipts and secrets, which he turned to a profit; nearly all the trees in the orchard were wild stocks, but he grafted them and made them produce excellent fruit.

Cosette had permission to spend an hour daily with him, and as the sisters were sad and he was kind, the child compared them and adored him. At the fixed hour she ran to the cottage, and when she entered it filled it with paradise.

Jean Valjean expanded, and felt his own happiness grow with the happiness which he caused Cosette. The joy which we inspire has this charming thing about it, that far from being weakened, like ordinary reflections, it returns to us more radiant than before. In her hours of recreation Jean Valjean watched her from a distance, playing and running, and distinguished her laugh from that of the others.

For Cosette now laughed.

Her face had also changed to a certain extent, for laughter is the sun which drives winter from the human face.

When Cosette returned to her studies Jean Valjean watched the windows of her school-room, and at night would rise to gaze at the windows of her dormitory.

God has His inscrutable designs, and the convent contributed, like Cosette, to maintain and complete the bishop's work in Jean Valjean. It is certain that one of the sides of virtue leads to pride, and there is a bridge built there by the demon. Jean Valjean was perhaps unconsciously very near this bridge when Providence threw him into the convent of the Little Picpus. So long as he only compared himself with the bishop, he had found himself unworthy, and had been humble, but for some time past he had been beginning to compare himself with men, and pride was growing up. Who knows whether he might not have ended by gently returning to hatred?

The convent checked him on this slope.

It was the second place of captivity which he had seen. In his youth, in what had been to him the commencement of life, and again very recently he had seen another, a frightful spot, a terrible spot, whose severities had ever appeared to him to be the iniquity of justice and the crime of the law. At the present day after the hulks he saw the convent, and reflecting that he had been a member of the galleys and was now, so to speak, a spectator of the convent, he anxiously confronted them in his thoughts.

At times he leaned on his spade, and fell into a profound reverie.

He recalled his old comrades, how wretched they were! They rose at dawn and worked till night; they were scarce granted time to sleep; they lay down on camp-beds and were only allowed mattresses two inches thick; their rooms were only warmed in the severest months of the year; they were dressed in hideous red jackets; they were allowed, as an indulgence, canvas trousers in the great heat, and a woolen bandage on their back in the severe cold; they only ate meat and drank wine when they worked on fatigue parties; they lived without names, solely designated by numbers, lowering their eyes, lowering their voice, with shorn hair, under the stick, and in disgrace.

Then his thoughts turned to the beings whom he had before him.

These beings also lived with cropped hair, downcast eyes, and a low voice, not in disgrace, but amid the mockery of the world, and if their backs were not bruised by a stick, their shoulders were lacerated by the discipline. Their names had vanished, too, among human beings, and they only existed under severe appellations. They never ate meat nor drank wine; they often remained without food till night; they were dressed, not in a red jacket, but in a black woolen pall, heavy in summer and light in winter, and were unable to reduce it or add to it at all, and they wore for six months in the year serge chemises, which caused them a fever. They slept not in rooms warmed merely in the severe cold, but in cells in which fires were never kindled; they slept not on mattresses two inches thick, but on straw; lastly, they were not even allowed to sleep; every night, after a day of labor, they were compelled to get up, dress themselves, and go and pray in a freezing dark chapel, with their knees upon the stones.

On certain days, moreover, each of these beings was obliged, in turn, to remain for twelve hours prostrate on the ground, with her arms extended like a cross.

The former were men; the latter were women.

What had the men done? They had robbed, violated, plundered, killed, assassinated. They were bandits, forgers, poisoners, incendiaries, murderers, and parricides. What had these women done? Nothing.

On one side, brigandage and fraud, cozening, violence, lubricity, homicide, every sort of sacrilege, every variety of crime; on the other, only one thing,—innocence, perfect innocence, which was still attached to the earth by virtue, and already attached to Heaven by holiness.

On one side confessions of crimes made in a whisper; on the other, confessions of faults made aloud. And what crimes and what faults!

On one side miasmas, on the other an ineffable perfume; on one side a mortal pestilence, closely guarded, held down by cannon, and slowly devouring its plague-sufferers; on the other, a chaste kindling of all the souls on the same hearth. There darkness, here shadow, but a shadow full of light, and light full of radiance.

They were two places of slavery, but in the former there was a possible deliverance, a constantly visible legal limit, and, besides, escape; in the second perpetuity, the only hope being that gleam of liberty which men call death, upon the extreme horizon.

In the former people were only held by chains, in the latter by faith.

What emerged from the former? An immense curse, gnashing of

teeth, hatred, desperate wickedness, a cry of rage against human society, and sarcasms hurled at Heaven.

What issued from the latter? blessings, love.

And in these two places which were so similar, and yet so varying, these two so different species of beings accomplished the same work of expiation.

Jean Valjean perfectly understood the expiation of the former, as personal, but he did not understand the expiation of the others, of these creatures who were without reproach or stain, and he asked himself with trembling, "Expiation for what?"

A voice answered his conscience: "The most divine proof of human generosity, expiation for others."

Here we lay aside any and every personal theory; we are only the narrator, we are standing in Jean Valjean's place, and transferring his impressions.

He had before his eyes the sublime summit of abnegation, the highest pinnacle of possible virtue, that innocence which forgives men their faults, and expiates them in their place; servitude endured, torture accepted, punishment demanded by souls which have not sinned, that they may absolve souls which have erred; the love of humanity swallowed up in the love of God, but remaining distinct and suppliant in it; gentle, feeble beings who have the wretchedness of those who are punished and the smile of those who are rewarded.

And he remembered that he had dared to complain.

He often rose in the middle of the night to listen to the grateful song of these innocent creatures weighed down by severity, and his blood ran cold when he thought that men who were justly chastised only raised their voices to Heaven to blaspheme, and that he, wretch as he was, had threatened God.

It was a striking thing, which made him reflect deeply and imagine it a warning of Providence, that all the things he had done to escape from the other place of expiation, such as climbing walls, difficulties, dangerous adventures, and risks of death, he had gone through again, in entering the present place. Was it a symbol of his destiny?

This house was a prison, too, and bore a mournful likeness to the other abode from which he had fled, and yet he had never had such an idea here.

He saw again the bars, bolts, and iron bars, to guard whom? Angels.

The lofty walls which he had seen around tigers he saw again around lambs.

It was a place of expiation, and not of punishment, and yet it was even more austere, gloomy, and pitiless than the other. These virgins were more harshly bowed than the galley-slaves; a rough, cold wind, the wind which had chilled his youth, blew through the barred and padlocked cage of the vultures; but a sharper and more painful wind passed through the cotes of these doves.

Why was this?

When he thought of these things, all within him bowed down before this mystery of sublimity.

In these meditations pride vanished; he felt himself insignificant, and wept many times; all that had entered his life during the past six months led him back to the bishop's holy injunction,—Cosette by love, the convent by humility.

At times, in those hours of the night when the garden was deserted, he might have been seen kneeling in front of that window through which he had gazed on the night of his arrival, turned toward the spot where he knew that the sister who was making reparation was prostrated in prayer. He prayed thus kneeling before this sister.

It seemed as if he dared not kneel directly to God.

All that surrounded him, this peaceful garden, these fragrant flowers, these children uttering merry cries, these grave and simple women, these silent cloisters, slowly penetrated him, and gradually his soul was composed of silence like this cloister, of perfume like these flowers, of peace like this garden, of simplicity like these women, and of joy like these children. And then he thought how two houses of God had in turn received him at the two critical moments of his life, the first when all doors were closed and human society repulsed him, the second at the moment when human society was beginning to hunt him down again, and the hulks were yawning for him; and that, had it not been for the former, he would have fallen back into crime, and but for the latter, into punishment.

All his heart melted into gratitude, and he loved more and more.

Several years passed thus, and Cosette grew.

VOLUME THREE

Marius

CONTENTS · VOLUME III

BOOK I—STUDY OF AN ATOM OF PARIS

BOOK II—LE GRAND BOURGEOIS

BOOK III—GRANDFATHER AND GRANDSON

BOOK VII—PATRON-MINETTE

BOOK VIII—THE BAD POOR MAN

MARIUS

BOOK I

STUDY OF AN ATOM OF PARIS

1. PARVULUS

Paris has a child and the forest has a bird; the bird is called a sparrow, the child is called a gamin.

Couple these two ideas, the one which is all furnace, the other all dawn; bring the two sparks, Paris and childhood, into collision, and a little being is produced, a homuncio, as Plautus would say.

This little being is joyous; he does not eat every day, and he goes to the theater every night if he thinks proper. He has no shirt on his body, no shoes on his feet, and no covering on his head; he is like the flies, which have none of these things. He is from seven to thirteen years of age, lives in troops, lodges in the open air, wears an old pair of his father's trousers, which descend lower than his heels, an old hat belonging to some other father, which comes below his ears, and one yellow list brace. He runs, watches, begs, kills time, colors pipes, swears like a fiend, haunts the wine-shop, knows thieves, speaks familiarly to the street-girls, talks slang, sings filthy songs, and has nothing bad in his heart; for he has in his soul a pearl, Innocence; and pearls are not dissolved by mud. So long as the man is a child, God desires that he should be innocent.

If we were to ask the enormous city, "What is this creature?" it would reply, "It is my little one."

2. *SOME OF HIS CHARACTERISTICS*

THE gamin of Paris is the dwarf of the giantess. Let us not exaggerate; this cherub of the gutter has sometimes a shirt, but in that case has only one; he has shoes at times, but then they have no soles; he has at times a home, and likes it, for he finds his mother there; but he prefers the street, because he finds liberty there. He has games of his own, and his own tricks, of which hatred of the bourgeois class constitutes the basis, and he has metaphors of his own,—thus to be dead, he calls eating dandelions by the root. He has trades of his own, fetching hackney coaches, letting down steps, collecting toll for ferriage across the gutters in heavy showers, which he calls building the *Pont des Arts,* and shouting out speeches made by the authorities in favor of the French people. He has also a currency of his own, composed of all the little pieces of copper that can be picked up in the streets. This curious money, which takes the name of *loques,* has an unvarying and well-established value in this childish Bohemia.

Lastly, he has a fauna of his own, which he studiously observes in every hole and corner,—the lady-bird, the death's-head moth, the daddy long-legs, and the "devil," a black insect which threatens by writhing his tail, and which is armed with two horns. He has his fabulous monster, which has scales on its belly, and is not a lizard, and spots on its back, but is not a frog; it lives in holes in old lime-kilns and dried-up wells; it is black, hairy, slimy, and crawls about, at one moment slowly, at another quickly; it utters no sound, but looks so terrible that no one has ever seen it. This monster he calls the "deaf one," and looking for it under stones is a pleasure of a formidable nature. Another pleasure is suddenly to raise a paving-stone and look at the wood-lice. Every region of Paris is interest-

4

ing for the celebrated "finds" which may be in them; thus, there are earwigs in the timber-yards of the Ursulines, centipedes at Pantheon, and tad-poles in the ditches of the Champ de Mars.

As for witticisms, this child is as full of them as Talleyrand; but, though no less cynical, he is more honest. He is gifted with an unforeseen joviality, and startles the shopkeeper by his mad laugh. His range extends from genteel comedy to farce.

A funeral passes, and among the persons following is a physician. "Hilloh!" shouts a gamin, "when did the doctors begin to carry home their own work?"

Another is in a crowd. A serious man, adorned with spectacles and watch-seals, turns indignantly: "You scoundrel, what do you mean by taking my wife's waist?" "I, sir? search me!"

3 . HE IS AGREEABLE

AT night, thanks to a few half-pence which he always contrives to procure, the homuncio enters a theater. On crossing this magical threshold, he becomes transfigured; he was a gamin, and he becomes the *titi*. Theaters are like overturned vessels, which have their hold in the air, and the titis congregate in the hold. The titi is to the gamin as the butterfly to the chrysalis,—the same being, but now flying and hovering. It is sufficient for him to be present, with his radiant happiness, his power of enthusiasm and delight, and the clapping of his hands, which resembles the flapping of wings—and the narrow, fetid, obscure, dirty, unhealthy, hideous, abominable hold is at once called Paradise.

Give a being what is useless and deprive him of what is necessary, and you will have the gamin.

He possesses some literary intuition, and his tastes—we confess it with

5

all proper regret—are not classical. He is by nature but little of an academician.

This beings bawls, shouts, ridicules, and fights; wears patches like a babe, and rags like a philosopher; fishes in the gutter, sports in the sewers, extracts gayety from filth, grins and bites, whistles and sings, applauds and hisses, tempers the Hallelujah with Matanturlurette, hums every known tune, finds without looking, knows what he is ignorant of, is a Spartan in filching, is foolish even to wisdom, is lyrical even to filth, would sprawl on Olympus, wallows on the dung-heap, and emerges covered with stars. The gamin of Paris is the boy Rabelais.

He is not satisfied with his trousers, if they have no watch-pockets.

He is surprised at little and frightened by less; he sings down superstitions, reduces exaggerations, puts out his tongue at ghosts, depoetizes stilts, and introduces caricature into most serious affairs. It is not that he is prosaic, far from it, but he substitutes a farcical phantasmagoria for solemn vision. If Adamastor were to appear to him, the gamin would say, "Hilloh, old Boguey!"

4. *HE MAY BE USEFUL*

PARIS begins with the Badaud and ends with the gamin, two beings of which no other city is capable; the passive acceptance which is satisfied with looking, and the inexhaustible initiative, Prudhomme and Fouillou. Paris alone has that in its natural history; all the monarchy is in the Badaud, all the anarchy is in the gamin.

This pale child of the faubourgs of Paris lives and is developed, and grows up in suffering, a thoughtful witness in the presence of social realities and human things. He believes himself reckless, but is not so; he looks on, ready to laugh, but also ready for something else. Whoever you may be who call yourself prejudice, abuse, ignominy, oppression, iniquity, despotism, injustice, fanaticism or tyranny, take care of the yawning gamin.

This little fellow will grow.

Of what clay is he made? of anything; take a handful of mud, a breath, and you have Adam; it is sufficient for a God to pass, and a God has ever passed over the gamin. Fortune toils for this little being, though by the word fortune we mean to some extent luck. Will this pigmy, molded in the coarse common clay, ignorant, uneducated, brutal, violent, and of the populace, be an Ionian or a Bœotian? Wait awhile, *dum currit rota,* and the genius of Paris, that demon which creates children of accident and men of destiny, will behave exactly contrary to the Latin potter, and make an amphora out of the earthenware jar.

5. *HIS FRONTIERS*

THE gamin loves the town, but he loves solitude as well, for there is something of the sage in him; he is *urbis amator* like Fuscus, and *ruris amator* like Flaccus.

To wander about dreamily, that is, to loaf, is an excellent employment of time for the philosopher, particularly in that sort of slightly bastard country, ugly enough, but strange and composed of two natures, that surrounds certain large cities, and notably Paris. Observing the suburbs is looking at an amphibious scene; it is the end of the trees and the beginning of the roofs, the end of the grass and the beginning of the pavement, the end of the furrows and the beginning of the shops, the end of ruts and the beginning of passions, the end of the divine murmur and the beginning of human reason, and all this produces an extraordinary interest.

7

Such is the motive of the apparently objectless walks of the dreamer in those unattractive parts, which the passerby at once brands with the title of "dreary."

The author of these lines was for a long time a prowler about the suburbs of Paris, and it is a source of profound recollection for him. The worn grass, the stony path, the chalk, the marl, the plaster, the rough monotony of plowed and fallow land, the young plants in the market-garden suddenly noticed in a hollow, the mixture of the wild and the tame, the vast deserted nooks in which the garrison drummers hold their noisy school, these Thebaïds by day and cut-throat dens by night, the tottering mill turning in the wind, the windlasses of the quarries, the wine-shops at the corners of the cemeteries, the mysterious charm of the tall dark walls cutting at right angles immense open fields bathed in sunshine and full of butterflies—all this attracted him.

Hardly any one knows those singular spots, la Glacière, la Cimette, the hideous wall of Grenelle pock-marked with bullets, the Mont Parnasse, the Fosse aux Loups, Les Aubiers on the bank of the Marne, Mont Souris, the Tombe Issoire, or the Pierre Plate de Chatillon, where there is an old exhausted quarry, which is now only employed to grow mushrooms, and is closed by a heap of rotten board flush with the ground. The Campagna of Rome is an idea, and the banlieue of Paris is another. To see in what a horizon offers us naught but fields, houses, or trees is to remain on the surface; for all the aspects of things are the thoughts of God. The spot where a plain forms its junction with a town is always imprinted with a species of penetrating melancholy; for nature and humanity address you simultaneously, and local peculiarities make their appearance there.

Any one who has wandered like we have in those solitudes contiguous to our suburbs, which might be called the Limbos of Paris, has seen here and there, at the most deserted spot, and at the most unexpected moment, behind a scrubby hedge, or in the corner of some melancholy wall, children grouped tumultuously, fetid, muddy, dusty, unkempt, and ragged, playing together, crowned with corn-flowers. They are the little runagates of poor families; this external boulevard is their breathing medium, and the banlieue belongs to them, and they eternally play truant in it. They ingenuously sing there their repertory of unclean songs. They are there, or, to speak more correctly, they dwell there, far from any eye, in the gentle warmth of May or June. Circling round a hole in the ground and playing at marbles, squabbling for farthings, like irresponsible, freed,

8

and happy beings, so soon as they perceive you, they remember that they have a trade and must gain their livelihood, and they offer to sell you an old woolen stocking full of May-bugs or a spray of lilac. Such a meeting with chance children is one of the charming, and yet poignant, graces of the environs of Paris.

Sometimes there are girls among the heap of boys,—are they their sisters?—almost grown up, thin, feverish, sunburned, and freckled, crowned with wheat-ears and poppies; gay, haggard, and barefooted. You may see them eating cherries among the wheat, and at night hear them laugh. These groups, warmly illumined by the bright light of midday, or seen in the twilight, for a long time occupy the dreamer, and these visions are mingled with his dreams.

Paris is the center, the banlieue is the circumference—that is, the whole earth for these children. They never venture beyond it, and can no more leave the Parisian atmosphere than fish can live out of water. With them there is nothing beyond two leagues from the barrière; Ivry, Gentilly, Arcueil, Belleville, Aubervilliers, Ménilmontant, Choisy le Roi, Billancourt, Meudon, Issy, Vanvre, Sevres, Puteaux, Neuilly, Gennevilliers, Colombes, Romainville, Chatou, Asnières, Bougival, Nanterre, Enghien, Noisy-le-Sec, Nogent, Gourney, Drancy, and Gonesse—at these places their universe ends.

6. *A SMALL BIT OF HISTORY*

AT the almost contemporary period when this story happened, there was not, as at the present day, a policeman at every street-corner (a blessing which we have no time to discuss), and wandering children abounded in Paris. Statistics give us an average of two hundred and sixty shelterless children, picked up annually by the police of that day, in uninclosed

9

fields, in houses building, and under the arches of bridges. One of these nests, which became famous, produced "the swallows of the Rue d'Arcole." This, by the way, is the most disastrous of social symptoms, for all the crimes of the man begin with the vagabondage of the lad.

We must except Paris, however, and in a relative degree, and, in spite of the statistics we have just quoted, the exception is fair. While in any other great city a vagabond child is a ruined man, while nearly everywhere the boy left to himself is, to some extent, devoted and left to a species of fatal immersion in public vice, which destroys honor and conscience within him, the gamin of Paris, though externally so marred and dinted, is internally almost intact. It is a magnificent thing to be able to say, and one revealed in the splendid probity of our popular revolutions, that a certain incorruptibility emanates from the idea which is in the atmosphere of Paris, as from the salt which is in the ocean water. Breathing Paris preserves the soul.

But what we have just stated does not in any way decrease the heart-contraction which we feel every time we meet one of these lads, around whom we fancy that we can see the threads of the broken family fluttering. In our present civilization, which is still so incomplete, it is not a very abnormal fact, that families thus broken up should not know what becomes of their children, and allow their offspring to fall upon the public way. Hence come these obscure destinies, and this sad thing has become proverbial, and is known as "being cast on the pavement of Paris."

Let us remark parenthetically that such desertion of children was not discouraged by the old monarchy. A little of the Bohemian and Egyptian element in the lower classes suited the higher spheres, and the powerful ones profited by it. Hatred of national education was a dogma; of what good were half-lights? Such was the sentence, and the vagabond boy is the corollary of the ignorant boy.

Besides, the monarchy sometimes wanted lads, and then it skimmed the streets.

In the reign of Louis XIV, to go no further back, the king wished, rightly enough, to create a fleet. The idea was good, but let us look at the means. No fleet is possible, unless you have by the side of the sailing vessels, which are the playthings of the winds, vessels which can be sent wherever may be necessary, or be used as tugs, impelled by oars or steam; and in those days galleys were to the navy what steam-vessels now are. Hence galleys were needed, but galleys are only moved through the galley-slave, and hence the latter must be procured. Colbert ordered the provincial intendants and parliaments to produce as many convicts as they could, and the magistrates displayed great complaisance in the matter. A man kept on his hat when a procession passed; that was a Huguenot attitude, and he was sent to the galleys. A boy was met in the street; provided that he was fifteen years of age, and had no place to sleep in, he was sent to the galleys. It was a great reign—a great age.

In the reign of Louis XV, children disappeared in Paris; the police carried them off, and no one knew for what mysterious employment. Monstrous conjectures were whispered as to the king's purple baths. It sometimes happened that when boys ran short, the exempts seized such as had parents, and the parents, in their despair, attacked the exempts. In such a case parliament interfered and hanged—whom? the exempts? no—the fathers.

7. *THE GAMIN WOULD HAVE HIS PLACE*
IN THE CASTES OF INDIA

THE Parisian gamin almost forms a caste, and we might say that a boy does not become so by wishing. The word *gamin* was printed for the first time, and passed from the populace into literature, in 1834. It made its first appearance in a work called "Claude Gueux"; the scandal was great, but the word has remained.

The elements that constitute the consideration of gamins among one another are very varied. We knew and petted one who was greatly respected and admired because he had seen a man fall off the towers of Notre Dame; another because he had managed to enter the back-yard in which the statues of the dome of the Invalides were temporarily deposited, and filched lead off them; another, because he had seen a diligence upset; another, because he knew a soldier who had all but put out the eye of a civilian.

This explains the exclamation of the Parisian gamin, at which the vulgar laughed without understanding its depth: "Dieu de Dieu! how unlucky I am! just think that I never saw anybody fall from a fifth floor!"

Assuredly it was a neat remark of the peasant's: "Father So-and-so, your wife has died of her illness; why did you not send for a doctor?"—"What would you have, sir? we poor people die of ourselves." But if all the passiveness of the peasant is contained in this remark, all the free-thinking anarchy of the faubourien will be found in the following: A man condemned to death is listening to the confessor in the cart and the child of Paris protests, "He is talking to the skull-cap. Oh, the capon!"

A certain boldness in religious matters elevates the gamin, and it is important for him to be strong-minded.

Being present at executions is a duty with him. He points at the guillotine and laughs at it, and calls it by all sorts of pet names—end of the soup; the grumbler; the sky-blue mother; the last mouthful, etc. In order to lose none of the sight, he climbs up walls, escalades balconies, mounts trees, hangs to gratings, clings to chimney-pots. The gamin is born to be a slater, as he is to be a sailor, and he is no more frightened at a roof than at a mast. No holiday is equal to the Grève, and Samson and the Abbé Montes are the real popular fêtes. The sufferer is hooted to encourage him, and is sometimes admired. Lacenaire, when a gamin, seeing the frightful Dautun die bravely, uttered a remark in which lay a future: "I was jealous of him." In gamindom, Voltaire is unknown, but Papavoine is famous. Politicians and murderers are mingled in the same legend, and traditions exist as to the last garments of all. They know that Tolleron had a night-cap on; Avril a fur cap, Louvel a round hat; that old Delaporte was bald and bareheaded; Castaing rosy-cheeked and good-looking, and that Bories had a romantic beard; Jean Martin kept his braces on, and Lecouffé and his mother abused each other: "Don't quarrel about your basket," a gamin shouted to them. Another little fellow climbed up a lamp-post on the quay, in order to watch Debacker pass; and a gendarme posted there frowned at him. "Let me climb up, M'sieu le Gendarme," and to soften the man in authority, he added: "I shall not fall." "What do I care whether you fall or not?" the gendarme replied.

Among the gamins a memorable accident is highly esteemed and a lad attains the summit of consideration if he gives himself a deep cut "to the bone."

The fist is no small element of success, and one of the things which a gamin is very fond of saying is, "I am precious strong." To be left-handed renders you enviable, while squinting is held in great esteem.

8. *AN ANECDOTE OF THE LAST KING*

In summer the gamin is metamorphosed into a frog, and leaps off the coal-barges and the washerwomen's boats in front of the Jena and Austerlitz bridges into the Seine and into all possible infractions of the laws of decency. Still the police are on the watch, and hence results a highly dramatic situation, which once gave rise to a paternal and memorable cry. This cry, which became celebrated about 1830, is a strategic warning from gamin to gamin; it can be scanned like a verse of Homer, with a notation almost as indescribable as the Eleusiac song of the Panathenæa, in which the ancient Evohé may be traced,—"Ohé, Titi, ohéée, here's the cop, pick up your duds, and be off through the sewer!"

Sometimes this gadfly—that is the name he gives himself—can read, sometimes he can write and draw after a fashion. He does not hesitate to acquire, by some mysterious mutual instruction, all the talents which may be useful to the public cause. From 1815 to 1830 he imitated the cry of a turkey; from 1830 to 1848 he drew a pear upon the walls. One summer evening, Louis Philippe, returning home on foot, saw a very little scamp struggling to raise himself high enough to draw with charcoal a gigantic pear on the pillar of the Neuilly gates, and the king, with that kindness which he inherited from Henry IV, helped the gamin to finish the pear and gave him a louis, saying, "The pear is on that too." The gamin likes a commotion, and any violent condition pleases him. He execrates the curés. One day a young scamp was seen taking a sight at the gate-way of No. 69, Rue de l'Université. "Why are you doing that to that gate?" a passerby asked him; the lad answered, "A curé lives there." The Papal Nuncio, in fact, resided there.

Still, however great the gamin's Voltaireanism may be, if the opportunity is offered him of being a chorister, he may possibly accept, and in that case serves mass gracefully. There are two things of which he is the Tantalus, and which he constantly desires without ever being able to attain them,—to overthrow the government and have his trousers reseated.

The gamin, in a perfect state, is acquainted with all the police of Paris, and when he meets one, can always give a name to his face. He numbers them on his fingers, studies their names, and has his special notes about each. He reads the minds of the police like an open book, and will say curiously and without hesitating,—"So-and-so is a *traitor*, So-and-so is *very wicked*, So-and-so is *great*, So-and-so is *ridiculous*" (the italicized words have all a peculiar meaning in his mouth). This one believes that the Pont Neuf belongs to him, and prevents the *world* from walking on the cornice, outside the parapet; another has a mania for pulling the ears of *persons*, etc., etc.

9. *THE OLD SOUL OF GAUL*

THIS lad may be traced in Poquelin, a son of the Halles, and again in Beaumarchais, for gaminerie is a tinge of the Gallic temper. When blended with common sense, it at times adds strength in the same way as alcohol when mixed with wine; at other times it is a fault. Homer, it is true, repeats himself, and we might say that Voltaire plays the gamin. Camille Desmoulins was a faubourien. Championnet, who abused miracles, issued from the pavement of Paris; when quite a lad, he "inundated the porticoes" of Saint Jean de Beauvais and Saint Etienne du Mont, and was on such familiar terms with the shrine of Saint Geneviève as eventually to give his orders to the vial of St. Januarius.

The Parisian gamin is respectful, ironical, and insolent. He has bad teeth because he is badly fed and his stomach suffers, and fine eyes because he has talent. He would hop up the steps of Paradise in the very presence of Jehovah. He is clever at the savate, and all creeds are possible to him. He plays in the gutter, and draws himself up at the sound of an émeute; his effrontery cannot be subdued by grape-shot; he was a vaga-bond and becomes a hero, and, like the little Theban, he shakes the lion's skin. Barra the drummer was a Parisian gamin; he shouted, "Forward!" as the horse in Scripture says "Ha! Ha!" and in an instant became a giant.

This child of the mud is also the child of the ideal; to see this we need only measure the distance between Molière and Barra.

In a word, the gamin is a being who amuses himself because he is unhappy.

10. *ECCE PARIS, ECCE HOMO*

THE gamin of Paris at the present day, like the Græculus of Rome in former time, is the youthful people with the wrinkle of the Old World on its forehead.

The gamin is a grace for a nation, and at the same time a malady, a malady which must be cured. In what way? By light.

Light is sanitary and illumining.

All the generous social irradiations issue from science, letters, the arts, and instruction. Make men, make men! Enlighten them in order that they may warm you. Sooner or later the splendid question of universal instruction will be asked with the irresistible authority of absolute truth; and then those who govern under the surveillance of French ideas will have to make a choice between children of France and gamins of Paris, between flames in light or will-o'-the-wisps in the darkness.

The gamin expresses Paris, and Paris expresses the world.

For Paris is a total; it is the ceiling of the human race, and the whole of this prodigious city is an epitome of dead manners and living manners. The man who sees Paris imagines that he sees universal history, with sky and constellations in the intervals. Paris has a capital in the Town Hall, a Parthenon in Notre Dame, a Mons Aventinus in the Faubourg St. Antoine, an Asinarium in the Sorbonne, a Pantheon in the Pantheon, a Via Sacra in the Boulevard des Italiens, a Tower of the Winds in public opinion, and ridicule has been substituted for the Gemoniæ. Its *majo* is called the "faraud," its Trasteverino is called the faubourien, its *hammal* the "fort de la Halle," its *lazzarone* the "pegre," and its *cockney* the "gandin." All that is elsewhere is in Paris. Dumarsais' fish-hag can give a reply to the herb-seller of Euripides, Vejanus the discobolus lives again in the rope-dancer Forioso; Therapontiginus Miles could walk arm-in-arm with Grenadier Vadeboncœur; Damasippus the broker would be happy among the dealers in *bric-à-brac;* Vincennes would hold Socrates under lock, just as the Agora would pounce on Diderot; Grimod de la Reynière discovered roast-beef with tallow, in the same way as Curtillus invented roast hedge-hog. We have seen the trapeze of which we read in Plautus re-appear under the balloon of the Arc de l'Etoile; the sword swallower of the Pœcile met by Apuleius, is a swallower of sabers on the Pont Neuf; Rameau's nephew and Curculion the parasite form a pair; Ergasilus would have himself introduced to Cambacérès by d'Aigrefeuille; the four fops of Rome, Alcesimarchus, Phædromus, Dicabolus, and Argiryppus, descend the Courtille in Labatut's post-chaise; Aulus Gellius stopped before Congrio no longer than Charles Nodier did before Punchinello; Marton is not a tigress, but Pardalisca was not a dragon. Pantolabus the jester humbugs Nomentamus, the gourmet, at the café Anglais; Hermogenes is the Tenor in the Champs Elysées, and Thrasius the beggar, dressed as Bobéche, carries round the hat for him; the troublesome fellow who catches hold of your coat-button in the Tuileries makes you repeat after two thousand years the apostrophe of Thesprion,— *Quis properantem me prehendit pallio?* The wine of Suresne is a parody of the wine of Alba; Père Lachaise exhales in the night showers the same gleams as the Esquiliæ; and the poor man's grave bought for five years is quite equal to the hired coffin of the slave.

Seek for anything which Paris has not. The tun of Trophonius contains nothing which is not in Mesmer's trough; Ergaphilas is resuscitated in Cagliostro; the Brahmin Vasaphanta is incarnated in the Count de St. Germain; and the cemetery of Saint Medard performs quite as good miracles as the Oumoumié Mosque at Damascus.

Paris has an Esop in Mayeux, and a Canidia in Mademoiselle Lenormand; it is startled as Delphi was by the flaming realities of the vision; it makes tables turn as Dodona did tripods; it places a grisette upon a throne as Rome placed a courtesan; and, after all, if Louis Quinze is worse than Claudius, Madame Dubarry is better than Messalina. Paris combines in an extraordinary type what is dead and what we have rubbed elbows against,—Greek nudity, the Hebrew ulcer, and Gascon puns. It mixes up Diogenes, Job, and Paillasse, dresses a ghost in old numbers of the *Constitutionnel,* and makes Shadrach a Duclos.

Although Plutarch says that "the tyrant never grows old," Rome, under Sylla as under Domitian, was resigned, and liked to mix water with its wine. The Tiber was a Lethe, if we may believe the somewhat doctrinaire eulogium which Varus Vibiscus made of it: *Contra Gracchos Tiberim habemus. Bibere Tiberim, id est seditionem oblivisci.* Paris drinks a million quarts of water a day, but that does not prevent it from beating the tattoo and ringing the alarm-bell when the opportunity offers.

With this exception, Paris is good-natured; it accepts everything royally; it is not difficult in the matter of its Venus; its Callipyge is a Hottentot; provided that it laughs, it forgives; ugliness amuses it, deformity does it good, and vice distracts it; if you are droll you may be a scoundrel; even hypocrisy, that supreme cynicism, does not revolt it; it is so literary that it does not hold its nose on passing Basile, and is no more scandalized by Tartuffe's prayer than Horace was terrified by the "hiccough" of Priapus. No feature of the human face is wanting in the profile of Paris; the Bal Mabille is not the Polyhymnian dance of the Janiculum, but the hirer out of dresses has her eyes fixed on the Lorette there, exactly as the procuress Staphyla watched the Virgin Planesium. The Barrière du Combat is not a Coliseum, but people are as ferocious there as if Cæsar were looking on. The Syrian hostess has more grace than Mother Saguet, but if Virgil frequented the Roman wine-shop, David of Angers, Balzac, and Charlet have seated themselves in Parisian pot-houses. Paris reigns, geniuses flash in it, and red-tails prosper. Adonaïs passes through it in his twelve-wheeled car of thunder and lightning; and Silenus makes his entrance on his barrel. For Silenus read Ramponneau.

Paris is the synonym of Cosmos; Paris is Athens, Rome, Sybaris, Jerusalem, and Pantin. All civilizations are found there abridged, but so are all barbarisms. Paris would be very sorry not to have a guillotine.

A little of the Place de Grève is useful, for what would this eternal festival be without that seasoning? The laws have wisely provided for that, and, thanks to them, the knife drains drops of blood upon this Mardi Gras.

11. *THE REIGN OF RIDICULE*

THERE are no limits to Paris, and no other city has held this sway which at times derides those whom it holds in subjection. "To please you, O Athenians!" Alexander exclaimed. Paris makes more than the law, for it sets the fashion; and it makes more than fashion, for it produces routine. Paris may be stupid, if it think proper; at times it indulges in that luxury, and then the universe is stupid with it; but Paris soon wakes up, rubs its eyes, says "How stupid I am," and laughs in the face of the human race. What a marvel such a city is! how strange it is to find this grandeur and this buffoonery side by side, to see how all this majesty is not deranged by this parody; and the same mouth to-day blowing the trumpet of the last judgment, and to-morrow a penny whistle! Paris has a sovereign gayety, but the gayety is lightning, and its farce holds a scepter. Its hurricane at times issues from a furnace; its explosions, its days, its masterpieces, its prodigies, its epics, go to the end of the world, and so do its cock-and-bull tales. Its laugh is the crater of a volcano which bespatters the world; and its jokes are sparkles of fire. It imposes upon nations its caricatures as well as its ideal, and the loftiest monuments of human civilization accept its ironies and lend their eternity to its jokes. It is superb; it has a prodigious July 14, which delivers the glove; its night of August 4 dissolves in three hours a thousand years of feudalism; it makes its logic the muscle of the unanimous will; it multiplies itself in every form of sublimity; it fills with its luster Washington, Kosciusco, Bolivar, Botzaris, Riego, Bem, Manin, Lopez, John Brown, and Garibaldi. It is found wherever the future bursts into a flash,—at Boston in 1779, at the Isle of Leon in 1820, at Pesth in 1848, at Palermo in 1860; it whispers the powerful watchword "Liberty" in the ear of the American abolitionists assembled at Harper's Ferry, and in that of the patriots of Ancona assembled in the darkness before the Gozzi inn, on the sea-shore; it creates Canaris, it creates Quiroga, it creates Pisacane, it radiates grandeur upon the earth; it was by going whither its blast impelled him that Byron died at Missolonghi, and Mazet at Barcelona; it is a tribune under the feet of Mirabeau, and a crater under those of Robespierre; its books, plays, art, science, literature, and philosophy are the manuals of the human race; it has Pascal, Regnier, Corneille, Descartes, and Jean Jacques; Voltaire for every moment, Molière for all ages; it makes the universal mouth speak its language, and that language becomes the word; it constructs in every mind the idea of progress; the liberating dogmas which it fuses are the "pistol under the pillow" of generations, and it is with the mind of its thinkers and its poets that all the heroes of all nations have been formed since 1789. Still this does not prevent it from playing the gamin, and the enormous genius which is called Paris, while transfiguring the world with its light, draws Bouginier's nose with charcoal on the wall of the Temple of Theseus, and writes Crédeville Voleur upon the Pyramids.

Paris constantly shows its teeth, and when it is not scolding it is laughing,—such is Paris.

The smoke from its chimneys constitutes the ideas of the universe; it is a pile of mud and stones if you like, but it is, before all, a moral being. It is more than grand, it is immense; and why? Because it dares.

Daring is the price paid for progress.

All sublime contests are more or less the rewards of boldness. For the Revolution to take place, it was not enough that Montesquieu should foresee it, Diderot preach it, Beaumarchais announce it, Condorcet calculate it, Arouet prepare it, and Rousseau premeditate it,—it was necessary that Danton should dare it.

The cry *Audace!* is a *fiat lux*. In order that the human race may progress, it must have proved lessons of courage permanently before it. Rashness dazzles history, and is one of the brightnesses of man. The dawn dares when it breaks. To attempt, to brave, persist, and persevere, to be faithful to one's self, to wrestle with destiny, to astound the catastrophe by the slight fear which it causes us, at one moment to confront unjust power, at another to insult intoxicated victory, to hold firm and withstand—such is the example which people need and which electrifies them. The same formidable flash goes from the torch of Prometheus to the short clay pipe of Cambronne.

12. THE FUTURE LATENT IN THE PEOPLE

As for the Parisian people, even when full grown, it is always the gamin. Depicting the lad is depicting the city, and that is the reason why we have studied the eagle in the sparrow.

The Parisian race, we say again, is found most truly in the Faubourg; there it is pure-blooded, there we find the real physiognomy, there the people work and suffer, and toil and suffering are the two faces of the man. There are immense numbers of strange beings, among whom may be found the wildest type, from the porter of la Râpée to the quarryman of Montfaucon. *Fæx urbis,* Cicero exclaims; *mob,* Burke adds, indignantly; a crowd, a multitude, a population, these words are quickly uttered: but no matter! what do I care that they go about barefoot? They cannot read; all the worse. Will you abandon them on that account? Will you convert their distress into a curse? Cannot light penetrate these masses? Let us revert to that cry of light, and insist upon it. Light, light, who knows whether this opaqueness may not become transparent? for are not revolutions themselves transfigurations? Come, philosophers, teach, enlighten, illumine, think aloud, speak loudly, run joyfully into the sunshine, fraternize with the public places, announce the glad tidings, spread alphabets around, proclaim the right, sing the Marseillaise, sow enthusiasm, and pluck green branches from the oaks. Make a whirlwind of the idea. This crowd may be sublimated, so let us learn how to make use of that vast conflagration of principles and virtues which crackles and bursts into a flame at certain hours. These bare feet, these naked arms, these rags, this ignorance, this abjectness, this darkness, may be employed for the conquest of the ideal. Look through the people, and you will perceive the truth; the vile sand which you trample under foot, when cast into the furnace and melted, will become splendid crystal, and by its aid Galileo and Newton discover stars.

13. *LITTLE GAVROCHE*

Eight or nine years after the events recorded in the second portion of this story, there might be noticed on the Boulevard du Temple and in the regions of the Château d'Eau, a boy about eleven or twelve years of age, who would have tolerably well realized the ideal of a gamin as sketched above, had he not had, with the smile of his age on his lips, a heart absolutely gloomy and void. This child was dressed in a man's trousers, but he had not got them from his father, and a woman's jacket, which did not come from his mother. Some persons had clothed him in rags out of charity. Yet he had a father and a mother, but his father did not think of him, and his mother did not love him.

He was one of those children worthy of pity before all who have father and mother and are orphans.

This child was never so comfortable anywhere as in the street, for the paving-stones were less hard to him than his mother's heart.

His parents had kicked him out into life, and he had simply tried his wings.

He was a noisy, pale, active, sharp, impudent lad, with a cunning and sickly look. He came and went, sang, played at hopscotch, searched the gutters, pilfered a little, but gayly, like cats and sparrows, laughed when he was called a scamp, and felt angry when called a thief.

He had no bed, no bread, no fire, no love; but he was happy because he was free.

When these poor beings are men the mill of social order nearly always crushes them, but so long as they are children they escape because they are small. The slightest hole saves them.

Still, so abandoned as this child was, it happened every two or three months that he said, "Well, I'll go and see mamma." Then he quitted the Boulevard, the Circus, the Porte St. Martin, went along the quay, crossed the bridge, reached the Salpetrière, and arrived—where? Exactly at that double No. 50-52, which the reader knows, the Maison Gorbeau.

At this period No. 50-52, which was habitually deserted and eternally decorated with a bill of "Lodgings to Let," was, strange to say, inhabited by several persons who had no acquaintance with each other, as is always the case in Paris. All belonged to that indigent class which begins with the last small tradesman in difficulties, and is prolonged from wretchedness to wretchedness to those two beings to whom all material things of civilization descend, the scavenger and the ragpicker.

The chief lodger of Jean Valjean's day was dead, and her place had been taken by another exactly like her. I forget now what philosopher said, "There is never any want of old women."

This new old woman was called Madame Burgon, and had nothing remarkable in her life save a dynasty of three parrots, which had successively reigned over her soul.

The most wretched of all persons inhabiting the house were a family of four persons, father, mother, and two nearly grown-up daughters, all four living in the same attic, one of the cells to which we have alluded.

This family offered at the first glance nothing very peculiar beyond its destitution; and the father, on hiring the room, stated that his name was Jondrette. A short time after he moved in, which had borne a striking resemblance—to employ the memorable remark of the chief lodger—to the coming in of nothing at all, this Jondrette had said to the woman, who, like her predecessor, was also portress and swept the stairs, "Mother So-and-so, if any one were to ask by chance for a Pole or an Italian, or perhaps a Spaniard, I am the party."

This was the family of the merry little vagabond. He joined it, and found distress, and, what is sadder still, not a smile: a cold hearth and cold heart. When he entered, they asked him, "Where do you come from?" and he answered "From the street"; when he went away, "Where are you going?" and he answered, "To the street." His mother would say to him, "What do you want here?"

The boy lived in this absence of affection like the pale grass which grows in cellars. He was not hurt by it being so, and was not angry with any one; he did not know exactly how a father and mother ought to be.

Moreover, his mother loved his sisters.

We have forgotten to mention that on the boulevard the lad was called Little Gavroche. Why was he called Gavroche?

Probably because his father's name was Jondrette.

Breaking the thread seems the instinct of some wretched families.

The room which the Jondrettes occupied at the Maison Gorbeau was the last in the passage, and the cell next to it was occupied by a very poor young man of the name of Monsieur Marius.

Let us state who this Monsieur Marius was.

BOOK II

LE GRAND BOURGEOIS

1. *NINETY YEARS OLD, AND TWO-AND-THIRTY TEETH*

THERE are still a few persons residing in the Rue Boucherat, Rue de Normandie, and Rue de Saintonge, who can remember a gentleman of the name of M. Gillenormand, and speak kindly about him; he was old when they were young. This dim figure has not entirely disappeared, with those who look sadly at the vague congregation of shadows called the past, from the labyrinth of streets near the Temple, which in the reign of Louis XIV received the names of all the provinces of France, exactly in the same way as in our time the names of all the capitals of Europe have been given to the streets in the new Tivoli quarter; a progression, by the bye, in which progress is visible.

M. Gillenormand, who was most lively in 1831, was one of those men who have become curious to look on, solely because they have lived a long time, and are strange, because they once resembled every body and now no longer resemble any one. He was a peculiar old man, and most certainly the man of another age, the true complete bourgeois, rather haughty, of the eighteenth century, who carried his honest old bourgeoisie with the same air as marquises did their marquisate. He had passed his ninetieth year, walked upright, talked loudly, saw clearly, drank heartily, and ate, slept, and snored. He still had his two-and-thirty teeth, and only wore spectacles to read with. He was of an amorous temper, but said for the last ten years he had decidedly and entirely given up the sex. "He could not please," he said; and he did not add "I am too old," but "I am too poor. If I were not ruined—he, hé, he!" In fact, all that was left him was an income of about fifteen thousand francs. His dream was to drop into a large inheritance, and have one hundred thousand francs a year, in order to keep mistresses. As we see, he did not belong to that weak variety of octogenarians who, like M. de Voltaire, were dying all their life; his longevity was not that of a cracked jug, and this jolly old gentleman had constantly enjoyed good health. He was superficial, rapidly and easily angered, and he would storm at the slightest thing, most usually an absurd trifle. When he was contradicted, he raised his cane and thrashed his people, as folks used to do in the great age. He had a daughter upward of fifty years of age and unmarried, whom he gave a hearty thrashing to when he was in a passion, and whom he would have liked to whip, for he still fancied her eight years of age. He boxed his servant's ears energetically, and would say, "Ah, carrion!" One of his oaths was, "By the *pantoufloche* of the *pantouflochade!*" His tranquillity was curious; he was shaved every morning by a barber who had been mad and who detested him, for he was jealous of M. Gillenormand on account of his wife, who was a pretty little coquette. M. Gillenormand admired his own discernment in everything, and declared himself extremely sagacious. Here is one of his remarks: "I have, in truth, some penetration. I am able to say, when a flea bites me, from what woman I caught it." The words he employed most frequently were "the sensitive man" and "nature," but he did not give to the latter word the vast acceptation of our age. But there was a certain amount of homeliness in his satirical remarks. "Nature," he would say, "anxious that civilization may have a little of everything, even gives it specimens of amusing barbarism. Europe has specimens of Asia and Africa, in a reduced size; the cat is a drawing-room tiger, the lizard a pocket crocodile. The ballet girls at the opera are pink savagesses; they do not eat men, but they live on them; the little magicians change them into oysters and swallow them. The Caribs only leave the bones, and they only leave the shells. Such are our manners; we do not devour, but we nibble; we do not exterminate, but we scratch."

2 . *LIKE MASTER LIKE HOUSE*

HE lived in the Marais, at No. 6, Rue des Filles du Calvaire, and the house belonged to him. This house has since been pulled down and rebuilt, and the number has probably been changed in the numbering revolutions which the streets of Paris undergo. He occupied an old and vast suite of rooms on the first floor, furnished up to the ceiling with large Gobelins and Beauvais tapestry representing shepherd scenes; the subjects of the ceiling and panels were repeated in miniature upon the chairs. He surrounded his bed with an immense screen of Coromandel lacquer-work; long curtains hung from the windows and made very splendid, large, broken folds. The garden immediately under the windows was reached by a flight of twelve or fifteen steps running from one of them, which the old gentleman went up and down very nimbly. In addition to a library adjoining his bedroom, he had a boudoir which he was very fond of, a gallant withdrawing-room, hung with a magnificent fleur-de-lised tapestry, made in the galleys of Louis XIV, which M. de Vivonne had ordered of his convicts for his mistress. M. Gillenormand inherited this from a stern maternal great-aunt who died at the age of one hundred. He had had two wives. His manners were midway between those of the courtier which he had never been, and of the barrister which he might have been. He was gay and pleasing when he liked; in his youth he had been one of those men who are always deceived by their wives and never by their mistresses, because they are at once the most disagreeable husbands and the most charming lovers imaginable. He was a connoisseur of pictures, and had in his bedroom a marvelous portrait of somebody unknown, painted by Jordaens with bold sweeps of the brush, and with an infinitude of details. M. Gillenormand's coat was not in the style of Louis

29

XV or even Louis XVI, but it was in the style of the Incroyables of the Directory. He had believed himself quite a youth at that time, and followed the fashions. His coat was of light cloth with large flaps, with a long swallow-tail and large steel buttons. Add to these knee-breeches and buckle-shoes. He always had his hands in his fobs, and said authoritatively, "The French Revolution is a collection of ragamuffins."

3. *LUKE ESPRIT*

AT the age of sixteen, when at the opera one night, he had the honor of being examined simultaneously by two beauties at that time celebrated and sung by Voltaire—la Camargo and la Salle. Caught between two fires, he beat a heroic retreat upon a little dancing-girl of the name of Nahenry, sixteen years of age, like himself, obscure as a cat, of whom he was enamored. He abounded in recollections, and would exclaim, "How pretty that Guimard-Guimardini-Guimardinette was, the last time I saw her at Longchamps, with her hair dressed in 'sustained feelings,' her 'come and see them' of turquoises, her dress of the color of 'newly arrived people,' and her muff of 'agitation'." He had worn in his youth a jacket of Nain-Lóndrin, to which he was fond of alluding: "I was dressed like a Turk of the Levantine Levant." Madame Boufflers, seeing him accidentally when he was twenty years of age, declared him to be "a charming madcap." He was scandalized at all the names he saw in politics and power, and considered them low and bourgeois. He read the journals, the *newspapers,* the *gazettes,* as he called them, and burst into a laugh. "Oh!" he would say, "who are these people? Corbière! Humann! Casimir Périer! there's a ministry for you! I can imagine this in a paper, M. Gillenormand, minister; it would be a farce, but they are so stupid that it might easily happen." He lightly called everything by its proper or improper name, and was not checked by the presence of ladies; and he uttered coarseness, obscenity, and filth with a peculiarly calm and slightly amazed accent in which was elegance. That was the fashion, the careless way of his age, for we may draw attention to the fact that the season of paraphrases in verse was that of crudities in prose. His grandfather had predicted that he would be a man of genius, and gave him the two significant Christian names Luke Esprit.

4. AN ASPIRING CENTENARIAN

HE gained prizes in his youth at the college of Moulins, in which town he was born, and was crowned by the hand of the Duc de Nivernais, whom he called the Duc de Nevers. Neither the convention, the death of Louis XVI, Napoleon, nor the return of the Bourbons had effaced the recollection of this coronation. The Duc de Nevers was to him the grand figure of the age. "What a charming nobleman," he would say, "and how well his blue ribbon became him!" In the eyes of M. Gillenormand, Catherine II repaired the crime of the division of Poland by purchasing of Bestucheff, for three thousand roubles, the secret of the elixir of gold, and on this point he would grow animated. "The elixir of gold!" he would exclaim. "Bestucheff's yellow tincture and the drops of General Lamotte were, in the eighteenth century, at one louis the half-ounce bottle, the grand remedy for love catastrophes, the panacea against Venus. Louis XV sent two hundred bottles of it to the Pope." He would have been greatly exasperated had he been told that the gold elixir is nothing but perchloride of iron. M. Gillenormand adored the Bourbons, and held 1789 in horror; he incessantly described in what way he had escaped during the reign of terror, and how he had been obliged to display great gayety and wit in order not to have his head cut off. If any young man dared in his presence to praise the republic, he turned blue and grew so angry as almost to faint. Sometimes he alluded to his ninety years, and said, "I trust that I shall not see '93 twice." At other times, though, he informed persons that he intended to live to be a hundred.

5 . *BASQUE AND NICOLETTE*

HE had his theories; here is one of them: "When a man passionately loves women, and himself has a wife for whom he cares little, for she is ugly, legitimate, full of her rights, reliant on the code, and jealous when she likes to be so, he has only one way of getting out of the hobble and living at peace,—it is to leave his purse-strings to his wife. This abdication renders him free; the wife is henceforth occupied, grows passionately fond of handling specie, verdigrises her fingers, undertakes to instruct the peasants and train the farmers, harangues the notaries, visits their officers, follows the course of lawsuits, draws up leases, dictates contracts, feels herself queen-like, sells, buys, regulates, orders, promises and compromises, yields, concedes and recedes, arranges, deranges, saves and squanders; she commits follies, which is a supreme and personal happiness, and that consoles her. While her husband despises her, she has the satisfaction of ruining her husband." This theory M. Gillenormand applied to himself, and it became his history. His wife, the second one, managed his fortune in such a manner that one fine day when he found himself a widower he had just enough to live on by buying an annuity, three-fourths of which would expire with him. He had not hesitated, for he did not care much about leaving anything to his heir, and besides, he had seen that patrimonies had their adventures, and, for instance, became "national property"; he had seen the avatars of the three per cent. consols, and put but little faith in the great book. "All this is Rue Quincampoix!" he would say. His house in the Rue des Filles du Calvaire belonged, as we stated, to him, and he had two servants, "a he and a she." When a servant came into his house M. Gillenormand rechristened him and gave the men the name of their province, Nîmois, Comtois, Poitevin, or Picard. His last valet was a fat, cunning man of fifty-five, incapable of running twenty yards, but, as he was born at Bayonne, M. Gillenormand called him Basque. As for the maid-servants, he called them all Nicolette (even la Magnon, to whom we shall allude directly). One day a proud cook, a Cordon Bleu, of the lofty porter race, presented herself. "What wages do you expect a month?" M. Gillenormand asked her. "Thirty francs." "What is your name?" "Olympie." "I will give you forty and call you Nicolette."

6. A GLIMPSE AT MAGNON AND HER LITTLE ONES

IN Gillenormand sorrow was translated into passion; he was furious at being in despair. He had every prejudice and took every license. One of the things of which he composed his external relief and internal satisfaction was, as we have indicated, having remained a gay fellow, and passing energetically for such. He called this having a "royal renown," but this royal renown at times brought him singular presents. One day a big baby, wrapped in rags and crying lustily, was brought to him in a basket, which a maid-servant, discharged six months previously, attributed to him. M. Gillenormand was at that time past his eighty-fourth year, and people around him became indignant and clamorous. "Does the impudent wench expect to make anybody believe this? What audacity! what an abominable calumny!" M. Gillenormand, however, did not feel at all angry. He looked at the brat with the amiable smile of a man flattered by the calumny, and said to the company, "Well, what is the matter? Is there anything so wonderful in it, that you should stand there like stuck pigs and display your ignorance? M. le Duc d'Angoulême, bastard of his Majesty Charles IX, married at the age of eighty-five a girl of fifteen; Monsieur Virginal, Marquis d'Alleuze, and brother of Cardinal de Sourdis, archbishop of Bordeaux, had, at the age of eighty-three, by the lady's maid of Madame Jacquin, the president's wife, a genuine love-child, who was a Knight of Malta and member of the Privy Council. One of the great men of this age, Abbé Tabaraud, is the son of a man of eighty-seven years of age. These things are common enough; and then take the Bible! After this, I declare that this little gentleman is none of mine, but take care of him, for it is not his fault." The creature, the aforesaid Magnon, sent him a second parcel the next year, also a boy, and M. Gillenormand thought it time to capitulate. He sent the two brats to their mother, agreeing to pay eighty francs a month for their support, but on condition that the mother was not to begin again. He added, "I expect that the mother will treat them well, and I shall go and see them now and then," which he did. He had a brother, a priest, who was for three-and-thirty years rector of the Poitiers academy, and died at the age of seventy-nine. "I lost him when quite young," he would say. This brother, who is not much remembered, was a great miser, who, as he was a priest, thought himself bound to give alms to the poor he met, but he never gave them aught but bad or called-in money, thus finding means of going to Hades by the road to Paradise. As for M. Gillenormand the elder, he gave alms readily and handsomely; he was benevolent, brusque, and charitable, and had he been rich his declining years would have been magnificent. He liked everything that concerned him to be done grandly; even when he was swindled one day, having been plundered in the matter of an inheritance by a man of business in a clumsy and evident way, he made the solemn remark, "Sir, that was done very awkwardly, and I feel ashamed of such clumsiness. Everything has degenerated in this age, even the swindlers. Morbleu! a man of my stamp ought not to be robbed in that way; I was plundered as if I were in a wood, but clumsily plundered, *sylvæ sint consule dignæ!*" He had married twice, as we said; by his first wife he had a girl, who did not marry, and by the second another girl who died at the age of thirty, and who married through love, or chance, or otherwise, a soldier of fortune who had served in the armies of the republic and the empire, won the cross at Austerlitz and his colonel's commission at Waterloo. "He is the disgrace of my family," the old gentleman used to say. He took a great deal of snuff, and had a peculiarly graceful way of shaking his shirt-frill with the back of his hand. He believed very little in God.

7. RULE: NEVER RECEIVE EXCEPT IN THE EVENING

SUCH was M. Luke Esprit Gillenormand, who had not lost his hair, which was rather gray than white, and always wore it in dog's-ears. Altogether he was venerable. He was a man of the eighteenth century, frivolous and grand.

In 1814 and the early years of the Restoration, M. Gillenormand, who was still a youth,—he was only seventy-four,—resided in the Rue Sirvandoni, near St. Sulpice, Faubourg St. Germain. He only retired to the Marais on leaving society; that is to say, long after the eightieth year.

On leaving the world he immured himself in his habits; the chief one, and in that he was invariable, was to keep his door closed by day and receive nobody, no matter the nature of his business, till night. He dined at five and then his door was thrown open; it was the fashion of his century, and he did not like to give it up. "Day is low," he would say, "and only deserved closed shutters." People of fashion light up their wit when the zenith illumines its stars; and he barricaded himself against everybody, even had it been the king,—such was the old fashionable style of his day.

8. *TWO DO NOT MAKE A PAIR*

As for M. Gillenormand's two daughters, they were born at an interval of ten years. In their youth they had been very little alike, and both in character and face were as little sisters as was possible. The younger was a charming creature, who turned to the light, loved flowers, poetry, and music, was enthusiastic, ethereal, and mentally betrothed from her youth up to some heroic figure. The elder had a chimera too; she saw in the azure an army-contractor, some fat and very rich man, a splendidly stupid husband, a million converted into a man or else a prefect, the receptions at the prefecture, and the usher in the anteroom with a chain round his neck, the official balls, the addresses at the mansion-house to be "Madame la Préfète,"—all this buzzed in her imagination. The two sisters wandered each in her own reverie at the period when they were girls, and both had wings,—the one those of an angel, the other those of a goose.

No ambition is fully realized, at least not in this nether world, and no paradise becomes earthly in our age. The younger married the man of her dreams, but she was dead, while the elder did not marry.

At the period when she enters into our narrative she was an old virtue, an incombustible prude, with one of the most acute noses and most obtuse intellects imaginable. It is a characteristic fact that beyond her family no one had ever known her familiar name; she was called Mademoiselle Gillenormand the elder.

In the matter of cant, Mademoiselle Gillenormand could have given points to a Miss, and she was modesty carried to the verge of blackness. She had one frightful reminiscence in her life—one day a man saw her garter.

Age had only heightened this pitiless modesty,—her chemisette was never sufficiently opaque, and never was high enough. She multiplied brooches and pins at places where no one dreamed of looking. The peculiarity of prudery is to station the more sentries the less the fortress is menaced.

Still, let who will explain these old mysteries of innocence, she allowed herself to be kissed without displeasure by an officer in the Lancers, who was her grand nephew, and Théodule by name.

In spite of this favored Lancer, however, the ticket of "Prude" which we have set upon her suited her exactly. Mademoiselle Gillenormand's was a species of twilight soul, and prudery is a semi-virtue and a semi-vice.

She added to prudery the congenial lining of bigotry; she belonged to the Sisterhood of the Virgin, wore a white veil on certain saints' days, muttered special orisons, revered "the holy blood," venerated "the sacred heart," remained for hours in contemplation before a rococo-Jesuit altar in a closed chapel, and allowed her soul to soar among the little marble clouds and through the large beams of gilt wood.

She had a chapel friend, an old maid like herself, of the name of Mlle. Vaubois, absolutely imbecile, and by whose side Mlle. Gillenormand had the pleasure of being an eagle. Beyond Agnus Deis and Ave Marias, Mlle. Vaubois knew nothing except the different ways of making preserves. Perfect of her genius, she was the ermine of stupidity without a single spot of intelligence.

We must add that Mlle. Gillenormand, as is the case with passive natures, rather gained than lost by growing old. She had never been wicked, which is a relative goodness; and, then, years abrade angles. The softening influence of time had touched her. She had an obscure melancholy of which she did not herself possess the secret, and about her entire person there was the stupor of a finished life which has not begun.

She kept house for her father; such families, consisting of an old man and an old maid, are not rare, and have the ever-touching appearance of two weaknesses supporting each other.

There was also in this house a child, a little boy, who was always trembling and dumb in the old gentleman's presence. M. Gillenormand never spoke to this boy except with a stern voice, and at times with upraised cane. "Come here, sir,—scamp, scoundrel, come here,—answer me, fellow,—Let me see you, vagabond!" etc., etc. He adored him.

It was his grandson, and we shall meet him again.

BOOK III

GRANDFATHER AND GRANDSON

1 . *AN OLD DRAWING-ROOM*

WHEN M. Gillenormand lived in the Rue Sirvandoni, he frequented several very good and highly noble salons. Although a bourgeois, M. Gillenormand was welcome in them, and as he had a twofold stock of wit, namely, that which he had and that attributed to him, he was sought after and made much of. There are some people who desire influence and to be talked about, no matter what price they pay; and when they cannot be oracles they make themselves buffoons. M. Gillenormand was not of that nature; and his domination in the royalist drawing-rooms which he frequented did not cost him any of his self-respect. He was an oracle everywhere, and at times he held his own against M. de Bonald, and even M. Bengy-Puy-Vallée.

About 1817, he invariably spent two afternoons a week at the house of the Baronne de T. . . . , a worthy and respectable person, whose husband had been under Louis XVI ambassador to Berlin. The Baron de T. . . . , who, when alive, was passionately devoted to magnetic ecstasies and visions, died abroad a ruined man, leaving as his sole fortune ten MS. volumes bound in red morocco and gilt-edged, which contained very curious memoirs about Mesmer and his trough. Madame de T. . . . did not publish these memoirs through dignity, and lived on a small annuity which had escaped no one knew how. Madame de T. . . . lived away from court, "which was a very mixed society," as she said, in noble, proud and poor isolation. Some friends collected twice a week round her widow's fire, and this constituted a pure royalist salon. Tea was drunk, and people uttered there, according as the wind blew to elegiacs or dithyrambics, groans or cries of horror, about the age, the charter, the Bonapartists, the prostitution of the Blue Ribbon to untitled persons, and the Jacobinism of Louis XVIII; and they also whispered about the hopes which monsieur, afterward Charles X, produced.

Low songs, in which Napoleon was called Nicholas, were greeted here with transports of delight. Duchesses, the most charming and delicate of ladies, went into ecstasies there about couplets like the following, which were addressed to the "Federals":

> *"Renfoncez dans vos culottes*
> *Le bout d'chemis' qui vous pend.*
> *Qu'on n' dis pas qu'les patriotes*
> *Ont arboré l'drapeau blanc!"*

They amused themselves with puns which they fancied tremendous, with innocent jokes which they supposed venomous, with quatrains and even distichs; here is one on the Dessolles Ministry, the moderate cabinet of which MM. Decazes and Deserre formed part:

> *"Pour raffermir le trone ébranlé sur sa base,*
> *Il faut changer de sol, et de serre et de case";*

or else they played upon the list of the House of Peers, "An abominably Jacobin chamber," and combined names on this list so as to form, for instance, phrases like the following: "Damas, Sabran, Gouvion de St. Cyr."

In this society the Revolution was parodied, and they had some desire to sharpen the same passions in the contrary sense, and sang their *ça ira.*

> *"Ah! ça ira! ça ira! ça ira!*
> *Les Buonapartist' à la lanterne!"*

Songs are like the guillotine,—they cut off indiscriminately to-day this head, and to-morrow that. It is only a variation.

In the Fualdès affair, which belongs to this period, 1816, they sided with Bastide and Jausion, because Fualdès was a "Bonapartist." They called the Liberals "friends and brothers," and that was the last degree of insult.

Like some church-steeples, the salon of the Baronne de T. . . . had two cocks; one was M. Gillenormand, the other Comte de Lamothe Valois, of whom they whispered with a species of respect, "You know? the Lamothe of the necklace business,"—parties have these singular amnesties.

Let us add this: in the bourgeoisie, honored situations are lessened by too facile relations, and care must be taken as to who is admitted. In the same as there is a loss of caloric in the vicinity of cold persons, there is a diminution of respect on the approach of despised persons. The old high society held itself above this law, as above all others; Marigny, brother of the Pompadour, visited the Prince de Soubise, not although, but because he was her brother. Du Barry, godfather of the Vaubrenier, is most welcome at the house of the Maréchal de Richelieu. That world is Olympus, and Mercury and the Prince de Guéménée are at home in it. A robber is admitted to it, provided he be a god.

The Comte de Lamothe, who, in 1815, was seventy-five years of age, had nothing remarkable about him beyond his silent and sententious air, his angular and cold face, his perfectly polite manners, his coat buttoned up to the chin, and his constantly crossed legs, covered with trousers of the color of burnt sienna. His face was the same color as his trousers.

This M. de Lamothe was esteemed in this salon on account of his "celebrity," and, strange to say, but true, on account of his name of Valois.

As for M. Gillenormand, the respect felt for him was of perfectly good alloy. He was an authority; in spite of his levity, he had a certain imposing worthy, honest, and haughty manner which did not at all injure his gayety, and his great age added to it. A man is not a century with impunity, and years eventually form a venerable fence around a head.

He made remarks, too, which had all the sparkle of the old régime. Thus, when the king of Prussia, after restoring Louis XVIII, paid him a visit under the name of the Comte de Ruppin, he was received by the descendant of Louis XIV somewhat as if he were Marquis de Brandebourg, and with the most delicate impertinence. M. Gillenormand approved of it. "All kings who are not king of France," he said, "are provincial kings." One day the following question was asked, and answer given in his presence: "What has been done about the editor of the *Courrier Français?*" "He is to be changed." "There's a *c* too much," M. Gillenormand dryly observed.

At an anniversary Te Deum for the return of the Bourbons, on seeing M. de Talleyrand pass, he said: "There's his excellency, the Evil."

M. Gillenormand was generally accompanied by his daughter, a tall young lady, who at that time was forty and looked fifty; and by a pretty boy nine years of age, red and white, fresh, with happy, confident eyes, who never appeared in this drawing-room without hearing all the voices buzz around him,—"How pretty he is! what a pity! poor boy!" This lad was the one to whom we referred just now, and he was called "poor boy" because he had for father "a brigand of the Loire."

This brigand was that son-in-law of M. Gillenormand who has already been mentioned, and whom the old gentleman called the "disgrace of his family."

2. *A RED SPECTER OF THAT DAY*

ANY one who had passed at that period through the little town of Vernon and walked on the handsome stone bridge, which let us hope, will soon be succeeded by some hideous wire bridge, would have noticed, on looking over the parapet, a man of about fifty, wearing a leathern cap and trousers and jacket of coarse gray cloth to which something yellow, which had been a red ribbon, was sewn, with a face tanned by the sun and almost black, and hair almost white, with a large scar on his forehead and running down his cheek, bowed and prematurely aged, walking almost every day, spade and pick in hand, in one of the walled inclosures near the bridge which border, like a belt of terraces, the left bank of the Seine. There are delicious inclosures full of flowers, of which you might say, were they much larger, "they are gardens," and if they were a little smaller, "they are bouquets." All these inclosures join the river at one end and a house at the other. The man in the jacket and wooden shoes, to whom we have alluded, occupied in 1817 the narrowest of these inclosures and the smallest of these houses. He lived there alone and solitary, silently and poorly, with a woman who was neither young nor old, neither pretty nor ugly, neither peasant nor bourgeoise, who waited on him. The square of land which he called his garden was celebrated in the town for the beauty of the flowers he cultivated, and they were his occupation.

Through his toil, perseverance, attention, and watering-pot, he had succeeded in creating after the Creator; and he had invented sundry tulips and dahlias which seemed to have been forgotten by nature. He was ingenious, and preceded Soulange Bodin in the formation of small patches of peat-soil for the growth of the rare and precious shrubs of America and China. From daybreak in summer he was in his walks, pricking out, clipping, hoeing, watering, or moving among his flowers, with an air of kindness, sorrow, and gentleness. At times he would stand thoughtful and motionless for hours, listening to the song of a bird in a tree, the prattle of a child in a house, or else gazing at a drop of dew on a blade of grass, which the sun converted into a carbuncle. He lived very poorly, and drank more milk than wine; a child made him give way, and his servant scolded him. He was timid to such an extent that he seemed stern, went out rarely, and saw no one but the poor who tapped at his window, and his curé, Abbé Mabœuf, a good old man. Still, if the inhabitants of the town or strangers, curious to see his roses or tulips, came and tapped at his little door, he opened it with a smile. He was the brigand of the Loire.

Any one who at the same time read military Memoirs and Biographies, the *Moniteur,* and the bulletins of the great army, might have been struck by a name which pretty often turns up, that of George Pontmercy. When quite a lad this Pontmercy was a private in the Saintonge regiment, and when the Revolution broke out this regiment formed part of the army of the Rhine, for the regiments of the monarchy kept their provincial names even after the fall of the monarchy, and were not brigaded till 1794. Pontmercy fought at Spires, Worms, Neustadt, Turkheim, Alzey, and at Mayence, where he was one of the two hundred who formed Houchard's rear-guard. He, with eleven others, held out against the corps of the Prince of Hesse behind the old rampart of Andernach, and did not fall back on the main body until the enemy's guns had opened a breach from the parapet to the talus. He was under Kleber at Marchiennes, and at the fight of Mont Palissel, where his arm was broken by a rifle-ball; then he went to the frontier of Italy, and was one of the thirty who defended the Col de Tenda with Joubert. Joubert was appointed adjutant-general, and Pontmercy sub-lieutenant; he was by Berthier's side in the middle of the musketry on that day of Lodi which made Bonaparte say, "Berthier was gunner, trooper, and grenadier."

He saw his own general Joubert fall at Novi at the moment when he was shouting, with uplifted saber, "Forward!" Having embarked with

45

his company on board a cutter which sailed from Genoa to some little port of the coast, he fell into a wasps' nest of seven or eight English sail. The Genoese commandant wished to throw his guns into the sea, hide the soldiers in the hold, and pass like a merchant vessel, but Pontmercy had the tricolor flag hoisted at the peak, and proudly passed under the guns of the British frigates. Twenty leagues further on, his audacity increasing, he attacked and captured a large English transport conveying troops to Sicily, and so laden with men and horses that the vessel's deck was almost flush with the sea. In 1805 he belonged to Malher's division, which took Günzburg from the Archduke Ferdinand, and at Wettingen he caught in his arms, amid a shower of bullets, Colonel Maupetit, who was mortally wounded at the head of the 9th Dragoons. He distinguished himself at Austerlitz in that admirable march in columns of companies performed under the enemy's fire; and when the Russian Imperial Horse Guards destroyed one of the battalions of the 4th line Infantry, Pontmercy was among those who took their revenge and drove back these Guards. For this the emperor gave him a cross. Pontmercy saw in turn Wurmser made prisoner at Mantua, Mélas at Alessandria, and Mack at Ulm, and he belonged to the eighth corps of the grand army which Mortier commanded, and which took Hamburg. Then he joined the 55th regiment of the line, which was the old regiment of Flanders; at Eylau, he was in the cemetery where the heroic Captain Louis Hugo, uncle of the author of this book, withstood with his company of eighty-three men, for two hours, the whole effort of the enemy's army. Pontmercy was one of the three who left this cemetery alive. He was at Friedland; then he saw Moscow, the Beresina, Lutzen, Bautzen, Dresden, Wachau, Leipsic, and the defiles of Gelenhausen; then at Montmirail, Chateau-Thierry, Craon, the banks of the Marne, the banks of the Aisne, and the formidable position of Laon. At Arnay le Duc, as captain, he sabered ten Cossacks, and saved not his general, but his corporal; he was cut to pieces on this occasion, and seven-and-twenty splinters were taken out of his left arm alone. Eight days before the capitulation of Paris he exchanged with a comrade and entered the cavalry; for he had what was called under the old régime a "double hand," that is to say, an equal aptitude in handling, as private, a saber or musket, as officer, a squadron or a company. From this aptitude, improved by military education, special arms sprang; for instance, the dragoons, who are at once cavalry and infantry. He accompanied Napoleon to Elba, and at Waterloo was a major of the cuirassiers in Dubois' brigade. It was he who took the colors of the Limburg battalion, and himself threw them at the emperor's feet. He was covered with blood, for, on seizing the colors, he received a saber cut across the face. The emperor, who was pleased, cried out to him, "You are a colonel, a baron, and officer of the Legion of Honor!" Pontmercy answered, "Sire, I thank you on behalf of my widow." An hour later he fell into the ravine of Ohain. And now who was this George Pontmercy? He was the same brigand of the Loire.

We have already seen some portion of his history. After Waterloo, Pontmercy, drawn, as we remember, out of the hollow way of Ohain, succeeded in rejoining the army, and dragged himself from ambulance to ambulance as far as the cantonments of the Loire.

The Restoration put him on half-pay, and then sent him to Vernon under honorable surveillance. King Louis XVIII, regarding all that was done in the Hundred Days as if it had not happened, recognized neither his quality as officer of the Legion of Honor, nor his commission as colonel, nor his title as baron. He for his part neglected no opportunity to sign himself "Colonel Baron de Pontmercy." He had only one old blue coat, and never went out without attaching to it the rosette of the Legion of Honor. The king's attorney advised him that he would be tried for illegally wearing this decoration, and when this hint was given him by an officious intermediator, Pontmercy replied, with a bitter smile, "I do not know whether it is that I no longer understand French, or whether you are not speaking it but the fact remains the same—I do not understand you." Then he went out for eight days in succession with his rosette, and the authorities did not venture to interfere with him. Twice or thrice the minister of war or the general commanding the department wrote to him with the following superscription: "M. le Commandant Pontmercy," and he sent back the letters unopened. At the same moment Napoleon at St. Helena was treating in the same fashion the missives of Sir Hudson Lowe, addressed to "General Bonaparte." If we may be forgiven the remark, Pontmercy finished by having the same saliva in his mouth as the emperor.

There were also at Rome Carthaginian prisoners who refused to salute Flaminius, and had a little of Hannibal's soul in them.

One morning he met the king's attorney in a street of Vernon, went up to him, and said, "Monsieur le Procureur du Roi, am I allowed to wear my scar?"

He had nothing but his scanty half-pay as major, and he had taken the smallest house in Vernon, where he lived alone, in what way we have just seen. Under the empire and between two wars he found time to marry Mlle. Gillenormand. The old bourgeois, who was indignant in his heart, concluded with a sigh and saying, "The greatest families are forced into it." In 1815, Madame Pontmercy, a most admirable woman in every respect, and worthy of her husband, died, leaving a child. This child would have been the colonel's delight in his solitude, but the grandfather imperiously claimed him, declaring that if he were not given up to him he would disinherit him. The father yielded for the sake of the little one, and, unable to love his son, he took to loving flowers.

He had, however, given up everything, and did not join the opposition or conspire. He shared his thoughts between the innocent things he did and the great things he had done, and he spent his time in hoping for a carnation or calling to mind Austerlitz.

M. Gillenormand kept up no relations with his son-in-law; the colonel was to him a "bandit," and he was for the colonel an "ass." M. Gillenormand never spoke about the colonel, except at times to make mocking allusions to "his barony." It was expressly stipulated that Pontmercy should never attempt to see his son or speak to him, under penalty of having him thrown on his hands disinherited. To the Gillenormands, Pontmercy was a plague patent, and they intended to bring up the child after their fashion. The colonel perhaps did wrong in accepting these terms, but he endured them in the belief that he was acting rightly and only sacrificing himself.

The inheritance of the grandfather was a small matter, but that of Mlle. Gillenormand the elder was considerable, for this aunt was very rich on her mother's side, and her sister's son was her natural heir. The boy, who was called Marius, knew that he had a father, but nothing more, and no one opened his lips to him on the subject. Still, in the society to which his grandfather took him, the whisperings and winks eventually produced light in the boy's mind; he understood something at last, and, as he naturally accepted, by a species of infiltration and slow penetration, the ideas and opinions which were, so to speak, his breathing medium, he gradually came to think of his father only with shame.

While he was thus growing up in this way, the colonel every two or three months came furtively to Paris, like a convict who is breaking his ban, and posted himself at St. Sulpice at the hour when Aunt Gillenormand took Marius to mass. Trembling lest the aunt should turn round, concealed behind a pillar, motionless, and scarce daring to breathe, he looked at this boy. The scarred warrior was frightened at this old maid.

From this very circumstance emanated his friendship with the Abbé Mabœuf, curé of Vernon.

This worthy priest had a brother, churchwarden of St. Sulpice, who had several times noticed this man contemplating his child, and the scar on his cheek, and the heavy tear in his eye. This man, who looked so thoroughly a man and who wept like a child, struck the churchwarden, and this face adhered to his memory. One day when he went to Vernon to see his brother, he met on the bridge Colonel Pontmercy, and recognized this man of St. Sulpice. The churchwarden told the affair to the curé, and both made some excuse to pay a visit to the colonel. This visit led to others, and the colonel, though at first very close, eventually opened his heart, and the curé and the churchwarden learned the whole story, and how Pontmercy sacrificed his own happiness to the future of his child. The result was that the curé felt a veneration and tenderness for him, and the colonel, on his side, took the curé into his affection. By the way, when both are equally sincere and good, no men amalgamate more easily than an old priest and an old soldier, for they are the same men at the bottom. One devotes himself to his country down here, the other to his country up there; that is the sole difference.

Twice a year, on January 1 and St. George's day, Marius wrote his father letters dictated by his aunt, and which looked as if copied from a hand-book, for that was all M. Gillenormand tolerated; and the father sent very affectionate replies, which the grandfather thrust into his pocket without reading.

3. REQUIESCANT!

THE salon of Madame de T. was all that Marius Pontmercy knew of
the world, and it was the sole opening by which he could look out into
life. This opening was gloomy, and more cold than heat, more night
than day, reached him through this trap. This boy, who was all joy and
light on entering the strange world, became thus, in a short time, sad,
and, what is more contrary still to his age, serious. Surrounded by all
these imposing and singular persons, he looked about him with serious
astonishment, and all contributed to augment his stupor. There were in
Madame de T.'s drawing-room old, noble, and very venerable ladies, who
called themselves Mathan, Noé, Levis, pronounced Levi, and Cambis,
pronounced Cambyse. These ancient faces and these biblical names were
mingled in the boy's mind with his Old Testament, which he learned
by heart; and when they were all present, seated in a circle round an
expiring fire, scarce illumined by a green-shaded lamp, with their severe
faces, their gray or white hair, their long dresses of another age, in which
only mournful colors could be seen, and uttering at lengthened intervals
words at once majestic and stern, little Marius regarded them with wondering eyes and fancied that he saw not women, but patriarchs and Magi,
—not real beings, but ghosts.

With these ghosts were mingled several priests, habitués of this old
salon, and a few gentlemen, the Marquis de Sass. . . . , secretary to
Madame de Berry; the Vicomte de Val. . . . , who published odes under
the pseudonym of Charles Antoine; the Prince de Beauff. . . . , who,
though still young, had a gray head and a pretty, clever wife, whose dress
of scarlet velvet, with gold embroidery, cut very low in the neck, startled
this gloom; the Marquis de C. . . . , d'E. . . . , the Frenchman who

was most acquainted with "graduated politeness"; the Comte d'Am...., a gentleman with a benevolent chin; and the Chevalier de Port de Guy, the pillar of the library of the Louvre, called the King's Cabinet. M. de Port de Guy, bald and rather aging than old, used to tell how, in 1793, when he was sixteen years of age, he was placed in the hulks as refractory, and chained to an octogenarian, the bishop of Mirepoix, also a refractory, but as priest, while he was so as soldier. It was at Toulon, and their duty was to go at night to collect on the scaffold the heads and bodies of persons guillotined during the day. They carried these dripping trunks on their backs, and their red jackets had behind the nape of the neck a crust of blood which was dry in the morning and moist at night. These tragical narratives abounded in the salon of Madame de T., and through cursing Marat they came to applaud Trestaillon. A few deputies of the "introuvable" sort played their rubber of whist there; for instance, M. Thibord du Chalard, M. Lemarchant de Gomicourt, and the celebrated jester of the right division, M. Cornet Dincourt. The Bailli de Ferrette, with his knee-breeches and thin legs, at times passed through this room when proceeding to M. de Talleyrand's; he had been a companion of the Comte d'Artois, and, acting in the opposite way to Aristotle crouching under Campaspe, he had made the Guimard crawl on all fours, and thus displayed to ages a philosopher avenged by a Bailli.

As for the priests there was the Abbé Halma, the same to whom M. Larose, his fellow-contributer on *la Foudre,* said, "Stuff, who is not fifty years of age? a few hobble-de-hoys, perhaps." Then came the Abbé Letourneur, preacher to the king; the Abbé Frayssinous, who at that time was neither bishop, count, minister, nor peer, and who wore a soutane from which buttons were absent, and the Abbé Keravenant, curé of St. Germain des Prés. To them must be added the Papal Nuncio, at that date Monsignore Macchi, archbishop of Nisibis, afterward cardinal, and remarkable for his long pensive nose; and another monsignore, whose titles ran as follows: Abbate Palmieri, domestic prelate, one of the seven acting prothonotaries of the holy see, canon of the glorious Liberian Basilica, and advocate of the saints, *postulatore di Santi*—an office relating to matters of canonization, and meaning, very nearly, referendary to the department of Paradise. Finally, there were two cardinals, M. de la Luzerne and M. de Cl. ... T..... The Cardinal de la Luzerne was an author, and was destined to have the honor a few years later of signing articles in the *Conservateur* side by side with Chateaubriand, while M. de Cl. ... T.... was archbishop of Toulouse, and frequently spent the summer in Paris with his nephew, the Marquis de T. . . . , who had been minister of the navy and of war. This cardinal was a merry little old gentleman who displayed his red stockings under his ragged cassock. His specialty was hating the encyclopedia and playing madly at billiards; and persons who on summer evenings passed along the Rue M. . . . , where the Marquis de T. . . . resided, stopped to listen to the sound of the balls and the sharp voice of the cardinal crying to his conclavist Monseigneur Cottret, bishop *in partibus* of Caryste, "Mark me a carom, abbé." The Cardinal de C. . . . T. . . . had been introduced to Madame de T. . . . by his most intimate friend, M. de Roquelaure, ex-bishop of Senlis and one of the Forty. M. de Roquelaure was remarkable for his great height and his assiduity at the Academy. Through the glass door of the room adjoining the library, in which the French Academy at that time met, curious persons could contemplate every Thursday the ex-bishop of Senlis, usually standing with hair freshly powdered, in violet stockings, and turning his back to the door, apparently to display his little collar the better. All these ecclesiastics, although mostly courtiers as much as churchmen, added to the gravity of the salon, to which five peers of France, the Marquis de Vib. . . . , the Marquis de Tal. . . . , the Marquis d'Herb. . . . , the Vicomte Damb. . . . , and the Duc de Val. . . . , imparted the lordly tone. This Duc de Val. . . . , though Prince de Monaco, that is to say, a foreign sovereign prince, had so lofty an idea of France and the peerage that he looked at everything through them. It was he who said, "The cardinals are the peers of France of Rome, and the lords are the peers of France of England." Still, as in the present age the Revolution must be everywhere, this feudal salon was ruled, as we have seen, by M. Gillenormand, a bourgeois.

It was the essence and quintessence of white Parisian society, and reputations, even royalist ones, were kept in quarantine there, for there is always anarchy in reputation. Had Chateaubriand come in he would have produced the effect of Père Duchesne. Some converts, however, entered this orthodox society through a spirit of toleration. Thus the Comte de Beug. . . . was admitted for the purpose of correction.

The "noble" salons of the present day in no way resemble the one which I am describing, for the royalists of to-day, let us say it in their praise, are demagogues.

At Madame de T.'s the society was superior, and the taste exquisite and haughty beneath a grand bloom of politeness. The habits there displayed all sorts of involuntary refinement, which was the ancient régime itself, which lived though interred. Some of these habits, especially in conversation, seemed whimsical, and superficial persons would have taken for provincialism what was merely antiquated. They called a lady "Madame la Générale," and "Madame la Colonelle" had not entirely been laid aside. The charming Madame de Léon, doubtless remembering the Duchesses de Longueville and de Chevreuse, preferred that appellation to her title of princess, and the Marquise de Créquy was also called "Madame la Colonelle."

It was this small high society which invented at the Tuileries the refinement of always speaking to the king in the third person, and never saying "Your majesty," as that qualification had been "sullied by the usurper."

Facts and men were judged there, and the age was ridiculed—which saved the trouble of comprehending it. They assisted one another in amazement, and communicated mutually the amount of enlightenment they possessed. Methusalem instructed Epimenides, and the deaf man put the blind man straight. The time which had elapsed since Coblenz was declared not to have passed, and in the same way as Louis XVIII was *Dei gratia* in the twenty-fifth year of his reign, the *emigrés* were *de jure* in the twenty-fifth year of their adolescence.

Everything harmonized here: no one was too lively, the speech was like a breath, and the newspapers, in accordance with the salon, seemed a papyrus. The liveries in the ante-room were old, and these personages who had completely passed away were served by footmen of the same character. All this had the air of having lived a long time and obstinately struggling against the tomb. To conserve, conservation, conservative, represented nearly their entire dictionary, and the question was "to be in good odor." There were really aromatics in the opinions of these venerable groups, and their ideas smelt of vervain. It was a mummy world, in which the masters were embalmed and the servants stuffed.

A worthy old marchioness, ruined by the emigration, who had only one woman-servant left, continued to say, "My people."

What did they do in Madame de T.'s salon? They were ultra.

This remark, though what it represents has possibly not disappeared, has no meaning at the present day, so let us explain it.

To be ultra is going beyond; it is attacking the specter in the name of the throne, and the miter in the name of the altar; it is mismanaging the affair you have in hand; it is kicking over the traces; it is quarreling with the stake as to the degree of cooking which heretics should undergo; it is reproaching the idol for its want of idolatry; it is insulting through excess of respect; it is finding in the pope insufficient papism, in the king too little royalty, and too much light in the night; it is being dissatisfied with alabaster, snow, the swan, and the lily, on behalf of whiteness; it is being a partisan of things to such a pitch that you become their enemy; it is being so strong for, that you become against.

The ultra spirit specially characterizes the first phase of the Restoration.

Nothing in history ever resembled that quarter of an hour which begins in 1814 and terminates in 1820, with the accession of M. de Villèle, the practical man of the Right. These six years were an extraordinary moment, at once noisy and silent and gloomy, enlightened, as it were, by a beam of dawn, and covered at the same time by the darkness of the great catastrophe which still filled the horizon and was slowly sinking into the past. There was in this light and this shadow an old society and a new society, buffoon and melancholy, juvenile and senile, and rubbing its eyes, for nothing is so like a re-awakening as a return. There were groups that regarded France angrily and which France regarded ironically; the streets full of honest old marquis-owls, "ci-devants," stupefied by everything; brave and noble gentlemen smiling at being in France and also weeping at it, ravished at seeing their country again and in despair at not finding their monarchy; the nobility of the crusades spitting on the nobility of the empire, that is to say, of the sword; historic races that had lost all feeling of history, the sons of the companions of Charlemagne disdaining the companions of Napoleon. The swords, as we have said, hurled insults at one another: the sword of Fontenoy was ridiculous, and only a bar of rusty iron; the sword of Marengo was odious, and only a saber. The olden times misunderstood yesterday, and no one had a feeling of what is great or what is ridiculous. Some one was found to call Bonaparte Scapin. This world no longer exists, and nothing connected with it, let us repeat, remains at the present day. When we draw out of it some figure hap-hazard, and try to bring it to bear again mentally, it seems to us as strange as the antediluvian world, and in fact it was also swallowed up by a deluge and disappeared under two revolutions. What waves ideas are! how quickly do they cover whatever they have a mission to destroy and bury, and how promptly do they produce unknown depths!

Such was the physiognomy of the salon in those distant and candid days when M. Martainville had more wit than Voltaire.

These salons had a literature and politics of their own: people in them believed in Fiévée, and M. Agier laid down the law there. M. Colnet, the publisher and bookseller of the Quai Malaquais, was commented on, and Napoleon was fully the ogre of Corsica there. At a later date the introduction into history of the Marquis de Buonaparté, lieutenant-general of the armies of the king, was a concession to the spirit of the age.

These salons did not long remain pure, and in 1818 a few doctrinaires, a very alarming tinge, began to culminate in them. In matters of which the ultras were very proud, the doctrinaires were somewhat ashamed; they had wit, they had silence, their political dogma was properly starched with hauteur, and they must succeed. They carried white neckcloths and buttoned coats to an excessive length, though it was useful. The fault or misfortune of the doctrinaire party was in creating old youth: they assumed the posture of sages and dreamed of grafting a temperate power upon the absolute and excessive principle. They opposed, and at times with rare sense, demolishing liberalism by conservative liberalism, and they might be heard saying, "Have mercy on royalism, for it has rendered more than one service. It brought back traditions, worship, religion, and respect. It is faithful, true, chivalrous, loving, and devoted, and has blended, though reluctantly, the secular grandeurs of the monarchy with the new grandeurs of the nation. It is wrong in not understanding the Revolution, the empire, glory, liberty, young ideas, young generations, and the age,—but do we not sometimes act quite as wrongly against it? The Revolution of which we are the heirs ought to be on good terms with everything. Attacking the royalists is the contrary of liberalism; what a fault and what blindness! Revolutionary France fails in its respect to historic France, that is to say, to its mother, to itself. After September 5 the nobility of the monarchy were treated like the nobility of the empire after July 8; they were unjust to the eagle and we are unjust to the *fleur-de-lis*. There must be, then, always something to proscribe! is it very useful to ungild the crown of Louis XIV and scratch off the escutcheon of Henry IV? We sneer at M. de Vaublanc, who effaced the N's from the bridge of Jena, but he only did what we are doing. Bouvines belongs to us as much as Marengo, and the *fleurs-de-lis* are ours like the N's. They constitute our patrimony; then why should we diminish it? The country must be no more denied in the past than in the present; why should we not have a grudge with the whole of history? why should we not love the whole of France?"

It was thus that the doctrinaires criticised and protected the royalists, who were dissatisfied at being criticised, and furious at being protected.

The ultras marked the first epoch of the Revolution, and the congregation characterized the second; skill succeeded impetuosity. Let us close our sketch at this point.

In the course of his narrative, the author of this book found on his road this curious moment of contemporary history, and thought himself bound to take a passing glance at it and retrace some of the singular features of this society which is unknown at the present day. But he has done so rapidly, and without any bitter or derisive idea, for affectionate and respectful reminiscences connected with his mother attach him to this past. Moreover, let him add, this little world had a grandeur of its own, and though we may smile at it we cannot despise or hate it. It was the France of other days.

Marius Pontmercy, like most children, received some sort of education. When he left the hands of Aunt Gillenormand, his grandfather intrusted him to a worthy professor of the finest classical innocence. This young mind, just expanding, passed from a prude to a pedant.

Marius spent some years at college and then joined the law-school; he was a royalist, fanatic, and austere. He loved but little his grandfather, whose gayety and cynicism ruffled him, and he was gloomy as regarded his father.

In other respects, he was an ardent yet cold, noble, generous, proud, religious, and exalted youth: worthy almost to harshness, and fierce almost to savageness.

4. *THE END OF THE BRIGAND*

THE conclusion of Marius's classical studies coincided with M. Gillenormand's retirement from society; the old gentleman bade farewell to the Faubourg St. Germain and Madame de T.'s drawing-room, and withdrew to his house in the Marais. His servants were, in addition to the porter, that Nicolette who succeeded Magnon, and that wheezing, short-winded Basque to whom we have already alluded.

In 1827 Marius attained his seventeenth year; on coming home one evening, he saw his grandfather holding a letter in his hand.

"Marius," said M. Gillenormand, "you will start tomorrow for Vernon."

"What for?" Marius asked.

"To see your father."

Marius trembled, for he had thought of everything excepting this, that he might one day be obliged to see his father. Nothing could be more unexpected, more surprising, and, let us add, more disagreeable for him. It was estrangement forced into approximation, and it was not an annoyance so much as a drudgery.

Marius, in addition to his motives of political antipathy, was convinced that his father, the trooper, as M. Gillenormand called him in his good-tempered days, did not love him; that was evident, as he had abandoned him thus and left him to others. Not feeling himself beloved, he did not love: and he said to himself that nothing could be more simple.

He was so stupefied that he did not question his grandfather, but M. Gillenormand continued:

"It seems that he is ill, and asks for you."

And after a silence he added:

"Start to-morrow morning. I believe there is a coach which leaves at six o'clock and gets to Vernon at nightfall. Go by it, for he says that the matter presses."

Then he crumpled up the letter and put it in his pocket. Marius could have started the same night and have been with his father the next morning; a diligence at that time used to run at night to Rouen, passing through Vernon. But neither M. Gillenormand nor Marius dreamed of inquiring.

On the evening of the following day Marius arrived at Vernon and asked the first passer-by for the house of "Monsieur Pontmercy." For in his mind he was of the same opinion as the Restoration, and did not recognize either his father's barony or colonelcy.

The house was shown him; he rang, and a woman holding a small hand-lamp opened the door for him.

"Monsieur Pontmercy?" Marius asked.

The woman stood motionless.

"Is this his house?" Marius continued.

The woman nodded her head in the affirmative.

"Can I speak to him?"

The woman made a negative sign.

"Why, I am his son," Marius added; "and he expects me."

"He no longer expects you," the woman said.

Then he noticed that she was crying.

She pointed to the door of a parlor, and he went in.

In this room, which was lighted by a tallow candle placed on the mantel-piece, there were three men, one standing, one on his knees, and one lying full length upon the floor in his shirt. The one on the floor was the colonel; the other two were a physician and a priest praying.

The colonel had been attacked by a brain fever three days before, and, having a foreboding of evil, he wrote to M. Gillenormand, asking for his son. The illness grew worse, and on the evening of Marius's arrival at Vernon the colonel had an attack of delirium. He leaped out of bed, in spite of the maid-servant, crying, "My son does not arrive, I will go to meet him." Then he left his bedroom and fell on the floor of the ante-room;—he had just expired.

The physician and the curé were sent for, but both arrived too late; the son too had also arrived too late.

By the twilight gleam of the candle, a heavy tear, which had fallen from the colonel's dead eye, could be noticed on his pallid cheek. The eye was lusterless, but the tear had not dried up. This tear was his son's delay.

Marius gazed upon this man whom he saw for the first time and the last, upon this venerable and manly face, these open eyes which no longer saw, this white hair, and the robust limbs upon which could be distinguished here and there brown lines, which were saber cuts, and red stars, which were bullet holes. He gazed at the gigantic scar which imprinted heroism on this face, upon which God had imprinted gentleness. He thought that this man was his father, and that this man was dead, and he remained cold.

The sorrow he felt was such as he would have felt in the presence of any other man whom he might have seen lying dead before him.

Mourning and lamentation were in this room. The maid-servant was weeping in a corner, the priest was praying, and could be heard sobbing, the physician wiped his eyes, and the corpse itself wept.

The physician, priest, and woman looked at Marius through their affliction without saying a word, for he was the stranger. Marius, who was so little affected, felt ashamed and embarrassed at his attitude, and he let the hat which he held in his hand fall on the ground, in order to induce a belief that sorrow deprived him of the strength to hold it.

At the same time he felt a species of remorse, and despised himself for acting thus. But was it his fault? he had no cause to love his father.

The colonel left nothing, and the sale of the furniture scarce covered the funeral expenses.

The maid-servant found a scrap of paper, which she handed to Marius. On it were the following lines, written by the colonel:

"For my son: The emperor made me a baron on the field of Waterloo, and as the Restoration contests this title, which I purchased with my blood, my son will assume it and wear it. Of course he will be worthy of it."

On the back the colonel had added:

"At this same battle of Waterloo a sergeant saved my life; his name is Thénardier, and I believe that he has recently kept a small inn, in a village near Paris, either Chelles or Montfermeil. If my son meet this Thénardier he will do all he can for him."

Not through any affection for his father, but owing to that vague respect for death which is ever so imperious in the heart of man, Marius took the paper and put it away.

Nothing was left of the colonel. M. Gillenormand had his sword and uniform sold to the Jews; the neighbors plundered the garden and carried off the rare flowers, while the others became brambles and died.

Marius only remained forty-eight hours in Vernon. After the funeral he returned to Paris and his legal studies, thinking no more of his father than if he had never existed. In two days the colonel was buried, and in three forgotten.

Marius had a crape on his hat, and that was all.

5 . MARIUS MEETS A CHURCHWARDEN

MARIUS had retained the religious habits of his childhood. One Sunday, when he went to hear mass at St. Sulpice, in the same Lady's chapel to which his aunt took him when a boy, being on that day more than usually absent and thoughtful, he placed himself behind a pillar, and knelt, without paying attention to the fact, upon a Utrecht velvet chair, on the back of which was written, "Monsieur Mabœuf, Churchwarden." The mass had scarce begun when an old gentleman presented himself and said to Marius:

"This is my place, sir."

Marius at once stepped aside, and the old gentleman took his seat.

When mass was ended Marius stood pensively for a few moments till the old gentleman came up to him and said:

"I ask your pardon, sir, for having disturbed you just now, and for troubling you afresh at this moment, but you must have considered me ill-bred, and so I wish to explain the matter to you."

"It is unnecessary, sir," said Marius.

"No, it is not," the old man continued, "for I do not wish you to have a bad opinion of me. I am attached to this seat, and it seems to me that the mass is better here, and I will tell you my reason. To this spot I saw during ten years, at regular intervals of two or three months, a poor worthy father come, who had no other opportunity of or way of seeing his son, because they were separated through family arrangements. He came at the hour when he knew that his son would be brought to mass. The boy did not suspect that his father was here—perhaps did not know, the innocent, that he had a father. The latter kept behind a pillar so that he might not be seen, looked at his child and wept; for the poor man

60

adored him, as I could see. This spot has become, so to speak, sanctified for me, and I have fallen into the habit of hearing mass here. I prefer it to the bench to which I should have a right as churchwarden. I even knew the unfortunate gentleman slightly. He had a father-in-law, a rich aunt, and other relatives, who threatened to disinherit the boy if the father ever saw him, and he sacrificed himself that his son might one day be rich and happy. They were separated through political opinions, and though I certainly approve of political opinions, there are persons who do not know where to stop. Good gracious! because a man was at Waterloo he is not a monster; a father should not be separated from his child on that account. He was one of Bonaparte's colonels, and is dead, I believe. He lived at Vernon, where I have a brother who is curé, and his name was something like Pontmarie, Montpercy—he had, on my word, a splendid saber cut."

"Pontmercy," Marius said, turning pale.

"Precisely, Pontmercy; did you know him?"

"He was my father, sir."

The old churchwarden clasped his hands and exclaimed:

"Ah! you are the boy! Yes, yes, he would be a man now. Well, poor boy, you may say that you had a father who loved you dearly."

Marius offered his arm to the old gentleman, and conducted him to his house.

The next day he said to M. Gillenormand:

"Some friends of mine have arranged a shooting party; will you allow me to go away for three days?"

"Four," the grandfather answered, "go and amuse yourself."

He whispered to his daughter with a wink:

"Some love affair."

6. THE RESULT OF MEETING A CHURCHWARDEN

WHERE Marius went we shall learn presently.

He was away three days, then returned to Paris, went straight to the Library of the Law-School, and asked for a file of the *Moniteur*.

He read it, he read all the histories of the republic and the empire; the Memorial of St. Helena, all the memoirs, journals, bulletins, and procla-mations—he fairly devoured them. The first time he came across his father's name in a bulletin of the grand army, he had a fever for a whole week. He called upon the generals under whom George Pontmercy had served; among others, Count H. . . . . The churchwarden, whom he saw again, told him of the life at Vernon, the colonel's retirement, his flowers, and his solitude. Marius had at last a perfect knowledge of this rare, sublime, and gentle man, this·species of lion-lamb—who had been his father.

While occupied with this study, which filled all his moments as well as his thoughts, he scarce ever saw the Gillenormands. He appeared at meals, but when sought for after them he could not be found. His aunt sulked, but old Gillenormand smiled. "Stuff, stuff, it is the right age." At times the old man would add, "Confound it, I thought that it was an affair of gallantry, but it seems that it is a passion."

It was a passion, in truth, for Marius was beginning to adore his father.

At the same time an extraordinary change took place in his ideas, and the phases of this change were numerous and successive. As this is the history of many minds in our day, we deem it useful to follow these phases step by step, and indicate them all.

The history he had just read startled him, and the first effect was bedazzlement.

The republic, the empire, had hitherto been to him but monstrous words,—the republic a guillotine in the twilight; the empire a saber in the night. He had looked into it, and where he had only expected to find a chaos of darkness he had seen, with a species of extraordinary surprise mingled with fear and delight, stars flashing,—Mirabeau, Vergniaud, St. Just, Robespierre, Camille Desmoulins, and Danton,—and a sun rise, Napoleon. He knew not where he was, and he recoiled, blinded by the brilliancy. Gradually, when the first surprise had worn off, he accustomed himself to this radiance. He regarded the deed without dizziness, and examined persons without terror; the Revolution and the empire stood out in luminous perspective before his visionary eyeballs; he saw each of these two groups of events and facts contained in two enormous facts— the Revolution in the sovereignty of civic right restored to the masses, the empire in the sovereignty of the French idea imposed on Europe; he saw the great figure of the people emerge from the Revolution, the great figure of France from the empire, and he declared to himself on his conscience that all this was good.

What his bedazzlement neglected in this first appreciation, which was far too synthetical, we do not think it necessary to indicate here. We are describing the state of a mind advancing, and all progress is not made in one march. This said, once for all, as to what precedes and what is to follow, we will continue.

He then perceived that up to this moment he had no more understood his country than he did his father. He had known neither the one nor the other, and he had spread a species of voluntary night over his eyes. He now saw, and on one side he admired, on the other he adored.

He was full of regret and remorse, and he thought with despair that he could only tell to a tomb all that he had in his mind. Oh, if his father were alive, if he had him still, if God in his compassion and his goodness had allowed this father to be still alive, how he would have flown, how he would have cried to his father: "Father, here I am, it is I! I have the same heart as you! I am your son!" How he would have kissed his white head, bathed his hair with his tears, gazed at his scar, pressed his hand, adored his clothes and embraced his feet! Oh, why did this father die so soon, before justice had been done him, before he had known his son's love? Marius had a constant sob in his heart, which said at every moment, "Alas!" At the same time he became more truly serious, more truly grave, more sure of his faith and his thoughts. At each instant beams of light arrived to complete his reason, and a species of internal growth went on within him. He felt a natural aggrandizement produced by the two things so new to him—his father and his country.

As a door can be easily opened when we hold the key, he explained to himself what he had hated, and understood what he had abhorred. Henceforth he saw clearly the providential, divine, and human meaning, the great things which he had been taught to detest, and the great men whom he had been instructed to curse. When he thought of his previous opinions, which were but of yesterday, and which yet seemed to him so old, he felt indignant and smiled.

From the rehabilitation of his father he had naturally passed to that of Napoleon, but the latter, we must say, was not effected without labor.

From childhood he had been imbued with the judgments of the party of 1814 about Bonaparte; now all the prejudices of the Restoration, all its interests and all its instincts, tended to disfigure Napoleon, and it execrated him even more than Robespierre. It had worked rather cleverly upon the weariness of the nation and the hatred of mothers. Bonaparte had become a species of almost fabulous monster, and in order to depict him to the imagination of the people, which, as we said just now, resembles that of children, the party of 1814 brought forward in turn all the frightful masques, from that which is terrible while remaining grand, down to that which is terrible while becoming grotesque, from Tiberius down to old Boguey. Hence, in speaking of Bonaparte, people were at liberty to sob or burst with laughter, provided that hatred sung the bass. Marius had never had on the subject of—that man, as he was called—any other ideas but these in his mind, and they were combined with his natural tenacity. He was a headstrong little man, who hated Napoleon.

On reading history, on studying, before all, documents and materials, the veil which hid Napoleon from Marius's sight was gradually rent asunder, he caught a glimpse of something immense, and suspected that up to this moment he had been mistaken about Bonaparte, as about all the rest; each day he saw more clearly, and he began climbing slowly, step by step, at the beginning almost reluctantly, but then with intoxication, and as if attracted by an irresistible fascination, first, the gloomy steps, then the dimly lighted steps, and at last the luminous and splendid steps of enthusiasm.

One night he was alone in his little garret, his candle was lighted, and he was reading at a table by the open window. All sorts of reveries reached him from the space and were mingled with his thoughts. What a spectacle is night! We hear dull sounds and know not whence they come; we see Jupiter, which is twelve hundred times larger than the earth, glowing like a fire-ball; the blue is black, the stars sparkle, and the whole forms a formidable sight.

He was reading the bulletins of the grand army, those Homeric strophes written on the battle-field; he saw in them at intervals the image of his father, and ever that of the emperor; the whole of the great empire was before him; he felt, as it were, a tide within him swelling and mounting; it seemed at moments as if his father passed close to him like a breath, and whispered in his ear; strange feelings gradually came over him; he fancied he could hear drums, cannon, and bugles, the measured tread of the battalions and the hollow distant gallop of the cavalry; from time to time his eyes were raised and surveyed the colossal constellations flashing in the profundities, and then they fell again upon the book, and he saw in that other colossal things stirring confusedly. His heart was contracted, he was transported, trembling and gasping; and all alone, without knowing what was within him or what he obeyed, he rose, stretched his arms out of the window, looked fixedly at the shadow, the silence, the dark infinitude, the eternal immensity, and shouted, "Long live the emperor!"

From this moment it was all over. The ogre of Corsica, the usurper, the tyrant, the monster, who was the lover of his own sisters, the actor who took lessons of Talma, the poisoner of Jaffa, the tiger, Bonaparte,—all this faded away and made room in his mind for a radiance in which the pale marble phantom of Cæsar stood out serenely at an inaccessible height. The emperor had never been to his father more than the beloved captain whom a man admires and for whom he devotes himself, but to Marius he was far more. He was the predestined constructor of the French group which succeeded the Roman group in the dominion of the universe; he was the prodigious architect of an earthquake, the successor of Charlemagne, Louis XI, Henry IV, Richelieu, Louis XIV, and the committee of public safety; he had doubtless his spots, his faults, and even his crimes; that is to say, he was a man, but he was august in his faults, brilliant in his spots, and powerful in his crime.

He was the predestined man who compelled all nations to say,—The great nation. He was even more, he was the very incarnation of France, conquering Europe by the sword he held, and the world by the luster which he emitted. Marius saw in Bonaparte the dazzling specter which will ever stand on the frontier and guard the future. He was a despot, but a dictator,—a despot resulting from a republic and completing revolution.

Napoleon became for him the man-people, as the Saviour is the man-God.

As we see, after the fashion of all new converts to religion, his conversion intoxicated him, and he dashed into faith and went too far. His nature was so; once upon an incline, it was impossible to check himself. Fanaticism for the swords seized upon him, and complicated in his mind the enthusiasm for the idea; he did not perceive that he admired force as well as genius; that is to say, filled up the two shrines of his idolatry, —on one side that which is divine, on the other that which is brutal. He also deceived himself on several other points, though in a different way; he admitted everything. There is a way of encountering error by going to meet truth, and by a sort of violent good faith which accepts everything unconditionally. Upon the new path he had entered, while judging the wrongs of the ancient régime and measuring the glory of Napoleon, he neglected attenuating circumstances.

However this might be, a prodigious step was made; where he had once seen the downfall of monarchy he now saw the accession of France. The points of his moral compass were changed, and what had once been sunset was now sunrise.

All these revolutions took place in turns, without his family suspecting it.

When, in this mysterious labor, he had entirely lost his old Bourbonic and ultra skin, when he had pulled off the aristocrat, the Jacobite, and the royalist, when he was a perfect revolutionist, profoundly democratic, and almost republican, he went to an engraver's and ordered one hundred cards, with the address, "Baron Marius Pontmercy."

This was but the logical consequence of the change which had taken place in him, a change in which everything gravitated round his father.

Still, as he knew nobody and could not leave his cards at any porter's lodge, he put them in his pocket.

By another natural consequence, in proportion as he drew nearer to his father, his memory, and the things for which the colonel had fought during five-and-twenty years, he drew away from his grandfather. As we said, M. Gillenormand's humor had not suited him for a long time past, and there already existed between them all the dissonances produced by the contact of a grave young man with a frivolous old man. The gayety of Géronte offends and exasperates the melancholy of Werther. So long as the same political opinions and ideas had been common to them, Marius met his grandfather upon them as on a bridge, but when the bridge fell there was a great gulf between them; and then, before all else, Marius had indescribable attacks of revolt when he reflected that it was M. Gillenormand, who, through stupid motives, pitilessly tore him from the colonel, thus depriving father of son and son of father.

Through his reverence for his father, Marius had almost grown into an aversion for his grandfather.

Nothing of this, however, was revealed in his demeanor; he merely became colder than before, laconic at meals, and rarely at home. When his aunt scolded him for it he was very gentle, and alleged as excuse his studies, examinations, conferences, etc. The grandfather, however, still adhered to his infallible diagnostic.—"He is in love; I know the symptoms."

Marius was absent every now and then.

"Where can he go?" the aunt asked.

In one of his trips, which were always very short, he went to Montfermeil in order to obey his father's intimation, and sought for the ex-sergeant of Waterloo, Thénardier, the landlord. Thénardier had failed, the public-house was shut up, and no one knew what had become of him. In making this search Marius remained away for four days.

"He is decidedly getting out of order," said the grandfather.

They also fancied they could notice that he wore under his shirt something fastened round his neck by a black ribbon.

7. SOME PETTICOAT

WE have alluded to a lancer.

He was a great-grand-nephew of M. Gillenormand's, on the father's side, who led a garrison life, far away from the domestic hearth. Lieutenant Théodule Gillenormand fulfilled all the conditions required for a man to be a pretty officer; he had a young lady's waist, a victorious way of clanking his victorious saber, and turned-up mustaches. He came very rarely to Paris, so rarely that Marius had never seen him, and the two cousins only knew each other by name. Théodule was, we think we said, the favorite of Aunt Gillenormand, who preferred him because she never saw him; for not seeing people allows of every possible perfection being attributed to them.

One morning Mlle. Gillenormand the elder returned to her apartments as much affected as her general placidity would allow. Marius had again asked his grandfather's permission to make a short trip, adding that he wished to start that same evening. "Go," the grandfather answered; and he added to himself, as he pursed up his eye, "Another relapse of sleeping from home." Mlle. Gillenormand went up to her room greatly puzzled, and cast to the staircase this exclamation, "It's too much!" and this question, "But where is it that he goes?" She caught a glimpse of some more or less illicit love adventure, of a woman in the shadow, a meeting, a mystery, and would not have felt vexed to have a closer peep at it through her spectacles. Scenting a mystery is like the first bite at a piece of scandal, and holy souls do not detest it. In the secret compartments of bigotry there is some curiosity for scandal.

She was, therefore, suffering from a vague appetite to learn a story.

In order to distract this curiosity, which agitated her a little beyond her wont, she took refuge in her talents, and began festooning with cotton upon cotton one of those embroideries of the empire and the Restoration, in which there are a great many cabriolet wheels. It was a clumsy job, and the workwoman was awkward. She had been sitting over it for some hours when the door opened. Mlle. Gillenormand raised her nose, and saw Lieutenant Théodule before her making his regulation salute. She uttered a cry of delight; for a woman may be old, a prude, devout, and an aunt, but she is always glad to see a lancer enter her room.

"You here, Théodule!" she exclaimed.

"In passing, my dear aunt."

"Well, kiss me."

"There," said Théodule, as he kissed her. Aunt Gillenormand walked to her secretaire and opened it. "You will stop the week out?"

"My dear aunt, I am off again to-night."

"Impossible!"

"Mathematically."

"Stay, my dear Théodule, I beg of you."

"The heart says Yes, but duty says No. The story is very simple; we are changing garrison; we were at Melun and are sent to Gaillon. In order to go to the new garrison we were obliged to pass through Paris, and I said to myself, 'I will go and see my aunt'."

"And here's for your trouble."

And she slipped ten louis into his hand.

"You mean to say for my pleasure, dear aunt."

Théodule kissed her a second time, and she had the pleasure of having her neck slightly grazed by his gold-laced collar.

"Are you traveling on horseback with your regiment?"

"No, my aunt; I have come to see you by special permission. My servant is leading my horse, and I shall travel by the diligence. By the way, there is one thing I want to ask you."

"What is it?"

"It appears that my cousin Marius Pontmercy is going on a journey, too."

"How do you know that?" the aunt said, her curiosity being greatly tickled.

"On reaching Paris I went to the coach-office to take my place in the coupé."

"Well?"

"A traveler had already taken a seat in the Impériale, and I saw his name in the way-bill; it was Marius Pontmercy."

"Oh, the scamp," the aunt exclaimed. "Ah! your cousin is not a steady lad like you. To think that he is going to pass the night in a diligence!"

"Like myself."

"You do it through duty, but he does it through disorder."

"The deuce!" said Théodule.

Here an event occurred to Mlle. Gillenormand the elder: she had an idea. If she had been a man she would have struck her forehead. She addressed Théodule:

"You are aware that your cousin does not know you?"

"I have seen him, but he never deigned to notice me."

"Where is the diligence going to?"

"To Andelys."

"Is Marius going there?"

"Unless he stops on the road, like myself. I get out at Vernon, to take the Gaillon coach. I know nothing about Marius's route."

"Marius! what an odious name! what an idea it was to call him that! well, your name, at least, is Théodule."

"I would rather it was Alfred," the officer said.

"Listen, Théodule; Marius absents himself from the house."

"Eh, eh!"

"He goes about the country."

"Ah, ah!"

"He sleeps out."

"Oh, oh!"

"We should like to know the meaning of all this."

Théodule replied, with the calmness of a bronze man, "Some petticoat!"

And with that inward chuckle which evidences a certainty, he added, "Some gurl!"

"That is evident!" the aunt exclaimed, who believed that she heard M. Gillenormand speaking, and who felt his conviction irresistibly from that word "gurl," accentuated almost in the same way by grand-uncle and grand-nephew. She continued:

"Do us a pleasure by following Marius a little. As he does not know you, that will be an easy matter. Since there is a girl in the case, try to get a look at her, and write and tell us all about it, for it will amuse your grand-uncle."

Théodule had no excessive inclination for this sort of watching, but he was greatly affected by the ten louis, and he believed he could see a possible continuation of such gifts.

He accepted the commission, and said, "As you please, aunt," and added in an aside, "I am a Duenna now!"

Mlle. Gillenormand kissed him.

"You would not play such tricks as that, Théodule, for you obey discipline, are the slave of duty, and a scrupulous man, and would never leave your family to go and see a creature."

The lancer made the satisfied grimace of Cartouche when praised for his probity.

Marius, on the evening that followed this dialogue, got into the diligence, not suspecting that he was watched. As for the watcher, the first thing he did was to fall asleep, and his sleep was complete and conscientious. Argus snored the whole night.

At daybreak the guard shouted, "Vernon; passengers for Vernon, get out here!" and Lieutenant Théodule awoke.

"All right," he growled, still half asleep, "I get out here."

Then, his memory growing gradually clearer, he thought of his aunt, the ten louis, and the account he had promised to render of Marius's sayings and doings. This made him laugh.

"He is probably no longer in the coach," he thought, while buttoning up his jacket. "He may have stopped at Pacy, he may have stopped at Triel, if he did not get out at Meulan, he may have done so at Mantes, unless he stopped at Rolleboise, or only went as far as Pacy, with the choice of turning on his left to Evreux, or on his right to La Rocheguyon. Run after him, aunty. What the deuce shall I write to the old lady?"

At this moment the leg of a black trouser appeared against the window-pane of the *coupé*. "Can it be Marius?" the lieutenant said.

It was Marius.

A little peasant girl was offering flowers to the passengers, and crying, "Bouquets for your ladies."

Marius went up to her, and bought the finest flowers in her basket.

"By Jove," said Théodule, as he leaped out of the *coupé,* "the affair is growing piquant. Who the deuce is he going to carry those flowers to? she must be a deucedly pretty woman to deserve so handsome a bouquet. I must have a look at her."

And he then began following Marius, no longer by order, but through personal curiosity, like those dogs which hunt on their own account.

Marius paid no attention to Théodule. Some elegant women were getting out of the diligence, but he did not look at them; he seemed to see nothing around him.

"He must be preciously in love," Théodule thought.

Marius proceeded toward the church.

"That's glorious!" Théodule said to himself, "the church, that's the thing. Rendezvous spiced with a small amount of mass are the best. Nothing is so exquisite as an ogle exchanged in the presence of the Virgin."

On reaching the church, Marius did not go in, but disappeared behind one of the buttresses of the apse.

"The meeting outside," Théodule said; "now for a look at the gurl."

And he walked on tiptoe up to the corner which Marius had gone round. On reaching it, he stopped in stupefaction.

Marius, with his forehead in both his hands, was kneeling in the grass upon a tomb, and had spread his flowers out over it. At the head of the grave was a cross of black wood, with this name in white letters: "COLONEL BARON PONTMERCY." Marius could be heard sobbing.

.The girl was a tomb.

8. MARBLE AGAINST GRANITE

It is hither that Marius had come the first time that he had absented himself from Paris; it was to this spot he retired each time that M. Gillenormand said, "He sleeps out."

Lieutenant Théodule was absolutely discountenanced by this unexpected elbowing of a tomb, and felt a disagreeable and singular sensation, which he was incapable of analyzing, and which was composed of respect for a tomb mingled with respect for a colonel. He fell back, leaving Marius alone in the cemetery, and there was discipline in this retreat; death appeared to him wearing heavy epaulettes, and he almost gave it a military salute. Not knowing what to write to his aunt, he resolved not to write at all; and there would probably have been no result from Théodule's discovery of Marius's amour had not, by one of those mysterious arrangements so frequent in accident, the scene at Vernon had almost immediately a sort of counterpart in Paris.

Marius returned from Vernon very early in the morning of the third day, and wearied by two nights spent in a diligence, and feeling the necessity of repairing his want of sleep by an hour at the swimming-school, he hurried up to his room, only took the time to take off his traveling coat and the black ribbon which he had round his neck, and went to the bath.

M. Gillenormand, who rose at an early hour like all old men who are in good health, heard him come in, and hastened as quick as his old legs would carry him up the stairs leading to Marius's garret, in order to welcome him back and try and discover his movements.

But the young man had taken less time in descending than the octogenarian in ascending, and when Father Gillenormand entered the garret Marius was no longer there.

The bed had been unoccupied, and on it lay the coat and black ribbon unsuspectingly.

"I prefer that," said M. Gillenormand.

A moment later he entered the drawing-room, where Mlle. Gillenormand the elder was already seated embroidering her cabriolet wheels.

The entrance was triumphant. M. Gillenormand held in one hand the coat, and in the other the neck-ribbon, and shouted:

"Victory! we are going to penetrate the mystery, we are going to know the cream of the joke, we are going to lay our hands on the libertinage of our cunning gentleman. Here is the romance itself, for I have the portrait."

In fact, a box of shagreen leather, much like a miniature, was suspended from the ribbon.

The old man took hold of this box and looked at it for some time without opening, with the air of pleasure, eagerness, and anger of a poor starving fellow who sees a splendid dinner, of which he will have no share, carried past under his nose.

"It is evidently a portrait, and I am up to that sort of thing. It is worn tenderly on the heart,—what asses they are! some abominable gorgon, who will probably make me shudder, for young men have such bad taste nowadays."

"Let us look, father," the old maid said.

The box opened by pressing a spring, but they only found in it a carefully folded-up paper.

"*From the same to the same,*" said M. Gillenormand, bursting into a laugh. "I know what it is—a billet-doux!"

"Indeed! let us read it," said the aunt.

She put on her spectacles. They unfolded the paper and read as follows:

"*For my son.* The emperor made me a baron on the field of Waterloo, and as the Restoration contests this title, which I purchased with my blood, my son will assume it and wear it. Of course he will be worthy of it."

What the father and daughter felt it is not possible to describe; but they were chilled as if by the breath of a death's-head. They did not exchange a syllable.

M. Gillenormand merely said in a low voice, and as if speaking to himself: "It is that trooper's handwriting."

The aunt examined the slip of paper, turned it about in all directions, and then placed it again in the box.

At the same instant, a small square packet, wrapped up in blue paper, fell from a pocket of the great-coat. Mlle. Gillenormand picked it up and opened the blue paper.

It contained Marius's one hundred cards, and she passed one to M. Gillenormand, who read, "Baron Marius Pontmercy."

The old man rang, and Nicolette came in. M. Gillenormand took the ribbon, the box, and the coat, threw them on the ground in the middle of the room, and said:

"Remove that rubbish."

A long hour passed in the deepest silence; the old man and the old maid were sitting back to back and thinking, probably both of the same things.

At the end of this hour, Mlle. Gillenormand said:

"Very pretty!"

A few minutes after, Marius came in; even before he crossed the threshold he perceived his grandfather holding one of his cards in his hand. On seeing Marius he exclaimed, with his air of bourgeois and grimacing superiority, which had something crushing about it:

"Stay! stay! stay! stay! stay! You are a baron at present; I must congratulate you. What does this mean?"

Marius blushed slightly, and answered:

"It means that I am my father's son."

M. Gillenormand left off laughing, and said harshly, "I am your father."

"My father," Marius continued, with downcast eyes and a stern air, "was an humble and heroic man who gloriously served the republic of France, who was great in the greatest history which men have ever made, who lived for a quarter of a century in a bivouac, by day under a shower of grapeshot and bullets, and at night in snow, mud, wind, and rain. He was a man who took two flags, received twenty wounds, died in forgetfulness and abandonment, and who had never committed but one fault, that of loving too dearly two ungrateful beings—his country and myself."

This was more than M. Gillenormand could hear; at the word republic he had risen, or, more correctly, sprung up. Each of the words that Marius had just uttered had produced on the old gentleman's face the same effect as the blast of a forge-bellows upon a burning log. From gloomy he became red, from red, purple, and from purple, flaming.

"Marius," he shouted, "you abominable boy! I know not who your father was, and do not wish to know. I know nothing about it, but what I do know is, that there never were any but scoundrels among all those people; they were all rogues, assassins, red caps, robbers! I say all, I say all! I know nobody! I say all; do you understand me, Marius? You must know that you are as much a baron as my slipper is! They were all bandits who served Robespierre! they were all brigands who served B-u-o-naparté! all traitors who betrayed, betrayed, betrayed their legitimate king! all cowards who ran away from the Prussians and the English at Waterloo. That is what I know. If your father was among them, I am ignorant of the fact, and am sorry for it. I am your humble servant!"

In his turn, Marius became the brand, and M. Gillenormand the bellows. Marius trembled all over, he knew not what to do, and his head was aglow. He was the priest who sees his consecrated wafers cast to the wind, the Fakir who notices a passer-by spit on his idol. It was impossible that such things could be said with impunity in his presence, but what was he to do? His father had just been trampled under foot and insulted in his presence, but by whom? by his grandfather. How was he to avenge the one without outraging the other? It was impossible for him to insult his grandfather, and equally impossible for him to avenge his father. On one side was a sacred tomb, on the other was white hair.

He tottered for a few moments like a drunken man, then raised his eyes, looked fixedly at his grandfather, and shouted in a thundering voice:

"Down with the Bourbons and that great pig of a Louis XVIII!"

Louis XVIII had been dead four years, but that made no difference to him.

The old man, who had been scarlet, suddenly became whiter than his hair. He turned to a bust of the Duc de Berry which was on the mantel-piece, and bowed to it profoundly with a sort of singular majesty. Then he walked twice, slowly and silently, from the mantel-piece to the window, and from the window to the mantel-piece, crossing the whole room, and making the boards creak as if he were a walking marble statue.

The second time he bent over his daughter, who was looking at the disturbance with the stupor of an old sheep, and said to her with a smile which was almost calm:

"A baron like this gentleman and a bourgeois like myself can no longer remain beneath the same roof."

And suddenly drawing himself up, livid, trembling, and terrible, with

75

his forehead dilated by the fearful radiance of passion, he stretched out his arm towards Marius, and shouted:

"Begone!"

Marius left the house.

On the next day M. Gillenormand said to his daughter:

"You will send every six months sixty pistoles to that blood-drinker, and never mention his name to me."

Having an immense amount of fury to expend, and not knowing what to do with it, he continued to address his daughter as "you" instead of "thou" for upward of three months.

Marius, on his side, left the house indignant, and a circumstance aggravated his exasperation. There are always small fatalities of this nature to complicate domestic dramas; the anger is augmented although the wrongs are not in reality increased. In hurriedly conveying, by the grandfather's order, Marius's rubbish to his bedroom, Nicolette, without noticing the fact, let fall, probably on the attic stairs, which were dark, the black shagreen case in which was the paper written by the colonel. As neither could be found, Marius felt convinced that "Monsieur Gillenormand"—he never called him otherwise from that date—had thrown "his father's will" into the fire. He knew by heart the few lines written by the colonel, and, consequently, nothing was lost; but the paper, the writing, this sacred relic,—all this was his heart. What had been done with it?

Marius went away without saying where he was going and without knowing, with thirty francs, his watch, and some clothes in a carpet-bag. He jumped into a cabriolet, engaged it by the hour, and proceeded at all risk toward the Pays Latin.

What would become of Marius?

BOOK IV

THE FRIENDS OF THE A. B. C.

1. A GROUP THAT NEARLY BECAME HISTORICAL

At this epoch, which was apparently careless, a certain revolutionary quivering was vaguely felt. There were breezes in the air which returned from the depths of '89 and '92; and the young men, if we may be forgiven the expression, were in the molting stage. Men became transformed, almost without suspecting it, by the mere movement of time, for the hand which moves round the clock-face also moves in the mind. Each took the forward step he had to take; the royalists became liberals, and the liberals democrats. It was like a rising tide complicated by a thousand ebbs, and it is the peculiarity of ebbs to cause things to mingle. Hence came very singular combinations of ideas, and men adored liberty and Napoleon at the same time. We are writing history here, and such were the mirages of that period. Opinions pass through phases, and Voltairean royalism, a strange variety, had a no less strange pendant in Bonapartist liberalism.

Other groups of minds were more serious; at one spot principles were sounded, and at another men clung to their rights. They became impassioned for the absolute, and obtained glimpses of infinite realizations; for the absolute, through its very rigidity, causes minds to float in the illimitable ether. There is nothing like dogma to originate a dream, and nothing like a dream to engender the future: the Utopia of to-day is flesh and bone to-morrow.

Advanced opinions had a false bottom, and a commencement of mystery threatened "established order," which was suspected and cunning. This is a most revolutionary sign. The after-thought of the authorities meets in the sap the after-thought of the people, and the incubation of revolution is the reply to the premeditation of coups d'état.

There were not as yet in France any of those vast subjacent organizations, like the Tugendbund of Germany or the Carbonari of Italy; but here and there were dark subterranean passages with extensive ramifications. The Cougourde was sketched out at Aix; and there was at Paris, among other affiliations of this nature, the society of the friends of the A. B. C.

Who were the friends of the A. B. C.? A society, whose ostensible object was the education of children, but the real one the elevation of men.

They call themselves friends of the A. B. C., and the people were the *Abaissés* whom they wished to raise. It would have been wrong to laugh at this pun, for puns at times are serious in politics; witnesses of this are the *Castratus ad castra,* which made Narses general of an army; the *Barbari* and *Barberini; fueros y fuegos; tu es Petrus et super hanc Petram,* etc., etc.

The friends of the A. B. C. were few in number; it was a secret society, in a state of embryo, and we might almost call it a coterie, if coteries produced heroes. They assembled at two places in Paris,—at a cabaret called *Corinthe* near the Halles, to which we shall revert hereafter, and near the Pantheon in a small café on the Place St. Michel, known as the Café Musain, and now demolished; the first of these meeting-places was contiguous to the workmen, and the second to the students.

The ordinary discussions of the friends of the A. B. C. were held in a back room of the Café Musain.

This room, some distance from the coffee-room, with which it communicated by a very long passage, had two windows and an issue by a secret staircase into the Little Rue des Grès. They smoked, drank, played, and laughed there; they spoke very loudly about everything, and in a whisper about the other thing. On the wall hung an old map of France under the Republic, which would have been a sufficient hint for a police agent.

Most of the friends of the A. B. C. were students, who maintained a cordial understanding with a few workmen. Here are the names of the principal members, which belong in a certain measure to history: Enjolras, Combeferre, Jean Prouvaire, Feuilly, Courfeyrac, Bahorel, Lesgle or Laigle, Joly, and Grantaire.

These young men formed a species of family through their friendship, and all came from the south, excepting Laigle.

This group is remarkable, although it has vanished in the invisible depths which are behind us. At the point of this drama which we have now attained, it will not be labor lost, perhaps, to throw a ray of light upon these heads before the reader watches them enter the shadows of a tragical adventure.

Enjolras, whom we named first, it will be seen afterward why, was an only son, and rich.

He was a charming young man, capable of becoming terrible; he was angelically beautiful, and looked like a stern Antinous. On noticing the pensive depth of his glance, you might have fancied that he had gone through the revolutionary apocalypse in some preceding existence. He knew the traditions of it like an eye-witness, and was acquainted with all the minor details of the great thing. His was a priestly and warlike nature, strange in a young man; he was a churchman and a militant; from the immediate point of view a soldier of democracy, but, above the contemporary movement, a priest of the ideal. He had a slightly red eyelid, a thick and easily disdainful lower lip, and a lofty forehead; a good deal of forehead on a face is like a good deal of sky in an horizon. Like certain young men of the beginning of the present century and the end of the last, who became illustrious at an early age, he looked excessively young, and was as fresh as a school-girl though he had his hours of pallor. Although a man, he seemed still a boy, and his two-and-twenty years looked like only seventeen; he was serious, and did not appear to know that there was on the earth a being called woman. He had only one passion, justice, and only one thought, overthrowing the obstacle. On the Mons Aventinus he would have been Gracchus; in the convention he would have been St. Just. He scarcely noticed roses, was ignorant of spring, and did not hear the birds sing; the bare throat of Evadne would have affected him as little as it did Aristogiton; to him, as to Harmodius, flowers were only good to conceal the sword. He was stern in his joy, and before all that was not the republic he chastely lowered his eyes—he was the marble lover of liberty. His language had a sharp inspiration and a species of rhythmic strain. He had unexpected expansions of soul. Woe to the girl who ventured to ensnare him! If any grisette of the Place Cambray, or the Rue St. Jean de Beauvais, seeing this face so like that of a collegian out of bounds, this figure of a page, his long light lashes, his blue eyes, his hair floating wildly in the breeze, his pink cheeks, cherry lips, and exquisite teeth, had felt a longing for all this dawn and tried the effect of her charms upon Enjolras, a formidable look of surprise would have suddenly shown her the abyss and taught her not to confound the avenging cherub of Ezekiel with the gallant cherub of Beaumarchais.

By the side of Enjolras, who represented the logic of the Revolution, Combeferre represented its philosophy. Between the logic and the philosophy of revolutions there is this difference, that the logic may conclude in war while its philosophy can only lead to peace. Combeferre completed and rectified Enjolras; he was not so tall, but broader. He wished that the extended principles of general ideas should be poured over minds, and said, "Revolution but civilization!" and he opened the vast blue horizon around the peaked mountain. Hence there was something accessible and practicable in all Combeferre's views; and the Revolution with him was more respectable than with Enjolras. Enjolras expressed its divine right, and Combeferre its natural right, and while the former clung to Robespierre the latter bordered on Condorcet. Combeferre loved more than Enjolras the ordinary life of mankind; and if these two young men had gained a place in history, the one would have been the just man, the other the sage. Enjolras was more manly, Combeferre more humane, and the distinction between them was that between *homo* and *vir*. Combeferre was gentle as Enjolras was stern, through natural whiteness; he loved the word citizen, but preferred man, and would have gladly said *Hombre,* like the Spaniards. He read everything, went to the theaters, attended the public lectures, learned from Arago the polarization of light, and grew quite excited about a lecture in which Geoffroy St. Hilaire explained the double functions of the external and internal carotid arteries, the one which makes the face and the other which produces the brain; he was conversant with, and followed, science step by step, confronted St. Simon with Fourier, deciphered hieroglyphics, broke pebbles which he found, drew from memory a bombyx butterfly, pointed out the errors in French in the dictionary of the Academy, studied Puységur and Deleuze, affirmed nothing, not even miracles, denied nothing, not even ghosts, turned over the file of the *Moniteur* and reflected. He declared that the future is in the hand of the schoolmaster, and busied himself with educational questions. He wished that society should labor without relaxation at the elevation of the intellectual and moral standard, at coining science, bringing ideas into circulation, and making the minds of youth grow; and he feared that the present poverty of methods, the wretchedness from the literary point of view of confining studies to two or three centuries called classical, the tyrannical dogmatism of official pedants, scholastic prejudices, and routine would in the end convert our colleges into artificial oyster-beds. He was learned, a purist, polite, and polytechnic, a delver, and at the same time pensive, "even to a chimera," as his friend said. He believed in all dreams, railways, the suppression of suffering in surgical operations, fixing the image of the camera obscura, electric telegraphy, and the steering of balloons. He was slightly terrified by the citadels built on all sides against the human race by superstitions, despotisms, and prejudices, for he was one of those men who think that science will, in the end, turn the position. Enjolras was a chief, and Combeferre a guide; you would have liked to fight under one and march with the other. Not that Combeferre was incapable of fighting, he did not refuse to seize obstacles round the waist and attack them by main force; but it pleased him better to bring the human race into harmony with its destiny, gradually, by the instruction of axioms and the promulgation of positive laws; and with a choice between two lights, his inclination was for illumination rather than fire. A fire may certainly produce a dawn, but why not wait for daybreak? A volcano illumines, but the sun does so far better. Combeferre, perhaps, preferred the whiteness of the beautiful to the flashing of the sublime, and a brightness clouded by smoke; a progress purchased by violence only half satisfied his tender and serious mind. A headlong hurling of a people into the truth, a '93, startled him; still, stagnation was more repulsive to him, for he smelt in it putrefaction and death. Altogether he liked foam better than miasma, and preferred the torrent to the sewer, and the Falls of Niagara to the Lake of Montfaucon. In a word, he desired neither halt nor haste, and while his tumultuous friends, who were chivalrously attracted by the absolute, adored and summoned the splendid revolutionary adventurer, Combeferre inclined to leave progress, right progress, to act—it might be cold but it was pure, methodical but irreproachable, and phlegmatic but imperturbable. Combeferre would have knelt down and prayed that this future might arrive with all its candor, and that nothing might disturb the immense virtuous evolution of the peoples. *The good must be innocent,* he repeated incessantly. And in truth, if the grandeur of the Revolution is to look fixedly at the dazzling ideal, and fly toward it through the lightning, with blood and fire in the claws, the beauty of progress is to be unspotted; and there is between Washington, who represents the one, and Danton, who is the incarnation of the other, the same difference as that which separates the angel with the swan's wings from the angel with the eagle's wings.

Jean Prouvaire was of an even softer tinge than Combeferre; he was called "Jehan," through that little momentary fantasy which was blended with the powerful and profound movement from which issued the most necessary study of the middle ages. Jean Prouvaire was always in love, cultivated a pot of flowers, played a flute, wrote verses, loved the people, pitied women, wept over children, confounded in the same confidence the future and God, and blamed the Revolution for having caused a royal head to fall, that of André Chénier. He had a voice which was habitually delicate, and suddenly became masculine; he was erudite, and almost an Orientalist. He was good before all, and through a motive which those will easily understand who know how closely goodness borders on grandeur,—he loved immensity in poetry. He knew Italian, Latin, Greek, and Hebrew, and he employed his knowledge to read only four poets,—Dante, Juvenal, Æschylus, and Isaiah. In French he preferred Corneille to Racine, and Agrippa d'Aubigné to Corneille. He was fond of strolling about the fields of wild oats and corn-flowers, and occupied himself with clouds almost as much as with events. His mind had two attitudes,—one turned to man, the other to God; he either studied or contemplated. The whole day long he studied social questions,—wages, capital, credit, marriage, religion, liberty of thought, liberty of love, education, the penal code, wretchedness, partnership, property, production, and division, that enigma of the lower world which casts a shadow over the human ant-heap, and at night he looked at the stars, those enormous beings. Like Enjolras, he was rich, and an only son; he talked softly, hung his head, looked down, smiled with an embarrassed air, dressed badly, had an awkward gait, blushed at a nothing, and was very timid; with all that, he was intrepid.

Feuilly was a journeyman fan-maker, doubly an orphan, who laboriously earned three francs a day, and had only one idea—to deliver the world. He had another preoccupation as well, instructing himself, which he called self-deliverance. He had taught himself to read and write; and all that he knew he had learned alone. Feuilly had a generous heart and hugged the world. This orphan had adopted the peoples, and as he had no mother he meditated on his country. He had wished that there should not be in the world a man who had no country, and he brooded over what we now call the "idea of nationalities" with the profound divination of the man of the people. He had studied history expressly that he might be indignant with the knowledge of the fact, and in this youthful assembly of Utopians, who were specially interested about France, he represented the foreign element. His specialty was Greece, Poland, Roumania, Hungary, and Italy; he pronounced these names incessantly, in season and out of season, with the tenacity of right. The violations committed by Turkey, on Greece and Thessaly, of Russia on Warsaw, and Austria on Venice, exasperated him, and above all the great highway robbery of 1772 aroused him. There can be no more sovereign eloquence than truth in indignation, and he was eloquent with that eloquence. He never left off talking about the infamous date 1772, the noble and valiant people suppressed by treachery, this crime committed by three accomplices, and the monstrous ambush, which is the prototype and pattern of all those frightful suppressions of states which have since struck several nations, and have, so to speak, erased their name from the baptismal register. All the social assaults of the present day emanate from the division of Poland, and it is a theorem to which all our political crimes are corollaries. There is not a despot or a traitor who for a century past has not revised, confirmed, countersigned, and margined with the words *ne varietur* the division of Poland. When we consult the list of modern treasons this appears the first, and the Congress of Vienna consulted this crime ere it consummated its own; 1772 sounds the View-halloo, and 1815 witnesses the *curée* of the stag. Such was Feuilly's usual text. This poor workman had made himself the guardian of justice, and she rewarded him by making him grand. In truth, there is an eternity in justice, and Warsaw can no more be Tartar than Venice German. Kings lose their time and their honor over such things. Sooner or later, the submerged country floats on the surface and re-appears. Greece becomes Greece once more, and Italy Italy. The protest of right against deeds persists forever, and there is no law of prescription for the robbery of a nation. Such high acts of pilfering have no future, and the mark cannot be taken out of a nation like a handkerchief.

Courfeyrac had a father who was known as M. de Courfeyrac. One of the incorrect ideas of the bourgeoisie of the Restoration in the matter of the aristocracy and the nobility was a belief in the particle. The particle, as we know, has no meaning, but the bourgeois of the time of the *Minerve* esteemed this poor *de* so highly that persons thought themselves obliged to abdicate it. M. de Chauvelin called himself M. Chauvelin; M. de Caumartin, M. Caumartin; M. de Constant de Rebecque, Benjamin Constant, and M. de Lafayette, M. Lafayette. Courfeyrac was unwilling to remain behindhand, and called himself Courfeyrac quite short.

As concerns this gentleman, we might almost stop here and content ourselves with saying as to the rest, *for* Courfeyrac *read* Tholomyès; Courfeyrac, in fact, had those sallies of youth which might be called a mental *beauté du diable*. At a latter date this expires like the prettiness of the kitten; and all this grace produces, upon two feet the bourgeois, and on four paws the tom-cat.

The generations which pass through the schools, and the successive levies of youth, transmit this species of wit from one to the other, and pass it from hand to hand, *quasi cursores,* nearly always the same; so that, as we have said, the first-comer who had listened to Courfeyrac in 1828 might have fancied he was hearing Tholomyès in 1817. The only thing was that Courfeyrac was an honest fellow, and beneath an apparent external similitude the difference between Tholomyès and himself was great, and the latent man who existed within them was very different in the former from what it was in the latter. In Tholomyès there was an attorney, and in Courfeyrac a Paladin.

Enjolras was the chief, Combeferre the guide, and Courfeyrac the center. The others gave more light, but he produced more heat; and he had in truth all the qualities of a center, in the shape of roundness and radiation.

Bahorel had been mixed up in the sanguinary tumult of June, 1822, on the occasion of the burial of young Lallemand. Bahorel was a being of good temper and bad company, an honest fellow and a spendthrift, prodigal and reaching generosity, chattering and reaching eloquence, bold and reaching effrontery, and the very best clay for the devil's molding imaginable. He displayed daring waistcoats and scarlet opinions. He was a turbulent on a grand scale; that is to say, that he liked nothing so much as a quarrel unless it were an émeute, and nothing so much as an émeute except a revolution. He was ever ready to break a pane of glass, tear up the paving-stones, and demolish a government, in order to see the effect—he was a student in his eleventh year. He sniffed at the law, but did not practice it, and he had taken as his motto, "never a lawyer" and as his coat of arms a night-table surmounted by a square cap. Whenever he passed in front of the law-school, which rarely happened to him, he buttoned up his frock-coat and took hygienic precautions. He said of the school gate, "What a fierce old man!" and of the Dean M. Devincourt, "What a monument!" He found in his lectures a subject for coarse songs, and in his professors an occasion for laughter. He spent in doing nothing a very considerable allowance, something like three thousand francs.

His parents were peasants in whom he had inculcated a respect for their son. He used to say of them, "They are peasants, and not towns-people; that is why they are so intelligent."

Bahorel, as a capricious man, visited several cafés; and while the others had habits; he had none. He strolled about; if *errare* is human, strolling is Parisian. Altogether, he had a penetrating mind, and thought more than people fancied.

He served as the connecting link between the friends of the A. B. C. and other groups which were still unformed, but which were to be con-stituted at a later date.

There was in this assembly of young men a bald-headed member.

The Marquis d'Avaray, whom Louis XVIII made a duke because he helped him to get into a hired cab on the day when he emigrated, used to tell how, when the king landed in 1814 at Calais, upon his return to France, a man handed him a petition.

"What do you want?" the king said.

"A postmastership, sire."

"What is your name?"

"L'Aigle."

The king frowned, but looked at the signature of the petition, and read the name thus written, LESGLE. This, anything but Bonapartist orthog-raphy, touched the king, and he began smiling. "Sire," the man with the petition went on, "my ancestor was a whipper-in of the name of Les-gueules, and my name came from that. I called myself Lesgueules, by contraction Lesgle, and by corruption L'Aigle." This remark caused the king to smile still more, and at a later date he gave the man the post-office at Meaux, purposely or through a mistake.

The bald Mentor of the group was son of this Lesgle or Lègle, and signed himself Lègle (of Meaux). His comrades, to shorten this, called him Bossuet, who, as everybody knows, was christened the Eagle of Meaux.

Bossuet was a merry fellow, who was unlucky, and his specialty was to succeed in nothing. *Per contra,* he laughed at everything. At the age of five-and-twenty he was bald; his father left him a house and a field, but the son knew nothing so pressing as to lose them both in a swindling speculation, and nothing was left him. He had learning and sense, but they were abortive; he failed in everything and everything cozened him; whatever he built up broke down under him. If he chopped wood, he cut his fingers; and if he had a mistress, he speedily discovered that she had also a friend. At every moment some misfortune happened to him, and hence came his joviality; and he used to say, "I live under the roof of falling tiles." Feeling but slight astonishment, for every accident was foreseen by him, he accepted ill luck serenely, and smiled at the pinpricks of destiny like a man who is listening to a good joke. He was poor, but his wallet of good temper was inexhaustible; he speedily reached his last half-penny, but never his last laugh. When adversity entered his room, he bowed to his old acquaintance cordially; he tickled catastrophes in the ribs, and was so familiar with fatality as to call it by a nickname—"Good-day, ill luck!" said he.

These persecutions of fate had rendered him inventive, and he was full of resources. He had no money, but contrived to make a "frenzied outlay" whenever he thought proper. One night he went so far as to devour a hundred francs in a supper with a girl, which inspired him in the middle of the orgy with the memorable remark, "Fille de cinq Louis, pull off my boots."

Bossuet was advancing slowly to the legal profession, and studied law much after the fashion of Bahorel. Bossuet had but little domicile, at times none at all, and he lived first with one and then with the other, but most frequently with Joly.

Joly was a student of medicine, of two years' younger standing than Bossuet.

Joly was the young *Malade imaginaire*. What he had gained by his medical studies was to be more a patient than a doctor, for at the age of twenty-three he fancied himself a valetudinarian, and spent his life in looking at his tongue in a mirror. He declared that a man becomes magnetized like a needle, and in his room he placed his bed with the head to the south and the feet to the north, so that at night the circulation of his blood might not be impeded by the great magnetic current of the globe. In storms he felt his pulse, but for all that was the gayest of all. All these incoherences, youth, mania, dyspepsia, and fun, lived comfortably together and the result was an eccentric and agreeable being, whom his comrades, lavish of liquid consonants, called "Joly."

Joly was accustomed to touch his nose with the end of his cane, which is the sign of a sagacious mind.

All these young men who differed so greatly, and of whom after all, we must speak seriously, had the same religion,—Progress.

They were all the direct sons of the French Revolution and the lightest among them became serious when pronouncing the date of '89. Their fathers in the flesh were, or had been, feuilletants, royalists, or doctrinaires, but that was of little consequence; this pell-mell, anterior to themselves, who were young, did not concern them, and the pure blood of principles flowed in their veins; they attached themselves without any intermediate tinge, to incorruptible right and absolute duty.

Affiliated and initiated, they sketched out the ideal in their subterranean meetings.

Amid all these impassioned hearts and convinced minds there was a skeptic; how did he get there? through juxtaposition. The name of this skeptic was Grantaire, and he usually wrote it after the manner of a charade,—R.* Grantaire was a man who carefully avoided believing anything; he was, however, one of those students who had learned the most during a Parisian residence. He knew that the best coffee was at Lemblier's and the best billiard-table at the Café Voltaire; that excellent cakes and agreeable girls could be found at the Hermitage on the Boulevard du Maine, spatch-cocks at Mother Saquet's, excellent matelottes at the Barrière de la Cunette, and a peculiar white wine at the Barrière Combat. Besides all this, he was a mighty drinker. He was abominably ugly, and Irma Boissy, the prettiest boot-binder of that day, in her indignation at his ugliness, passed the verdict, "Grantaire is impossible." But Grantaire's fatuity was not disconcerted by this. He looked tenderly and fixedly at every woman, and assumed an expression of "If I only liked!" and he tried to make his companions believe that he was in general request with the sex.

All such words as rights of the people, rights of man, the social contract, the French Revolution, republic, democracy, humanity, civilization, progress, had as good as no meaning with Grantaire, and he smiled at them. Skepticism, that curse of the intellect, had not left him one whole idea in his mind. He lived in irony, and his axiom was, "There is only one thing certain—my full glass." He ridiculed every act of devotion in every party,—the brother as much as the father, young Robespierre as heartily as Loizerolles. "They made great progress by dying," he would exclaim; and would say of the crucifix, "There is a gallows which was successful." Idler, gambler, libertine, and often intoxicated, he annoyed these young democrats by incessantly singing, *"J'aimons les filles et j'aimons le bon vin,"* to the tune of "Long live Henri IV."

This skeptic, however, had a fanaticism; it was neither an idea, a dogma, an act, nor a sense; it was a man,—Enjolras. Grantaire admired, loved, and revered Enjolras. Whom did this anarchical doubter cling to

*Grantaire=Grand R.

in this phalanx of absolute minds? to the most absolute. In what way did Enjolras subjugate him? by ideas? No, but by character. This is a frequently observed phenomenon, and a skeptic who clings to a believer is as simple as the law of complementary colors. What we do not possess attracts us; no one loves daylight like the blind man; the dwarf adores her drum-major, and the frog has its eyes constantly fixed on heaven to see the bird fly. Grantaire, in whom doubt groveled, liked to see faith soaring in Enjolras, and he felt the want of him, without clearly understanding it, or even dreaming of explaining the fact to himself. This chaste, healthy, firm, upright, harsh and candid nature charmed him, and he instinctively admired his contrary. His soft, yielding, dislocated, sickly and shapeless ideas attached themselves to Enjolras as to a vertebra, and his moral spine supported itself by this firmness. Grantaire, by the side of Enjolras, became somebody again; and he was, moreover, himself composed of two apparently irreconcilable elements,—he was ironical and cordial. His mind could do without belief, but his heart could not do without friendship. This is a profound contradiction, for an affection is a conviction, but his nature was so. There are some men apparently born to be the reverse of the coin, and the names are Pollux, Patroclus, Nisus, Eudamidas, Hephestion, and Pechmeja. They only live on the condition of being backed by another man; their name is a continuation, and is never written except preceded by the conjunction *and;* their existence is not their own, but is the other side of a destiny which is not theirs. Grantaire was one of these men.

We might almost say that affinities commence with the letters of the alphabet, and in the series O and P are almost inseparable. You may, as you please, say O and P, or Orestes and Pylades.

Grantaire, a true satellite of Enjolras, dwelt in this circle of young men: he lived there, he solely enjoyed himself there and he followed them everywhere. His delight was to see their shadows coming and going through the fumes of wine, and he was tolerated for his pleasant humor.

Enjolras, as a believer, disdained this skeptic, and as a sober man loathed this drunkard, but he granted him a little haughty pity. Grantaire was an unaccepted Pylades: constantly repulsed by Enjolras, harshly rejected, and yet returning, he used to say of him, "What a splendid statue!"

2. A FUNERAL ORATION BY BOSSUET

On a certain afternoon, which, as we shall see, has some coincidence with the events recorded above, Laigle de Meaux was sensually leaning against the door-post of the Café Musain. He looked like a caryatid out for a holiday, and having nothing to carry but his reverie. Leaning on one's shoulder is a mode of lying down upright which is not disliked by dreamers. Laigle de Meaux was thinking, without melancholy, of a slight misadventure which had occurred to him on the previous day but one at the law-school, and modified his personal plans for the future, which, as it was, were somewhat indistinct.

Reverie does not prevent a cabriolet from passing, or a dreamer from noticing the cabriolet. Laigle, whose eyes were absently wandering, saw through this somnambulism a two-wheeled vehicle moving across the Place St. Michel at a foot-pace and apparently undecided. What did this cab want? why was it going so slowly? Laigle looked at it, and saw inside a young man seated by the side of the driver, and in front of the young man a carpet-bag. The bag displayed to passersby this name, written in large black letters on the card sewn to the cloth, MARIUS PONTMERCY.

This name made Laigle change his attitude; he drew himself up, and shouted to the young man in the cab,

"M. Marius Pontmercy."

The cab stopped, on being thus hailed, and the young man, who also appeared to be thinking deeply, raised his eyes.

"Hilloh!" he said.

"Are you M. Pontmercy?"

"Yes."

"I was looking for you," Laigle of Meaux continued.

"How so?" asked Marius, for it was really he, who had just left his grandfather's, and had before him a face which he saw for the first time. "I do not know you."

"And I don't know you, either."

Marius fancied that he had to do with a practical joker, and, as he was not in the best of tempers at the moment, frowned. Laigle imperturbably continued:

"You were not at lecture the day before yesterday."

"Very possibly."

"It is certain."

"Are you a student?" Marius asked.

"Yes, sir, like yourself. The day before yesterday I entered the law-school by chance; as you know, a man has an idea like that sometimes. The professor was engaged in calling over, and you are aware how ridiculously strict they are in the school at the present moment. Upon the third call remaining unanswered, your name is erased from the list, and sixty francs are gone."

Marius began to listen, and Laigle continued:

"It was Blondeau who was calling over. You know Blondeau has a pointed and most malicious nose, and scents the absent with delight. He craftily began with the letter P, and I did not listen, because I was not compromised by that letter. The roll-call went on capitally, there was no erasure, and the universe was present. Blondeau was sad, and I said to myself aside, 'Blondeau, my love, you will not perform the slightest execution to-day.' All at once Blondeau calls out, 'Marius Pontmercy.' No one answered, and so Blondeau, full of hope, repeats in a louder voice, 'Marius Pontmercy,' and takes up his pen. I have bowels, sir, and said to myself hurriedly, 'The name of a good fellow is going to be erased. Attention! he is not a proper student, a student who studies, a reading man, a pedantic sap, strong in science, literature, theology, and philosophy. No, he is an honorable idler, who lounges about, enjoys the country, cultivates the grisette, pays his court to the ladies, and is perhaps with my mistress at this moment. I must save him; death to Blondeau!' At this moment Blondeau dipped his pen, black with erasures, into the ink, looked around his audience, and repeated for the third time, 'Marius Pontmercy!' I answered, 'Here!' and so your name was not erased."

"Sir—" Marius exclaimed.

"And mine was," added Laigle of Meaux.

"I do not understand you," said Marius.

Laigle continued:

"And yet it was very simple. I was near the desk to answer, and near the door to bolt. The professor looked at me with a certain fixedness, and suddenly Blondeau, who must be the crafty nose to which Boileau refers, leaps to the letter L, which is my letter, for I come from Meaux, and my name is L'Esgle."

"L'Aigle!" Marius interrupted, "what a glorious name."

"Blondeau arrives, sir, at that glorious name, and exclaims 'L'Aigle!' I answer, 'Here!' Then Blondeau looks at me with the gentleness of a tiger, smiles, and says, 'If you are Pontmercy you are not Laigle,' a phrase which appears offensive to you, but which was only lugubrious for me. After saying this, he erased me."

Marius exclaimed:

"I am really mortified, sir—"

"Before all," Laigle interrupted, "I ask leave to embalm Blondeau in a few phrases of heart-felt praise. I will suppose him dead, and there will not be much to alter in his thinness, paleness, coldness, stiffness, and smell, and I say, *Erudimini qui judicatis terram.* Here lies Blondeau, the nosy, Blondeau Nasica, the ox of discipline, *bos disciplinæ,* the mastiff of duty, the angel of the roll-call, who was straight, square, exact, rigid, honest, and hideous. God erased him as he erased me."

Marius continued, "I am most grieved—"

"Young man," said Laigle, "let this serve you as a lesson; in future be punctual."

"I offer a thousand apologies."

"And do not run the risk of getting your neighbor erased."

"I am in despair—"

Laigle burst into a laugh.

"And I am enchanted. I was on the downward road to become a lawyer, and this erasure saves me. I renounce the triumphs of the bar. I will not defend the orphan or attack the widow. I have obtained my expulsion, and I am indebted to you for it, M. Pontmercy. I intend to pay you a solemn visit of thanks; where do you live?"

"In this cab," said Marius.

"A sign of opulence," Laigle remarked calmly; "I congratulate you, for you have apartments at nine thousand francs a year."

At this moment Courfeyrac came out of the café.

Marius smiled sadly.

"I have been in this lodging for two hours, and am eager to leave it, but I do not know where to go."

"Come home with me," Courfeyrac said to him.

"I ought to have the priority," Laigle observed, "but then I have no home."

"Hold your tongue, Bossuet," Courfeyrac remarked.

"Bossuet," said Marius, "why, you told me your name was Laigle."

"Of Meaux," Laigle answered; "metaphorically Bossuet."

Courfeyrac got into the cab.

"Hotel de la Porte St. Jacques, driver," he said.

The same evening Marius was installed in a room in this house, next door to Courfeyrac.

3. *MARIUS IS ASTONISHED*

In a few days Marius was a friend of Courfeyrac, for youth is the season of prompt weldings and rapid cicatrizations. Marius by the side of Courfeyrac breathed freely, a great novelty for him. Courfeyrac asked him no questions, and did not even think of doing so, for at that age faces tell everything at once, and words are unnecessary. There are some young men of whose countenances you may say that they gossip—you look at them and know them. One morning, however, Courfeyrac suddenly asked him the question:

"By the way, have you any political opinion?"

"Eh! what!" said Marius, almost offended by the question.

"What are you?"

"Bonapartist—democrat."

"Gray shade of quiet mouse," Courfeyrac remarked.

On the next day he led Marius to the Café Musain, and whispered in his ear with a smile, "I must introduce you to the Revolution," and he led him to the room of the friends of the A. B. C. He introduced him to his companions, saying in a low voice, "a pupil," which Marius did not at all comprehend.

Marius had fallen into a mental wasp's nest, but, though he was silent and grave, he was not the less winged and armed.

Marius, hitherto solitary, and muttering soliloquies and asides through habit and taste, was somewhat startled by the swarm of young men around him. The tumultuous movement of all these minds at liberty and at work made his ideas whirl, and at times, in his confusion, they flew so far from him that he had a difficulty in finding them again. He heard philosophy, literature, art, history, and religion spoken of in an unexpected way; he caught a glimpse of strange aspects, and as he did not place them in perspective, he was not sure that he was not gazing at chaos. On giving up his grandfather's opinions for those of his father, he believed himself settled, but he now suspected, anxiously, and not daring to confess it to himself, that it was not so. The angle in which he looked at everything was beginning to be displaced afresh, and a certain oscillation shook all the horizons of his brain. It was a strange internal moving of furniture, and it almost made him ill.

It seemed as if there were no "sacred things" for these young men, and Marius heard singular remarks about all sorts of matters which were offensive to his still timid mind.

A play-bill came under notice, adorned with the title of an old stock tragedy of the so-called classical school. "Down with the tragedy dear to the bourgeois!" Bahorel shouted, and Marius heard Combeferre reply:

"You are wrong, Bahorel. The cits love tragedy, and they must be left at peace upon that point. Periwigged tragedy has a motive, and I am not one of those who for love of Æschylus contest its right to exist. There are sketches in nature and ready-made parodies in creation; a beak which is no beak, wings which are no wings, gills which are no gills, feet which are no feet, a dolorous cry which makes you inclined to laugh—there you have the duck. Now, since poultry exists by the side of the bird, I do not see why classic tragedy should not exist face to face with ancient tragedy."

Or else it happened accidentally that Marius passed along the Rue Jean Jacques Rousseau between Enjolras and Courfeyrac, and the latter seized his arm.

"Pay attention! this is the Rue Plâtrière, now called Rue Jean Jacques Rousseau, on account of a singular family that lived here sixty years back,

95

and they were Jean Jacques and Thérèse. From time to time little creatures were born; Thérèse brought them into the world, and Jean Jacques brought them to the Foundling."

And Enjolras reproved Courfeyrac.

"Silence before Jean Jacques! for I admire that man. I grant that he abandoned his children, but he adopted the people."

Not one of these young men ever uttered the words—the emperor; Jean Prouvaire alone sometimes said Napoleon; all the rest spoke of Bonaparte. Enjolras pronounced it Buonaparte.

Marius was vaguely astonished. *Initium sapientœ.*

4. *THE BACK ROOM OF THE CAFE MUSAIN*

ONE of the conversations among the young men at which Marius was present, and in which he mingled now and then, was a thorough shock for his mind.

It came off in the back room of the Café Musain, and nearly all the friends of the A. B. C. were collected on that occasion, and the chandelier was solemnly lighted. They talked about one thing and another, without passion and with noise, and with the exception of Enjolras and Marius, who were silent, each harangued somewhat hap-hazard. Conversations among chums at times display these peaceful tumults. It was a game and a skirmish as much as a conversation; words were thrown and caught up, and students were talking in all the four corners.

No female was admitted into this back room, excepting Louison, the washer-up of cups, who crossed it from time to time to go from the wash-house to the "laboratory."

Grantaire, who was quite intoxicated, was deafening the corner he had seized upon, by shouting things, reasonable and unreasonable, in a thundering voice:

"I am thirsty, mortals; I have dreamt that the tun of Heidelberg had a fit of apoplexy, and I was one of the dozen leeches applied to it. I want to drink, for I desire to forget life. Life is a hideous invention of somebody whom I am unacquainted with. It lasts no time and is worth nothing, and a man breaks his neck to live. Life is a scenery in which there are no practicables, and happiness is an old side-scene only painted on one side. The Ecclesiastes says, All is vanity; and I agree with the worthy gentleman, who possibly never existed. Zero, not liking to go about naked, clothed itself in vanity. O vanity! the dressing up of everything in big words! A kitchen is a laboratory, a dancer a professor, a mountebank a gymnast, a boxer a pugilist, an apothecary a chemist, a barber an artist, a bricklayer an architect, a jockey a sportsman, and a wood-louse a pterygibranch. Vanity has an obverse and a reverse; the obverse is stupid,—it is the negro with his glass beads; the reverse is ridiculous,—it is the philosopher in his rags. I weep over the one and laugh at the other. What are called horrors and disasters, and even honor and dignity, are generally made of mosaic. Kings make a toy of human pride. Caligula made a horse a consul, and Charles II knighted a sirloin of beef. Drape yourselves, therefore, between Incitatus Consul and Sir Roastbeef. As to the intrinsic value of people, it is not one bit more respectable; just listen to the panegyric which one neighbor makes of another. White against white is ferocious. If the lily could talk, how it would run down the dove; and the bigoted woman talking of a pious woman is more venomous than the asp and the whip-snake. It is a pity that I am an ignoramus, for I would quote a multitude of things, but I know nothing. But for all that I have always had sense: when I was a pupil of Gros, instead of daubing sketches I spent my time in prigging apples. So much for myself, but you others are as good as I, and I have no use for your perfections, excellency, and qualities, for every quality has its corresponding defect. The saving man is akin to the miser, the generous man is very nearly related to the prodigal, and the brave man trenches on the braggart. When you call a man very pious, you mean that he is a little bigoted, and there are just as many vices in virtue as there are holes in the mantle of Diogenes. Which do you admire—the killed or the killer, Cæsar or Brutus? People generally stick up for the killer. Long live Brutus! for he was a murderer. Such is virtue; it may be virtue, but it is folly at the same time. There are some queer spots on these great men;

the Brutus who killed Cæsar was in love with the statue of a boy. This statue was made by the Greek sculptor Strongylion who also produced that figure of an Amazon called Finelegs, Eucnemys, which Nero carried about with him when travelling. This Strongylion only left two statues, which brought Brutus and Nero into harmony; Brutus was in love with one and Nero with the other. History is but one long repetition, and one century is a plagiarism of another. The battle of Marengo is a copy of the battle of Pydna, and the Tolbiac of Clovis and the Austerlitz of Napoleon are as much alike as two drops of blood. I set but little value on victory; nothing is so stupid as conquering, true glory is to convince. But try to prove anything! you satisfy yourself with success, what mediocrity! and with conquering, what a wretched trifle! Alas! vanity and cowardice are everywhere, and everything obeys success, even grammar. *Si volet usus,* as Horace says. Hence I despise the whole human race. Suppose we descend from universals to particulars? would you wish me to begin admiring the peoples? what people, if you please? Is it Greece?—The Athenians, those Parisians of former time killed Phocion, as you might say Coligny, and adulated tyrants to such a pitch that Anacephorus said of Pisistratus, 'his urine attracts the bees.' The most considerable man in Greece for fifty years was the grammarian Philetas, who was so short and small that he was obliged to put lead in his shoes to keep the wind from blowing him away. On the great square of Corinth there was a statue sculptured by Silanion, and catalogued by Pliny, and it represented Episthatus. What did Episthatus achieve? He invented the cross-buttock. There you have a summary of Greece and glory, and now let us pass to others. Should I admire England? should I admire France? France, why? on account of Paris? I have just told you my opinion of the Athenians. England, why? on account of London? I hate Carthage, and, besides, London, the metropolis of luxury, is the headquarters of misery: in Charing Cross parish alone one hundred persons die annually of starvation. Such is Albion, and I will add, as crowning point, that I have seen an Englishwoman dancing in a wreath of roses and with blue spectacles. So, a groan for England. If I do not admire John Bull, ought I to admire brother Jonathan with his peculiar institution? Take away 'Time is money,' and what remains of England? take away 'Cotton is king,' and what remains of America? Germany is lymph and Italy bile. Shall we go into ecstasies about Russia? Voltaire admired that country, and he also admired China. I allow Russia has its beauties, among others a powerful despotism: but I pity the despots, for they have a delicate health. An Alexis decapitated, a Peter stabbed, a Paul strangled, another Paul flattened out with boot-heels, sundry Ivans butchered, several Nicholases and Basils poisoned—all this proves that the palace of the emperor of Russia is in a flagrantly unhealthy condition. All the civilized nations offer to the admiration of the thinker one detail, war. Now war, civilized war, exhausts and collects all the forms of banditism, from the brigandages of the trabuceros in the gorges of Mont Jaxa down to the forays of the Comanche Indians in the Doubtful Pass. Stuff, you will say to me, Europe is better than Asia, after all. I allow that Asia is absurd, but I do not exactly see what cause you have to laugh at the grand lama, you great western nations, who have blended with your fashions and elegances all the complicated filth of majesty, from the dirty chemise of Queen Isabelle down to the *chaise-percée* of the dauphin. At Brussels the most beer is consumed, at Stockholm the most brandy, at Madrid the most chocolate, at Amsterdam the most gin, at London the most wine, at Constantinople the most coffee, and at Paris the most absinthe,—these are all useful notions. Paris, after all, bears away the bell, for in that city the very rag-pickers are sybarites; and Diogenes would as soon have been a rag-picker on the Place Maubert as a philosopher at the Piræus. Learn this fact also; the wine-shops of the rag-pickers are called 'bibines,' and the most celebrated are the *Casserole* and the *Abattoir*. O pot-houses, sample-rooms, bar-rooms, grog-shops, rum-holes, gin-mills, dives, saloons, boozing-dens, wine-shops of the rag-pickers, caravanserais for caliphs, I call you to witness. I am a voluptuary. I dine at Richard's for fifty sous, and I want Persian carpets in which to roll the naked Cleopatra. Where is Cleopatra? ah, it is you. Louison? Good-evening."

Thus poured forth Grantaire, more than drunk, as he seized the plate-washer as she passed his corner.

Bossuet, stretching out his hand toward him, strove to make him be silent, but Grantaire broke out afresh.

"Eagle of Meaux, down with your paws; you produce no effect upon me with your gesture of Hippocrates refusing the *bric-a-brac* of Artaxerxes. You need not attempt to calm me and besides I am melancholy. What would you have me say? man is bad, man is a deformity; the butterfly is a success, but man is a mistake. God made a failure with that animal. A crowd is a choice of uglinesses; the first-comer is a scoundrel, and woman rhymes with human; yes, I have the spleen, complicated with melancholy, homesickness, and a dash of hypochondria, and I rage, and I yawn, and I am killing myself, I make myself horribly dull. To the Devil with God."

"Silence, big R," Bossuet remarked again, who was discussing a legal point with some chums, and was sunk to his waist in a sentence of judicial slang, of which the following is the end:

"For my part, although I am scarce an authority, and at the most an amateur lawyer, I assert this, that, according to the terms of the customs of Normandy, upon the Michaelmas day and in every year an equivalent must be paid to the lord of the manor, by all and singular, both by proprietors and by tenants for life, and that for every lease, copyhold, allodium, mortgage—"

"Echo, plaintive nymph!" Grantaire hummed.

Close to Grantaire, at an almost silent table, a quire of paper, an inkstand, and a pen between two small glasses announced that a farce was being sketched out.

This great affair was discussed in a low voice, and the heads of the workers almost touched.

"Let us begin with the names, for when you have the names you have the plot."

"That is true: dictate, and I will write."

"Monsieur Dorimon?"

"An annuitant?"

"Of course. His daughter Celestine."

"—Tine. Who next?"

"Colonel Sainval."

"Sainval is worn out. Say Valsin."

By the side of these theatrical aspirants another group, which also took advantage of the noise to talk low, were discussing a duel. An old student of thirty was advising a young man of eighteen, and explaining with what sort of adversary he had to deal.

"Hang it! you will have to be careful, for he is a splendid swordsman. He can attack, makes no useless feints, has a strong wrist, brilliancy, and mathematical parries. And then he is left-handed."

In the corner opposite to Grantaire, Joly and Bahorel were playing at dominoes and talking of love affairs.

"You are happy," said Joly, "you have a mistress who is always laughing."

"It is a fault she commits," Bahorel answered; "a man's mistress does wrong to laugh, for it encourages him to deceive her, for seeing her gay saves you from remorse. If you see her sad, you have scruples of conscience."

"Ungrateful man! a woman who laughs is so nice, and you never quarrel."

"That results from the treaty we made; on forming our little holy alliance, we gave each other a frontier which we never step beyond. Hence comes peace."

"Peace is happiness digesting."

"And you, Joly, how does your quarrel stand with Mamselle—you know whom I mean?"

"Oh, she still sulks with a cruel patience."

"And yet you are a lover of most touching thinness."

"Alas!"

"In your place, I would leave her."

"It's easy to say that."

"And to do. Is not her name Musichetta?"

"Yes, ah! my dear Bahorel, she is a superb girl, very literary, with little hands and feet, dresses with taste, is white and plump, and has eyes like a gypsy fortune-teller. I am wild about her."

"Then you must please her, dress well, buy fashionable trousers."

"For how much?" cried Grantaire.

In the third corner a poetical discussion was going on, and Pagan Mythology was quarreling with Christian Mythology. The point was Olympus, whose defeat Jean Prouvaire undertook through his romantic nature.

Jean Prouvaire was only timid when in repose; once excited, he broke out in a species of gayety, accentuated his enthusiasm, and he was at once laughing and lyrical.

"Let us not insult the gods," he said, "for perhaps they have not all departed, and Jupiter does not produce the effect of a dead man upon me. The gods are dreams, you say; well, even in nature such as it is at the present day, and after the flight of these dreams, we find again all the old Pagan myths. A mountain with the profile of a citadel, like the Vignemale, for instance, is still for me the head-dress of Cybele. It has not yet been proved to me that Pan does not come at night to whistle in the hollow trunks of the willows, while stopping their holes with his fingers in turn, and I have ever believed that Io had some connection with the cascade of Pissevache."

In the last corner politics were being discussed, and the Charter was pulled to pieces. Combeferre supported it feebly, while Courfeyrac attacked it energetically. There was on the table an unlucky copy of the Charte Touquet. Courfeyrac had seized it, and was shaking it, mixing with his arguments the rustling of this sheet of paper.

"In the first place, I do not want kings; even from the economic point of view alone I do not want them, for a king is a parasite, and there are no gratis monarchs. Listen to this, kings are an expensive luxury. On the death of Francis I the public debt of France was thirty thousand livres, on the death of Louis XIV it was two milliards six hundred millions, at twenty-eight livres the marc, which in 1740 was equivalent, according to Desmarets, to four milliards five hundred millions, and at the present day would be equal to twelve milliards. In the second place, no offense to Combeferre, a conceded charter is a bad expedient of civilization, for saving the transaction, softening the passage, deadening the shock, making the nation pass insensibly from monarchy to democracy by the practice of constitutional fictions—all these are detestable fictions. No, no, let us never give the people a false light, and principles pine and grow pale in your constitutional cellar. No bastardizing, no compromise, no concession, from king to people! In all these concessions there is an article XIV, and by the side of the hand that gives is the claw that takes back again. I distinctly refuse your charter, for a charter is a mask, and there is falsehood behind it. A people that accepts a charter abdicates, and right is only right when entire. No charter, then, I say."

It was winter-time, and two logs were crackling on the hearth; this was tempting, and Courfeyrac did not resist. He crumpled up the poor Charte Touquet and threw it in the fire,—the paper blazed, and Combeferre philosophically watched the masterpiece of Louis XVIII burning, contenting himself with saying:

"The charter metamorphosed into flame."

And sarcasms, sallies, jests, that French thing which is called *entrain,* that English thing which is called humor, good taste and bad, sound and unsound reasoning, all the rockets of dialogue ascending together and crossing each other in all parts of the room, produced above their heads a species of merry explosion.

5 · ENLARGEMENT OF THE HORIZON

The collision of young minds has this admirable thing about it, that the spark can never be foreseen or the lightning divined. What will shoot forth presently? no one knows. The burst of laughter is heard, and at the next moment seriousness makes its entrance.

The impulse is given by some chance word, a pun opens the way to the unexpected. The dialogue has sharp turns when the view suddenly changes. Hazard is the scene-shifter in each conversation. A stern thought, which strangely issued from a clash of words, suddenly flashed through the medley in which Grantaire, Bahorel, Prouvaire, Bossuet, Combeferre, and Courfeyrac were blindly slashing and pointing.

How is it that a phrase suddenly springs up in conversation and underlines itself at once in the attention of those who trace it? as we have just said, no one knows. In the midst of the general confusion Bossuet concluded some remark he made to Combeferre with the date,

"June 18, 1815, Waterloo."

At this name of Waterloo, Marius, who had been leaning over a glass of water, removed his hand from under his chin, and began looking intently at the company.

"Pardieu!" Courfeyrac exclaimed (*Parbleu* at this period was beginning to grow out of fashion). "That number eighteen is strange, and strikes me, for it is Bonaparte's fatal number. Place Louis before and Brumaire behind, and you have the man's whole destiny, with this expressive peculiarity, that the beginning has its heel rubbed by the end."

Enjolras, who had hitherto been dumb, now broke the silence, and said:

"Courfeyrac, you mean the crime by the expiation."

This word *crime* exceeded the measure which Marius, who was already greatly affected by this sudden reference to Waterloo, could accept. He rose, walked slowly to the map of France hanging on the wall, on the bottom of which could be seen an island in a separate compartment; he placed his finger on this and said:

"Corsica, a small island, which made France very great."

This was the breath of frozen air; all broke off, for they felt that something was about to begin.

Bahorel, who was assuming a victorious attitude in answering Bossuet, gave it up in order to listen.

Enjolras, whose blue eye was fixed on no one and seemed to be examining space, answered without looking at Marius:

"France requires no Corsica to be great. France is great because she is France, *quia nominor leo.*"

Marius felt no desire to give way; he turned to Enjolras, and his voice had a strange vibration, produced by his internal emotion.

"Heaven forbid that I should diminish France; but it is not diminishing her to amalgamate Napoleon with her. Come, let us talk; I am a new-comer among you, but I confess that you astonish me. Where are we? who are we? who are you? who am I? Let us come to an understanding about the emperor. I hear you call him Buonaparte, laying a stress on the *u,* like the royalists, but I must tell you that my grandfather does better still, for he says 'Buonaparté.' I fancied you young men, but where do you keep your enthusiasm, and what do you do with it? whom do you admire, if it is not the emperor? and what more do you want? if you will not have that great man, what great man would you have? He had everything, he was complete, and in his brain was the cube of human faculties. He made codes like Justinian, and dictated like Cæsar; his conversation blended the lightning of Pascal with the thunder of Tacitus; he made history and wrote it, and his bulletins are Iliads; he combined the figures of Newton with the metaphor of Mahomet. He left behind him in the East words great as the Pyramids; at Tilsit he taught majesty to emperors, at the Academy of Sciences he answered Laplace, at the Council of State he held his own against Merlin,—he gave a soul to the geometry of the one and to the sophistry of the other, for he was legist with the lawyers, sidereal with the astronomers. Like Cromwell, blowing out one of two candles, he went to the Temple to bargain for a curtain tassel; he saw everything, knew everything, but that did not prevent him from laughing heartily by the cradle of his new-born son. And, all at once, startled Europe listened, armies set out, parks of artillery rolled along, bridges of boats were thrown over rivers, clouds of cavalry galloped in the hurricane, and shouts, bugles, and the crashing of thrones could be heard all around. The frontiers of kingdoms oscillated on the map, the sound of a superhuman sword being drawn from its scabbard could be heard, and he was seen, standing erect on the horizon, with a gleam in his hand and a splendor in his eyes, unfolding in the thunder his two wings, the grand army and the Old Guard. He was the archangel of war."

All were silent, and Enjolras hung his head. Silence always produces to some extent the effect of acquiescence, or a species of setting the back against the wall. Marius, almost without drawing breath, continued with increased enthusiasm:

"Let us be just, my friends. What a splendid destiny it is for a people to be the empire of such an emperor, when that people is France and adds its genius to the genius of that man! To appear and reign; to march and triumph; to have as bivouacs every capital; to select grenadiers and make kings of them; to decree the downfall of dynasties; to transfigure Europe at double-quick step; to feel when you threaten that you lay your hand on the sword-hilt of God; to follow in one man Hannibal, Cæsar, and Charlemagne; to be the people of a ruler who accompanies your every daybreak with the brilliant announcement of a battle gained; to be aroused in the morning by the guns of the Invalides; to cast into the abysses of light prodigious words which are eternally luminous,—Marengo, Arcola, Austerlitz, Jena, and Wagram!—to produce at each moment on the zenith of centuries constellations of victories; to make the French empire a pendant of the Roman empire; to be the great nation, and give birth to the great army; to send legions all over the world, as the mountain sends its eagles in all directions, to conquer, rule, and crush; to be in Europe a people gilt by glory; to sound a Titanic flourish of trumpets through history; to conquer the world twice, by conquest and by amazement—all this is sublime, and what is there greater?"

"To be free," said Combeferre.

Marius in his turn hung his head. This simple and cold remark had traversed his epical effusion like a steel blade, and he felt it fainting away within him. When he raised his eyes Combeferre was no longer present; probably satisfied with his reply to the apotheosis, he had left the room, and all, excepting Enjolras, had followed him. Enjolras, alone with Marius, was looking at him gravely. Marius, however, having slightly collected his ideas, did not confess himself defeated, and he was in all probability about to begin afresh upon Enjolras, when he suddenly heard some one singing on the staircase. It was Combeferre, and this is what he sang:

> *"Si César m'avait donné*
> *La gloire et la guerre,*
> *Et qu'il me fallût quitter*
> *L'amour de ma mère,*
> *Je dirais au grand César:*
> *Reprends ton sceptre et ton char,*
> *J'aime mieux ma mère, ô gué!*
> *J'aime mieux ma mère!"*

The tender and solemn accent with which Combeferre sang this couplet imparted to it a species of strange grandeur. Marius, with his eye pensively fixed on the ceiling, repeated almost mechanically, "my mother!"

At this moment he felt Enjolras's hand on his shoulder.

"Citizen," he said to him, "my mother is the republic."

6 · *RES ANGUSTA*

THIS evening left a sad obscurity and a profound shock in the mind of Marius, and he felt what the earth probably feels when it is opened by the plowshare that the grain may be deposited; it only feels the wound, and the joy of giving birth does not arrive till later.

Marius was gloomy; he had only just made himself a faith, and must he reject it again? He declared to himself that he would not; he resolved not to doubt, and began doubting involuntarily. To stand between two religions, one of which you have not yet lost, and the other of which you have not yet entered, is unendurable, and twilight only pleases bat-like souls. Marius was an open eyeball and wanted true light; and the semi-luster of doubt hurt him. Whatever might be his desire to remain where he was and cling to it, he was invincibly constrained to continue, to advance, to think, to go further. Whither would this lead him? He feared lest, after taking so many steps which had drawn him near his father, he was now going to take steps which would carry him away from him. His discomfort increased with all the reflections that occurred to him, and a rampart was drawn around him. He agreed neither with his grandfather nor his friends; he was rash for the one and behindhand for the others; and he found himself doubly isolated, on the side of old age and on the side of youth. He left off going to the Café Musain.

In the troubled state of his conscience he did not think at all of certain serious sides of existence, but the realities of life will not allow themselves to be forgotten, and so they suddenly came to jog his memory. One morning the landlord came into Marius's room, and said to him:

"Monsieur Courfeyrac recommended you?"

"Yes."

"But I want my money."

"Ask Courfeyrac to come and speak to me," said Marius.

When Courfeyrac arrived the landlord left them, and Marius told his friend what he had not dreamed of telling him yet,—that he was, so to speak, alone in the world, and had no relations.

"What will become of you?" said Courfeyrac.

"I do not know," Marius answered.

"What do you intend doing?"

"I do not know."

"Have you any money?"

"Fifteen francs."

"Are you willing to borrow from me?"

"Never."

"Have you clothes?"

"There they are."

"And jewelry?"

"A gold watch."

"I know a second-hand clothes-man who will take your overcoat and a pair of trousers."

"Very good."

"You will only have a pair of trousers, a waistcoat, a hat, and coat left."

"And my boots."

"What? you will not go barefoot? what opulence!"

"That will be enough."

"I know a jeweler who will buy your watch."

"All right."

"No, it is not all right; what will you do after?"

"Anything I can that is honest."

"Do you know English?"

"No."

"Or German?"

"No."

"All the worse."

"Why so?"

"Because a friend of mine, a publisher, is preparing a sort of Encyclopedia, for which you could have translated English or German articles. The pay is bad, but it is possible to live on it."

"I will learn English and German."

"And in the meanwhile?"

"I will eat my clothes and my watch."

The clothes-dealer was sent for, and gave twenty francs for the coat and trousers; next they went to the jeweler's, who bought the watch for forty-five francs.

"That's not so bad," said Marius to Courfeyrac on returning to the hotel; "with my fifteen francs, that makes eighty."

"And your bill here?" Courfeyrac observed.

"Oh, I forgot that," said Marius.

The landlord presented his bill, which Marius was bound to pay at once; it amounted to seventy francs.

"I have ten francs left," said Marius.

"The deuce," Courfeyrac replied; "you will spend five francs while learning English, and five while learning German. That will be swallowing a language very quickly or a five-franc piece very slowly."

Aunt Gillenormand, who was not a bad-hearted woman in cases of distress, discovered her nephew's abode.

One morning, when Marius returned from college, he found a letter from his aunt and the "sixty pistoles," that is to say, six hundred francs in gold, in a sealed-up box.

Marius sent the thirty louis back to his aunt with a respectful note, in which he stated that he would be able in future to take care of himself; at that moment he had just three francs left.

The aunt did not tell grandpapa of this refusal, through fear of raising his exasperation to the highest pitch; besides, had he not said, "Never mention that blood-drinker's name in my presence."

Marius quitted the hotel of the Porte St. Jacques, as he did not wish to run into debt.

BOOK V

THE GOOD OF BAD LUCK

1. MARIUS IS INDIGENT

LIFE became severe for Marius; eating his clothes and his watch was nothing, but he also went through that indescribable course which is called "chewing the cud." This is a horrible thing which contains days without bread, nights without sleep, evenings without candle, a house without fire, weeks without work, a future without hope, a threadbare coat, an old hat at which the girls laugh, the door which you find locked at night because you have not paid your rent, the insolence of the porter and the eating-house keeper, the grins of neighbors, humiliations, dignity trampled under foot, any work taken, disgust, bitterness, and desperation. Marius learned how all this is devoured, and how it is often the only thing which a man has to eat. At that moment of life when a man requires pride because he requires love, he felt himself derided because he was meanly dressed, and ridiculous because he was poor. At the age when youth swells the heart with an imperial pride, he looked down more than once at his worn-out boots, and knew the unjust shame and the burning blushes of wretchedness. It is an admirable and terrible trial, from which the weak come forth infamous and the strong sublime. It is the crucible into which destiny throws a man whenever it wishes to have a scoundrel or a demi-god.

For man's great actions are performed in minor struggles. There are obstinate and unknown braves who defend themselves inch by inch in the shadows against the fatal invasion of want and turpitude. They are noble and mysterious triumphs which no eye sees, no renown rewards, and no flourish of trumpets salutes. Life, misfortune, isolation, abandonment, and poverty are battle-fields which have their heroes—obscure heroes who are at times greater than illustrious heroes.

Firm and exceptional natures are thus created: misery, which is nearly always a step-mother, is at times a mother; destitution brings forth the power of soul and mind; distress is the nurse of pride, and misfortune is an excellent milk for the magnanimous.

There was a time in Marius's life when he swept his own landing, when he bought a half-pennyworth of Brie cheese of the fruiterer, when he waited till nightfall to go into the baker's and buy a loaf, which he carried stealthily to his garret as if he had stolen it. At times there might have been seen slipping into the butcher's shop at the corner, among the gossiping cooks who elbowed him, a young, awkward man with books under his arm, who had a timid and wild air, who on entering removed his hat from his dripping forehead, made a deep bow to the astonished butcher's wife, another to the foreman, asked for a mutton-chop, paid three or four pence, wrapped the chop in paper, placed it between two books under his arm, and went away. It was Marius, and on this chop, which he cooked himself, he lived for three days.

On the first he ate the lean, on the second he ate the fat, and on the third he gnawed the bone. Several times did Aunt Gillenormand make tentatives and send him the sixty pistoles, but Marius always returned them, saying that he wanted for nothing.

He was still in mourning for his father when the revolution we have described took place within him, and since then he had not left off black clothes, but the clothes left him. A day arrived when he had no coat, though his trousers would still pass muster. What was he to do? Courfeyrac, to whom he on his side rendered several services, gave him an old coat. For thirty sous Marius had it turned by some porter, and it became a new coat. But it was green, and Marius henceforth did not go out till nightfall, which caused his coat to appear black. As he still wished to be in mourning, he wrapped himself in the night.

Through all this he contrived to pass his examination. He was supposed to inhabit Courfeyrac's rooms, which were decent, and where a certain number of legal tomes, supported by broken-backed volumes of novels, represented the library prescribed by the regulations. He had his letters addressed to Courfeyrac's lodgings.

When Marius was called to the bar, he informed his grandfather of the fact in a cold letter, which, however, was full of submission and respect. M. Gillenormand took the letter with a trembling hand, read it, tore it in four parts, and threw them into the basket. Two or three days later, Mlle. Gillenormand heard her father, who was alone in his room, talking aloud, which always happened when he was agitated. She listened and heard the old gentleman say, "If you were not an ass, you would know that you cannot be at the same time a baron and a lawyer."

2 · MARIUS POOR

It is the same with misery as with everything else,—in the end it becomes possible, it assumes a shape. A man vegetates, that is to say, is developed in a certain poor way, which is, however, sufficient for life. This is the sort of existence which Marius Pontmercy had secured.

He had got out of the narrowest part, and the defile had grown slightly wider before him. By labor, courage, perseverance, and his will, he contrived to earn about seven hundred francs a year by his work. He had taught himself English and German, and, thanks to Courfeyrac, who introduced him to his friend the publisher, he filled the modest post of hack in his office. He wrote prospectuses, translated newspapers, annotated editions, compiled biographies, and, one year with the other, his net receipts were seven hundred francs. He lived upon them—how? not badly, as we shall show.

Marius occupied at No. 50-52, for the annual rent of thirty francs, a garret without a fire-place, which was called a "cabinet," and only contained the indispensable articles of furniture, and this furniture was his own. He paid three francs a month to the old principal lodger for sweeping out his room, and bringing him every morning a little hot water, a new-laid egg, and a half-penny roll. On this roll and egg he breakfasted, and the outlay varied from a penny to two-pence, according as eggs were dear or cheap. At six in the evening he went to the Rue St. Jacques to dine at Rousseau's, exactly opposite Basset's, the print-shop at the corner of the Rue des Mathurins. He did not eat soup, but he ordered a plate of meat for six sous, half a plate of vegetables for three sous, and dessert three sous. For three sous he had as much bread as he liked, and for wine he drank water. On paying at the bar, where Madame Rousseau, at that period a fat and still good-looking dame, was majestically enthroned, he gave a sou for the waiter, and Madame Rousseau gave him a smile. Then he went away; for sixteen sous he had a smile and a dinner.

This Rousseau restaurant, where so few bottles and so many waterjugs were emptied, was rather a sedative than a restorer. It no longer exists, but the master used to have a wonderful nickname,—he was called Rousseau the aquatic.

Thus, with breakfast four sous, dinner sixteen, his food cost him three hundred and sixty-five francs a year. Add thirty francs for rent and the thirty-six francs for the old woman and a few minor expenses, and for four hundred and fifty francs, Marius was boarded, lodged and served. His clothes cost him a hundred francs, his linen fifty, his washing fifty, but the whole did not exceed six hundred and fifty francs. He had fifty left, and was rich; at times he would lend ten francs to a friend, and Courfeyrac once actually borrowed sixty francs of him. As for firing, as Marius had no chimney, he "simplified" it.

Marius always had two complete suits: one old, for everyday wear, and the other new, for occasions, and both were black. He had but three shirts,—one on, one in the drawer, and one at the wash, and he renewed them as they became worn out. As they were usually torn he had a fashion of buttoning up his coat to the chin.

It had taken Marius years to reach this flourishing condition, rude and difficult years, in which he underwent great struggles, but he had not failed to himself a single day. As regarded want, he had suffered everything and he had done everything except run into debt. He gave himself the credit of never having owed a farthing to any one, for to him debt was the beginning of slavery. He said to himself that a creditor is worse than a master; for a master holds only your person, while a creditor holds your dignity and may insult it. Sooner than borrow he did not eat, and he had known many days of fasting. Knowing that unless a man is careful, reduction of fortune may lead to baseness of soul, he jealously watched over his pride: many a remark or action which, under other circumstances, he would have regarded as deference, now seemed to him platitudes, and he refrained from them. He ventured nothing, as he did not wish to fall back; he had on his face a stern blush, and he was timid almost to rudeness.

In all his trials he felt encouraged, and to some extent supported, by a secret force within him; for the soul helps the body and at times raises it, and is the only bird that upholds its cage.

By the side of his father's name another name was engraved on Marius's heart, that of Thénardier. Marius, in his grave and enthusiastic nature, enveloped in a species of glory the man to whom he owed his father's life, that intrepid sergeant who saved his colonel among the balls and bullets of Waterloo. He never separated the memory of this man from that of his father, and he associated them in his veneration; it was a species of shrine with two steps, the high altar for the colonel, the low one for Thénardier. What doubled the tenderness of his gratitude was the thought of the misfortune into which he knew that Thénardier had fallen and was swallowed up. Marius had learned at Montfermeil the ruin and bankruptcy of the unfortunate landlord, and since then had made extraordinary efforts to find his trail and try to reach him in the frightful abyss of misery through which Thénardier had disappeared. Marius went everywhere: he visited Chelles, Bondy, Gournay Nogent, and Lagny, and obstinately continued his search for three years, spending in these explorations the little money he saved. No one was able to give him the slightest information of Thénardier, and it was supposed he had gone to a foreign country. His creditors had sought him too, with less love, but quite as much perseverance, as Marius, and had been unable to lay hands on him. Marius accused and felt angry with himself for not succeeding in his search; it was the only debt the colonel left him, and he felt in honor bound to pay it. "What," he thought, "when my father lay dying on the battle-field, Thénardier contrived to find him in the midst of the smoke and grape-shot, and carried him off on his shoulders, although he owed him nothing, while I, who owe so much to Thénardier, am unable to come up with him in the shadow where he is dying of want, and in my turn bring him back from death to life. Oh, I will find him!" In fact, Marius would have given one of his arms to find Thénardier, and his last drop of blood to save him from want; and his sweetest and most magnificent dream was to see Thénardier, do him some service and say to him, "You do not know me, but I know you; I am here, dispose of me as you please."

3. *MARIUS GROWN UP*

At this period Marius was twenty years of age, and he had left his grandfather's house for three. They remained on the same terms, without attempting reconciliation or trying to meet. What good would it have been to meet?—to come into collision again? Which of them would have got the better? Marius was the bronze vessel, but Father Gillenormand was the iron pot.

We are bound to say that Marius was mistaken as to his grandfather's heart; he imagined that M. Gillenormand had never loved him, and that this sharp, harsh, laughing old gentleman, who cursed, shouted, stormed, and raised his cane, only felt for him at the most that light and severe affection of the Gérontes of comedy. Marius was mistaken: there are fathers who do not love their children; but there is not a grandfather who does not adore his grandson. In his heart, as we said, M. Gillenormand idolized Marius; he idolized him, it is true, after his fashion, with an accompaniment of abuse and even of blows, but when the lad had disappeared he felt a black gap in his heart; he insisted upon his name not being mentioned, but regretted that he was so strictly obeyed. At the outset he hoped that this Bonapartist, this Jacobin, this terrorist, this septembrist, would return, but weeks passed, months passed, years passed, and, to the great despair of M. Gillenormand, the drinker of blood did not re-appear. "I could not do otherwise, though, than turn him out," the grandfather said; and asked himself, "If it were to be done again, would I do it?" His pride at once answered Yes, but his old head, which he silently shook, sorrowfully answered No. He had his hours of depression, for he missed Marius, and old men require affection as much as they do the sun to warm them. However strong he might naturally be, the absence of Marius had changed something in him; for no consideration in the world would he have taken a step toward the "little scamp," but he suffered. He lived in greater retirement than ever at the Marais; he was still gay and violent as of yore, but his gayety had a convulsive harshness, as if it contained grief and passion, and his violence generally terminated with a sort of gentle and sombre depression. He would say to himself at times, "Oh, if he were to come back, what a hearty box of the ears I would give him!"

As for the aunt, she thought too little to love much; to her Marius was only a black and vague profile, and in the end she paid much less attention to him than to the cat or the parrot which she probably had. What added to Father Gillenormand's secret suffering was that he shut it up within himself, and did not allow it to be divined. His chagrin was like one of those newly invented furnaces which consume their own smoke. At times it happened that officious friends would speak to him about Marius, and ask, "How is your grandson, and what is he doing?" The old bourgeois would answer, with a sigh if he were sad, or with a flip to his frill if he wished to appear gay, "Baron Pontmercy is playing the lawyer in some corner."

While the old gentleman regretted, Marius applauded himself. As is the case with all good hearts, misfortune had freed him from bitterness; he thought of M. Gillenormand gently, but he was resolved never to accept anything from a man *who had been unjust to his father.* This was the mitigated translation of his first indignation. Moreover, he was glad that he had suffered, and was still suffering, for he did so for his father. The hardness of his life satisfied and pleased him, and he said to himself with a sort of joy that it was the least he could do, and that it was an expiation; that, were it not so, he would have been punished, otherwise and hereafter, for his impious indifference toward his father, and such a father,—that it would not have been just for his father to have all the suffering and he none; and, besides, what were his toil and want when compared with the colonel's heroic life? Lastly, that his only way of approaching his father, and resembling him, was to be valiant against indigence, as he had been brave against the enemy, and that this was doubtless what the colonel meant by the words, *he will be worthy of it*— words which Marius continued to bear, not on his chest, as the colonel's letter had disappeared, but in his heart.

And then, again, on the day when his grandfather turned him out he was only a boy, while now he was a man and felt he was so. Misery (we lay a stress on the fact) had been kind to him, for poverty in youth, when it succeeds, has the magnificent result of turning the whole will to effort, and the whole soul to aspiration. Poverty at once lays bare material life and renders it hideous; and hence come indescribable soarings toward the ideal life. The rich young man has a thousand brilliant and coarse amusements,—races, shooting, dogs, tobacco, gambling, good dinners, and so on, which are occupations of the lower part of the mind at the expense of the higher and more delicate part. The poor young man has to work for his bread, and when he has eaten he has only reverie left him. He goes to the gratis spectacles which God gives him; he looks at the sky, space, the stars, the flowers, the children, the humanity in which he is suffering, and the creation in which he radiates. He looks so much at humanity that he sees the soul, and so much at creation that he sees God. He dreams, and feels himself great; he dreams again, and feels himself tender. From the egotism of the man who suffers, he passes to the compassion of the man who contemplates, and an admirable feeling is aroused in him—forgetfulness of self, and pity for all. On thinking of the numberless enjoyments which nature offers, gives, and lavishes on open minds, and refuses to closed minds, he, the millionaire of intellect, learns to pity the millionaire of money. Hatred departs from his heart in proportion as brightness enters his mind. Moreover, was he unhappy? no, for the wretchedness of a young man is never wretched. Take the first lad who passes, however poor he may be, with his health, his strength, his quick step, his sparkling eyes, his blood circulating warmly, his black hair, his ruddy cheeks, his coral lips, his white teeth, and his pure breath—and he will ever be an object of envy to an old emperor. And then, each morning he goes to earn his livelihood, and while his hands can earn bread his backbone gains strength, and his brain ideas. When his work is ended he returns to ineffable ecstasy, to contemplation and joy; he lives with his feet in affliction, in obstacles, on the pavement, in the brambles, or at times in the mud, but his head is in the light. He is firm, serene, gentle, peaceful, attentive, serious, satisfied with a little, and benevolent, and he blesses God for having given him two riches which rich men often want—labor which makes him free, and thought that renders him worthy.

This is what went on in Marius, and, truth to tell, he inclined almost too much to the side of contemplation. From the day when he felt tolerably certain of a livelihood, he stopped there, thinking it good to be poor, and taking from labor hours which he gave to thought. That is to say, he spent entire days now and then in dreaming, plunged like a vision-ary into the silent delights of ecstasy. He had thus arranged the problem of this life; to toil as little as possible at the material task, in order to work as much as possible on the impalpable task—in other words, to devote a few hours to real life, and throw the rest into infinity. He did not per-ceive, as he fancied that he wanted for nothing, that contemplation, thus understood, ended by becoming one of the forms of indolence; that he had contented himself with subduing the absolute necessities of life, and that he was resting too soon.

It was evident that for such a generous and energetic nature as his this could only be a transitional state, and that at the first collision with the inevitable complications of destiny Marius would wake up.

In the meanwhile, though, he was called to the bar, and, whatever Father Gillenormand might think, he did not play the pleader, for reverie had turned him away from pleas. It was a bore to flatter attorneys, attend regularly at the Palais de Justice, and seek for briefs. And why should he do so? he saw no reason to change his means of existence; his obscure task was certain, he had but little labor over it, and, as we have explained, he considered his income satisfactory.

One of the publishers for whom he worked, M. Magimel, I think, offered to take him into his house, lodge him comfortably, find him regular work, and pay him one thousand five hundred francs a year. To be comfortably lodged and have one thousand five hundred francs a year! doubtless agreeable things, but then, to resign his liberty, to be a hired servant, a sort of literary clerk! In the opinion of Marius, if he accepted, his position would become better and worse; he would gain comfort and lose dignity; he would exchange a complete and fine mis-fortune for an ugly and ridiculous constraint; it would be something like a blind man who became one-eyed. So he declined the offer.

Marius lived in solitude; through the inclination he had to remain outside everything, and also through the commotion he had undergone, he held aloof from the society presided over by Enjolras. They remained excellent friends, and ready to help each other when the opportunity offered, but nothing more. Marius had two friends, one, young Courfey-rac, the other, old M. Mabœuf, and he inclined to the latter. In the first place, he owed to him the revolution which had taken place in him, and his knowledge and love of his father. "He operated on me for the cata-ract," he would say

Certainly, this churchwarden had been decisive.

For all that, M. Mabœuf had only been in this affair the calm and impassive agent of Providence. He had enlightened Marius accidentally and unconsciously, just as a candle does which some one brings into a room; but he had been the candle, and not the some one.

As for the internal political revolution which had taken place in Marius, M. Mabœuf was entirely incapable of understanding, wishing, or directing it.

As we shall meet M. Mabœuf again, hereafter, a few remarks about him will not be thrown away.

4 . M. MABOEUF

ON the day when M. Mabœuf said to Marius, "I certainly approve of political opinions," he expressed the real state of his mind. All political opinions were a matter of indifference to him, and he approved of them all without distinction, that they might leave him at peace, just as the Greeks called the Furies "the lovely, the kind, the exquisite," the Eumenides. M. Mabœuf's political opinion was to love plants passionately, and books even more. He possessed, like everybody else, his termination in *ist*, without which no one could have lived at that day, but he was neither royalist, Bonapartist, chartist, Orleanist, nor anarchist,—he was a botanist.

He did not understand how men could come to hate each other for trifles like the charter, democracy, legitimacy, monarchy, the republic, etc., when there were in the world all sorts of mosses, grasses, and plants which they could look at, and piles of folios, and even 32 mos, whose pages they could turn over. He was very careful not to be useless; his having books did not prevent him reading them, and being a botanist did not prevent him being a gardener. When he knew Colonel Pontmercy, there was this sympathy between them, that the colonel did

for flowers what he did for fruits. M. Mabœuf had succeeded in producing pears as sweet as those of St. Germain; it is one of those combinations from which sprang, as it seems, the autumn Mirabelle, which
is still celebrated, and no less perfumed than the summer one. He
attended mass more through gentleness than devotion, and because,
while he loved men's faces but hated their noise, he found them at church
congregated and silent, and feeling that he must hold some position in
the state, he selected that of churchwarden. He had never succeeded in
loving any woman so much as a tulip bulb, or any man so much as an
Elzevir. He had long passed his sixtieth year, when some one asked him
one day, "How is it that you never married?" "I forgot it," he said. When
he happened to say—and to whom does it not happen?—"Oh, if I were
rich!" it was not when ogling a pretty girl, like Father Gillenormand,
but when contemplating a quarto. He lived alone with an old housekeeper; he was rather gouty, and when he slept his old chalk-stoned
fingers formed an arch in the folds of the sheets. He had written and
published a "Flora of the Environs of Cauteretz," with colored plates, a
work of some merit, of which he possessed the plates, and sold it himself.
People rang at his door in the Rue Mézières two or three times a day to
buy a copy; he made a profit of about two thousand francs a year by the
book, and that was nearly his whole fortune. Although poor, he had
contrived by patience and privations, and with time, to form a valuable
collection of all sorts of rare examples. He never went out without a
book under his arm, and frequently returned with two. The sole ornaments of his four rooms on the ground floor, which, with a small garden,
formed his lodging, were herbals and engravings by old masters. The
sight of a musket or a saber froze him, and in his life he had never walked
up to a cannon, not even at the Invalides. He had a tolerable stomach, a
brother a curé, very white hair, no teeth left in his mouth or in his mind,
a tremor all over him, a Picard accent, a childish laugh, and the air of
an old sheep. Withal, he had no other friend among the living than an
old bookseller at the Porte St. Jacques of the name of Royol; and the
dream of his life was to naturalize indigo in France.

His maid-servant was also a variety of innocence. The good woman
was an old maid, and Sultan, her tom-cat, who might have miauled the
Miserere of Allegri in the Sistine Chapel, filled her heart, and sufficed
for the amount of passion within her. Not one of her dreams had ever
gone so far as a man, and had not got beyond her cat; like him, she had
mustaches. Her glory was perfectly white caps, and she spent her time

on Sunday, after mass, in counting the linen in her box, and spreading on her bed the gowns which she bought in the piece and never had made up. She knew how to read, and M. Mabœuf had christened her Mother Plutarch.

M. Mabœuf had taken a fancy to Marius, because the young man, being young and gentle, warmed his old age without startling his timidity. Youth, combined with gentleness, produces on aged people the effect of sun without wind. When Marius was saturated with military glory, gunpowder, marches and countermarches, and all the prodigious battles in which his father gave and received such mighty saber cuts, he went to see M. Mabœuf, who talked to him about the hero in his connection with flowers.

About the year 1830 his brother, the curé, died, and almost immediately after, as when night arrives, the entire horizon became dark for M. Mabœuf. The bankruptcy of a notary despoiled him of ten thousand francs, all he possessed of his brother's capital and his own, while the revolution of July produced a crisis in the book trade. In times of pressure the first thing which does not sell is a *Flora,* and the "Flora of the Environs of Cauteretz" stopped dead. Weeks passed without a purchaser. At times M. Mabœuf started at the sound of the house-bell, but Mother Plutarch would say to him sadly, "It is the water-carrier, sir." In a word, M. Mabœuf left the Rue Mézières one day, abdicated his office as church-warden, gave up St. Sulpice, sold a portion, not of his books, but of his engravings, for which he cared least, and installed himself in a small house on the boulevard Montparnasse, where, however, he only remained three months, for two reasons—in the first place, the ground-floor and garden cost three hundred francs, and he did not dare set aside more than two hundred francs for rent; and secondly, as he was close to the Fatou shooting-gallery, he heard pistol-shots, which he could not endure.

He carried off his *Flora,* his copper-plates, his herbals, portfolios, and books, and settled down near the Salpetrière, in a sort of hut, in the village of Austerlitz, where he rented for fifty crowns a year three rooms, a garden inclosed by a hedge, and a well. He took advantage of this removal to sell nearly all his furniture. On the day when he entered his new house he was in very good spirits, and drove in with his own hands the nails on which to hang the engravings; he dug in his garden for the rest of the day, and at night, seeing that Mother Plutarch had an anxious look and was thoughtful, he tapped her on the shoulder and said with a smile, "We have the indigo."

Only two visitors, the publsher and Marius, were allowed admission to his hut in Austerlitz, a noisy name, by the way, which was most disagreeable to him.

As we have remarked, things of this world permeate very slowly brains absorbed in wisdom, or mania, or, as often happens, in both at once. Their own destiny is remote from them. The result of such concentrations is a passiveness which, were it of a reasoning nature, would resemble philosophy. Men sink, pass away, drift away, even crumble away without exactly noticing, though this always ends with a re-awakening, but a tardy one. In the meanwhile, it appears as if they are neutral in the game which is being played between their happiness and misery; they are the stakes, and look on at the game with indifference.

It was thus that M. Mabœuf remained rather childishly but most profoundly serene, in the obscurity that was enveloping him gradually, and while his hopes were being extinguished in turn. The habits of his mind had the regular movement of a clock, and when he was once wound up by an illusion he went for a very long time, even when the illusion had disappeared. A clock does not stop at the precise moment when the key is lost.

M. Mabœuf had innocent pleasures, which cost but little and were unexpected, and the slightest accident supplied him with them. One day Mother Plutarch was reading a novel in the corner of the room; she was reading aloud, for she fancied that she understood better in that way. There are some persons who read very loud, and look as if they were pledging themselves their word of honor about what they are reading.

Mother Plutarch read her novel with an energy of this nature, and M. Mabœuf listened to her without hearing.

While reading, Mother Plutarch came to the following passage, relating to a bold dragoon and a gushing young lady:

"La belle bouda, et le Dragon—"

Here she broke off to wipe her spectacles.

"Bouddha and the dragon," M. Mabœuf repeated in a low voice; "yes, that is true; there was a dragon, which lived in a cavern, belched flames, and set fire to the sky. Several stars had already been burned up by this monster, which had tiger claws, by the bye, when Bouddha went into its den and succeeded in converting the dragon. That is an excellent book you are reading, Mother Plutarch, and there cannot be a finer legend."

And M. Mabœuf fell into a delicious reverie.

Marius felt a liking for this candid old man who saw himself slowly assailed by poverty and yet was not depressed by it. Marius met Courfeyrac and sought M. Mabœuf—very rarely, however—once or twice a month at the most.

Marius's delight was to take long walks alone, either on the external boulevards at the Champ de Mars, or in the least-frequented walks of the Luxembourg. He often spent half a day in looking at a kitchen-garden, the patches of lettuce, the fowls on the dung-heap, and the horse turning the pump-wheel. Passers-by looked at him with surprise, and some thought his dress suspicious and face dangerous, while it was only a poor young man thinking without an object.

It was in one of these walks that he discovered the Maison Gorbeau, and, the isolation and the cheapness tempting him, he took a room there. He was only known by the name of M. Marius.

Some of his father's old generals and old comrades invited him to come and see them, when they knew him, and Marius did not refuse, for they were opportunities to speak about his father. He called thus from time to time upon Count Pajol, General Bellavesne, and General Fririon at the Invalides. There was generally music and dancing, and on such evenings Marius put on his best suit; but he never went to such parties except on days when it was freezing tremendously hard, for he could not pay for a vehicle, and he would not go unless his boots were like looking-glasses.

He would say at times, though not at all bitterly, "Men are so constituted that in a drawing-room you may have mud everywhere except on your boots. In order to give you a proper reception, only one irreproachable thing is expected from you—is it your conscience? no, your boots."

All passions, saving those of the heart, are dissipated in reverie. The political fever of Marius had vanished, and the revolution of 1830 had aided in this, by satisfying and calming him. He had remained the same, except in his passion; he still held the same opinions, but they were softened down. Properly speaking, he no longer had opinions but sympathies; to what party did he belong? to that of humanity. For humanity he selected France; in the nation he chose the people; and in the people woman, and his pity was mainly given to her. At the present time he preferred an idea to a fact, a poet to a hero, and he admired a book like Job even more than an event like Marengo; and when after a day of meditation he returned along the boulevard and saw through the trees the illimitable space, the nameless gleams, the abyss, shadow, and mystery, all that was only human seemed to him infinitely little.

He believed that he had—and probably he had—reached the truth of life and of human philosophy, and he ended by gazing at nothing but the sky, the only thing which truth can see from the bottom of her well.

This did not prevent him from multiplying plans, combinations, scaffolding, and projects for the future. In this state of reverie, any eye which had seen into Marius's interior would have been dazzled by the purity of his mind. In fact, if our eyes of the flesh were allowed to peer into the consciences of our neighbor, a man could be judged far more surely from what he dreams than from what he thinks. There is a volition in thought, but there is none in a dream, and the latter, which is entirely spontaneous, assumes and retains, even in the gigantic and the ideal, the image of our mind. Nothing issues more directly and more sincerely from the bottom of our soul than our unreflecting and disproportioned aspirations for the splendors of destiny. The true character of every man could be found in these aspirations far more certainly than in arranged, reasoned, and coördinated ideas. Our chimeras are the things which most resemble ourselves, and each man dreams of the unknown and the impossible according to his nature.

About the middle of the year 1831 the old woman who waited on Marius told him that his neighbors, the wretched Jondrette family, were going to be turned out. Marius, who spent nearly his whole time out-of-doors, scarce knew that he had neighbors.

"Why are they turned out?" he asked.

"Because they do not pay their rent, and owe two quarters."

"How much is it?"

"Twenty francs," said the old woman.

Marius had thirty francs in reserve in a drawer.

"Here are twenty-five francs," he said to the woman; "pay the rent of the poor people, give them five francs, and do not tell them where the money comes from."

6. *THE SUBSTITUTE*

ACCIDENT decreed that the regiment to which Lieutenant Théodule belonged should be quartered in Paris. This was an opportunity for Aunt Gillenormand to have a second idea; her first one had been to set Théodule watching Marius, and she now plotted to make him succeed him.

In the event of the grandfather feeling a vague want for a youthful face in the house,—for such rays of dawn are sometimes sweet to ruins, —it was expedient to find another Marius. "Well," she thought, "it is only a simple erratum, such as I notice in books; for *Marius* read *Théodule*."

A grand-nephew is much the same as a grandson, after all, and in default of a barrister you can take a lancer.

One morning when M. Gillenormand was going to read something like the *Quotidienne,* his daughter came in and said in her softest voice, for the interests of her favorite were at stake:

"Papa, Théodule is coming this morning to pay his respects to you."

"Who's Théodule?"

"Your grand-nephew."

"Ah!" said the old gentleman.

Then he began reading, thought no more of the grand-nephew, who was only some Théodule, and soon became angry, which nearly always happened when he read. The paper he held (a royalist one, we need hardly say) announced for the morrow, without any softening of words, one of the daily events of Paris at that day. "The pupils of the schools of law and medicine were going to assemble in the Pantheon Square—to deliberate." The affair was one of the questions of the moment, the artillery of the national guard, and a conflict between the war minister and the "Citizen Militia," on the subject of guns parked in the court-yard of the Louvre. The students were going to "deliberate" on this, and it did not require much more to render M. Gillenormand furious.

He thought of Marius, who was a student, and who would probably go, like the others, "to deliberate at midday in the Pantheon Square."

While he was making these painful reflections Lieutenant Théodule came in, dressed in mufti, which was clever, and was discreetly introduced by Mlle. Gillenormand. The lancer had reasoned thus: "The old Druid has not sunk all his money in annuities, and so it is worth the while to disguise one's self as a *pékin* now and then."

Mlle. Gillenormand said aloud to her father:

"Théodule, your grand-nephew."

And in a whisper to the lieutenant:

"Assent to everything."

And retired.

The lieutenant, but little accustomed to such venerable meetings, stammered, with some timidity, "Good-morning, uncle," and gave a greeting which was composed of the involuntary and mechanical military salute, terminating in the bow of the citizen.

"Ah, it's you; very good, sit down," said the old gentleman; and after saying this he utterly forgot the lancer.

Théodule sat down, and M. Gillenormand got up.

He began walking up and down the room with his hands in his pockets, talking aloud, and feeling, with his old irritated fingers, the two watches which he wore in his two fobs.

"That heap of scamps! so they are going to meet in the Pantheon Square! *Vertu de ma mie!* little ragamuffins who were at nurse yesterday! if you were to squeeze their noses the milk would run out! and they are going to deliberate to-morrow! Where are we going? where are we going? it is clear that we are going to the abyss, and the descamisados have led us to it. The citizen artillery! deliberate about the citizen artillery! go and chatter in the open air about the squibs of the National Guard, and whom will they meet there? Just let us see to what Jacobinism leads. I will wager whatever you like, a million against a counter, that there will be only liberated convicts and pick-pockets there, for the republicans and the galley-slaves are like one nose and one handkerchief. Carnot used to say, 'Where do you want me to go, traitor?' and Fouché answer, 'Wherever you like, imbecile!' That is what the republicans are."

"That is true," said Théodule.

M. Gillenormand half turned his head, saw Théodule, and went on:

"And then to think that that scamp had the villainy to become a republican! why did you leave my house to become a republican? Pest! in the first place the people do not want your republic, for they are sensible, and know very well that there always have been kings, and always will be, and they know, after all, that the people are only the people, and they laugh at your republic, do you hear, Cretin? Is not such a caprice horrible? to fall in love with Père Duchesne, to ogle the guillotine, to sing romances, and play the guitar under the balcony of '93—why, all these young men ought to be spat upon, for they are so stupid! They are all caught, and not one escapes, and they need only inhale the air of the street to go mad. The nineteenth century is poison; the first-comer lets his goat's beard grow, believes himself a scoundrel for the truth, and bolts from his old parents. That is republican, it is romantic; just be good enough to tell me what that word romantic means?—every folly possible. A year ago they went to see *Hernani*. Just let me ask you, *Hernani!* antitheses, abominations, which are not even written in French. And then there are cannon in the court-yard of the Louvre; such is the brigandage of the present age."

"You are right, uncle," said Théodule.

M. Gillenormand continued:

"Guns in the court-yard of the Museum! what to do? Cannon, what do you want of me? do you wish to fire grape-shot at the Apollo Belvidere? What have cartridges to do with the Venus de Medici? Oh! the young men of the present day are ragamuffins, and this Benjamin Constant is not much. And those who are not villains are gawkies! they do all they can to make themselves ugly,—they dress badly, they are afraid of women, and they have near petticoats an air of begging which makes the girls laugh; on my word of honor, you might call them love's shamefaced poor. They are deformed, and perfect it by being stupid; they repeat the jokes of Tiercelin and Potier; they wear sack-coats, hostlers' waist-coats, trousers of coarse cloth, boots of coarse leather, and their chatter resembles their plumage—their jargon might be employed to sole their boots. And all these silly lads have political opinions, and it ought to be strictly prohibited. They manufacture systems, they remodel society, they demolish the monarchy, upset all laws, put the garret in the place of the cellar, and my porter in the place of the king; they upset Europe from one end to the other, build up the world again, and their amours consist in looking sheepishly at the legs of the washerwomen as they get into their carts. Ah, Marius! ah, scoundrel! to go and vociferate in the public square! to discuss, debate, and form measures—they call them measures. Great gods! why, disorder is decreasing and becoming silly. I have seen chaos and I now see a puddle. Scholars deliberating about the National Guard! why, that could not be seen among the Ojibways or the Cadodaches! The savages who go about naked, with their noddles dressed like a racket-bat and with a club in their paw, are less of brutes than these bachelors, two-penny-half-penny brats, who dare to decree and order, deliberate and argue! Why, it is the end of the world; it is evidently the end of this wretched globe; it wanted a final shove, and France has given it. Deliberate, my scamps! These things will happen so long as they go to read the papers under the arcades of the Odéon; it costs them a half-penny, and their common sense and their intelligence, and their heart, and their soul, and their mind. They leave that place, and then bolt from their family. All the newspapers are poison, even the *Drapeau Blanc!* and Martainville was a Jacobin at heart. Ah, just Heaven! you can boast of having rendered your grandfather desperate!"

"That is quite plain," said Théodule.

And taking advantage of the moment, during which M. Gillenormand was recovering breath, the lancer added magisterially:

"There ought to be no other paper but the *Moniteur,* and no other book but the 'Army List'."

M. Gillenormand went on:

"It is just like their Sieyès! a regicide who became a senator! for they always end with that. They scar themselves with their thee-ing and thou-ing, so that they may be called in the long run Monsieur le Comte—, Monsieur le Comte, as long as the arm of the slaughterers of September. The philosopher Sieyès! I do myself the justice of saying that I never cared any more for the philosophy of all these philosophers than I did for the spectacles of the grimacer at the Tivoli. One day I saw the senators pass along the Quay Malaquais, in violet velvet cloaks studded with bees, and wearing Henri IV hats; they were hideous and looked like the apes of the tigers' court. Citizens, I declare to you that your progress is a madness, that your humanity is a dream, that your revolution is a crime, that your republic is a monster, that your young virgin France emerges from a brothel, and I sustain it against you all, no matter whether you are journalists, social economists, lawyers, and greater connoisseurs of liberty, equality, and fraternity than the cut-throat of the guillotine! I tell you this plainly, my good fellows."

"Parbleu!" the lieutenant cried, "that is admirably true!"

M. Gillenormand interrupted a gesture which he had begun, turned round, gazed intently at Théodule the lancer between the eyes, and said to him:

"You are an ass."

BOOK VI

CONJUNCTION OF TWO STARS

I. NICKNAMES AND FAMILY NAMES

MARIUS at this period was a handsome young man of middle height, with very black hair, a lofty and intelligent forehead, open and impassioned nostrils, a sincere and calm air, and something haughty, pensive, and innocent was spread over his whole face. His profile, in which all the lines were rounded without ceasing to be firm, had that Germanic gentleness which entered France through Alsace and Lorraine, and that absence of angles which rendered it so easy to recognize the Sicambri among the Romans, and distinguishes the leonine from the aquiline race. He had reached the season of life when the mind of men is composed of depth and simplicity in nearly equal proportions. A serious situation being given, he had all that was necessary to be stupid, but, with one more turn of the screw, he could be sublime. His manner was reserved, cold, polite, and unexpansive; but, as his mouth was beautiful, his lips bright vermilion, and his teeth the whitest in the world, his smile corrected any severity in his countenance. At certain moments, this chaste forehead and voluptuous smile offered a strange contrast. His eye was small, his look great.

In the period of his greatest need he remarked that the people turned to look at him when he passed, and he hurried away or hid himself, with death in his soul. He thought that they were looking at his shabby clothes and laughing at them; but the fact is, they were looking at his face, and thinking about it.

This silent misunderstanding between himself and pretty passers-by had rendered him savage, and he did not select one, from the simple reason that he fled from all. He lived thus indefinitely—stupidly, said Courfeyrac.

Courfeyrac added, "Do not aspire to be venerable, and take one bit of advice, my dear fellow. Do not read so many books, and look at the wenches a little more, for they have some good about them. O Marius! you will grow brutalized if you go on shunning women and blushing."

On other occasions, Courfeyrac, when he met him, would say, "Good-morning, Abbé."

When Courfeyrac had made any remark of this nature, Marius for a whole week would shun women, young and old, more than ever, and Courfeyrac in the bargain.

There were, however, in the whole immense creation, two women whom Marius did not shun, or to whom he paid no attention. To tell the truth, he would have been greatly surprised had any one told him that they were women. One was the hairy-faced old woman who swept his room, and induced Courfeyrac to remark, "Seeing that his servant wears her beard, Marius does not wear his"; the other was a young girl whom he saw very frequently and did not look at.

For more than a year Marius had noticed in a deserted walk of the Luxembourg, the one which is bordered by the Parapet de la Pépinière, a man and a very young lady nearly always seated side by side at the most solitary end of the walk, near the Rue de l'Ouest. Whenever that accident, which mingles with the promenades of people whose eye is turned inwards, led Marius to this walk, and that was nearly daily, he met this couple again.

The man seemed to be about sixty years of age; he appeared sad and serious, and the whole of his person offered the robust and fatigued appearance of military men who have retired from service. If he had worn a decoration, Marius would have said, "He is an old officer." He looked kind, but unapproachable, and never fixed his eye on that of another person. He wore blue trousers, a coat of the same color, and a broad-brimmed hat, all of which seemed constantly new, a black cravat, and a Quaker's, that is to say, dazzlingly white, but very coarse shirt. A grisette who passed him one day said, "What a clean old widower." His hair was very white.

The first time that the young lady who accompanied him sat down with him upon the bench which they seemed to have adopted, she was about thirteen or fourteen, so thin as to be almost ugly, awkward, insignificant, and promising to have perhaps very fine eyes some day; still they were always raised with a species of displeasing assurance. She wore the garb, at once old and childish, of boarders at a convent,—a badly cut dress of coarse black merino. They looked like father and daughter.

Marius examined for two or three days the old man, who was not yet aged, and this little girl, who was not yet a woman, and then paid no further attention to them. They, on their side, seemed not even to see him, and talked together with a peaceful and careless air. The girl talked incessantly and gayly, the old man spoke but little, and at times he fixed upon her eyes filled with ineffable paternity. Marius had formed the mechanical habit of walking in this alley, and invariably found them there.

This is how matters went on:

Marius generally arrived by the end of the walk furthest from the bench; he walked the whole length, passed them, then turned back to the end by which he had arrived, and began again. He took this walk five or six times nearly every day in the week, but these persons and himself never even exchanged a bow. The man and the girl, though they appeared, and perhaps because they appeared, to shun observation, had naturally aroused to some little extent the attention of some students who walked from time to time along La Pépinière; the studious after lectures, the others after their game of billiards. Courfeyrac, who belonged to the latter, had watched them for some time, but, finding the girl ugly, he got away from them very rapidly, firing at them like a Parthian a sobriquet. Being solely struck by the dress of the girl and the old man's hair, he christened the former Mlle. Lanoire, and the father Monsieur Leblanc, so that, as no one knew them otherwise, this name adhered to them in the absence of a better one. The students said, "Ah, M. Leblanc is at his bench," and Marius, like the rest, found it convenient to call this strange gentleman M. Leblanc.

We will follow their example, and speak of him as M. Leblanc.

Marius saw them nearly daily, at the same hour, during a year; he considered the man to his liking, but the girl rather unpleasant.

2. *LUX FACTA EST*

In the second year, just at the point of our story which the reader has now reached, it happened that Marius broke off his daily walk in the Luxembourg, without exactly knowing why, and was nearly six months without setting foot in the garden. One day, however, he returned to it; it was a beauteous summer's day, and Marius was joyous as men are when the weather is fine. He felt as if he had in his heart all the birds' songs that he heard, and all the patches of blue sky of which he caught a glimpse between the leaves.

He went straight to "his" walk, and when he reached the end he noticed the well-known couple seated on the same bench, but when he drew near he found that, while it was the same man, it did not seem to be the same girl. The person he now saw was a tall and lovely creature, possessing the charming outlines of the woman at the precise moment when they are still combined with the most simple graces of the child— a fugitive and pure moment which can alone be rendered by the two words "fifteen years." He saw admirable auburn hair tinted with veins of gold, a forehead that seemed made of marble, cheeks that seemed made of a rose-leaf, pale flesh tints, a flushing whiteness, an exquisite mouth, from which a smile issued like a flash, and words like music, and a head which Raffaelle would have given to a Virgin, set upon a neck which Jean Goujon would have given to a Venus. And, that nothing might be wanting in this ravishing face, the nose was not beautiful, but pretty, neither straight nor bent, neither Italian nor Greek; it was the Parisian nose,—that is to say, something witty, fine, irregular, and pure, which is the despair of painters and the charm of poets.

When Marius passed her, he could not see her eyes, which she constantly drooped; he only saw her long chestnut eyelashes, penetrated with shade and modesty.

This did not prevent the lovely girl from smiling while she listened to the white-haired man who was speaking to her, and nothing could be so ravishing as this fresh smile with the downcast eyes.

At the first moment Marius thought that it was another daughter of the gentleman's, a sister of the former. But when the invariable habit of his walk brought him again to the bench, and he examined her attentively, he perceived that it was the same girl. In six months the child had become a woman, that was all, and nothing was more frequent than this phenomenon. There is a moment in which girls become roses instantly,—yesterday you left them children, to-day you find them objects of anxiety.

This girl had not only grown, but was idealized; as three days in April suffice to cover some trees with flowers, six months had sufficed to clothe her with beauty—her April had arrived.

We sometimes see poor and insignificant persons suddenly wake up, pass from indigence to opulence, lay out money in all sorts of extravagance, and become brilliant, prodigal, and magnificent. The reason is that they have just received their dividends; and the girl had been paid six months' income.

And then she was no longer the boarding-school miss, with her plush bonnet, merino dress, thick shoes, and red hands; taste had come to her with beauty, and she was well dressed, with a species of simple, rich, and unaffected elegance. She wore a black brocade dress, a cloak of the same material, and a white crape bonnet; her white gloves displayed the elegance of her hand, which was playing with the ivory handle of a parasol, and her satin boot revealed the smallness of her foot; when you passed her, her whole toilet exhaled a youthful and penetrating perfume.

As for the man, he was still the same.

The second time that Marius passed, the girl raised her eyelids, and he could see that her eyes were of a deep cærulean blue, but in this veiled azure there was only the glance of a child. She looked at Marius carelessly, as she would have looked at the child playing under the sycamores, or the marble vase that threw a shadow over the bench; and Marius continued his walk, thinking of something else.

He passed the bench four or five times, but did not once turn his eyes toward the young lady.

On the following days he returned as usual to the Luxembourg; as usual he found the "father and daughter" there, but he paid no further attention to them. He thought no more of the girl now that she was lovely than he had done when she was ugly, and though he always passed very close to the bench on which she was sitting, it was solely the result of habit.

3. *THE EFFECT OF SPRING*

ONE day the air was warm, the Luxembourg was inundated with light and shade, the sky was as pure as if the angels had washed it that morning, the sparrows were twittering shrilly in the foliage of the chestnut-trees, and Marius opened his whole soul to nature. He was thinking of nothing, he loved and breathed, he passed by the bench, the young lady raised her eyes to him, and their two glances met.

What was there this time in her look? Marius could not have said; there was nothing and there was everything, it was a strange flash.

She let her eyes fall, and he continued his walk.

What he had just seen was not the simple and ingenuous eye of a child, but a mysterious gulf, the mouth of which had opened and then suddenly closed again.

There is a day on which every maiden looks in this way, and woe to the man on whom her glance falls!

This first glance of a soul which does not yet know itself is like dawn in the heavens; it is the awakening of something radiant and unknown. Nothing could render the mysterious charm of this unexpected flash which suddenly illumines the adorable darkness, and is composed of all the innocence of the present and all the passion of the future. It is a sort of undecided tenderness, which reveals itself accidentally and waits; it is a snare which innocence sets unconsciously, and in which it captures hearts without wishing or knowing it.

It is a virgin who looks at you like a woman.

It is rare for a profound reverie not to spring up wherever this flame falls; all purity and all candor are blended in this heavenly and fatal beam which possesses, more than the best-managed ogles of coquettes, the magic power of suddenly causing that dangerous flower, full of perfume and poison, called love, suddenly to expand in the soul.

On returning to his garret in the evening, Marius took a glance at his clothes, and perceived for the first time that he had been guilty of the extraordinary impropriety and stupidity of walking in the Luxembourg in his "every-day dress"; that is to say, with a broken-brimmed hat, clumsy boots, black trousers, white at the knees, and a black coat pale at the elbows.

4. BEGINNING OF A GRIEVOUS MALADY

THE next day, at the accustomed hour, Marius took out of the drawers his new coat, his new trousers, his new hat, and his new boots; he dressed himself in this complete panoply, put on gloves, an extraordinary luxury, and went off to the Luxembourg.

On the road he met Courfeyrac, and pretended not to see him. Courfeyrac on reaching home said to his friends:

"I have just met Marius's new hat and new coat and Marius inside them. He was going, I fancy, to pass some examination for he looked so stupid."

On reaching the Luxembourg, Marius walked round the basin and gazed at the swans; then he stood for a long time contemplating a statue all black with mold, and which had lost one hip. Near the basin was a comfortable bourgeois of about forty, holding by the hand a little boy, and saying to him, "Avoid all excesses, my son; keep at an equal distance from despotism and anarchy." Marius listened to this bourgeois, then walked once again round the basin, and at length proceeded toward "his" walk slowly, and as if regretfully. He seemed to be at once forced and prevented from going, but he did not explain this to himself, and fancied he was behaving as he did every day.

On turning into the walk he saw M. Leblanc and the young lady at the other end, seated on "their" bench. He buttoned up his coat to the top, pulled it down so that it should make no creases, examined with some complacency the luster of his trousers, and marched upon the bench. There was attack in this march, and assuredly a desire for conquest, and hence I say that he marched upon this bench, as I would say Hannibal marched on Rome.

Still, all his movements were mechanical, and he had not in any way altered the habitual preoccupation of his mind and labors. He was thinking at this moment that the "Manuel du Baccalauréat" was a stupid book, and that it must have been edited by wondrous ignoramuses, who analyzed as masterpieces of the human mind three tragedies of Racine and only one comedy of Molière. He had a shrill whistling in his ear, and while approaching the bench he pulled down his coat, and his eyes were fixed on the maiden. He fancied that she filled the whole end of the walk with a vague blue light.

As he drew nearer, his pace gradually decreased. On coming within a certain distance of the bench, though still some distance from the end of the walk, he stopped, and did not know how it was that he turned back. The young lady was scarce able to notice him and see how well he looked in his new suit. Still he held himself very erect, for fear any one behind might be looking at him.

He reached the opposite end, then returned, and this time approaching a little nearer to the bench. He even got within the distance of three trees, but then he felt an impossibility of going further, and hesitated. He fancied he could see the young lady's face turned toward him; however, he made a masculine, violent effort, subdued his hesitation, and continued to advance. A few moments after he passed in front of the bench, upright and firm, but red up to the ears and not daring to take a glance either to the right or left, and with his hand thrust into his coat like a statesman. At the moment when he passed under the guns of the fort, he felt his heart beat violently. She was dressed as on the previous day, and he heard an ineffable voice which must "be her voice." She was talking quietly, and was very beautiful; he felt it, though he did not attempt to look at her. "And yet," he thought, "she could not fail to have esteem and consideration for me if she knew that I am the real author of the dissertation on Marcos Obregon de La Ronda, which M. François de Neufchateau appropriated and made a preface to his edition of Gil Blas."

He passed the bench, went to the end of the walk which was close by, then turned and again passed the young lady. This time he was very pale, and his feelings were most disagreeable. He went away from the bench and the maiden, and while turning his back he fancied that she was looking at him, and this made him totter.

He did not again attempt to pass the bench; he stopped at about the middle of the walk and then sat down, a most unusual thing for him, taking side glances, and thinking in the innermost depths of his mind that after all it was difficult for a person whose white bonnet and black dress he admired to be absolutely insensible to his showy trousers and new coat.

At the end of a quarter of an hour he rose, as if about to walk toward this bench which was surrounded by a glory, but he remained motionless. For the first time in fifteen months he said to himself that the gentleman who sat there daily with his daughter must have noticed him, and probably considered his assiduity strange.

For the first time, too, he felt that it was rather irreverent to designate this stranger, even in his own thoughts, by the nickname of M. Leblanc.

He remained thus for some minutes with hanging head, making sketches in the sand with the stick he held in his hand.

Then he suddenly turned in the direction opposed to the bench and went home.

That day he forgot to go to dinner; he noticed the fact at eight in the evening, and, as it was too late to go to the Rue St. Jacques, he ate a lump of bread.

He did not go to bed till he had brushed and carefully folded up his coat.

5. MAME BOUGON IS THUNDERSTRUCK

THE next day, Mame Bougon—it was thus that Courfeyrac called the old portress, principal lodger, and charwoman of No. 50-52, though her real name was Madame Burgon, as we have stated, but that scamp of a Courfeyrac respected nothing—Mame Bougon, to her stupefaction, noticed that Marius again went out in his best coat.

He returned to the Luxembourg, but did not go beyond his half-way bench; he sat down there, as on the previous day, regarding from a distance, and seeing distinctly, the white bonnet, the black dress, and, above all, the blue radiance. He did not move or return home till the gates of the Luxembourg were closed. He did not see M. Leblanc and his daughter go away, and hence concluded that they left the garden by the gate in the Rue de l'Ouest. Some weeks after, when reflecting on the subject, he could never remember where he dined that day.

On the next day, the third, Mame Bougon received another thunderstroke: Marius went out in his new coat. "Three days running!" she exclaimed.

She tried to follow him, but Marius walked quickly, and with immense strides; it was a hippopotamus attempting to catch up with a chamois. She lost him out of sight in two minutes, and went back panting, three parts choked by her asthma, and furious. "What sense is there," she growled, "in putting on one's best coat every day, and making people run like that!"

Marius had gone to the Luxembourg.

M. Leblanc and the young lady were there already. Marius approached as near to them as he could, while pretending to read his book, though still a long distance off, and then returned to sit down on his bench, where he spent four hours in watching the sparrows, which he fancied were ridiculing him, hopping about in the walk.

A fortnight passed in this way; Marius no longer went to the Luxembourg to walk, but always to sit down at the same spot, without knowing why. When he had arrived there, he did not stir. He every morning put on his new coat, not to show himself, and began again on the morrow.

She was decidedly, marvelously beautiful; the sole remark resembling a criticism that could be made was, that the contradiction between her glance, which was sad, and her smile, which was joyous, gave her face a slightly startled look, which at times caused this gentle face to become strange without ceasing to be charming.

6. *TAKEN PRISONER*

On one of the last days of the second week, Marius was, as usual, seated on his bench, holding in his hand an open book in which he had not turned a page for several months, when he suddenly started—an event was occurring at the end of the walk. M. Leblanc and the girl had left their bench, the girl was holding her father's arm, and both were proceeding slowly toward the middle of the walk where Marius was. He shut his book, then opened it again and tried to read, but he trembled, and the glory came straight toward him. "Oh, heaven!" he thought, "I shall not have the time to throw myself into an attitude." The white-haired man and the girl, however, advanced; it seemed to him as if this lasted a century, and was only a second. "What do they want here?" he asked himself. "What! she is going to pass here; her feet will tread this walk, two paces from me?" He was quite upset, he would have liked to have been very handsome, and have the Cross of the Legion of Honor. He heard the soft, measured sound of their footsteps approaching him, and he imagined that M. Leblanc was taking an angry glance at him. "Is this gentleman going to speak to me?" he thought. He hung his head, and when he raised it again they were close to him. The girl passed, and in passing looked at him,—looked at him intently, with a thoughtful gentleness which made Marius shudder from head to foot. It seemed to him as if she reproached him for keeping away from her so long, and was saying, "I have come instead." Marius was dazzled by these eyeballs full of beams and abysses.

He felt that his brain was on fire. She had come toward him, what joy! and then, she had looked at him. She appeared to him lovelier than she had ever been, lovely with a beauty at once feminine and angelic, a perfect beauty, which would have made Petrarch sing and Dante kneel. He felt as if he were floating in the blue sky, but, at the same time, he was horribly annoyed because he had dust on his boots.

He felt sure that she had looked at his boots, too.

He looked after her till she disappeared, and then walked about the garden like a maniac. He probably at times laughed to himself and talked along. He was so pensive among the nurse girls that each of them fancied him in love with her.

He left the Luxembourg in hopes of seeing her in the street.

He met Courfeyrac under the arcades of the Pantheon, and said to him, "Come and dine with me." They went to Rousseau's and spent six francs. Marius ate like an ogre, and gave six sous to the waiter. After dinner he said to Courfeyrac, "Have you read the papers! what a fine speech Audry de Puyraveau made!"

He was distractedly in love.

He then said to Courfeyrac, "Let us go to the theater,—I'll pay." They went to the Porte St. Martin to see Frederick in the "Auberge des Adrets," and Marius was mightily amused.

At the same time he became more virtuous than ever. On leaving the theater he refused to look at the garter of a dressmaker who was striding across a gutter, and Courfeyrac happening to say, "I should like to place that woman in my collection," he almost felt horrified.

Courfeyrac invited him to breakfast next morning at the café Voltaire. He went there, and ate even more than on the previous day. He was thoughtful and very gay, and seemed to take every opportunity to laugh noisily. A party of students collected round the table and spoke of the absurdities paid for by the state, which are produced from the pulpit of the Sorbonne, and then the conversation turned to the faults and gaps in dictionaries. Marius interrupted the discussion by exclaiming, "And yet it is very agreeable to have the Cross of the Legion."

"That is funny!" Courfeyrac whispered to Jean Prouvaire.

"No, it is serious," the other answered.

It was, in truth, serious; Marius had reached that startling and charming hour which commences great passion.

A look had effected all this.

When the mine is loaded, when the fire is ready, nothing is more simple, and a glance is a spark.

It was all over; Marius loved a woman, and his destiny was entering the unknown.

The glance of a woman resembles certain trains of wheels which are apparently gentle, but are formidable; you daily pass by their side with impunity, and without suspecting anything, and the moment arrives when you even forget that the thing is there. You come, you go, you dream, you speak, you laugh, and all in a minute you feel yourself caught, and it is all over with you. The wheel holds you, the glance has caught you; it has caught, no matter where or how, by some part of your thought which dragged after you, or by some inattention on your part. You are lost, and your whole body will be drawn in; a series of mysterious forces seizes you, and you struggle in vain, for human aid is no longer possible. You pass from cog-wheel to cog-wheel, from agony to agony, from torture to torture—you and your mind, your fortune, your future, and your soul; and, according as you are in the power of a wicked creature, or of a noble heart, you will issue from this frightful machinery either disfigured by shame or transfigured by passion.

7. ADVENTURES OF THE LETTER U LEFT TO CONJECTURE

ISOLATION, detachment from everything, pride, independence, a taste for nature, the absence of daily and material labor, life in himself, the secret struggles of chastity, and his benevolent ecstasy in the presence of creation, had prepared Marius for that possession which is called passion. His reverence for his father had gradually become a religion, and, like all religions, withdrew into the depths of the soul; something was wanting for the foreground, and love came.

A whole month passed, during which Marius went daily to the Luxembourg; when the hour arrived nothing could stop him. "He is on duty," Courfeyrac said. Marius lived in transports, and it is certain that the young lady looked at him.

In the end he had grown bolder and went nearer the bench; still he did not pass in front of it, obeying at once the timid instincts and prudent instincts of lovers. He thought it advisable not to attract the father's attention, and hence arranged his stations behind trees and the pedestals of statues, with profound Machiavelism, so as to be seen as much as possible by the young lady and as little as possible by the old gentleman. At times he would be standing for half an hour motionless in the shadow of some Leonidas or Spartacus, holding in one hand a book, over which his eyes, gently raised, sought the lovely girl, and she, for her part, turned her charming profile toward him with a vague smile. While talking most naturally and quietly with the white-haired man, she fixed upon Marius all the reveries of a virginal and impassioned glance. It is an old and immemorial trick which Eve knew from the first day of the world, and which every woman knows from the first day of her life. Her mouth replied to one and her eye answered the other.

It must be supposed, however, that M. Leblanc eventually noticed something, for frequently when Marius arrived, he got up and began walking. He left their accustomed seat, and adopted at the other end of the walk the bench close to the Gladiator, as if to see whether Marius would follow them. Marius did not understand it, and committed this fault. "The father" began to become unpunctual, and no longer brought his "daughter" every day. At times he came alone and then Marius did not stop, and this was another fault.

Marius paid no attention to these symptoms; from the timid phase he had passed by a natural and fatal progress into a blind phase. His love was growing, and he dreamed of it every night, and then an unexpected happiness occurred to him, like oil on fire, and redoubled the darkness over his eyes. One evening at twilight he found on the bench which "M. Leblanc and his daughter" had just quitted, a simple, unembroidered handkerchief, which, however, was white and pure, and seemed to him to exhale ineffable odors. He seized it with transport, and noticed that it was marked with the letters U. F. Marius knew nothing about the lovely girl, neither her family, her name, nor her abode; these two letters were the first thing of hers which he seized, adorable initials, upon which he at once begun to erect his scaffolding. U. was evidently the Christian name: "Ursule!" he thought, "what a delicious name!" He kissed the handkerchief, smelt it, placed it on his heart during the day, and at night upon his lips to go to sleep.

"I can feel her whole soul!" he exclaimed.

This handkerchief belonged to the old gentleman, who had simply let it fall from his pocket.

On the days following the treasure-trove Marius only appeared at the Luxembourg, kissing the handkerchief and pressing it to his heart. The lovely girl did not understand what this meant, and expressed her surprise by imperceptible signs.

"O modesty!" said Marius.

8. EVEN THE INVALIDS MAY BE LUCKY

SINCE we have uttered the word modesty, and as we conceal nothing, we are bound to say, however, that on one occasion "his Ursule" caused him serious vexation in the midst of his ecstasy. It was on one of the days when she induced M. Leblanc to leave the bench and walk about. There was a sharp spring breeze which shook the tops of the plane trees; and father and daughter, arm in arm, had just passed in front of Marius, who rose and watched them, as was fitting for a man in his state of mind.

All at once a puff of wind, more merry than the rest, and probably ordered to do the business of spring, dashed along the walk, enveloped the maiden in a delicious rustling worthy of the nymphs of Virgil and the Fauns of Theocritus, and raised her dress, that dress more sacred than that of Isis, almost as high as her garter. A leg of exquisite shape became visible. Marius saw it, and he was exasperated and furious.

The maiden rapidly put down her dress, with a divinely startled movement, but he was not the less indignant. There was no one in the walk, it was true, but there might have been somebody; and if that somebody had been there! Is such a thing conceivable? what she has just done is horrible! Alas! the poor girl had done nothing, and there was only one culprit, the wind, but Marius, in whom there quivered the Bartholo which is in Cherubino, was determined to be dissatisfied, and was jealous of his shadow; it is thus, in fact, that the bitter and strange jealousy of the flesh is aroused in the human heart, and dominates it, even unjustly. Besides, apart from his jealousy, the sight of this charming leg was not at all agreeable to him, and any other woman's white stocking would have caused him more pleasure.

When "his Ursule," after reaching the end of the walk, turned back with M. Leblanc, and passed in front of the bench on which Marius was sitting, he gave her a stern, savage glance. The girl drew herself slightly up, and raised her eyelids, which means, "Well, what is the matter now?"

This was their first quarrel.

Marius had scarce finished upbraiding her in this way, with his eyes, when some one crossed the walk. It was a bending invalid, all wrinkled and white, wearing the uniform of Louis XV, having on his coat the little oval patch of red cloth with the crossed swords, the soldier's cross of St. Louis, and, in addition, decorated with coat-sleeves in which there was no arm, a silver chin, and a wooden leg. Marius fancied he could notice that this man had an air of satisfaction; it seemed to him that the old cynic, while hobbling past him, gave him a fraternal and extremely jovial wink, as if some accident had enabled them to enjoy in common some good thing. Why was this relic of Mars so pleased? what had occurred between this wooden leg and the other? Marius attained the paroxysm of jealousy. "He was perhaps there," he said to himself; "perhaps he saw," and he felt inclined to exterminate the invalid.

With the help of time every point grows blunted, and Marius's anger with "Ursule," though so just and legitimate, passed away. He ended by pardoning her, but it was a mighty effort, and he sulked for three days.

Still, through all this, and owing to all this, his passion increased, and became insane.

9. ECLIPSE

WE have seen how Marius discovered, or fancied he had discovered, she was named Ursule.

Appetite comes while loving, and to know that her name was Ursule was a great deal already, but it was little. In three or four weeks Marius had devoured this happiness and craved another; he wished to know where she lived.

He had made one mistake in falling into the trap of the Gladiator's bench; he had committed a second by not remaining at the Luxembourg when M. Leblanc went there alone; and he now committed a third, an immense one—he followed "Ursule."

She lived in the Rue de l'Ouest, in the most isolated part, in a new three-storied house of modest appearance.

From this moment Marius added to his happiness of seeing her at the Luxembourg the happiness of following her home.

His hunger increased; he knew what her name was, her Christian name at least, the charming, the real name of a woman; he knew where she lived, and now he wanted to know who she was.

One evening, after following them home and watching them disappear in the gate-way, he went in after them, and valiantly addressed the porter.

"Is that the gentleman of the first-floor who has just come in?"

"No," the porter answered; "it is the gentleman of the third-floor."

Another step made! This success emboldened Marius.

"Front?" he asked.

"Hang it," said the porter, "our rooms all look on the street."

"And what is this gentleman?" Marius continued.

"He lives on his property. He is a very good man, who does a deal of good to the unfortunate, though he is not rich."

"What is his name?" Marius added.

The porter raised his head and said:

"Are you a detective?"

Marius went off much abashed, but highly delighted, for he was progressing.

"Good," he thought, "I know that her name is Ursule, that she is a daughter of a retired gentleman, and that she lives there, on a third-floor in the Rue de l'Ouest."

On the morrow M. Leblanc and his daughter made but a short appearance at the Luxembourg, and went away in broad daylight. Marius followed them to the Rue de l'Ouest, as was his habit, and on reaching the gate-way M. Leblanc made his daughter go in first, then stopped, turned, and looked intently at Marius.

The next day they did not come to the Luxembourg, and Marius waited in vain the whole day.

At nightfall he went to the Rue de l'Ouest, and noticed a light in the third-floor windows, and he walked about beneath these windows till the light was extinguished.

The next day there was no one at the Luxembourg, Marius waited all day, and then went to keep his night-watch under the windows.

This took him till ten o'clock, and his dinner became what it could, for fever nourishes the sick man, and love the lover.

Eight days passed in this way, and M. Leblanc and his daughter did not again appear at the Luxembourg.

Marius made sorrowful conjectures, for he did not dare to watch the gate-way by day; he contented himself with going at night to contemplate the reddish brightness of the window-panes. He saw shadows pass now and then, and his heart beat.

On the eighth day, when he arrived beneath the windows, there was no light. "What," he said to himself, "the lamp is not lighted; can they have gone out?" He waited till ten o'clock, till midnight, till one o'clock, but no light was kindled at the third-floor windows, and nobody entered the house.

He went away with very gloomy thoughts.

On the morrow—for he only lived from morrow to morrow, and he had no to-day, so to speak—he saw nobody at the Luxembourg, as he expected, and at nightfall he went to the house.

There was no light at the windows, the shutters were closed, and the third-floor was all darkness.

Marius rapped, walked in, and said to the porter:

"The gentleman on the third-floor?"

"Moved," the porter answered.

Marius tottered, and asked feebly:

"Since when?"

"Yesterday."

"Where is he living now?"

"I do not know."

"Then he did not leave his new address?"

"No."

And the porter, raising his nose, recognized Marius.

"What? it's you, is it?" he said; "why, you must really be a detective!"

BOOK VII

PATRON-MINETTE

I. MINES AND MINERS

HUMAN societies have ever what is called in theaters "a third mezza-nine," and the social soil is everywhere undermined, here for good and there for evil. These works are upon one another; there are upper mines and lower mines, and there is a top and bottom in this obscure subsoil, which at times gives way beneath the weight of civilization, and which our indifference and carelessness trample under foot. The Ency-clopedia was in the last century an almost open mine; the darkness, that gloomy brooder of primitive Christianity, only awaited an occasion to explode beneath the Cæsars and inundate the human race with light. For in the sacred darkness there is latent light, and the volcanoes are full of a shadow which is capable of flashing. Every specter begins by being night. The catacombs in which the first mass was read were not merely the cellar of Rome, but also the vault of the world.

There are all sorts of excavations beneath the social building, that mar-vel complicated by a hovel; there is the religious mine, the philosophic mine, the political mine, the social economic mine, and the revolutionary mine. One man picks with the idea, another with figures, another with anger, and they call to and answer each other from the catacombs. Utopias move beneath the surface in the sewers, and ramify in all direc-tions; they meet there at times and fraternize. Jean Jacques lends his pick to Diogenes, who lends him his lantern in turn; at times, though, they fight, and Calvin clutches Socinus by the hair. But nothing arrests or interrupts the tension of all their energies toward the object, and the vast simultaneous energy, which comes and goes, ascends, descends, and reascends in the obscurity, and which slowly substitutes top for bottom and inside for out; it is an immense and unknown ant-heap. Society hardly suspects this excavation, which leaves no traces on its surface and yet changes its interior organs, and there are as many different works and varying excavations as there are subterranean adits. What issues from all these profound diggings?—the future.

The deeper we go the more mysterious the miners become. To a certain point which the social philosopher is able to recognize, the labor is good; beyond that point it is doubtful and mixed; and lower still it becomes terrible. At a certain depth the excavations can no longer be endured by the spirit of civilization, and man's limit of breathing is passed: a commencement of monsters becomes possible.

The descending ladder is strange, and each rung corresponds with a stage upon which philosophy can land and meet one of these miners, who are sometimes divine, at others deformed. Below John Huss there is Luther; below Luther, Descartes; below Descartes, Voltaire; below Voltaire, Condorcet; below Condorcet, Robespierre; below Robespierre, Marat; and below Marat, Babeuf, and so it goes on. Lower still we notice confusedly, at the limit which separates the indistinct from the invisible, other gloomy men, who perhaps do not yet exist; those of yesterday are specters, those of the morrow, grubs. The mental eye can only distinguish them obscurely, and the embryonic labor of the future is one of the visions of the philosopher.

A world in limbo in the fœtus stage—what an extraordinary sketch!

Saint Simon, Owen, and Fourier are also there in the side-passages.

Assuredly, although a divine and invisible chain connects together without their cognizance all these subterranean miners, who nearly always fancy themselves isolated but are not so, their labors vary greatly, and the light of the one contrasts with the dazzle of the other; some are paradisaic and other tragical. Still, however great the contrast may be, all these laborers, from the highest to the most nocturnal, from the wisest down to the maddest, have a similitude in their disinterestedness; they leave themselves on one side, omit themselves, do not think of themselves, and see something different from themselves. They have a glance, and that glance seeks the absolute; the first has heaven in his eyes, and the last, however enigmatical he may be, has beneath his eyebrow the pale brightness of infinity. Venerate every man, no matter what he may be doing—any man who has the sign, a starry eyeball.

The shadowy eyeball is the other sign, and with it evil begins.

Reflect and tremble in the presence of the man who does not look you in the face, for social order has its black miners.

There is a point where profundity is burial and where light is extinguished.

Below all these mines which we have indicated,—below all these galleries, below all this immense subterranean arterial system of progress and Utopia, far deeper in the ground below Marat, below Babeuf, much, much lower, there is the last passage, which has no connection with the upper drifts. It is a formidable spot, and what we termed the third mezzanine.

It is the grave of darkness and the cave of the blind, *Inferi*.

It communicates with the abysses.

2. *THE BOTTOM*

HERE disinterestedness fades away, and the dream is vaguely sketched. Every one for himself. The eyeless I yells, seeks, gropes, and groans; the social Ugolino is in this gulf.

The ferocious shadows which prowl about this grave, almost brutes, almost phantoms, do not trouble themselves about human progress; they are ignorant of the idea and the word, and thus they care for naught beyond individual gratification. They are almost unconscious, and there is within them a species of frightful obliteration. They have two mothers, both step-mothers, ignorance and wretchedness; they have for their guide want, and for all power of satisfaction appetite; they are brutally voracious, that is to say, ferocious,—not after the fashion of the tyrant, but that of the tiger. From suffering these grubs pass to crime,—it is a fatal affiliation, a ghastly propagation, the logic of darkness; what crawls in the lowest passage is no longer the stifled demand of the absolute, but the protest of matter. Man becomes a dragon then; his starting-point is to be hungry and thirsty, and his terminus is to be Satan: Lacenaire issued from this cave.

We have just seen one of the compartments of the upper mine, the great political, revolutionary, and philosophic sap. There, as we said, all is noble, pure, worthy, and honest; men may be mistaken in it, and are mistaken, but the error must be revered, because it implies so much heroism, and the work performed there has a name—Progress.

The moment has now arrived to take a glance at other and hideous depths.

There is beneath society, and there ever will be till the day when ignorance is dissipated, the great cavern of evil.

This cavern is below all the rest, and the enemy of all, it is hatred without deception. This cavern knows no philosophers, and its dagger never made a pen, while its blackness bears no relation with the sublime blackness of the inkstand. The fingers of night, which clench beneath this asphyxiating roof, never opened a book or unfolded a newspaper. Babeuf is to Cartouche a person who takes advantage of his knowledge, and Marat an aristocrat in the sight of Schinderhannes, and the object of this cavern is the overthrow of everything.

Of everything,—including the upper levels which it execrates. It not only undermines in its hideous labor the existing social order, but it undermines philosophy, science, the law, human thought, civilization, revolution, and progress, and it calls itself most simply robbery, prostitution, murder, and assassination. It is darkness, and desires chaos, and its roof is composed of ignorance.

All the other mines above it have only one object, to suppress it; and philosophy and progress strive for this with all their organs simultaneously, by the amelioration of the real as well as the contemplation of the ideal. Destroy the cave, Ignorance, and you destroy the mole, Crime.

Let us condense in a few words a portion of what we have just written.

The sole social evil is darkness; humanity is identity, for all men are of the same clay, and in this nether world, at least, there is no difference in predestination; we are the same shadow before, the same flesh during, and the same ashes afterward; but ignorance, mixed with the human paste, blackens it, and this incurable blackness enters man and becomes Evil there.

3. *BABET, GUEULEMER, CLAQUESOUS, AND MONTPARNASSE*

A QUARTETTE of bandits, Babet, Gueulemer, Claquesous, and Mont-parnasse, governed, from 1830 to 1835, the lowest depths of Paris.

Gueulemer was a Hercules out of place, and his den was the Arche-Marion sewer. He was six feet high, had lungs of marble, muscles of bronze, the respiration of a cavern, the bust of a colossus, and a bird's skull. You fancied you saw the Farnèse Hercules, attired in ticking trousers and cotton-velvet jacket. Gueulemer built in this mold might have subdued monsters, but he had found it easier to be one. A low forehead, wide temples, under forty years of age, yet with crows' feet, rough short hair, and a bushy beard—you can see the man. His muscles demanded work, and his stupidity would not accept it; he was a great slothful strength, and an assassin through nonchalance. People believed him to be a Creole, and he had probably laid his hands upon Marshal Brune when massacred, as he was a porter at Avignon in 1815. From that stage he had become a bandit.

Babet's transparency contrasted with the meat of Gueulemer: he was thin and learned,—transparent but impenetrable; you might see the light through his bones, but not through his eyes. He called himself a chemist, he had been a clown with Bobino, a bar-keeper with Bobêche, and had played in the vaudeville at St. Mihiel. He was a man of intentions, and a fine speaker, who underlined his smiles and placed his gestures between inverted commas. His trade was to sell in the open air plaster busts and portraits of the "chief of the State," and, in addition, he pulled teeth out. He had shown phenomena at fairs, and possessed a booth with a trumpet and the following show-board,—"Babet, dentist, and member of the academies, performs physical experiments on metals and metalloids, extirpates teeth, and undertakes stumps given up by the profession. Terms, —one tooth, one franc fifty centimes; two teeth, two francs; three teeth, two francs fifty centimes. Take advantage of the opportunity." (The last sentence meant, Have as many teeth pulled out as possible.) He was married and had children, but did not know what had become of wife or children; he had lost them, just as another man loses his handkerchief. Babet was a high exception in the obscure world to which he belonged, for he read the newspapers. One day, at the time when he still had his family with him in his caravan, he read in the *Moniteur* that a woman had just been delivered of a child with a calf's snout, and exclaimed, "There's a fortune! my wife would not have the sense to produce me a child like that!"

Since then he had given up everything to "undertake Paris"—the expression is his own.

What was Claquesous? he was night, and never showed himself till the sky was bedaubed with blackness. In the evening he emerged from a hole, to which he returned before daybreak. Where was this hole? no one knew. In the greatest darkness, and when alone with his accomplices, he turned his back when he spoke to them. Was his name Claquesous? no; he said, "My name is Not-at-all." If a candle were brought in he put on a mask, and he was a ventriloquist in the bargain, and Babet used to say, "Claquesous is a night bird with two voices." Claquesous was vague, wandering, and terrible; no one was sure that he had a name, for Claquesous was a nickname; no one was sure that he had a voice, for his stomach spoke more frequently than his mouth; and no one was sure that he had a face, as nothing had ever been seen but his mask. He disappeared like a ghost, and when he appeared he seemed to issue from the ground.

Montparnasse was a sad thing to contemplate. He was a lad not yet twenty, with a pretty face, lips that resembled cherries, beautiful black hair, and the brightness of spring in his eyes; he had every vice, and aspired to every crime, and the digestion of evil gave him an appetite for worse. He was the gamin turned pickpocket, and the pickpocket had become a garroter. He was genteel, effeminate, graceful, robust, soft, and ferocious. The left-hand brim of his hat was turned up to make room for the tuft of hair, in the style 1829. He lived by robbery committed with violence, and his coat was cut in the latest fashion, though worn at the seams. Montparnasse was an engraving of the fashions, in a state of want, and committing murders. The cause of all the attacks made by this young man was a longing to be well dressed; the first grisette who said to him, "You are handsome," put the black spot in his heart, and made a Cain of this Abel. Finding himself good-looking, he wished to be elegant, and the first stage of elegance is idleness; but the idleness of the poor man is crime. Few toughs were so grand as Montparnasse, and at the age of eighteen he had several corpses behind him. More than one wayfarer lay in the shadow of this villain with outstretched arms and with his face in a pool of blood. Curled, pomaded, with his waist pinched in, the hips of a woman, the bust of a Prussian officer, the buzz of admiration of the girls of the boulevard around him, a carefully tied cravat, a slung-shot in his pocket, and a flower in his button-hole—such was this dandy of the tomb.

4. *COMPOSITION OF THE TROOP*

THESE four bandits formed a species of Proteus, winding through the police ranks and striving to escape the indiscreet glances of Vidocq "under various faces, trees, flame, and fountain," borrowing each other's names and tricks, asylums for one another, laying aside their personality as a man removes a false nose at a masquerade; at times simplifying themselves so as to be only one man, at others multiplying themselves to such an extent that Coco-Latour himself took them for a mob.

These four men were not four men; they were a species of four-headed robber working Paris on a grand scale; the monstrous polyp of evil inhabiting the crypt of society.

Owing to their ramifications and the subjacent net-work of their relations, Babet, Gueulemer, Claquesous, and Montparnasse had the general direction of all the ambush work in the department of the Seine. The finders of ideas in this style, the men with nocturnal imaginations, applied to them to execute them; the four villains were supplied with the canvas, and they produced the scenery. They were always in a position to supply a proportionate and proper staff for every robbery which was sufficiently lucrative and required a stout arm. If a crime were in want of persons to carry it, they sublet the accomplices, and they always had a band of actors at the service of all the tragedies of the caverns.

They generally met at nightfall, the hour when they awoke, on the steppes that border the Salpêtrière. There they conferred, and as they had the twelve dark hours before them, they settled their employment.

Patron-Minette was the name given in the subterranean lurking-places to the association of these four men. In the old and fantastic popular language, which is daily dying out, Patron-Minette signifies the morning, just as "between dog and wolf" signifies night. This appellation was probably derived from the hour when their work finished, for dawn is the moment for specters to fade away and for bandits to part. These four men were known by this title. When the president of the assizes visited Lacenaire in prison, he questioned him about a crime which the murderer denied. "Who committed it?" the president asked, and Lacenaire gave this answer, which was enigmatical for the magistrate but clear for the police, "Perhaps Patron-Minette."

The plot of a play may be at times divined from the list of names, and a party of bandits may, perhaps, be appreciated in the same way. Here are the names to which the principal members of Patron-Minette answered, exactly as they survive in special memoirs:

Panchaud, called Spring, *alias* Bigrenaille.

Brujon (there was a dynasty of Brujons, about whom we may still say a word).

Boulatruelle, the road-mender, of whom we have caught a glimpse.

Laveuve.

Finistère.

Homer-Hogu, a negro.

Tuesday night.

Make haste.

Fauntleroy, *alias* Flower-girl.

Glorious, a liberated convict.

Stop the coach, *alias* Monsieur Dupont.

The southern Esplanade.

Poussàgrive.

Carmagnolet.

Kruideniers, *alias* Bizarro.

Lace-eater.

Feet in the air.

Half farthing, *alias* Two Milliards, etc., etc.

These names have faces, and express not merely beings but species. Each of these names responds to a variety of poisonous fungi which grows beneath civilization.

These beings, very careful about showing their faces, were not of those whom we may see passing by day, for at that period, weary of their night-wanderings, they went to sleep in the lime-kilns, the deserted quarries of Montmartre or Montrouge, or even in the snow. They ran to earth.

What has become of these men? they still exist, and have ever existed. Horace alludes to them in his *Ambubaiarum collegia, pharmacopolæ, mendici, mimi,* and so as long as society is what it is they will be what they are. Under the obscure vault of their cellar they are even born again from the social leakage, they return as specters, but ever identical; the only difference is that they no longer bear the same names, and are no longer in the same skins.

The individuals are extirpated, the tribe exists.

They have always the same qualities, and from beggar to prowler the race ever remains pure. They guess purses in pockets and scent watches in fobs; and gold and silver have a peculiar smell for them. There are simple cits of whom we might say that they have a robbable look, and these men patiently follow these cits. When a foreigner or a countryman passes, they quiver like the spider in its web.

These men, when we catch a glimpse of them upon a deserted boulevard at midnight, are frightful; they do not seem to be men, but forms made of living fog; we might say that they are habitually a portion of the darkness, that they are not distinct, that they have no other soul but shadow and that they have become detached from night momentarily, and in order to live a monstrous life for a few moments.

What is required to make these phantoms vanish? light, floods of light. Not a single bat can resist the dawn. Light up the lower strata of society.

BOOK VIII

THE BAD POOR MAN

1. *A MAN'S CAP INSTEAD OF A GIRL'S BONNET*

SUMMER passed away, then autumn and winter arrived. Neither
M. Leblanc nor the young lady had set foot again in the Luxembourg, while Marius had but one thought, that of seeing again this sweet
and adorable face. He sought it ever, he sought it everywhere, but found
nothing. He was no longer Marius, the enthusiastic dreamer, the resolute,
ardent, and firm man, the bold challenger of destiny, the brain that built
up future upon future, the young mind encumbered with plans, projects,
pride, ideas, and resolves,—he was a lost dog. He fell into a dark sorrow,
and it was all over with him; work was repulsive, walking fatigued him
and solitude wearied him. Mighty nature, once so full of forms, brightness, voices, counsel, perspectives, horizons, and instruction, was now a
vacuum before him; and he felt as if everything had disappeared.

He still thought, for he could not do otherwise, but no longer took
pleasure in his thoughts. To all that they incessantly proposed to him in
whispers, he answered in the shadow: "What use is it?"

He made himself a hundred reproaches. "Why did I follow her? I was
so happy merely in seeing her! She looked at me, and was not that immense? She looked as if she loved me, and was not that everything? I
wanted to have what? there is nothing beyond that, and I was absurd. It
is my fault," etc., etc. Courfeyrac, to whom he confided nothing, as was
his nature, but who guessed pretty nearly all, for that was his nature too,
had begun by congratulating him on being in love, and made sundry bad
jokes about it. Then, on seeing Marius in this melancholy state, he ended
by saying to him, "I see that you have simply been an animal; come to
the Chaumière."

Once putting confidence in a splendid September sun, Marius allowed himself to be taken to the ball of Sceaux by Courfeyrac, Bossuet, and Grantaire, hoping—what a dream!—that he might find her there. Of course he did not see the lady whom he sought—"and yet this is the place where all the lost women can be found," Grantaire growled aside. Marius left his friends at the ball, and returned afoot, alone, tired, feverish, with eyes troubled and sad, in the night, stunned with noise and dust by the many vehicles full of singing beings who were returning from the holiday, and who passed him. He was discouraged, and in order to relieve his aching head inhaled the sharp smell of the walnut-trees on the roadside.

He began living again more than ever in solitude, crushed, giving way to his internal agony, walking up and down like a wolf caught in a trap, everywhere seeking the absent one, and brutalized by love.

Another time he had a meeting which produced a strange effect upon him. In the little streets adjoining the Boulevard des Invalides he passed a man dressed like a workman and wearing a deep-peaked cap, under which white locks peered out. Marius was struck by the beauty of his white hair, and looked at the man, who was walking slowly and as if absorbed in painful meditation. Strange to say, he fancied that he could recognize M. Leblanc,—it was the same hair, the same profile, as far as the peak allowed him to see, and the same gait, though somewhat more melancholy. But why this workman's clothing? What was the meaning of this disguise? Marius was greatly surprised, and when he came to himself again, his first impulse was to follow this man, for he might, perhaps, hold the clew which he had so long been seeking; at any rate, he must have a close look at the man and clear up the enigma; but he hit on this idea too late, for the man was no longer there. He had turned into some side street, and Marius was unable to find him again. This meeting troubled him for some days, and then faded away. "After all," he said to himself, "it is probably only a resemblance."

2. MARIUS FINDS SOMETHING

MARIUS still lived at No. 50-52, but he paid no attention to his fellow-lodgers.

At this period, in truth, here were no other tenants in the house but himself and those Jondrettes whose rent he had once paid without ever having spoken to father, mother, or daughters. The other lodgers had removed, were dead, or turned out for not paying their rent.

On one day of this winter the sun had shown itself a little during the afternoon, but it was February 2, that old Candlemas day, whose treacherous sun, the precursor of a six weeks' frost, inspired Matthew Laensberg with these two lines, which have justly become classical:

> *"Qu'il luise ou qu'il luiserne,*
> *L'ours rentre à sa caverne."*

Marius had just left his cavern, for night was falling. It was the hour to go and dine, for he had been obliged to revert to that practice, such is the infirmity of ideal passions.

He had just crossed the threshold of his door, which Mame Bougon was sweeping at this very moment, while uttering the memorable soliloquy:

"What is there cheap at present? everything is dear. There is only trouble which is cheap, and it may be had for nothing."

Marius walked along the boulevard, in the direction of the Rue St. Jacques. He walked thoughtfully with hanging head.

All at once he felt himself elbowed in the fog. He turned and saw two girls in rags, one tall and thin, the other not quite so tall, who passed hurriedly, panting, frightened, and as if running away; they were coming toward him, and, not seeing him, ran against him as they passed. Marius noticed in the twilight their livid faces, uncovered heads, disheveled hair, their ragged petticoats, and bare feet. While running they talked together, and the elder said:

"The cops came, and nearly caught me."

And the other answered, "I saw them, and so I bolted, bolted, bolted."

Marius understood that the police had nearly caught the two girls, and that they had managed to escape.

They buried themselves beneath the trees behind him, and for a few minutes produced a sort of vague whiteness in the obscurity.

Marius had stopped for a moment, and was just going on, when he noticed a small gray packet lying at his feet. He stooped down and picked it up; it was a sort of envelope, apparently containing papers.

"Why," he said, "these poor girls must have let it fall."

He turned back and called to them, but could not find them. He thought they must be some distance off, so he thrust the parcel into his pocket and went to dinner.

On his way he saw, in a lane turning out of the Rue Mouffetard, a child's coffin, covered with a black pall, laid on three chairs, and illumined by a candle. The two girls in the twilight reverted to his thoughts.

"Poor mothers!" he thought, "there is something even more sad than to see one's children die,—it is to see them live badly."

Then these shadows, which varied his melancholy, passed from his thoughts, and he fell back into his usual reflections. He began thinking of his six months of love and happiness in the open air and broad daylight under the glorious Luxembourg trees.

"How sad my life has become!" he said to himself; "girls constantly appear to me, but formerly they were angels, and now they are ghouls."

3 · QUADRIFRONS

At night, as he undressed to go to bed, his hand felt in his coat-pocket the parcel which he had picked up in the boulevard and forgotten. He thought that it would be as well to open it, as the packet might contain the girls' address, if it belonged to them, or in any case the necessary information to restore it to the person to whom it belonged.

He opened the envelope, which was not sealed, and contained four letters, also unsealed.

The addresses were on all four, and they exhaled a frightful perfume of tobacco.

The first letter was addressed to *Madame, Madame la Marquise de Grucheray, on the Square opposite the Chamber of Deputies.*

Marius said to himself that he would probably find the information he wanted, and as the letter was not sealed he could read it without impropriety. It was drawn up as follows:

Madame la Marquise,

The virtue of clemency and piety is that which unites sosiety most closely. Move your Christian feelings, and dain a glance of compassion at this unfortunate Spaniard, a victim to his loyalty and attachment to the sacred cause of legitimacy, who shed his blood, devoted awl his fortune to defend this cause, and is now in the greatest missery. He does not doubt that you, honored lady, will grant some asistence to preserve an existence entirely painful for a soldier of honor and edducation, covered with wounds, and he reckons before hand on the humanity which annimates you, and the interest which your ladyship takes in so unhappy a nacion. Their prayer will not be in vain, and their gratitude will retain her charming memory.

With the most respectful feelings, I have the honor to be, Madame,

Don Alvares,

Spanish captain of cavvalry, a Royalist refugee in France, who is travelling for his country, and who wants the means to continue his jurney.

No address was attached to the signature, but Marius hoped to find it in the second letter, of which the subscription was: *"To Madame, Madame la Comtesse de Montvernet, No. 9, Rue Cassette."* This is what Marius read:

My Lady Comtesse,

It is a unhappy mother of a familly of six children, of which the yungest is only eight months old; I ill since my last confinement, deserted by my husband, and havving no ressourse in the world, the most fright-ful indijance.

Trusting in your ladyship, she has the honor to be, madame, with profound respect,

Mrs. Balizard.

Marius passed to the third letter, which was, like the preceding, a petition, and he read in it:

Monsieur Pabourgeot, *Elector, wholesale dealer in caps, Rue St. Denis, at the corner of the Rue Aux-Fers.*

I venture to adress this letter to you, to ask you to grant me the pretious favor of your simpathies, and to interest you in a litterary man, who has just sent a drama to the Theatre Français. The subject is histori-cal, and the scene takes place in Auvergne in the time of the empire; the style, I believe, is natural, laconic, and may possess some merit. There are couplets for singing at four places. The comic, the serious, and the un-expected elements are blended in it with a variety of characters, and a tinge of romance is lightly spread through the whole plot, which moves misteriously, and the finale takes place amid several brilliant tableaux. My principal desire is to sattisfy the desire which progressively animates sosiety, that is to say, fashion, that capritious and vague whirligig which changes with nearly every wind.

In spite of these quallities, I have reason to fear that jealousy and the selfishness of privileged authors may obtain my exclusion from the stage, for I am not unaware of the vexation which is caused to new comers.

*Monsieur Pabourgeot, your just reputation as the enlightened protec-
tor of litterary men, emboldens me to send to you my daughter, who will
explain to you our indijant situation, wanting for bread and fire in this
winter s* son. *To tell you that I wish you to accept the homage which I
desire to make to you of my drama, and all those that may succeed it, is
to prove to you how much I desire the honor of sheltering myself under
your ægus, and adorning my writings with your name. If you dain to
honor me with the most modest offering, I will at once set to work writing a coppy of verses, by which to pay you my debt of grattitude. These
verses, which I will try to render as perfect as possible, will be sent to you
before they are insirted in the beginning of the drama and produced on
the stage.*

My most respectful homage to Monsieur and Madame Pabourgeot,

GENFLOT, *Man of Letters.*

*P. S.—If it was only forty sous. I appologize for sending my daughter,
and not paying my respects personaly, but sad reasons of dress do not
allow me, alas! to go out.*

Marius then opened the last letter, which was addressed to—*The
Benevolent gentleman of the church of St. Jacques du Haut-pas,* and it
contained the following few lines:

BENEVOLENT MAN,—

*If you will dain to accompany my daughter you will witness a mis-
serable calamity, and I will show you my certificates.*

*At the sight of these dokuments your generous soul will be moved
by a feeling of sensitive benevolence, for true philosophers always experience lively emotions.*

*Allow, compasionate man, that a man must experience the most cruel
want, and that it is very painful to obtain any relief, by having it attested
by the authorities, as if a man were not at liberty to suffer and die of
inanicion, while waiting till our missery is releaved. Fate is too cruel to
some and too lavish or protecting for others. I await your presence or
your offering, if you dain to make one, and I beg you to believe in the
grateful feelings with which I have the honor of being, really magnanimous sir,*

Your very humble and most obedient servant,

P. FABANTOU, *dramatic artist.*

After reading these four letters, Marius did not find himself much more advanced than before.

In the first place, not one of the writers gave his address.

In the next, they appeared to come from four different individuals, "Don Alvares, Madame Balizard, Genflot the poet, and Fabantou the dramatic artist"; but these letters offered this peculiarity, that they were all in the same handwriting.

What could be concluded from this, save that they came from the same person?

Moreover,—and this rendered the conjecture even more probable,—the paper, which was coarse and yellow, was the same for all four, the tobacco smell was the same, and though an attempt had evidently been made to vary the handwriting, the same orthographical mistakes were reproduced with the most profound tranquillity, and Genflot, the literary man, was no more exempt from them than the Spanish captain.

To strive and divine this mystery was time thrown away, and if he had not picked it up it would have looked like a mystification; Marius was too sad to take kindly even a jest of accident, and lend himself to a game which the street pavement appeared desirous to play with him. He felt as if he were playing at blind man's buff among these four letters and they were mocking him.

Nothing, besides, indicated that these letters belonged to the girls whom Marius had met in the boulevard. After all they were papers evidently of no value. Marius returned them to the envelope, threw the lot into a corner, and went to bed.

At about seven in the morning he had got up and breakfasted, and was trying to set to work, when there came a gentle tap at the door.

As he possessed nothing, he never took out his key, except very rarely, when he had a pressing job to finish. As a rule, even when out, he left the key in the lock. "You will be robbed," said Mame Bougon. "Of what?" Marius asked. It is a fact, however, that one day, a pair of old boots were stolen, to the great triumph of Mame Bougon.

There was a second knock, quite as gentle as the first.

"Come in," said Marius.

The door opened.

"What is the matter, Mame Bougon?" Marius continued, without taking his eyes off the books and MSS. on his table.

A voice, which was not Mame Bougon's, replied: "I beg your pardon, sir."

It was a hollow, cracked, choking, rattling voice, the voice of an old man, rendered hoarse by dram-drinking and exposure to the cold.

Marius turned sharply and noticed a girl.

4. *A ROSE IN WRETCHEDNESS*

A very young girl was standing in the half-open door. The sky-light, through which light entered, was exactly opposite the door, and threw upon this face a sallow gleam. She was a wretched, tanned, fleshless creature, and had only a chemise and a petticoat upon her shivering and frozen nudity. For waist-belt she had a piece of string, for head-dress another; pointed shoulders emerged from her chemise; she was of a lymphatic pallor, earthy collar-bones, hands red, mouth half open, some teeth out, eye sunken and hollow, and she had the outline of an abortive girl, and the look of a corrupted old woman, or fifty years blended with fifteen. She was one of those beings who are at once weak and horrible, and who make those shudder whom they do not cause to weep.

Marius had risen, and was gazing with a species of stupor at this being, who almost resembled the shadows that traverse dreams.

What was most crushing of all was that this girl had not come into the world to be ugly, and in her childhood she must even have been pretty. The grace of youth was still struggling with the hideous and premature senility of debauchery and poverty. A remnant of beauty was expiring on this countenance of sixteen, like the pallid sun which dies out under the frightful clouds on the dawn of a winter's day.

This face was not absolutely strange to Marius, and he fancied that he had already seen it somewhere.

"What do you want, miss?" he asked.

The girl replied, with her drunken galley-slave's voice:

"It is a letter for you, Monsieur Marius."

She addressed him by name, and hence he could not doubt but that her business was with him; but who was this girl, and how did she know his name?

Without waiting for any authority, she walked in, walked in boldly, looking around, with a sort of assurance that contracted the heart, at the whole room, and the unmade bed. Her feet were bare, and large holes in her petticoat displayed her long legs and thin knees.

She was shivering, and held in her hand a letter, which she offered to Marius.

On opening the letter, he noticed that the large clumsy wafer was still damp, which proved that the missive had not come a long distance, and he read:

My amiable neighbor and young sir,

I have herd of your kindness to me, and that you paid my half-year's rent six months ago. I bless you for it, young sir. My eldest daughter will tell you that we have been without a morsel of bread for two days,—four persons, and my wife ill. If I am not deceived in my opinion, I dare to hope that your generous heart will be affected by this statement, and will sudjest in you a desire to be propicious to me, by daining to lavish on me a trifling charity.

I am, with the distinguished consideration which is due to the benefactors of humanity,

JONDRETTE.

P. S. My daughter will wait for your orders, my dear Monsieur Marius.

This letter, in the midst of the obscure adventure which had been troubling Marius since the previous evening, was like a candle in a cellar; all was suddenly lit up.

This letter came from where the other letters came. It was the same handwriting, the same style, the same orthography, the same paper, and the same tobacco smell.

They were five letters, five stories, five names, five signatures, and only one writer. The Spanish captain Don Alvares, the unhappy mother Balizard, the dramatic author Genflot, and the old comedian Fabantou were all four Jondrette, if, indeed, Jondrette's name were really Jondrette.

During the lengthened period that Marius had inhabited this No. 50-52, he had, as we stated, but rare occasions to see, or even catch a glance of, his very low neighbors. His mind was elsewhere, and where the mind is there is the eye. He must have passed the Jondrettes more than once in the passage and on the stairs, but they were to him merely shadows. He had paid so little attention to them, that on the previous evening he had run against the Jondrette girls on the boulevard without recognizing them, for it was evidently they, and it was with great difficulty that the girl who had just entered the room aroused in him, through disgust and pity, a vague fancy that he had met her somewhere before.

Now he saw everything clearly. He comprehended that his neighbor Jondrette had hit upon the trade, in his distress, of working upon the charity of benevolent persons; that he procured addresses and wrote under supposititious names, to people whom he supposed to be rich and charitable, letters which his children delivered at their risk and peril, for this father had attained such a stage that he hazarded his daughters; he was gambling with destiny and staked them. Marius comprehended that in all probability, judging from their flight of the previous evening, their panting, their terror, and the slang words he overheard, these unfortunates carried on some other dark trades, and the result of all this was, in the heart of human society such as it is constituted, two wretched beings, who were neither children nor girls nor women, but a species of impure and innocent monsters, which were the product of wretchedness.

Melancholy beings without age, name, or sex, to whom neither good nor evil is any longer possible, and who, on emerging from childhood, have nothing left in the world, not liberty, nor virtue, nor responsibility; souls that expanded yesterday and are faded to-day, like the flowers that have fallen in the street and are splashed by the mud, while waiting till a wheel crushes them.

While Marius was bending on the young girl an astonished and painful glance, she was walking about the garret with the boldness of a specter, and without troubling herself in the slightest about her state of nudity. At some moments her unfastened and torn chemise fell almost to her waist. She moved the chairs about, disturbed the toilet articles on the chest of drawers, felt Marius's clothes, and rummaged in every corner.

"Why," she said, "you have a looking-glass!"

And she hummed, as if she had been alone, bits of vaudeville songs and wild choruses, which her guttural and hoarse voice rendered mournful.

But beneath this boldness there was something constrained, alarmed, and humiliated, for effrontery is a disgrace.

Nothing could well be more sad than to see her fluttering about the room with the movement of a broken-winged bird startled by a dog. It was palpable that with other conditions of education and destiny the gay and free demeanor of this girl might have been something gentle and charming. Among animals, the creature born to be a dove is never changed into an osprey; that is only possible with men.

Marius was thinking, and left her alone, and she walked up to the table.

"Ah!" said she, "books."

A gleam darted from her glassy eye; she continued, and her accent expressed the attitude of being able to boast of something to which no human creature is insensible:

"I know how to read."

She quickly seized the book lying on the table, and read rather fluently:

"General Bauduin received orders to carry with the five battalions of his brigade the Chateau of Hougomont, which is in the center of the plain of Waterloo—"

She broke off.

"Ah, Waterloo, I know all about that. It was a battle in which my father was engaged, for he served in the army. We are thorough Bonapartists, we are. Waterloo was fought against the English."

She laid down the book, took up a pen, and exclaimed:

"And I can write, too."

She dipped the pen in the ink, and turned to Marius, saying:

"Would you like a proof? stay, I will write a line to show you."

And ere he had time to answer, she wrote on a sheet of white paper in the middle of the table, *"Here are the cops."*

Then, throwing down the pen, she added:

"There are no errors in spelling, as you can see, for my sister and I were well educated. We have not always been what we are now; we were not made—"

Here she stopped, fixed her glassy eyes on Marius, and burst into a laugh, as she said, with an intonation which contained every possible agony blended with every possible cynicism:

"Bah!"

And then she began humming these words to a lively air.

> *J'ai faim, mon père.*
> *Pas de fricot.*
> *J'ai froid, ma mère.*

Pas de tricot.
Grelotte,
Lolotte!
Sanglote,
Jacquot!

She had scarce completed this couplet ere she exclaimed:

"Do you ever go to the play, Monsieur Marius? I do so. I have a brother, who is a friend of the actors, and gives me tickets every now and then. I don't care for the gallery much, though, for you are so squeezed up; at times, too, there are noisy people there, and others who smell bad."

Then she stared at Marius, gave him a strange look, and said to him:

"Do you know, M. Marius, that you are a very good-looking fellow?"

And at the same moment the same thought occurred to both, which made her smile and him blush.

She walked up to him and laid a hand on his shoulder: "You don't pay any attention to me, but I know you, M. Marius. I meet you here on the staircase, and then I see you go in to a swell of the name of M. Mabœuf, who lives over at Austerlitz, when I am out that way. Your curly hair becomes you very well."

Her voice tried to be very soft, and only succeeded in being very low; a part of her words was lost in the passage from the larynx to the lips, as on a pianoforte some keys of which are broken.

Marius had gently recoiled.

"I have a packet," he said, with his cold gravity, "which, I believe, belongs to you. Allow me to deliver it to you."

And he handed her the envelope which contained the four letters; she clapped her hands and said:

"We looked for it everywhere."

Then she quickly seized the parcel and undid the envelope, while saying:

"Lord of lords! how my sister and I *did* look for it! And so you found it? on the boulevard, did you not? it must have been there. You see, it was dropped while we were running and it was my brat of a sister who was such an ass. When we got home we could not find it, and, as we did not wish to be beaten, which is unnecessary, which is entirely unnecessary, which is absolutely unnecessary, we said at home that we had delivered the letters, and that the answer was, Nix! and here are the poor letters! Well, and how did you know that they were mine? oh, yes, by the writing. So, then, it was you that we ran against last night? We could not see anything, and I said to my sister, 'Is it a gentleman?' and she answered, 'Yes, I think it is a gentleman'."

While saying this she had unfolded the petition addressed to the "benevolent gentleman of the church of St. Jacques du Haut-pas."

"Hilloh!" she said, "this is the one for the old swell who goes to mass. Why, 'tis just the hour, and I will carry it to him. He will perhaps give us something for breakfast."

Then she burst into a laugh, and added:

"Do you know what it will be if we breakfast to-day? we shall have our breakfast of the day before yesterday, our dinner of the day before yesterday, our breakfast of yesterday, our dinner of yesterday, all at once this morning. Well, hang it all! if you are not satisfied, rot, dogs!"

This reminded Marius of what the hapless girl had come to get from him; he fumbled in his waistcoat, but found nothing.

The girl went on, and seemed speaking as if no longer conscious of the presence of Marius:

"Sometimes I go out at night. Sometimes I do not come home. Before we came here last winter we lived under the arches of the bridges, and kept close together not to be frozen. My little sister cried. How sad the water is. When I thought of drowning myself, I said 'No, it is too cold.' I go about all alone when I like, and sleep at times in ditches. Do you know, at night, when I walk along the boulevard, I see trees like forks, I see black houses as tall as the towers of Notre Dame, I fancy that the white walls are the river, and I say to myself, 'Why, there is water!' The stars are like illumination lamps, and you might say that they smoke and the wind puts them out. I feel stunned, as if my hair was lashing my ears; however the night may be, I hear barrel-organs and spinning machinery, but what do I know? I fancy that stones are being thrown at me, and I run away unconsciously, for all turns round me. When you have not eaten, it is funny."

And she gazed at him with haggard eyes.

After feeling in the depths of his pockets, Marius succeeded in getting together five francs sixteen sous; it was at this moment all that he possessed in the world. "Here is my to-day's dinner," he thought, "and to-morrow will take care of itself." He kept the sixteen sous, and gave the girl the five-franc piece.

She eagerly clutched the coin.

"Good!" she said, "there is sunshine."

And, as if the sunshine had the property of melting in her brain avalanches of slang, she went on:

"Five francs! a shiner! a monarch! ain't that stunning? Well, you are a jolly cock, and I do the humble to you. Hurrah for the brick! two days' grub; here's a feed; beans and bacon and a bellyful; you're a daisy!"

She pulled her chemise up over her shoulders, gave Marius a deep courtesy and a familiar wave of the hand, and walked toward the door, saying: "Good-day, sir; but no matter, I'll go and find my old swell."

As she passed she noticed on the drawers an old crust of dry bread moldering in the dust; she caught it up, and bit into it savagely, grumbling:

"It is good, it is hard; it breaks my teeth!"

Then she left the room.

5. *A PROVIDENTIAL SPY-HOLE*

MARIUS had lived for the past five years in poverty, want, and even distress, but he now saw that he had never known what real misery was, and he had just witnessed it—it was the phantom which had just passed before him. For, in truth, he who has only seen man's misery has seen nothing, he must see woman's misery; while he who has seen woman's misery has seen nothing, for he must see the misery of the child.

When man has reached the last extremity, he has also reached the limit of his resources; and, then, woe to the defenseless beings that surround him! Work, wages, bread, fire, courage, and food will all fail him at once; the light of day seems extinguished outside, the moral light is extinguished within him. In these shadows man comes across the weakness of the wife and child, and violently bends them to ignominy.

In such a case, every horror is possible, and despair is surrounded by thin partitions which all open upon vice and crime.

Health, youth, honor, the sacred and retiring delicacy of the still innocent flesh, heart, virginity, modesty, that epidermis of the soul, are
foully clutched by this groping hand, which seeks resources, finds opprobrium, and puts up with it.

Fathers, mothers, brothers, sisters, men, women, and girls adhere and
are aggregated, almost like a mineral formation, in this misty promiscuity of sexes, relations, ages, infamies, and innocencies. Leaning against
each other, they crouch back to back in a species of den of destiny, and
look at each other lamentably. Oh! the unfortunates! how pale they are!
how cold they are! it seems as if they belong to a planet much farther
from the sun than our own.

This girl was to Marius a sort of emissary from the darkness, and she
revealed to him a hideous side of night.

Marius almost reproached himself for the preoccupations of reverie
and passion which, up to this day, had prevented him from taking a
glance at his neighbors. To have paid their rent was a mechanical impulse, which any one might have had; but he, Marius, ought to have done
better. What! only a wall separated himself from these abandoned creatures, who lived groping in night, beyond the pale of other living beings.
He elbowed them, he was to some extent the last link of the human race
which they could touch; he heard them living, or rather dying, by his
side, and he paid no attention to them! Every moment of the day he
heard them, through the wall, coming, going, and talking—and he did
not listen! and in their words were groans, and he did not hear them!
His thoughts were elsewhere,—engaged with dreams, impossible sunbeams, loves in the air, and follies; and yet, human creatures, his brethren
in Christ, his brethren in the people, were slowly dying by his side, dying
unnecessarily! He even formed part of their misfortune, and he aggravated it. For, if they had had another neighbor, a neighbor more attentive, less chimerical, an ordinary and charitable man, their indigence
would evidently have been noticed, their signals of distress perceived, and
they might, perhaps, have been picked up and saved long before. They
doubtless seemed very depraved, very corrupt, very vile, and indeed very
odious; but persons who fall without being degraded are rare; besides,
there is a stage where the unfortunate and the infamous are mingled and
confounded in one word, a fatal word, LES MISÉRABLES; and with whom
lies the fault? And then, again, should not the charity be the greater the
deeper the fall is?

While reading himself this lecture, for there were occasions on which

Marius was his own pedagogue and reproached himself more than he deserved, he looked at the wall which separated him from the Jondrettes, as if his pitying glance could pass through the partition and warm the unhappy beings. The wall was a thin coating of plaster, supported by laths and beams, and which, as we have stated, allowed the murmurs of words and voices to be distinctly heard. A man must be a dreamer like Marius not to have noticed the fact before. No paper was hung on either side of the wall, and its clumsy framework was plainly visible. Almost unconsciously Marius examined this partition; for at times reverie examines, scrutinizes, and observes much like thought does. All at once he rose, for he had just noticed near the ceiling a triangular hole produced by the gap between three laths. The plaster which once covered this hole had fallen off, and by getting on his chest of drawers he could see through this aperture into the room of the Jondrettes. Commiseration has, and should have, its curiosity, and it is permissible to regard misfortune traitorously when we wish to relieve it.

"Let me see," thought Marius, "what these people are like, and what state they are in." He clambered on the drawers, put his eye to the hole, and looked.

6. . . *THE WILD-BEAST MAN IN HIS LAIR*

CITIES, like forests, have their dens, in which everything that is most wicked and formidable conceals itself. The only difference is, that what hides itself thus in cities is ferocious, unclean, and little,—that is to say, ugly; what conceals itself in the forest is ferocious, savage, and grand,— that is to say, beautiful. Den for den, those of the beasts are preferable to those of men; and caverns are better than hiding-places.

What Marius saw was a hiding-place.

Marius was poor, and his room was indigent; but, in the same way as his poverty was noble, his room was clean. The garret into which he was now looking was abject, dirty, fetid, infectious, dark, and sordid. The furniture only consisted of a straw-bottomed chair, a rickety table, a few old bits of crockery, and in the corners two indescribable beds. The only light came through a sky-light with four panes of glass and festooned with spider-webs. Through this came just sufficient light for the face of a man to see the face of a specter. The walls had a leprous look, and were covered with gashes and scars, like a face disfigured by some horrible disease, and a filthy damp oozed from them. Obscene designs, clumsily drawn in charcoal, could be distinguished on them.

The room which Marius occupied had a broken-brick flooring, but in this one, without bricks or planks, people walked on the old plaster, which had grown black under the feet. Upon this uneven flooring, in which the dust was, so to speak, incrusted, and which had but one virginity, that of the broom, were capriciously grouped constellations of old shoes, boots, and frightful rags; this room, however, had a chimney, and for this reason was let at forty francs a year. There was something of everything in this fire-place,—a chafing-dish, a pot, some broken planks, rags hanging from nails, a bird-cage, ashes, and even a little fire, for two logs were smoking there sadly.

A thing which augmented the horror of this garret was the fact of its being large; it had angles, nooks, black holes under the roof, bays and promontories. Hence came frightful inscrutable corners, in which it seemed as if spiders large as a fist, wood-lice as large as a foot, and possibly some human monsters, must lurk.

One of the beds was near the door, the other near the window, but the ends of both ran down to the mantel-piece, and faced Marius. In a corner near the hole through which Marius was peeping, a colored engraving in a black frame, under which was written in large letters, THE DREAM, was hung against the wall. It represented a sleeping woman and a sleeping child, the child lying on the woman's knees, an eagle in the clouds with a crown in its beak, and the woman removing the crown from the child's head, without awakening it, however; in the background Napoleon, surrounded by a glory, was leaning against a dark blue column, with a yellow capital, that bore the following inscription:

MARINGO. IENA. WAGRAMME.
AUSTERLITS. ELOT.

Below this frame a sort of wooden panel, longer than it was wide, was placed on the ground and leaning against the wall. It looked like a picture turned from the spectator, or some sign-board detached from a wall and forgotten there while waiting to be hung again.

At the table, on which Marius noticed pen, ink, and paper, a man about sixty years of age was seated, short, thin, livid, haggard, with a sharp, cruel, and listless look, a hideous scamp.

If Lavater had examined this face, he would have found in it the vulture blended with the attorney's clerk; the bird of prey and the man of trickery rendering each other more ugly and more perfect—the man of trickery rendering the bird of prey ignoble, and the bird of prey rendering the man of trickery horrible.

This man had a long gray beard, and wore a woman's chemise, which allowed his hairy chest and naked arms, bristling with gray hairs, to be seen. Under this chemise might be noticed muddy trousers, and boots out of which his toes stuck.

He had a pipe in his mouth, and was smoking; there was no bread in the garret, but there was still tobacco.

He was writing, probably some letter like those which Marius had read.

On one corner of the table could be seen an old, broken-backed volume, the form of which, the old 12mo of circulating libraries, indicated a romance; on the cover figured the following title, printed in large capitals: "GOD, THE KING, HONOR, AND THE LADIES. BY DUCRAY DUMINIL, 1814."

While writing, the man was talking aloud, and Marius heard his words:

"Only to think that there is no equality, even when a man is dead! Just look at Père Lachaise! The great ones, those who are rich, are up above, in the Acacia avenue, which is paved, and reach it in a coach. The little folk, the poor people, the wretched—they are put down at the bottom, where there is mud up to your knees, in holes and damp, and they are placed there that they may rot all the sooner. You can't go to see them without sinking into the ground."

Here he stopped, smote the table with his fist, and added, while he gnashed his teeth:

"Oh! I could eat the world!"

A stout woman, who might be forty or one hundred, was crouched up near the chimney-piece on her naked heels.

She, too, was only dressed in a chemise and a cotton petticoat pieced

187

with patches of old cloth, and an apron of coarse canvas concealed one-half of the petticoat. Though this woman was sitting all of a heap, you could see that she was very tall and a species of giantess by her husband's side. She had frightful hair, of a reddish auburn, beginning to turn gray, which she thrust back every now and then with the enormous strong hands with flat nails.

By her side, on the ground, was lying an open volume of the same form as the other, probably part of the same romance.

On one of the beds Marius caught a glimpse of a tall, young, unhealthy-looking girl, sitting up almost naked, and with hanging feet, who did not seem to hear, see, or live.

She was, doubtless, the younger sister of the one who had come to him.

She appeared to be eleven or twelve years of age, but, on examining her attentively, it could be seen that she was at least fourteen; it was the girl who said on the boulevard the previous night, "I bolted, bolted, bolted."

She was of that sickly class who keep down for a long time and then shoot up quickly and suddenly. It is indigence which produces these human plants, and these creatures have neither infancy nor adolescence. At fifteen they seem twelve, and at sixteen they appear twenty; to-day it is a little girl, to-morrow a woman; we might almost say that they stride through life in order to reach the end more rapidly.

At this moment, however, she had the look of a child.

In this lodging there was not the slightest sign of work; not a loom, a spinning-wheel, or a single tool, but in one corner were some iron implements of dubious appearance. It was that dull indolence which follows despair and precedes death.

Marius gazed for some time at this mournful interior, which was more terrifying than the interior of a tomb, for the human soul could be seen stirring in it and life palpitating.

The garret, the cellar, the hole, in which some indigent people crawl in the lowest part of the social edifice, is not exactly the sepulcher, but it is the antechamber to it; but, like those rich men who display their greatest magnificence at the entrance to their palace, it seems that death, which is close at hand, places all its greatest wretchedness in this vestibule.

The man was silent, the woman did not speak, and the girl did not seem to breathe; the pen could be heard moving across the paper.

The man growled, without ceasing to write, "Scoundrels, scoundrels, all are scoundrels."

The variation upon Solomon's exclamation drew a sigh from the wife.

"Calm yourself, my love," she said, "do not hurt yourself, darling. You are too good to write to all those people, dear husband."

In misery bodies draw more closely together, as in cold weather, but hearts are estranged. This woman, to all appearance, must have loved this man with the amount of love within her, but probably this had been extinguished in the daily and mutual reproaches of the frightful distress that pressed upon the whole family, and she now only had the ashes of affection for her husband within her. Still, caressing appellations, as frequently happens, had survived; she called him *darling, pet, husband,* with her lips, but her heart was silent.

The man continued to write.

7. STRATEGY AND TACTICS

MARIUS, with an aching heart, was just going to descend from the species of observatory which he had improvised, when a noise attracted his attention and made him remain at his post.

The door of the garret was suddenly opened, and the elder daughter appeared on the threshold. She had on her feet clumsy men's shoes covered with mud, which had even splashed her red ankles, and she was covered with an old ragged cloak, which Marius had not noticed an hour previously and which she had probably left at his door, in order to inspire greater sympathy, and put on again when she went out. She came in, shut the door after her, stopped to fetch breath, for she was panting, and then cried, with an expression of triumph and joy:

"He is coming!"

The father turned his eyes to her, the mother turned her head, and the little girl did not move.

"Who?" the father asked.

"The gentleman."

"The philanthropist?"

"Yes."

"From the church of St. Jacques?"

"Yes. He is following me."

"Are you sure?"

"I am sure."

"Sure he is coming?"

"He is coming in a hackney coach, I tell you."

"A hackney coach! why, it is Rothschild!"

The father rose.

"Why are you sure? if he is coming in a coach, how is it that you got here before him? did you give him the address, and are you certain you told him the last door on the right in the passage? I only hope he will not make a mistake. Did you find him at church? did he read my letter, and what did he say to you?"

"Ta, ta, ta," said the girl, "how you gallop, my good man. I went into the church, he was at his usual place, I made a courtesy and handed him the letter, he read it, and said to me, 'Where do you live, my child?' I said, 'I will show you the way, sir'; he said, 'No, give me your address, for my daughter has some purchases to make. I will take a hackney coach and be at your abode as soon as you.' I gave him the address, and when I mentioned the house he seemed surprised, and hesitated for a moment, but then said, 'No matter, I will go.' When mass was over I saw him leave the church and get into a coach with his daughter. And I carefully told him the last door on the right at the end of the passage."

"And what tells you that he will come?"

"I have just seen the coach turn into the Rue du Petit Banquier, and that is why I ran."

"How do you know it is the same coach?"

"Because I noticed the number, of course."

"What was it?"

"Four hundred and forty."

"Good, you are a clever girl."

The girl looked boldly at her father, and said, as she pointed to the shoes on her feet:

"It is possible that I am a clever girl; but I say that I will not put on those shoes again; in the first place, on account of my health, and, secondly, for the sake of decency. I know nothing more annoying than shoes which are too big for you, and go, gji, gji, gji, along the road. I would sooner be barefooted."

"You are right," the father replied, in a gentle voice, which contrasted with the girl's rudeness; "but the poor are not admitted into churches unless they wear shoes; God's presence must not be entered barefoot," he added bitterly.

Then he returned to the object that occupied him.

"And so you are sure that he will come?"

"He is at my heels," she replied.

The man drew himself up, and there was a species of illumination on his face.

"Wife," he cried, "you hear! Here is the philanthropist; put out the fire."

The stupefied mother did not stir.

The father, with the agility of a mountebank, seized the cracked pot which stood on the chimney-piece, and threw water on the logs.

Then he said to his elder daughter:

"Pull the straw out of the chair."

As his daughter did not understand him, he seized the chair and kicked the seat out; his leg passed through it.

While drawing it out he asked the girl: "Is it cold?"

"Very cold; it is snowing."

The father turned to the younger girl, who was on the bed near the window, and shouted in a thundering voice:

"Come off the bed, directly, idler; you never will do anything; break a pane of glass!"

The girl jumped off the bed, shivering.

"Break a pane!" he continued.

The girl was quite stunned, and did not move.

"Do you hear me?" the father repeated, "I tell you to break a pane."

The child, with a sort of terrified obedience, stood on tip-toe and broke a pane with her fist; the glass fell with a great clash.

"All right," said the father.

He was serious and active, and his eye rapidly surveyed every corner of the garret.

He was like a general who makes his final preparations at the moment when an action is about to begin.

The mother, who had not yet said a word, rose and asked in a slow, dull voice, the words seeming to issue as if frozen:

"Darling, what do you intend to do?"

"Go to bed," the man replied.

The tone admitted of no deliberation; the mother obeyed, and threw herself heavily on one of the beds.

A sobbing was now audible in a corner.

"What is that?" the father cried.

The younger girl, without leaving the gloom in which she was crouching, showed her bleeding hand. In breaking the glass she had cut herself; she had crawled close to her mother's bed, and was now crying silently.

It was the mother's turn to draw herself up and cry:

"You see what nonsensical acts you commit! she has cut herself in breaking the window."

"All the better," said the man, "I expected it."

"How all the better?" the woman continued.

"Silence!" the father replied, "I suppress the liberty of the press."

Then, tearing the chemise which he wore, he made a bandage, with which he quickly wrapped up the girl's bleeding hand.

This done, his eye settled on the torn shirt with satisfaction.

"And the shirt too!" he said, "all this looks well."

An icy blast blew through the pane and entered the room. The external fog penetrated it, and dilated like a white piece of wadding pulled open by invisible fingers. The snow could be seen falling through the broken pane, and the cold promised by the Candlemas sun had already arrived.

The father took a look around him, as if to make sure that he had forgotten nothing; then he fetched an old shovel and strewed the ashes over the wet logs so as to conceal them entirely.

Then, getting up and leaning against the chimney-piece, he said:

"Now we can receive the philanthropist."

8. A SUNBEAM IN THE GARRET

THE elder girl walked up to her father and laid her hand in his.

"Just feel how cold I am!" she said.

"Stuff!" the father answered, "I am much colder than that."

The mother cried impetuously:

"You always have everything better than the others, the bad even."

"Down!" the man said.

The mother, looked at by him in a certain way, held her tongue, and there was a momentary silence in the den.

The elder girl was carelessly removing the mud from the edge of her cloak, and her younger sister continued to sob. The mother had taken her head between her hands, and covered it with kisses, while whispering:

"Pray do not go on so, my treasure, it will be nothing, so don't cry, or you will vex your father."

"No," the father cried, "on the contrary, sob away, for that does good."

Then he turned to the elder girl:

"Why, he is not coming! suppose he were not to come! I should have broken my pane, put out my fire, unseated my chair, and torn my shirt all for nothing."

"And hurt the little one," the mother murmured.

"Do you know," the father continued, "that it is infernally cold in this devil's own garret? Suppose the man did not come! but no, he is keeping us waiting, and says to himself, 'Well, they will wait my pleasure; they are sent into the world for that!' Oh! how I hate the rich, and with what joy, jubilation, enthusiasm, and satisfaction would I strangle them all! All the rich, I say, those pretended charitable men who play the devout, attend mass, keep in with the priests, and believe themselves above us, and who come to humiliate us, and bring us 'clothes,' as they say! They bring us old rubbish not worth four sous, and bread; but it is not that I want, you pack of scoundrels, but money. Ah, money! never! because they say that we would go and drink, and that we are drunkards and idlers. And they, what are they, pray, and what have they been in their time? Thieves, for they could not have grown rich without that. Oh! society ought to be tossed in a blanket, and the whole lot thrown into the air! all would be broken, very possibly, but at any rate no one would have anything, and that would be so much gained! But what is your humbug of a benevolent gentleman about! will he come? perhaps the animal has forgotten the address. I will bet that the old brute—"

At this moment there was a gentle tap at the door; the man rushed forward and opened it, while exclaiming with deep bows and smiles of adoration:

"Come in, sir; deign to enter, my respected benefactor, as well as your charming daughter."

A man of middle age and a young lady stood in the doorway.

Marius had not left his post, and what he felt at this moment is beyond the human tongue.

It was She.

Any one who has loved knows the radiant meaning conveyed in the three letters that form the word She.

It was certainly she, though Marius could hardly distinguish her through the luminous vapor which had suddenly spread over his eyes. It was the gentle creature he had lost, the star which had gleamed on him for six months; it was the forehead, the mouth, the lovely mouth which had produced night by departing. The eclipse was over, and she now re-appeared.

She re-appeared in the darkness, in this attic, in this filthy den, in this horror.

Marius trembled. What! it was she! the palpitation of his heart affected his sight, and he felt ready to burst into tears! What! he saw her again after seeking her so long! it seemed to him as if he had lost his soul and had just found it again.

She was still the same, though perhaps a little paler; her delicate face was framed in a violet velvet bonnet, and her waist was hidden by a black satin pelisse; a glimpse of her little foot in a silk boot could be caught under her long dress.

She was accompanied by M. Leblanc, and she walked into the room and placed a rather large parcel on the table.

The elder girl had withdrawn behind the door, and looked with a jealous eye at the velvet bonnet, the satin pelisse, and the charming, happy face.

9. JONDRETTE ALMOST WEEPS

THE garret was so dark that persons who came into it felt much as if they were going into a cellar. The two new-comers, therefore, advanced with some degree of hesitation, scarce distinguishing the vague forms around them, while they were perfectly seen and examined by the eyes of the denizens in the attic, who were accustomed to this gloom.

M. Leblanc walked up to Father Jondrette, with his sad and gentle smile, and said:

"You will find in this parcel, sir, new apparel, woolen stockings, and blankets."

"Our angelic benefactor overwhelms us," Jondrette said, bowing to the ground.

Then, bending down to the ear of his elder daughter, he added in a hurried whisper, while the two visitors were examining this lamentable interior:

"Did I not say so? clothes, but no money. They are all alike. By the way, how was the letter to the old ass signed?"

"Fabantou."

"The actor, all right."

It was lucky that Jondrette asked this, for at the same moment M. Leblanc turned to him, and said, with the air of a person who is trying to remember the name:

"I see that you are much to be pitied, Monsieur—"

"Fabantou," Jondrette quickly added.

"Monsieur Fabantou; yes, that is it, I remember."

"An actor, sir, who has been successful in his time."

Here Jondrette evidently believed the moment arrived to catch his philanthropist, and he shouted in a voice which had some of the bombast of the country showman, and the humility of the professional beggar:

"A pupil of Talma, sir! I am a pupil of Talma! fortune smiled upon me formerly, but now, alas! the turn of misfortune has arrived. You see, my benefactor, we have no bread, no fire. My poor brats have no fire. My sole chair without a seat! a pane of glass broken! in such weather as this! my wife in bed, ill!"

"Poor woman!" said M. Leblanc.

"My child hurt," Jondrette added.

The child, distracted by the arrival of the strangers, was staring at the "young lady," and ceased sobbing.

"Cry, I tell you; roar!" Jondrette whispered to her.

At the same time he squeezed her injured hand. All this was done with the talent of a conjurer.

The little one uttered piercing cries, and the adorable girl whom Marius called in his heart "his Ursule" eagerly went up to her.

"Poor, dear child!" she said.

"You see, respected young lady," Jondrette continued, "her hand is bleeding. It is the result of an accident which happened to her while working at a factory to earn six sous a day. It is possible that her arm will have to be cut off."

"Really?" the old gentleman said in alarm.

The little girl, taking this remark seriously, began sobbing again her loudest.

"Alas, yes, my benefactor!" the father answered.

For some minutes past, Jondrette had been looking at the "philanthropist" in a peculiar way, and while speaking seemed to be scrutinizing him attentively, as if trying to recall his recollections. All at once, profiting by a moment during which the new-comers were questioning the little girl about her injured hand, he passed close to his wife, who was lying in her bed with a surprised and stupid air, and said to her, in a hurried whisper:

"Look at that man!"

Then he turned to M. Leblanc and continued his lamentations.

"Look, sir! my sole clothing consists of a chemise of my wife's, all torn, in the heart of winter. I cannot go out for want of a coat, and if I had the smallest bit of a coat I would go and call on Mademoiselle Mars, who knows me, and is much attached to me; does she still live in the Rue de la Tour des Dames? Do you know, sir, that we played together in the provinces, and that I shared her laurels? Célimène would come to my help, sir, and Elmire give alms to Belisarius. But no, nothing! and not a half-penny piece in the house! my wife ill, not a sou! my daughter dangerously injured, not a sou! my wife suffers from shortness of breath —it comes from her age, and then the nervous system is mixed up in it. She requires assistance and so does my daughter. But the physician and the apothecary, how are they to be paid? I have not a farthing! I would kneel down before a decime, sir. You see to what the arts are reduced! And do you know, my charming young lady, and you, my generous protector, who exhale virtue and goodness, and who perfume the church where my poor child sees you daily when she goes to say her prayers! for I am bringing up my daughters in religion, sir, and do not wish them to turn to the stage. Ah, the little rogues, just let me see them swerve! I do not jest, sir; I sling into them lectures on honor, morality, and virtue. Just ask them! they must go straight, for they have a father. They are not wretched girls who begin by having no family, and finish by marrying the public. Such a girl is Miss Nobody, and becomes Madame All-the-world. There must be nothing of that sort in the Fabantou family! I intend to educate them virtuously, and they must be respectable, and honest, and believe in God, by Jesus! Well, sir, worthy sir, do you know what will happen to-morrow? To-morrow is the fatal 4th February, the last respite my landlord has granted me, and if I do not pay my rent by to-night, my eldest daughter, myself, my wife with her fever, my child with her wound, will be all four of us turned out of here into the street, shelterless in the rain and snow. That is the state of the case, sir! I owe four quarters, a year's rent; that is to say, sixty francs."

Jondrette lied, for four quarters would only have been forty francs, and he could not owe four, as it was not six months since Marius had paid two for him. M. Leblanc took a five-franc piece from his pocket and threw it on the table.

Jondrette had time to growl in his grown-up daughter's ear:

"The scamp! what does he expect me to do with his five francs? They will not pay for the chair and pane of glass. There's the result of making an outlay."

In the meanwhile, M. Leblanc had taken off a heavy brown coat which he wore over his blue one, and thrown it on the back of a chair.

"Monsieur Fabantou," he said, "I have only these five francs about me, but I will take my daughter home and return to-night. Is it not to-night that you have to pay?"

Jondrette's face was lit up with a strange expression, and he hurriedly answered:

"Yes, respected sir, I must be with my landlord by eight o'clock."

"I will be here by six, and bring you the sixty francs."

"My benefactor!" Jondrette exclaimed wildly, and he added in a whisper:

"Look at him carefully, wife."

M. Leblanc had given his arm to the lovely young lady and was turning to the door.

"Till this evening, my friends," he said.

"At six o'clock?" Jondrette asked.

"At six o'clock precisely."

At this moment the overcoat left on the back of the chair caught the eye of the elder girl.

"Sir," she said, "you are forgetting your great-coat."

Jondrette gave his daughter a crushing glance, accompanied by a formidable shrug of the shoulders, but M. Leblanc turned and replied smilingly:

"I do not forget it, I'll leave it."

"Oh, my protector," said Jondrette, "my august benefactor, I am melting into tears! permit me to conduct you to your vehicle."

"If you go out," M. Leblanc remarked, "put on that overcoat, for it is really very cold."

Jondrette did not let this be said twice, but eagerly put on the brown coat. Then they all three went out, Jondrette preceding the two strangers.

10. *THE TARIFF OF CAB-FARES*

MARIUS had lost nothing of all this scene, and yet in reality he had seen nothing. His eyes remained fixed on the maiden; his heart had, so to speak, seized and entirely enfolded her from her first step into the garret. During the whole time she had been there he had lived that life of ecstasy which suspends material perceptions and concentrates the whole mind upon one point. He contemplated not the girl, but the radiance which was dressed in a satin pelisse and a velvet bonnet. Had the planet Sirius entered the room he would not have been more dazzled.

While she was opening the parcel and unfolding the clothes and blankets, questioning the sick mother kindly and the little wounded girl tenderly, he watched her every movement, and tried to hear her words. Though he knew her eyes, her forehead, her beauty, her waist, and her walk, he did not know the sound of her voice. He fancied that he had caught a few words once at the Luxembourg, but he was not absolutely sure. He would have given ten years of his life to hear her, and to carry off in his soul a little of this music, but all was lost in the lamentable braying of Jondrette's trumpet. This mingled a real anger with Marius's ravishment, and he devoured her with his eyes, for he could not imagine that it was really this divine creature whom he perceived among these unclean beings in this monstrous den; he fancied that he saw a humming-bird among frogs.

When she left the room he had but one thought,—to follow her, to attach himself to her trail, not to leave her till he knew where she lived, or at least not to lose her again after having so miraculously found her. He leaped off the drawers and seized his hat, but just as he laid his hand on the latch and was going out, a reflection arrested him; the passage was long, the staircase steep, Jondrette chattering and M. Leblanc had doubtless not yet got into his coach again. If, turning in the passage or on the stairs, he were to perceive him, Marius, in this house, he would assuredly be alarmed, and find means to escape him again, and so all would be over for the second time. What was to be done? wait awhile? but during this delay the vehicle might start off. Marius was perplexed, but at length risked it, and left the room.

There was no one in the passage, and he ran to the stairs, and as there was no one upon them he hurried down and reached the boulevard just in time to see a hackney coach turning the corner of the Rue du Petit Banquier, on its road to Paris.

Marius rushed in that direction, and, on reaching the corner of the boulevard, saw the hackney coach again rapidly rolling along the Rue Mouffetard; it was already some distance off, and he had no means of catching it up. Running after it was an impossibility; and, besides, a man running at full speed after the vehicle would be seen from it, and the father would recognize him. At this moment, by an extraordinary and marvelous accident, Marius perceived a cab passing along the boulevard, empty. There was only one thing to be done,—get into this cab and follow the hackney coach; that was sure, efficacious, and without danger.

Marius made the driver a sign to stop, and shouted to him:

"By the hour!"

Marius had no cravat on; he wore his old working coat, from which buttons were missing, and one of the plaits of his shirt was torn.

The driver stopped, winked, and held out to Marius his left hand, as he gently rubbed his forefinger with his thumb.

"What do you mean?" Marius asked.

"Payment in advance," said the coachman.

Marius remembered that he had only sixteen sous in his pocket.

"How much is it?"

"Forty sous."

"I will pay on returning."

The driver, in reply, whistled the air of La Palisse, and lashed his horse.

Marius watched the cab go off with a haggard look; for the want of twenty-four sous he lost his joy, his happiness, his love! he fell back into night! he had seen, and was becoming blind again. He thought bitterly, and, we must add, with deep regret, of the five francs which he had given that very morning to the wretched girl. If he had still had them, he would be saved, would emerge from limbo and darkness, and be drawn from isolation, spleen, and widowhood; he would have re-attached the black thread of his destiny to the beauteous golden thread which had just floated before his eyes, only to be broken again! He returned to his garret in despair.

He might have said to himself that M. Leblanc had promised to return that evening, and that then he must contrive to follow him better; but in his contemplation he had scarce heard him.

Just as he was going up the stairs he noticed on the other side of the wall, and against the deserted wall of the Rue de la Barrière des Gobelins, Jondrette, wrapped up in the "philanthropist's" overcoat and conversing with one of those ill-looking men who are usually called prowlers at the barrière; men with equivocal faces and suspicious soliloquies, who look as if they entertain evil thoughts, and most usually sleep by day, which leads to the supposition that they work at night.

These two men standing to talk in the snow, which was falling heavily, formed a group which a policeman would certainly have observed, but which Marius scarce noticed.

Still, though his preoccupation was so painful, he could not help saying to himself that the man to whom Jondrette was talking was like a certain Panchaud, *alias* Printanier, *alias* Bigrenaille, whom Courfeyrac had once pointed out to him, and who was regarded in the quarter as a very dangerous night-bird. This Panchaud afterward figured in several criminal trials, and eventually became a celebrated villain, though at this time he was only a famous villain. At the present day he is in a traditionary state among the bandits and burglars. He was the model toward the end of the last reign, and people used to talk about him in the Lion's den at La Force, at nightfall, at the hour when groups assemble and converse in whispers. In this prison, and at the exact spot where the sewer, which served as the unheard-of way of escape in broad daylight for the thirty prisoners in 1843, opened, this name, PANCHAUD, might be seen, daringly cut in the wall over the sewer in one of his attempted escapes. In 1832 the police already had their eye on him, but he had not yet fairly made a start.

11. *WRETCHEDNESS HELPS SORROW*

MARIUS ascended the stairs slowly, and at the moment when he was going to enter his cell he perceived behind him in the passage, the elder of Jondrette's girls following him.

This girl was odious in his sight, for it was she who had his five francs, but it was too late to ask them back from her, for both the hackney coach and the cab were now far away. Besides, she would not return them to him. As for questioning·her about the abode of the persons who had been here just now, that was useless, and it was plain that she did not know, for the letter signed Fabantou was addressed to the "benevolent gentleman of the church of St. Jacques du Haut-pas."

Marius went into his room and threw the door to after him, but it did not close; he turned and saw a hand in the aperture.

"Who's that?" he asked.

It was the girl.

"Oh! it's you!" Marius continued almost harshly, "always you. What do you want of me?"

She seemed thoughtful, and made no answer, and she no longer had her boldness of the morning; she did not come in, but stood in the dark passage, where Marius perceived her through the half-open door.

"Well, answer," said Marius, "what do you want of me?"

She raised her dull eye, in which a sort of luster seemed to be vaguely illumined, and said:

"Monsieur Marius, you look sad; what is the matter with you?"

"Nothing."

"Yes, there is!"

"Leave me alone."

Marius pushed the door again, but she still held it.

"Stay," she said, "you are wrong. Though you are not rich, you were kind this morning, and be so again now. You gave me food, and now tell me what is the matter with you. It is easy to see that you are in sorrow, and I do not wish you to be so. What can I do to prevent it, and can I be of any service to you? Employ me; I do not ask for your secrets, and you need not tell them to me, but I may be of use to you. Surely I can help you, as I help my father. When there are any letters to deliver, or any address to be found by following people, or asking from door to door, I am employed. Well, you can tell me what is the matter with you, and I will go and speak to persons. Now and then it is sufficient for some one to speak to persons in order to find out things, and all is arranged. Employ me."

An idea crossed Marius's mind, for no branch is despised when we feel ourselves falling.

He walked up to the girl.

"Listen to me," he said; "you brought an old gentleman and his daughter here."

"Yes."

"Do you know their address?"

"No."

"Find it for me."

The girl's eye, which was dull, had become joyous, but now it became gloomy.

"Is that what you want?" she asked.

"Yes."

"Do you know them?"

"No."

"That is to say," she added quickly, "you don't know her, but you would like to know her."

This *them,* which became *her,* had something most significant and bitter about it.

"Well, can you do it?" Marius said.

"You shall have the 'lovely young lady's' address."

In these words there was again a meaning which annoyed Marius, so he went on:

"Well, no matter! the father and daughter's address, their address, I say."

She looked at him fixedly.

"What will you give me for it?"

"Whatever you like."

"Whatever I like?"

"Yes."

"You shall have the address."

She hung her head, and then closed the door with a hurried gesture. Marius was alone again.

He fell into a chair, with his head and elbows on his bed, sunk in thoughts which he could not grasp, and suffering from a dizziness. All that had happened since the morning—the apparition of the angel, her disappearance, and what this creature had just said to him, a gleam of hope floating in an immense despair—this is what confusedly filled his brain.

All at once he was violently dragged out of his reverie, for he heard Jondrette's loud, hard voice uttering words full of the strangest interest for him.

"I tell you that I am sure, and that I recognized him."

Of whom was Jondrette talking, and whom had he recognized? M. Leblanc, the father of his "Ursule." What! did Jondrette know him? Was Marius going to obtain in this sudden and unexpected fashion all the information without which his life was obscure for himself? Was he at last going to know who she was whom he loved, and who her father was? Was the thick cloud that covered them on the point of clearing off? Would the veil be rent asunder? O heavens.

He bounded rather than ascended upon the chest of drawers and resumed his place at the aperture in the partition.

Once more he saw the interior of Jondrette's den.

12. THE FIVE FRANCS OF M. LEBLANC

THERE was no change in the appearance of the family, save that mother and daughters had put on stockings and flannel waistcoats taken out of the parcel, and two new blankets were thrown on the beds.

The man had evidently just returned, for he was out of breath; his daughters were seated near the chimney-piece on the ground, the elder tying up the younger's hand. The mother was crouching on the bed near the fire-place, with an astonished face, while Jondrette was walking up and down the room with long strides and extraordinary eyes.

The woman, who seemed frightened and struck with stupor before him, ventured to say:

"What, really, are you sure?"

"Sure! it is eight years ago, but I can recognize him! I recognized him at once. What! did it not strike you?"

"No."

"And yet I said to you, 'Pay attention!' Why, it is his figure, his face, very little older—for there are some people who never age, though I do not know how they manage it, and the sound of his voice. He is better dressed, that's all! Ah! you mysterious old villain, I have got you!"

He stopped and said to his daughters:

"Be off, you two!—It is funny that it did not strike you."

They rose to obey.

The mother stammered:

"With her bad hand?"

"The air will do it good," said Jondrette. "Off with you."

It was evident that this man was one of those who are not answered.

The girls went out, but just as they passed the door the father clutched the elder by the arm, and said, with a peculiar accent:

205

"You will be here at five o'clock precisely, both of you, for I shall want you."

Marius redoubled his attention.

When left alone with his wife, Jondrette began walking up and down the room again, and took two or three turns in silence. Then he spent several minutes thrusting the tail of the chemise which he wore into his trousers.

All at once he turned to his wife, folded his arms, and exclaimed: "And shall I tell you something? the young lady—"

"Well, what?" the wife retorted.

Marius could not doubt they were really talking about her. He listened with ardent anxiety, and all his life was in his ears.

But Jondrette had stooped down and was whispering to his wife. Then he rose, and ended aloud:

"It is she."

"That one?" the wife asked.

"That one!" said the husband.

No expression could render all there was in the mother's *that one;* it was surprise, rage, hatred, and passion mingled and combined in a monstrous intonation. A few words, doubtless a name which her husband whispered in her ear, were sufficient to arouse this fat, sluggish woman, and to make her more than repulsive and frightful.

"It is not possible," she exclaimed; "when I think that my daughters go about barefooted and have not a gown to put on! What! a satin pelisse, a velvet bonnet, clothes worth more than two hundred francs, so that you might take her for a lady! no! you are mistaken! and then, the other was hideous, while this one is not ugly; indeed, rather good-looking. Oh, it cannot be!"

"And I tell you that it is; you will see."

At this absolute assertion the woman raised her large red and white face and looked at the ceiling with a hideous expression. At this moment she appeared to Marius even more formidable than her husband, for she was a sow with the glance of a tigress.

"What!" she continued, "that horrible young lady who looked at my daughters with an air of pity is that vagabond! Oh! I should like to burst her belly with my wooden shoes."

She leaped off the bed, and stood for a moment unkempt, with swollen nostrils, parted lips, and clenched fists; then she fell back again on the bed. The husband walked up and down and paid no attention to his wife.

After a short silence he went up to her, and stood in front of her with folded arms, as he had done a few moments previously.

"And shall I tell you something else?"

"What?" she asked.

He replied in a low, guttural voice:

"That my fortune is made."

The wife looked at him in the way which means, "Can the man who is talking to me have suddenly gone mad?"

He continued:

"Thunder! I have been a long time a parishioner of the parish of die-of-hunger-if-you-are-cold, and die-of-cold-if-you-have-bread! I have had enough of that misery! I am not jesting, for I no longer consider this comical. I have had enough jokes, good God! and want no more farces, by the Eternal Father! I wish to eat when I am hungry, and drink when I am thirsty; to gorge, sleep, and do nothing. I want to have my turn now, and mean to be a bit of a millionaire before I rot!"

He walked up and down the room, and added: "Like the rest!"

"What do you mean?" his wife asked.

He shook his head, winked, and raised his voice like a street quack who is going to make an exhibition.

"What I mean? listen!"

"Not so loud," said his wife, "if it is business which ought not to be overheard."

"Nonsense! by whom? by the neighbor? I saw him go out just now. Besides, what does that long-legged ass listen to? and then I tell you I saw him go out."

Still, by a species of instinct, Jondrette lowered his voice, though not so low that his remarks escaped Marius. A favorable circumstance was that the fallen snow deadened the sound of the vehicles on the boulevard.

This is what Marius heard:

"Listen carefully. The Crœsus is trapped, or as good as trapped. It is done, arranged, and I have seen the people. He will come at six this evening to bring the sixty francs, the vagabond! Did you notice how I piped him off about my landlord on February 4th? Why, it is not a quarter-day, the ass. Well, he will come at six o'clock, and at that hour the neighbor has gone to dinner, and Mother Bougon is washing up dishes in town, so there will be no one in the house. The neighbor never comes in before eleven o'clock. The little ones will be on the watch, you will help us, and he will do it."

"And suppose he does not?" the wife asked.

Jondrette made a sinister gesture, and said:

"We will do it for him."

And he burst into a laugh. It was the first time that Marius saw him laugh, and this laugh was cold and quiet, and produced a shudder.

Jondrette opened a cupboard near the fire-place, and took out an old cap, which he put on his head, after brushing it with his cuff.

"Now," he said, "I am going out, for I have some more people to see, good men. I shall be away as short a time as possible, for it is a famous affair; and do you keep house."

And he stood thoughtfully with his hands in his trousers-pockets, and suddenly exclaimed:

"Do you know that it is very lucky he did not recognize me, for if he had done so he would not have returned, and would have slipped from us. It was my beard that saved us, my romantic beard, my pretty little beard."

And he laughed again.

He went to the window; the snow was still falling and striping the gray sky.

"What filthy weather!" he said.

Then he buttoned up his great-coat.

"The skin is too big, but no matter," he added; "it was devilish lucky that the old villain left it for me, for had he not I could not have gone out, and the whole affair would have been spoiled. On what slight accidents things depend!"

And, pulling his cap over his eyes, he went out.

He had only gone a short distance when the door opened again, and his sharp, intelligent face re-appeared in the aperture.

"I forgot," he said, "you will get a brazier of charcoal ready."

And he threw into his wife's apron the five-franc piece which the "philanthropist" left him.

"How many bushels of charcoal?" the wife asked.

"Two, at least."

"That will cost thirty sous, and with the rest I will buy some grub."

"Hang it, no."

"Why?"

"Don't spend the five *balls*."

"Why not?"

"Because I have something to buy, too."

"What?"

"Something."

"How much do you want?"

"Where is the nearest ironmonger's?"

"In the Rue Mouffetard."

"Ah, yes! at the corner of a street. I remember the shop."

"But tell me how much you want for what you have to buy."

"From fifty sous to three francs."

"There won't be much left for dinner."

"Don't bother about eating to-day; there is something better to do."

"That's enough, my jewel."

Jondrette closed the door again, and then Marius heard his steps as he went along the passage and down the stairs.

It struck one at this moment from St. Medard's.

13. *SOLOS CUM SOLO, IN LOCO REMOTO, NON COGITABUNTUR ORARE PATER NOSTER*

MARIUS, dreamer though he was, possessed, as we have said, a firm and energetic nature. His habits of solitary contemplation, by developing compassion and sympathy within him, had perhaps diminished the power of being irritated, but left intact the power of becoming indignant: he had the benevolence of a Brahmin and the sternness of a judge, and while he pitied a toad he crushed a viper.

At present he had a nest of vipers before him, and he said, "I must set my foot upon these villains."

Not one of the enigmas which he hoped to see cleared up was solved; on the contrary, they had become rather denser, and he had learned no more about the pretty girl of the Luxembourg and the man whom he called M. Leblanc, save that Jondrette knew them. Through the dark words which had been uttered he only saw one thing distinctly, that a snare was preparing, an obscure but terrible snare; that they both ran an imminent danger, she probably, and the father certainly, and that he must save them, and foil the hideous combinations of the Jondrettes by destroying their spider's web.

He watched the woman for a moment; she had taken an old iron furnace from the corner and was rummaging among the old scraps of iron

He got off the chest of drawers as gently as he could, and careful not to make any noise.

In his terror at what was preparing, and the horror with which the Jondrettes filled him, he felt a species of joy at the idea that it might perhaps be in his power to render such service to her whom he loved.

But what was he to do? should he warn the menaced persons? where was he to find them? for he did not know their address. They had reappeared to him momentarily, and then plunged again into the immense profundities of Paris. Should he wait for M. Leblanc at the gate at the moment when he arrived that evening and warn him of the snare? But Jondrette and his comrades would see him on the watch. The place was deserted, they would be stronger than he, they would find means to get him out of the way, and the man whom Marius wished to save would be lost. It had just struck one, and as the snare was laid for six o'clock Marius had five hours before him.

There was only one thing to be done.

He put on his best coat, tied a handkerchief round his neck, took his hat, and went out, making no more noise than if he were walking barefoot on moss; besides, the woman was still rummaging the old iron.

Once outside the house, he turned into the Rue du Petit Banquier.

About the middle of the street he found himself near a very low wall, which it was possible to bestride in some places, and which surrounded unoccupied ground. He was walking slowly, deep in thought as he was, and the snow deadened his footsteps, when all at once he heard voices talking close to him. He turned his head, but the street was deserted; it was open day, and yet he distinctly heard the voices.

He thought of looking over the wall, and when he did so saw two men seated in the snow and conversing in a low voice.

They were strangers to him: one was a bearded man in a blouse, and the other a hairy man in rags. The bearded man wore a Greek cap, while the other was bareheaded and had snow in his hair.

By thrusting out his head over them Marius could hear the hairy man say to the other, with a nudge:

"With Patron-Minette it cannot fail."

"Do you think so?" asked the bearded man.

The hairy man added:

"It will be five hundred balls for each, and the worst that can happen is five years, six years, or ten at the most."

The other replied with some hesitation, and shuddering under his Greek cap:

"That is a reality; and people must not go to meet things of that sort."

"I tell you that the affair cannot fail," the hairy man continued. "Father What's-his-name's trap will be all ready."

Then they began talking of a melodrama which they had seen on the previous evening at the Gaîté.

Marius walked on.

It seemed to him that the obscure remarks of these men, so strangely concealed behind this wall and crouching in the snow, must have some connection with Jondrette's abominable scheme; that must be the *affair*.

He went toward the Faubourg St. Marceau, and asked at the first shop he came to where he could find a police commissary.

He was told at No. 14, Rue de Pontoise, and he proceeded there.

As he passed a baker's he bought a two-sous roll and ate it, as he foresaw that he should not dine.

On the way he rendered justice to Providence. He thought that if he had not given that five francs in the morning to the girl he should have followed M. Leblanc's hackney coach, and consequently known nothing. There would in that case have been no obstacle to Jondrette's ambuscade, and M. Leblanc would have been lost, and doubtless his daughter with him.

14. *WHERE A POLICE OFFICER GIVES TWO KNOCK-ME-DOWNS TO A LAWYER*

On reaching No. 14, Rue de Pontoise, he went up to the second-floor and asked for the commissary.

"He is not in at present," said some clerk, "but there is an inspector to represent him. Will you speak to him? is your business pressing?"

"Yes," said Marius.

The clerk led him to the commissary's office. A very tall man was leaning here against the fender of a stove, and holding up with both hands the skirts of a mighty coat with three capes. He had a square face, thin and firm lips, thick grayish whiskers, and a look which seemed as if it was turning your pockets inside out. Of this look you might have said, not that it pierced, but that it searched.

This man did not appear much less ferocious or formidable than Jondrette; for sometimes it is just as dangerous to meet the dog as the wolf.

"What do you want?" he asked Marius, without adding sir.

"The police commissary."

"He is absent, but I represent him."

"It is a very secret affair."

"Then speak."

"And very urgent."

"In that case, speak quick."

This man, who was calm and quick, was at once terrifying and reassuring. He inspired both fear and confidence. Marius told him of his adventure—that a person whom he only knew by sight was to be drawn that very evening into a trap; that he, Marius Pontmercy, barrister, residing in the next room to the den, had heard the whole plot through the partition; that the scoundrel's name who invented the snare was Jondrette; that he would have accomplices, probably prowlers at the barrières, among others one Panchaud, *alias* Printanier, *alias* Bigrenaille; that Jondrette's daughter would be on the watch; that there was no means of warning the threatened man, as not even his name was known; and that, lastly, all this would come off at six in the evening, at the most deserted spot on the Boulevard de l'Hôpital, in the house No. 50-52.

At this number the inspector raised his head, and said coldly:

"It must be, then, in the room at the end of the passage."

"Exactly," Marius replied, and added, "do you know the house?"

The inspector remained silent for a moment, and then answered, while warming his boot-heel at the door of the stove:

"Apparently so."

He went on between his teeth, talking less to Marius than his cravat: "Patron-Minette must be mixed up in this."

This remark struck Marius.

"Patron-Minette!" he said, "yes, I heard that name mentioned."

And he told the inspector of the dialogue between the hairy man and the bearded man in the snow behind the wall in the Rue du Petit Banquier. The inspector growled:

"The hairy man must be Brujon, and the bearded man Demi-liard, *alias* Deux Milliards."

He was again looking down and meditating. "As for Father What's-his-name, I guess who he is. There, I have burnt my great-coat; they always make too large a fire in these cursed stoves. No. 50-52, formerly the property of one Gorbeau."

Then he looked at Marius.

"You only saw the hairy man and the bearded man?"

"And Panchaud."

"You did not see a small dandy prowling about there?"

"No."

"Nor a heavy lump of a fellow resembling the elephant in the Jardin des Plantes?"

"No."

"Nor a scamp who looks like an old red-tail?"

"No."

"As for the fourth, no one sees him, not even his pals, chums, and assistants. It is not surprising, therefore, that you did not perceive him."

"No. Who are all these men?" Marius asked.

The inspector continued:

"Besides, it is not their hour." He fell into silence, and presently added:

"50-52. I know the barrack! It is impossible for us to hide ourselves in the interior without the actors perceiving us, and then they would escape by cutting off the farce. They are so modest, and frightened at an audience. That won't do, for I want to hear them sing and make them dance."

This soliloquy ended, he turned to Marius, and asked, as he looked at him searchingly:

"Would you be afraid?"

"Of what?" Marius asked.

"Of these men."

"No more than I am of you," Marius answered roughly, for he was beginning to notice that this policeman had not yet said "sir."

The inspector looked at Marius more intently still, and continued, with a sort of sententious solemnity:

"You speak like a brave man and like an honest man. Courage does not fear crime, nor honesty the authorities."

Marius interrupted him:

"That is all very well, but what do you intend doing?"

The inspector restricted himself to saying:

"The lodgers in that house have latch-keys to let themselves in at night. You have one?"

"Yes," said Marius.

"Have you it about you?"

"Yes."

"Give it to me," the inspector said.

Marius took the key out of his waistcoat-pocket, handed it to the inspector, and added:

"If you take my advice, you will bring a strong force."

The inspector gave Marius such a glance as Voltaire would have given a provincial academician who proposed a rhyme to him; then he thrust both hands into his immense coat-pockets and produced two small steel pistols, of the sort called "knock-me-downs." He handed them to Marius, saying sharply and quickly:

"Take these. Go home. Conceal yourself in your room, and let them suppose you out. They are loaded; both with two bullets. You will watch, as you tell me there is a hole in the wall. People will come; let them go on a little. When you fancy the matter ripe, and you think it time to stop it, you will fire a pistol, but not too soon. The rest concerns me. A shot in the air, in the ceiling, I don't care where,—but mind, not too soon. Wait till they begin to put the screw on. You are a lawyer, and know what that means."

Marius took the pistols, and placed them in a side pocket of his coat.

"They bulge like that, and attract attention," said the inspector; "put them in your trousers-pockets."

Marius did so.

"And now," the inspector continued, "there is not a moment for any one to lose. What o'clock is it? Half-past two. You said seven?"

"Six o'clock," Marius corrected.

"I have time," the inspector added; "but only just time. Do not forget anything I have said to you. A pistol-shot."

"All right," Marius replied.

And as he put his hand on the latch to leave the room, the inspector shouted to him:

"By the way, if you should want me between this and then, come or send here. Ask for Inspector Javert."

15. *JONDRETTE MAKES HIS PURCHASE*

SOME minutes later, at about three o'clock, Courfeyrac happened to pass along the Rue Mouffetard, accompanied by Bossuet. The snow was thicker than ever, and filled the air, and Bossuet had just said to Courfeyrac:

"To see all these flakes of snow fall, we might say that the sky is suffering from a plague of white butterflies."

All at once Bossuet noticed Marius coming up the street toward the barrière with a peculiar look.

"Hilloh!" said Bossuet, "there's Marius."

"I saw him," said Courfeyrac; "but we won't speak to him."

"Why not?"

"He is busy."

"At what?"

"Do you not see that he looks as if he were following someone?"

"That is true," said Bossuet.

"Only see what eyes he makes!" Courfeyrac added.

"But whom the deuce is he following?"

"Some Mimi-Goton with flowers in her cap. He is in love."

"But," Bossuet observed, "I do not see any Mimi or any Goton, or any cap trimmed with flowers in the street. There is not a single woman."

Courfeyrac looked, and exclaimed: "He is following a man."

A man wearing a cap, and whose gray beard could be distinguished, although his back was turned, was walking about twenty yards ahead of Marius.

The man was dressed in a perfectly new great-coat, which was too large for him, and a frightful pair of ragged trousers, all black with mud.

Bossuet burst into a laugh.

"Who can the man be?"

"That?" Courfeyrac replied, "oh, he is a poet. Poets are fond of wearing the trousers of rabbit-skin buyers and the coats of the peers of France."

"Let us see where Marius is going," said Bossuet, "and where this man is going. Suppose we follow them, eh?"

"Bossuet!" Courfeyrac exclaimed, "Eagle of Meaux, you are a prodigious brute to think of following a man who is following a man."

They turned back.

Marius had really seen Jondrette in the Rue Mouffetard, and was following him.

Jondrette was walking along, not at all suspecting than an eye was already fixed upon him.

He left the Rue Mouffetard, and Marius saw him enter one of the most hideous lodging houses in the Rue Gracieuse, where he remained for about a quarter of an hour, and then returned to the Rue Mouffetard. He stopped at an iron-monger's shop, which was at that period at the corner of the Rue Pierre-Lombard; and a few minutes after Marius saw him come out of the shop, holding a large cold-chisel set in a wooden handle, which he hid under his great-coat. He then turned to his left and hurried toward the Rue du Petit Banquier. Day was drawing in; the snow, which had ceased for a moment, had begun again, and Marius concealed himself at the corner of Rue du Petit Banquier, which was deserted as usual, and did not follow Jondrette. It was lucky that he acted thus, for Jondrette, on reaching the spot where Marius had listened to the conversation of the hairy man and the bearded man, looked round, made sure that he was not followed, clambered over the wall, and disappeared.

The unused ground which this wall inclosed communicated with the back yard of a livery-stable keeper of bad repute, who had been a bankrupt, and still had a few vehicles standing under sheds.

Marius thought it would be as well to take advantage of Jondrette's absence and return home. Besides, time was slipping away, and every evening Mame Bougon, when she went to wash up dishes in town, was accustomed to close the gate, and, as Marius had given his latch-key to the inspector, it was important that he should be in time.

Night had nearly set in along the whole horizon, and in the whole immensity there was only one point still illumined by the sun, and that was the moon, which was rising red behind the low dome of the Salpêtrière.

Marius hurried to No. 50-52, and the gate was still open when he arrived. He went up the stairs on tiptoe, and glided along the passage-way to his room. This passage, it will be remembered, was bordered on either side by rooms which were now to let, and Mame Bougon, as a general rule, left the doors open. While passing one of these doors, Marius fancied that he could see in the uninhabited room four men's heads vaguely lit up by a remnant of daylight which fell through a window. Marius did not attempt to see, as he did not wish to be seen himself; and he managed to reënter his room noiselessly and unseen. It was high time, for a moment after he heard Mame Bougon going out, and the house-gate shutting.

16. *A SONG TO AN ENGLISH TUNE FASHIONABLE IN* 1832

MARIUS sat down on his bed; it might be about half-past five and only half an hour separated him from what was about to happen. He heard his arteries beat as you hear the ticking of a clock in the darkness, and he thought of the double march which was taking place at this moment in the shadows,—crime advancing on one side, and justice coming up on the other. He was not frightened, but he could not think without a certain tremor of the things that were going to happen, like all those who are suddenly assailed by a surprising adventure. This whole day produced on him the effect of a dream, and in order not to believe himself the prey of a nightmare he was obliged to feel in his pockets the cold barrels of the pistols.

It no longer snowed; the moon, now very bright, dissipated the mist, and its rays, mingled with the white reflection from the fallen snow, imparted a twilight appearance to the room.

There was a light in Jondrette's room, and Marius could see the hole in the partition glowing with a ruddy brilliancy that appeared to him the color of blood.

It was evident that this light could not be produced by a candle. There was no movement in the den, no one stirred there, no one spoke, there was not a breath, the silence was chilling and profound, and, had it not been for the light, Marius might have fancied himself close to a grave.

He gently took off his boots and thrust them under the bed.

Several minutes elapsed, and then Marius heard the house gate creaking on its hinges; a heavy, quick step ran up the stairs and along the passage, the hasp of the door was noisily raised,—it was Jondrette returned home.

All at once several voices were raised, and it was plain that the whole family were at home. They were merely silent in the master's absence, like the whelps in the absence of the wolves.

"It is I," he said.

"Good-evening, pappy," the girls yelped.

"Well?" the wife asked.

"All is well," Jondrette answered, "but I am cold as a starved dog. That's right; I am glad to see that you are dressed, for it inspires confidence."

"All ready to go out."

"You will not forget anything that I told you? You will do it all right."

"Of course."

"Because—" Jondrette began, but did not complete the sentence.

Marius heard him lay something heavy on the table, probably the chisel which he had bought.

"Well," Jondrette continued, "have you been eating here?"

"Yes," said the mother; "I bought three large potatoes and some salt. I took advantage of the fire to roast them."

"Good," Jondrette remarked; "to-morrow you will dine with me; we will have a duck and trimmings, and you will feed like Charles the Tenths."

Then he added, lowering his voice:

"The mouse-trap is open, and the cats are here."

He again lowered his voice and said:

"Put this in the fire."

Marius heard the click of some charcoal-bars stirred with a pair of iron pincers, or some steel instrument, and Jondrette ask:

"Have you greased the hinges of the door, so that they may make no noise?"

"Yes," the mother answered.

"What o'clock is it?"

"Close on six. It has struck the half-hour at St. Medard."

"Hang it!" said Jondrette, "the girls must go on the watch. Come here and listen to me."

There was a whispering, and then Jondrette's voice was again uplifted:

"Has Mame Bougon gone?"

"Yes," the mother answered.

"Are you sure there is nobody in the neighbor's room?"

"He has not come in all day, and you know that this is his dinner hour."

"Are you sure?"

"Quite."

"No matter," Jondrette added, "there is no harm in going to see whether he is in. Daughter, take the candle and go."

Marius fell on his hands and knees, and silently crawled under the bed. He had scarce done so ere he saw light through the cracks of his door.

"Papa," a voice exclaimed, "he is out."

He recognized the elder girl's voice.

"Have you been in his room?" the father asked.

"No," the girl replied, "but as his key is in his door, he has gone out."

The father shouted:

"Go in, all the same."

The door opened, and Marius saw the girl come in, candle in hand. She was the same as in the morning, save that she was even more fearful in this light.

She walked straight up to the bed, and Marius suffered a moment of intense anxiety, but there was a looking-glass hanging from a nail by the bedside, and it was to that she proceeded. She stood on tiptoe and looked at herself; a noise of iron being moved could be heard in the other room.

She smoothed her hair with her hand, and smiled in the glass, while singing, in her cracked and sepulchral voice:

> *Nos amours ont duré toute une semaine,*
> *Mais que du bonheur les instants sont courts!*
> *S'adorer huit jours c'était bien la peine!*
> *Le temps des amours devrait durer toujours!*
> *Devrait durer toujours! devrait durer toujours!*

Still Marius trembled, for he thought that she could not help hearing his breathing.

She walked to the window and looked out, while saying aloud with the half-insane look she had:

"How ugly Paris is when it has put on a white shirt!"

She returned to the glass, and began taking a fresh look at herself, first full face and then three-quarters.

"Well?" asked the father, "what are you doing there?"

"I am looking under the bed and the furniture," she said, as she continued to smooth her hair; "but there is nobody."

"You she-devil," the father yelled. "Come here directly, let us lose no time."

"Coming, coming," she said; "there's no time to do anything here." Then she hummed:

> *Vous me quittez pour aller à la gloire,*
> *Mon triste cœur suivra partout vos pas.*

She took a parting glance at the glass and went off, closing the door after her.

A moment later Marius heard the sound of the girls' naked feet pattering along the passage, and Jondrette's voice shouting to them:

"Pay attention! one at the barrière, and the other at the corner of the Rue du Petit Banquier. Do not let the gate of this house out of sight, and if you see anything, come back at once—at once; you have a key to let yourselves in."

The elder daughter grumbled:

"To stand sentry barefooted in the snow, what a treat!"

"To-morrow you shall have beetle-colored silk boots," the father said.

They went down the stairs, and a few seconds later the sound of the gate closing below announced that they had reached the street.

The only persons in the house now were Marius, the Jondrettes, and probably, too, the mysterious beings of whom Marius had caught a glimpse in the gloom behind the door of the unoccupied room.

17. *MARIUS'S FIVE-FRANC PIECE*

MARIUS judged that the moment had arrived for him to return to his observatory. In a second, and with the agility of his age, he was at the hole in the partition, and peeped through.

The interior of Jondrette's lodging offered a strange appearance, and Marius was able to account for the peculiar light he had noticed. A candle was burning in a verdigrised candlestick, but it was not this which really illumined the room; the whole den was lit up with the ruddy glow of a brazier standing in the fire-place, and filled with incandescent charcoal—it was the brazier which the wife had prepared in the morning. The charcoal was glowing, the brazier red, a bluish flame played round it and rendered it easy to recognize the shape of the chisel purchased by Jondrette, which was heating in the fire. In a corner, near the door, could be seen two heaps, one apparently of old iron, the other of ropes, arranged for some anticipated purpose. All this, to a person who did not know what was going to occur, would have made his mind vacillate between a very simple and a very sinister idea. The room, thus lit up, resembled a forge more than a mouth of Hades, but Jondrette, in this light, was more like a demon than a blacksmith.

The heat of the brazier was so great that the candle on the table was melted and guttering on the side turned toward it. An old copper dark-lantern, worthy of a Diogenes who had turned Cartouche, was standing on the mantel-piece.

The brazier which stood in the fire-place, close to the decaying logs, sent its smoke up the chimney, and thus produced no smell.

The moon, which found its way through the sky-light, poured its whiteness on the purple and flashing garret, and to the poetic mind of Marius, who was a dreamer even in the moment of action, it was like a thought of heaven mingled with the shapeless dreams of earth.

A breath of air that penetrated through the broken pane also helped to dissipate the smell of charcoal and conceal the presence of the brazier.

Jondrette's den, if our readers remember what we have said about the house, was admirably selected to serve as the scene of a violent and dark deed, and as a covert for crime. It was the furthest room in the most isolated house on the most deserted boulevard in Paris, and if ambushes had not existed they would have been invented there.

The whole length of a house and a number of uninhabited rooms separated this lair from the boulevard, and the only window in it looked out on fields inclosed by walls and boardings.

Jondrette had lit his pipe, was seated on the bottomless chair smoking, and his wife was speaking to him in a low voice.

If Marius had been Courfeyrac, that is to say, one of those men who laugh at every opportunity, he would have burst into a roar when his eye fell on Mother Jondrette. She had on a bonnet with black feathers, like the hats worn by the heralds at the coronation of Charles X, an immense tartan shawl over her cotton skirt, and the man's shoes which her daughter had disdained in the morning. It was this attire which drew from Jondrette the exclamation, "That's right; I am glad to see that you are dressed, for it inspires confidence."

As for Jondrette, he had not taken off the new coat which M. Leblanc had given him, and his dress continued to offer that contrast between trousers and coat which constituted in Courfeyrac's sight the ideal of the poet.

All at once Jondrette raised his voice.

"By the way, in such weather as this he will come in a hackney coach. Light your lamp and go down, and keep behind the front door; and when you hear the vehicle stop you will open the gate at once, light him upstairs and along the passage, and when he has come in here, you will go down as quickly as you can, pay the coachman, and discharge him."

"Where's the money to come from?" the woman asked.

Jondrette felt in his pocket, and gave her five francs.

"What is this?" she exclaimed.

He replied with dignity:

"The monarch which our neighbor gave us this morning," and added: "We shall want two chairs, though."

"What for?"

"Why, to sit down."

Marius shuddered on hearing the woman make the quiet answer:

"Well, I will go and fetch our neighbor's."

And with a rapid movement she opened the door and stepped into the passage.

Marius had not really the time to get off the drawers and hide under his bed.

"Take the candle," Jondrette shouted.

"No," she said, "it would bother me, for I have two chairs to carry. Besides, the moon is shining."

Marius heard the heavy hand of Mother Jondrette fumbling for his key in the darkness. The door opened, and he remained nailed to his post by alarm and stupor. The woman came in.

The sky-light sent a moonbeam between two large patches of shade, and one of these patches entirely covered the wall against which Marius was standing, so that he was invisible.

Mother Jondrette did not see Marius, took the two chairs, the only two that Marius possessed, and went off, noisily slamming the door after her.

She reëntered the den.

"Here are the two chairs."

"And here is the lantern," the husband said; "make haste down."

She hastened to obey, and Jondrette remained alone.

He placed the chairs on either side of the table, turned the chisel in the brazier, placed in front of the fire-place an old screen, which concealed the charcoal-pan, and then went to the corner where the heap of rope lay, and stooped down as if examining something. Marius then perceived that what he had taken for a shapeless heap was a rope ladder, very well made with wooden rungs, and two hooks to hang it by.

This ladder and a few large tools, perfect crowbars, which were mingled with the heap of old iron in the corner, had not been there in the morning, and had evidently been brought in the afternoon, during the absence of Marius.

"They are smith's tools," Marius thought.

Had he been a little better acquainted with the trade, he would have recognized, in what he took for tools, certain instruments that could force or pick a lock and others that could cut or pierce, the two families of sinister tools which burglars call "cadets" and "fauchants."

The fire-place, the table, and the two chairs were exactly opposite Marius, and, as the charcoal-pan was concealed, the room was only illumined by the candle, and the smallest article on the table or the chimney-piece cast a long shadow; a cracked water-jug hid half a wall. There was in this room a hideous and menacing calm, and an expectation of something awful could be felt.

Jondrette had let his pipe go out, a sign of deep thought, and had just sat down again. The candle caused the stern and fierce angles of his face to stand out; he was frowning, and suddenly thrust out his right hand now and then, as if answering the final counsels of a dark internal soliloquy. In one of the obscure replies he made to himself, he opened the table drawer, took out a long carving-knife hidden in it, and felt its edge on his thumb-nail. This done, he put the knife in the drawer, which he closed again.

Marius, on his side, drew the pistol from his pocket, and cocked it, which produced a sharp, clicking sound.

Jondrette started, and half rose from his chair.

"Who's there?" he shouted.

Marius held his breath. Jondrette listened for a moment, and then said, laughingly:

"What an ass I am! it is the partition creaking."

Marius held the pistol in his hand.

18. *THE TWO CHAIRS OPPOSITE EACH OTHER*

AT this moment the distant and the melancholy vibration of a bell shook the windows; six o'clock was striking at St. Medard's.

Jondrette marked each stroke by a shake of the head, and when he had counted the last he snuffed the candle with his fingers.

Then he began walking up and down the room, listened at the door, began walking again, and then listened once more.

"Provided he come," he growled, and then returned to his chair.

He was hardly seated ere the door opened.

Mother Jondrette had opened it, and remained in the passage making a horrible grimace, which one of the holes in the dark lantern lit up from below.

"Step in, sir," she said.

"Enter, my benefactor!" Jondrette repeated, as he hurriedly rose.

M. Leblanc appeared with that air of serenity which rendered him singularly venerable.

He laid four louis on the table.

"Monsieur Fabantou, here is the money for your rent, and something more to put you a little straight. After that we will see."

"May heaven repay you! my generous benefactor," said Jondrette.

Then rapidly approaching his wife:

"Dismiss the hackney coach."

She slipped away, while the husband made an infinitude of bows and offered a chair to M. Leblanc. A moment after she returned and whispered in his ear:

"All right."

The snow, which had not ceased to fall since morning, was now so thick that neither the arrival nor the departure of the coach had been heard.

M. Leblanc had seated himself, and Jondrette now took possession of the chair opposite to him.

And now the reader, in order to form an idea of the scene which is about to be acted, will kindly imagine the freezing night, the solitudes of the Salpêtrière covered with snow and white in the moonlight, like an immense winding-sheet, and the light of the lamps throwing a red glow here and there over these tragic boulevards and the long rows of black elms, not a passer-by for a quarter of a league round, and the Maison Gorbeau at its highest point of silence, horror, and night. In this house, amid this solitude and darkness, is Jondrette's spacious garret lit by a candle, and in this den two men are sitting at a table,—M. Leblanc calm, Jondrette smiling and terrible. Mother Jondrette, the she-wolf, is in a corner, and behind the partition, Marius, invisible, but not losing a word or a movement, with his eye on the watch and pistols in hand.

Marius, however, only felt an emotion of horror, but no fear; he clutched the butt of the pistol, and said to himself, feeling re-assured, "I can stop the scoundrel whenever I like."

He felt that the police were somewhere in ambush, waiting for the appointed signal, and all ready to stretch out arm.

In addition, he hoped that from this violent encounter between Jondrette and M. Leblanc some light would be thrown on all that he had an interest in knowing.

19. *DARK DEPTHS*

M. LEBLANC was scarce seated ere he turned his eyes to the beds, which were empty.

"How is the poor little wounded girl?" he asked.

"Very bad," Jondrette replied with a heart-broken and grateful smile. "Very bad, my good sir. Her elder sister has taken her to La Bourbe to have her hand dressed. But you will see them, as they will return almost immediately."

"Madame Fabantou seems to me better?" M. Leblanc continued, taking a glance at the strange garb of Mother Jondrette, who, standing between him and the door, as if already guarding the outlet, was looking at him in a menacing and almost combative posture.

"She is dying," Jondrette said, "but what would you have, sir? that woman has so much courage. She is not a woman, but an ox."

Mother Jondrette, affected by the compliment, protested with the affectation of a flattered monster:

"You are always too kind to me, Monsieur Jondrette."

"Jondrette?" said M. Leblanc, "why I thought your name was Fabantou."

"Fabantou, *alias* Jondrette," the husband quickly replied,—"a professional name."

And, giving his wife a shrug, which M. Leblanc did not see, he continued with an emphatic and caressing inflection of voice:

"Ah! that poor dear and I have ever lived happily together, for what would be left us if we had not that! we are so wretched, respectable sir. I have arms but no labor, a heart but no work. I do not know how the government manages it, but, on my word of honor, sir, I am no Jacobin, I wish them no harm, but if I were the ministers, on my most sacred word, things would go differently. For instance, I wished my daughters to learn the trade of making paper boxes. You will say to me: 'What! a trade?' Yes, a trade, a simple trade, a bread-winner. What a fall, my benefactor! what degradation, after persons have been in such circumstances as we were, but, alas! nothing is left us from our prosperous days. Nothing but one article—a picture, to which I cling, but which I am ready to part with, as we must live."

While Jondrette was saying this with a sort of apparent disorder, which did not in any way alter the thoughtful and sagacious expression of his face, Marius raised his eyes and saw some one at the back of the room, whom he had not seen before. A man had just entered, but so softly that the hinges had not been heard to creak. This man had on an old worn-out, torn, stained, violet knitted jacket, gapping at every seam, wide cotton-velvet trousers, thick socks on his feet, and no shirt; his neck was bare, his arms were naked and tattooed, and his face was daubed with black. He seated himself silently, and with folded arms, on the nearest bed, and, as he was behind Mother Jondrette, he could be but dimly distinguished.

That sort of magnetic instinct which warns the eye caused M. Leblanc to turn almost at the same moment as Marius. He could not suppress a start of surprise, which Jondrette noticed.

"Ah, I see," Jondrette exclaimed, as he buttoned his coat complacently, "you are looking at your surtout? It fits me, really fits me capitally."

"Who is that man?" M. Leblanc asked.

"That?" said Jondrette, "oh, a neighbor; pay no attention to him."

The neighbor looked singular, but chemical factories abound in the Faubourg St. Marceau, and a workman may easily have a black face.

M. Leblanc's whole person displayed a confident and intrepid candor, as he continued:

"I beg your pardon, but what were you saying, M. Fabantou?"

"I was saying, sir, and dear protector," Jondrette replied as he placed his elbows on the table and gazed at M. Leblanc with fixed and tender eyes, very like those of a boa-constrictor, "I was saying that I had a picture to sell."

There was a slight noise at the door; a second man came in and seated himself on the bed behind Mother Jondrette.

Like the first, he had bare arms and a mask, either of ink or soot.

Though this man literally glided into the room he could not prevent M. Leblanc noticing him.

"Take no heed," said Jondrette, "they are men living in the house. I was saying that I had a valuable picture left; look here, sir."

He rose, walked to the wall, against which the panel to which we have already referred was leaning, and turned it round, while still letting it rest on the wall. It was something, in fact, that resembled a picture, and which the candle almost illumined. Marius could distinguish nothing, as Jondrette was standing between him and the picture, but he fancied he could catch a glimpse of a coarse daub, and a sort of principal character standing out of the canvas, with the bold crudity of a showman's pictures or a sign-board.

"What is that?" M. Leblanc asked.

Jondrette exclaimed:

"A masterpiece, a most valuable picture, my benefactor! I am as attached to it as I am to my daughters, for it recalls dear memories; but, as I told you, and I will not go back from my word, I am willing to dispose of it, as we are in such poverty."

Either by accident or some vague feeling of anxiety, M. Leblanc's eye, while examining the picture, returned to the end of the room.

There were now four men there, three seated on the bed and one leaning against the door-post, but all four bare-armed, motionless, and with blackened faces. One of those on the bed was leaning against the wall with closed eyes and apparently asleep; this one was old, and the white hair on the blackened face was horrible. The other two were young; one was hairy, the other bearded. Not a single one had shoes, and those who did not wear socks were barefooted.

Jondrette remarked that M. Leblanc's eyes rested on these men.

"They are friends, neighbors," he said, "their faces are black because they work in charcoal, they look after smoky flues. Do not trouble yourself about them, sir, but buy my picture. Have pity on my misery. I will not ask much for it; what value do you set upon it?"

"Well," M. Leblanc said, looking Jondrette full in the face, like a man setting himself on guard, "it is some pothouse sign, and worth about three francs."

Jondrette replied gently: "Have you your pocket-book about you? I shall be satisfied with a thousand crowns."

M. Leblanc rose, set his back against the wall, and took a hurried glance round the room. He had Jondrette on his left by the window, and on his right the woman and the four men by the door. The four men did not stir, and did not even appear to see him.

Jondrette had begun talking again with a plaintive accent, and with such a wandering eye that M. Leblanc might fairly believe that he simply had before him a man driven mad by misery.

"If you do not buy my picture, dear benefactor," Jondrette said, "I have no resource remaining, and nothing is left me but to throw myself into the river. When I think that I wished my two daughters to learn how to make paper boxes for New-Year's gifts. Well, for that you require a table with a backboard to prevent the glasses falling on the ground, a stove made expressly, a pot with three compartments for the three different degrees of strength which the glue must have, according as it is used for wood, paper, and cloth; a board to cut pasteboard on, a hammer, a pair of pincers, and the deuce knows what, and all that to gain four sous a day! and you must work fourteen hours! and each box passes thirteen times through the hands of the work-girl! and moistening the paper! and not spoiling anything! and keeping the glue hot! the devil! I tell you, four sous a day! How do you expect them to live?"

While speaking, Jondrette did not look at M. Leblanc, who was watching him. M. Leblanc's eye was fixed on Jondrette, and Jondrette's on the door, while Marius's gasping attention went from one to the other. M. Leblanc seemed to be asking himself, Is he a lunatic? and Jondrette repeated twice or thrice with all sorts of varied inflections in the suppliant style, "All that is left me is to throw myself into the river! the other day I went for that purpose down three steps by the side of the bridge of Austerlitz."

All at once his eyes glistened with a hideous radiance, the little man drew himself up and became frightful; he walked a step toward M. Leblanc and shouted, in a thundering voice:

"That is not the point! Do you recognize me?"

THE attic door was torn open, and three men in blue cloth blouses and wearing masks of black paper came in. The first was thin, and carried an iron-shod cudgel; the second, who was a species of colossus, held a pole-axe by the middle, with the head down; while the third, a broad-shouldered fellow, not so thin as the first, but not so stout as the second, was armed with an enormous key stolen from some prison-gate.

It seemed as if Jondrette had been awaiting the arrival of these men, and a hurried conversation took place between him and the man with the cudgel.

"Is all ready?" asked Jondrette.

"Yes," the thin man replied.

"Where is Montparnasse?"

"He's stopped to talk to your eldest daughter."

"Is there a cab down below?"

"Yes."

"Is the hack ready?"

"Yes."

"With two good horses?"

"Excellent."

"Is it waiting where I ordered?"

"Yes."

"All right," said Jondrette.

M. Leblanc was very pale. He looked all round the room like a man who understands into what a snare he has fallen, and his head, turned toward all the heads that surrounded him, moved on his neck with an attentive and surprised slowness, but there was nothing in his appearance that resembled fear. He had formed an improvised bulwark of the table, and this man, who a moment before merely looked like an old man, had suddenly become an athlete, and laid his robust fist on the back of his chair with a formidable and surprising gesture.

This old man, so firm and brave in the presence of such a danger, seemed to possess one of those natures which are courageous in the same way as they are good—easily and simply. The father of a woman we love is never a stranger to us, and Marius felt proud of this unknown man.

Three of the men whom Jondrette called chimney-sweeps had taken from the mass of iron, one a large chisel, another a pair of heavy pincers, and the third a hammer, and posted themselves in front of the door, without saying a word. The old man remained on the bed, merely opening his eyes, and Mother Jondrette was sitting by his side.

Marius thought that the moment for interference was at hand, and raised his right hand to the ceiling in the direction of the passage, ready to fire his pistol. Jondrette, after finishing his colloquy with the three men, turned again to M. Leblanc, and repeated the question, with that low, restrained, and terrible laugh of his:

"Do you not recognize me?"

M. Leblanc looked him in the face and answered:

"No."

Jondrette then went up to the table; he bent over the candle with folded arms, and placed his angular and ferocious face as close as he could to M. Leblanc's placid face, and in this posture of a wild beast which is going to bite he exclaimed:

"My name is not Fabantou or Jondrette, but my name is Thénardier, the landlord of the inn at Montfermeil! Do you hear me? Thénardier. Now do you recognize me?"

An almost imperceptible flush shot athwart M. Leblanc's forehead, and he answered, with his ordinary placidity, and without the slightest tremor in his voice:

"No more than before."

Marius did not hear this answer, and any one who had seen him at this moment in the darkness would have found him haggard, stunned, and crushed. At the moment when Jondrette said, *My name is Thénardier,* Marius trembled in all his limbs, and he leaned against the wall, as if he felt a cold sword-blade thrust through his heart. Then his right hand, raised in readiness to fire, dropped, slowly and at the moment when Jondrette repeated, *Do you hear me? Thénardier.* Marius's relaxing fingers almost let the pistol fall. Jondrette, by revealing who he was, did not affect M. Leblanc, but he stunned Marius, for he knew this name of Thénardier, which was apparently unknown to M. Leblanc. Only remember what that name was for him! He had carried it in his heart, recorded in his father's will! he bore it in the deepest shrine of his memory in the sacred recommendation,—"A man of the name of Thénardier saved my life; if my son meet this man he will do all he can for him." This name, it will be remembered, was one of the pieties of his soul, and he blended it with his father's name in his worship. What! This man was Thénardier, the landlord of Montfermeil, whom he had so long and so vainly sought! He found him now, and in what a state! His father's saviour was a bandit! this man, to whom Marius burned to devote himself, was a monster! the liberator of Colonel Pontmercy was on the point of committing a crime, whose outline Marius could not yet see very distinctly, but which resembled an assassination! And on whom? Great heaven, what a fatality, what a bitter mockery of fate! His father commanded him from his tomb to do all in his power for Thénardier. During four years Marius had had no other idea but to pay this debt of his father's, and at the very moment, when he was about to deliver over to justice a brigand in the act of crime, destiny cried to him, "It is Thénardier!" and he was at length about to requite this man for saving his father's life, amid a hail-storm of grape-shot, on the heroic field of Waterloo, by sending him to the scaffold! He had vowed that, if ever he found this Thénardier, he would throw himself at his feet, and he had found him, but for the purpose of handing him over to the executioner! His father said to him, "Help Thénardier," and he was about to answer that adored and sacred voice by crushing Thénardier! To show his father in his grave the spectacle of the man who had dragged him from death, at the peril of his own life, being executed on the Place St. Jacques, by the agency of his son, that Marius to whom he bequeathed this name! And then what a derision it was to have so long carried in his heart the last wishes of his father, in order to perform exactly the contrary! but, on the other hand, how could he witness a murder, and not prevent it? What, should he condemn the victim and spare the assassin? could he be bound by any ties of gratitude to such a villain? All the ideas which Marius had entertained for four years were, as it were, run through the body by this unexpected stroke.

He trembled, all depended on him, and he held in his hands the unconscious beings who were moving before his eyes. If he fired the pistol, M. Leblanc was saved and Thénardier lost; if he did not fire, M. Leblanc was sacrificed and Thénardier might perhaps escape. Must he hunt down the one, or let the other fall? there was remorse on either side.

What should he do? which should he choose? be a defaulter to the most imperious recollections, to so many profound pledges taken to himself, to the most sacred duty, to the most venerated commands, disobey his father's will, or let a crime be accomplished? On one side he fancied he could hear "his Ursule" imploring him for her father; on the other, the colonel recommending Thénardier to him. He felt as if he were going mad. His knees gave way under him, and he had not even time to deliberate, as the scene he had before him was being performed with such furious precipitation. It was a tornado of which he had fancied himself the master, but which was carrying him away; he was on the verge of fainting.

In the meanwhile Thénardier (we will not call him otherwise in future) was walking up and down before the table, with a sort of wild and frenzied triumph.

He seized the candlestick and placed it on the chimney-piece with such a violent blow that the candle nearly went out, and the tallow spattered the wall.

Then he turned round furiously to M. Leblanc and spat forth these words:

"Done brown! grilled, fricasseed! spatch-cocked!"

And he began walking again with a tremendous explosion.

"Ah! I have found you again, my excellent philanthropist! my millionaire with the threadbare coat! the giver of dolls! the old niggard! Ah, you do not recognize me. I suppose it wasn't you who came to my inn at Montfermeil just eight years ago, on the Christmas night of 1823: it wasn't you who carried off Fantine's child, the Lark! it wasn't you who wore a yellow watchman's coat, and had a parcel of clothes in your hand, just as you had this morning. Look here, wife! It is his mania, it appears, to carry to houses bundles of woolen stockings, the old charitable humbug! Are you a cap-maker, my lord millionaire? You give your profits to the poor; what a holy man! what a mountebank! Ah, you do not recognize me! well, I recognize you, and did so directly you thrust your muzzle in here. Ah, you will be taught that it is not a rosy game to go like that to people's houses, under the excuse that they are inns, with such a wretched coat and poverty-stricken look that they feel inclined to give you a sou and then, to play the generous, rob them of their bread-winner and threaten them in the woods. I'll teach you that you won't get off by bringing people when they are ruined a coat that is too large, and two paltry hospital blankets, you old scamp, you child-stealer!"

He stopped, and for a moment seemed to be speaking to himself. It appeared as if his fury fell into some hole, like the Rhone; then, as if finishing aloud the things he had just been saying to himself, he struck the table with his fist, and cried:

"With his simple look!"

Then he apostrophized M. Leblanc.

"By heaven! you made a fool of me formerly, and are the cause of all my misfortunes. You got for fifteen hundred francs a girl who certainly belonged to rich parents, who had already brought me in a deal of money, and from whom I should have got an annuity! That girl would have made up to me all I lost in that wretched pot-house, where I threw away, like an ass, all my blessed savings! Oh, I wish that what was drunk at my house were poison to those who drank it! However, no matter! Tell me, I suppose you thought me a precious fool when you went off with the Lark. You had your cudgel in the forest, and were the stronger. To-day I shall have my revenge, for I hold all the trumps; you are done, my good fellow. Oh! how I laugh when I think that he fell into the trap! I told him that I was an actor, that my name was Fabantou, that I had played with Mamselle Mars, and that my landlord insisted on being paid the next day, and he did not even remember that Jan. 8th, and not Feb. 4th, is quarter-day. The absurd idiot, and these four paltry philippes he has brought me, the ass! He had not the pluck to go as far as five hundred francs; and how he swallowed my platitudes! it amused me, and I said to myself, 'There's an ass for you!' Well, I have got you; this morning I licked your paws, and to-night I shall gnaw your heart!"

Thénardier stopped, out of breath; his little narrow chest panted like a forge-bellows. His eye was full of the ignoble happiness of a weak, cruel, and cowardly creature who is at length able to trample on the man he feared, and insult him whom he flattered; it is the joy of a dwarf putting his heel on the head of Goliath, the joy of a jackal beginning to rend a sick bull, dead enough to be unable to defend itself, but still alive enough to suffer. M. Leblanc did not interrupt him, but said, when he ceased speaking:

"I do not know what you mean, and you are mistaken. I am a very poor man, and anything but a millionaire. I do not know you, and you take me for somebody else."

"Ah!" Thénardier said hoarsely, "a fine dodge! So you adhere to that joke, eh, old fellow? Ah, you do not remember, you do not see who I am!"

"Pardon me, sir," M. Leblanc replied with a polite accent, which had something strange and grand about it at such a moment, "I see that you are a bandit."

We may remind those who have not noticed the fact, that odious beings possess a susceptibility, and that monsters are ticklish. At the word "bandit," Mother Thénardier leaped from the bed, and her husband clutched a chair as if about to break it in his hand. "Don't stir, you," he shouted to his wife, and then, turning to M. Leblanc, said:

"Bandit! yes, I know that you rich swells call us so. It is true that I have been bankrupt. I am hiding, I have no bread, I have not a farthing, and I am a bandit! For three days I have eaten nothing, and I am a bandit! Ah, you fellows warm your toes, you wear pumps made by Sakoski, you have wadded coats like archbishops, you live on the first-floors of houses where a porter is kept, you eat truffles, asparagus at forty francs the bundle in January, and green peas. You stuff yourselves, and when you want to know whether it is cold you look in the newspapers to see what Chevalier's thermometer marks; but we, we are the thermometers. We have no call to go and look at the corner of the Jour d'Horloge how many degrees of cold there are, for we feel the blood stopped in our veins and the ice reach our hearts, and we say, 'There is no God!' and you come into our caverns, yes, our caverns, to call us bandits! But we will eat you, we will devour you, poor little chaps! Monsieur le Millionaire, learn this: I was an established man, I held a license, I was an elector, and am still a citizen, while you, perhaps, are not one."

Here Thénardier advanced a step toward the men near the door, and added with a quiver:

"When I think that he dares to come and address me like a cobbler."

Then he turned upon M. Leblanc with a fresh outburst of frenzy:

"And know this, too, my worthy philanthropist, I am not a doubtful man, nor one whose name is unknown and carries off children from houses! I am an ex-French soldier, and ought to have the cross! I was at Waterloo, and in the battle I saved the life of a general called the Comte Something or Other. He told me his name, but his dog of a voice was so weak that I did not catch it. I only caught *Mercy!* His name would have been better than his thanks. It would have helped me to find him. The picture you see here, and which was painted by David at Bruqueselles, do you know whom it represents? it represents me, for David wished to immortalize the exploit. I have the general on my back, and I am carrying him through the grape-shot. That is the story! the general never did anything for me, and he is no better than the rest, but, for all that, I saved his life at the peril of my own, and I have my pockets filled with certificates of the fact. I am a soldier of Waterloo, by all that's holy! And now that I have had the goodness to tell you all this, let us come to a finish; I want money, I want a deal of money, an enormous amount of money, or I shall exterminate you, by the thunder of heaven."

Marius had gained a little mastery over his agony, and was listening. The last possibility of doubt had vanished, and it was really the Thénardier of the will. Marius shuddered at the charge of ingratitude cast at his father, and which he was on the point of justifying so fatally, and his perplexities were redoubled.

Besides, there was in Thénardier's every word, in his accent and gestures, in his glance, which caused flames to issue from every word, in this explosion of an evil nature displaying everything, in this admixture of boasting and abjectness, pride and meanness, rage and folly, in this chaos of real griefs and false sentiments, in this impudence of a wicked man enjoying the pleasure of violence, in this daring nudity of an ugly soul, and in this blazing out of all possible suffering, combined with all possible hatred, something which was hideous as evil and poignant as truth.

The masterpiece, the picture by David, which he offered M. Leblanc, was, as the reader will have perceived, naught else than his public-house sign, painted by himself, and the sole relic he had preserved from his shipwreck at Montfermeil.

As he had stepped aside Marius was now enabled to look at this thing, and in the daub he really recognized a battle, a background of smoke, and one man carrying another. It was the group of Thénardier and Pontmercy—the saviour sergeant and the saved colonel. Marius felt as if intoxicated, for this picture represented to some extent his loving father; it was no longer an inn sign-board, but a resurrection; a tomb opened, a phantom rose. Marius heard his heart beating at his temples; he had the guns of Waterloo in his ears; his bleeding father vaguely painted on this ill-omened board startled him, and he fancied that the shapeless figure was gazing fixedly at him.

When Thénardier regained breath he fastened his bloodshot eyes on M. Leblanc, and said to him in a low, sharp voice:

"What have you to say before we put the screw on you?"

M. Leblanc was silent.

In the midst of this silence a husky voice uttered this mournful sarcasm in the passage:

"If there's any wood to be chopped, I'm your man."

It was the fellow with the pole-axe amusing himself.

At the same time an immense, hairy, earth-colored face appeared at the door with a frightful grin, which displayed not teeth but tusks.

It was the face of the man with the pole-axe.

"Why have you taken off your mask?" Thénardier asked him furiously.

"To laugh," the man answered.

For some minutes past M. Leblanc seemed to be watching and following every movement of Thénardier, who, blinded and dazzled by his own rage, was walking up and down the room, in the confidence of knowing the door guarded, of holding an unarmed man, and of being nine against one, even supposing that his wife only counted for one man.

In this speech to the man with the pole-axe he turned his back to M. Leblanc.

M. Leblanc took advantage of the opportunity, upset the chair with his foot, the table with his fist, and with one bound, ere Thénardier was able to turn, he was at the window. To open it and bestride the sill only took a second, and he was half out when six powerful hands seized him and energetically dragged him back into the room. The three "chimney-sweeps" had rushed upon him, and at the same time Mother Thénardier seized him by the hair.

At the noise which ensued the other bandits ran in from the passage, and the old man on the bed, who seemed the worse for liquor, came up tottering with a road-mender's hammer in his hand.

One of the sweeps, whose blackened face the candle lit up, and in whom Marius recognized, in spite of the blackening, Panchaud, *alias* Printanier, *alias* Bigrenaille, raised above M. Leblanc's head a species of life-preserver, made of two lumps of lead at the end of an iron bar.

Marius could not resist the sight. "My father," he thought, "forgive me," and his finger sought the trigger.

He was on the point of firing when Thénardier cried:

"Do not hurt him."

This desperate attempt of the victim, far from exasperating Thénardier, had calmed him.

There were two men in him, the ferocious man, and the skillful man. Up to this moment, in the exuberance of triumph, and while standing before his motionless victim, the ferocious man had prevailed, but when the victim made an effort and appeared inclined to struggle, the skillful man re-appeared and took the mastery.

"Do him no harm!" he repeated, and his first service was, though he little suspected it, that he stopped the discharge of the pistol and paralyzed Marius, to whom the affair did not appear so urgent, and who in the presence of this new phase saw no harm in waiting a little longer.

Who knew whether some accident might not occur which would deliver him from the frightful alternative of letting Ursule's father perish or destroying the colonel's saviour?

A herculean struggle had commenced. With one blow of his fist in the chest M. Leblanc sent the old man rolling in the middle of the room, and then with two back-handers knocked down two other assailants, and held one under each of his knees. The villains groaned under this pressure as under a granite mill-stone, but the four others had seized the formidable old man by the arms and neck and were holding him down upon the two "sweeps."

Thus, master of two, and mastered by the others, crushing those beneath him and crushed by those above him, M. Leblanc disappeared beneath this horrible group of bandits, like a boar attacked by a howling pack of dogs.

They succeeded in throwing him on to the bed nearest the window, and held him down. Mother Thénardier did not once let go his hair.

"Don't you interfere," Thénardier said to her, "you will tear your shawl."

The woman obeyed, as the she-wolf obeys the wolf, with a snarl.

"You fellows," Thénardier continued, "search him."

M. Leblanc appeared to have given up all thought of resistance, and they searched him.

He had nothing about him but a leather purse containing six francs and his handkerchief. Thénardier put the latter in his own pocket.

"What! no pocket-book?" he asked.

"No, and no watch," one of the sweeps replied.

"No matter," the masked man who held the large key muttered in the voice of a ventriloquist, "he is a tough old bird."

Thénardier went to the corner near the door, and took up some ropes, which he threw to them.

"Fasten him to the foot of the bed," he said.

Then, noticing the old man whom M. Leblanc had knocked down still motionless on the floor, he asked:

"Is Boulatruelle dead?"

"No," Bigrenaille answered, "he's drunk."

"Sweep him into a corner," Thénardier said.

Two of the sweeps thrust the drunkard with their feet to the side of the old iron.

"Babet, why did you bring so many?" Thénardier said in a whisper to the man with the cudgel, "it was unnecessary."

"They all wanted to be in it," the man answered, "for the season is bad, and there's nothing doing."

The bed upon which M. Leblanc had been thrown was a sort of hospital bed on four clumsy wooden legs.

M. Leblanc offered no resistance.

The bandits tied him firmly in an upright posture to the end of the bed furthest from the window and nearest to the chimney-piece.

When the last knot was tied Thénardier took a chair and sat down almost facing the prisoner.

He was no longer the same man; in a few minutes his countenance had passed from frenzied violence to tranquil and cunning gentleness.

Marius had a difficulty in recognizing in this polite smile of an official the almost bestial mouth which had been foaming a moment previously; he regarded this fantastic and alarming metamorphosis with stupor, and he felt as a man would feel who saw a tiger changed into an attorney.

"Sir," said Thénardier, and made a sign to the bandits who still held M. Leblanc to fall back.

"Leave me to talk with the gentleman," he said.

All withdrew to the door, and he resumed:

"You did wrong to try and jump out of the window, for you might have broken a leg. Now, with your permission, we will talk quietly; and, in the first place, I will communicate to you a thing I have noticed, that you have not yet uttered the slightest cry."

Thénardier was right; the fact was so, although it had escaped Marius in his trouble. M. Leblanc had merely said a few words without raising his voice, and even in his struggle near the window with the six bandits he had preserved the profoundest and most singular silence.

Thénardier went on:

"Good heavens! you might have tried to call Thieves! and I should not have thought it improper. Such a thing as Murder! is shouted on such occasions; I should not have taken it in ill part. It is very simple that a man should make a bit of a row when he finds himself with persons who do not inspire him with sufficient confidence. If you had done so we should not have interfered with you or thought of gagging you, and I will tell you the reason why. This room is very deaf; it has only that in its favor, but it has that. It is a cellar; you might explode a bomb-shell here, and it would not produce the effect of a drunkard's snore at the nearest post. Here cannon would go boum and thunder pouf. It is a convenient lodging. But still you did not cry out; all the better, and I compliment you on it, and will tell you what conclusion I draw from the fact. My dear sir, when a man cries for help, who come? the police; and after the police? justice. Well, you did not cry out, and so you are no more desirous than we are for the arrival of the police. The fact is—and I have suspected it for some time—that you have some interest in hiding something; for our part, we have the same interest, and so we may be able to come to an understanding."

While saying this, Thénardier was trying to drive the sharp points that issued from his eyes into his prisoner's conscience. Besides, his language, marked with a sort of moderate and cunning insolence, was reserved and almost chosen, and in this villain who was just before only a bandit could now be seen "the man who had studied for the priesthood."

The silence which the prisoner had maintained, this precaution which went so far as the very forgetfulness of care for his life, this resistance so opposed to the first movement of nature, which is to utter a cry, troubled and painfully amazed Marius so soon as his attention was drawn to it.

Thénardier's well-founded remark but rendered denser the mysterious gloom behind which was concealed the grave and peculiar face to which Courfeyrac had given the sobriquet of M. Leblanc.

But, whoever this man might be, though bound with cords, surrounded by bandits, and half buried, so to speak, in a grave where the earth fell upon him at every step—whether in the presence of Thénardier furious or of Thénardier gentle—he remained impassive, and Marius could not refrain from admiring this face so superbly melancholy at such a moment. He was evidently a soul inaccessible to terror, and ignorant of what it is to be alarmed. He was one of those men who dominate the amazement produced by desperate situations. However extreme the crisis might be, however inevitable the catastrophe, he had none of the agony of the drowning man who opens horrible eyes under water.

Thénardier rose without any affectation, removed the screen from before the fire-place, and thus unmasked the brazier full of burning charcoal, in which the prisoner could perfectly see the chisel at a white heat, and studded here and there with small red stars.

Then he came back and sat down near M. Leblanc.

"I will continue," he said; "we can come to an understanding, so let us settle this amicably. I did wrong to let my temper carry me away just now, I do not know where my senses were, I went much too far and uttered absurdities. For instance, because you are a millionaire, I told you that I insisted on money, a great deal of money, an immense sum of money, and that was not reasonable. Good heavens! you may be rich, but you have burdens, for who is there that has not? I do not wish to ruin you, for I am not a sheriff's officer after all. I am not one of those men who, because they have advantage of position, employ it to be ridiculous. Come, I will make a sacrifice on my side, and be satisfied with two hundred thousand francs."

M. Leblanc did not utter a syllable.

Thénardier continued:

"You see that I put plenty of water in my wine. I do not know the amount of your fortune, but I am aware that you do not care for money, and a benevolent man like you can easily give two hundred thousand francs to an unfortunate parent. Of course you are reasonable too; you cannot have supposed that I would take all that trouble this morning, and organize this affair to-night, which is a well-done job in the opinion of these gentlemen, merely to ask you for enough money to go and drink fifteen-sous wine and eat veal at Desnoyer's. But two hundred thousand francs, that's worth the trouble; once that trifle has come out of your pocket, I will guarantee that you have nothing more to apprehend. You will say, 'But I have not two hundred thousand francs about me.' Oh, I am not exorbitant and I do not insist on that. I only ask one thing of you; be good enough to write what I shall dictate."

Here Thénardier stopped, but added, laying a stress on the words and casting a smile at the brazier:

"I warn you that I shall not accept the excuse that you cannot write."

A grand inquisitor might have envied that smile.

Thénardier pushed the table close up to M. Leblanc, and took pen, ink, and paper out of the drawer, which he left half open, and in which the long knife-blade flashed.

He laid the sheet of paper before M. Leblanc. "Write!" he said.

The prisoner at last spoke.

"How can you expect me to write? my arms are tied."

"That is true; I beg your pardon," said Thénardier, "you are quite right."

And turning to Bigrenaille he added:

"Unfasten the gentleman's right arm."

Panchaud, *alias* Printanier, *alias* Bigrenaille, obeyed Thénardier's orders.

When the prisoner's hand was free, Thénardier dipped the pen in the ink and handed it to him.

"Make up your mind, sir, that you are in our absolute power, no human interference can liberate you, and we should really be sorry to be forced to proceed to disagreeable extremities. I know neither your name nor your address, but I warn you that you will remain tied up here until the person commissioned to deliver the letter you are going to write has returned. Now be good enough to write."

"What?" the prisoner asked.

Thénardier began dictating: "My daughter."

The prisoner started, and raised his eyes to Thénardier, who went on:

"Put 'My dear daughter'," said Thénardier.

M. Leblanc obeyed.

Thénardier continued:

"Come to me at once, for I want you particularly. The person who delivers this letter to you has instructions to bring you to me. I am waiting. Come in perfect confidence."

M. Leblanc wrote this down.

Thénardier resumed:

"By the way, efface that *'Come in perfect confidence,'* for it might lead to a supposition that the affair is not perfectly simple, and create distrust."

M. Leblanc erased the words.

"Now," Thénardier added, "sign it; what is your name!" The prisoner laid down the pen, and asked:

"For whom is this letter?"

"You know very well," Thénardier answered; "for the little one; I just told you so."

It was evident that Thénardier avoided mentioning the name of the girl in question; he called her "the Lark," he called her "the little one," but he did not pronounce her name. It was the precaution of a clever man who keeps his secret from his accomplices, and mentioning the name would have told them the whole affair and taught them more than there was any occasion for them to know.

So he repeated:

"Sign it. What is your name?"

"Urbain Fabre," said the prisoner.

Thénardier, with the movement of a cat, thrust his hand into his pocket and drew out the handkerchief found on M. Leblanc. He sought for the mark, and held it to the candle.

"U. F.; all right, Urbain Fabre. Well, sign it U. F."

The prisoner did so.

"As two hands are needed to fold a letter, give it to me and I will do so."

This done, Thénardier added:

"Write the address to *Mademoiselle Fabre* at your house. I know that you live somewhere near here in the neighborhood of St. Jacques du Haut-pas, as you attend mass there every day, but I do not know in what street. I see that you understand your situation, and as you have not told a falsehood about your name you will not do so about your address. Write it yourself."

The prisoner remained pensive for a moment, and then took up the pen and wrote:

"Mademoiselle Fabre, at M. Urbain Fabre's, No. 17, Rue St. Dominique d'Enfer."

Thénardier seized the letter with a sort of feverish convulsion.

"Wife," he shouted, and the woman came up.

"Here is the letter, and you know what you have to do. There is a hackney coach down below, so be off at once, and return ditto."

Then he turned to the man with the pole-axe, and said: "As you have taken off your false nose you can accompany her. Get up behind the coach. You know where you left the hack?"

"Yes," said the man.

And, depositing the axe in a corner, he followed the woman.

As they were going away, Thénardier thrust his head out of the door and shouted down the passage:

"Mind and do not lose the letter! Remember, you have two hundred thousand francs about you."

The woman's hoarse voice replied:

"Don't be frightened, I've put it in my stomacher—"

A minute had not elapsed when the crack of a whip could be heard rapidly retiring.

"All right," Thénardier growled, "they are going at a good pace; with a gallop like that she will be back in three-quarters of an hour."

He drew up a chair to the fireside, and sat down with folded arms, and holding his muddy boots to the brazier.

"My feet are cold," he said.

Only five bandits remained in the den with Thénardier and the prisoner.

These men, through the masks or soot that covered their faces and rendered them, with a choice of horror, charcoal-burners, negroes, or demons, had a heavy, dull look, and it was plain that they performed a crime like a job, tranquilly, without passion or pity, and with a sort of weary air. They were heaped up in a corner like brutes, and were silent.

Thénardier was warming his feet.

The prisoner had fallen back into his taciturnity; a sinister calmness had succeeded the formidable noise which had filled the garret a few moments previously.

The candle, on which a large mushroom had formed, scarce lit up the immense room; the brazier had grown black, and all these monstrous heads cast misshapen shadows upon the walls and the ceiling.

No other sound was audible save the regular breathing of the old drunkard, who was asleep.

Marius was waiting in a state of anxiety, which everything tended to augment. The enigma was more impenetrable than ever; who was this "little one," whom Thénardier had also called "the Lark,"—was she "his Ursule"? The prisoner had not seemed affected by this name of "the Lark," and had answered with the most natural air in the world, "I do not know what you mean." On the other hand, the two letters U. F. were explained; they were Urbain Fabre, and Ursule's name was no longer Ursule. This is what Marius saw most clearly.

A sort of frightful fascination kept him nailed to the spot, whence he surveyed and commanded the whole scene. He stood there almost incapable of reflection and movement, as if annihilated by the frightful things which he saw close to him; and he waited, hoping for some incident, no matter its nature, unable to collect his thoughts, and not knowing what to do.

"In any case," he said, "if she is the Lark, I shall see her, for Mother Thénardier will bring her here. In that case I will give my life and blood, should it be necessary, to save her, and nothing shall stop me."

Nearly half an hour passed in this way; Thénardier seemed absorbed in dark thoughts, and the prisoner did not stir. Still Marius fancied that he could hear at intervals a low, dull sound in the direction of the prisoner. All at once Thénardier addressed his victim.

"By the way, M. Fabre," he said, "I may as well tell you something at once."

As these few words seemed the commencement of an explanation, Marius listened carefully. Thénardier continued:

"My wife will be back soon, so do not be impatient. I believe that the Lark is really your daughter, and think it very simple that you should keep her, but listen to me for a moment. My wife will go to her with your letter, and I told Madame Thénardier to dress herself in the way you saw, that your young lady might make no difficulty about following her. They will both get into the hackney coach with my comrade behind; near a certain barrier there is a trap drawn by two excellent horses; your young lady will be driven up to it in the hackney coach, and get into the trap with my pal, while my wife returns here to report progress. As for your young lady, no harm will be done her; she will be taken to a place where she will be all safe, and so soon as you have handed me the trifle of two hundred thousand francs she will be restored to you. If you have me arrested my pal will settle the Lark, that's all."

The prisoner did not utter a word, and after a pause Thénardier continued:

"It is simple enough, as you see, and there will be no harm, unless you like to make harm. I have told you all about it, and warned you, that you might know."

He stopped, but the prisoner did not interrupt the silence, and Thénardier added:

"So soon as my wife has returned and said to me, 'The Lark is on the way,' we will release you, and you can sleep at home if you like. You see that we have no ill intentions."

Frightful images passed across the mind of Marius. What! they were not going to bring the girl here! One of the monsters was going to carry her off in the darkness! where? Oh, if it were she!

It was plain that it was she. Marius felt the beating of his heart stop.

What should he do? fire the pistol and deliver all these villains into the hands of justice? But the hideous man with the pole-axe could not be the less out of reach with the girl, and Marius thought of Thénardier's words, whose sanguinary meaning he could read: *If you have me arrested, my pal will settle the Lark.*

Now he felt himself checked, not only by the colonel's will, but by his love and the peril of her whom he loved.

The frightful situation, which had already lasted above an hour, changed its aspect at every moment.

Marius had the strength to review in turn all the most frightful conjectures, while seeking a hope and finding none.

The tumult of his thoughts contrasted with the lugubrious silence of the den.

In the midst of this silence the sound of the staircase door being opened and shut became audible. The prisoner gave a start in his bonds.

"Here's my wife," said Thénardier.

He had scarce finished speaking when Mother Thénardier rushed into the room, red, out of breath, and with flashing eyes, and shouted as she struck her thighs with her two big hands:

"A false address."

The brigand who had accompanied her appeared behind, and took up his pole-axe again.

"A false address?" Thénardier repeated, and she went on:

"No Monsieur Urbain Fabre known at No. 17, Rue St. Dominique. They never heard of him."

She stopped to snort, and then continued:

"Monsieur Thénardier, that old cove has made a fool of you; for you are too good-hearted, I keep on telling you. I would have cut his throat to begin with! and if he had sulked I would have boiled him alive! that would have made him speak and tell us where his daughter is, and where he keeps his pile. That is how I should have managed the affair. People are right when they say that men are more stupid than women. Nobody at No. 17; it is a large gate-way. No Monsieur Fabre at No. 17, and we went at a gallop, with a fee for the driver and all! I spoke to the porter and his wife, who is a fine, tall woman, and they did not know anybody of the name."

Marius breathed again.

She, Ursule, or the Lark—he no longer knew her name—was saved.

While the exasperated woman was vociferating Thénardier sat down at the table; he remained for some minutes without saying a word, balancing his right leg and looking at the brazier with an air of savage reverie.

At last he said to the prisoner slowly, and with a peculiarly ferocious accent:

"A false address? why, what did you expect?"

"To gain time!" the prisoner thundered.

And at the same moment he shook off his bonds, which were cut through: the prisoner was only fastened to the bed by one leg.

Ere the seven men had time to look about them and rush forward, he had stretched out his hand toward the fire-place, and the Thénardiers and the brigands, driven back by surprise to the end of the room, saw him almost free, and in a formidable attitude, waving round his head the red-hot chisel, from which a sinister glare shot.

In the judicial inquiry that followed this affair it was stated that a large sou, cut and worked in a peculiar manner, was found in the garret when the police made their descent upon it. It was one of those marvels in industry which the patience of the galleys engenders in the darkness, and for the darkness—marvels which are naught but instruments of escape. These hideous and yet delicate products of a prodigious art are in the jewelry trade what slang metaphors are in poetry; for there are Benvenuto Cellinis at the bagne, in the same way as there are Villons in language. The wretch who aspires to deliverance finds means, without tools, or, at the most, with an old knife, to saw a sou in two, hollow out the two parts without injuring the dies, and form a thread in the edge of each part, so that they fit together. It screws and unscrews at pleasure, and is a box; and in this box a watch-spring saw is concealed, which, if well managed, will cut through fetters and iron bars. It is believed that the unhappy convict possesses only a sou; but, not at all, he possesses liberty. It was a sou of this nature which was found by the police under the bed near the window, and a small saw of blue steel, which could be easily concealed in the sou, was also discovered.

It is probable that at the moment when the bandits searched the prisoner he had the double sou about him, and hid it in his palm; and his right hand being at liberty afterward, he unscrewed it, and employed the saw to cut the ropes. This would explain the slight noise and the almost imperceptible movements which Marius had noticed.

As, however, he was unable to stoop down for fear of betraying himself, he had not cut the cord on his left leg.

The bandits gradually recovered from their surprise.

"Be easy," said Bigrenaille to Thénardier, "he is still held by one leg, and will not fly away. I put the pack-thread round that paw."

Here the prisoner raised his voice:

"You are villains, but my life is not worth so much trouble to defend.

As for imagining that you could make me speak, make me write what I do not wish to write, or make me say what I do not intend to say—"

He pulled up the sleeve of his left arm and added:

"Look here!"

At the same time he stretched out his arm, and placed on the naked flesh the red-hot chisel, which he held in his right hand by the wooden handle.

Then could be heard the frizzling of the burned flesh, and the smell peculiar to torture-rooms spread through the garret.

Marius tottered in horror, and the brigands themselves shuddered; but the face of the strange old man was scarce contracted, and while the red-hot steel was burying itself in the smoking wound, he—impassive and almost august—fixed on Thénardier his beautiful glance, in which there was no hatred, and in which suffering disappeared in a serene majesty.

For in great and lofty natures the revolt of the flesh and of the senses when suffering from physical pain, makes the soul appear on the brow, in the same way as the mutiny of troops compels the captain to show himself.

"Villains," he said, "be no more frightened of me than I am of you."

And, tearing the chisel out of the wound, he hurled it through the window which had been left open. The horrible red-hot tool whirled through the night and fell some distance off in the snow, which hissed at the contact.

The prisoner continued:

"Do to me what you like."

He was defenseless.

"Seize him," said Thénardier.

Two of the brigands laid their hands on his shoulders, and the masked man with the ventriloquist voice stood in front of him, ready to dash out his brains with a blow of the key at the slightest movement on his part. At the same time Marius heard below him, but so close that he could not see the speakers, the following remarks exchanged in a low voice:

"There is only one thing to be done."

"Cut his throat!"

"Exactly."

It was the husband and wife holding council.

Thénardier walked slowly to the table, opened the drawer, and took out the knife.

249

Marius clutched the handle of the pistol in a state of extraordinary perplexity. For above an hour he had heard two voices in his conscience, one telling him to respect his father's will, while the other cried to him to succor the prisoner. These two voices continued their struggle uninterruptedly, and caused him an agony. He had vaguely hoped up to this moment to find some mode of reconciling those two duties, but nothing possible had occurred to him.

Still the peril pressed; the last moment of delay was passed, for Thénardier, knife in hand, was reflecting a few paces from the prisoner.

Marius looked wildly around him, which is the last mechanical resource of despair. All at once he started.

At his feet on his table a bright moonbeam lit up and seemed to point out to him a sheet of paper. On this sheet he read this line, written in large letters that very morning by the elder of Thénardier's daughters:

"HERE ARE THE COPS."

An idea, a flash, crossed Marius's mind; this was the solution of the frightful problem that tortured him, sparing the assassin and saving the victim.

He knelt down on the chest of drawers, stretched forth his arm, seized the paper, softly detached a lump of plaster from the partition, wrapped it up in the paper, and threw it through the hole into the middle of the den.

It was high time, for Thénardier had overcome his last fears, or his last scruples, and was going toward the prisoner.

"There's something falling," his wife cried.

"What is it?" her husband asked.

The woman had bounded forward and picked up the lump of plaster wrapped in paper, which she handed to her husband.

"How did it get here?" Thénardier asked.

"Why hang it," his wife asked, "how do you expect that it did? through the window, of course."

"I saw it pass," said Bigrenaille.

Thénardier rapidly unfolded the paper and held it close to the candle.

"Eponine's handwriting—the devil!"

He made a signal to his wife, who hurried up to him and showed her the line written on the paper, then added in a hollow voice:

"Quick, the ladder! we must leave the bacon in the trap and clear out!"

"Without cutting the man's throat?" asked Mother Thénardier.

"We haven't the time."

"Which way?" Bigrenaille remarked.

"By the window," Thénardier replied; "as 'Ponine threw the stone through the window, that's a proof that the house is not beset on that side."

The mask with the ventriloquist voice laid his key on the ground, raised his arms in the air, and opened and shut his hands thrice rapidly, without saying a word.

This was like the signal for clearing for action aboard ship; the brigands who held the prisoner let him go, and in a twinkling the rope ladder was dropped out of the window and securely fastened to the sill by the two iron hooks.

The prisoner paid no attention to what was going on around him; he seemed to be thinking or praying. So soon as the ladder was fixed, Thénardier cried:

"The lady first."

And he dashed at the window.

But, as he was stepping out, Bigrenaille roughly seized him by the collar.

"No, no, my old joker; after us!" he said.

"After us!" the bandits yelled.

"You are children," said Thénardier; "we are losing time and the police are at our heels."

"Very well, then," said one of the bandits, "let us draw lots as to who shall go first."

Thénardier exclaimed:

"Are you mad? are you drunk? why, what a set of humbugs; lose time, I suppose, draw lots, eh? with a wet finger? a short straw? write our names and put them in a cap—?"

"May I offer my hat?" a voice said at the door.

All turned; it was Javert.

He held his hat in his hand and offered it smilingly.

21. *THE PROPER WAY TO BEGIN IS TO ARREST THE VICTIM*

JAVERT posted his men at nightfall, and ambushed himself behind the trees of the Rue de la Barrière des Gobelins, which joins No. 50-52 on the other side of the boulevard. He had begun by opening his "pocket," in order to thrust into it the two girls ordered to watch the approaches to the den, but he had only "nailed" Azelma; as for Eponine, she was not at her post, she had disappeared, and he had not been able to seize her. Then Javert took up his post and listened for the appointed signal. The departure and return of the hackney coach greatly perplexed him; at length he grew impatient, and feeling sure that there "was a nest there," and of being in "luck's way," and having recognized several of the bandits who went in, he resolved to enter without waiting for the pistol-shot.

It will be remembered that he had Marius's latch-key.

He arrived just in time.

The startled bandits dashed at the weapons which they had thrown into corners at the moment of their attempted escape; and in less than a second these seven men, formidable to look at, were grouped in a posture of defense, one with his pole-axe, another with his key, a third with his life-preserver, the others with chisels, pincers, and hammer, and Thénardier with his knife in his fist. The woman picked up an enormous paving-stone which lay in the angle of the room and served her daughter as a foot-stool.

Javert restored his hat to his head, and walked into the room, with folded arms, his cane under his arm and his sword in its scabbard.

"Halt!" he shouted, "you will not leave by the window, but by the door, which is not so unhealthy. You are seven and we are fifteen, so do not let us quarrel like water-carriers, but behave as gentlemen."

Bigrenaille drew his pistol from under his blouse and placed it in Thénardier's hand, as he whispered:

"It is Javert, and I dare not fire at that man. Dare you?"

"I should think so," Thénardier answered.

"Well, fire."

Thénardier took the pistol and aimed at Javert.

The inspector who was only three paces from him, looked at him fixedly, and contented himself with saying:

"Don't fire, for the pistol won't go off."

Thénardier pulled the trigger; there was a flash in the pan.

"Did I not tell you so?" Javert remarked.

Bigrenaille threw his life-preserver at Javert's feet.

"You are the emperor of the devils, and I surrender."

"And you?" Javert asked the other bandits.

They answered, "We too."

Javert remarked calmly:

"That is all right; I begged you to behave like gentlemen."

"I only ask one thing," Bigrenaille remarked, "that my baccy mayn't be stopped while I'm in solitary confinement."

"Granted," said Javert.

Then he turned and shouted:

"You can come in now."

A squad of police, sword in hand, and agents armed with bludgeons and sticks, rushed in at Javert's summons and bound the robbers.

This crowd of men, scarce illumined by the candle, filled the den with shadows.

"Handcuff them all," Javert cried.

"Just come this way if you dare," a voice shouted, which was not that of a man, but of which no one could have said, "It is a woman's voice."

Mother Thénardier had intrenched herself in one of the angles of the window, and it was she from whom this roar had come.

The police and the agents fell back.

She had thrown off her shawl, and kept her bonnet on; her husband, crouching behind her, almost disappeared under the fallen shawl, and she covered him with her body, while raising the paving-stone above her head with both hands, like a giantess about to heave a rock.

"Heads below!" she screeched.

All fell back upon the passage, and there was a large open space in the center of the garret.

The hag took a glance at the bandits, who had suffered themselves to be bound, and muttered in a hoarse and guttural voice:

"The cowards!"

Javert smiled and walked into the open space which the woman guarded with her eyes.

"Don't come nearer," she shrieked, "or I'll smash you. Be off!"

"What a grenadier!" said Javert, "Mother! you have a beard like a man, but I have claws like a woman."

And he continued to advance.

Mother Thénardier, with flying hair and terrible looks, straddled her legs, bent back, and wildly hurled the paving-stone at Javert. He stooped, the stone passed over him, struck the wall, from which it dislodged a mass of plaster, and then ricochetted from angle to angle till it fell exhausted at Javert's feet.

At the same moment Javert reached the Thénardiers: one of his large hands settled on the wife's shoulder, the other on the husband's head.

"Handcuffs here!" he shouted.

The policemen flocked in, and in a few seconds Javert's orders were carried out.

The woman, quite crushed, looked at her own and her husband's manacled hands, fell on the ground, and, bursting into tears, cried:

"My daughters."

"Oh, they are all right," said Javert.

By this time the police had noticed the drunken man sleeping behind the door, and shook him. He woke up and stammered:

"Is it all over, Jondrette?"

"Yes," Javert answered.

The six bound bandits were standing together, with their spectral faces, three daubed with black, and three masked.

"Keep on your masks," said Javert.

And passing them in review, like a Frederick II at a Potsdam parade, he said to the three "sweeps":

"Good-day, Bigrenaille." "Good-day, Brujon." "Good-day, Deux Milliards."

Then, turning to the three masks, he said to the man with the pole-axe, "Good-day, Gueulemer," and to the man with the cudgel, "Good-day, Babet," and to the ventriloquist, "Here's luck, Claquesous."

At this moment he noticed the prisoner, who had not said a word since the arrival of the police, and held his head down.

"Untie the gentleman," said Javert, "and let no one leave the room."

After saying this he sat down in a lordly way at the table on which the candle and the inkstand were still standing, took a stamped paper from his pocket, and began writing his report.

When he had written a few lines, which are always the same formula, he raised his eyes.

"Bring the gentleman here whom these gentlemen had tied up."

The agents looked around.

"Well," Javert asked, "where is he?"

The prisoner of the bandits, M. Leblanc, M. Urbain Fabre, the father of Ursule or the Lark, had disappeared.

The door was guarded, but the window was not. So soon as he found himself released, and while Javert was writing, he took advantage of the trouble, the tumult, the crowd, the darkness, and the moment when attention was not fixed upon him, to rush to the window.

An agent ran up and looked out; he could see nobody; but the rope ladder was still trembling.

"The devil!" said Javert between his teeth, "he must have been the best of the lot."

22. *THE LITTLE ONE WHO CRIED IN VOLUME SECOND*

On the day after that in which these events occurred in the house on the Boulevard de l'Hôpital, a lad, who apparently came from the bridge of Austerlitz, was trudging along the right-hand walk in the direction of the Barrière de Fontainebleau, at about nightfall.

This boy was pale, thin, dressed in rags, wearing canvas trousers in the month of February, and singing at the top of his lungs.

At the corner of the Rue du Petit Banquier, an old woman was stooping down and fumbling in a pile of garbage by the lamplight; the lad ran against her as he passed, and fell back, with the exclamation:

"My eye! why I took that for an enormous, an enormous dog."

He uttered the word *enormous* the second time with a sonorous twang, which might be expressed by capitals, "an enormous, an ENORMOUS dog."

The old woman drew herself up furiously.

"You young devil!" she growled, "if I had not been stooping, I know where my foot would have been now."

The lad was already some distance off.

"K'ss! k'ss!" he said; "after all, I may not have been mistaken."

The old woman, choked with indignation, drew herself up to her full height, and the street lantern fully lit up her livid face, which was hollowed by angles and wrinkles, and crows'-feet connecting the corners of the mouth. The body was lost in the darkness, and her head alone could be seen; she looked like a mask of decrepitude lit up by a flash darting through the night.

The lad looked at her.

"Madame," he said, "yours is not the style of beauty which would suit me."

He went his way, and began singing again:

> *Le Roi Coupdesabot*
> *S'en allait à la chasse,*
> *A la chasse aux corbeaux.*

At the end of these three lines he broke off. He had reached No. 50-52, and, finding the gate closed, he began giving it reëchoing and heroic kicks, which indicated rather the shoes of the man which he wore than the feet of the boy which he had.

By this time the same old woman whom he had met at the corner of the Rue du Petit Banquier ran up after him, uttering shouts and making the most extraordinary gestures.

"What's the matter? what's the matter? O Lord to God! the gate is being broken down and the house broken into."

The kicks continued, and the old woman puffed:

"Is that the way to treat a house?"

All at once she stopped, for she had recognized the gamin.

"Why, it is that Satan!"

"Hilloh! it's the old woman," said the boy. "Good-evening, my dear Burgonmuche, I have come to see my ancestors."

The old woman answered with a composite grimace, an admirable instance of hatred taking advantage of old age and ugliness, which was unfortunately lost in the darkness: "There's nobody here, scamp."

"Nonsense," the boy said, "where's father?"

"At La Force."

"Hilloh! and mother?"

"At Saint Lazare."

"Very fine! and my sisters?"

"At the Madelonnettes."

The lad scratched the back of his ear, looked at Mame Bougon, and said, "Ah!"

Then he turned on his heels, and a moment later the old woman, who was standing in the gate-way, heard him singing in his clear young voice, as he went off under the elms which were quivering in the winter breeze:

Le Roi Coupdesabot
S'en allait à la chasse,
A la chasse aux corbeaux,
Monté sur des échasses.
Quand on passait dessous,
On lui payait deux sous.

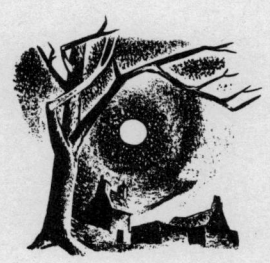

VOLUME FOUR

The Idyll of the Rue Plumet and the Epic of the Rue Saint Denis

CONTENTS · VOLUME IV

BOOK I—SOME PAGES OF HISTORY

BOOK II—EPONINE

BOOK III—THE HOUSE OF THE RUE PLUMET

BOOK IV—SUCCOR FROM BELOW MAY BE SUCCOR FROM ON HIGH

BOOK XIV—THE GRANDEUR OF DESPAIR

BOOK XV—RUE DE L'HOMME ARMÉ

The Idyll of the Rue Plumet

BOOK I

SOME PAGES OF HISTORY

I. EXCELLENTLY CUT OUT

THE two years 1831 and 1832, immediately attached to the revolution of July, contain the most peculiar and striking moments of history, and these two years, amid those that precede and follow them, stand out like mountains. They possess the true revolutionary grandeur, and precipices may be traced in them. The social masses, the very foundations of civilization, the solid group of superimposed and adherent interests, and the secular profiles of the ancient Gallic formations appear and disappear every moment through the stormy clouds of systems, passions, and theories. These appearances and disappearances were called resistance and movement, but, at intervals, truth, the daylight of the human soul, flashes through all.

This remarkable epoch is so circumscribed, and is beginning to become so remote from us, that we are able to seize its principal outlines. We will make the attempt. The Restoration was one of those intermediate phases which are so difficult to define, in which are fatigue, buzzing murmurs, sleep and tumult, and which, after all, are naught but the arrival of a great nation at a halting-place. These epochs are peculiar, and deceive the politician who tries to take advantage of them. At the outset the nation only demands repose; there is but one thirst, for peace, and only one ambition, to be small—which is the translation of behaving quietly. "Great events, great accidents, great adventures, great men,—O Lord! we have had enough of these; we are over head and ears in them." Cæsar would be given for Prusias, and Napoleon for the Roi d'Yvetôt, who was "such a merry little king." Folk have been marching since daybreak and arrive at the evening of a long and rough journey; they made their first halt with Mirabeau, the second with Robespierre, and the third with Napoleon, and they are exhausted. Everybody insists on a bed.

Worn-out devotions, crying heroisms, gorged ambitions, and made fortunes seek, claim, implore, and solicit, what?—a resting-place, and they have it. They take possession of peace, tranquillity, and leisure, and feel satisfied. Still, at the same time, certain facts arise, demand recognition, and knock at doors on their side. These facts have emerged from revolutions and wars. They exist, they live, and have the right of installing themselves in society, which they do, and in the majority of instances facts are the quartermasters that only prepare a billet for principles.

In such a case, this is what occurs to political philosophers. At the same time that wearied men claim rest, accomplished facts demand guarantees, for guarantees for facts are the same thing as repose for men. It is this that England asked of the Stuart after the Protector, and what France asked of the Bourbons after the empire. These guarantees are a necessity of the times, and they must be granted. The princes concede them, but in reality it is the force of things that gives them. This is a profound truth and worth knowing, which the Stuarts did not suspect in 1662, and of which the Bourbons did not even gain a glimpse in 1814.

The predestined family which returned to France when Napoleon collapsed, had the fatal simplicity of believing that it gave, and that it could take back what it had once given; that the Bourbon family possessed the right divine, and France possessed nothing, and that the political right conceded in the charter of Louis XVIII was nothing else but a branch of the divine right, detached by the House of Bourbon and graciously given to the people up to the day when the king thought proper to clutch it again. Still, from the displeasure which the gift caused it, the Bourbon family ought to have felt that it did not emanate from it. It behaved in a grudging way to the nineteenth century, and looked with an ugly smile at every expansion of the nation. To employ a trivial, that is to say, a popular and true phrase, it was crabbed, and the people noticed it.

The government believed it had strength because the empire had been removed before it, like a stage scene, but it did not perceive that it had been produced in the same way, nor see that it was held in the same hand which had removed Napoleon. It believed that it had roots because it was the past. It was mistaken; it formed a portion of the past, but the whole of the past was France; and the roots of French society were not in the Bourbons, but in the nation. These obscure and perennial roots did not constitute the right of a family, but the history of a people, and were everywhere, except under the throne. The House of Bourbon had been for France the illustrious and blood-stained knot of her history, but was no longer the principal element of her destiny nor the necessary basis of her political structure. She could do without the Bourbons as she had done for two-and-twenty years; there was a solution of continuity, but they did not suspect it. And how could they suspect it, when they imagined that Louis XVII reigned at the 9th Thermidor, and that Louis XVIII was reigning at the day of Marengo? Never, since the origin of history, have princes been so blind in the presence of history, and that portion of the divine authority which facts contain and promulgate. Never had the nether claim which is called the right of kings, denied to such a pitch the supreme right. It was a capital error that led this family to lay their hand again on the "granted" guarantees in 1814, or on the concessions as they entitled them. It is a sad thing that what they called their concessions were our conquests, and what they called our encroachments were our rights. When the hour appeared to have arrived, the Restoration, supposing itself victorious over Bonaparte, and rooted in the country, that is to say, believing itself strong and profound, suddenly made up its mind, and risked its stake. One morning it rose in the face of France, and, raising its voice, contested the collective title and the individual title, the sovereignty of the nation and the liberty of the citizen. In other terms, it denied the nation what made it a nation, and the citizen what made him a citizen. This is the substratum of those famous decrees which are called the "Ordonnances" of July. The Restoration fell, and fell justly. Still, let us add, it was not absolutely hostile to all the forms of progress, and grand things were accomplished, while it stood aloof. During the Restoration the nation had grown accustomed to calm discussion, which the republic had been deficient in, and to grandeur in peace, which was not known under the empire. France, strong and free, had been an encouraging example for the other nations of Europe. Under Robespierre the revolution ruled; under Bonaparte cannon; while in the reigns of Louis XVIII and Charles X the turn arrived for intellect to speak. The wind ceased, and the torch was re-illumined, while a pure mental light played around the serene crests. It was a magnificent, useful, and delightful spectacle; and for fifteen years those great principles, which are so old for the thinker, so new for the statesman,—equality before the law, liberty of conscience, freedom of the press and speech, and the accessibility of all fitting men to office,— could be seen at work in a reign of peace, and publicly. Things went on

5

thus till 1830, and the Bourbons were an instrument of civilization which broke in the hands of Providence.

The. fall of the Bourbons was full of grandeur, not on their side, but on that of the nation. They left the throne with gravity, but without authority; their descent into night was not one of those solemn disappearances which impart a somber emotion to history; it was neither the spectral calmness of Charles I nor the eagle cry of Napoleon. They went away, that was all. They laid down the crown and did not retain the glory, and though they were dignified, they were not august, and they were to a certain extent false to the majesty of their misfortune. Charles X, having a round table cut square during the Cherbourg voyage, seemed more anxious about the imperiled etiquette than the crumbling monarchy. This pettiness saddened the devoted men who were attached to the Bourbons personally, and the serious men who honored their race. The people behaved admirably, however, and the nation, attacked one morning by a species of royalist insurrection, felt themselves so strong that they displayed no anger. They defended themselves, restrained themselves, and restored things to their place; the government in the law, the Bourbons in exile, alas! and stopped there. They took the old King Charles X off the daïs which had sheltered Louis XIV, and gently placed him on the ground. They touched the royal persons cautiously and sorrowfully. It was not one man, or a few men, but France, united France, France victorious and intoxicated by its victory, which appeared to remember, and which practiced in the eyes of the whole world, the serious remarks of Guillaume du Vair after the day of the barricades. "It is easy for those who have been accustomed to obtain the favors of the great, and leap like a bird from branch to branch, from a low to a flourishing fortune, to show themselves harsh against their prince in his misfortunes; but for my part the fortune of my kings will be ever venerable to me, and principally of those who are in affliction." The Bourbons bore away with them respect, but not regret; as we have said, their misfortune was greater than themselves, and they faded away on the horizon.

The revolution of July at once found friends and enemies in the whole world; the former rushed toward it enthusiastically and joyfully, while the latter turned away, each according to his nature. The princes of Europe, the owls of this dawn, at the first moment closed their eyes, which were hurt and stupefied, and only opened them again to menace— it is a terror easy to understand and a pardonable anger. This strange revolution had been scarce a shock, and had not even done conquered royalty the honor of treating it as an enemy and shedding its blood. In the sight of despotic governments, which always have an interest in liberty calumniating itself, the revolution of July had the fault of being formidable and remaining gentle. No attempt, moreover, was made or prepared against it. The most dissatisfied and irritated persons saluted it, for whatever their selfishness or rancor may be, men feel a mysterious respect issue from events in which they are sentient of the cooperation of some power that labors high above mankind. The revolution of July is the triumph of right overthrowing fact, and is a thing full of splendor. The right overthrowing the fact—hence came the brilliancy of the three days, and at the same time their mansuetude; for right that triumphs has no need to be violent. Right is justice and truth. It is the property of right to remain eternally beautiful and pure. Fact, even the most necessary in appearance and best accepted by contemporaries, if it only exist as fact and contain too little right, is no right at all, and is infallibly destined to become, with the duration of time, misshapen, foul, and perhaps even monstrous. If we wish to discover at one glance what a degree of ugliness fact can attain, when looked at through the distance of centuries, let us regard Machiavelli. He is not an evil genius, a demon, or a cowardly and servile writer; he is nothing but the fact, and not merely the Italian fact, but the European fact, the fact of the sixteenth century. He appears hideous, and is so, in the presence of the moral idea of the nineteenth century. This struggle between right and fact has endured since the origin of societies. It is the task of wise men to terminate the duel, amalgamate the pure idea with human reality, and to make right penetrate fact and fact right pacifically.

2. *BADLY STITCHED*

But the task of wise men differs greatly from that of clever men, and the revolution of 1830 quickly stopped, for when a revolution has run ashore, the clever men plunder the wreck. Clever men in our century have decreed themselves the title of statesmen, so that the phrase has eventually become a bit of slang. For it must not be forgotten that where there is only cleverness, littleness necessarily exists, and to say "the clever" is much like saying the "mediocres." In the same way the word statesman is often equivalent to saying "traitor." If we believe clever men, then revolutions like that of July are severed arteries, and a rapid ligature is required. Right, if too loudly proclaimed, begins to give way, and hence so soon as right is substantiated the state must be strengthened, and when liberty is injured attention must be turned to power. At this point wise men do not yet separate from clever men, but begin to suspect them. Power, very good! but, in the first place, what is power? and, secondly, whence does it come? The clever men do not appear to hear the muttered objection and continue their maneuvers. According to politicians who ingeniously place a mask of necessity upon profitable fiction, the first want of a people after revolution, if that people form part of a monarchical continent, is to obtain a dynasty. In this way they say peace is secured after the revolution; that is to say, the necessary time for repairing the house and dressing the wounds. A dynasty hides the scaffolding and covers the hospital. Now, it is not always easy to obtain a dynasty. Strictly speaking, the first man of genius or the first adventurer met with is sufficient to make a king. You have in the first case Bonaparte, and in the second Iturbide. But the first family come across is not sufficient to form a dynasty, for there is necessarily a certain amount of antiquity required as a race, and the wrinkle of centuries cannot be improvised.

If we place ourselves at the stand-point of statesmen, with all due reserves, of course, what are the qualities of a king who issues from a revolution? He may be, and it is useful that he should be, revolutionary; that is to say, have played a personal part in the revolution, have had a hand in it, have become either compromised or renowned in it, and have wielded the axe or drawn the sword. What are the qualities of a dynasty? it must be national; that is to say, remotely revolutionary, not through acts done, but through ideas accepted. It must be composed of the past and be historical, and of the future and be sympathetic. All this explains why the first revolutions are satisfied with finding a man, Napoleon or Cromwell, while the second are determined on finding a family, like the House of Brunswick or the House of Orléans. Royal houses resemble those Indian fig-trees, each branch of which bends down, becomes rooted in the ground, and grows into a fig-tree. Each branch of the family may become a dynasty, on the sole condition that it bends down to the people. Such is the theory of clever men.

This, then, is the great art; to give success the sound of a catastrophe, so that those who profit by it may also tremble at it; to season every step taken with fear, to increase the curve of the transition until progress is checked, to bedim the dawn, denounce and retrench the roughness of enthusiasm, to cut angles and nails, to swathe the triumph in wadding, to wrap up the right, roll the giant people in flannel and put it to bed at full speed, to place this excess of health under medical treatment, and regard Hercules as a convalescent, to dilute the event in expediency and offer to minds thirsting for the ideal this weak nectar, to take precautions against extreme success, and provide the revolution with a sun-shade. 1830 practiced this theory, which had already been applied to England by 1688. 1830 is a revolution arrested half-way, and a moiety of progress is almost right. Now, logic ignores this as absolutely as the sun ignores a rushlight. Who check revolutions half-way? The bourgeoisie. Why? Because the bourgeoisie represent satisfied self-interest. Yesterday appetite was felt, to-day fullness, and to-morrow satiety. The phenomenon of 1814, after Napoleon, was reproduced in 1830 after Charles X. Attempts have been made, though wrongly, to convert the bourgeoisie into a class, but they are merely the contented portion of the population. The bourgeois is a man who has at last time to sit down, and a chair is not a caste. But, through a desire to sit down too soon, the progress of the human race may be arrested, and this has frequently been the fault of the bourgeoisie, and people are not a class because they commit a fault, and selfishness is not one of the divisions of the social order. However, as we must be just even toward selfishness, the condition for which that portion of the nation called the bourgeoisie aspired after the shock of 1830 was not inactivity, which is complicated with indifference and sloth, and contains a little shame, nor was it sleep, which presupposes a momentary oblivion accessible to dreams, but it was a halt. This word contains a double, singular, and almost contradictory meaning, for it implies troops on the march, that is to say, movement, and a stopping-place, that is to say, rest. A halt is the restoration of strength, it is repose armed and awake, it is the accomplished fact posting its sentries and standing on guard. A halt presupposes a combat yesterday and a combat to-morrow. It is the interlude between 1830 and 1848.

What we here call combat may also be called progress. Hence the bourgeoisie as well as the statesmen required a man who expressed the idea of a halt, an "although-because," a composite individuality signifying revolution and stability; in other words, strengthening the present by the evident compatibility of the past with the future. This man was found "ready-made," and his name was Louis Philippe d'Orléans. The 221 made Louis Philippe king, and Lafayette undertook the coronation. He named him *the best of Republics,* and the Town Hall of Paris was substituted for the Cathedral of Rheims. This substitution of a half throne for a complete throne was "the work of 1830." When the clever men had completed their task, the immense fault of their solution was apparent; all this had been done beyond the pale of absolute right, which shouted, "I protest!" and then—formidable fact—fell back into its darkness.

3 . *LOUIS PHILIPPE*

REVOLUTIONS have a terrible arm and a lucky hand; they hit hard and choose well. Even when incomplete, bastardized, and reduced to the state of a younger revolution, like that of 1830, they nearly always retain sufficient providential light not to fall badly, and their eclipse is never an abdication. Still we must not boast too loudly, for revolutions themselves are mistaken, and grave errors have been witnessed ere now. Let us return to 1830, which was fortunate in its deviation. In the establishment which was called order after the revolution was cut short, the king was worth more than the royalty. Louis Philippe was a rare man.

Son of a father to whom history will certainly grant extenuating circumstances, but as worthy of esteem as his father was of blame; possessing all the private virtues and several of the public virtues, careful of his health, his fortune, his person, and his business affairs; knowing the value of a minute, but not always the value of a year; sober, serious, peaceful, and patient; a good man and a good prince; sleeping with his wife, and having in his palace lackeys whose business it was to show the conjugal couch to the cits—a regular ostentation which had grown useful after the old illegitimate displays of the elder branch; acquainted with all the languages of Europe, and, what is rarer still, with all the languages of all the interests, and speaking them; an admirable representative of the "middle class," but surpassing it, and in every way greater; possessing the excellent sense, while appreciating the blood from which he sprang, of claiming merit for his personal value, and very particular, even on the question of his race, declaring himself an Orléans and not a Bourbon; a thorough first prince of the blood, so long as he had only been most serene highness, but a frank bourgeois on the day when he became his majesty; diffuse in public, and concise in private life; branded as a miser, but not proved to be one; in reality, one of those saving men who are easily prodigal to satisfy their caprices or their duty; well read, and caring but little for literature; a gentleman, but not a cavalier; simple, calm, and strong; adored by his family and his household; a seductive speaker, a statesman who had no illusions, cold in heart, swayed by the immediate interest, governing from hand to mouth; incapable of rancor and of gratitude; pitilessly employing superiorities upon mediocrities, and clever in confounding by parliamentary majorities those mysterious unanimities which growl hoarsely beneath thrones; expansive, at times imprudent in his expansiveness, but displaying marvelous skill in his imprudence; fertile in expedients, faces, and masks; terrifying France by Europe, and Europe by France; loving his country undeniably, but preferring his family; valuing domination more than authority, and authority more than dignity; a temperament which has this mournful feature about it, that, by turning everything to success, it admits of craft and does not absolutely repudiate baseness, but at the same time has this advantage, that it preserves politics from violent shocks, the state from fractures, and society from catastrophes; minute, correct, vigilant, attentive, sagacious, and indefatigable; contradicting himself at times, and belying himself; bold against Austria at Ancona, obstinate against England in Spain, bombarding Antwerp and paying Pritchard; singing the Marseillaise with conviction; inaccessible to despondency, to fatigue, to a taste for the beautiful and ideal, to rash generosity, to Utopias, chimeras, anger, vanity, and fear; possessing every form of personal bravery; a general at Valmy, a private at Jemmapes; eight times attacked by regicides, and constantly smiling; brave as a grenadier, and courageous as a thinker; merely anxious about the chances of an European convulsion, and unfitted for great political adventures; ever ready to risk his life, but not his work; making his will seem his influence for the sake of being obeyed rather as an intellect than as king; gifted with observation and not with divination; paying but slight attention to minds but with a thorough knowledge of men, that is to say, requiring to see ere he could judge; endowed with prompt and penetrating sense, practical sagacity, fluent tongue, a prodigious memory, incessantly drawing on that memory, his sole similitude with Cæsar, Alexander, and Napoleon; knowing facts, details, dates, and proper names, but ignorant of the various passions and tendencies of the crowd, the internal aspirations and concealed agitation of the minds—in one word, of all that may be called the invisible currents of consciences; accepted by the surface, but agreeing little with the lower strata of French society; getting out of scrapes by skill; governing too much and not reigning sufficiently; his own prime minister; excellent in the art of setting up the littleness of realities as an obstacle to the immensity of ideas; mingling with a true creative faculty of civilization, order, and organization, I do not know what petti-fogging temper and chicanery; the founder of a family and at the same time its man-of-law; having something of Charlemagne and something of an attorney in him; but, on the whole a lofty and original figure, a prince who managed to acquire power for himself in spite of the anxiety of France, and power for his country in spite of the jealousy of Europe—Louis Philippe will be ranked among the eminent men of his age, and would be classed among the most illustrious governors known in history, if he had loved glory a little, and had a feeling for what is grand to the same extent as he had a feeling for what is useful.

Louis Philippe had been handsome, and when aged, remained graceful; though not always admired by the nation, he was always so by the mob, for he had the art of pleasing and the gift of charm. He was deficient in majesty, and neither wore a crown though king, nor displayed white hair though an old man. His manners belonged to the ancient régime, and his habits to the new, a mixture of the noble and the citizen which suited 1830. Louis Philippe was transition on a throne, and retained the old pronunciation and orthography, which he placed at the service of modern opinions; he was fond of Poland and Hungary, but he wrote "les Polonois," and pronounced "les Hongrais." He wore the uniform of the National Guard like Charles X, and the ribbon of the Legion of Honor like Napoleon. He went but rarely to mass, not at all to the chase, and never to the opera; he was incorruptible by priests, whippers-in, and ballet girls, and this formed part of his citizen popularity. He had no court, and went out with an umbrella under his arm, and this umbrella for a long time formed part of his *nimbus*. He was a bit of a mason, a bit of a gardener, and a bit of a surgeon; he bled a postilion who had fallen from his horse, and no more thought of going out without his lancet than Henry III would without his dagger. The royalists ridiculed this absurd king, the first who shed blood to cure.

A deduction must be made in the charges which history brings against Louis Philippe: one accusing royalty, the second the reign, and the third the king; three different columns, each of which gives a different total.

Democratic right confiscated, progress made the second interest, the protests of the streets violently repressed, the military execution of insurrections, revolt made to run the gauntlet, the Rue Transnonain, the councils of war, the absorption of the real country in the legal country, and the "government at half price," with three hundred thousand privileged persons—are the deeds of royalty: Belgium refused, Algeria too harshly conquered with more of barbarity than civilization, like India by the English, the breach of faith to Abd-el-Kader, Blaye, Deutz bought and Pritchard paid, are chargeable to the reign—while the policy which cares more for the family than the nation belongs to the king. As we see, when the deductions have been made, the charge against the king is reduced; but his great fault was that he was modest in the name of France. Whence comes this fault?

Louis Philippe was a king who was too much a father, and this incubation of a family which is intended to produce a dynasty is frightened at everything and does not like to be disturbed. Hence arises excessive timidity, which is offensive to a nation which has July 14 in its civil traditions, and Austerlitz in its military annals. However, when we abstract public duties which should ever be first fulfilled, the family deserved Louis Philippe's profound tenderness for it. This domestic group was admirable, and combined virtue with talent. One of the daughters of Louis Philippe, Marie d'Orléans, placed the name of her race among artists as Charles d'Orléans had done among the poets, and she threw all her soul into a statue which she called Joan of Arc. Two of Louis Philippe's sons drew from Metternich this demagogic praise: "They are young men whose like can be found nowhere, and such princes as were never seen before." Here is the truth, without extenuating or setting down aught in malice, about Louis Philippe. It was his good fortune to be in 1830 the Prince Egalité, to bear within him the contradiction between the Restoration and the Revolution, and to possess that alarming side of the revolutionist which becomes re-assuring in the governor; and there was never a more complete adaptation of the man to the event, for one entered the other and the incarnation took place. Louis Philippe is 1830 made man, and he had also on his side that great title to a throne, exile. He had been proscribed, wandering, and poor, and had lived by his own labor. In Switzerland, this heir to the richest princely domains of France was obliged to sell a horse in order to eat; at Reichenau, he had given mathematical lessons while his sister Adelaide was embroidering and sewing. These souvenirs blended with a king rendered the bourgeoisie enthusiastic. With his own hands he had demolished the last iron cage at Mont St. Michel, erected by Louis XI, and employed by Louis XV. He was the companion of Dumouriez and the friend of Lafayette; he had belonged to the Jacobin club, and Mirabeau had tapped him on the shoulder, and Danton said to him, "Young man." At the age of twenty-four, in '93, when M. de Chartres, he had witnessed from an obscure gallery in the Convention the trial of Louis XVI, so well named *that poor tyrant*. The blind clairvoyance of the Revolution, breaking royalty in the king, and the king with royalty, while scarce noticing the man in the stern crushing out of the idea; the vast storm of the assembly who constituted the judges; public anger cross-examining; Capet not knowing what to answer; the frightful and stupefied vacillation of this royal head before the raging blast; the relative innocence of all mixed up in this catastrophe, of those who condemned as well as of him who was condemned—he, Louis Philippe, had looked at these things and contemplated this madness; he had seen centuries appear at the bar of the Convention; he had seen behind Louis XVI, that unfortunate and responsible victim, the real terrible culprit, monarchy, emerging from the darkness, and he retained in his mind a respectful dread of this immense justice of the people which is almost as impersonal as the justice of God. The traces which the Revolution left upon him were prodigious, and his memory was a living imprint of these great years, minute by minute. One day, in the presence of a witness whose statements we cannot doubt, he corrected from memory the entire letter A in the list of the Constituent Assembly.

Louis Philippe was an open-air king; during his reign the press was free, debates were free, conscience and speech were free. The laws of September were transparent. Though he knew the corrosive power of light upon privileges he left his throne exposed to the light, and history will give him credit for this honorable behavior. Louis Philippe, like all historic men who have quitted the stage, is at the present day being tried by the human conscience, but this trial has not yet gone through its first stage. The hour when history speaks with its venerable and free accent has not yet arrived for him; the moment has not yet come for the final judgment. Even the stern and illustrious historian Louis Blanc, has recently toned down his first verdict. Louis Philippe was elected by the two hundred and twenty-one deputies in 1830, that is to say, by a semi-parliament and a semi-revolution; and, in any case, we cannot judge him here philosophically, without making some reservations in the name of the absolute democratic principle. In the sight of the absolute, everything is usurpation which lies outside the rights of man first, and the rights of the people secondly; but what we are able to say at present is that, in whatever way we may regard him, Louis Philippe, taken by himself, and looked at from the stand-point of human goodness, will remain, to employ the old language of old history, one of the best princes that ever sat on a throne. What has he against him? this throne; take the king away from Louis Philippe and the man remains. This man is good, at times so good as to be admirable; often in the midst of the gravest cares, after a day's struggle against the whole diplomacy of the continent, he returned to his apartments at night, and then, though exhausted by fatigue and want of sleep,—what did he? He would take up a list of sentences, and spend the night in revising a criminal trial, considering that it was something to hold his own against Europe, but even greater to tear a culprit from the hands of the executioner. He obstinately resisted his keeper of the seals, and disputed the scaffold inch by inch with his attorney-generals, those *chatterers of the law,* as he called them. At times piles of sentences covered his table, and he examined them all, and felt an agony at the thought of abandoning these wretched condemned heads. One day he said to the witness whom we just now quoted: "I gained seven of them last night." During the earlier years of his reign the penalty of death was, as it were, abolished, and the reërection of the scaffold was a violence done to the king. As the Grève disappeared with the elder branch, a bourgeois Grève was established under the name of the Barrière St. Jacques, for "practical men" felt the necessity of a quasi-legitimate guillotine. This was one of the victories of the Casimir Périer, who represented the narrow side of the Bourgeoisie, over Louis Philippe, who represented the liberal side. The king annotated Beccaria with his own hand, and after the Fieschi machine he exclaimed: *What a pity that I was not wounded, for then I could have shown mercy.* Another time, alluding to the resistance offered by his ministers, he wrote with reference to a political culprit, who is one of the most illustrious men of the day: *His pardon is granted, and all that I have to do now is to obtain it.* Louis Philippe was as gentle as Louis IX, and as good as Henri IV. In our opinion any man deemed good by history, in which goodness is a rare pearl, is almost superior to one who was grand.

As Louis Philippe has been sternly judged by some, and perhaps harshly by others, it is very simple that a man, himself a phantom at the present day, who knew that king, should offer his testimony for him in the presence of history; this testimony, whatever its value may be, is evidently, and before all, disinterested. An epitaph written by a dead man is sincere. One shadow may console another shadow, for sharing the same darkness gives the right to praise, and there is no fear that it will ever be said of two tombs in exile, This one flattered the other.

4. *CRACKS IN THE FOUNDATION*

AT this moment, when the drama we are recounting is about to enter one of these tragic clouds which cover the beginning of the reign of Louis Philippe, it was quite necessary that this book should give an explanation about that king. Louis Philippe had entered upon the royal authority without violence or direct action on his part, through a revolutionary change of wind, which was evidently very distinct from the real object of the Revolution, but in which he, the Duc d'Orléans, had no personal initiative. He was born a prince, and believed himself elected a king; he had not given himself these functions, nor had he taken them; they were offered to him and he accepted, convinced, wrongly as we think, but still convinced, that the offer was in accordance with right, and acceptance in harmony with duty. Hence came honest possession, and we say in all conscience that, as Louis Philippe was honest in the possession, and democracy honest in its attack, the amount of terror disengaged from social struggles cannot be laid either on the king or the democracy. A collision of principles resembles a collision of elements; ocean defends the water and the hurricane the air; the king defends royalty, democracy defends the people; the relative, which is monarchy, resists the absolute, which is the republic; society bleeds from this conflict, but what is its suffering to-day will be its salvation at a later date; and, in any case, those who struggle must not be blamed, for one party must be mistaken. Right does not stand, like the Colossus of Rhodes, on two shores at once, with one foot in the republic, the other in royalty, but is indivisible, and entirely on one side; those who are mistaken are so in all sincerity, and a blind man is no more a culprit than a Vendean is a brigand. We must, therefore, only impute these formidable collisions to the fatality of things, and, whatever these tempests may be, human irresponsibility is mixed up with them.

Let us finish our statement! The government of 1830 had a hard life of it from the beginning, and born yesterday, it was obliged to combat to-day. Scarce installed, it felt everywhere the vague moments of faction beneath the foundation of July, which had so recently been laid, and was still anything but solid. Resistance sprang up on the morrow, and might, perhaps, have been born on the day before, and from month to month the hostility increased, and instead of being dull became patent. The Revolution of July, frowned upon by kings out of France, was diversely interpreted in France. God imparts to men His will visible in events, an obscure text written in a mysterious language. Men at once make themselves translations of it, hasty, incorrect translations, full of errors, gaps, and misunderstandings. Very few minds comprehend the divine language; the more sagacious, the calmer, and the more profound decipher slowly, and when they arrive with their version the work has been done long before; there are already twenty translations offered for sale. From each translation springs a party, and from each misunderstanding a failure, and each party believes that it has the only true text, and each faction believes that it possesses the light. Often power itself is a faction. There are in revolutions men who swim against the current,—they are the old parties. As revolutions issue from the right to revolt, the old parties that cling to heirdom by grace of God fancy that they have a right to revolt against them, but this is an error, for in revolutions the rebel is not the people but the king. Revolution is precisely the contrary of revolt; every revolution, being a normal accomplishment, contains its legitimacy within itself, which false revolutionists at times dishonor, but which endures even when sullied, and survives even when bleeding. Revolutions issue, not from an accident, but from a necessity, for they are a return from the factitious to the real, and they take place because they must take place.

The old legitimist parties did not the less assail the revolution of 1830 with all the violence which springs from false reasoning. Errors are excellent projectiles, and they skillfully struck it at the spot where it was vulnerable,—the flaw in its cuirass, its want of logic,—and they attacked this revolution in its royalty. They cried to it, "Revolution, why this king?" Factions are blind men who take good aim. This cry the revolutionists also raised, but coming from them it was logical. What was blindness in the legitimists was clear-sightedness in the democrats; 1830 had made the people bankrupt, and indignant democracy reproached it with the deed. The establishment of July struggled between these attacks, made by the past and the future; it represented the minute contending on one side with monarchical ages, on the other with eternal right. Then, again, 1830 being no longer a revolution, and becoming a monarchy, was obliged to take precedence of Europe, and it was a further difficulty to maintain peace, for a harmony desired against the grain is often more onerous than a war. From this sullen conflict, ever muzzled but ever growling, emerged armed peace, that ruinous expedient of civilization suspecting itself. The royalty of July reared in the team of European cabinets, although Metternich would have liked to put a kicking-strap upon it. Impelled by progress in France, it impelled in its turn the slowly moving European monarchies, and while towed, it towed too.

At home, however, pauperism, beggary, wages, education, the penal code, prostitution, the fate of woman, wealth, misery, production, consumption, division, exchange, money, capital, the rights of capital and the rights of labor,—all these questions were multiplied above society, and formed a crushing weight. Outside of political parties, properly so called, another movement became manifest, and a philosophic fermentation responded to the democratic fermentation, and chosen minds felt troubled like the crowd, differently, but quite as much. Thinking men meditated, while the soil, that is to say, the people, traversed by revolutionary currents, trembled beneath them with vague epileptic shocks. These thinkers, some isolated, but others assembled in families and almost in communities, stirred up social questions, peacefully but deeply; they were impassive miners, who quietly hollowed their galleries beneath volcanoes, scarce disturbed by the dull commotions and the fires of which they caught a glimpse. This tranquillity was not the least beautiful spectacle of this agitated epoch, and these men left to political parties the question of rights to trouble themselves about the question of happiness. What they wished to extract from society was the welfare of man; hence they elevated material questions, and questions about agriculture, trade, and commerce, almost to the dignity of a religion. In civilization, such as it has been constituted a little by God and a great deal by man, instincts are combined, aggregated, and amalgamated so as to form a real hard rock, by virtue of a law of dynamics which is carefully studied by social economists, those geologists of politics. These men, who grouped themselves under different appellations, but who may all be designated by the generic title of socialists, tried to pierce this rock and cause the living waters of human felicity to gush forth. Their labors embraced all questions, from that of the scaffold to that of war, and they added to the rights of man, proclaimed by the French revolutions, the rights of the woman and the child.

For various reasons we cannot thoroughly discuss here, from the theoretical point of view, the questions raised by socialism, and we limit ourselves to an indication of them. All the questions which the socialists proposed—laying aside cosmogonic visions, reverie, and mysticism—may be carried back to two original problems. The first problem to produce wealth; the second to distribute it. The first problem contains the question of labor, the second the question of wages; in the first the point is the employment of strength, and in the second the distribution of enjoyments. From a good employment of strength results public power, and from a good distribution of enjoyments individual happiness. By good distribution we mean not equal, but equitable distribution, for the first equality is equity. From these two things combined, public power abroad and individual happiness at home, results social prosperity; that is to say man happy, the citizen free, and the nation great.

England solves the first of these two problems,—she creates wealth admirably, but distributes it badly. This solution, which is completely on one side, fatally leads her to these two extremes, monstrous opulence and monstrous misery; all the enjoyments belong to the few, all the privations to the rest, that is to say, to the people, and privileges, exceptions, monopoly, and feudalism spring up from labor itself. It is a false and dangerous situation to base public power on private want, and to root the grandeur of the state in the sufferings of the individual; it is a badly composed grandeur in which all the material elements are combined, in which no moral element enters. Communism and the agrarian law fancy that they solve the second question, but they are mistaken. Their distribution kills production, and equal division destroys emulation, and consequently labor. It is a distribution made by the butcher who slaughters what he divides. Hence it is impossible to be satisfied with these pretended solutions, for killing riches is not distributing them. The two problems must be solved together in order to be properly solved; the two solutions demand to be combined and only form one. If you solve but the first of these problems, you will be Venice, you will be England, you will have, like Venice, an artificial power, like England, a material power, and you will be the wicked rich man; you will perish by violence, as Venice died, or by bankruptcy, as England will fall; and the world will leave you to die and fall, because it allows everything to die and fall which is solely selfishness, and everything which does not represent a virtue or an idea to the human race. Of course it will be understood that by the words Venice and England we do not mean the peoples, but the social constructions, the oligarchies that weigh down the nations, but not the nations themselves. Nations ever have our respect and sympathy. Venice, as a people, will live again; England, as the aristocracy, will fall, but England the nation is immortal. Having said this, let us proceed.

Solve the two problems, encourage the rich and protect the poor, suppress misery, put an end to the unjust exhaustion of the weak by the strong, bridle the iniquitous jealousy which the man still on the road feels for him who has reached the journey's end; adjust mathematically and fraternally the wage to the labor, blend gratuitous and enforced education with the growth of childhood, and render science the basis of manhood; develop intelligence while occupying the arms, be at once a powerful people and a family of happy men; democratize property, not by abolishing, but by universalizing it, so that every citizen, without exception, may be a land-owner, an easier task than it may be supposed; in two words, know how to produce wealth and to distribute it, and you will possess at once material greatness and moral greatness, and be worthy to call yourself France. Such was what socialism, above and beyond a few mistaken sects, said; this is what it sought in facts and stirred up in minds. They were admirable efforts and sacred attempts!

These doctrines, theories, and resistances, the unexpected necessity for the statesman of settling with the philosophers; glimpses caught of confused visions, a new policy to create, agreeing with the Old World, while not disagreeing too greatly from the revolutionary ideal; a situation in which Lafayette must be used to oppose Polignac, the intuition of progress apparent behind the riot, the chambers, and the street, the king's faith in the Revolution, the rivalries around him to be balanced, possibly some eventual resignation sprung from the vague acceptance of a definite and superior right; his wish to remain one of his race, his family affections, his sincere respect for the people, and his own honesty—all these painfully affected Louis Philippe, and at times, though he was so strong and courageous, crushed him beneath the difficulty of being a king. He felt beneath his feet a formidable disintegration which however, was not a crumbling to dust, as France was more France than ever. Dark storm-clouds were collected on the horizon; a strange, gradually-increasing shadow was extended over men, things, and ideas; it was a shadow that sprang from anger and systems. Everything that had been hastily suppressed stirred and fermented, and at times the conscience of the honest man held its breath, as there was such an uneasy feeling produced by this atmosphere, in which sophisms were mixed with truths. Minds trembled in the social anxiety, like leaves on the approach of a storm, the electric tension was such that at some moments the first-comer, a stranger, would produce a flash, then the twilight obscurity fell over the whole scene again. At intervals, deep and muttered rolling allowed one to judge what amount of lightning the cloud must contain.

Twenty months had scarce elapsed since the Revolution of July, and the year 1832 opened, with an imminent and menacing appearance. The distress of the people, workmen without bread; the Prince of Condé suddenly departed from the world; Brussels expelling the Nassaus, as Paris had done the Bourbons; Belgium offering itself to a French prince and given to an English prince; the Russian hatred of Nicholas; behind us two demons of the south—Ferdinand in Spain and Miguel in Portugal; the earth trembling in Italy; Metternich stretching out his hand over Bologna; France confronting Austria at Ancona; in the north the sinister sound of a hammer, inclosing Poland again in its coffin; throughout Europe angry eyes watching France; England, a suspicious ally, prepared to push any one who staggered, and to throw herself on him who fell; the peerage taking refuge behind Beccaria to refuse four heads to the law; the fleurs-de-lis erased from the king's coaches; the cross dragged from Notre Dame; Lafayette enfeebled, Lafitte ruined; Benjamin Constant dead in poverty; Casimir Périer dead in the exhaustion of power; a political and a social disease declaring themselves simultaneously in the two capitals of the kingdom; one the city of thought, the other the city of toil; in Paris a civil war, in Lyons a servile war; and in both cities the same furnace-glow, a volcanic purple on the brow of the people; the south fanaticized, the west troubled, the Duchesse de Berry in the Vendée; plots, conspiracies, insurrections, and cholera added to the gloomy rumor of ideas the gloomy tumult of events.

5. *FACTS FROM WHICH HISTORY SPRINGS, BUT WHICH HISTORY IGNORES*

TOWARD the end of April matters became aggravated, and the fermentation assumed the proportions of an ebullition. Since 1830 there had been small partial revolts, quickly suppressed, but breaking out again, which were the sign of a vast subjacent conflagration, and of something terrible smoldering. A glimpse could be caught of the lineaments of a possible revolution, though it was still indistinct and badly lighted. France was looking at Paris, and Paris at the Faubourg St. Antoine. The Faubourg St. Antoine, slowly heated, had reached the boiling-point. The wine-shops in the Rue de Charonne were grave and stormy, though the conjunction of these two epithets applied to wine-shops appears singular. The government was purely and simply put upon its trial there; and men publicly discussed whether *they should fight or remain quiet.* There were back rooms in which workmen swore to go into the streets at the first cry of alarm, "and fight without counting their enemies." Once they had taken the pledge, a man seated in a corner of the wine-shop shouted in a sonorous voice, *You hear! You have sworn!* Sometimes they went to a private room on the upper-floor, where scenes almost resembling masonic ceremonies took place, and the novice took oaths, *in order to render a service to himself as well as to the fathers of families,*—such was the formula. In the tap-rooms, "subversive" pamphlets were read, and, as a secret report of the day says, *they spurned the government.* Remarks like the following could be heard, *I do not know the names of the chiefs; we shall not know the day till two hours beforehand.* A workman said, *We are three hundred; let us each subscribe ten sous, and we shall have one hundred and fifty francs with which to manufacture bullets and gunpowder.* Another said, "I do not ask for six months, I do not ask for two. Within a fortnight we shall be face to face with the government, for it is possible to do so with twenty-five thousand men." Another said, *I do not go to bed at nights now, for I am making cartridges.* From time to time well-dressed men came, pretending to be embarrassed, and having an air of command, and shook hands with the *more important* and then went away, never staying longer than ten minutes, and significant remarks were exchanged in whispers, *The plot is ripe, the thing is ready;* to borrow the remarks of one of the audience, "this was buzzed by all present." The excitement was so great, that one day a workman said openly in a wine-shop, *But we have no weapons,* to which a comrade replied, *The soldiers have them,* unconsciously parodying Bonaparte's proclamation to the army of Italy. "When they had any very great secret," a report adds, "they did not communicate it there," though we do not understand what they could conceal after what they had said. The meetings were sometimes periodical; at certain ones there were never more than eight or ten members present, and they were always the same, but at others any one who liked went in, and the room was so crowded that they were obliged to stand; some went there through enthusiasm and passion, others *because it was the road to their work.* In the same way as during the Revolution, there were female patriots in these wine-shops, who kissed the new-comers.

Other expressive facts were collected. A man went into a wine-shop, drank, went away, saying *Wine-dealer, the Revolution will pay what is due.* Revolutionary agents were nominated at a wine-shop opposite the Rue de Charonne, and the ballot was made in caps. Workmen assembled at a fencing-master's who gave lessons in the Rue de Cotte. There was a trophy of arms, made of wooden sabers, canes, cudgels, and foils. One day the buttons were removed from the foils. A workman said, *We are five-and-twenty, but they do not reckon upon me, as they consider me a machine.* This man was at a later date Quénisset. Things that were premeditated gradually assumed a strange notoriety; a woman who was sweeping her door said to another woman, *They have been working hard at cartridges for a long time past.* In the open streets proclamations addressed to the National Guards of the departments were read aloud, and one of them was signed, *Burot, wine-dealer.*

One day a man with a large beard and an Italian accent leaped on a bench at the door of a dram-shop, in the Marché Lenoir, and began reading a singular document, which seemed to emanate from some occult power. Groups assembled round him and applauded, and the passages which most excited the mob were noted down at the time. "Our doctrines are impeded, our proclamations are torn down, our bill-stickers watched and cast into prison. . . . The fall in cottons has converted many middle-class men. . . . The future of the people is being worked out in our obscure ranks. . . . These are the terms laid down, action or reaction, revolution or counter-revolution, for in our age no one still believes in inertia or immobility. For the people, or against the people, that's the question, and there is no other. . . . On the day when we no longer please you, break us, but till then aid us to progress." All this took place in broad daylight. Other facts, of even a more audacious nature, appeared suspicious to the people, owing to their very audacity. On April 4, 1832, a passer-by leaped on the bench at the corner of the Rue Sainte Marguerite, and shouted, *I am a Babouviste,* but the people scented Gisquet under Babœuf. Among other things, this man said, "Down with property! the opposition of the Left is cowardly and treacherous; when they wish to gain their point they preach the Revolution; they are democratic that they may not be defeated, and royalist so that they need not fight. The republicans are feathered beasts; distrust the republicans, citizen-work-men!" "Silence, citizen-spy!" a workman shouted, and this put an end to the speech.

Mysterious events occurred. At nightfall a workman met a "well-dressed" man near the canal, who said to him, "Where art thou going, citizen?" "Sir," the workman answered, "I have not the honor of know-ing you." "I know thee, though"; and the man added, "Fear nothing, I am the agent of the committee, and it is suspected that thou art not to be trusted. But thou knowest that there is an eye upon thee if thou darest to reveal anything." Then he shook the workman's hand and went away saying, "We shall meet again soon." The police, who were listening, overheard singular dialogues, not only in the wine-shops, but in the streets. "Get yourself ready soon," said a weaver to a cabinet-maker. "Why so?" "There will be shots to fire." Two passers-by in rags exchanged the following peculiar remarks, which were big with an apparent Jacquerie: "Who governs us?" "It is Monsieur Philippe." "No, the bourgeoisie." It would be an error to suppose that we attach a bad sense to the word *Jacquerie;* the Jacques were the poor. Another time a man was heard saying to his companion: "We have a famous plan of attack." Only the following fragment was picked up at a private conversation between four men seated in a ditch, near the Barrière du Trône: "Everything possible will be done to prevent him walking about Paris any longer." Who is the *he?* there is a menacing obscurity about it. The "principal

25

chiefs," as they were called in the faubourg, kept aloof, but were supposed to assemble to arrange matters at a wine-shop near the Point St. Eustache. A man of the name of Aug—, chief of the society for the relief of tailors, was supposed to act as central intermediary between the chiefs and the Faubourg St. Antoine. Still, a considerable amount of obscurity hangs over these chiefs, and no fact could weaken the singular pride in the answer made at a later date, by a prisoner brought before the Court of Peers.

"Who was your chief?"

"I did not know any, or recognize any."

As yet they were but words, transparent but vague, at times mere rumors and hear-says, but other signs arrived ere long. A carpenter engaged in the Rue de Reuilly in nailing up a fence round a block of ground on which a house was being built, found on the ground a piece of a torn letter, on which the following lines were still legible: " . . . The committee must take measures to prevent recruiting in the sections for the different societies;" and as a postscript, "We have learned that there are guns at No. 5, Rue du Faubourg Poissonnière, to the number of five or six thousand, at a gun-maker's in the yard. The Section possesses no arms." What startled the carpenter, and induced him to show the thing to his neighbors, was that a few paces further on he found another paper, also torn, and even more significant, of which we reproduce the shape, owing to the historic interest of these strange documents.

Q	C	D	E	*Apprenez cette liste par cœur, après, vous la déchirerez: Les hommes admis en feront autant lorsque vous leur aurez transmis des ordres.*
				Salut et Fraternité
			u. og. a¹. fe.	*L*

Persons at that time in the secret of this discovery did not learn till a later date the meaning of the four capitals: *quinturions, centurions, décurions,* and *eclaireurs,* and the sense of the letters: *u. og. a¹. fe.,* which were a date, and indicated *this 15th April,* 1832. Under each capital letter were written names, followed by very characteristic remarks. Thus, Q

Bannerel, 8 guns, 83 cartridges. A safe man.—C *Boubière,* 1 pistol, 40 cartridges.—D *Rollet,* 1 foil, 1 pistol, 1 lb. gunpowder.—E *Tessin,* 1 saber, 1 cartridge-box. Punctual. *Tessier,* 8 guns, brave &c. Lastly, this carpenter found in the same inclosure a third paper on which was written in pencil, but very legibly, this enigmatical list:

Unité: Blanchard, Arbre sec. 6.

Barra. Sixteen. Salle au Comte.

Kosciusko, Aubrey, the butcher?

J. J. R.

Caius Gracchus.

Right of revision. Dufond. Four.

Downfall of the Girondists. Derbac. Maubuée.

Washington. Pinson, 1 pist., 86 cart.

Marseillaise.

Sover. of the people. Michel. Quincampoix. Saber.

Hoche.

Marceau, Plato. Arbre sec.

Warsaw, Tilly, crier, of the *Populaire.*

The honest citizen in whose hands this list remained learned its purport. It seemed that the list was the complete nomenclature of the sections of the fourth arrondissement of the Society of the Rights of Man, with the names and addresses of the chiefs of sections. At the present day, when these obscure facts have become historic, they may be published. We may add that the foundation of the Society of the Rights of Man seems to have been posterior to the date on which this paper was found, and so it was possibly only a sketch. After propositions and words and written information, material facts began to pierce through. In the Rue Popincourt, at the shop of a broker, seven pieces of paper, all folded alike, were found in a drawer; these papers contained twenty-six squares of the same gray paper, folded in the shape of cartridges, and a card on which was written:

Saltpeter	12	*oz.*
Sulphur	2	”
Charcoal	2½	”
Water	8	”

The report of the seizure showed that there was a strong smell of gunpowder in the drawer.

A mason returning home after his day's work left a small parcel on the bench near the bridge of Austerlitz; it was carried to the guard-house and opened, and from it were taken two printed dialogues signed *Lahautière,* a song called *Workmen, combine!* and a tin box full of cartridges. A workman drinking with his comrade bade him feel how hot he was; and the other noticed a pistol under his jacket. In the ditch on the boulevard between Père la Chaise and the Barrière du Trône, some children, playing at the most deserted spot, discovered under a heap of rubbish a bag containing a bullet-mold, a mandril for making cartridges, a pouch, in which there were some grains of gunpowder, and an iron ladle, on which were evident signs of melted lead. Some police agents, suddenly entering at five A. M. the room of one Pardon, who was at a later date a sectionist belonging to the Merry Barricade section, and killed in the insurrection of 1834, found him standing near his bed and holding in his hand some cartridges he was making. At the hour when workmen are generally resting, two men were noticed to meet between the Picpus and Charenton barrières, in a lane running between two walls. One took a pistol from under his blouse, which he handed to the other; as he gave it him he noticed that the perspiration on his chest had damped the gunpowder; he therefore filled the pan afresh, and the two men thereupon parted. A man by the name of Gallais, afterward killed in the April affair in the Rue Beaubourg, used to boast that he had at home seven hundred cartridges and twenty-four gun-flints. One day the government received information that arms and two hundred thousand cartridges had just been distributed in the faubourg, and the next week thirty thousand further cartridges were given out. The remarkable thing was that the police could not seize any of them. An intercepted letter stated: "The day is not far distant when eighty thousand patriots will be under arms in four hours."

All this fermentation was public, we might almost say calm, and the impending insurrection prepared its storm quietly in the face of the government. No singularity was lacking in this crisis, which was still subterranean, but already perceptible. The citizens spoke peacefully to the workmen of what was preparing. They said, "How is the revolt going on?" in the same tone as they could have said, "How is your wife?" A furniture broker in the Rue Moreau asked, "Well, when do you attack?" Another shop-keeper said, "They will attack soon; I know it. A month ago there were fifteen thousand of you, and now there are twenty-five thousand." He offered his gun, and a neighbor offered a pocket-pistol which was marked for sale at seven francs. The revolutionary fever spread, and no point of Paris or of France escaped it. The artery throbbed everywhere, and the network of secret societies began spreading over the country like the membranes which spring up from certain inflammations and are formed in the human body. From the Association of the Friends of the People, which was at the same time public and secret, sprang the Society of the Rights of Man, which thus dated one of its orders of the day, *Pluviôse, year 40 of the republican era,*—a society which was destined to even survive the decrees that suppressed it, and did not hesitate to give to its sections significant titles like the following:

Pikes. The tocsin. The alarm gun. The Phrygian cap. January 21. The beggars. The mendicants. March forward. Robespierre. The level. Ca ira.

The Society of the Rights of Man engendered the Society of Action, composed of impatient men who detached themselves and hurried forward. Other associations tried to recruit themselves in the great mother societies; and the sectionists complained of being tormented. Such were the *Gaulish Society* and the *Organizing Committee of the Municipalities;* such the associations for the *Liberty of the Press,* for *Individual Liberty,* for the *Instruction of the People,* and *Against Indirect Taxes.* Next we have the Society of Equalitarian workmen divided into three factions—the equalitarians, the communists, and the reformers. Then, again, the army of the Bastilles, a cohort possessing military organization, four men being commanded by a corporal, ten by a sergeant, twenty by a sublieutenant, and forty by a lieutenant; there were never more than five men who knew each other. This is a creation which is boldly combined, and seems to be marked with the genius of Venice. The central committee, which formed the head, had two arms—the Society of Action and the Army of the Bastilles. A legitimist association, the "Knights of Fidelity," agitated among these republican affiliations, but was denounced and repudiated. The Parisian societies ramified through the principal cities; Lyons, Nantes, Lille, had their Society of the Rights of Man, The Charbonnière, and the Free Men. Aix had a revolutionary society called the Cougourde. We have already mentioned that name.

At Paris the Faubourg Marceau buzzed no less than the Faubourg St. Antoine, and the schools were quite as excited as the faubourgs. A coffeeshop in the Rue Saint Hyacinthe, and the Estaminet des Sept Billiards in the Rue des Mathurins St. Jacques, served as the gathering-place for the students. The Society of the Friends of the A. B. C. affiliated with the

Mutualists of Angers, and the Cougourde of Aix assembled, as we have seen, at the Café Musain. The same young men met, as we have also said, at a wine-shop and eating-house near the Rue Montdétour, called Corinthe. These meetings were secret, but others were as public as possible, and we may judge of their boldness by this fragment from an examination that was held in one of the ulterior trials. "Where was the meeting held?" "In the Rue de la Paix." "At whose house?" "In the street." "What sections were there?" "Only one." "Which one?" "The Manuel section." "Who was the chief?" "Myself." "You are too young to have yourself formed this serious resolve of attacking the government. Whence came your instructions?" "From the central committee." The army was undermined at the same time as the population, as was proved at a later date by the movements of Belfort, Lunéville, and Epinal. Hopes were built on the 52d, 5th, 8th, and 37th regiments, and on the 20th light infantry. In Burgundy and the southern towns the *tree of liberty* was planted; that is to say, a mast surmounted by a red cap.

Such was the situation.

This situation was rendered more sensible and marked by the Faubourg St. Antoine, as we remarked at the commencement, than by any other group of the population. There was the stitch in the side. This old faubourg, people like an ant-heap, laborious, courageous, and passionate as a hive of bees, quivered in expectation and the desire of a commotion. All was agitation there, but labor was not suspended on that account. Nothing could give an idea of these sharp and somber faces, for there are in this faubourg crushing distress hidden under the roofs of houses, and also ardent and rare minds. In cases in which distress and intellect are mingled, it is extremely dangerous for extremes to meet. The Faubourg St. Antoine had other causes for excitement, as it received the counter-stroke of commercial crises, bankruptcies, stoppages, and cessation of work, which are inherent in all political convulsions. In revolutionary times misery is at once the cause and the effect, and the blow which it deals falls upon itself again. This population, full of haughty virtue, capable of the highest amount of latent caloric, ever ready to take up arms, prompt to explode, irritated, profound, and undermined, seemed to be only waiting for the fall of a spark. Whenever certain sparks float about the horizon, driven by the wind of events, we cannot help thinking of the Faubourg St. Antoine and the formidable chance which has placed at the gates of Paris this powder-magazine of sufferings and ideas.

The wine-shops of the *Faubourg Antoine,* which have been more than once referred to in this sketch, possess an historic notoriety. In times of trouble people grow intoxicated in them more on words than wine; and a species of prophetic spirit and an effluvium of the future circulates there, swelling hearts and ennobling minds. These wine-shops resemble the taverns on the Mons Aventinus, built over the Sibyl's cave and communicating with the sacred blasts of the depths below; taverns, in which the tables were almost tripods, and people drank what Ennius calls the Sibylline wine. The Faubourg St. Antoine is a reservoir of the people. The revolutionary earthquake makes fissures in it, through which the sovereignty of the people flows. This sovereignty can act badly, it deceives itself like other things, but even when led astray it remains grand. We may say of it, as of the blind Cyclops, *Ingens.* In '93, according as the idea that floated was good or bad, or according as it was the day of fanaticism or enthusiasm, savage legions or heroic bands issued from this faubourg. Savage,—let us explain that word. What did these bristling men want, who, in the genesis of the revolutionary chaos, rushed upon old overthrown Paris in rags, yelling and ferocious, with uplifted clubs and raised pikes? They wanted the end of oppression, the end of tyranny, the end of the sword, work for the man, instruction for the child, social gentleness for the woman, liberty, equality, fraternity, bread for all, the idea for all, the Edenization of the world, and progress; and this holy, good, and sweet thing called progress, they, driven to exasperation, claimed terribly with upraised weapons and curses. They were savages, we grant, but the savages of civilization. They proclaimed the right furiously, and wished to force the human race into Paradise, even were it through trembling and horror. They seemed barbarians, and were saviours; they demanded light while wearing the mask of night. With regard to these men who are stern and terrifying, but stern and terrifying for good, there are other men, smiling, embroidered, gilded, beribboned, in silk stockings, with white feathers, yellow gloves, and kid shoes, who, leaning upon a velvet-covered table near a marble chimney-piece, gently insist on the maintenance and preservation of the past, of the middle ages, of divine right, of fanaticism, of ignorance, of slavery, of the punishment of death, and of war, and who glorify in a low voice and with great politeness the saber, the pyre, and the scaffold. For our part, were we compelled to make a choice between the barbarians of civilization and the civilized of barbarians, we would choose the barbarians. But, thanks be to Heaven, another choice is possible; no fall down an abyss is required, either in front or behind, neither despotism nor terrorism. We wish for progress on a gentle incline. God provides for this, for reducing inclines is all the policy of God.

6. ENJOLRAS AND HIS LIEUTENANTS

SHORTLY after this period Enjolras made a sort of mysterious census, as if in the view of a possible event. All were assembled in council at the Café Musain. Enjolras spoke, mingling a few half-enigmatical but significant metaphors with his words.

"It behoves us to know where we are, and on whom we can count. If we want combatants we must make them; and there is no harm in having weapons to strike with. Passersby always run a greater chance of being gored when there are bulls in the road than when there are none. So, suppose we count the herd. How many are there of us? This task must not be deferred till tomorrow, for revolutionists must always be in a hurry, as progress has no time to lose. Let us distrust the unexpected, and not allow ourselves to be taken unawares; we have to go over all the seams which we have sewn, and see whether they hold, and the job must be done today. Courfeyrac, you will see the Polytechnic students, for this is their day for going out. Feuilly, you will see those of La Glacière, and Combeferre has promised to go to the Picpus. Bahorel will visit the Estrapade. Prouvaire, the masons are growing lukewarm, so you will obtain us news from the lodge in the Rue de Grenelle St. Honoré. Joly will go to Dupuytren's clinical lecture and feel the pulse of the medical scholars, while Bossuet will stroll round the court-house and talk with the law students. I take the Cougourde myself."

"That is all settled," said Courfeyrac.

"No. There is another very important matter."

"What is it?" Combeferre asked.

"The Barrière du Maine."

Enjolras was absorbed in thought for a moment, and then continued:
"At the Barrière du Maine are stone-cutters and painters, an enthusiastic body, but subject to chills. I do not know what has been the matter with them for some time past, but they are thinking of other things. They are dying out, and they spend their time in playing at dominoes. It is urgent to go and talk to them rather seriously, and they meet at Richefeu's, where they may be found between twelve and one o'clock. Those ashes must be blown up, and I had intended to intrust the task to that absent fellow Marius, who is all right, but no longer comes here. I need some one for the Barrière du Maine, and have no one left."

"Why, I am here," said Grantaire.

"What, you?"

"Yes, me."

"What! You indoctrinate republicans? you warm up chilled hearts in the name or principles?"

"Why not?"

"Can you possibly be fit for anything?"

"Well, I have a vague ambition to be so."

"You believe in nothing."

"I believe in you."

"Grantaire, will you do a service?"

"Any one; clean your boots."

"Well, do not interfere in our affairs, but sleep off your absinthe."

"You are an ungrateful fellow, Enjolras!"

"You the man capable of going to the Barrière du Maine!"

"I am capable of going down the Rue des Grès, crossing St. Michael's Square, cutting through the Rue Monsieur le Prince, taking the Rue de Vaugirard, passing the Carmelites, turning into the Rue d'Assas, arriving at the Rue Cherche Midi, leaving behind me the Council of War, stepping across the Rue des Vieilles-Tuileries, following the main road, going through the gate, and entering Richefeu's. I am capable of all that, and so are my shoes."

"Do you know the men at Richefeu's?"

"Not much."

"What will you say to them?"

"Talk to them about Robespierre, Danton, and principles."

"You!"

"I. You really do not do me justice, for when I make up my mind to it I am terrible. I have read Prudhomme, I know the social contract, and have by heart my constitution of the year II. 'The liberty of the citizen ends where the liberty of another citizen begins.' Do you take me for a brute? I have an old assignat in my drawer: The Rights of Man, the sovereignty of the people. Sapristi! I am a bit of a Herbertist myself. I can discourse splendid things for six hours at a stretch, watch in hand."

"Be serious," said Enjolras.

"I am stern," Grantaire answered.

Enjolras reflected for a few seconds, and then seemed to have made up his mind.

"Grantaire," he said gravely, "I consent to try you. You shall go to the Barrière du Maine."

Grantaire lived in a furnished room close to the Café Musain. He went away, and returned five minutes after—he had been home to put on a waistcoat of the Robespierre cut.

"Red," he said, on entering, and looked intently at Enjolras.

Then he energetically turned back on his chest the two scarlet points of the waistcoat, and walking up to Enjolras, whispered in his ear: "Never fear!" He boldly cocked his hat, and went out. A quarter of an hour after, the back room of the Café Musain was deserted, and all the friends of the A. B. C. were going in various directions about their business. Enjolras, who had reserved the Cougourde for himself, was the last to leave. The members of the Aix Cougourde who were in Paris assembled at that period on the plain of Issy, in one of the abandoned quarries so numerous on that side of Paris.

Enjolras, while walking toward the meeting-place, took a mental review of the situation. The gravity of the events was visible, for when the facts, which are the forerunners of latent social disease move heavily, the slightest complication checks and impedes their action. It is a phenomenon from which collapse and regeneration issue. Enjolras caught a glimpse of a luminous upheaving behind the dark clouds of the future. Who knew whether the moment might not be at hand when the people would seize their rights once again? What a splendid spectacle! the Revolution majestically taking possession of France once more, and saying to the world, "To be continued tomorrow!" Enjolras was satisfied, for the furnace was aglow, and he had at that self-same moment a gunpowder train of friends scattered over Paris. He mentally compared Combeferre's philosophic and penetrating eloquence, Feuilly's cosmopolitan enthusiasm, Courfeyrac's humor, Bahorel's laugh, Jean Prouvaire's melancholy, Joly's learning, and Bossuet's sarcasms, to a species of electrical flash, which produced fire, everywhere simultaneously. All were at work, and most certainly the result would respond to the effort. That was good, and it made him think of Grantaire. "Ah," he said to himself, "the Barrière du Maine is hardly at all out of my way, so suppose I go to Richefeu's, see what Grantaire is doing, and how far he has got."

It was striking one by the Vaugirard church when Enjolras reached Richefeu's. He pushed open the door, went in, folded his arms, and looked about the room, which was full of tables, men, and tobacco-smoke. A voice was audible in this fog, sharply interrupted by another voice; it was Grantaire talking with some opponent of his. Grantaire was seated opposite another man, at a marble table covered with sawdust and studded with dominoes. He smote the marble with his fist, and this is what Enjolras heard:

"Double-six."

"A four."

"The pig! I haven't any left."

"You are dead. A two."

"A six."

"A three."

"An ace."

"Me to play."

"Four points."

"Hardly."

"It is yours."

"I made an enormous mistake."

"You are getting on all right."

"Fifteen."

"Seven more."

"That makes me twenty-two (pensively), twenty-two!"

"You did not expect the double-six. Had I played it at first, it would have changed the whole game."

"Double-two."

"An ace."

"An ace! well, a five!"

"I haven't one."

"You played first, I believe?"

"Yes."

"A blank."

"What luck he has! Ah! you have a luck. (A long reverie.) A two."

"An ace."

"I've neither a five nor an ace. It is stupid for you."

"Domino!"

"Oh, the deuce!"

BOOK II

EPONINE

1. *THE LARK'S FIELD*

MARIUS witnessed the unexpected dénouement of the snare upon whose track he had placed Javert, but the inspector had scarce left the house, taking his prisoners with him in three hackney coaches, ere Marius stepped out of the house in his turn. It was only nine in the evening, and Marius went to call on Courfeyrac, who was no longer the imperturbable inhabitant of the Pays Latin. He had gone to live in the Rue de la Verrière, "for political reasons," and this district was one of those in which insurrectionists of the day were fond of installing themselves. Marius said to Courfeyrac: "I am going to sleep here," and Courfeyrac pulled off one of his two mattresses, laid it on the ground, and said: "There you are!" At seven o'clock the next morning, Marius returned to No. 50-52, paid his quarter's rent and what he owed to Mame Bougon, had his books, bed, table, chest of drawers, and two chairs placed on a truck, and went away, without leaving his address, so that when Javert returned in the morning to question Marius about the events of the previous evening, he only found Mame Bougon, who said to him: "Gone away." Mame Bougon was convinced that Marius was in some way an accomplice of the robbers arrested the previous evening. "Who would have thought it!" she exclaimed to the portresses of the quarter, "a young man whom you might have taken for a girl!"

Marius had two reasons for moving so promptly; the first was that he now felt a horror of this house in which he had seen so closely, and in all its most repulsive and ferocious development, a social ugliness more frightful still, perhaps, than the wicked rich man—the wicked poor man. The second was that he did not wish to figure at the trial, which would in all probability ensue, and be obliged to give evidence against Thénardier.

Javert believed that the young man, whose name he forgot, had been frightened and had run away, or else had not even returned home; he made some efforts however, to find him, which were unsuccessful. A month elapsed, then another. Marius was still living with Courfeyrac, and had learned from a young barrister, an habitual walker of the Salle des Pas Perdus, that Thénardier was in solitary confinement, and every Monday he left a five-franc piece for him at the wicket of La Force. Marius, having no money left, borrowed the five francs of Courfeyrac; it was the first time in his life that he borrowed money. These periodical five francs were a double enigma for Courfeyrac, who gave them, and for Thénardier, who received them. "Where can they go to?" Courfeyrac thought. "Where can they come from?" Thénardier asked himself.

Marius, however, was heart-broken, for everything had disappeared again under a trap-door. He saw nothing ahead of him, and his life was once more plunged into the mystery in which he had been groping. He had seen again momentarily and very closely the girl whom he loved, the old man who appeared her father, the strange beings who were his only interest and sole hope in this world, and at the moment when he fancied he should grasp them a breath had carried off all these shadows. Not a spark of certainty and truth had flashed even from that most terrific collision, and no conjecture was possible. He no longer knew the name of which he had felt so certain, and it certainly was not Ursule, and the Lark was a nickname; and then, what must he think of the old man? did he really hide himself from the police? The white-haired workman whom Marius had met in the vicinity of the Invalides reverted to his mind, and it now became probable that this workman and M. Leblanc were one and the same. He disguised himself, then, and this man had his heroic side and his equivocal side. Why did he not call for help? why did he fly? was he, yes or no, the father of the girl? and, lastly, was he really the man whom Thénardier fancied he recognized? Thénardier might have been mistaken. These were all so many insoluble problems. All this, it is true, in no way lessened the angelic charm of the maiden of the Luxembourg, and hence arose the poignant distress. Marius had a passion in his heart, and night over his eyes. He was impelled, he was attracted, and he could not stir; all had vanished, except love, and he had lost the sudden instincts and illuminations of even that love. Usually this flame which burns us enlightens us a little, and casts some useful light without, but Marius no longer even heard the dumb council of passion. He never said to himself, suppose I were to go there, or try this thing or the other? She whom he could no longer call Ursule was evidently somewhere, but nothing advised Marius in what direction he should seek her. All his life was now summed up in two words,—absolute uncertainty, in an impenetrable fog,—and though he still longed to see her, he no longer hoped it. As a climax, want returned, and he felt its icy breath close to him and behind him. In all these torments, and for a long time, he had discontinued his work, and nothing is more dangerous than discontinued work, for it is a habit which a man loses—a habit easy to give up, but difficult to re-acquire.

A certain amount of reverie is good, like a narcotic taken in discreet doses. It lulls to sleep the at times harsh fevers of the working brain, and produces in the mind a soft and fresh vapor which corrects the too sharp outlines of pure thought, fills up gaps and spaces here and there, and rounds the angles of ideas. But excess of reverie submerges and drowns, and woe to the mental workman who allows himself to fall entirely from thinking into reverie! he believes that he can easily rise again, and says that, after all, it is the same thing; but it is an error! Thought is the labor of the intellect, and reverie its voluptuousness; substituting reverie for thought is like confounding poison with nutriment. Marius, it will be remembered, began with that; passion arrived, and finished by hurling him into objectless and bottomless chimeras. In such a state a man only leaves his home to go and dream, and it is an indolent childishness, a tumultuous and stagnant gulf, and in proportion as work diminishes, necessities increase. This is a law; man in a dreamy state is naturally lavish and easily moved, and the relaxed mind can no longer endure the contracted life. There is, in this mode of existence, good mingled with evil, for if the softening be mournful, the generosity is healthy and good. But the poor, generous, and noble-minded man, who does not work, is ruined, the resources dry up, and necessity arises. This is a fatal incline, on which the most honest and the strongest men are dragged down like the weakest and the most vicious, and which leads to one of two holes,— suicide or crime. Through going out to dream, a day arrives when a man goes out to throw himself into the water. Excess of dreaminess produces such men as Escousse and Lebras. Marius went down this incline slowly, with his eyes fixed upon her whom he no longer saw. What we have just written seems strange, and yet it is true,—the recollection of an absent being is illumined in the gloom of the heart; the more it disappears the more radiant it appears, and the despairing and obscure soul sees this light on its horizon, the star of its inner night. She was Marius's entire thought; he dreamed of nothing else. He felt confusedly that his old coat was becoming an impossible coat, and that his new coat was growing an old coat, that his boots were wearing out, that his hat was wearing out, that his shirts were wearing out,—that is to say, that his life was wearing out; and he said to himself, Could I but see her again before I die!

One sole sweet idea was left him, and it was that She had loved him, that her glance had told him so, and that she did not know his name, but that she knew his soul, and that, however mysterious the spot might be where she now was, she loved him still. Might she not be dreaming of him as he was dreaming of her? At times in those inexplicable hours which every loving heart knows, as he had only reason to be sad, and yet felt within him a certain quivering of joy, he said to himself, "Her thoughts are visiting me," and then added, "Perhaps my thoughts also go to her." This illusion at which he shook his head a moment after, sometimes, however, contrived to cast rays which resembled hope into his soul at intervals. Now and then, especially at that evening hour which most saddens dreamers, he poured out upon virgin paper the pure, impersonal, and ideal reveries with which love filled his brain. He called this "writing to her." We must not suppose, however, that his reason was in disorder; quite the contrary. He had lost the faculty of working and going firmly toward a determined object, but he retained clear-sightedness and rectitude more fully than ever. Marius saw by a calm and real, though singular, light all that was taking place before him, even the most indifferent men and facts, and spoke correctly of everything with a sort of honest weariness and candid disinterestedness. His judgment, almost detached from hope, soared far above him. In this state of mind nothing escaped him, nothing deceived him, and he discovered at each moment the bases of life—humanity and destiny. Happy, even in agony, is the man to whom God has granted a soul worthy of love and misfortune! He who has not seen the things of this world and the heart of man in this double light, has seen nothing of the truth and knows nothing. The soul that loves and suffers is in a sublime state. Days succeeded each other, and nothing new occurred; it really seemed to him that the gloomy space which he still had to traverse was becoming daily reduced. He fancied that he could already see distinctly the brink of the bottomless abyss.

"What!" he repeated to himself, "shall I not see her again before that takes place?"

After going up the Rue St. Jacques, leaving the barrière on one side, and following for some distance the old inner boulevard, you reach the

Rue de la Santé, then the Glacière, and just before coming to the small stream of the Gobelins you notice a sort of field, the only spot on the long and monotonous belt of Parisian boulevards where Ruysdael would be tempted to sit down. I know not whence the picturesque aspect is obtained, for you merely see a green field crossed by ropes on which rags hang to dry; an old house built in the time of Louis XIII, with its high-pitched roof quaintly pierced with garret-windows; broken-down gratings; a little water between poplar-trees; women, laughter, and voices; on the horizon you see the Pantheon, the tree of the Deafmutes, the Val de Grâce, black, stunted, fantastic, amusing, and magnificent, and far in the back-ground the stern square towers of Notre Dame. As the place is not worth seeing, no one goes to it: scarce a cart or a wagon passes in a quarter of an hour. It once happened that Marius's solitary rambles led him to this field, and on that day there was a rarity on the boulevard, a passer-by. Marius, really struck by the almost savage grace of the field, asked him, "What is the name of this spot?"

The passer-by answered, "It is the Lark's field"; and added, "It was here that Ulbach killed the shepherdess of Ivry."

But, after the words "The Lark," Marius heard no more, for a word at times suffices to produce a congelation in a man's dreamy condition: the whole thought is condensed round an idea, and is no longer capable of any other perception. The Lark, that was the appellation which had taken the place of Ursule in the depths of Marius's melancholy. "Stay," he said, with that sort of unreasoning stupor peculiar to such mysterious asides, "this is her field; I shall learn where she lives." This was absurd but irresistible, and he came daily to this field of the Lark.

2. CRIMES IN EMBRYO, HATCHED IN PRISON

JAVERT's triumph at the Maison Gorbeau had seemed complete, but was not so. In the first place, and that was his chief anxiety, Javert had not been able to make a prisoner of the prisoner: the assassinated man who escapes is more suspicious than the assassin, and it was probable that this man who escaped, such a precious capture for the bandits, might be equally so for the authorities. Next, Montparnasse slipped out of Javert's clutches. He must wait for another opportunity to lay hands on "that cursed little fop." Montparnasse, in fact, having met Eponine on the boulevard keeping watch, went off with her, preferring to play the Nemorino with the daughter rather than Schinderhannes with the father, and it was lucky for him that he did so, as he was now free. As for Eponine, Javert "nailed" her, but it was a poor consolation, and sent her to join Azelma at the Madelonnettes. Lastly, in the drive from No. 50-52 to La Force, one of the chief men arrested, Claquesous, had disappeared; no one knew how he did it, and the sergeants and agents did not at all understand it. He had turned into vapor, slipped through the handcuffs, and passed through a crack in the coach; but no one could say anything, except that on reaching the prison there was no Claquesous. There was in this either enchantment or a police trick. Had Claquesous melted away in the darkness like a snow-flake in the water? was there an un-avowed connivance on the part of the agents? did this man belong to the double enigma of disorder and order? Had this Sphinx its front paws in crimes and its hind paws in the police? Javert did not accept these com-binations, and struggled against such compromises; but his squad con-tained other inspectors beside himself, and, though his subordinates, perhaps more thoroughly initiated in the secrets of the prefecture, and, Claquesous was such a villain that he might be a very excellent agent. To be on such intimate juggling relations with the night is capital for rogues and admirable for the police, and there are double-edged rogues of the sort. However this might be, Claquesous was lost and could not be found, and Javert seemed more irritated than surprised. As for Marius, "that scrub of a barrister who was probably frightened," and whose name he had forgotten, Javert did not trouble himself much about him, and, besides, a barrister can always be found. But, was he only a barrister?

The examination began. The magistrate thought it advisable not to put one of the members of the Patron-Minette in solitary confinement, as it was hoped he might chatter. This was Brujon, the hairy man of the Rue du Petit Banquier; he was turned into the Charlemagne Court, and the eyes of the spies were kept upon him. This name of Brujon is one of the recollections of La Force. In the hideous yard called the new building —which the government named the Court of St. Bernard, and the robbers christened the Lion's den—and on the wall covered with filth and leprosy that rose on the left to the height of the roof, and close to a rusty old iron gate which led to the old chapel of the Hotel de la Force, converted into a dormitory for prisoners, there might have been seen, twelve years ago, a species of Bastille, clumsily engraved with a nail in the stone, and beneath it this signature:

BRUJON, 1811

The Brujon of 1811 was the father of the Brujon of 1832. The latter, of whom we could only catch a glimpse in the garret, was a very crafty and artful young fellow, with a downcast and plaintive air. It was in consequence of this air that the magistrate turned him loose, believing him more useful in the Charlemagne yard than in a secret cell. Robbers do not interrupt their labors because they are in the hands of justice, and do not trouble themselves about such a trifle. Being in prison for one crime does not prevent another being commenced. There are artists who have a picture in the Exhibition, but for all that work at a new one in their studio. Brujon seemed stupefied by prison; he might be seen standing for hours in the yard near the canteen man's stall, gazing like an idiot at the duty list of prices, which began with *garlic, fifty-two centimes,* and ended with *cigar, five centimes.* Or else he passed his time in trembling, shaking his teeth, declaring he had the fever, and inquiring whether one of the twenty-six beds in the Infirmary were vacant.

All at once, toward the second half of February, 1832, it was discovered that Brujon, the sleepy-looking man, had had three messages delivered, not in his own name, but in those of his comrades, by the prison porters.

These messages had cost him fifty sous altogether, an exorbitant sum, which attracted the turnkey's attention. After making inquiries and consulting the tariff of messages hung up in the prisoners' visiting-room, this authority found out that the fifty sous were thus divided,—one message to the Pantheon, ten sous; one to Val de Grâce, fifteen sous; and one to the Barrière de Grenelle, twenty-five sous, the latter being the dearest in the whole list. Now at these very places resided these very dangerous prowlers at the barrière, Kruideniers alias Bizarro, Glorious, an ex-convict, and Stop-the-coach; and the attention of the police was directed to these through this incident. It was assumed that these men belonged to the Patron-Minette, of which band two chiefs, Babet and Gueulemer, were locked up. It was supposed that Brujon's messages, which were not delivered at the houses, but to persons waiting in the street, contained information about some meditated crime. The three ruffians were arrested, and the police believed they had scented some machination of Brujon's.

A week after these measures had been taken, a night watchman, who was inspecting the ground-floor sleeping-ward of the New Building was just placing his chestnut in the box,—this was the method employed to make sure that the turnkeys did their duty properly; every hour a chestnut must be dropped into all the boxes nailed on the doors of the sleeping-wards,—when he saw through the trap Brujon sitting up in bed and writing something. The turnkey went in, Brujon was placed in solitary confinement for a month, but what he had written could not be found. Hence the police were just as wise as before. One thing is certain that on the next day a "Postillion" was thrown from Charlemagne into the Lion's den over the five-storied building that separated the two yards. Prisoners gave the name of "postillion" to a ball of artistically molded bread, which is sent to "Ireland"; that is to say, thrown from one yard into another. This ball falls into the yard; the man who picks it up opens it and finds in it a note addressed to some prisoner in the yard. If it be a prisoner who finds the note he delivers it to the right address; if it be a turnkey, or one of those secretly bought prisoners, called "sheep" in prisons, and "foxes" at the galleys, the note is carried to the wicket and delivered to the police. This time the postillion reached its address, although the man for whom it was intended was at the time in a separate cell. This person was no other than Babet, one of the four heads of Patron-Minette. It contained a rolled-up paper, on which only two lines were written.

"Babet, there's a job to be done in the Rue Plumet, a gate opening on the garden."

It was what Brujon had written during the night. In spite of male and female searchers, Babet contrived to send the note from La Force to the Salpetrière to a "lady friend" of his locked up there. She in turn handed the note to a girl she knew of the name of Magnon, whom the police were actively watching, but had not yet arrested. This Magnon, of whose name the reader has already caught a glimpse, was closely connected with the Thénardiers, as we shall show presently, and by going to see Eponine was able to serve as a bridge between the Salpetrière and the Madelonnettes. At this very period Eponine and Azelma were discharged for want of evidence, and when Eponine went out, Magnon, who was watching for her at the gate of the Madelonnettes, handed her the note from Brujon to Babet, with instructions to look into the affair. Eponine went to the Rue Plumet, recognized the grating and the garden, observed the house, watched for some days, and then carried to Magnon a biscuit, which the latter sent to Babet's mistress at the Salpetrière. A biscuit, in the dark language of the prisons, means, "Nothing to be done."

In less than a week from this, Babet and Brujon happened to meet, as one was going before the magistrate, the other returning. "Well," Brujon asked, "the Rue P.?" "Biscuit," Babet answered. Thus the fœtus of crime engendered by Brujon at La Force became abortive. This abortion had consequences, for all that, perfectly strange to Brujon's plans, as will be seen. In fancying we are tying one thread, we often tie another.

3. *PÈRE MABOEUF SEES AN APPARITION*

MARIUS no longer called on any one, but at times he came across Father Mabœuf. While Marius was slowly descending the mournful steps which might be called the cellar stairs, and lead to places without light, on which you hear the footsteps of the prosperous above your head, M. Mabœuf was also descending. The *Flora of Cauteretz* did not sell at all now, and the indigo experiments had not been successful in the little garden of Austerlitz, which looked in a bad direction. M. Mabœuf could' only cultivate in it a few rare plants which are fond of moisture and shade. For all that, though, he was not discouraged: he had obtained a strip of ground at the Jardin des Plantes, with a good aspect, on which to carry on his experiments "at his own charge." To do this he pledged the plates of his *Flora,* and he reduced his breakfast to two eggs, of which he left one for his old servant, whose wages he had not paid for fifteen months past. And very frequently his breakfast was his sole meal. He no longer laughed with his childish laugh, he had grown morose and declined to receive visitors, and Marius did well not to call on him. At times, at the hour when M. Mabœuf proceeded to the Jardin des Plantes, the old man and the young man passed each other on the Boulevard de l'Hôpital; they did not speak, and merely shook their heads sorrowfully. It is a sad thing that the moment arrives when misery parts friends!

Royol the publisher was dead, and now M. Mabœuf knew nothing but his books, his garden, and his indigo; these were the three shapes which happiness, pleasure, and hope had assumed for him. They were sufficient to live, and he would say to himself: "When I have made my blue-balls, I shall be rich; I will redeem my plates from the Mont de Piété, bring my *Flora* into fashion again with charlatanism, the big drum, and advertisements in the papers, and buy, I know where, a copy of Pierre de Medine's 'Art of Navigation,' with wood-cuts, edition 1539." In the meanwhile, he toiled all day at his indigo patch, and at night went home to water his garden and read his books. M. Mabœuf at this period was close on eighty years of age.

One evening he had a strange apparition. He had returned home while it was still daylight, and found that Mother Plutarch, whose health was not so good as it might be, had gone to bed. He dined upon a bone on which a little meat remained and a lump of bread which he had found on the kitchen-table, and was seàted on a stone post which acted as a bench in his garden. Near this bench there was, after the fashion of old kitchen-gardens, a sort of tall building of planks in a very rickety condition, a hutch on the ground-floor, and a store-room on the first-floor. There were no rabbits in the hutch, but there were a few apples, the remnant of the winter stock, in the store-room. M. Mabœuf was reading, with the help of his spectacles, two books in which he took great interest, and which, a grave matter at his age, preoccupied him. His natural timidity rendered him prone to accept superstitions. The first of these books was the celebrated treatise of President Delancre, "On the Inconstancy of Delusions," and the other was the quarto work of Mutor de la Rubaudière, "On the Demons of Vauvert and the Goblins of la Bièvre." The latter book interested him the more, because his garden had been in olden times one of the places haunted by the goblins. Twilight was beginning to whiten what is above and blacken what is below. While reading, M. Mabœuf looked over the book which he held in his hand at his plants, and among others at a magnificent rhododendron, which was one of his consolations. Four scorching days of wind and sun had passed without a drop of rain, the stems were bending, the buds drooping, the leaves falling, and they all required watering; this rhododendron especially looked in a very sad way. M. Mabœuf was one of those men for whom plants have souls; he had been at work all day in his indigo patch, and was worn out with fatigue, but for all that he rose, laid his books on the bench, and walked in a bent posture and with tottering steps up to the well. But when he seized the chain he had not sufficient strength to unhook it; he then turned and took a glance of agony at the sky, which was glittering with stars. The evening had that serenity which crushes human sorrow under a lugubrious and eternal joy. The night promised to be as dry as the day had been.

"Stars everywhere!" the old man thought, "not the smallest cloud! not a drop of water!"

And his head, which had been raised a moment before fell again on his chest; then he looked once more at the sky, murmuring:

"A little dew! a little pity!"

He tried once again to unhook the well-chain, but could not succeed; at this moment he heard a voice saying:

"Father Mabœuf, shall I water the garden for you?" At the same time a sound like that of a wild beast breaking through was heard in the hedge, and he saw a tall thin girl emerge, who stood before him looking at him boldly. She looked less like a human being than some form engendered of the darkness. Ere Father Mabœuf, who easily took alarm, and who, as we said, was a trifle terrified, found time to answer a syllable, this creature, whose movements had in the gloom a sort of strange suddenness, had unhooked the chain, let down and drawn up the bucket, and filled the watering-pot; and the old gentleman saw this apparition,

THE IDYLL OF THE RUE PLUMET

which was barefooted and wore a ragged skirt, running along the flower-beds and distributing life around her. The sound of the water pattering on the leaves filled M. Mabœuf's soul with a ràvishment, and the rhododendron now seemed to him to be happy. The first bucket emptied, the girl drew a second, then a third, and watered the whole garden. To see her moving thus along the walks in which her outline appeared quite black, and waving on her long thin arms her ragged shawl, she bore a striking resemblance to a bat.

When she had finished, Father Mabœuf went up to her with tears in his eyes, and laid his hand on her forehead.

"God will bless you," he said; "you are an angel, since you take care of flowers."

"No," she replied, "I am the devil; but I don't care."

The old man continued, without waiting for or hearing the reply:

"What a pity that I am so unhappy and so poor, and can do nothing for you!"

"You can do something," she said.

"What is it?"

"Tell me where M. Marius lives."

The old man did not understand.

"What Monsieur Marius?"

He raised his glassy eyes and seemed seeking something which had vanished.

"A young man who used to come here."

"Ah, yes," he exclaimed, "I know whom you mean. Wait a minute? Monsieur Marius, Baron Pontmercy, pardieu! lives, or rather he does not live—well, I do not know."

While speaking, he had stooped to straighten a rhododendron branch, and continued:

"Ah, yes, I remember now. He passes very frequently along the boulevard, and goes in the direction of the Lark's field in the Rue Croule Barbe. Look for him there; he will not be difficult to find."

When M. Mabœuf raised his head again, he was alone, and the girl had disappeared. He was decidedly a little frightened.

"Really," he thought, "if my garden were not watered, I should fancy that it was a ghost."

An hour after, when he was in bed, this idea returned to him, and while falling asleep he said to himself confusedly at the disturbed moment when thought gradually assumes the form of dream in order to pass through sleep, like the fabulous bird which metamorphoses itself into a fish to cross the sea: "Really, now, this affair greatly resembles what la Rubaudière records about the goblins. Could it have been a ghost?"

4. *MARIUS SEES AN APPARITION*

A FEW days after this visit of a ghost to Father Mabœuf,—it was on a Monday, the day of the five-franc piece which Marius borrowed of Courfeyrac for Thénardier,—Marius placed the coin in his pocket, and before carrying it to the prison resolved to "take a little walk," hoping that on his return this would make him work. It was, however, everlastingly so. As soon as he rose, he sat down before a book and paper to set about some translation, and his job at this time was the translation into French of a celebrated German quarrel, the controversy between Gans and Savigny. He took up Gans, he took up Savigny, read four pages, tried to write one but could not, saw a star between his paper and himself, and got up from his chair, saying, "I will go out; that will put me in the humor," and he proceeded to the Lark's field, where he saw the star more than ever, and Gans and Savigny less. He went home, tried to resume his task, and did not succeed; he could not join a single one of the threads broken in his brain, and so said to himself, "I will not go out to-morrow, for it prevents me from working." But he went out every day.

He lived in the Lark's field more than at Courfeyrac's lodging, and his right address was Boulevard de la Santé at the seventh tree past the Rue Croule Barbe. On this morning he had left the seventh tree and was seated on the parapet of the bridge over the little stream. The merry sunbeams were flashing through the expanded and luminous leaves. He thought of "her," and his reverie, becoming a reproach, fell back on himself; he thought bitterly of the indolence and mental paralysis which were gaining on him, and of the night which constantly grew denser before him, so that he could no longer even see the sun. Still, through this painful disentangling of indistinct ideas which was not even a soliloquy, so weak action was in him, that he had no longer the strength to try and feel sad; through this melancholy absorption, we say, sensations from without reached him. He heard behind, below, and on both sides of him, the washer-women of the Gobelins beating their linen, and above him the birds twittering and singing in the elms,—on one side the sound of liberty, happy carelessness, and winged leisure; on the other the sound of labor. Two joyous sounds made him think deeply and almost reflect. All at once he heard amid his poignant ecstasy a familiar voice saying:

"Ah! here he is!"

He raised his eyes and recognized the unhappy girl who had come to him one morning, Eponine, the elder of Thénardier's daughters; he now knew what her name was. Strange to say, she had grown poorer and more beautiful, two things which he had not thought possible. She had accomplished a double progress, toward light and toward distress. Her feet were bare and her clothes torn, as on the day when she so boldly entered his room, but the rags were two months older and the holes larger. She had the same hoarse voice, the same forehead wrinkled and bronzed by exposure, the same free, absent, and wandering look, but she had, in addition, on her countenance, something startled and lamentable, which the passing through prison adds to misery. She had pieces of straw and hay in her hair, not that, like Ophelia, she had gone mad through contagion with Hamlet's lunacy, but because she had slept in some stable-loft. With all that she was beautiful. O youth, what a star art thou! She had stopped in front of Marius with a little joy on her livid face, and something like a smile, and it was some moments ere she could speak.

"I have found you!" she said at last. "Father Mabœuf was right, it was in this boulevard! How I have sought you! If you only knew! Do you know that I have been in quod for a fortnight! They let me go, as there was no charge against me; and, besides, I had not attained years of discretion by two months. Oh, how I have looked for you the last six weeks! So you no longer live down there?"

"No," said Marius.

"Ah, I understand, on account of that thing; well, such disturbances are unpleasant, and you moved. Hilloh, why do you wear an old hat like that? a young man like you ought to be handsomely dressed. Do you know, Monsieur Marius, that M. Mabœuf calls you Baron Marius—I forget what; but you are not a baron, are you? Barons are old swells, who walk in front of the Luxembourg palace, where there is the most sun, and read the *Quotidienne* for a sou. I went once with a letter for a baron who was like that, and more than a hundred years of age. Tell me, where do you live now?"

Marius did not answer.

"Ah," she added, "you have a hole in your shirt-front; I must mend it for you."

Then she continued, with an expression which gradually grew gloomier:

"You do not seem pleased to see me?"

Marius held his tongue. She was also silent for a moment, and then exclaimed:

"If I liked, I could compel you to look pleased."

"What do you mean?" Marius asked.

She bit her lip, and apparently hesitated, as if suffering from some internal struggle. At length she seemed to make up her mind.

"All the worse, but no matter, you look sad, and I wish you to be pleased; only promise me, though, that you will laugh, for I want to see you laugh and hear you say: 'Ah! that is famous!' Poor M. Marius! you know you promised you would give me all I wanted."

"Yes, but speak, can't you?"

She looked at M. Marius intensely and said, "I have the address."

Marius turned pale, and all his blood flowed to his heart. "What address?"

"The address which you asked me for." She added, as if with a great effort, "The address—you know?"

"Yes," Marius stammered.

"The young lady's."

These words uttered, she heaved a deep sigh. Marius leaped from the parapet on which he was sitting and wildly seized her hand.

"Oh! lead me to it! tell me! ask of me what you please! where is it?"

"Come with me," she answered; "I don't exactly know the street or the number, and it is quite on the other side of town, but I know the house well, and will take you to it."

She withdrew her hand, and continued in a tone which would have made an observer's heart bleed, but did not at all affect the intoxicated and transported lover:

"Oh, how pleased you are!"

A cloud passed over Marius's forehead, and he clutched Eponine's arm.

"Swear one thing."

"Swear?" she said, "what do you mean by that? what would you have me swear?"

And she burst into a laugh.

"Your father! promise me, Eponine, swear to me that you will never tell your father that address."

She turned to him with an air of stupefaction. "Eponine! how do you know that is my name?"

"Promise me what I ask you."

But she did not seem to hear him.

"That is nice! you called me Eponine!"

Marius seized both her arms.

"Answer me, in Heaven's name! pay attention to what I am saying; swear to me that you will not tell your father the address which you know."

"My father?" she remarked, "oh, yes, my father. He's all right in a secret cell. Besides, what do I care for my father!"

"But you have not promised!" Marius exclaimed.

"Let me go!" she said, as she burst into a laugh, "how you are shaking me! Yes, yes, I promise it, I swear it! how does it concern me? I will not tell my father the address. There, does that suit you, is that it?"

"And no one else?" said Marius.

"And no one else."

"Now," Marius continued, "lead me there."

"At once?"

"Yes."

"Come on! Oh, how glad he is!" she said.

A few yards further on she stopped.

"You are following me too closely, M. Marius; let me go on in front, and do you follow me as if you were not doing so. A respectable young man like you must not be seen with such a woman as I am."

No language could render all that was contained in the word "woman," thus pronounced by this child. She went a dozen paces and stopped again. Marius rejoined her, and she said to him aside without turning to him:

"By the bye, you know that you promised me something?"

Marius felt in his pocket; he had nothing in the world but the five-franc piece destined for Father Thénardier, but he laid the coin in Eponine's hand. She let it slip through her fingers on the ground, and, looking at him frowningly, said:

"I do not want your money."

BOOK III

THE HOUSE OF THE RUE PLUMET

1. THE MYSTERIOUS HOUSE

About the middle of the last century a president of the parliament of Paris who kept a mistress under the rose (for at that day the nobility displayed their mistresses and the bourgeois concealed theirs) had a "small house," built in the Faubourg St. Germain, in the deserted Rue de Blomet, which is now called Rue Plumet, and not far from the spot which was formerly known as the *Combat des Animaux*. This house consisted of a pavilion only one story in height, two sitting-rooms on the ground-floor, two bedrooms on the first, a kitchen below, a boudoir above, a garret beneath the roof, and the whole was surrounded by a large garden with railings looking out on the street. This was all that passers-by could see. But behind the pavilion was a narrow yard, with an outhouse containing two rooms, where a nurse and a child could be concealed if necessary. In the back of this outhouse was a secret door leading into a long, paved winding passage, open to the sky, and bordered by two lofty walls. This passage, concealed with prodigious art, and, as it were, lost between the garden walls, whose every turn and winding it followed, led to another secret door, which opened about a quarter of a mile off almost in another quarter, at the solitary end of the Rue de Babylone. The president went in by this door, so that even those who might have watched him, and observed that he mysteriously went somewhere every day, could not have suspected that going to the Rue de Babylone was going to the Rue Blomet. By clever purchases of ground, the ingenious magistrate had been enabled to make this hidden road upon his own land, and consequently uncontrolled. At a later date he sold the land bordering the passage in small lots for gardens, and the owners of these gardens on either side believed that they had a parting-wall before them, and did not even suspect the existence of this long strip of pavement winding between two walls among their flower-beds and orchards. The birds alone saw this curiosity, and it is probable that the linnets and the tomtits of the last century gossiped a good deal about the president.

The pavilion, built of stone, in the Mansard taste, and paneled and furnished in the Watteau style, rock-work outside, periwig within, and begirt by a triple hedge of flowers, had something discreet, coquettish, and solemn about it, befitting a caprice of love and the magistracy. This house and this passage, which have now disappeared, still existed fifteen years ago. In '93 a brazier bought the house for the purpose of demolishing it, but, as he could not pay, the nation made him bankrupt, and thus it was the house that demolished the brazier. Since then the house had remained uninhabited, and fell slowly into ruins, like every residence to which the presence of man no longer communicates life. The old furniture was left in it, and the ten or twelve persons who pass along the Rue Plumet were informed that it was for sale or lease by a yellow and illegible placard which had been fastened to the garden gate since 1810. Toward the end of the Restoration the same passers-by might have noticed that the bill had disappeared, and even that the second-floor shutters were open. The house was really occupied, and there were short curtains at the windows, a sign that there was a lady in the house. In October, 1829, a middle-aged man presented himself and took the house as it stood, including, of course, the outhouse and the passage leading to the Rue de Babylone, and he had the two secret doors of this passage put in repair. The house was still furnished much as the president had left it, so the new tenant merely ordered a few necessary articles, had the paving of the yard put to rights, new stairs put in, and the windows mended, and eventually installed himself there with a young girl and an old woman, without any disturbance, and rather like a man slipping in than one entering his own house. The neighbors, however, did not chatter, for the simple reason that he had none.

The tenant was in reality Jean Valjean, and the girl was Cosette. The domestic was a female of the name of Toussaint, whom Jean Valjean had saved from the hospital and wretchedness, and who was old, rustic and stammered, three qualities which determined Jean Valjean on taking her with him. He hired the house in the name of M. Fauchelevent, annuitant. In all we have recently recorded the reader will have doubtless recognized Jean Valjean even sooner than Thénardier did. Why had he left the convent of the Little Picpus, and what had occurred there? Nothing had occurred. It will be borne in mind that Jean Valjean was happy in the convent, so happy that his conscience at last became disturbed by it. He saw Cosette daily, he felt paternity springing up and being developed in him more and more; he set his whole soul on the girl; he said to himself that she was his, that no power on earth could rob him of her, that it would be so indefinitely, that she would certainly become a nun, as she was daily gently urged to it, that henceforth the convent was the world for him as for her, that he would grow old in it and she grow up, that she would grow old and he die there; and that, finally, no separation was possible. While reflecting on this, he began falling into perplexities; he asked himself if all this happiness were really his, if it were not composed of the happiness of this child, which he confiscated and deprived her of, and whether this were not a robbery? He said to himself that this child had the right to know life before renouncing it, that depriving her beforehand, and without consulting her, of all joys under the pretext of saving her from all trials, and profiting by her ignorance and isolation to make an artificial vocation spring up in her, was denaturalizing a human creature and being false to God. And who knew whether Cosette, some day meditating on this, and feeling herself a reluctant nun, might not grow to hate him? It was a last thought, almost selfish, and less heroic than the others, but it was insupportable to him. He resolved to leave the convent.

He resolved, and recognized with a breaking heart that he must do so. As for objections, there were none; for six years of residence between these walls, and of disappearance, had necessarily destroyed or dispersed the element of fear. He could return to human society at his ease, for he had grown old, and all had changed. Who would recognize him now? And then, looking at the worst, there was only danger for himself, and he had not the right to condemn Cosette to a cloister, for the reason that he had been condemned to the galleys; besides, what is danger in the presence of duty? Lastly, nothing prevented him from being prudent and taking precautions. As for Cosette's education, it was almost completed and terminated. Once the resolution was formed, he awaited the opportunity, which soon offered: old Fauchelevent died. Jean Valjean requested an audience of the reverend prioress, and told her that as he had inherited a small property by his brother's death, which would enable him to live without working, he was going to leave the convent and take his daughter with him; but as it was not fair that Cosette, who was not going to profess, should have been educated gratuitously, he implored the reverend prioress to allow him to offer the community, for the five years which Cosette had passed among them, the sum of five thousand francs. It was thus that Jean Valjean quitted the convent of the Perpetual Adoration.

On leaving it, he carried with his own hands, and would not intrust to any porter, the small valise, of which he always had the key about him. This valise perplexed Cosette, owing to the aromatic smell which issued from it. Let us say at once that this trunk never quitted him again; he always hid it in his bedroom, and it was the first, and at times the only, thing which he carried away in his removals. Cosette laughed, called this valise the inseparable, and said, "I am jealous of it." Jean Valjean, however, felt a profound anxiety when he returned to the outer air. He discovered the house in the Rue Plumet, and hid himself in it, henceforth remaining in possession of the name of Ultime Fauchelevent. At the same time he hired two other lodgings in Paris, so that he might attract less attention than if he had always remained in the same quarter; that he might, if necessary, absent himself for a while if anything alarmed him; and, lastly, that he might not be taken unawares, as on the night when he so miraculously escaped from Javert. These two lodgings were of a very mean appearance, and in two quarters very distinct from each other, one being in the Rue de l'Ouest, the other in the Rue de l'Homme-armé. He spent a few weeks now and then at one or the other of these lodgings, taking Cosette with him, and leaving Toussaint behind. He was waited on by the porters, and represented himself as a person living in the country, who had a lodging in town. This virtuous man had three domiciles in Paris in order to escape the police.

2. JEAN VALJEAN A NATIONAL GUARD

PROPERLY speaking, however, Jean Valjean's house was at the Rue
Plumet, and he had arranged his existence there in the following fashion.
Cosette and the servant occupied the pavilion; she had the best bedroom,
with the painted press, the boudoir with the gilt beading, the president's
drawing-room with its hangings and vast easy-chairs, and the garden.
Jean Valjean placed in Cosette's room a bed with a canopy of old damask
in three colors, and an old and handsome Persian carpet, purchased at
Mother Gaucher's in the Rue Figuier Saint Paul, while, to correct the
sternness of these old splendors, he added all the light gay furniture of
girls, an étagère, book-shelves with gilt books, a desk and blotting-case,
a work-table inlaid with mother-of-pearl, a silver dressing-case, and
toilet articles of Japanese china. Long damask curtains of three colors,
like those on the bed, festooned the second-floor windows, while on the
ground-floor they were of tapestry. All through the winter Cosette's
small house was warmed from top to bottom, while Valjean himself
lived in the sort of porter's lodge at the end of the back yard, which was
furnished with a mattress and common bedstead, a deal table, two straw-
bottomed chairs, an earthen-ware water-jug, a few books on a plank,
and his dear valise in a corner, but he never had any fire. He dined with
Cosette, and black bread was put on the table for him, and he had said
to Toussaint, when she came, "This young lady is mistress of the house."
"And you, sir?" Toussaint replied, quite stupefied. "Oh! I am much
better than the master,—I am the father."

Cosette had been taught housekeeping in the convent, and checked the
expenses, which were very small. Daily Jean Valjean took Cosette for a
walk, leading to the most sequestered allée of the Luxembourg, and

63

every Sunday they attended mass at the church of St. Jacques du Haut-pas, because it was a long distance off. As it is a very poor district, he gave away a considerable amount of alms, and the wretched flocked around him in the church, which caused Thénardier to head his letter to him in the way we have seen: *The benevolent gentleman of the church of St. Jacques du Haut-pas.* He was fond of taking Cosette to visit the indigent and the sick, but no stranger ever entered the house in the Rue Plumet. Toussaint bought the provisions, and Jean Valjean himself fetched the water from a fountain close by, on the boulevard. The wood and wine were kept in a semi-subterranean building covered with rock-work, near the door in the Rue Babylone, and which had formerly served the president as a grotto, for in the age of the Follies and Petites-Maisons, love was not possible without a grotto. In the door opening on the Rue Babylone there was a letter-box, but, as the inhabitants of the house in the Rue Plumet received no letters, this box, once on a time the go-between in amourettes, and the confidant of a love-sick lawyer, was now only of service to receive the tax-papers and the guard-summonses; for M. Fauchelevent, annuitant, belonged to the National Guard, and had been unable to escape the close meshes of the census of 1831. The municipal inquiries made at that period extended even to the convent of the Little Picpus, whence Jean Valjean emerged venerable in the sight of the mayor, and consequently worthy of mounting guard. Three or four times a year Jean Valjean donned his uniform and went on duty, and did so readily enough, for it was a disguise which enabled him to mix with everybody, while himself remaining solitary. Jean Valjean had attained his sixtieth year, or the age of legal exemption, but he did not look more than fifty; besides, he had no wish to escape his sergeant-major and cheat Count Lobau. He had no civil status, hid his name, his identity, his age, everything, and, as we just said, he was a willing National Guard; all his ambition was to resemble the first-comer who pays taxes. The ideal of this man was internally an angel, externally a bourgeois.

Let us mention one fact, by the way. When Jean Valjean went out with Cosette, he dressed himself in the way we have seen, and looked like a retired officer, but when he went out alone, and he did so usually at night, he was attired in a workman's jacket and trousers, and a cap whose peak was pulled over his eyes. Was this precaution or humility? Both at once. Cosette was accustomed to the enigmatical side of her destiny, and hardly noticed her father's singularities; as for Toussaint, she revered Jean Valjean, and considered everything he did right. One day her butcher, who got a glimpse of her master, said: "He's a queer-looking stick," and she replied, "He's a—a—a—saint." All three never left the house except by the gate in the Rue de Babylone; and unless they were noticed through the garden gate, it would be difficult to guess that they lived in the Rue Plumet. This gate was always locked, and Jean Valjean left the garden untended, that it might not be noticed. In this, perhaps, he deceived himself.

3. *FOLIIS AC FRONDIBUS*

THIS garden, left to itself for more than half a century, had become extraordinary and charming; passers-by forty years ago stopped in the street to gaze at it, without suspecting the secrets which it hid behind its fresh green screen. More than one dreamer at that day allowed his eyes and thoughts indiscreetly to penetrate the bars of the old locked, twisted, shaky gate, which hung from two mold-covered pillars and was quaintly surmounted by a pediment covered with undecipherable arabesques. There was a stone bank in a corner, there were one or two moldering statues, and some trellis-work, unnailed by time, was rotting against the walls; there was no turf or walk left, but there was dog-grass everywhere. The artificiality of gardening had departed, and nature had returned; weeds were abundant, and the festival of the gillyflowers was splendid there. Nothing in this garden impeded the sacred efforts of things toward life, and growth was at home there and held high holiday. The trees had bent down to the briars, the briars had mounted toward the trees; the plants had clambered up, the branches had bent down. What crawls on the ground had gone to meet what expands in the air, and what floats in the wind stooped down to what drags along the moss; brambles, branches, leaves, fibers, tufts, twigs, tendrils, and thorns were mixed together, tangled, wedded, and confounded; vegetation had celebrated and accomplished here, in a close and profound embrace, and beneath the satisfied eye of the Creator, the holy mystery of its fraternity, which is a symbol of human fraternity. This garden was no longer a garden, but a colossal thicket; that is to say, something which is as impenetrable as a forest, as populous as a city, as rustling as a nest, as dark as a cathedral, as fragrant as a bouquet, as solitary as a tomb, and as lively as a crowd.

In spring this enormous thicket, at liberty within its four walls, played its part in the dull task of universal germination, and quivered in the rising sun almost like the animal that exhales the effluvia of cosmic love and feels the sap of April ascending and boiling in its veins. Shaking in the wind its prodigious locks of verdure, the thicket scattered over the damp ground, the weather-beaten statues, the crumbling steps of the pavilion, and even over the pavement of the deserted street, constellations of flowers, pearls of dew, fecundity, beauty, life, joy, and perfumes. At midday thousands of white butterflies took refuge in it, and it was a divine sight to watch this living snow of summer falling in flakes through the shadows. In the pleasant gloom of the foliage a multitude of soft voices gently addressed the soul, and what the twittering forgot to say the buzzing completed. At night a dreamy vapor rose from the garden and enveloped it; a cerecloth of mist, a celestial and calm melancholy, covered it; the intoxicating smell of the honeysuckle and the bindweed ascended from all sides like an exquisite and subtle poison; the last appeals of the woodpeckers and the goldfinches could be heard ere they fell asleep under the branches, and the sacred intimacy between the bird and the trees was felt, for by day wings gladden the leaves, and at night the leaves protect the wings. In winter the thicket was black, dank, bristling, and shivering, and allowed a glimpse at the house to be taken. Instead of flowers among the stalks and dew upon the flowers, the long silvery trail of the snails could be seen on the cold, thick bed of yellow leaves; but in any case, under any aspect, and at all seasons, spring, summer, autumn, and winter, this little inclosure exhales melancholy contemplation, solitude, liberty, the absence of man and the presence of God, and the old rusty railings had an air of saying, "This garden is mine."

Although the pavement of Paris was all around, the classical and splendid mansions of the Rue de Varennes two yards off, the dome of the Invalides close by, and the Chamber of Deputies no great distance; although the carriages from the Rues de Bourgogne and St. Dominique rolled along luxuriously in the vicinity, and yellow, brown, white, and red omnibuses crossed the adjoining square, the Rue Plumet was a desert; and the death of the old proprietors, a revolution which had passed, the overthrow of old fortunes, absence, forgetfulness, and forty years of desertion and widowhood, had sufficed to bring back to this privileged spot ferns, torch-wheels, hemlock, ragwort, tall grass, large plants with wide leaves of pale green, lizards, beetles, and restless and rapid insects. A savage and stern grandeur had re-appeared between these four walls, and nature, who disconcerts all the paltry arrangements of man, and is as perfect in the ant as in the man, had displayed herself in a poor little Parisian garden with as much roughness and majesty as in a virgin forest of the New World. Nothing, in fact, is small, and any one who is affected by the profound penetrations of nature is aware of this fact. Although no absolute satisfaction is granted to philosophy, and though it can no more circumscribe the cause than limit the effect, the contemplator falls into unfathomable ecstasy when he watches all the decomposition of forces which result in unity. Everything labors for everything. Algebra is applied to the clouds, the irradiation of the planet benefits the rose, and no thinker would dare to say that the perfume of the hawthorn is useless to the constellations. Who can calculate the passage of a particle? who among us knows whether the creation of worlds is not determined by the fall of grains of sand? Who is acquainted with the reciprocal ebb and flow of the infinitely great and the infinitely little? A maggot is of importance, the little is great and the great little, all is in a state of equilibrium in nature, and this is a terrific vision for the mind. There are prodigious relations between beings and things, and in this inexhaustible total, from the flea to the sun, nothing despises the other, for all have need of each other. Light does not bear into the sky terrestrial perfumes without knowing what to do with them, and night distributes the planetary essence to the sleepy flowers. Every bird that flies has round its foot the thread of infinity; germination is equally displayed in the outburst of a meteor and the peck of the swallow breaking the egg, and it places the birth of a worm and the advent of Socrates in the same parallel; where the telescope ends, the microscope begins, and which of the two has the grandest sight? You can choose. A patch of green mold is a pleiad of flowers, and a nebula is an ant-hill of stars. There is the same and even a more extraordinary promiscuity of things of the intellect and the facts of the substance, elements and principles are mingled, combined, wedded together, and multiply each other till they lead both the moral and the material world into the same light. In the vast cosmic exchanges universal life comes and goes in unknown quantities, revolving everything in the invisible mystery of effluvia, employing everything, losing not a single dream of a sleep, sowing an animalcule here, crumbling away a star there, oscillating and winding, making of light a force, and of thought an element, disseminated and invisible, and dissolving everything save that geometrical point, the I; bringing back everything to the atom-soul, expanding everything in God; entangling all activities from the highest to the lowest in the obscurity of a vertiginous mechanism, attaching the flight of an insect to the movement of the earth, and subordinating, perhaps, if only through the identity of the law, the evolution of the comet in the firmament to the rotary movement of the infusoria in the drop of water. A machine made of spirit; an enormous machinery of cog-wheels, in which the first mover is the gnat, and the last wheel is the Zodiac.

4. *A CHANGE OF BARS*

It seemed as if this garden, created in former times to conceal libertine mysteries, had been transformed and become fitting to shelter chaste mysteries. There were no longer any cradles, bowling-greens, covered walks, or grottoes; but there was a magnificent tangled obscurity which fell all round, and Paphos was changed into Eden. A penitent feeling had refreshed this retreat, and the coquettish garden, once on a time so compromised, had returned to virginity and modesty. A president, assisted by a gardener, a good fellow who believed himself the successor of Lamoignon, and another good fellow who fancied himself the successor of Lenôtre, had turned it about, clipped it, and prepared it for purposes of gallantry, but nature had seized it again, filled it with shadow, and prepared it for love. There was, too, in this solitude a heart which was quite ready, and love had only to show itself; for there was here a temple composed of verdure, grass, moss, the sighs of birds, gentle shadows, waving branches, and a soul formed of gentleness, faith, candor, hope, aspirations, and illusions.

Cosette had left the convent while still almost a child. She was but little more than fourteen, and at the "ungrateful age," as we have said. With the exception of her eyes, she seemed rather ugly than pretty; still she had no ungraceful feature, but she was awkward, thin, timid and bold at the same time; in short, a grown-up little girl. Her education was finished, that is to say, she had been taught religion, and more especially devotion, also "history," that is to say, the thing so called in a convent; geography, grammar, the participles, the kings of France, and a little music, drawing, etc.; but in other respects she was ignorant of everything which is at once a charm and a peril. The mind of a young girl ought not to be left in darkness, for at a later date mirages too sudden and too quick are produced in it as a *camera obscura*. She should be gently and discreetly enlightened, rather by the reflection of realities than by their direct and harsh light; for this is a useful and graceful obscure semi-light which dissipates childish fears and prevents falls. There is only the maternal instinct, that admirable intuition into which the recollections of the virgin and the experience of the wife enter, that knows how or of what this semi-light should be composed. Nothing can take the place of this instinct, and in forming a girl's mind all the nuns in the world are not equal to one mother. Cosette had had no mother, she had only had a great many mothers. As for Jean Valjean, he had within him every possible tenderness and every possible anxiety; but he was only an old man who knew nothing at all. Now, in this work of education in this serious matter of preparing a woman for life, what knowledge is needed to contend against the other great ignorance which is called innocence. Nothing prepares a girl for passions like the convent, for it directs her thoughts to the unknown. The heart is driven back on itself, and hence come visions, suppositions, conjectures, romances sketched, adventures longed for, fantastic constructions, and edifices built entirely on the inner darkness of the mind, gloomy and secret dwellings in which the passions alone find a lodging so soon as passing through the convent bars allows it. The convent is a compression which must last the whole life, if it is to triumph over the human heart. On leaving the convent Cosette could not have found anything sweeter or more dangerous than the house in the Rue Plumet. It was the commencement of solitude with the commencement of liberty, a closed garden, but a rich, sharp, voluptuous, and fragrant soul; there were the same dreams as in the convent, but glimpses could be caught of young men,—the grating had bars, but it looked on the street. Still, we repeat, when Cosette first came here she was but a child. Jean Valjean gave over to her this uncultivated garden, and said to her, "Do what you like with it." This amused Cosette; she moved all the tufts and all the stones in search of "beasts"; she played about while waiting till the time came to think, and she loved this garden for the sake of the insects which she found in the grass under her feet, while waiting till she should love it for the sake of the stars she could see through the branches above her head.

And then, too, she loved her father, that is to say, Jean Valjean, with all her soul, with a simple, filial passion, which rendered the worthy man a desired and delightful companion to her. Our readers will remember that M. Madeleine was fond of reading, and Jean Valjean continued in the same track; he had learned to speak well, and he possessed the secret wealth and eloquence of a humble, true, and self-cultivated intellect. He had retained just sufficient roughness to season his kindness, and he had a rough mind and a soft heart. During their *tête-à-têtes* in the Luxembourg garden he gave her long explanations about all sorts of things, deriving his information from what he had read, and also from what he had suffered. While Cosette was listening to him her eyes vaguely wandered around. This simple man was sufficient for Cosette's thoughts in the same way as the wild garden was for her eyes. When she had chased the butterflies for a while she would run up to him panting, and say: "Oh! how tired I am!" and he would kiss her forehead. Cosette adored this good man, and she was ever at his heels, for wherever Jean Valjean was, happiness was. As he did not live either in the pavilion or the garden, she was more attached to the paved back yard than to the flower-laden garden, and preferred the little outhouse with the straw chairs to the large drawing-room hung with tapestry, along which silk-covered chairs were arranged. Jean Valjean at times said to her with a smile of a man who is delighted to be annoyed: "Come, go to your own rooms! leave me at peace for a little while."

She scolded him in that charming, tender way which is so graceful when addressed by a daughter to a parent.

"Father, I feel very cold in your room; why don't you have a carpet and a stove?"

"My dear child, there are so many persons more deserving than myself who have not even a roof to cover them."

"Then, why is there fire in my room and everything that I want?"

"Because you are a woman and a child."

"Nonsense! then men must be cold and hungry?"

"Some men."

"Very good! I'll come here so often that you will be obliged to have a fire." Or else it was: "Father, why do you eat such wretched bread as that?"

"Because I do, my daughter."

"Well, if you eat it, I shall eat it, too."

And so to prevent Cosette from eating black bread, Jean Valjean ate white. Cosette remembered her childhood but confusedly, and she prayed night and morning for the mother whom she had never known. The Thénardiers were like two hideous beings seen in a dream, and she merely remembered that she had gone "one day at night" to fetch water in a wood—she thought that it was a long distance from Paris. It seemed to her as if she had commenced life in an abyss, and that Jean Valjean had drawn her out of it, and her childhood produced on her the effect of a time when she had naught but centipedes, spiders, and snakes around her. When she thought at night before she fell asleep, as she had no very clear idea of being Jean Valjean's daughter, she imagined that her mother's soul had passed into this good man, and had come to dwell near her. When he was sitting down she rested her cheek on his white hair, and silently dropped a tear, while saying to herself, "Perhaps this man is my mother!" Cosette, strange though it is to say, in her profound ignorance, as a girl educated in a convent, and as, too, maternity is absolutely unintelligible to virginity, eventually imagined that she had had as little of a mother as was possible. This mother's name she did not know, and whenever it happened that she spoke to Jean Valjean on the subject, he held his tongue. If she repeated her question, he answered by a smile, and once, when she pressed him, the smile terminated in a tear. This silence on his part cast a night over Fantine. Was it through prudence? was it through respect? or was it through a fear of intrusting this name to the chances of another memory besides his own?

So long as Cosette was young, Jean Valjean readily talked to her about her mother, but when she grew up it was impossible for him to do so— he felt as if he dared not do it. Was is on account of Cosette or of Fantine? He felt a species of religious horror at making this shadow enter Cosette's thoughts and rendering a dead woman a third person in their society. The more sacred this shade was to him, the more formidable was it. He thought of Fantine, and felt himself overwhelmed by the silence. He saw vaguely in the darkness something that resembled a finger laid on a lip. Had all the modesty which was in Fantine, and which, during her existence, came out of her violently, returned after death, to watch indignantly over the dead woman's peace, and sternly guard her in the tomb? was Jean Valjean himself unconsciously oppressed by it? We who believe in death are not prepared to reject this mysterious explanation. Thence arose the impossibility of pronouncing, even to Cosette, the name of Fantine. One day Cosette said to him:

"Father, I saw my mother last night in a dream. She had two large wings, and in life she must have been a sainted woman."

"Through martyrdom," Jean Valjean replied. Altogether, though, he was happy; when Cosette went out with him she leaned on his arm, proudly and happily, in the fullness of her heart. Jean Valjean felt his thoughts melt into delight at all these marks of such exclusive tenderness, so satisfied with himself alone. The poor wretch, inundated with an angelic joy, trembled; he assured himself with transports that this would last his whole life; he said to himself that he had not really suffered enough to deserve such radiant happiness, and he thanked God, in the depths of his soul, for having allowed him, wretched as he was, to be loved by this innocent being.

5. *THE ROSE DISCOVERS THAT SHE IS A WEAPON OF WAR*

ONE day Cosette happened to look at herself in the glass, and said, "Good gracious!" She fancied that she was almost pretty, and this threw her into a singular trouble. Up to this moment she had not thought of her face, and though she saw herself in the mirror she did not look at herself. And, then, she had often been told that she was ugly; Jean Valjean alone would say gently, "Oh, no, oh, no!" However this might be, Cosette had always believed herself ugly, and had grown up in this idea with the facile resignation of childhood. And now all at once her looking-glass said to her, as Jean Valjean had done, "Oh, no!" She did not sleep that night. "Suppose I were pretty," she thought, "how droll it would be if I were pretty!" and she remembered those of her companions whose beauty produced an effect in the convent, and said to herself, "What! I might be like Mademoiselle So-and-so!"

On the next day she looked at herself, but not accidentally, and doubted. "Where was my sense?" she said; "no, I am ugly." She had simply slept badly, her eyes were heavy and her cheeks pale. She had not felt very joyous on the previous day when she fancied herself pretty, but was sad at no longer believing it. She did not look at herself again, and for upward of a fortnight tried to dress her hair with her back to the glass. In the evening, after dinner, she usually worked at her embroidery in the drawing-room, while Jean Valjean read by her side. Once she raised her eyes from her work, and was greatly surprised by the anxious way in which her father was gazing at her. Another time she was walking along the street, and fancied she heard some one behind her, whom she did not see, say, "A pretty woman, but badly dressed." "Nonsense," she thought, "it is not I, for I am well dressed and ugly." At that time she wore her plush bonnet and merino dress. One day, at last, she was in the garden, and heard poor old Toussaint saying, "Master, do you notice how pretty our young lady is growing?" Cosette did not hear her father's answer, for Toussaint's words produced a sort of commotion in her. She ran out of the garden up to her room, looked in the glass, which she had not done for three months, and uttered a cry—she had dazzled herself.

She was beautiful and pretty, and could not refrain from being of the same opinion as Toussaint and her glass. Her figure was formed, her skin had grown white, her hair was glossy, and an unknown splendor was lit up in her blue eyes. The consciousness of her beauty came to her fully in a minute, like the sudden dawn of day; others, besides, noticed her, Toussaint said so; it was evidently to herself that the passerby alluded, and no doubt was possible. She returned to the garden, believing herself a queen, hearing the birds sing, though it was winter, seeing the golden sky, the sun amid the trees, flowers on the shrubs; she was wild, distraught, and in a state of ineffable rapture. On his side, Jean Valjean experienced a profound and inexplicable contraction of the heart. For some time past, in truth, he had contemplated with terror the beauty which daily appeared more radiant in Cosette's sweet face. It was a laughing dawn for all, but most mournful for him.

Cosette had been for a long time beautiful ere she perceived the fact, but, from the first day, this unexpected light which slowly rose and gradually developed the girl's entire person hurt Jean Valjean's somber eyes. He felt that it was a change in a happy life, so happy that he did not dare stir in it, for fear of deranging it somewhere. This man, who had passed through every possible distress, who was still bleeding from the wounds dealt him by his destiny, who had been almost wicked, and had become almost a saint, who, after dragging the galley-chain, was now dragging the invisible but weighty chain of indefinite infamy; this man whom the law had not liberated, and who might at any moment be recaptured and taken from the obscurity of virtue to the broad daylight of public opprobrium—this man accepted everything, excused everything, pardoned everything, blessed everything, wished everything well, and only asked one thing of Providence, of men, of the laws, of society, of nature, of the world: that Cosette should love him; that Cosette might continue to love him; that God would not prevent the heart of this child turning to him and remaining with him! Loved by Cosette, he felt cured, at rest, appeased, overwhelmed, rewarded, and crowned. With Cosette's love all was well, and he asked no more. Had any one said to him, "Would you like to be better off?" he would have answered, "No." Had God said to him, "Do you wish for heaven?" he would have answered, "I should lose by it." All that could affect this situation, even on the surface, appeared to him the beginning of something else. He had never known thoroughly what a woman's beauty was, but he understood instinctively that it was terrible. This beauty, which continually expanded more triumphantly and superbly by his side, upon the ingenuous and formidable brow of the child, from the depth of his ugliness, old age, misery, reprobation, and despondency, terrified him, and he said to himself, "How beautiful she is! what will become of me?" Here lay the difference between his tenderness and that of a mother; what he saw with agony a mother would have seen with joy.

The first symptoms speedily manifested themselves. From the day when Cosette said to herself, "I am decidedly good-looking," she paid attention to her toilet. She remembered the remark of the passer-by,—pretty, but badly dressed,—a blast of the oracle which passed by her and died out, after depositing in her heart one of those two germs which are destined at a later period to occupy a woman's entire life,—coquettishness; the other is love. With faith in her beauty, all her feminine soul was expanded within her; she had a horror of merinos, and felt ashamed of plush. Her father never refused her anything, and she knew at once the whole science of the hat, the dress, the mantle, the slipper, and the sleeve, of the fabric that suits, and the color that is becoming, the science which makes the Parisian woman something so charming, profound, and dangerous. The expression *"femme capiteuse"* was invented for the Parisian. In less than a month little Cosette was in this Thebaïs of the Rue de Babylone, not only one of the prettiest women, which is something, but one of the best dressed in Paris, which is a great deal more. She would have liked to meet "her passer-by," to see what he would say, and teach him a lesson. The fact is, that she was in every respect ravishing, and could admirably distinguish a bonnet of Gérard's from one of Herbaut's. Jean Valjean regarded these ravages with anxiety, and while feeling that he could never do more than crawl, or walk at the most, he could see Cosette's wings growing. However, by the simple inspection of Cosette's toilet, a woman would have seen that she had no mother. Certain small proprieties and social conventionalisms were not observed by Cosette; a mother, for instance, would have told her that an unmarried girl does not wear brocade.

The first day that Cosette went out in her dress and cloak of black brocade, and her white crape bonnet, she took Jean Valjean's arm, gay, radiant, blushing, proud, and striking. "Father," she said, "how do you think I look?" Jean Valjean replied, in a voice which resembled the bitter voice of envy, "Charming." During the walk he was as usual, but when he returned home he asked Cosette:

"Will you not put on that dress and bonnet, you know which, again?"

This took place in Cosette's room; she returned to the wardrobe in which her boarding-school dress was hanging.

"That disguise?" she said; "how can you expect it, father? oh, no, indeed, I shall never put on those horrors again; with that thing on my head I look a regular dowdy."

Jean Valjean heaved a deep sigh.

From that moment he noticed that Cosette, who hitherto had wished to stay at home, saying, "Father, I amuse myself much better here with you," now constantly asked to go out. In truth, what good is it for a girl to have a pretty face and a delicious toilet if she does not show them?

He also noticed that Cosette no longer had the same liking for the back yard, and at present preferred remaining in the garden, where she walked without displeasure, near the railings. Jean Valjean never set foot in the garden, but remained in the back yard, like the dog. Cosette, knowing herself to be beautiful, lost the grace of being ignorant of the fact, an exquisite grace, for beauty heightened by simplicity is ineffable, and nothing is so adorable as a beauteous innocent maiden, who walks along unconsciously, holding in her hand the key of a Paradise. But what she lost in ingenuous grace she regained in a pensive and serious charm. Her whole person, impregnated with the joys of youth, innocence, and beauty, exhaled a splendid melancholy. It was at this period that Marius saw her again at the Luxembourg, after an interval of six months.

6. THE BATTLE BEGINS

COSETTE was in her shadow, as Marius was in his, ready prepared to be kindled. Destiny, with its mysterious and fatal patience, brought slowly together these two beings, all charged with, and pining in, the stormy electricity of the passion, these two souls which bore love as the clouds bore thunder, and were destined to come together and be blended in a glance like the clouds in a flash. The power of a glance has been so abused in love romances that it has been discredited in the end, and a writer dares hardly assert nowadays that two beings fell in love because they looked at each other. And yet that is the way, and the sole way, in which people fall in love; the rest is merely the rest, and comes afterward. Nothing is more real than the mighty shocks which two souls give each other by exchanging this spark. At the hour when Cosette unconsciously gave that glance which troubled Marius, Marius did not suspect that he too gave a glance which troubled Cosette. For a long time she had seen and examined him in the way girls see and examine, while looking elsewhere. Marius was still thinking Cosette ugly, when Cosette had already considered Marius handsome, but, as the young man paid no attention to her, he was an object of indifference. Still she could not refrain from saying to herself that he had silky hair, fine eyes, regular teeth, an agreeable voice, when she heard him talking with his companions; that he perhaps walked with a bad carriage if you liked, but with a grace of his own; that he did not appear at all silly, that his whole person was noble, gentle, simple, and proud, and, lastly, that though he seemed poor he had the bearing of a gentleman.

On the day when their eyes met, and at length suddenly said to each other the first obscure and ineffable things which the eye stammers, Cosette did not understand it at first. She returned pensively to the house in the Rue de l'Ouest, where Jean Valjean was spending six weeks, according to his wont. When she awoke the next morning she thought of the young stranger, so long indifferent and cold, who now seemed to pay attention to her, and this attention did not appear at all agreeable to her; on the contrary, she felt a little angry with the handsome, disdainful man. A warlike feeling was aroused, and she felt a very childish joy at the thought that she was at length about to be avenged. Knowing herself to be lovely, she felt, though in an indistinct way, that she had a weapon. Women play with their beauty as lads do with knives, and cut themselves with it. Our reader will remember Marius's hesitations, palpitations, and terrors; he remained on his bench and did not approach, and this vexed Cosette. One day she said to Jean Valjean, "Father, suppose we take a walk in that direction?" Seeing that Marius did not come to her, she went to him, for, in such cases, every woman resembles Mahomet. And then, strange it is, the first symptom of true love in a young man is timidity; in a girl it is boldness. This will surprise, and yet nothing is more simple; the two sexes have a tendency to approach, and each assumes the qualities of the other. On this day Cosette's glance drove Marius mad, while his glance made Cosette tremble. Marius went away confiding, and Cosette restless. Now they adored each other. The first thing that Cosette experienced was a confused and deep sorrow: it seemed to her that her soul had become black in one day, and she no longer recognized herself. The whiteness of the soul of maidens, which is composed of coldness and gayety, resembles snow: it melts before love, which is its sun.

Cosette knew not what love was, and she had never heard the word uttered in its earthly sense. In the books of profane music which entered the convent, *tambour* or *pandour* was substituted for *amour*. This produced enigmas which exercised the imagination of the big girls, such as: "Ah! how agreeable the drummer is!" or, "Pity is not a pandour!" But Cosette left the convent at too early an age to trouble herself about the "drummer," and hence did not know what name to give to that which now troubled her. But are we the less ill through being ignorant of the name of our disease? She loved with the more passion, because she loved in ignorance; she did not know whether it is good or bad, useful or dangerous, necessary or mortal, eternal or transient, permitted or prohibited,—she loved. She would have been greatly surprised had any one said to her, "You do not sleep? that is forbidden. You do not eat? that is very wrong. You have an oppression and beating of the heart? that cannot be tolerated. You blush and turn pale when a certain person dressed in black appears at the end of a certain green walk? why, that is abominable!" She would not have understood, and would have replied, "How can I be to blame in a matter in which I can do nothing, and of which I know nothing?"

It happened that the love which presented itself was the one most in harmony with the state of her soul; it was a sort of distant adoration, a dumb contemplation, the deification of an unknown man. It was the apparition of youth to youth, the dream of nights become a romance and remaining a dream, the wished-for phantom at length realized and incarnated, but as yet having no name, or wrong, or flaw, or claim, or defect; in a way, the distant lover who remained idealized, a chimera which assumed a shape. Any more palpable and nearer meeting would at this first stage have startled Cosette, who was still half plunged in the magnifying fog of the cloister. She had all the fears of children and all the fears of nuns blended together, and the essence of the convent, with which she had been impregnated for five years, was still slowly evaporating from her whole person and making everything tremble around her. In this situation, it was not a lover she wanted, not even an admirer, but a vision, and she began adoring Marius as something charming, luminous, and impossible.

As extreme simplicity trenches on extreme coquetry, she smiled upon him most frankly. She daily awaited impatiently the hour for the walk; she saw Marius, she felt indescribably happy, and sincerely believed that she was expressing her entire thoughts when she said to Jean Valjean,

"What a delicious garden the Luxembourg is!" Marius and Cosette were still in the dark, to each other: they did not speak, they did not bow, they did not know each other, but they met; and, like the stars in the heavens, which are millions of leagues separate, they lived by looking at each other. It is thus that Cosette gradually became a woman, and was developed into a beautiful and loving woman conscious of her beauty and ignorant of her love. She was a coquette into the bargain, through her innocence.

7. JEAN VALJEAN IS VERY SAD

ALL situations have their instincts, and old and eternal mother Nature warned Jean Valjean darkly of the presence of Marius. Jean Valjean trembled in the depth of his mind: he saw nothing, knew nothing, and yet regarded with obstinate attention the darkness in which he was, as if he felt on one side something being built up, on the other something crumbling away. Marius, who was also warned by the same mother Nature, did all in his power to conceal himself from the father, but, for all that, Jean Valjean sometimes perceived him. Marius's manner was no longer wise; he displayed clumsy prudence and awkward temerity. He no longer came quite close to them, as he had formerly done; he sat down at a distance and remained in an ecstasy; he had a book, and pretended to read it; why did he pretend? Formerly he came in an old coat, and now he came every day in his new one. Jean Valjean was not quite sure whether he did not have his hair dressed; he had a strange way of rolling his eyes, and wore gloves; in short, Jean Valjean cordially detested the young man. Cosette did not allow anything to be guessed. Without knowing exactly what was the matter with her, she had a feeling that it was something which must be hidden. There was parallelism which annoyed Jean Valjean between the taste for dress which had come to Cosette, and the habit of wearing new clothes displayed by this stranger. It was an accident, perhaps,—of course it was,—but a menacing accident.

He never opened his mouth to Cosette about this stranger. One day, however, he could not refrain, and said, with that vague despair which suddenly thrusts the probe into its own misfortune, "That young man looks like a pedant." Cosette, a year previously, when still a careless little girl, would have answered, "Oh, no, he is very good-looking." Ten years later, with the love of Marius in her heart, she would have replied, "An insufferable pedant; you are quite right." At the present moment of her life and heart, she restricted herself to saying with supreme calmness, "That young man!" Just as if she looked at him for the first time in her life. "How stupid I am," Jean Valjean thought, "she had not even noticed him, and now I have pointed him out to her." Oh, simplicity of old people! oh, depth of children! It is another law of these first years of suffering and care, of these sharp struggles of first love with first obstacles, that the maiden cannot be caught in any snare, while the young man falls into all. Jean Valjean had begun a secret war against Marius, which Marius, in the sublime stupidity of his passion and his age, did not guess. Jean Valjean laid all sorts of snares for him. He changed his hours, he changed his bench, he forgot his handkerchief, and went alone to the Luxembourg, and Marius went headlong into the trap, and to all these notes of interrogation which Jean Valjean planted in the road he ingenuously answered "Yes." Cosette, however, remained immured in her apparent carelessness and imperturbable tranquillity, so that Jean Valjean arrived at this conclusion, "That humbug is madly in love with Cosette, but Cosette does not even know that he exists."

For all that, though, he had a painful tremor in his heart, for the minute when Cosette would love might arrive at any instant. Does not all this commence with indifference? Only once did Cosette make a mistake and startle him; he arose from his bench to go home after three hours' sitting, and she said, "What, already?" Jean Valjean did not give up his walks at the Luxembourg, as he did not wish to do anything singular or arouse Cosette's attention, but during the hours so sweet for the two lovers, while Cosette was sending her smile to the intoxicated Marius, who only perceived this, and now saw nothing more in the world than a radiant, adored face, Jean Valjean fixed on Marius flashing and terrible eyes. He who had ended by no longer believing himself capable of a malevolent feeling, had moments when he felt, if Marius were present, as if he were growing savage and ferocious, and those old depths of his soul which had formerly contained so much anger opened again against this young man. It seemed to him as if unknown craters were again being formed within him. What! the fellow was there! What did he come to do? he came to sniff, examine, and attempt; he came to say, Well, why not? he came to prowl round his, Jean Valjean's life; to prowl round his happiness and carry it away from him. Jean Valjean added, "Yes, that is it! what does he come to seek? an adventure. What does he want? a love affair. A love affair! and I! What? I was first the most wretched of men, and then the most unhappy. I have spent sixty years on my knees, I have suffered all that a man can suffer, I have grown old without ever having been young; I have lived without family, parents, friends, children, or wife; I have left some of my blood on every stone, on every bramble, on every wall; I have been gentle, though men were harsh to me, and good though they were wicked; I have become an honest man again, in spite of everything; I have repented of the evil I did, and pardoned the evil done to me, and at the moment when I am rewarded, when all is finished, when I touched my object, when I have what I wish, and it is but fair, as I have paid for it and earned it— all this is to fade away, and I am to lose Cosette, my love, my joy, my soul, because it has pleased a long-legged ass to saunter about the Luxembourg garden!"

Then his eyeballs were filled with a mournful and extraordinary brilliancy; he was no longer a man looking at a man, no longer an enemy looking at an enemy,—he was a dog watching a robber. Our readers know the rest. Marius continued to act madly, and one day followed Cosette to the Rue de l'Ouest. Another day he spoke to the porter, and the porter spoke in his turn and said to Jean Valjean, "Do you happen to know, sir, a curious young man who has been making inquiries about you?" The next day Jean Valjean gave Marius that look which Marius at length noticed, and a week later Jean Valjean went away. He made a vow that he would never again set foot in the Rue de l'Ouest or the Luxembourg, and returned to the Rue Plumet. Cosette did not complain, she said nothing, she asked no questions, she did not attempt to discover any motive, for she had reached that stage when a girl fears that her thoughts may be perused, or she may betray herself. Jean Valjean had no experience of these miseries, the only ones which are charming, and the only ones he did not know, and on this account he did not comprehend the grave significance of Cosette's silence. Still he noticed that she became sad, and he became gloomy. Inexperience was contending on both sides. Once he made an essay, by asking Cosette, "Will you go to the Luxembourg?" A beam illuminated Cosette's pale face. "Yes," she said. They went there,—but three months had elapsed, and Marius no longer went there,—there was no Marius present. The next day Jean Valjean again asked Cosette, "Will you go to the Luxembourg?" She answered sadly and gently, "No." Jean Valjean was hurt by the sadness, and heart-broken by the gentleness.

What was taking place in this young and already so impenetrable mind? what was going to be accomplished? what was happening to Cosette's soul? Sometimes, instead of going to bed, Jean Valjean would remain seated by his bedside with his head between his hands, and spent whole nights in asking himself, "What has Cosette on her mind?" and in thinking of the things of which she might be thinking. Oh! at such moments what sad glances he turned toward the convent, that chaste summit, that abiding place of angels, that inaccessible glacier of virtue! With what despairing ravishment did he contemplate that garden, full of ignored flowers and immured virgins, where all the perfumes and all the souls ascend direct to heaven! How he adored that Eden, now closed against him forever, and which he had voluntarily and madly left! How he lamented his self-denial and his madness in bringing Cosette back to the world. He was the poor hero of the sacrifice, seized and hurled down by his own devotion! How he said to himself, What have I done! However, nothing of this was visible to Cosette—neither temper, nor roughness; it was ever the same serene, kind face. Jean Valjean's manner was even more tender and paternal than before; and if anything could have evidenced his joy, it was more gentleness.

On her side, Cosette was pining; she suffered from Marius's absence, as she had reveled in his presence, singularly, and not exactly knowing why. When Jean Valjean ceased taking her for her usual walk, a feminine instinct had whispered to her heart that she must not appear to be attached to the Luxembourg, and that if she displayed indifference in the matter her father would take her back to it. But days, weeks, and months succeeded each other, for Jean Valjean had tacitly accepted Cosette's tacit consent. She regretted it, but it was too late, and on the day when they returned to the Luxembourg, Marius was no longer there. He had disappeared then; it was all over. What could she do? would she ever see him again? She felt a contraction of the heart which nothing dilated and which daily increased; she no longer knew whether it were summer or winter, sunshine or rain, whether the birds were singing, whether it was the dahlia or the daisy season, whether the Luxembourg was more charming than the Tuileries, whether the linen brought home by the washerwoman was too much or insufficiently starched, or if Toussaint had gone to market well or ill; and she remained crushed, absorbed, attentive to one thought alone, with a vague and fixed eye, like a person gazing through the darkness at the deep, black spot where a phantom has just vanished. Still she did not allow Jean Valjean to see anything but her pallor, and her face was ever gentle to him. This pallor, though, was more than sufficient to render Jean Valjean anxious, and at times he would ask her:

"What is the matter with you?"

And she answered:

"Nothing."

After a silence, she would add, as if guessing that he was sad too:

"And, father, is there anything the matter with you?"

"With me? oh, nothing," he would reply.

These two beings, who had loved each other so exclusively, and one of them with such a touching love, and had lived for a long time one through the other, were now suffering side by side, one on account of the other, without confessing it, without anger, and with a smile.

8. *THE CHAIN-GANG*

THE more unhappy of the two was Jean Valjean, for youth, even in its sorrow, has always a brilliancy of its own. At certain moments Jean Valjean suffered so intensely that he became childish, for it is the peculiarity of grief to bring out a man's childish side. He felt invincibly that Cosette was slipping from him; and he would have liked to struggle, hold her back, and excite her enthusiasm by some external and brilliant achievement. These ideas, childish as we said, but at the same time senile, gave him, through their very childishness, a very fair notion of the influence of gold lace upon the imagination of girls. One day Count Coutard, commandant of Paris, passed along the street on horseback, and in full-dress uniform. He envied this gilded man, and said to himself what a happiness it would be to be able to put on that coat, which was an undeniable thing; that if Cosette saw him in it it would dazzle her, and when he passed before the Tuileries gates the sentinels would present arms to him, and that would be sufficient for Cosette, and prevent her looking at young men.

An unexpected shock was mingled with his sad thoughts. In the isolated life they led, and since they had gone to reside in the Rue Plumet, they had one habit. They sometimes had the pleasure of going to see the sun rise, a species of sweet joy which is agreeable to those who are entering life and those who are leaving it. To walk about at daybreak is equivalent, with the man who loves solitude, to walking about at night with the gayety of nature added. The streets are deserted and the birds sing. Cosette, herself a bird, generally woke at an early hour. These morning excursions were arranged on the previous evening; he proposed and she accepted. This was arranged like a plot; they went out before day, and it was a delight for Cosette, as these innocent eccentricities please youth. Jean Valjean had, as we know, a liking to go out to but little frequented places, to solitary nooks, and forgotten spots. There were at that time, in the vicinity of the gates of Paris, poor fields, almost forming part of the city, where sickly wheat grew in summer, and which in autumn, after the harvest was got in did not look as if they had been reaped, but skinned. Jean Valjean had a predilection for these fields, and Cosette did not feel wearied there; it was solitude for him and liberty for her. There she became a little girl again, she ran about and almost played, she took off her bonnet, laid it on Jean Valjean's knees, and plucked flowers. She watched the butterflies, but did not catch them, for humanity and tenderness spring up with love, and the maiden who has in her heart a trembling and fragile ideal feels pity for the butterfly's wing. She twined poppies into wreaths, which she placed on her head, and when the sun poured its beams on them and rendered them almost purple, they formed a fiery crown for her fresh pink face.

Even after their life had grown saddened they kept up their habit of early walks. One October morning, then, tempted by the perfect serenity of the autumn of 1831, they went out, and found themselves just before daybreak near the Barrière du Maine. It was not quite morning yet, but it was dawn, a ravishing and wild minute. There were a few stars in the pale azure sky, the earth was all black, the heavens all white, a shiver ran along the grass, and all around displayed the mysterious influence of twilight. A lark, which seemed mingled with the stars, was singing at a prodigious height, and it seemed as if this hymn of littleness to infinitude calmed the immensity. In the east the dark mass of Val de Grace stood out against the bright steel-blue horizon, and glittering Venus rose behind the dome and looked like a soul escaping from a gloomy edifice. All was peace and silence, there was no one in the highway, and a few workmen going to their daily toil could be indistinctly seen in the distance.

Jean Valjean was seated on some planks deposited at the gate of a timber-yard, his face was turned to the road, and his back to the light; he forgot all about the sunrise, for he had fallen into one of those profound reveries in which the mind is concentrated, which imprison even the glance and are equivalent to four walls. There are meditations which may be called wells, and when you are at the bottom it takes some time to reach the ground again. Jean Valjean had descended into one of these reveries; he was thinking of Cosette, of the possible happiness if nothing came betwixt him and her, of that light with which she filled his life, and which was the breath of his soul. He was almost happy in this reverie, and Cosette, standing by his side, was watching the clouds turn rose-hued. All at once Cosette exclaimed, "Father, there is something coming down there!" Jean Valjean raised his eyes. Cosette was correct. The road which leads to the old Barrière du Maine is a prolongation of the Rue de Sèvres, and is intersected at right angles by the inner boulevard. At the spot where the roads cross, a sound difficult to explain at such an hour could be heard, and a sort of confused mass appeared. Some shapeless thing coming along the boulevard was turning into the main road. It grew larger and seemed to be moving in an orderly way; although it shook and heaved, it seemed to be a vehicle, but its load could not be distinguished. There were horses, wheels, shouts, and the cracking of whips. By degrees the lineaments became fixed, though drowned in darkness; it was really a vehicle coming toward the barrière near which Jean Valjean was seated; a second resembling it followed, then a third, then a fourth; seven carts debouched in turn, the heads of the horses touching the backs of the vehicles. Figures moved on these carts, sparks could be seen in the gloom, looking like bare sabers, and a clang could be heard resembling chains being shaken; all this advanced, the voices became louder, and it was a formidable thing, such as issues from the cavern of dreams.

On drawing nearer this thing assumed a shape, and stood out behind the trees with the lividness of an apparition: the mass grew whiter, and the gradually dawning day threw a ghastly gleam over this mass, which was at once sepulchral and alive,—the heads of the shadows became the faces of corpses, and this is what it was. Seven vehicles were moving in file along the road, and the first six had a singular shape; they resembled brewers' drays, and consisted of long ladders laid upon two wheels, and forming a shaft at the front end. Each dray, or, to speak more correctly, each ladder, was drawn by a team of four horses, and strange clusters of men were dragged along upon these ladders. In the faint light these men could not be seen so much as divined. Twenty-four on each ladder, twelve on either side, leaning against each other, had their faces turned to the passers-by, and their legs hanging down; and they had behind their back something which rang, and was a chain, and something that glistened, which was a collar. Each man had his collar, but the chain was for all so that these twenty-four men if obliged to get down from the dray and walk, were seized by a species of inexorable unity, and were obliged to wind on the ground with the chain as backbone, very nearly like centipedes. At the front and back of each cart stood two men armed with guns, who stood with their feet on the end of the chain. The seventh vehicle, a vast fourgon, with rack sides but no hood, had four wheels and six horses, and carried a resounding mass of coppers, boilers, chafing-dishes, and chains, among which were mingled a few bound men lying their full length, who seemed to be ill. This fourgon, which was quite open, was lined with broken-down hurdles, which seemed to have been used for old punishments.

These vehicles held the crown of the causeway, and on either side marched a double file of infamous-looking guards, wearing three-cornered hats, like the soldiers of the Directory, and dirty, torn, stained uniforms, half gray and blue, a coat of the Invalides and the trousers of the undertaker's men, red epaulettes, and yellow belts, and were armed with short sabers, muskets, and sticks. These sbirri seemed compounded of the abjectness of the beggar and the authority of the hangman, and the one who appeared leader held a postillion's whip in his hands. All these details grew more and more distinct in the advancing daylight, and at the head and rear of the train marched mounted gendarmes with drawn sabers. The train was so long, that at the moment when the first vehicle reached the barrière, the last had scarce turned out of the boulevard. A crowd, which came no one knew whence and formed in a second, as is so common in Paris, lined both sides of the road, and looked. In the side lanes could be heard the shouts of people calling to each other, and the wooden shoes of the kitchen-gardeners running up to have a peep.

The men piled upon the drays allowed themselves to be jolted in silence, and were livid with the morning chill. They all wore canvas trousers, and their naked feet were thrust into wooden shoes, but the rest of their attire was left to the fancy of wretchedness. Their accouterments were hideously discordant, for nothing is more mournful than the harlequin garb of rags. There were crushed hats, oilskin caps, frightful woolen night-caps, and, side by side with the blouse, an out-at-elbow black coat; some wore women's bonnets, and others had baskets as headgear; hairy chests were visible and through the rents of the clothes tattooing could be distinguished,—temples of love, burning hearts, and cupids,—but ringworm and other unhealthy red spots might also be noticed. Two or three had passed a straw rope through the side rail of the dray, which hung down like a stirrup and supported their feet, while one of them held in his hand and raised to his mouth something like a black stone, which he seemed to be gnawing; it was bread he was eating. All the eyes were dry, and either dull or luminous with a wicked light. The escort cursed, but the chained men did not breathe a syllable; from time to time the sound of a blow dealt with a stick on shoulder-blades or heads could be heard; some of these men yawned; the rags were terrible; their feet hung down, their shoulders oscillated, their heads struck against each other, their irons rattled, their eyeballs flashed ferociously, their fists clenched or opened inertly like the hands of death, and in the rear of the chain a band of children burst into a laugh.

This file of vehicles, whatever their nature might be, was lugubrious. It was plain that within an hour a shower might fall, that it might be followed by another, and then another, that the ragged clothing would be drenched, and that, once wet through, these men would not dry again, and, once chilled, would never grow warm any more; that their canvas trousers would be glued to their bones by the rain, the water would fill their wooden shoes, that lashes could not prevent the chattering teeth, that the chain would continue to hold them by the neck, and their feet would continue to hang; and it was impossible not to shudder on seeing these human creatures thus bound and passive beneath the cold autumnal clouds, and surrendered to the rain, the breezes, and all the furies of the atmosphere, like trees and stones. The blows were not even spared the sick who lay bound with rope and motionless in the seventh vehicle, and who seemed to have been thrown there like sacks filled with wretchedness.

All at once the sun appeared, the immense beam leaped up in the east, and it seemed as if it set fire to all these ferocious heads. Tongues became untied, and a storm of furies, oaths, and songs exploded. The wide horizontal light cut the whole file in two, illumining the heads and bodies, and leaving the feet and wheels in obscurity. Thoughts appeared on faces, and it was a fearful thing to see demons with their masks thrown away, and ferocious souls laid bare. Some of the merrier ones had in their mouths quills, through which they blew vermin on the crowd, selecting women; the dawn caused their lamentable faces to stand out in the darkness of the shadows. Not one of these beings but was misshapen through wretchedness, and it was so monstrous that it seemed to change the light of the sun into the gleam of a lightning flash. The first cart-load heading the train struck up a tune and were now loudly singing with a haggard joviality a potpourri of Désaugiers, at that time famous, under the title of *la Vestale;* the trees shook mournfully, while in the sidewalks bourgeois faces were listening with an idiotic beatitude to these comic songs chanted by specters. All destinies could be found in this gang, like a chaos; there were the facial angles of all animals—old men, youths, naked skulls, gray beards, cynical monstrosities, sulky resignation, savage grins, wild attitudes, youth, girlish heads with corkscrew curls on their temples, infantine, and for that reason horrible faces, and then countenances of skeletons, which only lacked death. On the first dray could be seen a negro, who had been a slave probably, and was enabled to compare the chains. The frightful leveler, shame, had passed over all these foreheads; at this stage of abasement the last transformations were undergone by all in the lowest depths; and ignorance changed into dullness was the equal of intellect changed into despair. No choice was possible among these men, who appeared to be the pick of the mud; and it was clear that the arranger of this unclean procession had not attempted to classify them. These beings had been bound and coupled pell-mell, probably in alphabetical disorder, and loaded haphazard on the vehicles. Still, horrors, when grouped, always end by disengaging a resultant; every addition of wretched men produces a total;—a common soul issued from each chain, and each dray-load had its physiognomy. By the side of the man who sang was one who yelled; a third begged; another could be seen gnashing his teeth; another threatened the passers-by; another blasphemed God, and the last was silent as the tomb. Dante would have fancied that he saw the seven circles of the Inferno in motion. It was the march of the damned to punishment, performed in a sinister way, not upon the formidable flashing car of the Apocalypse, but, more gloomy still, in the hangman's cart.

One of the keepers, who had a hook at the end of his stick, from time to time attempted to stir up this heap of human ordure. An old woman in the crowd pointed them to a little boy five years of age, and said to him, "You scamp, that will teach you!" As the songs and blasphemy grew louder, the man who seemed the captain of the escort cracked his whip, and at the signal a blind, indiscriminate bastinado fell with the sound of hail upon the seven cart-loads. Many yelled and foamed at the lips, which redoubled the joy of the gamins who had come up like a cloud of flies settling upon wounds. Jean Valjean's eye had become frightful; it was no longer an eyeball, but that profound glass bulb which takes the place of the eye in some unfortunate men, which seems unconscious of reality, and in which the reflection of horrors and catastrophes flashes. He was not looking at a spectacle, but going through a vision; he had to rise, fly, escape, but could not move his foot. At times, things which you see seize you and root you in the ground. He remained petrified and stupid, asking himself through a confused and inexpressible agony what was the meaning of this sepulchral persecution, and whence came this Pandemonium that pursued him. All at once he raised his hand to his forehead, the usual gesture of those to whom memory suddenly returns; he remembered that this was really the road taken, that this détour was usual to avoid any meeting with royalty, which was always possible on the Fontainebleau road, and that five-and-thirty years before he had passed through that barrière. Cosette was not the less horrified, though in a different way; she did not understand, her breath failed her, and what she saw did not appear to her possible. At length she exclaimed:

"Father! what is there in those vehicles?"

Jean Valjean answered:

"Convicts."

"Where are they going?"

"To the galleys."

At this moment the bastinado, multiplied by a hundred hands, became tremendous; strokes of the flat of the saber were mingled with it, and it resembled a tornado of whips and sticks—the galley-slaves bowed their heads, a hideous obedience was produced by the punishment, and all were silent, with the look of chained wolves. Cosette, trembling in all her limbs, continued:

"Father, are they still men?"

"Sometimes," the wretched man replied.

It was, in fact, the chain, which, leaving Bicêtre before daybreak, was taking the Mans road, to avoid Fontainebleau, where the king then was. This détour made the fearful journey last three or four days longer; but it surely may be prolonged to save a royal personage the sight of a punishment. Jean Valjean went home crushed, for such encounters are blows, and the recollections they leave behind resemble a concussion. While walking along the Rue de Babylone, Jean Valjean did not notice that Cosette asked him other questions about what they had just seen; perhaps he was himself too absorbed in his despondency to notice her remarks and answer them. At night, however, when Cosette left him to go to bed, he heard her say in a low voice, and as if speaking to herself, "I feel that if I were to meet one of those men in the street, I should die only from being so close to him."

Luckily, the next day after this tragic interlude there were festivals in Paris on account of some official solemnity which I have forgotten, a review at the Champ de Mars, a quintain on the Seine, theaters in the Champs Elysées, fireworks at the Etoile, and illuminations everywhere. Jean Valjean, breaking through his habits, took Cosette to these rejoicings, in order to make her forget the scene of the previous day, and efface, beneath the laughing tumult of all Paris, the abominable thing which had passed before her. The review, which seasoned the fête, rendered uniforms very natural; hence Jean Valjean put on his National Guard coat, with the vague inner feeling of a man who is seeking a refuge. However, the object of this jaunt seemed to be attained. Cosette, who made it a law to please her father, and to whom any festival was a novelty, accepted the distraction with the easy and light good-will of adolescents, and did not make too disdainful a pout at the porringer of joy which is called a public holiday. Hence Jean Valjean might believe that he had succeeded, and that no trace of the hideous vision remained. A few days after, one morning when the sun was shining, and both were

on the garden steps,—another infraction of the rules, which Jean Valjean seemed to have imposed on himself, and that habit of remaining
in her chamber which sadness had caused Cosette to assume,—the girl,
wearing a combing jacket, was standing in that morning negligé which
adorably envelops maidens, and looks like a cloud over a star; and with
her head in the light, her cheeks pink from a good night's rest, and gazed
at softly by the old man, she was plucking the petals of a daisy. She did
not know the delicious legend of "I love you, a little, passionately," etc.,
for who could have taught it to her? She handled the flower instinctively
and innocently without suspecting that plucking a daisy to pieces is
questioning a heart. If there were a fourth grace called melancholy, she
had the air of that grace when smiling. Jean Valjean was fascinated by
the contemplation of these little fingers on this flower, forgetting everything in the radiance which surrounded the child. A red-breast was
twittering in a bush hard by, and white clouds crossed the sky so gayly
that you might have said that they had just been set at liberty. Cosette
continued to pluck her flower attentively; she seemed to be thinking of
something, but that something must be charming. All at once she turned
her head on her shoulder, with the delicate slowness of a swan, and said
to Jean Valjean, "Tell me, father, what the galleys are."

BOOK IV

SUCCOR FROM BELOW MAY BE SUCCOR
FROM ON HIGH

1. *AN EXTERNAL WOUND AND AN INTERNAL CURE*

THEIR life thus gradually became overcast. Only one amusement was left them which had formerly been a happiness, and that was to carry bread to those who were starving and clothes to those who were cold. In these visits to the poor, in which Cosette frequently accompanied Jean Valjean, they found again some portion of their old expansiveness, and, at times, when the day had been good, when a good deal of distress had been relieved, and many children warmed and reanimated, Cosette displayed a little gayety at night. It was at this period that they paid the visit to Jondrette's den. The day after that visit Jean Valjean appeared at an early hour in the pavilion, calm as usual, but with a large wound in his left arm, which was inflamed and venomous, that resembled a burn, and which he accounted for in some way or other. This wound kept him at home with a fever for a whole month, without going out, for he would not see any medical man, and when Cosette dressed him, he said, "Call in the dog-doctor." Cosette dressed his wound morning and night with an air of such divine and angelic happiness at being useful to him, that Jean Valjean felt all his old joy return, his fears and anxieties dissipated, and he gazed at Cosette saying, "Oh, the excellent wound! the good evil!"

Cosette, seeing her father ill, had deserted the pavilion and regained her taste for the little outhouse and the back court. She spent nearly the whole day by the side of Jean Valjean, and read to him any books he chose, which were generally travels. Jean Valjean was regenerated; his happiness returned with ineffable radiance; the Luxembourg, the young unknown prowler, Cosette's coldness, all these soul-clouds disappeared, and he found himself saying, "I imagined all that; I am an old fool!" His happiness was such that the frightful discovery of the Thénardiers in the Jondrette den, which was so unexpected, had to some extent glided over him. He had succeeded in escaping, his trail was lost, and what did he care for the rest! he only thought of it to pity those wretches. They were in prison, and henceforth incapable of mischief, he thought, but what a lamentable family in distress! As for the hideous vision of the Barrière du Maine, Cosette had not spoken again about it. In the convent Sister Ste. Mechtilde had taught Cosette music; she had a voice such as a linnet would have if it possessed a soul, and at times she sang, in the wounded man's obscure room, melancholy songs which Jean Valjean was delighted with. Spring arrived, and the garden was so delicious at that season of the year that Jean Valjean said to Cosette, "You never go out, and I wish you to take a stroll." "As you please, father," said Cosette. And, to obey her father, she resumed her walks in the garden, generally alone, for, as we have mentioned, Jean Valjean, who was probably afraid of being seen through the railing, hardly ever entered it.

Jean Valjean's wound had been a diversion. When Cosette saw that her father suffered less, and was recovering and seemed happy, she felt a satisfaction which she did not even notice, for it came so softly and naturally. Then, too, it was the month of March, the days were drawing out, winter was departing, and it always takes with it some portion of our sorrow; then came April, that daybreak of summer, fresh as every dawn, and gay like all childhoods, and somewhat tearful at times, like the new-born babe it is. Nature in that month has charming beams which pass from the sky, the clouds, the trees, the fields, and the flowers into the human heart. Cosette was still too young for this April joy, which resembled her, not to penetrate her; insensibly, and without suspecting it, the dark cloud departed from her mind. In spring there is light in sad souls, as there is midday in cellars. Cosette was no longer so very sad; it was so, but she did not attempt to account for it. In the morning, after breakfast, when she succeeded in drawing her father into the garden for a quarter of an hour, and walked him up and down, while supporting his injured arm, she did not notice that she laughed every moment and was happy. Jean Valjean was delighted to see her become ruddy-cheeked and fresh once more.

"Oh! the famous wound!" he repeated to himself in a low voice.

And he was grateful to the Thénardiers. So soon as his wound was cured he recommenced his solitary night-rambles; and it would be a mistake to suppose that a man can walk about alone in the uninhabited regions of Paris without meeting with some adventure.

2. MOTHER PLUTARCH ACCOUNTS FOR A MIRACLE

ONE evening little Gavroche had eaten nothing; he remembered that he had not dined either on the previous day, and that was becoming ridiculous, so he formed the resolution to try and sup. He went prowling about at the deserted spots beyond the Salpetrière, for there are good windfalls there; where there is nobody something may be found. He thus reached a suburb which seemed to him to be the village of Auster-litz. In one of his previous prowls he had noticed there an old garden frequented by an old man and an old woman, and in this garden a passable apple-tree. By the side of this tree was a sort of badly closed fruit-loft, whence an apple might be obtained. An apple is a supper, an apple is life, and what ruined Adam might save Gavroche. The garden skirted a solitary unpaved lane, bordered by shrubs, while waiting for houses, and a hedge separated it from the lane. Gavroche proceeded to the garden; he found the lane again, he recognized the apple-tree, saw the fruit-loft, and examined the hedge; a hedge is but a stride. Day was declining, there was not a cat in the lane, and the hour was good. Gavroche was preparing to clamber over the hedge when he stopped short—some people were talking in the garden. Gavroche looked through one of the interstices in the hedge. Two paces from him, at the foot of the hedge, exactly at the spot where the hole he intended to make would have ended, lay a stone, which formed a species of bench, and on this bench the old man of the garden was seated, with the old woman standing in front of him. The old woman was grumbling, and Gavroche, who was not troubled with too much discretion, listened.

"Monsieur Mabœuf!" the old woman said.

"Mabœuf," Gavroche thought, "that's a rum name."

The old man thus addressed did not stir, and the old woman repeated: "Monsieur Mabœuf!"

The old man, without taking his eyes off the ground, resolved to answer:

"Well, Mother Plutarch!"

"Mother Plutarch!" Gavroche thought, "that's another rum name."

Mother Plutarch continued, and the old gentleman was compelled to accept the conversation.

"The landlord is not satisfied."

"Why so?"

"There are three quarters owing."

"In three months more we shall owe four."

"He says that he will turn you out."

"I will go."

"The greengrocer wants to be paid, or she will supply no more fagots. How shall we warm ourselves this winter if we have no wood?"

"There is the sun."

"The butcher has stopped our credit, and will not supply any more meat."

"That is lucky, for I cannot digest meat; it is heavy."

"But what shall we have for dinner?"

"Bread."

"The baker insists on receiving something on account; 'No money, no bread,' he says."

"Very good."

"What will you eat?"

"We have the apples from the apple-tree."

"But, really, sir, we cannot live in that way without money."

"I have none."

The old woman went away and left the old gentleman alone. He began thinking, and Gavroche thought too; it was almost night. The first result of Gavroche's reflection was that, instead of climbing over the hedge, he lay down under it. The branches parted a little at the bottom. "Hilloh," said Gavroche to himself, "it's an alcove," and he crept into it. His back was almost against the octogenarian's bench, and he could hear him breathe. Then, in lieu of dining, Gavroche tried to sleep. It was the sleep of a cat, with one eye open; while dozing Gavroche watched. The whiteness of the twilight lit up the ground, and the lane formed a livid line between two rows of dark thickets. All at once two figures appeared on this white strip; one was in front and the other a little distance behind.

"Here are two coves," Gavroche growled.

The first figure seemed to be some old bowed citizen, more than simply attired, who walked slowly, owing to his age, and was strolling about in the starlight. The second was straight, firm, and slim; he regulated his steps by those of the man in front; but suppleness and agility could be detected in his voluntary slowness. This figure had something ferocious and alarming about it, and the appearance of what was called a dandy in those days; the hat was of good shape, and the coat was black, well cut, probably of fine cloth, and tight at the waist. He held his head up with a sort of robust grace, and under the hat a glimpse could be caught of a pale, youthful profile in the twilight. This profile had a rose in its mouth, and was familiar to Gavroche, for it was Montparnasse. As for the other, there was nothing to be said save that he was a respectable old man. Gavroche at once began observing, for it was evident that one of these men had projects upon the other. Gavroche was well situated to see the finale, and the alcove had opportunely become a hiding-place. Montparnasse hunting at such an hour and such a spot, that was menacing. Gavroche felt his gamin entrails moved with pity for the old gentleman. What should he do? interfere? one weakness helping another! Montparnasse would have laughed at it, for Gavroche did not conceal from himself that the old man first, and then the boy, would be only two mouthfuls for this formidable bandit of eighteen. While Gavroche was deliberating, the attack, a sudden and hideous attack, took place; it was the attack of a tiger on an onager, of a spider on a fly. Montparnasse suddenly threw away the rose, leaped upon the old man, grappled him and clung to him, and Gavroche had difficulty in repressing a cry. A moment after, one of these men was beneath the other, crushed, gasping, and struggling, with a knee of marble on his chest. But it was not exactly what Gavroche had anticipated; the man on the ground was Montparnasse, the one on top the citizen. All this took place a few yards from Gavroche. The old man received the shock, and repaid it so terribly that in an instant the assailant and the assailed changed parts.

"That's a tough invalide," Gavroche thought. And he could not refrain from clapping his hands, but it was thrown away; it was not heard by the two combatants, who feared one another, and mingled their breath in the struggle. At length there was a silence, and Montparnasse ceased writhing; Gavroche muttered this aside, "Is he dead?" The worthy man had not uttered a word or given a cry; he rose, and Gavroche heard him say to Montparnasse, "Get up."

Montparnasse did so, but the citizen still held him. Montparnasse had the humiliated and furious attitude of a wolf snapped at by a sheep. Gavroche looked and listened, making an effort to double his eyes with his ears; he was enormously amused. He was rewarded for his conscientious anxiety, for he was able to catch the following dialogue, which borrowed from the darkness a sort of tragic accent; the gentleman questioned, and Montparnasse answered.

"What is your age?"

"Nineteen."

"You are strong and healthy; why do you not work?"

"It is a bore."

"What is your trade?"

"Idler."

"Speak seriously. Can anything be done for you? what do you wish to be?"

"A robber."

There was a silence, and the old gentleman seemed to be in profound thought, but he did not loose his hold of Montparnasse. Every now and then the young bandit, who was vigorous and active, gave starts like a wild beast caught in a snare; he shook himself, attempted a trip, wildly writhed his limbs, and tried to escape. The old gentleman did not appear to notice it, and held the ruffian's two arms in one hand with the sovereign indifference of absolute strength. The old man's reverie lasted some time; then, gazing fixedly at Montparnasse, he mildly raised his voice and addressed to him, in the darkness where they stood, a sort of solemn appeal, of which Gavroche did not lose a syllable.

"My boy, you are entering by sloth into the most laborious of existences. Ah! you declare yourself an idler; then prepare yourself for labor. Have you ever seen a formidable machine which is called a rolling-mill? You must be on your guard against it, for it is a crafty and ferocious thing, and if it catch you by the skirt of the coat it drags you under it entirely. This machine is indolence. Stop while there is yet time, and save yourself; otherwise it is all over with you, and ere long you will be among the cog-wheels. Once caught, hope for nothing more. You will be forced to fatigue yourself, idler, and no rest will be allowed you, for the iron hand of implacable toil has seized you. You refuse to earn your livelihood, have a calling, and accomplish a duty; it bores you to be like the rest. Well, you will be different. Labor is the law, and whoever repels it as a bore must have it as a punishment. You do not wish to be a laborer, and you will be a slave; toil only lets loose on one side to seize you again on the other; you do not wish to be its friend, and you will be its negro. Ah, you did not care for the honest fatigue of men, and you are about to know the sweat of the damned; while others sing, you will groan. You will see other men working in the distance, and they will seem to you to be resting. The digger, the reaper, the sailor, the blacksmith, will appear to you in the light like the blessed inmates of a paradise. What a radiance there is in the anvil! what joy it is to guide the plow and tie up the sheaf; what a holiday to fly before the wind in a boat! But you, idler, dig, drag, roll, walk! Pull at your halter, for you are a beast of burden in the team of hell! So your desire is to do nothing? Well, you will not have a week, a day, an hour without feeling crushed. You will not be able to lift anything without agony, and every passing minute will make your muscles crack. What is a feather for others will be a rock for you, and the most simple things will grow rugged. Life will become a monster around you, and coming, going, breathing, will be so many terrible tasks for you. Your lungs will feel like a hundred-pound weight, and going there rather than here will be a problem to solve. Any ordinary man who wishes to go out merely opens his door and finds himself in the street; but if you wish to go out, you must pierce through your wall. What do honest men do to reach the street? they go downstairs; but you will tear up your sheets, make a cord of them fiber by fiber, then pass through your window and hang by this thread over an abyss, and it will take place at night, in the storm, the rain, or the hurricane, and if the cord be too short you will have one way of descending, by falling—falling haphazard into the gulf, and from any height, and on what? on some unknown thing beneath. Or you will climb up a chimney at the risk of burning yourself; or crawl through a sewer at the risk of drowning. I will say nothing of the holes which must be masked; of the stones which you will have to remove and put back twenty times a day, or of the plaster you must hide under your mattress. A lock presents itself, and the citizen has in his pocket the key for it, made by the locksmith, but you, if you wish to go out, are condemned to make a terrible masterpiece. You will take a double sou and cut it asunder. With tools, you will invent them; that is your business. Then you will hollow out the interior of the two parts, being careful not to injure the outside, and form a thread all round the edge, so that the two parts may fit closely like a box and its cover. When they are screwed together, there will be nothing suspicious to the watchers, for you will be watched; it will be a double sou, but for yourself a box. What will you place in this box? a small piece of steel, a watch-spring, in which you have made teeth, and which will be a saw. With this saw, about the length of a pin, you will be obliged to cut through the bolt of the lock, the padlock of your chain, the bar at your window, and the fetter on your leg. This masterpiece done, this prodigy accomplished, all the miracles of art, skill, cleverness, and patience executed, what will be your reward if you are detected?—a dungeon. Such is the future. What precipices are sloth and pleasure! To do nothing is a melancholy resolution; are you aware of that? To live in indolence on the social substance! to be useless; that is to say, injurious! This leads straight to the bottom of misery. Woe to the man who wishes to be a parasite, for he will be a vermin! Ah! it does not please you to work! Ah! you have only one thought, to drink well, to eat well, and sleep well. You will drink water; you will eat black bread; you will sleep on a plank, with fetters riveted to your limbs, and feel their coldness at night in your flesh! You will break these fetters and fly; very good. You will drag yourself on your stomach into the shrubs and eat grass like the beasts of the field; you will be recaptured, and then you will pass years in a dungeon, chained to the wall, groping in the dark for your water-jug, biting at frightful black bread which dogs would refuse, and eating beans which maggots have eaten before you. You will be a wood-louse in a cellar. Ah! ah! take pity on yourself, wretched boy, still so young, who were at your nurse's breast not twenty years ago, and have doubtless a mother still! I implore you to listen to me. You will want fine black cloth, polished shoes, to scent your head with fragrant oil, to please the girls, and be a pretty fellow; you will have your hair close shaved, and wear a red jacket and wooden shoes. You want a ring on your finger; you shall wear a collar on your neck, and if you look at a woman you will be beaten. And you will go in there at twenty and come out at fifty years of age. You will go in young, red-cheeked, healthy, with your sparkling eyes, and all your white teeth and your curly locks, and you will come out again broken, bent, wrinkled, toothless, horrible, and gray-headed! Ah, my poor boy, you are on the wrong road, and indolence is a bad adviser, for robbery is the hardest of labors. Take my advice, and do not undertake the laborious task of being an idler. To become a rogue is inconvenient. It is not nearly so hard to be an honest man. Now, go and think over what I have said to you. By the bye, what did you want of me? my purse? here it is."

And the old man, releasing Montparnasse, placed his purse in his hand, which Montparnasse weighed for a moment; after which, with the same mechanical precaution as if he had stolen it, Montparnasse let it glide gently into the back-pocket of his coat. All this said and done, the old gentleman turned his back and quietly resumed his walk.

"Old humbug!" Montparnasse muttered. Who was the old gentleman? the reader has doubtless guessed. Montparnasse, in his stupefaction, watched him until he disappeared in the gloom, and this contemplation was fatal for him. While the old gentleman retired Gavroche advanced. Gavroche had assured himself by a glance that Father Maboeuf was still on his bench, and was probably asleep; then the gamin left the bushes, and began crawling in the shadow behind the motionless Montparnasse. He thus got up to the young bandit unnoticed, gently insinuated his hand into the back-pocket of the fine black cloth, seized the purse, withdrew his hand, and crawled back into the shadow like a lizard. Montparnasse, who had no reason to be on his guard, and who was thinking for the first time in his life, perceived nothing, and Gavroche, when he had returned to the spot where Father Maboeuf was sitting, threw the purse over the hedge and ran off at full speed. The purse fell on Father Maboeuf's foot and awoke him. He stooped down and picked up the purse, which he opened, without comprehending anything. It was a purse with two compartments; in one was some change, in the other were six napoleons. M. Maboeuf, greatly startled, carried the thing to his housekeeper.

"It has fallen from heaven," said Mother Plutarch.

BOOK V

THE END OF WHICH DOES NOT RESEMBLE THE BEGINNING

1. SOLITUDE AND THE BARRACKS COMBINED

Cosette's sorrow, so poignant and so sharp four or five months previously, had, without her knowledge, attained the convalescent stage. Nature, spring, youth, love for her father, the gayety of the flowers and birds, filtered gradually, day by day and drop by drop, something that almost resembled oblivion into her virginal and young soul. Was the fire entirely extinguished? or were layers of ashes merely formed? The fact is, that she hardly felt any longer the painful and burning point. One day when she suddenly thought of Marius, "Why," she said, "I had almost forgotten him." This same week she noticed, while passing the garden gate, a very handsome officer in the Lancers, with a wasp-like waist, a delightful uniform, the cheeks of a girl, a saber under his arm, waxed mustaches, and lacquered schapska. In other respects, he had light hair, blue eyes flush with his head, a round, vain, insolent, and pretty face; he was exactly the contrary of Marius. He had a cigar in his mouth, and Cosette supposed that he belonged to the regiment quartered in the barracks of the Rue de Babylone. The next day she saw him pass again, and remarked the hour. From this moment—was it an accident? —she saw him pass nearly every day. The officer's comrades perceived that there was in this badly kept garden, and behind this poor, old-fashioned railing, a very pretty creature, who was nearly always there when the handsome lieutenant passed, who is no stranger to the reader, as his name was Théodule Gillenormand.

"Hilloh!" they said to him, "there's a little girl making eyes at you; just look at her."

"Have I the time," the lancer replied, "to look at all the girls who look at me?"

It was at this identical time that Marius was slowly descending to the death-struggle, and said, "If I could only see her again before I die!" If his wish had been realized, if he had at that moment seen Cosette looking at a lancer, he would have been unable to utter a word, but expired of grief. Whose fault would it have been? nobody's. Marius possessed one of those temperaments which bury themselves in chagrin and abide in it. Cosette was one of those who plunge into it and again emerge. Cosette, however, was passing through that dangerous moment, the fatal phase of feminine reverie left to itself, in which the heart of an isolated maiden resembles those vine tendrils which cling, according to chance, to the capital of a marble column or to the sign-post of a pot-house. It is a rapid and decisive moment, critical for every orphan, whether she be poor or rich, for wealth does not prevent a bad choice, and misalliances take place in very high society. But the true misalliance is that of souls; and in the same way as many an unknown young man, without name, birth, or fortune, is a marble capital supporting a temple of grand sentiments and grand ideas, so such and such a man of the world, satisfied and opulent, who has polished boots and varnished words, if we look not at the exterior but at the interior, that is to say, what is reserved for the wife, is naught but a stupid log obscurely haunted by violent, unclean, and drunken passions—the sign-post of the pot-house.

What was there in Cosette's soul? passion calmed or lulled to sleep, love in a floating state; something which was limpid and brilliant, perturbed at a certain depth, and somber lower still. The image of the handsome officer was reflected on the surface, but was there any reminiscence at the bottom, quite at the bottom? perhaps so, but Cosette did not know.

A singular incident occurred.

2. FEARS OF COSETTE

In the first fortnight in April Jean Valjean went on a journey: this, as we know, occurred from time to time at very lengthened intervals, and he remained away one or two days at the most. Where did he go? no one knew, not even Cosette; once only she had accompanied him in a hackney coach, upon the occasion of one of these absences, to the corner of a little lane, which was called, *L'Impasse de la blanchette*. He got out there, and the coach carried Cosette back to the Rue de Babylone. It was generally when money ran short in the house that Jean Valjean took these trips. Jean Valjean, then, was absent, and he had said, "I shall be back in three days." At night Cosette was alone in the drawing-room, and in order to while away the time she opened her piano and began singing to her own accompaniment the song of Euryanthe, "Hunters wandering in the wood," which is probably the finest thing we possess in the shape of music. When she had finished she remained pensive. Suddenly she fancied she heard some one walk in the garden. It could not be her father, for he was away, and it could not be Toussaint, as she was in bed, for it was ten o'clock at night. Cosette went up to the drawing-room shutters, which were closed, and put her ear to them; and it seemed to her that it was the footfall of a man who was walking very gently. She hurried up to her room on the upper-floor, opened a Venetian frame in her shutter, and looked out into the garden. The moon was full and was shining bright as day, and there was nobody in it. She opened her window; the garden was perfectly calm, and all that could be seen of the street was as deserted as usual.

Cosette thought that she was mistaken. She had supposed that she heard the noise; it was an hallucination produced by Weber's gloomy and prodigious chorus, which opens before the mind prodigious depths, which trembles before the eye like a dizzy forest, in which we hear the cracking of the dead branches under the restless feet of the hunters, of whom we catch a glimpse in the obscurity. She thought no more of it. Moreover, Cosette was not naturally very timid: she had in her veins some of the blood of the gypsy and the adventuress who goes about barefooted. As we may remember, she was rather a lark than a dove, and she had a stern and brave temper.

The next evening, at nightfall, she was walking about the garden. In the midst of the confused thoughts which occupied her mind, she fancied she could distinguish now and then a noise like that of the previous night, as if some one was walking in the gloom under the trees not far from her, but she said to herself that nothing so resembles the sound of a footfall on grass as the grating of two branches together, and she took no heed of it—besides, she saw nothing. She left the "thicket," and had a small grass-plat to cross ere she reached the house. The moon, which had just risen behind her, projected Cosette's shadow, as she left the clump of bushes, upon the grass in front of her. She stopped in terror. By the side of her shadow the moon distinctly traced on the grass another singularly startling and terrible shadow—a shadow with a hat on its head. It was like the shadow of a man standing at the edge of the clump a few paces behind Cosette. For a moment she was unable to speak, or cry, or call out, or stir, or turn her head, but at last she collected all her courage and boldly turned round. There was nobody. She looked on the ground and the shadow had disappeared. She went back into the shrubs, bravely searched in every corner, was as far as the railings, and discovered nothing. She felt really chilled: was it again an hallucination? what! two days in succession? one hallucination might pass, but two! The alarming point was, that the shadow was most certainly not a ghost, for ghosts never wear round hats.

The next day Jean Valjean returned, and Cosette told him what she fancied she had seen and heard. She expected to be re-assured, and that her father would shrug his shoulders and say, "You are a little goose." Jean Valjean became anxious.

"Perhaps it is nothing," he said to her. He left her with some excuse, and went into the garden, where she saw him examine the railings with considerable attention. In the night she woke up; this time she was certain, and she distinctly heard someone walking just under her windows. She walked to her shutter and opened it. There was in the garden really a man holding a large stick in his hand. At the moment when she was going to cry out, the moon lit up the man's face—it was her father. She went to bed again, saying, "He seems really very anxious!" Jean Valjean passed that and the two following nights in the garden, and Cosette saw him through the hole in her shutter. On the third night the moon was beginning to rise later, and it might be about one in the morning when she heard a hearty burst of laughter, and her father's voice calling her:

"Cosette!"

She leaped out of bed, put on her dressing-gown, and opened her window; her father was standing on the grass-plat below.

"I have woke you up to re-assure you," he said; "look at this,—here's your shadow in the round hat."

And he showed her on the grass a shadow, which the moon designed, and which really looked rather like the specter of a man wearing a round hat. It was an outline produced by a zinc chimney-pot with a cowl, which rose above an adjoining roof. Cosette also began laughing, all her mournful suppositions fell away, and the next morning at breakfast she jested at the ill-omened garden, haunted by the ghosts of chimney-pots. Jean Valjean quite regained his ease; as for Cosette, she did not notice particularly whether the chimney-pot were really in the direction of the shadow which she had seen, or fancied she saw, and whether the moon were in the same part of the heavens. She did not cross-question herself as to the singularity of a chimney-pot which is afraid of being caught in the act, and retires when its shadow is looked at, for the shadow did retire when Cosette turned round, and she fancied herself quite certain of that fact. Cosette became quite re-assured, for the demonstration seemed to her perfect, and the thought that there could have been any one walking about the garden by night left her brain. A few days after, however, a fresh incident occurred.

3 · *THE COMMENTS OF TOUSSAINT*

IN the garden, near the railings, looking out on the street, there was a stone bench, protected from the gaze of passers-by by a hedge, but it would have been an easy task to reach it by thrusting an arm through the railings and the hedge. One evening in this same month of April, Jean Valjean had gone out, and Cosette, after sunset, was seated on this bench. The wind was freshening in the trees, and Cosette was reflecting; an objectless sorrow was gradually gaining on her, the invincible sorrow which night produces and which comes, perhaps,—for who knows?— from the mystery of the tomb which is yawning at the moment. Possibly Fantine was in that shadow.

Cosette rose and slowly went round the garden, walking on the dew-laden grass, and saying to herself through the sort of melancholy somnambulism in which she was plunged, "I ought to have wooden shoes to walk in the garden at this hour; I shall catch cold." She returned to the bench, but at the moment when she was going to sit down she noticed at the place she had left a rather large stone, which had evidently not been there a moment before. Cosette looked at the stone, asking herself what it meant; all at once the idea that the stone had not reached the bench of itself, that some one had placed it there, and that an arm had been passed through the grating, occurred to her, and frightened her. This time it was a real fear, for there was the stone. No doubt was possible; she did not touch it, but fled without daring to look behind her, sought refuge in the house, and at once shuttered, barred, and bolted the French window opening on the steps. Then she asked Toussaint:

"Has my father come in?"

"No, miss."

(We have indicated once for all Toussaint's stammering, and we ask leave no longer to accentuate it, as we feel a musical notation of an infirmity to be repulsive.)

Jean Valjean, a thoughtful man, and stroller by night, often did not return till a late hour.

"Toussaint," Cosette continued, "be careful to put up the bars to the shutters looking on the garden, and to place the little iron things in the rings that close them."

"Oh, I am sure I will, miss."

Toussaint did not fail, and Cosette was well aware of the fact, but she could not refrain from adding:

"For it is so desolate here."

"Well, that's true," said Toussaint; "we might be murdered before we had the time to say Ouf! and then, too, master does not sleep in the house. But don't be frightened, miss, I fasten up the windows like Bastilles. Lone women! I should think that is enough to make a body shudder. Only think! to see men coming into your bedroom and hear them say 'Silence!' and then they begin to cut your throat. It is not so much the dying, for everybody dies, and we know that we must do so, but it is the abomination of feeling those fellows touch you; and then their knives are not sharp, perhaps; O Lord!"

"Hold your tongue," said Cosette, "and fasten up everything securely."

Cosette, terrified by the drama improvised by Toussaint, and perhaps too by the apparitions of the last week, which returned to her mind, did not even dare to say to her, "Just go and look at the stone laid on the bench," for fear of having to open the garden gate again, and the men might walk in. She had all the doors and windows carefully closed, made Toussaint examine the whole house from cellar to attic, locked herself in her bedroom, looked under the bed, and slept badly. The whole night through she saw the stone as large as a mountain and full of caverns. At sunrise—the peculiarity of sunrise is to make us laugh at all our terrors of the night, and our laughter is always proportioned to the fear we have felt—at sunrise, Cosette, on waking, looked at her terror as a nightmare, and said to herself, "What could I be thinking about? it was like the steps which I fancied I heard last week in the garden at night! It is like the shadow of the chimney-pot; am I going to turn coward now?" The sun, which poured through the crevices of her shutters and made the damask curtains one mass of purple, re-assured her so fully that all faded away in her mind, even to the stone.

"There was no more a stone on the bench than there was a man in a round hat in the garden. I dreamed of the stone, like the rest."

She dressed herself, went down into the garden, and felt a cold perspiration all over her—the stone was there. But this only lasted for a moment, for what is terror by night is curiosity by day.

"Nonsense!" she said, "I'll see."

She raised the stone, which was of some size, and there was something under it that resembled a letter; it was an envelope of white paper. Cosette seized it; there was no address on it, and it was not sealed up. Still, the envelope, though open, was not empty, for papers could be seen inside. Cosette no longer suffered from terror, nor was it curiosity; it was a commencement of anxiety. Cosette took out a small quire of paper, each page of which was numbered and bore several lines written in a very nice and delicate hand, so Cosette thought. She looked for a name, but there was none; for a signature, but there was none either. For whom was the packet intended? probably for herself, as a hand had laid it on the bench. From whom did it come? An irresistible fascination seized upon her; she tried to turn her eyes away from these pages, which trembled in her hand. She looked at the sky, the street, the acacias all bathed in light, the pigeons circling round an adjoining roof, and then her eye settled on the manuscript, and she said to herself that she must know what was inside it. This is what she read:

4. *A HEART BENEATH A STONE*

THE *reduction of the universe to a single being, the dilatation of a single being as far as God, such is love.*

Love is the salutation of the angels to the stars.

How sad the soul is when it is sad through love.—What a void is the absence of the being who of her own self fills the world. Oh! how true it is that the beloved being becomes God! we might understand how God might be jealous, had not the Father of all evidently made creation for the soul, and the soul for love.

The soul only needs to see a smile in a white crape bonnet in order to enter the palace of dreams.

God is behind everything, but everything conceals God. Things are black and creatures are opaque, but to love a being is to render her transparent.

Certain thoughts are prayers. There are moments when the soul is kneeling, no matter what the attitude of the body may be.

Separated lovers cheat absence by a thousand chimerical things, which, however, have their reality. They are prevented seeing each other, and they cannot write, but they find a number of mysterious ways to correspond. They send to each other the song of birds, the light of the sun, the sighs of the breeze, the rays of the stars, and the whole creation; and why should they not? All the works of God are made to serve love. Love is sufficiently powerful to interest all nature with its messages.

O spring, thou art a letter which I write to her.

The future belongs even more to hearts than to minds. Loving is the only thing which can occupy and fill the immensity, for the infinite needs the inexhaustible.

Love is a portion of the soul itself, and is of the same nature as it. Like it, it is the divine spark; like it, it is incorruptible, indivisible, and imperishable. It is a point of fire within us, which is immortal and infinite, which nothing can limit, and nothing extinguish; we feel it burning even in the marrow of our bones, and see its flashing in the depths of the heavens.

O Love! adoration! voluptuousness of two minds which comprehend each other, of two hearts which are exchanged, of two glances that penetrate each other. You will come to me, O happiness, will you not? Walks with her in the solitudes, blest and radiant days! I have dreamed that from time to time hours were detached from the lives of the angels, and came down here to pass through the destinies of men.

God can add nothing to the happiness of those who love, except giving them endless duration. After a life of love, an eternity of love is in truth an augmentation; but it is impossible even for God to increase in its intensity the ineffable felicity which love gives to the soul in this world. God is the fullness of heaven; love is the fullness of man.

You gaze at a star for two motives, because it is luminous and because it is impenetrable. You have by your side a sweeter radiance and greater mystery—woman.

All of us, whoever we may be, have our respirable beings. If they fail us, air fails us, and we stifle and die. Dying through want of love is frightful, for it is the asphyxia of the soul.

When love has blended and molded two beings in an angelic and sacred union, they have found the secret of life; henceforth they are only the two terms of the same destiny, the two wings of one mind. Love and soar!

On the day when a woman who passes before you emits light as she walks, you are lost, for you love! You have from that moment but one thing to do,—think of her so intently that she will be compelled to think of you.

What love begins can only be completed by God.

True love is in despair, or enchanted by a lost glove or a found handkerchief, and it requires eternity for its devotion and its hopes. It is composed at once of the infinitely great and the infinitely little.

If you are a stone, be a magnet; if you are a plant, be sensitive; if you are a man, be love.

Nothing is sufficient for love. You have happiness, and you wish for paradise. You have paradise, and you crave for heaven. O ye who love each other, all this is contained in love; hence try to find it in it. Love has, equally with heaven, contemplation, and more than heaven voluptuousness.

Does she still go to the Luxembourg? No, sir.—Does she attend mass in that church? She does not go there any longer.—Does she still live in this house? She has removed—Where has she gone to live? She did not leave her address.

What a gloomy thing it is not to know where to find one's soul!

Love has its childishness, and other passions have their littleness. Shame on the passions that make a man little! Honor to the one which makes him a child!

It is a strange thing; are you aware of it? I am in the night. There is a being who carried off heaven with her when she flew away.

Oh! to lie side by side in the same tomb hand in hand, and to gently caress a finger from time to time in the darkness, would suffice for my eternity.

You who suffer because you love, love more than ever. To die of love is to live through it.

Love, a gloomy, starry transfiguration, is mingled with this punishment, and there is ecstasy in the agony.

Oh, joy of birds! they sing because they have the nest.

Love is a celestial breathing of the atmosphere of paradise.

Profound hearts, wise minds, take life as God makes it; it is a long trial, an unintelligible preparation for the unknown destiny. This destiny, the true one, begins for man with the first step in the interior of the tomb. Then something appears to him, and he begins to distinguish the definite. The definite; reflect on that word. The living see the infinite, but the definite only shows itself to the dead. In the meanwhile love and suffer, hope and contemplate. Woe, alas! to the man who has only loved bodies, shapes, and appearances! Death will strip him of all that. Try to love souls, and you will meet them again.

I have met in the street a very poor young man who was in love. His hat was old, his coat worn, his coat was out at elbows, the water passed through his shoes, and the stars through his soul.

What a grand thing it is to be loved! what a grander thing still to love! The heart becomes heroic by the might of passion. Henceforth it is composed of naught but what is pure, and is only supported by what is elevated and great. An unworthy thought can no more germinate in it than a nettle on a glacier. The lofty and serene soul, inaccessible to emotions and vulgar passions, soaring above the clouds and shadows of the world, follies, falsehoods, hatreds, vanities, and miseries, dwells in the azure of the sky, and henceforth only feels the profound and subterranean heavings of destiny as the summits of the mountains feel earthquakes.

If there were nobody who loved, the sun would be extinguished.

5 . COSETTE AFTER THE LETTER

WHILE reading these lines Cosette gradually fell into a reverie, and at the moment when she raised her eyes from the last page the pretty officer passed triumphantly in front of the gate, for it was his hour. Cosette found him hideous. She began gazing at the roll of paper again; it was in an exquisite handwriting, Cosette thought, all written by the same hand, but with different inks, some very black, others pale, as when ink is put in the stand, and consequently on different days. It was, therefore, a thought expanded on the paper, sigh by sigh, irregularly, without order, without choice, without purpose, accidentally. Cosette had never read anything like it; this manuscript, in which she saw more light than obscurity, produced on her the effect of the door of a shrine left ajar. Each of these mysterious lines flashed in her eyes, and inundated her heart with a strange light. The education which she had received had always spoken to her of the soul, and not of love, much as if a person were to speak of the burning log and say nothing about the flame. This manuscript of fifteen pages suddenly and gently revealed to her the whole of love, sorrow, destiny, life, eternity, the beginning and the end. It was like a hand which opened and threw upon her a handful of beams. She felt in these few lines an impassioned, ardent, generous, and honest nature, a sacred will, an immense grief and an immense hope, a contracted heart, and an expanded ecstasy. What was the manuscript? a letter. A letter without address, name, or signature, pressing and disinterested, an enigma composed of truths, a love-message fit to be borne by an angel and read by a virgin; a rendezvous appointed off the world, a sweet love-letter written by a phantom to a shadow. It was a tranquil and crushed absent man who seemed ready to seek a refuge in death, and who sent to the absent one the secret of destiny, the key of life—love. It had been written with one foot in the grave and the hand in heaven; and these lines, which had fallen one by one on the paper were what might be called drops of the soul.

And now, from whom could these pages come? Who could have written them? Cosette did not hesitate for a moment,—only from one man, from *him!* Daylight had returned to her mind, and everything reappeared. She experienced an extraordinary joy and a profound agony. It was he! he who wrote to her! he had been there! his arm had been passed through the railings! while she was forgetting him, he had found her again! But had she forgotten him? no, never! she was mad to have thought so for a moment, for she had ever loved, ever adored him. The fire was covered and had smoldered for a while, but, as she now plainly saw, it had spread its ravages and again burst into a flame which entirely kindled her. This letter was like a spark that had fallen from the other soul into hers; she felt the fire begin again. She was penetrated by every word of the manuscript. "Oh, yes," she said to herself, "how well I recognize all this; I had read it all already in his eyes."

As she finished reading it for the third time Lieutenant Théodule returned past the railings, and clanked his spurs on the pavement. Cosette was obliged to raise her eyes, and she found him insipid, silly, stupid, useless, fatuous, displeasing, impertinent, and very ugly. The officer thought himself bound to smile. She turned away ashamed and indignant; she would have gladly thrown something at his head. She ran away, reëntered the house, and locked herself in her bedroom, to reread the letter, learn it by heart, and dream. When she had read it thoroughly she kissed it and hid it in her bosom. It was all over. Cosette had fallen back into the profound seraphic love, the Paradisaic abyss had opened again. The whole day through Cosette was in a state of bewilderment; she hardly thought, and her ideas were confused in her brain; she could not succeed in forming any conjectures, and she hoped, through her tremors, what? vague things. She did not dare promise herself anything, and she would not refuse herself anything. A pallor passed over her face, and a quiver over her limbs, and she fancied at moments that it was all a chimera, and said to herself, "Is it real?" then she felt the well-beloved paper under her dress, pressed it to her heart, felt the corners against her flesh, and if Jean Valjean had seen her at that moment he would have shuddered at the luminous and strange joy which over-flowed from her eyelids. "Oh, yes," she thought, "it is certainly his! this comes from him for me!" And she said to herself that an intervention of the angels, a celestial accident, had restored him to her. Oh, transfigura-tion of love! oh, dreams! this celestial accident, this intervention of angels, was the ball of bread cast by one robber to another from the Charlemagne yard to the Lion's den over the buildings of La Force.

6. THE OLD PEOPLE CONVENIENTLY GO OUT

WHEN night came Jean Valjean went out, and Cosette dressed herself. She arranged her hair in the way that best became her, and put on a dress whose body, having received a cut of the scissors too much, displayed the whole of the neck, and was therefore, as girls say, "rather indecent." It was not the least in the world indecent, but it was prettier than the former fashion. She dressed herself in this way without knowing why. Was she going out? No. Did she expect a visitor? No. She went down into the garden as it grew dark; Toussaint was engaged in her kitchen, which looked out on the back yard. Cosette began walking under the branches, removing them from time to time with her hand, as some were very low, and thus reached the bench. The stone was still there and she sat down and laid her beautiful white hand on the stone, as if to caress and thank it. All at once she had that indescribable feeling which people experience even without seeing, when some one is standing behind them. She turned her head and rose—it was he. He was bareheaded, and seemed pale and thin, and his black clothes could be scarce distinguished. The twilight rendered his glorious forehead livid, and covered his eyes with darkness, and he had, beneath a veil of incomparable gentleness, something belonging to death and night. His face was lit up by the flush of departing day, and by the thoughts of an expiring soul. He seemed as if he were not yet a specter, but was no longer a man. His hat was thrown among the shrubs a few paces from him. Cosette, though ready to faint, did not utter a cry; she slowly recoiled as she felt herself attracted, but he did not stir. Through the ineffable sadness that enveloped him she felt the glance of the eyes which she could not see. Cosette, in recoiling, came to a tree, and leaned against it; had it not been for this tree she would have fallen. Then she heard his voice, that voice which she had really never heard before, scarce louder than the rustling of the foliage, as he murmured:

"Pardon me for being here; my heart is swollen. I could not live as I was, and I have come. Have you read what I placed on that bench? do you recognize me at all? do not be frightened at me. Do you remember that day when you looked at me, now so long ago? It was in the Luxembourg garden, near the Gladiator, and the days on which you passed before me were June 16 and July 2; it is nearly a year ago. I have not seen you again for a very long time. I inquired of the woman who lets out chairs, and she said that you no longer came there. You lived in the Rue de l'Ouest on the third-floor front of a new house. You see that I know. I followed you,—what else could I do? and then you disappeared. I fancied that I saw you pass once as I was reading the papers under the Odéon Arcade, and ran after you,—but no; it was a person wearing a bonnet like yours. At night I came here—fear nothing, no one sees me; I come to look at your window, and I walk very softly that you may not hear me, for you might be alarmed. The other evening I was behind you, you turned round, and I fled. Once I heard you sing, and I was happy; does it harm you that I should listen to you through the shutters while singing? no, it cannot harm you. You see you are my angel, so let me come now and then, and I believe that I am going to die. If you only knew how I adore you! But forgive me, I am speaking to you, I know not what I am saying, perhaps I offend you—do I offend you?"

"Oh, my mother!" she said.

And she sank down as if she were dying. He seized her in his arms and pressed her to his heart, not knowing what he did. He supported her while himself tottering. He felt as if his head were full of smoke; flashes passed between his eyelashes; his ideas left him, and it seemed to him as if he were accomplishing a religious act, and yet committing a profanation. However, he had not the least desire for this ravishing creature, whose form he felt against his chest; he was distractedly in love. She took his hand and laid it on her heart; he felt the paper there, and stammered:

"You love me, then?"

She answered, in so low a voice that it was almost an inaudible breath: "Silence! you know I do."

And she hid her blushing face in the chest of the proud and intoxicated young man. He fell on to the bench, and she by his side. They no longer found words, and the stars were beginning to twinkle. How came it that their lips met? how comes it that the bird sings, the snow melts, the rose opens, May bursts into life, and the dawn grows white behind the black trees on the rustling tops of the hills? One kiss, and that was all; both trembled and gazed at each other in the darkness with flashing eyes. They neither felt the fresh night nor the cold stone, nor the damp grass, nor the moist soil,—they looked at each other, and their hearts were full of thoughts. Their hands were clasped without their cognizance. She did not ask him, did not even think of it, how he had managed to enter the garden, for it seemed to her so simple that he should be there. From time to time Marius's knee touched Cosette's knee, and both quivered. At intervals Cosette stammered a word; for her soul trembled on her lips like the dew-drop on a flower.

Gradually they conversed, and expansiveness succeeded the silence which is plenitude. The night was serene and splendid above their heads, and these two beings, pure as spirits, told each other everything,—their dreams, their intoxication, their ecstasy, their chimeras, their depressions, how they had adored and longed for each other at a distance, and their mutual despair when they ceased to meet. They confided to each other, in an ideal intimacy which nothing henceforth could increase, all their most hidden and mysterious thoughts. They told each other, with a candid faith in their illusions, all that love, youth, and the remnant of childhood which they still had, brought to their minds; their two hearts were poured into each other, so that at the end of an hour the young man had the maiden's soul and the maiden his. They were mutually penetrated, enchanted, and dazzled. When they had finished, when they had told each other everything, she laid her head on his shoulder and asked him:

"What is your name?"

"Marius," he said; "and yours?"

"Mine is Cosette."

BOOK VI

LITTLE GAVROCHE

1. A MALICIOUS TRICK OF THE WIND

SINCE 1823, while the public-house at Montfermeil was sinking, and gradually being swallowed up, not in the abyss of a bankruptcy, but in the sewer of small debts, the Thénardiers had had two more children, both male. These made five, two daughters and three boys, and they were a good many. The mother had got rid of the latter while still babies by a singular piece of good luck. Got rid of, that is exactly the term, for in this woman there was only a fragment of nature; it is a phenomenon, however, of which there is more than one instance. Like the Maréchale de Lamothe-Houdancourt, the Thénardier was only a mother as far as her daughters, and her maternity ended there. Her hatred of the human race began with her sons: on that side was a precipice of cruelty, and her heart had a lugubrious escarpment there. As we have seen, she detested the eldest and execrated the two others. Why? because she did. The most terrible of motives and most indisputable of answers is, Because. "I do not want a pack of squalling brats," this mother said.

Let us explain how the Thénardiers managed to dispose of their two last children, and even make a profit of them. That girl Magnon, to whom we referred a few pages back, was the same who continued to get an annuity out of old Gillenormand for the two children she had. She lived on the Quai des Celestins, at the corner of that ancient Rue du Petit-Musc, which has done all it could to change its bad reputation into a good odor. Our readers will remember the great croup epidemic which, thirty-five years ago, desolated the banks of the Seine in Paris, and of which science took advantage to make experiments on a grand scale as to the efficacy of inhaling alum, for which the external application of tincture of iodine has been so usefully substituted in our day. In this epidemic Magnon lost her two boys, still very young, on the same day,—one in the morning, the other in the evening. It was a blow, for these children were precious to their mother, as they represented eighty francs a month. These eighty francs were very punctually paid by the receiver of M. Gillenormand's rents, a M. Barge, a retired bailiff, who lived in the Rue de Sicile. When the children were dead the annuity was buried, and so Magnon sought an expedient. In the dark free-masonry of evil of which she formed part, everything is known, secrets are kept, and people help each other. Magnon wanted two children, and Madame Thénardier had two of the same size and age; it was a good arrangement for one, and an excellent investment for the other. The little Thénardiers became the little Magnons, and Magnon left the Quai des Celestins and went to live in the Rue Cloche-Percée. In Paris the identity which attaches an individual to himself is broken by moving from one street to another. The authorities, not being warned by anything, made no objections, and the substitution was effected in the simplest way in the world. Thénardier, however, demanded for this loan of children ten francs a month, which Magnon promised, and even paid. We need not say that M. Gillenormand continued to fulfill his promise and went every six months to see the children. He did not notice the change. "Oh, sir," Magnon would say to him, "how like you they are, to be sure."

Thénardier, to whom avatars were an easy task, seized this opportunity to become Jondrette. His two daughters and Gavroche had scarcely had time to perceive that they had two little brothers, for in a certain stage of misery people are affected by a sort of spectral indifference and regard human beings as ghosts. Your nearest relatives are often to you no more than vague forms of the shadow, hardly to be distinguished from the nebulous back-ground of life, and which easily become blended again with the invisible. On the evening of the day when Mother Thénardier handed over her two babes to Magnon, with the well-expressed will of renouncing them forever, she felt, or pretended to feel, a scruple, and said to her husband, "Why, that is deserting one's children!" but Thénardier, magisterial and phlegmatic, cauterized the scruple with this remark, "Jean Jacques Rousseau did better." From scruple the mother passed to anxiety. "But suppose the police were to trouble us? tell me, Monsieur Thénardier, whether what we have done is allowable?" Thénardier replied, "Everything is allowable. It is all serene. Besides, no one has any interest in inquiring closely after children that have not a cent." Magnon was a sort of she-dandy in crime, and dressed handsomely. She shared her rooms, which were furnished in a conventional and miserable way, with a very clever Gallicized English thief. This Englishwoman, a naturalized Parisian recommended by very wealthy connections, who was closely connected with medals of the library and diamonds of Mademoiselle Mars, was at a later date celebrated in the annals of crime; she was called *Mamselle Miss.* The two little ones who had fallen into Magnon's clutches had no cause to complain; recommended by the eighty francs, they were taken care of, like everything which brings in a profit; they were not badly clothed, not badly fed, treated almost like "little gentlemen," and better off with their false mother than the true one. Magnon acted the lady, and never talked slang in their presence. They spent several years there, and Thénardier augured well of it. One day he happened to say to Magnon as she handed him the monthly ten francs, "The 'father' must give them an education."

All at once these two poor little creatures, hitherto tolerably well protected, even by their evil destiny, were suddenly hurled into life, and forced to begin it. An arrest of criminals *en masse,* like that in the Jondrette garret, being necessarily complicated with researches and ulterior incarcerations, is a veritable disaster for that hideous and occult countersociety which lives beneath public society, and an adventure of this nature produces all sorts of convulsions in the gloomy world. The catastrophe of the Thénardiers was the catastrophe of Magnon. One day, a little while after Magnon had given Eponine the note relating to the Rue Plumet, the police made a sudden descent on the Rue Cloche-Percée. Magnon was arrested, as was Mamselle Miss, and all the inhabitants of the house who were suspected were caught in the haul. The two little boys were playing at the time in the back yard, and saw nothing of the razzia, but when they tried to go in they found the door locked and the house empty. A cobbler whose stall was opposite called to them and gave them a paper which "their mother" had left for them. On the paper was this address, "M. Barge, receiver of rents, No. 8, Rue du Roi de Sicile." The cobbler said to them, "You no longer live here. Go there; it is close by,—the first street on your left. Ask your way with that paper." The boys set off, the elder leading the younger, and holding in his hand the paper which was to serve as their guide. It was cold, and his little numbed fingers held the paper badly, and at the corner of a lane a puff of wind tore it from him, and as it was night the boy could not find it again. They began wandering about the streets hap-hazard.

2. *GAVROCHE TO THE RESCUE*

SPRING in Paris is very frequently traversed by sharp, violent breezes, which, if they do not freeze, chill; these breezes which sadden the brightest days, produce exactly the same effect as the blasts of cold wind which enter a warm room through the crevices of a badly closed door or window. It seems as if the gloomy gate of winter has been left ajar, and that a wind comes from there. In the spring of 1832, the period when the first great epidemic of this century broke out in Europe, these breezes were sharper and more cutting than ever, and some door even more icy than that of winter had been left ajar. It was the door of the sepulcher, and the breath of cholera could be felt in these breezes. From a meteorological point of view, these cold winds had the peculiarity that they did not exclude a strong electric tension, and frequent storms, accompanied by thunder and lightning, broke out at this period.

One evening when these breezes were blowing sharply, so sharply that January seemed to have returned, and the citizens had put on their cloaks again, little Gavroche, still shivering gayly under his rags, was standing as if in ecstasy in front of a hair-dresser's shop in the vicinity of the Orme-Saint Gervais. He was adorned with a woman's woolen shawl, picked up no one knew where, of which he had made a muffler. Little Gavroche appeared to be lost in admiration of a waxen image of a bride, wearing a very low-necked dress, and a wreath of orange flowers in her hair, which revolved between two lamps and lavished its smiles on the passer-by; but in reality he was watching the shop to see whether he could not "bone" a cake of soap, which he would afterward sell for a half-penny to a barber in the suburbs. He frequently breakfasted on one of these cakes, and he called this style of work, for which he had a talent, "shaving the barber." While regarding the bride, and casting sheep's-eyes on the cake of soap, he growled between his teeth, "Tuesday—This is not Tuesday—Is it Tuesday?—It is perhaps Tuesday; yes, it is Tuesday." What this soliloquy referred to was never known, but if it was the last time he had dined, it was three days ago, for the present day was a Friday. The barber in his shop, warmed with a good stove, was shaving a customer and taking every now and then a side glance at this enemy, this shivering and impudent gamin, who had his two hands in his pockets, but his mind evidently ready for anything.

While Gavroche was examining the bride, the window, and the Windsor soap, two boys of unequal height, very decently dressed, and younger than himself, one apparently seven, the other five years of age, timidly turned the handle and entered the shop, asking for something, charity possibly, in a plaintive murmur, which was more like a sob than a prayer. They both spoke together, and their words were unintelligible, because sobs choked the voice of the younger boy, and cold made the teeth of the elder rattle. The barber turned with a furious face, and, without laying down his razor, drove one into the street with his left hand, the other with his knee, and closed the door again, saying:

"To come and chill people for nothing!"

The two lads set out again, crying: a cloud had come up in the meanwhile, and it began raining. Little Gavroche ran up to them, and accosted them thus:

"What's the matter with you, babes?"

"We don't know where to sleep," the elder replied.

"Is that all?" said Gavroche, "that's a great matter to cry about, you babes in the wood." And assuming an accent of tender affection and gentle protection, which was visible through his somewhat pompous superiority, he said:

"Come with me, brats."

"Yes, sir," said the elder boy.

And the two children followed him as they would have done an archbishop, and left off crying. Gavroche led them along the Rue St. Antoine, in the direction of the Bastille, and while going off took an indignant and retrospective glance at the barber's shop.

"That whiting has no heart," he growled; "he's an Englishman."

A girl seeing the three walking in file, Gavroche at the head, burst into a loud laugh. This laugh was disrespectful to the party.

"Good-day, Mamselle Omnibus," Gavroche said to her.

A moment after, the hair-dresser returning to his mind, he added:

"I made a mistake about the brute: he is not a whiting, but a snake. Barber, I'll go and fetch a locksmith, and order him to put a bell on your tail."

This barber had made him aggressive; as he stepped across a gutter, he addressed a bearded portress, worthy to meet Faust on the Brocken, and who was holding her broom in her hand:

"Madame," he said to her, "I see that you go out with your horse."

And after this he splashed the varnished boots of a passer-by.

"Scoundrel!" the gentleman said furiously. Gavroche raised his nose out of the shawl.

"Have you a complaint to make, sir?"

"Yes, of you," said the gentleman.

"The office is closed," Gavroche remarked. "I don't receive any more complaints to-day."

As he went along the street he noticed a girl of thirteen or fourteen, shivering in a gate-way, in such short petticoats that she showed her knees. But the little girl was beginning to get too tall a girl for that; growth plays you such tricks, and the petticoat begins to become short when nudity grows indecent.

"Poor girl," said Gavroche, "she hasn't even a pair of breeches. Here, collar this."

And taking off all the good wool which he had round his neck, he threw it over the thin, violet shoulders of the beggar-girl, when the muffler became once again a shawl. The little girl looked at him with an astonished air, and received the shawl in silence. At a certain stage of distress, a poor man in his stupor no longer groans at evil, and gives no thanks for kindness. This done:

"Brr!" said Gavroche, colder than St. Martin, who, at any rate, retained one-half his cloak. On hearing this brr, the shower, redoubling its passion, poured down; those wicked skies punish good actions.

"Hilloh!" Gavroche shouted, "What's the meaning of this? it is raining again. My God, if this goes on, I shall withdraw my subscription."

And he set out again.

"No matter," he said, as he took a glance at the beggar-girl crouching under her shawl, "she's got a first-rate skin."

And, looking at the clouds, he cried, "Sold, you are!"

The two children limped after him, and as they passed one of those thick, close gratings which indicate a baker's (for bread, like gold, is placed behind a grating), Gavroche turned round. "By the bye, brats, have you dined?"

"We have had nothing to eat, sir, since early this morning," the elder answered.

"Then you haven't either father or mother?" Gavroche continued, majestically.

"I beg your pardon, sir, we have a pa and a ma, but we don't know where they are."

"Sometimes that is better than knowing," said Gavroche, who was a philosopher in his small way.

"We have been walking about for two hours," the lad continued, "and looked for things at the corners of the streets, but found nothing."

"I know," said Gavroche, "the dogs eat everything." He resumed:

"And so we have lost the authors of our being. We don't know what we have done with them. That isn't the right thing, brats, and you oughtn't to turn grown-up people loose like that. Well, I suppose I must find them a shakedown."

He did not ask them any more questions, for what could be more simple than to have no home? The elder of the boys, who had almost entirely recovered the happy carelessness of childhood, made this remark, "It is funny, for all that, for mamma said she would take us to look for some blessed box on Palm Sunday. Mamma is a lady who lives with Mamselle Miss."

"—Tanflûte!" Gavroche added.

He stooped, and for some minutes searched all sorts of corners which he had in his rags. At length he raised his head with an air which only wished to express satisfaction, but which was in reality triumphant.

"Calm yourselves, my infants; here is supper for three."

And he drew a sou from one of his pockets, without giving the lads time to feel amazed; he pushed them both before him into the baker's shop, and laid his sou on the counter, exclaiming:

"Boy, five centimes' worth of bread."

The baker, who was the master in person, took up a loaf and a knife.

"In three pieces, my boy," Gavroche remarked. He added with dignity: "We are three."

And seeing that the baker, examining the three suppers, had taken a loaf of brown bread, he thrust his finger into his nose, with as imperious a sniff as if he had the great Frederick's pinch of snuff on his thumb, and cast in the baker's face this indignant remark:

"Keksekça?"

Those of our readers who might be tempted to see in this remark of Gavroche's to the baker a Russian or Polish word, or one of the savage cries which the Iowas or the Botocudos hurl at each other across the deserted streams, are warned that this is a phrase which they (our readers) employ daily, and which signifies, *"qu'est-ce que c'est que cela?"* The baker perfectly comprehended, and replied:

"Why, it is bread; very good seconds bread."

"You mean black bread," Gavroche remarked, with a calm and cold disdain. "White bread, my lad; I stand treat."

The baker could not refrain from smiling, and while cutting some white bread gazed at them in a compassionate way, which offended Gavroche.

"Well," he said, "what is there about us that you size us up in that way?"

All the three, put end to end, would not have sized up six feet.

When the bread was cut, the baker put the sou in the till, and Gavroche said to the two boys:

"Grub away."

The boys looked at him in surprise. Gavroche burst into a laugh.

"Oh, yes, that's true, they don't understand yet, they are so little."

And he continued, "Eat."

At the same time he gave each of them a lump of bread. Thinking that the elder, who appeared to him more worthy of his conversation, merited some special encouragement, and ought to have any hesitation about satisfying his hunger removed, he added, as he gave him the larger lump:

"Shove that into your gun."

There was one piece smaller than the two others, and he took that for himself. The poor boys, Gavroche included, were starving; while tearing the bread with their teeth, they blocked up the baker's shop, who, now that he was paid, looked at them angrily.

"Let us return to the street," said Gavroche.

They started again in the direction of the Bastille. From time to time, as they passed lighted shops, the younger boy stopped to see what o'clock it was by the leaden watch hung round his neck by a string.

"Well, he is a baby," said Gavroche.

Then he thoughtfully growled between his teeth, "No matter, if I had brats of my own I would take more care of them than that."

As they were finishing their bread, they reached the corner of that gloomy Rue de Ballet at the end of which the low and hostile wicket of La Force is visible.

"Hilloh, is that you, Gavroche?" some one said.

"Hilloh, is that you, Montparnasse?" said Gavroche.

It was a man who accosted Gavroche, no other than Montparnasse disguised with blue spectacles, but recognizable by Gavroche.

"My eye!" Gavroche went on, "you have a skin of the color of a linseed poultice and blue spectacles like a doctor. You're putting on style, on the word of an old man!"

"Silence," said Montparnasse, "not so loud." He quickly dragged Gavroche out of the light of the shops: the two little boys followed mechanically, holding each other by the hand. When they were under the black arch of a gate-way, protected from eyes and rain, Montparnasse remarked:

"Do you know where I am going?"

"To the abbey of Mount-with-regret,"* said Gavroche.

"Joker!"

And Montparnasse added:

"I am going to meet Babet."

"Ah!" said Gavroche, "her name is Babet, is it?"

Montparnasse lowered his voice:

"It is not a she, but a he."

"I thought he was buckled up."

"He has unfastened the buckle," Montparnasse replied.

And he hurriedly told the boy that, on that very morning, Babet, while being removed to the Conciergerie, escaped by turning to the left instead of the right in the "police office passage."

Gavroche admired his skill.

"What a dentist!" he said.

Montparnasse added a few details about Babet's escape, and ended with, "Oh, that is not all."

Gavroche, while talking, had seized a cane which Montparnasse held in his hand: he mechanically pulled at the upper part, and a dagger-blade became visible.

"Ah!" he said, as he quickly thrust it back, "you have brought your gendarme with you disguised as a civilian."

Montparnasse winked.

*The Scaffold.

"The deuce!" Gavroche continued, "are you going to have a turn-up with the cops?"

"There's no knowing," Montparnasse answered carelessly, "It's always as well to have a pin about you."

Gavroche pressed him.

"What are you going to do to-night?"

Montparnasse again became serious, and said, mincing his words: "Some things."

And he suddenly changed the conversation.

"By the bye—"

"What?"

"Something that happened the other day. Just fancy. I meet a bourgeois, and he makes me a present of a sermon and a purse. I put it in my pocket, a moment later I feel for it, and there was nothing there."

"Only the sermon," said Gavroche.

"But where are you going now?" Montparnasse continued.

Gavroche pointed to his two protégés, and said:

"I am going to put these two children to bed."

"Where?"

"At my house."

"Have you a lodging?"

"Yes."

"Where?"

"Inside the elephant," said Gavroche.

Montparnasse, though naturally not easy to astonish, could not refrain from the exclamation:

"Inside the elephant?"

"Well, yes, kekçaa?"

This is another word belonging to the language which nobody reads and everybody speaks; kekçaa signifies, *qu'est-ce que cela a?*

The gamin's profound remark brought Montparnasse back to calmness and good sense; he seemed to entertain a better opinion of Gavroche's lodgings.

"Ah, yes," he said, "elephant. Are you comfortable there?"

"Very," Gavroche replied. "Most comfortable. There are no draughts as there are under the bridges."

"How do you get in—is there a hole?"

"Of course there is, but you have no need to mention it; it's between the front legs, and the detectives don't know it."

"And you climb in? yes, I understand."

"One turn, cric crac, it's done, and there's no one to be seen."

After a pause Gavroche added:

"I shall have a ladder for these young ones."

Montparnasse burst into a laugh.

"Where the devil did you pick up those brats?"

Gavroche answered with simplicity:

"A barber made me a present of them."

In the meanwhile Montparnasse had become pensive.

"You recognized me very easily," he said.

He took from his pocket two small objects, which were quills wrapped in cotton, and thrust one into each nostril; they made him quite a different nose.

"That changes you," said Gavroche; "you are not so ugly now, and you ought to keep them in for good."

Montparnasse was a handsome fellow, but Gavroche was fond of a joke.

"Without any humbug," Montparnasse asked; "what do you think of me now?"

It was also a different sound of voice; in a second Montparnasse had become unrecognizable.

"Oh! Play Porrichinelle for us!" Gavroche exclaimed.

The two lads, who had heard nothing up to this moment, engaged as they were themselves in thrusting their fingers up their noses, drew nearer on hearing this name, and gazed at Montparnasse with a beginning of joy and admiration. Unhappily Montparnasse was in no humor for jesting; he laid his hand on Gavroche's shoulder, and said with a stress on each word:

"Listen to what I tell you, boy; if I were on the plaza, with my dog, my knife, and my wife, and you were to offer me ten double sous I would not refuse to work, but we are not at Shrove Tuesday."*

This strange sentence produced a singular effect on the gamin; he turned round sharply, looked with his little bright eyes all around, and noticed a few yards off a policeman with his back turned to them. Gavroche let an "all right" slip from him, which he at once repressed, and shook Montparnasse's hand.

---

*Ecoute ce que te dis, garcon, si j'etais sur la place, avec mon dogue, ma dague, et ma digue, et si vous me prodiguiez dix gros sous, je ne refuserais d'y goupiner, mais nous sommes pas le Mardi-gras.

"Well, good-night," he said; "I am off to my elephant with my brats. Should you happen to want me any night, you'll find me there. I lodge in the *entresol,* and there's no porter; ask for Monsieur Gavroche."

"All right," said Montparnasse.

And they parted, Montparnasse going toward the Grève, and Gavroche toward the Bastille. The youngest boy, dragged on by his brother, whom Gavroche dragged along in his turn, looked round several times to watch Porrichinelle go away.

The enigmatical sentence by which Montparnasse informed Gavroche of the presence of the policeman contained no other talisman but the sound *dig* repeated five or six times under various forms. This syllable, not pronounced separately, but artistically mingled with the words of a sentence, means "take care, we cannot speak freely." There was also in Montparnasse's remark a literary beauty which escaped Gavroche's notice, that is *"mon dogue, ma dague, et ma digue,"* a phrase of the Temple slang greatly in use among the rufflers and slashers of the great age in which Molière wrote and Callot designed.

Twenty years back there might have been seen in the south-eastern corner of the square of the Bastille, near the canal dock, dug in the old moat of the citadel prison, a quaint monument, which has already been effaced from the memory of Parisians, and which should have left some trace, as it was an idea of the "member of the Institute commander-in-chief of the army of Egypt." We say monument, though it was only a plaster cast; but this cast itself, a prodigious sketch, the grand corpse of a Napoleonic idea which two or three successive puffs of wind carried away each time further from us, had become historic, and assumed something definitive, which formed a contrast with its temporary appearance. It was an elephant, forty feet high, constructed of carpentry and masonry, bearing on its back a castle which resembled a house, once painted green by some plasterer, and now painted black by the heavens, the rain, and time. In this deserted and uncovered corner of the square the wide forehead of the colossus, its trunk, its tusks, its castle, its enormous back, and its four feet like columns produced at night upon the starlit sky a surprising and terrible outline. No one knew what it meant, and it seemed a sort of symbol of the popular strength. It was gloomy, enigmatical, and immense; it looked like a powerful phantom visible and erect by the side of the invisible specter of the Bastille. Few strangers visited this edifice, and no passer-by looked at it. It was falling in ruins, and each season, plaster becoming detached from its flanks made horrible wounds upon it. The "Ediles," as they were called in the fashionable slang, had forgotten it since 1814; it stood there in its corner, gloomy, sickly, crumbling away, surrounded by rotting palings, which were sullied every moment by drunken drivers; there were yawning cracks in its stomach, a lath issued from its tail, and tall grass grew between its legs; and as the level of the square had risen during the last thirty years through that slow and continuous movement which insensibly elevates the soil of great cities, it was in a hollow and it seemed as if the earth were giving way beneath it. It was unclean, despised, repulsive, and superb; ugly in the eyes of cits, but melancholy in the eyes of the thinker. It had something about it of the ordure which is swept away, and something of the majesty which is decapitated.

As we said, at night its appearance changed; for night is the real medium of everything which is shadow. So soon as twilight set in the old elephant was transfigured; and it assumed a placid and redoubtable appearance in the formidable serenity of darkness. As it belonged to the past it belonged to night, and this obscurity suited its grandeur. This monument, rude, broad, heavy, rough, austere, and almost shapeless, but most assuredly majestic, and imprinted with a species of magnificent and savage gravity, has disappeared to allow the sort of gigantic stove, adorned with its stove-pipe, to reign in peace, which was substituted for the frowning fortalice with its nine towers, much in the same way as the bourgeoisie are substituted for feudalism. It is very simple that a stove should be the symbol of an epoch in which a stew-pan contains the power. This period will pass away,—it is already passing away; people are beginning to understand that if there may be strength in a boiler, there can only be power in a brain; in other words, that what leads and carries away the world is not locomotives but ideas. Attach locomotives to ideas, and then it is all right; but do not take the horse for the rider.

However this may be, to return to the Bastille square, the architect of the elephant managed to produce something grand with plaster, while the architect of the stove-pipe has succeeded in making something little out of bronze. This stove-pipe, which was christened a sonorous name, and called the Column of July, this spoiled monument of an abortive revolution, was still wrapped up, in 1832, in an immense sheet of carpentry-work which we regret for our part, and a vast inclosure of planks, which completed the isolation of the elephant. It was to this corner of this square, which was scarce lighted by the reflection of a distant oil-lamp, that the gamin led the two children.

Allow us to interrupt our narrative here and remind our readers that we are recording the simple truth, and that twenty years ago a boy, who was caught sleeping in the inside of the elephant of the Bastille, was brought before the police on the charge of vagabondage and breaking a public monument.

On coming near the colossus, Gavroche understood the effect which the infinitely great may produce on the infinitely little, and said:

"Don't be frightened, brats."

Then he went through a hole in the palings into the ground round the elephant, and helped the children to pass through the breach. The lads, a little frightened, followed Gavroche without a word, and confided in this little Providence in rags who had given them bread and promised them a bed. A ladder, employed by workmen at the column by day, was lying along the palings; Gavroche raised it with singular vigor, and placed it against one of the elephant's fore legs. At the point where the ladder ended, a sort of black hole could be distinguished in the belly of the colossus. Gavroche pointed out the ladder and the hole to his guests, and said, "Go up, and go in." The two little boys looked at each other in terror.

"You are frightened, brats!" Gavroche exclaimed, and added, "You shall see."

He clung round the elephant's wrinkled foot, and in a twinkling, without deigning to employ the ladder, he reached the hole. He went in like a lizard gliding into a crevice, and a moment after the two boys saw his head appear vaguely, like a white, livid form, on the edge of the hole, which was full of darkness.

"Well," he cried, "come up, my blessed babes. You will see how snug it is. Come up, you," he said to the elder. "I will hold out my hand."

The little boys nudged each other, for the gamin at once frightened and re-assured them, and then it was raining very hard. The elder boy ventured, and the younger, on seeing his brother ascending and himself left alone between the feet of this great beast, felt greatly inclined to cry, but did not dare. The elder climbed up the rungs of the ladder in a very tottering way, and as he did so Gavroche encouraged him by exclamations of a fencing-master to his pupils, or of a muleteer to his mules.

"Don't be frightened—that's it—keep on moving—set your foot there —now, your hand here—bravo!"

And when he was within reach he quickly and powerfully seized him by the arm, and drew him to him.

"Swallowed!" he said.

The boy had passed through the crevice.

"Now," said Gavroche, "wait for me. Pray sit down, sir."

And, leaving the hole in the same way as he entered it, he slid down the elephant's leg with the agility of a marmoset, fell on his feet in the grass, seized the youngest boy round the waist and planted him on the middle of the ladder; then he began ascending behind him, shouting to the elder boy:

"I'll push him, and you'll pull him."

In a second the little fellow was pushed up, dragged, pulled, and drawn through the hole before he knew where he was, and Gavroche, entering after him, kicked away the ladder, which fell in the grass, and clapped his hands as he shouted. "There we are! long live General La-fayette." This explosion over, he added, "Brats, you are in my house."

Gavroche was, in fact, at home. Oh! unexpected utility of the useless! oh, charity of great things—! oh, goodness of the giants! this huge monument, which had contained a thought of the emperor, had become the lodging of a gamin; the brat had been accepted and sheltered by the colossus. The cits in their Sunday clothes who passed by the elephant of the Bastille were prone to say, as they measured it with a contemptuous look from the eyes flush with their head, "Of what service is that?" It served to save from cold, from frost, from damp and rain, to protect from the winter wind, to preserve from sleeping in the mud, which entails fever, and from sleeping in the snow, which causes death, a little fatherless and motherless boy, without bread, clothes, or shelter. It served to shelter the innocent boy whom society repulsed. It served to diminish the public wrong. It was a lair opened to him against whom all doors were closed. It seemed as if the old wretched mastodon, attacked by vermin and oblivion, covered with warts, mold, and ulcers, tottering, crumbling, abandoned, and condemned, a species of colossal mendicant asking in vain the alms of a benevolent glance in the midst of the high-way, had taken pity on this other beggar, the poor pigmy who walked about without shoes on his feet, without a ceiling over his head, blowing his fingers, dressed in rags, and supporting life on what was thrown away. This is what use the elephant of the Bastille was, and this idea of Napoleon's, disdained by men, had been taken up again by God; what had only been illustrious had become august. The emperor would have needed, in order to realize what he meditated, porphyry, bronze, iron, gold, and marble, but for God the old collection of planks, beams, and plaster was sufficient. The emperor had had a dream of genius; in this Titanic elephant, armed, prodigious, raising its trunk, and spouting all around glad and living waters, he wished to incarnate the people, and God had made a greater thing of it, for He lodged a child in it.

The hole by which Gavroche entered was a breach scarce visible from the outside, as it was concealed, as we said, under the elephant's belly, and so narrow that only cats and boys could pass through it.

"Let us begin," said Gavroche, "by telling the porter that we are not at home."

And plunging into the darkness with certainty, like a man who knows every corner of the room, he took a plank and stopped up the hole. Gavroche plunged again into the darkness, the children heard the fizzing of a match dipped into the bottle of phosphorus,—for chemical matches did not yet exist,—and the Fumade fire-producer represented progress at that day. A sudden light made them wink. Gavroche had lit one of those bits of string dipped in pitch which are called "cellar rats"; and this thing, which smoked more than it illumined, rendered the inside of the elephant indistinctly visible. Gavroche's two guests looked around them, and had much such a feeling as any one would feel if shut up in the Heidelberg tun, or, better still, what Jonas must have experienced in the biblical belly of the whale. An entire gigantic skeleton was visible to them and enveloped them; above their heads a long brown beam, from which sprang at regular distances massive cross-bars, represented the spine with the ribs, stalactites of plaster hung down like viscera, and vast spider-webs formed from one side to the other dusty diaphragms. Here and there in corners could be seen large black spots which seemed alive, and changed places rapidly, with a quick and startled movement. The pieces which had fallen from the elephant's back on its belly had filled up the concavity, so that it was possible to walk on it as on a flooring.

The youngest lad nudged his brother, and said:

"It is black."

This remark caused Gavroche to object, for the petrified air of the two lads rendered a shock necessary.

"What are you giving us?" he shouted; "what's that nonsense, eh? you're showing your disgust, are you? I suppose you want the Tuileries? are you brutes? if you are, say so, but I warn you that I'm not a fellow to put up with any humbug. Ah, ah, to hear you talk one would think that your father was a prince of the blood."

A little roughness is good in terror, for it re-assures; the two children drew nearer to Gavroche, who, affected paternally by this confidence passed from sternness to gentleness, and addressing the younger lad:

"You little goose," he said,—toning down the insult with a caressing inflection of the voice,—"it is outside that it's black. Outside it rains, and here it does not rain; outside it is cold, and here there is not a breath of wind; outside there is a heap of people, and here there's nobody; outside there's not even the moon, and here there's a candle, the deuce take it all."

The two lads began looking round the apartment with less terror, but Gavroche did not allow them any leisure for contemplation.

"Quick," he said.

And he thrust them toward what we are very happy to call the end of the room, where his bed was. Gavroche's bed was perfect; that is to say, there was a mattress, a coverlet, and an alcove with curtains. The mattress was a straw mat, and the coverlet was a rather wide wrapper of coarse, gray wool, very warm, and nearly new. This is what the alcove was: Three long props were driven securely into the plaster soil, that is to say, the elephant's belly, two in front and one behind, and were fastened by a cord at the top, so as to form a hollow pyramid. This pyramid supported a grating of brass wire, simply laid upon it, but artistically fastened with iron wire, so that it entirely surrounded the three poles. A row of large stones fastened the lattice-work down to the ground, so that nothing could pass. This lattice was merely a piece of the brass-work put up in aviaries and menageries. Gavroche's bed was under the wire-work as in a cage, and the whole resembled an Esquimaux's tent. Gavroche moved a few of the stones that held down the lattice-work in front, and shouted to the lads:

"Now, then, on all fours."

He made his guests enter the cage cautiously, then went in after them, brought the stones together again, and hermetically closed the opening. They lay down all three on the mat, and though they were all so short, not one of them could stand upright in the alcove. Gavroche still held the "cellar rat" in his hand.

"Now," he said, "to roost; I am going to suppress the chandelier."

"What is that, sir?" the elder of the lads asked Gavroche, pointing to the brass grating.

"That," said Gavroche gravely, "is on account of the rats. Go to roost!"

Still he thought himself obliged to add a few words of instruction for these young creatures, and continued:

"It comes from the Jardin des Plantes, and is employed to guard ferocious animals. There is a whole store-house full; you have only to climb over a wall, crawl through a window, and pass under a door, and you can have as much as you like."

While speaking he wrapped up the little boy in the blanket, who murmured:

"Oh, that is nice; it's so warm!"

Gavroche took a glance of satisfaction at the coverlet.

"That also comes from the Jardin des Plantes," he said; "I took it from the monkeys."

And pointing out to the elder one the straw mat on which he was lying, which was very thick and admirably made, he added:

"That belonged to the giraffe."

After a pause he continued:

"The beasts had all this, and I took it from them, and they were not at all angry, for I told them that I wanted it for the elephant."

There was another interval of silence, after which he continued, "You climb over walls and pipe off the government; that's the racket."

The two lads gazed with a timid and stupefied respect at this intrepid and inventive being, a vagabond like them, isolated like them, weak like them, who had something admirable and omnipotent about him, who appeared to them supernatural, and whose face was composed of all the grimaces of an old mountebank, mingled with the simplest and most charming smile.

"Then, sir," the elder lad said, timidly, "you are not afraid of the police?"

Gavroche limited himself to answering:

"Brat! you mustn't say 'police,' but 'cops'."

The younger had his eyes wide open, but said nothing. As he was at the edge of the mat, the elder being in the center, Gavroche tucked in the coverlet round him as a mother would have done, and raised the mat under his head with old rags, so as to make him a pillow. Then he turned to the elder boy:

"Well, it is jolly here, eh?"

"Oh, yes!" the lad answered, as he looked at Gavroche with the expression of a saved angel.

The two poor little fellows, who were wet through, began to grow warm again.

"By the bye," Gavroche went on, "why were you blubbering?"

And, pointing to the younger boy, he said to his brother:

"A kid like that, I don't say no; but a tall chap like you to cry,—why, it is idiotic; one looks like a stuck pig."

"Well, sir," the lad said, "we hadn't any lodging to go to."

"Brat," Gavroche remarked, "you mustn't say 'lodging,' but 'ken'."

"And then we felt afraid of being all alone like that in the night."

"People don't say 'night,' but 'gropus'."

"Thank you, sir," said the boy.

"Listen to me," Gavroche went on. "You must never blubber for anything. I'll take care of you, and you'll see what fun we shall have. In summer we'll go to the Glacière with Navet, a pal of mine; we'll bathe in the dock, and run about naked on the timber-floats in front of the bridge of Austerlitz, for that puts the washerwomen in a rage. They yell, they kick, and, Lord! if you only knew how ridiculous they are! We'll go and see the skeleton-man; he's all alive at the Champs Elysées, and that citizen is as thin as all outside. And then I will take you to the play, and let you see Frederick Lemaître; I get tickets, for I know some actors, and even performed myself once in a piece; we were a lot of boys who ran about under a canvas, and that made the sea. I will get you an engagement at my theater. We will go and see the savages, but they ain't real savages; they wear pink fleshing which forms creases, and you can see repairs made at their elbows with white thread. After that we will go to the opera, and enter with the claqueurs, who are very well selected at the opera, though I wouldn't care to be seen with them on the boulevard. At the opera, just fancy, they're people who pay their twenty sous, but they are asses, and we call them dishclouts. And then we will go and see a man guillotined, and I'll point out the executioner to you; he lives in the Rue de Marais, and his name's Sanson, and he's got a letter-box at his door. Ah! we shall amuse ourselves famously."

At this moment a drop of pitch fell on Gavroche's hand and recalled him to the realities of life.

"The devil," he said, "the match is wearing out. Pay attention! I can't afford more than a sou a month for lighting, and when people go to bed they are expected to sleep. We haven't the time to read Monsieur Paul de Kock's romances. Besides, the light might pass through the crevices of the gate, and the cops might see it."

"And then," said the elder lad, who alone dared to speak to Gavroche and answer him, "a spark might fall on the straw and we must be careful not to set the house on fire."

"You mustn't say 'set a house afire'," Gavroche remarked, "but 'blaze a crib'."

The storm grew more furious, and through the thunder-peals the rain could be heard pattering on the back of the colossus.

"The rain's sold!" said Gavroche. "I like to hear the contents of the water-bottle running down the legs of the house. Winter's an ass; it loses its time, it loses its trouble, it can't drown us, and so that is the reason why the old water-carrier up there is so growling with us."

This allusion to the thunder, whose consequences Gavroche, in his quality as a nineteenth-century philosopher, accepted, was followed by a lengthened flash so dazzling that a portion of it passed through the hole in the elephant's belly. Almost at the same moment the thunder roared, and very furiously; the two little boys uttered a cry and rose so quickly that the brass grating was almost thrown down; but Gavroche turned toward them his bold face, and profited by the thunder-clap to burst into a laugh.

"Be calm, my children, and do not upset the edifice. That's fine thunder of the right sort, and it isn't like that humbugging lightning. Dog gone it! It's almost as fine as at the Ambigu."

This said, he restored order in the grating, softly pushed the two lads on to the bed, pressed their knees to make them lie full length, and cried:

"Since Providence is lighting his candle, I can put out mine. Children, my young humans, we must sleep, for it's very bad not to sleep. It makes you stink in the throat, as people say in fashionable society. Wrap yourselves well up in the blanket, for I am going to put the light out. Are you all right?"

"Yes," said the elder boy, "I'm all right and feel as if I had a feather pillow under my head."

"You mustn't say 'head'," Gavroche cried, "but 'nut'."

The two lads crept close together; Gavroche made them all right on the mat, and pulled the blanket up to their ears; then he repeated for the third time in the hieratic language, "Roost."

And he blew out the rope's end. The light was scarce extinguished ere a singular trembling began to shake the trellis-work under which the three children were lying. It was a multitude of dull rubbings which produced a metallic sound, as if claws and teeth were assailing the copper wire, and this was accompanied by all sorts of little shrill cries. The little boy five years of age, hearing this noise above his head, and chilled with terror, nudged his elder brother, but he was "roosting" already, as

Gavroche had ordered him; then the little one, unable to hold out any longer for fright, dared to address Gavroche, but in a very low voice and holding his breath.

"Sir?"

"Hilloh!" said Gavroche, who had just closed his eyes.

"What is that?"

"It's the rats," Gavroche answered.

And he laid his head again on the mat. The rats, which were really by thousands in the elephant's carcass, and were the live black spots to which we have alluded, had been held in check by the flame of the link so long as it was alight, but so soon as this cavern, which was, so to speak, their city, had been restored to night, sniffing what that famous story-teller, Perrault, calls "fresh meat," they rushed in bands to Gavroche's tent, climbed to the top, and were biting the meshes, as if trying to enter this novel sort of trap. In the meanwhile the little one did not sleep.

"Sir?" he began again.

"Well?" Gavroche asked.

"What are rats?"

"They're mice."

This explanation slightly re-assured the child, for he had seen white mice in his life, and had not been afraid of them; still he raised his voice again.

"Sir?"

"Well?" Gavroche repeated.

"Why don't you keep a cat?"

"I had one," Gavroche answered; "I brought it here, but they ate it for me."

This second explanation undid the work of the first, and the child began trembling once more; the dialogue between him and Gavroche was resumed for the fourth time.

"Sir?"

"Well?"

"What was eaten?"

"The cat."

"What ate the cat?"

"The rats."

"The mice?"

"Yes, the rats."

The child, terrified by these mice which ate the cat, continued:

"Would those mice eat us?"

"O Lord, yes!" Gavroche said.

The child's terror was at its height, but Gavroche added:

"Don't be frightened, they can't get in. And then I am here. Stay, take my hand, hold your tongue, and sleep."

Gavroche at the same time took the boy's hand across his brother, and the child pressed the hand against his body and felt re-assured, for courage and strength have mysterious communications. Silence had set in again around them, the sound of voices had startled and driven away the rats, and when they returned a few minutes later and furiously attacked, the three boys, plunged in sleep, heard nothing more. The night hours passed away; darkness covered the immense Bastille square; a winter wind, which was mingled with the rain, blew in gusts; the patrols examined doors, inclosures, and dark corners, and, while searching for nocturnal vagabonds, passed silently before the elephant; the monster, erect and motionless, with its eyes open in the darkness, seemed to be dreaming, as if satisfied at its good deed, and sheltered from the sky and rain the three poor sleeping children. In order to understand what is going to follow, it must be remembered that at this period the main-guard of the Bastille was situated at the other end of the square, and that what took place near the elephant could neither be prevented nor heard by the sentry. Toward the end of the hour which immediately precedes day-break, a man came running out of the Rue St. Antoine, crossed the square, went round the great inclosure of the Column of July, and slipped through the palings under the elephant's belly. If any light had fallen on this man, it might have been guessed from his thoroughly drenched state that he had passed the night in the rain. On getting under the elephant he uttered a peculiar cry, which belongs to no human language and which a parrot alone could reproduce. He repeated twice this cry, of which the following orthography scarce supplies any idea: "Kiri-kikiou!" At the second cry a clear, gay, and young voice answered from the elephant's belly, "Yes!" almost immediately the plank that closed the hole was removed, and left a passage for a lad, who slid down the elephant's leg and fell at the man's feet. It was Gavroche, and the man was Montparnasse. As for the cry of *Kirikikiou*, it was doubtless what the lad meant to say by, "You will ask for Monsieur Gavroche." On hearing it he jumped up with a start, crept out of his alcove by moving the grating a little, and then carefully closing it again, after which he opened the trap and went down.

The man and the child silently recognized each other in the night, and Montparnasse confined himself to saying:

"We want you; come and give us a help."

The gamin asked for no other explanation. "Here I am," he said.

And the pair proceeded toward the Rue St. Antoine, whence Montparnasse had come, winding rapidly through the long file of market-carts which were coming into town at the time. The gardeners, lying on their wagons among their salads and vegetables, half asleep, and rolled up to their eyes in their great-coats, owing to the beating rain, did not even look at these strange passers-by.

3. INCIDENTS OF AN ESCAPE

THIS is what occurred on this same night at La Force. An escape had been concerted between Babet, Brujon, Gueulemer, and Thénardier, although Thénardier was in secret confinement. Babet had managed the affair on his own account during the day, as we heard from Montparnasse's narrative to Gavroche, and Montparnasse was to help them outside. Brujon, while spending a month in a punishment-room, had time, first, to make a rope, and, secondly, to ripen a plan. Formerly, these severe places, in which prison discipline leaves the prisoner to himself, were composed of four stone walls, a stone ceiling, a brick pavement, a camp-bed, a grated skylight, and a gate lined with iron, and were called dungeons; but the dungeon was considered too horrible, so now it is composed of an iron gate, a grated skylight, a camp-bed, a brick pavement, a stone ceiling, four stone walls, and it is called a "punishment-room." A little daylight is visible about midday. The inconvenience of these rooms, which, as we see, are not dungeons, is to leave beings to think who ought to be set to work. Brujon, therefore, reflected, and he left the punishment-room with a cord. As he was considered very dangerous in the Charlemagne yard, he was placed in the New Building, and the first thing he found there was Gueulemer, the second a nail; Gueulemer, that is to say, crime, and a nail, that is to say, liberty.

Brujon, of whom it is time to form a complete idea, was, with the appearance of a delicate complexion and a deeply premeditated languor, a polished, intelligent robber, who possessed a caressing look and an atrocious smile. His look was the result of his will, and his smile the result of his nature. His first studies in his art were directed to roofs, and he had given a great impulse to the trade of lead-stealers, who strip roofs and carry away gutters by the process called *au gras double*. What finally rendered the moment favorable for an attempted escape was that workmen were at this very moment engaged in relaying and retipping a portion of the prison slates. The Saint Bernard was not absolutely isolated from the Charlemagne and St. Louis yards. Up there, on the roof, there were scaffolding and ladders,—in other words, bridges and staircases, on the side of deliverance. The New Building, which was the most cracked and decrepit affair possible to imagine, was the weak point of the prison. Saltpeter had so gnawed the walls that it had been found necessary to prop up and shore the ceilings of the dormitories, because stones became detached and fell on the prisoners' beds. In spite of this antiquity, the error was committed of confining in the New Building the most dangerous prisoners, and placing in it the "heavy cases," as is said in the prison jargon. The New Building contained four sleeping-wards, one above the other, and a garret-floor called the "Fine Air." A large chimney, probably belonging to some old kitchen of the Ducs de la Force, started from the ground-floor, passed through the four stories, cut in two the sleeping-wards, in which it figured as a sort of flattened pillar, and issued through a hole in the roof. Gueulemer and Brujon were in the same ward, and had been placed through precaution on the ground-floor. Accident willed it that the head of their beds rested against the chimney. Thénardier was exactly above their heads in the attic called Fine Air.

The passer-by who stops in the Rue Culture Sainte Catherine, after passing the fireman's barracks, and in front of the bath-house gate-way, sees a court-yard full of flowers and shrubs in boxes, at the end of which is a small white rotunda with two wings, enlivened by green shutters, the bucolic dream of Jean Jacques. Not ten years ago there rose above this rotunda a black, enormous, frightful, naked wall, which was the outer wall of La Force. This wall behind this rotunda was like a glimpse of

Milton caught behind Berquin. High though it was, this wall was surmounted by an even blacker roof, which could be seen beyond,—it was
the roof of the New Building.

Four dormer windows protected by bars could be seen in it, and they
were the windows of Fine Air. A chimney passed through the roof,
which was the chimney of the sleeping-wards. Fine Air, the attic-floor of
the New Building, was a species of large hall, closed with triple gratings
and iron-lined doors, starred with enormous nails. When you entered by
the north end, you had on your left the four dormers, and on your right,
facing these, four square and spacious cages, separated by narrow passages, built up to breast-height of masonry, and the rest to the roof of
iron bars. Thénardier had been confined in solitary punishment since
the night of February 3. It was never discovered how, or by what connivance, he succeeded in procuring and concealing a bottle of that prepared wine, invented, so 'tis said, by Desrues, in which a narcotic is
mixed, and which the band of the *Endormeurs* rendered celebrated.
There are in many prisons treacherous turnkeys, half jailers, half robbers,
who assist in escapes, sell to the police a faithless domesticity, and "make
the handle of the salad-basket dance."

On this very night, then, when little Gavroche picked up the two
straying children, Brujon and Gueulemer, who knew that Babet, who
had escaped that same morning, was waiting for them in the street with
Montparnasse, gently rose, and began breaking open with a nail which
Brujon had found, the chimney against which their beds were. The rubbish fell on Brujon's bed, so that it was not heard, and the gusts of wind
mingled with the thunder shook the doors on their hinges, and produced
a frightful and hideous row in the prison. Those prisoners who awoke
pretended to fall asleep again, and left Brujon and Gueulemer to do as
they pleased; and Brujon was skillful, and Gueulemer was vigorous.
Before any sound had reached the watchman sleeping in the grated cell
which looked into the ward, the wall was broken through, the chimney
escaladed, the iron trellis-work which closed the upper opening of the
chimney forced, and the two formidable bandits were on the roof. The
rain and the wind were tremendous, and the roof was slippery.

"What a fine night for an escape!" said Brujon.

An abyss of six feet in width and eighty feet deep separated them from
the surrounding wall, and at the bottom of this abyss they could see a
sentry's musket gleaming in the darkness. They fastened to the ends of
the chimney-bars which they had just broken the rope which Brujon had

woven in the cell, threw the other end over the outer wall, crossed the abyss at a bound, clung to the coping of the wall, bestraddled it, glided one after the other along the rope to a little roof which joins the bath-house, pulled their rope to them, jumped into the yard of the bath-house, pushed open the porter's half-door near which his cord was hanging, pulled the cord, opened the gate-way, and found themselves in the street. Not three-quarters of an hour had elapsed since they were standing on the bed, nail in hand, and with their plan in their heads. A few minutes after, they had rejoined Babet and Montparnasse, who were prowling in the neighborhood. On drawing the cord to them they broke it, and a piece had remained fastened to the chimney on the roof, but they had met with no other accident beyond almost entirely skinning their fingers. On this night Thénardier was warned, though it was impossible to discover how, and did not go to sleep. At about one in the morning, when the night was very black, he saw two shadows passing, in the rain and gusts, the window opposite his cage. One stopped just long enough to give a look; it was Brujon. Thénardier saw him, and understood—that was enough for him. Thénardier, reported to be a burglar, and detained on the charge of attempting to obtain money at night by violence, was kept under constant watch, and a sentry, relieved every two hours, walked in front of his cage with a loaded musket. The Fine Air was lighted by a sky-light, and the prisoner had on his feet a pair of fetters weighing fifty pounds. Every day at four in the afternoon, a turnkey, escorted by two mastiffs,—such things still happened at that day,— entered his cage, placed near his bed a black loaf of two pounds weight, a water-jug, and a bowl of very weak broth in which a few beans floated, inspected his fetters, and tapped the bars. This man with his dogs returned twice during the night.

Thénardier had obtained permission to keep a sort of iron pin which he used to nail his bread to the wall, in order, as he said, "to preserve it from the rats." As Thénardier was under a constant watch, this pin did not seem dangerous; still it was remembered at a later day that a turnkey said, "It would have been better only to leave him a wooden skewer." At two in the morning, the sentry, who was an old soldier, was changed, and a recruit substituted for him. A few minutes after, the man with the dogs paid his visit, and went away without having noticed anything, except the youth and peasant look of the "Tourlourou." Two hours after, when they came to relieve this conscript, they found him asleep, and lying like a log by the side of Thénardier's cage. As for the prisoner, he was no longer there; his severed fetters lay on the ground, and there was a hole in the ceiling of his cage, and another above it in the roof. A plank of his bed had been torn out and carried off, for it could not be found. In the cell was also found the half-empty bottle, containing the rest of the drugged wine with which the young soldier had been sent to sleep. The soldier's bayonet had disappeared. At the moment when all this was discovered, Thénardier was supposed to be out of reach; the truth was, that he was no longer in the New Building, but was still in great danger. Thénardier, on reaching the roof of the New Building, found the remainder of Brujon's rope hanging from the chimney-bars, but as the broken cord was much too short, he was unable to cross the outer wall as Brujon and Gueulemer had done.

When you turn out of the Rue des Ballets into the Rue du Roi de Sicile, you notice almost directly on your right a dirty hole. In the last century a house stood here, of which only the back wall exists, a perfect ruin of a wall which rises to the height of a third-story between the adjacent buildings. This ruin can be recognized by two large square windows, still visible; the center one, the one nearest the right-hand gable, is barred by a moldy beam placed slanting like a prop, and through these windows could be seen formerly a lofty lugubrious wall, which was a portion of the outer wall of La Force. The gap which the demolished house has left in the street is half filled up with a hoarding of rotten planks, supported by five stone pillars, and inside is a small hut built against the still standing ruin. The boarding has a door in it which, a few years ago, was merely closed with a latch. It was the top of this ruin which Thénardier had attained a little after three in the morning. How did he get there? This was never explained or understood. The lightning-flashes must at once have impeded and helped him. Did he employ the ladders and scaffolding of the slaters to pass from roof to roof, over the buildings of the Charlemagne yard, those of the St. Louis yard, the outer, and thence reach the ruined wall in the Rue du Roi de Sicile? But there were gaps in this passage which seemed to render it impossible. Had he laid the plank from his bed as a bridge from the roof of Fine Air to the outer wall, and crawled on his stomach along the coping, all round the prison till he reached the ruin? But the outer wall of La Force was very irregular; it rose and sank; it was low at the sappers' barracks, and rose again at the bath-house; it was intersected by buildings, and had everywhere drops and right angles; and then, too, the sentries must have seen the fugitive's dark outline,—and thus the road taken by Thénardier remains almost inexplicable. Had he, illumined by that frightful thirst for liberty which changes precipices into ditches, iron bars into reeds, a cripple into an athlete, a gouty patient into a bird, stupidity into instinct, instinct into intellect, and intellect into genius, invented and improvised a third mode of escape? No one ever knew.

It is not always possible to explain the marvels of an escape; the man who breaks prison is, we repeat, inspired, there is something of the star, something of a flash in the mysterious light of the flight; the effort made for deliverance is no less surprising than the soaring toward the sublime, and people say of an escaped robber, "How did he manage to scale that roof?" in the same way as they say of Corneille, "Where did he find his *qu'il mourût?*" However this may be, Thénardier, dripping with perspiration, wet through with rain, with his clothes in rags, his hands torn, his elbows bleeding, and his knees lacerated, reached the ruined wall, lay down full length on it, and then his strength failed him. A perpendicular wall as high as a three-storied house separated him from the street. The rope he had was too short. He waited there, pale, exhausted, despairing, though just now so hopeful, still covered by night, but saying to himself that day would soon come; horrified at the thought that he should shortly hear it strike four from the neighboring clock of St. Paul, the hour when the sentry would be changed and be found asleep under the hole in the roof, gazing, with stupor, at such a terrible depth below, and in the light of the lamps, at the wet black pavement—that desired and terrific pavement which was death and which was liberty. He asked himself whether his three accomplices had succeeded in escaping, whether they were waiting for him, and if they would come to his help? He listened: excepting a patrol, no one had passed through the street since he had been lying there. Nearly all the market carts from Montreuil, Charonne, Vincennes, and Bercy came into town by the Rue St. Antoine.

Four o'clock struck, and Thénardier trembled. A few minutes after, the startled and confused noise which follows the discovery of an escape broke out in the prison. The sound of doors being opened and shut, the creaking of gates on their hinges, the tumult at the guard-room, and the clang of musket-butts on the pavement of the yards reached his ears; lights flashed past the grated windows of the sleeping-wards, a torch ran along the roof of the New Building, and the sappers were called out. Three caps, which the torch lit up in the rain, came and went along the roofs, and at the same time Thénardier saw, in the direction of the Bastille, a livid gleam mournfully whitening the sky. He was on top of a wall ten inches wide, lying in the pitiless rain, with a gulf on his right hand and on his left, unable to stir, suffering from the dizziness of a possible fall and the horror of a certain arrest, and his mind, like the clapper of a bell, went from one of these ideas to the other: "Dead if I fall, caught if I remain." In this state of agony he suddenly saw in the still perfectly dark street a man, who glided along the walls and came from the Rue Pavée, stop in the gap over which Thénardier was, as it were, suspended. This man was joined by a second, who walked with similar caution, then by a third, and then by a fourth. When these men were together, one of them raised the hasp of the hoarding gate, and all four entered the inclosure where the hut is, and stood exactly under Thénardier. These men had evidently selected this place to consult in, in order not to be seen by passers-by or the sentry guarding the wicket of La Force a few paces distant. We must say, too, that the rain kept this sentry confined to his box. Thénardier, unable to distinguish their faces, listened to their remarks with the desperate attention of a wretch who feels himself lost. He felt something like hope pass before his eyes when he heard these men talking slang. The first said in a low voice, but distinctly, something which we had better translate.

"Let us be off. What are we doing here?"

The second replied:

"It is raining hard enough to put out the fire of hell. And then the police will pass soon; besides, there is a sentry on. We shall get ourselves arrested here."

Two words employed, *icigo,* and *icicaille,* which both mean "here," and which belong, the first to the flash language of the barrières, and the second to that of the Temple, were rays of light for Thénardier. By *icigo* he recognized Brujon, who was a prowler at the barrières, and by *icicaille* Babet, who, among all his other trades, had been a second-hand clothes dealer at the Temple. The antique slang of the great century is only talked now at the Temple, and Babet was the only man who spoke it in its purity. Had it not been for the *icicaille,* Thénardier could not have recognized him, for he had completely altered his voice. In the meanwhile the third man had interfered.

"There is nothing to hurry us, so let us wait a little. What is there to tell us that he does not want us?"

Through this, which was only French, Thénardier recognized Montparnasse, whose pride it was to understand all the slang dialects and not speak one of them. As for the fourth man, he held his tongue, but his wide shoulders betrayed him, and Thénardier did not hesitate; it was Gueulemer. Brujon replied almost impetuously, but still in a low voice:

"What is that you are saying? The landlord has not been able to escape. He does not know the trade! A man must be a clever hand to tear up his shirt and cut his sheets in slips to make a rope; to make holes in doors; manufacture false papers; make false keys; file his fetters through; hang his rope out of the window; hide and disguise himself. The old chap cannot have done this, for he does not know how to work."

Babet added, still in the correct classic slang which Poulailler and Cartouche spoke, and which is to the new, bold and colored slang which Brujon employed what the language of Racine is to that of André Chénier.

"Your landlord has been caught in the act, for he is only an apprentice. He has let himself be duped by a spy, perhaps by a sheep, who played the pal. Listen, Montparnasse; do you hear those shouts in the prison? You saw all those candles; he is caught again. Well, he will get off with twenty years. I am not frightened, I am no coward, as is well known, but there is nothing to be done, and we shall be trapped. Do not feel offended, but come with us, and let us drink a bottle of old wine together."

"Friends must not be left in a difficulty," Montparnasse growled.

"I tell you he is caught again," Brujon resumed, "and at this moment the landlord is not worth a cent. We can do nothing for him, so let us be off. I feel at every moment as if a policeman were holding me in his hand."

Montparnasse resisted but feebly; the truth is that these four men, with the fidelity which bandits have of never deserting each other, had prowled the whole night round La Force, in spite of the peril they incurred, in the hope of seeing Thénardier appear on the top of some wall. But the night, which became really too fine, a down-pour which rendered all the streets deserted, the cold which attacked them, their dripping clothes, their worn-out shoes, the alarming noises which had broken out in the prison, the hours which had elapsed, the patrols they had met, the hope which departed and the fear that returned,—all this urged them to retreat. Montparnasse himself, who was perhaps Thénardier's son-in-law in a certain sense, yielded, and in a moment they would be gone. Thénardier gasped on his wall like the shipwrecked crew of the *Méduse* did on their raft when they watched the ship which they had sighted fade away on the horizon. He did not dare to call to them, for a cry overheard might ruin everything, but he had an idea, a last idea, an inspiration,—he took from his pocket the end of Brujon's rope, which he had detached from the chimney of the New Building, and threw it at their feet.·

"A cord!" said Babet.

"My cord!" said Brujon.

"The landlord is there," said Montparnasse. They raised their eyes, and Thénardier thrust out his head a little.

"Quiet," said Montparnasse; "have you the other end of the rope, Brujon?"

"Yes."

"Fasten the two ends together; we will throw the rope to him, he will attach it to the wall, and it will be long enough for him to come down."

Thénardier ventured to raise his voice:

"I am wet through."

"We'll warm you."

"I cannot stir."

"You will slip down and we will catch you."

"My hands are swollen."

"Only just fasten the rope to the wall."

"I can't."

"One of us must go up," said Montparnasse.

"Three stories!" Brujon ejaculated.

An old plaster conduit pipe, which had served as a chimney for a stove formerly lit in the hut, ran along the wall almost to the spot where Thénardier was lying. This pipe, which at that day was full of cracks and holes, has since fallen down, but its traces may be seen. It was very narrow.

"It would be possible to mount by that," said Montparnasse.

"By that pipe?" Babet exclaimed; "a man? oh, no, a boy is required."

"Yes, a boy," Brujon said in affirmative.

"Where can we find one?" Gueulemer said.

"Wait a minute," Montparnasse said; "I have it."

He gently opened the hoarding door, assured himself that there was no passer-by in the street, went out, shut the door cautiously after him, and ran off in the direction of the Bastille. Seven or eight minutes elapsed, eight thousand centuries for Thénardier; Babet, Brujon and Gueulemer did not open their lips; the door opened again, and Montparnasse came in, panting and leading Gavroche. The rain continued to make the street completely deserted. Little Gavroche stepped into the inclosure and looked calmly at the faces of the bandits. The rain was dripping from his hair, and Gueulemer said to him:

"Brat, are you a man?"

Gavroche shrugged his shoulders, and replied:

"A child like me is a man, and men like you are children."

"What a well-hung tongue the brat has!" Babet exclaimed.

"The boy of Paris is not made of wet paste," Brujon added.

"What do you want of me?" said Gavroche.

Montparnasse answered:

"Climb up that pipe."

"With this rope," Babet remarked.

"And fasten it," Brujon continued.

"At the top of the wall," Babet added.

"To the cross-bar of the window," Brujon said, finally.

"What next?" asked Gavroche.

"Here it is," said Gueulemer.

The gamin examined the rope, the chimney, the wall, and the window, gave that indescribable and disdainful smack of the lips which signifies, "What is it?"

"There is a man up there whom you will save," Montparnasse continued.

"Are you willing?" Brujon said.

"Ass!" the lad replied, as if the question seemed to him extraordinary, and took off his shoes.

Gueulemer seized Gavroche by one arm, placed him on the roof of the pent-houses, where moldering planks bent under the boy's weight, and handed him the rope which Brujon had joined again during the absence of Montparnasse. The gamin turned to the chimney, which it was an easy task to enter by a large crevice close to the roof. At the moment when he was going to ascend, Thénardier, who saw safety and life approaching, leaned over the edge of the wall; the first gleam of day whitened his dark forehead, his livid cheek-bones, his sharp savage nose, and his bristling gray beard, and Gavroche recognized him.

"Hilloh!" he said, "it's my father; well, that won't stop me."

And, taking the rope between his teeth, he resolutely commenced his ascent. He reached the top of the wall, straddled across it like a horse, and securely fastened the rope to the topmost cross-bar of the window. A moment after, Thénardier was in the street; so soon as he touched the pavement, so soon as he felt himself out of danger, he was no longer wearied, chilled, or trembling; the terrible things he had passed through were dissipated like smoke, and all his strange and ferocious intellect was re-aroused, and found itself erect and free, ready to march onward. The first remark this man made was:

"Well, whom are we going to eat?"

It is unnecessary to explain the meaning of this frightfully transparent sentence, which signifies at once killing, assassinating, and robbing. The real meaning of *to eat* is to *devour*.

"We must get into hiding," said Brujon. "We will understand each other in three words, and then separate at once. There was an affair that seemed good in the Rue Plumet, a deserted street, an isolated house, old rust-eaten railings looking on a garden, and lone women."

"Well, why not try it?" Thénardier asked.

"Your daughter Eponine went to look at the thing," Babet answered.

"And gave Magnon a biscuit," Brujon added; "there's nothing to be done there."

"The girl's no fool," said Thénardier; "still, we must see."

"Yes, yes," Brujon remarked, "we must see."

Not one of the men seemed to notice Gavroche, who during this colloquy was sitting on one of the posts; he waited some minutes, perhaps in the hope that his father would turn to him, and then put on his shoes again, saying:

"Is it all over? you men don't want me any more, I suppose, as I've got you out of the scrape? I'm off, for I must go and wake my brats."

And he went off. The five men left the inclosure in turn. When Gavroche had disappeared round the corner of the Rue des Ballets, Babet took Thénardier on one side.

"Did you notice that brat?" he asked him.

"What brat?"

"The one who climbed up the wall and handed you the rope."

"Not particularly."

"Well, I don't know, but I fancy it's your son."

"Nonsense," said Thénardier; "do you think so?"

BOOK VII

SLANG

1. THE ORIGIN OF SLANG

Pigritia is a terrible word. It engenders a world, *la pègre,* for which read—*robbery;* and a Hades, *la pégrenne,* for which read—*hunger.* Hence indolence is a mother, and has a son, robbery, and a daughter, hunger. Where are we at this moment? in slang. What is slang? It is at once the nation and the idiom, it is robbery in its two species,—people and language. Four-and-thirty years ago, when the narrator of this grave and somber history introduced into the middle of a work written with the same object as this one* a robber speaking slang, there was amazement and clamor. "Why! what! slang! why, it is frightful, it is the language of the chain-gang, of hulks and prisons, of everything that is the most abominable in society," etc., etc. We could never understand objections of this nature. Since that period two powerful romance-writers, of whom one was a profound observer of humanity, the other an intrepid friend of the people, Balzac and Eugène Sue, having made bandits talk in their natural tongue, as the author of *Le dernier Jour d'un Condamné* did in 1828, the same objections were raised, and people repeated, "What do writers want with this repulsive patois? slang is odious, and produces a shudder." Who denies it? of course it does. When the object is to probe a wound, a gulf, or a society, when did it become a fault to drive the probe too deep? We have always thought that it was sometimes an act of courage, and at the very least a simple and useful action, worthy of the sympathetic attention which a duty accepted and carried out deserves. Why should we not explore and study everything, and why stop on the way? Stopping is the function of the probe, and not of the prober.

*Le dernier Jour d'un Condamné.

163

Certainly it is neither an attractive nor an easy task to seek in the lowest depths of social order, where the earth leaves off and mud begins, to grope in these vague densities, to pursue, seize, and throw quivering on the pavement that abject idiom which drips with filth when thus brought to light, that pustulous vocabulary of which each word seems an unclean ring of a monster of the mud and darkness. Nothing is more mournful than thus to contemplate, by the light of thought, the frightful vermin swarm of slang in its nudity. It seems, in fact, as if you have just drawn from its sewer a sort of horrible beast made for the night, and you fancy you see a frightful, living, and bristling polype, which shivers, moves, is agitated, demands the shadow again, menaces, and looks. One word resembles a claw, another a lusterless and bleeding eye, and some phrases seem to snap like the pincers of a crab. All this lives with the hideous vitality of things which are organized in disorganization. Now, let us ask, when did horror begin to exclude study? or the malady drive away the physician? Can we imagine a naturalist who would refuse to examine a viper, a bat, a scorpion, a scolopendra, or a tarantula, and throw them into the darkness, saying, "Fie, how ugly they are!" The thinker who turned away from slang would resemble a surgeon who turned away from an ulcer or a wart. He would be a philologist hesitating to examine a fact of language, a philosopher hesitating to scrutinize a fact of humanity. For we must tell all those ignorant of the fact, that slang is at once a literary phenomenon and a social result. What is slang, properly so called? it is the language of misery.

Here we may, perhaps, be stopped; the fact may be generalized, which is sometimes a way of attenuating it; it may be observed that every trade, every profession, we might also say all the accidents of the social hierarchy, and all the forms of intelligence, have their slang. The merchant who says, *Montpellier in demand, Marseilles fine quality;* the broker who says, *carrying stock* and *going long;* the gambler who says, *pique, repique, and capote;* the bailiff of the Norman isles who says, *the feoffee cannot make any claim on the fruits of the fee during the hereditary seizure of the realty by the tenant;* the playwright who says, *the piece was goosed;* the actor who says, *I made a hit;* the philosopher who says, *phenomenal triplicity;* the sportsman who says, *a covey of partridges, a leash of woodcocks;* the phrenologist who says, *amativeness, combativeness, secretiveness;* the infantry soldier who says, *my clarionette;* the dragoon who says, *my turkey-cock;* the fencing-master who says, *tierce, quarte, disengage;* the printer who says, *hold a chapel;* all—printer, fencing-master, dragoon, infantry man, phrenologist, sportsman, philosopher, actor, playwright, gambler, stockbroker, and merchant—talk slang. The painter who says, *my grinder;* the attorney who says, *my gutter-jumper;* the barber who says, *my clerk;* and the cobbler who says, *my scrub,*—all talk slang. Rigorously taken, all the different ways of saying right and left, the sailor's larboard and starboard, the scene-shifter's off-side and prompt side, and the parson's Epistle-side and Gospel-side, are slang. There is the slang of affectation as there was the slang of the précieuses, and the Hôtel de Rambouillet bordered to some slight extent the Cour des Miracles. There is the slang of duchesses, as is proved by this sentence, written in a note by a very great lady and very pretty woman of the Restoration: *Vous trouverez dans ces potains-là une foultitude de raisons pour que je me libertise.** Diplomatic ciphers are slang, and the pontifical chancery, writing 26 for "Rome," *grkztntgzyal* for "Envoy," and *abfxustgrnogrkzu tu* XI. for "the Duke of Modena," talk slang. The mediæval physicians who, in order to refer to carrots, radishes, and turnips, said *opoponach, perfroschinum, reptitalmus, dracatholicum angelorum,* and *postmegorum,* talk slang. The sugar-baker who says, *clarified lumps, molasses, bastard, common, burned, loaf,* this honest manufacturer talks slang. A certain school of critics, who twenty years ago said, "one half of Shakespere is puns and playing on words," spoke slang. The poet and the artist who with profound feeling would call M. de Montmorency a bourgeois, if he were not a connoisseur in verses and statues, talk slang. The classic academician who calls flowers *Flora,* the fruits *Pomona,* the sea *Neptune,* love the *Flames,* beauty the *Charms,* a horse a *charger,* the white or tricolor cockade *the rose of Bellona,* the three-cornered hat *the triangle of Mars,*—that classic academician talks slang. Algebra, medicine, and botany have their slang. The language employed on shipboard, that admirable sea-language so complete and picturesque, which Jean Bart, Duquesne, Suffren, and Duperré spoke, which is mingled with the straining of the rigging, the sound of the speaking-trumpets, the clang of boarding axe, the rolling, the wind, the gusts, and the cannon—is an heroic and brilliant slang, which is to the ferocious slang of robbers what the lion is to the jackal.

All this is perfectly true, but, whatever people may say, this mode of comprehending the word slang is an extension which everybody will not be prepared to admit. For our part, we perceive the precise circumscribed and settled acceptation of the word, and restrict slang to slang.

*"You will find in that tittle-tattle a multitude of reasons why I should take my liberty."

The true slang, the slang *par excellence,* if the two words can be coupled, the immemorial slang which was a kingdom, is nothing else, we repeat, than the ugly, anxious, cunning, treacherous, venomous, cruel, blear-eyed, vile, profound, and fatal language of misery. There is at the extremity of all abasements and all misfortunes a last depth of misery, which revolts and resolves to contend with the ensemble of fortunate facts and reigning rights; a frightful struggle, in which, at one moment crafty, at another violent, at once unhealthy and ferocious, it attacks the social order with pin-pricks by vice, and with club-blows by crime. For the necessities of this struggle, misery has invented a fighting language, which is called slang. To hold up on the surface and keep from forgetfulness, from the gulf, only a fragment of any language which man has spoken, and which would be lost, that is to say, one of the elements, good or bad, of which civilization is composed and complicated, is to extend the data of social observation and serve civilization itself. Plautus rendered this service, whether voluntarily or involuntarily, by making two Carthaginian soldiers speak Phœnician; Molière rendered it also by making so many of his characters talk Levantine and all sorts of patois. Here objections crop out afresh; Phœnician, excellent, Levantine, very good, and even patois may be allowed, for they are languages which have belonged to nations or provinces—but slang? of what service is it to preserve slang and help it to float on the surface?

To this we will only make one remark. Assuredly, if the language which a nation or a province has spoken is worthy of interest, there is a thing still more worthy of attention and study, and that is the language which a wretchedness has spoken. It is the language which has been spoken in France, for instance, for more than four centuries, not only by a wretchedness, but by every wretchedness, by every human wretchedness possible. And, then, we insist upon the fact, to study social deformities and infirmities, and point them out for cure, is not a task in which choice is permissible. The historian of morals and ideas has a mission no less austere than the historian of events. The latter has the surface of civilization, the struggles of crowned heads, the births of princes, the marriages of kings, battles, assemblies, great public men and revolutions,—all the external part: the other historian has the interior, the basis, the people that labors, suffers, and waits, the crushed woman, the child dying, the dull warfare of man with man, obscure ferocities, prejudices, allowed iniquities, the subterranean counterstrokes of the law, the secret evolutions of minds, the indistinct shivering of multitudes, those who die of hunger, the bare-footed, the bare-armed, the disinherited, the orphans, the unhappy, the infamous, and all the ghosts that wander about in obscurity. He must go down with his heart full of charity and severity, at once as a brother and as a judge, into the impenetrable casements in which crawl pell-mell those who bleed and those who wound, those who weep and those who cure, those who fast and those who devour, those that endure evil and those who commit it. Are the duties of the historians of hearts and souls inferior to those of the historians of external facts? can we believe that Dante has less to say than Machiavelli? is the lower part of civilization, because it is deeper and more gloomy, less important than the upper? Do we know the mountain thoroughly if we do not know the caverns?

We will notice, by the way, that from our previous remarks a marked separation, which does not exist in our mind, might be inferred between the two classes of historians. No one is a good historian of the patent, visible, brilliant, and public life of a people, unless he is at the same time and to a certain extent the historian of their profound and hidden life, and no one is a good historian of the interior unless he can be, whenever it is required, historian of the exterior. The history of morals and ideas penetrates the history of events, and *vice versâ;* they are two orders of different facts which answer to each other, are always linked together, and often engender one another. All the lineaments which providence traces on the surface of a nation have their gloomy but distinct parallels at the base, and all the convulsions of the interior produce upheavings on the surface. As true history is a medley of everything, the real historian attends to everything. Man is not a circle with only one center; he is an ellipse with two foci, facts being the one, and ideas the other. Slang is nothing but a vestiary in which language, having some wicked action to commit, disguises itself. It puts on these masks of words and rags of metaphors. In this way it becomes horrible. It can scarce be recognized. Is it really the French language, the great human tongue? Here it is, ready to go on the stage and take up the cue of crime, and suited for all the parts in the repertory of evil. It no longer walks, but shambles; it limps upon the crutch of the Cour des Miracles, a crutch which may be metamorphosed into a club; all the specters, its dressers, have daubed its face, and it crawls along and stands erect with the double movement of the reptile. It is henceforth ready for any part, for it has been made to squint by the forger, has been verdigrised by the prisoner, blackened by the soot of the incendiary, and rouged by the murderer.

When you listen at the door of society, on the side of honest men, you catch the dialogue of those outside. You distinguish questions and answers, and notice, without comprehending it, a hideous murmur, sounding almost like the human accent, but nearer to a yell than to speech. It is slang; the words are deformed, wild, imprinted with a species of fantastic bestiality. You fancy that you hear hydras conversing. It is unintelligibility in darkness, it gnashes its teeth and talks in whispers, supplementing the gloom by enigmas. There is darkness in misfortune, and greater darkness still in crime, and these two darknesses amalgamated compose slang. There is obscurity in the atmosphere, obscurity in the deeds, obscurity in the voices. It is a horrifying, frog-like language, which goes, comes, hops, crawls, slavers, and moves monstrously in that common gray mist composed of crime, night, hunger, vice, falsehood, injustice, nudity, asphyxia, and winter, which is the high noon of the wretched.

Let us take compassion on the chastised, for, alas! what are we ourselves? who am I, who am speaking to you? who are you, who are listening to me? whence do we come? and is it quite sure that we did nothing before we were born? The earth is not without a resemblance to a jail, and who knows whether man is not the ticket-of-leave of Divine justice? If we look at life closely we find it so made that there is punishment everywhere to be seen. Are you what is called a happy man? Well, you are sad every day, and each of them has its great grief or small anxiety. Yesterday you trembled for a health which is dear to you, to-day you are frightened about your own, to-morrow it will be a monetary anxiety, and the day after the diatribe of a calumniator, and the day after that again the misfortune of some friend; then the weather, then something broken or lost, or a pleasure for which your conscience and your backbone reproach you; or, another time, the progress of public affairs, and we do not take into account heart-pangs. And so it goes on; one cloud is dissipated, another forms, and there is hardly one day in one hundred of real joy and bright sunshine. And you are one of that small number who are happy; as for other men, the stagnation of night is around them. Reflecting minds rarely use the expressions the happy and the unhappy, for in this world, which is evidently the vestibule of another, there are no happy beings. The true human division is into the luminous and the dark. To diminish the number of the dark, and augment that of the luminous, is the object, and that is why we cry, "Instruction and learning!" Learning to read is lighting the fire, and every syllable spelt is a spark. When we say light, however, we do not necessarily mean joy; for men suffer in light, and excess of light burns. Flame is the enemy of the wings, and to burn without ceasing to fly is the prodigy of genius. When you know and when you love, you will still suffer, for the day is born in tears, and the luminous weep, be it only for the sake of those in darkness.

2. ROOTS OF SLANG

SLANG is the language of those in darkness. Thought is affected in its gloomiest depths, and social philosophy is harassed in its most poignant undulations, in the presence of this enigmatical dialect, which is at once branded and in a state of revolt. There is in this a visible chastisement, and each syllable looks as if it were marked. The words of the common language appear in it, as if branded and hardened by the hangman's red-hot irons, and some of them seem to be still smoking; some phrases produce in you the effect of a robber's fleur-de-lised shoulder suddenly exposed, and ideas almost refuse to let themselves be represented by these convict substantives. The metaphors are at times so daring that you feel that they have worn fetters. Still, in spite of all this, and in consequence of all this, this strange patois has by right its compartment in that great impartial museum, in which there is room for the oxydized cent as well as the gold medal, and which is called toleration. Slang, whether people allow it or no, has its syntax and poetry, and is a language. If, by the deforming of certain words, we perceive that it has been chewed by Mandrin, we feel from certain metonyms that Villon spoke it. That exquisite and so celebrated line:

Mais où sont les neiges d'antan?

is a verse of slang. "Antan"— *ante annum,* is a slang word of Thunes, which signified "the past year," and, by extension, "formerly." Five-and-thirty years ago, on the departure of the great chain-gang, in 1827, there might be read in one of the dungeons of Bicêtre this maxim, engraved with a nail upon the wall by a king of Thunes condemned to the galleys, "les dabs d'antan trimaient siempre pour la pierre du Coësre," which means, "the kings of former days used always to go to be consecrated." In the thought of that king, the consecration was the galleys. The word *décarade,* which expresses the departure of a heavy coach at a gallop, is attributed to Villon, and is worthy of him. This word, which strikes fire, contains in a masterly onomatopœia the whole of Lafontaine's admirable line:

Six forts chevaux tiraient un coche.

From a purely literary point of view, few studies would be more curious or fertile than that of slang. It is an entire language within a language, a sort of sickly grafting which has produced a vegetation, a parasite which has its roots in the old Gaulish trunk, and whose sinister foliage crawls up the whole of one side of the language. This is what might be called the first or common notion of slang, but to those who study the language as it should be studied, that is to say, as geologists study the earth, slang appears like a real alluvium. According as we dig more or less deeply, we find in slang, beneath the old popular French Provençal, Spanish, Italian, Levantine, that language of the Mediterranean ports, English, and German, Romanic, in its three varieties of French, Italian, and Roman Latin, and, finally, Basque and Celtic. It is a deep and strange formation, a subterranean edifice built up in common by all scoundrels. Each accursed race has deposited its stratum, each suffering has let its stone fall, each heart has given its pebble. A multitude of wicked, low, or irritated souls who passed through life, and have faded away in eternity, are found there almost entire, and to some extent still visible, in the shape of a monstrous word.

Do you want Spanish? the old Gothic slang swarms with it. Thus we have *boffette,* a box of the ears, which comes from *bofeton; vantane,* a window (afterward vanterne), from *vantana; gat,* a cat, from *gato; acite,* oil, from *aceyte.* Do you want Italian? we have *spade,* a sword, which comes from *spada,* and *carvel,* a boat, which comes from *caravella.* From the English we have *bichot,* the *bishop; raille,* a spy, from *rascal;* and *pilche,* a case, from *pilcher,* a scabbard. Of German origin are *calner*, the waiter, *kellner; hers*, the master, *herzog*, or duke. In Latin, we find *frangir*, to break, from *frangere; affurer*, to steal, from *fur*, and *cadène*, a chain, from *catena*. There is one word which is found in all continental language with a sort of mysterious power and authority, and that is the word *magnus*; Scotland makes of it, for instance, *mac*, and slang reduces it to *muk*, afterward *Meg*, that is to say, the Deity. Do you wish for Basque? here is *gahisto*, the devil, which is derived from *fiaiztoa*, bad; and *sorgabon*, good-night, which comes from *gabon*, good-evening. In Celtic we find *blavin*, a handkerchief, derived from *blavet*, running water; *ménesse*, a woman (in a bad sense), from *meinec*, full of stones; *barant*, a stream, from *baranton*, a fountain; *goffeur*, a lock-smith, from *goff*, a blacksmith; and *guédouze*, death, which comes from *guenn-du*, white and black. Lastly, do you wish for a bit of history? Slang calls crowns "the Maltese" in memory of the change which was current aboard the Maltese galleys.

In addition to the philological origins which we have indicated, slang has other and more natural roots, which issue, so to speak, directly from the human mind. In the first place, there is the direct creation of words, for it is the mystery of language to paint with words which have, we know not how or why, faces. This is the primitive foundation of every human language, or what might be called the granite. Slang swarms with words of this nature, immediate words created all of one piece, it is impossible to say when, or by whom, without etymologies, analogies, or derivatives,—solitary, barbarous, and at times, hideous words, which have a singular power of expression, and are alive. The executioner, *le taule;* the forest, *le sabri;* fear or flight, *taf;* the footman, *le larbin;* the general, prefect, or minister, *pharos;* and the devil, *le rabouin*. Nothing can be stranger than these words, which form transparent masks; some of them, *le rabouin*, for instance, are at the same time grotesque and terrible, and produce the effect of a Cyclopean grimace. In the second place, there is metaphor, and it is the peculiarity of a language which wishes to say everything and conceal everything to abound in figures. Metaphor is an enigma in which the robber who is scheming a plot, or the prisoner arranging an escape, takes the refuge. No idiom is more metaphorical than slang; *dévisser le coco*, to twist the neck, *tortiller*, to eat; *être gerbé*, to be tried; *un rat*, a stealer of bread; *il lansquine*, it rains—an old striking figure, which bears to some extent its date with it, assimilates the long, oblique lines of rain to the serried, sloping pikes of the lansquenets, and contains in one word the popular adage, "It is raining Halberts." At times, in proportion as slang passes from the first to the second stage, words pass from the savage and primitive state to the metaphorical sense. The devil ceases to be *le rabouin,* and becomes "the baker," or he who puts in the oven. This is wittier, but not so grand; something like Racine after Corneille, or Euripides after Æschylus. Some slang phrases which belong to both periods, and have at once a barbarous and a metaphorical character, resemble phantasmagorias: *Les sorgueurs vont sollicter les gails à la lune.* (The prowlers are going to steal horses at night.) This passes before the mind like a group of specters, and we know not what we see. Thirdly, there is expediency: slang lives upon the language, uses it as it pleases, and when the necessity arises limits itself to denaturalizing it summarily and coarsely. At times, with the ordinary words thus deformed and complicated with pure slang, picturesque sentences are composed, in which the admission of the two previous elements, direct creation and metaphor, is visible— *le cab jaspine, je marronne que la roulette Pantin trime dans le sabri* (the dog barks, I suspect that the Paris diligence is passing through the wood); *le dab est sinve, la dabuge est merloussière, la fée est bative* (the master is stupid, the mistress is cunning, and the daughter pretty). Most frequently, in order to throw out listeners, slang confines itself to adding indistinctly to all the words of the language a species of ignoble tail, a termination in *aille, orgue, iergue,* or *uche.* Thus: *Vouziergue trouvaille bonorgue ce gigotmuche?* Do you find that leg of mutton good? This was a remark made by Cartouche to a jailer, in order to learn whether the sum offered him for an escape suited him. The termination in *mar* has been very recently added.

Slang, being the idiom of corruption, is itself quickly corrupted. Moreover, as it always tries to hide itself, so soon as it feels that it is understood, it transforms itself. Exactly opposed to all other vegetables, every sunbeam kills what it falls on in it. Hence slang is being constantly decomposed and recomposed and this is an obscure and rapid labor which never ceases, and it makes more way in ten years than language does in ten centuries. Thus *larton* (head) becomes *lartif, gail* (a horse) *gaye, fertanche* (straw) *fertillé, momignard* (the child) *momaque, fiques* (clothes) *frusques, chique* (the church) *l'egrugeoir,* and *colabre* (the neck) *colas.* The devil is first *gahisto,* then *le rabouin,* and next the "baker," a priest is the *ratichon,* and then the *sanglier;* a dagger is the *vingtdeux,* next a *surin,* and lastly a *lingre;* the police are *railles,* then *roussins,* then *marchands de lacet,* then *coqueurs,* and lastly *cognes;* the executioner is the *taule,* then *Charlot,* then the *atigeur,* and then the *becquillard.* In the seventeenth century, to fight, was to "take snuff"; in the nineteenth, it is "to have a quid in the throat," but twenty different names have passed away between these two extremes, and Cartouche would speak Hebrew to Lacenaire. All the words of this language are perpetually in flight, like the men who employ them. Still, from time to time, and owing to this very movement, the old slang reappears and becomes new again. It has its head-quarters where it holds its ground: the Temple preserved the slang of the seventeenth century, and Bicêtre, when it was a prison, that of Thunes. There the termination in *anche* of the old Thuners could be heard: *Boyanches-tu?* (do you drink?) *il croyanche* (he believes). But perpetual motion does not the less remain the law. If the philosopher succeeds in momentarily fixing, for the purpose of observation, this language, which is necessarily evaporating, he falls into sorrowful and useful meditations, and no study is more efficacious or more fertile and instructive. There is not a metaphor or an etymology of slang which does not contain a lesson. Among these men, *fighting* means *pretending:* they "fight" a disease, for cunning is their strength. With them the idea of man is not separated from the idea of a shadow. Night is called *la sorgue* and man *l'orgue:* man is a derivative of night. They have formed the habit of regarding society as an atmosphere which kills them, as a fatal force, and they talk of their health. A man arrested is a "patient"; a man sentenced is a "corpse." The most terrible thing for the prisoner within the four stone walls which form his sepulcher is a sort of freezing chastity, and hence he always calls the dungeon the *castus.* In this funereal place external life will appear under its most smiling aspect. The prisoner has irons on his feet, and you may perhaps fancy that he thinks how people walk with their feet; no, he thinks that they dance with them, hence, if he succeed in cutting through his fetters, his first idea is that he can now dance, and he calls the saw a *bastringue.* A name is a *center,* a profound assimilation. The bandit has two heads,—the one which revolves his deeds and guides him through life, the other which he has on his shoulders on the day of his death; he calls the head which counsels him in crime, the *sorbonne,* and the one that expiates it, the *tronche.* When a man has nothing but rags on his body and vices in his heart,—when he has reached that double moral and material degradation which the word *gueux* characterizes in its two significations,—he is ripe for crime: he is like a well-sharpened blade; he has two edges,—his distress and his villainy, and hence slang does not call him a *gueux*, but a *rêguisé*. What is the bagne? a furnace of damnation, a hell, and the convict calls himself a *faggot*. Lastly, what name do malefactors give to the prison? the *college*. A whole penitentiary system might issue from this word.

Would you like to know whence came most of the galley songs,— those choruses called in the special vocabularies the *lirlonfa*? Listen to this:

There was at the Chatelet of Paris, a large, long cellar, which was eight feet below the level of the Seine. It had neither windows nor gratings, and the sole opening was the door; men could enter it, but air not. This cellar had for ceiling a stone arch, and for floor ten inches of mud; it had been paved, but, owing to the leakage of the water, the paving had rotted and fallen to pieces. Eight feet above the ground, a long massive joist ran from one end to the other of this vault; from this joist hung at regular distances chains, three feet long, and at the end of these chains were collars. In this cellar men condemned to the galleys were kept until the day of their departure for Toulon; they were thrust under this beam, where each had his fetters oscillating in the darkness and waiting for him. The chains, like pendent arms, and the collars, like open hands, seized these wretches by the neck; they were riveted and left there. As the chain was too short, they could not lie down; they remained motionless in this cellar, in this night, under this beam, almost hung, forced to make extraordinary efforts to reach their loaf or water-jug, with the vault above their heads and mud up to their knees, drawn and quartered by fatigue, giving way at the hips and knees, hanging on by their hands to the chain to rest themselves, only able to sleep standing, and awakened every moment by the choking of the collar: some did not awake. To eat they were compelled to draw up their bread, which was thrown into the mud, with the heel all along the thigh to their hand. How long did they remain in this state? one month, two months, sometimes six months; one man remained a year. It was the antechamber of the galleys, and men were put in it for stealing a hare from the king. In this hellish sepulcher, what did they? they died by inches as people can do in a sepulcher, and sang, which they can do in a hell, for when there is no longer hope, song remains; in the Maltese waters, when a galley was approaching, the singing was heard before the sound of the oars. The poor poacher Survincent, who passed through the cellar-prison of the Châtelet, said, *rhymes sustained me*. Poetry is useless; what is the good of rhymes? In this cellar nearly all the slang songs were born, and it is from the dungeon of the great Châtelet of Paris that comes the melancholy chorus of Montgomery's galley: *Timaloumisaine, timoulamison.* Most of the songs are sad, some are gay, and one is tender:

Icicaille est le théâtre
*du petit dardant.**

Do you what you will, you cannot destroy that eternal relic of man's heart, love.

In this world of dark deeds secrets are kept, for secrets are a thing belonging to all, and with these wretches secrecy is the unity which serves as the basis of union. To break secrecy is to tear from each member of this ferocious community something of himself. To denounce is called, in the energetic language of slang, "to eat the piece" as if the denouncer took a little of the substance of each, and supported himself on a piece of the flesh of each. What is receiving a buffet? the conventional metaphor answers, "It is seeing six-and-thirty candles." Here slang interferes and reads *camoufle* for candle; life in its ordinary language takes *camouflet* as a synonym for a box on the ears. Hence, by a sort of penetration from bottom to top, and by the air of metaphor, that incalculable trajectory, slang ascends from the cellar to the academy, and Poulailler saying, "I light my *camoufle*," makes Voltaire write, "Langleviel la Beaumelle deserves a hundred *camouflets*." Searching in slang is a discovery at every step, and the study and investigation of this strange idiom lead to the point of intersection of regular with accursed society. The robber has also his food for powder, or stealable matter, in you, in me, in the first passer-by, the *pantre (pan,* everybody). Slang is the word converted into a convict. It produces a consternation to reflect that the thinking principle of man can be hurled down so deep that it can be dragged there and bound by the obscure tyranny of fatality, and be fastened to some unknown rivets on this precipice. Alas! will no one come to the help of the human soul in this darkness? Is it its destiny ever to await the mind, the liberator, the immense tamer of Pegasuses and hippogriffs, the dawn-colored combatant, who descends from the azure sky between two wings, the radiant knight of the future? will it ever call in vain to its help the lance of the light of idealism? is it condemned always to look down into the gulf of evil and see closer and closer to it beneath the hideous water the demoniac head, the slavering

*The Archer Cupid.

mouth, and this serpentine undulation of claws, swellings, and rings? Must it remain there without a gleam of hope, left to the horror of this formidable and vaguely smelt approach of the monster, shuddering, with disheveled hair, wringing its arms and eternally chained to the rock of night, like a somber Andromeda, white and naked in the darkness?

3. *LAUGHING SLANG AND CRYING SLANG*

As we see, the whole of slang, the slang of four hundred years ago, as well as that of the present day, is penetrated by that gloomy symbolic spirit which gives to every word at one moment a suffering accent, at another a menacing air; we see in it the old ferocious sorrow of those mumpers of Cour des Miracles, who played at cards with packs of their own, some of which have been preserved for us. The eight of clubs, for instance, represented a tall man bearing eight enormous clover leaves, a sort of fantastic personification of the forest. At the foot of this tree could be seen a lighted fire, at which three hares were roasting a gamekeeper on a spit, and behind, over another fire, a steaming caldron from which a dog's head emerged. Nothing can be more lugubrious than these reprisals in painting upon a pack of cards, in the face of the pyres for smugglers and the caldron for coiners. The various forms which thought assumed in the kingdom of slang, singing, jests, and menaces, all had this impotent and crushed character. All the songs of which a few melodies have come down to us were humble and lamentable enough to draw tears. The *pègre* calls himself the poor *pègre,* for he is always the hare that hides itself, the mouse that escapes, or the bird that flies away. He hardly protests, but restricts himself to sighing, and one of his groans has reached us: *Je n'entrave que le dail comment meck, le daron des orgues, peut atiger ses mômes et ses momignards, et les locher criblant sans etre atigé lui-même.** The wretch whenever he has time to think, makes himself little before the law and paltry before society; he lies down on his stomach, supplicates, and implores pity, and we can see that he knows himself to be in the wrong.

Toward the middle of the last century a change took place; the person, songs, and choruses of the robbers assumed, so to speak, an insolent and jovial gesture. The *larifla* was substituted for the plaintive *maluré,* and we find in nearly all the songs of the galleys, the hulks, and the chaingangs, a diabolical and enigmatical gayety. We hear in them that shrill and leaping chorus which seems illumined by a phosphorescent gleam, and appears cast into the forest by a will-o'-the-wisp playing the fife.

> *Mirlababi surlababo*
> *Mirliton ribonribette,*
> *Surlababi mirlababo*
> *Mirliton ribonribo.*

They sang this while cutting a man's throat in a cellar or a thicket. It is a serious symptom that in the eighteenth century the old melancholy of these desponding classes is dissipated, and they begin to laugh; they mock the grand "meg" and the grand "Dab," and, Louis XV being given, they call the king of France the Marquis de Pantin. The wretches are nearly gay, and a sort of dancing light issues from them, as if their conscience no longer weighed them down. These lamentable tribes of darkness no longer possess the despairing audacity of deeds, but the careless audacity of the mind; this is a sign that they are losing the feeling of their criminality, and finding some support of which they are themselves ignorant, among the thinkers and dreamers. It is a sign that robbery and plunder are beginning to be filtered even into doctrines and sophisms, so as to lose a little of their ugliness, and give a good deal of it to the sophisms and the doctrine. Lastly, it is a sign of a prodigious and speedy eruption, unless some diversion arise. Let us halt here for a moment. Whom do we accuse? is it the eighteenth century? is it its philosophy? certainly not. The work of the eighteenth century is healthy and good, and the encyclopædists, with Diderot at their head, the physiocrats under Turgot, the philosophers led by Voltaire, and the Utopists

*I do not understand how God, the father of men, can torture His children and His grandchildren, and hear them cry, without being tortured Himself.

177

commanded by Rousseau, are four sacred legions. The immense advance of humanity toward the light is due to them, and they are the four advance guards of the human races, going toward the four cardinal points of progress—Diderot toward the beautiful, Turgot toward the useful, Voltaire toward truth, and Rousseau toward justice. But by the side of and below the philosophers were the sophists, a venomous vegetation mingled with a healthy growth, a hemlock in the virgin forest. While the hangman was burning on the grand staircase of the Palace of Justice the grand liberating books of the age, writers now forgotten were publishing, with the royal privilege, strangely disorganizing books, which were eagerly read by scoundrels. Some of these publications, patronized, strange to say, by a prince, will be found in the *Bibliothèque secrète*. These facts, profound but unknown, were unnoticed on the surface, but at times the very obscurity of a fact constitutes its danger, and it is obscure because it is subterranean. Of all the writers, the one who perhaps dug the most unhealthy gallery at that day in the masses was Restif de la Bretonne.

This work, peculiar to all Europe, produced greater ravages in Germany than anywhere else. In Germany, during a certain period which was summed up by Schiller in his famous drama of the Robbers, robbery and plunder were raised into a protest against property and labor; they appropriated certain elementary ideas, specious and false, apparently just, and in reality absurd, wrapped themselves up in these ideas, and to some extent disappeared in them, assumed an abstract name, and passed into a theoretical state, and in this way circulated among the laborious, suffering, and honest masses, without even the cognizance of the imprudent chemists who prepared the mixture, and the masses that accepted it. Whenever a fact of this nature is produced, it is serious; suffering engenders passion; and while the prosperous blind themselves, or go to sleep, the hatred of the unfortunate classes kindles its torch at some sullen or ill-constituted mind, which is dreaming in a corner, and sets to work examining society. The examination of hatred is a terrible thing. Hence come, if the misfortune of the age desires it, those frightful commotions, formerly called Jacqueries, by the side of which purely political commotions are child's play, and which are no longer the struggle of the oppressed with the oppressor, but the revolt of want against comfort. Everything is overthrown at such a time. Jacqueries are the earthquakes of nations.

The French Revolution, that immense act of probity, cut short this peril, which was perhaps imminent in Europe toward the close of the eighteenth century. The French Revolution, which was nothing but the ideal armed with a sword, rose, and by the same sudden movement closed the door of evil and opened the door of good. It disengaged the question, promulgated the truth, expelled the miasma, ventilated the age, and crowned the people. We may say that it created man a second time by giving him a second soul—justice. The nineteenth century inherits and profits by its work, and at the present day the social catastrophe which we just now indicated is simply impossible. Blind is he who denounces it! fool is he who fears it! for the Revolution is the vaccine of Jacquerie. Thanks to the Revolution, the social conditions are altered, and the feudal and monarchical diseases are no longer in our blood. There is no middle age left in our constitution, and we are no longer at the time when formidable internal commotions broke out, when the obscure course of a dull sound could be heard beneath the feet; when the earth thrown out from the mole-holes appeared on the surface of civilization, when the soil cracked, when the roofs of caverns opened, and monstrous heads suddenly emerged from the ground. The revolutionary sense is a moral sense, and the feelings of right being developed, develops the feeling of duty. The law of all is liberty, which ends where the liberty of another man begins, according to Robespierre's admirable definition. Since 1789 the whole people has been dilated in the sublimated individual; there is no poor man who, having his right, has not his radiance; the man, dying of hunger, feels within himself the honesty of France. The dignity of the citizen is an internal armor; the man who is free is scrupulous, and the voter reigns. Hence comes incorruptibility; hence comes the abortion of unhealthy covetousness, and hence eyes heroically lowered before temptation. The revolutionary healthiness is so great, that on a day of deliverance, a 14th of July or a 10th of August there is no populace, and the first cry of the enlightened and progressing crowds is, "Death to the robbers!" Progress is an honest man, and the ideal and the absolute do not steal pocket-handkerchiefs. By whom were the carriages containing the wealth of the Tuileries escorted in 1848? by the rag-pickers of the Faubourg St. Antoine. Tatters mounted guard over the treasure, and virtue rendered these ragamuffins splendid. In these carts, in barely closed chests,—some, indeed, still opened,—there was, amid a hundred dazzling cases, that old crown of France, all made of diamonds, surmounted by the royal carbuncle and the Regent diamonds, worth thirty millions of francs. Barefooted they guarded this crown. Hence Jacquerie is no longer possible, and I feel sorry for the clever men; it is an old fear which has made its last effort, and could no longer be employed in politics. The great spring of the red specter is now broken, and every bird is aware of the fact, the scare-crow no longer horrifies. The birds treat the mannikin familiarly, and deposit their guano upon it, and the bourgeois laugh at it.

4. TWO DUTIES. WATCHING AND HOPING

THIS being the case, is every social danger dissipated? certainly not. There is no Jacquerie, and society may be reassured on that side; the blood will not again rush to its head, but it must pay attention to the way in which it breathes. Apoplexy is no longer to be apprehended, but there is consumption, and social consumption is called wretchedness. People die as well when undermined as when struck by lightning. We shall never grow weary of repeating, that to think before all of the disinherited and sorrowful classes, to relieve, ventilate, enlighten, and love them, to magnificently enlarge their horizon, to lavish upon them education in every shape, to offer them the example of labor, and never that of indolence, to lessen the weight of the individual burden by increasing the notion of the universal object, to limit poverty without limiting wealth, to create vast fields of public and popular activity, to have, like Briareus, a hundred hands to stretch out on all sides to the crushed and the weak, to employ the collective power in opening workshops for every arm, schools for every aptitude and laboratories for every intellect, to increase wages, diminish the toil, and balance the debit and credit,— that is to say, proportion the enjoyment to the effort, and the satisfaction to the wants; in a word, to evolve from the social machine, on behalf of those who suffer and those who are ignorant, more light and more comfort,—is (and sympathetic souls must not forget it) the first of brotherly obligations; and, let egotistic hearts learn the fact, the first of political necessities. And all this, we are bound to add, is only a beginning, and the true question is this, labor cannot be law without being a right. But this is not the place to dwell on such a subject.

If nature is called providence, society ought to call itself foresight. Intellectual and moral growth is no less indispensable than natural amelioration; knowledge is a viaticum; thinking is a primary necessity, and truth is nourishment, like wheat. A reasoning faculty fasting for knowledge and wisdom grows thin, and we must lament for minds that do not eat quite as much as stomachs. If there be anything more poignant than a body pining away for want of bread, it is a mind that dies of hunger for enlightenment. The whole of our progress tends toward the solution, and some day people will be stupefied. As the human race ascends, the deepest strata will naturally emerge from the zone of distress, and the effacement of wretchedness will be effected by a simple elevation of the level. We should do wrong to doubt this blessed solution. The past, we grant, is very powerful at the present hour, and is beginning again. This rejuvenescence of a corpse is surprising, yet here it is, marching straight toward us. The dead man appears a victor, and is a conqueror; he arrives with his legion, superstitions; with his sword, despotism; with his banner, ignorance; and during sometime past he has gained ten battles. He advances, he threatens, he laughs, he is at our gates. But we have no reason to despair; let us sell the field on which Hannibal is encamped. What can we, who believe, fear? A recoil of ideas is no more possible than it is for a river to flow up a hill. But those who desire no future ought to reflect; by saying no to progress they do not condemn the future, but themselves, and they give themselves a deadly disease by inoculating themselves with the past. There is only one way of refusing to-morrow, and that is by dying. We wish for death,— that of the body, as late as possible, and that of the soul, never. Yes, the sphinx will speak, the enigma will be guessed, and the problem will be solved; the people sketched by the eighteenth century will be finished by the nineteenth. He is an idiot who doubts it. The future, the speedy bursting into flower of universal welfare, is a divinely fatal phenomenon. Immense and combined impulsions pushing together govern human facts, and lead them all within a given time to the logical state, that is to say, to equilibrium, or, in other words, to equity. A force composed of earth and heaven results from humanity and governs it; this force is a performer of miracles, and marvelous denouements are as easy to it as extraordinary incidents. Aided by science, which comes from man, and the event, which comes from another source, it is but little frightened by those contradictions in the setting of problems which seem to the vulgar herd impossibilities. It is no less skillful in producing a solution from the approximation of ideas than in producing instruction from the approximation of facts, and we may expect anything and everything from the mysterious power of progress, which one fine day confronts the east and the west in a sepulcher, and makes the Imams hold conference with Bonaparte in the interior of the great Pyramid. In the meanwhile, there is no halt, no hesitation, no check, in the grand forward march of minds. Social philosophy is essentially the source of peace; it has for its object, and must have as result, the dissolution of passions by the study of antagonisms. It examines, scrutinizes, and analyzes, and then it recomposes; and it proceeds by the reducing process, by removing hatred from everything.

It has more than once occurred that a society has been sunk by the wind which is let loose on men; history is full of the shipwrecks of peoples and empires; one day that stranger, the hurricane, passes, and carries away manners, laws, and religions. The civilizations of India, Chaldæa, Persia, Assyria, and Egypt have disappeared in turn; why? we are ignorant. What are the causes of these disasters? we do not know. Could those societies have been saved? was it any fault of their own? did they obstinately adhere to some fatal vice which destroyed them? What amount of suicide is there in these terrible deaths of a nation and a race? These are unanswerable questions, for darkness covers the condemned civilizations. They have been under water, since they sank, and we have no more to say, and it is with a species of terror that we see in the background of that sea which is called the past, and behind those gloomy waves, the centuries, those immense vessels, Babylon, Nineveh, Tarsus, Thebes, and Rome, sunk by the terrific blast which blows from all the mouths of the darkness. But there was darkness then, and we have light; and if we are ignorant of the diseases of ancient civilizations, we know the infirmities of our own, and we contemplate its beauties and lay bare its deformities. Wherever it is wounded we probe it, and at once the suffering is decided, and the study of cause leads to the discovery of the remedy. Our civilization, the work of twenty centuries, is at once the monster and the prodigy, and is worth saving; it will be saved. To solace it is much, and to enlighten it is also something. All the labors of modern social philosophy ought to converge to this object, and the thinker of the present day has a grand duty to apply the stethoscope to civilization. We repeat it, this auscultation is encouraging; and we intend to finish these few pages, which are an austere interlude in a mournful drama, by laying a stress on this encouragement. Beneath the social mortality the human imperishableness is felt, and the globe does not die, because here and there are wounds in the shape of craters, and ring-worms in the shape of solfatari, and a volcano which breaks out and scatters its fires around. The diseases of the people do not kill the man.

And yet some of those who follow the social clinics shake their heads at times, and the strongest, the most tender, and the most logical have their hours of despondency. Will the future arrive? it seems as we may almost ask this question on seeing so much terrible shadow. There is a somber, face-to-face meeting of the egotists and the wretched. In the egotist we trace prejudices, the cloudiness of a caste education, appetite growing with intoxication, and prosperity that stuns, a fear of suffering which in some goes so far as an aversion from the sufferers, an implacable satisfaction, and the feeling of self so swollen that it closes the soul. In the wretched we find covetousness, envy, the hatred of seeing others successful, the profound bounds of the human wild beast at satisfaction, and hearts full of mist, sorrow, want, fatality, and impure and simple ignorance. Must we still raise our eyes to heaven? is the luminous point which we notice there one of those which die out? The ideal is frightful to look on thus lost in the depths, small, isolated, imperceptible, and brilliant, but surrounded by all those great black menaces monstrously collected around it; for all that, though, it is in no more danger than a star in the yawning throat of the clouds.

BOOK VIII

ENCHANTMENTS AND DESOLATIONS

1. BRIGHT LIGHT

THE reader has, of course, understood that Eponine, on recognizing through the railings the inhabitant of the house in the Rue Plumet, to which Magnon sent her, began by keeping the bandits aloof from the house, then led Marius to it, and that, after several days of ecstasy before the railings, Marius, impelled by that force which attracts iron to the loadstone and the lover toward the stones of the house in which she whom he loves resides, had eventually entered Cosette's garden, as Romeo did Juliet's. This had been even an easier task for him than for Romeo, for Romeo was obliged to escalade a wall, while Marius had merely to move one of the bars of the decrepit railing, which was loose in its rusty setting, after the fashion of the teeth of old people. As Marius was thin, he easily passed. As there never was anybody in the street, and as Marius never entered the garden save at night, he ran no risk of being seen. From that blessed and holy hour when a kiss affianced these two souls, Marius went to the garden every night. If, at this moment of her life, Cosette had fallen in love with an unscrupulous libertine, she would have been lost, for there are generous natures that surrender themselves, and Cosette was one of them. One of the magnanimities of a woman is to yield, and love, at that elevation where it is absolute, is complicated by a certain celestial blindness of modesty. But what dangers you incur, ye noble souls! you often give the heart and we take the body; your heart is left you, and you look at it in the darkness with a shudder. Love has no middle term; it either saves or destroys, and this dilemma is the whole of human destiny. No fatality offers this dilemma of ruin or salvation more inexorably than does love, for love is life, if it be not death: it is a cradle, but also a coffin. The same feeling says yes and no in the human heart, and of all the things which God has made the human heart is the one which evolves the most light, and, alas! the most dark-ness. God willed it that the love which Cosette came across was one of those loves which save. So long as the month of May of that year, 1832, lasted, there were every night in this poor untrimmed garden, and un-der this thicket which daily became more fragrant and more thick, two beings composed of all the chastities and all the innocences overflowing with all the felicities of heaven, nearer to the arch-angels than to man, pure, honest, intoxicated, and radiant, and who shone for each other in the darkness. It seemed to Cosette as if Marius had a crown, and to Marius as if Cosette had a glory. They touched each other, they looked at each other, they took each other by the hand, they drew close to each other; but there was a distance which they never crossed. Not that they respected it, but they were ignorant of it. Marius felt a barrier in Cosette's purity, and Cosette felt a support in the loyalty of Marius. The first kiss had also been the last; since then Marius had never gone beyond touch-ing Cosette's hand, or neckerchief, or a curl, with his lips. Cosette was to him a perfume, and not a woman, and he inhaled her. She refused nothing, and he asked for nothing; Cosette was happy and Marius sat-isfied. They lived in that ravishing state which might be called the be-dazzlement of a soul by a soul; it was the ineffable first embrace of two virginities in the ideal, two swans meeting on the Jungfrau. At this hour of love, the hour when voluptuousness is absolutely silenced by the om-nipotence of ecstasy, Marius, the pure and seraphic Marius, would have sooner been able to go home with a street-walker than raise Cosette's gown as high as her ankle. Once in the moonlight, Cosette stooped to pick up something on the ground, and her dress opened and displayed her neck. Marius turned his eyes away.

What passed between these two lovers? Nothing; they adored each other. At night, when they were there, this garden seemed a living and sacred spot. All the flowers opened around them and sent them their incense; and they opened their souls and spread them over the flowers. The wanton and vigorous vegetation quivered, full of sap and intoxica-tion, around these two innocents, and they uttered words of love at which the trees shivered. What were these words? Mere breaths, and nothing more, but they were sufficient to trouble and affect all this nature. It is a magic power which it would be difficult to understand, were we to read in a book this conversation made to be carried away and dissipated like smoke beneath the leaves by the wind. Take away from these whispers of two lovers the melody which issues from the soul, and accompanies them like a lyre, and what is left is only a shadow, and you say, "what! is it only that?" Well, yes, child's play, repetitions, laughs at nothing, absurdities, foolishness, all that is the most sublime and profound in the world! the only things which are worth the trouble of being said and being listened to. The man who has never heard, the man who has never uttered, these absurdities and poor things is an imbecile and a wicked man. Said Cosette to Marius:

"Do you know that my name is Euphrasie?"

"Euphrasie? no, it is Cosette."

"Oh! Cosette is an ugly name, which was given me when I was little, but my real name is Euphrasie. Don't you like that name?"

"Yes, but Cosette is not ugly."

"Do you like it better than Euphrasie?"

"Well—yes."

"In that case, I like it better, too. That is true, Cosette is pretty. Call me Cosette."

Another time she looked at him intently, and exclaimed:

"You are handsome, sir, you are good-looking, you have wit, you are not at all stupid, you are much more learned than I, but I challenge you with, 'I love you.'"

And Marius fancied that he heard a strophe sung by a star. Or else she gave him a little tap because he coughed, and said:

"Do not cough, sir; I do not allow anybody to cough in my house without permission. It is very wrong to cough and frighten me. I wish you to be in good health, because if you were not I should be very unhappy, and what would you have me do?"

And this was simply divine.

Once Marius said to Cosette:

"Just fancy! I supposed for a while that your name was Ursule."

This made them laugh the whole evening. In the middle of another conversation, he happened to exclaim:

"Oh! one day at the Luxembourg I felt disposed to settle an invalid!"

But he stopped short, and did not complete the sentence, for he would have been obliged to allude to Cosette's garter, and that was impossible. There was a strange feeling connected with the flesh, before which this immense, innocent love recoiled with a sort of holy terror. Marius imagined life with Cosette like this, without anything else; to come every evening to the Rue Plumet, remove the old complacent bar of the president's railings, sit down elbow to elbow on this bench, look through the trees at the scintillation of the commencing night, bring the fold in his trouser-knee into co-habitation with Cosette's ample skirts, to caress her thumb-nail, and to inhale the same flower in turn forever and indefinitely. During this time the clouds passed over their heads, and each time the wind blows it carries off more of a man's thoughts than of clouds from the sky. We cannot affirm that this chaste, almost stern love was absolutely without gallantry. "Paying compliments" to her whom we love is the first way of giving caresses and an attempted semi-boldness. A compliment is something like a kiss through a veil, and pleasure puts its sweet point upon it, while concealing itself. The heart retires to love more. The cajoleries of Marius, all saturated with chimera, were, so to speak, of an azure blue. The birds when they fly in the direction of the angels must hear words of the same nature; still life, humanity, and the whole amount of positivism of which Marius was capable were mingled with it. It was what is said in the grotto, as a prelude to what will be said in the alcove; a lyrical effusion, the strophe and the sonnet commingled, the gentle hyperboles of cooing, all the refinements of adoration arranged in a posy, and exhaling a subtle and celestial perfume, an ineffable prattling of heart to heart.

"Oh!" Marius muttered, "how lovely you are! I dare not look at you, and that is the reason why I contemplate you. You are a grace, and I know not what is the matter with me. The hem of your dress, where the end of your slipper passes through, upsets me. And then, what an enchanting light when your thoughts become visible, for your reason astonishes me, and you appear to me for instants to be a dream. Speak; I am listening to you, and admiring you. O Cosette, how strange and charming it is; I am really mad. You are adorable, and I study your feet in the microscope, and your soul with the telescope."

And Cosette made answer:

"And I love you a little more through all the time which has passed since this morning."

Questions and answers went on as they could in this dialogue, which always agreed in the subject of love, like the elder-pith balls on the nail. Cosette's entire person was simplicity, ingenuousness, whiteness, candor, and radiance, and it might have been said of her that she was transparent. She produced on every one who saw her a sensation of April and daybreak, and she had dew in her eyes. Cosette was a condensation of the light of dawn in a woman's form. It was quite simple that Marius, as he adored, should admire. But the truth is that this little boarding-school miss, just freshly turned out of a convent, talked with exquisite penetration, and made at times all sorts of true and delicate remarks. Her chattering was conversation, and she was never mistaken about anything, and conversed correctly. Woman feels and speaks with the infallibility which is the tender instinct of the heart. No one knows like a woman how to say things which are at once gentle and deep. Gentleness and depth,—in those things the whole of woman is contained, and it is heaven. And in this perfect felicity tears welled in their eyes at every moment. A lady-bird crushed, a feather that fell from a nest, a branch of hawthorn broken, moved their pity, and then ecstasy, gently drowned by melancholy, seemed to ask for nothing better than to weep. The most sovereign symptom of love is a tenderness which becomes at times almost insupportable. And by the side of all this—for contradictions are the lightning sport of love—they were fond of laughing with a ravishing liberty, and so familiarly that, at times, they almost seemed like two lads. Still, even without these two hearts intoxicated with chastity being conscious of it, unforgettable nature is ever there, ever there with its brutal and sublime object, and, whatever the innocence of souls may be, they feel in the most chaste *tête-à-tête* the mysterious and adorable distinction which separates a couple of lovers from a couple of friends.

They idolized each other. The permanent and the immutable exist; a couple love, they laugh, they make little pouts with their lips, they intertwine their fingers, and that does not prevent eternity. Two lovers conceal themselves in a garden in the twilight, in the invisible, with the birds and the roses; they fascinate each other in the darkness with their souls which they place in their eyes, they mutter, they whisper, and during this period immense constellations of planets fill infinity.

2. PERFECT HAPPINESS

COSETTE and Marius lived vaguely in the intoxication of their happiness, and they did not notice the cholera which was decimating Paris in that very month. They had made as many confessions to each other as they could, but they had not extended very far beyond their names. Marius had told Cosette that he was an orphan, Pontmercy by name, a barrister by profession, and gaining a livelihood by writing things for publishers; his father was a colonel, a hero, and he, Marius, had quarreled with his grandfather, who was rich. He also incidentally remarked that he was a baron, but this did not produce much effect on Cosette. Marius a baron? she did not understand it, and did not know what the word meant, and Marius was Marius to her. For her part, she confided to him that she had been educated at the convent of the Little Picpus, that her mother was dead, like his, that her father's name was Fauchelevent, that he was very good and gave a great deal to the poor, but was himself poor, and deprived himself of everything, while depriving her of nothing. Strange to say, in the species of symphony in which Marius had lived since he found Cosette again, the past, even the most recent, had become so confused and distant to him that what Cosette told him completely satisfied him. He did not even dream of talking to her about the nocturnal adventure in the garret, the Thénardiers, the burning, the strange attitude and singular flight of her father. Marius momentarily forgot all this; he did not know at night what he had done in the morning, where he had breakfasted or who had spoken to him; he had a song in his ears which rendered him deaf to every other thought, and he only existed during the hours when he saw Cosette. As he was in heaven at that time, it was perfectly simple that he should forget the earth. Both of them bore languidly the undefinable weight of immaterial joys; that is the way in which those somnambulists called lovers live.

Alas! who is there that has not experienced these things? Why does an hour arrive when we emerge from this azure, and why does life go on afterward? To love almost takes the place of thinking. Love is an ardent forgetfulness, moreover. It is absurd to ask passion for logic, for there is no more an absolute logical concatenation in the human heart than there is a perfect geometric figure in the celestial mechanism. For Cosette and Marius nothing more existed than Marius and Cosette; the whole universe around them had fallen into a gulf, and they lived in a golden moment, with nothing before them, nothing behind them. Marius scarce remembered that Cosette had a father, and in his brain there was the effacement of bedazzlement. Of what did these lovers talk? as we have seen, of flowers, swallows, the setting sun, the rising moon, and all the important things. They had told themselves everything except everything, for the everything of lovers is nothing. Of what use would it be to talk of her father, the realities, that den, those bandits, that adventure? and was it quite certain that the nightmare had existed? They were two, they adored each other, and there was only that, there was nothing else. It is probable that this evanishment of death behind us is inherent to the arrival in Paradise. Have we seen demons? are there any? have we trembled? have we suffered? we no longer know, and there is a roseate cloud over it all.

Hence these two beings lived in this way, very high up, and with all the unverisimilitude which there is in nature; neither at the nadir nor at the zenith, but between man and the seraphs, above the mud and below the ether, in the clouds; they were not so much flesh and bone as soul and ecstasy from head to foot, already too sublimated to walk on earth, and still too loaded with humanity to disappear in ether, and held in suspense like atoms which are waiting to be precipitated; apparently beyond the pale of destiny, and ignorant of that rut, yesterday, to-day, and to-morrow; amazed, transported, and floating at moments with a lightness sufficient for a flight in the infinitude, and almost ready for the eternal departure. They slept awake in this sweet lulling; oh splendid lethargy of the real overpowered by the ideal! At times Cosette was so beautiful that Marius closed his eyes before her. The best way of gazing at the soul is with closed eyes. Marius and Cosette did not ask themselves to what this would lead them, and looked at each other as if they had already arrived. It is a strange claim on the part of men to wish that love should lead them somewhere.

193

3. *THE BEGINNING OF THE SHADOW*

JEAN VALJEAN suspected nothing, for Cosette, who, not quite such a dreamer as Marius, was gay, and that sufficed to render Jean Valjean happy. Cosette's thoughts, her tender preoccupations, and the image of Marius which filled her soul, removed none of the incomparable purity of her splendid, chaste, and smiling forehead. She was at the age when the virgin wears her love as the angel wears its lily. Jean Valjean was, therefore, happy; and, besides, when two lovers understand each other, things always go well, and any third party who might trouble their love is kept in a perfect state of blindness by a small number of precautions, which are always the same with all lovers. Hence Cosette never made any objections; if he wished to take a walk, very good, my little papa, and if he stayed at home, very good, and if he wished to spend the evening with Cosette, she was enchanted. As he always went to his outhouse at ten o'clock at night, on those occasions Marius did not reach the garden till after that hour, when he heard from the street Cosette opening the door. We need hardly say that Marius was never visible by day, and Jean Valjean did not even remember that Marius existed. One morning, how-ever, he happened to say to Cosette, "Why, the back of your dress is all white!" On the previous evening Marius, in a transport, had pressed Cosette against the wall. Old Toussaint, who went to bed at an early hour, only thought of sleeping so soon as her work was finished, and was ignorant of everything, like Jean Valjean.

Marius never set foot in the house. When he was with Cosette, they concealed themselves in a niche near the steps, so as not to be seen or heard from the street, and sat there, often contenting themselves with the sole conversation of pressing hands twenty times a minute, and gazing at the branches of the trees. At such moments, had a thunderbolt fallen within thirty feet of them, they would not have noticed it, so profoundly was the reverie of the one absorbed and plunged in the reverie of the other. It was a limpid purity, and the hours were all white, and nearly all alike. This kind of love is a collection of lily leaves and dove's feathers. The whole garden was between them and the street, and each time that Marius came in and out he carefully restored the bar of the railings, so that no disarrangement was visible. He went away generally at midnight, and went back to Courfeyrac's lodgings. Courfeyrac said to Bahorel:

"Can you believe it? Marius returns home at present at one in the morning."

Bahorel answered:

"What would you have? There is always a bomb-shell inside a seminarist."

At times Courfeyrac crossed his arms, assumed a stern air, and said to Marius:

"Young man, you are becoming irregular in your habits."

Courfeyrac, who was a practical man, was not pleased with this reflection of an invisible paradise cast on Marius. He was but little accustomed to unpublished passions; hence he grew impatient, and at times summoned Marius to return to reality. One morning he cast this admonition to him:

"My dear fellow, you produce on me the effect at present of being a denizen of the moon, in the kingdom of dreams, the province of illusion, whose chief city is soap-bubble. Come, don't play the prude,—what is her name?"

But nothing could make Marius speak, and his nails could have been dragged from him more easily than one of these three sacred syllables of which the ineffable name *Cosette* was composed. True love is luminous as the dawn, and silent as the tomb. Still Courfeyrac found this change in Marius, that he possessed a radiant taciturnity. During the sweet month of May, Marius and Cosette knew this immense happiness. To quarrel and become reconciled, to talk for a long time, and with the most minute details, about people who did not interest them the least in the world,—a further proof that in that ravishing opera which is called love, the libretto is nothing. For Marius, it was heaven to listen to Cosette talking of dress; for Cosette, to listen to Marius talking politics,—to listen, knee against knee, to the vehicles passing along the Rue de Babylone, to look at the same planet in space, or the same worm glistening in the grass, to be silent together a greater pleasure still than talking, etc., etc., etc.

Still, various complications were approaching. One evening Marius was going to the rendezvous along the Boulevard des Invalides; he was walking as usual with his head down, and as he was turning the corner of the Rue Plumet, he heard some one say close to him:

"Good-evening, Monsieur Marius."

He raised his head, and recognized Eponine. This produced a singular effect; he had not once thought of this girl since the day when she led him to the Rue Plumet; he had not seen her again, and she had entirely left his mind. He had only motives to be grateful to her; he owed her his present happiness, and yet it annoyed him to meet her. It is an error to believe that passion, when it is happy and pure, leads a man to a state of perfection; it leads him simply, as we have shown, to a state of forget-fulness. In this situation, man forgets to be wicked, but he also forgets to be good, and gratitude, duty, and essential and material recollections fade away. At any other time Marius would have been very different to Eponine, but, absorbed by Cosette, he had not very clearly compre-hended that this Eponine was Eponine Thénardier, and that she bore a name written in his father's will—that name to which he would have so ardently devoted himself a few months previously. We show Marius as he was, and his father himself slightly disappeared in his mind be-neath the splendor of his love. Hence he replied with some embarrass-ment:

"Ah, is it you, Eponine?"

"Why do you treat me so coldly? Have I done you any injury?"

"No," he answered.

Certainly he had no fault to find with her; on the contrary. Still, he felt that he could not but say "you," to Eponine now that he said "thou" to Cosette. As he remained silent, she exclaimed:

"Tell me—"

Then she stopped, and it seemed as if words failed this creature, who was formerly so impudent and bold. She tried to smile and could not, so continued:

"Well?"

Then she was silent again, and looked down on the ground.

"Good-night, Monsieur Marius," she suddenly said, and went away.

4. *A CAB RUNS IN ENGLISH AND BARKS IN SLANG*

THE next day—it was June 3, 1832, a date to which we draw attention owing to the grave events which were at that moment hanging over the horizon of Paris in the state of lightning-charged clouds—Marius at nightfall was following the same road as on the previous evening, with the same ravishing thoughts in his heart, when he saw between the boulevard trees Eponine coming toward him. Two days running—that was too much; so he sharply turned back, changed his course, and went to the Rue Plumet by the Rue Monsieur. This caused Eponine to follow him as far as the Rue Plumet, a thing she never had done before; hitherto she had contented herself with watching him as he passed along the boulevard, without attempting to meet him; last evening was the first time she ventured to address him. Eponine followed him, then, without his suspecting it; she saw him move the railing-bar aside and step into the garden.

"Hilloh!" she said, "he enters the house."

She went up to the railing, felt the bars in turn, and easily distinguished the one which Marius had removed; and she muttered in a low voice, and with a lugubrious accent, "None of that, Lisette!"

She sat down on the stone-work of the railing, close to the bar, as if she were guarding it. It was exactly at the spot where the railings joined the next wall, and there was there a dark corner, in which Eponine entirely disappeared. She remained thus for more than an hour without stirring or breathing, absorbed in thought. About ten o'clock at night, one of the two or three passers along the Rue Plumet, an old belated citizen, who was hurrying along the deserted and ill-famed street, while passing the railing, heard a dull, menacing voice saying:

"I am not surprised now that he comes every evening."

The passer-by looked around him, saw nobody, did not dare to peer into this dark corner, and felt horribly alarmed. He redoubled his speed, and was quite right in doing so, for in a few minutes, six men, who were walking separately and at some distance from each other under the walls, and who might have been taken for a drunken patrol, entered the Rue Plumet. The first who reached the railings stopped and waited for the rest, and a second after all six were together. They began talking in whispered slang:

"It's here," said one of them.

"Is there a dog in the garden?" another asked.

"I don't know. In any case I have brought a ball which we will make it swallow."

"Have you got some mastic to break a pane?"

"Yes."

"The railings are old," remarked the fifth man, who seemed to have the voice of a ventriloquist.

"All the better," said the second speaker; "it will make no noise when sawn, and won't be so hard to cut through."

The sixth, who had not yet opened his mouth, began examining the railings as Eponine had done an hour ago, grasping every bar and shaking it cautiously. He thus reached the bar which Marius had unfastened. Just as he was about to seize this bar, a hand, suddenly emerging from the darkness, clutched his arm; he felt himself roughly thrust back, and a hoarse voice whispered to him, "There's a *cab*" (a dog). At the same time he saw a pale girl standing in front of him. The man had that emotion which is always produced by things unexpected; his hair stood hideously on end. Nothing is more formidable to look at than startled wild beasts. Their air of terror is terrible. He fell back and stammered:

"Who is this she-devil?"

"Your daughter."

It was, in truth, Eponine speaking to Thénardier. Upon her apparition, the other five men, that is to say, Claquesous, Gueulemer, Babet, Montparnasse, and Brujon, approached noiselessly, without hurry or saying a word, but with the sinister slowness peculiar to these men of the night. Some hideous tools could be distinguished in their hands, and Gueulemer held a pair of those short pincers which burglars call *fauchons*.

"Well, what are you doing here? what do you want? are you mad?" Thénardier exclaimed, as far as is possible to exclaim in a whisper. "Have you come to prevent us from working?"

Eponine burst into a laugh and leaped on his neck. "I am here, my dear little pappy, because I am here; are not people allowed to sit down on stones at present? it is you who oughtn't to be here; and what have you come to do, since it is a biscuit? I told Magnon so, and there is nothing to be done here. But embrace me, my dear pappy; it is such a time since I saw you. You are out, then!"

Thénardier tried to free himself from Eponine's arms, and growled:

"There, there, you have embraced me. Yes, I am out and not in. Now be off."

But Eponine did not loose her hold, and redoubled her caresses.

"My dear pappy, how ever did you manage? You must have been very clever to get out of that scrape, so tell me all about it. And where is mamma? give me some news of her."

Thénardier answered:

"She's all right. I don't know; leave me and be off, I tell you."

"I do not exactly want to go off," Eponine said, with the pout of a spoiled child; "you send me away, though I haven't seen you now for four months, and I have scarce had time to embrace you."

And she caught her father again around the neck.

"Oh, come, this is a bore," said Babet.

"Make haste," said Gueulemer; "the police may pass."

The ventriloquial voice hummed:

> *Nous n'sommes pas le jour de l'an,*
> *A bécoter papa, maman.*

Eponine turned to the five bandits:

"Why, that's Monsieur Brujon. Good-evening, Monsieur Babet; good-evening, Monsieur Claquesous. What, don't you know me, Monsieur Gueulemer? How are you, Montparnasse?"

"Yes, they know you," said Thénardier; "but now, good-night, good-night, and be off; leave us alone."

"It is the hour of the foxes, and not of the chickens," said Montparnasse.

"Don't you see that we have work here?" Babet added.

Eponine took Montparnasse by the hand. "Mind," he said, "you will cut yourself, for I have an open knife."

"My dear Montparnasse," Eponine replied very gently, "confidence ought to be placed in people, and I am my father's daughter, perhaps. Monsieur Babet, Monsieur Gueulemer, I was ordered to examine into this affair."

It is remarkable that Eponine did not speak slang; ever since she had known Marius that frightful language had become impossible to her. She pressed Gueulemer's great coarse fingers in her little bony hand, which was as weak as that of a skeleton, and continued: "You know very well that I am no fool, and people generally believe me. I have done you a service now and then; well, I have made inquiries, and you would run a needless risk. I swear to you that there is nothing to be done in this house."

"There are lone women," said Gueulemer.

"No, they have moved away."

"Well, the candles haven't," Babet remarked. He pointed over the trees to a light which was moving about the garret; it was Toussaint who was up so late in order to hang up some linen to dry. Eponine made a final effort.

"Well," she said, "they are very poor people, and there isn't a penny piece in the house."

"Go to the devil," cried Thénardier; "when we have turned the house topsy-turvy, and placed the cellar at top and the attics at the bottom, we will tell you what there is inside, and whether they are francs, sous, or liards."

And he thrust her away that he might pass.

"My kind M. Montparnasse," Eponine said, "I ask you, who are a good fellow, not to go in."

"Take care, you'll cut yourself," Montparnasse replied.

Thénardier remarked with that decisive accent of his:

"Decamp, fairy, and leave men to do their business."

Eponine let go Montparnasse's hand, which she had seized again, and said:

"So you intend to enter this house?"

"A little," the ventriloquist said with a grin.

She leaned against the railings, faced these six men armed to the teeth, to whom night gave demoniac faces, and said in a firm, low voice:

"Well, I will not let you!"

They stopped in stupefaction, but the ventriloquist completed his laugh. She continued:

"Friends, listen to me, for it's now my turn to speak. If you enter this garden, or touch this railing, I will scream, knock at doors, wake people; I will have you all six seized, and call the police."

"She is capable of doing it," Thénardier whispered to the ventriloquist and Brujon.

She shook her head, and added:

"Beginning with my father."

Thénardier approached her.

"Not so close, my good man," she said.

He fell back, growling between his teeth, "Why, what is the matter?" and added, "the b—."

She burst into a terrible laugh.

"As you please, but you shall not enter; but I am not the daughter of a dog, since I am the whelp of a wolf. You are six, but what do I care for that? You are men and I am a woman. You won't frighten me, I can tell you, and you shall not enter this house because it does not please me. If you come nearer I bark, and I told you there was a dog, and I am it. I do not care a farthing for you, so go your way, for you annoy me! Go where you like, but don't come here for I forbid it. Come on as you like, you with your knives, and I have my feet."

She advanced a step toward the bandits and said, with the same frightful laugh:

"Confound it! I'm not frightened. This summer I shall be hungry, and this winter I shall be cold. What asses these men must be to think they can frighten a girl! Afraid of what? You have got dolls of mistresses who crawl under the bed when you talk big, but I am afraid of nothing!"

She fixed her eye on Thénardier, and said: "Not even of you, father."

Then she continued, as she turned her spectral, blood-shot eyeballs on each of the bandits in turn:

"What do I care whether I am picked up to-morrow on the pavement of the Rue Plumet stabbed by my father, or am found within a year in the nets of St. Cloud or on Swan's island, among old rotting corks and drowned dogs!"

She was compelled to break off, for she was attacked by a dry cough, and her breath came from her weak, narrow chest like the death-rattle.

She continued:

"I have only to cry out and people will come right away. You are six, but I am all the world."

Thénardier moved a step toward her.

"Don't come near me," she cried.

He stopped, and said gently:

"Well, no, I will not approach you, but do not talk so loud. Do you wish to prevent us from working, my daughter? And yet we must earn a livelihood. Do you no longer feel any affection for your father?"

"You bore me," said Eponine.

"Still we must live, we must eat—"

"Rot of hunger."

This said, she sat down on the coping of the railings and sang:

Mon bras si dodu,
Ma jambe bien faite,
Et le temps perdu.

She had her elbow on her knee, and her chin in her hand, and balanced her foot with a careless air. Her ragged gown displayed her thin shoulder-blades, and the neighboring lamp lit up her profile and attitude. Nothing more resolute or more surprising could well be imagined. The six burglars, amazed and savage at being held in check by a girl, went under the shadow of the lamp and held council, with humiliated and furious shrugs of their shoulders. She, however, looked at them with a peaceful and stern air.

"There's something the matter with her," said Babet, "some reason for it. Can she be in love with the dog? and yet, it's a pity to miss the affair. There are two women who live alone, an old cove who lives in a yard, and very decent curtains up to the windows. The old swell must be a Jew, and I consider the affair a good one."

"Well, do you fellows go in," Montparnasse exclaimed, "and do the trick. I will remain here with the girl, and if she stirs—"

He let the knife which he held in his hand glisten in the lamp-light. Thénardier did not say a word, and seemed ready for anything they pleased. Brujon, who was a bit of an oracle, and who, as we know, "put up the job," had not yet spoken, and seemed thoughtful. He was supposed to recoil at nothing, and it was notorious that he had plundered a police office through sheer bravado. Moreover, he wrote verses and songs, which gave him a great authority. Babet questioned him:

"Have you nothing to say, Brujon?"

Brujon remained silent for a moment, then tossed his head in several different ways, and at length decided on speaking.

"Look here. I saw this morning two sparrows fighting, and to-night I stumble over a quarrelsome woman; all that is bad, so let us be off."

They went away. While doing so, Montparnasse muttered:

"No matter, if you had been agreeable, I would have cut her throat." Babet replied:

"I wouldn't, for I never strike a lady."

At the corner of the street they stopped and exchanged in a low voice this enigmatical dialogue.

"Where shall we go and sleep to-night?"

"Under Paris."

"Have you your key about you, Thénardier?"

"Of course."

Eponine, who did not take her eyes off them, saw them return by the road along which they had come. She arose and crawled after them along the walls and the houses. She followed them thus along the boulevard. There they separated, and she saw the six men bury themselves in the darkness, where they seemed to fade away.

5. THINGS OF THE NIGHT

AFTER the departure of the bandits the Rue Plumet resumed its calm, nocturnal aspect. What had just taken place in this street would not have astonished a forest, for the thickets, the coppices, the heather, the interlaced branches, and the tall grass exist in a somber way; the savage swarm catches glimpses there of the sudden apparitions of the invisible world. What there is below man distinguishes there through the mist what there is beyond man; and things unknown to us living beings confront each other there in the night. Bristling and savage nature is startled by certain approaches in which it seems to feel the supernatural; the forces of the shadow know each other and maintain a mysterious equilibrium between themselves. Teeth and claws fear that which is unseizable, and blood-drinking bestiality, voracious, starving appetites in search of prey, the instincts armed with nails and jaws, which have for their source and object the stomach, look at and sniff anxiously the impassive spectral lineaments prowling about in a winding-sheet, or standing erect in this vaguely rustling robe, and which seems to them to live a dead and terrible life. These brutalities, which are only matter, have a confused fear at having to deal with the immense condensed obscurity in an unknown being. A black figure barring the passage stops the wild beast short; what comes from the cemetery intimidates and disconcerts what comes from the den; ferocious things are afraid of sinister things, and wolves recoil on coming across a ghoul.

6. *MARIUS GIVES HIS ADDRESS TO COSETTE*

WHILE this sort of human-faced dog was mounting guard against the railings, and six bandits fled before a girl, Marius was by Cosette's side. The sky had never been more star-spangled and more charming, the trees more rustling, or the smell of the grass more penetrating; never had the birds fallen asleep beneath the frondage with a softer noise; never had the universal harmonies of serenity responded better to the internal music of the soul; never had Marius been more enamored, happier, or in greater ecstasy. But he had found Cosette sad; she had been crying, and her eyes were red. It was the first cloud in this admirable dream. Marius's first remark was:

"What is the matter with you?"

And she replied:

"I will tell you."

Then she sat down on the bench near the house, and while he took his seat, all trembling, by her side, she continued:

"My father told me this morning to hold myself in readiness, for he had business to attend to, and we were probably going away."

Marius shuddered from head to foot. When we reach the end of life, death signifies a departure, but at the beginning departure means death. For six weeks past Marius had slowly and gradually taken possession of Cosette; it was a perfectly ideal, but profound, possession. As we have explained, in first love men take the soul long before the body; a later date they take the body before the soul, and at times they do not take the soul at all,—the Faublas and Prudhommes add, because there is no such thing, but the sarcasm is fortunately a blasphemy. Marius, then, possessed Cosette in the way that minds possess; but he enveloped her with his entire soul, and jealousy seized her with an incredible conviction. He possessed her touch, her breath, her perfume, the deep flash of her blue eyes, the softness of her skin when he touched her hand, the charming mark which she had on her neck, and all her thoughts. They had agreed never to sleep without dreaming of each other, and had kept their word. He, therefore, possessed all Cosette's dreams. He looked at her incessantly, and sometimes breathed on the short hairs which she had on her neck, and said to himself that there was not one of those hairs which did not belong to him. He contemplated and adored the things she wore, her bows, her cuffs, her gloves, and slippers, like sacred objects of which he was the master. He thought that he was the lord of the small tortoise-shell combs which she had in her hair, and he said to himself, in the confused stammering of dawning voluptuousness, that there was not a seam of her dress, not a mesh of her stockings, not a wrinkle in her bodice, which was not his. By the side of Cosette he felt close to his property, near his creature, who was at once his despot and his slave. It seemed that they had so blended their souls that, if they had wished to take them back, it would have been impossible for them to recognize them. This is mine—no, it is mine—I assure you that you are mistaken. This is really I—what you take for yourself is myself; Marius was something which formed part of Cosette, and Cosette was something that formed part of Marius. Marius felt Cosette live in him; to have Cosette, to possess Cosette, was to him not different from breathing. It was in the midst of this faith, this intoxication, this virginal, extraordinary, and absolute possession, and this sovereignty, that the words, "We are going away," suddenly fell on him, and the stern voice of reality shouted to him,

"Cosette is not thine." Marius awoke. For six weeks, as we said, he had been living out of life, and the word "depart" made him roughly re-enter it. He could not find a word to say, and Cosette merely noticed that his hand was very cold. She said to him in her turn:

"What is the matter with you?"

He answered, in so low a voice that Cosette could scarce hear him:

"I do not understand what you said."

She continued:

"This morning my father told me to prepare my clothes and hold myself ready, that he would give me his linen to put in a portmanteau, that he was obliged to make a journey, that we were going away, that we must have a large trunk for myself and a small one for him, to get all this ready within a week, and that we should probably go to England."

"Why, it is monstrous!" Marius exclaimed.

It is certain that, at this moment, in Marius's mind, no abuse of power, no violence, no abomination of the most prodigious tyrants, no deed of Busiris, Tiberius, or Henry VIII, equaled in ferocity this one,—M. Fauchelevent taking his daughter to England because he had business to attend to. He asked in a faint voice:

"And when will you start?"

"He did not say when."

"And when will you return?"

"He did not tell me."

And Marius rose and said coldly:

"Will you go, Cosette?"

Cosette turned to him, her beautiful eyes full of agony, and answered, with a species of wildness:

"Where?"

"To England; will you go?"

"What can I do?" she said, clasping her hands.

"Then you will go?"

"If my father goes."

"So you are determined to go?"

Cosette seized Marius's hand, and pressed it as sole reply.

"Very well," said Marius, "in that case I shall go else where."

Cosette felt the meaning of this remark even more than she comprehended it; she turned so pale that her face became white in the darkness, and stammered:

"What do you mean?"

Marius looked at her, then slowly raised his eyes to heaven, and replied:

"Nothing."

When he looked down again he saw Cosette smiling at him; the smile of the woman whom we love has a brilliancy which is visible at night.

"How foolish we are! Marius, I have an idea."

"What is it?"

"Follow us if we go away! I will tell you whither! and you can join me where I am."

Marius was now a thoroughly wide-awake man, and had fallen back into reality; hence he cried to Cosette:

"Go with you! are you mad? why, it would require money, and I have none! Go to England! why I already owe more than ten louis to Courfeyrac, one of my friends, whom you do not know! I have an old hat, which is not worth three francs, a coat with buttons missing in front, my shirt is all torn, my boots let in the water, I am out at elbows, but I have not thought of it for six weeks, and did not tell you. Cosette, I am a wretch; you only see me at night and give me your love; were you to see me by day you would give me a half-penny. Go to England! Why I have not enough to pay for a passport!"

He threw himself against a tree, with his arms over his head, and his forehead pressed to the bark, neither feeling the wood that grazed his skin nor the fever which spotted his temples, motionless and ready to fall, like the statue of despair. He remained for a long time in this state—people would remain for an eternity in such abysses. At length he turned and heard behind a little stifled, soft and sad sound; it was Cosette sobbing; she had been crying for more than two hours by the side of Marius, who was reflecting. He went up to her, fell on his knees, seized her foot, which peeped out from under her skirt, and kissed it. She let him do so in silence, for there are moments when a woman accepts, like a somber and resigned duty, the worship of love.

"Do not weep," he said.

She continued:

"But I am, perhaps, going away, and you are not able to come with me."

He said, "Do you love me?"

She replied by sobbing that Paradisaic word, which is never more charming than through tears, "I adore you."

He pursued, with an accent which was an inexpressible caress:

"Do not weep. Will you do so much for me as to check your tears?"

"Do you love me?" she said.

He took her hand.

"Cosette, I have never pledged my word of honor to any one, because it frightens me, and I feel that my father is by the side of it. Well, I pledge you my most sacred word of honor that if you go away I shall die."

There was in the accent with which he uttered these words such a solemn and calm melancholy that Cosette trembled, and she felt that chill which is produced by the passing of a somber and true thing. In her terror she ceased to weep.

"Now listen to me," he said; "do not expect me tomorrow."

"Why not?"

"Do not expect me till the day after."

"Oh, why?"

"You will see."

"A day without your coming!—oh, it is impossible."

"Let us sacrifice a day to have, perhaps, one whole life."

And Marius added in a low voice and aside: "He is a man who makes no change in his habits, and he never received anybody before the evening."

"What man are you talking about?" Cosette asked.

"I? I did not say anything."

"What do you hope for then?"

"Wait till the day after to-morrow."

"Do you desire it?"

"Yes, Cosette."

He took her head between his two hands, as she stood on tiptoe to reach him and tried to see his hopes in his eyes. Marius added:

"By the bye, you must know my address, for something might happen; I live with my friend Courfeyrac, at No. 16, Rue de la Verrerie."

He felt in his pockets, took out a knife, and scratched the address on the plaster of the wall. In the meanwhile, Cosette had begun looking in his eyes again.

"Tell me your thought, Marius, for you have one. Tell it to me. Oh, tell it to me, so that I may pass a good night."

"My thought is this; it is impossible that God can wish to separate us. Expect me the day after to-morrow."

"What shall I do till then?" Cosette said. "You are in the world, and come and go; how happy men are; but I shall remain all alone. Oh, I shall be so sad! what will you do to-morrow night, tell me?"

"I shall try something."

"In that case I shall pray to Heaven, and think of you, so that you may succeed. I will not question you any more, as you do not wish it, and you are my master. I will spend my evening in singing the song from *Euryanthe,* of which you are so fond, and which you heard one night under my shutters. But you will come early the next evening, and I shall expect you at nine o'clock exactly. I warn you. Oh, good Heaven! how sad it is that the days are so long! You hear: I shall be in the garden as it is striking nine."

"And I too."

And without saying a word, moved by the same thought, carried away by those electric currents which place two lovers in continual communication, both intoxicated with voluptuousness, even in their grief, they fell into each other's arms without noticing that their lips were joined together, while their upraised eyes, overflowing with ecstasy and full of tears, contemplated the stars. When Marius left, the street was deserted, for it was the moment when Eponine followed the bandits into the boulevard. While Marius dreamed with his head leaning against a tree an idea **had** crossed his mind, an idea, alas! which himself considered **mad and impossible.** He had formed a violent resolution.

7. *AN OLD HEART AND A YOUNG HEART*
FACE EACH OTHER

FATHER GILLENORMAND at this period had just passed his ninety-first birthday, and still lived with his daughter at No. 6, Rue des Filles du Calvaire, in the old house, which was his own property. He was, it will be remembered, one of those antique old men, who await death erect, whom age falls on without bending, and whom even sorrow cannot bow. Still, for some time past, his daughter had said, "My father is breaking." He no longer boxed the ears of the maid-servants, or banged with his cane so violently the staircase railing when Basque kept him waiting. The revolution of July had not exasperated him for more than six months, and he had seen almost with tranquility in the *Moniteur* this association of words, M. Humblot-Conté, Peer of France. The truth is, that the old man was filled with grief; he did not bend, he did not surrender, for that was not possible, either with his moral or physical nature; but he felt himself failing inwardly. For four years he had been awaiting Marius with a firm foot—that is really the expression—with the conviction that the wicked young scamp would ring his bell some day, and now he had begun to say to himself, in hours of depression, that Marius might remain away a little too long. It was not death that was insupportable to him, but the idea that perhaps he might not see Marius again. This idea had never occurred to him till one day, and at present it rose before him constantly, and chilled him to death. Absence, as ever happens in natural and true feelings, had only heightened the grandfather's love for the ungrateful boy who had gone away like that. It is on December nights, when the thermometer is almost down at zero, that people think most of the sun. M. Gillenormand was, or fancied himself, utterly incapable of taking a step toward his grandson; "I would rot first," he said to himself. He did not think himself at all in the wrong, but he only thought of Marius with profound tenderness and the dumb despair of an old man who is going down in the valley of the shadows. He was beginning to lose his teeth, which added to his sorrow. M. Gillenormand, without confessing it to himself, however, for he would have been furious and ashamed of it, had never loved a mistress as he loved Marius. He had hung up in his room, as the first thing he might see on awaking, an old portrait of his other daughter, the one who was dead, Madame de Pontmercy, taken when she was eighteen. He incessantly regarded this portrait, and happened to say one day, while gazing at it: "I can notice a likeness."

"To my sister?" Mlle. Gillenormand remarked; "oh, certainly."

The old man added, "And to him, too."

When he was once sitting, with his knees against each other and his eyes almost closed, in a melancholy posture, his daughter ventured to say to him:

"Father, are you still so furious against—?" She stopped, not daring to go further.

"Against whom?" he asked.

"That poor Marius."

He raised his old head, laid his thin wrinkled fist on the table, and cried in his loudest and most irritated accent:

"Poor Marius, you say! that gentleman is a scoundrel, a scamp, a little vain ingrate, without heart or soul, a proud and wicked man!"

And he turned away so that his daughter might not see a tear which he had in his eyes. Three days later he interrupted a silence which had lasted four hours to say to his daughter gruffly:

"I had had the honor of begging Mademoiselle Gillenormand never to mention his name to me."

Aunt Gillenormand gave up all attempts, and formed this profound diagnostic: "My father was never very fond of my sister after her folly. It is clear that he detests Marius." "After her folly" meant "since she married the colonel." Still, as may be conjectured, Mademoiselle Gillenormand failed in her attempt to substitute her favorite, the officer of lancers, in Marius's place. Théodule had met with no success, and M. Gillenormand refused to accept the *quid pro quo;* for the vacuum in the heart cannot be stopped by a bung. Théodule, on his side, while sniffing the inheritance, felt a repugnance to the task of pleasing, and the old gentleman annoyed the lancer, while the lancer offended the old gentleman. Lieutenant Théodule was certainly gay but gossiping, frivolous but vulgar, a good liver but bad company; he had mistresses, it is true, and he talked a good deal about them, it is also true, but then he talked badly. All his qualities had a defect, and M. Gillenormand was worn out with listening to the account of the few amours he had had round his barracks in the Rue Babylone, and then Lieutenant Théodule called sometimes in uniform with the tricolor cockade, which rendered him simply impossible. M. Gillenormand eventually said to his daughter, "I have had enough of Théodule, for I care but little for a warrior in peace times. You can receive him if you like, but for my part I do not know whether I do not prefer the wielders to the trailers of sabers, and the clash of blades in battle is less wretched, after all, than the noise of scabbards on the pavement. And, then, to throw up one's head like a king of clubs, and to lace one's self like a woman, to wear stays under a cuirass, is doubly ridiculous. When a man is a real man he keeps himself at an equal distance from braggadocio and foppishness. So keep your Théodule for yourself." Though his daughter said to him, "After all he is your grandnephew," it happened that M.˙ Gillenormand, who was grandfather to the end of his nails, was not a granduncle at all. The fact is, that as he was a man of sense and comparison, Théodule only served to make him regret Marius the more.

On the evening of June 4, which did not prevent Father Gillenormand from having an excellent fire in his chimney, he had dismissed his daughter, who was sewing in the adjoining room. He was alone in his apartment with the pastoral hangings, with his feet on the andirons, half enveloped in his nine-leaved Coromandel screen, sitting at a table on which two candles burned under a green shade swallowed up in his needle-worked easy chair, and holding a book in his hand, which he was not reading. He was dressed, according to his wont, as an "Incroyable," and resembled an old portrait of Garat. This would have caused him to be followed in the streets, but, whenever he went out, his daughter wrapped him up in a sort of episcopal wadded coat, which hid his dress. At home he never wore a dressing-gown, save when he got up and went to bed. "It gives an old look," he was wont to say. Father Gillenormand was thinking of Marius bitterly and lovingly, and, as usual, bitterness gained the upper hand. His savage tenderness always ended by boiling over and turning into indignation, and he was at the stage when a man seeks to make up his mind and accept that which is to be. He was explaining to himself that there was no longer any reason for Marius's return, that if he had meant to come home he would have done so long before, and all idea of it must be given up. He tried to form the idea that it was all over, and that he should die without seeing that "gentleman" again. But his whole nature revolted, and his old paternity could not consent. "What," he said, and it was his mournful burden, "he will not come back!" and his old bald head fell on his chest, and he vaguely fixed a lamentable and irritated glance upon the ashes of his hearth. In the depth of this reverie his old servant Basque came in and asked:

"Can you receive M. Marius, sir?"

The old man sat up, livid, and like a corpse which is roused by a galvanic shock. All his blood flowed to his heart, and he stammered:

"M. Marius! who?"

"I do not know," Basque replied, intimidated and disconcerted by his master's air, "for I did not see him. It was Nicolette who said to me just now, 'there is a young man here, say it is M. Marius.'"

Father Gillenormand stammered in a low voice, "Show him in."

And he remained in the same attitude, with hanging head and eye fixed on the door. It opened, and a young man appeared—it was Marius. He stopped in the door-way as if waiting to be asked in. His almost wretched clothes could not be seen in the obscurity produced by the shade, and only his calm, grave, but strangely sorrowful face could be distinguished. Father Gillenormand, as if stunned by stupor and joy, remained for a few minutes, seeing nothing but a brilliancy, as when an apparition rises before us. He was ready to faint, and perceived Marius through a mist. It was really he, it was really Marius! At length, after four years! He took him in entirely, so to speak, at a glance, and found him handsome, noble, distinguished, grown, a thorough man, with a proper attitude and a charming air. He felt inclined to open his arms and call the boy to him, his heart swelled with ravishment, affectionate words welled up and overflowed his bosom. At length all this tenderness burst forth and reached his lips, and through the contrast which formed the basis of his character a harshness issued from it. He said roughly:

"What do you want here?"

Marius replied, with an embarrassed air:

"Sir——"

Monsieur Gillenormand would have liked for Marius to throw himself into his arms, and he was dissatisfied both with Marius and himself. He felt that he was rough and Marius cold, and it was an insupportable and irritating anxiety to the old gentleman to feel himself so tender and imploring within, and unable to be otherwise than harsh externally. His bitterness returned, and he abruptly interrupted Marius.

"In that case why do you come?"

The "in that case" meant *"if you have not come to embrace me."* Marius gazed at his ancestor's marble face.

"Sir——"

The old gentleman resumed in a stern voice:

"Have you come to ask my pardon? have you recognized your error?"

He believed that he was putting Marius on the right track, and that "the boy" was going to give way. Marius trembled, for it was a disavowal of his father that was asked of him, and he lowered his eyes and replied: "No, sir."

"Well, in that case," the old man exclaimed impetuously, and with a sharp sorrow full of anger, "what is it you want of me?"

Marius clasped his hands, advanced a step, and said in a weak, trembling voice:

"Take pity on me, sir."

This word moved M. Gillenormand; had it come sooner it would have softened him, but it came too late. The old gentleman rose, and rested both hands on his cane; his lips were white, his head shook, but his lofty stature towered over the stooping Marius.

"Pity on you, sir! the young man asks pity of an old man of ninety-one! You are entering life, and I am leaving it; you go to the play, to balls, to the coffee-house, the billiard-table; you are witty, you please women, you are a pretty fellow, while I spit on my logs in the middle of summer; you are rich with the only wealth there is, while I have all the poverty of old age, infirmity, and isolation. You have your two-and-thirty teeth, a good stomach, a quick eye, strength, appetite, health, gayety, a forest of black hair, while I have not even my white hair left. I have lost my teeth, I am losing my legs, I am losing my memory, for there are three names of streets which I incessantly confound, the Rue Charlot, the Rue du Chaume, and the Rue St. Claude. Such is my state; you have a whole future before you, full of sunshine, while I am beginning to see nothing, as I have advanced so far into night. You are in love, that is a matter of course, while I am not beloved by a soul in the world, and yet you ask me for pity! By Jove, Molière forgot that. If that is the way you barristers jest at the palace of justice, I compliment you most sincerely upon it, for you are droll fellows."

And the octogenarian added, in a serious and wrathful voice: "Well, what is it you want of me?"

"I am aware, sir," said Marius, "that my presence here displeases you, but I have only come to ask one thing of you, and then I shall go away at once."

"You are a fool," the old man said; "who told you to go away?"

This was the translation of the tender words which he had at the bottom of his heart. "Ask my pardon, why don't you? and throw your arms round my neck." M. Gillenormand felt that Marius was going to leave him in a few moments, that his bad reception offended him, and that his harshness expelled him; he said all this to himself, and his grief was augmented by it; as his grief immediately turned into passion and his harshness grew the greater. He had wished that Marius should understand, and Marius did not understand, which rendered the old gentleman furious. He continued:

"What? you insulted me, your grandfather; you left my house to go the Lord knows whither; you broke your aunt's heart; you went away to lead a bachelor's life, of course that's more convenient, to play the fop, come home at all hours, and amuse yourself; you have given me no sign of life, you have incurred debts without even asking me to pay them, you have been a breaker of windows and a brawler, and at the end of four years you return to my house and have nothing more to say to me than that!"

This violent way of forcing the grandson into tenderness only produced silence on the part of Marius. M. Gillenormand folded his arms, a gesture which with him was peculiarly imperious, and bitterly addressed Marius:

"Let us come to an end. You have come to ask something of me, you say! well, what is it? speak."

"Sir," said Marius, with the look of a man who feels that he is going to fall over a precipice, "I have come to ask your permission to marry."

M. Gillenormand rang the bell, and Basque popped his head into the door.

"Send my daughter here."

A second later the door opened again, and Mlle. Gillenormand did not enter, but showed herself. Marius was standing silently, with drooping arms and the face of a criminal, while M. Gillenormand walked up and down the room. He turned to his daughter and said to her:

"It is nothing. That is M. Marius, wish him good-evening. This gentleman desires to marry, that will do. Be off."

The sound of the old man's sharp, hoarse voice announced a strange fury raging within him. The aunt looked at Marius in terror, seemed scarce to recognize him, did not utter a syllable, and disappeared before her father's breath like a straw before a hurricane. In the meanwhile M. Gillenormand had turned back and was now leaning against the mantel-piece.

"You marry! at the age of one-and-twenty! you have settled all that, and you have only a permission to ask, a mere formality! Sit down, sir. Well, you have had a revolution since I had the honor of seeing you last, the Jacobins had the best of it, and you are of course pleased; are you not a republican since you became a baron? those two things go famously together, and the republic is a sauce for the barony. Are you one of the decorated of July? did you give your small aid to take the Louvre, sir? Close by, in the Rue St. Antoine, opposite the Rue des Nonaindières, there is a cannon-ball imbedded in the wall of a house three stories up, with the inscription, July 28, 1830. Go and look at it, for it produces a fine effect. Ah! your friends do very pretty things! By the way, are they not erecting a fountain on the site of the Duc de Berry's monument? So you wish to marry? May I ask without any indiscretion who the lady is?"

He stopped, and before Marius had time to answer he added violently:

"Ah! have you a profession, a fortune? how much do you earn by your trade as a lawyer?"

"Nothing," said Marius, with a sort of fierceness and almost stern resolution.

"Nothing? then you have only the twelve hundred livres which I allow you to live on?"

Marius made no reply, and M. Gillenormand continued:

"In that case, I presume that the young lady is wealthy?"

"Like myself."

"What? no dowry?"

"No."

"Any expectations?"

"I do not think so."

"Quite naked! and what is the father?"

"I do not know."

"And what is her name?"

"Mademoiselle Fauchelevent."

"Mademoiselle Fauchewhat?"

"Fauchelevent."

"Ptt!" said the old gentleman.

"Sir!" Marius exclaimed.

M. Gillenormand interrupted him, with the air of a man who is talking to himself:

"That is it, one-and-twenty, no profession, twelve hundred livres a year, and the Baroness Pontmercy will go and buy a penn'orth of parsley at the green-grocer's."

"Sir," Marius replied in the wildness of the last vanishing hope, "I implore you, I conjure you in Heaven's name, with clasped hands I throw myself at your feet,—sir, permit me to marry her!"

The old man burst into a sharp, melancholy laugh, through which he coughed and spoke:

"Ah, ah, ah! you said to yourself, 'I'll go and see that old periwig, that absurd ass! What a pity that I am not five-and-twenty yet, how I would fling at him a respectful summons!' 'Old fool, you are too glad to see me, I feel inclined to marry Miss Lord-knows-who, the daughter of M. Lord-knows-what. She has no shoes, and I have no shirt, that matches; I am inclined to throw into the river my career, my youth, my future, my life, and take a plunge into wretchedness with a wife round my neck—that is my idea, and you must consent; and the old fossil will consent.' Go in, my lad, fasten your paving-stone round your neck, marry your Pousselevent, your Coupelevent—never, sir, never!"

"Father—"

"Never!"

Marius lost all hope through the accent with which this "never" was pronounced. He crossed the room slowly, with hanging head, tottering, and more like a man that is dying than one who is going away. M. Gillenormand looked after him, and at the moment when the door opened and Marius was about to leave the room, he took four strides with the senile vivacity of an impetuous and spoiled old man, seized Marius by the collar, pulled him back energetically in the room, threw him into an easy-chair and said:

"Tell me all about it."

The word *father* which had escaped from Marius's lips produced this revolution. Marius looked at M. Gillenormand haggardly, but his flexible features expressed naught now but a rough and ineffable goodness. The ancestor had made way for the grandfather.

"Well, speak; tell me of your love episodes, tell me all. Sapristi! how stupid young men are!"

"My father!" Marius resumed.

The old gentleman's entire face was lit up with an indescribable radiance.

"Yes, that is it, call me father, and you'll see."

There was now something so gentle, so good, so open, and so paternal, in this sharpness, that Marius, in this sudden passage from discouragement to hope, was, as it were, stunned and intoxicated. As he was seated near the table, the light of the candles fell on his seedy attire, which Father Gillenormand studied with amazement.

"Well, father," said Marius.

"What," M. Gillenormand interrupted him, "have you really no money? You are dressed like a thief."

He felt in a drawer and pulled out a purse, which he laid on the table. "Here are one hundred louis to buy a hat with."

"My father," Marius continued, "my kind father. If you only knew how I love her! You cannot imagine it. The first time I saw her was at the Luxembourg, where she came to walk. At the beginning I paid no great attention to her, and then, I know not how it happened, but I fell in love with her. Oh! how wretched it made me. I see her now every day at her own house, and her father knows nothing about it; just fancy, they are going away; we see each other at night in the garden, but her father means to take her to England, and then I said to myself, 'I will go and see my grandfather and tell him about it.' I should go mad first, I should die, I should have a brain fever, I should throw myself into the water. I must marry her, or else I shall go mad. That is the whole truth, and I do not believe that I have forgotten anything. She lives in a garden with a railing to it, in the Rue Plumet; it is on the side of the Invalides."

Father Gillenormand was sitting radiantly by Marius's side; while listening and enjoying the sound of his voice he enjoyed at the same time a lengthened pinch of snuff. At the words Rue Plumet, he interrupted his snuff-taking, and allowed the rest of the snuff to fall on his knees.

"Rue Plumet! did you say Rue Plumet? only think! is there not a barrack down there? oh; yes, of course there is. Your cousin, Théodule, the officer, the lancer, told me about it—a girl, my dear fellow, a girl! By Jove, yes, Rue Plumet, which used formerly to be called Rue Blomet. I remember it all now, and I have heard about the little girl behind the railings in the Rue Plumet. In a garden. A Pamela. Your taste is not bad. I am told she is very tidy. Between ourselves, I believe that ass of a lancer has courted her a little; I do not exactly know how far matters have gone, but, after all, that is of no consequence. Besides, there is no believing him, for he brags, Marius! I think it very proper that a young man like you should be in love, for it becomes your age, and I would sooner have you in love than a Jacobin. I would rather know you caught by a petticoat, ay, by twenty petticoats, than by Monsieur de Robespierre. For my part, I do myself the justice of saying, that, as regards sans-culottes, I never loved any but the women. Pretty girls are pretty girls, hang it all! and there is no harm in that. And so she receives you behind her father's back, does she? that's all right, and I had affairs of the same sort, more than one. Do you know what a man does in such cases? he does not regard the matter ferociously, he does not hurl himself into matrimony, or conclude with marriage and M. le Maire in his scarf. No, he is very simply a sharp fellow, and a man of common sense. Glide, mortals, but do not marry. Such a young man goes to his grandfather, who is well inclined after all, and who has always a few rolls of louis in an old drawer, and he says to him, 'Grandpapa, that's how matters stand,' and grandpapa says, 'It is very simple; youth joy must take, and old age must break.' I have been young, and you will be old. All right, my lad, you will requite it to your grandson. Here are two hundred pistoles, go and amuse yourself, confound you! That is the way in which the matter should be arranged; a man does not marry, but that is no obstacle: do you understand?"

Marius, petrified and incapable of uttering a word, shook his head in the negative. The old gentleman burst into a laugh, winked his aged eyelid, tapped him on the knee, looked at him straight in the eyes with a mysterious and radiant air, and said with the tenderest shrug of the shoulders possible:

"You goose! make her your mistress!"

Marius turned pale; he had understood nothing of what his grand-father had been saying, and this maundering about the Rue Blomet, Pamela, the barracks, the lancer, had passed before Marius like a phantasmagoria. Nothing of all this could affect Cosette, who was a lily, and the old gentleman was wandering. But this wandering had resulted in a sentence which Marius understood, and which was a mortal insult to Cosette, and the words, *make her your mistress,* passed through the grave young man's heart like a sword-blade. He rose, picked up his hat which was on the ground, and walked to the door with a firm, assured step. Then he turned, gave his grandfather a low bow, drew himself up again, and said:

"Five years ago you outraged my father; to-day you outraged my wife. I have nothing more to ask of you, sir; farewell!"

Father Gillenormand, who was stupefied, opened his mouth, stretched out his arms, strove to rise, and ere he was able to utter a word the door had closed again, and Marius had disappeared. The old gentleman remained for a few minutes motionless, and as if thunderstruck, unable to speak or breathe, and as though a garroter's hand were compressing his throat. At length he tore himself out of his easy-chair, ran to the door as fast as a man can run at ninety-one, opened it, and cried:

"Help! help!"

His daughter appeared, and then his servants; he went on with a lamentable rattle in his throat:

"Run after him! catch him up! how did I offend him? he is mad and going away! O Lord, O Lord! this time he will not return."

He went to the window which looked on the street, opened it with his old trembling hands, bent half his body out of it, while Basque and Nicolette held his skirts, and cried:

"Marius! Marius! Marius! Marius!"

But Marius could not hear him, for at this very moment he was turning the corner of the Rue St. Louis. The octogenarian raised his hand twice or thrice to his temples with an expression of agony, tottered back, and sank into an easy-chair, pulseless, voiceless, and tearless, shaking his head and moving his lips with a stupid air, and having nothing left in his eyes or heart but a profound and gloomy rigidity which resembled night.

BOOK IX

WHERE ARE THEY GOING?

I. JEAN VALJEAN

THAT same day, about four in the afternoon, Jean Valjean was seated on one of the most solitary slopes of the Champ de Mars. Either through prudence, a desire to reflect, or simply in consequence of one of those insensible changes of habits which gradually introduce themselves into all existences, he now went out very rarely with Cosette. He had on his workman's jacket and gray canvas trousers, and his long-peaked cap concealed his face. He was at present calm and happy by Cosette's side; what had startled and troubled him for a while was dissipated; but, during the last week or fortnight, anxieties of a fresh nature had sprung up. One day, while walking along the boulevard, he noticed Thénardier; thanks to his disguise, Thénardier did not recognize him, but after that Jean Valjean saw him several times again, and now felt a certainty that Thénardier was prowling about the quarter. This was sufficient to make him form a grand resolution, for Thénardier present was every peril at once. Moreover, Paris was not quiet, and political troubles offered this inconvenience to any man who had something in his life to hide, that the police had become very restless and suspicious, and, when trying to find a man like Pepin or Morey, might very easily discover a man like Jean Valjean. He, therefore, resolved to leave Paris, even France, and go to England; he had warned Cosette, and hoped to be off within a week. He was sitting on the slope, revolving in his mind all sorts of thoughts,—Thénardier, the police, the journey, and the difficulty of obtaining a passport. From all these points of view he was anxious. Lastly, an inexplicable fact, which had just struck him, and from which he was still hot, added to his alarm. On the morning of that very day he, the only person up in the house, and walking in the garden before Cosette's

223

shutters were opened, suddenly perceived this line on the wall, probably scratched with a nail:

16, *Rue de la Verrerie.*

It was quite recent, the lines were white on the old black mortar, and a bed of nettles at the foot of the wall was powdered with fine fresh plaster. This had probably been inscribed during the night. What was it? an address? a signal for others, or a warning for himself? In any case, it was evident that the secrecy of the garden was violated, and that strangers entered it. He remembered the strange incidents which had already alarmed the house, and his mind was at work on this subject; but he was careful not to say a word to Cosette about the line written on the wall, for fear of alarming her. In the midst of his troubled thoughts he perceived, from a shadow which the sun threw, that some one was standing on the crest of the slope immediately behind him. He was just going to turn, when a folded paper fell on his knees, as if a hand had thrown it over his head. He opened the paper, and read these words, written in large characters, and in pencil:

LEAVE YOUR HOUSE

Jean Valjean rose smartly, but there was no longer any one on the slope; he looked round him, and perceived a person, taller than a child and shorter than a man, dressed in a gray blouse and dust-colored cotton-velvet trousers, bestriding the parapet, and slipping down into the moat of the Champ de Mars. Jean Valjean at once went home very pensively.

2. MARIUS

MARIUS had left M. Gillenormand's house in a wretched state; he had gone in with very small hopes, and came out with an immense despair. However,—those who have watched the first movements of the human heart will comprehend it,—the lancer, the officer, the fop, cousin Théodule, had left no shadow on his mind, not the slightest. The dramatic poet might apparently hope for some complications to be produced by this revelation, so coarsely made to the grandson by the grandfather, but what the drama would gain by it truth would lose. Marius was at that age when a man believes nothing that is wrong; later comes the age when he believes everything. Suspicions are only wrinkles, and early youth has none; what upsets Othello glides over Candide. Suspect Cosette? Marius could have committed a multitude of crimes more easily. He began walking about the streets, the resource of those who suffer, and he thought of nothing which he might have remembered. At two in the morning he went to Courfeyrac's lodging, and threw himself on his mattress full dressed; it was bright sunshine when he fell asleep, with that frightful oppressive sleep which allows ideas to come and go in the brain. When he awoke he saw Courfeyrac, Enjolras, Feuilly, and Combeferre, all ready to go out, and extremely busy. Courfeyrac said to him:

"Are you coming to General Lamarque's funeral?"

It seemed to him as if Courfeyrac were talking Chinese. He went out shortly after them, and put in his pockets the pistols which Javert had intrusted to him at the affair of February 3, and which still remained in his possession. They were still loaded, and it would be difficult to say what obscure notion he had in his brain when he took them up. The

225

whole day he wandered about, without knowing where; it rained at times, but he did not perceive it; he bought for his dinner a half-penny roll, put it in his pocket, and forgot it. It appears that he took a bath in the Seine without being conscious of it; for there are moments when a man has a furnace under his skull, and Marius had reached one of those moments. He hoped for nothing, feared nothing now, and had taken this step since the previous day. He awaited the evening with a feverish impatience, for he had but one clear idea left, that at nine o'clock he should see Cosette. This last happiness was now his sole future; after that came the shadow. At times, while walking along the most deserted boulevards, he imagined that he could hear strange noises in Paris; then he thrust his head out of his reverie, and said: "Can they be fighting?" At nightfall, at nine o'clock precisely, he was at the Rue Plumet, as he had promised Cosette. He had not seen her for eight-and-forty hours, he was about to see her again. Every other thought was effaced, and he only felt an extraordinary and profound joy. Those minutes in which men live ages have this sovereign and admirable thing about them, that, during their passing, they entirely occupy the heart.

Marius removed the railings and rushed into the garden. Cosette was not at the place where she usually waited for him, and he crossed the garden, and went to the niche near the terrace. "She is waiting for me there," he said; but Cosette was not there. He raised his eyes and saw that the shutters of the house were closed; he walked round the garden, and the garden was deserted. Then he returned to the garden, and, mad with love, terrified, exasperated with grief and anxiety, he rapped at the shutters, like a master who returns home at a late hour. He rapped, he rapped again, at the risk of seeing the window open and the father's frowning face appear, and ask him, "What do you want?" This was nothing to what he caught a glimpse of. When he had rapped, he raised his voice, and called Cosette. "Cosette!" he cried; "Cosette!" he repeated imperiously. There was no answer, and it was all over; there was no one in the garden, no one in the house. Marius fixed his desperate eyes on this mournful house, which was as black, as silent, and more empty than a tomb. He gazed at the stone bench on which he had spent so many adorable hours by Cosette's side; then he sat down on the garden steps, with his heart full of gentleness and resolution; he blessed his love in his heart, and said to himself that since Cosette was gone all left him was to die. All at once he heard a voice which seemed to come from the street, crying through the trees:

"Monsieur Marius!"

He drew himself up.

"Hilloh?" he said.

"Are you there, M. Marius?"

"Yes."

"Monsieur Marius," the voice resumed, "your friends are waiting for you at the barricade in the Rue de la Chanvrerie."

This voice was not entirely strange to him, and resembled Eponine's rough, hoarse accents. Marius ran to the railings, pulled aside the shifting bar, passed his head through, and saw some one, who seemed to be a young man, running away in the gloaming.

3 · M. MABOEUF

JEAN VALJEAN's purse was useless to M. Mabœuf, who, in his venerable childish austerity, had not accepted the gift of the stars; he had not allowed that a star could coin itself into louis d'or, and he had not guessed that what fell from heaven came from Gavroche. Hence he carried the purse to the police commissary of the district, as a lost object, placed by the finder at the disposal of the claimants. The purse was really lost; we need hardly say that no one claimed it, and it did not help M. Mabœuf. In other respects M. Mabœuf had continued to descend. The indigo experiments had succeeded no better at the Jardin des Plantes than in his garden of Austerlitz. The previous year he owed his housekeeper her wages, and now, as we have seen, he owed his landlord his rent. The government pawnbroker's office sold the copper-plates of his *Flora,* at the expiration of thirteen months, and some brazier had made stew-pans of them. When his plates had disappeared, as he could no longer complete the unbound copies of his *Flora* which he still possessed, he sold off plates and text to a second-hand book-seller, as defective. Nothing was then left him of the labor of his whole life, and he began eating the money produced by the copies. When he saw that this poor resource was growing exhausted he gave up his garden, and did not attend to it; before, and long before, he had given up the two eggs and slice of beef which he ate from time to time, and now dined on bread and potatoes. He had sold his last articles of furniture, then everything he had in duplicate in linen, clothes, and coverlids, and then his herbals and plates, but he still had his most precious books, among them being several of great rarity, such as the *Les Quadrains Historiques de la Bible,* the edition of 1560; *La Concordance des Bibles,* of Pierre de Besse; *Les Marguerites de la Marguerite,* of Jean de la Haye, with a dedication to the Queen of Navarre; the work on the *Duties and Dignity of an Ambassador,* by the Sieur de Villiers Hotman; a *Florilegium Rabbinicum,* of 1644; a *Tibullus,* of 1567, with the splendid imprint, *Venetiis, in ædibus Manutianis,* and lastly a *Diogenes Laertius,* printed at Lyons in 1644, in which were the famous various readings of the Vatican MS. 411, of the thirteenth century, and those of the two Venetian *codices* 393 and 394, so usefully consulted by Henri Estienne, and all the passages in the Doric dialect, only to be found in the celebrated twelfth-century MS. of the Naples library. M. Mabœuf never lit a fire in his room, and went to bed with the sun, in order not to burn a candle; it seemed as if he no longer had neighbors, for they shunned him when he went out, and he noticed it. The wretchedness of a child interests a mother, the wretchedness of a youth interests an old man, but the wretchedness of an old man interests nobody, and it is the coldest of all distresses. Still M. Mabœuf had not entirely lost his childlike serenity; his eye acquired some vivacity when it settled on his books, and he smiled when he regarded the *Diogenes Laertius,* which was an unique copy. His glass case was the only furniture which he had retained beyond what was indispensable. One day Mother Plutarch said to him:

"I have no money to buy dinner with."

What she called dinner consisted of a loaf and four or five potatoes.

"Can't you get it on credit?" said M. Mabœuf.

"You know very well that it is refused me."

M. Mabœuf opened his book-case, looked for a long time at all his books in turn, like a father obliged to decimate his children would look at them before selecting, then took one up quickly, put it under his arm, and went out.

He returned two hours later with nothing under his arm, laid thirty sous on the table, and said:

"You will get some dinner."

From this moment, Mother Plutarch saw a dark veil, which was not raised again, settle upon the old gentleman's candid face. The next day, the next after that, and every day, M. Mabœuf had to begin again; he went out with a book and returned with a piece of silver. As the second-hand booksellers saw that he was compelled to sell they bought for twenty sous books for which he had paid twenty francs, and frequently to the same dealers. Volume by volume his whole library passed away, and he said at times, "and yet I am eighty years of age," as if he had some lurking hope that he should reach the end of his days ere he reached the end of his books. His sorrow grew, but once he had a joy; he went out with a Robert Estienne, which he sold for thirty-five sous on the Quai Malaquais, and came home with an Aldus which he had bought for forty sous on the Rue de Grès. "I owe five sous," he said quite radiantly to Mother Plutarch, but that day he did not dine. He belonged to the Horticultural Society, and his poverty was known. The president of the society called on him, promised to speak about him to the minister of commerce and agriculture, and did so. "What do you say?" the minister exclaimed; "I should think so! an old savant! a botanist! an inoffensive man! we must do something for him." The next day M. Mabœuf received an invitation to dine with the minister, and, trembling with joy, showed the letter to Mother Plutarch. "We are saved!" he said. On the appointed day he went to the minister, and noticed that his ragged cravat, his long, square-cut coat, and shoes varnished with white of egg astounded the footman. No one spoke to him, not even the minister, and at about ten in the evening, while still waiting for a word, he heard the minister's wife, a handsome lady in a low-necked dress, whom he had not dared to approach, ask, "Who can that old gentleman be?" He went home afoot at midnight through the pouring rain; he had sold an Elzevir to pay his hackney coach in going.

Every evening, before going to bed, he had fallen into the habit of reading a few pages of his *Diogenes Laertius;* for he knew enough of Greek to enjoy the peculiarities of the text which he possessed, and had no other joy now left him. A few weeks passed away, and all at once Mother Plutarch fell ill. There is one thing even more sad than having no money to buy bread at a baker's, and that is, not to have money to buy medicine at the chemist's. One night, the doctor had ordered a most expensive potion, and then the disease grew worse, and a nurse was necessary. M. Mabœuf opened his book-case, but there was nothing left in it; the last volume had departed, and the only thing left him was the *Diogenes Laertius.*

He placed the unique copy under his arm and went out—it was June 4, 1832; he proceeded to Royol's successor at the Porte St. Jacques, and returned with one hundred francs. He placed the pile of five-franc pieces on the old servant's table, and entered his bedroom without uttering a syllable.

At dawn of the next day he seated himself on the overturned post in his garden, and over the hedge he might have been seen the whole morning, motionless, with drooping head, and eyes vaguely fixed on the faded flower-beds. It rained every now and then, but the old man did not seem to notice it.

In the afternoon extraordinary noises broke out in Paris, resembling musket-shots and the clamor of a multitude.

Father Mabœuf raised his head, noticed a gardener passing, and said: "What is the matter?"

The gardener replied, with the spade on his back, and with the most peaceful accent:

"It's the riots."

"What! riots?"

"Yes, they are fighting."

"Why are they fighting?"

"The Lord alone knows," said the gardener.

"In what direction?"

"Over by the arsenal."

Father Mabœuf went into his house, took his hat, mechanically sought for a book to place under his arm, found none, said, "Ah, it is true!" and went out with a wandering look.

BOOK X

THE FIFTH OF JUNE, 1832

1. THE SURFACE OF THE QUESTION

OF what is a revolt composed? of nothing and of everything, of an electricity suddenly disengaged, of a flame which suddenly breaks out, of a wandering strength and a passing breath. This breath meets with heads that talk, brains that dream, souls that suffer, passions that burn, and miseries which yell, and carries them off with it. Whither? it is chance work; through the state, through the laws, through prosperity and the insolence of others. Irritated convictions, embittered enthusiasms, aroused indignations, martial instincts suppressed, youthful courage exalted, and generous blindnesses; curiosity, a taste for a change, thirst for something unexpected, the feeling which causes us to find pleasure in reading the announcement of a new piece, or on hearing the machinist's whistle; vague hatreds, rancors, disappointments, every vanity which believes that destiny has been a bankrupt to it; straightened circumstances, empty dreams, ambitions surrounded with escarpments, every man who hopes for an issue from an overthrow, and lastly, at the very bottom, the mob, that mud which takes fire—such are the elements of riot. The greatest and the most infamous, beings who prowl about beyond the pale of everything, while awaiting an opportunity; gypsies, nameless men, highway vagabonds, the men who sleep o' nights in a desert of houses with no other roof but the cold clouds of heaven, those who daily ask their bread of chance, and not of toil; the unknown men of wretchedness and nothingness, bare arms and bare feet, belong to the riot. Every man who has in his soul a secret revolt against any act of the state, of life, or of destiny is on its border line, and so soon as it appears he begins to quiver and to feel himself lifted by the whirlwind.

Riot is a species of social atmospheric waterspout, which is suddenly formed in certain conditions of temperature, and which in its revolutions mounts, runs, thunders, tears up, razes, crushes, demolishes, and uproots, bearing with it grand and paltry natures, the strong man and the weak mind, the trunk of a tree and the wisp of straw. Woe to the man whom it carries as well as to the one it dashes at, for it breaks one against the other. It communicates to those whom it seizes a strange and extraordinary power; it fills the first-comer with the force of events and converts everything into projectiles; it makes a cannon-ball of a stone, and a general of a porter. If we may believe certain oracles of the crafty policy, a little amount of riot is desirable from the governing point of view. The system is, that it strengthens those governments which it does not overthrow; it tries the army; it concentrates the bourgeoisie, strengthens the muscles of the police, and displays the force of the social frame-work. It is a lesson in gymnastics, and almost in hygiene, and power feels better after a riot, as a man does after a rubbing down. Riot, thirty years ago, was also regarded from other standpoints. There is for everything a theory which proclaims itself as "common sense," a mediation offered between the true and the false: explanation, admonition, and a somewhat haughty extenuation which, because it is composed of blame and apology, believes itself wisdom, and is often nothing but pedantry. An entire political school, called the "Juste milieu," emanated from this, and between the cold water and hot water there is the lukewarm water party. This school, with its false depths entirely superficial, which dissects effects without going back to the causes, scolds, from the elevation of semi-science, the agitations of the public streets.

If we listen to this school we hear: "The riots which complicated the deed of 1830 deprived that grand event of a portion of its purity. The revolution of July was a fine blast of the popular wind, suddenly followed by a blue sky, and the riots caused a cloudy sky to re-appear, and compelled the revolution, originally so remarkable through unanimity, to degenerate into a quarrel. In the revolution of July, as in every progress produced by a jerk, there were secret fractures which the riots cause to be noticed. One could say, 'Ah, that is broken!' After the revolution of July only the deliverance was felt, but after the riots the catastrophe was felt. Every riot closes shops, depresses funds, consternates the Stock Exchange, suspends trade, checks business, and entails bankruptcies: there is no money, trade is disconcerted, capital is withdrawn, labor is at a discount, there is fear everywhere, and counterstrokes take place in every city, whence come gulfs. It is calculated that the first day of riot costs France twenty millions of francs, the second forty, and the third sixty. Hence a riot of three days costs one hundred and twenty millions, that is to say, if we only regard the financial result, is equivalent to a disaster, shipwreck, or lost action, which might annihilate a fleet of sixty vessels of the line. Indubitably, riots, historically regarded, had their beauty: the war of the paving-stones is no less grand or pathetic than the war of the thickets; in the one there is the soul of forests, in the other the heart of cities; one has Jean Chouan, the other has Jeanne. Riots lit up luridly but splendidly all the most original features of the Parisian character,—generosity, devotion, stormy gayety, students proving that bravery forms a part of intellect, the National Guard unswerving, bivouacs formed by shop-keepers, fortresses held by gamins, and contempt of death in the passers-by. Schools and legions came into collision, but, after all, there was only the difference of age between the combatants, and they are the same race; the same stoical men who die at the age of twenty for their ideas, and at forty for their families; the army, ever sad in civil wars, opposed prudence to audacity; and the riots, while manifesting the popular intrepidity, were the education of the bourgeois courage. That is all very well, but is all this worth the bloodshed? And then add to the bloodshed the future darkened, progress compromised, anxiety of the better classes, honest liberals despairing, foreign absolutism delighted at these wounds dealt to revolution by itself, and the conquered of 1830 triumphing and shouting, 'Did we not say so?' Add Paris possibly aggrandized, France assuredly diminished. Add—for we must tell the whole truth—the massacres which too often dishonored the victory of order, which became ferocious, over liberty which went mad, and we must arrive at the conclusion that riots have been fatal."

Thus speaks that almost-wisdom with which the bourgeoisie, that almost-people, are so readily contented. For our part, we regret the word riots, as being too wide, and consequently too convenient, and make a distinction between one popular movement and another; we do not ask ourselves whether a riot costs as much as a battle. In the first place, why a battle? here the question of war arises. Is war less a scourge than riot is a calamity? and, then, are all riots calamities? and supposing that July 14 cost one hundred and twenty millions, the establishment of Philip V in Spain cost France two billions, and even were the price equal, we should prefer the 14th July. Besides, we reject these figures, which seem reasons and are only words, and a riot being given, we ex-

amine it in itself. In all that the doctrinaire objection we have just reproduced says, the only question is about effect and we are seeking for
the cause. We give a definition.

2. *THE BOTTOM OF THE QUESTION*

THERE is riot, and there is resurrection; they are two passions, one of
which is just, the other unjust. In democratic states, the only ones based
on justice, it sometimes happens that the fraction usurps power; in that
case, the whole people rises, and the necessary demand for its rights
may go so far as taking up arms. In all the questions which result from
collective sovereignty the war of all against the fraction is insurrection,
and the attack of the fraction on the masses is a riot; according as the
Tuileries contain the king or the convention they are justly or unjustly
attacked. The same guns pointed at the mob are in the wrong on August
14, and in the right on the 14th Vendemiaire. Their appearance is alike,
but the base is different: the Swiss defend what is false, and Bonaparte
what is true. What universal suffrage has done in its liberty and its
sovereignty cannot be undone by the street. It is the same in matters of
pure civilization, and the instinct of the masses, clear-sighted yesterday,
may be perturbed to-morrow. The same fury is legitimate against Terray
and absurd against Turgot. Smashing engines, pillaging storehouses,
tearing up rails, the demolition of docks, the false roads of multitude,
the denial of popular justice to progress, Ramus assassinated by the
scholars, and Rousseau expelled from Switzerland by stones—all this
is riot. Israel rising against Moses, Athens against Phocion, Rome against
Scipio, are riots, while Paris attacking the Bastille is insurrection. The
soldiers opposing Alexander, the sailors mutinying against Christopher
Columbus, are the same revolt, an impious revolt. Why? because Alex-

ander does for Asia with the sword what Columbus does for America with the compass; Alexander, like Columbus, finds a world. These gifts of a world to civilization are such increments of light that any resistance in such a case is culpable. At times the people breaks its fidelity to itself, and the mob behaves treacherously to the people. Can anything, for instance, be stranger than the long and sanguinary protest of the "false salters," a legitimate chronic revolt which at the decisive moment, on the day of salvation, and in the hour of the popular victory, espouses the throne, turns into chouannerie, and from an insurrection against the government becomes a riot for it? These are gloomy masterpieces of ignorance! The false salter escapes from the royal gallows, and with the noose still round his neck mounts the white cockade. "Death to the salt taxes" brings into the world "Long live the king." The killers of St. Bartholomew, the murderers of September, the massacrers of Avignon, the assassins of Coligny, of Madame de Lamballe, the assassins of Brune, the Miquelets, the Verdets, and the Cadenettes, the companions of Jehu, and the Chevaliers du Brassard—all this is riot. The Vendée is a grand Catholic riot. The sound of right in motion can be recognized, and it does not always come from the trembling of the overthrown masses; there are mad furies and cracked bells, and all the tocsins do not give the sound of bronze. The commotion of passions and ignorances differs from the shock of progress. Rise, if you like, but only to grow, and show me in what direction you are going, for insurrection is only possible with a forward movement. Any other uprising is bad, every violent step backward is riot, and recoiling is an assault upon the human race. Insurrection is the outburst of the fury of truth; the paving-stones which insurrection tears up emit the spark of right, and they only leave to riot their mud. Danton rising against Louis XVI, is insurrection; Hébert against Danton is riot.

Hence it comes that if insurrection in given cases may be, as Lafayette said, the most holy of duties, riot may be the most fatal of attacks. There is also some difference in the intensity of caloric; insurrection is often a volcano, a riot often a straw fire. Revolt, as we have said, is sometimes found in the power. Polignac is a rioter, and Camille Desmoulins is a government. At times insurrection is a resurrection. The solution of everything by universal suffrage being an absolutely modern fact, and all history anterior to that fact being for four thousand years filled with violated right and the suffering of the peoples, each epoch of history brings with it the protest which is possible to it. Under the Cæsars there was no insurrection, but there was Juvenal. The *facit indignatio* takes the place of the Gracchi. Under the Cæsars there is the Exile of Syene, and there is also the man of the "Annals." We will not refer to the awful Exile of Patmos; he also crushes the real world with a protest in the name of the ideal world, converts a vision into an enormous satire, and casts on Rome-Nineveh, Rome-Babylon, and Rome-Sodom the flashing reflection of the Apocalypse. John on his rock is the sphinx on its pedestal. We cannot understand him, for he is a Jew and writes in Hebrew, but the man who writes the Annals is a Latin, or, to speak more correctly, a Roman. As the Neros reign in the black manner, they must be painted in the same. Work produced by the graver alone would be pale, and so a concentrated biting prose must be poured into the lines. Despots are of some service to thinkers, for chained language is terrible language, and the writer doubles and triples his style when silence is imposed by a master on the people. There issues from this silence a certain mysterious fullness which filters and fixes itself in bronze in the thought. Compression in history produces conciseness in the historian, and the granitic solidity of certain celebrated prose is nothing but a pressure put on by the tyrant. Tyranny forces the writer into contraction of the diameter, which is increase of strength. The Ciceronean period, scarce sufficient for Verres, would be blunted upon a Caligula. Though there is less breadth in the sentence, there is more intensity in the blow, and Tacitus thinks with a drawn-back arm. The honesty of a great heart condensed in justice and truth is annihilating.

We must observe, by the way, that Tacitus is not historically superimposed on Cæsar, and the Tiberii are reserved for him. Cæsar and Tacitus are two successive phenomena, whose meeting seems to be mysteriously prevented by Him who regulates the entrances and exits on the stage of centuries. Cæsar is great, Tacitus is great and God spares these two grandeurs by not bringing them into collision. The judge, in striking Cæsar, might strike too hard and be unjust, and God does not wish that. The great wars of Africa and Spain, the Cilician pirates destroyed, civilization introduced into Gaul, Britain, and Germany— all this glory covers the Rubicon. There is in this a species of delicacy on the part of Divine justice, hesitating to let loose on the illustrious usurper the formidable historian, saving Cæsar from the sentence of a Tacitus, and granting extenuating circumstances to genius. Assuredly despotism remains despotism, even under the despot of genius. There is corruption under illustrious tyrants, but the moral plague is more hideous still under infamous tyrants. In such reigns nothing veils the shame; and the producers of examples, Tacitus like Juvenal, buffet more usefully in the presence of this human race this ignominy, which has no reply to make. Rome smells worse under Vitellius than under Sylla; under Claudius and Domitian there is a deformity of baseness corresponding with the ugliness of the tyrant. The foulness of the slaves is the direct product of the despots; a miasma is extracted from these crouching consciences in which the master is reflected; the public power is unclean, heads are small, consciences flat, and souls vermin; this is the case under Caracalla, Commodus, and Heliogabalus, while from the Roman senate under Cæsar there only issues the smell peculiar to eagles' nests. Hence the apparently tardy arrival of Juvenal and Tacitus, for the demonstrator steps in at the hour for the experiment to be performed.

But Juvenal or Tacitus, like Isaiah in biblical times and Dante in the middle ages, is the man; riot and insurrection are the multitude, which is sometime wrong, sometime right. In the most general cases riot issues from a material fact, but insurrection is always a moral phenomenon. Riot is Masaniello; insurrection is Spartacus. Insurrection is related to the mind, riot to the stomach; Gaster is irritated, but Gaster is certainly not always in the wrong. In questions of famine, riot, the Buzançais one, for instance, has a true, pathetic, and just starting-point, and yet it remains a riot. Why? because, though right in the abstract, it is wrong in form. Ferocious though legitimate, violent though strong, it has marched hap-hazard, crushing things in its passage like a blind elephant; it has left behind it the corpses of old men, women, and children, and has shed, without knowing why, the blood of the unoffending and the innocent. Feeding the people is a good end, but massacre is a bad means.

All armed protests, even the most legitimate, even August 10 and July 14, set out with the same trouble, and before right is disengaged there are tumult and scenes. At the outset an insurrection is a riot, in the same way as the river is a torrent, and generally pours itself into that ocean, Revolution. Sometimes, however, insurrection, which has come from those lofty mountains which command the moral horizon, justice, wisdom, reason, and right, and is composed of the purest snow of the ideal, after a long fall from rock to rock, after reflecting the sky in its transparency, and being swollen by a hundred confluents in its majestic course, suddenly loses itself in some bourgeois bog, as the Rhine does in the marshes. All this belongs to the past, and the future will be different, for universal suffrage has this admirable thing about it, that it dissolves riot in its origin, and, by giving insurrection a vote, deprives it of the weapon. The disappearance of war, street wars as well as frontier wars, such is the inevitable progress, and, whatever to-day may be, peace is the to-morrow. However, the bourgeois, properly so called, makes but a slight distinction between insurrection and riot. To him everything is sedition, pure and simple rebellion, the revolt of the dog against the master, an attempt to bite, which must be punished with the chain and the kennel, a barking, until the day when the dog's head, suddenly enlarged, stands out vaguely in the shadow with a lion's face. Then the bourgeois shouts, "Long live the people!"

This explanation given, how does the movement of 1832 stand to history? Is it a riot or an insurrection? It is an insurrection. It may happen that in the course of our narrative of a formidable event we may use the word "riot," but only to qualify surface facts, and while still maintaining the distinction between the form riot and the basis insurrection. The movement of 1832 had in its rapid explosion and mournful extinction so much grandeur than even those who only see a riot in it speak of it respectfully. To them it is like a remnant of 1830, for, as they say, excited imaginations cannot be calmed in a day, and a revolution does not stop short with a precipice, but has necessarily a few undulations before it returns to a state of peace, like a mountain in redescending to the plain. There are no Alps without a Jura, no Pyrenees without Asturias. This pathetic crisis of contemporary history, which the memory of the Parisians calls the *"time of the riots,"* is assuredly a characteristic hour among the stormy hours of this age. One last word before we return to our story.

The facts which we are going to record belong to that dramatic and living reality which the historian sometimes neglects through want of time and space, but they contain, we insist upon it, life, palpitation, and human quivering. Small details, as we think we have said, are, so to speak, the foliage of great events, and are lost in the distance of history. The period called the riots abounds in details of this nature, and the judicial inquiries, through other than historic reasons, have not revealed everything, or perhaps studied it. We are, therefore, going to bring into light, among the peculiarities known and published, things which are not known and facts over which the forgetfulness of some and the death of others have passed. Most of the actors in these gigantic scenes have disappeared. On the next day they held their tongues, but we may say that we saw what we are about to narrate. We will change a few names, for history recounts and does not denounce, but we will depict true things. The nature of our book will only allow us to display one side and one episode, assuredly the least known, of the days of June 5 and 6, 1832, but we will do so in such a way that the reader will be enabled to catch a glimpse of the real face of this frightful public adventure behind the dark veil which we are about to lift.

3. *A BURIAL GIVES OPPORTUNITY FOR A REVIVAL*

In the spring of 1832, although for three months cholera had chilled minds and cast over their agitation a species of dull calm, Paris had been for a long time ready for a commotion. As we have said, the great city resembles a piece of artillery when it is loaded,—a spark need only fall and the gun goes off. In June, 1832, the spark was the death of General Lamarque. Lamarque was a man of renown and of action, and had displayed in succession, under the Empire and the Restoration, the two braveries necessary for the two epochs, the bravery of the battle-field and the bravery of the oratorical tribune. He was eloquent as he had been valiant, and a sword was felt in his words; like Foy, his predecessor, after holding the command erect, he held liberty erect; he sat between the Left and the extreme Left, beloved by the people because he accepted the chances of the future, and beloved by the mob because he had served the emperor well. He was with Gérard and Drouet, one of Napoleon's marshals *in petto,* and the hiatus of 1815 affected him like a personal insult. He hated Wellington with a direct hatred, which pleased the multitude, and for the last seventeen years, scarcely paying attention to intermediate events, he had majestically nursed his grief for Waterloo. In his dying hour he pressed to his heart a sword which the officers of the hundred days had given him, and while Napoleon died uttering the word *army,* Lamarque died pronouncing the word *country.* His death, which was expected, was feared by the people as a loss, and by the government as an opportunity. This death was a mourning, and, like everything which is bitter, mourning may turn into revolt. This really happened. On the previous evening, and on the morning of June 5, the day fixed for the interment of Lamarque, the Faubourg St. Antoine, close to which the procession would pass, assumed a formidable aspect. This tumultuous net-work of streets was filled with rumors, and people armed themselves as they could. Carpenters carried off the bolts of their shop "to break in doors with"; one of them made a dagger of a stocking-weaver's hook, by breaking off the hook and sharpening the stump. Another, in his fever "to attack," slept for three nights in his clothes. A carpenter of the name of Lombier met a mate, who asked him, "Where are you going?" "Why, I have no weapon, so I am going to my shop to fetch my compasses." "What to do?" "I don't know," Lombier said. A porter of the name of Jacqueline arrested any workman who happened to pass, and said, "Come with me." He paid for a pint of wine, and asked, "Have you work?" "No." "Go to Filspierre's, between the Montreuil and Charonne barrières, and you will find work." At Filspierre's cartridges and arms were distributed. Some well-known chiefs went the rounds, that is to say, ran from one to the other to collect their followers. At Barthelemy's, near the Barrière du Trone, and at Capel's, the Petit Chapeau, the drinkers accosted each other with a serious air, and could be heard saying, *Where is your pistol? Under my blouse; and yours? Under my shirt.* In the Rue Traversière, in front of Roland's workshop, and in the yard of the Burnt House, before the workshop of Bernier, the tool-maker, groups stood whispering. The most ardent among them was a certain Mavot, who never stopped longer than a week at a shop, for his masters sent him away, "as they were obliged to quarrel with him every day." Mavot was killed the next day on the barricade of the Rue Menilmontant. Pretot, who was also destined to die in the struggle, seconded Mavot, and replied to the question *"What is your object?"* "Insurrection." Workmen assembled at the corner of the Rue de Berry, awaiting a man of the name of Lemarin, revolutionary agent for the Faubourg St. Marceau, and pass-words were exchanged almost publicly.

On June 5, then, a day of sunshine and shower, the funeral procession of General Lamarque passed through Paris with the official military pomp, somewhat increased by precautions. Two battalions with covered drums and reversed muskets, ten thousand of the National Guard with their sabers at their side, and the batteries of the artillery of the National Guard escorted the coffin, and the hearse was drawn by young men. The officers of the Invalides followed immediately after, bearing laurel branches, and then came a countless, agitated, and strange multitude, the sectionists of the friends of the people, the school of law, the school of medicine, refugees of all nations, Spanish, Italian, German, Polish flags, horizontal tricolor flags, every banner possible, children waving green branches, stone-cutters and carpenters out of work at this very time, and printers easy to recognize by their paper caps, marching two and two, three and three, uttering cries, nearly all shaking sticks, and some sabers, without order, but with one soul, at one moment a mob, at another a column. Squads selected their chiefs, and a man armed with a brace of pistols, which were perfectly visible, seemed to pass others in review, whose files made way for him. On the sidewalks of the boulevards, on the branches of the trees, in the balconies, at the windows and on the roofs, there was a dense throng of men, women, and children, whose eyes were full of anxiety. An armed crowd passed, and a startled crowd looked at it. On its side government was observing, with its hand on the sword-hilt. Four squadrons of carbineers, mounted, and with their trumpeters at the head, with their cartridge-boxes full, and their musketoons loaded, might be seen on the Place Louis XV, in the Pays Latin, and at the Jardin des Plantes; the municipal guard were echelonned from street to street; at the Halle-aux-Vins was a squadron of dragoons, at the Grève one-half of the 12th Light Infantry, while the other half was at the Bastille; the 6th Dragoons were at the Celestins, and the court of the Louvre was crammed with artillery; all the rest of the troops were confined to barracks, without counting the regiments in the environs of Paris. The alarmed authorities held suspended over the threatening multitude twenty-four thousand soldiers in the city, and thirty thousand in the suburbs.

Various rumors circulated in the procession, legitimist intrigues were talked about, and they spoke about the Duke of Reichstadt, whom God was marking for death at the very moment when the crowd designated him for emperor. A person who was never discovered announced that at appointed hours two overseers, gained over, would open to the people the gates of a small-arm factory. An enthusiasm blended with despondency was visible in the uncovered heads of most of the persons present, and here and there too in this multitude, suffering from so many violent but noble emotions, might be seen criminal faces and ignoble lips that muttered, "Let us plunder." There are some agitations which stir up the bottom of the marsh and bring clouds of mud to the surface of the water; this is a phenomenon familiar to a well-constituted police force. The procession proceeded with feverish slowness from the house of death along the boulevards to the Bastille. It rained at intervals, but the rain produced no effect on this crowd. Several incidents, such as the coffin carried round the Vendôme column, stones thrown at the Duc de Fitz-james, who was noticed in a balcony with his hat on his head, the Gallic cock torn from a popular flag and dragged in the mud, a policeman wounded by a sword-thrust at the Porte St. Martin, an officer of the 12th Light Infantry saying aloud, "I am a republican," the Polytechnic school coming up, after forcing its gates, and the cries of "Long live the Polytechnic school!" "Long live the republic!" marked the passage of the procession. At the Bastille long formidable files of spectators, coming down from the Faubourg St. Antoine, effected their junction with the procession, and a certain terrible ebullition began to agitate the crowd. A man was heard saying to another, "You see that fellow with the red beard; he will say when it is time to fire." It seems that this red beard re-appeared with the same functions in a later riot, the Quénisset affair.

The hearse passed the Bastille, followed the canal, crossed the small bridge, and reached the esplanade of the bridge of Austerlitz, where it halted. At this moment a bird's-eye view of the crowd would have offered the appearance of a comet, whose head was on the esplanade, and whose tail was prolonged upon the boulevard as far as the Porte St. Martin. A circle was formed round the hearse, and the vast crowd was hushed. Lafayette spoke, and bade farewell to Lamarque: it was a touching and august moment,—all heads were uncovered, and all hearts beat. All at once a man on horseback, dressed in black, appeared in the middle of the group with a red flag, though others say with a pike surmounted by a red cap. Lafayette turned his head away, and Exelmans left the procession. This red flag aroused a storm and disappeared in it: from the boulevard Bourdon to the bridge of Austerlitz one of these clamors which resemble billows stirred up the multitude, and two prodigious cries were raised, *Lamarque to the Pantheon!—Lafayette to the Hotel de Ville!* Young men, amid the acclamations of the crowd, began dragging Lamarque in the hearse over the bridge of Austerlitz, and Lafayette in a hackney coach along the Quai Morland. In the crowd that surrounded and applauded Lafayette people noticed and pointed out to each other a German of the name of Ludwig Snyder, who has since died a centenarian, who also went through the campaign of 1776, and had fought at Trenton under Washington, and under Lafayette at Brandywine.

The municipal cavalry galloped along the left bank to stop the passage of the bridge, while on the right the dragoons came out of the Celestins and deployed along the Quai Morland. The people who were drawing Lafayette suddenly perceived them at a turning of the quay, and cried, "The dragoons!" The troops advanced at a walk, silently, with their pistols in the holsters, sabers undrawn, and musketoons slung with an air of gloomy expectation. Two hundred yards from the little bridge they halted, the coach in which Lafayette was went up to them, they opened their ranks to let it pass, and then closed up again. At this moment the dragoons and the crowd came in contact, and women fled in terror. What took place in this fatal minute? no one could say, for it is the dark moment when two clouds clash together. Some state that a bugle-call sounding the charge was heard on the side of the Arsenal, others that a dragoon was stabbed with a knife by a lad. The truth is, that three shots were suddenly fired, one killing Major Cholet, the second an old deaf woman who was closing her window in the Rue Contrescarpe, while the third grazed an officer's shoulder. A woman cried, "They have begun too soon!" and all at once the squadron of dragoons was seen galloping up on the opposite side with drawn sabers, and sweeping everything before it.

At such a moment the last word is said, the tempest is unchained, stones shower, the fusillade bursts forth; many rush to the water's edge and cross the small arm of the Seine, which is now filled up; the timber-yards on Isle Louviers, that ready-made citadel, bristle with combatants, stakes are pulled up, pistols are fired, a barricade is commenced, the young men, driven back, pass over the bridge of Austerlitz with the hearse at the double, and charge the municipal guard; the carbineers gallop up, the dragoons saber, the crowd disperses in all directions, a rumor of war flies to the four corners of Paris; men cry "To arms!" and run, overthrow, fly, and resist. Passion spreads the riot as the wind does fire.

4 · THE EBULLITIONS OF OTHER DAYS

NOTHING is more extraordinary than the commencement of a riot, for everything breaks out everywhere at once. Was it foreseen? yes. Was it prepared? no. Where does it issue from? from the pavement. Where does it fall from? the clouds. At one spot the insurrection has the character of a plot, at another of an improvisation. The first-comer grasps a current of the mob, and leads it whither he pleases. It is a beginning full of horror, with which a sort of formidable gayety is mingled. First there is a clamor; shops are closed, and the goods disappear from the tradesmen's windows; then dropping shots are heard; people fly, gateways are assailed with the butts of muskets, and servant-maids may be heard laughing in the yards of the houses, and saying: *There's going to be a row.*

A quarter of an hour had not elapsed: this is what was going on simultaneously at twenty different points in Paris. In the Rue St. Croix de la Bretonnerie, twenty young men, with beards and long hair, entered a wine-shop, and came out a moment after carrying a horizontal tricolor flag covered with crape, and having at their head three men armed, one with a saber, the second with a gun, and the third with a pike. In the Rue des Nonaindières, a well-dressed bourgeois, who had a large stomach, a sonorous voice, bald head, lofty forehead, black beard, and one of those rough mustaches which cannot be kept from bristling, publicly offered cartridges to passers-by. In the Rue St. Pierre Montmartre, bare-armed men carried about a black flag, on which were read these words, in white letters: *Republic or death.* In the Rue des Jeûneurs, Rue du Cadran, Rue Montorgueil, and Rue Mandar, groups appeared waving flags, on which could be distinguished the word *section* in gold letters with a number. One of these flags was red and blue, with an imperceptible parting line of white. A small-arm factory, on the Boulevard St. Martin, and three gunsmiths' shops, one on the Rue Beaubourg, the second, Rue Michel le Comte, the third, Rue du Temple, were plundered, and in a few minutes the thousand hands of the mob seized and carried off two hundred and thirty guns, nearly all double-barreled, sixty-four sabers, and eighty-three pistols. In order to arm as many persons as possible, one took the musket, the other the bayonet. Opposite the Quai de la Grève young men armed with muskets stationed themselves in the rooms of some ladies in order to fire; one of them had a wheel-lock gun. They rang, went in, and began making cartridges, and one of the ladies said afterward: "I did not know what cartridges were till my husband told me." A crowd broke into a curiosity shop on the Rue des Vieilles-Haudriettes, and took from it yataghans and Turkish weapons. The corpse of a mason killed by a bullet lay in the Rue de la Perle. And then, on the right bank and the left bank, on the quays, on the boulevards, in the Quartier Latin, and on the Quartier of the Halles, panting men, workmen, students, and sectionists read proclamations, shouted: "To arms!" broke the lanterns, unharnessed vehicles, tore up the pavement, broke in the doors of houses, uprooted trees, searched cellars, rolled up barrels, heaped up paving-stones, furniture, and planks, and formed barricades.

Citizens were forced to lend a hand; the rioters went to the wives, compelled them to surrender the saber and musket of their absent husbands, and then wrote on the door in chalk, *The arms are given up*. Some signed with their own names receipts for musket and saber, and said, *Send for them to-morrow at the Mayoralty*. Isolated sentries and National Guards proceeding to their gathering-place were disarmed in the streets. Epaulettes were torn from the officers, and in the Rue du Cimitière St. Nicholas, an officer of the National Guard, pursued by a party armed with sticks and foils, found refuge with great difficulty in a house, where he was compelled to remain till night, and then went away in disguise. In the Quartier St. Jacques the students came out of their lodging-houses in swarms, and went up the Rue Ste. Hyacinthe to the Café du Progres or down to the Café des Sept Billiards in the Rue des Mathurins, there the young men stood on benches and distributed arms; and the timber-yard in the Rue Transnonain was pillaged to make barricades. Only at one spot did the inhabitants offer resistance, at the corner of the Rue St. Avoye and Simon-le-Franc, where they themselves destroyed the barricade. Only at one point, too, did the insurgents give way; they abandoned a barricade begun in the Rue du Temple, after firing at a detachment of the National Guard, and fled along the Rue de la Corderie. The detachment picked up on the barricade a red flag, a packet of cartridges, and three hundred pistol bullets; the National Guards tore up the flag and carried off the strips on the point of their bayonets. All this, which we are describing here slowly and successively, was going on simultaneously at all parts of the city, in the midst of a vast tumult, like a number of lightning flashes in a single peal of thunder. In less than an hour twenty-seven barricades issued from the ground in the single quarter of the Halles; in the center was that famous No. 50, which was the fortress of Jeanne and her hundred-and-six companions, and which, flanked on one side by a barricade at St. Merry, and on the other by a barricade in the Rue Maubuée, commanded the three streets, des Arcis, St. Martin, and Aubry le Boucher, the last of which it faced. Two barricades at right angles extended one from the Rue Montorgueil to the Grand Truanderie, the other from the Rue Geoffroy-Langevin to the Rue Sainte Avoye. This is without counting innumerable barricades in twenty other districts of Paris, as the Marais and the Montagne Ste. Geneviève; one in the Rue Menilmontant, in which a gate could be seen torn off its hinges; and another near the little bridge of the Hotel Dieu, made of an overthrown vehicle, three hundred yards from the prefecture of police. At the barricade in the Rue des Ménétriers a well-dressed man distributed money to the artisans; at the barricade in the Rue Grenéta a horseman rode up and handed to the man who seemed to be chief of the barricade a roll, which looked like money. "Here," he said, "is something to pay the expenses,—the wine, etc." A light-haired young man, without a cravat, went from one barricade to another, carrying the passwords, and another, with drawn saber and a blue forage-cap on his head, stationed sentries. In the interior, within the barricades, the wine-shops and cabarets were converted into guard-rooms, and the riot was managed in accordance with the most skillful military tactics. The narrow, uneven, winding streets, full of corners and turnings, were admirably selected,—the vicinity of the Halles more especially, a network of streets more tangled than a forest. The society of the Friends of the People had, it was said, taken the direction of the insurrection in the St. Avoye district, and a plan of Paris was found on the body of a man killed in the Rue du Ponceau.

What had really assumed the direction of the insurrection was a sort of unknown impetuosity that was in the atmosphere. The insurrection had suddenly built barricades with one hand, and with the other seized nearly all the garrison posts. In less than three hours the insurgents, like a powder-train fired, had seized and occupied on the right bank the Arsenal, the Place Royal, the Marais, the Popincourt arms factory, the Galiote, the Château d'Eau, and all the streets near the Halles; on the left bank the veterans' barracks, Ste. Pelagie, the Place Maubert, the powder manufactory of the Two-mills, and all the barrières. At five in the evening they were masters of the Bastille, the Lingerie, and the Blanc-Manteaux; while their scouts were close to the Place de Victoires and menaced the bank, the barracks of the Petits-Pères, and the post-office. One-third of Paris was in the hands of the revolt. On all points the struggle had begun on a gigantic scale, and the result of the disarmaments, the domiciliary visits, and the attack on the gunsmiths' shops was that the fight which had begun with stone-throwing was continued with musket-shots.

About six in the evening the Passage du Sauman became the battle-field; the rioters were at one end and the troops at the other, and they fired from one gate at the other. An observer, a dreamer, the author of this book, who had gone to have a near look at the volcano, found himself caught between two fires in the passage, and had nothing to protect him from the bullets but the projecting semi-columns which used to separate the shops; he was nearly half an hour in this delicate position. In the meanwhile the tattoo was beaten, the National Guards hurriedly dressed and armed themselves, the legions issued from the mayoralties, and the regiments from the barracks. Opposite Passage de l'Ancre a drummer was stabbed; another was attacked in the Rue de Cygne by thirty young men, who ripped up his drum and took his saber, while a third was killed in the Rue Grenier St. Lazare. In the Rue Michel le Comte three officers fell dead one after the other, and several municipal guards, wounded in the Rue des Lombards, recoiled. In front of the Cour Batave, a detachment of National Guards found a red flag, bearing this inscription, *"Republican Revolution, No. 127."* Was it really a revolution? The insurrection had made of the heart of Paris a sort of inextricable, tortuous, and colossal citadel; there was the nucleus, there the question would be solved; all the rest was merely skirmishing. The proof that all would be decided there lay in the fact that fighting had not yet begun there.

In some regiments the troops were uncertain, which added to the startling obscurity of the crisis; and they remembered the popular ovation which, in July, 1830, greeted the neutrality of the 53rd line. Two intrepid men, tried by the great wars, Marshal de Lobau and General Bugeaud, commanded—Bugeaud under Lobau. Enormous patrols, composed of battalions of the line inclosed in entire companies of the National Guard, and preceded by the police commissary in his scarf, went to reconnoiter the insurgent streets. On their side the insurgents posted videttes at the corner of the streets, and audaciously sent patrols beyond the barricades. Both sides were observing each other; the government, with an army in its hand, hesitated; night was setting in, and the tocsin of St. Merry was beginning to be heard. Marshal Soult, the minister of war at that day, who had seen Austerlitz, looked at all this with a gloomy air. These old sailors, habituated to correct maneuvers, and having no other resource and guide but tactics, the compass of battles, are completely thrown out when in the presence of that immense foam which is called the public anger. The wind of revolutions is not favorable for sailing. The National Guards of the suburbs ran up hastily and disorderly; a battalion of the 12th Light Infantry came at the double from St. Denis; the 14th line arrived from Courbevoie, the batteries of the military school had taken up position at the Carrousel, and guns were brought in from Vincennes.

At the Tuileries there was not an additional sentry posted, and Louis Philippe was full of serenity.

5. ORIGINALITY OF PARIS

DURING the two past years Paris, as we have said, had seen more than one insurrection. With the exception of the insurgent districts, as a rule, nothing is more strangely calm than the physiognomy of Paris during a riot. Paris very soon grows accustomed to everything—it is only a riot—

and Paris has so much to do that it does not put itself out of the way for such a trifle. These colossal cities alone can offer such spectacles. These immense inclosures alone can contain simultaneously civil war and a strange tranquillity. Usually, when the insurrection begins, when the drum, the tattoo, and the assembly are heard, the shopkeeper confines himself to saying:

"Ah, there seems to be a row in the Rue St. Martin."

Or: "The Faubourg St. Antoine."

And he often adds, negligently: "Somewhere over that way."

At a later date, when the heart-rending and mournful sound of musketry and platoon fire can be distinguished, the shopkeeper says: "Bless me, it is growing hot."

A moment later, if the riot approaches and spreads, he precipitately closes his shop and puts on his uniform, that is to say, places his wares in safety and risks his person. Men shoot one another on a square, in a passage, or a blind alley; barricades are taken, lost, and retaken, blood flows, the grape-shot pockmark the fronts of the houses, bullets kill people on their beds, and corpses encumber the pavement. A few yards off you hear the click of the billiard-balls in the coffee-houses. The theaters open their doors and play farces; and gossips talk and laugh two yards from these streets full of war. Hackney coaches roll along, and their fares are going to dine out, sometimes in the very district where the fighting is. In 1831 a fusillade was interrupted in order to let a wedding pass. During the insurrection of May 12, 1839, in the Rue St. Martin, a little old infirm man, dragging a hand truck surmounted by a tricolor rag, and carrying bottles full of some fluid, came and went from the barricade to the troops, and from the troops to the barricade, impartially offering glasses of cocoa, first to the government and then to anarchy. Nothing can be stranger, and this is the peculiar character of Parisian riots, which is not found in any other capital, as two things are required for it—the grandeur of Paris and its gayety, the city of Voltaire and of Napoleon. This time, however, in the insurrection of June 5, 1832, the great city felt something which was perhaps stronger than itself, and was frightened. Everywhere, in the most remote and "disinterested" districts, doors, windows, and shutters were closed in broad daylight. The courageous armed, the cowardly hid themselves, and the careless and busy passengers disappeared. Many streets were as empty as at four in the morning. Alarming details were hawked about, and fatal news spread—that *they* were masters of the bank—that at the cloisters of St. Merry alone, they were six hundred, intrenched with loopholes in a church—that the line was sure—that Armand Carrel had been to see Marshal Clausel, and the latter said to him, *Have a regiment first*—that Lafayette, though ill, had said to them, *I am with you and will follow you wherever there is room for a chair*—that people must be on their guard, for at night burglars would plunder isolated houses in the deserted corners of Paris (in this could be recognized the imagination of the police, that Anne Ratcliffe blended with authority)—that a battery had been established in the Rue Aubry-le-Boucher—that Lobau and Bugeaud were agreed, and that at midnight, or at daybreak at the latest, four columns would march together on the center of the revolt, the first coming from the Bastille, the second from the Porte St. Martin, the third from the Grève, and the fourth from the Halles—that perhaps, too, the troops would evacuate Paris, and retire on the Champ de Mars—that no one knew what would happen, but this time it was certainly very serious. People were alarmed, too, by the hesitation of Marshal Soult; why did he not attack at once? It is certain that he was greatly absorbed, and the old lion seemed to scent an unknown monster in the darkness.

Night came, and the theaters were not opened, the patrols went their rounds with an air of irritation, passers-by were searched and suspected persons were arrested. At nine o'clock there were more than eight hundred persons taken up, and the Prefecture of Police, the Conciergerie, and La Force were crowded. At the Conciergerie, especially, the long vault called the Rue de Paris was strewn with trusses of straw, on which lay a pile of prisoners, whom Lagrange, the man of Lyons, valiantly harangued. All this straw, moved by all these men, produced the sound of a shower. Elsewhere the prisoners slept in the open air on lawns. There was anxiety everywhere, and a certain trembling, not at all usual to Paris. People barricaded themselves in the houses; wives and mothers were alarmed, and nothing else but this was heard, *Oh heavens! he has not come in!* Only the rolling of a few vehicles could be heard in the distance, and the people listened in the doorways to the noises, cries, tumults, and dull, indistinct sounds, of which they said, *That is the cavalry,* or *It is the galloping of tumbrils;* to the bugles, the drums, the firing, and before all to the lamentable tocsin of St. Merry. They waited for the first sound of artillery, and men rose at the corner of the streets and disappeared, after shouting "Go in." And they hastened to bolt their doors, saying, *How will it all end?* From moment to moment, as the night became darker, Paris seemed to be more lugubriously colored by formidable flashes of revolt.

BOOK XI

THE ATOM FRATERNIZES WITH THE HURRICANE

1. EXPLANATIONS OF THE ORIGIN OF GAVROCHE'S POETRY

AT the moment when the insurrection, breaking out through the collision between the people and the troops in front of the arsenal, produced a retrograde movement in the multitude that followed the hearse, and which pressed with the whole length of the boulevards upon the head of the procession, there was a frightful reflux. The ranks were broken, and all ran or escaped, some with cries of attack, others with the pallor of flight. The great stream which covered the boulevards divided in a second, overflowed on the right and left, and spread in torrents over two hundred streets at once as if a dyke had burst. At this moment a ragged lad who was coming down the Rue Menilmontant, holding in his hand a branch of flowering laburnum which he had picked on the heights of Belleville, noticed in the shop of a seller of curiosities an old holster-pistol. He threw his branch on the pavement and cried:

"Mother What's-your-name, I'll borrow your machine."

And he ran off with the pistol. Two minutes after a crowd of frightened cits flying through the Rue Basse met the lad, who was brandishing his pistol and singing:

> *La nuit on ne voit rien,*
> *Le jour on voit très bien,*
> *D'un écrit apocryphe*
> *Le bourgeois s'ébouriffe*
> *Pratiquez la vertu,*
> *Tutu chapeau pointu!*

It was little Gavroche going to the wars. On the boulevard he noticed that his pistol had no hammer. Who was the composer of this couplet which served to punctuate his march, and all the other songs which he was fond of singing when he had a chance? who knows? himself, perhaps. Besides, Gavroche was acquainted with all the popular tunes in circulation, and mingled with them his own chirping, and, as a young vagabond, he made a *pot-pourri* of the voices of nature and the voices of Paris. He combined the repertory of the birds with that of the workshops, and he was acquainted with artists' grinders, a tribe contiguous to his own. He had been for three months, it appears, apprenticed to a painter, and had one day delivered a message for M. Baour Lormian, one of the forty; Gavroche was a lettered gamin. Gavroche did not suspect, however, that on that wretched rainy night when he offered the hospitality of his elephant to the two boys he was performing the offices of Providence to his two brothers. His brothers in the evening, his father in the morning,—such had been his night. On leaving the Rue des Ballets at dawn, he hurried back to the elephant, artistically extracted the two boys, shared with them the sort of breakfast which he had invented, and then went away, confiding them to that good mother, the street, who had almost brought himself up. On leaving them he arranged to meet them on the same spot at night and left them this speech as farewell,—"I am breaking a cane, *alias* my name's Walker, or, as they say at court, I am going to hook it. My brats, if you do not find papa and mamma, come here again to-night. I will give you your supper and put you to bed." The two lads, picked up by some policeman and placed at the depôt, or stolen by some mountebank, or simply lost in that Chinese puzzle, Paris, did not return. The substrata of the existing social world are full of such lost traces. Gavroche had not seen them again, and ten or twelve weeks had elapsed since that night. More than once he had scratched his head and asked himself, "Where the deuce are my two children?"

He reached the Rue du Pont aux Choux, and noticed that there was only one shop still open in that street, and it was worthy of reflection that it was a confectioner's. It was a providential opportunity to eat one more apple-puff before entering the unknown. Gavroche stopped, felt in his pockets, turned them inside out, found nothing, not even a sou, and began shouting, "Help!" It is hard to go without the last cake, but for all that Gavroche went on his way. Two minutes after he was in the Rue St. Louis, and on crossing the Rue du Parc Royal he felt the necessity of compensating himself for the impossible apple-puff, and gave himself the immense treat of tearing down in open daylight the play-bills. A little further on, seeing a party of stout gentry who appeared to him to be retired from business, he shrugged his shoulders and spat out this mouthful of philosophic bile:

"How fat annuitants are! they wallow in good dinners. Ask them what they do with their money, and they don't know. They eat it, eat their bellyful."

2. GAVROCHE ON THE MARCH

HOLDING a pistol without a cock in the streets is such a public function, that Gavroche felt his audacity increase at every step. He cried between the scraps of the Marseillaise which he sang:

"All goes well. I suffer considerably in my left paw. I have broken my rheumatism, but I am happy, citizens. The bourgeois have only to hold firm, and I am going to sing them some subversive couplets. What are the police? dogs; after all," he added thinking of the hammer* missing from his pistol, "we must not treat all dogs disrespectfully. I have just come from the boulevard, my friends, where it is getting warm, and the soup is simmering; it is time to skim the pot. Forward, my men, and let an impure blood inundate the furrows! I give my days for my country. I shall not see my concubine again, it's all over. Well, no matter! long live joy! let us fight, crebleu, for I have had enough of despotism!"

At this moment the horse of a lancer, in the National Guard, who was passing, fell. Gavroche laid his pistol on the pavement, helped the man up, and then helped to raise the horse, after which he picked up his pistol, and went his way again. In the Rue de Thorigny all was peace

* An untranslatable pun, as the hammer of a pistol is called a dog in France.

and silence; and this apathy, peculiar to the Marais, contrasted with the vast surrounding turmoil. Four gossips were conversing on the step of a door; Scotland has trios of witches, but Paris has quartettes of gossips, and the "thou shalt be king" would be as lugubriously cast at Bonaparte at the Baudoyer crossway, as to Macbeth on the Highland heath—it would be much the same croak. The gossips in the Rue de Thorigny only trouble themselves about their own affairs; they were three port-resses, and a rag-picker with her dorser and her hook. They seemed to be standing all four at the four corners of old age, which are decay, de-crepitude, ruin, and sorrow. The rag-picker was humble, for in this open-air world the rag-picker bows, and the portress protects. The things thrown into the street are fat and lean, according to the fancy of the person who makes the pile, and there may be kindness in the broom. This rag-picker was grateful, and she smiled, what a smile! at the three portresses. They were making remarks like the following:

"So your cat is as ill-tempered as ever?"

"Well, good gracious, you know that cats are naturally the enemy of dogs. It's the dogs that complain."

"And people too."

"And yet cats' fleas do not run after people."

"Dogs are really dangerous. I remember one year when there were so many dogs that they were obliged to put it in the papers. It was at that time when there were large sheep at the Tuileries to drag the little carriage of the king of Rome. Do you remember the king of Rome?"

"I liked the Duc de Bordeaux better."

"Well, I know Louis XVII, and I like him better."

"How dear meat is, Mame Patagon!"

"Oh, don't talk about it, butcher's meat is a horror, a horrible horror. It is only possible to buy coarse pieces now."

Here the rag-picker interposed:

"Ladies, trade does not go on well at all, and the rubbish is abominable. People do not throw away anything now, but eat it all."

"There are poorer folk than you, Vargoulême."

"Ah, that's true," the rag-picker replied deferentially, "for I have a profession."

There was a pause, and the rag-picker, yielding to that need of display which is at the bottom of the human heart, added:

"When I go home in the morning I empty out my basket and sort the articles; that makes piles in my room. I put the rags in a box, the cabbage-stalks in a tub, the pieces of linen in my cupboard, the woolen rags in my chest of drawers, old papers on the corner of the window, things good to eat in my porringer, pieces of glass in the fire-place, old shoes behind the door, and bones under my bed."

Gavroche had stopped and was listening.

"Aged dames," he said, "What right have you to talk politics?"

A broadside, composed of a quadruple yell, assailed him.

"There's another of the villains."

"What's that he has in his hand? a pistol?"

"Just think, that rogue of a boy!"

"They are never quiet unless when they are overthrowing the authorities."

Gavroche disdainfully limited his reprisals to lifting the tip of his nose with his thumb, and opening his hand to the full extent. The rag-picker exclaimed:

"The barefooted scamp!"

The one who answered to the name of Mame Patagon struck her hands together with scandal.

"There are going to be misfortunes, that's safe. The young fellow with the beard round the corner, I used to see him pass every morning with a girl in a pink bonnet on his arm; but this morning I saw him pass, and he was giving his arm to a gun. Mame Bacheux says there was a revolution last week at, at, at, at,—where do the calves come from?— at Pontoise. And then, just look at this atrocious young villain's pistol. It seems that the Celestins are full of cannon. What would you have the government do with these vagabonds who can only invent ways to upset the world, after we were beginning to get over all the misfortunes which fell, good gracious! on that poor queen whom I saw pass in a cart? and all this will raise the price of snuff. It is infamous, and I will certainly go and see you guillotined, malefactor."

"You snuffle, my aged friend," said Gavroche, "blow your promontory."

And he passed on. When he was in the Rue Pavée his thoughts reverted to the rag-picker, and he had this soliloquy:

"You are wrong to insult the Revolutionists, Mother Cornerpost. This pistol is on your behalf, and it is for you to have in your basket more things good to eat."

All at once he heard a noise behind; it was the portress Patagon, who had followed him and now shook her fist at him, crying:

"You are only a bastard."

"At that I scoff with all my heart," said Gavroche.

A little later he passed the Hotel Lamoignon, where he burst into this appeal:

"Let us haste to the battle."

And he was attacked by a fit of melancholy; he regarded his pistol reproachfully, and said to it:

"I am going off, but you will not go off."

One dog may distract from another,* a very thin whelp passed, and Gavroche felt pity for it.

"My poor little creature," he said to it, "you must have swallowed a barrel, as you show all the hoops."

Then he proceeded toward the Orme St. Gervais.

3. *JUST INDIGNATION OF A WIG-MAKER*

THE worthy barber who had turned out the two children for whom Gavroche had opened the elephant's paternal intestines, was at this moment in his shop, engaged in shaving an old legionary who had served under the empire. The barber had naturally spoken to the veteran about the riot, then about General Lamarque, and from Lamarque they had come to the emperor. Hence arose a conversation between the barber and the soldier, which Prudhomme, had he been present, would have enriched with arabesques, and entitled, *A dialogue between a razor and a saber.*

"How did the emperor ride, sir?" the barber asked.

"Badly. He did not know how to fall off, and so he never fell off."

* Another allusion to the hammer (chien) of the pistol.

"Had he fine horses? he must have had fine horses!"

"On the day when he gave me the cross I noticed his beast. It was a white mare. It had its ears very far apart, a deep saddle, a fine head, marked with a black star, a very long neck, prominent knees, projecting flanks, oblique shoulders, and a strong crupper. It was a little above fifteen hands high."

"A fine horse," said the barber.

"It was his majesty's animal."

The barber felt that after this remark a little silence was befitting; then he went on:

"The emperor was only wounded once, I believe, sir?"

The old soldier replied, with the calm and sovereign accent of the man who has felt wounds:

"In the heel, at Ratisbon. I never saw him so well dressed as on that day. He was as clean as a half-penny."

"And you, sir, I suppose, have received sword-wounds?"

"I," said the soldier, "oh, a mere flea-bite. I received two saber-cuts on my neck at Marengo, I got a bullet in my right arm at Jena, another in the left hip at Jena; at Friedland a bayonet-thrust—there; at the Muskowa seven or eight lance-prods, never mind where; at Lützen, a piece of shell carried off a finger, and—oh yes! at Waterloo a bullet from a case-shot in my thigh. That's all."

"How glorious it is," the barber exclaimed, with a Pindaric accent, "to die on the battle-field! on my word of honor, sooner than die on a bed of disease, slowly, a bit every day, with drugs, cataplasms, clysters, and medicine, I would sooner have a cannon-ball in my stomach!"

"And you're right," said the soldier. He had scarce ended ere a frightful noise shook the shop; a great pane of glass was suddenly smashed. The barber turned livid.

"Good Lord," he cried, "it is one."

"What?"

"A cannon-ball."

"Here it is."

And he picked up something which was rolling on the ground—it was a pebble. The barber ran to his broken pane, and saw Gavroche flying at full speed toward the Marché St. Jean. On passing the barber's shop Gavroche, who had the two lads at his heart, could not resist the desire of wishing him good-evening, and threw a stone through his window.

"Just look," the barber yelled, who had become blue instead of livid, "he does harm for harm's sake. What had I done to that villain?"

4. THE CHILD ASTONISHES THE OLD MAN

ON reaching the Marché Saint Jean, the post at which he had been disarmed already, Gavroche effected his junction with a band led by Enjolras, Courfeyrac, Combeferre, and Feuilly. They were all more or less armed, and Bahorel and Prouvaire had joined them and swelled the group. Enjolras had a double-barreled fowling-piece, Combeferre a National Guard's musket bearing the number of a legion, and in his waist-belt two pistols, which his unbuttoned coat allowed to be seen; Jean Prouvaire an old cavalry musketoon, and Bahorel a carbine; Courfeyrac brandished a sword drawn from a cane, while Feuilly, with a naked saber in his hand, walked along shouting, "Long live Poland!" They reached the Quai Morland without neckcloths or hats, panting for breath, drenched with rain, but with lightning in their eyes. Gavroche calmly approached them:

"Where are we going?"

"Come," said Courfeyrac.

Behind Feuilly marched or rather bounded Bahorel, a fish in the water of revolt. He had a crimson waistcoat, and uttered words which smash everything. His waistcoat upset a passer-by, who cried wildly, "Here are the reds!"

"The reds, the reds," Bahorel answered, "that's a funny fear, citizen. For my part, I do not tremble at a poppy, and the little red cap does not inspire me with any terror. Citizen, believe me, let us leave a fear of the red to horned cattle."

He noticed a corner wall, on which was placarded the most peaceful piece of paper in the world, a permission to eat eggs, a Lent mandamus addressed by the archbishop of Paris to his "flock." Bahorel exclaimed:

"A flock! a polite way of saying geese." And he tore the paper down. This conquered Gavroche and from this moment he began studying Bahorel.

"Bahorel," Enjolras observed, "you are wrong, you should have left that order alone, for we have nothing to do with it, and you needlessly expended your passion. Keep your stock by you; a man does not fire out of the ranks any more with his mind than with his gun."

"Every man has his own way, Enjolras," Bahorel replied: "the bishop's prose offends me, and I insist on eating eggs without receiving permission to do so. Yours is the cold burning style, while I amuse myself; moreover I am not expending myself, but getting the steam up, and if I tore that order down, Hercle! it is to give me an appetite."

This word *hercle* struck Gavroche, for he sought every opportunity of instructing himself, and this tearing down of posters possessed his esteem. Hence he asked:

"What's the meaning of *hercle*?"

Bahorel answered:

"It means cursed name of a dog in Latin."

Here Bahorel noticed at a window a young pale man, with a black beard, who was watching them pass, probably a friend of the A. B. C. He shouted to him:

"Quick with the cartridges, *para bellum*."

"A handsome man (bel homme), that's true," said Gavroche, who now comprehended Latin.

A tumultuous crowd accompanied them—students, artists, young men affiliated to the Cougourde of Aix, artisans, and lightermen, armed with sticks and bayonets, and some, like Combeferre, with pistols passed through their trouser-belt. An old man, who appeared very aged, marched in this band. He had no weapon, and hurried on, that he might not be left behind, though he looked thoughtful.

Gavroche caught sight of him.

"What's dat?" he said to Courfeyrac.

"An old man."

It was M. Mabœuf.

5. *THE OLD MAN*

WE will tell what had occurred. Enjolras and his friends were on the Bourdon Boulevard near the granaries, at the moment when the dragoons charged, and Enjolras, Courfeyrac, and Combeferre were among those who turned into the Rue Bassompierre shouting "To the barricades!" In the Rue Lesdiguières they met an old man walking along, and what attracted their attention was that he was moving very irregularly, as if intoxicated. Moreover, he had his hat in his hand, although it had rained the whole morning and was raining rather hard at that very moment. Courfeyrac recognized Father Mabœuf, whom he knew through having accompanied Marius sometimes as far as his door. Knowing the peaceful and more than timid habits of the churchwarden and bibliomaniac, and stupefied at seeing him in the midst of the tumult, within two yards of cavalry charges, almost in the midst of the musketry fire, bareheaded in the rain, and walking about among bullets, he accosted him, and the rebel of five-and-twenty and the octogenarian exchanged this dialogue.

"Monsieur Mabœuf, you had better go home."

"Why so?"

"There is going to be a row."

"Very good."

"Saber-cuts and shots, M. Mabœuf."

"Very good."

"Cannon-shots."

"Very good. Where are you gentlemen going?"

"To upset the government."

"Very good."

And he began following them, but since that moment had not said a word. His step had become suddenly firm, and when workmen offered him an arm, he declined it with a shake of the head. He walked almost at the head of the column, having at once the command of a man who is marching and the face of a man who is asleep.

"What a determined old fellow!" the students muttered, and the rumor ran along the party that he was an ex-conventionalist, an old regicide. The band turned into the Rue de la Verrerie, and little Gavroche marched at the head, singing at the top of his voice, which made him resemble a bugler. He sang:

> Voici la lune qui paraît,
> Quand irons-nous dans la forêt?
> Demandait Charlot à Charlotte.
>
> Tou tou tou
> Pour Chatou,
> Je n'ai qu'un Dieu, qu'un roi, qu'un liard, et
> qu'une botte.
>
> Pour avoir bu de grand matin
> La rosée à même le thym,
> Deux moineaux étaient en ribotte.
>
> Zi zi zi
> Pour Passy.
> Je n'ai qu'un Dieu, qu'un roi, qu'un liard, et
> qu'une botte.
>
> Et ces deux pauvres petits loups
> Comme deux grives étaient soûls;
> Un tigre en riait dans sa grotte.
>
> Don don don
> Pour Meudon.
> Je n'ai qu'un Dieu, qu'un roi, qu'un liard, et
> qu'une botte.
>
> L'un jurait et l'autre sacrait,
> Quand irons-nous dans la forêt?
> Demandait Charlot à Charlotte.

Tin tin tin
Pour Pantin
Je n'ai qu'un Dieu, qu'un roi, qu'un liard, et
qu'une botte.

They were going toward St. Merry.

6. *RECRUITS*

THE band swelled every moment, and near the Rue des Billettes, a tall, grayish-haired man, whose rough bold face Courfeyrac, Enjolras, and Combeferre noticed, though not one of them knew him, joined them. Gavroche, busy singing, whistling, and shouting, and rapping on the window-shutters with his pistol-butt, paid no attention to this man. As they went through the Rue de la Verrerie they happened to pass Courfeyrac's door.

"That's lucky," said Courfeyrac, "for I have forgotten my purse and lost my hat."

He left the band and bounded upstairs, where he put on an old hat and put his purse in his pocket. He also took up a large square box of the size of a portmanteau, which was concealed among his dirty linen. As he was running downstairs again his portress hailed him:

"Monsieur de Courfeyrac!"

"Portress, what is your name?" Courfeyrac retorted.

She stood in stupefaction.

"Why, you know very well, sir, that my name is Mother Veuvain."

"Well, then, if ever you call me M. de Courfeyrac again, I shall call you Mother de Veuvain; now speak, what is it?"

"Some one wishes to speak to you."

266

"Who is it?"

"I don't know."

"Where is he?"

"In my lodge."

"Oh, the devil!" said Courfeyrac.

"Why, he has been waiting for more than an hour for you to come in."

At the same time a species of a young workman, thin, livid, small, marked with freckles, dressed in an old blouse and a pair of patched cotton-velvet trousers, who looked more like a girl attired as a boy than a man, stepped out of the lodge and said to Courfeyrac in a voice which was not the least in the world a feminine voice:

"Monsieur Marius, if you please?"

"He is not here."

"Will he come to-night?"

"I do not know."

And Courfeyrac added, "I shall not be in to-night."

The young man looked at him intently and asked:

"Why not?"

"Because I shall not."

"Where are you going?"

"How does that concern you?"

"Shall I carry your chest for you?"

"I am going to the barricades."

"May I go with you?"

"If you like," Courfeyrac replied; "the street is free, and the pavement. belongs to everybody."

And he ran off to join his friends again; when he had done so, he gave one of them the box to carry, and it was not till a quarter of an hour after that he noticed that the young man was really following them. A band does not go exactly where it wishes, and we have explained that a puff of wind directs it. They passed St. Merry, and found themselves, without knowing exactly why, in the Rue St. Denis.

BOOK XII

CORINTH

I. HISTORY OF CORINTH FROM ITS FOUNDATION

THE Parisians, who at the present day on entering the Rue Rambu-teau from the side of the Halles notice on their right, opposite the Rue de Mondétour, a basket-maker's shop having for sign a basket in the shape of Napoleon the Great, with this inscription:

NAPOLEON EST FAIT
TOUT EN OSIER,—

do not suspect the terrible scenes which this very site saw hardly thirty years ago. Here were the Rue de la Chanvrerie, which old title-deeds write Chanvrerie, and the celebrated wine-shop called Corinth. Our readers will remember all that has been said about the barricade erected at this spot, and eclipsed, by the way, by the St. Merry barricade. It is on this famous barricade of the Rue de la Chanvrerie, which has now fallen into deep night, that we are going to throw a little light.

For the clearness of our narrative, we may be permitted to have re-course to the simple mode which we employed for Waterloo. Those persons who wish to represent to themselves in a tolerably exact manner the mass of houses which at that day stood at the north-east corner of the Halles, at the spot where the opening of the Rue Rambuteau now is, need only imagine an N whose two vertical strokes are the Rue de la Grande Truanderie, and the Rue de la Chanvrerie, and of which the Rue de la Petite Truanderie would be the cross-stroke. The old Rue Mondétour intersected the three strokes with the most tortuous angles, so that the Dædalian entanglement of these four streets was sufficient to make upon a space of one hundred square yards, between the Halles

and the Rue St. Denis on one side, between the Rue du Cygne and the
Rue des Prêcheurs on the other side, seven islets of houses, strangely cut,
of different heights, standing sideways, and as if accidentally, and scarce
separated by narrow cracks, like the blocks of stone in a dock. We say
narrow cracks and cannot give a fairer idea of these obscure, narrow,
angular lanes, bordered by tenements eight stories in height. These
houses were so decrepit that in the Rues de la Chanvrerie and La Petite
Truanderie the frontages were supported by beams running across from
one house to the other. The street was narrow and the gutter wide; the
passer-by walked on a constantly damp pavement, passing shops like
cellars, heavy posts shod with iron, enormous piles of filth, and gates
armed with extraordinarily old palings. The Rue Rambuteau has devas-
tated all this. The name of Mondétour exactly describes the windings
of all this laystall. A little further on it was found even better expressed
by the Rue Pirouette, which threw itself into the Rue Mondétour. The
wayfarer who turned out of the Rue St. Denis into the Rue de la
Chanvrerie saw it gradually contract before him, as if he had entered
an elongated funnel. At the end of the street, which was very short,
he found the passage barred on the side of the Halles by a tall row of
houses, and he might have fancied himself in a blind alley had he not
perceived on his right and left two black cuts through which he could
escape. It was the Rue Mondétour, which joined on one side the Rue des
Prêcheurs, on the other the Rue du Cygne. At the end of this sort of blind
alley, at the corner of the right-hand cutting, a house lower than the
rest, forming a species of cape in the street, might be noticed. It is in this
house, only two stories high, that an illustrious cabaret had been installed
for more than three hundred years. This inn produced a joyous noise
at the very spot which old Théophile indicated in the two lines:

Là branle le squelette horrible
D'un pauvre amant qui se pendit.

The spot was good, and the landlords succeeded each other from
father to son. In the time of Mathurin Régnier this inn was called the
"Rose-pot," and as rebuses were fashionable, it had as sign a post painted
pink, which represented a "Poteau rose," hence the pot-aux-roses. In
the last century worthy Natoire, one of the fantastic masters disdained
at the present day by the stiff school, having got tipsy several times in
this inn at the same table where Régnier had got drunk, painted out of

gratitude a bunch of currants on the pink post. The landlord, in his delight, changed his sign, and had the words gilt under the bunch, *au raisin de Corinthe,* hence the name of Corinth. Nothing is more natural to drunkards than ellipses, for they are the zigzags of language. Corinth had gradually dethroned the rose-pot, and the last landlord of the dynasty, Father Hucheloup, being not acquainted with the tradition, had the post painted blue.

A ground-floor in which was the bar, a second-floor room in which was a billiard-table, a spiral wooden staircase piercing the ceiling, wine on the tables, smoke on the walls, and candles by daylight—such was the inn. A staircase with a trap in the ground-floor room led to the cellar, and the apartments of the Hucheloups were on the third-floor, reached by a staircase more like a ladder, and through a door hidden in the wall of a large second-floor room. Under the roof were two garrets, the nests of the maid-servants, and the kitchen shared the ground-floor with the bar. Father Hucheloup might have been born a chemist, but was really a cook, and customers not only drank but ate in his wine-shop. Hucheloup had invented an excellent dish, which could only be eaten at his establishment; it was stuffed carp, which he called *carpes au gras.* This was eaten by the light of a tallow candle or a lamp of the Louis XVI style, on tables on which oil-cloth was nailed in lieu of a table-cloth. People came from a long distance, and Hucheloup one fine morning had thought it advisable to inform passers-by of his "specialty"; he dipped a brush in a pot of blacking, and as he had an orthography of his own, he improvised on his wall the following remarkable inscription,

CARPES HO GRAS.

One winter the showers and the hail amused themselves with effacing the s which terminated the first word, and the G which began the last, and the following was left,

CARPE HO RAS.

By the aid of time and rain an humble gastronomic notice had become a profound counsel. In this way it happened that Hucheloup, not knowing French, had known Latin, had brought philosophy out of the kitchen, and, while simply wishing to efface Carême, equaled Horace. And the striking thing was that this also meant "Enter my inn." Nothing of all this exists at the present day; the Mondétour labyrinth was gutted and widened in 1847, and probably is no longer to be found at the present day. The Rue de la Chanvrerie and Corinth have disappeared under the pavement of the Rue Rambuteau. As we have said, Corinth was a meeting-place, if not a gathering-place, of Courfeyrac and his friends, and it was Grantaire who discovered it. He went in for the sake of the *carpe ho ras* and returned for the sake of the carp *au gras*. People drank there, ate there, and made a row there; they paid little, paid badly, or paid not at all, but were always welcome. Father Hucheloup was a worthy fellow. Hucheloup, whom we have just called a worthy fellow, was an eating-house keeper with a mustache, an amusing variety. He always looked ill-tempered, appeared wishful to intimidate his customers, growled at persons who came in, and seemed more disposed to quarrel with them than serve them. And yet we maintain people were always welcome. This peculiarity filled his bar, and brought to him young men who said, "Let us go and have a look at Father Hucheloup." He had been a fencing-master, and would suddenly break out into a laugh; he had a rough voice, but was a merry fellow. His was a comic foundation with a tragic look; and he asked for nothing better than to frighten you, something like the snuff-boxes which had the shape of a pistol—the detonation produces a sneeze. He had for wife a Mother Hucheloup, a bearded and very ugly being. About 1830 Father Hucheloup died, and with him disappeared the secret of the carp *au gras*. His widow, who was almost inconsolable, carried on the business, but the cooking degenerated and became execrable, and the wine, which had always been bad, was frightful. Courfeyrac and his friends, however, continued to go to Corinth—through pity, said Bossuet.

Widow Hucheloup was short of breath and shapeless, and had rustic recollections, which she deprived of their insipidity by her pronunciation. She had a way of her own of saying things which seasoned her reminiscences of her village and the spring; it had formerly been her delight, she declared, to hear "the red-beasts singing in the awe-thorns."* The second-floor room, where the restaurant was, was a large, long apartment, crowded with stools, chairs, benches, and tables, and an old rickety billiard-table. It was reached by the spiral staircase which led to a square hole in the corner of the room, like a ship's hatchway. This apartment,

---

*The original malapropism, "les loups-de-gorge chanter dans les ogrépines," is utterly untranslatable. The above is only an attempt to convey some approximate idea.

lighted by only one narrow window and a constantly burning lamp, had a garret-look about it, and all the four-legged articles of furniture behaved as if they had only three. The white-washed wall had for sole ornament, the following quatrain in honor of Mame Hucheloup:

Elle étonne a dix pas, elle épouvante à deux
Une verrue habite en son nez hasardeux;
On tremble à chaque instant qu'elle ne vous la mouche,
Et qu'un beau jour son nez ne tombe dans sa bouche.

This was written in charcoal on the wall. Mame Hucheloup, very like her description, walked past this quatrain from morning till night, with the most perfect tranquillity. Two servant girls, called Matelote and Gibelotte, and who were never known by other names, helped Mame Hucheloup in placing on the tables bottles of blue wine, and the various messes served to the hungry guests in earthenware bowls. Matelote, stout, round, red-haired, and noisy, an ex-favourite sultana of the defunct Hucheloup, was uglier than the ugliest mythological monster; and yet, as it is always proper that the servant should be a little behind the mistress, she was not so ugly as Mame Hucheloup. Gibelotte, tall, delicate, white with a lymphatic whiteness, with blue circles round her eyes, and drooping lids, ever exhausted and oppressed, and suffering from what may be called chronic lassitude, the first to rise, the last to go to bed, waited on everybody, even to the other servants, silently and gently, and smiling a sort of vague, sleepy smile through her weariness. Before entering the restaurant the following line written by Courfeyrac in chalk was legible:

"Feast if you can, and eat if you dare."

2. PRELIMINARY GAYETIES

LAIGLE of Meaux, as we know, liked to live better with Joly than any one else, and he had a lodging much as the bird has a branch. The two friends lived together, ate together, slept together, and had everything in common, Musichetta perhaps included. They were, to use the expression of the schools, *bini,* or twins. On the morning of June 5 they went to breakfast at Corinth. Joly had a cold in his head, and Laigle's coat was threadbare, while Joly was well dressed. It was about nine in the morning when they pushed open the door of Corinth. They went up to the first-floor room, where they were received by Matelote and Gibelotte.

"Oysters, cheese, and ham," said Laigle.

They sat down at the table. The room was empty, there was no one in it but themselves. Gibelotte, recognizing Joly and Laigle, placed a bottle of wine on the table. As they attacked the first dozen of oysters, a head appeared in the hatchway and a voice said:

"As I was passing I smelt a delicious perfume of Brie cheese, so I stepped in."

It was Grantaire. He took a stool and sat down at the table. Gibelotte, on seeing Grantaire, placed two bottles of wine on the table, which made three.

"Are you going to drink these two bottles?" Laigle asked Grantaire, who replied:

"All men are ingenious, but you alone are ingenuous. Two bottles never yet astonished a man."

The others began with eating, but Grantaire began with drinking; a pint was soon swallowed.

"Why, you must have a hole in your stomach," said Laigle.

"Well, you have one in your elbow," Grantaire retorted. And after emptying his glass, he added:

"Oh, yes, Laigle of the funeral orations, your coat is old."

"I should hope so," Laigle replied, "for my coat and I live comfortably together. It has assumed all my wrinkles, does not hurt me anywhere, has molded itself on my deformities and is complacent to all my movements, and I only feel its presence because it keeps me warm. Old coats are old friends."

"Grantaire," Laigle asked, "have you come from the boulevard?"

"No."

"Joly and I have just seen the head of the procession pass."

"It is a marvelous sight," said Joly.

"How quiet this street is," Laigle exclaimed. "Who could suspect that Paris is turned topsy-turvy? How easy it is to see that formerly there were monasteries all round here! Du Breuil and Sauval give a list of them, and so does the Abbé Lebœuf. There was all around where we are now sitting a busy swarm of monks, shod and barefooted, tonsured and bearded, gray, black, white, Franciscans, Minims, Capuchins, Carmelites, little Augustines, great Augustines, old Augustines——"

"Don't talk about monks," Grantaire interrupted, "for it makes me feel to want to scratch myself." Then he exclaimed:

"Bouh! I have just swallowed a bad oyster, and that has brought back my hypochondria. Oysters are spoiled, servant girls are ugly, and I hate the human race. I passed just now before the great public library in the Rue Richelieu, and that pile of oyster-shells, which is called a library, disgusts me with thinking. What paper! what ink! what pothooks and hangers! all that has been written! what ass was it that said man was a featherless biped? And then, too, I met a pretty girl I know, lovely as spring, and worthy to be called Floreal, who was ravished, transported, happy in Paradise, the wretch, because yesterday a hideous banker spotted with small-pox deigned to throw his handkerchief to her! Alas! woman looks out for a keeper quite as much as for a lover; cats catch mice as well as birds. This girl not two months ago was living respectably in a garret, and fitted little copper circles into the eyelet-holes of stays; what do you call it? She sewed, she had a flock bed, she lived by the side of a pot of flowers, and was happy. Now she is a bankeress, and the transformation took place last night. I met the victim this morning perfectly happy, and the hideous thing was that the wretched creature was quite as pretty this morning as she was yesterday, and there was no sign of the financier on her face. Roses have this more or less than women, that the traces which the caterpillars leave on them are visible. Ah! there is no morality left in the world, and I call as witnesses the myrtle, symbol of love, the laurel, symbol of war, the olive, that absurd symbol of peace, the apple-tree, which nearly choked Adam with its pips, and the fig-tree, the grandfather of petticoats. As for justice, do you know what justice is? The Gauls covet Clusium, Rome protects Clusium and asks what wrong Clusium has done them. Brennus answers, 'The wrong which Alba did to you, the wrong that Fidène did to you, the wrong that the Equi, Volscians, and Sabines did to you. They were your neighbors, and the Clusians are ours. We understand neighborhood in the same way as you do. You stole Alba, and we take Clusium.' Rome says, 'You shall not take Clusium,' and Brennus took Rome, and then cried *Væ victis!* That is what justice is! Oh, what birds of prey there are in the world! What eagles, what eagles! the thought makes my flesh creep."

He held out his glass to Joly, who filled it, then drank, and continued, almost uninterrupted by the glass of wine, which no one noticed, not even himself:

"Brennus who takes Rome is an eagle; the banker who takes the grisette is an eagle; and there is no more shame in one than the other. So let us believe nothing; there is only one reality, drinking. Of whatever opinion you may be, whether you back the lean cock, like the canton of Uri, or the fat cock, like the canton of Glarus, it is of no consequence, drink. You talk to me about the boulevard, the procession, etc.; what, are we going to have another revolution? this poverty of resources astonishes me on the part of le bon Dieu; and He must at every moment set to work greasing the groove of events. Things stick and won't move,—look sharp, then, with a revolution; le bon Dieu has always got his hands black with that filthy cart-wheel grease. In his place I should act more simply, I should not wind up my machinery at every moment, but lead the human race evenly; I should knit facts mesh by mesh without breaking the thread; I should have no temporary substitutes, and no extraordinary repertory. What you fellows call progress has two motive powers, men and events, but it is a sad thing that something exceptional is required every now and then. For events as for men the ordinary stock company is not sufficient; among men there must be geniuses, and among events revolutions. Great accidents are the law, and the order of things cannot do without them; and, judging from the apparition of comets, we might be tempted to believe that heaven itself feels a want of leading actors. At the moment when it is least expected, God bills the wall of the firmament with a meteor, and some strange star follows, underlined by an enormous tail. And that causes the death of Cæsar; Brutus gives him a dagger-thrust, and God deals him a blow with a comet. Crac! here is an aurora borealis, here is a revolution, here is a great man: '93 in big letters, Napoleon in a display heading, and the comet of 1811 at the head of the bill. Ah! what a fine blue poster, spangled all over with unexpected flashes! Boum! boum! an extraordinary sight. Raise your eyes, idlers. Everything is disheveled, the star as well as the drama. O Lord! it is too much and not enough, and these resources, drawn from exceptional circumstances, seem magnificence and are only poverty. My friends, Providence has fallen into the stage of expedients. What does a revolution prove? that God is running short: He produces a coup d'état, because there is a solution of continuity between the present and the future, and He is unable to join the ends. In fact, this confirms me in my conjectures as to the state of Jehovah's fortune; and on seeing so much discomfort above and below, so much paltriness and pinching and saving and distress, both in heaven and on earth, from the bird which has not a seed of grain to myself who have not one hundred thousand francs a year,—on seeing human destiny which is very much worn, and even royal destiny which is threadbare, as witness the Prince de Condé hung—on seeing winter, which is only a rent in the zenith, through which the wind blows,—on seeing so many rags, even in the brand-new morning purple on the tops of the hills,— on seeing drops of dew, those false pearls, and hoar-frost, that *strass*— on seeing humanity unripped and events patched, and so many spots on the sun, so many holes in the moon, and so much wretchedness everywhere—I suspect that God is not rich. There is an appearance, it is true, but I see the pressure, and He gives a revolution just as a merchant whose cash-box is empty gives a ball. We must not judge the gods by appearances, and under the gilding of heaven I catch a glimpse of a poor universe. There is a bankruptcy in creation, and that is why I am dissatisfied. Just see, this is June 5, and it is almost night; I have been waiting since morning for day to come, and it has not come, and I will wager that it does not come at all. It is the irregularity of a badly paid clerk. Yes, everything is badly arranged, nothing fits into anything, this old world is thrown out of gear, and I place myself in the ranks of the opposition. Everything goes crooked, and the Universe is close-fisted; it is like the children,—those who ask get nothing, and those who don't ask get something. And then, again, it afflicts me to look at that bald-headed Laigle of Meaux, and I am humiliated by the thought that I am of the same age as that knee. However, I criticise but do not insult; the Universe is what it is, and I speak without any evil meaning, and solely to do my duty by my conscience. Ah! by all the saints of Olympus, and by all the Gods of Paradise, I was not made to be a Parisian, that is to say, to be constantly thrown like a shuttle-cock between two battle-dores, from a group of idlers to a group of noisy fellows. No! I was meant to be a Turk, looking all day at Egyptian damsels performing those exquisite dances which are as lubricous as the dreams of a chaste man, or a Beauceron peasant, or a Venetian gentleman surrounded by gentildonnes, or a small German prince, supplying one-half a soldier to the Confederation, and employing his leisure hours in drying his stockings on his hedge, that is to say, his frontier! Such were the destinies for which I was born. Yes, I said Turk, and I will not recall it. I do not understand why the Turks are usually looked upon askance, for Mahom has some good points; let us respect the inventor of harems of houris, and Paradises of Odalisques, and we ought not to insult Mahometism, the only religion adorned with a hen-coop! After this, I insist on drinking, for the earth is a great piece of stupidity. And it appears that all those asses are going to fight, to break each other's heads and massacre one another in the heart of summer, in the month of June, when they might go off with a creature on their arm to inhale in the fields the perfume of that immense cup of tea of cut hay. Really too many follies are committed. An old broken lantern, which I saw just now at a broker's, suggests a reflection to me, 'it is high time to enlighten the human race.' Yes, I am sad again, and it has come from an oyster and a revolution sticking in my throat. I am growing lugubrious again. Oh, frightful old world! on your surface people strive, are destitute, prostitute themselves, kill themselves, and grow accustomed to it!"

And after this burst of eloquence Grantaire had a burst of coughing, which was well deserved.

"Talking of a revolution," said Joly, "it seems that Marius is decidedly in love."

"Do you know with whom?" Laigle asked.

"Do."

"No?"

"Do, I tell you."

"The loves of Marius!" Grantaire exclaimed, "I can see them from here. Marius is a fog, and will have found a vapor. Marius belongs to the poetic race, and poet and madman are convertible terms. *Thymbræus Apollo*. Marius, and his Marie, or his Maria, or his Mariette, or his Marion, must be a funny brace of lovers. I can fancy what it is; ecstasies in which kissing is forgotten. Chaste on earth, but connected in the infinitude. They are souls that have feelings, and they sleep together in the stars."

Grantaire was attacking his second bottle, and perhaps his second harangue, when a new head emerged from the staircase hatchway. It was a boy under ten years of age, ragged, very short, and yellow, with a bull-dog face, a quick eye, and an enormous head of hair: he was dripping with wet, but seemed happy. The lad, choosing without hesitating among the three, though he knew none of them, addressed Laigle of Meaux.

"Are you Monsieur Bossuet?"

"I am called so," Laigle replied; "what do you want?"

"A tall, light-haired gent said to me on the boulevard, 'Do you know Mother Hucheloup's?' I said, 'Yes, in the Rue Chanvrerie, the old one's widow.' Says he to me, 'Go there, you will find Monsieur Bossuet there, and say to him from me, A—B—C.' I suppose it's a trick played on you, eh? he gave me ten sous."

"Joly, lend me ten sous," said Laigle; and, turning to Grantaire, "Grantaire, lend me ten sous."

This made twenty sous, which Laigle gave the lad. "Thank you, sir," he said.

"What is your name?" Laigle asked.

"Navet, Gavroche's friend."

"Stay with us," Laigle said.

"Breakfast with us," Grantaire added.

The lad replied, "I can't, for I belong to the procession, and have to cry, 'Down with Polignac.'"

And, drawing his foot slowly after him, which is the most respectful of bows possible, he went away. When he was gone Grantaire remarked:

"That is pure gamin, and there are many varieties in the gamin genus. The notary-gamin is called 'gutter jumper'; the cook-gamin is called 'scullion'; the baker-gamin is called 'doughey'; the footman-gamin is called 'tiger'; the sailor-gamin is called 'powder monkey'; the soldier-gamin is called 'a child of the regiment'; the tradesman-gamin is called 'errand boy'; the courtier-gamin is called 'page'; the royal-gamin is called 'dauphin'; and the divine-gamin is called 'Bambino.'"

In the meanwhile Laigle meditated, and said in a low voice:

"A—B—C, that is to say, funeral of General Lamarque."

"The tall, fair man," Grantaire observed, "is Enjolras, who has sent to warn you."

"Shall we go?" asked Bossuet.

"It's raibing," said Joly; "I have sworn to go through fire but dot through water, and I do dot wish to bake by cold worse."

"I shall stay here," Grantaire remarked; "I prefer breakfast to a hearse."

"Conclusion, we remain," Laigle continued; "in that case let us drink. Besides, we may miss the funeral without missing the row."

"Ah, the row!" cried Joly, "I'b id that."

Laigle rubbed his hands.

"So the revolution of 1830 is going to begin over again. In fact it annoys people with corners."

"I do not care a rap for your revolution," Grantaire remarked, "and I do not execrate the present government, for it is the crown tempered by the cotton night-cap, a scepter terminating in an umbrella. In such weather as this Louis Philippe might use his royalty for two objects, stretch out the scepter-end against the people, and open the umbrella-end against the sky."

The room was dark, and heavy clouds completely veiled the daylight. There was no one in the wine-shop nor in the streets, for everybody had gone "to see the events."

"Is it midday or midnight?" Bossuet asked; "I can see nothing; bring a candle, Gibelotte."

Grantaire was drinking sorrowfully.

"Enjolras disdains me," he muttered. "Enjolras said to himself, 'Joly is ill and Grantaire is drunk,' and so he sent Navet to Bossuet. And yet, if he fetched me, I would have followed him. All the worse for Enjolras! I will not go to his funeral."

This resolution formed, Bossuet, Grantaire, and Joly did not stir from the wine-shop, and at about 2 P. M. the table at which they sat was covered with empty bottles. Two candles burned on it, one in a perfectly green copper candle-stick, the other in the neck of a cracked water-bottle. Grantaire had led Joly and Bossuet to wine, and Bossuet and Joly had brought Grantaire back to joy. As for Grantaire, he gave up wine at midday as a poor inspirer of dreams. Wine is not particularly valued by serious sots, for inebriety there is white magic and dark magic, and wine is only the white magic. Grantaire, a bold drinker of dreams, was attracted rather than arrested by the blackness of a formidable intoxication yawning before him, and he had given up bottles and taken to the dram glass, which is an abyss. Not having at hand either opium or hasheesh, and willing to fill his brain with darkness, he turned to that frightful mixture of brandy, stout, and absinthe, which produces such terrible lethargies. Of these three vapors, beer, brandy, and absinthe, the lead of the soul is made; there are three darknesses in which the celestial butterfly is drowned; and three dumb furies, nightmare, night, and death, which hover over the sleeping Psyche, are produced in a membranous smoke vaguely condensed into a bat's wing. Grantaire had not yet reached that phase, far from it; he was prodigiously gay, and Bossuet and Joly kept even with him. Grantaire added to the eccentric accentuation of words and ideas the divagation of gestures; he laid his left hand on his knee with a dignified air, and with his neck-cloth unloosed, straddling his stool, and with his full glass in his right hand, he threw these solemn words at the stout servant girl, Matelote:

"Open the gates of the palace! Let every man belong to the French Academy and have the right of embracing Madame Hucheloup! Let us drink."

And turning to the landlady, he added:

"Antique female, consecrated by custom, approach, that I may contemplate thee."

And Joly exclaimed:

"Batelote and Gibelotte, don't give Grantaire ady bore drink. He is spending a frightful sum, and odly since this borning has devoured in shabeful prodigality two francs, dwenty-five centibes."

And Grantaire went on:

"Who has unhooked the stars without my leave, in order to place them on the table in the lieu of candles?"

Bossuet, who was very drunk, had retained his calmness. He was sitting on the sill of the open window, letting the rain drench his back, while he gazed at his two friends. All at once he heard behind him a tumult, hurried footsteps, and shouts of *To arms!* He turned, and noticed in the Rue St. Denis, at the end of the Rue Chanvrerie, Enjolras passing, carbine in hand, Gavroche with his pistol, Feuilly with his saber, Courfeyrac with his sword, Jean Prouvaire with his musketoon, Combeferre with his fowling-piece, Bahorel with his, and the whole armed and stormy band that followed them. The Rue de la Chanvrerie was not a pistol-shot in length, so Bossuet improvised a speaking trumpet with his mouth and shouted:

"Courfeyrac! Courfeyrac! hilloh!"

Courfeyrac heard the summons, perceived Bossuet, and walked a few steps down the Rue de la Chanvrerie, exclaiming, "What do you want?" which was crossed by a "Where are you going?"

"To make a barricade," Courfeyrac answered.

"Well, why not make it here? the spot is good."

"That is true, Eagle," Courfeyrac remarked.

And at a sign from Courfeyrac the band rushed into the Rue de la Chanvrerie.

3. *THE NIGHT BEGINS TO FALL ON GRANTAIRE*

THE ground was, in fact, admirably suited: the entrance of the street was wide, the end narrowed, and, like a blind alley, Corinth formed a contraction in it; the Rue de Mondétour could be easily barred right and left, and no attack was possible save by the Rue St. Denis, that is to say, from the front and in the open. Bossuet drunk had had the inspiration of Hannibal sober. At the sound of the band rushing on, terror seized on the whole street, and not a passer-by but disappeared. More quickly than a flash of lightning, shops, stalls, gates, doors, Venetian blinds, and shutters of every size were shut from the ground-floor to the roofs, at the end on the right, and on the left. An old terrified woman fixed up a mattress before her window with clothes-props, in order to deaden the

musketry, and the public-house alone remained open—and for an excellent reason, because the insurgents had rushed into it.

"O Lord, O Lord!" Mame Hucheloup sighed.

Bossuet ran down to meet Courfeyrac, and Joly, who had gone to the
window, shouted:

"Courfeyrac, you ought to have brought an umbrella. You will catch
cold."

In a few minutes twenty iron bars were pulled down from the railings
in front of the inn, and ten yards of pavement dug up. Gavroche and
Bahorel seized, as it passed, the truck of a lime-dealer, of the name of
Anceau, and found in it three barrels of lime, which they placed under
the piles of paving-stones; Enjolras had raised the cellar-flap, and all
Mame Hucheloup's empty casks went to join the barrels of lime; Feuilly,
with his fingers accustomed to illumine the delicate sticks of fans, re-
enforced the barrels and the trucks with two massive piles of stones.
Stones improvised like everything else and taken no one knew whence.
The supporting shores were pulled away from the frontage of an adjoining house and laid on the casks. When Courfeyrac and Bossuet turned
round one half the street was already barred by a rampart taller than
a man, for there is nothing like the hand of the people to build up anything that is built by demolishing. Matelote and Gibelotte were mixed
up with the workmen, and the latter went backward and forward,
loaded with rubbish, and her lassitude helped at the barricade. She
served paving-stones, as she would have served wine, with a sleepy look.
An omnibus drawn by two white horses passed the end of the street;
Bossuet jumped over the stones, ran up, stopped the driver, ordered the
passengers to get out, offered his hand to the "ladies," dismissed the con-
ductor, and returned, pulling the horses on by the bridles.

"Omnibuses," he said, "must not pass before Corinth. *Non licet omnibus adire Corinthum.*"

A moment after the unharnessed horses were straggling down the
Rue Mondétour, and the omnibus lying on its side completed the barricade. Mame Hucheloup, quite upset, had sought refuge on the second-
floor, her eyes were wandering and looked without seeing, and her
cries of alarm dared not issue from her throat.

"It is the end of the world," she muttered.

Joly deposited a kiss on Mame Hucheloup's fat, red, wrinkled neck,
and said to Grantaire: "My dear fellow, I have always considered a
woman's neck an infinitely delicate thing." But Grantaire had reached

the highest regions of dithyramb. When Matelote came up to the first-floor he seized her round the waist, and burst into loud peals of laughter at the window.

"Matelote is ugly," he cried, "Matelote is the ideal of ugliness, she is a chimera. Here is the secret of her birth: a Gothic Pygmalion, who was carving cathedral gargoyles, fell in love on a fine morning with the most horrible of them. He implored love to animate it, and this produced Matelote. Look at her, citizens! She has chromate-of-lead-colored hair, like Titian's mistress, and is a good girl; I will answer that she fights well, for every good girl contains a hero. As for Mother Hucheloup, she is an old brave; look at her mustachios, she inherited them from her husband. She will fight too, and the couple will terrify the whole of the suburbs. Comrades, we will overthrow the government so truly as there are fifteen intermediate acids between margaric acid and formic acid; however, it is a matter of perfect indifference to me. My father always detested me because I could not understand mathematics; I only understand love and liberty. I am Grantaire, the good fellow; never having had any money, I have not grown accustomed to it and for that reason have never wanted it; but, had I been rich, there would be no poor left! you would have seen! Oh, if good hearts had large purses, how much better things would be! I can imagine the Saviour with Rothschild's fortune! what good he would do! Matelote, embrace me! You are voluptuous and timid; you have cheeks that claim the kiss of a sister, and lips that claim the kiss of a lover!"

"Hold your tongue, barrel!" Courfeyrac said.

Grantaire replied:

"I am the capitoul and master of the Floral games!"

Enjolras, who was standing on the top of the barricade, gun in hand, raised his handsome, stern face. Enjolras, as we know, blended the Spartan with the Puritan; he would have died at Thermopylæ with Leonidas, and burned Drogheda with Cromwell.

"Grantaire," he cried, "go and sleep off your wine elsewhere; this is the place for intoxication, and not for drunkenness. Do not dishonor the barricade."

These angry words produced on Grantaire a singular effect, and it seemed as if he had received a glass of cold water in his face. He appeared suddenly sobered. He sat down near the window, gazed at Enjolras with inexpressible tenderness, and said to him:

"Let me sleep here."

"Go and sleep elsewhere," Enjolras cried.

But Grantaire, still fixing on him his tender and misty eyes, answered: "Let me sleep here till I die here."

Enjolras looked at him disdainfully.

"Grantaire, you are incapable of believing, thinking, wishing, living, and dying."

Grantaire replied in a grave voice:

"You will see."

He stammered a few more unintelligible words, then his head fell noisily on the table, and—as is usually the effect of the second period of ebriety into which Enjolras had roughly and suddenly thrust him—a moment later he was asleep.

4. *AN EFFORT TO CONSOLE THE WIDOW HUCHELOUP*

BAHOREL, delighted with the barricade, exclaimed: "How well the street looks in a low-cut dress!"

Courfeyrac, while gradually demolishing the public-house, tried to console the widowed landlady.

"Mother Hucheloup, were you not complaining the other day that you had been summoned by the police, because Gibelotte shook a counterpane out of the window?"

"Yes, my good Monsieur Courfeyrac. Ah! good gracious! are you going to put that table too in your horror? Yes, and the government also condemned me to a fine of one hundred francs on account of a flower-pot that fell out of the garret into the street. Is that not abominable?"

"Well, Mother Hucheloup, we are going to avenge you."

Mother Hucheloup did not exactly see the advantage accruing to her from the reparation made her. She was satisfied after the fashion of the Arab woman who, having received a box on the ear from her husband, went to complain to her father, crying vengeance, and saying, "Father, you owe my husband affront for affront." The father asked, "On which cheek did you receive the blow?". "On the left cheek." The father boxed her right cheek, and said, "Now you must be satisfied. Go and tell your husband that he buffeted my daughter, but I have buffeted his wife." The rain had ceased, and recruits began to arrive. Artisans brought under their blouses a barrel of gunpowder, a hamper containing carboys of vitriol, two or three carnival torches, and a basket full of lamps, "remaining from the king's birthday," which was quite recent, as it was celebrated on May 1. It was said that this ammunition was sent by a grocer in the Faubourg St. Antoine, of the name of Pepin. The only lantern in the Rue de la Chanvrerie, and the corresponding one in the Rue Saint Denis, and all those in the surrounding streets, were broken. Enjolras, Combeferre, and Courfeyrac directed everything, and now two barricades were erected simultaneously, both of which were supported by Corinth and formed a square; the larger one closed the Rue de la Chanvrerie, and the smaller Rue Mondétour on the side of the Rue du Cygne. This latter barricade, which was very narrow, was merely made of barrels and paving-stones. There were about fifty workmen there, of whom three were armed with guns, for on the road they had borrowed a gunsmith's entire stock.

Nothing could be stranger or more motley than this group: one had a sleeved waistcoat, a cavalry saber, and a pair of holster pistols; another was in shirt sleeves, with a round hat, and a powder-flask hung at his side, while a third was cuirassed with nine sheets of gray paper, and was armed with a saddler's awl. There was one who shouted, *Let us exterminate to the last, and die on the point of our bayonet!* This man had no bayonet. Another displayed over his coat the belts and pouch of a national guard, with these words sewed in red worsted on the cover— *public order*. There were many muskets, bearing the number of legions, few hats, no neck-ties, a great many bare arms, and a few pikes; add to this all ages, all faces, short pale youths, and bronzed laborers at the docks. All were in a hurry, and, while assisting each other, talked about the possible chances—that they were sure of one regiment, and Paris would rise. These were terrible remarks, with which a sort of cordial joviality was mingled; they might have been taken for brothers, though they did not know each other's names. Great dangers have this beauty about them, that they throw light on the fraternity of strangers.

A fire was lighted in the kitchen, and men were melting, in a bullet-mold, bowls, spoons, forks, and all the pewter articles of the public-house. They drank while doing this, and caps and slugs lay pell-mell on the table with glasses of wine. In the billiard-room Mame Hucheloup, Matelote, and Gibolette, variously affected by terror,—as one was brutal-ized by it, another had her breath stopped, while the third was awakened, —were tearing up old sheets and making lint; three insurgents helped them, three hairy, bearded, and mustached fellows, who pulled the linen asunder with the fingers of a sempstress, and made them tremble. The tall man, whom Courfeyrac, Combeferre, and Enjolras had noticed, as he joined the band at the corner of the Rue des Billettes, was working at the small barricade, and making himself useful. Gavroche was work-ing at the large one, and as for the young man who had waited for Courfeyrac at his lodgings and asked after M. Marius, he disappeared just about the time when the omnibus was overthrown.

Gavroche, who was perfectly radiant, had taken the arrangements on himself; he came, went, ascended, descended, went up again, rustled and sparkled. He seemed to be there for the encouragemnt of all; had he a spur? certainly in his misery; had he wings? certainly in his joy. Gavroche was a whirlwind: he was seen incessantly and constantly heard, and he filled the air, being everywhere at once. He was a sort of almost irritating ubiquity, and it was impossible to stop with him. The enormous barricade felt him on its crupper; he annoyed the idlers, excited the slothful, re-animated the fatigued, vexed the thoughtful, rendered some gay and gave others time to breathe, set some in passion, and all in motion; he piqued a student and stung a workman, he halted, then started again, flew over the turmoil and the efforts, leaped from one to the other, murmured, buzzed, harassed the whole team; he was the fly of the immense revolutionary coach. Perpetual movement was in his little arms, and perpetual clamor in his little lungs.

"Push ahead; more paving-stones, more barrels, more vehicles! where are there any? We want a hod-load of plaster to stop up this hole. Your barricade is very small, and must mount. Put everything into it, smash up the house; a barricade is Mother Gibou's tea. Hilloh! there's a glass door."

This made the workmen exclaim:

"A glass door! what would you have us to do with that, tubercle?"

"Hercules yourselves," Gavroche retorted: "a glass door in a barricade is excellent, for, though it does not prevent the attack, it makes it awkward to take it. Have you never boned apples over a wall on which there was broken glass? A glass door cuts the corns of the National Guards when they try to climb up the barricade. By Jove! glass is treacherous. Well, you fellows have no very bright imagination."

He was furious with his useless pistol, and went from one to the other saying: "A gun! I want a gun! Why don't you give me a gun?"

"A gun for you?" said Combeferre.

"Well, why not?" Gavroche answered; "I had one in 1830, when we quarreled with Charles X."

Enjolras shrugged his shoulders.

"When all the men have guns we will give them to the boys."

Gavroche turned firmly, and answered him:

"If you are killed before me I will take yours."

"Gamin!" said Enjolras.

"Puppy!" said Gavroche.

A dandy lounging past the end of the street created a diversion; Gavroche shouted to him:

"Come to us, young man! what, will you do nothing for your old country?"

The dandy fled.

5 . *THE PREPARATIONS*

THE journals of the day which stated that the barricade in the Rue de la Chanvrerie, that *almost impregnable fortress,* as they called it, reached the level of a second-floor, are mistaken, for the truth is, that it did not exceed an average height of six or seven feet. It was so built that the combatants could, at will, either disappear behind it or ascend to its crest, by means of a quadruple row of pairing-stalls arranged like steps inside.

Externally the front of the barricade, composed of piles of paving-stones and barrels, held together by joists and planks, passed through the wheels of the truck and the omnibus, had a bristling and inextricable appearance. A gap, sufficiently wide for one man to pass, was left between the house wall and the end of the barricade furthest from the wine-shop, so that a sortie was possible. The pole of the omnibus was held upright by ropes, and a red flag fixed to this pole floated over the barricade. The small Mondétour barricade, concealed behind the wine-shop, could not be seen, but the two barricades combined formed a real redoubt. Enjolras and Courfeyrac had not thought it advisable to barricade the other portion of the Rue Mondétour, which opens onto the Halles, as they doubtless wished to maintain a possible communication with the outside, and had but little fear of being attacked by the difficult and dangerous Rue des Prêcheurs. With the exception of this issue left free, which constituted what Folard would have called in a strategic style, a zigzag, and of the narrow passage in the Rue de la Chanvrerie, the interior of the barricade, in which the wine-shop formed a salient angle, presented an irregular quadrilateral, inclosed on all sides. There was a space of twenty yards between the great barricade and the tall houses which formed the end of the street, so that it might be said that the barricade leaned against these houses, which were all inhabited, but closed from top to bottom.

All this labor was completed without any obstacle in less than an hour, during which this handful of men had not seen a single bear-skin cap or bayonet. The few citizens who still ventured at this moment of riot into the Rue St. Denis took a glance into the Rue de la Chanvrerie, perceived the barricade, and doubled their pace. When the two barricades were completed and the flag was hoisted, a table was pulled from the wine-shop into the street, and Courfeyrac got upon it. Enjolras brought up the square chest, which Courfeyrac opened, and it proved to be full of cartridges. When they saw these cartridges the bravest trembled, and there was a moment's silence. Courfeyrac distributed the cartridges smilingly, and each man received thirty; many had powder, and began making others with the bullets which had been cast; as for the powder barrel, it was on a separate table, near the door, and was held in reserve. The drum-beat, which was traversing the whole of Paris, did not cease, but in the end it had become a monotonous sound, to which they no longer paid any attention. This noise at one moment retired, at another came nearer, with lugubrious undulations. The guns and carbines were loaded all together, without precipitation and with a solemn gravity.

Enjolras then stationed three sentries outside the barricades—one in the Rue de la Chanvrerie, the second in the Rue des Prêcheurs, the third at the corner of the Petite Truanderie. Then, when the barricades were built, the posts assigned, the guns loaded, the sentries set, the insurgents alone in these formidable streets, through which no one now passed, surrounded by dumb and, as it were, dead houses, in which no human movement palpitated, enveloped in the menacing darkness, in the midst of that silence and obscurity in which they felt something advancing, and which had something tragical and terrifying about it, isolated, armed, determined, and tranquil—waited.

6. WAITING

DURING the hours of waiting, what did they? We are bound to tell it, because this is historical. While the men were making cartridges and the women lint, while a large stew-pan full of melted tin and lead, intended for the bullet-mold, was smoking on a red-hot chafing-dish, while the vedettes were watching with shouldered guns on the barricade, while Enjolras, whom it was impossible to distract, watched the vedettes, Combeferre, Courfeyrac, Jean Prouvaire, Feuilly, Bossuet, Joly, Bahorel, and a few others assembled, as in the most peaceful days of their student conversations, and in one corner of the wine-shop converted into a casemate, two paces from the barricade which they had raised, and with their loaded and primed muskets leaning against the back of their chairs, these fine young men, so near their last hour, wrote love verses.

What kind of verses? Here they are:

Vous rappelez-vous notre douce vie,
Lorsque nous étions si jeunes tous deux,

Et que nous n'avions au cœur d'autre envie
Que d'être bien mis et d'être amoureux,

Lorsqu'en ajoutant votre âge à mon âge,
Nous ne comptions pas à deux quarante ans,
Et que, dans notre humble et petit ménage,
Tout, même, l'hiver, nous était printemps?

(Translation.)

Do you remember our charming times,
When we were both so young, and knew
Of naught on earth that was worth a wish
But love, and to look your best,—we two;

When all your birthdays, added to mine,
A total of forty would not bring,
And when, in our humble and cosey roost,
All, even the Winter, to us was Spring?

———

Beaux jours! Manuel était fier et sage,
Paris s'asseyait à de saints banquets,
Foy lançait la foudre, et votre corsage
Avait une épingle où je me piquais.

Tout vous contemplait. Avocat sans causes,
Quand je vous menais au Prado dîner,
Vous étiez jolie, au point que les roses
Me faisaient l'effet de se retourner.

Je les entendais dire: Est-elle belle!
Comme elle sent bon! Quels cheveux à flots!
Sous son mantelet elle cache une aile.
Son bonnet charmant est à peine éclos.

J'errais avec toi, pressant ton bras souple.
Les passants croyaient que l'amour charmé
Avait marié, dans notre heureux couple,
Le doux mois d'avril au beau mois de mai.

293

Nous vivions cachés, contents, porte close,
Dévorant l'amour, bon fruit défendu,
Ma bouche n'avait pas dit une chose
Que déjà ton cœur avait répondu.

(Translation.)

Rare days! Then prudish Manuel stalked,
  Paris a godly life essayed,
Foy thundered, and yes, 'twas then a pin
  In your bodice pricked my hand that strayed!

Everything ogled you. At Prado's
  Where you and your briefless barrister dined,
You were so pretty, the roses, I thought,
  Turned to look at you from behind.

They seemed to whisper: "How handsome she is!
  What wavy tresses! what sweet perfume!
Under her mantle she hides her wings;
  Her flower of a bonnet is just in bloom!"

I roamed with you, pressing your dainty arm,
  And the passers thought that Love, in play,
Had mated, in unison so sweet,
  . The gallant April with gentle May.

We lived so merrily, all by ourselves,
  On love,—that choice forbidden fruit,—
And never a word my mouth could speak
  But your heart already had followed suit.

———————

La Sorbonne était l'endroit bucolique
Où je t'adorais du soir au matin.
C'est ainsi qu'une âme amoureuse applique
La carte du Tendre au pays latin.

O place Maubert! ô place Dauphine!
Quand, dans le taudis frais et printanier,

Tu tirais ton bas sur ta jambe fine,
Je voyais un astre au fond du grenier.

J'ai fort lu Platon, mais rien ne m'en reste;
Mieux que Malebranche et que Lamennais
Tu me démontrais la bonté céleste
Avec une fleur que tu me donnais.

Je t'obéissais, tu m'étais soumise;
O grenier doré! te lacer! te voir
Aller et venir dès l'aube, en chemise,
Mirant ton front jeune à ton vieux miroir!

Et qui donc pourrait perdre la mémoire
De ces temps d'aurore et de firmament,
De rubans, de fleurs, de gaze et de moire,
Où l'amour bégaye un argot charmant?

(Translation.)

The Sorbonne was that bucolic place
  Where night till day my passion throve:
'Tis thus that an ardent youngster makes
  The Latin Quarter a Land of Love.

O Place Maubert! O Place Dauphine!
  Sky-parlor reaching heavenward far,
In whose depths, when you drew your stocking on,
  I saw, methought, a shining star.

Hard-learned Plato I've long forgot:
  Neither Malebranche nor Lamennais
Taught me such faith in Providence
  As the flower which in your bosom lay.

You were my servant and I your slave:
  O golden attic! O joy, at morn,
To lace you—watch you dressing, and viewing
  Your girlish face in that glass forlorn!

Ah! who indeed could ever forget
  The sky and dawn commingling still;
That ribbony, flowery, gauzy glory,
  And love's sweet nonsense talked at will?

———————

Nos jardins étaient un pot de tulipe;
Tu masquais la vitre avec un jupon;
Je prenais le bol de terre de pipe,
Et je te donnais la tasse en japon.

Et ces grands malheurs qui nous faisaient rire!
Ton manchon brulé, ton boa perdu!
Et ce cher portrait du divin Shakspeare
Qu'un soir pour souper nous avons vendu!

J'étais mendiant et toi charitable.
Je baisais au vol tes bras frais et ronds.
Dante in-folio nous servait de table
Pour manger gaiment un cent de marrons.

La première fois qu'en mon joyeux bouge
Je pris un baiser à ta lèvre en feu,
Quand tu t'en allas décoiffé et rouge,
Je restai tout pale et je crus en Dieu!

Te rappelles-tu nos bonheurs sans nombre,
Et tous ces fichus changés en chiffons?
Oh! que de soupirs, de nos cœurs pleins d'ombre,
Se sont envolés dans les cieux profonds!

(Translation.)

Our garden a pot of tulips was;
  Your petticoat curtained the window-pane;
I took for myself the earthen bowl,
  And passed you the cup of porcelain.

What huge disasters to make us fun!
  Your muff afire; your tippet lost;

And that cherished portrait of Shakspeare, sold,
One hungry evening, at half its cost.

I was a beggar and you were kind:
A kiss from your fair round arms I'd steal,
While the folio-Dante we gaily spread
With a hundred chestnuts, our frugal meal.

And oh! when first my favored mouth
A kiss to your burning lips had given,
You were disheveled and all aglow;
I, pale with rapture, believed in Heaven.

Do you remember our countless joys?
Those neckerchiefs rumpled every day?
Alas, what sighs from our boding hearts
The infinite skies have borne away!

The hour, the spot, the recollections of youth recalled a few stars which were beginning to glisten in the sky, the funereal repose of these deserted streets, the imminence of the inexorable adventure which was preparing, gave a pathetic charm to these verses murmured in a low voice in the twilight by Jean Prouvaire, who, as we said, was a gentle poet.

In the meanwhile, a lamp had been lit on the small barricade, and on the large one one of those wax torches such as may be seen on Shrove Tuesday in front of the vehicles crowded with masks that are proceeding to the Courtille. These torches, we know, came from the Faubourg St. Antoine. The torch was placed in a species of lantern of paving-stones, closed on three sides to protect it from the wind, and arranged so that the entire light should fall on the flag. The street and the barricade remained plunged in darkness, and nothing was visible save the red flag formidably illumined, as if by an enormous dark lantern. This light added a strange and terrible purple to the scarlet of the flag.

297

NIGHT had quite set in, and nothing occurred, only confused rumors and fusillades now and then could be heard, but they were rare, badly maintained, and distant. This respite, which was prolonged, was a sign that the government was taking its time and collecting its strength. These fifty men were waiting for the coming of sixty thousand. Enjolras was attacked by that impatience which seizes on powerful minds when they stand on the threshold of formidable events. He looked up Gavroche, who was busy manufacturing cartridges in the ground-floor room by the dubious light of two candles placed on the bar for precaution, on account of the gunpowder sprinkled over the tables. These two candles threw no rays outside, and the insurgents allowed no light in the upper floors. Gavroche was at this moment greatly occupied, though not precisely with his cartridge.

The recruit from the Rue des Billettes had come into the room and seated himself at the least-lighted table. A Brown Bess of the large model had fallen to his share, and he held it between his legs. Gavroche up to this moment, distracted by a hundred "amusing" things, had not even seen this man. When he entered Gavroche looked after him, mechanically admiring his musket, but when the man was seated the gamin suddenly rose. Those who might have watched this man would have noticed him observe everything in the barricade, and the band of insurgents, with singular attention, but when he entered the room he fell into a state of contemplation, and seemed to see nothing of what was going on. The gamin approached this pensive man, and began walking round him on tiptoe, in the same way as people move round a man whom they are afraid of awaking. At the same time all the grimaces of an old man passed over his childish face, at once so impudent and so serious, so giddy and so profound, so gay and so affecting, and these grimaces signified, "Oh stuff! it is not possible, I must see double—I am dreaming—can it be?—no, it is not—yes, it is—no, it is not." Gavroche balanced himself on his heels, clenched his fists in his pockets, moved his neck like a bird, and expended on an enormously outstretched lip all the sagacity of a lower lip. He was stupefied, uncertain, convinced, and dazzled. He looked like the chief of the eunuchs at the slave-market discovering a Venus among the girls, and the air of an amateur recognizing a Raphael in a pile of daubs. Everything in him was at work, the instinct that scents and the intellect that combines; it was plain that an event was happening to Gavroche. It was when he was deepest in thought that Enjolras accosted him.

"You are little," he said, "and will not be seen. Go out of the barricades, slip along the houses, pass through as many streets as you can, and come back to tell me what is going on."

Gavroche drew himself up.

"So little ones are good for something? that's lucky! I'm off. In the meanwhile trust to the little and distrust the big," and Gavroche, raising his head and dropping his voice, added, as he pointed to the man of the Rue des Billettes:

"You see that tall fellow?"

"Well?"

"He's a spy."

"Are you sure?"

"Not a fortnight back he pulled me down by the ear from the cornice of the Point Royal where I was taking the air."

Enjolras hurriedly left the gamin and whispered a few words to a laborer from the wine-docks who was present. The laborer went out and returned almost immediately, followed by three others. The four men, four broad-shouldered porters, stationed themselves silently behind the table at which the man was seated, in evident readiness to fall upon him, and then Enjolras walked up to the man and asked him:

"Who are you?"

At this sudden question the man started; he looked into the depths of Enjolras's candid eyeballs, and seemed to read his thoughts. He gave a smile, which was at once the most disdainful, energetic, and resolute possible, and answered, with a haughty gravity:

"I see what you mean,—well, yes!"

"Are you a spy?"

"I am an agent of the authority!"

"And your name is—?"

"Javert."

Enjolras gave the four men a sign, and in a twinkling, before Javert had time to turn round, he was collared, thrown down, bound, and searched. They found on him a small round card fixed between two pieces of glass, and bearing on one side the arms of France, with the motto, "Surveillance and vigilance," and on the other this notice, "Javert, Police Inspector, fifty-two years of age," and the signature of the prefect of police of that day, M. Gisquet. He also had a watch and a purse containing some pieces of gold, and both were left him. Behind his watch at the bottom of his fob a paper was found, which Enjolras unfolded, and on which he read these lines, written by the prefect of police himself:

"So soon as his political mission is concluded, Javert will assure himself by a special watch whether it is true that criminals assemble on the slope of the right bank of the Seine, near the bridge of Jena."

When the search was ended, Javert was raised from the ground, his arms were tied behind his back, and he was fastened in the middle of the room to the celebrated post which in olden times gave its name to the wine-shop. Gavroche, who had watched the whole scene and approved of everything with a silent shake of the head, went up to Javert, and said:

"The mouse has trapped the cat."

All this took place so quickly that it was completed before those outside the wine-shop were aware of it. Javert had not uttered a cry. On seeing him fastened to the post, Courfeyrac, Bossuet, Combeferre, Joly, and the men scattered over the two barricades flocked in. Javert, who was surrounded with cords so that he could not stir, raised his head with the intrepid serenity of a man who has never told a falsehood.

"It is a spy," said Enjolras, and, turning to Javert, "You will be shot two minutes before the barricade is taken."

Javert replied, with his most imperious accent:

"Why not at once?"

"We are saving powder."

"Then settle the affair with a knife."

"Spy," said the beautiful Enjolras, "we are judges, and not assassins." Then he called Gavroche.

"You be off now and do what I told you."

"I am off," Gavroche cried, but stopped just as he reached the door.

"By the way, you will give me his gun. I leave you the musician, but I want his clarinet."

The gamin gave a military salute, and gaily slipped around the large barricade.

8. *WAS LE CABUC THE NAME OF THE MAN WHO CALLED HIMSELF LE CABUC?*

THE tragical picture we have undertaken would not be complete, the reader would not see in their exact and real relief those great moments of social lying-in and revolutionary giving birth, in which there are throes blended with effort, if we were to omit in our sketch an incident full of an epic and stern horror, which occurred almost immediately after Gavroche's departure.

Bands of rioters, it is well known, resemble a snow-ball, and, as they roll along, agglomerate many tumultuous men, who do not ask each other whence they come. Among the passers-by who joined the band led by Enjolras, Combeferre, and Courfeyrac, there was a man wearing a porter's jacket, much worn at the shoulders, who gesticulated and vociferated, and had the appearance of a drunken savage. This man, whose name or nickname was Le Cabuc, and entirely unknown to those who pretended to know him, was seated, in a state of real or feigned intoxication, with four others, round a table which they had dragged out of the wine-shop. This Cabuc, while making the others drink, seemed to be gazing thoughtfully at the large house behind the barricade, whose five stories commanded the whole street and faced the Rue St. Denis. All at once he exclaimed:

"Do you know what, comrades? we must fire from that house. When we are at the windows, hang me if any one can come up the street."

"Yes, but the house is closed," said one of the drinkers.

"We'll knock."

"They won't open."

"Then we'll break in the door."

Le Cabuc ran up to the door, which had a very massive knocker, and rapped; as the door was not opened he rapped again, and, no one answering, he gave a third rap, but the silence continued.

"Is there any one in here?" Le Cabuc shouted. But nothing stirred, and so he seized a musket and began hammering the door with the butt end. It was an old, low, narrow, solid door, made of oak, lined with sheet-iron inside and a heavy bar, and a thorough postern gate. The blows made the whole house tremble, but did not shake the door. The inhabitants, however, were probably alarmed, for a little square trap-window was at length lit up and opened on the third story, and a candle and the gray-haired head of a terrified old man, who was the porter, appeared in the orifice. The man who was knocking left off.

"What do you want, gentlemen?" the porter asked.

"Open the door!" said Le Cabuc.

"I cannot, gentlemen."

"Open, I tell you!"

"It is impossible, gentlemen."

Le Cabuc raised his musket and took aim at the porter, but as he was below and it was very dark the porter did not notice the fact.

"Will you open? yes or no."

"No, gentlemen."

"You really mean it?"

"I say no, my kind——"

The porter did not finish the sentence, for the musket was fired, the bullet entered under his chin and came out of his neck after passing through the jugular vein. The old man fell in a heap, without heaving a sigh, the candle went out, and nothing was visible save a motionless head lying on the sill of the window, and a small wreath of smoke ascending to the roof.

"There," said Le Cabuc, as he let the butt of the pistol fall on the pavement again.

He had scarce uttered the word ere he felt a hand laid on his shoulder with the tenacity of an eagle's talon, and he heard a voice saying to him:

"On your knees!"

The murderer turned, and saw before him Enjolras's white, cold face. Enjolras held a pistol in his hand, and hurried up on hearing the shot fired, and clutched with his left hand Le Cabuc's blouse, shirt, and braces.

"On your knees!" he repeated.

And with a sovereign movement the frail young man of twenty bent like a reed the muscular and robust porter, and forced him to kneel in the mud. Le Cabuc tried to resist, but he seemed to have been seized by a superhuman hand. Enjolras, pale, bare-necked, with his disheveled hair and feminine face, had at this moment I know not what of the ancient Themis. His dilated nostrils, his downcast eyes, gave to his implacable Greek profile that expression of wrath, and that expression of chastity, which in the opinion of the world, are becoming to justice. All the insurgents had hurried up, and then ranged themselves in a circle at a distance, feeling that it was impossible for them to utter a word in the presence of what they were going to see. Le Cabuc, conquered, no longer attempted to struggle, and trembled all over. Enjolras loosed his grasp and took out his watch.

"Pray or think!" he said; "you have one minute to do so."

"Mercy!" the murderer stammered, then hung his head and muttered a few inarticulate execrations.

Enjolras did not take his eyes off the watch; he let the minute pass, and then put the watch again in his fob. This done, he seized Le Cabuc by the hair, who clung to his knees with a yell, and placed the muzzle of the pistol to his ear. Many of these intrepid men, who had so tranquilly entered upon the most frightful adventures, turned away their heads. The explosion was heard, the assassin fell on his head on the pavement, and Enjolras drew himself up and looked round him with a stern air of conviction. Then he kicked the corpse and said:

"Throw this outside."

Three men raised the body of the wretch, which was still writhing in the last mechanical convulsions of expiring life, and threw it over the small barricade into the Mondétour lane. Enjolras stood pensive; some grand darkness was slowly spreading over his formidable serenity. Presently he raised his voice, and all were silent.

"Citizens," said Enjolras, "what that man did is frightful, and what I have done is horrible; he killed, and that is why I killed, and I was obliged to do so, as insurrection must have its discipline. Assassination is even more of a crime here than elsewhere, for we stand under the eye of the revolution, we are the priests of the republic, we are the sacred victims to duty, and we must not do aught that would calumniate our combat. I, therefore, tried and condemned this man to death, for my part, constrained to do what I have done, but, abhorring it, I have also tried myself, and you will shortly see what sentence I have passed."

All who listened trembled.

"We will share your fate," Combeferre exclaimed.

"Be it so!" Enjolras continued. "One word more. In executing that man I obeyed Necessity; but Necessity is a monster of the old world, and its true name is Fatality. Now, it is the law of progress that monsters should appear before angels, and Fatality vanish before Fraternity. It is a bad moment to utter the word love, but, no matter, I utter it, and I glorify it. Love, thou hast a future; Death, I make use of thee, but I abhor thee. Citizens, in the future there will be no darkness, no thunder-claps; neither ferocious ignorance nor bloodthirsty retaliation; and as there will be no Satan left, there will be no St. Michael. In the future no man will kill another man, the earth will be radiant, and the human race will love. The day will come, citizens, when all will be concord, harmony, light, joy, and life, and in order that it may come we are going to die."

Enjolras was silent, his virgin lips closed, and he stood for some time at the spot where he had shed blood, in the motionlessness of a marble statue. His fixed eyes caused people to talk in whispers around him. Jean Prouvaire and Combeferre shook hands silently, and, leaning against each other in an angle of the barricade, gazed, with an admiration in which there was compassion, at this grave young man, who was an executioner and priest, and had at the same time the light and the hardness of crystal. Let us say at once that after the action, when the corpses were conveyed to the morgue and searched, a police-agent's card was found on Le Cabuc; the author of this work had in his hands in 1848 the special report on this subject made to the prefect of police in 1832. Let us add that, if we may believe a strange but probably well-founded police tradition Le Cabuc was Claquesous. It is certainly true that after the death of Cabuc, Claquesous was never heard of again, and left no trace of his disappearance. He seemed to have become amalgamated with the invisible; his life had been gloom, and his end was night. The whole insurgent band were still suffering from emotion of this tragical trial, so quickly begun and so quickly ended, when Courfeyrac saw again at the barricade the short young man who had come to his lodgings to ask for Marius. This lad, who had a bold and reckless look, had come at night to rejoin the insurgents.

BOOK XIII

MARIUS ENTERS INTO THE SHADOW

1. *FROM THE RUE PLUMET TO THE RUE SAINT DENIS*

THE voice which summoned Marius through the twilight to the barricade in the Rue de la Chanvrerie had produced on him the effect of the voice of destiny. He wished to die, and the opportunity offered; he rapped at the door of the tomb, and a hand held out the key to him from the shadows. Such gloomy openings in the darkness just in front of despair are tempting; Marius removed the bar which had so often allowed him to pass, left the garden, and said, "I will go." Mad with grief, feeling nothing fixed and solid in his brain, incapable of accepting anything henceforth of destiny, after the two months spent in the intoxication of youth and love, and crushed by all the reveries of despair at once, he had only one wish left,—to finish with it all at once. He began walking rapidly, and he happened to be armed, as he had Javert's pistols in his pocket. The young man whom he fancied that he had seen had got out of his sight in the streets.

Marius, who left the Rue Plumet by the boulevard, crossed the esplanade and bridge of the Invalides, the Champs Elysées, the square of Louis XV, and reached the Rue de Rivoli. The shops were open there, the gas blazed under the arcades, ladies were making purchases, and people were eating ices at the Café Laiter and cakes at the English pastrycook's. A few post-chaises, however, were leaving at a gallop the Hotel des Princes and Meurice's. Marius entered the Rue St. Honoré by the passage Delorme. The shops were closed there, the tradesmen were conversing before their open doors, people walked along, the lamps were lighted, and from the second-floors upward the houses were illumined as usual. Cavalry were stationed on the square of the Palais Royal. Marius followed the Rue St. Honoré, and the further he got from the Palais

Royal the fewer windows were lit up; the shops were entirely closed, nobody was conversing on the thresholds, the street grew darker, and at the same time the crowd denser, for the passers-by had now become a crowd. No one could be heard speaking in the crowd, and yet a hollow, deep buzzing issued from it. Near the Arbre Sec Fountain there were mobs, motionless and somber groups standing among the comers and goers like stones in the middle of a running stream. At the entrance of the Rue des Prouvaires, the crowd no longer moved; it was a resisting, solid, compact, almost impenetrable mob of persons packed together and conversing in a low voice. There were hardly any black coats or round hats present, only fustian jackets, blouses, caps, and bristling beards. This multitude undulated confusedly in the night mist, and its whispering had the hoarse accent of a rustling, and, though no one moved, a tramping in the mud could be heard. Beyond this dense crowd there was not a window lit up in the surrounding streets, and the solitary and decreasing rows of lanterns could only be seen in them. The street-lanterns of that day resembled large red stars suspended from ropes, and cast on to the pavement a shadow which had the shape of a large spider. These streets, however, were not deserted, and piled muskets, moving bayonets, and troops bivouacking could be distinguished in them. No curious person went beyond this limit, and circulation ceased there; there the mob ended and the army began.

Marius wished with the will of a man who no longer hopes; he had been summoned and was bound to go. He found means to traverse the crowd and bivouacking troops; he hid himself from the patrols and avoided the sentries. He made a circuit, came to the Rue de Béthisy, and proceeded in the direction of the Halles; at the corner of the Rue des Bourdonnais the lanterns ceased. After crossing the zone of the mob he had left the border of troops, and now found himself in something frightful. There was not a wayfarer, nor a soldier, nor a light, nothing but solitude, silence, and night, and a strangely piercing cold; entering a street was like entering a cellar. Still he continued to advance; some one ran close past him; was it a man? a woman? were there more than one? He could not have said, for it had passed and vanished. By constant circuits he reached a lane, which he judged to be the Rue de la Poterie, and toward the middle of that lane came across an obstacle. He stretched out his hands and found that it was an overturned cart, and his feet recognized pools of water, holes, scattered and piled-up paving-stones—it was a barricade which had been begun, and then abandoned. He clambered over the stones, and soon found himself on the other side of the obstacle; he walked very close to the posts, and felt his way along the house walls. A little beyond the barricade he fancied that he could see something white before him, and on drawing nearer it assumed a form. It was a pair of white horses, the omnibus horses unharnessed by Bossuet in the morning, which had wandered, hap-hazard, from street to street all day, and at last stopped here, with the stolid patience of animals which no more comprehend the actions of man than man comprehends the actions of Providence. Marius left the horses behind him, and as he entered a street which seemed to be the Rue du Contrat-social, a musket-shot, which came no one could say whence, and traversed the darkness at hazard, whizzed close past him, and pierced above his head a copper shaving-dish hanging from a hair-dresser's shop. In 1846, this dish with the hole in it was still visible at the corner of the pillars of the Halles. This shot was a trace of life, but from this moment nothing further occurred. The whole itinerary resembled a descent down black steps. For all that Marius did not the less advance.

2. *AN OWL'S-EYE VIEW OF PARIS*

ANY being hovering over Paris at this moment, with the wings of a bat or an owl, would have had a gloomy spectacle under his eyes. The entire old district of the Halles, which is like a city within a city, which is traversed by the Rues St. Denis and St. Martin, and by a thousand lanes which the insurgents had converted into their redoubt and arsenal, would have appeared like an enormous black hole dug in the center of Paris. Here the eye settled on an abyss, and, owing to the broken lamps and the closed shutters, all brilliancy, life, noise, and movement had ceased in it. The invisible police of the revolt were watching everywhere and maintaining order, that is to say, night. To hide the small number in a vast obscurity, and to multiply each combatant by the possibilities which this obscurity contains, is the necessary tactics of the insurrection, and at nightfall every window in which a candle gleamed received a bullet; the light was extinguished, and sometimes the occupant killed. Hence, nothing stirred; there was naught but terror, mourning, and stupor in the houses, and in the streets a sort of sacred horror. Not even the long rows of windows and floors, the net-work of chimneys and roofs, and the vague reflections which glisten on the muddy and damp pavement could be perceived. The eye which had looked down from above on this mass of shadow might perhaps have noticed here and there indistinct gleams, which made the broken and strange lines, and the profile of singular buildings, stand out, something like flashes flitting through ruins—at such spots were the barricades. The rest was a lake of darkness and mystery, oppressive and funereal, above which motionless and mournful outlines rose, the tower of St. Jacques, the Church of St. Merry, and two or three other of those grand edifices of which man makes giants and night phantoms. All around this deserted and alarming labyrinth, in those districts where the circulation of Paris was not stopped, and where a few lamps glistened, the aerial observer would have distinguished the metallic scintillation of bayonets, the dull rolling of artillery, and the buzz of silent battalions, which was augmented every moment—it was a formidable belt, slowly contracting and closing in on the revolt.

The invested district was now but a species of monstrous cavern; everything seemed there asleep or motionless, and, as we have seen, each of the streets by which it could be approached only offered darkness. It was a stern darkness, full of snares, full of unknown and formidable collisions, into which it was terrifying to penetrate, and horrible to remain, where those who entered shuddered before those who awaited them, and those who awaited shuddered before those who were about to come. Invisible combatants were entrenched at the corner of every street, like sepulchral traps hidden in the thickness of the night. It was all over,—no other light could be hoped for there henceforth save the flash of musketry, no other meeting than the sudden and rapid apparition of death. Where? how? when? they did not know, but it was certain and inevitable: there, at the spot marked out for the contest, the government and the insurrection, the National Guards and the popular society, the bourgeoisie and the rioters, were about to grope their way toward each other. There was the same necessity for both sides, and the only issue henceforth possible was to be killed or conquer. It was such an extreme situation, such a powerful obscurity, that the most timid felt resolute and the most daring terrified. On both sides, however, there was equal fury, obstinacy, and determination; on one side advancing was death, and no one dreamed of recoiling; on the other remaining was death, and no one thought of flying. It was necessary that all should be over by the morrow, that the victory should be with one side or the other, and the insurrection either become a revolution or a riot. The government understood this as well as the partisans, and the smallest tradesman felt it. Hence came an agonizing thought with the impenetrable gloom of this district, where all was about to be decided; hence came a redoubled anxiety around this silence, whence a catastrophe was going to issue. Only one sound could be heard, a sound as heart-rending as a death-rattle, and as menacing as a malediction, the tocsin of St. Merry. Nothing could be so chilling as the clamor of this distracted and despairing bell as it lamented in the darkness.

As often happens, nature seemed to have come to an understanding with what men were going to do, and nothing deranged the mournful harmonies of the whole scene. The stars had disappeared, and heavy clouds filled the entire horizon with their melancholy masses. There was a black sky over these dead streets, as if an intense pall were cast over the immense tomb. While a thoroughly political battle was preparing on the same site which had already witnessed so many revolutionary events,—while the youth, the secret associations, and the schools, in the name of principles, and the middle classes in the name of interests, were coming together to try a final fall,—while everybody was hurrying up and appealing to the last and decisive hour of the crisis, in the distance and beyond that fatal district, at the lowest depths of the unfathomable cavities of that old wretched Paris, which is disappearing under the splendor of happy and opulent Paris, the gloomy voice of the people could be heard hoarsely growling. It is a startling and sacred voice, composed of the yell of the brute and the word of God, which terrifies the weak and warns the wise, and which at once comes from below like the voice of the lion, and from above like the voice of thunder.

3 . THE EXTREME BRINK

MARIUS had reached the Halles. There all was calmer, darker, and even more motionless than in the neighboring streets. It seemed as if the frozen piece of the tomb had issued from the ground and spread over the sky. A ruddy tinge, however, brought out from the black background the tall roofs of the houses which barred the Rue de la Chanvrerie on the side of St. Eustache. It was the reflection of the torch burning on the Corinth barricade, and Marius walked toward that ruddy hue; it led him to the Marché-aux-Poirées, and he caught a glimpse of the Rue des Prêcheurs, into which he turned. The sentry of the insurgents watching at the other end did not notice him; he felt himself quite close to what he was seeking, and he walked on tiptoe. He thus reached the corner of that short piece of the Mondétour lane which was, as will be remembered, the sole communication which Enjolras had maintained with the outer world. At the corner of the last house on his left, he stopped and peeped into the lane. A little beyond the dark corner formed by the lane and the Rue de la Chanvrerie, which formed a large patch of shadow, in which he was himself buried, he noticed a gleam on the pavement, a portion of a wine-shop, a lamp flickering in a sort of shapeless niche, and men crouching down with guns on their knees,—all this was scarce ten yards away from him, and was the interior of the barricade. The houses that lined the right-hand side of the lane hid him from the rest of the wine-shop, the large barricade, and the flag. Marius had but one step to take, and then the unhappy young man sat down on a post, folded his arms, and thought of his father.

He thought of that heroic Colonel Pontmercy who had been such a proud soldier, who had defended under the republic the frontier of

France, and touched under the empire the frontier of Asia; who had seen Genoa, Alessandria, Milan, Turin, Madrid, Vienna, Dresden, Berlin, and Moscow; who had left on all the victorious battle-fields of Europe drops of the same blood which Marius had in his veins; who had grown gray before age in discipline and command; who had lived with his waist-belt buckled, his epaulettes falling on his chest, his cockade blackened by smoke, his brow wrinkled by his helmet, in barracks, in camp, in bivouacs, and in hospitals, and who, at the expiration of twenty years, had returned from the great wars with his scarred cheek and smiling face, simple, tranquil, admirable, pure as an infant, having done everything for France, and nothing against her. He said to himself that his own day had now arrived, that his hour had at length struck, that after his father he, too, was going to be brave, intrepid, and bold, to rush to meet bullets, offer his chest to the bayonets, shed his blood, seek the enemy, seek death; that he in his turn was about to wage war and go into the battle-field, and that the battle he would enter was the street, and the war he was about to wage civil war. He saw civil war opening like a gulf before him, and that he was going to fall into it; then he shuddered.

He thought of his father's sword, which his grandfather had sold to the old clothes-dealer, and which he had so painfully regretted. He said to himself that this valiant and chaste sword had done well to escape from him and disappear angrily in the darkness; that it fled away thus because it was intelligent, and foresaw the future,—the riots, the war of gutters, the war of paving-stones, fusillades from cellar-traps, and blows dealt and received from behind; that, coming from Marengo and Austerlitz, it was unwilling to go to the Rue de la Chanvrerie, and after what it had done with the father refused to do that with the son! He said to himself that if that sword had been here, if, after receiving it at his dead father's bedside, he had dared to take it and carry it into this nocturnal combat between Frenchmen in the streets, it would assuredly have burned his hands, and have flashed before him like the glaive of the archangel! He said to himself that it was fortunate it was not there, but had disappeared,—that this was well, this was just, that his grandfather had been the true guardian of his father's glory, and that it was better for the colonel's sword to have been put up to auction, sold to the second-hand dealer, or broken up as old iron, than come to-day to make the flank of the country bleed. And then he began weeping bitterly. It was horrible, but what was he to do? he could not live without Cosette, and since she had departed, all left him was to die. Had he not pledged her his word of honor that he would die? She had gone away knowing this, and it was plain that she was pleased with Marius's dying; and then it was clear that she no longer loved him, since she had gone away thus without warning him, without a word, without a letter, and yet she knew his address! Of what use was it to live? and why should he live now? And then; to have come so far and then recoil! to have approached the danger and run away! to have come to look at the barricade and then slip off! to slip off, trembling, and saying, "After all I have had enough of that. I have seen it, that is sufficient; it is civil war, and I will be off." To abandon his friends who expected him, who perhaps had need of him, and who were a handful against an army! To be false to everything at once,—to love, to friendship, to his word! to give his poltroonery the pretext of patriotism! Oh, that was impossible; and if his father's phantom was there in the shadows, and saw him recoil, it would lash him with the flat of its saber, and cry to him, "Forward, coward!"

A prey to this oscillation of his thoughts, he hung his head, but suddenly raised it again, for a species of splendid rectification had just taken place in his mind. There is a dilatation of thought peculiar to the vicinity of the tomb; and to be near death makes a man see correctly. The vision of the action upon which he saw himself perhaps on the point of entering no longer appeared to him lamentable, but superb; the war of the street was become transfigured by some internal labor of the soul before his mental eye. All the tumultuous notes of interrogation of reverie crowded back upon him, but without troubling him, and he did not leave a single one unanswered. Why would his father be indignant? are there not cases in which insurrection attains to the dignity of duty? what was there degrading for the son of Colonel Pontmercy in the combat which was about to commence? It is no longer Montmirail or Champaubert, it is something else; it is no longer a question of a sacred territory but of a holy idea. The country complains; be it so, but humanity applauds. Is it true, besides, that the country complains? France bleeds, but liberty smiles, and on seeing the smile of liberty France forgets her wound. And then, regarding things from a higher point still, what did people mean by talking of a civil war?

What is the meaning of civil war? is there such a thing as a foreign war? Is not every war between men a war between brothers? War can only be qualified by its object, and there is neither foreign war nor civil war, there is only just or unjust war. Up to the day when the great human

concordat is concluded, war, at least that which is the effort of the hurrying future against the laggard past, may be necessary. What reproach
can be urged against such a war? war does not become a disgrace, or the
sword a dagger, until it assassinates right, progress, reason, civilization,
and truth. In such a case, whether civil war or foreign war, it is iniquitous, and is called crime. Beyond that holy thing, justice, what right
would one form of war have to despise another? by what right would
the sword of Washington ignore the pike of Camille Desmoulins?
Which is the greater, Leonidas contending against the foreigner or
Timoleon against the tyrant? one is the defender, the other is the liberator. Must we brand, without investigating the object, every taking up
of arms in the interior of a city? if so, mark with contumely Brutus,
Marcel, Arnould of Blankenheim, and Coligny. A war of thickets? a
street war? why not? such was the war of Ambiorix, of Artevelde, of
Marnix, and Pelagius. But Ambiorix struggled against Rome, Artevelde
against France, Marnix against Spain, and Pelagius against the Moors,
all against the foreigner. Well, monarchy is the foreigner, oppression is
the foreigner, divine right is the foreigner, and despotism violates the
moral frontier as invasion does the geographical frontier. Expelling the
tyrant or expelling the English is, in either case, a re-conquest of territory.
An hour arrives when a protest is insufficient; after philosophy action is
needed, living strength completes what the idea has sketched out.
Prometheus Bound begins, Aristogiton ends, the Enyclopædia enlightens minds, and August 10 electrifies them. After Æschylus, Thrasybulus;
after Diderot, Danton. Multitudes have a tendency to accept the master,
and their mass deposits apathy. A crowd is easily led into habits of obedience. These must be stirred up, impelled, and roughly treated by the
very blessing of their deliverance, their eyes be hurt by the truth, and
light hurled at them in terrible handfuls. They must themselves be to
some extent thunderstruck by their own salvation, for such a dazzling
awakes them. Hence comes the necessity of tocsins and wars; it is necessary that great combatants should rise, illumine nations by audacity,
and shake up that sorry humanity over which divine right, Cæsarian
glory, strength, fanaticism, irresponsible power, and absolute majesties
cast a shadow,—a mob stupidly occupied in contemplating these gloomy
triumphs of the night in their crepuscular splendor. But what? whom
are you talking of? do you call Louis Philippe the tyrant? no, no more
than Louis XVI. These are both what history is accustomed to call good
kings, but principles cannot be broken up, the logic of truth is rectilinear,

and its peculiarity to be deficient in complaisance; no concession therefore; every encroachment on man must be repressed: there is the right
divine in Louis XVI, there is the "because a Bourbon" in Louis Philippe;
both represent to a certain extent the confiscation of right, and they
must be combated in order to sweep away universal usurpation; it must
be so, for France is always the one who begins, and when the master
fails in France he fails everywhere. In a word, what cause is more just,
and consequently what war is greater, than to reëstablish social truth,
give back its throne to liberty, restore the people to the people and the
sovereignty to man, to replace the crown on the head of France, to restore
reason and equity in their plenitude, to suppress every germ of antago-
nism by giving back individuality, to annihilate the obstacle which the
royalty offers to the immense human concord, and to place the human
race once again on a level with right? Such wars construct peace. An
enormous fortalice of prejudice, privileges, superstitions, falsehoods,
exactions, abuses, violences, iniquities, and darknesses is still standing
on the earth with its towers of hatred, and it must be thrown down, and
the monstrous mass crumble away. To conquer at Austerlitz is great,
but to take the Bastille is immense.

No one but will have noticed in himself that the mind—and this is the
marvel of its unity complicated with ubiquity—has the strange aptitude
of reasoning almost coldly in the most violent extremities, and it often
happens that weird passions and deep despair, in the very agony of their
blackest soliloquies, handle subjects and discuss these. Logic is mingled
with the convulsions, and the thread of syllogism runs without breaking
through the storm of thoughts:—such was Marius's state of mind. While
thinking thus, crushed, but resolute, and yet hesitating and shuddering
at what he was going to do, his eyes wandered about the interior of the
barricade. The insurgents were conversing in whispers, without moving,
and that almost silence which marks the last phase of expectation was
perceptible. Above them, at a third-floor window, Marius distinguished
a species of spectator or of witness, who seemed singularly attentive,—
it was the porter killed by Le Cabuc. From below this head could be
vaguely perceived in the reflection of the torch burning on the barricade,
and nothing was stranger in this dense and vacillating light than this
motionless, livid, and amazed face, with its bristling hair, open and fixed
eyes and gaping mouth, bending over the street in an attitude of curiosity. It might be said that this dead man was contemplating those who
were going to die. A long stream of blood which had flowed from his
head, descended from the window to the first-floor, where it stopped.

BOOK XIV

THE GRANDEUR OF DESPAIR

1. THE FLAG—ACT FIRST

NOTHING came yet: it had struck ten by St. Merry's, and Enjolras and Combeferre were sitting, musket in hand, near the sally-port of the great barricade. They did not speak, but were listening, trying to catch the dullest and most remote sound of marching. Suddenly, in the midst of this lugubrious calm, a clear, young, gay voice, which seemed to come from the Rue St. Denis, burst forth, and began singing distinctly, to the old popular tune of *Au clair de la lune,* these lines terminating with a cry that resembled a cock-crow.

> *Mon nez est en larmes,*
> *Mon ami Bugeaud,*
> *Prêt'-moi tes gendarmes*
> *Pour leur dire un mot.*
> *En capote bleue,*
> *La poule au shako,*
> *Voici la banlieue!*
> *Co-cocorico!*

They shook hands.

" 'Tis Gavroche," said Enjolras.

"He is warning us," said Combeferre.

Hurried footsteps troubled the deserted streets, and a being more active than a clown was seen climbing over the omnibus, and Gavroche leaped into the square, out of breath, and saying:

"My gun! here they are."

An electric shudder ran along the whole barricade, and the movement of hands seeking guns was heard.

"Will you have my carbine?" Enjolras asked the gamin.

"I want the big gun," Gavroche answered, and took Javert's musket. Two sentries had fallen back and came in almost simultaneously with Gavroche; they were those from the end of the street and the Petite Truanderie. The vedette in the lane des Prêcheurs remained at his post, which indicated that nothing was coming from the direction of the bridges and the Halles. The Rue de la Chanvrerie, in which a few paving-stones were scarce visible in the reflection of the light cast on the flag, offered to the insurgents the aspect of a large black gate vaguely opened in a cloud of smoke. Every man proceeded to his post. Forty-three insurgents among whom were Enjolras, Combeferre, Courfeyrac, Bossuet, Joly, Bahorel, and Gavroche, knelt behind the great barricade, with the muzzles of their guns and carbines thrust out between paving-stones as through loop-holes, attentive, silent, and ready to fire. Six, commanded by Feuilly, installed themselves at the upper windows of Corinth. Some minutes more elapsed, and then a measured, heavy tramp of many feet was distinctly heard from the direction of St. Leu; this noise, at first faint, then precise, and then heavy and reëchoing, approached slowly without halt or interruption, and with a tranquil and terrible continuity. Nothing was audible but this; it was at once the silence and noise of the statue of the Commander, but the stormy footfall had something enormous and multiple about it which aroused the idea of a multitude at the same time as that of a specter; you might have fancied that you heard the fearful statue Legion on the march. The tramp came nearer, nearer still, and then ceased; and the breathing of many men seemed to be audible at the end of the street. Nothing, however, was visible, though quite at the end in the thick gloom could be distinguished a multitude of metallic threads, fine as needles and almost imperceptible, which moved about like that indescribable phosphoric net-work which we perceive under our closed eyelids just at the moment when we are falling asleep. These were bayonets and musket barrels on which the reflection of the torch confusedly fell. There was another pause, as if both sides were waiting. All at once a voice, which was the more sinister because no one could be seen, and it seemed as if the darkness itself was speaking, shouted:

"Who goes there?"

At the same time the click of muskets being cocked could be heard. Enjolras replied with a sonorous and haughty accent:

"The French Revolution."

"Fire!" the voice commanded.

A flash lit up all the frontages in the street, as if the door of a furnace had been suddenly opened and shut, and a frightful shower of bullets hurled against the barricade, and the red flag fell. The discharge had been so violent and dense that it cut the staff asunder, that is to say, the extreme point of the omnibus pole. Bullets ricochetting from the corners of the houses penetrated the barricade and wounded several men. The impression produced by this first discharge was chilling; the attack was rude, and of a nature to make the boldest think. It was plain that they had to do with a whole regiment at the least.

"Comrades," Courfeyrac cried, "let us not waste our powder, but wait till they have entered the street before returning their fire."

"And before all," Enjolras said, "let us hoist the flag again!"

He picked up the flag which had fallen just at his feet; outside the ring of ramrods in barrels could be heard,—the troops were reloading. Enjolras continued:

"Who has a brave heart among us? who will plant the flag on the barricade again?"

Not one replied, for to mount the barricade at this moment, when all the guns were doubtless aimed at it, was simply death, and the bravest man hesitates to condemn himself. Enjolras even shuddered as he repeated:

"Will no one offer?"

2. *THE FLAG—ACT SECOND*

SINCE the arrival at Corinth and the barricade had been begun no one paid any further attention to Father Mabœuf. M. Mabœuf, however, had not quitted the insurgents; he had gone into the ground-floor room of the wine-shop and seated himself behind the bar, where he was, so to speak, annihilated in himself. He seemed no longer to see or think. Courfeyrac and others had twice or thrice accosted him, warning him of the peril and begging him to withdraw, but he had not appeared to hear them. When no one was speaking to him his lips moved as if he were answering some one, and as soon as people addressed him his lips left off moving, and his eyes no longer seemed alive. A few hours before the barricade was attacked he had assumed a posture which he had not quitted since, with his two hands on his knees, and his head bent forward, as if he were looking into a precipice. Nothing could have drawn him out of this attitude, and it did not appear as if his mind were in the barricade. When every one else went to his post the only persons left in the room were Javert tied to the post, an insurgent with drawn saber watching over Javert, and Mabœuf. At the moment of the attack, at the detonation, the physical shock affected and, as it were, awoke him; he suddenly rose, crossed the room, and at the moment when Enjolras repeated his appeal, "Does no one offer?" the old man was seen on the threshold of the wine-shop. His presence produced a series of commotion in the groups, and the cry was raised:

"It is the voter, the conventionalist, the representative of the people!"

He probably did not hear it. He walked straight up to Enjolras, the insurgents making way for him with a religious fear, tore the flag from Enjolras, who recoiled with petrifaction, and then, no one daring to arrest or help him, this old man of eighty, with shaking head, but firm step, slowly began ascending the staircase of paving-stones formed inside the barricade. This was so gloomy and so grand that all around him cried, "Off with your hats." With each step he ascended the scene became more frightful; his white hair, his decrepit face, his tall, bald, and wrinkled forehead, his hollow eyes, his amazed and open mouth, and his old arm raising the red banner, stood out from the darkness and were magnified in the sanguinary brightness of the torch, and the spectators fancied they saw the specter of '93 issuing from the ground, holding the flag of terror in its hand. When he was on the last step, when this trembling and terrible phantom, standing, on the pile of ruins, in the presence of twelve hundred invisible gun-barrels, stood facing death, and as if stronger than it, the whole barricade assumed in the darkness a supernatural and colossal aspect. There was one of those silences which only occur at the sight of prodigies, and in the midst of the silence the old man brandished the red flag, and cried:

"Long live the revolution! long live the republic! fraternity! equality! and death!"

A low and quick talking, like the murmur of a hurried priest galloping through a mass, was heard,—it was probably the police commissary making the legal summons at the other end of the street. Then the same loud voice which had shouted "Who goes there?" cried: "Withdraw!"

M. Mabœuf, livid, haggard, with his eyeballs illumined by the mournful flames of mania, raised the flag above his head and repeated:

"Long live the republic!"

"Fire!" the voice commanded.

A second discharge, resembling a round of grape-shot, burst against the barricade. The old man sank on his knees, then rose again, let the flag slip from his hand, and fell back on the pavement like a log, with his arms stretched out like a cross. Streams of blood flowed under him, and his old, pale, melancholy face seemed to be gazing at heaven. One of those emotions stronger than man, which makes him forget self-defense, seized on the insurgents, and they approached the corpse with respectful horror.

"What men these regicides are!" said Enjolras.

Courfeyrac whispered in Enjolras's ear:

"This is only between ourselves, as I do not wish to diminish the enthusiasm, but this man was anything rather than a regicide. I knew him, and his name was Mabœuf. I do not know what was the matter with him to-day, but he was a brave idiot. Look at his head."

"The head of an idiot and the heart of Brutus!" Enjolras replied, then he raised his voice.

"Citizens! such is the example which the old give to the young. We hesitated and he came; we recoiled and he advanced. This is what those who tremble with old age teach those who tremble with fear! This aged man is august before his country; he has had a long life and a magnificent death! Now let us place his corpse under cover, let each of us defend this dead old man as he would defend his living father, and let his presence in the midst of us render the barricade impregnable!"

A murmur of gloomy and energetic adhesion followed these words. Enjolras bent down, raised the old man's head, and sternly kissed him on the forehead; then, stretching out his arms and handling the dead man with tender caution, as if afraid of hurting him, he took off his coat, pointed to the blood-stained holes, and said:

"This is our flag now."

3. *GAVROCHE HAD BETTER HAVE TAKEN THE CARBINE OF ENJOLRAS*

A LONG black shawl of Widow Hucheloup's was thrown over Father Mabœuf: six men made a litter of their muskets, the corpse was laid on them, and they carried it with bare heads and solemn slowness to a large table in the ground-floor room. These men, entirely engaged with the grave and sacred thing they were doing, did not think of the perilous situation in which they were, and when the corpse was carried past the stoical Javert, Enjolras said to the spy:

"Your turn will come soon."

During this period little Gavroche, who alone had not left his post, and had remained on the watch, fancied he could see men creeping up to the barricade: all at once he cried, "Look out!" Courfeyrac, Enjolras, Jean Prouvaire, Combeferre, Joly, Bahorel, and Bossuet, all hurried tumultuously out of the wine-shop, but it was almost too late; for they saw a flashing line of bayonets undulating on the crest of the barricade. Municipal Guards of tall stature penetrated, some by striding over the omnibus, others through the sally-port, driving before them the gamin, who fell back, but did not fly. The moment was critical; it was that first formidable minute of inundation when the river rises to the level of the dam and the water begins to filter through the fissures of the dyke. One second more and the barricade was captured. Bahorel dashed at the first Municipal Guard who entered, and killed him with a shot from his carbine; the second killed Bahorel with a bayonet-thrust. Another had already leveled Courfeyrac, who was shouting Help! while the tallest of all of them, a species of Colossus, was marching upon Gavroche, with his bayonet at the charge. The gamin raised in his little arms Javert's enormous musket, resolutely aimed at the giant, and pulled the trigger. But the gun did not go off, as Javert had not loaded it; the Municipal Guard burst into a laugh, and advanced upon the lad. Before the bayonet had reached Gavroche, however, the musket fell from the soldier's hands, for a bullet struck him in the middle of the forehead, and he fell on his back. A second bullet struck the other guard, who had attacked Courfeyrac, in the middle of the chest, and laid him low.

The shots were fired by Marius, who had just entered the barricade.

4. *THE BARREL OF GUNPOWDER*

MARIUS, still concealed at the corner of the Rue Mondétour, had watched the first phase of the combat with shuddering irresolution. Still he was unable to resist for any length of time that mysterious and sovereign dizziness which might be called the appeal from the abyss; and at the sight of the imminence of the peril, of M. Mabœuf's death, that mournful enigma, Bahorel killed, Courfeyrac shouting, this child menaced, and his friends to succor or revenge, all hesitation vanished, and he rushed into the medley, pistols in hand. With the first shot he saved Gavroche, and with the second delivered Courfeyrac. On hearing the shots and the cries of the guards, the assailants swarmed up the intrenchment, over the crest of which could now be seen more than half the bodies of Municipal Guards, troops of the line, and National Guards from the suburbs, musket in hand. They already covered more than two-thirds of the barricade, but no longer leaped down into the inclosure, and hesitated, as if they feared some snare. They looked down into the gloomy space as they would have peered into a lion's den; and the light of the torch only illumined bayonets, bear-skin shakos, and anxious and irritated faces.

Marius had no longer a weapon, as he had thrown away his discharged pistols, but he had noticed the barrel of gunpowder near the door of the ground-floor room. As he half turned to look in that direction a soldier leveled his musket at him, and at the moment when the soldier was taking steady aim at Marius, a hand was laid on the muzzle of his musket and stopped it up; the young workman in the velvet trousers had rushed forward. The shot was fired, the bullet passed through the hand, and probably through the workman, for he fell, but did not hit Marius. Marius, who was entering the wine-shop, hardly noticed this; still he had confusedly seen the gun pointed at him, and the hand laid on the muzzle, and had heard the explosion. But in minutes like this things that men see vacillate, and they do not dwell on anything, for they feel themselves obscurely impelled toward deeper shadows still, and all is mist. The insurgents, surprised but not terrified, had rallied, and Enjolras cried, "Wait, do not throw away your shots!" and, in truth, in the first moment of confusion they might wound each other. The majority had gone up to the second-floor and attic windows, whence they commanded the assailants, but the more determined, with Enjolras, Courfeyrac, Jean Prouvaire, and Combeferre, were haughtily standing against the houses at the end, unprotected, and facing the lines of soldiers and guards who crowned the barricade. All this was done without precipitation, and with that strange and menacing gravity which precedes a combat; on both sides men were aiming at each other within point-blank range, and they were so near that they could converse. When they were at the point where the spark was about to shoot forth, an officer wearing a gorget and heavy epaulettes stretched out his sword and cried:

"Throw down your arms!"

"Fire!" Enjolras commanded.

The two detonations took place at the same moment, and everything disappeared in smoke, a sharp and stifling smoke, in which the dying and the wounded writhed, with faint and hollow groans. When the smoke dispersed, the two lines of combatants could be seen thinned, but at the same spot, and silently reloading their guns. All at once a thundering voice was heard shouting:

"Begone, or I will blow up the barricade!"

All turned to the quarter whence the voice came.

Marius had entered the wine-shop, fetched the barrel of gunpowder, and then, taking advantage of the smoke and obscure mist which filled the intrenched space, glided along the barricade up to the cage of paving-stones in which the torch was fixed. To tear out the torch, place in its stead the barrel of powder, throw down the pile of paving-stones on the barrel, which was at once unheaded with a sort of terrible obedience, had only occupied so much time as stooping and rising again; and now all, National Guards, Municipal Guards, officers and privates, collected at the other end of the barricade, gazed at him in stupor, as he stood with one foot on the paving-stones, the torch in his hand, his haughty face illumined by a fatal resolution, approaching the flame of the torch to the formidable heap, in which the broken powder-barrel could be distinguished, and uttering the terrifying cry:

"Begone, or I will blow up the barricade!"

Marius, on this barricade after the octogenarian, was the vision of the young revolution after the apparition of the old one.

"Blow up the barricade!" a sergeant said, "and yourself, too!"

Marius answered, "And myself, too!"

And he lowered the torch toward the barrel of gunpowder, but there was no one left on the barricade; the assailants, leaving their dead and their wounded, fell back pell-mell and in disorder to the end of the street, and disappeared again in the night. It was a *sauve qui peut*. The barricade was saved.

5. *END OF THE VERSES OF JEAN PROUVAIRE*

ALL surrounded Marius, and Courfeyrac fell on his neck.

"Here you are!"

"What happiness!" said Combeferre.

"You arrived just in time," said Bossuet.

"Were it not for you I should be dead!" Courfeyrac remarked.

"Without you I should have been gobbled up," Gavroche added.

Marius added: "Who is the leader?"

"Yourself," Enjolras replied.

Marius, the whole day through, had had a furnace in his brain, but now it was a tornado, and this tornado which was in him produced on him the effect of being outside him and carrying him away. It seemed to him as if he were already an immense distance from life; and his two luminous months of joy and love suddenly terminated at this frightful precipice. Cosette lost to him, this barricade, M. Mabœuf letting himself be killed for the republic, himself chief of the insurgents—all these things seemed to him a monstrous nightmare, and he was obliged to make a mental effort in order to remind himself that all which surrounded him was real. Marius had not lived long enough yet to know that nothing is so imminent as the impossible, and that what must be always foreseen is the unforeseen. He witnessed the performance of his own drama, as if it were a piece of which he understood nothing. In his mental fog he did not recognize Javert, who, fastened to his post, had not made a movement of his head during the attack on the barricade, and saw the revolt buzzing round him with the resignation of a martyr and the majesty of a judge. Marius did not even see him. In the meanwhile the assailants no longer stirred; they could be heard marching and moving at the end of the street, but did not venture into it either because they were waiting for orders, or else required reënforcements, before rushing again upon this impregnable redoubt. The insurgents had posted sentries, and some who were medical students had begun dressing wounds. All the tables had been dragged out of the wine-shop, with the exception of the two reserved for the lint and the cartridges, and the one on which Father Mabœuf lay; they had been added to the barricade, and the mattresses off the beds of Widow Hucheloup and the girls had been put in their place. On these mattresses the wounded were laid; as for the three poor creatures who inhabited Corinth, no one knew what had become of them, but they were at length found hidden in the cellar.

A poignant emotion darkened the joy of the liberated barricade. The roll-call was made, and one of the insurgents was missing. Who was he? one of the dearest and most valiant, Jean Prouvaire. He was sought for among the dead, but was not there; he was sought for among the wounded, and was not there; he was evidently a prisoner. Combeferre said to Enjolras:

"They have our friend, but we have their agent; do you insist on the death of this spy?"

"Yes," Enjolras replied, "but less than the life of Jean Prouvaire."

This was said in the bar-room close to the post where Javert was tied.

"Well," Combeferre continued, "I will fasten a handkerchief to my cane, and go as a flag of truce to offer to give them their man for our man."

"Listen," said Enjolras, as he laid his hand on Combeferre's arm.

There was a meaning click of guns at the end of the street, and a manly voice could be heard crying:

"Long live France! long live the future!"

They recognized Prouvaire's voice; a flash passed and a detonation burst forth; then the silence returned.

"They have killed him," Combeferre exclaimed.

Enjolras looked at Javert and said to him:

"Your friends have just shot you."

6. *THE AGONY OF DEATH AFTER THE AGONY OF LIFE*

IT is a singularity of this sort of war, that the attack on barricades is almost always made in the front, and that the assailants generally refrain from turning positions, either because they suspect ambuscades, or are afraid to enter winding streets. The whole attention of the insurgents was, consequently, directed to the great barricade, which was evidently the constantly threatened point, and the contest would infallibly recommence there. Marius, however, thought of the little barricade, and went to it; it was deserted, and only guarded by the lamp which flickered among the paving-stones. However, the Mondétour lane and the branches of the little Truanderie were perfectly calm. As Marius, after making his inspection, was going back, he heard his name faintly uttered in the darkness:

"Monsieur Marius!"

He started, for he recognized the voice which had summoned him two hours back through the garden railings in the Rue Plumet, but this voice now only seemed to be a gasp. He looked around him and saw nobody. Marius fancied that he was mistaken, and that it was an illusion added by his mind to the extraordinary realities which were pressing round him. He took a step to leave the remote angle in which the barricade stood.

"Monsieur Marius!" the voice repeated. This time he could not doubt, for he had heard distinctly; he looked around but saw nothing.

"At your feet," the voice said.

He stooped down and saw in the shadow a form crawling toward him on the pavement. It was the speaker. The lamp enabled him to distinguish a blouse, torn cotton-velvet trousers, bare feet, and something that resembled a pool of blood; Marius also caught a glimpse of a pale face raised to him, and saying:

"Do you not recognize me?"

"No."

"Eponine."

Marius eagerly stooped down; it was really that hapless girl dressed in male clothes.

"What brought you here? what are you doing?"

"Dying," she said to him.

There are words and incidents that wake up crushed beings; Marius cried, with a start:

"You are wounded? wait, I will carry you into the wine-shop! your wound will be dressed! is it serious? how shall I catch hold of you so as not to hurt you? where is it you suffer? Help, good God! but what did you come to do here?"

And he tried to pass his hand under her to lift her, and as he did so he touched her hand—she uttered a faint cry.

"Have I hurt you?" Marius asked.

"A little."

"But I only touched your hand."

She raised her hand to Marius's eyes, and he could see a hole right through it.

"What is the matter with your hand?" he said.

"It is pierced."

"Pierced?"

"Yes."

"What with?"

"A bullet."

"How?"

"Did you see a musket aimed at you?"

"Yes, and a hand laid on the muzzle."

"It was mine."

Marius shuddered.

"What madness! poor child! but all the better, if that is your wound, it is nothing, so let me carry you to a bed. Your wound will be dressed, and people do not die of a bullet through the hand."

She murmured:

"The bullet passed through my hand but came out of my back, so it is useless to move me from here. I will tell you how you can do me more good than a surgeon; sit down by my side on that stone."

He obeyed; she laid her head on his knees, and, without looking at him, said:

"Oh, how good that is, how comforting! There! I do not suffer now."

She remained silent for a moment, then turned her head with an effort and gazed at Marius.

"Do you know what, M. Marius? it annoyed me that you entered that garden, though it was very foolish of me, as I showed you the house, and then, too, I ought to have remembered that a young gentleman like you——"

She broke off, and, leaping over the gloomy transitions which her mind doubtless contained, she added with a heart-rending smile:

"You thought me ugly, did you not?"

Then she continued:

"You are lost, and no one will leave the barricade now. I brought you here, you know, and you are going to die; I feel sure of it. And yet when I saw the soldier aiming at you, I laid my hand on the muzzle of his gun. How droll that is, but the reason was that I wished to die with you. When I received that bullet I dragged myself here, and as no one saw me I was not picked up. I waited for you and said, 'Will he not come?' Oh, if you only knew how I bit my blouse, for I was suffering so terribly, but now I feel all right. Do you remember the day when I came into your room and looked at myself in your glass, and the day when I met you on the boulevard near the washer-women? how the birds sang, and it is not so very long ago. You gave me five francs, and I said to you, 'I do

333

not want your money.' I hope you picked up your coin, for you are not rich, and I did not think of telling you to pick it up. The sun was shining, and it was not at all cold. Do you remember, M. Marius? Oh, I am so happy, for everybody is going to die."

She had a wild, grave and heart-rending look, and her ragged blouse displayed her naked throat. While speaking she laid her wounded hand on her chest, in which was another hole, and whence every moment a stream of blood spurted like a jet of wine from an open bung. Marius gazed at this unfortunate creature with profound compassion.

"Oh!" she suddenly continued, "it is coming back; I choke!"

She raised her blouse and bit it, and her limbs stiffened on the pavement. At this moment Gavroche's crowing voice could be heard from the barricade; the lad had got on to a table to load his musket, and was gayly singing the song so popular at that day:

> *"En voyant Lafayette,*
> *Le gendarme répète:*
> *Sauvons-nous! sauvons-nous! sauvons-nous!"*

Eponine raised herself and listened; then she muttered:

"It is he."

And, turning to Marius, added:

"My brother is here, but he must not see me, or he will scold me."

"Your brother?" Marius asked, as he thought most bitterly and sadly of the duties toward the Thénardiers which his father had left him; "which is your brother?"

"That little fellow."

"The one who is singing?"

"Yes."

Marius made a move.

"Oh, do not go away," she said; "it will not be long just now."

She was almost sitting up, but her voice was very low, and every now and then interrupted by the death-rattle. She put her face as close as she could to that of Marius, and added with a strange expression:

"Come, I will not play you a trick; I have had a letter addressed to you in my pocket since yesterday: I was told to put it in the post, but kept it, as I did not wish it to reach you. But, perhaps, you will not be angry with me when we meet again ere long, for we shall meet again, shall we not? Take your letter."

She convulsively seized Marius's hand with her wounded hand, but seemed no longer to feel the suffering. She placed Marius's hand in her blouse-pocket, and he really felt a paper.

"Take it," she said.

Marius took the letter, and she gave a nod of satisfaction and consent.

"Now, for my trouble; promise me——"

And she stopped.

"What?" Marius asked.

"Promise me!"

"I do promise!"

"Promise to kiss me on the forehead when I am dead—I shall feel it."

She let her head fall again on Marius's knees, and her eyes closed—he fancied the poor soul departed. Eponine remained motionless, but all at once, at the moment when Marius believed her eternally asleep, she slowly opened her eyes, on which the gloomy profundity of death was visible, and said to him with an accent whose gentleness seemed already to come from another world:

"And then, Monsieur Marius, I think that I was a little bit in love with you."

She tried to smile once more, and expired.

7. GAVROCHE CALCULATES DISTANCES

MARIUS kept his promise; he deposited a kiss on this livid forehead, upon which an icy perspiration beaded. It was not an infidelity to Cosette, but a pensive and sweet farewell to an unhappy soul. He had not taken without a quiver the letter which Eponine gave him; for he at once suspected an event in it, and was impatient to read it. The heart of man is so constituted,—and the unfortunate child had scarce closed her eyes ere Marius thought of unfolding the paper. He gently laid her on the ground and went off, for something told him that he could not read this letter in the presence of that corpse. He walked up to a candle in the ground-floor room; it was a little note folded and sealed with the elegant care peculiar to women. The address was in a feminine hand-writing, and ran:

"To Monsieur, Monsieur Marius Pontmercy, at Courfeyrac's, No. 16, Rue de la Verrerie."

He broke the seal and read:

"MY WELL-BELOVED: *Alas! my father insists on our going away at once. We shall be this evening at No. 7, Rue de l'Homme Armé, and within a week in London.*—COSETTE.—*June 4.*"

Such was the innocence of their love that Marius did not even know Cosette's handwriting.

What had happened may be told in a few words. Eponine had done it all. After the night of June 3 she had had a double thought,—to foil the plans of her father and the bandits upon the house in the Rue Plumet, and separate Marius and Cosette. She had changed rags with the first scamp she met, who thought it amusing to dress up as a woman, while Eponine disguised herself as a man. It was she who gave Jean Valjean the expressive warning, *Change your house,* and he had gone straight home and said to Cosette: "We shall start this evening, and go to the Rue de l'Homme Armé with Toussaint. Next week we shall be in London." Cosette, startled by this unexpected blow, had hastily written two lines to Marius, but how was she to put the letter in the post? She never went out alone, and Toussaint, surprised by such an errand, would certainly show the letter to M. Fauchelevent. In this state of anxiety, Cosette noticed through the railings Eponine in male clothes, who now incessantly prowled round the garden. Cosette had summoned "this young workman," and gave him the letter and a five-franc piece, say-ing, "Carry this letter at once to its address," and Eponine put the letter in her pocket. The next day she went to Courfeyrac's and asked for Marius, not to hand him the letter, but "to see," a thing which every jealous, loving soul will understand. There she waited for Marius, or at any rate Courfeyrac—always "to see." When Courfeyrac said to her, "We are going to the barricades," an idea crossed her mind—to throw herself into this death as she would have done into any other, and thrust

Marius into it. She followed Courfeyrac, assured herself of the spot where the barricade was being built; and, feeling certain, since Marius had not received the letter, that he would go at night-fall to the usual meeting-place, she went to the Rue Plumet, waited for Marius there, and gave him that summons in the name of his friends, which, as she thought, must lead him to the barricade. She reckoned on Marius's despair when he did not find Cosette, and she was not mistaken, and then she returned to the Rue de la Chanvrerie. We have just seen what she did there; she died with the tragic joy of jealous hearts which drag the beloved being down to death with them and say, "No one shall have him!"

Marius covered Cosette's letter with kisses; she loved him, then! and for a moment he had an idea that he ought not to die, but then he said to himself: "Her father is taking her to England, and my grandfather will not give his consent to the marriage; no change has taken place in fatality." Dreamers like Marius undergo such supreme despondencies, and desperate resolves issue from them; the fatigue of living is insupportable, and death is sooner over. Then he thought that two duties were left him to accomplish: inform Cosette of his death, and send her his last farewell, and save from the imminent catastrophe which was preparing that poor boy, Eponine's brother and Thénardier's son. He had a pocket-book about him, the same which had contained the paper on which he had written so many love-thoughts for Cosette; he tore out a leaf, and wrote in pencil these few lines:

"Our marriage was impossible; I asked my grandfather's consent, and he refused to give it; I have no fortune, nor have you. I ran to your house, and did not find you there; you remember the pledge I made you, and I have kept it. I die. I love you, and when you read this my soul will be near you, and smile upon you."

Having nothing with which to seal this letter, he merely folded it, and wrote on it the address:

"To Mademoiselle Cosette Fauchelevent, at M. Fauchelevent's, No. 7, Rue de l'Homme Armé."

The letter folded, he stood for a moment in thought, then opened his pocket-book again, and wrote with the same pencil these lines on the first-page:

"My name is Marius Pontmercy. Carry my body to my grandfather, M. Gillenormand, No. 6, Rue des Filles du Calvaire, in the Marais."

He returned the book to his coat-pocket, and then summoned Gavroche. The lad, on hearing Marius's voice, ran up with his joyous and devoted face.

"Will you do something for me?"

"Everything," said Gavroche, "God of gods! my goose would have been cooked without you."

"You see this letter?"

"Yes."

"Take it. Leave the barricade at once (Gavroche began scratching his ear anxiously), and to-morrow morning you will deliver it at its address, No. 7, Rue de l'Homme Armé."

The heroic lad replied:

"Well, but during that time the barricade will be attacked, and I shall not be here."

"The barricade will not be attacked again until daybreak, according to all appearances, and will not be taken till to-morrow afternoon."

The new respite which the assailants granted to the barricade was really prolonged; it was one of those intermissions frequent in night fights, which are always followed by redoubled obstinacy.

"Well," said Gavroche, "suppose I were to deliver your letter to-morrow morning?"

"It will be too late, for the barricade will probably be blockaded, all the issues guarded, and you will be unable to get out. Be off at once."

Gavroche could not find any reply, so he stood there undecided, and scratching his head sorrowfully. All at once he seized the letter with one of those bird-like movements of his.

"All right," he said.

And he ran off toward the narrow Rue Mondétour. Gavroche had an idea which decided him, but which he did not mention; it was the following:

"It is scarce midnight, the Rue de l'Homme Armé is no great distance off. I will deliver the letter at once, and be back in time."

BOOK XV

RUE DE L'HOMME ARMÉ

1 . *THE TREACHEROUS BLOTTING-BOOK*

WHAT are the convulsions of a city compared with the convulsions of a soul? man is even a greater profundity than the people. Jean Valjean at this very moment was suffering from a frightful internal earthquake, and all the gulfs were re-opened within him. He too was quivering, like Paris, on the threshold of a formidable and obscure revolution. A few hours had sufficed to cover his destiny and his conscience with shadows, and of him, as of Paris, it might be said, "The two principles are face to face." The white angel and the black angel are about to wrestle with each other on the brink of the abyss; which will hurl the other down? which will triumph?

On the evening of the same day, Jean Valjean, accompanied by Cosette and Toussaint, proceeded to the Rue de l'Homme Armé, where a tremendous incident was fated to take place. Cosette had not left the Rue Plumet without an attempt at resistance, and, for the first time since they had lived together, the will of Cosette and the will of Jean Valjean had shown themselves distinct, and had contradicted each other, though they did not come into collision. There was objection on one side and inflexibility on the other; for the abrupt advice, "move," thrown to Jean Valjean by a stranger, had alarmed him to such a point as to render him absolute. He fancied himself tracked and pursued, and Cosette was compelled to yield. The pair reached the Rue de l'Homme Armé without exchanging a syllable, for each was deep in personal thought, while Jean Valjean was so anxious that he did not notice Cosette's sadness, and Cosette was so sad that she did not notice Jean Valjean's anxiety. Jean Valjean had brought Toussaint with him, which he had never done in his previous absences, but he foresaw that he might possibly never return to the Rue Plumet, and he could neither leave Toussaint behind him nor tell her his secret. Moreover, he felt her to be devoted and sure; the treachery of a servant to a master begins with curiosity, and Toussaint, as if predestined to be Jean Valjean's servant, was not curious. She was wont to say while stammering in her patois of a Barneville peasant, "I am so, I do my work, and the rest does not concern me." In his departure from the Rue Plumet, which was almost a flight, Jean Valjean took away with him nothing but the fragrant little portmanteau, christened by Cosette the *inseparable*. Packed trunks would have required porters, and porters are witnesses; a hackney-coach had been called to the gate in the Rue de Babylone, and they went away in it. It was with great difficulty that Toussaint obtained permission to pack up a little stock of linen and clothes, and a few toilet articles; Cosette, herself, only took her desk and blotting-book. Jean Valjean, in order to heighten the solitude and mystery of this disappearance, had so arranged as to leave the Rue Plumet at nightfall, which had given Cosette the time to write her note to Marius. They reached the Rue de l'Homme Armé when it was quite dark, and went to bed in perfect silence.

The apartments in this street were situated on a third-floor in a back yard, and consisted of two bedrooms, a dining-room, and a kitchen adjoining, with a closet in which was a flock-bed that fell to the lot of Toussaint. The dining-room was at the same time anteroom and separated the two bed-rooms, and the apartments were provided with the necessary articles of furniture. Human nature is so constituted that men become re-assured almost as absurdly as they are alarmed; hence Jean Valjean had scarce reached the Rue de l'Homme Armé ere his anxiety cleared away and was gradually dissipated. There are calming places which act to some extent mechanically on the mind, and when a street is obscure the inhabitants are peaceful. Jean Valjean felt a contagious tranquillity in this lane of old Paris, which is so narrow that it is barred against vehicles by a cross-beam, which is dumb and deaf amid the noisy town, full of twilight in broad day-light, and, so to speak, incapable of feeling emotions between its two rows of high, century-old houses, which are silent, like the old folk they are. There is in this street a stagnant oblivion, and Jean Valjean breathed again in it, for how was it possible that he could be found there? His first care was to place the *inseparable* by his side. He slept soundly. Night counsels; we might add, night appeases. The next morning he woke up almost gay. He considered the dining-room charming, though it was hideous, for it was furnished with an old round table, a low sideboard, surmounted by a mirror, a rickety easy-chair, and a few chairs encumbered with Toussaint's parcels. In one of these parcels Jean Valjean's National Guard uniform could be seen through an opening.

As for Cosette, she ordered Toussaint to bring a basin of broth to her bedroom, and did not make her appearance till evening. At about five o'clock, Toussaint, who went about very busy settling this little household, placed a cold fowl on the dinner-table, which Cosette consented to look at, through deference for her father. This done, Cosette, protesting headache, said good-night to Jean Valjean, and shut herself up in her bedroom. Jean Valjean ate a wing of the fowl with appetite, and with his elbows on the table, and gradually growing re-assured, regained his feelings of security. While he was eating this modest dinner, he vaguely heard twice or thrice stammering Toussaint say to him, "There is a disturbance, sir, and people are fighting in Paris." But, absorbed in a multitude of internal combinations, he had paid no attention to her; truth to tell, he had not heard her. He rose and began walking from the door to the window, and from the window to the door, with calmness. Cosette, his sole preoccupation, reverted to his mind; not that he was alarmed by this headache, a slight nervous attack, a girl's pouting, a momentary cloud which would disappear in a day or two, but he thought of the future, and, as usual, thought of it gently. After all, he saw no obstacle to his happy life resuming its course; at certain hours everything seems impossible, at others everything appears easy, and Jean Valjean was in one of those good hours. They usually arrive after bad hours, as day does after night, through that law of succession and contrast which is the basis of our nature, and which superficial minds call antithesis. In this peaceful street where he had sought shelter, Jean Valjean freed himself from all that had troubled him for some time past, and from the very fact that he had seen so much darkness he was beginning to perceive a little azure. To have left the Rue Plumet without any complication of incident was a good step gained, and perhaps it would be wise to leave the country, were it only for a few months, and go to London. Well, they would go; what did he care whether he were in England or France, provided that he had Cosette by his side? Cosette was his nation. Cosette sufficed for his happiness, and the idea that he perhaps did not suffice for Cosette's happiness, that idea which had formerly been his fever and sleeplessness, did not even present itself to his mind. All his past sorrows had collapsed, and he was in the center of optimism. Cosette, being by his side, seemed to be his, and this is an optical effect which everybody has experienced. He arranged in his mind, and with all possible facility, the departure for England with Cosette, and he saw his felicity reconstructed, no matter where, in the perspectives of his reverie.

While slowly walking up and down, his eye suddenly fell on something strange. He noticed, facing him in the inclined mirror over the sideboard, and read distinctly:

"MY WELL-BELOVED: *Alas! my father insists on our going away at once. We shall be this evening at No. 7, Rue de l'Homme Armé, and within a week in London.*

"COSETTE.— June, 4."

Jean Valjean stopped with haggard gaze. Cosette, on arriving, had laid her blotting-book on the sideboard facing the mirror, and, immersed in her painful thoughts, had forgotten it there, without even noticing that she had left it open at the very page on which she had dried the few lines she had written and intrusted to the young workman passing along the Rue Plumet. The writing was imprinted on the blotting-paper, and the mirror reflected the writing. The result was what is called in geometry a symmetric image, so that the writing reversed on the blotting-paper was placed straight in the mirror, and offered its natural direction, and Jean Valjean had before his eyes the letter written on the previous evening by Cosette to Marius. It was simple and crushing. Jean Valjean walked up to the mirror and read the lines again, but did not believe in them. They produced on him the effect of appearing in a flash of lightning: it was an hallucination—it was impossible—it could not be. Gradually his perception became more precise; he looked at Cosette's blotting-book, and the feeling of the real fact returned to him. He took up the blotting-book, said, "It comes from that." He feverishly examined the lines imprinted on the blotting-paper, but as they ran backward he could see no meaning in the strange scrawl. Then he said to himself, "Why, it means nothing, there is nothing written there." And he drew a long breath with inexpressible relief. Who has not felt such wild delight in horrible moments? the soul does not surrender to despair till it has exhausted every illusion.

He held the book in his hand and gazed at it, stupidly happy, almost ready to laugh at the hallucination of which he had been the dupe. All at once his eyes fell again on the mirror, and he saw the vision again; the lines stood on it with inexorable clearness. This time it was no mirage, it was palpable, it was the writing turned straight in the mirror, and he comprehended the fact. Jean Valjean tottered, let the blotting-book slip from his grasp, and fell into the old easy-chair by the side of the sideboard with hanging head and glassy, wandering eye. He said to himself that it was evident that the light of this world was eclipsed, and that Cosette had written that to somebody. Then he heard his soul, which had become terrible again, utter a hoarse roar in the darkness. Just attempt to take from the lion the dog he has in his cage! Strange, and sad to say, at that moment Marius had not yet received Cosette's letter, and accident had treacherously carried it to Jean Valjean before delivering it to Marius. Jean Valjean up to that day had never been conquered by a trial; he had been subjected to frightful assaults, not a blow of evil fortune had been spared him, and the ferocity of fate, armed with all social revenge and contempt, had taken him for its victim and ferociously attacked him. He had accepted, when it was necessary, every extremity; he had surrendered his re-acquired inviolability as man, given up his liberty, risked his head, lost everything and suffered everything, and he had remained disinterested and stoical, to such an extent that at times he seemed to be oblivious of self like a martyr. His conscience, hardened to all possible assaults of adversity, might seem quite impregnable, but any one who had now gazed into his heart would have been compelled to allow that it was growing weak. In truth, of all the tortures he had undergone in this long trial to which fate subjected him, this was the most formidable, and never had such a vise held him before. He felt the mysterious movement of all his latent sensibilities; he felt the thrilling of the unknown fiber. Alas! the supreme trial, we may say the sole trial, is the loss of the being whom we love.

Poor old Jean Valjean did not assuredly love Cosette otherwise than as a father, but, as we have already remarked, the very widowhood of his life had introduced all the forms of love into his paternity; he loved Cosette as his daughter, loved her as his mother, and loved her as his sister, and, as he had never had a mistress or a wife, that feeling, too, the most clinging of all, was mingled with the others, vague, ignorant, pure with the purity of blindness, unconscious, heavenly, angelic, and divine, less as a feeling than an instinct, less as an instinct than an attraction, imperceptible, invisible, but real; and love, properly so called, was in his enormous tenderness for Cosette as the vein of gold is in the mountain, dark and virginal. Our readers must study for a moment this state of the heart; no marriage was possible between them, not even that of souls, and yet it is certain that their destinies were wedded. Excepting Cosette, that is to say, excepting a childhood, Jean Valjean, during the whole of his life, had known nothing about things that may be loved. Those passions and loves which succeed each other had not produced in him those successive stages of green, light green, or dark green which may be noticed on leaves that survive the winter, and in men who pass their fiftieth year. In fine, as we have more than once urged, this internal fusion, all this whole, whose resultant was a lofty virtue, ended by making Jean Valjean a father to Cosette. A strange father, forged out of the grandsire, the son, the brother, and the husband which were in Jean Valjean; a father in whom there was even a mother; a father who loved Cosette and adored her, and who had this child for his light, his abode, his family, his country, and his Paradise. Hence, when he saw that it was decidedly ended, that she was escaping from him, slipping through his fingers, concealing herself, that she was a cloud, that she was water, when he had before his eyes this crushing evidence, another is the object of her heart, another is the wish of her life, she has a lover, I am only the father, I no longer exist,—when he could no longer doubt, when he said to himself, "She is leaving me," the sorrow he experienced went beyond the limits of the possible. To have done all that he had done to attain this! and to be nothing! Then, as we have just stated, he had a quivering of revolt from head to foot; he felt even in the roots of his hair the immense re-awakening of selfishness, and the "I" yelled in the depths of this man's soul.

There are such things as internal landslides; the penetration of a desperate certainty into a man is not effected without removing and breaking certain profound elements which are at times the man himself. Grief, when it attains that pitch, is a frantic flight of all the forces of the conscience, and such crises are fatal. Few among us emerge from them equal to ourselves and firm in our duty, for when the limit of suffering is exceeded the most imperturbable virtue is disconcerted. Jean Valjean took up the blotting-book and convinced himself afresh; he bent down as if petrified, and with fixed eye, over the undeniable lines, and such a cloud collected within him that it might be believed that the whole interior of his soul was crumbling down. He examined this revelation through the exaggeration of reverie with an apparent and startling calmness, for it is a formidable thing when a man's calmness attains the coldness of a statue. He measured the frightful step which his destiny had taken without any suspicion on his part; he recalled his fears of the past summer, so madly dissipated; he recognized the precipice, it was still the same, but Jean Valjean was no longer at the top but at the bottom. It was an extraordinary and crushing fact that he had fallen without perceiving it. The whole light of his life had fled while he still fancied he could see the sun. His instinct did not hesitate; he brought together certain circumstances, certain dates, certain blushes, and certain palenesses of Cosette, and said to himself, "It is he!" The divination of despair is a species of mysterious bow which never misses its mark, and with its first shaft it hit Marius. He did not know the name, but at once found the man; he perceived distinctly at the bottom of the implacable evocation of memory the unknown prowler of the Luxembourg, that villainous seeker of amourettes, that romantic idler, that imbecile, that coward, for it is cowardice to exchange loving glances with girls who have by their side a father who loves them. After feeling quite certain that this young man was at the bottom of the situation, and that all this came from him, Jean Valjean, the regenerated man, the man who had toiled so heavily in his soul, the man who made so many efforts to resolve his whole life, his whole misery, and his whole misfortune into love, looked into himself and saw there a specter—Hatred.

Great griefs contain exhaustion, and discourage us with life; the man into whom they enter feels something retire from him. In youth their visit is mournful, at a later date sinister. Alas! when the blood is hot, when the hair is black, when the head is upright on the body like the flame on the candle, when the heart, full of a yearning love, still has palpitations which may be given to it in return, when a man has time to recover from the wound, when all women are there, and all the smiles, and all the future, and the whole horizon, when the strength of life is complete—if despair be a frightful thing under such circumstances, what is it then in old age, when years are growing more and more livid, at that twilight hour when the stars of the tomb are beginning to become visible? While Jean Valjean was thinking, Toussaint came in; he rose and asked her:

"Do you know whereabout it is?"

Toussaint, in her stupefaction, could only answer:

"I beg your pardon, sir."

Jean Valjean continued:

"Did you not say just now that they were fighting?"

"O yes, sir," Toussaint replied; "over at St. Merry."

There are some mechanical movements which come to us, without our cognizance, from our deepest thoughts. It was doubtless under the impulse of a movement of this nature, of which he was scarce conscious, that Jean Valjean found himself five minutes later in the street. He was bare-headed, and sat down on the bench before his house, seemingly listening.

Night had set in.

2. GAVROCHE, THE ENEMY OF LAMPS

How long did he remain there? what was the ebb and flow of this tragical meditation? did he draw himself up? did he remain bowed down? had he been bent till he was broken? could he recover himself and stand again upon something solid in his conscience? Probably he could not have said himself. The street was deserted; and a few anxious citizens who hurriedly returned home scarce noticed him, for each for himself is the rule in times of peril. The lamp-lighter came as usual to light the lamp which was exactly opposite the door of No. 7 and went away. Jean Valjean would not have appeared to be a living man to any one who might have examined him in this gloom, and he sat on his bench motionless, like a statue of ice. His despair had got beyond congelation. The tocsin and vague stormy noises could be heard, and in the midst of all these convulsions of the bell blended with the riot, the clock of St. Paul struck the eleventh hour, solemnly and without hurrying; for the tocsin is man, the hour is God. The passing of the hour produced no effect on Jean Valjean, and he did not stir. Almost immediately after, however, a sudden detonation broke out in the direction of the Halles, followed by a second even more violent,—it was probably that attack on the barricade of the Rue de la Chanvrerie which we have just seen repulsed by Marius. At this double discharge, whose fury seemed increased by the stupor of the night, Jean Valjean started; he turned in the direction whence the sound came, but then fell back on his bench, crossed his arms, and his head slowly bent down again on his chest. He resumed his dark dialogue with himself.

All at once he raised his eyes, for there was some one in the street; he heard footsteps close to him, and by the light of the lamp he perceived a livid, young, and radiant face, in the direction of the street which runs past the Archives. It was Gavroche, who had just arrived from the Rue de la Chanvrerie. Gavroche was looking up in the air, and appeared to be seeking. He saw Jean Valjean distinctly, but paid no attention to him. Gavroche, after looking up in the air, looked down on the ground; he stood on tiptoe, and felt the doors and ground-floor windows,—they were all shut, bolted, and barred. After examining the fronts of several houses barricaded in this way, the gamin shrugged his shoulders, and then resumed his self-colloquy with himself, thus, "By Jove!" Then he looked up in the air again. Jean Valjean, who a moment previously in his present state of mind would neither have spoken to nor answered any one, felt an irresistible impulse to address this lad.

"My little boy," he said, "what is the matter with you?"

"Why, I'm hungry," Gavroche answered, bluntly. And he added, "Little yourself."

Jean Valjean felt in his pocket and pulled out a five-franc piece. But Gavroche, who was a species of wagtail, and rapidly passed from one gesture to another, had just picked up a stone. He had noticed the lamp.

"Hilloh!" he said, "you have still got lights here. You are not acting rightly, my friends; that is disorderly conduct. Break it for me."

And he threw the stone at the lamp, whose glass fell with such a noise that the citizens concealed behind their curtains in the opposite house cried, "It is as bad as '93!" The lamp oscillated violently and went out; the street suddenly became dark.

"That's it, old street," said Gavroche, "put on your night-cap." Then, turning to Jean Valjean, he said:

"What do you call that gigantic monument which you have there at the end of the street? it's the Archives, isn't it? let's pull down some of those great brutes of columns and make a tidy barricade."

Jean Valjean walked up to Gavroche.

"Poor creature," he said in a low voice, and as if speaking to himself, "he is hungry."

And he placed the five-franc piece in his hand. Gavroche raised his nose, amazed at the size of this double sou; he looked at it in the darkness, and the whiteness of the double sou dazzled him. He was acquainted with five-franc pieces by hearsay, and their reputation was agreeable to him; he was delighted to see one so closely, and said, "Let us contemplate the tiger." He looked at it for some moments in ecstasy; then, turning to Jean Valjean, he held out the coin to him, and said majestically:

"Citizen, I prefer breaking lamps. Take back your ferocious animal, for I am not to be corrupted. It has five claws, but can't scratch me."

"Have you a mother?" Jean Valjean asked.

Gavroche replied: "Perhaps more than you."

"Well," Jean Valjean continued, "keep that money for your mother."

Gavroche was affected. Moreover, he had noticed that the man who was addressing him had no hat on, and this inspired him with confidence.

"Really, then," he said, "it is not to prevent me breaking the lamps?"

"Break as many as you like."

"You are a worthy man," said Gavroche.

And he put the five-franc piece in one of his pockets. Then, with increasing confidence, he added:

"Do you belong to this street?"

"Yes; why?"

"Can you point me out No. 7?"

"What do you want at No. 7?"

Here the lad stopped, for he feared that he had said too much. He energetically plunged his nails into his hair, and confined himself to answering:

"Ah, there it is."

An idea flashed across Jean Valjean's mind, for agony has lucidities of that nature. He said to the boy:

"Have you brought me the letter which I am expecting?"

"You?" said Gavroche, "you ain't a woman."

"The letter is for Mlle. Cosette, is it not?"

"Cosette?" Gavroche grumbled; "yes, I think it is that absurd name."

"Well," Jean Valjean continued, "you have to deliver the letter to me, so give it here."

"In that case you must be aware that I am sent from the barricade?"

"Of course," said Jean Valjean.

Gavroche thrust his hand into another of his pockets, and produced a square folded letter. Then he gave the military salute.

"Respect for the dispatch," he said; "it comes from the provisional government."

"Give it to me," said Jean Valjean.

Gavroche held the paper above his head.

"You must not imagine that it is a love-letter, though it is for a woman; it is for the people we are fighting, and we respect the sex; we are not like people in the world of fashion, where there are lions that send love-letters to camels."

"Give it to me."

"After all," Gavroche continued, "you look like an honest man."

"Make haste."

"Here it is."

And he handed the paper to Jean Valjean.

"And make haste, Monsieur Chose, since Mamselle Chosette is waiting."

Gavroche felt pleased at having made this pun. Jean Valjean added: "Must the answer be taken to St. Merry?"

"You would make in that way," Gavroche exclaimed, "one of those cakes vulgarly called *brioches*. The letter comes from the barricade in the Rue de la Chanvrerie, and I am going back to it. Good-night, citizen."

This said, Gavroche went away, or, to speak more correctly, resumed his bird-like flight to the spot whence he had escaped. He plunged again into the darkness, as if there were a hole there, with the rigid rapidity of a projectile; the lane of l'Homme Armé became once again silent and solitary. In a twinkling, this strange lad, who had shadow and dreams within him, buried himself in the gloom of these rows of black houses, and was lost in it like smoke in darkness, and it might have been fancied that he was dispersed, had vanished, had not, a few minutes after his disappearance, a noisy breakage of glass, and the splendid echo of a lamp falling on the pavement, suddenly re-awakened the indignant citizens. It was Gavroche passing along the Rue du Chaume.

3. *WHILE COSETTE AND TOUSSAINT ARE ASLEEP*

Jean Valjean reëntered with Marius's letter. He groped his way upstairs, pleased with the darkness like an owl that holds its prey, gently opened and closed the door, listened whether he could hear any sound, convinced himself that Cosette and Toussaint were, according to all appearances, asleep, and plunged into the Fumade lighting-bottle three or four matches before he could procure a spark, for his hand trembled so, as what he had just done was a robbery. At last his candle was lit, he sat down at the table, opened the letter, and read. In such violent emotions men do not read; they hurl down, so to speak, the paper they hold, clutch it like a victim, crumple it, bury it in the nails of their fury or delight, they run to the end, they dash at the beginning; the attention is feverish, it understands the essential facts, it seizes on one point, and all the rest disappears. In the note from Marius to Cosette Jean Valjean only saw these words:

"—I die; when you read this my soul will be near you."

In the presence of this line he felt a horrible bedazzlement; he remained for a moment as if crushed by the change of emotion which took place in him. He gazed at Marius's letter with a species of drunken amazement; he had before his eyes this splendor, the death of the hated being. He uttered a frightful cry of infernal joy. So all was over, and the denouement arrived more quickly than he could have dared to hope. The being that encumbered his destiny was disappearing; he went away of his own accord, freely and willingly, without his doing anything in the matter, without any fault on the part of him, Jean Valjean; "that man" was going to die, perhaps was already dead. Here his fever made its calculations: "No, he is not yet dead. The letter was evidently written to be read by Cosette on the next morning, since the two volleys he had heard between eleven o'clock and midnight nothing had occurred; the barricade would not be seriously attacked till daybreak, but no matter, from the moment when 'that man' is mixed up in this war he is lost, he is caught in the cog-wheels." Jean Valjean felt himself delivered; he was going to find himself once more alone with Cosette, the rivalry ceased and the future begun again. He need only keep the note in his pocket, and Cosette would never know what had become of 'that man'; "I have only to let things take their course. That man cannot escape, and if he is not dead yet it is certain that he is going to die. What happiness!" All this said internally, he became gloomy. Then he went down and aroused the porter. About an hour later Jean Valjean left the house in the uniform of a National Guard and armed. The porter had easily obtained for him in the neighborhood the articles to complete his equipment; he had a loaded musket and a full cartridge-box. He proceeded in the direction of the Halles.

4. GAVROCHE'S EXCESS OF ZEAL

IN the meanwhile an adventure had happened to Gavroche. After conscientiously stoning the lamp in the Rue du Chaume, he approached the Rue des Vieilles-Haudriettes, and, not seeing a "cat" there, found the opportunity excellent for striking up a song at the full pitch of his lungs. His march, far from being checked by the singing, became accelerated, and he sowed along the sleeping or terrified houses the following incendiary couplets:

> *L'oiseau médit dans les charmilles,*
> *Et prétend qu'hier Atala*

Avec un Russe s'en alla.

> *Où vont les belles filles,*
> *Lon la.*

Mon ami Pierrot, tu babilles,
Parce que l'autre jour Mila
Cogna sa vitre, et m'appela.

> *Où vont les belles filles,*
> *Lon la.*

Les drôlesses sont fort gentilles;
Leur poisson qui m'ensorcela
Griserait Monsieur Orfila.

> *Où vont les belles filles,*
> *Lon la.*

J'aime l'amour et ses bisbilles,
J'aime Agnes, j'aime Paméla,
Lise en m'allumant se brula.

> *Où vont les belles filles,*
> *Lon la.*

Jadis, quand je vis les mantilles,
De Suzette et de Zeila,
Mon âme à leurs plis se mêla.

> *Où vont les belles filles,*
> *Lon la.*

Amour, quand, dans l'ombre où tu brilles,
Tu coiffes de roses, Lola,
Je me damnerais pour cela.

> *Où vont les belles filles,*
> *Lon la.*

Jeanne, à ton miroir tu t'habilles!
Mon cœur un beau jour s'envola;
Je crois que c'est Jeanne qui l'a.

Où vont les belles filles,
Lon la.

Le soir, en sortant des quadrilles,
Je montre aux étoiles, Stella,
Et je leur dis, regardez-la.

Où vont les belles filles,
Lon la.

Gavroche, while singing, was lavish of his pantomime, for gesture is the mainstay of a chorus. His face, an inexhaustible repertory of masks, made grimaces more convulsive and more fantastic than the mouths of a torn sheet in a stiff breeze. Unluckily, he was alone and in the dark, this was neither seen nor visible. Much wealth is lost in this way. Suddenly he stopped short.

"We must interrupt the song," he said.

His cat-like eye had just distinguished inside a gate-way what is called in painting an ensemble, that is to say, a being and a thing: the thing was a hand-cart, the being an Auvergnat sleeping inside it. The shafts of the cart were upon the pavement, and the Auvergnat's head leaned on the backboard of the truck. His body lay along this inclined plane, and his feet touched the ground. Gavroche, with his experience of the things of this world, recognized a drunkard; it was some street-corner porter who had drunk too much and was sleeping too much.

"Such is the use," Gavroche thought, "to which summer nights may be turned. The Auvergnat sleeps in his truck. I take the truck for the republic, and leave the Auvergnat for the monarchy."

His mind had just been illumined by this flash.

"That truck would be famous on our barricade!"

The Auvergnat was snoring. Gavroche gently pulled the truck behind and the Auvergnat in front, that is to say, by the feet, and in a second the porter was lying imperturbably flat on the pavement. The truck was empty. Gavroche, accustomed constantly to face unexpected events, had always everything about him. He felt in one of his pockets and

355

pulled out a scrap of paper and a piece of red pencil, stolen from some carpenter. He wrote:

"République Française
Received this truck."

And he signed, GAVROCHE.

This done, he placed the paper in the snoring porter's velvet waistcoat-pocket, seized the hand-cart, and started in the direction of the Halles, thrusting the truck before him at a gallop with a glorious triumphal row. This was dangerous, for there was a post at the royal printing-office, and Gavroche did not think of that. This post was held by suburban National Guards; a certain amount of alarm was beginning to arouse the squad, and heads were raised in the guard-beds. Two lamps broken so shortly after each other, and this singing at the pitch of the lungs, were a good deal for these cowardly streets, which like to go to bed at sunset, and put the extinguisher on their candle at so early an hour. For an hour past the gamin had been making in this peaceful district the noise of a fly in a bottle. The sergeant of the district listened and waited, for he was a prudent man. The wild rolling of the truck filled up the measure of possible awaiting, and determined the sergeant to attempt a reconnoissance.

"There must be a whole band of them," he said, "so we will advance gently."

It was clear that the hydra of anarchy had emerged from its box, and was playing the deuce in the quarter, so the sergeant ventured out of the guard-house on tiptoe. All at once, Gavroche, pushing his truck, found himself, just as he was turning out of the Rue des Vieilles-Haudriettes, face to face with a uniform, a shako, a pompon, and a musket. For a second he stopped short.

"Hilloh," he said, "it's he. Good-day, public order."

Gavroche's surprises were short and rapidly thawed.

"Where are you going, scamp?" the sergeant cried.

"Citizen," said Gavroche, "I have not yet called you a bourgeois, so why do you insult me?"

"Where are you going, scoundrel?"

"Sir," Gavroche continued, "it is possible that you were a man of sense yesterday, but you must have sent in your resignation this morning."

"I ask you where you are going, villain?"

Gavroche answered: "You speak politely. Really, no one would fancy you that age. You ought to sell your hair at one hundred francs apiece, and that would bring you in five hundred francs."

"Where are you going? where are you going? where are you going, bandit?"

Gavroche answered:

"Those are ugly words. The first time they give you the breast they ought to wash your mouth out better."

The sergeant leveled his bayonet.

"Will you tell me where you are going, or not, wretch?"

"My general," said Gavroche, "I am going to fetch the doctor for my wife, who is taken in labor."

"To arms!" the sergeant shouted.

It is the masterpiece of powerful minds to save themselves by what has ruined them; and Gavroche measured the whole situation at a glance. It was the truck that had compromised him, and so the truck must now protect him. At the moment when the sergeant was going to rush on Gavroche, the truck, converted into a projectile and launched at full speed, rolled upon him furiously, and the sergeant, struck in the stomach, fell back into the gutter, while his musket was discharged in the air. On hearing their sergeant's cry, the guard hurried forth pell-mell; the shot produced a general discharge blindly, after which the guns were reloaded, and they began again. This blindman's-buff firing lasted a good quarter of an hour, and killed sundry panes of glass. In the meanwhile, Gavroche, who had turned back, stopped five or six streets off, and sat down panting on the bench at the corner of the En-fants Rouges, and listened. After breathing for a few minutes, he turned in the direction where the musketry was raging, raised his left hand to the level of his nose, and thrust it out thrice, while striking the back of his head with his right hand,—a sovereign gesture, in which the Parisian gamins have condensed French irony, and which is evidently effective, as it has already lasted more than half a century. This gayety was troubled by a bitter reflection.

"Yes," he said, "I am delighted, I overflow with joy, I crack my sides, but I am losing my road, and shall be obliged to steer a roundabout course. I only hope I shall reach the barricade betimes."

After saying this he ran off again. While running he asked himself, "Where was I?" Then he began his song again, which gradually died out in the darkness of the streets.

Mais il reste encore des bastilles,
Et je vais mettre le holà
Dans l'ordre public que voilà.

> *Où vont les belles filles,*
> *Lon la.*

Quelqu'un veut-il jouer aux quilles?
Tout le vieux monde s'écroula,
Quand la grosse boule roula.

> *Où vont les belles filles,*
> *Lon la.*

Vieux bon peuple, à coups de béquilles,
Cassons ce Louvre où s'étala
La monarchie en falbala.

> *Où vont les belles filles,*
> *Lon la.*

Nous en avons forcé les grilles
Le roi Charles Dix ce jour-là
Tenait mal, et se décolla.

> *Où vont les belles filles,*
> *Lon la.*

The turn-out of the guard produced some results, for a truck was captured and the drunkard made prisoner. The first was placed in the barrack-yard, while the second was afterward brought before a court-martial as an accomplice. The public minister of that day displayed in this circumstance his indefatigable zeal in the defense of society. Gavroche's adventure, which has remained as a tradition in the Temple quarter, is one of the most terrible reminiscences of the old bourgeois of the Marais, and is entitled in their memory, "The night attack on the guard-house of the royal printing-office."

VOLUME FIVE

Jean Valjean

CONTENTS · VOLUME V

BOOK I—WAR WITHIN FOUR WALLS

BOOK II—THE INTERIOR OF LEVIATHAN

BOOK III—MUD, BUT SOUL

BOOK IV—JAVERT DERAILED

BOOK V—GRANDSON AND GRANDFATHER

JEAN VALJEAN

BOOK I

WAR WITHIN FOUR WALLS

1. THE CHARYBDIS OF THE FAUBOURG ST. ANTOINE AND THE SCYLLA OF THE FAUBOURG DU TEMPLE

THE two most memorable barricades which the observer of social diseases can mention do not belong to the period in which the action of this book is laid. These two barricades, both symbols under different aspects of a formidable situation, emerged from the earth during the fatal insurrection of June, 1848, the greatest street-war which history has seen.

It happens sometimes that the canaille, that great despairing crowd, contrary to principles, even contrary to liberty, equality, and fraternity, even contrary to the universal vote, the government of all by all, protests, in the depths of its agony, its discouragement, its deprivations, its fevers, its distresses, its miasmas, its ignorance, and its darkness, and the populace offers battle to the people. The beggars attack the common right, the ochlocracy rises in insurrection against the demos.

Those are mournful days; for there is always a certain amount of right even in this mania, there is suicide in this duel, and these words, intended to be insults, such as beggars, canaille, ochlocracy, the populace, prove, alas! rather the fault of those who reign than the fault of those who suffer; rather the fault of the privileged than the fault of the disinherited. For our part, we never pronounce these words without grief and respect, for when philosophy probes the facts with which they correspond it often finds much grandeur by the side of misery. Athens was an ochlocracy; the beggars produced Holland; the populace more than once saved Rome; and the canaille followed the Saviour. There is no thinker who has not at times contemplated the magnificence below. St.

3

Jerome doubtless thought of this canaille, of all these poor people, all these vagabonds, and all the wretches whence the apostles and martyrs issued, when he uttered the mysterious words, *Faex urbis, lex orbis.*

The exasperations of this mob, which suffers and which bleeds, its unwilling violence against the principles which are its life, its assaults upon the right, are coups d'état of the populace, and must be repressed. The just man devotes himself, and, through love for this very mob, combats it. But how excusable he finds it while resisting it; how he venerates it, even while opposing it! It is one of these rare moments in which a man while doing his duty feels something that disconcerts him and almost dissuades him from going further; he persists, and must do so, but the satisfied conscience is sad, and the accomplishment of the duty is complicated by a contraction of the heart.

June, 1848, was, let us hasten to say, a separate fact, and almost impossible to classify in the philosophy of history. All the words we have uttered must be laid aside when we have to deal with this extraordinary riot, in which the holy anxiety of labor claiming its right was felt. It must be combated, and it was a duty to do so, for it attacked the republic; but, in reality, what was June, 1848? a revolt of the people against itself.

When the subject is not left out of sight there is no digression, and hence we may be permitted to concentrate the reader's attention momentarily upon the two absolutely unique barricades to which we have alluded, and which characterized this insurrection. The one blocked up the entrance to the Faubourg St. Antoine, the other defended the approaches to the Faubourg du Temple; those before whom these two frightful masterpieces of civil war were raised in the dazzling June sun will never forget them.

The St. Antoine barricade was monstrous; it was three stories high and seven hundred feet in width. It barred from one corner to the other the vast mouth of the Faubourg, that is to say, three streets; ravined, slashed, serrated, surmounted by an immense jagged line, supported by heaps which were themselves bastions, pushing out capes here and there, and powerfully reënforced by the two great promontories of the houses of the Faubourg, it rose like a Cyclopean wall at the back of the formidable square which had seen July 14. There were nineteen barricades erected in the streets behind the mother barricade, only on seeing it you felt in the Faubourg the immense agonizing suffering which had reached that extreme stage in which misery desires to become a catas-

4

trophe. Of what was this barricade made? of three six-storied houses demolished expressly, some say; of the prodigy of all anger, others say. It possessed the lamentable aspect of all the buildings of hatred, ruin. You might ask who built this? and you might also ask who destroyed this? It was the improvisation of the ebullition. Here with that door, that grating, that awning, that chimney, that broken stove, that cracked stew-pan. Give us anything, throw everything in! push, roll, pick, dismantle, overthrow, and pull down everything! it was a collaboration of the pavement-stones, beams, iron bars, planks, broken windows, unseated chairs, cabbage-stalks, rags, tatters, and curses. It was great and it was little; it was the abyss parodied by formless chaos. It was the mass side by side with the atom, a pulled-down wall and a broken pipkin, a menacing fraternization of all fragments, into which Sisyphus had cast his rock and Job his potsherds. Altogether it was terrible, it was the acropolis of the barefooted. Over-turned carts studded the slope; an immense wain spread out across it, with its wheels to the sky, and looked like a scar on this tumultuous façade; an omnibus gayly hoisted by strength of arm to the very top of the pile, as if the architects of this savage edifice had wished to add mockery to the horror, offered its bare pole to the horses of the air. This gigantic mound, the alluvium of the riot, represented to the mind an Ossa upon Pelion of all revolutions, '93 upon '89, the 9th Thermidor upon the 10th August, the 18th Brumaire upon January 21, Vendemiaire upon Prairial, 1848 upon 1830. The place was worth the trouble, and this barricade was worthy of appearing upon the very spot whence the Bastille had disappeared. If the ocean made dykes it would build them in this way, and the fury of the tide was stamped on this shapeless incumbrance. What tide? the people. You fancied that you saw a petrified riot, and heard the enormous dark bees of violent progress humming about this barricade as if they had their hive there. Was it a thicket? was it a Bacchanalian feast? was it a fortress? Vertigo seemed to have built it with the flapping of its wings. There was a sewer in this redoubt, and something Olympian in this mass. You saw there in a confusion full of desperation, gables of roofs, pieces of garrets with their painted paper, window-frames with all their panes planted in the mass awaiting the cannon, pulled down mantel-pieces, chests of drawers, tables, benches, a howling topsy-turvy, and those thousand wretched things cast away even by a beggar which contain at once fury and nothingness. It may be said that it was the rags of a people, rags of wood, of iron, of bronze, of stone; that the Faubourg

St. Antoine had swept them to their door with a gigantic broom, and made a barricade of their misery. Logs resembling executioners' blocks, broken chains, anvil frames of the shape of gallows, horizontal wheels emerging from the heap produced on this edifice of anarchy the representation of the old punishments suffered by the people. The St. Antoine barricade made a weapon of everything. All that civil war can throw at the head of society came from it; it was not a fight, but a paroxysm: the muskets which defended this redoubt, among which were several blunderbusses, discharged stones, bones, coat-buttons, and even the casters of night commodes, very dangerous owing to the copper. This barricade was furious; it hurled an indescribable clamor into the clouds; at certain moments when challenging the army it was covered with a crowd and a tempest; it had a prickly crest of guns, sabers, sticks, axes, pikes, and bayonets; a mighty red flag fluttered upon it in the breeze, and the cries of command, the songs of attack, the rolling of the drums, the sobs of women, and the sardonic laughter of men dying of starvation could be heard there. It was immeasurable and living, and a flash of lightning issued from it as from the back of an electric animal. The spirit of revolution covered with its cloud this summit, where that voice of the people, which resembles the voice of God, was growling, and a strange majesty was disengaged from this Titanic mass of stones. It was a dung-heap, and it was Sinai.

As we said above, it attacked in the name of the revolution, what? the revolution. It, this barricade, an accident, a disorder, a misunderstanding, an unknown thing, had facing it the constituent assembly, the sovereignty of the people, universal suffrage, the nation, the republic; and it was Carmagnole defying the Marseillaise. It was a mad but heroic challenge, for this old faubourg is a hero. The faubourg and its redoubt supported each other; the faubourg formed the epaulement of the redoubt, and the redoubt leaned upon the faubourg. The vast barricade was like a cliff against which the strategy of the African generals was broken. Its caverns, its excrescences, its warts, its humps, made grimaces, if we may employ the expression, and grinned behind the smoke. The grape-shot vanished in the shapeless heap; shells buried themselves in it, and were swallowed up; cannon-balls only succeeded in forming holes, for of what use is it bombarding chaos? and the regiments, accustomed to the sternest visions of war, gazed with anxious eye at this species of wild-beast redoubt, which was a boar through its bristling and a mountain through its enormity.

6

A quarter of a league further on, at the corner of the Rue Vieille du Temple which debouches on the boulevard near the Château d'Eau, if you boldly advanced your head beyond the point formed by the projection of the magazine Dallemagne, you could see in the distance across the canal, and at the highest point of the ascent to Belleville, a strange wall rising to the third-floor and forming a sort of connecting link between the houses on the right and those on the left, as if the street had folded back its highest wall in order to close itself up. This was built of paving-stones; it was tall, straight, correct, cold, perpendicular, and leveled with the plumb-line and the square; of course there was no cement, but, as in some Roman walls, this in no way disturbed its rigid architecture. From its height, its thickness could be guessed, for the entablature was mathematically parallel to the basement. At regular distances almost invisible loop-holes, resembling black threads, could be distinguished in the gray wall, separated from each other by equal intervals. This street was deserted throughout its length, and all the windows and doors were closed. In the background rose this bar which converted the street into a blind alley; it was a motionless and tranquil wall,—no one was seen, nothing was heard, not a cry, nor a sound, nor a breath. It was a sepulcher. The dazzling June inundated this terrible thing with a light,—it was the barricade of the Faubourg du Temple. So soon as you reached the ground and perceived it, it was impossible even for the boldest not to become pensive in the presence of this mysterious apparition. It was adjusted, clamped, imbricated, rectilinear, symmetrical, and funereal; science and darkness were both there. You felt that the chief of this barricade was a geometrician or a specter, and as you gazed you spoke in a whisper. From time to time if any one, private, officer, or representative of the people, ventured to cross the solitary road, a shrill faint whistling was heard, and the passer-by fell wounded or dead, or, if he escaped, a bullet could be seen to bury itself in some shutter or the stucco of the wall. Sometimes it was a grape-shot, for the man of the barricade had made out of gas-pipes, stopped up at one end with tow and clay, two small cannon. There was no useless expenditure of gunpowder, and nearly every shot told. There were a few corpses here and there, and patches of blood on the pavement. I remember a white butterfly that fluttered up and down the street; summer does not abdicate. All the gate-ways in the vicinity were crowded with corpses, and you felt in this street that you were covered by some one you could not see, and that the whole street was under the marksman's aim.

The soldiers of the attacking column, massed behind the species of ridge which the canal-bridge forms at the entrance of the Faubourg du Temple, watched gravely and thoughtfully this mournful redoubt, this immobility, this impassiveness, from which death issued. Some crawled on their stomachs to the top of the pitch of the bridge, while careful not to let their shakos pass beyond it. Brave Colonel Monteynard admired this barricade with a tremor. "*How it is built,*" he said to a representative; "*not a single paving-stone projects beyond the other. It is made of china.*" At this moment a bullet smashed the cross on his chest, and he fell. "The cowards!" the troops shouted, "Why do they not show themselves? they dare not! they hide!" The barricade of the Faubourg du Temple, defended by eighty men and attacked by ten thousand, held out for three days, and on the fourth day the troops acted as they had done at Zaatcha and Constantine,—they broke through houses, passed along roofs, and the barricade was taken. Not one of the eighty cowards dreamed of flying; all were killed with the exception of Barthelemy, the chief, to whom we shall allude directly. The barricade of St. Antoine was the tumult of the thunder; the barricade of the Temple was the silence. There was between the two barricades the same difference as exists between the formidable and the sinister. The one seemed a throat, the other a mask. Admitting that the gigantic and dark insurrection of June was composed of a fury and an enigma, the dragon was seen in the first barricade and the sphinx behind the second.

These two fortresses were built by two men, Cournet and Barthelemy: Cournet made the St. Antoine barricade, Barthelemy the Temple barricade, and each of them was the image of the man who built it. Cournet was a man of tall stature; he had wide shoulders, a red face, a smashing fist, a brave heart, a loyal soul, a sincere and terrible eye. He was intrepid, energetic, irascible, and stormy; the most cordial of men, and the most formidable of combatants. War, contests, medley, were the air he breathed, and put him in good temper. He had been an officer in the navy, and from his gestures and his voice it could be divined that he issued from the ocean and came from the tempest; he continued the hurricane in battle. Omitting the genius, there was in Cournet something of Danton, as, omitting the divinity, there was in Danton something of Hercules. Barthelemy, thin, weak, pale, and taciturn, was a species of tragical gamin, who, having been struck by a policeman, watched for him, waited for him, and killed him, and at the age of seventeen was sent to the galleys. He came out and built this barricade. At a later date, when both were exiles in London, Barthelemy killed Cournet; it was a melancholy duel. Some time after that, Barthelemy, caught in the cog-wheels of one of those mysterious adventures in which passion is mingled, catastrophes in which French justice sees extenuating circumstances, and English justice only sees death, was hanged. The gloomy social edifice is so built that, owing to maternal denudation and moral darkness, this wretched being, who had an intellect, certainly firm and possibly great, began with the galleys in France and ended with the gibbet in England. Barthelemy only hoisted one flag,—it was the black one.

2. WHAT CAN ONE DO IN THE ABYSS, BUT TALK?

SIXTEEN years count in the subterranean education of revolt, and June, 1848, knew a great deal more than June, 1832. Hence the barricade in the Rue de la Chanvrerie was only a sketch and an embryo when compared with the two colossal barricades which we have just described, but for the period it was formidable. The insurgents, under the eye of Enjolras, for Marius no longer looked at anything, had turned the night to good account: the barricade had not only been repaired, but increased. It had been raised two feet, and iron bars planted in the paving-stones resembled lances in rest. All sorts of rubbish, added and brought from all sides, complicated the external confusion, and the redoubt had been cleverly converted into a wall inside and a thicket outside. The staircase of paving-stones, which allowed the top of the barricade to be reached, was restored, the ground-floor of the room of the inn was cleared out, the kitchen converted into an infirmary, the wounds were dressed, the powder scattered about the tables and floor was collected, bullets were cast, cartridges manufactured, lint plucked, the fallen arms distributed; the dead were carried off and laid in a heap, in the Mondétour lane, of which they were still masters. The pavement remained for a long time red at that spot. Among the dead were four suburban National Guards, and Enjolras ordered their uniforms to be laid on one side. Enjolras had advised two hours' sleep, and his advice was an order; still, only three or four took advantage of it, and Feuilly employed the two hours in engraving this inscription on the wall facing the wine-shop: "LONG LIVE THE PEOPLES."

These four words, carved in the stone with a nail, could still be read on this wall in 1848. The three women took advantage of the respite to disappear entirely, which allowed the insurgents to breathe more at their ease; and they contrived to find refuge in some neighboring house. Most of the wounded could and would still fight. There were, on a pile of mattresses and trusses of straw laid in the kitchen converted into an infirmary, five men seriously wounded, of whom two were Municipal Guards; the wounds of the latter were dressed first. No one remained in the ground-floor room, save Mabœuf under his black cere-cloth and Javert fastened to the post.

"This is the charnel-house," said Enjolras.

In the interior of this room, which was scarce lighted by a solitary candle, the mortuary table at the end being behind the post like a horizontal bar, a sort of large vague cross resulted from Javert standing and Mabœuf lying down. Although the pole of the omnibus was mutilated by the bullets, sufficient remained for a flag to be attached to it. Enjolras, who possessed that quality of a chief of always doing what he said, fastened to it the bullet-pierced and blood-stained coat of the killed old man. No meal was possible, for there was neither bread nor meat. The fifty men during the sixteen hours they had stood at the barricade speedily exhausted the scanty provisions of the inn. At a given moment every barricade that holds out becomes the raft of the *Medusa,* and the combatants must resign themselves to hunger. They had reached the early hours of that Spartan day, June 6, when, at the barricade of St. Merry, Jeanne, surrounded by insurgents who cried for bread, answered, "What for? it is three o'clock; at four we shall be dead." As they could no longer eat, Enjolras prohibited drinking; he put the wine under an interdict, and served out the spirits in rations. Some fifteen full bottles, hermetically sealed, were found in the cellar, which Enjolras and Combeferre examined. Combeferre on coming up again said, "It belongs to Father Hucheloup's stock at the time when he was a grocer." "It must be real wine," Bossuet observed; "it is lucky that Grantaire is asleep, for, if he were up, we should have a difficulty in saving those bottles." Enjolras, in spite of the murmurs, put his veto on the fifteen bottles, and in order that no one might touch them, and that they should be to some extent sacred, he had placed them under the table on which Father Mabœuf lay.

At about two in the morning they counted their strength; there were still thirty-seven. Day was beginning to appear, and the torch, which had been returned to its stone socket, was extinguished. The interior of the barricade, that species of small yard taken from the street, was bathed in darkness, and resembled, through the vague twilight horror, the deck of a dismantled ship. The combatants moved about like black forms. Above this frightful nest of gloom the floors of the silent houses stood out lividly, and above them again the chimney-pots were assuming a roseate hue. The sky had that charming tint which may be white and may be blue, and the birds flew about in it with twitterings of joy. The tall house which formed the background of the barricade looked to the east, and had a pink reflection on its roof. At the third-floor window the morning breeze blew about the gray hair on the head of the dead man.

"I am delighted that the torch is put out," Courfeyrac said to Feuilly. "That flame flickering in the breeze annoyed me, for it seemed to be frightened. The light of torches resembles the wisdom of cowards; it illumines badly because it trembles."

The dawn arouses minds like birds, and all were talking. Joly, seeing a cat stalking along a gutter, extracted this philosophy from the fact.

"What is the cat?" he exclaimed; "it is a correction. God, having made a mouse, said to himself, 'Hilloh, I have done a foolish trick,' and he made the cat, which is the erratum of the mouse. The mouse plus the cat is the revised and corrected proof of creation."

Combeferre, surrounded by students and workmen, was talking of the dead, of Jean Prouvaire, of Bahorel, of Mabœuf, and even of Le Cabuc and the stern sorrow of Enjolras. He said:

"Harmodius and Aristogiton, Brutus, Chereas, Stephanus, Cromwell, Charlotte Corday, and Sand, all had their moment of agony after the blow was struck. Our heart is so quivering, and human life such a mystery, that even in a civic murder, even in a liberating murder, if there be such a thing, the remorse at having struck a man exceeds the joy of having benefited the human race."

And, such are the meanderings of conversation, a moment later, by a transition which came from Jean Prouvaire's verses, Combeferre was comparing together the translators of the Georgics, Raux with Cournand, Cournand with Delille, and pointing out the few passages translated by Malfilâtre, especially the prodigies on the death of Cæsar, and at that name the conversation reverted to Brutus.

"Cæsar," said Combeferre, "fell justly. Cicero was severe to Cæsar, and was in the right, for such severity is not a diatribe. When Zoilus insults Homer, when Mævius insults Virgil, when Visé insults Molière, when Pope insults Shakespeare, when Fréron insults Voltaire, it is an old law of envy and hatred being carried out; for genius attracts insult, and great men are all barked at more or less. But Zoilus and Cicero are different. Cicero is a justiciary with thought in the same way as Brutus is a justiciary with the sword. For my part, I blame that last justice, the glaive; antiquity allowed it. Cæsar, the violator of the Rubicon, conferring, as if coming from him, dignities that came from the people and not rising on the entrance of the senate, acted, as Eutropius said, like a king, and almost like a tyrant, *regia ac pœne tyrannica*. He was a great man, all the worse or all the better, the lesson is the more elevated. His three-and-twenty wounds affect me less than the spitting on the brow of Christ. Cæsar is stabbed by the senators, Christ is buffeted by soldiers. The God is seen in the greater amount of the outrage."

Bossuet, standing on a pile of stones, and overlooking the speakers exclaimed, gun in hand:

"Oh! Cydathenæum, oh! Myrrhinus, oh! Probalynthus, oh! graces of Eanthus, oh! who will give me power to utter, to pronounce the verses of Homer like a Greek of Laurium or Edapteon?"

3 · *LAUGHS AND SHADOWS*

ENJOLRAS had gone out to reconnoiter, and had left by the Mondé-tour lane, keeping in the shadow of the houses. The insurgents, we must state, were full of hope; the way in which they had repulsed the night attack almost made them disdain beforehand the attack at daybreak. They waited for it and smiled at it, and no more doubted of their success than of their cause; moreover, help was evidently about to reach them, and they reckoned on it. With that facility of triumphant prophecy which is a part of the strength of the fighting Frenchman, they divided into three certain phases the opening day,—at six in the morning a regiment, which had been "worked upon," would turn; at midday insurrection all over Paris; at sunset the revolution. The tocsin of St. Merry, which had not ceased once since the previous evening, could be heard, and this was a proof that the other barricade, the great one, Jeanne's, still held out. All these hopes were interchanged by the groups with a species of gay and formidable buzzing, which resembled the war-hum of a swarm of bees. Enjolras re-appeared, returning from his gloomy walk in the external darkness. He listened for a moment to all this joy with his arms folded, and then said, fresh and rosy in the growing light of dawn:

"The whole army of Paris is out, and one-third of that army is preparing to attack the barricade behind which you now are. There is, too, the National Guard. I distinguish the shakos of the fifth regiment of the line, and the guidons of the sixth legion. You will be attacked in an hour; as for the people, they were in a state of ferment yesterday, but this morning do not stir. There is nothing to wait for, nothing to hope; no more a faubourg than a regiment. You are abandoned."

13

These words fell on the buzzing groups, and produced the same effect as the first drops of a storm do on a swarm. All remained dumb, and there was a moment of inexpressible silence, in which death might have been heard flying past. This moment was short, and a voice shouted to Enjolras from the thickest of the crowd:

"Be it so. Let us raise the barricade to a height of twenty feet, and all fall upon it. Citizens, let us offer the protest of corpses, and show that if the people abandon the republicans, the republicans do not abandon the people."

These words disengaged the thoughts of all from the painful cloud of individual anxieties, and an enthusiastic shout greeted them. The name of the man who spoke thus was never known; he was some unknown blouse-wearer, an unknown man, a forgotten man, a passing hero, that great anonymous always mixed up in human crises and social geneses, who at the given moment utters the decisive word in a supreme fashion, and who fades away into darkness, after having represented for a minute, in the light of a flash, the people and God. This inexorable resolution was so strongly in the air of June 6, 1832, that almost at the same hour the insurgents of the St. Merry barricade uttered this cry, which became historical, "Whether they come to our help or whether they do not, what matter? Let us all fall here, to the last man." As we see, the two barricades, though materially isolated, communicated.

4. *FIVE LESS AND ONE MORE*

AFTER the man, whoever he might be, who decreed the "protest of corpses," had spoken, and given the formula of the common soul, a strangely satisfied and terrible cry issued from every mouth, funereal in its meaning, and triumphal in its accent.

"Long live death! Let us all remain here."

"Why all?" Enjolras asked.

"All, all!"

Enjolras continued:

"The position is good and the barricade fine. Thirty men are sufficient; then why sacrifice forty?"

They replied:

"Because not one of us will go away."

"Citizens," Enjolras cried, and there was in his voice an almost irritated vibration. "the republic is not rich enough in men to make an unnecessary outlay. If it be the duty of some to go away, that duty must be performed like any other." Enjolras, the man-principle, had over his co-religionists that species of omnipotence which is evolved from the absolute. Still, however great that omnipotence might be they murmured. A chief to the tips of his fingers, Enjolras, on seeing that they murmured, insisted. He continued haughtily:

"Let those who are afraid to be only thirty say so."

The murmurs were redoubled.

"Besides," a voice in the throng remarked, "it is easy to say, Go away; but the barricade is surrounded."

"Not on the side of the Halles," said Enjolras. "The Rue Mondétour is free, and the Marché des Innocents can be reached by the Rue des Prêcheurs."

"And then," another voice in the group remarked, "we should be caught by falling in with some grand rounds of the line or the National Guard. They will see a man passing in blouse and cap: 'Where do you come from, don't you belong to the barricade?' and they will look at your hands; you smell of powder, and will be shot."

Enjolras, without answering, touched Combeferre's shoulder and both entered the ground-floor room. They came out again a moment after, Enjolras holding in his outstretched hands the four uniforms which he had laid on one side, and Combeferre followed him, carrying the cross-belts and shakos.

"In this uniform," Enjolras said, "it is easy to enter the ranks and escape. Here are four, at any rate."

And he threw the uniforms on the unpaved ground; but, as no one moved in the stoical audience, Combeferre resolved to make an appeal.

"Come," he said, "you must show a little pity. Do you know what the question is here? it is about women. Look you, are there wives,—

yes or no? are there children,—yes or no? are these nothing, who rock
a cradle with their foot and have a heap of children around them? let
him among you who has never seen a nurse's breast hold up his hand.
Ah, you wish to be killed. I wish it too, I who am addressing you, but
I do not wish to feel the ghosts of women twining their arms around
me. Die,—very good, but do not cause people to die. Suicides like the
one which is about to take place here are sublime, but suicide is restricted and does not allow of extension, and so soon as it affects your
relations, suicide is called murder. Think of the little fair heads, and
think, too, of the white hair. Listen to me,—Enjolras tells me that just
now he saw at the corner of the Rue du Cygne a candle at a poor window
on the fifth-floor, and on the panes the shaking shadow of an old woman
who appeared to have spent the night in watching at the window; she
is perhaps the mother of one of you. Well, let that man go and hasten
to say to his mother, 'Mother, here I am!' Let him be easy in his mind,
for the work will be done here all the same. When a man supports his
relatives by his toil, he has no longer any right to sacrifice himself, for
that is deserting his family. And then, too, those who have daughters,
and those who have sisters! only think of them. You let yourselves be
killed, you are dead, very good; and to-morrow? it is terrible when
girls have no bread, for a man begs, but a woman sells. Oh, those charming, graceful, and gentle creatures with flowers in their caps, who fill
the house with chastity, who sing, who prattle, who are like a living
perfume, who prove the existence of angels in heaven by the purity
of virgins on earth, that Jeanne, that Lise, that Mimi, those adorable
and honest creatures, who are your blessing and your pride,—ah, my
God! they will starve. What would you have me say to you? There is a
human flesh-market, and you will not prevent them entering it with
your shadowy hands trembling around them. Think of the street, think
of the pavement covered with strollers, think of the shops before which
women in low-necked dresses come and go in the mud. Those women,
too, were pure. Think of your sisters, you who have any; misery, prostitution, the police. Saint Lazare, that is what these delicate maidens,
these fragile marvels of chastity, modesty, and beauty, fresher than the
lilies in May, will fall to. Ah! you have let yourselves be killed! ah! you
are no longer there! that is very good, you have wished to withdraw the
people from royalty, and you give your daughters to the police. My
friends, take care and have compassion; we are not wont to think much
about women, hapless women; we trust to the fact that women have

not received the education of men. They are prevented reading, thinking, or occupying themselves with politics; but will you prevent them
going to-night to the Morgue and recognizing your corpses? Come,
those who have families must be good fellows, and shake our hand and
go away, leaving us to do the job here all alone. I am well aware that
courage is needed to go away, and that it is difficult, but the more difficult, the more meritorious it is. You say, 'I have a gun and am at the
barricade; all the worse, I remain.' All the worse is easily said. My
friends, there is a morrow, and that morrow you will not see, but your
families will see it. And what sufferings! Stay, do you know what becomes of a healthy child with cheeks like an apple, who chatters, prattles,
laughs, and smiles as fresh as a kiss, when he is abandoned? I saw one,
quite little, about so high; his father was dead and poor people had
taken him in through charity, but they had not bread for themselves.
The child was always hungry; it was winter-time, but though he was
always hungry he did not cry. He was seen to go close to the stove, whose
pipe was covered with yellow earth. The boy detached with his fingers
a piece of this earth and ate it,—his breathing was hoarse, his face livid,
his legs soft, and his stomach swollen. He said nothing, and when spoken
to made no answer. He is dead, and was brought to die at the Necker
hospice, where I saw him, for I was a student there. Now, if there be
any fathers among you, fathers who take a delight in taking a walk on
Sunday, holding in their powerful hand a child's small fingers, let each
of these fathers fancy this lad his own. The poor brat I can remember
perfectly; I fancy I see him now; and when he lay on the dissecting-
table, his bones stood out under his skin like the tombs under the grass
of a cemetery. We found a sort of mud in his stomach, and he had ashes
between his teeth. Come, let us examine our conscience and take the
advice of our heart; statistics prove that the mortality among deserted
children is fifty-five per cent. I repeat, it is a question of wives, of mothers,
of daughters, and babes. Am I saying anything about you? I know very
well what you are. I know that you are all brave. I know that you have
all in your hearts the joy and the glory of laying down your lives for the
great cause. I know very well that you feel yourselves chosen to die usefully and magnificently, and that each of you clings to his share of
the triumph. Very good. But you are not alone in this world, and there
are other things of whom you must think; you should not be selfish."

All hung their heads with a gloomy air, strange contradictions of the
human heart in the sublimest moments. Combeferre, who spoke thus,

was not an orphan; he remembered the mothers of others and forgot his own; he was going to let himself be killed, and was "selfish." Marius, fasting and feverish, who had successively given up all hope, cast ashore on grief, the most mournful of shipwrecks, saturated with violent emotions, and feeling the end coming, had buried himself deeper and deeper in that visionary stupor which ever precedes the fatal and voluntarily accepted hour. A physiologist might have studied on him the growing symptoms of that febrile absorption which is known and classified by science, and which is to suffering what voluptuousness is to pleasure, for despair also has its ecstasy. Marius had attained that stage; as we have said, things which occurred before him appeared to him remote; he distinguished the ensemble, but did not perceive the details. He saw people coming and going before him in a flash, and he heard voices speaking as from the bottom of an abyss. Still this affected him, for there was in this scene a point which pierced him and aroused him. He had but one idea,—to die,—and he did not wish to avert his attention from it, but he thought in his gloomy somnambulism that in destroying himself he was not prohibited from saving somebody. He raised his voice:

"Enjolras and Combeferre are right," he said; "let us have no useless sacrifice. I join them, and we must make haste. Combeferre has told you decisive things; there are men among you who have families, mothers, sisters, wives, and children. Such must leave the ranks."

Not a soul stirred.

"Married men and supporters of families will leave the ranks," Marius repeated.

His authority was great, for, though Enjolras was really the chief of the barricade, Marius was its saviour.

"I order it," Enjolras cried.

"I implore it," Marius said.

Then these heroic men, stirred up by Combeferre's speech, shaken by Enjolras's order, and moved by Marius's entreaty, began denouncing one another. "It is true," a young man said to a grown-up man, "you are a father of a family; begone!" "No! you ought to do so rather," the man replied, "for you have two sisters to support;" and an extraordinary contest broke out, in which each struggled not to be thrust out of the tomb.

"Make haste," said Combeferre; "in a quarter of an hour there will no longer be time."

18

"Citizens," Enjolras added, "we have a republic here, and universal suffrage reigns. Point out yourselves the men who are to leave us."

They obeyed, and at the end of a few minutes five were unanimously pointed out and left the ranks.

"There are five of them!" Marius exclaimed.

There were only four uniforms.

"Well," the five replied, "one will have to remain behind."

And then came who should remain, and who should find reason for others not to remain. The generous quarrel began again.

"You have a wife who loves you—you have your old mother—you have neither father nor mother; so what will become of your three little brothers?—you are the father of five children—you have a right to live, for you are only seventeen, and it is too early to die."

These great revolutionary barricades were meeting-places of heroisms. The improbable was simple there, and these men did not astonish one another.

"Make haste," Courfeyrac repeated.

Cries to Marius came from the groups.

"You must point out the one who is to remain."

"Yes!" the five said, "do you choose, and we will obey you."

Marius did not believe himself capable of any emotion; still at this idea of choosing a man for death, all the blood flowed back to his heart, and he would have turned pale could he have grown paler. He walked up to the five, who smiled upon him, and each, with his eyes full of that great flame which gleams through history on Thermopylæ, cried to him:

"I! I! I!"

And Marius stupidly counted them. There were still five! then his eyes settled on the four uniforms. All at once a fifth uniform fell, as if from heaven, on the other four; the fifth man was saved. Marius raised his eyes, and recognized M. Fauchelevent. Jean Valjean had just entered the barricade; either through information he had obtained, through instinct, or through accident, he arrived by the Mondétour lane, and, thanks to his National Guard uniform, passed without difficulty. The vedette stationed by the insurgents in the Rue Mondétour had no cause to give the alarm signal for a single National Guard, and had let him enter the street, saying to himself, "He is probably a re-enforcement, or at the worst a prisoner." The moment was too serious for a sentry to turn away from his duty or his post of observation. At the moment when Jean Valjean entered the redoubt, no one noticed him, for all eyes were

fixed on the five chosen men and the four uniforms. Jean Valjean, however, had seen and heard, and silently took off his coat and threw it on
the pile formed by the other coats. The emotion was indescribable.

"Who is this man?" Bossuet asked.

"He is a man," Combeferre replied, "who saves his fellow-man."

Marius added in a grave voice:

"I know him."

This bail was sufficient for all, and Enjolras turned to Jean Valjean:
"Citizen, you are welcome."

And he added:

"You are aware that you will die."

Jean Valjean, without answering, helped the men he was saving to
put on his uniform.

5. THE VIEW FROM THE TOP OF A BARRICADE

THE situation of the whole party in this fatal hour, and at this inexorable spot, had as resultant and summit the supreme melancholy of Enjolras. Enjolras had within him the plenitude of the revolution; he was
imperfect, however, so far as the absolute can be so; he had too much
of St. Just and not enough of Anacharsis Clootz; still his mind, in the
society of the friends of the A. B. C., had eventually received a certain
magnetism of Combeferre's ideas. For some time past he had been gradually emerging from the narrow form of dogmatism and yielding to the
expansion of progress, and in the end he had accepted, as the definitive
and magnificent evolution, the transformation of the great French republic into the immense human republic. As for the immediate means,
given a violent situation, he wished them to be violent; in that he did not

vary, and he still belonged to that epic and formidable school which is summed up in the words " '93."

Enjolras was standing on the paving-stone steps, with one of his elbows on the muzzle of his gun. He was thinking, he trembled, as men do when a blast passes, for spots where death lurks produce this tripod effect. A sort of stifled fire issued from beneath his eyelashes, which were full of the internal glance. All at once he raised his head, his light hair fell back like that of the angel on the dark quadriga composed of stars; it was like the mane of a roused lion surrounded by a flaming glory; and he cried:

"Citizens, do you represent the future to yourselves? the streets of towns inundated with light, green branches on the thresholds; nations sisters; men just; old men blessing children; the past loving the present; men thinking at perfect liberty; believers enjoying perfect equality; for religion, heaven; God, without the intervention of the priest, the human conscience converted into an altar; no more hatred, the fraternity of the workshop and the school, notoriety the sole punishment and reward, work for all, right for all, peace for all; no more bloodshed, no more wars, and happy mothers! To subdue matter is the first step; to realize ideal is the second. Reflect on what progress has already done; formerly the first human races saw with terror the hydra that breathed upon the waters, the dragon that vomited fire, the griffin which was the monster of the air, and which flew with the wings of an eagle and the claws of a tiger, pass before their eyes, frightful beasts which were below man. Man, however, set his snares, the sacred snares of intellect, and ended by catching the monsters. We have subdued the hydra, and it is called the steamboat; we have tamed the dragon, and it is called the locomotive; we are on the point of taming the griffin, we hold it already, and it is called the balloon. The day on which that Promethean task is terminated and man has definitely attached to his will the triple antique chimera, the dragon, the hydra, and the griffin, he will be master of water, fire, and air, and he will be to the rest of animated creation what the ancient gods were formerly to him. Courage, and forward! Citizens, whither are we going? to science made into government, to the strength of things converted into the sole public strength, to the natural law having its sanction and penalty in itself and promulgating itself by evidence, and to a dawn of truth corresponding with the dawn of day. We are proceeding to a union of the peoples; we are proceeding to a unity of man. No more fictions, no more parasites. The real governed by the true is our object. Civilization will hold its assize on the summit of Europe, and eventually in the center of the continent, in a great parliament of intellect. Something like this has been seen already; the Amphictyons held two sessions a year, one at Delphi, the place of the gods, the other at Thermopylæ, the place of heroes. Europe will have her Amphictyons, the globe will have its Amphictyons, France bears the sublime future within her, and this is the gestation of the nineteenth century. What Greece sketched out is worthy of being finished by France. Listen to me. Feuilly, valiant workman, man of the people, man of the peoples, I venerate thee; yes, thou seest clearly future times, yes, thou art right. Thou hast neither father nor mother, Feuilly, and thou hast adopted humanity as thy mother and right as thy father. Thou art about to die here; that is to say, to triumph. Citizens, whatever may happen to-day, we are about to make a revolution, by our defeat as well as by our victory. In the same way as fires light up a whole city, revolutions light up the whole human race. And what a revolution shall we make? I have just told you, the revolution of the True. From the political point of view, there is but one principle, the sovereignty of man over himself. This sovereignty of me over me is called Liberty, and where two or three of these liberties are associated the state begins. But in this association there is no abdication, and each sovereignty gives up a certain amount of itself to form the common right. This quality is the same for all, and this identity of concession which each makes to all, is called Equality. The common right is naught but the protection of all radiating over the right of each. This protection of all over each is termed Fraternity. The point of intersection of all aggregated sovereignties is called Society, and this intersection being a junction, the point is a knot. Hence comes what is called the social tie; some say the social contract, which is the same thing, as the word contract is etymologically formed with the idea of a tie. Let us come to an understanding about equality, for if liberty be the summit, equality is the base. Equality, citizens, is not the whole of society on a level, a society of tall blades of grass and small oaks, or a number of entangled jealousies; it is, civilly, every aptitude having the same opening for a career; politically, all votes having the same weight, and, religiously, all consciences having the same right. Equality has an organ in gratuitous and compulsory education, and it should begin with the right to the alphabet. The primary school imposed on all, the secondary offered to all; such is the law, and from the identical school issues equal instruction. Yes, instruction! light, light! everything comes from light and everything returns to it. Citizens, the nineteenth century is great, but the twentieth century will be happy. Then there will be nothing left resembling ancient history; there will be no cause to fear, as at the present day, conquest, invasion, usurpation, armed rivalry of nations, an interruption of civilization depending on a marriage of kings, a birth in hereditary tyrannies, a division of peoples by a congress, a dismemberment by the collapse of dynasties, a combat of two religions, clashing like two goats in the darkness on the bridge of infinity; there will be no cause longer to fear famine, exhaustion, prostitution through distress, misery through stoppage of work, and the scaffold, and the sword, and battles, and all the brigandage of accident in the forest of events;—we might almost say there will be no more events: we shall be happy; the human race will accomplish its law as the terrestrial globe does its law; harmony will be restored between the soul and the planet, and the soul will gravitate round the truth as the planet does round light. Friends, the hour we are now standing in is a gloomy hour, but there are such terrible purchases of the future! Oh! the human race will be delivered, relieved, and consoled! We affirm it on this barricade, and where should the cry of love be raised if not on the summit of the sacrifice? Oh, my brothers, this is the point of junction between those who think and those who suffer; this barricade is not made of paving-stones, beams, and iron bars: it is made of two aggregations,—one of ideas and one of sufferings. Misery meets there the ideal; day embraces the night there, and says to it, 'I am about to die with thee, and thou shalt be born again with me.' Faith springs from the embrace of all the desolations; sufferings bring hither their agony and ideas their immortality. This agony and this immortality are about to be mingled and compose one death. Brothers, the man who dies here dies in the radiance of the future, and we shall enter a tomb all filled with dawn."

Enjolras interrupted himself, rather than was silent; his lips moved silently as if he were talking to himself, which attracted attention, and in order still to try to hear him they held their tongues. There was no applause, but they whispered together for a long time. Language being breath, the rustling of intellects resembles the rustling of leaves.

23

6. MARIUS HAGGARD, JAVERT LACONIC

LET us describe what was going on in Marius's thoughts; our readers will remember his state of mind, for, as we just now said, everything was only a vision to him. His appreciation was troubled, for he was (we urge the fact) beneath the shadow of the great gloomy wings opened above the dying. He felt that he had entered the tomb, he fancied that he was already on the other side of the wall, and he only saw the faces of the living with the eyes of a dead man. How was M. Fauchelevent present? why was he here, and what did he come to do? Marius did not ask himself all these questions. Moreover, as our despair has this peculiar thing about it that it develops others as it does ourselves, it appeared to him logical that everybody should die. Still, he thought of Cosette with a contraction of the heart. However, M. Fauchelevent did not speak to him, did not look at him, and did not even seem to hear Marius when he raised his voice, saying, "I know him." As for Marius, this attitude of M. Fauchelevent relieved him, and if such a word were permissible for such impressions, we might say that it pleased him. He had ever felt an absolute impossibility in addressing this enigmatical man, who was at once equivocal and imposing to him. It was a very long time, too, since he had seen him; and this augmented the impossibility for a timid and reserved nature like Marius's.

The five men selected left the barricade by the Mondétour lane, perfectly resembling National Guards. One of them wept as he went away, and before doing so they embraced those who remained. When the five men sent back to life had left, Enjolras thought of the one condemned to death. He went to the ground-floor room, where Javert, tied to the post, was reflecting.

"Do you want anything?" Enjolras asked him.

Javert answered:

"When will you kill me?"

"Wait. We require all our cartridges at this moment."

"In that case, give me some drink," Javert said.

Enjolras himself held out to him a glass of water, and, as Javert was bound, helped him to drink.

"Is that all?" Enjolras resumed.

"I feel uncomfortable at this post," Javert replied; "you did not act kindly in leaving me fastened to it the whole night. Bind me as you please, but you might surely lay me on a table, like the other man."

And, with a nod of the head, he pointed to M. Mabœuf's corpse.

It will be remembered that there was at the end of the room a long wide table on which bullets had run and cartridges made. All the cartridges being made, and all the powder expended, this table was free. By Enjolras's order four insurgents unfastened Javert from the post, and while they did so a fifth held a bayonet to his chest. His hands remained fastened behind his back, a thin strong cord was attached to his feet, which enabled him to step fifteen inches, like those who are going to ascend the scaffold, and he was forced to walk to the table at the end of the room, on which they laid him, securely fastened round the waist. For greater security, a system of knotting was employed by means of a cord fastened to the neck, which rendered any escape impossible; it was the sort of fastening called in prisons, a martingale, which starts from the nape of the neck, is crossed on the stomach, and is turned round the hands after passing between the legs.

While Javert was being bound, a man standing in the doorway regarded him with singular attention, and the shadow this man cast caused Javert to turn his head. He raised his eyes and recognized Jean Valjean; but he did not even start,—he merely looked down haughtily and restricted himself to saying, "It is quite simple."

7. *THE SITUATION BECOMES WORSE*

DAY grew rapidly, but not a window opened, not a door was ajar; it was the dawn, not an awaking. The end of the Rue de la Chanvrerie opposed to the barricade had been evacuated by the troops, as we stated; it appeared to be free and open for passers-by with sinister tranquillity. The Rue St. Denis was dumb as the Avenue of the Sphinxes at Thebes; there was not a living being on the square, which a sun-beam whitened. Nothing is so melancholy as this brightness of deserted streets; nothing could be seen, but something could be heard, and there was a mysterious movement at a certain distance off. It was evident that the critical moment was arriving, and, as on the previous evening, the vedettes fell back, but this time all of them did so. The barricade was stronger than at the prior attack, for since the departure of the five it had been heightened. By the advice of the vedette who had been watching the region of the Halles, Enjolras, through fear of a surprise in the rear, formed a serious resolution. He barricaded the small passage of the Mondétour lane, which had hitherto remained free, and for this purpose a further portion of the street was unpaved. In this way the barricade, built up on three sides,—in front on the Rue de la Chanvrerie, on the left on the Rue du Cygne, and on the right on the Rue Mondétour,—was truly almost impregnable, but it is true that they were fatally inclosed within it. It had three fronts but no issue, it was a fortress but a mouse-trap, as Courfeyrac said with a smile. Enjolras had some thirty paving-stones piled up by the door of the inn, which, as Bossuet said, have been "removed over and above." The silence was now so profound in that direction whence the attack must come, that Enjolras ordered all his

26

men to return to their fighting-posts, and a ration of brandy was distributed to each man.

Nothing is more curious than a barricade preparing for an assault; every man chooses his place, as at the theater. They crowd, elbow, and shoulder one another, and some make stalls of paving-stones. Here an angle of the wall is in the way, and they leave it; there is a redan which may offer protection, and they seek shelter in it. Left-handed men are precious, for they take places inconvenient for others. Many arrange so as to fight seated, for they wish to be at their ease to kill, and comfortable in dying. In the fatal war of June, 1848, an insurgent, who was a wonderful marksman, and who fought from a terraced roof, had a Voltaire easy-chair carried there, and was knocked over in it by a volley of grape-shot. So soon as the chief has given the signal for action, all disorderly movements cease; there is no longer any sharp-shooting, any conversations, or asides: all that minds contain converges, and is changed into the waiting for the assailant. A barricade before danger is a chaos; in danger discipline, for peril produces order. So soon as Enjolras had taken his double-barreled gun, and placed himself at a species of parapet which he reserved for himself, all were silent; a quick, sharp, crackling ran confusedly along the wall of paving-stones,—it was the muskets being cocked. However, the attitudes were haughtier and more confident than ever, for an excess of sacrifice strengthens, and though they no longer had hope, they had despair—despair, that last weapon, which at times gives victory, as Virgil tells us. Supreme resources issue from extreme resolutions. To embark on death is at times the means of escaping the shipwreck, and the cover of the coffin becomes a plank of salvation. As on the previous evening, all their attention was turned upon the end of the street, which was now lighted up and visible. They had not long to wait ere the movement began again distinctly in the direction of St. Leu, but it did not resemble the sound of the first attack. A rattling of chains, the alarming rolling of a heavy weight, a clang of bronze leaping on the pavement, and a species of solemn noise announced that a sinister engine was approaching; there was a tremor in the entrails of these old peaceful streets, pierced and built for the fruitful circulation of interests and ideas, and not made for the monstrous rolling of the wheels of war. The fixity of the eyes turned toward the end of the street became stern, as a cannon appeared. The gunners pushed the gun on; the limber was detached, and two men supported the carriage, while four were at the wheels; others followed with the tumbril, and the lighted match could be seen smoking.

"Fire!" shouted Enjolras.

The whole barricade burst into a flame, and the detonation was frightful; an avalanche of smoke covered and concealed the gun and the men. A few seconds after, the cloud was dispersed, and the gun and the men re-appeared; the gunners were bringing it up to the front of the barricade, slowly, correctly, and without hurry; not one had been wounded. Then the captain of the gun, hanging with his whole weight on the breech to elevate the muzzle, began pointing the gun, with the gravity of an astronomer setting a telescope.

"Bravo for the artillery!" cried Bossuet.

And all the men at the barricade clapped their hands. A moment after the gun, standing in the very center of the street across the gutter, was in position, and a formidable mouth yawned at the barricade.

"Come, we are going to be gay," said Courfeyrac; "here is brutality; after the fillip the blow with the fist. The army is extending its heavy paw toward us, and the barricade is going to be seriously shaken. The musketry fire feels, and the cannon takes."

"It is an eight-pounder of the new pattern in bronze," Combeferre added. "Those guns, if the proportion of ten parts of tin to one hundred of copper is exceeded, are liable to burst, for the excess of tin renders them too soft. It thus happens that they have holes and cavities in the vent, and in order to obviate this danger and be able to load, it would perhaps be advisable to revert to the process of the fourteenth century, circling and reënforcing the gun with a series of steel rings, without any welding from the breech to the trunnions. In the meanwhile they remedy the defect as well as they can, and they manage to discover where the holes are in the vent of the gun by means of a searcher; but there is a better method in Gribeauval's movable star."

"In the sixteenth century," Bossuet observed, "guns were rifled."

"Yes," Combeferre replied, "that augments the ballistic force, but lessens the correctness of aim. At short distances the trajectory has not all the desirable rigidness, the parabola is exaggerated, the path of the projectile is not sufficiently rectilinear for it to hit intermediate objects, though that is a condition of fighting whose importance grows with the proximity of the enemy and the precipitation of the firing. This defective tension of the curve of the projectile in rifled cannon of the sixteenth century emanated from the weakness of the charge; weak charges for such engines are imposed by the ballistic necessities—such, for instance, as the preservation of the carriage. After all, the cannon, that despot, cannot do all that it wishes, and strength is a great weakness. A cannon-ball only goes six hundred leagues an hour, while light covers seventy thousand leagues per second. Such is the superiority of our Saviour over Napoleon."

"Reload your guns," said Enjolras.

In what manner would the revetment of the barricade behave against a cannon-ball? would a breach be formed? that was the question. While the insurgents were reloading their guns, the artillery-men loaded their cannon. The anxiety within the redoubt was profound; the shot was fired, and the detonation burst forth.

"Present!" a joyous voice cried.

And at the same time as the cannon-ball struck the barricade, Gavroche bounded inside it. He came from the direction of the Rue du Cygne, and actively clambered over the accessory barricade which fronted the labyrinth of the little Truanderie. Gavroche produced greater effect at the barricade than the cannon-ball did; for the latter was lost in the heap of rubbish. It had broken a wheel of the omnibus and finished the old truck, on seeing which the insurgents burst into a laugh.

"Pray go on," Bossuet cried to the gunners.

8. *THE ARTILLERY-MEN SET SERIOUSLY TO WORK*

GAVROCHE was surrounded, but he had no time to report anything, as Marius, shuddering, drew him on one side.

"What have you come to do here?"

"What a question!" the boy said; "and you, pray?"

And he gazed fixedly at Marius with his epic effrontery; his eyes were dilated by the proud brightness which they contained. It was with a stern accent that Marius continued:

"Who told you to return? I only trust that you have delivered my letter at its address."

Gavroche felt some degree of remorse in the matter of the letter; for, in his hurry to return to the barricade, he had got rid of it rather than delivered it. He was forced to confess to himself that he had confided somewhat too lightly in this stranger, whose face he had not even been able to distinguish. It is true that this man was bareheaded, but that was not enough. In short, he reproached himself quietly for his conduct, and feared Marius's reproaches. He took the simplest process to get out of the scrape,—he told an abominable falsehood.

"Citizen, I delivered the letter to the porter. The lady was asleep, and she will have the letter when she wakes."

Marius had two objects in sending the letter, to bid Cosette farewell and save Gavroche. He was obliged to satisfy himself with one-half of what he wanted. The connection between the sending of the letter and M. Fauchelevent's presence at the barricade occurred to his mind, and he pointed him out to Gavroche.

"Do you know that man?"

"No," said Gavroche.

Gavroche, in truth, as we know, had only seen Jean Valjean by night. The troubled and sickly conjectures formed in Marius's mind were dissipated; did he know M. Fauchelevent's opinions? perhaps he was a republican. Hence his presence in the action would be perfectly simple. In the meanwhile, Gavroche had run to the other end of the barricade, crying, "My gun!" and Courfeyrac ordered it to be given to him. Gavroche warned "his comrades," as he called them, that the barricade was invested; and he had found great difficulty in reaching it. A battalion of the line, with their arms piled in the little Truanderie, was observing on the side of the Rue du Petit Cygne; on the opposite side the Municipal Guard occupied the Rue des Prêcheurs, while in front of them they had the main body of the army. This information given, Gavroche added:

"I authorize you to give them a famous pill."

Enjolras was in the meanwhile watching at his loop-hole with open ears; for the assailants, doubtless little satisfied with the gunshot, had not repeated it. A company of line infantry had come up to occupy the extremity of the street, behind the gun. The soldiers unpaved the street, and erected with the stones a small, low wall, a species of epaulement, only eighteen inches high, and facing the barricade. At the left-hand angle of this work could be seen the head of a suburban column, massed in the Rue St. Denis. Enjolras, from his post, fancied he could hear the peculiar sound produced by canister when taken out of its box, and he saw the captain of the gun change his aim and turn the gun's muzzle slightly to the left. Then the gunners began loading, and the captain of the gun himself took the port-fire and walked up to the vent.

"Fall on your knees all along the barricade," Enjolras shouted.

The insurgents scattered in front of the wine-shop, and who had left their posts on Gavroche's arrival, rushed pell-mell toward the barricade; but ere Enjolras's order was executed, the discharge took place with the frightful rattle of a round of grape-shot; it was one, in fact. The shot was aimed at the opening in the redoubt, and ricocheted against the wall, killing two men and wounding three. If this continued, the barricade would be no longer tenable, for the grape-shot entered it. There was a murmur of consternation.

"Let us stop a second round," Enjolras said; and, leveling his gun, he aimed at the firer, who was leaning over the breech and rectifying the aim. The firer was a handsome young sergeant of artillery, fair, gentle-faced, and having the intelligent look peculiar to that predestined and formidable arm which, owing to its constant improvement, must end by killing war. Combeferre, who was standing by Enjolras's side, gazed at this young man.

"What a pity," said Combeferre; "what a hideous thing such butchery is! Well, when there are no kings left there will be no war. Enjolras, you aim at that sergeant, but do not notice him. Just reflect that he is a handsome young man; he is intrepid. You can see that he is a thinker, and these young artillery-men are well educated; he has a father, mother, and family; he is probably in love; he is but twenty-five years of age at the most, and might be your brother."

"He is so," said Enjolras.

"Yes," Combeferre added, "and mine too. Do not kill him."

"Let me alone. It must be."

And a tear slowly coursed down Enjolras's marble cheek. At the same time he pulled the trigger, and the fire flashed forth. The artillery-man turned twice on his heel, with his arms stretched out before him, and his head raised as if to breathe the air, and then fell across the cannon motionless. His back could be seen, from the middle of which a jet of blood gushed forth; the bullet had gone right through his chest, and he was dead. It was necessary to bear him away and fill up his place, and thus a few minutes were gained.

9. *THE POACHER'S SKILL AND THE UNERRING SHOT*
WHICH HAD AN INFLUENCE AT THE TRIAL IN 1796

OPINIONS varied in the barricade, for the firing of the piece was going to begin again, and the barricade could not hold out for a quarter of an hour under the grape-shot; it was absolutely necessary to deaden the rounds. Enjolras gave the command:

"We must have a mattress there."

"We have none," said Combeferre; "the wounded are lying on them."

Jean Valjean, seated apart on a bench, near the corner of the wine-shop, with his gun between his legs, had not up to the present taken any part in what was going on. He did not seem to hear the combatants saying around him, "There is a gun that does nothing." On hearing the order given by Enjolras, he arose. It will be remembered that on the arrival of the insurgents in the Rue de la Chanvrerie, an old woman in her terror of the bullets, placed her mattress in front of her window. This window, a garret window, was on the roof of a six-storied house, a little beyond the barricade. The mattress, placed across it, leaning at the bottom upon two clothes-props, was held above by two ropes, which, at a distance, seemed two pieces of pack-thread, and were fastened to nails driven into the cornice of the roof. These cords could be distinctly seen on the sky, like hairs.

"Can any one lend me a double-barreled gun?" Jean Valjean asked.

Enjolras, who had just reloaded his, handed it to him. Jean Valjean aimed at the garret-window and fired; one of the two cords of the mattress was cut asunder, and it only hung by one thread. Jean Valjean fired the second shot, and the second cord lashed the garret-window;

the mattress glided between the two poles and fell into the street. The insurgents applauded, and every voice cried:

"There is a mattress."

"Yes," said Combeferre, "but who will go and fetch it?"

The mattress, in truth, had fallen outside the barricade, between the besiegers and the besieged. Now, as the death of the sergeant of artillery had exasperated the troops, for some time past they had been lying flat behind the pile of paving-stones which they had raised; and in order to make up for the enforced silence of the gun, they had opened fire on the barricade. The insurgents, wishing to save their ammunition, did not return this musketry; the fusillade broke against the barricade, but the street which it filled with bullets was terrible. Jean Valjean stepped out of the gap, entered the street, traversed the hail of bullets, went to the mattress, picked it up, placed it on his back, and, re-entering the barricade, himself placed the mattress in the gap, and fixed it against the wall so that the gunners should not see it. This done, they waited for the next round, which was soon fired. The gun belched forth its canister with a hoarse roar, but there was no ricochet, and the grape-shot was checked by the mattress. The expected result was obtained, and the barricade saved.

"Citizen," Enjolras said to Jean Valjean, "the republic thanks you."

Bossuet admired, and laughingly said:

"It is immoral for a mattress to have so much power; it is the triumph of what yields over that which thunders. But no matter, glory to the mattress that annuls a cannon."

10. *DAWN*

AT this moment Cosette awoke; her bedroom was narrow, clean, modest, with a long window on the east side looking out into the courtyard of the house. Cosette knew nothing of what was going on in Paris, for she had returned to her bedroom at the time when Toussaint said, "There is a row." Cosette had slept but a few hours, though well. She had had sweet dreams, which resulted, perhaps, from the fact that her small bed was very white. Somebody, who was Marius, appeared to her in light; and she rose with the sun in her eyes, which at first produced the effect of a continuation of her dream upon her. Her first thought on coming out of the dream was of a smiling nature, and she felt quite re-assured. Like Jean Valjean a few hours before, she was passing through that reaction of the soul which absolutely desires no misfortune. She began hoping with all her strength, without knowing why, and then suffered from a contraction of the heart. She had not seen Marius for three days, but she said to herself that he must have received her letter, that he knew where she was, and that he was so clever, and would find means to get to her,—and most certainly to-day, and perhaps that very morning. It was bright day, but the sunbeam was nearly horizontal, and so she thought that it must be early, but that she ought to rise in order to receive Marius. She felt that she could not live without Marius, and that consequently this was sufficient, and Marius would come.. No objection was admissible, all this was certain. It was monstrous enough to have suffered for three days; Marius absent for three days! that was horrible on the part of Providence. Now this cruel suspense sent from on high was a trial passed through; Marius was about to come and bring good news. Thus is youth constituted; it wipes away its tears quickly, and, finding sorrow useless, does not accept it. Youth is the smile of the

34

future before an unknown thing, which is itself; it is natural for it to be happy, and it seems as if its breath were made of hope.

However, Cosette could not succeed in recalling to mind what Marius had said to her on the subject of this absence, which was only to last one day, and what explanation he had given her about it. Every one will have noticed with what skill a coin let fall on the ground runs to hide itself, and what art it has in rendering itself invisible. There are thoughts which play us the same trick; they conceal themselves in a corner of our brain; it is all over, they are lost, and it is impossible to recall them to memory. Cosette felt somewhat vexed at the little, useless effort her memory made, and said to herself that it was very wrong and culpable of her to forget words pronounced by Marius. She left her bed, and performed the two ablutions of the soul and the body, her prayers and her toilet.

We may, if absolutely required, introduce a reader into a nuptial chamber, but not into a virgin's room. Verse could scarce venture it, but prose durst not do so. It is the interior of a still closed flower, a whiteness in the gloaming, the inner cell of a closed lily, which must not be gazed at by man till it has been gazed at by the sun. Woman in the bud is sacred: this innocent bud, which discovers itself, this adorable semi-nudity which is afraid of itself, this white foot which takes refuge in a slipper, this throat which veils itself before a mirror as if the mirror were an eye, this chemise which hurriedly rises and covers the shoulder at the sound of a piece of furniture creaking or a passing vehicle, these knotted strings, this stay-lace, this tremor, this shudder of cold and shame, this exquisite shyness in every movement, this almost winged anxiety when there is nothing to fear, the successive phases of the apparel, which are as charming as the clouds of dawn—it is not befitting that all this should be described, and it is too much to have merely indicated it. The eye of man must be even more religious before the rising of a maiden than before the rising of a star. The possibility of attaining ought to be turned into augmented respect. The down of the peach, the bloom of the plum, the crystal radiated with snow, the butterfly's wing powdered with feathers, are but coarse things by the side of this chastity, which does not know itself that it is chaste. The maiden is only the flesh of a dream, and is not yet a statue; her alcove is concealed in the shadowy part of the ideal, and the indiscreet touch of the eye brutalizes this vague, transparent penumbra. In this case contemplation is profanation. We will therefore say nothing about the sweet awaking and rising of Cosette. An eastern fable tells us that the rose was made white by God, but that

Adam having looked at it for a moment when it opened, it felt shamed and turned red. We are of those who feel themselves abashed in the presence of maidens and flowers, for we find them venerable.

Cosette dressed herself very rapidly, and combed and dressed her hair, which was very simple at that day, when women did not swell their ringlets and plaits with cushions and pads, and placed no crinoline in their hair. Then she opened the window and looked all around, hoping to see a piece of the street, an angle of a house, a corner of the pavement, to watch for Marius there. But nothing could be seen of the outside; the court-yard was surrounded by rather lofty walls, and was bounded by other gardens. Cosette declared these gardens hideous, and for the first time in her life considered flowers ugly. The paltriest street gutter would have suited her purpose better; and she resolved to look up to heaven, as if she thought that Marius might possibly come thence. Suddenly she burst into tears, not through any fickleness of temperament, but her situation consisted of hopes dashed with despondency. She confusedly felt something horrible. In truth, things are in the air. She said to herself that she was sure of nothing, that letting herself out of sight was losing herself, and the idea that Marius might return to her from heaven appeared to her no longer charming, but lugubrious. Then—for such these clouds are—calmness returned, and hope and a species of unconscious smile, which trusted in God, however.

Everybody was still asleep in the house, and a provincial silence prevailed. No shutter was opened, and the porter's lodge was still closed. Toussaint was not up, and Cosette naturally thought that her father was asleep. She must have suffered greatly, and must still be suffering, for she said to herself that her father had been unkind, but she reckoned on Marius. The eclipse of such a light was decidedly impossible. At moments she heard, some distance off, a sort of heavy shock, and thought how singular it was that gates were opened and shut at so early an hour; it was the sound of the cannon-balls battering the barricade. There was a martin's nest a few feet below Cosette's window in the old smoke-blackened cornice, and the mouth of the nest projected a little beyond the cornice, so that the interior of this little paradise could be seen from above. The mother was there, expanding her wings like a fan over her brood; the male bird fluttered round, went away, and then returned, bringing in his bill food and kisses. The rising day gilded this happy thing; the great law, increase and multiply, was there, smiling and august, and the sweet mystery was unfolded in the glory of the morn,

Cosette, with her hair in the sunshine, her soul in flames, enlightened by love within and the dawn without, bent forward as if mechanically, and, almost without daring to confess to herself that she was thinking at the same time of Marius, she began looking at these birds, this family, this male and female, this mother and her little ones, with all the profound trouble which the sight of a nest occasions a virgin.

11. *THE SHOT WHICH HITS AND KILLS NOBODY*

THE fire of the assailants continued, and the musketry and grape-shot alternated, though without producing much mischief. The upper part of Corinth alone suffered, and the second-floor and garret windows pierced by slugs and bullets, gradually lost their shape. The combatants posted there were compelled to withdraw; but, in fact, such are the tactics of an attack on a barricade, to skirmish for a long time and exhaust the ammunition of the insurgents, if they commit the error of returning the fire. When it is discovered by the slackening of their fire that they have no powder or ball left, the assault is made. Enjolras had not fallen into this trap, and the barricade did not reply. At each platoon fire, Gavroche thrust his tongue into his cheek, a sign of supreme disdain.

"That's good," he said; "tear up the linen, for we require lint."

Courfeyrac addressed the grape-shot on its want of effect, and said to the cannon:

"You are becoming diffuse, my good fellow."

In battle, intrigues take place as at a ball; and it is probable that the silence of the redoubt was beginning to render the assailants anxious, and made them fear lest some unexpected incident had occurred. They felt a need of seeing clearly through this pile of paving-stones, and what was going on behind this impassive wall, which received shots without answering them. The insurgents suddenly perceived a helmet glistening in the sun upon an adjoining roof; a sapper was leaning against a tall chimney-pot and apparently a sentry there. He looked down into the barricade.

"That's a troublesome spy," said Enjolras.

Jean had returned Enjolras his fowling-piece, but still had his own musket. Without saying a word he aimed at the sapper, and a second later the helmet, struck by a bullet, fell noisily into the street. The soldier disappeared with all possible haste. A second watchman took his place, and it was an officer. Jean Valjean, who had reloaded his musket, aimed at the new-comer, and sent the officer's helmet to join the private's. The officer was not obstinate, but withdrew very quickly. This time the hint was understood, and no one again appeared on the roof.

"Why did you not kill the man?" Bossuet asked Jean Valjean, who, however, made no reply.

12. *DISORDER THE PARTISAN OF ORDER*

BOSSUET muttered in Combeferre's ear:

"He has not answered my question."

"He is a man who does kind actions with musket-shots," said Combeferre.

Those who have any recollection of this now distant epoch know that the suburban National Guards were valiant against the insurrection, and they were peculiarly brave and obstinate in the days of June, 1832. Any worthy landlord whose establishment the insurrection closed, became leonine on seeing his dancing-room deserted, and let himself be killed in order to save order as represented by the bar. At this time, which was at once heroic and bourgeois, in the presence of ideas which had their knights, interest had its Paladins, and the prosaicism of the motive took away none of the bravery of the movement. The decrease of a pile of crowns made bankers sing the Marseillaise; men lyrically shed their blood for the till, and defended with Lacedæmonian enthusiasm the shop, that immense diminutive of the country. Altogether there was a good deal that was very serious in all this; social interests were entering in a contest while awaiting the day when they would enter a state of equilibrium. Another sign of this time was the anarchy mingled with the governmentalism (a barbarous term of the orthodox party), and men were for order without discipline. The drums played unexpectedly fancy calls at the command of some colonel of the National Guard; one captain went under fire through inspiration, while some National Guards fought "for the idea," and on their own account. In moments of a crisis during "the days" men followed the advice of their chiefs less than their own instincts, and there were in the army of order real guerrilleros, some of the sword, like Fannicot, and others of the pen, like Henry Fonfrède. Civilization, unhappily represented at this period more by an aggregation of interests than by a group of principles, was, or believed itself to be, in danger; it uttered the alarm cry, and every man, constituting himself a center, defended, succored, and protected it in his own way, and the first-comer took on himself to save society.

Zeal sometimes went as far as extermination; a platoon of National Guards constituted themselves of their own authority a council of war, and tried and executed in five minutes an insurgent prisoner. It was an improvisation of this nature which killed Jean Prouvaire. It is that ferocious Lynch-law with which no party has the right to reproach another, for it is applied by the republic in America as by monarchy in Europe. This Lynch-law was complicated by mistakes; on a day of riot a young poet of the name of Paul Aimé Garnier was pursued on the Palace Royale at the bayonet's point, and only escaped by taking shelter under the gate-way at No. 6. *There's another of those St. Simonians,* they shouted, and wished to kill him. Now he had under his arm a volume of the Memoirs of the Duc de St. Simon; a National Guard read on the back the words *Saint Simon,* and shouted, "'Death to him!'" On June 6, 1832, a company of suburban National Guards, commanded by Captain Fannicot, to whom we have already referred, decimated the Rue de la Chanvrerie for his own good pleasure, and on his own authority. This fact, singular though it is, was proved by the judicial report drawn up in consequence of the insurrection of 1832. Captain Fannicot, an impatient and bold bourgeois, a species of condottiere of order, and a fanatical and insubmissive governmentalist, could not resist the attraction of firing prematurely, and the ambition of taking the barricade all by himself; that is to say, with his company. Exasperated at the successive apparition of the red flag and the old coat, which he took for the black flag, he loudly blamed the generals and commanders of corps, who were holding councils, as they did not think the decisive moment for assault had arrived, but were "letting the insurrection stew in its own gravy," according to a celebrated expression of one of them. As for him, he thought the barricade ripe, and as everything that is ripe is bound to fall, he made the attempt.

He commanded men as resolute as himself. "Madmen," a witness called them. His company, the same which had shot Jean Prouvaire, was the first of the battalion posted at the street-corner. At the moment when it was least expected, the captain dashed his men at the barricade, but this movement, executed with more good-will than strategy, cost Fannicot's company dearly. Before it had covered two-thirds of the street, a general discharge from the barricade greeted it; four, the boldest men of all, running at the head, were shot down in point-blank range at the very foot of the barricade, and this courageous mob of National Guards, very brave men, but not possessing the military tenacity, was compelled to fall back after a few moments, leaving fifteen corpses in the street. The momentary hesitation gave the insurgents time to reload, and a second and most deadly charge assailed the company before the men were able to regain their shelter at the corner of the street. In a moment they were caught between two fires, and received the volley from the cannon, which, having no orders to the contrary, did not cease firing. The intrepid and imprudent Fannicot was one of those killed by this round of grape-shot; he was laid low by the cannon. This attack, which was more furious than serious, irritated Enjolras.

"The asses!" he said; "they have their men killed and expend our ammunition for nothing."

Enjolras spoke like the true general of the riot that he was: insurrection and repression do not fight with equal arms; for the insurrection, which can be soon exhausted, has only a certain number of rounds to fire and of combatants to expend. An expended cartridge-box and a killed man cannot have their place filled up. Repression, on the other hand, having the army, does not count men, and having Vincennes does not count rounds. Repression has as many regiments as the barricade has men, and as many arsenals as the barricade has cartridge-boxes. Hence these are always contests of one man against a hundred, which ever end by the destruction of the barricade, unless revolution, suddenly dashing up, casts into the balance its flashing arch-angel's glaive. Such things happen, and then everything rises, paving-stones get into a state of ebullition, and popular redoubts swarm. Paris has a sovereign tremor, the *quid divinum* is evolved; there is an August 10 or a July 29 in the air, a prodigious light appears, the yawning throat of force recoils, and the army, that lion, sees standing erect and tranquil before it that prophet, France.

13. *PASSING FLASHES*

In the chaos of feelings and passions which defend a barricade, there is everything,—bravery, youth, the point of honor, enthusiasm, the ideal, conviction, the obstinacy of the gambler, and above all intermitting gleams of hope. One of these intermissions, one of these vague quiverings of hope, suddenly ran along the Chanvrerie barricade at the most unexpected moment.

"Listen," Enjolras, who was ever on the watch, exclaimed, "I fancy that Paris is waking up."

It is certain that on the morning of June 6th the insurrection had for an hour or two a certain reanimation. The obstinacy of the tocsin of St. Merry aroused a few inclinations, and barricades were begun in the Rue de Poirier and in the Rue du Graulliers. In front of the Porte St. Martin, a young man armed with a gun attacked a squadron of cavalry, alone, unprotected, and on the open boulevard he knelt down, raised his gun, fired and killed the major, and then turned away, saying, *There's another who will do us no more mischief*. He was cut down. In the Rue St. Denis a woman fired at the National Guard from behind a Venetian shutter, and the wooden laths could be seen to tremble every moment. A boy of fourteen was arrested in the Rue de la Cossonnerie with his pockets full of cartridges, and several guard-houses were attacked. At the entrance of the Rue Bertin-Poirée, a very sharp and quite unexpected fusillade greeted a regiment of cuirassiers, at the head of which rode General Cavaignac de Barague. In the Rue Planche Milbray, old crockery and household utensils were thrown from the roofs down on the troops; this was a bad sign, and when Marshal Soult was informed of the fact, Napoleon's old lieutenant became pensive, for he remembered Suchet's remark at Saragossa: *We are lost when old women empty their pots de chambre on our heads.* These general symptoms manifested at a moment when the riots were supposed to be localized, this fever of anger which regained the upper hand, these Will-o'-the-wisps flying here and there over the profound masses of combustible matter which are called the faubourgs of Paris, and all the accompanying facts, rendered the chiefs anxious, and they hastened to extinguish the first outbreak of the fire. Until these sparks were quenched, the attacks on the barricade Maubuée, de la Chanvrerie, and St. Merry were deferred, so that all might be finished at one blow. Columns of troops were sent through the streets in fermentation, sweeping the large streets and probing the smaller ones, on the right and on the left, at one moment slowly and cautiously, at another at the double. The troops broke open the doors of the houses whence firing was heard, and at the same time cavalry maneuvers dispersed the groups on the boulevards. This repression was not effected without turmoil and that tumultuous noise peculiar to collisions between the army and the people, and it was this that had attracted Enjolras's attention in the intervals between the cannonading and the platoon fire. Moreover, he had seen wounded men carried along the end of the street on litters, and said to Courfeyrac, "Those wounded are not our handiwork."

The hope lasted but a short time, and the gleam was quickly eclipsed. In less than half an hour what there was in the air vanished; it was like a flash of lightning without thunder, and the insurgents felt that leaden pall, which the indifference of the people casts upon abandoned, obstinate men, fall upon them again. The general movement, which seemed to have been obscurely designed, failed, and the attention of the minister of war and the strategy of the generals could now be concentrated on the three or four barricades that remained standing. The sun rose on the horizon, and an insurgent addressed Enjolras:

"We are hungry here. Are we really going to die like this, without eating?"

Enjolras, still leaning at his parapet, made a nod of affirmation, without taking his eyes off the end of the street.

14. *WHERE WE READ THE NAME OF THE MISTRESS OF ENJOLRAS*

COURFEYRAC, seated on a stone by the side of Enjolras, continued to insult the cannon, and each time that the gloomy shower of projectiles which is called a grape-shot passed with its monstrous noise he greeted it with an ironical remark.

"You are wasting your breath, my poor old brute, and I feel sorry for you, as your row is thrown away. That is not thunder, but a cough."

And those around him laughed. Courfeyrac and Bossuet, whose valiant good-humor increased with danger, made up for the want of food, like Madame Scarron, by jests, and, as wine was short, poured out gayety for all.

"I admire Enjolras," Bossuet said, "and his temerity astonishes me. He lives alone, which, perhaps, renders him a little sad; and Enjolras is to be pitied for his greatness, which attaches him to widowhood. We fellows have all, more or less, mistresses, who make us mad, that is to say, brave; and when a man is as full of love as a tiger, the least he can do is to fight like a lion. That is a way of avenging ourselves for the tricks which our grisettes play us. Roland lets himself be killed to vex Angelique, and all our heroism comes from our women. A man without a woman is like a pistol without a hammer, and it is the woman who makes a man go off. Well, Enjolras has no woman, he is not in love, and

43

finds means to be intrepid. It is extraordinary that a man can be as cold as ice and daring as fire."

Enjolras did not appear to listen; but any one who had been near him might have heard him murmur, in a low voice, *Patria*. Bossuet laughed again, when Courfeyrac shouted:

"Here's something fresh."

And assuming the voice of a groom of the chambers who announces a visitor, he added:

"Mr. Eight-pounder."

In fact, a new character had come on the stage; it was a second piece of artillery. The gunners rapidly got it into position by the side of the first one, and this was the beginning of the end. A few minutes later both guns, being actively served, were at work against the barricade, and the platoon fire of the line and the suburban National Guards supported the artillery. Another cannonade was audible some distance off. At the same time as the two guns were furiously assaulting the redoubt in the Rue de la Chanvrerie, two other pieces placed in position, one in the Rue St. Denis, the other in the Rue Aubrey-le-Boucher, were pounding the St. Merry barricade. The four guns formed a lugubrious echo to each other, and the barks of the grim dogs of war responded to each other. Of the two guns now opened on the barricade of the Rue de la Chanvrerie, one fired shell and the other solid shot. The gun which fired the latter was pointed at a slight elevation, and the firing was so calculated that the ball struck the extreme edge of the crest of barricades, and hurled the broken paving-stones on the heads of the insurgents. This mode of fire was intended to drive the combatants from the top of the redoubt, and compel them to close up in the interior; that is to say, it announced the assault. Once the combatants were driven from the top of the barricade by the cannon and from the windows of the public-house by the canister, the columns of attack could venture into the street without being aimed at, perhaps without even being seen, suddenly escalade the barricade, as on the previous evening, and take it by surprise.

"The annoyance of the guns must be reduced," said Enjolras, and he shouted, "Fire at the artillery-men."

All were ready,—the barricade, which had so long been silent, was belted with flame; seven or eight rounds succeeded each other with a sort of rage and joy; the street was filled with a blinding smoke, and at the expiration of a few minutes there might be confusedly seen through the mist, all striped with flame, two-thirds of the artillery-men lying under the gun-wheels. Those who remained standing continued to serve the guns with stern tranquillity, but the fire was reduced.

"Things are going well," said Bossuet to Enjolras, "that is a success." Enjolras shook his head, and replied:

"Another quarter of an hour of that success, and there will not be a dozen cartridges left in the barricade."

It appears that Gavroche heard the remark.

15. *GAVROCHE OUTSIDE*

COURFEYRAC all at once perceived somebody in the street, at the foot of the barricade, amid the shower of bullets. Gavroche had fetched a hamper from the pot-house, passed through the gap, and was quickly engaged in emptying into it the full cartridge-boxes of the National Guards killed on the slope of the barricade.

"What are you doing there?" Courfeyrac said.

Gavroche looked up.

"Citizen, I am filling my hamper."

"Do you not see the grape-shot?"

Gavroche replied:

"Well, it is raining; what then?"

Courfeyrac cried, "Come in."

"Directly," said Gavroche.

And with one bound he reached the street. It will be borne in mind that Fannicot's company, in retiring, left behind it a number of corpses; some twenty dead lay here and there all along the pavement of the street. That made twenty cartridge-boxes for Gavroche, and a stock of cartridges for the barricade. The smoke lay in the street like a fog; any one who has seen a cloud in a mountain gorge, between two precipitous escarpments, can form an idea of this smoke, contracted, and, as it were, rendered denser by the two dark lines of tall houses. It rose slowly, and was incessantly renewed; whence came a gradual obscurity, which dulled even the bright daylight. The combatants could scarce see each other from either end of the street, which was, however, very short. This darkness, probably desired and calculated on by the chiefs who were about to direct the assault on the barricade, was useful for Gavroche. Under the cloak of this smoke, and thanks to his shortness, he was enabled to advance a considerable distance along the street unnoticed, and he plundered the first seven or eight cartridge-boxes without any great danger. He crawled on his stomach, galloped on all-fours, took his hamper in his teeth, writhed, glided, undulated, wound from one corpse to another, and emptied the cartridge-box as a monkey opens a nut. They did not cry to him from the barricade, to which he was still rather close, to return, for fear of attracting attention to him. On one corpse, which was a corporal's, he found a powder-flask.

"For thirst," he said, as he put it in his pocket.

While moving forward, he at length reached the point where the fog of the fire became transparent, so that the sharp-shooters of the line drawn up behind their parapet of paving-stones, and the National Guard at the corner of the street, all at once pointed out to each other something stirring in the street. At the moment when Gavroche was taking the cartridges from a sergeant near a post, a bullet struck the corpse.

"Oh! for shame," said Gavroche; "they are killing my dead for me."

A second bullet caused the stones to strike fire close to him, while a third upset his hamper. Gavroche looked and saw that it came from the National Guards. He stood upright, with his hair floating in the breeze, his hand on his hip, and his eyes fixed on the National Guards who were firing, and he sang:

> On est laid à Nanterre,
> C'est la faute à Voltaire,
> Et bête à Palaisseau,
> C'est la faute à Rousseau.

Then he picked up his hamper, put into it the cartridges scattered around without missing one, and walked toward the firing party, to despoil another cartridge-box. Then a fourth bullet missed him. Gavroche sang:

Je ne suis pas notaire,
C'est la faute à Voltaire,
Je suis petit oiseau,
C'est la faute à Rousseau.

A fifth bullet only succeeded so far as to draw a third couplet from him:

Joie est mon caractère,
C'est la faute à Voltaire:
Misère est mon trousseau,
C'est la faute à Rousseau.

They went on for some time longer, and the sight was at once terrific and charming; Gavroche, while fired at, ridiculed the firing, and appeared to be greatly amused. He was like a sparrow deriding the sportsmen, and answered each discharge by a couplet. The troops aimed at him incessantly and constantly missed him, and the National Guards and the soldiers laughed, while covering him. He lay down, then rose again, hid himself in a door-way, then bounded, disappeared, reappeared, ran off, came back, replied to the grape-shot with his thumb to his nose, and all the while plundered cartridges, emptied boxes, and filled his hamper. The insurgents watched him, as they panted with anxiety, but while the barricade trembled he sang. He was not a child, he was not a man, he was a strange goblin gamin, and he resembled the invulnerable dwarf of the combat. The bullets ran after him, but he was more active than they; he played a frightful game of hide-and-seek with death; and each time that the snub-nosed face of the specter approached, the gamin gave it a fillip. One bullet, however, better aimed or more treacherous than the rest, at length struck the Will-o'-the-wisp lad; Gavroche was seen to totter and then sink. The whole barricade uttered a cry, but there was an Antæus in this pigmy; for a gamin to touch the pavement is like the giant touching the earth; and Gavroche had only fallen to rise again. He remained in a sitting posture, a long jet of blood ran down his face, he raised both arms in the air, looked in the direction whence the shot had come, and began singing:

Je suis tombé par terre,
C'est la faute à Voltaire:
Le nez dans le ruisseau,
C'est la faute à ——

47

He did not finish, for a second shot from the same marksman stopped him short. This time he lay with his face on the pavement, and did not stir again. This little great soul had fled away.

16. HOW A BROTHER BECOMES A FATHER

THERE were at this very moment in the Luxembourg garden—for the eye of the drama must be everywhere present—two lads holding each other's hand. One might be seven, the other, five years of age. As they were wet through with the rain, they walked along sunshiny paths; the elder led the younger, both were in rags and pale, and they looked like wild birds. The younger said: "I am very hungry." The elder, who had already a protecting air, led his brother with the left hand, and had a switch in his right. They were alone in the garden, which was deserted, as the gates were closed by police order on account of the insurrection. The troops who had bivouacked there had issued forth for the exigencies of the combat. How were these children here? Perhaps they had escaped from some guard-room where the door was left ajar; perhaps in the vicinity, at the Barrière l'Enfer, on the esplanade of the observatory, or in the neighboring square overshadowed by the cornice, on which may be read, *invenerunt parvulum pannis involutum,* there was some mountebank's booth from which they had fled; perhaps they had on the previous evening kept out of sight of the keepers at the Luxembourg, and had spent the night in one of those summer-houses in which people read the papers; the fact is, that they were wandering about and seemed to be free. To be a wanderer, and to appear free, is to be lost, and these poor little creatures were really lost. The two lads were the same about whom Gavroche had been in trouble, and whom, the reader will remember, were sons of Thénardier, let out to Magnon, attributed to M. Gillenormand, and now leaves fallen from all these rootless branches, and rolled along the ground by the wind.

Their clothes, clean in the time of Magnon, and which served her as a prospectus to M. Gillenormand, had become rags; and these beings henceforth belonged to the statistics of "deserted children," whom the police pick up, lose, and find again on the pavement of Paris. It needed the confusion of such a day as this for these two poor little wretches to be in this garden. If the keepers had noticed these rags they would have expelled them, for poor little lads do not enter public gardens, and yet it ought to be remembered that as children they have a right to flowers. They were here, thanks to the locked gates, and were committing an offense; they had stepped into the garden and remained there. Though locked gates do not give a holiday to the keepers, and their surveillance is supposed to continue, it grows weaker and rests; and the keepers, also affected by the public affairs, and more busied about the outside than the inside, did not look at the garden, and had not seen the two delinquents. It had rained on the previous evening, and even slightly on this morning, but in June showers are of no great consequence. People hardly perceive, an hour after a storm, that this fair beauteous day has wept, for the earth dries up as rapidly as a child's cheek. At this period of the solstice the midday light, is so to speak, poignant, and it seizes everything. It clings to and spreads itself over the earth with a sort of suction, and we might say that the sun is thirsty. A shower is a glass of water, and rain is at once drunk up. In the morning everything glistens, in the afternoon everything is dusty. Nothing is so admirable as verdure cleansed by the rain and dried by the sun; it is warm freshness. Gardens and fields, having water in their roots and sunshine in their flowers, become censers of incense, and smoke with all their perfumes at once. Everything laughs, sings, and offers itself, and we feel softly intoxicated; summer is a temporary paradise, and the sun helps man to be patient.

There are beings who ask no more, living creatures who, having the azure of heaven, say, it is enough, dreamers absorbed in the prodigy of the world, drawing from the idolatry of nature indifference to good and evil, contemplators of the Cosmos, radiantly distracted from man, who do not understand how people can trouble themselves about the hunger of one person, the thirst of another, the nudity of the poor man in winter, the lymphatic curvature of a small backbone, the truckle bed, the garret, the cell, and the rags of young shivering girls, when one can dream under the trees: they are peaceful and terrible minds, pitilessly satisfied, and, strange to say, infinitude suffices them. They ignore that great want of man, the finite which admits of an embrace, and do not dream of the finite which admits of progress, that sublime toil. The indefinite, which springs from the divine and human combination of the infinite and the finite, escapes them, and, provided that they can be face to face with immensity, they smile. They never feel joy, but always ecstasy, and their life is one of abstraction. The history of humanity is to them but a grand detail; the All is not in it, the All remains outside of it. Of what use is it to trouble one's self about that item man? Man suffers, it is possible; but just look at Aldebaran rising! The mother has no milk left, the new-born babe is dying. I know nothing of all that, but just look at the marvelous rose made by a sprig of hawthorn; when looked at through a microscope, just compare the finest Mechlin lace with that. These thinkers forget to love, and the zodiac has such an attraction over them that it prevents them seeing the weeping child. God eclipses their soul, and they are a family of minds at once great and little. Homer belonged to it, so did Goethe, and possibly La Fontaine, magnificent egotists of the infinite, calm spectators of sorrow, who do not see Nero if the weather be fine; from whom the sun hides the pyre; who would look at a guillotining to seek an effect of light in it; who hear neither cries nor sobs, nor death-rattle nor the tocsin, for whom everything is good, since there is the month of May; who so long as they have clouds of purple and gold above their heads declare themselves satisfied, and who are determined to be happy until the radiance of the stars and the song of birds are exhausted.

These are dark radiances, and they do not suspect that they are to be pitied. But they are certainly so, for the man who does not weep does not see. We must admire and pity them, as we would pity and admire a being at once night and day, who had no eyes under his brows, but a star in the center of his forehead. The indifference of these thinkers is, according to some, a grand philosophy. Be it so, but in this superiority there is infirmity. A man may be immortal and limp, as witness Vulcan, and he may be more than man and less than man; there is immense incompleteness in nature, and who knows whether the sun be not blind? but in that case, whom to trust? *Solem quis dicere falsum audeat?* Hence, certain geniuses, certain human deities, starmen, might be mistaken? What is above, at the summit, at the zenith, which pours so much light on the earth, might see little, see badly, not see at all? is not that desperate? no; but what is there above the sun? God.

On June 6, 1832, at about eleven in the forenoon, the Luxembourg, solitary and depopulated, was delicious. The quincunxes and flower-beds sent balm and dazzlement into the light, and the branches, wild in the brilliancy of midday, seemed trying to embrace each other. There was in the sycamores a twittering of linnets, the sparrows were triumphal, and the woodpeckers crept along the chestnuts, gently tapping the holes in the bark. The flower-beds accepted the legitimate royalty of the lilies, for the most august of perfumes is that which issues from whiteness. The sharp odor of the carnations was inhaled, and the old rooks of Marie de Medicis made love on the lofty trees. The sun gilded, purpled, and illumined the tulips, which are nothing but all the varieties of flame made into flowers. All around the tulip-beds hummed the bees, the flashes of these fire-flowers. All was grace and gayety; even the coming shower, for that relapse, by which the lilies of the valley and honeysuckles would profit, had nothing alarming about it, and the swallows made the delicious menace of flying low. What was there drank in happiness; life had a pleasant perfume, and all this nature exhaled candor, help, assistance, paternity, caresses, and dawn. The thoughts that fell from heaven were as soft as a little child's hand that we kiss. The statues under the trees, nude and white, were robed in dresses of shadow shot with light: these goddesses were all ragged with sunshine, and rags hung from them on all sides. Around the great basin the earth was already so dry as to be parched, and there was a breeze sufficiently strong to create here and there small riots of dust. A few yellow leaves remaining from last autumn joyously pursued each other, and seemed to be sporting.

The abundance of light had something strangely re-assuring about it; life, sap, heat, and exhalations overflowed, and the immensity of the source could be felt beneath creation. In all these blasts penetrated with love, in this movement of reflections and gleams, in this prodigious expenditure of rays, and in this indefinite outpouring of fluid gold, the prodigality of the inexhaustible could be felt, and behind this splendor, as behind a curtain of flames, glimpses of God, that millionaire of the stars, could be caught. Thanks to the sand, there was not a speck of mud, and, thanks to the rain, there was not a grain of dust. The bouquets had just performed their ablutions, and all the velvets, all the satins, all the varnish, and all the gold, which issue from the earth in the shape of flowers, were irreproachable. This magnificence was free from stain, and the grand silence of happy nature filled the garden,—a heavenly silence, compatible with a thousand strains of music, the fondling tones from the nests, the buzzing of the swarms, and the palpitations of the wind. The whole harmony of the season was blended into a graceful whole, the entrances and exits of spring took place in the desired order, the lilacs were finishing and the jessamine beginning, a few flowers were behind and a few insects before their time, and the vanguard of the red butter-flies of June fraternized with the rear-guard of the white butterflies of May. The plane trees were putting on a fresh skin, and the breeze formed undulations in the magnificent enormity of the chestnut-trees. It was splendid. A veteran from the adjoining barracks who was looking through the railings said, "Nature is presenting arms in full-dress uniform."

All nature was breakfasting, and creation was at table; it was the hour; the great blue cloth was laid in heaven, and the great green one on earth, while the sun gave an *à giorno* illumination. God was serving his univer-sal meal, and each being had its pasture or its pasty. The wood-pigeon found hemp-seed, the greenfinch found millet, the gold-finch found chick-weed, the redbreast found worms, the bee found flowers, the fly found infusoria, and the swallow found flies. They certainly devoured each other to some extent, which is the mystery of evil mingled with good, but not a single animal had an empty stomach. The two poor abandoned boys had got near the great basin, and, somewhat confused by all this light, tried to hide themselves, which is the instinct of the poor and the weak in the presence of magnificence, even when it is impersonal, and they kept behind the swan's house. Now and then, at intervals when the wind blew, confused shouts, a dull roar, a sort of noisy death-rattle which was musketry, and dull blows which were cannon-shots, could be heard. There was smoke above the roofs in the direction of the Halles, and a bell which seemed to be summoning sounded in the distance. The children did not seem to notice the noises, and the younger lad repeated every now and then in a low voice, "I am hungry."

Almost simultaneously with the two boys another couple approached the basin, consisting of a man of about fifty, leading by the hand a boy six years of age. It was doubtless a father with his son. The younger of the two had a cake in his hand. At this period certain contiguous houses in the Rue Madame and the Rue d'Enfer had keys to the Luxembourg, by which the lodgers could let themselves in when the gates were locked, but this permission has since been withdrawn. This father and son evidently came from one of these houses. The two poor little creatures saw "this gentleman" coming, and hid themselves a little more. He was a citizen, and perhaps the same whom Marius through his love-fever had one day heard near the same great basin, counseling his son "to avoid excesses." He had an affable and haughty look, and a mouth which, as it did not close, always smiled. This mechanical smile, produced by too much jaw and too little skin, shows the teeth rather than the soul. The boy with the bitten cake, which he did not finish, seemed uncomfortably full; the boy was dressed in a National Guard's uniform, on account of the riots, and the father remained in civilian garb for the sake of prudence. Father and son had halted near the great basin, in which the two swans were disporting. This bourgeois appeared to have a special admiration for the swans, and resembled them in the sense that he walked like them. At this moment the swans were swimming, which is their principal talent, and were superb. Had the two little fellows listened, and been of an age to comprehend, they might have overheard the remarks of a serious man; the father was saying to his son:

"The sage lives contented with little. Look at me, my son; I do not care for luxury. You never see me in a coat glistening with gold and precious stones; I leave that false luster to badly organized minds."

Here the deep shouts which came from the direction of the Halles broke out, with a redoublement of bells and noise.

"What is that?" the lad asked.

The father replied:

"That is the saturnalia."

All at once he perceived the two little ragged boys standing motionless behind the swan's green house.

"Here is the beginning," he said.

And after a silence he added:

"Anarchy enters this garden."

In the meanwhile the boy bit the cake, spat it out again, and suddenly began crying.

"Why are you crying?" the father asked.

"I am no longer hungry," said the boy.

The father's smile became more marked than ever.

"You need not be hungry to eat a cake."

"I am tired of cake. It is so filling."

"Don't you want any more?"

"No."

The father showed him the swans.

"Throw it to those palmipedes."

53

The boy hesitated, for if he did not want any more cake, that was no reason to give it away.

The father continued:

"Be humane; you ought to have pity on animals."

And, taking the cake from his son, he threw it into the basin, when it fell rather near the bank. The swans were some distance off, near the center of the basin, and engaged with some prey; they had seen neither the citizen nor the cake. The citizen, feeling that the cake ran a risk of being lost, and affected by this useless shipwreck, began a telegraphic agitation, which eventually attracted the attention of the swans. They noticed something floating on the surface, tacked, like the vessels they are, and came toward the cake slowly, with the majesty that befits white beasts.

"Swans understand signs," the bourgeois, pleased at his own cleverness, said.

At this moment the distant tumult of the city was suddenly swollen. This time it was sinister, and there are some puffs of wind which speak more distinctly than others. The one which blew at this moment distinctly brought up the rolling of drums, shouts, platoon fires, and the mournful replies of the tocsin and the cannon. This coincided with a black cloud which suddenly veiled the sky. The swans had not yet reached the cake.

"Let us go home," the father said: "they are attacking the Tuileries."

He seized his son's hand again, and then continued:

"From the Tuileries to the Luxembourg there is only the distance which separates the royalty from the peerage; and that is not far. It is going to rain musketry."

He looked at the cloud.

"And perhaps we shall have rain of the other sort, too; heaven is interfering; the younger branch is condemned. Let us make haste home."

"I should like to see the swans eat the cake," said the boy.

"It would be imprudent," the father answered; and he led away his little bourgeois. The son, regretting the swans, turned his head toward the basin until an elbow of the quincunxes concealed it from him. The two little vagabonds had in the meanwhile approached the cake simultaneously with the swans. It was floating on the water; the smaller boy looked at the cake; the other looked at the citizen, who was going off. Father and son entered the labyrinth of trees that runs to the grand staircase of the clump of trees in the direction of the Rue Madame. When they were no longer in sight, the elder hurriedly lay down full length on the rounded bank of the basin, and holding by his left hand, while bending over the water, till he all but fell in, he stretched out his switch toward the cake with the other. The swans, seeing the enemy, hastened up, and in hastening their breasts produced an effect useful to the little fisher; the water flowed back in front of the swans, and one of the gentle, concentric undulations softly impelled the cake toward the boy's switch. When the swans got up, the stick was touching the cake; the lad gave a quick blow, startled the swans, seized the cake, and got up. The cake was soaking, but they were hungry and thirsty. The elder boy divided the cake into two parts, a large one and a small one, kept the small one for himself, and gave the larger piece to his brother, saying:

Shove that into your gun.

17. MORTUUS PATER FILIUM MORITORUM EXPECTAT

MARIUS rushed out of the barricade, and Combeferre followed him; but it was too late, and Gavroche was dead. Combeferre brought in the hamper of cartridges, and Marius the boy. Alas! he thought he was requiting the son for what the father had done for his father; but Thénardier had brought in his father alive, while he brought in the lad dead. When Marius reëntered the barricade with Gavroche in his arms, his face was inundated with blood, like the boy's; for, at the very instant when he stooped to pick up Gavroche, a bullet had grazed his skull, but he had not noticed it. Courfeyrac took off his neckcloth and bound Marius's forehead; Gavroche was deposited on the same table with Mabœuf, and the black shawl was spread over both bodies; it was large enough for the old man and the child. Combeferre distributed the cartridges which he had brought in, and they gave each man fifteen rounds to fire. Jean Valjean was still at the same spot, motionless on his bench. When Combeferre offered him his fifteen cartridges he shook his head.

"That is a strange eccentric," Combeferre said in a whisper to Enjolras. "He manages not to fight inside this barricade."

"Which does not prevent him from defending it," Enjolras answered.

"Heroism has its original characters," Combeferre resumed.

And Courfeyrac, who overheard him, said:

"He is a different sort from Father Mabœuf."

It is a thing worth mentioning, that the fire which struck the barricade scarce disturbed the interior. Those who have never passed the tornado of a warfare of this nature cannot form any idea of the singular moments of calmness mingled with these convulsions. Men come and go; they talk, they jest, they idle. A friend of ours heard a combatant say to him, in the midst of the grape-shot, *It is like being at a bachelor's breakfast here.* The redoubt in the Rue de la Chanvrerie, we repeat, appeared internally most calm; and all the incidents and phases were, or would shortly be exhausted. From critical the position had become menacing, and from menacing was probably about to become desperate. In proportion as the situation grew darker, an heroic gleam more and more purpled the barricade. Enjolras commanded it in the attitude of a young Spartan devoting his bare sword to the gloomy genius, Epidotas. Combeferre, with an apron tied round him, was dressing the wounded. Bossuet and Feuilly were making cartridges with the powder-flask found by Gavroche on the dead corporal, and Bossuet was saying to Feuilly, *We are soon going to take the diligence for another planet.* Courfeyrac, seated on the few paving-stones which he had set aside near Enjolras, was preparing and arranging an entire arsenal—his sword-cane, his gun, two holster-pistols, and a club—with the ease of a girl setting a small dunkerque in order. Jean Valjean was silently looking at the wall facing him, and a workman was fastening on his head, with a piece of string, a broad-brimmed straw bonnet of Mother Hucheloup's, *for fear of sun-strokes,* as he said. The young men of the Aix Cougourde were gayly chatting together, as if desirous to talk patois for the last time. Joly, who had taken down Widow Hucheloup's mirror, was examining his tongue in it; while a few combatants, who had discovered some nearly moldering crusts of bread in a drawer, were eating them greedily. Marius was anxious about what his father would say to him.

18. *THE VULTURE BECOMES THE PREY*

WE must lay a stress upon a psychological fact peculiar to barricades, for nothing which characterizes this surprising war of streets ought to be omitted. Whatever the internal tranquillity to which we have just referred may be, the barricade does not the less remain a vision for those who are inside it. There is an apocalypse in a civil war; all the darkness of the unknown world is mingled with these stern flashes, revolutions are sphinxes, and any one who has stood behind a barricade believes that he has gone through a dream. What is felt at these spots we have shown in the matter of Marius, and the consequences thereof we shall see. It is more and it is less than life. On leaving a barricade, a man no longer knows what he has seen; he may have been terrible, but he is ignorant of the fact. He has been surrounded there by combating ideas which possessed human faces, and had his head in the light of futurity. There were corpses laid low, and phantoms standing upright; and the hours were colossal, and seemed hours of eternity. A man has lived in death, and shadows have passed. What was it? he has seen hands on which was blood; it was a deafening din, but at the same time a startling silence; there were open mouths that cried, and other open mouths which were silent, and men were in smoke, perhaps in night. A man fancies he has touched the sinister dripping of unknown depths, and he looks at something red which he has in his nails, but he no longer recollects anything.

Let us return to the Rue de la Chanvrerie. Suddenly, between two discharges, the distant sound of a clock striking was heard.

"It is midday," said Combeferre.

The twelve strokes had not died out ere Enjolras drew himself up to his full height and hurled the loud cry from the top of the barricade:

"Take up the paving-stones into the house, and line the windows with them. One-half of you to the stones, the other half to the muskets. There is not a moment to lose."

A party of sappers, with their axes on their shoulders, had just appeared in battle array at the end of the street. This could only be the head of a column; and of what column? evidently the column of attack; for the sappers ordered to demolish the barricade always precede the troops told off to escalade it. Plainly, the moment was at hand which M. Clermont Tonnerre called in 1822, "putting your weight in the collar."

Enjolras's order was carried out with that correct speed peculiar to ships and barricades, the only two battle-fields whence escape is impossible. In less than a minute two-thirds of the paving-stones which Enjolras had ordered to be piled up against the door of Corinth were carried to the first-floor and attic, and before a second minute had passed, these paving-stones, artistically laid on one another, walled up one-half of the window. A few spaces carefully arranged by Feuilly, the chief constructor, allowed the gun-barrels to pass through. This armament of the windows was the more easily effected because the grape-shot had ceased. The two cannon were now firing solid shot at the center of the barricade, in order to make a hole, and, if possible, a breach, for the assault. When the stones intended for the final assault were in their places, Enjolras carried to the second-floor the bottles he had placed under the table on which Mabœuf lay.

"Who will drink that?" Bossuet asked him.

"They will," Enjolras answered.

Then the ground-floor window was also barricaded, and the iron bars which closed the door at night were held in readiness. The fortress was complete, the barricade was the rampart, and the wine-shop the keep. With the paving-stones left over, the gap was stopped up. As the defenders of a barricade are always obliged to save their ammunition, and the besiegers are aware of the fact, the latter combine their arrangements with a sort of irritating leisure, expose themselves before the time to the fire, though more apparently than in reality, and take their ease. The preparations for the attack are always made with a certain methodical slowness, and after that comes the thunder. This slowness enabled Enjolras to revise and render everything perfect. He felt that since such men were about to die, their death must be a masterpiece. He said to Marius:

"We are the two chiefs. I am going to give the final orders inside, while you remain outside and watch."

Marius posted himself in observation on the crest of the barricade, while Enjolras had the door of the kitchen, which, it will be remembered, served as an ambulance, nailed up.

"No spattering on the wounded," he said.

He gave his final instructions in the ground-floor room in a sharp but wonderfully calm voice, and Feuilly listened and answered in the name of all.

"Have axes ready on the second-floor to cut down the stairs. Have you them?"

"Yes," Feuilly answered.

"How many?"

"Two axes and a crowbar."

"Very good. In all twenty-six fighting-men left. How many guns are there?"

"Thirty-four."

"Eight too many. Keep those guns loaded like the others, and within reach. Place your sabers and pistols in your belts. Twenty men to the barricade. Six will ambush themselves in the garret and at the first-floor window, to fire on the assailants through the loop-holes in the paving-stones. There must not be an idle workman here. Presently, when the drummer sounds the charge, the twenty men below will rush to the barricade, and the first to arrive will be the best placed."

These arrangements made, he turned to Javert, and said to him:

"I have not forgotten you."

And, laying a pistol on the table, he added:

"The last man to leave here will blow out this spy's brains."

"Here?" a voice answered.

"No, let us not have this corpse near ours. It is easy to stride over the small barricade in Mondétour lane, as it is only four feet high. This man is securely bound, so lead him there and execute him."

Some one was at this moment even more stoical than Enjolras,—it was Javert. Here Jean Valjean appeared; he was mixed up with the group of insurgents, but stepped forward and said to Enjolras:

"Are you the commandant?"

"Yes."

"You thanked me just now."

"In the name of the Republic. The barricade has two saviours, Marius Pontmercy and yourself."

"Do you think that I deserve a reward?"

"Certainly."

"Well, then, I ask one."

"What is it?"

"To let me blow out that man's brains myself."

Javert raised his head, saw Jean Valjean, gave an imperceptible start, and said: "It is fair."

As for Enjolras, he was reloading his gun. He looked around him.

"Is there no objection?"

And he turned to Jean Valjean.

"Take the spy."

Jean Valjean took possession of Javert by seating himself on the end of the table. He seized the pistol, and a faint clink showed that he had cocked it. Almost at the same moment the bugle-call was heard.

"Mind yourselves," Marius shouted from the top of the barricade.

Javert began laughing that noiseless laugh peculiar to him, and looking intently at the insurgents, said to them:

"You are no healthier than I am."

"All outside," Enjolras cried.

The insurgents rushed tumultuously forth, and as they passed, Javert smote them on the back, so to speak, with the expression, "We shall meet again soon."

19. *THE VENGEANCE OF JEAN VALJEAN*

So soon as Jean Valjean was alone with Javert, he undid the rope which fastened the prisoner round the waist, the knot of which was under the table. After this he made him a signal to rise. Javert obeyed with that indefinable smile in which the supremacy of enchained authority is condensed. Jean Valjean seized Javert by the martingale, as he would have taken an ox by its halter, and, dragging him after him, quitted the wine-shop slowly, for Javert, having his feet hobbled, could only take very short steps. Jean Valjean held the pistol in his hand, and they thus crossed the inner trapeze of the barricade; the insurgents, prepared for the imminent attack, turned their backs.

Marius alone, placed at the left extremity of the barricade, saw them pass. This group of the victim and his executioner was illumined by the sepulchral gleams which he had in his soul. Jean Valjean forced Javert to climb over the barricade with some difficulty, but did not loosen the cord. When they had crossed the bar, they found themselves alone in the lane, and no one could now see them, for the elbow formed by the houses hid them from the insurgents. The corpses removed from the barricade formed a horrible pile a few paces from them. Among the dead could be distinguished a livid face, disheveled hair, a pierced hand, and a half-naked female bosom; it was Eponine. Javert looked askance at this dead girl, and said with profound calmness:

"I fancy I know that girl."

Then he turned to Jean Valjean, who placed the pistol under his arm and fixed on Javert a glance which had no need of words to say, "Javert, it is I."

Javert answered, "Take your revenge."

Jean Valjean took a knife from his pocket and opened it.

"A clasp-knife," Javert exclaimed. "You are right; that suits you better."

Jean Valjean cut the martingale which Javert had around his neck, then he cut the ropes on his wrists, and then, stooping down, those on his feet; then rising again, he said, "You are free."

It was not easy to astonish Javert; still, master though he was of himself, he could not suppress his emotion. He stood gaping and motionless, while Jean Valjean continued:

"I do not believe that I shall leave this place. Still, if by accident I do, I live under the name of Fauchelevent, at No. 7, Rue de l'Homme Armé."

Javert gave a tigerish frown, which opened a corner of his mouth, and muttered between his teeth:

"Take care."

"Begone," said Jean Valjean.

Javert added:

"You said Fauchelevent, Rue de l'Homme Armé?"

"No. 7."

Javert repeated in a low voice, "No. 7."

He rebuttoned his frock-coat, restored his military stiffness between his shoulders, made a half turn, crossed his arms while supporting his chin with one of his hands, and walked off in the direction of the Halles. Jean Valjean looked after him. After going a few yards, Javert turned and said: "You annoy me. I would sooner be killed."

Javert did not even notice that he no longer addressed Jean Valjean in the second person singular.

"Begone," said Valjean.

Javert retired slowly, and a moment after turned the corner of the Rue des Prêcheurs. When Javert had disappeared, Jean Valjean discharged the pistol in the air, and then returned to the barricade, saying: "It is all over."

This is what had taken place in the meanwhile. Marius, more occupied with the outside than the inside, had not hitherto attentively regarded the spy fastened up at the darkened end of the ground-floor room. When he saw him in the open daylight bestriding the barricade, he recognized him, and a sudden hope entered his mind. He remembered the inspector of the Rue de Pontoise, and the two pistols he had given him, which he, Marius, had employed at this very barricade, and he not only remembered his face, but his name.

This recollection, however, was foggy and disturbed, like all his ideas. It was not an affirmation he made, so much as a question which he asked himself—"Is that not the police inspector, who told me that his name was Javert?" Marius shouted to Enjolras, who had just stationed himself at the other end of the barricade.

"Enjolras!"

"Well?"

"What is that man's name?"

"Which man?"

"The police agent. Do you know his name?"

"Of course I do, for he told it to us."

"What is it?"

"Javert."

Marius started, but at this moment a pistol-shot was heard, and Jean Valjean reappeared, saying, "It is all over." A dark chill crossed Marius's heart.

20. THE DEAD ARE RIGHT AND THE LIVING ARE NOT WRONG

THE death-agony of the barricade was about to begin, and everything added to the tragical majesty of this supreme moment; a thousand mysterious sounds in the air, the breathing of armed masses set in motion in streets which could not be seen, the intermittent gallop of cavalry, the heavy roll of artillery, the platoon firing and the cannonade crossing each other in the labyrinth of Paris; the smoke of the battle rising golden above the roofs, distant and vaguely terrible cries, flashes of menace everywhere, the tocsin of St. Merry, which now had the sound of a sob, the mildness of the season, the splendor of the sky full of sunshine and clouds, the beauty of the day, and the fearful silence of the houses; for, since the previous evening, the two rows of houses in the Rue de la Chanvrerie had become two walls, ferocious walls, with closed doors, closed windows, and closed shutters.

At that day, so different from the present time, when the hour arrived in which the people wished to end with a situation which had lasted too long, with a charter granted from a king or a country defined by law, not by nature, when the universal wrath was diffused in the atmosphere, when the city consented to an upheaving of paving-stones, when the insurrection made the bourgeoisie smile by whispering its watchword in their ear, then the inhabitant, impregnated with riot, so to speak, was the auxiliary of the combatant, and the house fraternized with the improvised fortress which it supported. When the situation was not ripe, when the insurrection was not decidedly accepted, when the masses disavowed the movement, it was all over with the combatant; the town was changed into a desert round the revolt, minds were chilled, asylums were walled up, and the street became converted into a defile to help the army in taking the barricade. A people cannot be forced to move faster than it wishes by a surprise, and woe to the man who tries to compel it; a people will not put up with it, and then it abandons the insurrection to itself. The insurgents become lepers; a house is a precipice, a door is a refusal, and a façade is a wall. This wall sees, hears, and will not; it might open and save you, but no,—the wall is a judge, and it looks at you and condemns you. What gloomy things are these closed houses! they seem dead though they are alive, and life, which is, at it were, suspended, clings to them. No one has come out for the last four-and-twenty hours, but no one is absent. In the interior of this rock people come and go, retire to bed and rise again; they are in the bosom of their family; they eat and drink, and are afraid, terrible to say. Fear excuses this formidable inhospitality, and the alarm offers extenuating circumstances. At times even, and this has been witnessed, the fear becomes a passion, and terror may be changed into fury, and prudence into rage; hence the profound remark, *The enraged moderates*. There are flashes of supreme terror, from which passion issues like a mournful smoke. "What do these people want? they are never satisfied, they compromise peaceable men. As if we had not had revolutions of that nature! what have they come to do here? let them get out of it as they can. All the worse for them, it is their fault, and they have only what they deserve. That does not concern us. Look at our poor street torn to pieces by cannon; they are a heap of scamps, and be very careful not to open the door." And the house assumes the aspect of a tomb; the insurgent dies a lingering death before their door; he sees the grape-shot and naked sabers arrive; if he cries out, he knows there are people who hear him, but will not help him; there are walls which might protect him, and men who might save him, and these walls have ears of flesh, and these men have entrails of stone.

Whom should we accuse? nobody and everybody, the imperfect times in which we live. It is always at its own risk and peril that Utopia converts itself into an insurrection, and becomes an armed protest instead of a philosophic protest, a Pallas and no longer a Minerva. The Utopia which grows impatient and becomes a riot knows what awaits it, and it nearly always arrives too soon. In that case it resigns itself, and stoically accepts the catastrophe, in lieu of a triumph. It serves, without complaining, and almost exculpating them, those who deny it, and its magnanimity is to consent to abandonment. It is indomitable against obstacles, and gentle toward ingratitude. Is it ingratitude, after all? yes, from the human point of view; no, from the individual point of view. Progress is the fashion of man; the general life of the human race is called progress; and the collective step of the human race is also called progress. Progress marches; it makes the great terrestrial and human journey toward the celestial and divine; it has its halts where it rallies the straying flock; it has its stations where it meditates, in the presence of some splendid Canaan suddenly unveiling its horizon; it has its nights when it sleeps; and it is one of the poignant anxieties of the thinker to see the shadow on the human soul, and to grope in the darkness for sleeping progress, without being able to awaken it.

God is perhaps dead, Gerard de Nerval said one day to the writer of these lines, confounding progress with God, and taking the interruption of the movement for the death of the Being. The man who despairs is wrong; progress infallibly reawakens, and we might say that it moves even when sleeping, for it has grown. When we see it upright again, we find that it is taller. To be peaceful depends no more on progress than on the river; do not raise a bar, or throw in a rock, for the obstacle makes the water foam, and humanity boil. Hence come troubles, but after these troubles we notice that way has been made. Until order, which is naught else than universal peace, is established, until harmony and unity reign, progress will have revolutions for its halting-places. What, then, is progress? We have just said, the permanent life of the peoples. Now, it happens at times that the momentary life of individuals offers a resistance to the eternal life of the human race.

Let us avow without bitterness that the individual has his distinct interest, and can, without felony, stipulate for that interest and defend it; the present has its excusable amount of egotism; momentary right has its claims, and cannot be expected to sacrifice itself incessantly to the future. The generation which at the present moment has its turn of passing over the earth is not forced to abridge it for the generations, its equals after all, whose turn will come at a later date. "I exist," murmurs that some one, who is everybody. "I am young and in love, I am old and wish to rest, I am a father of a family, I work, I prosper, I do a good business, I have houses to let, I have money in the funds, I am happy, I have wife and children, I like all that, I wish to live; and so, leave us in peace." Hence at certain hours a profound coldness falls on the magnanimous vanguard of the human race. Utopia, moreover, we confess it, deserts its radiant sphere in waging war. It, the truth of to-morrow, borrows its process, battle, from the falsehood of yesterday. It, the future, acts like the past; it, the pure idea, becomes an assault. It complicates its heroism with a violence for which it is but fair that it should answer—a violence of opportunity and expediency, contrary to principles, and for which it is fatally punished. Utopia, when in a state of insurrection, combats with the old military code in its hand; it shoots spies, executes traitors, suppresses living beings, and hurls them into unknown darkness. It makes use of death, a serious thing. It seems that Utopia no longer puts faith in the radiance, which is its irresistible and incorruptible strength. It strikes with the sword, but no sword is simple; every sword has two edges, and the man who wounds with one wounds himself with the other.

This reservation made, and made with all severity, it is impossible for us not to admire, whether they succeed or no, the glorious combatants of the future, the confessor of Utopia. Even when they fall they are venerable, and it is perhaps in ill success that they possess most majesty. Victory, when in accordance with progress, deserves the applause of the peoples, but an heroic defeat merits their tenderness. The one is magnificent, the other sublime. With us who prefer martyrdom to success, John Brown is greater than Washington, and Pisacane greater than Garibaldi.

There should be somebody to take the part of the conquered, and people are unjust to these great essayers of the future when they fail.

Revolutionists are accused of sowing terror, and every barricade appears an attack. Their theory is incriminated, their object is suspected, their afterthought is apprehended, and their conscience is denounced. They are reproached with elevating and erecting against the reigning social fact a pile of miseries, griefs, iniquities, and despair, and with pulling down in order to barricade themselves behind the ruins and combat. People shout to them: "You are unpaving Hades," and they might answer: "That is the reason why our barricade is made of good intentions." The best thing is certainly the pacific solution; after all, let us allow, when people see the pavement, they think of the bear, and it is a good-will by which society is alarmed. But it depends on society to save itself, and we appeal to its own good-will. No violent remedy is necessary; study the evil amicably, and then cure it,—that is all we desire.

However this may be, those men, even when they have fallen, and especially then, are august, who at all points of the universe, with their eyes fixed on France, are struggling for the great work with the inflexible logic of the ideal; they give their life as a pure gift for progress, they accomplish the will of Providence, and perform a religious act. At the appointed hour, with as much disinterestedness as an actor who takes up his cue, they enter the tomb in obedience to the divine scenario, and they accept this hopeless combat and this stoical disappearance in order to lead to its splendid and supreme universal consequences. The magnificent human movement irresistibly began on July 14. These soldiers are priests, and the French revolution is a deed of God. Moreover, there are—and it is proper to add this distinction to the distinctions already indicated in another chapter—there are accepted insurrections which are called revolutions; and there are rejected revolutions which are called riots. An insurrection which breaks out is an idea which passes its examination in the presence of the people. If the people drops its blackball, the idea is dry fruit, and the insurrection is a street-riot. Waging war at every appeal and each time that Utopia desires it, is not the act of the peoples; for nations have not always, and at all hours, the temperament of heroes and martyrs. They are positive; *a priori* insurrection is repulsive to them, in the first place, because it frequently has a catastrophe for result, and, secondly, because it always has an abstraction as its starting-point.

For, and this is a grand fact, those who devote themselves do so for the ideal, and the ideal alone. An insurrection is an enthusiasm, and enthusiasm may become a fury, whence comes an uprising of muskets. But every insurrection which aims at a government or a régime aims higher. Hence, for instance, we will dwell on the fact that what the chiefs of the insurrection of 1832, and especially the young enthusiasts of the Rue de la Chanvrerie, combated was not precisely Louis Philippe. The majority, speaking candidly, did justice to the qualities of this king who stood between monarchy and revolution, and not one of them hated him. But they attacked the younger branch of the right divine in Louis Philippe, as they had attacked the elder branch in Charles X, and what they wished to overthrow in overthrowing the monarchy in France was, as we have explained, the usurpation of man over man, and privilege opposing right throughout the universe. Paris without a king has as its counterstroke the world without despots. They reasoned in this way, and though their object was doubtless remote, vague perhaps, and recoiling before the effort, it was grand.

So it is. And men sacrifice themselves for these visions, which are for the sacrificed nearly always illusions, but illusions with which the whole of human certainty is mingled. The insurgent poeticizes and gilds the insurrection, and men hurl themselves into these tragical things, intoxicating themselves upon what they are about to do. Who knows? perhaps they will succeed; they are the minority; they have against them an entire army; but they are defending the right, natural law, the sovereignty of each over himself which allows of no possible abdication, justice, and truth, and, if necessary, they die like the three hundred Spartans. They do not think of Don Quixote, but of Leonidas, and they go onward, and once the battle has begun they do not recoil, but dash forward, head downward, having for hope an extraordinary victory, the revolution completed, progress restored to liberty, the aggrandizement of the human race, universal deliverance, and at the worst a Thermopylæ. These combats for progress frequently fail, and we have explained the cause. The mob is restive against the impulse of the Paladins; the heavy masses, the multitudes fragile on account of their very heaviness, fear adventures, and there is adventure, in the ideal. Moreover, it must not be forgotten that these are interests which are no great friends of the ideal and the sentimental. Sometimes the stomach paralyzes the heart. The greatness and beauty of France are, that she does not grow so stout as other nations, and knots the rope round her hips with greater facility; she is the first to wake and the last to fall asleep; she goes forward and seeks. The reason of this is because she is artistic.

The ideal is naught else than the culminating point of logic, in the same way as the beautiful is only the summit of the true. Artistic peoples are also consistent peoples; to love beauty is to see light. The result of this is, that the torch of Europe, that is to say, of civilization, was first borne by Greece, who passed it to Italy, who passed it to France. Divine illuminating nations. *Vita lampada tradunt.* It is an admirable thing that the poesy of a people is the element of its progress, and the amount of civilization is measured by the amount of imagination. Still, a civilizing people must remain masculine; Corinth yes, but Sybaris no, for the man who grows effeminate is bastardized. A man must be neither dilettante nor virtuoso, but he should be artistic. In the matter of civilization, there must not be refinement, but sublimation, and on that condition the pattern of the ideal is given to the human race.

The modern ideal has its type in art, and its means in science. It is by science that the august vision of the poet, the social beauty, will be realized, and Eden will be remade by A + B. At the point which civilization has reached, exactitude is a necessary element of the splendid, and the artistic feeling is not only served but completed by the scientific organ; the dream must calculate. Art, which is the conqueror, ought to have science, which is the mover, as its base. The strength of the steed is an important factor, and the modern mind is the genius of Greece, having for vehicle the genius of India—Alexander mounted on an elephant. Races petrified in dogma, or demoralized by time, are unsuited to act as guides to civilization. Genuflection before the idol or the dollar ruins the muscle which moves and the will that goes. Hieratic or mercantile absorption reduces the radiance of a people, lowers its horizon by lowering its level, and withdraws from it that intelligence, at once human and divine, of the universal object, which renders nations missionaries. Babylon has no ideal, nor has Carthage, while Athens and Rome have, and retain, even through all the nocturnal density of ages, a halo of civilization.

France is of the same quality, as a people, as Greece and Rome; she is Athenian through the beautiful, and Roman through the grand. Besides, she is good, and is more often than other nations in the humor for devotion and sacrifice. Still, this humor takes her and leaves her; and this is the great danger for those who run when she merely wishes to walk, or who walk when she wishes to halt. France has her relapses into materialism, and at seasons the ideas which obstruct this sublime brain have nothing that recalls French grandeur, and are of the dimensions of a Missouri or a South Carolina. What is to be done? the giantess plays the dwarf, and immense France feels a fancy for littleness. That is all.

To this nothing can be said, for peoples, like planets, have the right to be eclipsed. And that is well, provided that light return and the eclipse does not degenerate into night. Dawn and resurrection are synonymous, and the re-appearance of light is synonymous with the existence of the Ego.

Let us state these facts calmly. Death on a barricade or a tomb in exile is an acceptable occasion for devotion, for the real name of devotion is disinterestedness. Let the abandoned be abandoned, let the exiles be exiled, and let us confine ourselves to imploring great nations not to recoil too far when they do recoil. Under the pretext of returning to reason, it is not necessary to go too far down the incline. Matter exists, the moment exists, interests exist, the stomach exists, but the stomach must not be the sole wisdom. Momentary life has its rights, we admit, but permanent life has them also. Alas! to have mounted does not prevent falling, and we see this in history more frequently than we wish; a nation is illustrious, it tastes of the ideal, then it bites into the mud and finds it good, and when we ask it why it abandons Socrates for Falstaff, it replies, because I am fond of statesmen.

One word before returning to the barricade. A battle like the one which we are describing at this moment is only a convulsion for the ideal. Impeded progress is sickly, and has such tragic attacks of epilepsy. This malady of progress, civil war, we have met as we passed along, and it is one of the fatal phases, at once act and interlude, of that drama whose pivot is a social condemnation, and whose true title is *Progress*.

Progress! this cry, which we raise so frequently, is our entire thought, and at the point of our drama which we have reached, as the idea which it contains has still more than one trial to undergo, we may be permitted, even if we do not raise the veil, to let its gleams pierce through clearly. The book which the reader has before him at this moment is, from one end to the other, in its entirety and its details, whatever its intermissions, exceptions, and short-comings may be, the progress from evil to good, from injustice to justice, from falsehood to truth, from night to day, from appetite to conscience, from corruption to life, from bestiality to duty, from hell to heaven, and from nothingness to God. The starting-point is matter, the terminus the soul; the hydra at the commencement, the angel at the end.

21. *THE HEROES*

SUDDENLY the drum beat the charge, and the attack was a hurricane. On the previous evening the barricade had been silently approached in the darkness as by a boa, but, at present, in broad daylight, within this empty street, surprise was impossible; besides, the armed force was unmasked, the cannon began the roaring, and the troops rushed upon the barricade. Fury was now skill. A powerful column of line infantry, intersected at regular intervals by National Guards and dismounted Municipal Guards, and supported by heavy masses, that could be heard if not seen, debouched into the street at the double, with drums beating, bugles braying, bayonets leveled, and sappers in front, and imperturbable under the shower of projectiles, dashed straight at the barricade with all the weight of a bronze battering-ram. But the wall held out firmly, and the insurgents fired impetuously; the escaladed barricade displayed a flashing mane. The attack was so violent that it was in a moment inundated by assailants; but it shook off the soldiers as the lion does the dogs, and it was only covered with besiegers as the cliff is with foam, to re-appear a minute later scarped, black, and formidable.

The columns, compelled to fall back, remained massed in the street, exposed but terrible, and answered the redoubt by a tremendous musketry-fire. Any one who has seen fireworks will remember the piece composed of a cross-fire of lightnings, which is called a bouquet. Imagine this bouquet, no longer vertical but horizontal, and bearing at the end of each jet a bullet, slugs, or iron balls, and scattering death. The barricade was beneath it. On either side was equal resolution; the bravery was almost barbarous, and was complicated by a species of heroic ferocity which began with self-sacrifice. It was the epoch when a National Guard fought like a Zouave. The troops desired an end, and the insurrection wished to struggle. The acceptance of death in the height of youth and health, converts intrepidity into a frenzy, and each man in this action had the grandeur of the last hour. The street was covered with corpses. The barricade had Marius at one of its ends, and Enjolras at the other. Enjolras, who carried the whole barricade in his head, reserved and concealed himself; three soldiers fell under his loop-hole without even seeing him, while Marius displayed himself openly, and made himself a mark. More than once half his body rose above the barricade. There is no more violent prodigal than a miser who takes the bit between his teeth, and no man more startling in action than a dreamer. Marius was formidable and pensive, and was in action as in a dream. He looked like a firing ghost. The cartridges of the besieged were exhausted, but not their sarcasms; and they laughed in the tornado of the tomb in which they stood. Courfeyrac was bareheaded.

"What have you done with your hat?" Bossuet asked him and Courfeyrac answered:

"They carried it away at last with cannon-balls."

Or else they made haughty remarks.

"Can you understand," Feuilly exclaimed bitterly, "those men" (and he mentioned names, well-known and even celebrated names, that belonged to the old army) "who promised to join us and pledged their honor to aid us, and who are generals, and abandon us?"

Combeferre restricted himself to replying with a grave smile:

"They are people who observe the rules of honor as they do the stars, a long distance off."

The interior of the barricade was so sown with torn cartridges that it seemed as if there had been a snow-storm. The assailants had the numbers, and the insurgents the position. They were behind a wall, and crushed at point-blank range the soldiers who were stumbling over the dead and wounded. This barricade, built as it was, and admirably strengthened, was really one of those situations in which a handful of men holds a legion in check. Still, constantly recruited and growing beneath a shower of bullets, the column of attack inexorably approached and now gradually, step by step, little by little but certainly, compressed like a vise the barricade.

The assaults succeeded each other, and the horror became constantly greater. Then there broke out on this pile of paving-stones, in the Rue de la Chanvrerie, a struggle worthy of the wall of Troy. These sallow, ragged, and exhausted men, who had not eaten for four-and-twenty hours, who had not slept, who had only a few rounds more to fire, who felt their empty pockets for cartridges—these men, nearly all wounded, with head or arm bound round with a blood-stained blackish rag, having holes in their coats from which the blood flowed, scarce armed with bad guns and old rusty sabers, became Titans. The barricade was ten times approached, assaulted, escaladed, and never captured. To form an idea of the contest it would be necessary to imagine a heap of terrible courages set on fire, and that you are watching the flames. It was not a combat, but the interior of a furnace; mouths breathed flames there, and the faces were extraordinary. The human form seemed impossible there, the combatants flashed, and it was a formidable sight to see these salamanders of the fight flitting about in this red smoke. The successive and simultaneous scenes of this butchery are beyond our power to depict, for epic poetry alone has the right to fill ten thousand verses with a battle. It might have been called that Inferno of Brahminism, the most formidable of the seventeen abysses, which the Veda calls the forest of swords. They fought foot to foot, body to body, with pistol-shots, saber-cuts, and fists, close by, at a distance, above, below, on all sides, from the roof of the house, from the wine-shop, and even from the traps of the cellars into which some had slipped. The odds were sixty to one, and the frontage of Corinth half demolished was hideous. The window, pock-marked with grape-shot, had lost glass and frame, and was only a shapeless hole, tumultuously stopped up with paving-stones. Bossuet was killed, Feuilly was killed, Courfeyrac was killed, Joly was killed. Combeferre, traversed by three bayonet-stabs in the breast at the moment when he was raising a wounded soldier, had only time to look up to heaven, and expired. Marius, still fighting, had received so many wounds, especially in the head, that his face disappeared in blood and looked as if it were covered by a red handkerchief. Enjolras alone was not wounded; when he had no weapon, he held out his arm to the right or left, and an insurgent placed some instrument in his hand. He had only four broken sword-blades left, one more than Francis I had at Marignano.

Homer says, "Diomed slew Axylus, son of Teuthranis, who dwelt in happy Arisbe; Euryalus, son of Mecisteus, killed Dresos and Opheltios, Æsepos, and that Pedasus whom the naiad Abarbarea bore to the blameless Bucolion; Ulysses overthrew Pidytas of Percose; Antilochus, Ablerus; Polypoetes, Astyalus; Polydamas, Otus of Cyllene; and Teucer, Aretaon; Meganthius died by the spear of Euripylus; Agamemnon, king of men, laid low Elatas, born in the rocky town which is loved by sounding Satnoeis." In our old poems of the Gestes, Esplandian attacks with a flaming falchion the Marquis Géant Swantibore, who defends himself by storming the knight with towers which he uproots. Our old mural frescoes show us the two Dukes of Brittany and Bourbon armed for war and mounted, and approaching each other, axe in hand, masked with steel, shod with steel, gloved with steel, one caparisoned with ermine and the other draped in azure; Brittany with his lion between the two horns of his crown, and Bourbon with an enormous *fleur-de-lis* at his vizor. But, in order to be superb, it is not necessary to wear, like Yvon, the ducal morion, or to have in one hand a living flame, like Esplandian; it is sufficient to lay down one's life for a conviction or a loyal deed. This little simple soldier, yesterday a peasant of Beauce or the Limousin, who prowls about, cabbage-knife by his side, round the nurse-maids in the Luxembourg, this young pale student bowed over an anatomical study or book, a fair-haired boy who shaves himself with a pair of scissors,— take them both, breathe duty into them, put them face to face in the Carrefour Boucherat or the Planche Mibray blind alley, and let one fight for his flag and the other combat for his ideal, and let them both imagine that they are contending for their country, and the struggle will be colossal; and the shadow cast by these two contending lads on the great epic field where humanity is struggling, will be equal to that thrown by Megarion, King of Lycia, abounding in tigers, as he wrestles with the immense Ajax, the equal of the gods.

22. *FOOT TO FOOT*

WHEN there were no chiefs left but Enjolras and Marius at the two ends of the barricade, the center, which had so long been supported by Courfeyrac, Bossuet, Joly, Feuilly, and Combeferre, yielded. The cannon, without making a practicable breach, had severely injured the center of the redoubt; then the crest of the wall had disappeared under the balls and fallen down, and the fragments which had collected both inside and out had in the end formed two slopes, the outer one of which offered an inclined plane by which to attack. A final assault was attempted thus, and this assault was successful; the bristling mass of bayonets, hurled forward at a run, came up irresistibly, and the dense line of the attacking column appeared in the smoke on the top of the scarp. This time it was all over, and the band of insurgents defending the center recoiled pell-mell.

Then the gloomy love of life was rekindled in some; covered by this forest of muskets, several did not wish to die. It is the moment when the spirit of self-preservation utters yells, and when the beast re-appears in man. They were drawn up against the six-storied house at the back of the barricade, and this house might be their salvation. This house was barricaded, as it were, walled up from top to bottom, but before the troops reached the interior of the redoubt, a door would have time to open and shut, and it would be life for these desperate men, for at the back of this house were streets, possible flight, and space. They began kicking and knocking at the door, while calling, crying, imploring, and clasping their hands. But no one opened. The dead head looked down on them from the third-floor window. But Marius and Enjolras, and seven or eight men who rallied round them, had rushed forward to protect them. Enjolras shouted to the soldiers, "Do not advance," and as an officer declined to obey he killed the officer. He was in the inner yard of the redoubt, close to Corinth, with his sword in one hand and carbine in the other, holding open the door of the wine-shop, which he barred against the assailants. He shouted to the desperate men, "There is only one door open, and it is this one"; and covering them with his person, and alone facing a battalion, he made them pass behind him. All rushed in, and Enjolras, whirling his musket round his head, drove back the bayonets and entered the last, and there was a frightful moment, during which the troops tried to enter and the insurgents to bar the door. The latter was closed with such violence that the five fingers of a soldier who had caught hold of the door-post were cut off clean, and remained in the crevice. Marius remained outside; a bullet broke his collar-bone, and he felt himself fainting and falling. At this moment, when his eyes were already closed, he felt the shock of a powerful hand seizing him, and his fainting-fit scarce left him time for this thought, blended with the supreme recollection of Cosette, "I am made prisoner, and shall be shot."

Enjolras, not seeing Marius among those who had sought shelter in the house, had the same idea, but they had reached that moment when each could only think of his own death. Enjolras put the bar on the door, bolted and locked it, while the soldiers beat it with musket-butts and the sappers attacked it with their axes outside. The assailants were grouped round this door, and the siege of the wine-shop now began. The soldiers, let us add, were full of fury; the death of the sergeant of artillery had irritated them, and then, more mournful still, during the few hours that preceded the attack a whisper ran along the ranks that the insurgents were mutilating their prisoners, and that there was the headless body of a soldier in the cellar. This species of fatal rumor is the general accompaniment of civil wars, and it was a false report of the same nature which at a later date produced the catastrophe of the Rue Transnonain. When the door was secured, Enjolras said to the others:

"Let us sell our lives dearly."

Then he went up to the table on which Mabœuf and Gavroche were lying; under the black cloth two forms could be seen straight and livid, one tall, the other short, and the two faces were vaguely designed under the cold folds of the winding-sheet. A hand emerged from under it, and hung toward the ground; it was the old man. Enjolras bent down and kissed this venerable hand, in the same way as he had done the forehead on the previous evening. They were the only two kisses he had ever given in his life.

Let us be brief. The barricade had resisted like a gate of Thebes, and the wine-shop resisted like a house of Saragossa. Such resistances are violent, and there is no quarter, and a flag of truce is impossible; people are willing to die provided that they can kill. When Suchet says, "Capitulate," Palafox answers, "After the war with cannon, the war with the knife." Nothing was wanting in the attack on the Hucheloup wine-shop; neither paving-stones showering from the window and roof on the assailants, and exasperating the troops by the frightful damage they committed, nor shots from the attics and cellar, nor the fury of the attack, nor the rage of the defense, nor, finally, when the door gave way, the frenzied mania of extermination. When the assailants rushed into the wine-shop, their feet entangled in the panels of the broken door which lay on the ground, they did not find a single combatant. The winding staircase, cut away with axes, lay in the middle of the ground-floor room, a few wounded men were on the point of dying, all who were not killed were on the second-floor, and a terrific fire was discharged thence through the hole in the ceiling which had been the entrance to the restaurant. These were the last cartridges, and when they were expended and nobody had any powder or balls left, each man took up two of the bottles reserved by Enjolras, and defended the stairs with these frightfully fragile weapons. They were bottles of aqua fortis. We describe the gloomy things of carnage exactly as they are: the besieged makes a weapon of everything. Greek fire did not dishonor Archimedes, boiling pitch did not dishonor Bayard; every war is a horror, and there is no choice. The musketry-fire of the assailants, though impeded and discharged from below, was murderous; and the brink of the hole was soon lined with dead heads, whence dripped long red and streaming jets. The noise was indescribable, and a compressed burning smoke almost threw night over the combat. Words fail to describe horror when it has reached this stage. There were no men in this now infernal struggle, there were no longer giants contending against Titans. It resembled Milton and Dante more than Homer, for demons attacked and specters resisted.

It was a monster heroism.

23. ORESTES SOBER AND PYLADES DRUNK.

AT length, by employing the skeleton of the staircase, by climbing up the walls, clinging to the ceiling and killing on the very edge of the trap the last who resisted, some twenty assailants, soldiers, National and Municipal Guards, mostly disfigured by wounds in the face received in this formidable ascent, blinded by blood, furious and savage, burst into the second-floor room. There was only one man standing there—Enjolras; without cartridges or sword, he only held in his hand the barrel of his carbine, whose butt he had broken on the heads of those who entered. He had placed the billiard-table between himself and his assailants, he had fallen back to the end of the room, and there, with flashing eyes and head erect, holding the piece of a weapon in his hand, he was still sufficiently alarming for a space to be formed round him. A cry was raised:

"It is the chief; it was he who killed the artillery-man; as he has placed himself there, we will let him remain there. Shoot him on the spot."

"Shoot me," Enjolras said.

And, throwing away his weapon and folding his arms, he offered his chest. The boldness of dying bravely always moves men. So soon as Enjolras folded his arms, accepting the end, the din of the struggle ceased in the room, and the chaos was suddenly appeased in a species of sepulchral solemnity. It seemed as if the menacing majesty of Enjolras, disarmed and motionless, produced an effect on the tumult, and that merely by the authority of his tranquil glance, this young man who alone was unwounded, superb, blood-stained, charming, and indifferent, like one invulnerable, constrained this sinister mob to kill him respectfully. His beauty, heightened at this moment by his haughtiness, was dazzling, and as if he could be no more fatigued than wounded after the frightful four-

and-twenty hours which had elapsed, he was fresh and rosy. It was to
him that the witness referred when he said at a later date before the
court-martial, "There was an insurgent whom I heard called Apollo." A
National Guard who aimed at Enjolras lowered his musket, saying, "I
feel as if I were going to kill a flower." Twelve men formed into a platoon
in the corner opposite the one in which Enjolras stood, and got their
muskets ready in silence. Then a sergeant shouted, "Present."

An officer interposed.

"Wait a minute."

And, addressing Enjolras:

"Do you wish to have your eyes bandaged?"

"No."

"It was really you who killed the sergeant of artillery?"

"Yes."

Grantaire had been awake for some minutes past. Grantaire, it will be
remembered, had been sleeping since the past evening in the upper room,
with his head lying on a table. He realized in all its energy the old metaphor, dead drunk. The hideous philter of absinthe, stout, and alcohol had
thrown him into a lethargic state, and as his table was small, and of no
use at the barricade, they had left it him. He was still in the same posture,
with his chest upon the table, his head reeling on his arms, and surrounded by glasses and bottles. He was sleeping the deadly sleep of the
hibernating bear or the filled leech. Nothing had roused him,—neither
the platoon fire, nor the cannon-balls, nor the canister which penetrated
through the window into the room where he was, nor the prodigious
noise of the assault. Still he at times responded to the cannon by a snore.
He seemed to be waiting for a bullet to save him the trouble of waking;
several corpses lay around him, and, at the first glance, nothing distinguished him from these deep sleepers of death.

Noise does not wake a drunkard, but silence arouses him, and this
peculiarity has been more than once observed. The fall of anything near
him increased Grantaire's lethargy, and noise lulled him. The species of
halt which the tumult made before Enjolras was a shock to this heavy
sleep. It is the effect of a galloping coach which stops short. Grantaire
started up, stretched out his arms, rubbed his eyes, looked, yawned and
understood. Intoxication wearing off resembles a curtain that is rent, and
a man sees at once, and at a single glance, all that is concealed. Everything
offers itself suddenly to the memory, and the drunkard, who knows
nothing of what has happened during the last twenty-four hours, has

scarce opened his eyes ere he understands it all. Ideas return with a sudden lucidity; the species of suds that blinded the brain is dispersed and makes way for a clear and distinctive apprehension of the reality.

Concealed, as he was, in a corner, and sheltered, so to speak, by the billiard-table, the soldiers, who had their eyes fixed on Enjolras, had not even perceived Grantaire, and the sergeant was preparing to give the order to fire, when all at once they heard a powerful voice crying at their side:

"Long live the Republic! I belong to it."

Grantaire had risen; and the immense gleam of all the combat which he had missed appeared in the flashing glance of the transfigured drunkard. He repeated, "Long live the Republic!" crossed the room with a firm step, and placed himself before the muskets by Enjolras's side.

"Kill us both at once," he said.

And turning gently to Enjolras, he asked him:

"Do you permit it?"

Enjolras pressed his hand with a smile, and this smile had not passed away ere the detonation took place. Enjolras, traversed by eight bullets, remained leaning against the wall, as if nailed to it; he merely hung his head; Grantaire was lying stark dead at his feet. A few minutes later the soldiers dislodged the last insurgents who had taken refuge at the top of the house, and were firing through a partition in the garret. They fought desperately, and threw bodies out of windows, some still alive. Two voltigeurs, who were trying to raise the smashed omnibus, were killed by two shots from the attics; a man in a blouse rushed out with a bayonet-thrust in his stomach, and lay on the ground expiring. A private and insurgent slipped together down the tiles of the roof, and, as they would not loosen their hold, fell into the street, holding each other in a ferocious embrace. There was a similar struggle in the cellar: cries, shots, and a fierce clashing; then a silence. The barricade was captured, and the soldiers began searching the adjacent houses and pursuing the fugitives.

24. PRISONER!

MARIUS was really a prisoner, prisoner to Jean Valjean; the hand which had clutched him behind at the moment when he was falling, and of which he felt the pressure as he lost his senses, was Jean Valjean's.

Jean Valjean had taken no other part in the struggle than that of exposing himself. Had it not been for him, in the supreme moment of agony, no one would have thought of the wounded. Thanks to him who was everywhere present in the carnage like a Providence, those who fell were picked up, carried to the ground-floor room, and had their wounds dressed, and in the intervals he repaired the barricade. But nothing that could resemble a blow, an attack, or even personal defense, could be seen with him, and he kept quiet and succored. However, he had only a few scratches; and the bullets had no billet for him. If suicide formed part of what he dreamed of when he came to this sepulcher, he had not been successful, but we doubt whether he thought of suicide, which is an irreligious act. Jean Valjean did not appear to see Marius in the thick of the combat, but in truth he did not take his eyes off him. When a bullet laid Marius low, Jean Valjean leaped upon him with the agility of a tiger, dashed upon him as on a prey, and carried him off.

The whirlwind of the attack was at this moment so violently concentrated on Enjolras and the door of the wine-shop that no one saw Jean Valjean, supporting the fainting Marius in his arms, cross the unpaved ground of the barricade, and disappear round the corner of Corinth. Our readers will remember this corner, which formed a sort of cape in the street, and protected a few square feet of ground from bullets and grapeshot, and from glances as well. There is thus at times in fires a room which does not burn, and in the most raging seas, beyond a promontory, or at the end of a reef, a little quiet nook. It was in this corner of the inner trapeze of the barricade that Eponine drew her last breath. Here Jean Valjean stopped, let Marius slip to the ground, leaned against a wall, and looked around him.

The situation was frightful; for the instant, for two or three minutes perhaps, this piece of wall was a shelter, but how to get out of this massacre? He recalled the agony he had felt in the Rue Polonceau, eight years previously, and in what way he had succeeded in escaping; it was difficult then, but now it was impossible. He had in front of him that implacable and silent six-storied house, which only seemed inhabited by the dead man leaning out of his window; he had on his right the low barricade which closed the Petite Truanderie; to climb over this obstacle appeared easy, but a row of bayonet-points could be seen over the crest of the barricade; they were line troops posted beyond the barricade and on the watch. It was evident that crossing the barricade was seeking a platoon fire, and that any head which appeared above the wall of paving-stones would serve as a mark for sixty muskets. He had on his left the battle-field, and death was behind the corner of the wall.

What was he to do? a bird alone could have escaped from this place. And he must decide at once, find an expedient, and make up his mind. They were fighting a few paces from him, but fortunately all were obstinately engaged at one point, the wine-shop door, but if a single soldier had the idea of turning the house or attacking it on the flank all would be over. Jean Valjean looked at the house opposite to him, he looked at the barricade by his side, and then looked on the ground, with the violence of supreme extremity, wildly, and as if he would have liked to dig a hole with his eyes. By force of looking, something vaguely discernible in such an agony was to be traced, and assumed a shape at his feet, as if the eyes had the power to produce the thing demanded. He perceived a few paces from him, at the foot of the small barricade so pitilessly guarded and watched from without, and beneath a pile of paving-stones which almost concealed it an iron grating, laid flat and flush with the ground. This grating, made of strong cross-bars, was about two feet square, and the framework of paving-stones which supported it had been torn out, and it was, as it were, dismounted. Through the bars a glimpse could be caught of an obscure opening, something like a chimney-pot or the cylinder of a cistern. Jean Valjean dashed up, and his old skill in escapes rose to his brain like a beam of light. To remove the paving-stones, tear up the grating, take Marius, who was inert as a dead body, on his shoulders, descend with this burden on his loins, helping himself with his elbows and knees, into this sort of well, which was fortunately of no great depth, to let the grating fall again over his head, to set foot on a paved surface, about ten feet below the earth, all this was executed like something done in delirium, with a giant's strength and the rapidity of an eagle. It occupied but a few minutes. Jean Valjean found himself with the still fainting Marius in a sort of long subterranean corridor, where there was profound peace, absolute silence, and night. The impression which he had formerly felt in falling out of the street into the convent recurred to him; still, what he now carried was not Cosette, but Marius.

He had scarce heard above his head like a vague murmur the formidable tumult of the wine-shop being taken by assault.

BOOK II

THE INTERIOR OF LEVIATHAN

Paris casts twenty-five millions of francs annually into the sea, and we assert this without any metaphor. How so, and in what way? by day and night. For what object? for no object. With what thought? without thinking. What to do? nothing. By means of what organ? its intestines. What are its intestines? its sewers. Twenty-five millions are the most moderate of the approximative amounts given by the estimates of modern science. Science, after groping for a long time, knows now that the most fertilizing and effective of manures is human manure. The Chinese, let us say it to our shame, knew this before we did; not a Chinese peasant—it is Eckeberg who states the fact—who goes to the city but brings back at each end of his bamboo a bucketful of what we call filth. Thanks to the human manure the soil in China is still as youthful as in the days of Abraham, and Chinese wheat yields just one-hundred-and-twenty-fold the sowing. There is no guano comparable in fertility to the detritus of a capital, and a large city is the most important of dung-heaps. To employ the town in manuring the plain would be certain success, for if gold be dross, on the other hand our dross is gold.

What is done with this golden dung? it is swept into the gulf. We send, at a great expense, fleets of ships to collect at the southern pole the guano of petrels and penguins, and cast into the sea the incalculable element of wealth which we have under our hand. All the human and animal manure which the world loses, if returned to the land instead of being thrown into the sea, would suffice to nourish the world. Do you know what those piles of ordure are, collected at the corners of streets, those carts of mud carried off at night from the streets, the frightful barrels of the night-man, and the fetid streams of subterranean mud which the pavement conceals from you? All this is a flowering field; it is green grass, it is mint and thyme and sage, it is game, it is cattle, it is the satisfied lowing of heavy kine at night, it is perfumed hay, it is gilded wheat, it is bread on your table, it is warm blood in your veins, it is health, it is joy, it is life. So desires that mysterious creation, which is transformation on earth, and transfiguration in heaven; restore this to the great crucible, and your abundance will issue from it, for the nutrition of the plains produces the nourishment of men. You are at liberty to lose this wealth and consider me ridiculous in the bargain; that would be the master-piece of your ignorance. Statistics have calculated that France alone pours every year into the Atlantic a sum of half a milliard. Note this: with these five hundred millions one-quarter of the expenses of the budget would be paid. The cleverness of man is so great that he prefers to get rid of these five hundred millions in the gutter. The very substance of the people is borne away, here drop by drop, and there in streams, by the wretched vomiting of our sewers into the rivers and the gigantic vomit-ing of our rivers into the ocean. Each eructation of our drains costs us one thousand francs, and this has two results,—the earth impoverished and the water poisoned; hunger issuing from the furrow and sickness from the river. It is notorious that at this very hour the Thames poisons Lon-don! and as regards Paris, it has been found necessary to remove most of the mouths of the sewers down the river below the last bridge.

A double tubular apparatus supplied with valves and flood-gates, a system of elementary drainage as simple as the human lungs, and which is already in full work in several English parishes, would suffice to bring into our towns the pure water of the fields and ·send to the fields the rich water of the towns; and this easy ebb and flow, the most simple in the world, would retain among us the five hundred millions thrown away. But people are thinking of other things. The present process does mischief while meaning well. The intention is good, but the result is sorrowful; they believe they are draining the city, while they are destroy-ing the population. A sewer is a misunderstanding, and when drainage, with its double functions, restoring what it takes, is everywhere substi-tuted for the sewer, that simple and impoverishing washing, and is also combined with the data of a new social economy, the produce of the soil will be increased tenfold, and the problem of misery will be singu-larly attenuated. Add the suppression of parasitisms, and it will be solved. In the meanwhile the public wealth goes to the river, and a sinking takes place,—sinking is the right word, for Europe is being ruined in this way by exhaustion. As for France, we have mentioned the figures. Now, as Paris contains one twenty-fifth of the whole French population, and the Parisian guano is the richest of all, we are beneath the truth when we estimate at twenty-five millions the share of Paris in the half-milliard which France annually refuses. These twenty-five millions, employed in assistance and enjoyment, would double the splendor of Paris, and the city expends them in sewers. So that we may say, the great prodigality of Paris, its marvelous fête, its Folie Beaujon, its orgy, its lavishing of gold, its luxury, splendor, and magnificence, is its sewerage. It is in this way that, in the blindness of a bad political economy, people allow the comfort of all to be drowned and wasted in the water; there ought to be St. Cloud nets to catch the public fortunes.

Economically regarded, the fact may be resumed thus; Paris is a sieve. Paris, that model city, that pattern of well-conducted capitals, of which every people strives to have a copy, that metropolis of the ideal, that august home of initiative, impulse, and experiment, that center and gathering-place of minds, that nation city, that bee-hive of the future, that marvelous composite of Babylon and Corinth, would make a peasant of Fo-Kian shrug his shoulders, from our present point of view. Imitate Paris, and you will ruin yourself; moreover, Paris imitates itself particularly in this immemorial and insensate squandering. These surprising follies are not new; it is no youthful nonsense. The ancients acted like the moderns. "The drains of Rome," says Liebig, "absorbed the entire welfare of the Roman peasant." When the Campagna of Rome was ruined by the Roman drains, Rome exhausted Italy, and when it had placed Italy in its cloaca, it poured into it Sicily, and then Sardinia, and then Africa. The drains of Rome swallowed up the world, and this cloaca offered its tunnels to the city and to the world. *Urbi et orbi.* Eternal city and unfathomable drain.

For these things as for others, Rome gives the example, and this example Paris follows with all the folly peculiar to cities of talent. For the requirements of the operation which we have been explaining, Paris has beneath it another Paris, a Paris of Sewers, which has its streets, squares, lanes, arteries, and circulation, which is mud, with the human form at least. For nothing must be flattered, not even a great people; where there is everything, there is ignominy by the side of sublimity, and if Paris contain Athens, the city of light, Tyre, the city of power, Sparta, the city of virtue, Nineveh, the city of prodigies, it also contains Lutetia, the city of mud. Moreover, the stamp of its power is there too, and the Titanic sewer of Paris realizes among monuments the strange ideal realized in humanity by a few men like Machiavelli, Bacon, and Mirabeau; the grand abject. The subsoil of Paris, if the eye could pierce the surface, would offer the aspect of a gigantic madrepore; a sponge has not more passages and holes than the piece of ground, six leagues in circumference, upon which the old great city rests. Without alluding to the catacombs, which are a separate cellar, without speaking of the inextricable net of gas-pipes, without referring to the vast tubular system for the distribution of running water, the drains alone form on either bank of the river a prodigious dark ramification, a labyrinth which has its incline for its clew.

In the damp mist of this labyrinth is seen the rat, which seems the produce of the accouchement of Paris.

2. THE OLD HISTORY OF THE SEWER

If we imagine Paris removed like a cover, the subterranean net-work of drains regarded from a bird's-eye view would represent on either bank a sort of large branch grafted upon the river. On the right bank the encircling sewer will be the trunk of this branch, the secondary tubes the branches, and the blind alleys the twigs. This figure is only summary and half correct, as the right angle, which is the usual angle in subterranean ramifications of this nature, is very rare in vegetation. Our readers will form a better likeness of this strange geometric plan by supposing that they see lying on a bed of darkness some strange Oriental alphabet as confused as a thicket, and whose shapeless letters are welded to each other in an apparent confusion, and, as if accidentally, here by their angles and there by their ends. The sewers and drains played a great part in the middle ages, under the Lower Empire and in the old East. Plague sprang from them and despots died of it. The multitudes regarded almost with a religious awe these beds of corruption, these monstrous cradles of death. The vermin-ditch at Benares is not more fearful than the Lion's den at Babylon. Tiglath-Pileser, according to the rabbinical books, swore by the sink of Nineveh. It was from the drain of Munster that John of Leyden produced his false moon, and it was from the cesspool-well of Kekhscheb that his Oriental double, Mokannah, the veiled prophet of Korassan, brought his false sun.

The history of men is reflected in the history of the sewers, and the Gemoniae narrated the story of Rome. The drain of Paris is an old formidable thing; it has been a sepulcher, and it has been an asylum. Crime, intellect, the social protest, liberty of conscience, thought, robbery, all that human laws pursue or have pursued, have concealed themselves in this den,—the Maillotins, in the fourteenth century, the cloak-stealers in the fifteenth, the Huguenots in the sixteenth, the illuminé of Morin in the seventeenth, and the Chauffeurs in the eighteenth. One hundred years ago the nocturnal dagger issued from it, and the rogue in danger glided into it; the forest had the cave and Paris had the drain. The Truanderie, that Gallic *picareria,* accepted the drain as an annex of the Court of Miracles, and at night, cunning and ferocious, entered beneath the Maubuée vomitory as into an alcove. It was very simple that those who had for their place of daily toil the Vide-Gousset lane, or the Rue Coupe-Gorge, should have for their nightly abode the Ponceau of the Chemin-Vert or the Hurepoix cagnard. Hence comes a swarm of recollections, all sorts of phantoms haunt these long solitary corridors, on all sides are putridity and miasma, and here and there is a trap through which Villon inside converses with Rabelais outside.

The drain in old Paris is the meeting-place of all exhaustions and of all experiments; political economy sees there a detritus, and social philosophy a residuum. The drain is the conscience of the city, and everything converges and is confronted there. In this livid spot there is darkness, but there are no secrets. Each thing has its true form, or at least its definitive form. The pile of ordure has this in its favor, that it tells no falsehood, and simplicity has taken refuge there. Basile's mask is found there, but you see the pasteboard, the threads, the inside and out, and it is marked with honest filth. Scapin's false nose is lying close by. All the uncleanlinesses of civilization, where no longer of service, fall into this pit of truth; they are swallowed up, but display themselves in it. This pell-mell is a confession; there no false appearance nor is any plastering possible, order takes off its shirt, there is an absolute nudity, a rout of illusions and mirage, and there nothing but what is assuming the gloomy face of what is finishing. Reality and disappearance. There a bottle-heel confesses intoxication, and a basket-handle talks about domesticity; there the apple core which has had literary opinions becomes once again the apple core, the effigy on the double sou grows frankly verdigrised, the saliva of Caiphas meets the vomit of Falstaff, the louis-d'or which comes from the gambling-hell dashes against the nail whence hangs the end of the suicide's rope, a livid fœtus rolls along wrapped in spangles which danced last Shrove Tuesday at the opera, a wig which has judged men wallows by the side of a rottenness which was Margoton's petticoat; it is more than fraternity, it is the extremest familiarity. All that painted itself is bedaubed, and the last veil is torn away. The drain is a cynic and says everything. This sincerity of uncleanliness pleases us and reposes the mind. When a man has spent his time upon the earth in undergoing the great airs assumed by state reasons, the oath, political wisdom, human justice, professional probity, the austerities of the situation, and incorruptible robes, it relieves him to enter a drain and see there the mud which becomes it.

It is instructive at the same time, for, as we said just now, history passes through the drain. St. Bartholomew filters there drop by drop, through the paving-stones, and great public assassinations, political and religious butcheries, traverse this subterranean way of civilization, and thrust their corpses into it. For in the eye of the dreamer, all historical murderers are there, in the hideous gloom on their knees, with a bit of their winding-sheet for an apron, and mournfully sponging their task. Louis XI is there with Tristan, Francis I is there with Duprat, Charles IX is there with his mother, Richelieu is there with Louis XIII, Louvois is there, Letellier is there, Herbert and Maillard are there, scratching the stones, and trying to efface the trace of their deed. The brooms of these specters can be heard under these vaults and the enormous fetidness of social catastrophes is breathed there. You see in corners red flashes, and a terrible water flows there in which blood-stained hands have been washed.

The social observer should enter these shadows, for they form part of his laboratory. Philosophy is the microscope of thought; everything strives to fly from it, but nothing escapes it. Tergiversation is useless, for what side of himself does a man show in tergiversation? his ashamed side. Philosophy pursues evil with its upright glance, and does not allow it to escape into nothingness. It recognizes everything in the effacement of disappearing things, and in the diminution of vanishing things. It reconstructs the purple from the rags, and the woman from the tatters. With the sewer it remakes the town; with the mud it remakes manners. It judges from the potsherds whether it were an amphora or an earthen-ware jar. It recognizes by a nail-mark on a parchment the difference which separates the Jewry of the Judengasse from the Jewry of the Ghetto. It finds again in what is left what has been, the good, the bad, the false, the true, the patch of blood in the palace, the ink-stain of the cavern, the tallow-drop of the brothel, trials undergone, temptations welcome, orgies vomited up, the wrinkle which characters have formed in abasing themselves, the traces of prostitution in the souls which their coarseness rendered capable of it, and under the vest of the porters of Rome the mark of the elbow-nudge of Messalina.

3. *BRUNESEAU*

THE drain of Paris in the middle ages was legendary. In the sixteenth century Henry II attempted soundings which failed, and not a hundred years ago, as Mercer testifies, the sewer was abandoned to itself, and became what it could. Such was that ancient Paris, handed over to quarrels, indecisions, and groping. It was for a long time thus stupid, and a later period, '89, showed how cities acquire sense. But in the good old times the capital had but little head; it did not know how to transact its business either morally or materially, and could no more sweep away its ordure than its abuses. Everything was an obstacle, everything raised a question. The drain, for instance, was refractory to any itinerary, and people could no more get on under the city than they did in it. Above, everything was unintelligible; below, inextricable; beneath the confu-sion of tongues was the confusion of cellars, and Dædalus duplicated with

Babel. At times the drain of Paris thought proper to overflow, as if this misunderstood Nile had suddenly fallen into a passion. There were, infamous to relate, inundations of the drain. At moments this stomach of civilization digested badly, the sewer flowed back into the throat of the city, and Paris had the after-taste of its ordure. These resemblances of the drain to remorse had some good about them, for they were warnings, very badly taken, however; for the city was indignant that its mud should have so much boldness, and did not admit that the ordure should return. Better get rid of it.

The inundation of 1802 is in the memory of Parisians eighty years of age. The mud spread across the Place des Victoires, on which is the statue of Louis XIV; it entered Rue St. Honoré by the two mouths of the drain of the Champs Elysées, Rue St. Florentin by the St. Florentin drain, Rue Pierre à Poisson by the drain of the Sonnerie, Rue Popincourt by the Chemin-Vert drain, and Rue de la Roquette by the Rue de Lappe drain; it covered the level of the Rue des Champs Elysées, to a height of fourteen inches, and in the south, owing to the vomitory of the Seine performing its duties contrariwise, it entered Rue Mazarine, Rue de l'Echaudé, and Rue du Marais, where it stopped after running on a hundred and twenty yards, just a few yards from the house which Racine had inhabited, respecting in the seventeenth century the poet more than the king. It reached its maximum depth in the Rue St. Pierre, where it rose three feet above the gutter, and its maximum extent in the Rue St. Sabine, where it extended over a length of two hundred and fifty yards.

At the beginning of the present century the drain of Paris was still a mysterious spot. Mud can never be well famed, but here the ill reputation extended almost to terror. Paris knew confusedly that it had beneath it a gruesome cave; people talked about it as of that monstrous cesspool of Thebes, in which centipedes fifteen feet in length swarmed, and which could have served as a bathing-place for Behemoth. The heavy boots of the sewer-men never ventured beyond certain known points. It was still very close to the time when the scavengers' carts, from the top of which St. Foix fraternized with the Marquis de Créqui, were simply unloaded into the drain. As for the cleansing, the duty was intrusted to the showers, which choked up rather than swept away. Rome allowed some poetry to her cloaca, and called it the Gemoniæ, but Paris insulted its own, and called it the stench-hole. Science and superstition were agreed as to the horror, and the stench-hole was quite as repugnant to hygiene as to legend. The hobgoblin Monk saw light under the fetid arches of the

Mouffetard drain; the corpses of the Marmousets were thrown into the Barillerie drain. Fagot attributed the malignant fever of 1685 to the great opening of the Marais drain, which remained yawning until 1833 in the Rue St. Louis, nearly opposite the sign of the Messager Galant. The mouth of the drain in the Rue de la Mortellerie was celebrated for the pestilences which issued from it; with its iron-pointed grating that resembled a row of teeth, it yawned in this fatal street like the throat of a dragon breathing hell on mankind. The popular imagination seasoned the gloomy Parisian sewer with some hideous mixture of infinitude; the drain was bottomless, the drain was a Barathrum, and the idea of exploring these leprous regions never even occurred to the police. Who would have dared to cast a sound into this darkness, and go on a journey of discovery in this abyss? It was frightful, and yet some one presented himself at last, and the cloaca had its Christopher Columbus.

One day in 1805, during one of the rare apparitions which the emperor made in Paris, the minister of the interior attended at his master's *petit lever*. In the court-yard could be heard the clanging sabers of all the extraordinary soldiers of the great republic and the great empire; there was a swarm of heroes at Napoleon's gates: men of the Rhine, the Scheldt, the Adige, and the Nile; comrades of Joubert, of Desaix, of Marceau, Hoche, and Kleber; aeronauts of Fleurus, grenadiers of Mayence, pontooners of Genoa, hussars whom the Pyramids had gazed at, artillerymen who had been bespattered by Junot's cannon-balls, cuirassiers who had taken by assault the fleet anchored in the Zuyder Zee; some had followed Bonaparte upon the bridge of Lodi, others had accompanied Murat to the trenches of Mantua, while others had outstripped Lannes in the hollow way of Montebello. The whole army of that day was in the court of the Tuileries, represented by a squadron or a company, and guarding Napoleon in repose; and it was the splendid period when the great army had Marengo behind it and Austerlitz before it. "Sire," said the minister of the interior to Napoleon, "I have seen to-day the most intrepid man of your empire." "Who is the man?" the emperor asked sharply, "and what has he done?" "He wishes to do something, sire." "What is it?" "To visit the drains of Paris." This man existed, and his name was Bruneseau.

4. UNKNOWN DETAILS

The visit took place, and was a formidable campaign; a nocturnal battle against asphyxia and plague. It was at the same time a voyage of discovery, and one of the survivors of the exploration, an intelligent workman, very young at that time, used to recount a few years ago the curious details which Bruneseau thought it right to omit in his report to the prefect of police, as unworthy of the administrative style. Disinfecting processes were very rudimentary at that day, and Bruneseau had scarce passed the first articulations of the subterranean net-work ere eight workmen out of twenty refused to go further. The operation was complicated, for the visit entailed cleansing; it was, therefore, requisite to cleanse and at the same time take measurements; note the water entrances, count the traps and mouths, trace the branches, indicate the currents, recognize the respective dimensions of the different basins, sound the small drain grafted on the main sewer, measure the height under the keystone of each passage, and the width both at the bottom and the top; finally, to determine the levels for each affluent from the sewer and from the street. They advanced with difficulty, and it was not rare for the ladders to sink into three feet of mud. The lanterns would scarce burn in the mephitic atmosphere, and from time to time, a sewer-man was carried away in a fainting state. At certain spots there was a precipice; the soil had given way, the stones were swallowed up, and the drain was converted into a lost well; nothing solid could be found, and they had great difficulty in dragging out a man who suddenly disappeared. By the advice of Fourcroy, large cages filled with tow saturated with resin were set fire to at regular distances in spots sufficiently purified. The wall was covered in places with shapeless fungi which might have

94

been called tumors, and the stone itself seemed sick in this unbreathable medium.

Bruneseau, in his exploration, proceeded down-hill. At the point where the two water-pipes of the Grand Hurleur separate, he deciphered on a projecting stone the date 1550; this stone indicated the limit where Philibert Delorme, instructed by Henri II to inspect the subways of Paris, stopped. This stone was the mark of the sixteenth century in the drain, and Bruneseau found the handiwork of the seventeenth in the conduit du Ponceau and that of the Rue Vieille du Temple, which were arched between 1600 and 1650, and the mark of the eighteenth in the west section of the collecting canal, inclosed and arched in 1740. These two arches, especially the younger one, that of 1740, were more decrepit and cracked than the masonry of the belt drain, which dated from 1412, the period when the Ménilmontant stream was raised to the dignity of the grand drain of Paris, a promotion analogous to that of a peasant who became first valet to the king; something like Grand Jean transformed into Lebel.

They fancied they recognized here and there, especially under the Palais de Justice, the form of old dungeons formed in the drain itself, hideous *in pace*. An iron collar hung in one of these cells, and they were all bricked up. A few of the things found were peculiar; among others the skeleton of an orang-outang, which disappeared from the Jardin des Plantes in 1800, a disappearance probably connected with the famous and incontestable apparition of the fiend in the Rue des Bernardins in the last year of the eighteenth century. The poor animal eventually drowned itself in the drain. Under the long vaulted passage leading to the Arche Marion a rag-picker's *hotte* in a perfect state of preservation caused the admiration of connoisseurs. Everywhere the mud, which the sewer-men had come to handle intrepidly, abounded in precious objects: gold and silver, jewelry, precious stones, and coin. A giant who had filtered this cloaca would have found in his sieve the wealth of centuries. At the point where the two branches of the Rue du Temple and the Rue St. Avoye divide, a singular copper Huguenot medal was picked up, bearing on one side a pig wearing a cardinal's hat, and on the other a wolf with a tiara on its head.

The most surprising discovery was at the entrance of the Grand Drain. This entrance had been formerly closed by a gate, of which only the hinges now remained. From one of these hinges hung a filthy, shapeless rag, which doubtless caught there as it passed, floated in the shadow, and was gradually moldering away. Bruneseau raised his lantern and examined this fragment; it was of very fine linen, and at one of the corners, less gnawn than the rest, could be distinguished an heraldic crown embroidered above these seven letters, LAUBESP. The crown was a marquis's crown, and the seven letters signified *Laubespine*. What they had under their eyes was no less than a piece of Marat's winding-sheet. Marat, in his youth, had had amours, at the time when he was attached to the household of the Comte d'Artois in the capacity of physician to the stables. Of these amours with a great lady, which are historically notorious, this sheet had remained to him as a waif or a souvenir; on his death, as it was the only fine linen at his lodgings, he was buried in it. Old women wrapped up the tragic friend of the people for the tomb in this sheet which had known voluptuousness. Bruneseau passed on; the strip was left where it was. Was it through contempt or respect? Marat deserved both. And then destiny was so impressed on it that a hesitation was felt about touching it. Moreover, things of the sepulcher should be left at the place which they select. Altogether the relic was a strange one; a marquise had slept in it, Marat had rotted in it; and it had passed through the Pantheon to reach the sewer-rats. This rag from an alcove, every crease in which Watteau would have formerly joyously painted, ended by becoming worthy of the intent glance of Dante.

The visit to the subways of Paris lasted for seven years, from 1805 to 1812. While going along, Bruneseau designed, directed, and carried out considerable operations; in 1808 he lowered the Ponceau drain, and everywhere pushing out new lines, carried the sewer in 1809 under the Rue St. Denis to the Fountain of the Innocents; in 1810 under the Rue Froidmanteau and the Salpetrière; in 1811 under the Rue Neuve des Petits Pères, under the Rue du Mail, the Rue de l'Echarpe and the Place Royal; in 1812 under the Rue de la Paix and the Chaussée d'Antin. At the same time he disinfected and cleansed the entire net-work, and in the second year called his son-in-law Nargaud to his assistance. It is thus that at the beginning of this century the old society flushed its subway and performed the toilet of its drain. It was so much cleaned, at any rate. Winding, cracked, unpaved, full of pits, broken by strange elbows, ascending and descending illogically, fetid, savage, ferocious, submerged in darkness, with cicatrices on its stones and scars on its walls, and gruesome,—such was the old drain of Paris, retrospectively regarded. Ramifications in all directions, crossings of trenches, branches, dials and stars as in saps, blind guts and alleys, arches covered with saltpeter, infected pits, scabby exudations on the walls, drops falling from the roof, and darkness; nothing equaled the horror of this old excremental crypt; the digestive apparatus of Babylon, a den, a trench, a gulf pierced with streets, a Titanic mole-hill, in which the mind fancies that it sees, crawling in the shadows, amid the ordure which had once been splendor, that old enormous blind mole, the past.

Such, we repeat, was the sewer of the olden time.

5. *PRESENT PROGRESS*

At the present day the sewer is clean, cold, straight, and correct, and almost realizes the ideal of what is understood in England by the word "respectable." It is neat and gray; built with the plumb-line, we might almost say coquettishly. It resembles a contractor who has become a councilor of state. You almost see clearly in it, and the mud behaves itself decently. At the first glance you might be inclined to take it for one of those subterranean passages so common formerly, and so useful for the flights of monarchs and princes in the good old times "when the people loved its kings." The present sewer is a handsome sewer; the pure style prevails there; the classic rectilinear Alexandrine, which expelled from poetry, appears to have taken refuge in architecture, seems blended with all the stones of this long, dark, and white vault; each vomitory is an arcade, and the Rue de Rivoli sets the fashion even in the cloaca. However, if the geometric line be anywhere in its place, it is assuredly so in the stercoraceous trench of a great city, where everything must be subordinated to the shortest road. The sewer has, at the present day, assumed a certain official aspect, and the police reports of which it is sometimes the object are no longer deficient in respect to it. The words which characterize it in the administrative language are lofty and dignified: what used to be called a gut is now a gallery, and what used to be a hole is now a "look." Villon would no longer recognize old temporary lodgings. This net-work of cellars still has its population of rodents swarming more than ever; from time to time a rat, an old veteran, ventures his head at the window of the drain and examines the Parisians; but even these vermin are growing tame, as they are satisfied with their subterranean palace. The cloaca no longer retains its primitive ferocity, and the rain which sullied the drain of olden times washes that of the present day. Still, do not trust to it too entirely, for miasmas still inhabit it, and it is rather hypocritical than irreproachable. In spite of all the prefecture of police and the board of health have done, it exhales a vague, suspicious odor, like Tartuffe after confession.

Still we must allow that, take it altogether, finishing is an homage which the sewer pays to civilization, and as from this point of view Tartuffe's conscience is a progress upon the stable of Augeas, it is certain that the sewer of Paris has been improved.

It is more than a progress, it is a transmutation; between the old and the present sewer there is a revolution.

Who effected this revolution? the man whom every one forgets and whom we have named—Bruneseau.

6. FUTURE PROGRESS

DIGGING the sewer of Paris was no small task. The last ten centuries have toiled at it without being able to finish it more than they could finish Paris. The sewer, in fact, receives all the counterstrokes of the growth of Paris. It is in the ground a species of dark polyp with a thousand antennæ, which grows below, equally with the city above. Each time that the city forms a street, the sewer stretches out an arm. The old monarchy only constructed twenty-three thousand three hundred meters of drain, and Paris had reached that point on January 1, 1806. From this period, to which we shall presently revert, the work has been usefully and energetically taken up and continued. Napoleon built—and the figures are curious—four thousand eight hundred and four meters; Charles X, ten thousand eight hundred and thirty-six; Louis Philippe, eighty-nine thousand and twenty; the republic of 1848, twenty-three thousand three hundred and eighty-one; the present government, seventy thousand five hundred; altogether, two hundred and twenty-six thousand six hundred meters, or sixty leagues, of sewer, the enormous entrails of Paris,—an obscure ramification constantly at work, an unknown and immense construction. As we see, the subterranean labyrinth of Paris is, at the present day, more than tenfold what it was at the beginning of the century. It would be difficult to imagine all the perseverance and efforts required to raise this cloaca to the point of relative perfection at which it now is. It was with great trouble that the old monarchical provostry, and, in the last ten years of the eighteenth century, the revolutionary mayoralty, succeeded in boring the five leagues of drains which existed prior to 1806. All sorts of obstacles impeded this operation; some peculiar to the nature of the soil, others inherent in the prejudices of the working population of Paris. Paris is built on a stratum strangely rebellious to the pick, the spade, the borer, and human manipulation. Nothing is more difficult to pierce and penetrate than this geological formation on which the marvelous historical formation called Paris is superposed. So soon as labor in any shape ventures into this layer of alluvium, subterranean resistances abound. They are liquid clay, running springs, hard rocks, and that soft and deep mud which the special science calls "mustard." The pick advances laboriously in the calcareous layers alternating with very thin veins of clay and schistose strata incrusted with oyster-shells, which are contemporaries of the pre-Adamite oceans. At times a stream suddenly bursts into a tunnel just commenced, and inundates the workmen, or a slip of chalk takes place and rushes forward with the fury of a cataract, breaking like glass the largest supporting shores. Very recently at La Villette, when it was found necessary to carry the collecting sewer under the St. Martin canal without stopping the navigation or letting off the water, a fissure formed in the bed of the canal, and the water poured into the tunnel, deriding the efforts of the draining pumps. It was found neccessary to employ a diver to seek for the fissure which was in the mouth of the great basin, and it was only stopped up with great difficulty.

Elsewhere, near the Seine, and even at some distance from the river, as, for instance, at Belleville Grand Rue and the Passage Lunière, bottomless sands are found, in which men have been swallowed up. Add asphyxia by miasmas, interment by slips and sudden breaking in of the soil; add typhus, too, with which the workmen are slowly impregnated. In our days, after having hollowed the gallery of Clichy with a *banquette* to convey the main water-conduit of the Ourque, a work performed by trenches ten meters in depth; after having arched the Bièvre from the Boulevard de l'Hôpital to the Seine, in the midst of earth-slips, and by the help of trenching, often through putrid matter, and of shores; after having, in order to deliver Paris from the torrent-like waters of Montmartre, and give an outlet to the river-like pond of twenty-three acres which stagnated near the Barrière de Martyrs; after having, we say, constructed the line of sewers from the Barrière Blanche to the Aubervilliers road, in four months, by working day and night at a depth of eleven meters; and after having carried out subterraneously a drain in the Rue Barre du Bec without a cutting, a thing unknown before at a depth of six meters—the surveyor Monnot died. After arching three thousand meters of sewer in all parts of the city, from the Rue Traversière Saint Antoine to the Rue de l'Ourcine; after having, by the Arbalète branch, freed the Censier-Mouffetard square from pluvial inundations; after having constructed the St. George's drain through liquid sand upon rubble and beton, and after having lowered the formidable pitch of the Notre Dame de St. Lazarette branch—the engineer Duleau died. There are no bulletins for such acts of bravery, which are more useful, however, than the brutal butchery of battlefields.

The sewers of Paris were in 1832 far from being what they are now. Bruneseau gave the impulse, but it required the cholera to determine the vast reconstruction which has taken place since. It is surprising to say, for instance, that in 1821 a portion of the begirding sewer, called the Grand Canal, as at Venice, still stagnated in the open air, in the Rue des Gourdes. It was not till 1823 that the city of Paris found in its pocket the twenty-six thousand six hundred and eighty francs, six centimes, needed to cover in this turpitude. The three absorbing wells of the Combat, la Cunette, and St. Mandé, with their disgorging apparatus, draining wells, and deodorizing branches, merely date from 1836. The intestine canal of Paris has been remade, and, as we said, augmented more than tenfold during the last quarter of a century. Thirty years ago, at the period of the insurrection of June 5 and 6, it was still in many parts almost the old sewer. A great number of streets, now convex, were at that time broken causeways. There could be frequently seen, at the bottom of the watersheds of streets and squares, large square gratings, whose iron glistened from the constant passage of the crowd, dangerous and slippery for vehicles, and throwing horses down. The official language of the department of the roads and bridges gave these gratings the expressive name of *Cassis*. In 1832 in a number of streets—Rue de l'Etoile, Rue St. Louis, Rue du Temple, Rue Vieille du Temple, Rue Notre Dame de Nazareth, Rue Folie Méricourt, Quai aux Fleurs, Rue du Petit Musc, Rue de Normandie, Rue Pont aux Biches, Rue des Marais, Faubourg St. Martin, Rue Notre Dame des Pictoires, Faubourg Montmartre, Rue Grange Batelière, at the Champs Elysées, the Rue Jacob, and the Rue de Tournon—the old Gothic cloaca still cynically displayed its throats. They were enormous stone orifices, sometimes surrounded with posts, with a monumental effrontery. Paris in 1806 was much in the same state as regards drains as in May, 1663; five thousand three hundred and twenty-eight toises. After Bruneseau, on January 1, 1832, there were forty thousand three hundred meters. From 1806 to 1831 seven hundred and fifty meters were on the average constructed annually; since then eight and even ten thousand meters have been made every year in brick-work, with a coating of concrete on a foundation of beton. At two hundred francs the meter, the sixty leagues of drainage in the Paris of to-day represents forty-eight million francs.

In addition to the economic progress to which we alluded at the outset, serious considerations as to the public health are attached to this immense question,—the drainage of Paris. Paris is situated between two sheets, a sheet of water and a sheet of air. The sheet of water, lying at a very great depth, but already tapped by two borings, is supplied by the stratum of green sandstone situated between the chalk and the jurassic limestone; this stratum may be represented by a disk with a radius of twenty-five leagues; a multitude of rivers and streams drip into it, and the Seine, the Marne, the Yonne, the Oise, the Aisne, the Cher, the Vienne, and the Loire are drunk in a glass of water from the Grenelle well. The sheet of water is salubrious, for it comes from the sky first, and then from the earth, but the sheet of air is unhealthy, for it comes from the sewer. All the miasmas of the cloaca are mingled with the breathing of the city— hence this bad breath. The atmosphere taken from above a dungheap, it has been proved scientifically, is purer than the atmosphere taken from over Paris. Within a given time, by the aid of progress, improvements in

machinery, and enlightenment, the sheet of water will be employed to
purify the sheet of air; that is to say, to wash the sewer. It is known that
by washing the sewer we mean restoring the ordure to the earth by sending dung to the arable lands, the manure to the grass lands. Through this
simple fact there will be for the whole social community a diminution of
wretchedness and an augmentation of health. At the present hour the
radiation of the diseases of Paris extends for fifty leagues round, the
Louvre taken as the axle of this pestilential wheel.

We might say that for the last ten centuries the cloaca has been the
misery of Paris, and the sewer is the viciousness which the city has in its
blood. The popular instinct has never been deceived, and the trade of
the sewer-man was formerly almost as dangerous and almost as repulsive
to the people as that of the knacker which so long was regarded with
horror and left to the hangman. Great wages were required to induce a
bricklayer to disappear in the fetid sap; the ladder of the well-digger hesitated to plunge into it; it was said, proverbially, *Going into the sewer is
entering the tomb,* and all sorts of hideous legends, as we said, covered
this colossal cesspool with terrors. It is a formidable fosse which bears
traces of the revolutions of the globe as well as the revolutions of men,
and vestiges may be found there of every cataclysm from the shells of the
Deluge to the ragged sheet of Marat.

BOOK III

MUD, BUT SOUL

1. *THE SEWER AND ITS SURPRISES*

IT WAS in the sewer of Paris that Jean Valjean found himself. There is a further resemblance of Paris with the sea; as in the ocean the diver can disappear there. It was an extraordinary transition, in the very heart of the city. Jean Valjean had left the city, and in a twinkling, in the time required to lift a trap and let it fall again, he had passed from broad daylight to complete darkness, from midday to midnight, from noise to silence, from the uproar of thunder to the stagnation of the tomb, and, by an incident far more prodigious even than that of the Rue Polonceau, from the extremest peril to the most absolute security. A sudden fall into a cellar; disappearance in the oubliette of Paris; leaving this street where death was all around for this species of sepulcher in which was life; it was a strange moment. He stood for some minutes as if stunned, listening and amazed. The trap-door of safety had suddenly opened beneath him, and the kindness of heaven had to some extent snared him by treachery. Admirable ambuscades of Providence.

Still, the wounded man did not stir, and Jean Valjean did not know whether what he was carrying in this tomb were alive or dead.

His first sensation was blindness, for he all at once could see nothing. He felt, too, that in a moment he had become deaf, for he could hear nothing more. The frenzied storm of murder maintained a few yards above him only reached him confusedly and indistinctly, and like an echo in a deep place. He felt that he had something solid under his feet, but that was all; still it was sufficient. He stretched out one arm, then the other; he touched the wall on both sides, and understood that the passage was narrow; his foot slipped, and he understood that the pavement was damp. He advanced one foot cautiously, fearing a hole, a cesspool, or some gulf, and satisfied himself that the pavement went onward. A fetid gust warned him of the spot where he was.

At the expiration of a few minutes he was no longer blind, a little light fell through the trap by which he descended, and his eye grew used to this cavern. He began to distinguish something. The passage in which he had run to earth—no other word expresses the situation better—was walled up behind him; it was one of those blind alleys called in official language branches. Before him he had another wall, a wall of night. The light of the trap expired ten or twelve feet from the spot where Jean Valjean was, and scarce produced a livid whiteness on a few yards of the damp wall of the sewer. Beyond that, the opaqueness was massive; to penetrate it seemed horrible, and to enter it was like being swallowed up. Yet it was possible to bury one's self in this wall of fog, and it must be done, and must even be done quickly. Jean Valjean thought that the grating which he had noticed in the street might also be noticed by the troops, and that all depended on this chance. They might also come down into the well and search, so he had not a minute to lose. He had laid Marius on the ground and now picked him up, that is again the right expression,—took him on his shoulders, and set out. He resolutely entered the darkness.

The truth is that they were less saved than Jean Valjean believed; perils of another nature, but equally great, awaited them. After the flashing whirlwind of the combat came the cavern of miasmas and snares, after the chaos the cloaca. Jean Valjean had passed from one circle of the Inferno into another. When he had gone fifty yards he was obliged to stop, for a question occurred to him; the passage ran into another, which it intersected, and two roads offered themselves. Which should he take? ought he to turn to the left or right? how was he to find his way in this black labyrinth? This labyrinth, we have said, has a clew in its slope, and following the slope leads to the river. Jean Valjean understood this immediately: he said to himself that he was probably in the sewer of the Halles, that if he turned to the left and followed the incline, he would arrive in a quarter of an hour at some opening on the Seine between the Pont au Change and the Pont Neuf; that is to say, appear in broad daylight in the busiest part of Paris. Perhaps he might come at some street-opening, and passers-by would be stupefied at seeing two blood-stained men emerge from the ground at their feet. The police would come up and they would be carried off to the nearest guard-room; they would be prisoners before they had come out. It would be better, therefore, to bury himself in the labyrinth, confide in the darkness, and leave the issue to Providence.

He went up the incline and turned to the right; when he had gone round the corner of the gallery the distant light from the trap disappeared, the curtain of darkness fell on him again, and he became blind once more. For all that, he advanced as rapidly as he could; Marius's arms were passed round his neck, and his feet hung down behind. He held the two arms with one hand and felt the wall with the other. Marius's cheek touched his and was glued to it, as it was bloody, and he felt a warm stream which came from Marius drip on him and penetrate his clothing. Still, a warm breath in his ear, which touched the wounded man's mouth, indicated respiration, and consequently life. The passage in which Jean Valjean was now walking was not so narrow as the former, and he advanced with some difficulty. The rain of the previous night had not yet passed off, and formed a small torrent in the center, and he was forced to hug the wall in order not to have his feet in the water.

He went on thus darkly, resembling beings of the night groping in the invisible, and subterraneously lost in the veins of gloom. Still, by degrees, because either distant gratings sent a little floating light into this opaque mist or his eyes grew accustomed to the obscurity, he regained some vague vision, and began to notice confusedly at one moment the wall he was touching, at another the vault under which he was passing. The pupil is dilated at night, and eventually finds daylight in it, in the same way as the soul is dilated in misfortune and eventually finds God in it.

To direct himself was difficult, for the sewers represent, so to speak, the outline of the streets standing over them. There were in the Paris of that day two thousand two hundred streets, and imagine beneath them that forest of dark branches called the sewer. The system of drains existing at that day, if placed end on end, would have given a length of eleven leagues. We have already said that the present net-work, owing to the special activity of the last thirty years, is no less than sixty leagues. Jean Valjean began by deceiving himself: he fancied that he was under the Rue St. Denis; and it was unlucky that he was not so. There is under that street an old stone drain, dating from Louis XIII, which runs straight to the collecting sewer, called the Great sewer, with only one turn on the right, by the old Court of Miracles, and a single branch, the Saint Martin sewer, whose four arms cut each other at right angles. But the tunnel of the little Truanderie, whose entrance was near the Corinth wine-shop, never communicated with the sewer of the Rue St. Denis; it falls into the Montmartre drain, and that is where Jean Valjean now was. There opportunities for losing himself were abundant, for the Montmartre drain is one of the most labyrinthine of the old net-work. Luckily Jean Valjean had left behind him the drain of the Halles, whose geometrical plan represents a number of interlaced topmasts; but he had before him more than one embarrassing encounter, and more than one street-corner —for they are streets—offering itself in the obscurity as a note of interrogation. In the first place on his left, the vast Plâtrière drain, a sort of Chinese puzzle, thrusting forth and intermingling its chaos of T's and Z's under the Post-office, and the rotunda of the Halle au blé as far as the Seine, where it terminates in a Y; secondly, on his right the curved passage of the Rue du Cadran, with its three teeth, which are so many blind alleys; thirdly, on his left the Mail branch, complicated almost at the entrance by a species of fork, and running with repeated zigzags to the great cesspool of the Louvre, which ramifies in every direction; and lastly, on his right the blind alley of the Rue des Jeuneurs, without counting other pitfalls, ere he reached the belt drain which alone could lead him to some issue sufficiently distant to be safe.

Had Jean Valjean had any notion of all that we have just stated, he would have quickly perceived, merely by feeling the wall, that he was not in the subterranean gallery of the Rue St. Denis. Instead of the old carved stone, instead of the old architecture, haughty and royal even in the drain, with its arches and running courses of granite, which cost eight hundred livres the fathom, he would feel under his hand modern cheapness, the economic expedient, brick work supported on a layer of beton, which costs two hundred francs the meter, that bourgeois masonry known as *à petits matériaux;* but he knew nothing of all this. He advanced anxiously but calmly, seeing nothing, hearing nothing, plunged into chance; that is to say, swallowed up in Providence. By degrees, however, we are bound to state that a certain amount of horror beset him, and the shadow which enveloped him entered his mind. He was walking in an enigma. This aqueduct of the cloaca is formidable, for it intersects itself in a vertiginous manner, and it is a mournful thing to be caught in this Paris of Darkness. Jean Valjean was obliged to find, and almost invent, his road without seeing it. In this unknown region, each step that he ventured might be his last. How was he to get out of it? would he find an issue? would he find it in time? could he pierce and penetrate this colossal subterranean sponge with its channels of stone? would he meet there some unexpected knot of darkness? would he arrive at something inextricable and impassable? would Marius die of hemorrhage, and himself of hunger? would they both end by being lost there, and forming two skeletons in a corner of this night? He did not know; he asked himself all this, and could not find an answer. The intestines of Paris are a precipice, and like the prophet he was in the monster's belly.

He suddenly had a surprise; at the most unexpected moment, and without ceasing to walk in a straight line, he perceived that he was no longer ascending; the water of the gutter plashed against his heels instead of coming to his toes. The sewer was now descending; why? Was he about to reach the Seine suddenly? That danger was great, but the peril of turning back was greater still, and he continued to advance. He was not proceeding toward the Seine; the ridge which the soil of Paris makes on the right bank disembogues one of its water-sheds into the Seine, and the other in the great sewer. The crest of this ridge, which determines the division of the waters, designs a most capricious line; the highest point is in the St. Avoye sewer, beyond the Rue Michel-le-comte, in the Louvre sewer near the boulevards, and in the Montmarte drain near the Halles. This highest point Jean Valjean had reached, and he was proceeding toward the belt sewer, or in the right direction, but he knew it not. Each time that he reached a branch he felt the corners, and if he found the opening narrower than the passage in which he was, he did not enter, but continued his march, correctly judging that any narrower way must end in a blind alley, and could only take him from his object; that is to say, an outlet. He thus avoided the fourfold snare laid for him in the darkness by the four labyrinths which we have enumerated. At a certain moment he recognized that he was passing from under that part of Paris petrified by the riot, where the barricades had suppressed circulation, and returning under living and normal Paris. He suddenly heard above his head a sound like thunder, distant but continuous; it was the rolling of vehicles.

He had been walking about half an hour, at least that was the calculation he made, and had not thought of resting; he had merely changed the hand which held Marius up. The darkness was more profound than ever, but this darkness·re-assured him. All at once he saw his shadow before him; it stood out upon a faint and almost indistinct redness which vaguely empurpled the road-way at his feet and the vault above his head and glided along the greasy walls of the passage. He turned his head in stupefaction, and saw behind him, glistening at a distance which appeared immense, a sort of horrible star that seemed to be looking at him. It was the gloomy police star rising in the sewer. Behind this star there moved confusedly nine or ten black, upright, indistinct, and terrible forms.

2. EXPLANATION

ON the day of June 6 a battue of the sewers was ordered, for it was feared lest the conquered should fly to them as a refuge, and Prefect Gisquet ordered occult Paris to be searched, while General Bugeaud swept public Paris,—a double connected operation, which required a double strategy of the public force, represented above by the army and beneath by the police. Three squads of agents and sewer-men explored the subway of Paris,—the first the right bank, the second the left bank, and the third the cité. The agents were armed with carbines, bludgeons, swords, and daggers, and what was at this moment pointed at Jean Valjean was the lantern of the round of the right bank. This round had just inspected the winding gallery and three blind alleys which are under the Rue du Cadran. While the police were turning their light about these blind alleys, Jean Valjean in his progress came to the entrance of the gallery, found it narrower than the main gallery, and had not entered it. The police, on coming out of the Cadran gallery, fancied that they could hear the sound of footsteps in the direction of the outer drain, and they were really Jean Valjean's footsteps. The head sergeant of the round raised his lantern, and the squad began peering into the mist in the direction whence the noise had come.

It was an indescribable moment for Jean Valjean; luckily, if he saw the lantern well, the lantern saw him badly, for it was the light and he was the darkness. He was far off, and blended with the blackness of the spot, so he drew himself up against the wall and stopped. However, he did not explain to himself what was moving behind him; want of sleep and food and emotion had made him to pass into a visionary state. He saw a flash, and round this flash specters. What was it? he did not understand. When Jean Valjean stopped, the noise ceased; the police listened and heard nothing, they looked and saw nothing, and hence consulted together. There was at that period, at that point in the Montmartre drain, a sort of square called *de service,* which has since been removed on account of the small internal lake which the torrents of rain formed there. The squad assembled on this square. Jean Valjean saw the specters make a sort of circle, and their bull-dog heads came together and whispered. The result of this council held by the watch-dogs was that they were mistaken, that there had been no noise, that there was nobody there, that it was useless to enter the surrounding sewer, that it would be time wasted, but that they must hasten to the St. Merry drain, for if there was anything to be done and any "boussingot" to track, it would be there.

From time to time parties new-sole their old insults. In 1832, the word *boussingot* formed the transition between the word *jacobin,* no longer current, and the word *demagogue,* at that time almost unused, and which has since done excellent service.

The sergeant gave orders to left-wheel toward the water-shed of the Seine. Had they thought of dividing into two squads and going in both directions, Jean Valjean would have been caught. It is probable that the instructions of the Prefecture, fearing the chance of a fight with a large body of insurgents, forbade the round from dividing. The squad set out again, leaving Jean Valjean behind; and in all this movement he perceived nothing except the eclipse of the lantern, which was suddenly turned away.

Before starting, the sergeant, to satisfy his police conscience, discharged his carbine in the direction where Jean Valjean was. The detonation rolled echoing along the crypt, like the rumbling of these Titanic bowels. A piece of plaster which fell into the gutter and plashed up the water a few yards from Jean Valjean warned him that the bullet had struck the vault above his head. Measured and slow steps echoed for some time along the causeway, growing more and more deadened by the glowing distance; the group of black forms disappeared; a light oscillated and floated, forming on the vault a ruddy circle, which decreased and disappeared; the silence again became profound, the obscurity again became complete, and blindness and deafness again took possession of the gloom, and Jean Valjean, not daring yet to stir, remained leaning for a long time against the wall, with out-stretched ears and dilated eyeballs, watching the evanishment of the patrol of phantoms.

3. *THE TRACKED MAN*

WE must do the police of that day the justice of saying that even in the gravest public conjunctures they imperturbably accomplished their duties as inspectors and watchmen. A riot was not in their eyes a pretext to give a loose reign to malefactors, and to neglect society for the reason that the government was in danger. The ordinary duties were performed correctly, in addition to the extraordinary duties, and were in no way disturbed. In the midst of an incalculable political event, under the pressure of a possible revolution, an agent, not allowing himself to be affected by the insurrection and the barricade, would track a robber. Something very like this occurred on the afternoon of June 6, on the right bank of the Seine, a little beyond the Pont des Invalides. There is no bank there at the present day, and the appearance of the spot has been altered. On this slope two men, a certain distance apart, were observing each other; the one in front seemed to be trying to get away, while the one behind wanted to catch him up. It was like a game of chess played at a distance and silently; neither of them seemed to be in a hurry, and both walked slowly, as if they were afraid that increased speed on the part of one would be imitated by the other. It might have been called an appetite following a prey, without appearing to do so purposely; the prey was crafty, and kept on guard.

The proportions required between the tracked weasel and the tracking dog were observed. The one trying to escape was thin and mean-looking, the one trying to catch was a tall fellow, rough in aspect, and evidently a rough customer. The first, feeling himself the weaker, avoided the second, but did so with internal fury; any one who could have observed him would have seen in his eyes the gloomy hostility of flight, and all the threat which there is in fear; the slope was deserted, there were no passers-by, not even a boatman or raftsman in the boats moored here and there. They could only be noticed easily from the opposite quay, and any one who had watched them at that distance would have seen that the man in front appeared a bristling, ragged, and shambling fellow, anxious and shivering under a torn blouse, while the other was a classic and official personage, wearing the frock-coat of authority buttoned up to the chin. The reader would probably recognize these two men, were he to see them more closely. What was the object of the last one? probably he wished to clothe the other man more warmly. When a man dressed by the state pursues a man in rags, it is in order to make of him also a man dressed by the state. The difference of color is the sole question,—to be dressed in blue is glorious, to be dressed in red is disagreeable. There is a purple of the lower classes. It was probably some disagreeable thing, and some purple of this sort, which the first man desired to escape.

If the other allowed him to go on ahead, and did not yet arrest him, it was, in all appearance, in the hope of seeing him arrive at some significative rendezvous and some group worth capturing. This delicate operation is called tracking. What renders this conjecture highly probable is the fact that the buttoned-up man, perceiving from the slope an empty fiacre passing, made a sign to the driver; the driver understood, evidently perceived with whom he had to deal, turned round, and began following the two men along the quay. This was not perceived by the ragged, shambling fellow in front. The hackney-coach rolled along under the trees of the Champs Elysées, and over the parapet could be seen the shoulders of the driver, whip in hand. One of the secret instructions of the police to the agents is, "Always have a hackney-coach at hand in case of need." While each of these men maneuvered with irreproachable strategy, they approached an incline in the quay, which allowed drivers coming from Passy to water their horses in the river. This incline has since been suppressed for the sake of symmetry,—horses die of thirst, but the eye is flattered. It was probable that the man in the blouse would

ascend by this incline in order to try and escape in the Champs Elysées,
a place adorned with trees, but, to make up for that, much frequented
by police agents, where the other could easily procure assistance. This
point of the quay is a very little distance from the house brought from
Moret to Paris, in 1824, by Colonel Brack, and called the house of
Francis I. A picket is always stationed near there. To the great surprise
of his watcher, the tracked man did not turn up the road to the watering-
place, but continued to advance along the bank parallel with the quay.
His position was evidently becoming critical, for, unless he threw himself into the Seine, what could he do?

There were no means now left him of returning to the quay, no incline or steps, and they were close to the spot marked by the turn in the
Seine, near the Pont de Jena, where the bank, gradually contracting,
ended in a narrow strip and was lost in the water. There he must inevitably find himself blockaded between the tall wall on his right, the
river on his left and facing him, and authority at his heels. It is true
that this termination of the bank was masked from sight by a pile of
rubbish seven feet high, the result of some demolition. But did this man
hope to conceal himself profitably behind this heap? the expedient
would have been puerile. He evidently did not dream of it, for the innocence of robbers does not go so far. The pile of rubbish formed on
the water-side a sort of eminence extending in a promontory to the quay
wall; the pursued man reached this small mound and went around it,
so that he was no longer seen by the other. The latter, not seeing, was
not seen, and he took advantage of this to give up all dissimulation and
walk very fast. In a few minutes he reached the heap and turned it, but
stood there stupefied. The man he was pursuing was not there; it was
a total eclipse of the man in the blouse. The bank did not run more
than thirty yards beyond the heap, and then plunged under the water
which washed the quay wall. The fugitive could not have thrown himself into the Seine, or have climbed up the quay wall, without being seen
by his pursuer. What had become of him?

The man in the buttoned-up coat walked to the end of the bank and
stood there for a moment, thoughtfully, with clenched fists and scowl-
ing eye. All at once he smote his forehead; he had just perceived, at the
point where the ground ended and the water began, a wide, low, arched,
iron grating, provided with a heavy lock and three massive hinges. This
grating, a sort of gate pierced at the bottom of the quay, opened on the
river as much as on the bank, and a black stream poured from under it

into the Seine. Beyond the heavy rusty bars could be distinguished a sort of arched and dark passage. The man folded his arms and looked at the grating reproachfully, and, this look not being sufficient, he tried to push it open, he shook it, but it offered a sturdy resistance. It was probable that it had just been opened, although no sound had been heard, a singular thing with so rusty a gate, but it was certain that it had been closed again. This indicated that the man who had opened the gate had not a pick-lock but a key. This evidence at once burst on the mind of the man who was trying to open the grating, and drew from him this indignant apostrophe:

"That is strong! a government key!"

Then, calming himself immediately, he expressed a whole internal world of ideas by this outburst of monosyllables, marked by an almost ironical accent:

"Stay, stay, stay, stay."

This said, hoping we know not what, either to see the man come out or others enter, he posted himself on the watch behind the heap of rubbish, with the patient rage of a yard-mastiff. On its side, the hackney-coach, which regulated itself by all his movements, stopped above him near the parapet. The driver, foreseeing a long halt, put on his horses the nose-bag full of damp oats so well known to the Parisians upon whom the government, we may remark parenthetically, puts it sometimes. The few passers over the Pont de Jena, before going on, turned their heads to look for a moment at these motionless objects,—the man on the bank and the hackney-coach on the quay.

4. *HE TOO BEARS HIS CROSS*

JEAN VALJEAN had resumed his march, and had not stopped again. This march grew more and more laborious; for the level of these passages varies; the average height is about five feet six inches, and was calculated for a man's stature. Jean Valjean was compelled to stoop so as not to dash Marius against the roof, and was forced at each moment to bend down, then draw himself up and incessantly feel the wall. The dampness of the stones and of the flooring rendered them bad supports, either for the hand or the foot, and he tottered in the hideous dungheap of the city. The intermittent flashes of the street-gratings only appeared at lengthened intervals, and were so faint that the bright sunshine seemed to be moonlight; all the rest was fog, miasma, opaqueness, and blackness. Jean Valjean was hungry and thirsty, the latter most, and it was like the sea, there was water, water everywhere, but not a drop to drink. His strength, which, as we know, was prodigious, and but slightly diminished by age, owing to his chaste and sober life, was, however, beginning to give way; fatigue assailed him, and his decreasing strength increased the weight of his burden. Marius, who was perhaps dead, was heavy, like all inert bodies, but Jean Valjean held him so that his chest was not affected, and he could breathe as freely as possible. He felt between his legs the rapid gliding of rats, and one was so startled as to bite him. From time to time a gush of fresh air came through the gratings, which revived him.

It might be about three P. M. when he reached the external sewer, and was at first amazed by the sudden widening. He unexpectedly found himself in a gallery whose two walls his outstretched arms did not reach, and under an arch which his head did not touch. The grand sewer, in fact, is eight feet in width by seven high. At the point where the Montmartre drain joins the grand sewer, two other subterranean galleries, that of the Rue de Provence and that of the Abattoir, form cross-roads. Between these four ways a less sagacious man would have been undecided, but Jean Valjean selected the widest; that is to say, the encircling sewer. But here the question came back again,—Should he ascend or descend? He thought that the situation was pressing, and that he must at all risks now reach the Seine, in other words, descend, so he turned to the left. It was fortunate that he did so, for it would be an error to suppose that the encircling sewer has two issues, one toward Bercy, the other toward Passy, and that it is, as its name indicates, the subterranean belt of Paris on the right bank. The grand sewer, which is naught else, it must be borne in mind, than the old Ménilmontant stream, leads, if you ascend it, to a blind alley; that is to say, to its old starting-point, a spring at the foot of the Menilmontant mound. It has no direct communication with the branch which collects the waters of Paris after leaving the Popincourt quarter, and which falls into the Seine by the Amelot sewer above the old isle of Louviers. This branch, which completes the collecting sewer, is separated from it under the Rue Ménilmontant by masonry-work, which marks where the waters divide. If Jean Valjean had remounted the gallery, he would have arrived, exhausted by fatigue and dying, at a wall; he would have been lost.

Strictly speaking, by going back a little way, entering the passage of les Filles du Calvaire, on condition that he did not hesitate at the subterranean maze of the Boucherat cross-roads, by taking the St. Louis passage, then on the left the St. Gilles trench, then by turning to the right and avoiding the St. Sebastian gallery, he might have reached the Amelot sewer; and then, if he did not lose his way in the species of F which is under the Bastille, he would have reached the issue on the Seine near the arsenal. But for that he must have thoroughly known, in all its ramifications and piercings, the enormous madrepore of the sewer. Now we dwell on the fact that he knew nothing of this frightful labyrinth in which he was marching, and had he been asked where he was, he would have replied, "In night." His instinct served him well; going down, in fact, was the only salvation possible. He left on his right the two passages which ramify in the shape of a claw under the Rues Laffitte and St. Georges, and the long bifurcate corridor of the Chaussée d'Antin. A little beyond an affluent, which was, most likely, the Madeleine branch, he stopped, for he was very weary. A large grating, probably the one in the Rue d'Anjou, produced an almost bright light. Jean Valjean, with the gentle movements which a brother would bestow on a wounded brother, laid Marius on the *banquette* of the drain, and his white face gleamed under the white light of the trap as from the bottom of a tomb. His eyes were closed, his hair was attached to his forehead like painters' brushes dyed in blood, his hands were hanging and dead, his limbs cold, and blood was clotted at the corner of his lips. Coagulated blood had collected in his cravat-knot, his shirt entered the wounds, and the cloth of his coat rubbed the gaping edges of the living flesh. Jean Valjean, removing the clothes with the tips of his fingers, laid his hand on his chest,—the heart still beat. Jean Valjean tore up his shirt, bandaged the wounds as well as he could, and stopped the blood that was flowing; then, stooping down in this half daylight over Marius, who was still unconscious and almost breathless, he looked at him with indescribable hatred. In moving Marius's clothes, he had found in his pockets two things,—the loaf, which he had forgotten the previous evening, and his pocket-book. He ate the bread and opened the pocket-book. On the first page he read the lines written by Marius, as will be remembered:

My name is Marius Pontmercy. Carry my body to my grandfather's, M. Gillenormand, No. 6, Rue des Filles du Calvaire, in the Marais.

Jean Valjean read by the light of the grating these lines, and remained for a time, as it were, absorbed in himself, and repeating in a low voice, "Rue des Filles du Calvaire,—No. 6,—M. Gillenormand." He returned the portfolio to Marius's pocket; he had eaten, and his strength had come back to him. He raised Marius again, carefully laid his head on his right shoulder, and began descending the sewer.

The grand sewer, running along the channel of the valley of Ménilmontant, is nearly two leagues in length, and is paved for a considerable portion of the distance. This torch, formed of the names of the streets of Paris, with which we enlighten for the reader Jean Valjean's subterranean march, he did not possess. Nothing informed him what zone of the city he was traversing, nor what distance he had gone; still, the growing paleness of the flakes of light which he met from time to time indicated to him that the sun was retiring from the pavement, and that day would be soon ended, and the rolling of vehicles over his head, which had become intermittent instead of continuous, and then almost ceased, proved to him that he was no longer under central Paris, and was approaching some solitary region near the external boulevards or most distant quays, where there are fewer houses and streets, and the drain has fewer gratings. The obscurity thickened around Jean Valjean; still he continued to advance, groping his way in the shadow.

This shadow suddenly became terrible.

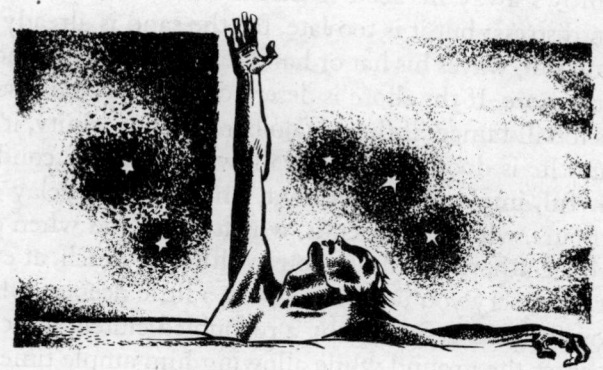

5. SAND, LIKE WOMAN, MAY BE SO FINE
AS TO BE PERFIDIOUS

HE felt that he was entering water, and that he had under his feet no longer stone, but mud. It often happens on certain coasts of Brittany or Scotland that a man, whether traveler or fisherman, traversing at low water the sands some distance from the coast, suddenly perceives that during the last few minutes he has found some difficulty in walking. The shore beneath his feet is like pitch, his heels are attached to it, it is no longer sand, but bird-lime; the bank is perfectly dry, but at every step taken, so soon as the foot is raised the imprint it leaves fills with water. The eye, however, has perceived no change, the immense expanse is smooth and calm, all the sand seems alike, nothing distinguishes the soil which is solid from that which is no longer so, and the little merry swarm of water-fleas continue to leap tumultuously round the feet of the wayfarer. The man follows his road, turns toward the land, and tries to approach the coast,—not that he is alarmed; alarmed at what? Still he feels as if the heaviness of his feet increased at every step he takes; all at once he sinks in, sinks in two or three inches. He is decidedly not on the right road, and stops to look about him. Suddenly he looks at his feet, but they have disappeared; the sand covers them. He draws his feet out of the sand and tries to turn back, but he sinks in deeper still. The sand comes up to his ankle; he pulls it out and turns to his left; when the sand comes to his knee, he turns to the right, and the sand comes up to his thigh; then he recognizes with indescribable terror that he is caught in a quicksand, and has under him the frightful medium in which a man can no more walk than a fish can swim. He throws away his load if he have one, and lightens himself like a ship in distress; but it is too late, for the sand is already above his knees. He calls out, waves his hat or handkerchief, but the sand gains on him more and more. If the shore is deserted, if land is too distant, if the quicksand is too ill-famed, if there is no hero in the vicinity, it is all over with him, and he is doomed to be swallowed up. He is condemned to that long, awful, implacable interment, impossible to delay or hasten, which lasts hours, which never ends, which seizes you when erect, free, and in perfect health, which drags you by the feet, which, at every effort you attempt, every cry you utter, drags you a little deeper; which seems to punish you for your resistance by a redoubled clutch, which makes a man slowly enter the ground while allowing him ample time to look at the houses, the trees, the green fields, the smoke from the villages on the plain, the sails of the vessels on the sea, the birds that fly and sing, the sun, and the sky. A quicksand is a sepulcher that converts itself into a tide, and ascends from the bottom of the earth toward a living man. Each minute is an inexorable grave-digger. The wretch tries to sit, to lie down, to walk, to crawl; all the movements that he makes bury him; he draws himself up, and only sinks deeper; he feels himself being swallowed up; he yells, implores, cries to the clouds, writhes his arms, and grows desperate. Then he is in the sand up to his waist; the sand reaches his chest, he is but a bust. He raises his hands, utters furious groans, digs his nails into the sand, tries to hold by this dust, raises himself on his elbows to grasp a weak sea-weed, and sobs frenziedly; but the sand mounts. It reaches his shoulders, it reaches his neck; the face alone is visible now. The mouth cries, and the sand fills it, and then there is a silence. The eyes still look, but the sand closes them, and there is night. Then the forehead sinks, and a little hair waves above the sand; a hand emerges, digs up the sand, is waved, and disappears. It is a sinister effacement of a man. At times the rider is swallowed up with his horse, at times the carter with his cart; it is a shipwreck otherwhere than in the water; it is the land drowning man. The land penetrated by the ocean becomes a snare; it presents itself as a plain, and opens like a wave. The abyss has its acts of treachery.

Such a mournful adventure, always possible on some sea-shore, was also possible some thirty years ago in the sewer of Paris. Before the important works began in 1833 the subway of Paris was subject to sudden breakings-in. The water filtered through a subjacent and peculiarly friable soil; and the road-way, if made of paving-stones, as in the old drains, or of concrete upon beton, as in the new galleries, having no support, bent. A bend in a road of this nature is a crevice, and a crevice is a bursting-in. The road-way broke away for a certain length, and such a gap, a gulf of mud, was called, in the special language of the sewer-men, *fontis*. What is a fontis? it is the quicksand of the sea-shore suddenly met with under-ground; it is the quicksand of Mount St. Michael in a sewer. The moistened soil is in a state of fusion, all its particles are held in suspense in a shifting medium; it is not land and it is not water. The depth is at times very great. Nothing can be more formidable than meeting with such a thing. If water predominate, death is quick, for a man is drowned; if earth predominate, death is slow, for he is sucked down.

Can our readers imagine such a death? if it be frightful to sink in a quicksand on the sea-shore, what is it in a cloaca? instead of fresh air, daylight, a clear horizon, vast sounds, the free clouds from which life rains, the bark perceived in the distance, that hope under every form, of possible passers-by, of possible help up to the last minute,—instead of all this, deafness, blindness, a black archway, the interior of a tomb already made, death in the mud under a tombstone! slow choking by ordure, a sarcophagus where asphyxia opens its claws in the filth and clutches you by the throat; fetidness mingled with the death-rattle, mud instead of sand, sulphureted hydrogen in lieu of the hurricane, a dung-heap instead of the ocean! and to call and gnash the teeth, and writhe and struggle and expire, with this enormous city which knows nothing of it above one's head.

Inexpressible the horror of dying thus! Death sometimes expiates its atrocity by a certain terrible dignity. On the pyre, in shipwreck, a man may be great; in the flames, as in the foam, a superb attitude is possible, and a man transfigures himself. But in this case it is not so; for the death is unclean. It is humiliating to expire in such a way, and the last floating visions are abject. Mud is the synonym of shame, and is little, ugly, and infamous. To die in a butt of Malmsey like Clarence—very well; but in a sewer like d'Escoubleau is horrible. To struggle in it is hideous, for at the same time as one is dying, one is wallowing. There is enough darkness for it to be Hell, and enough mud for it to be merely a slough, and the dying man does not know whether he is about to become a specter or a frog. Everywhere else the sepulcher is sinister, but here it is deformed.

The depth of the fontis varied, as did its length and its density, according to the nature of the subsoil. At times a fontis was three or four feet deep, at times eight or ten, and sometimes it was bottomless. In one the mud was almost solid, in another nearly liquid. In the Lunière fontis, a man would have taken a day in disappearing, while he would have been devoured in five minutes by the Phélippeaux slough. The mud bears more or less well according to its degree of density, and a lad escapes where a man is lost. The first law of safety is to throw away every sort of loading, and every sewer-man who felt the ground giving way under him began by getting rid of his basket of tools.

The fontis had various causes, friability of soil, some convulsion beyond man's depth, violent summer storms, the incessant winter rain, and long, fine showers. At times the weight of the surrounding houses upon a marshy or sandy soil broke the roofs of the subterranean galleries and made them shrink, or else it happened that the road-way broke and split up under the terrific pressure. The pile of the Pantheon destroyed in this way about a century ago a portion of the cellars in the Mount Ste. Geneviève. When a sewer gave way under the weight of the houses, the disorder was expressed above in the street by a sort of saw-toothed parting between the paving-stones. This rent was developed in a serpentine line along the whole length of the injured drain, and in such a case, the evil being visible, the remedy might be prompt. It often happened also that the internal ravage was not revealed by any scar outside, and in that case, woe to the sewer-men. Entering the injured drain incautiously, they might be lost in it. The old registers mention several sewer-men buried in this manner in the fontis. They give several names, among others that of the sewer-man swallowed up in a slough under the opening on the Rue Carême-Prenant, of the name of Blaise Poutrain; this Blaise was brother of Nicholas Poutrain, who was the last sexton of the cemetery called the Charnier des Innocents in 1785, when that cemetery expired. There was also the young and charming Vicomte d'Escoubleau, to whom we have alluded, one of the heroes of the siege of Lerida, where the assault was made in silk stockings and with violins at their head. D'Escoubleau, surprised one night with his cousin, the Duchesse de Sourdis, drowned himself in a cesspool of the Beautreillis drain, where he had taken refuge to escape the Duc. Madame de Sourdis, when informed of his death, asked for her smelling-bottle, and forgot to weep through inhaling her salts. In such a case, there is no love that holds out; the cloaca extinguishes it. Hero refuses to wash the corpse of Leander, the Thisbe stops her nose in the presence of Pyramus, saying, Peugh!

6. THE FONTIS

JEAN VALJEAN found himself in presence of a fontis: this sort of breaking-in was frequent at that day in the subsoil of the Champs Elysées, which was difficult to manage for hydraulic works, and most injurious to under-ground drains owing to its extreme fluidity. This fluidity exceeds even the looseness of sands of St. George's district, which could only be overcome by laying rubble on beton, and of the gas-infected clay strata in the Quartier des Martyrs, which are so liquid that a passage could only be effected under the Galerie des Martyrs by means of an iron tube. When in 1836 the authorities demolished and rebuilt under the Faubourg St. Honoré the old stone drain in which Jean Valjean is now engaged, the shifting sand which is the subsoil of the Champs Elysées as far as the Seine offered such an obstacle that the operation lasted six months, to the great annoyance of those living on the water-side, especially such as had mansions and coaches. The works were more than difficult, they were dangerous; but we must allow that it rained for four and a half months, and the Seine overflowed thrice.

The fontis which Jean Valjean came across was occasioned by the shower of the previous evening. A giving way of the pavement, which was badly supported by the subjacent sand, had produced a deposit of rain-water, and when the infiltration had taken place the ground broke in, and the road-way, being displaced, fell into the mud. How far? it was impossible to say, for the darkness was denser there than anywhere else; it was a slough of mud in a cavern of night. Jean Valjean felt the pavement depart from under him as he entered the slough; there was water at top and mud underneath. He must pass it, for it was impossible to turn back; Marius was dying, and Jean Valjean worn out. Where else could he go? Jean Valjean advanced; the slough appeared but of slight depth at the first few steps, but as he advanced his legs sank in. He soon had mud up to the middle of the leg, and water above the knee. He walked along, raising Marius with both arms as high as he could above the surface of the water; the mud now came up to his knees and the water to his waist. He could no longer draw back, and he sank in deeper and deeper. This mud, dense enough for the weight of one man, could not evidently bear two; Marius and Jean Valjean might have had a chance of getting out separately, but, for all that, Jean Valjean continued to advance, bearing the dying man, who was perhaps a corpse. The water came up to his armpits, and he felt himself drowning; he could scarce move in the depth of mud in which he was standing, for the density which was the support was also the obstacle. He still kept Marius up, and advanced with an extraordinary expenditure of strength, but he was sinking. He had only his head out of water and his two arms sustaining Marius. In some old paintings of the Deluge there is a mother holding her child in the same way. As he still sank, he threw back his face to escape the water and be able to breathe; any one who saw him in this darkness would have fancied he saw a mask floating on the gloomy waters. He vaguely perceived above him Marius's hanging head and livid face; he made a desperate effort, and advanced his foot, which struck against something solid, a resting-place. It was high time.

He drew himself up, and writhed and rooted himself with a species of fury upon this support. It produced on him the effect of the first step of a staircase re-ascending to life. This support met with in the mud, at the supreme moment, was the beginning of the other side of the road-way, which had fallen in without breaking, and bent under the water like a plank in a single piece. A well-constructed pavement forms a curve and possesses such firmness. This fragment of road-way, partly submerged, but solid, was a real incline, and once upon it they were saved. Jean Valjean ascended it, and attained the other side of the slough. On leaving the water his foot caught against a stone, and he fell on his knees. He found that this was just, and remained on them for some time, with his soul absorbed in words addressed to God.

He rose, shivering, chilled, bent beneath the dying man he carried, dripping with filth, but with his soul full of strange brightness.

7. WRECKED IN SIGHT OF PORT

HE set out once again; still, if he had not left his life in the fontis, he seemed to have left his strength there. This supreme effort had exhausted him, and his fatigue was now so great that he was obliged, every three or four paces, to take breath, and leaned against the wall. Once he had to sit down on the banquette in order to alter Marius's position, and believed that he should remain there. But if his vigor were dead, his energy was not so, and he rose again. He walked desperately, almost quickly, went thus one hundred yards without raising his head, almost without breathing, and all at once ran against the wall. He had reached an elbow of the drain, and on arriving head down at the turning came against the wall. He raised his eyes, and at the end of the passage down there, far, very far away, perceived a light. But this time it was no terrible light, but white, fair light. It was daylight. Jean Valjean saw the outlet. A condemned soul that suddenly saw from the middle of the furnace the issue from Gehenna would feel what Jean Valjean felt. It would fly wildly with the stumps of its burned wings toward the radiant gate. Jean Valjean no longer felt fatigue, he no longer felt Marius's weight, he found again his muscles of steel, and ran rather than walked. As he drew nearer, the outlet became more distinctly designed; it was an arch, not so tall as the roof, which gradually contracted, and not so wide as the gallery, which grew narrower at the same time as the roof became low-

ered. The tunnel finished inside in the shape of a funnel, a faulty reduction, imitated from the wickets of houses of correction, logical in a
prison, but illogical in a drain, and which has since been corrected.

Jean Valjean reached the issue and then stopped; it was certainly the
outlet, but they could not get out.

The arch was closed by a strong grating, and this grating, which apparently rarely turned on its oxidized hinges, was fastened to the stone
wall by a heavy lock, which, red with rust, seemed an enormous brick.
The key-hole was visible, as well as the bolt deeply plunged into its iron
box. It was one of those Bastille locks of which ancient Paris was so
prodigal. Beyond the gratings were the open air, the river, daylight, the
bank, very narrow, but sufficient to escape by; the distant quays, Paris,
that gulf in which a man hides himself so easily; the wide horizon, and
liberty. On the right could be distinguished, down the river, the Pont
de Jena, and up it the Pont des Invalides; the spot would have been a
favorable one to await night and escape. It was one of the most solitary
points in Paris, the bank facing the Gros-Caillou. The flies went in and
out through the grating-bars. It might be about half-past eight in the
evening, and day was drawing in; Jean Valjean laid Marius along the
wall on the dry part of the way, then walked up to the grating, and
seized the bars with both hands; the shock was frenzied, but the effect
null. The grating did not stir. Jean Valjean seized the bars one after the
other, hoping he might be able to break out the least substantial one,
and employ it as a lever to lift the gate off the hinges or break the lock,
but not a bar stirred. A tiger's teeth are not more solidly set in their
sockets. Without a lever it was impossible to open the grating, and the
obstacle was invincible.

Must he finish then, there? what should he do? what would become
of him? he had not the strength to turn back and recommence the
frightful journey which he had already made. Moreover, how was he
to cross again that slough from which he had only escaped by a miracle?
And after the slough, was there not the police squad, which he assuredly
would not escape twice; and then where should he go, and in what direction? following the slope would not lead to his object, for if he
reached another outlet he would find it obstructed by an iron plate or
a grating. All the issues were indubitably closed in that way; accident
had left the grating by which they entered open, but it was plain that
all the other mouths of the sewer were closed. They had only succeeded
in escaping into a prison.

It was all over, and all that Jean Valjean had done was useless: God opposed it. They were both caught in the dark and immense web of death, and Jean Valjean felt the fearful spider already running along the black threads in the darkness.

He turned his back to the grating and fell on the pavement near Marius, who was still motionless, and whose head had fallen between his knees. There was no outlet; that was the last drop of agony.

Of whom did he think in this profound despondency? Neither of himself nor of Marius! He thought of Cosette.

8. THE TORN COAT-SKIRT

In the midst of his annihilation a hand was laid on his shoulder and a low voice said:

"Half shares."

Some one in the shadow? As nothing so resembles a dream as despair, Jean Valjean fancied that he was dreaming. He had not heard a footstep. Was it possible? He raised his eyes, and a man was standing before him. This man was dressed in a blouse, his feet were naked, and he held his shoes in his hand; he had evidently taken them off in order to be able to reach Jean Valjean without letting his footsteps be heard. Jean Valjean had not a moment's hesitation; however unexpected the meeting might be, the man was known to him: it was Thénardier. Although, so to speak, aroused with a start, Jean Valjean, accustomed to alarms and to unexpected blows, which it is necessary to parry quickly, at once regained possession of all his presence of mind. Besides, the situation could not be worse; a certain degree of distress is not capable of any crescendo, and Thénardier himself could not add any blackness to this night. There was a moment's expectation. Thénardier, raising his right hand to the level of his forehead, made a screen of it; then he drew his eyebrows together with a wink, which, with a slight pinching of the lips, characterizes the sagacious attention of a man who is striving to recognize another. He did not succeed. Jean Valjean, as we said, was turning his back to the light, and was besides so disfigured, so filthy and blood-stained, that he could not have been recognized in broad daylight. On the other hand, Thénardier, with his face lit up by the light from the grating, a cellar brightness, it is true, livid but precise in his lividness, leaped at once into Jean Valjean's eyes, to employ the energetic popular metaphor. This inequality of conditions sufficed to insure some advantage to Jean Valjean in the mysterious duel which was about to begin between the two situations and the two men. The meeting took place between Jean Valjean masked and Thénardier unmasked. Jean Valjean at once perceived that Thénardier did not recognize him; and they looked at each other silently in this gloom, as if taking each other's measure. Thénardier was the first to break the silence.

"How do you mean to get out?"

Jean Valjean not replying, Thénardier continued:

"It is impossible to pick the lock; and yet you must get out of here."

"That is true," said Jean Valjean.

"Well, then, half shares."

"What do you mean?"

"You have killed the man, very good, and I have the key."

Thénardier pointed to Marius, and continued, "I do not know you, but you must be a friend, and I wish to help you."

Jean Valjean began to understand. Thénardier took him for an assassin. The latter continued:

"Listen, mate, you did not kill this man without looking to see what he had in his pockets. Give me my half and I open the gate."

And half drawing a heavy key from under his ragged blouse, he added: "Would you like to see how the 'key of the street' is made? Look here."

Jean Valjean was so astounded that he doubted whether what he saw was real. It was Providence appearing in a horrible form, and the good angel issuing from the ground in the shape of Thénardier. The latter thrust his hand into a wide pocket hidden under his blouse, drew out a rope, and handed it to Jean Valjean.

"There," he said, "I give you the rope in the bargain."

"What am I to do with a rope?"

"You also want a stone, but you will find that outside, as there is a heap of them."

"What am I to do with a stone?"

"Why, you ass, as you are going to throw the cove into the river, you want a rope and a stone, or else the body will float on the water."

Jean Valjean took the rope mechanically, and Thénardier snapped his fingers as if a sudden idea had occurred to him.

"Hilloh, mate, how did you manage to get through that slough? I did not dare venture into it. Peugh! you do not smell pleasant."

After a pause he added:

"I ask you questions, but you are right not to answer; it is an apprenticeship for the magistrate's ugly quarter of an hour. And then, by not speaking at all a man runs no risk of speaking too loud. No matter, though I cannot see your face and do not know your name, you would do wrong in supposing that I do not know who you are and what you want. I know all about it; you have smashed that swell a little, and now want to get rid of him somewhere. You prefer the river, that great nonsense-hider, and I will help you out of the hobble. It is my delight to aid a good fellow when in trouble."

While commending Jean Valjean for his silence, it was plain that he was trying to make him speak. He pushed his shoulder, so as to be able to see his profile, and exclaimed, though without raising the pitch of his voice:

"Talking of the slough, you are a precious ass. Why did you not throw the man into it?"

Jean Valjean preserved silence. Thénardier continued, raising his rag of a cravat to the Adam's apple, a gesture which completes the capable air of a serious man:

"Really, you may have acted sensibly, for the workmen coming to-morrow to stop up the hole would certainly have found the swell, and your trail would be followed up. Some one has passed through the sewer; who? how did he get out? was he seen to do so? The police are full of sense; the drain is a traitor, and denounces you. Such a find is a rarity, it attracts attention, for few people employ the sewer for their little business, while the river belongs to everybody, and is the real grave. At the end of a month your man is fished up at the nets of St. Cloud; well, who troubles himself about that? it's cold meat, that's all. Who killed the man? Paris, and justice makes no inquiries. You acted wisely."

The more loquacious Thénardier became, the more silent Jean Valjean was. Thénardier shook his shoulder again. "And now let's settle our business. You have seen my key, so show me your money."

Thénardier was haggard, firm, slightly menacing, but remarkably friendly. There was one strange fact: Thénardier's manner was not simple; he did not appear entirely at his ease; while not affecting any mysterious air, he spoke in a low voice. From time to time he laid his finger on his lip, and muttered, "Chut!" it was difficult to guess why, for there were only themselves present. Jean Valjean thought that other bandits were probably hidden in some corner no great distance off, and that Thénardier was not anxious to share with them. The latter continued:

"Now for a finish. How much had the swell about him?"

Jean Valjean felt in his pockets. It was, as will be remembered, always his rule to have money about him, for the gloomy life of expedients to which he was condemned rendered it a law for him. This time, however, he was unprovided. In putting on, upon the previous evening, his National Guard uniform, he forgot, mournfully absorbed as he was, to take out his pocket-book, and he had only some change in his waistcoat-pocket. He turned out his pocket, which was saturated with slime, and laid on the banquette a louis d'or, two five-franc pieces, and five or six double sous. Thénardier thrust out his lower lip with a significant twist of the neck.

"You did not kill him for much," he said.

He began most familiarly feeling in Jean Valjean's and Marius's pockets, and Jean Valjean, who was most anxious to keep his back to the light, allowed him to do so. While feeling in Marius's coat, Thénardier, with the dexterity of a conjurer, managed to tear off, without Jean Valjean perceiving the fact, a strip, which he concealed under his blouse; probably thinking that this piece of cloth might help him to recognize hereafter the assassinated man and the assassin. However, he found no more than the thirty francs.

"It is true," he said; "one with the other, you have no more than that."

And, forgetting his phrase half shares, he took all. He hesitated a little at the double sous, but on reflection he took them too, while grumbling, "I don't care; it is killing people too cheaply."

This done, he again took the key from under his blouse.

"Now, my friend, you must be off. It is here as at the fairs; you pay when you go out. You have paid, so you can go."

And he began laughing. We may be permitted to doubt whether he had the pure and disinterested intention of saving an assassin, when he gave a stranger the help of this key, and allowed any one but himself to pass through this gate. Thénardier helped Jean Valjean to replace Marius on his back, and then proceeded to the grating on the tips of his naked feet. After making Jean Valjean a sign to follow him, he placed his finger on his lip, and remained for some seconds as if in suspense; but when the inspection was over he put the key in the lock. The bolt slid, and the gate turned on its hinges without grinding or creaking. It was plain that this grating and these hinges, carefully oiled, opened more frequently than might be supposed. This ease was ill-omened; it spoke of furtive comings and goings, of the mysterious entrances and exits of night-men, and the crafty foot-fall of crime. The sewer was evidently an accomplice of some dark band, and this taciturn grating was a receiver.

Thénardier held the door ajar, left just room for Jean Valjean to pass, relocked the gate, and plunged back into the darkness, making no more noise than a breath; he seemed to walk with the velvety pads of a tiger.

A moment later this hideous providence had disappeared, and Jean Valjean was outside.

9. *MARIUS APPEARS DEAD TO AN EXPERT*

He let Marius slip down on to the bank. They were outside; the miasmas, the darkness, the horror were behind him; the healthy, pure, living, joyous, freely respirable air inundated him. All around him was silence, but it was the charming silence of the sun setting in the full azure. Twilight was passing, and night, the great liberator, the friend of all those who need a cloak of darkness to escape from an agony, was at hand. The sky presented itself on all sides like an enormous calm, and the river rippled up to his feet with the sound of a kiss. The aerial dialogue of the nests bidding each other good-night in the elms of the Champs Elysées was audible. A few stars, faintly studding the pale blue of the zenith, formed in the immensity little imperceptible flashes. Night unfolded over Jean Valjean's head all the sweetness of infinitude.

It was the undecided and exquisite hour which says neither yes nor no. There was already sufficient light for a man to lose himself in it a short distance off, and yet sufficient daylight to recognize any one close by.

Jean Valjean was for a few seconds irresistibly overcome by all this august and caressing serenity. There are minutes of oblivion in which suffering gives up harassing the wretch; all is eclipsed in thought; peace covers the dreamer like night, and under the gleaming twilight the soul shines starry in imitation of the sky which is becoming illumined. Jean Valjean could not refrain from contemplating the vast clear shade which he had above him, and pensively took a bath of ecstasy and prayer in the majestic silence of the eternal heavens. Then, as if the feeling of duty returned to him, he eagerly bent down over Marius, and, lifting some water in the hollow of his hand, softly threw a few drops into his face. Marius's eyelids did not move, but he still breathed through his parted lips. Jean Valjean was again about to plunge his hand into the river, when he suddenly felt that strange sensation as when we feel there is some one behind us though we cannot see him. He turned round, and there was really some one behind him, and there had been just before.

A man of tall stature, dressed in a long coat, with folded arms, and carrying in his right hand a cudgel, whose leaden knob could be seen, was standing a few paces behind Jean Valjean, who was leaning over Marius. It was, with the help of the darkness, a species of apparition. Any simple man would have been frightened at it owing to the twilight, and a thoughtful one on account of the bludgeon. Jean Valjean recognized Javert. The reader has doubtless guessed that the tracker of Thénardier was no other than Javert. Javert, after his unhoped-for escape from the barricade, went to the prefecture of police, made a verbal report to the prefect in person in a short audience, and then immediately returned to duty, which implied—the note found on him will be remembered—a certain surveillance of the right bank of the river at Champs Elysées, which had for some time past attracted the attention of the police. There he perceived Thénardier and followed him. The rest is known.

It will be also understood that the grating so obligingly opened for Jean Valjean was a clever trick on the part of Thénardier. He felt that Javert was still there; the man watched has a scent which never deceives him; and it was necessary to throw a bone to this greyhound. An assassin—what a chance! he could not let it slip. Thénardier, on putting Jean Valjean outside in his place, offered a prey to the policeman, made him loose his hold, caused himself to be forgotten in a greater adventure, recompensed Javert for his loss of time, which always flatters a spy, gained thirty francs, and fully intended, for his own part, to escape by the help of this diversion.

Jean Valjean had passed from one shoal to another; these two meetings, one upon the other, falling from Thénardier on Javert, were rude. Javert did not recognize Jean Valjean, who, as we have said, no longer resembled himself. He did not unfold his arms, but secured his grasp of his life-preserver by an imperceptible movement, and said in a sharp, calm voice:

"Who are you?"

"Myself."

"What do you mean?"

"I am Jean Valjean."

Javert placed his life-preserver between his teeth, bent his knees, bowed his back, laid his two powerful hands on Jean Valjean's shoulders, which they held as in two vises, examined and recognized him. Their faces almost touched, and Javert's glance was terrific. Jean Valjean remained inert under Javert's gripe, like a lion enduring the claw of a lynx.

"Inspector Javert," he said, "you have me. Besides, since this morning I have considered myself your prisoner. I did not give you my address in order to try and escape you. Take me, but grant me one thing."

Javert did not seem to hear, but kept his eyeballs fixed on Jean Valjean. His wrinkled chin thrust up his lips toward his nose, a sign of stern reverie. At length he loosed his hold of Jean Valjean, drew himself up, clutched his life-preserver, and, as if in a dream, muttered rather than asked this question:

"What are you doing here? who is that man?"

Jean Valjean replied, and the sound of his voice seemed to awaken Javert:

"It is of him that I wish to speak. Do with me as you please, but help me first to carry him home. I only ask this of you."

Javert's face was contracted in the same way as it always was when any one believed him capable of a concession; still he did not say no.

He stooped again, took from his pocket a handkerchief, which he dipped in the water, and wiped Marius's ensanguined forehead.

"This man was at the barricade," he said in a low voice, and as if speaking to himself, "he was the one whom they called Marius."

He was a first-class spy, who had observed everything, listened to everything, heard everything, and picked up everything when he believed himself about to die; who even in his death agony was a spy, and, standing on the first step of the sepulcher, took notes. He seized Marius's hand and felt his pulse.

"He is wounded," said Jean Valjean.

"He is a dead man," said Javert.

Jean Valjean replied:

"No; not yet."

"Then you brought him from the barricade here?" Javert observed.

His preoccupation must have been great for him not to dwell on this alarming escape through the sewers, and not even remark Jean Valjean's silence after his question. Jean Valjean, on his side, seemed to have a sole thought; he continued:

"He lives in the Marais, in the Rue des Filles du Calvaire, with his grandfather. I do not know his name."

Jean Valjean felt in Marius's pocket, took out the pocket-book, opened it at the page on which Marius had written in pencil, and offered it to Javert. There was still sufficient floating light in the air to be able to read, and Javert besides had in his eyes the feline phosphorescence of night-birds. He deciphered the few lines written by Marius, and growled, "Gillenormand, No. 6, Rue des Filles du Calvaire." Then he cried, "Driver!"

Our readers will remember the coachman waiting above in case of need. A moment after the hackney, which came down the incline leading to the watering-place, was on the bank. Marius was deposited on the back seat, and Javert sat down by Jean Valjean's side on the front one. When the door was closed the fiacre started off rapidly along the quays in the direction of the Bastille. They quitted the quay and turned into the streets; and the driver, a black outline on his seat, lashed his lean horses. There was an icy silence in the hackney-coach; Marius motionless, with his body reclining in one corner, his head on his chest, his arms pendent, and his legs stiff, appeared to be only waiting for a coffin; Jean Valjean seemed made of gloom, and Javert of stone; and in this fiacre full of night, whose interior, each time that it passed a lamp, seemed to be lividly lit up as if by an intermittent flash, accident united and appeared to confront the three immobilities of tragedy,— the corpse, the specter, and the statue.

10. *RETURN OF THE SON PRODIGAL OF HIS LIFE*

AT each jolt over the pavement a drop of blood fell from Marius's hair. It was quite night when the hackney-coach reached No. 6, Rue des Filles du Calvaire.

Javert got out first, examined at a glance the number over the gateway, and raising the heavy knocker of hammered steel, adorned in the old style with a goat and a satyr contending, gave a violent knock. The folding-door opened slightly, and Javert pushed it open. The porter half-showed himself, yawning, and scarce awake, candle in hand. All were asleep in the house, for people go to bed early at the Marais, especially on days of rioting. This good old district, terrified by the revolution, takes refuge in sleep, like children who, when they hear old Boguey coming, quickly hide their heads under the counterpane.

In the meanwhile Jean Valjean and the driver removed Marius from the hackney-coach, Valjean holding him under the armpits, and the coachman under the knees. While carrying Marius in this way, Jean Valjean passed his hands under his clothes, which were terribly torn, felt his chest, and assured himself that his heart still beat. It even beat a little less feebly, as if the motion of the vehicle had produced a certain return to life. Javert addressed the porter in the tone which becomes the government in the presence of the porter of a man who belongs to a faction.

"Any one live here of the name of Gillenormand?"

"It is here. What do you want with him?"

"We have brought home his son."

"His son?" the porter asked in amazement.

"He is dead."

Jean Valjean, who followed, ragged and filthy, behind Javert, and whom the porter regarded with some horror, made him a sign that it was not so. The porter seemed neither to understand Javert's remark nor Jean Valjean's motion. Javert continued:

"He has been to the barricade, and here he is."

"To the barricade!" the porter exclaimed.

"He has been killed. Go and wake his father."

The porter did not stir.

"Go!" Javert continued, and added, "There will be a funeral here to-morrow."

For Javert, the ordinary incidents of the streets were classified categorically, which is the commencement of foresight and surveillance, and each eventuality had its compartment; the possible facts were to some extent kept in drawers, whence they issued on occasions in variable quantities; there were in the streets, disturbance, riot, carnival, and interments.

The porter limited himself to awaking Basque; Basque awoke Nicolette; Nicolette awoke Aunt Gillenormand. As for the grandfather, he was left to sleep, as it was thought that he would know the affair quite soon enough.

Marius was carried to the second-floor, no one being acquainted with the fact in the rest of the house, and he was laid on an old sofa in M. Gillenormand's anteroom, and, while Basque went to fetch a physician and Nicolette opened the linen-presses, Jean Valjean felt Javert touch his shoulder. He understood, and went down, Javert following close at his heels. The porter saw them depart, as he had seen them arrive, with a startled sleepiness. They got into the hackney-coach, and the driver on his box.

"Inspector Javert," Jean Valjean said, "grant me one thing more."

"What is it?" Javert answered roughly.

"Let me go home for a moment, and you can then do with me what you please."

Javert remained silent for a few moments with his chin thrust into the collar of his great-coat, and then let down the front window.

"Driver," he said, "No. 7 Rue de l'Homme Armé."

11. *A SHOCK TO THE ABSOLUTE*

THEY did not speak during the entire ride. What did Jean Valjean want? to finish what he had begun; to warn Cosette, tell her where Marius was, give her perhaps some other useful information, and make, if he could, certain final arrangements. For his own part, as regarded what concerned him personally, it was all over; he had been arrested by Javert, and did not resist. Any other than he, in such a situation, would perhaps have vaguely thought of the rope which Thénardier had given him, and the bars of the first cell he entered; but since his meeting with the bishop Jean Valjean had within him a profound religious hesitation against every assault, even on himself. Suicide, that mysterious attack on the unknown, which may contain to a certain extent the death of the soul, was impossible to Jean Valjean.

On entering the Rue de l'Homme Armé the coach stopped, as the street was too narrow for vehicles to pass along it. Jean Valjean and Javert got out. The driver humbly represented to "Mr. Inspector" that the Utrecht velvet of his coach was quite spoiled by the blood of the assassinated man and the filth of the assassin,—that is how he understood the affair,—and he added that an indemnity was due to him. At the same time, taking his license-book from his pocket, he begged "Mr. Inspector" to have the kindness to write him a little bit of a certificate.

Javert thrust back the book which the driver offered him, and said:

"How much do you want, including the time you waited and the journey?"

"It's seven hours and a quarter," the driver answered, "and my velvet was brand-new. Eighty francs, 'Mr. Inspector'."

Javert took from his pocket four napoleons, and dismissed the hackney-coach. Jean Valjean thought that it was Javert's intention to take him on foot to the Blancs Manteaux post, or that of the Archives, which are close by. They entered the street, which was as usual deserted. Javert followed Jean Valjean, and, on reaching No. 7, the latter rapped, and the gate opened.

"Very good," said Javert, "go up."

He added, with a strange expression, and as if making an effort to speak as he was doing:

"I will wait for you here."

Jean Valjean looked at Javert, for this style of conduct was not at all a habit of Javert's. Still, it could not surprise him greatly that Javert should now place in him a sort of haughty confidence, the confidence of the cat which grants the mouse liberty to the length of its claw. Resolved, as he was, to have done with it all, this could not surprise him. He thrust open the gate, entered the house, shouted to the porter, who was in bed and had pulled the string, "It is I," and mounted the staircase. On reaching the first story he paused, for every Via Dolorosa has its stations. The window, a sash-window, was open, and, as is the case in many old houses, the staircase obtained light from, and looked out on, the street. The street-lantern, situated precisely opposite, threw some little light on the stairs, which caused a saving of a lamp. Jean Valjean, either to breathe, or mechanically, thrust his head out of this window and looked down into the street. It is short, and the lamp lit it from one end to the other. Jean Valjean had a bedazzlement of stupor; there was no one in it.

Javert had gone away.

12 . *THE GRANDFATHER*

BASQUE and the porter had carried Marius, who was still lying motionless on the sofa on which he had been laid on arriving, into the drawing-room. The physician, who had been sent for, hurried in, and Aunt Gillenormand had risen. Aunt Gillenormand came and went, horrified, clasping her hands, and incapable of doing anything, but saying, "Can it be possible?" She added at intervals, "Everything will be stained with blood." When the first horror had passed away, a certain philosophy of the situation appeared even in her mind, and was translated by the exclamation, "It must end in this way." She did not go so far, though, as *Did I not say so?* which is usual on occasions of this nature.

By the surgeon's orders a cot-bed was put up near the sofa. He examined Marius, and after satisfying himself that the pulse still beat, that the patient had no penetrating wound in the chest, and that the blood at the corners of the lips came from the nostrils, he had him laid flat on the bed, without a pillow, the head level with the body, and even a little lower, and with naked chest, in order to facilitate the breathing. Mademoiselle Gillenormand, seeing that Marius was being undressed, withdrew, and told her beads in her bedroom. The body had received no internal injury; a ball, deadened by the pocket-book, had deviated and passed around the ribs with a frightful gash, but as it was not deep it was, therefore, not dangerous. The long subterranean march had completed the dislocation of the broken collar-bone, and there were serious injuries there. The arms were covered with saber-cuts; no scar disfigured the face, but the head was cut all over with gashes; what would be the state of these wounds on the head? did they stop at the scalp or did they reach the brain? it was impossible to say yet. It was a serious symptom that they had caused the faintness. And men do not always awake from such fainting-fits; the hemorrhage, moreover, had exhausted the wounded man. From the waist downward the lower part of the body had been protected by the barricade.

Basque and Nicolette tore up linen and prepared bandages; Nicolette sewed them and Basque rolled them. As they had no lint, the physician had temporarily checked the effusion of blood with cakes of wadding. By the side of the bed, three candles burned on the table on which the surgeon's pocket-book lay open. He washed Marius's face and hair with cold water, and a bucketful was red in an instant. The porter, candle in hand, lighted him.

The surgeon seemed to be thinking sadly; from time to time he gave a negative shake of the head, as if answering some question which he mentally addressed to himself. Such mysterious dialogues of the physician with himself are a bad sign for the patient. At the moment when the surgeon was wiping the face and gently touching with his finger the still closed eyelids, a door opened at the end of the room, and a tall, pale figure appeared,—it was the grandfather. The riot during the last two days had greatly agitated, offended, and occupied M. Gillenormand; he had not been able to sleep on the previous night, and he had been feverish all day. At night he went to bed at a very early hour, bidding his people bar up the house, and had fallen asleep through weariness.

Old men have a fragile sleep. M. Gillenormand's bedroom joined the drawing-room, and, whatever precautions had been taken, the noise awoke him. Surprised by the crack of light which he saw in his door, he had got out of bed and groped his way to the door. He was standing on the threshold, with one hand on the handle, his head slightly bent forward and shaking, his body enfolded in a white dressing-gown, as straight and creaseless as a winding-sheet: he was surprised, and looked like a ghost peering into a tomb. He noticed the bed, and on the mattress this young bleeding man, of the whiteness of snow, with closed eyes, open mouth, livid cheeks, naked to the waist, marked all over with vermilion wounds, motionless, and brightly illumined.

The grandfather had from head to foot that shudder which ossified limbs can have. His eyes, whose cornea was yellow owing to their great age, were veiled by a sort of glassy stare; his entire face assumed in an instant the earthly angles of a skeleton's head; his arms fell pendent as if a spring had been broken in them, and his stupor was displayed by the outspreading of all the fingers of his two old trembling hands. His knees formed a salient angle, displaying through the opening of his dressing-gown his poor naked legs bristling with white hairs, and he murmured:

"Marius!"

"He has just been brought here, sir," said Basque; "he went to the barricade and—"

"He is dead," the old gentleman exclaimed, in a terrible voice. "Oh! the brigand!"

Then a sort of sepulchral transfiguration drew up this centenarian as straight as a young man.

"You are the surgeon, sir," he said; "begin by telling me one thing. He is dead, is he not?"

The surgeon, who was frightfully anxious, maintained silence, and M. Gillenormand writhed his hands with a burst of terrifying laughter.

"He is dead, he is dead! he has let himself be killed at the barricade through hatred of me; it was against me that he did it! ah, the blood-drinker, that is the way in which he returns to me. Woe of my life, he is dead!"

He went to a window, opened it quite wide, as if he were stifling, and standing there began speaking to the night in the street.

"Stabbed, sabered, massacred, exterminated, slashed, cut to pieces! Do you see that, the beggar! he knew very well that I expected him, and that I had his room ready, and that I had placed at my bed-head his portrait when he was a child! He knew very well that he need only return, and that for years I had been recalling him, and that I sat at night by my fireside with my hands on my knees, not knowing what to do, and that I was crazy about him! You knew that very well, you had only to return and say, 'It is I,' and you would be the master of the house, and I would obey you, and you could do anything you liked with your old ass of a grandfather! You knew it very well, and said, 'No, he is a royalist; I will not go!' and you went to the barricades, and have let yourself be killed out of spite! in order to revenge yourself for what I said on the subject of Monsieur le Duc de Berry! Is not that infamous? Go to bed and sleep quietly, for he is dead. This is my awaking."

The surgeon, who was beginning to be anxious for both, left Marius, and, going up to M. Gillenormand, took his arm. The grandfather turned, looked at him with eyes that seemed dilated and blood-shot, and calmly said:

"I thank you, sir, I am calm; I am a man; I saw the death of Louis XVI, and can endure events. There is one thing that is terrible,—it is the thought that it is your newspapers which do all the mischief. You have scribblers, speakers, lawyers, orators, tribunes, discussions, progress, lights, rights of man, liberty of the press; and this is the way in which your children are brought back to your houses. O Marius, it is abominable! killed! dead before me! a barricade! oh, the bandit! Doctor, you live in the quarter, I believe? Oh, yes, I know you well. From my window I see your cab pass. Well, I will tell you. You would do wrong to believe that I am in a passion, for people do not get in a passion with a dead man; that would be stupid. This is a boy I brought up; I was old when he was still quite little. He played in the Tuileries with his little spade and his little chair, and, in order that the inspectors should not scold, I used to fill up with my cane the holes which he made with his spade. One day he cried, 'Down with Louis XVIII!' and went off. It is not my fault. He was all pink and white, and his mother is dead; have you noticed that all little children are light-haired? Supposing that he is a son of one of those brigands of the Loire, children are innocent of their fathers' crimes. I remember him when he was so high, and he could never manage to pronounce a d. He spoke so sweetly and incomprehensibly that you might have fancied him a bird. I remember one day that a circle was formed in front of Farnese Hercules to admire that child, for he was so lovely. He had a head such as you see in pictures. I used to speak loud to him, and threaten him with my cane, but he knew very well that it was a joke. In the morning, when he entered my room, I scolded, but it produced the effect of sunshine upon me. It is not possible to defend yourself against these brats, for they take you, and hold you, and do not let you go again. It is the fact that there never was a Cupid like that child, and now what do you say of your Lafayette, your Benjamin Constant, and your Tirecuir de Corcelles, who kill him for me? oh, it cannot end like that."

He went up to Marius, who was still livid and motionless, and to whom the surgeon had returned, and he began wringing his arms again. The old gentleman's white lips moved, as it were, mechanically, and allowed indistinct sentences to pass, which were scarce audible. "Ah, heartless, ah! clubbist! ah, scoundrel! ah, Septembrist!" reproaches uttered in a low voice by a dying man to a corpse. By degrees, as such internal eruptions must always burst forth, the flood of words returned, but the grandfather seemed no longer to have the strength to utter them; his voice was so hollow and choked that it seemed to come from the other brink of an abyss.

"I do not care a bit, I will die too. And then to think there is not a she-devil in Paris who would not be happy to produce the happiness of that scoundrel, a scamp, who, instead of amusing himself and enjoying life, went to fight, and let himself be shot like a brute! and for whom, and for what? for the republic! instead of going to dance at the Chaumière, as is the duty of young men. It is really worth while being twenty years of age. The republic, a fine absurdity! Poor mothers bring pretty boys into the world for that! Well, he is dead; that will make two hearses under the gate-way. So you have got yourself served in that way for love of General Lamarque! What did General Lamarque do for you? a saberer! a chatterer! to get one's self killed for a dead man! is it not enough to drive one mad? Can you understand that? at twenty! and without turning his head to see whether he left anything behind him! Now, see the poor old fellows who are obliged to die all alone. Rot in your corner, owl! Well, after all, that is what I hoped for, and is for the best, as it will kill me right off. I am too old, I am one hundred, I am a hundred thousand, and I had a right to be dead long ago. Well, this blow settles it; it is all over, what happiness! what is the use of making him inhale ammonia and all that pile of drugs? you ass of a doctor, you are wasting your time. There, he's dead, quite dead. I know it, for I am dead too. He did not do the thing by halves. Yes, the present age is infamous, infamous, infamous, and that is what I think of you, your ideas, your systems, your masters, your oracles, your doctors, your scamps of writers, your rogues of philosophers, and all the revolutions which have startled the Tuileries ravens during the last sixty years. And since you were pitiless in letting yourself be killed so, I will not even feel sorry at your death; do you hear, assassin?"

At this moment Marius slowly opened his eyes, and his glance, still veiled by lethargic surprise, settled on M. Gillenormand.

"Marius!" the old man cried. "Marius, my little Marius! my child! my beloved son! you open your eyes! you look at me! you are alive! thanks!"

And he fell down in a fainting-fit.

BOOK IV

JAVERT DERAILED

1. JAVERT OFF THE TRACK

JAVERT retired slowly from the Rue de l'Homme Armé. He walked with drooping head for the first time in his life, and, equally for the first time in his life, with his hands behind his back. Up to that day Javert had only assumed, of Napoleon's two attitudes, the one which expresses resolution, the arms folded on the chest; the one indicating uncertainty, the arms behind the back, was unknown to him. Now a change had taken place, and his whole person, slow and somber, was stamped with anxiety. He buried himself in the silent streets, but followed a certain direction; he went by the shortest road to the Seine, reached the Quai des Ormes, walked along it, passed the Grève, and stopped, a little distance from the Châtelet Square, at the corner of the Pont Notre Dame. The Seine makes there, between that bridge and the Pont au Change on one side, and the Quai de la Mégisserie and the Quai aux Fleurs on the other, a species of square lake traversed by a rapid. This point of the Seine is feared by boatmen; nothing can be more dangerous than this rapid, which just then was contracted and irritated by the stakes of the mill-bridge, since demolished. The two bridges, so close to each other, heighten the danger, for the water hurries formidably through the arches. It rolls in large folds, it is heaped up and piled up; the stream strives to pull away the piles of the bridge with its strong liquid cords. Men who fall in there do not re-appear, and the best swimmers are drowned.

Javert leaned his elbows on the parapet, his chin on his hand, and while his hands mechanically closed on his thick whiskers, he reflected. A novelty, a revolution, a catastrophe had just taken place within him, and he must examine into it. Javert was suffering horribly, and for some hours past Javert had ceased to be simple. He was troubled; this brain, so limpid in its blindness, had lost its transparency, and there was a cloud in this crystal. Javert felt in his conscience that duty was doubled, and he could not hide the fact from himself. When he met Jean Valjean so unexpectedly on the Seine bank, he had something within him of the wolf that recaptures his prey and the dog that finds its master again.

He saw before him two roads, both equally straight, but he saw two of them, and this terrified him, as he had never known in his life but one straight line. And, poignant agony, these two roads were contrary, and one of these right lines excluded the other. Which of the two was the true one? His situation was indescribable: to owe his life to a malefactor, to accept this debt and repay him; to be, in spite of himself, on the same footing with an escaped convict, and requite one service with another service; to let it be said to him, Be off, and to say in his turn, Be free; to sacrifice to personal motives duty, that general obligation, and to feel in these personal motives something general too, and perhaps superior; to betray society in order to remain faithful to his conscience—that all these absurdities should be realized, and accumulated upon him, was what startled him.

One thing had astonished him—that Jean Valjean had shown him mercy; and one thing had petrified him—that he, Javert, had shown mercy to Jean Valjean.

Where was he? he sought and no longer found himself. What was he to do now? to give up Jean Valjean was bad, to leave Jean Valjean at liberty was bad. In the former case, the man of authority fell lower than the man of the galleys; in the second, a convict rose higher than the law, and set his foot upon it. In either case, dishonor for him, Javert. Whatever resolution he might form, there was a fall, for destiny has certain extremities projecting over the impossible, beyond which life is only a precipice. Javert had reached one of these extremities; one of his anxieties was to be constrained to think, and the very violence of all these contradictory emotions compelled him to do so. Now, thought was an unusual thing for him, and singularly painful. There is always in thought a certain amount of internal rebellion, and he was irritated at having that within him. Thought, no matter on what subject beyond the narrow circle of his duties, would have been to him in any case useless and wearisome, but thinking about the day which had just passed was a torture. And yet he must after such shocks look into his conscience and give himself an account of himself. What he had done caused him to shudder. He, Javert, had thought fit to decide against all police regulations, against all social and judicial organization, and against the entire codes, for a discharge: that had suited him; he had substituted his own affairs for public affairs,—was not that unjustifiable? Each time that he stood facing the nameless action which he had committed, he trembled from head to foot. What should he resolve on? Only one resource was left to him, to return at full speed to the Rue de l'Homme Armé and lock up Jean Valjean. It was clear that this was what he ought to do, but he could not do it. Something barred the way on that side. What! is there anything in the world besides sentences, the police, and the authorities? Javert was overwhelmed.

A sacred galley-slave! a convict impregnable by justice, and that through the deed of Javert! Was it not frightful that Javert and Jean Valjean, the man made to punish and the man made to endure, that these two men, who were both the property of the law, should have reached the point of placing themselves both above the law? What? such enormities could happen and no one be punished? Jean Valjean, stronger than the whole social order, would be free, and he, Javert, would continue to eat the bread of the government! His reverie gradually became terrible: he might through this reverie have reproached himself slightly on the subject of the insurgent carried home to the Rue des Filles du Calvaire, but he did not think of it. The slighter fault was lost in the greater, and besides, this insurgent was evidently a dead man, and, legally, death checks prosecution. Jean Valjean,—that was the weight which he had on his mind, and he disconcerted him. All the axioms which had been the support of his whole life crumbled away before this man, and the generosity of Jean Valjean to him, Javert, overwhelmed him. Other facts which he remembered, and which he had formerly treated as falsehoods and folly, now returned to his mind as realities. M. Madeleine reappeared behind Jean Valjean, and the two figures were blended into one, which was venerable. Javert felt that something horrible—admiration for a convict—was entering his soul. Respect for a galley-slave, is it possible? he shuddered at it, and could not escape from it, although he struggled! he was reduced to confess in his soul the sublimity of this villain, and this was odious. A benevolent malefactor, a compassionate, gentle, helping, and merciful convict, repaying good for evil, pardon for hatred, preferring pity to vengeance, ready to destroy himself sooner than his enemy, saving the man who had struck him, kneeling on the pinnacle of virtue, and nearer to the angels than to man. Javert was constrained to confess to himself that such a monster existed.

This could not last. Assuredly—and we lay stress on the fact—he had not yielded without resistance to this monster, to this infamous angel, to this hideous hero, at whom he felt almost as indignant as stupefied. Twenty times, while in that hackney-coach face to face with Jean Valjean, the legal tiger had roared within him. Twenty times he had felt tempted to hurl himself on Jean Valjean, to seize and devour him; that is to say, arrest him. What more simple, in fact! shout to the nearest post before which he passed, "Here is a convict who has broken his ban!" and then go away leaving the condemned man there, be ignorant of the rest, and interfere no further. This man is eternally the prisoner of the law, and the law will do what it pleases with him. What was fairer? Javert had said all this to himself, he had wished to go further, to act, to apprehend the man, and then, as now, he had been unable; and each time that his hand was convulsively raised to Jean Valjean's collar, it fell back as if under an enormous weight, and he heard in the bottom of his heart, a voice, a strange voice, crying to him, "That is well. Give up your saviour; then send for Pontius Pilate's basin, and wash your hands in it."

Then his thoughts reverted to himself, and by the side of Jean Valjean aggrandized he saw himself degraded. A convict was his benefactor, but why had he allowed that man to let him live? he had the right of being killed at that barricade, and should have employed that right. It would have been better to call the other insurgents to his aid against Jean Valjean, and have himself shot by force. His supreme agony was the disappearance of certainty, and he felt himself uprooted. The code was now only a stump in his hand, and he had to deal with scruples of an unknown species. There was within him a sentimental revelation entirely distinct from the legal affirmation, his sole measure hitherto, and it was not sufficient to remain in his old honesty. A whole order of unexpected facts arose and subjugated him, an entire new world appeared to his soul; benefits accepted and returned, devotion, mercy, indulgence, violence done by pity to austerity, no more definitive condemnation, no more damnation, the possibility of a tear in the eye of the law, and perhaps some justice according to God acting in an inverse ratio to justice according to man. He perceived in the darkness the rising of an unknown moral sun, and he was horrified and dazzled. He was an owl forced to look like the eagle.

He said to himself that it was true, then, that there were exceptions, that authority might be disconcerted, that the rule might fall short in the presence of a fact, that everything was not contained in the text of a code, that the unforeseen made itself obeyed, that the virtue of a convict might set a snare for the virtue of a functionary, that the monstrous might be divine, that destiny had such ambuscades, and he thought with despair that he had himself not been protected from a surprise. He was compelled to recognize that goodness existed; this galley-slave had been good, and he, too, extraordinary to say, had been good also. Hence he was becoming depraved. He felt that he was a coward, and it horrified him. The ideal for Javert was not to be human, grand, or sublime; it was to be irreproachable, and now he had broken down. How had he reached this stage? how had all this happened?—he could not have told himself. He took his head between his hands, but, whatever he might do, he could not succeed in explaining it. He certainly had had the intention of delivering Jean Valjean over to the law, of which Jean Valjean was the captive, and of which he was the slave. He had not confessed to himself for a single instant, while he held him, that he had a thought of letting him go; it was to some extent unconsciously that his hand had opened and allowed him to escape.

All sorts of enigmatic novelties passed before his eyes. He asked himself questions, and gave himself answers, and his answers terrified him. He asked himself, "What has this convict, this desperate man, whom I followed to persecution, and who had me under his heel, and could have avenged himself, and ought to have acted so, both to gratify his rancor and assure his security, what has he done in leaving me my life, and showing me mercy? his duty? no, something more. And what have I done in showing him mercy in my turn? my duty? no, something more. Is there, then, something more than duty?" Here he was terrified, he was thrown off his balance, one of the scales fell into the abyss, the other ascended to heaven; and Javert felt no less horror at the one above than at the one below. Without being the least in the world what is called a Voltairean, or philosopher, or an incredulous man, respectful, on the contrary, instinctively to the Established Church, he only knew it as an august fragment of the social *ensemble;* order was his dogma, and sufficient for him. Since he had attained man's age and office, he had set nearly all his religion in the police, being—and we employ the words without the slightest irony, and in their most serious acceptation,—being, as we have said, a spy as another man is a priest. He had a superior,

M. Gisquet, but he had never thought up to this day of that other superior, God. He felt the presence of this new Chief unexpectedly, and was troubled by Him. He was thrown out of gear by this person; he knew not what to do with this Superior, for he was not ignorant that the subordinate is bound always to bow the head, that he must neither disobey nor blame nor discuss, and that when facing a superior who astonishes him too much, the inferior has no other resource but his resignation. But how could he manage to give in his resignation to God?

However this might be, one fact to which he constantly returned, and which ruled everything else, was that he had just committed a frightful infraction of the law. He had closed his eyes to a relapsed convict who had broken his ban; he had set a galley-slave at liberty. He had stolen from the laws a man who belonged to them. He had done this, and no longer understood himself. He was not certain of being himself. The very reasons of his deed escaped him, and he only felt the dizziness it produced. He had lived, up to this moment, in that blind faith which engenders a dark probity; and this faith was leaving him, this probity had failed him. All that he had believed was dissipated, and truths which he did not wish for inexorably besieged him. He must henceforth be another man, and he suffered the strange pain of a conscience suddenly operated on for cataract. He saw what it was repulsive to him to see, and felt himself spent, useless, dislocated from his past life, discharged, and dissolved. Authority was dead within him, and he no longer had a reason for living. Terrible situation! to feel emotion! to be made of granite, and doubt! to be the statue of punishment cast all of one piece in the mold of the law, and to suddenly perceive that you have under your bronze bosom something absurd and disobedient, which almost resembles a heart! to have requited good for good, though you have said to yourself up to this day that such good is evil! to be the watch-dog and fawn! to be ice and melt! to be a pair of pincers, and become a hand! suddenly to feel your fingers opening! to lose your hold. Oh! what a frightful thing! The man projectile, no longer knowing his road, and recoiling! to be obliged to confess this. Infallibility is not infallible; there may be an error in dogma, all is not said when a code has spoken, society is not perfect, authority is complicated with vacillation, a crack in the immutable is possible, judges are men, the law may be deceived, the courts may make a mistake! to see a flaw in the immense blue window of the firmament.

What was taking place in Javert was the Fampoux of a rectilinear conscience, the overthrow of a mind, the crushing of a probity irresistibly hurled in a straight line, and breaking itself against God. It was certainly strange that the fireman of order, the engineer of authority, mounted on the blind iron horse, could be unsaddled by a beam of light! that the immutable, the direct, the correct, the geometrical, the passive, the perfect, could bend; that there should be for a locomotive a road to Damascus!

God, ever within man, and Himself the true conscience, refractory to the false conscience; the spark forbidden to expire, the ray ordered to remember the sun, the mind enjoined to recognize the true absolute when it confronts itself with the fictitious absolute; a humanity that cannot be thrown off, the human heart that cannot be cast aside—did Javert comprehend this splendid phenomenon, the most glorious, perhaps, of our internal prodigies? Did he penetrate it? Did he explain it to himself? Evidently no, but under the pressure of this incontestable incomprehensibility he felt his brain cracking. He was less transfigured than the victim of this prodigy; he endured it with exasperation, and only saw in all this an immense difficulty of living. It seemed to him as if henceforth his breathing was eternally impeded. He was not accustomed to have anything unknown over his head; hitherto everything he had above him had been to his eye a clear, simple, limpid surface; there was nothing unknown or obscure; nothing but what was definite, coördinated, enchained, precise, exact, circumscribed, limited, and closed; everything foreseen; authority was a flat surface, there was no fall in it or dizziness before it. Javert had never seen anything unknown except below him. Irregularity, unexpected things, the disorderly opening of the chaos, and a possible fall over a precipice,—all this was the state of the lower regions, of the rebels, the wicked and the wretched. Now Javert threw himself back, and was suddenly startled by this extraordinary apparition,—a gulf above him!

What, then! the world was dismantled from top to bottom and absolutely disconcerted! in what could men trust, when what they felt convinced of was crumbling away! What! the flaw in the cuirass of society could be formed by a magnanimous scoundrel! What! an honest servant of the law could find himself caught between two crimes, the crime of letting a man escape and the crime of arresting him! all was not certain, then, in the orders given by the state to the official! there could be blind alleys in duty! What, then! all this was real! was it true that an ex-bandit, bowed under condemnations, could draw himself up and end by being in the right? was this credible? were there, then, cases in which the law must retire before transfigured crime and stammer its apologies! Yes, it was so! and Javert saw it! and Javert touched it! and not only could he not deny it, but he had a share in it. These were realities, and it was abominable that real facts could attain such a deformity. If facts did their duty, they would restrict themselves to being proofs of the law; for facts are sent by God. Was, then, anarchy about to descend from on high?

Thus, both in the exaggeration of agony and the optical illusion of consternation, everything which might have restricted and corrected his impression faded away, and society, the human race, and the universe henceforth were contained for his eyes in a simple and hideous outline—punishment; the thing tried, the strength due to the legislature, the decrees of sovereign courts, the magistracy, the government, prevention and repression, official wisdom, legal infallibility, the principle of authority, all the dogmas on which political and civil security, sovereignty, justice, logic flowing from the code, public truth,—all were a heap of ruins, chaos; he himself, Javert, the watcher of order, incorruptibility in the service of the police, the Providence-dog of society, conquered and hurled to the ground, and on the summit of all this ruin stood a man in a green cap, and with a glory round his brow; such was the state of overthrow he had reached, such the frightful vision which he had in his mind. Was this endurable? no, it was a violent state, if there ever was one, and there were only two ways of escaping from it: one was to go resolutely to Jean Valjean and restore to the dungeon the man of the galleys; the other——

Javert left the parapet, and, with head erect this time, walked firmly toward the guard-room indicated by a lantern at one of the corners of the Châtelet Square. On reaching it, he saw through a window the policeman, and went in. The police recognize each other merely by the way in which they push open the door of a guard-room. Javert mentioned his name, showed his card to the sergeant, and sat down at the table on which a candle was burning. There were also on the table a pen, a leaden inkstand, and paper for drawing up reports, and the assignments of the night patrols. This table, always completed by a straw chair, is an institution; it exists in all police offices, it is always adorned with a boxwood saucer full of sawdust, and a box of red wafers, and it is the lower stage of the official style. It is here that the state literature commences.

Javert took the pen and a sheet of paper and began writing. This is what he wrote:

A FEW REMARKS FOR THE GOOD OF THE SERVICE.

1. *I beg M. le Préfet to cast his eyes on this.*

2. *Prisoners when they return from examination at the magistrate's office take off their shoes and remain barefoot on the slabs while they are being searched. Many have coughs when they return to prison. This entails infirmary expenses.*

3. *Tracking is good, with relays of agents at regular distances; but on important occasions two agents at the least should not let each other out of sight, because, if for any reason one agent were to fail in his duty, the other would watch him and take his place.*

4. *There is no explanation why the special rules of the prison of the Madelonnettes prohibit a prisoner from having a chair, even if he pay for it.*

5. *At the Madelonnettes there are only two gratings to the canteen, which allows the canteen woman to let the prisoners touch her hand.*

6. *The prisoners called barkers, who call the other prisoners to the visitors' room, demand two sous from each prisoner for crying his name distinctly. This is a robbery.*

7. *Ten sous are stopped from a prisoner working in the weaving-room for a running thread; this is an abuse on the part of the manager, as the cloth is not the less good.*

8. *It is annoying that visitors to La Force are obliged to pass through the boys' court in proceeding to the speaking-room of St. Marie l'Egyptienne.*

9. *It is certain that gendarmes are daily heard repeating in the courtyard of the prefecture, the examination of prisoners by the magistrates. For a gendarme, who ought to be sacred, to repeat what he has heard in the office is a serious breach of duty.*

10. *Madame Henry is an honest woman, her canteen is very clean, but it is wrong for a woman to hold the key of the secret cells. This is not worthy of the Conciergerie of a great civilization.*

Javert wrote these lines in his calmest and most correct handwriting, not omitting to cross a *t,* and making the paper cry firmly beneath his pen. Under the last line he signed,

J A V E R T,

Inspector of the 1st class,

At the post of the Châtelet Square, June 7, 1832,

about one in the morning.

Javert dried the ink on the paper, folded it like a letter, sealed it, wrote on the back, *Note for the Administration,* left it on the table, and quitted the guard-room. The glass door fell back after him. He again diagonally crossed the Place du Châtelet, reached the quay again, and went back with automatic precision to the same spot which he had left a quarter of an hour previously: he bent down and found himself again in the same attitude on the same parapet slab; it seemed as if he had not stirred. The darkness was complete, for it was the sepulchral moment which follows midnight, a ceiling of clouds hid the stars; the houses in the cité did not display a single light, no one passed, all the streets and quays that could be seen were deserted, and Notre Dame and the towers of the Palais de Justice appeared lineaments of the night. A lamp reddened the edge of the quay, and the shadows of the bridges looked ghostly one behind the other. Rains had swelled the river. The spot where Javert was leaning was, it will be remembered, precisely above the rapids of the Seine, and that formidable whirlpool which unrolls itself and rolls itself up again like an endless screw. Javert stooped down and looked; all was dark, and nothing could be distinguished. A sound of spray was audible, but the river was invisible. At moments in this dizzy depth a flash appeared and undulated, for water has the power, even on the darkest night, of obtaining light, no one knows whence, and changing itself into a lizard. The gleam faded away and all became indistinct again. Immensity seemed open there, and what was beneath was not water, but the gulf. The quay-wall, abrupt, confused, mingled with the vapor, then hidden, produced the effect of a precipice of infinitude.

Nothing could be seen, but the hostile coldness of the water and the sickly smell of the damp stones could be felt. A ferocious breath rose from this abyss, and the swelling of the river, divined rather than perceived, the tragic muttering of the water, the mournful vastness of the bridge arches, a possible fall into this gloomy vacuum—all this shadow was full of horror.

Javert remained for some moments motionless, gazing at this opening of the darkness, and considered the invisible with an intentness which resembled attention. All at once he took off his hat and placed it on the brink of the quay. A moment after a tall, black figure, which any belated passer-by might have taken at a distance for a ghost, appeared standing on the parapet, stooped toward the Seine, then drew itself up, and fell straight into the darkness. There was a dull plash, and the shadows alone were in the secret of this obscure form which had disappeared beneath the waters.

BOOK V

GRANDSON AND GRANDFATHER

1. *THE TREE WITH THE ZINC PLATE*

SOME time after the events which we have just recorded the Sieur Boulatruelle experienced a lively emotion. The Sieur Boulatruelle is the road-mender of Montfermeil of whom we have already caught a glimpse in the dark portions of this book. Boulatruelle, it will be perhaps remembered, was a man occupied with troubled and various things. He broke stones and plundered travelers on the high-way. Road-mender and robber, he had a dream; he believed in the treasures buried in the forest of Montfermeil. He hoped some day to find money in the ground at the foot of a tree, and in the meanwhile readily sought for some in the pockets of passers-by. Still, for the present, he was prudent, for he had just had a narrow escape. He was, as we know, picked up with the other ruffians in Jondrette's garret. There is some usefulness in a vice, for his drunkenness saved him, and it never could be cleared up whether he were there as a robber or as a robbed man. He was set at liberty on account of his proved intoxication on the night of the attack, and returned to the woods. He went back to his road from Gagny to Lagny, to break stones for the state, under surveillance, with hanging head and very thoughtful, slightly chilled by the robbery, which had almost ruined him, but turning with all the more tenderness to the wine which had saved him.

As for the lively emotion which he had a short time after his return beneath the turf-roof of his road-mender's cabin, it was this: One morning Boulatruelle, while going as usual to his work and to his lurking-place, possibly a little before daybreak, perceived among the branches a man whose back alone he could see, but whose shape, so he fancied, through the mist and darkness, was not entirely unknown to him. Boulatruelle, though a drunkard, had a correct and lucid memory, an indispensable defensive weapon for any man who is at all on bad terms with legal order.

"Where the deuce have I seen some one like that man?" he asked.

But he could give himself no reply, save that he resembled somebody of whom he had a confused recollection. Boulatruelle, however, made his guesses and calculations, though he was unable to settle the identity. This man did not belong to those parts, and had come there evidently afoot, as no public vehicle passed through Montfermeil at that hour; he must have been walking all night. Where did he come from? no great distance, for he had neither haversack nor bundle. Doubtless from Paris. Why was he in this wood? why was he there at such an hour? What did he want here? Boulatruelle thought of the treasure; by dint of racking his memory he vaguely remembered having had, several years previously, a similar alarm on the subject of a man, who might very well be this man. While meditating he had, under the very weight of his meditation, hung his head, a natural but not clever thing. When he raised it again, the man had disappeared in the forest and the mist.

"By the deuce," said Boulatruelle, "I will find him again, and discover to what district that fellow belongs. This walker of Patron-Minette has a motive, and I will know it. No one must have a secret in my forest without my being mixed up in it."

He took up his pick, which was very sharp. "Here's something," he growled, "with which to search the ground and a man."

And as one thread is attached to another thread, tracing the footsteps as fast as he could in the direction which the man must have followed, he began marching through the coppice. When he had gone about a hundred yards, day, which was beginning to break, aided him. Footsteps on the sand here and there, trampled grass, broken heather, young branches bent into the shrubs and rising with a graceful slowness, like the arms of a pretty woman, who stretches herself on waking, gave him a species of trail. He followed it and then lost it, and time slipped away; he got deeper into the wood, and reached a species of eminence. A matutinal sportsman passing at a distance along a path, and whistling the air of Guillery, gave him the idea of climbing up a tree, and, although old, he was active. There was on the mound a very large beech, worthy of Tityrus and Boulatruelle, and he climbed up the tree as high as he could. The idea was a good one, for, while exploring the solitude on the side where the wood is most entangled, Boulatruelle suddenly perceived the man, but had no sooner seen him than he lost him out of sight again. The man entered, or rather glided, into a rather distant clearing, masked by large trees, but which Boulatruelle knew very well, because he had noticed, near a large heap of stones, a sick chestnut-tree bandaged with a zinc belt nailed upon it. This clearing is what was formerly called the Blaru bottom, and the pile of stones, intended no one knows for what purpose, which could be seen there thirty years ago, is doubtless there still. Nothing equals the longevity of a heap of stones, except that of a plank hoarding. It is there temporarily; what a reason for lasting!

Boulatruelle, with the rapidity of joy, tumbled off the tree, rather than came down it. The lair was found, and now he had only to seize the animal. The famous treasure he had dreamed of was probably there. It was no small undertaking to reach the clearing by beaten paths which make a thousand annoying windings, it would take a good quarter of an hour; in a straight line through the woods, which is at that spot singularly dense, very thorny, and most aggressive, it would take half an hour at least. This is what Boulatruelle was wrong in not understanding; he believed in the straight line, a respectable optical illusion which has ruined many men. The wood, bristling though it was, appeared to him the right road.

"Let us go by the Rue de Rivoli of the wolves," he said.

Boulatruelle, accustomed to crooked paths, this time committed the error of going straight, and resolutely cast himself among the shrubs. He had to contend with holly, nettles, hawthorns, eglantines, thistles, and most irascible roots, and was fearfully scratched. At the bottom of the ravine he came to a stream, which he was obliged to cross, and at last reached the Blaru clearing after forty minutes, perspiring, wet through, blowing, and ferocious. There was no one in the clearing. Boulatruelle hurried to the heap of stones; it was still in its place, and had not been carried off. As for the man, he had vanished in the forest. He had escaped; where? in which direction? into which clump of trees? it was impossible to guess. And, most crushing thing of all, there was behind the heap of stones, and in front of the zinc-banded tree a pick, forgotten or abandoned, and a hole; but the hole was empty.

"Robber!" Boulatruelle cried, shaking his fists at heaven.

2. MARIUS, QUITTING CIVIL, PREPARES
FOR DOMESTIC WAR

MARIUS was for a long time neither dead nor alive. He had for several weeks a fever accompanied by delirium, and very serious brain symptoms caused by the effects of the wounds in the head rather than the wounds themselves.

He repeated Cosette's name for whole nights with the lugubrious loquacity of fever and the gloomy obstinacy of agony. The width of certain wounds was a serious danger, for the suppuration of wide wounds may always be absorbed into the system, and consequently kill the patient, under certain atmospheric influences; and at each change in the weather, at the slightest storm, the physician became anxious. "Mind that the patient suffers from no emotion," he repeated. The dressings were complicated and difficult, for the fixing of bandages and lint by the sparadrap had not been imagined at that period. Nicolette expended in lint a sheet "as large as a ceiling," she said; and it was not without difficulty that the chlorureted lotions and nitrate of silver reached the end of the gangrene. So long as there was danger, M. Gillenormand, broken-hearted by the bedside of his grandson, was like Marius, neither dead nor alive.

Every day, and sometimes twice a day, a white-haired and well-dressed gentleman—such was the description given by the porter—came to inquire after the wounded man, and left a large parcel of lint for the dressings. At length, on September 7, four months, day by day, from the painful night on which he had been brought home dying to his grandfather, the physician declared that he could answer for him, and that convalescence was setting in. Marius, however, would be obliged to lie for two months longer on a couch owing to the accidents produced by the fracture of the collar-bone. There is always a last wound like that which will not close, and eternizes the dressings, to the great annoyance of the patient. This long illness and lengthened convalescence, however, saved him from prosecution; in France there is no anger, even public, which six months does not extinguish. Riots, in the present state of society, are so much everybody's fault that they are followed by a certain necessity of closing the eyes. Let us add that Gisquet's unjustifiable decree, which ordered physicians to denounce their patients, having outraged opinion, and not merely opinion, but the king first of all, the wounded were covered and protected by this indignation, and, with the exception of those taken prisoners in the act of fighting, the courts-martial did not dare to molest any one. Hence Marius was left tranquil.

M. Gillenormand first passed through every form of agony and then through every form of ecstasy. Great difficulty was found in keeping him from passing the whole night by Marius's side; he had his large easy-chair brought to the bed, and he insisted on his daughter taking the finest linen in the house to make compresses and bandages. Mlle. Gillenormand, as a sensible and elderly lady, managed to save the fine linen, while making her father believe that he was obeyed. M. Gillenormand would not listen to any explanation that for the purpose of making lint fine linen is not so good as coarse, or new so good as worn. He was present at all the dressings, from which Mlle. Gillenormand modestly absented herself. When the dead flesh was cut away with scissors she said, Aïe, aïe! Nothing was so touching as to see him hand the wounded man a cup of broth with his gentle, senile trembling. He overwhelmed the surgeon with questions, and did not perceive that he constantly repeated the same.

On the day when the physician informed him that Marius was out of danger, he was beside himself. He gave his porter three louis d'or, and at night, when he went to his bedroom, danced a gavotte, making castanets of his thumb and fore-finger, and sang a song something like this:

> *Jeanne est née à Fougère,*
> *Vrai nid d'une bergère;*
> *J'adore son jupon*
> *Fripon.*

Amour, tu vis en elle;
Car c'est dans sa prunelle
Que tu mets ton carquois,
Narquois!

Moi, je la chante, et j'aime,
Plus que Diane même,
Jeanne et ses durs tetons
Bretons.

Then he knelt on a chair, and Basque, who was watching him through the crack of the door, felt certain that he was praying. Up to that day he had never believed in God. At each new phase in the improvement of the patient, which went on steadily, the grandfather was extravagant. He performed a multitude of mechanical actions full of delight; he went up and down stairs without knowing why. A neighbor's wife, who was very pretty, by the way, was stupefied at receiving one morning a large bouquet; it was M. Gillenormand who sent it to her, and her husband got up a jealous scene. M. Gillenormand tried to draw Nicolette on his knees; he called Marius Monsieur le Baron, and shouted, Long live the Republic! Every moment he asked the medical man, "There is no danger now, is there?" He looked at Marius with a grandmother's eyes, and gloated over him when he slept. He no longer knew himself, no longer took himself into account, Marius was the master of the house; there was abdication in his joy, and he was the grandson of his grandson. In his present state of merriment he was the most venerable of children; through fear of wearying or annoying the convalescent, he would place himself behind him in order to smile upon him. He was satisfied, joyous, ravished, charming, and young, and his white hair added a gentle majesty to the gay light which he had on his face. When grace is mingled with wrinkles, it is adorable; and there is a peculiar dawn in expansive old age.

As for Marius, while letting himself be nursed and petted, he had one fixed idea—Cosette. Since the fever and delirium had left him, he no longer pronounced this name, and it might be supposed that he had forgotten it, but he was silent precisely because his soul was there. He knew not what had become of Cosette; the whole affair of the Rue de la Chanvrerie was like a cloud in his memory; shadows, almost indistinct, floated in his mind. Eponine, Gavroche, Mabœuf, the Thénardiers, and all his friends mournfully mingled with the smoke of the barricade; the strange passage of M. Fauchelevent through that blood-stained adventure, produced upon him the effect of an enigma in a tempest; he understood nothing of his own life, he knew not how or by whom he had been saved, and no one about him knew it either. All they were able to tell him was that he had been brought there at night in a hackney-coach; past, present, and future,—all this was to him like the mist of a vague idea. But there was in this mist one immovable point, a clear and precise lineament, something made of granite, a resolution, a will—to find Cosette again. For him the idea of life was not distinct from the idea of Cosette; he had decreed in his heart that he would not receive one without the other, and he unalterably determined to demand of his grandfather, of destiny, of fate, of Hades itself, the restitution of his lost Eden.

He did not conceal the obstacles from himself. Here let us underline one fact: he was not won or greatly affected by all the anxiety and all the tenderness of his grandfather. In the first place he was not in the secret of them all, and next, in his sick man's reveries, which were perhaps still feverish, he distrusted this gentleness as a strange and new thing intended to subdue him. He remained cold to it, and the poor grandfather lavished his smiles all in vain. Marius said to himself that it was all very well so long as he did not speak and let matters rest, but when he came to Cosette, he should find another face, and his grandfather's real attitude would be unmasked. Then the affair would be troublesome; a warming up of family questions, a comparison of positions, every possible sarcasm and objection at once. Fauchelevent, Coupelevent, fortune, poverty, wretchedness, the stone on the neck, the future, a violent resistance, and the conclusion,—a refusal. Marius stiffened himself against it beforehand. And then, in proportion as he regained life, his old wrongs re-appeared, the old ulcers of his memory re-opened; he thought again of the past. Colonel Pontmercy placed himself once more between M. Gillenormand and him, Marius, and he said to himself that he had no real kindness to hope for from a man who had been so unjust and harsh to his father. And with health came back a sort of bitterness against his grandfather, from which the old man gently suffered. M. Gillenormand, without letting it be seen, noticed that Marius, since he had been brought home and regained consciousness, had never once called him father. He did not say Sir, it is true, but he managed to say neither one nor the other, by a certain way of turning his sentences.

A crisis was evidently approaching, and, as nearly always happens in such cases, Marius, in order to try himself, skirmished before offering battle; this is called feeling the ground. One morning it happened that M. Gillenormand, alluding to a newspaper which he had come across, spoke lightly of the Convention, and darted a Royalist epigram at Danton, St. Just, and Robespierre. "The men of '93 were giants," Marius said sternly; the old man was silent, and did not utter another syllable all the day. Marius, who had the inflexible grandfather of his early years ever present to his mind, saw in this silence a profound concentration of anger, augured from it an obstinate struggle, and augmented his preparations for the contest in the recesses of his mind. He determined that in case of refusal he would tear off his bandages, dislocate his collarbone, expose all the wounds still unhealed, and refuse all food. His wounds were his ammunition; he must have Cosette or die.

He awaited the favorable moment with the crafty impatience of sick persons, and the moment arrived.

3. *MARIUS ATTACKS*

ONE day M. Gillenormand, while his daughter was arranging the phials and cups on the marble slab of the sideboard, leaned over Marius, and said in his most tender accent:

"Look you, my little Marius, in your place I would rather eat meat than fish; a fried sole is excellent at the beginning of a convalescence, but a good cutlet is necessary to put the patient on his legs."

Marius, whose strength had nearly quite returned, sat up, rested his two clenched fists on his sheet, looked his grandfather in the face, assumed a terrible air, and said:

"That induces me to say one thing to you."

"What is it?"

"That I wish to marry."

"Foreseen," said the grandfather, bursting into a laugh.

"How foreseen?"

"Yes, foreseen. You shall have your little maid."

Marius, stupefied and dazzled, trembled in all his limbs, and M. Gillenormand continued:

"Yes, you shall have the pretty little dear. She comes every day in the form of an old gentleman to ask after you. Ever since you have been wounded she has spent her time in crying and making lint. I made inquiries; she lives at No. 7, Rue de l'Homme Armé. Ah! there we are! Ah, you want her, do you? well, you shall have her. There's a trick for you; you had made your little plot, and had said to yourself, 'I will tell it point-blank to that grandfather, that mummy of the Regency and the Directory, that old beau, that Dorante who has become Géronte. He has had his frolics too, and his amourettes, and his grisettes, and his Cosettes; he has had his fling, he has had his wings, and he has eaten the bread of spring; he must surely remember it, we shall see. Battle!' Ah, you take the cockchafer by the horns, very good. I offer you a cutlet, and you answer me, 'By the bye, I wish to marry.' By Jupiter Ammon, that is a transition! Ah, you made up your mind for a quarrel, but you did not know that I was an old coward. What do you say to that? You are sold, you did not expect to find your grandfather more stupid than yourself. You have lost the speech you intended to make me, master lawyer, and that is annoying. Well, all the worse, rage away; I do what you want, and that cuts the speech short. Listen, I have made my inquiries, for I too am cunning; she is charming, she is virtuous, the lancer does not speak the truth, she made heaps of lint. She is a jewel, she adores you; if you had died, there would have been three of us, and her coffin would have accompanied mine. I had the idea so soon as you were better of planting her there by your bedside, but it is only in romances that girls are introduced to the beds of handsome young wounded men in whom they take an interest. That would not do, for what would your aunt say? You are quite naked three parts of the time, sir: ask Nicolette, who never left you for a moment, whether it were possible for a female to be here? And then, what would the doctor have said? for a pretty girl does not cure a fever. Well, say no more about it, it is settled and done, take her; such is my cruelty. Look you, I saw that you did not love me, and I said, 'What can I do to make that animal love me?' I said, 'Stay, I have my little Cosette ready to hand. I will give her to him, and then he must love me a little, or tell me the reason why.' Ah, you believed that the old man would storm, talk big, cry no, and lift his cane against all this day-dawn. Not at all. Cosette, very good; love, very good; I ask for nothing better; take the trouble, sir, to marry, be happy, my beloved child."

After saying this the old man burst into sobs; he took Marius' head and pressed it to his old bosom, and both began weeping. That is one of the forms of supreme happiness.

"My father!" Marius exclaimed.

"Ah, you love me then!" the old man said.

There was an ineffable moment; they were choking and could not speak; at length the old man stammered:

"Come! the stopper is taken out of him! he called me father."

Marius disengaged his head from his grandfather's arms, and said, gently:

"Now that I am better, father, I fancy I could see her."

"Foreseen, too; you will see her to-morrow."

"Father?"

"Well, what?"

"Why not to-day?"

"Well, to-day; done for to-day. You have called me father thrice, and it's worth that. I will see about it, and she shall be brought here. Fore-seen, I tell you. That has already been put in verse, and it is the dénoue-ment of André Chénier's elegy, the 'Jeune malade,' André Chénier who was butchered by the vill—, by the giants of '93."

M. Gillenormand fancied he could see a light frown on Marius's face, though, truth to tell, he was not listening, as he had flown away into ecstasy, and was thinking much more of Cosette than of 1793. The grandfather, trembling at having introduced André Chénier so inop-portunely, hurriedly continued:

"Butchered is not the word. The fact is that the great revolutionary geniuses who were not wicked,—that is incontestable,—who were heroes, Pardi, found that André Chénier was slightly in their way, and they had him guillo——; that is to say, these great men on the 7th Thermidor, in the interest of the public safety, begged André Chénier to be kind enough to go——"

M. Gillenormand, garroted by his own sentence, could not continue; unable to terminate it or retract it, the old man rushed, with all the speed which his age allowed, out of the bedroom, shut the door after him, and

purple, choking, and foaming, with his eyes out of his head, found himself nose to nose with honest Basque, who was cleaning boots in the
anteroom. He seized Basque by the collar, and furiously shouted into
his face, "By the hundred thousand Javottes of the devil, those brigands
assassinated him!"

"Whom, sir?"

"André Chénier."

"Yes, sir," said the horrified Basque.

4. MLLE. GILLENORMAND HAS NO OBJECTIONS TO THE MATCH

COSETTE and Marius saw each other again. We will not attempt to
describe the interview, for there are things which we must not attempt
to paint; the sun is of the number. The whole family, Basque and Nicolette included, were assembled in Marius's chamber at the moment when
Cosette entered. She appeared in the door-way, and seemed to be surrounded by a halo; precisely at the moment this grandfather was going
to blow his nose, but he stopped short, holding his nose in his handkerchief and looking over it.

"Adorable!" he cried.

And then he blew a sonorous blast. Cosette was intoxicated, ravished,
startled, in heaven. She was as timid as a person can be through happiness; she stammered, turned pale and then pink, and wished to throw
herself into Marius's arms, but dared not. She was ashamed of loving
before so many people; for the world is merciless to happy lovers, and
always remains at the very moment when they most long to be alone.
And yet they do not want these people at all. With Cosette, and behind
her, had entered a white-haired man, serious, but still smiling, though

the smile was wandering and poignant. It was "Monsieur Fauchelevent,"
—it was Jean Valjean. He was *well dressed,* as the porter had said, in a
new black suit and a white cravat. The porter was a thousand leagues
from recognizing in this correct citizen, this probable notary, the frightful corpse-bearer who had risen at the gate on the night of June 7, ragged,
filthy, hideous, and haggard, with a mask of blood and mud on his face,
supporting in his arms the unconscious Marius; still his porter's instincts
were aroused. When M. Fauchelevent arrived with Cosette, the porter
could not refrain from confiding this aside to his wife: "I don't know
why, but I fancy that I have seen that face before." M. Fauchelevent remained standing by the door of Marius's room, as if afraid; he held under
his arm a packet rather like an octavo volume wrapped in paper. The
paper was green, apparently from mildew.

"Has this gentleman always got books under his arm like that?"
Mlle. Gillenormand, who was not fond of books, asked Nicolette in a
whisper.

"Well," M. Gillenormand, who had heard her, answered in the same
key, "he is a savant, is that his fault? Monsieur Boulard, whom I knew,
never went out without a book either, and always had one close to his
heart like that."

Then bowing, he said, in a loud voice:

"M. Tranchelevent."

Father Gillenormand did not do it purposely, but an inattention to
proper names was an aristocratic way of his.

"Monsieur Tranchelevent, I have the honor of requesting this lady's
hand for my grandson, M. le Baron Marius Pontmercy?"

Monsieur "Tranchelevent" bowed.

"All right," the grandfather said.

And turning to Marius and Cosette, with both arms extended in ben-
ediction, he cried:

"You have leave to adore each other."

They did not let it be said twice, and the prattling began. They talked
in a whisper, Marius reclining on his couch and Cosette standing by his
side. "Oh, Heaven!" Cosette murmured, "I see you again; it is you. To
go and fight like that! But why? it is horrible. For four months I have
been dead. Oh, how wicked it was of you to have been at that battle!
what had I done to you? I forgive you, but you will not do it again. Just
now, when they came to tell me to come to you, I thought again that I
was going to die, but it was of joy. I was so sad! I did not take the time to

dress myself, and I must look frightful; what will your relations say at seeing me in a tumbled collar? But speak! you let me speak all alone. We are still in the Rue de l'Homme Armé. It seems that your shoulder was terrible, and I was told that I could put my hand in it, and then it seems that your flesh was cut with scissors. How frightful that is! I wept so that I have no eyes left. It is strange that a person can suffer like that. Your grandfather has a very kind look. Do not disturb yourself, do not get on your elbow like that, or you will do yourself an injury. Oh! how happy I am! So our misfortunes are all ended! I am quite foolish. There were things I wanted to say to you which I have quite forgotten. Do you love me still? We live in the Rue de l'Homme Armé. There is no garden there. I made lint the whole time; look here, sir, it is your fault, my fingers are quite rough."

"Angel!" said Marius.

Angel is the only word in the language which cannot be worn out; no other word would resist the pitiless use which lovers make of it. Then, as there was company present, they broke off, and did not say a word more, contenting themselves with softly clasping hands. M. Gillenormand turned to all the rest in the room, and cried:

"Speak loudly, good people; make a noise, will you? Come, a little row, hang it all, so that these children may prattle at their ease."

And going up to Marius and Cosette, he whispered to them:

"Go on; don't put yourselves out of the way."

Aunt Gillenormand witnessed with stupor this irruption of light into her antiquated house. This stupor had nothing aggressive about it; it was not at all the scandalized and envious glance cast by an owl at two ring-doves; it was the stupid eye of a poor innocent of the age of fifty-seven; it was a spoiled life looking at that triumph, love.

"Mlle. Gillenormand the elder," her father said to her, "I told you that this would happen."

He remained silent for a moment, and added:

"Look at the happiness of others."

Then he turned to Cosette.

"How pretty she is! how pretty she is! she is a Greuze! So you are going to have all that for yourself, scamp? Ah, my boy, you have had a lucky escape from me; if I were not fifteen years too old, we would fight with swords and see who should have her. There, I am in love with you, mademoiselle; but it is very simple, it is your right. What a famous, charming little wedding we will have! Saint Denis du Saint-Sacrament is our parish; but I will procure a dispensation, so that you may be married at St. Paul, for the church is better. It was built for the Jesuits, and more coquettish. It is opposite Cardinal Birague's fountain. The masterpiece of Jesuit architecture is at Namur, and is called Saint Loup; you should go and see that when you are married, for it is worth the journey. Mademoiselle, I am entirely of your opinion; I wish girls to marry, for they are made for it. There is a certain Sainte Catharine whom I would always like to see unveiled. To remain a maid is fine, but it is cold. Multiply, says the Bible. To save the people, a Joan of Arc is wanted; but to make a people, we want Mother Gigogne. So marry, my darlings; I really do not see the use of remaining a maid. I know very well that they have a separate chapel in the church, and join the confraternity of the virgin; but, sapristi, a good-looking young husband, and at the end of a year a plump bantling, who sucks at you bravely, and who has rolls of fat on his thighs, and who clutches your bosom with his pink little paws, are a good deal better than holding a candle at vespers and singing *Turris Eburnea.*"

The grandfather pirouetted on his nonagenarian heels, and began speaking again, like a spring which has been wound up.

Ainsi, bornant le cours de tes rêvasseries,
Alcippe, il est donc vrai, dans peu tu te maries.

"By the bye!"
"What, father?"
"Had you not an intimate friend?"
"Yes; Courfeyrac."
"What has become of him?"
"He is dead."
"That is well."

He sat down by their side, made Cosette take a chair, and took their four hands in his old wrinkled hands.

"This darling is exquisite. This Cosette is a masterpiece! She is a very little girl and a very great lady. She will be only a baroness, and that is a derogation, for she is born to be a marchioness. What eyelashes she has! My children, drive it into your heads that you are on the right road. Love one another; be foolish over it, for love is the stupidity of men and the cleverness of God. So adore one another. Still," he added, suddenly growing sad, "what a misfortune! more than half I possess is sunk in annuities; so long as I live it will be all right, but when I am dead, twenty years hence, ah! my poor children, you will not have a farthing. Your pretty white hands, Madame la Baronne, will be wrinkled by work."

Here a serious and calm voice was heard saying:

"Mlle. Euphrasie Fauchelevent has six hundred thousand francs."

It was Jean Valjean's voice. He had not yet uttered a syllable; no one seemed to remember that he was present, and he stood motionless behind all these happy people.

"Who is the Mlle. Euphrasie in question?" the startled grandfather asked.

"Myself," said Cosette.

"Six hundred thousand francs!" M. Gillenormand repeated.

"Less fourteen or fifteen thousand, perhaps," Jean Valjean said.

And he laid on the table the parcel which Aunt Gillenormand had taken for a book. Jean Valjean himself opened the packet; it was a bundle of bank-notes. They were turned over and counted; there were five hundred bank-notes for a thousand francs, and one hundred and sixty-eight for five hundred, forming a total of five hundred and eighty-four thousand francs.

"That's a famous book," said M. Gillenormand.

"Five hundred and eighty-four thousand francs!" the aunt murmured.

"That arranges a good many things, does it not, Mlle. Gillenormand the elder?" the grandfather continued. "That devil of a Marius has found a millionaire grisette upon the tree of dreams! Now trust to the amourettes of young people! Students find studentesses with six hundred thousand francs. Cherubim works better than Rothschild."

"Five hundred and eighty-four thousand francs!" Mlle. Gillenormand repeated; "five hundred and eighty-four thousand francs! we may as well say six hundred thousand."

As for Marius and Cosette, they were looking at each other during this period, and hardly paid any attention to the circumstance.

5. *BETTER PLACE YOUR MONEY IN A FOREST THAN WITH A NOTARY*

OF course our readers have understood, and no lengthy explanation will be required, that Jean Valjean, after the Champmathieu affair, was enabled by his escape for a few days to come to Paris and withdraw in time from Lafitte's the sum he had gained under the name of M. Madeleine at Montreuil sur Mer; and that, afraid of being recaptured, which in fact happened to him shortly after, he buried this sum in the forest of Montfermeil, at the spot called the Blaru bottom. The sum, six hundred and thirty thousand francs, all in bank-notes, occupied but little space, and was contained in a box; but, in order to protect the box from damp, he placed it in an oak coffer filled with chips of chestnut-wood. In the same coffer he placed his other treasure, the bishop's candlesticks. It will be remembered that he carried off these candlesticks in his escape from Montreuil sur Mer. The man seen on one previous evening by Boulatruelle was Jean Valjean, and afterward, whenever Jean Valjean required money, he fetched it from the Blaru clearing, and hence his absences to which we have referred. He had a pick concealed somewhere in the shrubs, in a hiding-place known to himself alone. When he found Marius to be convalescent, feeling that the hour was at hand when this money might be useful, he went to fetch it; and it was also he whom Boulatruelle saw in the wood, but this time in the morning, and not at night. Boulatruelle inherited the pick.

The real sum was five hundred and eighty-four thousand five hundred francs, but Jean Valjean kept back the five hundred francs for himself. "We will see afterward," he thought. The difference between this sum and the six hundred and thirty thousand francs withdrawn from

Lafitte's represented the expenditure of ten years from 1823 to 1833. The five years' residence in the convent had only cost five thousand francs. Jean Valjean placed the two silver candle-sticks on the mantel-piece, where they glistened, to the great admiration of Toussaint.

Moreover, Jean Valjean knew himself freed from Javert; it had been stated in his presence, and he verified the fact in the *Moniteur,* which had published it, that an inspector of police of the name of Javert had been found drowned under a washer-woman's boat between the Pont-au-change and the Pont-Neuf, and that a letter left by this man, hitherto irreproachable and highly esteemed by his chiefs, led to the belief in an attack of dementia and suicide. "In truth," thought Jean Valjean, "since he let me go when he had me, he must have been mad at that time."

6. *THE TWO OLD MEN, EACH IN HIS WAY, DO ALL TO RENDER COSETTE HAPPY*

ALL preparations were made for the marriage, and the physician, on being consulted, declared that it might take place in February. It was now December, and a few ravishing weeks of perfect happiness slipped away. The least happy man was not the grandfather; he sat for a whole quarter of an hour contemplating Cosette. "The admirably pretty girl!" he would exclaim, "and she has so soft and kind an air! She is the most charming creature I have ever seen in my life. Presently she will have virtues with a violent scent. She is one of the Graces, on my faith! A man can only live nobly with such a creature. Marius, my lad, you are a baron, you are rich, so do not be a pettifogger, I implore you."

Cosette and Marius had suddenly passed from the sepulcher into paradise: the transition had not been prepared, and they would have been stunned if they had not been dazzled.

"Do you understand anything of all this?" Marius would say to Cosette.

"No," Cosette answered, "but it seems to me as if God were looking at us."

Jean Valjean did everything, smoothed everything, conciliated everything, and rendered everything easy. He hurried toward Cosette's happiness with as much eagerness, and apparently with as much joy, as Cosette herself. As he had been mayor, he was called to solve a delicate problem, the secret of which he alone possessed,—the civil status of Cosette. To tell her origin openly might have prevented the marriage, but he got Cosette out of all the difficulties. He arranged for her a family of dead people, a sure method of not incurring any inquiry. Cosette was the only one left of an extinct family. Cosette was not his daughter but the daughter of another Fauchelevent. Two brothers Fauchelevent had been gardeners at the convent of the Little Picpus; inquiries were made there, and the best testimonials and most satisfactory character were given; for the good nuns, little suited and but little inclined to solve questions of paternity, had never known exactly of which of the two Fauchelevents Cosette was the daughter. They said what was wanted, and said it zealously. A legal declaration was drawn up, and Cosette became by law Mademoiselle Euphrasie Fauchelevent, and was declared an orphan both on the father's and mother's side. Jean Valjean managed so as to be designated, under the name of Fauchelevent, as guardian of Cosette, with M. Gillenormand as supervising guardian. As for the five hundred and eighty-four thousand francs, they were a legacy left to Cosette by a dead person who wished to remain unknown; the original legacy had been five hundred and ninety-four thousand francs, but ten thousand had been spent in the education of Mademoiselle Euphrasie, five thousand of which had been paid to the convent. This legacy, deposited in the hands of a third party, was to be handed over to Cosette upon her majority, or at the period of her marriage. All this was highly acceptable, as we see, especially when backed up by more than half a million francs. There were certainly a few singular points here and there, but they were not seen, for one of the persons interested had his eyes bandaged by love, and the others by the six hundred thousand francs.

Cosette learned that she was not the daughter of the old man whom she had so long called father; he was only a relation and another Fauchelevent was her real father. At another moment this would have grieved her, but in the ineffable hour she had now reached it was only a slight shadow, a passing cloud; and she had so much joy that this cloud lasted but a short time. She had Marius; the young man came, the old man disappeared; life is so. And then, Cosette had been accustomed for many long years to see enigmas around her; every being who has had a mysterious childhood is ever ready for certain renunciations. Still she continued to call Jean Valjean "father." Cosette, who was among the angels, was enthusiastic about Father Gillenormand; it is true that he overwhelmed her with madrigals and presents. While Jean Valjean was constructing for Cosette an unassailable position in society, M. Gillenormand attended to the wedding trousseau. Nothing amused him so much as to be magnificent; and he had given Cosette a gown of Binche guipure, which he inherited from his own grandmother. "These fashions spring up again," he said, "antiquities are the great demand, and the young ladies of my old days dress themselves like the old ladies of my youth." He plundered his respectable round-bellied commodes of Coromandel lacquer, which had not been opened for years. "Let us shrive these dowagers," he said, "and see what they have in them." He noisily violated drawers full of the dresses of all his wives, all his mistresses, and all his female ancestry. He lavished on Cosette Chinese satins, damasks, lampas, painted moires, gros de Naples dresses, Indian handkerchiefs embroidered with gold that can be washed, Genoa and Alençon point lace, sets of old jewelry, ivory bonbon boxes adorned with microscopic battles, laces, and ribbons. Cosette, astounded, wild with love for Marius and with gratitude to M. Gillenormand, dreaming of an unbounded happiness, dressed in satin and velvet. Her trousseau seemed to her supported by seraphim, and her soul floated in ether with wings of Mechlin lace. The intoxication of the lovers was only equaled, as we stated, by the ecstasy of the grandfather, and there was something like a flourish of trumpets in the Rue des Filles du Calvaire. Each morning there was a new offering of *bric-à-brac* from the grandfather to Cosette, and all sorts of ornaments were spread out splendidly around her. One day Marius, who was fond of talking seriously amid his happiness, said, with reference to some incident which I have forgotten:

"The men of the revolution are so great that they already possess the prestige of centuries, like Cato and like Phocion, and each of them seems an antique memory."

"'Moire antique!" exclaimed the old gentleman; "thank you, Marius, that is the very idea which I was seeking for."

And on the morrow a splendid tea-colored moire antique dress was added to Cosette's outfit. The grandfather extracted a wisdom from this frippery:

"Love is all very well, but this is required with it. Something useless is required in happiness; happiness is only what is absolutely necessary, but season it, say I, with an enormous amount of superfluity. A palace and her heart; her heart and the Louvre. Her heart and the fountains of Versailles. Give me my shepherdess, and take care that she be a duchess. Bring me Phillis crowned with corn-flowers, and add to her one hundred thousand francs a year. Open for me an endless Bucolic under a marble colonnade. I consent to the Bucolic and also to the fairy scene in marble and gold. Dry happiness resembles dry bread; you eat it, but you do not dine. I wish for superfluity, for the useless, for extravagance, for that which is of no use. I remember to have seen in Strasbourg Cathedral a clock as tall as a three-storied house, which marked the hour, which had the kindness to mark the hour, but did not look as if it was made for the purpose; and which, after striking midday or midnight,—midday, the hour of the sun, and midnight, the hour of love, or any other hour you please,—gave you the moon and the stars, earth and sea, birds and fishes, Phœbus and Phœbe, and a heap of things that came out of a niche, and the twelve apostles, and the Emperor Charles V, and Eponine, and Sabinus, and a number of little gilt men, who played the trumpet, into the bargain, without counting the ravishing chimes which it scattered in the air on every possible occasion, without your knowing why. Is a wretched, naked clock, which only marks the hours, worth that? I am of the opinion of the great clock of Strasbourg, and prefer it to the Black Forest cuckoo clock."

M. Gillenormand talked of all sorts of nonsense about the marriage, and all the ideas of the eighteenth century passed pell-mell into his dithyrambs.

"You are ignorant of the art of festivals, and do not know how to get up a day's pleasure in these times," he exclaimed. "Your nineteenth century is soft, and is deficient in excess; it is ignorant of what is rich and noble. In everything it is close-shorn. Your third estate is insipid and has no color, smell, or shape. The dream of your bourgeoises who established themselves, as they call it, is a pretty boudoir freshly decorated with mahogany and calico. Make way there! the Sieur Grigou marries the demoiselle Grippesou. Sumptuousness and splendor. A louis d'or has been stuck to a wax candle. Such is the age. I insist on flying beyond the Sarmatians. Ah, so far back as 1787 I predicted that all was lost on the day when I saw the Duc de Rohan, Prince de Léon, Duc de Chabot, Duc de Montbazon, Marquis de Soubise, Vicomte de Thouars, and Peer of France, go to Longchamps in a *tapecul;* that bore its fruits. In this century men have a business, gamble on the Stock Exchange, win money, and are mean. They take care of and varnish their surface; they are carefully dressed, washed, soaped, shaved, combed, rubbed, brushed, and cleaned externally, irreproachable, as polished as a pebble, discreet, trim, and at the same time, virtue of my soul! they have at the bottom of their conscience dungheaps and cesspools at which a milkmaid who blows her nose with her fingers would recoil. I grant the present age this motto, —dirty propriety. Marius, do not be annoyed; grant me the permission to speak, for I have been saying no harm of the people, you see. I have my mouth full of your people, but do let me give the bourgeoisie a pill. I tell you point-blank that at the present day people marry, but no longer know how to marry.

"Ah, it is true, I regret the gentility of the old manners; I regret everything; that elegance, that chivalry, that courteous and dainty manner, that rejoicing luxury which every one possessed, the music forming part of the wedding, symphony above and tabors below stairs, the joyous faces seated at the table, the spicy madrigals, the songs, the fireworks, the hearty laugh, the devil and his train, and the large ribbon bows. I regret the bride's garter, for it is first cousin of the girdle of Venus. On what does the siege of Troy turn? Parbleu, on Helen's garter. Why do men fight? Why does the divine Diomedes smash on the head of Merioneus that grand brass helmet, with the ten points? Why do Achilles and Hector tickle each other with lances? Because Helen let Paris take her garter. With Cosette's garter Homer would write the Iliad; he would place in his poem an old chatterer like myself, and call him Nestor. My friends, in former times, in those amiable former times, people married learnedly; they made a good contract and then a good merrymaking. So soon as Cujas had gone out, Gamacho came in. Hang it all! the stomach is an agreeable beast that demands its due, and wishes to hold its wedding too. We supped well, and had at table a pretty neighbor without a neckerchief, who only concealed her throat moderately. Oh, the wide laughing mouths; and how gay people were in those days! Youth was a bouquet, every young man was a branch of lilac or a posy of roses; if he were a warrior, he was a shepherd, and if by chance he were a captain of dragoons, he managed to call himself Florian. All were anxious to be pretty fellows, and they wore embroidery and rouge. A bourgeois looked like a flower, and a marquis like a precious stone. They did not wear straps, they did not wear boots; they were flashing, lustrous, gilt, light, dainty, and coquettish, but it did not prevent them wearing a sword by their side; they were humming-birds with beak and nails. It was the time of the *Indes galantes*. One of the sides of that age was delicate, the other magnificent, and, by jingo, people amused themselves. At the present day folk are serious; the bourgeois is miserly, the bourgeoise prudish, and your age is out of shape. The graces would be expelled because their dresses were cut too low in the neck. Alas! beauty is concealed as an ugliness. Since the revolution, all wear trousers, even the ballet-girls; a ballet-girl must be serious, and your rigadoons are doctrinaire. A man must be majestic, and would feel very much annoyed at not having his chin in his cravat. The idea of a scamp of twenty who is about to marry, is to resemble Monsieur Royer-Collard. And do you know what people reach by this majesty? they are little. Learn this fact: joy is not merely joyous, it is grand. Be in love gayly, though, hang it all! marry, when you do marry, with fever and amazement and noise and the confusion of happiness. Gravity at church, if you will; but so soon as the mass is ended you ought to make a dream whirl round your wife. A marriage ought to be royal and chimerical, and display the ceremony from the Cathedral of Rheims to the Pagoda of Chanteloup. I have a horror of a scrubby marriage, confound it! be an Olympus at least upon that day. Be gods. Ah, people might be sylphs. Games and laughter, Argyraspides, but they are scrubs. My friends, every newly married man ought to be Prince Aldobrandini. Take advantage of this unique moment of life to fly into the Empyrean with the swans and the eagles, even if you fall to-morrow back into the bourgeoisie of frogs. Do not save upon the hymeneal rites; do not nibble at this splendor, nor split farthings on the day when you are radiant. A wedding is not housekeeping. Oh, if I had my way it should be a gallant affair, and violins should be heard in the trees. Here is my programme: sky-blue and silver. I would mingle in the fête the rustic divinities, and convene the Dryads and the Nereids. The wedding of Amphitrite, a pink cloud, nymphs with their hair carefully dressed and quite nude, an academician offering quatrains to the goddess, a car drawn by marine monsters.

Triton trottait devant, et tirait de sa conque,
Des sons si ravissants qu'il ravissait quiconque!

"There is a programme for a fête, or I'm no judge, egad!"

While the grandfather, in the heat of his lyric effusion, was listening to himself, Cosette and Marius were intoxicating themselves by looking freely at each other. Aunt Gillenormand regarded all this with her imperturbable placidity; she had, during the last five or six months, a certain amount of emotions; Marius returned, Marius brought back bleeding, Marius brought back from the barricade, Marius dead, then living, Marius reconciled, Marius affianced, Marius marrying a poor girl, Marius marrying a millionaire. The six hundred thousand francs had been her last surprise, and then her indifference returned to her. She went regularly to her mass, told her beads, read her euchology, whispered in one corner of the house her *Aves,* while *I love you* was being whispered in another, and saw Marius and Cosette vaguely like two shadows. The shadow was herself. There is a certain state of inert asceticism in which the mind, neutralized by torpor, and a stranger to what might be called the business of living, does not perceive, with the exception of earthquakes and catastrophes, any human impressions, either pleasant or painful. "This devotion," Father Gillenormand would say to his daughter, "resembles a cold in the head; you smell nothing of life, neither a good odor nor a bad one." However, the six hundred thousand francs had settled the old maid's indecision. Her father was accustomed to take her so little into account that he had not consulted her as to the consent to Marius's marriage. He had acted impetuously, according to his wont, having, as a despot who has become a slave, but one thought, that of satisfying Marius. As for the aunt, he had scarce remembered that the aunt existed, and that she might have an opinion of her own, and, sheep though she was, this had offended her. Somewhat roused internally, but externally impassive, she said to herself, "My father settles the marriage question without me, and I will settle the question of the inheritance without him." She was rich, in fact, and her father was not so, and it is probable that if the marriage had been poor she would have left it poor. "All the worse for my nephew! if he choose to marry a beggar, he may be a beggar too." But Cosette's half a million of francs pleased the aunt and changed her feelings with respect to the loving couple; consideration is due to six hundred thousand francs, and it was evident that she could not do otherwise than leave her fortune to these young people, because they no longer required it.

It was arranged that the couple should reside at M. Gillenormand's, and the grandfather insisted on giving them his bedroom, the finest room in the house. *It will make me younger,* he declared. *It is an old plan. I always had the idea that the wedding should take place in my room.* He furnished this room with a heap of old articles of gallantry; he had it hung with an extraordinary fabric which he had in the piece, and believed to be Utrecht, a gold satin ground with velvet auriculas. "It was with that stuff," he said, "that the bed of the Duchess d'Anville, at la Rocheguyon, was hung." He placed on the mantel-piece a figure in Saxon porcelain carrying a muff on its naked stomach. M. Gillenormand's library became the office, which Marius required; for an office, it will be borne in mind, is insisted upon by the bar.

7. DREAMS MINGLED WITH HAPPINESS

THE lovers saw each other daily; and Cosette came with M. Fauchelevent. "It is turning things topsy-turvy," said Mlle. Gillenormand, "that the lady should come to the gentleman's house to have court paid to her in that way." But Marius's convalescence had caused the adoption of the habit, and the easy chairs of the Rue des Filles du Calvaire, more convenient for a *tête-à-tête* than the straw-bottomed chairs of the Rue de l'Homme Armé, had decided it. Marius and M. Fauchelevent saw each other, but did not speak, and this seemed to be agreed on. Every girl needs a chaperon, and Cosette could not have come without M. Fauchelevent; and for Marius, M. Fauchelevent was the condition of Cosette's presence, and he accepted him. In discussing vaguely, and without any precision, political matters as connected with the improvement of all, they managed to say a little more than Yes and No. Once, on the subject of instruction, which Marius wished to be gratuitous and obligatory, multiplied in every form, lavished upon all like light and air, and, in a word, respirable by the entire people, they were agreed, and almost talked. Marius remarked on this occasion that M. Fauchelevent spoke well, and even with a certain elevation of language, though something was wanting. M. Fauchelevent had something less than a man of the world, and something more. Marius in his innermost thoughts surrounded with all sorts of questions this M. Fauchelevent, who was to him simple, well-wishing, and cold. At times doubts occurred to him as to his own recollections; he had a hole in his memory, a black spot, an abyss dug by four months of agony. Many things were lost in it, and he was beginning to ask himself whether it was the fact that he had seen M. Fauchelevent, a man so serious and so calm, at the barricade.

This was, however, not the sole stupor which the appearances and disappearances of the past had left in his mind. We must not believe that he was delivered from all those promptings of memory which compel us, even when happy and satisfied, to take a melancholy backward glance. The head which does not turn to effaced horizons contains neither thought nor love. At moments Marius buried his face in his hands, and the tumultuous and vague past traversed the fog which he had in his brain. He saw Mabœuf fall again, he heard Gavroche singing under the grape-shot, and he felt on his lips the coldness of Eponine's forehead; Enjolras, Courfeyrac, Jean Prouvaire, Combeferre, Bossuet, Grantaire, all his friends rose before him, and then disappeared. Were all these dear, dolorous, valiant, charming and tragic beings, dreams? had they really existed? The riot had robed everything in its smoke, and these great fevers have great dreams. He questioned himself, he felt himself, and had a dizziness from all these vanished realities. Where were they all, then? was it really true that everything was dead? a fall into the darkness had carried away everything, except himself; all this had disappeared, as it were, behind the curtain of a theater. There are such curtains which drop on life, and God passes on to the next act.

In himself, was he really the same man? He, poor, was rich; he, the abandoned man, had a family; he, the desperate man, was going to marry Cosette. He seemed to have passed through a tomb, and that he had gone in black and come out white. And in this tomb the others had remained. At certain times all these beings of the past, returning and present, formed a circle round him, and rendered him gloomy. Then he thought of Cosette and became serene again, but it required no less than this felicity to efface this catastrophe.

M. Fauchelevent had almost a place among these vanished beings.

Marius hesitated to believe that the Fauchelevent of the barricade was the same as that Fauchelevent in flesh and bone, so gravely seated by the side of Cosette. The first was probably one of those nightmares brought to him and carried away by his hours of delirium. However, as their two natures were widely sundered, it was impossible for Marius to ask any question of M. Fauchelevent. The idea had not even occurred to him; we have already indicated this characteristic detail. Two men who have a common secret, and who by a sort of tacit agreement do not exchange a syllable on the subject, are not so rare as may be supposed.

Once, however, Marius made an effort; he turned the conversation on the Rue de la Chanvrerie, and, turning to M. Fauchelevent, he said to him:

"Do you know that street well?"

"What street?"

"The Rue de la Chanvrerie."

"I have never heard the name of that street," M. Fauchelevent said, in the most natural tone in the world.

The answer, which related to the name of the street, and not to the street itself, seemed to Marius more conclusive than it really was.

"Decidedly," he thought, "I must have been dreaming. I had an hallucination. It was some one that resembled him, and M. Fauchelevent was not there."

8. *TWO MEN IMPOSSIBLE TO DISCOVER*

THE enchantment, great though it was, did not efface other thoughts from Marius's mind. While the marriage arrangements were being made and the fixed period was waited for, he made some difficult and scrupulous retrospective researches. He owed gratitude in several quarters; he owed it for his father, and he owed it for himself. There was Thénardier, and there was the stranger who had brought him back to M. Gillenormand's. Marius was anxious to find these two men again, as he did not wish to marry, be happy, and forget them, and feared lest these unpaid debts of honor might cast a shadow over his life, which would henceforth be so luminous.

It was impossible for him to leave all these arrears suffering behind him, and he wished, ere he entered joyously into the future, to obtain a receipt from the past.

That Thénardier was a villain took nothing from the fact that he had saved Colonel Pontmercy. Thénardier was a bandit for all the world excepting for Marius. And Marius, ignorant of the real scene on the battle-field of Waterloo, did not know this peculiarity, that his father stood to Thénardier in a strange situation of owing him life without owing him gratitude.

Not one of the agents whom Marius employed could find Thénardier's trail, and the disappearance seemed complete on that side. Mother Thénardier had died in prison before trial, and Thénardier and his daughter Azelma, the only two left of this lamentable group, had plunged again into the shadow. The gulf of the social unknown had silently closed again upon these beings. No longer could be seen on the surface that quivering, that tremor, and those obscure concentric circles which announce that something had fallen there, and that a grappling-iron may be thrown in.

Mother Thénardier being dead, Boulatruelle being out of the way, Claquesous having disappeared, and the principal accused having escaped from prison, the trial for the affair in the Gorbeau attic had pretty nearly failed. The affair had remained rather dark, and the assize court had been compelled to satisfy itself with two subalterns, Panchaud, *alias* Printanier, *alias* Bigrenaille, and Demi-Liard, *alias* Deux Milliards, who had been condemned to fourteen years at the galleys. Penal servitude for life was passed against their accomplices who escaped; Thénardier, as chief and promoter, was condemned to death, also in default. This condemnation was the only thing that remained of Thénardier, casting on this buried name its sinister gleam, like a candle by the side of a coffin.

However, this condemnation, by thrusting Thénardier back into the lowest depths through the fear of being recaptured, added to the dense gloom which covered this man.

As for the other, the unknown man who had saved Marius, the researches had at first some result, and then stopped short. They succeeded in finding again the hackney-coach which had brought Marius to the Rue des Filles du Calvaire on the night of June 6.

The driver declared that on the 6th of June, by the order of a police agent, he had stopped from three P. M. till nightfall on the quay of the Champs Elysées, above the opening of the great sewer; that at about nine in the evening the gate of the sewer which looks upon the river bank opened; that a man came out, bearing on his shoulders another man, who appeared to be dead; that the agent, who was watching at this point, had arrested the living man, and seized the dead man; that he, the coachman, had taken "all these people" into his hackney-coach; that they drove first to the Rue des Filles du Calvaire, and deposited the dead man there; that the dead man was M. Marius, and that he, the coachman recognized him thoroughly, though he was alive this time; that afterward they got into his coach again, and a few yards from the gate of the Archives he was ordered to stop; that he was paid in the street and discharged, and the agent took away the other man; that he knew nothing more, and that the night was very dark.

Marius, as we said, remembered nothing. He merely remembered that he had been seized from behind by a powerful hand at the moment when he fell backward from the barricade, and then all was effaced for him. He had only regained his senses when he was at M. Gillenormand's.

He lost himself in conjectures; he could not doubt as to his own identity, but how was it that he, who had fallen in the Rue de la Chanvrerie, had been picked up by the police agent on the bank of the Seine, near the bridge of the Invalides? Some one had brought him from the quarter of the Halles to the Champs Elysées, and how? by the sewer? Extraordinary devotion! Some one? who? it was this man whom Marius was seeking. Of this man, who was his saviour, he could find nothing, not a trace, not the slightest sign. Marius, though compelled on this side to exercise a great reserve, pushed on his inquiries as far as the prefecture of police, but there the information which he obtained led to no better result than elsewhere. The prefecture knew less about the matter than the driver of the hackney-coach; they had no knowledge of any arrest having taken place at the outlet of the great drain on June 6; they had received no report from the agent about this fact, which, at the prefecture, was regarded as a fable. The invention of this fable was attributed to the driver; for a driver anxious for drink-money is capable of anything, even imagination. The fact, however, was certain, and Marius could not doubt it, unless he doubted his own identity, as we have just said. Everything in this strange enigma was inexplicable; this man, this mysterious man, whom the driver had seen come out of the grating of the great drain, bearing the fainting Marius on his back, and whom the police agent caught in the act of saving an insurgent,—what had become of him? what had become of the agent himself? why had this agent kept silence? had the man succeeded in escaping? had he corrupted the agent? why did this man give no sign of life to Marius, who owed everything to him? the disinterestedness was no less prodigious than the devotion. Why did this man not reappear? perhaps he was above reward, but no man is above gratitude. Was he dead? who was the man? what did he look like? No one was able to say; the driver replied, "The night was very dark." Basque and Nicolette in their start had only looked at their young master, who was all bloody. The porter, whose candle had lit up Marius's tragic arrival, had alone remarked the man in question, and this was the description he gave of him: "The man was frightful."

In the hope of deriving some advantage from them for his researches, Marius kept his blood-stained clothes which he wore when he was brought to his grandfather's. On examining the coat, it was noticed that the skirt was strangely torn, and a piece was wanting. One evening Marius was speaking in the presence of Cosette and Jean Valjean about all this singular adventure, the countless inquiries he had made, and the inutility of his efforts; Monsieur Fauchelevent's cold face offended him, and he exclaimed with a vivacity which had almost the vibration of anger:

"Yes, that man, whoever he may be, was sublime! Do you know what he did, sir? He intervened like an arch-angel. He was obliged to throw himself into the midst of the contest, carry me away, open the sewer, drag me off, and carry me. He must have gone more than a league and a half through frightful subterranean galleries, bent and bowed in the darkness in the sewer, for more than half a league, sir, with a corpse on his back! And for what object? for the sole object of saving that corpse, and that corpse was myself. He said to himself: 'There is, perhaps, a gleam of life left here, and I will risk my existence for this wretched spark!' and he did not risk his existence once, but twenty times! and each step was a danger, and the proof is that on leaving the sewer he was arrested. Do you know, sir, that this man did all that! and he had no reward to expect. Who was I? An insurgent. Who was I? A conquered man. Oh! if Cosette's six hundred thousand francs were mine—"

"They are yours," Jean Valjean interrupted.

"Well, then," Marius continued, "I would give them to find that man."

Jean Valjean was silent.

BOOK VI

THE SLEEPLESS NIGHT

1. FEBRUARY 16, 1833

THE night of February 16 was a blessed night, for it had above its shadow the open sky. It was the wedding-night of Marius and Cosette.

The day had been adorable; it was not the blue feast dreamed of by the grandfather, a fairy scene, with a confusion of cherubim and cupids above the head of the married couple, a marriage worthy of being represented over a door; but it had been sweet and smiling.

The fashion of marrying in 1833 was not at all as it is now. France had not yet borrowed from England that supreme delicacy of carrying off one's wife, flying on leaving the church, hiding one's self as if ashamed of one's happiness, and combining the maneuvers of a bankrupt with the ravishment of the Song of Songs. We had not yet understood how chaste, exquisite, and decent it is to jolt one's paradise in a post-chaise, to vary the mystery with clic-clacs of the whip; to select an inn bed as the nuptial couch, and to leave behind one, at the conventional alcove at so much per night, the most sacred recollection of life, pell-mell with the *tête-à-têtes* of the guard of the diligence and the chamber-maid.

In the second half of the nineteenth century, in which we now are, the mayor and his scarf, the priest and his chasuble, the law and God, are no longer sufficient; they must be complemented by the postilion of Longjumeau; blue jacket with red facings and bell buttons, a leather-bound plate, green leather breeches, oaths to the Norman horses with their knotted tails, false lace, oil-skin hat, heavy, dusty horses, an enormous whip, and strong boots. France does not carry elegance to such an extent as to shower on the post-chaise, as the English nobility do, old shoes and battered slippers, in memory of Churchill, afterward Marlborough or Malbrouck, who was assailed on his wedding-day by the anger of an aunt, which brought him good luck. Shoes and slippers do not yet form part of our nuptial celebrations; but patience, with the spread of good taste we shall yet come to it.

In 1833, that is to say, one hundred years ago, marriage was not performed at a smart trot; people still supposed at that epoch, whimsically enough, that a marriage is a private and social festival; that a patriarchal banquet does not spoil a domestic solemnity; that gayety, even if it be excessive, so long as it is decent, does no harm to happiness; and, finally, that it is venerable and good, that the fusion of these two destinies from which a family will issue begin in the house, and that the household may have in future the nuptial chamber as a witness. And people were so immodest as to marry at home. The wedding took place, then, according to this fashion which is now antiquated, at M. Gillenormand's; and though this affair of marrying is so simple and natural, the publication of the bans, drawing up the deeds, the mayoralty, and the church always cause some complication, and they could not be ready before February 16. Now—we note this detail for the pure satisfaction of being exact—it happened that the 16th was Shrove Tuesday. There were hesitations and scruples, especially on the part of Aunt Gillenormand.

"A Shrove Tuesday!" the grandfather exclaimed: "all the better. There is a proverb that

Mariage un Mardi gras
N'aura point d'enfants ingrats.

All right. Done for the 16th. Do you wish to put it off, Marius?"

"Certainly not," said the amorous youth.

"We'll marry, then," said the grandfather.

The marriage, therefore, took place on the 16th, in spite of the public gayety. It rained on that day, but there is always in the sky a little blue patch at the service of happiness, which lovers see, even when the rest of creation is under its umbrellas. On the previous day, Jean Valjean had handed to Marius, in the presence of M. Gillenormand, the five hundred and eighty-four thousand francs.

As the marriage took place in the ordinary way, the deeds were very simple. Toussaint was henceforth useless to Jean Valjean, so Cosette inherited her, and promoted her to the rank of lady's-maid. As for Jean Valjean, a nice room was furnished expressly for him at M. Gillenormand's, and Cosette had said to him so irresistibly, "Father, I implore you," that she had almost made him promise that he would come and occupy it.

A few days before that fixed for the marriage, an accident happened to Jean Valjean; he slightly injured the thumb of his right hand. It was not serious, and he had not allowed any one to poultice it, or even see it, not even Cosette. Still, it compelled him to wrap up his hand in a bandage and wear his arm in a sling, and this, of course, prevented him from signing anything. M. Gillenormand, as supervising guardian to Cosette, took his place. We will not take the reader either to the mayoralty or to church. Two lovers are not usually followed so far, and we are wont to turn our back on the drama so soon as it puts a bridegroom's bouquet in its button-hole. We will restrict ourselves to noting an incident which, though unnoticed by the bridal party, marked the drive from the Rue des Filles du Calvaire to St. Paul's church.

The Rue Saint Louis was being repaired at the time, and it was blocked from the Rue du Parc Royal; hence it was impossible for the carriage to go direct to St. Paul's. As they were obliged to change their course, the most simple plan was to turn into the boulevard. One of the guests drew attention to the fact that, as it was Shrove Tuesday, there would be a block of vehicles. "Why so?" M. Gillenormand asked. "On account of the masks." "Famous," said the grandfather; "we will go that way. These young people are going to marry and see the serious side of life, and seeing a bit of masquerade will be a preparation for it." They turned into the boulevard; the first of the wedding-coaches contained Cosette and Aunt Gillenormand, M. Gillenormand and Jean Valjean. Marius, still separated from his bride, according to custom, was in the second. The nuptial procession, on turning out of the Rue des Filles du Calvaire, joined the long file of vehicles making an endless chain from the Madeleine to the Bastille, and from the Bastille to the Madeleine. Masks were abundant on the boulevard; and though it rained every now and then, Paillasse, Pantalon, and Gille were obstinate. In the good humor of that winter of 1833, Paris had disguised itself as Venus. We do not see such Shrove Tuesdays nowadays, for as everything existing is a widespread carnival, there is no carnival left. The sidewalks were thronged with pedestrians, and the windows with gazers; and the terraces crowning the peristyles of the theaters were covered with spectators. In addition to the masks, they looked at the file, peculiar to Shrove Tuesday as to Longchamp, of vehicles of every description, citadins' carts, curricles, and cabs, marching in order, rigorously riveted to each other by police regulations, and, as it were, running on rails. Any one who happens to be in one of these vehicles is at once spectator and spectacle. Policemen standing by the side of the boulevard kept in place these two interminable files moving in contrary directions, and watched that nothing should impede the double current of these two streams, one running up, the other down, one toward the Chaussée d'Antin, the other toward the Faubourg St. Antoine. The escutcheoned carriages of the peers of France and ambassadors held the crown of the causeway, coming and going freely; and certain magnificent and gorgeous processions, notably the Bœuf Gras, had the same privilege. In this Parisian gayety, England clacked its whip, for the post-chaise of Lord Seymour, at which a popular sobriquet was hurled, passed with a great noise.

In the double file, along which Municipal Guards galloped like watchdogs, honest family arks, crowded with great-aunts and grandmothers, displayed at windows healthy groups of disguised children, Pierrots of seven, and Pierrettes of six, ravishing little creatures, feeling that they officially formed part of the public merriment, penetrated with the dignity of their Harlequinade, and displaying the gravity of functionaries. From time to time a block occurred somewhere in the procession of vehicles; one or other of the two side files stopped until the knot was untied, for one impeded vehicle paralyzed the entire line. Then they started again. The wedding-carriages were in the file, going toward the Bastille on the right-hand side of the boulevard. Opposite the Rue du Pont-aux-Choux there was a stoppage, and almost at the same moment the file on the other side proceeding toward the Madeleine stopped too. At this point of the procession there was a carriage of masks. These carriages, or, to speak more correctly, these cart-loads of masks, are well known to the Parisians; if they failed on a Shrove Tuesday or at mid-Lent, people would say, *There's something behind it. Probably we are going to have a change of ministry.* A heap of Cassandras, Harlequins, and Columbines jolted above the heads of the passers-by—all possible grotesques, from the Turk to the savage. Hercules supporting Marquises, fish-fags who would make Rabelais stop his ears, as well as Mænads who would make Aristophanes look down, tow perukes, pink fleshings, three-cornered hats, pantaloons, spectacles, cries given to the pedestrians, fists akimbo, bold postures, naked shoulders, masked faces, and unmuzzled immodesty; a chaos of effronteries driven by a coachman in a head-dress of flowers—such is this institution. Greece felt the want of Thespis's cart, and France needs Vadé's fiacre.

All may be parodied, even parody; and the Saturnalia, that grimace of antique beauty, arrive by swelling and swelling at the Mardi gras; and the Bacchanal, formerly crowned with vine-leaves, inundated by sunshine, and displaying her marble breasts in a divine semi-nudity, which is now flabby under the drenched rags of the north, has ended in vulgar slang.

The tradition of the coaches of masks dates back to the oldest times of the monarchy; the accounts of Louis XI allow the palace steward "twenty sous tournois for three coaches of masquerades." In our time, these nosy piles of creatures generally ride in some old coucou of which they encumber the roof, or cover with their tumultuous group a landau of which the hood is thrown back. There are twenty where there is room for only six. You see them on the seat, on the front stool, on the springs of the hood, and on the pole, and they even straddle across the lamps. They are standing, lying down, or seated, cross-legged, or with pendent legs. The women occupy the knees of the men, and this wild pyramid is seen for a long distance over the heads of the crowd. These vehicles form mountains of merriment in the midst of the mob, and Collé, Panard, and Piron flow from them enriched with slang, and the fish-fag's catechism is expectorated from above upon the people. This fiacre, which has grown enormous through its burden, has an air of conquest; Brouhaha is in front and Tohubohu behind. People shout in it, sing in it, yell in it, and writhe with happiness in it; gayety roars there, sarcasm flashes, and joviality is displayed like a purple robe; two nags drag in it farce expanded into an apotheosis, and it is the triumphal car of laughter,—a laughter, though, too cynical to be frank, and in truth this laughter is suspicious. It has a mission, that of proving the existence of the carnival to the Parisians. These fish-fag vehicles, in which some strange darkness is perceptible, cause the philosopher to reflect; there is something of the government in them, and you lay your finger there on a curious affinity between public men and public women. It is certainly a sorry thought, that heaped-up turpitudes give a sum total of gayety; that a people can be amused by building up ignominy on opprobrium; that espionage, acting as a caryatid to prostitution, amuses the mob while affronting it; that the crowd is pleased to see pass on four wheels this monstrous living pile of beings, spangled rags, one-half ordure, one-half light, who bark and sing; that they should clap their hands at all this shame, and that no festival is possible for the multitude unless the police promenade in its midst these twenty-headed hydras of joy. Most sad this certainly is, but what is to be done? These tumbrils of beribboned and flowered slime are insulted and forgiven by the public laughter, and the laughter of all is the accomplice of universal degradation. Certain unhealthy festivals disintegrate the people and convert them into populace, but a populace, like tyrants, requires buffoons. The king has Roquelaure, and the people has Paillasse. Paris is the great mad city, wherever it is not the great sublime city, and the carnival there is political. Paris, let us confess it, willingly allows infamy to play a farce for its amusement, and only asks of its masters—when it has masters—one thing, Rouge the mud for me. Rome was of the same humor—she loved Nero, and Nero was a Titanic débardeur.

Accident willed it, as we have just said, that one of the shapeless groups of masked men and women collected in a vast barouche stopped on the left of the boulevard, while the wedding-party stopped on the right. The carriage in which the masks were, noticed across the road, opposite to it, the carriage in which was the bride.

"Hilloh!" said a mask, "a wedding."

"A false wedding," another retorted; "we are the true one."

And, as they were too far off to address the wedding-party, and as they also feared the interference of the police, the two masks looked elsewhere. The whole cart-load had plenty of work a moment after, for the mob began hissing it, which is the caress given by the mob to masquerades, and the two masks who had just spoken were obliged to face the crowd with their comrades, and found the projectiles from the arsenal of the Halles scarce sufficient to reply to the enormous yells of the people. A frightful exchange of metaphors took place between the masks and the crowd. In the meanwhile, two other masks in the same carriage, a Spaniard with an exaggerated nose, an oldish look, and enormous black mustaches, and a thin and very youthful fish-girl, wearing a half mask had noticed the wedding also, and while their companions and the spectators were insulting each other, held a conversation in a low voice.

Their aside was covered by the tumult and was lost in it. The showers had drenched the open carriage, the February wind is not warm, and so the fish-girl, while answering the Spaniard, shivered, laughed, and coughed.

This was the dialogue, which we translate from the original slang:

"Look here."

"What is it, pa?"

"Do you see that old man?"

"What old man?"

"There, in the wedding-coach, with his arm in a sling."

"Yes."

"Well?"

"I feel sure that I know him."

"Ah!"

"May my neck be cut, and I never have said you, thou, or I in my life, if I do not know that Parisian."*

"To-day Paris is Pantin."

"Can you see the bride by stooping?"

"No."

"And the bridegroom?"

"There is no bridegroom in·that coach."

"Nonsense."

"Unless it be the other old man."

"Come, try and get a look at the bride by stooping."

"I can't."

"No matter, that old fellow who has something the matter with his paw, I feel certain I know him."

"And what good will it do you, your knowing him?"

"I don't know. Sometimes!"

"I don't care a curse for old fellows."

"I know him."

"Know him as much as you like."

"How the deuce is he at the wedding?"

"Why, we are there too."

"Where does the wedding come from?"

"How do I know?"

"Listen."

"Well, what is it?"

"You must do something."

"What is it?"

"Get out of our trap and follow that wedding."

"What to do?"

"To know where it goes and what it is. Make haste and get down; run, my daughter, for you are young."

*Je veux qu'on me fauche le colabre et n'avoir de ma vioc dit vousaille, tonorgue ni mézig, si je ne colombe pas ce pantinois-là.

"I can't leave the carriage."

"Why not?"

"I am hired."

"Oh, the devil!"

"I owe the prefecture my day's work."

"That's true."

"If I leave the carriage, the first inspector who sees me will arrest me. You know that."

"Yes, I know it."

"To-day I am bought by Pharos" (the government).

"No matter, that old fellow bothers me."

"All old men bother you, and yet you ain't a chicken yourself."

"He is in the first carriage."

"Well, what then?"

"In the bride's carriage."

"What next?"

"So he is the father."

"How does that concern me?"

"I tell you he is the father."

"You do nothing but talk about that father."

"Listen."

"Well, what?"

"I can only go away masked, for I am hidden here, and no one knows I am here. But to-morrow there will be no masks, for it is Ash Wednesday, and I run a risk of being nailed. I shall be obliged to go back to my hole, but you are free."

"Not quite."

"Well, more so than I am."

"Well, what then?"

"You must try and find out where that wedding-party is going to."

"Going to?"

"Yes."

"Oh, I know."

"Where to, then?"

"To the Cadran Bleu."

"But that is not the direction."

"Well, then! to La Rapée."

"Or elsewhere."

"They can do as they like, for weddings are free."

"That is not the thing. I tell you that you must try and find out for me what that wedding is, and where it comes from."

"Of course! that would be funny. It's so jolly easy to find out a week after where a wedding-party has gone to that passed on Shrove Tuesday. A pin in a bundle of hay. Is it possible?"

"No matter, you must try. Do you hear, Azelma?"

The two files recommenced their opposite movement on the boulevard, and the carriage of masks lost out of sight that which contained the bride.

2. *JEAN VALJEAN STILL HAS HIS ARM IN A SLING*

To realize one's dream—to whom is this granted? There must be elections for this in heaven; we are the unconscious candidates, and the angels vote. Cosette and Marius had been elected.

Cosette, both at the mayoralty and at church, was brilliant and touching. Toussaint, helped by Nicolette, had dressed her. Cosette wore over a skirt of white taffetas her dress of Binche lace, a veil of English point, a necklace of fine pearls, and a crown of orange flowers; all this was white, and in this whiteness she was radiant. It was an exquisite candor expanding and becoming transfigured in light; she looked like a virgin on the point of becoming a goddess. Marius's fine hair was shining and perfumed, and here and there a glimpse could be caught under the thick curls of pale lines, which were the scars of the barricade. The grandfather, superb, with head erect, amalgamating in his toilet and manners all the elegances of the time of Barras, gave Cosette his arm. He took the place of Jean Valjean, who, owing to his wound, could not give his hand to the bride. Jean Valjean, dressed all in black, followed and smiled.

"Monsieur Fauchelevent," the grandfather said to him, "this is a glorious day, and I vote the end of afflictions and cares. Henceforth there must be no sorrow anywhere. By Heaven! I decree joy! misfortune has no right to exist, and it is a disgrace for the azure of heaven that there are unfortunate men. Evil does not come from man, who, at the bottom, is good; but all human miseries have their capital and central government in hell, otherwise called the Tuileries of the devil. There, I am making demagogic remarks at present. For my part, I have no political opinions left; and all I stick to is that men should be rich, that is to say, joyous."

When, at the end of all the ceremonies,—after pronouncing before the mayor and before the priest every possible yes, after signing the register at the municipality and in the sacristy, after exchanging rings, after kneeling side by side under the canopy of white moire in the smoke of the censer,—they arrived holding each other by the hand, admired and envied by all,—Marius in black, she in white, preceded by the beadle in the colonel's epaulettes, striking the flag-stones with his halbert, between two rows of dazzled spectators, at the church doors, which were thrown wide open, ready to get into their carriage,—and then all was over. Cosette could not yet believe it. She looked at Marius, she looked at the crowd, she looked at heaven; it seemed as if she were afraid of awaking. Her astonished and anxious air imparted something strangely enchanting to her. In returning, they both rode in the same carriage, Marius seated by Cosette's side, and M. Gillenormand and Jean Valjean forming their vis-à-vis. Aunt Gillenormand had fallen back a step and was in the second carriage. "My children," the grandfather said, "you are now M. le Baron and Madame la Baronne, with thirty thousand francs a year." And Cosette, pressing against Marius, caressed his ear with the angelic whisper, "It is true, then. My name is Marius and I am Madame Thou."

These two beings were resplendent; they had reached the irrevocable and irrecoverable moment, the dazzling point of intersection of all youth and all joy. They realized Jean Prouvaire's verses; together they did not count forty years. It was marriage sublimated; and these two children were two lilies. They did not see each other, but contemplated each other. Cosette perceived Marius in a glory, and Marius perceived Cosette upon an altar. And upon this altar, and in this glory, the two apotheoses blending behind a cloud for Cosette, and in a flashing for Marius, there was the ideal thing, the real thing, the meeting-place of kisses and of sleep, the nuptial pillow.

All the torments they had gone through returned to them in intoxication; it appeared to them as if the griefs, the sleeplessness, the tears, the anguish, the terrors, and the despair, by being converted into caresses and sunbeams, rendered more charming still the charming hour which was approaching; and that their sorrows were so many hand-maidens who performed the toilet of joy. How good it is to have suffered! their misfortunes made a halo for their happiness, and the long agony of their love ended in an ascension.

There was in these two souls the same enchantment, tinged with voluptuousness in Marius and with modesty in Cosette. They said to each other in a whisper, "We will go and see again our little garden in the Rue Plumet." The folds of Cosette's dress were upon Marius.

Such a day is an ineffable blending of dream and certainty; you possess and you suppose, and you still have time before you to divine. It is an indescribable emotion on that day to be at midday and think of midnight. The delight of these two hearts overflowed upon the crowd, and imparted merriment to the passers-by. People stopped in the Rue St. Antoine, in front of St. Paul's, to look through the carriage window—the orange flowers trembling on Cosette's head.

Then they returned to the Rue des Filles du Calvaire—home. Marius, side by side with Cosette, ascended, triumphantly and radiantly, that staircase up which he had been dragged in a dying state. The beggars collected before the gate, and, dividing the contents of their purses, blessed them. There were flowers everywhere, and the house was no less fragrant than the church: after the incense the rose. They fancied they could hear voices singing in infinitude; they had God in their hearts; destiny appeared to them like a ceiling of stars; they saw above their heads the flashing of the rising sun. Marius gazed at Cosette's charming bare arm and the pink things which could be vaguely seen through the lace of the stomacher, and Cosette, catching Marius's glance, blushed to the white of her eyes. A good many old friends of the Gillenormand family had been invited, and they thronged round Cosette, outvying each other in calling her Madame la Baronne. The officer, Théodule Gillenormand, now captain, had come from Chartres, where he was stationed, to be present at his cousin's marriage; Cosette did not recognize him. He, on his side, accustomed to be thought a pretty fellow by the women, remembered Cosette no more than any other.

"How right I was in not believing that story of the lancer's!" Father Gillenormand said to himself aside.

Cosette had never been more affectionate to Jean Valjean. She was in unison with Father Gillenormand; while he built up joy in aphorisms and maxims, she exhaled love and beauty like a perfume. Happiness wishes everybody to be happy. In talking to Jean Valjean, she renewed inflections of her voice from the time when she was a little girl, and caressed him with a smile. A banquet had been prepared in the dining-room; an illumination *à giorno* is the necessary seasoning of a great joy, and mist and darkness are not accepted by the happy. They do not consent to be black; night, yes; darkness, no; and if there be no sun, one must be made. The dining-room was a furnace of gay things; in the center, above the white glistening tables, hung a Venetian chandelier, with all sorts of colored birds, blue, violet, red, and green, perched among the candles; round the chandelier were girandoles, and on the walls were mirrors with three and four branches; glasses, crystal, plate, china, crockery, gold, and silver, all flashed and rejoiced. The spaces between the candelabra were filled up with bouquets, so that where there was not a light there was a flower. In the anteroom three violins and a flute played some of Haydn's quartettes.

Jean Valjean had seated himself on a chair in the drawing-room, behind the door, which, being thrown back, almost concealed him. A few minutes before they sat down to table, Cosette gave him a deep courtesy, while spreading out her wedding-dress with both hands, and with a tenderly mocking look asked him:

"Father, are you satisfied?"

"Yes," said Jean Valjean, "I am satisfied."

"Well, then, laugh."

Jean Valjean began laughing. A few minutes later Basque came in to announce that dinner was on the table. The guests, preceded by M. Gillenormand, who gave his arm to Cosette, entered the dining-room, and collected round the table in the prescribed order. There was a large easy-chair on either side of the bride, one for M. Gillenormand, the other for Jean Valjean. M. Gillenormand seated himself, but the other chair remained empty. All looked round for Monsieur Fauchelevent, but he was no longer there, and M. Gillenormand hailed Basque.

"Do you know where M. Fauchelevent is?"

"Yes, sir, I do," Basque replied. "Monsieur Fauchelevent requested me to tell you, sir, that his hand pained him, and that he could not dine with M. le Baron and Madame la Baronne. He therefore begged to be excused, but would call to-morrow. He has just left."

This empty chair momentarily chilled the effusion of the wedding feast; but, though M. Fauchelevent was absent, M. Gillenormand was there, and the grandfather shone for two. He declared that M. Fauchelevent acted rightly in going to bed early if he were in pain, but that it was only a small hurt. This declaration was sufficient; besides, what is a dark corner in such an overwhelming joy? Cosette and Marius were in one of those egotistic and blessed moments when people possess no other faculty than that of perceiving joy; and then M. Gillenormand had an idea, "By Jupiter! this chair is empty; come hither, Marius; your aunt, though she has a right to it, will permit you; this chair is for you; it is legal, and it is pretty—Fortunatus by the side of Fortunata." The whole of the guests applauded. Marius took Jean Valjean's place by Cosette's side, and things were so arranged that Cosette, who had at first been saddened by the absence of Jean Valjean, ended by being pleased at it. From the moment when Marius was the substitute, Cosette would not have regretted God. She placed her little white satin-slippered foot upon Marius's foot.

When the easy-chair was occupied, M. Fauchelevent was effaced, and nothing was wanting. And five minutes later all the guests were laughing from one end of the table to the other, with utter forgetfulness.

At dessert M. Gillenormand rose, with a glass of champagne in his hand, only half full, so that the trembling of ninety-two years might not upset it, and proposed the health of the newly married couple.

"You will not escape from two sermons," he exclaimed; "this morning you had the curé's, and this evening you will have grandpapa's; listen to me, for I am going to give you some advice: Adore each other. I do not beat around the bush, but go straight to the point; be happy. There are no sages in creation but the turtle-doves. Philosophers say, moderate your joys. But I say, throw the bridle on the neck of your joys. Love like fiends, be furious. The philosophers babble, and I should like to thrust their philosophy down their throats for them. Can we have too many perfumes, too many open rose-buds, too many singing nightingales, too many green leaves, and too much dawn in life? can we love too much? can we please one another too much? Take care, Estella, you are too pretty! take care, Nemorin, you are too handsome! What jolly nonsense! can people enchant each other, tease each other, and charm each other too much? can they be too loving? can they be too happy?

"Moderate your joys,—oh, stuff! down with the philosophers, for wisdom is jubilation. Do you jubilate; let us jubilate; are we happy because we are good, or are we good because we are happy? Is the Sancy diamond called the Sancy because it belonged to Harley de Sancy, or because it weighs one hundred and six carats? I do not know; and life is full of such problems: the important thing is to have the Sancy and happiness. Be happy without reserve, and let us blindly obey the sun. What is the sun? it is love; and when I say love, I mean woman. Ah, ah! woman is an omnipotence. Ask that demagogue, Marius, if he is not the slave of that little she-tyrant, Cosette? and willingly so, the coward. Woman! there is not a Robespierre who can stand, but woman reigns. I am now only a royalist of that royalty. What is Adam? the royalty of Eve. There is no '89 for Eve. There was the royal scepter surmounted by the fleur-de-lis, there was the imperial scepter surmounted by a globe, there was Charlemagne's scepter of iron, and the scepter of Louis the Great, which was of gold. The Revolution twisted them between its thumb and forefinger like straws. It is finished, it is broken, it lies on the ground,—there is no scepter left. But just make a revolution against that little embroidered handkerchief which smells of patchouli! I should like to see you at it. Try it. Why is it solid? because it is a rag. Ah! you are the nineteenth century. Well, what then? We were the eighteenth, and were as foolish as you. Do not suppose that you have made any tremendous change in the world because your epidemic is called cholera, and your bourrée the cachucha. After all, woman must always be loved, and I defy you to get out of that. These she-devils are our angels. Yes; love, woman, and a kiss form a circle from which I defy you to issue, and for my own part I should be very glad to enter it again. Who among you has seen the star Venus, the great coquette of the abyss, the Célimène of ocean, rise in infinite space, appeasing everything below her, and looking at the waves like a woman? The ocean is a rude Alcestis, and yet, however much he may growl, when Venus appears he is forced to smile. That brute-beast submits, and we all do so. Anger, tempest, thunderbolts, foam up to the ceiling. A woman comes upon the stage, a star rises, and you crawl in the dust. Marius was fighting six months ago, and is marrying to-day, and that is well done. Yes, Marius, yes, Cosette, you are right. Exist bravely one for the other, make us burst with rage because we cannot do the same, and idolize each other. Take in both your beaks the little straws of felicity which lie on the ground, and make of them a nest for life. By Jove! to love, to be loved, what a great miracle when a man is young. Do not suppose that you invented it. I too have dreamed and thought, and sighed. I too have a moonlit soul. Love is a child six thousand years of age, and has a right to a long white beard. Methuselah is a baby by the side of Cupid. Sixty centuries back man and woman got out of the scrape by loving. The devil, who is cunning, took to hating man; but man, who is more cunning still, took to loving woman. In this way he did himself more good than the devil did him harm. That trick was discovered simultaneously with the terrestrial paradise. My friends, the invention is old, but it is brand-new. Take advantage of it; be Daphnis and Chloe while awaiting till you are Baucis and Philemon. Manage so that, when you are together, you may want for nothing, and that Cosette may be the sun for Marius, and Marius the universe for Cosette. Cosette, let your fine weather be your husband's smiles. Marius, let your wife's tears be the rain, and mind that it never does rain in your household. You have drawn the good number in the lottery, love in the sacrament. You have the prize number, so keep it carefully under lock and key. Do not squander it. Adore each other, and a fig for the rest. Believe what I tell you, then, for it is good sense, and good sense cannot deceive. Be to one another a religion, for each man has his own way of adoring God. Saperlotte! the best way of adoring God is to love one's wife. I love you! that is my catechism; and whoever loves is orthodox. The oath of Henri IV places sanctity between guttling and intoxication. *Ventre Saint Gris!* I do not belong to the religion of that oath, for woman is forgotten in it, and that surprises me on the part of Henri IV's oath. My friends, long live woman! I am old, so people say; but it is amazing how disposed I feel to be young. I should like to go and listen to the bagpipes in the woods. These children, who succeed in being beautiful and satisfied, intoxicate me. I am quite willing to marry if anybody will have me. It is impossible to imagine that God has made us for anything else than this, to idolize, to purr, to adonize, to be a pigeon, to be a cock, to caress our loves from morning till night, to admire ourselves in our little wife, to be proud, to be triumphant, and to swell. Such is the object of life. That, without offense, is what we thought in our time, when we were young men. Ah, Heavens! what charming women there were in those days, what ducks! I carried on my ravages among them. So love each other. If men and women did not love, I really do not see what use there would be in having a spring. And, for my part, I would pray to God to lock up all the fine things he shows us and take them back from us, and to return to his box the flowers, the birds, and the pretty girls. My children, receive the blessing of an old man."

The evening was lively, gay, and pleasant; the sovereign good humor of the grandfather gave the tone to the whole festivity, and each was regulated by this almost centenary cordiality. There was a little dancing, and a good deal of laughter; it was a merry wedding, to which that worthy old fellow "Once on a time" might have been invited; however, he was present in the person of Father Gillenormand. There was a tumult, and then a silence; the married couple disappeared. A little after midnight the Gillenormand mansion became a temple. Here we stop, for an angel stands on the threshold of wedding-nights, smiling, and with finger on lip; the mind becomes contemplative before this sanctuary in which the celebration of love is held. There must be rays of light above such houses, and the joy which they contain must pass through the walls in brilliancy, and vaguely irradiate the darkness. It is impossible for this sacred and fatal festival not to send a celestial radiance to infinitude. Love is the sublime crucible in which the fusion of man and woman takes place; the one being, the triple being, the final being, the human trinity, issue from it. This birth of two souls in one must have emotion for the darkness. The lover is the priest, and the transported virgin feels an awe. A portion of this joy ascends to God. When there is really marriage, that is to say, when there is love, the ideal is mingled with it, and a nuptial couch forms in the darkness a corner of the dawn. If it was given to the mental eye to perceive the formidable and charming visions of higher life, it is probable that it would see the forms of night, the unknown winged beings, the blue wayfarers of the invisible, bending down round the luminous house, satisfied and blessing, pointing out to each other the virgin bride, who is gently startled, and having the reflection of human felicity on their divine countenances. If, at this supreme hour, the pair, dazzled with pleasure, and who believe themselves alone, were to listen, they would hear in their chamber a confused rustling of wings, for perfect happiness implies the guarantee of angels. This little obscure alcove has an entire heaven for its ceiling. When two mouths, which have become sacred by love, approach each other in order to create, it is impossible but that there is a tremor in the immense mystery of the stars above this ineffable kiss.

These felicities are the real ones, there is no joy beyond their joys, love is the sole ecstasy, and all the rest weeps.

To love or to have loved is sufficient; ask nothing more after that. There is no other pearl to be found in the dark folds of life, for love is a consummation.

3 · *THE INSEPARABLE*

WHAT had become of Jean Valjean?

Directly after he had laughed, in accordance with Cosette's request, as no one was paying any attention to him, Jean Valjean rose, and, unnoticed, reached the anteroom. It was the same room which he had entered eight months previously, black with mud and blood and gunpowder, bringing back the grandson to the grandfather. The old paneling was garlanded with flowers and leaves, the musicians were seated on the sofa upon which Marius had been deposited. Basque, in black coat, knee-breeches, white cravat, and white gloves, was placing wreaths of roses round each of the dishes which was going to be served up. Jean Valjean showed him his arm in the sling, requested him to explain his absence, and quitted the house. The windows of the dining-room looked out on the street, and Valjean stood for some minutes motionless in the obscurity of those radiant windows. He listened, and the confused sound of the banquet reached his ears; he heard the grandfather's loud and dictatorial voice, the violins, the rattling of plates and glasses, the burst of laughter, and in all this gay uproar he distinguished Cosette's soft, happy voice.

He left the Rue des Filles du Calvaire and returned to the Rue de l'Homme Armé.

In going home he went along the Rue Saint Louis, the Rue Culture Sainte Catherine, and the Blancs Manteaux; it was a little longer, but it was the road by which he had been accustomed to come with Cosette during the last three months, in order to avoid the crowd and mud of the Rue Vieille du Temple. This road, which Cosette had passed along, excluded the idea of any other itinerary for him. Jean Valjean returned home, lit his candle, and went upstairs. The apartments were empty, and not even Toussaint was in there now. Jean Valjean's footsteps made more noise in the rooms than usual. All the wardrobes were open; he entered Cosette's room and there were no sheets on the bed. The pillow, without a case or lace, was laid on the blankets folded at the foot of the bed, in which no one was going to sleep again. All the small feminine articles to which Cosette clung had been removed; only the heavy furniture and the four walls remained. Toussaint's bed was also unmade, and the only one made which seemed to be expecting somebody was Jean Valjean's.

Jean Valjean looked at the walls, closed some of the wardrobe drawers, and walked in and out of the rooms. Then he returned to his own room and set his candle on the table; he had taken his arm out of the sling, and used it as if he were suffering no pain in it.

He went up to his bed and his eyes fell—was it by accident or was it purposely?—on the *inseparable* of which Cosette had been jealous, the little valise which never left him. On June 4, when he arrived at the Rue de l'Homme Armé, he laid it on a table; he now walked up to this table with some eagerness, took the key out of his pocket, and opened the portmanteau.

He slowly drew out the clothes in which, ten years previously, Cosette had left Montfermeil: first the little black dress, then the black handkerchief, then the stout shoes, which Cosette could almost have worn still, so small was her foot; next the petticoat, then the apron, and, lastly, the woolen stockings. These stockings, in which the shape of a little leg was gracefully marked, were no longer than Jean Valjean's hand. All these articles were black, and it was he who took them for her to Montfermeil. He laid each article on the bed as he took it out, and he thought and remembered. It was in winter, a very cold December, she was shivering under her rags, and her poor feet were quite red in her wooden shoes. He, Jean Valjean, had made her take off these rags and put on this mourning garb; the mother must have been pleased in her tomb to see her daughter wearing mourning for her, and above all to see that she was well clothed and was warm. He thought of that forest of Montfermeil, he thought of the weather it was, of the trees without leaves, of the wood without birds, and the sky without sun; but no matter, it was charming. He arranged the little clothes on the bed, the handkerchief near the petticoat, the stockings along with the shoes, the apron by the side of the dress, and he looked at them one after the other. She was not much taller than that, she had her large doll in her arms, she had put her louis d'or in the pocket of this apron, she laughed, they walked along holding each other's hand, and she had no one but him in the world.

Then this venerable white head fell on the bed, his old stoical heart broke; his face was buried in Cosette's clothes, and had any one passed upstairs at that moment he would have heard frightful sobs.

4. *IMMORTALE JECUR*

The old formidable struggle, of which we have already seen several phases, began again. Jacob only wrestled with the angel for one night. Alas! how many times have we seen Jean Valjean caught round the waist in the darkness by his conscience, and struggling frantically against it!

An extraordinary struggle! at certain moments the foot slips, at others the ground gives way. How many times had that conscience, clinging to the right, strangled and crushed him! how many times had inexorable truth set its foot on his chest? how many times had he, felled by the light, cried for mercy! how many times had that implacable light, illumined within and over him by the bishop, dazzled him when he wished to be blinded! how many times had he risen again in the contest, clung to the rock, supported himself by sophistry, and been dragged through the dust, at one moment throwing his conscience under him, at another thrown by it! how many times, after an equivoque, after the treacherous and specious reasoning of egotism, had he heard his irritated conscience cry in his ears, "Tripper! scoundrel!" how many times had his refractory thoughts groaned convulsively under the evidence of duty! what secret wounds he had, which he alone felt bleeding! what excoriations there were in his lamentable existence! how many times had he risen, bleeding, mutilated, crushed, enlightened, with despair in his heart and serenity in his soul! and, though vanquished, he felt himself the victor, and after having dislocated, tortured, and broken him, his conscience erect before him, luminous and tranquil, would say to him, "Now go in peace!"

What a mournful peace, alas; after issuing from such a contest.

This night, however, Jean Valjean felt that he was fighting his last battle. A crushing question presented itself; predestinations are not all straight; they do not develop themselves in a rectilinear avenue before the predestined man; they have blind alleys, zigzags, awkward corners, and perplexing cross-roads. Jean Valjean was halting at this moment at the most dangerous of these cross-roads.

He had reached the supreme crossing of good and evil, and had that gloomy intersection before his eyes. This time again, as had already happened in other painful interludes, two roads presented themselves before him, one tempting, the other terrifying; which should he take? The one which frightened him was counseled by the mysterious pointing hand which we all perceive every time that we fix our eyes upon the darkness. Jean Valjean had once again a choice between the terrible haven and the smiling snare.

Is it true, then? the soul may be cured, but not destiny. What a frightful thing! an incurable destiny!

The question which presented itself was this: In what way was Jean Valjean going to behave with regard to the happiness of Cosette and Marius? That happiness he had willed, he had made; and at this hour, in gazing upon it, he could have the species of satisfaction which a cutler would have who recognized his trade-mark upon a knife, when he drew it, all smoking, from his chest.

Cosette had Marius, Marius possessed Cosette; they possessed everything, even wealth, and it was his doing. But, now that this happiness existed and was there, how was he, Jean Valjean, to treat it? should he force himself upon it, and treat it as if belonging to himself? Doubtless, Cosette was another man's; but should he, Jean Valjean, retain of Cosette all that he could retain? Should he remain the sort of father, scarce seen but respected, which he had hitherto been? should he introduce himself quietly into Cosette's house? should he carry his past to this future without saying a word? should he present himself there as one having a right, and should he sit down, veiled, at this luminous hearth? Should he smilingly take the hands of these two innocent creatures in his tragic hands? should he place on the andirons of the Gillenormand

drawing-room his feet which dragged after them the degrading shadow
of the law? Should he render the obscurity on his brow and the cloud
on theirs denser? should he join his catastrophe to their two felicities?
should he continue to be silent?—in a word, should he be the sinister
dumb man of destiny by the side of these two happy beings?

We must be accustomed to fatality and to meeting it, to raise our eyes
when certain questions appear to us in their terrible nudity. Good and
evil are behind this stern note of interrogation. "What are you going to
do?" the sphinx asks.

This habit of trial Jean Valjean had, and he looked at the sphinx
fixedly, and examined the pitiless problem from all sides.

Cosette, that charming existence, was the raft of this ship-wrecked
man; what should he do, cling to it or let it go? If he clung to it, he
issued from disaster, he remounted to the sunshine, he let the bitter water
drip off his clothes and hair, he was saved and lived.

Suppose he let it go? then there was an abyss.

He thus dolorously held counsel with his thoughts, or, to speak more
correctly, he combated; he rushed furiously within himself, at one moment against his will, at another against his convictions. It was fortunate for Jean Valjean that he had been able to weep, for that enlightened
him, perhaps. Still, the beginning was stern; a tempest, more furious
than that which had formerly forced him to Arras, was let loose within
him. The past returned to him in the face of the present; he compared
and sobbed. Once the sluice of tears was opened the despairing man
writhed. He felt himself arrested, alas! in the deadly fight between one
egotism and one duty. When we thus recoil inch by inch before our
ideal, wildly, obstinately, exasperated at yielding, disputing the ground,
hoping for a possible flight, and seeking an issue, what a sudden and
sinister resistance is the foot of a wall behind us! to feel the sacred shadow
forming an obstacle! The inexorable invisible, what a crushing force!

Hence we have never finished with our conscience. Make up your
mind, Brutus; make up your mind, Cato, it is bottomless, for it is God.
You cast into this pit the labor of your whole life, your fortune, your
wealth, your success, your liberty, or your country, your comfort, your
repose, your joy. More, more, more! empty the vase, tread over the urn,
you must end by throwing in your heart. There is a barrel like this somewhere in the Hades of old. Is it not pardonable to refuse at last? can that
which is inexhaustible have any claim? are not endless chains beyond
human strength? who, then, would blame Sisyphus and Jean Valjean
for saying, "It is enough."

The obedience of matter is limited by friction; is there not a limit to the obedience of the soul? If perpetual motion be impossible, why is perpetual devotion demanded? The first step is nothing; it is the last that is difficult. What was the Champmathieu affair by the side of Cosette's marriage? what did it bring with it? what is returning to the hulks by the side of entering nothingness? Oh, first step to descend, how gloomy thou art! oh, second step, how black thou art! How could he help turning his head away this time? Martyrdom is a sublimation, a corrosive sublimation; it is a torture which consecrates. A man may consent to it for the first hour; he sits on the throne of red-hot iron, the crown of red-hot iron is placed on his head, he accepts the red-hot globe, he takes the red-hot scepter, but he still has to don the mantle of flame; and is there not a moment when the miserable flesh revolts and the punishment is fled from?

At length Jean Valjean entered the calmness of prostration; he wished, thought over, and considered the alternations, the mysterious balance of light and shadow.

Should he force his galleys on these two dazzling children, or consummate his own irremediable destruction? On one side was the sacrifice of Cosette, on the other his own.

On which solution did he decide? what determination did he form? what was his mental definitive reply to the incorruptible interrogatory of fatality? what door did he resolve on opening? which side of his life did he make up his mind to close and condemn; amid all those unfathomable precipices that surrounded him, which was his choice? what extremity did he accept? to which of these gulfs did he nod his head? His confusing reverie lasted all night; he remained till day-break in the same position, leaning over the bed, prostrate before the enormity of fate, crushed perhaps, alas! his fists clenched, and arms extended at a right angle like an unnailed crucified man thrown with his face on the ground. He remained thus for twelve hours, the twelve hours of a long winter's night, frozen, without raising his head or uttering a syllable. He was motionless as a corpse, while his thoughts rolled on the ground or fled away, sometimes like a hydra, sometimes like the eagle. To see him thus, you would have thought him a dead man; but all at once he started convulsively, and his mouth, pressed to Cosette's clothes, kissed them; then one saw that he was alive.

One! who? For Jean Valjean was alone; nobody was there!

The *One* who is in the Darkness.

BOOK VII

THE LAST DROP IN THE CUP

1. THE SEVENTH CIRCLE AND THE EIGHTH HEAVEN

THE day after a wedding is solitary, for people respect the retirement of the happy, and to some extent their lengthened slumbers. The confusion of visits and congratulations does not begin again till a later date. On the morning of February 17, it was a little past midday when Basque, with napkin and feather-brush under his arm, was dusting the anteroom, when he heard a low tap at the door. There had not been a ring, which is discreet on such a day. Basque opened and saw M. Fauchelevent; he conducted him to the drawing-room, which was still encumbered and looked like the battle-field of the previous day's joys.

"Really, sir," observed Basque, "we woke late."

"Is your master up?" Jean Valjean asked.

"How is your hand, sir?" Basque replied.

"Better. Is your master up?"

"Which one? the old or the new?"

"Monsieur Pontmercy."

"Monsieur le Baron!" said Basque drawing himself up.

A baron is before all a baron to his servants; a portion of it comes to them, and they have what a philosopher would call a splash from the title, and that flatters them. Marius, we may mention in passing, a militant republican as he had proved, was now a baron, in spite of himself. A little revolution had taken place in the family with reference to this title; it was M. Gillenormand who was attached to it, and Marius who cared little for it. But Colonel Pontmercy had written, *My son will bear my title,* and Marius obeyed. And then Cosette, in whom the woman was beginning to germinate, was delighted at being a baroness.

"Monsieur le Baron?" repeated Basque, "I will go and see. I will tell him that Monsieur Fauchelevent is here."

"No, do not tell him it is I. Tell him that some one wishes to speak to him privately, and do not mention my name."

"Ah!" said Basque.

"I wish to surprise him."

"Ah!" Basque repeated, giving himself his second "Ah!" as an explanation of the first.

And he left the room, and Jean Valjean remained alone. The drawing-room, as we said, was all in disorder, and it seemed as if you could still hear the vague sounds of the wedding. On the floor were all sorts of flowers, which had fallen from garlands and head-dresses, and the candles burned down to the socket added wax stalactites to the crystal of the lusters. Not an article of furniture was in its place; in the corner three or four easy-chairs, drawn close together and forming a circle, looked as if they were continuing a conversation. The *ensemble* was laughing; there is a certain grace left in a dead festival, for it has been happy. Upon those disarranged chairs, amid those fading flowers, and under those extinguished lamps, persons have thought of joy. The sun succeeded the chandelier, and gayly entered the drawing-room. A few moments passed, during which Jean Valjean remained motionless at the spot where Basque left him. His eyes were hollow, and so sunk in their sockets by sleeplessness that they almost disappeared. His black coat displayed the fatigued creases of a coat which has been up all night, and the elbows were white with that down which friction with linen leaves on cloth. Jean Valjean looked at the window designed on the floor at his feet by the sun.

There was a noise at the door, and he raised his eyes.

Marius came in with head erect, laughing mouth, a peculiar light over his face, a smooth forehead, and a flashing eye. He, too, had not slept.

"It is you, father!" he exclaimed, on perceiving Jean Valjean; "why, that ass Basque affected the mysterious. But you have come too early, it is only half-past twelve, and Cosette is asleep."

That word, father, addressed to M. Fauchelevent by Marius, signified supreme felicity. There had always been, as we know, a gulf, a coldness, and constraint between them; ice to melt or break. Marius was so intoxicated that the gulf disappeared, the ice dissolved, and M. Fauchelevent was for him, as for Cosette, a father. He continued, the words overflowed with him, which is peculiar to these divine paroxysms of joy: "How delighted I am to see you! if you only knew how we missed you yesterday! Good-day, father; how is your hand? better, is it not?"

And, satisfied with the favorable answer which he gave himself, he went on:

"We both spoke about you, for Cosette loves you so dearly. You will not forget that you have a room here, for we will not hear a word about the Rue de l'Homme Armé. I do not know how you were able to live in that street, which is sick, and mean, and poor, which has a barrier at one end, where you feel cold, and which no one can enter! You will come and install yourself here, and from to-day, or else you will have to settle with Cosette. She intends to lead us both by the nose, I warn you. You have seen your room; it is close to ours, and looks out on the gardens. We have had the lock mended, the bed is made, it is all ready, and you have only to move in. Cosette has placed close to your bed a large old easy-chair of Utrecht velvet, to which she said, 'Hold out your arms to him!' Every spring a nightingale comes to the clump of acacias which faces your windows, and you will have it in two months. You will have its nest on your left and ours on your right; at night it will sing, and by day Cosette will talk. Your room faces due south; Cosette will arrange your books in it, the 'Travels of Captain Cook,' and the other, 'Vancouver's Travels,' and all your matters. There is, I believe, a valise to which you are attached, and I have arranged a corner of honor for it. You have won my grandfather, for you suit him; we will live together. Do you know whist? you will overwhelm my grandfather if you are acquainted with whist. You will take Cosette for a walk on the day when I go to the courts; you will give her your arm, as you used to do, you remember, formerly at the Luxembourg. We are absolutely determined to be very happy, and you will share in our happiness; do you hear, papa? By the bye, you will breakfast with us this morning?"

"I have one thing to remark to you, sir," said Jean Valjean; "I am an ex-convict."

The limit of the perceptible acute sounds may be as well exceeded for the mind as for the ear. These words, *I am an ex-convict,* coming from M. Fauchelevent's mouth and entering Marius's ear, went beyond possibility. Marius did not hear; it seemed to him as if something had been just said to him, but he knew not what. He stood with gaping mouth. Jean Valjean unfastened the black handkerchief that supported his right arm, undid the linen rolled round his hand, bared his thumb, and showed it to Marius.

"I have nothing the matter with my hand," he said.

Marius looked at the thumb.

"There was never anything the matter with it," Jean Valjean added. There was, in fact, no sign of a wound.

Jean Valjean continued: "It was proper that I should be absent from your marriage, and I was, so far as I could. I feigned this wound in order not to commit a forgery and render the marriage-deeds null and void."

Marius stammered: "What does this mean?"

"It means," Jean Valjean replied, "that I have been to the galleys."

"You are driving me mad," said the horrified Marius.

"Monsieur Pontmercy," said Jean Valjean, "I was nineteen years at the galleys for robbery. Then I was sentenced to them for life, for robbery and a second offense. At the present moment I am an escaped convict."

Although Marius recoiled before the reality, refused the facts, and resisted the evidence, he was obliged to yield to it. He was beginning to understand, and, as always happens in such a case, he understood too much. He had the shudder of a hideous internal flash; and an idea that made him shudder crossed his mind. He foresaw a frightful destiny for himself in the future.

"Say all, say all," he exclaimed; "you are Cosette's father!"

And he fell back two steps, with a movement of indescribable horror. Jean Valjean threw up his head with such a majestic attitude that he seemed to rise to the ceiling.

"It is necessary that you should believe me here, sir, although the oath of men like us is not taken in a court of justice—"

Here there was a silence, and then, with a sort of sovereign and sepulchral authority, he added, speaking slowly and laying a stress on the syllables:

"You will believe me. I Cosette's father! Before Heaven, no, Monsieur le Baron Pontmercy. I am a peasant of Faverolles, and earned my livelihood by pruning trees. My name is not Fauchelevent, but Jean Valjean. I am nothing to Cosette, so re-assure yourself."

Marius stammered: "Who proves it to me?"

"I do, since I say it."

Marius looked at this man; he was mournful and calm, and no falsehood could issue from such calmness. What is frozen is sincere, and the truth could be felt in this coldness of the tomb.

"I do believe you," said Marius.

Jean Valjean bowed his head, as if to note the fact, and continued: "What am I to Cosette? a passer-by. Ten years ago I did not know that she existed. I love her, it is true, for men love a child whom they have seen little when old themselves; when a man is old, he feels like a grandfather to all little children. You can, I suppose, imagine that I have something which resembles a heart. She was an orphan, without father or mother, and needed me, and that is why I came to love her. Children are so weak that the first-comer, even a man like myself, may be their protector. I performed this duty to Cosette. I cannot suppose that so small a thing can be called a good action; but if it be one, well, assume that I had done it. Record that extenuating fact. To-day Cosette leaves my life, and our two roads separate. Henceforth I can do no more for her; she is Madame Pontmercy; her providence has changed, and she has gained by the change, so all is well. As for the six hundred thousand francs, you say nothing of them, but I will meet your thought half-way; they are a deposit. How was it placed in my hands? no matter. I give up the deposit, and there is nothing more to ask of me. I complete the restitution by stating my real name, and this too concerns myself, for I am anxious that you should know who I am."

And Jean Valjean looked Marius in the face.

All that Marius experienced was tumultuous and incoherent, for certain blasts of the wind of destiny produce such waves in our soul. We have all had such moments of trouble in which everything is dispersed within us; we say the first things that occur to us, which are not always precisely those which we ought to say. There are sudden revelations which we cannot bear, and which intoxicate like a potent wine. Marius was stupefied by the new situation which appeared to him, and spoke to this man almost as if he were angry at the avowal.

"But why," he exclaimed, "do you tell me all this? who forces you to do so? you might have kept your secret to yourself. You are neither denounced, nor pursued, nor tracked. You have a motive for making the revelation so voluntarily. Continue; there is something else; for what purpose do you make this confession? for what motive?"

"For what motive?" Jean Valjean answered, in a voice so low and dull that it seemed as if he were speaking to himself rather than Marius. "For what motive? in truth, does this convict come here to say, I am a convict? Well, yes, the motive is a strange one; it is through honesty. The misfortune is that I have a thread in my heart which holds me fast, and it is especially when a man is old that these threads are most solid. The whole of life is undone around, but they resist. Had I been enabled to tear away that thread, break it, unfasten or cut the knot, and go a long way off, I would be saved, and needed only to start. There are diligences in the Rue du Bouloy; you are happy, and I am off. I tried to break that thread. I pulled at it, it held out, it did not break, and I pulled out my heart with it. Then I said, I cannot live anywhere else, and must remain. Well, yes, but you are right. I am a fool; why not remain simply? You offer me a bedroom in the house. Madame Pontmercy loves me dearly; she said to that fauteuil, 'Hold out your arms to him'; your grandfather asks nothing better than to have me. I suit him, we will live all together, have our meals in common, I will give my arm to Cosette, to Madame Pontmercy,—forgive me, but it is habit,—we will have only one roof, one table, one fire, the same chimney-corner in winter, the same walk in summer; that is joy, that is happiness, that is everything. We will live in one family."

At this word Jean Valjean became fierce. He folded his arms, looked at the board at his feet as if he wished to dig a pit in it, and his voice suddenly became loud.

"In one family? no. I belong to no family; I do not belong to yours; I do not even belong to the human family. In houses where people are together, I am in the way. There are families, but none for me; I am the unhappy man, I am outside. Had I a father and mother? I almost doubt it. On the day when I gave you that child in marriage, it was all ended. I saw her happy, and that she was with the man she loved; that there is a kind old gentleman here, a household of two angels, and every joy in this house; and I said to myself, 'Do not enter.' I could lie, it is true, deceive you all, and remain Monsieur Fauchelevent; so long as it was for her, I was able to lie, but now that it would be for myself, I ought not to do so. I only required to be silent, it is true, and all would have gone on. You ask me what compels me to speak? a strange sort of a thing—my conscience. It would have been very easy, however, to hold my tongue; I spent the night in trying to persuade myself into it. You are shriving me, and what I have just told you is so extraordinary that you have the right to do so. Well, yes, I spent the night in giving myself reasons. I gave myself excellent reasons; I did what I could. But there are two things in which I could not succeed,—I could neither break the string which holds me by the heart, fixed, sealed, and riveted here, nor silence some one who speaks to me in a low voice when I am alone. That is why I have come to confess all to you this morning,—all, or nearly all, for it is useless to tell what only concerns myself, and that I keep to myself. You know the essential thing. I took my mystery, then, and brought it to you, and ripped it up before your eyes. It was not an easy resolution to form, and I debated the point the whole night. Ah! you may fancy that I did not say to myself that this was not the Champmathieu affair, that in hiding my name I did no one any harm, that the name of Fauchelevent was given me by Fauchelevent himself in gratitude for a service rendered, and that I might fairly keep it, and that I should be happy, in this room which you offer me, that I should not be at all in the way, that I should be in my little corner, and that while you had Cosette I should have the idea of being in the same house with her; each would have his proportioned happiness. Continuing to be Monsieur Fauchelevent arranged everything. Yes, except my soul; there would be joy all around me, but the bottom of my soul would remain black. Thus I should have remained Monsieur Fauchelevent. I should have hidden my real face in the presence of your happiness; I should have had an enigma, and in the presence of your broad sunshine I should have had darkness; thus, without crying 'Look out,' I should have introduced the hulks to your hearth, I should have sat down at your table with the thought that if you knew who I was you would expel me; and let myself be served by the servants, who, had they known, would have said, 'What a horror!' I should have touched you with my elbow, which you have a right to feel offended at, and swindled you out of shakes of the hand. There would have been in your house a divided respect between venerable gray hairs and branded gray hairs; in your most intimate hours, when all hearts formed themselves to each other, when we were all four together,—the grandfather, you two, and I,—there would have been a stranger there. Hence I, a dead man, would have imposed myself on you who are living, and I should have sentenced her for life. You, Cosette, and I would have been three heads in the green cap! Do you not shudder? I am only the most crushed of men, but I should have been the most monstrous. And this crime I should have committed daily! and this falsehood I should have told daily! and this face of night I should have worn daily! and I should have given you daily, daily, a share in my stigma, to you, my beloved, to you, my children, to you my innocents. Holding one's tongue is nothing? keeping silence is simple? no, it is not simple, for there is a silence which lies, and my falsehood, and my fraud, and my indignity, and my cowardice, and my treachery, and my crime, I should have drunk drop by drop; I should have spat it out, and then drunk it again; I should have ended at midnight and begun again at midday, and my 'good-day' would have lied, and my 'good-night' would have lied, and I should have slept upon it, and eaten it with my bread; and I should have looked at Cosette, and responded to the smile of the angel with the smile of the condemned man, and I should have been an abominable scoundrel, and for what purpose? to be happy. I happy? have I the right to be happy? I am out of life, sir."

Jean Valjean stopped, and Marius listened, but such enchainments of ideas and agonies cannot be interrupted. Jean Valjean lowered his voice again, but it was no longer the dull voice, but the sinister voice.

"You ask why I speak? I am neither denounced nor pursued nor tracked, you say. Yes, I am denounced! Yes, I am pursued! Yes, I am tracked! By whom? by myself. It is I who bar my own passage, and I drag myself along, and I push myself, and I arrest myself, and execute myself; and when a man holds himself, he is securely held."

And seizing his own collar, and dragging it toward Marius, he continued:

"Look at this fist. Do you not think that it holds this collar so as not to let it go? Well, conscience is a very different hand! If you wish to be happy, sir, you must never understand duty; for, so soon as you have understood it, it is implacable. People may say that it punishes you for understanding it; but no, it rewards you for it, for it places you in a hell where you feel God by your side. A man has no sooner torn his entrails than he is at peace with himself."

And with an indescribable accent he added:

"Monsieur Pontmercy, this is not common sense. I am an honest man. It is by degrading myself in your eyes that I raise myself in my own. This has happened to me once before, but it was less painful; it was nothing. Yes, an honest man. I should not be one if you had, through my fault, continued to esteem me; but now that you despise me I am so. I have this fatality upon me, that as I am never able to have any but stolen consideration, this consideration humiliates and crushes me internally, and in order that I may respect myself people must despise me. Then I draw myself up. I am a galley-slave who obeys his conscience. I know very well that this is not likely, but what would you have me do? it is so. I have made engagements with myself, and keep them. There are accidents which bind us. There are hazards which drag us into duty. Look you, Monsieur Pontmercy, things have happened to me in my life."

Jean Valjean made another pause, swallowing his saliva with an effort, as if his words had a bitter after-taste, and he continued:

"When a man has such a horror upon him, he has no right to make

others share it unconsciously, he has no right to communicate his plague
to them, he has no right to make them slip over his precipice without
their perceiving it, he has no right to drag his red cap over them, and no
right craftily to encumber the happiness of another man with his misery.
To approach those who are healthy and touch them in the darkness with
his invisible ulcer is hideous. Fauchelevent may have lent me his name,
but I have no right to use it; he may have given it to me, but I was unable
to take it. A name is a self. Look you, sir, I have thought a little and read
a little, though I am a peasant; and you see that I express myself properly. I explain things to myself, and have carried out my own education.
Well, yes; to abstract a name and place one's self under it is dishonest.
The letters of the alphabet may be filched like a purse or a watch. To
be a false signature in flesh and blood, to be a living false key, to enter
among honest folk by picking their lock, never to look, but always to
squint, to be internally infamous,— no! no! no! no! It is better to suffer,
bleed, tear one's flesh with one's nails, pass the nights writhing in agony,
and gnaw one's stomach and soul. That is why I have come to tell you all
this,—voluntarily, as you remarked."

He breathed painfully, and uttered this last remark:

"Formerly I stole a loaf in order to live; to-day I will not steal a name
in order to live."

"To live!" Marius interrupted, "you do not require that name to live."

"Ah! I understand myself," Jean Valjean replied, raising and drooping
his head several times in succession. There was a silence; both were
speechless, sunk, as they were, in a gulf of thought. Marius was sitting
near a table and supporting the corner of his mouth in one of his fingers.
Jean Valjean walked backward and forward; he stopped before a glass
and remained motionless. Then, as if answering some internal reasoning, he said, as he looked in this glass, in which he did not see himself:

"For the present I am relieved."

He began walking again, and went to the other end of the room. At
the moment when he turned, he perceived that Marius was watching his
walk, and he said to him, with an indescribable accent:

"I drag my leg a little. You understand why now."

Then he turned round full to Marius.

"And now, sir, imagine this. I have said nothing. I have remained
Monsieur Fauchelevent. I have taken my place in your house. I am one
of your family. I am in my room. I come down to breakfast in my slippers; at night we go to the play, all three. I accompany Madame Pont-

mercy to the Tuileries and to the Place Royale; we are together, and you believe me your equal. One fine day I am here, you are there. We are talking and laughing, and you hear a voice cry this name, 'Jean Valjean!' and then that fearful hand, the police, issues from the shadow, and suddenly tears off my mask!"

He was silent again. Marius had risen with a shudder, and Jean Valjean continued:

"What do you say to that?"

Marius's silence replied, and Jean Valjean continued:

"You see very well that I did right in not holding my tongue. Be happy, be in heaven, be the angel of an angel, be in the sunshine and content yourself with it, and do not trouble yourself as to the way in which a poor condemned man opens his heart and does his duty; you have a wretched man before you, sir."

Marius slowly crossed the room, and when he was by Jean Valjean's side offered him his hand. But Marius was compelled to take this hand which did not offer itself. Jean Valjean let him do so, and it seemed to Marius that he was pressing a hand of marble.

"My grandfather has friends," said Marius. "I will obtain your pardon."

"It is useless," Jean Valjean replied; "I am supposed to be dead, and that is sufficient. The dead are not subjected to surveillance, and are supposed to rot quietly. Death is the same thing as pardon."

And, liberating the hand which Marius held, he added with a sort of inexorable dignity: "Moreover, duty, my duty, is the friend to whom I have recourse, and I only need one pardon—that of my conscience."

At this moment the door opened gently at the other end of the drawing-room, and Cosette's head appeared in the crevice. Only her sweet face was visible. Her hair was in charming confusion, and her eyelids were still swollen with sleep. She made the movement of a bird thrusting its head out of the nest, looked first at her husband, then at Jean Valjean, and cried to them laughingly—it looked like a smile issuing from a rose:

"I will bet that you are talking politics. How stupid that is, instead of being with me!"

Jean Valjean started.

"Cosette," Marius stammered, and he stopped. They looked like two culprits; Cosette, radiant, continued to look at them both, and there were in her eyes gleams of Paradise.

"I have caught you in the act," Cosette said; "I just heard through this,

Father Fauchelevent saying, Conscience, doing one's duty. That is politics, and I will have none of it. People must not talk politics on the very next day; it is not right."

"You are mistaken, Cosette," Marius replied; "we are talking of business. We are talking about the best way of investing your six hundred thousand francs."

"I am coming," Cosette interrupted. "Do you want me here?"

And, resolutely passing through the door, she entered the drawing-room. She was dressed in a large combing gown with a thousand folds and large sleeves, which descended from her neck to her feet. There are in the golden skies of old Gothic paintings these charming sacks to place an angel in. She contemplated herself from head to foot in a large mirror, and then exclaimed, with an ineffable outburst of ecstasy:

"There were once upon a time a king and queen. Oh! how delighted I am!"

This said, she courtesied to Marius and Jean Valjean.

"Then," she said, "I am going to install myself near you in an easy-chair; we shall breakfast in half an hour. You will say all you like, for I know very well that gentlemen must talk, and I shall be very good."

Marius took her by the arm and said to her, lovingly:

"We are talking about business."

"By the way," Cosette answered, "I have opened my window, and a number of sparrows (pierrots) have just entered the garden. Birds, not masks. To-day is Ash Wednesday, but not for the birds."

"I tell you that we are talking of business, so go, my little Cosette, leave us for a moment. We are talking figures, and they would only annoy you."

"You have put on a charming cravat this morning, Marius. You are very coquettish, monseigneur. No, they will not annoy me."

"I assure you that they will."

"No, since it is you, I shall not understand you, but I shall hear you. When a woman hears voices she loves, she does not require to understand the words they say. To be together is all I want, and I shall stay with you,—there!"

"You are my beloved Cosette! impossible."

"Impossible!"

"Yes."

"Very good," Cosette remarked, "I should have told you some news. I should have told you that grandpapa is still asleep, that your aunt is at mass, that the chimney of papa Fauchelevent's room smokes, that Nicolette has sent for the chimney-sweep, that Nicolette and Toussaint have already quarreled, and that Nicolette ridicules Toussaint's stammering. Well, you shall know nothing. Ah, it is impossible? you shall see, sir, that in my turn I shall say it is impossible. Who will be caught then? I implore you, my little Marius, to let me stay with you two."

"I assure you that we must be alone."

"Well, am I anybody?"

Jean Valjean did not utter a word, and Cosette turned to him.

"In the first place, father, I insist on your coming and kissing me. What do you mean by saying nothing, instead of taking my part? Did one ever see a father like that? That will show you how unhappy my marriage is, for my husband beats me. Come and kiss me at once."

Jean Valjean approached her, and Cosette turned to Marius.

"I make a face at you."

Then she offered her forehead to Jean Valjean, who moved a step toward her. All at once Cosette recoiled.

"Father, you are pale; does your arm pain you?"

"It is cured," said Jean Valjean.

"Have you slept badly?"

"No."

"Are you sad?"

"No."

"Kiss me. If you are well, if you slept soundly, if you are happy, I will not scold you."

And she again offered him her forehead, and Jean Valjean set a kiss on this forehead, upon which there was a heavenly reflection.

"Smile."

Jean Valjean obeyed, but it was the smile of a ghost.

"Now, defend me against my husband."

"Cosette—" said Marius.

"Be angry, father, and tell him I am to remain. You can talk before me. You must think me very foolish. What you are saying is very astonishing, then! business, placing money in a bank, that is a great thing. Men make mysteries for nothing. I mean to say I am very pretty this morning. Marius, look at me."

And, with an adorable shrug of the shoulders and an exquisite pout, she looked at Marius. Something like a flash passed between these two beings, and they cared little about a third party being present.

"I love you," said Marius.

"I adore you," said Cosette.

And they irresistibly fell into each other's arms.

"And now," Cosette continued, as she smoothed a crease in her dressing-gown, with a little triumphant pout, "I remain."

"No," Marius replied, imploringly, "we have something to finish."

"Again, no?"

Marius assumed a serious tone:

"I assure you, Cosette, that it is impossible."

"Ah, you are putting on your man's voice, sir; very good, I will go. You did not support me, father; and so you, my hard husband, and you, my dear papa, are tyrants. I shall go and tell grandpapa. If you believe that I intend to return and talk platitudes to you, you are mistaken. I am proud, and I intend to wait for you at present. You will see how wearisome it will be without me. I am going, very good."

And she left the room, but, two seconds after, the door opened again, her fresh, rosy face passed once again between the two folding doors, and she cried to them:

"I am very angry."

The door closed again, and darkness returned. It was like a straggling sunbeam which, without suspecting it, had suddenly traversed the night. Marius assured himself that the door was really closed.

"Poor Cosette," he muttered, "when she learns—"

At these words Jean Valjean trembled all over, and he fixed his haggard eyes on Marius.

"Cosette! oh, yes, it is true. You will tell Cosette about it. It is fair. Stay, I did not think of that. A man has strength for one thing, but not for another. I implore you, sir, I conjure you, sir, give me your most sacred word, do not tell her. Is it not sufficient for you to know it? I was able to tell it of my own accord, without being compelled. I would have told it to the universe, to the whole world, and I should not have cared; but she, she does not know what it is, and it would horrify her. A convict, what! you would be obliged to explain to her; tell her it is a man who has been to the galleys. She saw the chain-gang once; oh, my God!"

He sank into a chair and buried his face in his hands; it could not be heard, but from the heaving of his shoulders it could be seen that he was weeping. They were silent tears, terrible tears. There is choking in a sob. A species of convulsion seized on him, he threw himself back in his chair, letting his arms hang, and displaying to Marius his face bathed in tears, and Marius heard him mutter, so low that his voice seemed to come from a bottomless abyss: "Oh! I would like to die."

"Be at your ease," Marius said, "I will keep your secret to myself."

And less affected than perhaps he ought to have been, but compelled for more than an hour to listen to unexpected horrors, gradually seeing a convict taking M. Fauchelevent's place, gradually overcome by this mournful reality, and led by the natural state of the situation to notice the gap which had formed between himself and this man, Marius added:

"It is impossible for me not to say a word about the trust money which you have so faithfully and honestly given up. That is an act of probity, and it is but fair that a reward should be given you; fix the sum yourself, and it shall be paid you. Do not fear to fix it very high."

"I thank you, sir," Jean Valjean replied gently.

He remained pensive for a moment, mechanically passing the end of his forefinger over his thumb-nail, and then raised his voice:

"All is nearly finished; there is only one thing left me."

"What is it?"

Jean Valjean had a species of supreme agitation, and voicelessly, almost breathlessly, he stammered, rather than said:

"Now that you know, do you, sir, who are the master, believe that I ought not to see Cosette again?"

"I believe that it would be better," Marius replied coldly.

"I will not see her again," Jean Valjean murmured. And he walked toward the door; he placed his hand upon the handle, the door opened, Jean Valjean was going to pass out, when he suddenly closed it again, then opened the door again, and returned to Marius. He was no longer pale, but livid, and in his eyes was a sort of tragic flame, instead of tears. His voice had grown strangely calm again.

"Stay, sir," he said; "if you like I will come to see her, for I assure you that I desire it greatly. If I had not longed to see Cosette, I should not have made you the confession I have done, but have gone away; but, wishing to remain at the spot where Cosette is, and continue to see her, I was obliged to tell you everything honestly. You follow my reasoning, do you not? it is a thing easy to understand. Look you, I have had her with me for nine years; we lived at first in that hovel on the boulevard, then in the convent, and then near the Luxembourg. It was there that you saw her for the first time, and you remember her blue plush bonnet. Next we went to the district of the Invalides, where there was a railing and a garden, the Rue Plumet. I lived in a little back yard where I could hear her pianoforte. Such was my life, and we never separated. That lasted nine years and seven months; I was like her father, and she was my child. I do not know whether you understand me, M. Pontmercy, but it would be difficult to go away now, see her no more, speak to her no more, and have nothing left. If you have no objection, I will come and see Cosette every now and then, but not too often, and I will not remain long. You can tell them to show me into the little room on the ground-floor; I would certainly come in by the back door, which is used by the servants, but that might cause surprise, so it is better, I think, for me to come in by the front door. Really, sir, I should like to see Cosette a little, but as rarely as you please. Put yourself in my place; I have only that left. And then, again, we must be careful, and if I did not come at all it would have a bad effect, and appear singular. For instance, what I can do is to come in the evening, when it is beginning to grow dark."

"You can come every evening," said Marius, "and Cosette will expect you."

"You are kind, sir," said Jean Valjean.

Marius bowed to Jean Valjean, happiness accompanied despair to the door, and these two men parted.

2. THE OBSCURITY WHICH A REVELATION MAY CONTAIN

MARIUS was overwhelmed; the sort of estrangement which he had ever felt for the man with whom he saw Cosette was henceforth explained. There was in this person something enigmatic, against which his instinct warned him. This enigma was the most hideous of shames, the galleys. This M. Fauchelevent was Jean Valjean, the convict.

To find suddenly such a secret in the midst of his happiness is like discovering a scorpion in a turtle-dove's nest. Was the happiness of Marius and Cosette in future condemned to this proximity? was it an accomplished fact? did the acceptance of this man form part of the consummated marriage? could nothing else be done?

Had Marius also married the convict?

Although a man may be crowned with light and joy, though he be enjoying the grand hour of life's purple, happy love, such shocks would compel even the archangel in his ecstasy, even the demi-god in his glory, to shudder.

As ever happens in sudden transformation-scenes of this nature, Marius asked himself whether he ought not to reproach himself? Had he failed in foresight? had he been deficient in prudence? Had he voluntarily been headstrong? slightly so, perhaps. Had he entered, without taking sufficient precaution to light up all the surroundings, upon this love-adventure, which resulted in his marriage with Cosette? He verified—it is thus, by a series of verifications of ourselves on ourselves, that life is gradually corrected—he verified, we say, the visionary and chimerical side of his nature, a sort of internal cloud peculiar to many organizations, and which in the paroxysms of passion and grief expands, as the temperature of the soul changes, and invades the entire man to such an extent that he merely becomes a conscience enveloped in a fog. We have more than once indicated this characteristic element in Marius's individuality.

He remembered that during the intoxication of his love in the Rue Plumet, during those six or seven ecstatic weeks, he had not even spoken to Cosette about the drama in the Gorbeau hovel, during which the victim was so strangely silent both in the struggle and eventual escape. How was it that he had not spoken to Cosette about it? and yet it was so close and so frightful! how was it that he had not even mentioned the Thénardiers, and especially on the day when he met Eponine? he found almost a difficulty in explaining to himself now his silence at that period, but he was able to account for it. He remembered his confusion, his intoxication for Cosette, his love absorbing everything, the carrying off of one by the other into the ideal world, and perhaps, too, as the imperceptible amount of reason mingled with that violent and charming state of mind a vague and dull instinct to hide and efface in his memory that formidable adventure with which he feared contact, in which he wished to play no part, from which he stood aloof, and of which he could not be narrator or witness without being an accuser.

Moreover, these few weeks had been a flash, and they had had time for nothing, save loving.

In short, when all was revolved, and everything examined, supposing that he had described the Gorbeau trap to Cosette, had mentioned the Thénardiers to her, what would have been the consequence, even if he had discovered that Jean Valjean was a convict? would that have changed him, Marius, or his Cosette? would he have drawn back? would he have loved her less? would he have refused to marry her? No. Would it have made any change in what had happened? No. There was nothing, therefore, to regret, nothing to reproach, and all was well. There is a God for those drunkards who are called lovers, and Marius had blindly followed the road which he had selected with his eyes open. Love had bandaged his eyes to lead him, whither?—to paradise.

But this paradise was henceforth complicated by an infernal proximity, and the old estrangement of Marius for this man, for this Fauchelevent who had become Jean Valjean, was at present mingled with horror, but in this horror, let us say it, there was some pity, and even a certain degree of surprise. This robber, this relapsed robber, had given up a deposit, and what deposit? six hundred thousand francs. He alone held the secret of that deposit, he could have kept it all, but he gave it all up.

Moreover, he had revealed his situation of his own accord, nothing compelled him to do so, and if he, Marius, knew who he was, it was through himself. There was in this confession more than the acceptance of humiliation, there was the acceptance of peril. For a condemned man a mask is not a mask, but a shelter, and he had renounced that shelter. A false name is a security, and he had thrown away that false name. He, the galley-slave, could conceal himself forever in an honest family, and he had resisted that temptation, and for what motive? through scruples of conscience. He had explained himself with the irresistible accent of truth. In short, whoever this Jean Valjean might be, his was incontestably a conscience which was being awakened. Some mysterious rehabilitation had been begun, and according to all appearances, scruples had been master of this man for a long time past. Such attacks of justice and honesty are not the attributes of vulgar natures, and an awakening of the conscience is greatness of soul. Jean Valjean was sincere, and this sincerity, visible, palpable, irrefragable, and evident in the grief which it caused him, rendered his statements valuable, and gave authority to all that this man said.

Here, for Marius, was a strange inversion of situations. What issued from M. Fauchelevent? distrust; what was disengaged from Jean Valjean? confidence.

In the mysterious balance-sheet of this Jean Valjean which Marius mentally drew up, he verified the credit, he verified the debit, and tried to arrive at a balance. But all this was as in a storm, Marius, striving to form a distinct idea of this man, and pursuing Jean Valjean, so to speak, to the bottom of his thoughts, lost him, and found him again in a fatal mist.

The honest restoration of the trust money and the probity of the confession were good, and formed, as it were, a break in the cloud; but then the cloud became black again. However confused Marius's reminiscences might be, some shadows still returned to him.

What, after all, was that adventure in the Jondrette garret? why on the arrival of the police did that man, instead of complaining, escape? here Marius found the answer,—because this man was a convict who had broken his ban. Another question, why did this man come to the barricade? for at present Marius distinctly saw again that recollection, which re-appeared in his emotions like sympathetic ink before the fire. This man was at the barricade, and did not fight, what did he want there? Before this question a specter rose, and gave the answer, Javert. Marius perfectly remembered now the mournful vision of Jean Valjean dragging the bound Javert out of the barricade, and heard again behind the angle of the little Mondétour lane the frightful pistol-shot. There was, probably, a hatred between this spy and this galley-slave, and one annoyed the other. Jean Valjean went to the barricade to revenge himself; he arrived late, and was probably aware that Javert was a prisoner there.

The Corsican Vendetta has penetrated certain lower strata of society, and is the law with them; it is so simple that it does not astonish minds which have half returned to virtue, and their hearts are so constituted that a criminal, when on the path of repentance, may be scrupulous as to a robbery and not so as to a vengeance. Jean Valjean had killed Javert, or, at least, that seemed evident.

The last question of all admitted of no reply, and this question Marius felt like a pair of pincers. How was it that the existence of Jean Valjean had so long touched that of Cosette?

What was this gloomy sport of Providence which had brought this man and this child in contact? are there chains for two forged in heaven, and does God take pleasure in coupling the angel with the demon? a crime and an innocence can, then, be chamber companions in the mysterious hulks of misery? In that march past of condemned men which is called destiny, two foreheads may pass along side by side, one simple, the other formidable—one all bathed in the divine whiteness of dawn, the other eternally branded? who can have determined this inexplicable approximation? in what way, in consequence of what prodigy, could a community of life have been established between this celestial child and this condemned old man? What could have attached the lamb to the wolf, and even more incomprehensible still, the wolf to the lamb? for the wolf loved the lamb, the ferocious being adored the weak being, and for nine years the angel had leaned on the monster for support. The childhood and maidenhood of Cosette and her virgin growth toward life and light had been protected by this deformed devotion. Here questions exfoliated themselves, if we may employ the expression, into countless enigmas; abysses opened at the bottom of abysses, and Marius could no longer bend over Jean Valjean without feeling a dizziness; what could this man-precipice be?

The old genesiac symbols are eternal; in human society, such as it now exists until a greater light shall change it, there are even two men, one superior, the other subterranean: the one who holds to good is Abel, the one who holds to bad is Cain. What was this tender Cain? what was this bandit religiously absorbed in the adoration of a virgin, watching over her, bringing her up, guarding her, dignifying her, and, though himself impure, surrounding her with purity? What was this cloaca which had venerated this innocence so greatly as not to leave a spot upon it? what was this Valjean carrying on the education of Cosette? what was this figure of darkness, whose sole care it was to preserve from every shadow and every cloud the rising of a star?

That was Jean Valjean's secret; that was also God's secret, and Marius recoiled before this double secret.

The one, to some extent, re-assured him about the other, for God was as visible in this adventure as was Jean Valjean. God has his instruments, and employs whom He likes as tool and is not responsible to him. Do we know how God sets to work? Jean Valjean had labored on Cosette, and had to some extent formed her mind; that was incontestable. Well, what then? The workman was horrible, but the work was admirable, and God produces his miracles as He thinks proper. He had constructed that charming Cosette and employed Jean Valjean on the job, and it had pleased Him to choose this strange assistant. What explanation have we to ask of Him? is it the first time that manure has helped spring to produce the rose?

Marius gave himself these answers, and declared to himself that they were good. On all the points which we have indicated he had not dared to press Jean Valjean, though he did not confess to himself that he dared not. He adored Cosette, he possessed Cosette; Cosette was splendidly pure, and that was sufficient for him. What enlightenment did he require when Cosette was a light? does light need illumination? He had everything; what more could he desire? is not everything enough? Jean Valjean's personal affairs in no way concerned him, and in bending down over the fatal shadow of this wretched man he clung to his solemn declaration, *I am nothing to Cosette; ten years ago I did not know that she existed.* Jean Valjean was a passer-by; he had said so himself. Well, then, he passed, and, whoever he might be, his part was played out. Henceforth Marius would have to perform the functions of Providence toward Cosette; she had found again in ether her equal, her lover, her husband, her celestial male. In flying away, Cosette, winged and transfigured, left behind her on earth her empty and hideous chrysalis, Jean Valjean.

In whatever circle of ideas Marius might turn, he always came back to a certain horror of Jean Valjean; a sacred horror, perhaps, for, as we have stated, he felt a *quid divinum* in this man. But, though it was so, and whatever extenuating circumstances he might seek, he was always compelled to fall back on this: he was a convict, that is to say, a being who has not even a place on the social ladder, being beneath the lowest rung.

After the last of men comes the convict, who is no longer, so to speak, in the likeness of his fellow-men. The law has deprived him of the entire amount of humanity which it can strip off a man. Marius, in penal matters, democrat though he was, was still at the inexorable system, and he entertained all the ideas of the law about those whom the law strikes. He had not yet made every progress, we are forced to say; he had not yet learned to distinguish between what is written by man and what is written by God, between the law and the right. He had examined and weighed the claim which man sets up to dispose of the irrevocable, the irreparable, and the word *vindicta* was not repulsive to him. He considered it simple that certain breaches of the written law should be followed by eternal penalties, and he accepted social condemnation as a civilizing process. He was still at this point, though infallibly certain to advance at a later date, for his nature was good and entirely composed of latent progress.

In this medium of ideas Jean Valjean appeared to him deformed and repelling, for he was the punished man, the convict. This word was to him like the sound of the trumpet of the last judgment; and after regarding Jean Valjean for a long time his last gesture was to turn away his head—*vade retro*.

Marius,—we must recognize the fact and lay a stress on it,—while questioning Jean Valjean to such an extent that Jean Valjean himself said, *You are shriving me,* had not, however, asked him two or three important questions.

It was not that they had not presented themselves to his mind, but he had been afraid of them. The Jondrette garret? the barricade? Javert? Who knew where the revelations might have stopped? Jean Valjean did not seem the man to recoil, and who knows whether Marius, after urging him on, might not have wished to check him? In certain supreme conjunctures has it not happened to all of us, that after asking a question we have stopped our ears, in order not to hear the answer? a man is especially guilty of such an act of cowardice when he is in love. It is not wise to drive sinister situations into a corner, especially when the indissoluble side of our own life is fatally mixed up with them. What a frightful light might issue from Jean Valjean's desperate explanations, and who knows whether that hideous brightness might not have been reflected on Cosette? Who knows whether a sort of infernal gleam might not have remained on that angel's brow? Fatality knows such complications in which innocence itself is branded with crime by the fatal law of coloring reflections, and the purest faces may retain forever the impression of a horrible vicinity. Whether rightly or wrongly, Marius was terrified, for he already knew too much, and he had rather to deafen than to enlighten himself. He wildly bore off Cosette in his arms, closing his eyes upon Jean Valjean. This man belonged to the night, the living and terrible night; how could he dare to seek its foundation? It is a horrible thing to question the shadow, for who knows what it will answer? The dawn might be eternally blackened by it.

In this state of mind it was a crushing perplexity for Marius to think that henceforth this man would have any contact with Cosette; and he now almost reproached himself for not having asked these formidable questions before which he had recoiled, and from which an implacable and definitive decision might have issued. He considered himself too kind, too gentle, and, let us say it, too weak; and the weakness had led him to make a fatal concession. He had allowed himself to be affected, and had done wrong; he ought simply and purely to have rejected Jean Valjean. Jean Valjean was an incendiary, and he ought to have freed his house from the presence of this man.

He was angry with himself, he was angry with that whirlwind of emotions which had deafened, blinded, and carried him away. He was dissatisfied with himself.

What was he to do now? the visits of Jean Valjean were most deeply repulsive to him. Of what use was it that this man should come to his house? what did he want here? Here he refused to investigate the matter, he refused to study, and he was unwilling to probe his own heart. He had promised, he had allowed himself to be drawn into a promise; Jean Valjean held that promise, and he must keep his word even with a convict—above all with a convict. Still his first duty was toward Cosette. In brief, a repulsion, which overcame everything else, caused him a loathing. Marius confusedly revolved all these ideas in his mind, passing from one to the other, and shaken by all. Hence arose a deep trouble, which it was not easy to conceal from Cosette, but love is a talent, and Marius succeeded in doing it.

However, he asked, without any apparent motive, some questions of Cosette, who was as candid as a dove is white, and suspected nothing; he spoke to her of her childhood and her youth, and he convinced himself more and more that this convict had been to Cosette as good, paternal, and respectful as a man can be. Everything of which Marius had caught a glimpse and supposed, was real,—this sinister nettle had loved and protected this lily.

BOOK VIII

THE TWILIGHT DECLINE

1 . THE GROUND-FLOOR ROOM

ON the morrow, at night-fall, Jean Valjean tapped at the gate-way of the Gillenormand mansion, and it was Basque who received him. Basque was in the yard at the appointed time, as if he had had his orders. It sometimes happens that people say to a servant, "You will watch for Mr. So-and-so's arrival."

Basque, without waiting for Jean Valjean to come up to him, said: "Monsieur le Baron has instructed me to ask you, sir, whether you wish to go upstairs or stay down here?"

"Stay down here," Jean Valjean replied.

Basque, who, however, was perfectly respectful in his manner, opened the door of the ground-floor room, and said, "I will go and inform her ladyship."

The room which Jean Valjean entered was a damp, arched, basement-room, employed as a cellar at times, looking out on the street, with a flooring of red tiles, and badly lighted by an iron-barred window. This room was not one of those which are harassed by the broom and mop, and the dust was quiet there. No persecution of the spiders had been organized, and a fine web, extensively drawn out, quite black, and adorned with dead flies, formed a wheel on one of the window panes. The room, which was small and with a low ceiling, was furnished with a pile of empty bottles collected in a corner. The wall, covered with a yellow-ochre wash, crumbled off in large patches; at the end was a mantel-piece of paneled black wood, with a narrow shelf, and a fire was lighted in it, which indicated that Jean Valjean's reply, *Stay down here,* had been calculated on. Two chairs were placed, one in each chimney-corner, and between the chairs was spread, in guise of carpet, an old bedroom rug, which displayed more cord than wool. The room was illumined by the flickering of the fire and the twilight through the window. Jean Valjean was fatigued; for several days he had not eaten or slept, and he fell into one of the arm-chairs. Basque returned, placed a lighted candle on the mantelpiece, and withdrew. Jean Valjean, who was sitting with hanging head, did not notice either Basque or the candle, till all at once he started up, for Cosette was behind him; he had not seen her come in, but he felt that she was doing so. He turned round and contemplated her; she was adorably lovely. But what he gazed at with this profound glance was not the beauty, but the soul.

"Well, father," Cosette exclaimed, "I knew that you were singular, but I could never have expected this. What an idea! Marius told me that it was your wish to see me here."

"Yes, it is."

"I expected that answer, and I warn you that I am going to have a scene with you. Let us begin with the beginning; kiss me, father."

And she offered her cheek; but Jean Valjean remained motionless.

"You do not stir, I mark the fact! it is the attitude of a culprit. But I do not care, I forgive you. Christ said, 'Offer the other cheek'; here it is."

And she offered the other cheek, but Jean Valjean did not stir; it seemed as if his feet were riveted to the floor.

"This is growing serious," said Cosette. "What have I done to you? I am offended, and you must make it up with me; you will dine with us!"

"I have dined."

"That is not true, and I will have you scolded by M. Gillenormand. Grandfathers are made to lay down the law to fathers. Come, go with me to the drawing-room. Come at once."

"Impossible."

Cosette here lost a little ground; she ceased to order and began questioning.

"But why? and you choose the ugliest room in the house to see me in. It is horrible here."

"You know,"—Jean Valjean broke off,—"You know, madame, that I am peculiar, and have my fancies."

Cosette clapped her little hands together.

"Madame—*you* know—more novelties; what does this all mean?"

Jean Valjean gave her that heart-broken smile to which he sometimes had recourse.

"You wish to be madame, and are so."

"Not for you, father."

"Do not call me father any more."

"What?"

"Call me Monsieur Jean, or Jean, if you like."

"You are no longer father? I am no longer Cosette? Monsieur Jean? why, what does it mean? These are revolutions. What has happened? Look me in the face if you can. And you will not live with us! and you will not accept our bedroom! What have I done to offend you? Oh, what have I done? there must be something."

"Nothing."

"In that case, then?"

"All is as usual."

"Why do you change your name?"

"You have changed yours."

He smiled the same smile again and added:

"Since you are Madame Pontmercy, I may fairly be Monsieur Jean."

"I do not understand anything, and all this is idiotic. I will ask my husband's leave for you to be Monsieur Jean and I hope that he will not consent. You cause me great sorrow, and though you may have whims, you have no right to make your little Cosette grieve. That is wrong and you have no right to be naughty, for you are so good."

As he made no reply, she seized both his hands eagerly, and with an irresistible movement raising them to her face, she pressed them against her neck under her chin, which is a profound sign of affection.

"Oh," she said, "be kind to me."

And she continued:

"This is what I call being kind: to behave yourself, come and live here, for there are birds here as in the Rue Plumet; to live with us, leave that hole in the Rue de l'Homme Armé, give us no more riddles to guess; to be like everybody else, dine with us, breakfast with us, and be my father."

He removed her hands:

"You no longer want a father, as you have a husband."

Cosette broke out:

"I no longer want a father! Things like that have no common sense, and I really don't know what to say."

"If Toussaint were here," Jean Valjean continued, like a man seeking authorities, and who clings to every branch, "she would be the first to allow that I have always had strange ways of my own. There is nothing new in it, for I always loved my dark corner."

"But it is cold here, and we cannot see distinctly, and it is abominable to wish to be Monsieur Jean, and I shall not allow you to call me madame."

"As I was coming along just now," Jean Valjean replied, "I saw a very pretty piece of furniture at a cabinet-maker's in the Rue St. Louis. If I were a pretty woman, I should treat myself to it. It is a very nice toilet-table in the present fashion, made of rosewood, I think you call it, and inlaid. There is a rather large glass with drawers, and it is very nice."

"Hou! the ugly bear!" Cosette replied.

And clinching her teeth, and parting her lips in the most graceful way possible, she blew at Jean Valjean; it was a Grace imitating a cat. "I am furious," she went on, "and since yesterday you have all put me in a passion. I do not understand it at all; you do not defend me against Marius, Marius does not take my part against you, and I am all alone. I have a nice room prepared, and if I could have put the good God in it, I would have done so; but my room is left on my hands and my lodger makes me bankrupt. I order Nicolette to prepare a nice little dinner, and—they will not touch your dinner, madame. And my father Fauche-levent wishes me to call him Monsieur Jean, and that I should receive him in a frightful old, ugly, mildewed cellar, in which the walls wear a beard, and empty bottles represent the looking-glasses, and spiders' webs the curtains. I allow that you are a singular man, it is your way, but a truce is granted to newly married people, and you ought not to have begun to be singular again so soon. You are going to be very satisfied, then, in your horrible Rue de l'Homme Armé; well, I was very wretched there. What have I done to offend you? you cause me great sorrow. Fie!"

And suddenly growing serious, she looked intently at Jean Valjean and added:

"You are angry with me for being happy, is that it?"

Simplicity sometimes penetrates unconsciously very deep, and this question, simple for Cosette, was deep for Jean Valjean. Cosette wished to scratch, but she tore. Jean Valjean turned pale; he remained for a moment without answering, and then murmured with an indescribable accent, and speaking to himself:

"Her happiness was the object of my life, and at present God may order my departure. Cosette, thou art happy, and my course is run."

"Ah! you said *thou* to me," Cosette exclaimed, and leaped on his neck.

Jean Valjean wildly strained her to his heart, for he felt as if he were almost taking her back again.

"Thank you, father," Cosette said to him.

The excitement was getting too painful for Jean Valjean; he gently withdrew himself from Cosette's arms, and took up his hat.

"Well?" said Cosette.

Jean Valjean replied:

"I am going to leave you, madame, as you will be missed."

And on the threshold he added:

"I said to you *thou;* tell your husband that it shall not happen again. Forgive me."

Jean Valjean left Cosette stupefied by this enigmatical leave-taking.

2. *ANOTHER BACKWARD STEP*

THE next day Jean Valjean came at the same hour, and Cosette asked him no questions, was no longer astonished, no longer exclaimed that it was cold, no longer alluded to the drawing-room; she avoided saying either father or Monsieur Jean. She allowed herself to be called madame; there was only a diminution of her delight perceptible, and she would have been sad, had sorrow been possible.

It is probable that she had held with Marius one of those conversations in which the beloved man says what he wishes, explains nothing, and satisfies the beloved woman; for the curiosity of lovers does not extend far beyond their love.

The basement-room had been furbished up a little; Basque had suppressed the bottles, and Nicolette the spiders. Every following day brought Jean Valjean back at the same hour; he came daily, as he had not the strength to take Marius's permission otherwise than literally. Marius arranged so as to be absent at the hour when Jean Valjean came, and the house grew accustomed to M. Fauchelevent's new mode of behaving. Toussaint helped in it; *my master was always so,* she repeated. The grandfather issued this decree, He is an original, and everything was said. Moreover, at the age of ninety no connection is possible; everything is juxtaposition, and a new-comer is in the way; there is no place for him, for habits are unalterably formed. M. Fauchelevent, M. Tranchelevent, Father Gillenormand desired nothing better than to get rid of "that gentleman," and added, "Nothing is more common than such originals. They do all sorts of strange things without any motive. The Marquis de Canoples did worse, for he bought a palace in order to live in the garret."

No one caught a glimpse of the sinister reality, and in fact who could have divined such a thing? There are marshes like this in India; the water seems extraordinary, inexplicable, rippling when there is no breeze, and agitated when it ought to be calm. People look at the surface of this ebullition which has no cause, and do not suspect the hydra dragging itself along at the bottom. Many men have in this way a secret monster, an evil which they nourish, a dragon that gnaws them, a despair that dwells in their night. Such a man resembles others, comes and goes, and no one knows that he has within him a frightful parasitic pain with a thousand teeth, which dwells in the wretch and kills him. They do not know that this man is a gulf; he is stagnant, but deep. From time to time a trouble which no one understands is produced on his surface; a mysterious ripple forms, then fades away, then re-appears; a bubble rises and bursts. It is a slight thing, but it is terrible, for it is the respiration of the unknown beast. Certain strange habits, such as arriving at the hour when others go away, hiding one's self when others show themselves, wearing on all occasions what may be called the wall-colored cloak, seeking the solitary walk, preferring the deserted street, not mixing in conversation, avoiding crowds and festivities, appearing to be comfortably off and living poorly, having, rich though one is, one's key in one's pocket, and one's candle in the porter's lodge, entering by the small door, and going up the back stairs—all these insignificant singularities, ripples, air-bubbles, and fugitive marks on the surface frequently come from a formidable depth below.

Several weeks passed thus; a new life gradually seized on Cosette,— the relations which marriage creates, visits, the management of the household, and pleasures, that great business. The pleasures of Cosette were not costly; they consisted in only one, being with Marius. To go out with him, remain at home with him, was the great occupation of her life. It was for them an ever novel joy to go out arm in arm, in the sunshine, in the open streets, without hiding themselves, in the face of everybody, both alone.

Cosette had one vexation: Toussaint could not agree with Nicolette (for the welding of the two old maids was impossible), and left. The grandfather was quite well; Marius had a few briefs now and then; Aunt Gillenormand peacefully lived with the married pair that lateral life which sufficed her, and Jean Valjean came daily. The terms "Madame" and "Monsieur Jean," however, made him different to Cosette, and the care he had himself taken to detach himself from her succeeded. She was more and more gay, and less and less affectionate, and yet she loved him dearly still, and he felt it.

One day she suddenly said to him, "You were my father, you are no longer my father; you were my uncle, you are no longer my uncle; you were Monsieur Fauchelevent, and are now Jean. Who are you, then? I do not like all this. If I did not know you to be so good, I should be afraid of you."

He still lived in the Rue de l'Homme Armé, as he could not resolve to remove from the quarter in which Cosette lived. At first he only stayed a few minutes with Cosette, and then went away, but by degrees he grew into the habit of making his visits longer. It might be said that he took advantage of the lengthening days; he arrived sooner and went away later. One day, the word "father" slipped over Cosette's lips, and a gleam of joy lit up Jean Valjean's old, solemn face, but he chided her: "Say Jean."

"Ah, that is true," she replied, with a burst of laughter, "Monsieur Jean."

"That is right," he said, and he turned away that she might not see the tears in his eyes.

3. THEY REMEMBER THE GARDEN IN THE RUE PLUMET

THIS was the last occasion, and after this last flash total extinction took place. There was no more familiarity, no more good-day with a kiss, and never again that so deeply tender word "father"; he had been at his own request and with his own complicity, expelled from all those joys in succession, and he underwent this misery, that, after losing Cosette entirely on one day, he was then obliged to lose her again bit by bit. The eye eventually grows accustomed to cellar light, and he found it enough to have an apparition of Cosette daily. His whole life was concentrated in that hour; he sat down by her side, looked at her in silence, or else talked to her about former years, her childhood, the convent, and her little friends of those days. One afternoon—it was an early day in April, already warm, but still fresh, the moment of the sun's great gayety, the gardens that surrounded Marius's and Cosette's windows were rousing from their slumber, the hawthorn was about to bourgeon, a jewelry of wall-flowers was displayed on the old wall, there was on the grass a fairy carpet of daisies and buttercups, the white butterflies were springing forth, and the wind, that minstrel of the eternal wedding-feast, was trying in the trees the first notes of that great auroral symphony which the old poets called the "renewal"—Marius said to Cosette, "We said that we would go and see our garden in the Rue Plumet again. Come, we must not be ungrateful." And they flew off like two swallows toward the spring. This garden in the Rue Plumet produced on them the effect of a dawn, for they already had behind them in life something that resembled the springtime of their love. The house in the Rue Plumet, being taken on lease, still belonged to Cosette; they went to this garden and house, found themselves again, and forgot themselves there. In the evening Jean Valjean went to the Rue des Filles du Calvaire at the usual hour. "My lady went out with the Baron," said Basque, "and has not returned yet." He sat down silently and waited an hour, but Cosette did not come in; he hung his head and went away. Cosette was so intoxicated by the walk in "their garden," and so pleased at having "lived a whole day in her past," that she spoke of nothing else the next day. She did not remark that she had not seen Jean Valjean.

"How did you go there?" Jean Valjean asked her.

"On foot."

"And how did you return?"

"On foot too."

For some time Jean Valjean had noticed the close life which the young couple led, and was annoyed at it. Marius's economy was severe, and that word had its absolute meaning with Jean Valjean; he hazarded a question:

"Why do you not keep a carriage? A little coupé would not cost you more than five hundred francs a month, and you are rich."

"I do not know," Cosette answered.

"It is the same with Toussaint," Jean Valjean continued; "she has left, and you have engaged no one in her place. Why not?"

"Nicolette is sufficient."

"But you must want a lady's-maid?"

"Have I not Marius?"

"You ought to have a house of your own, servants of your own, a carriage, and a box at the opera. Nothing is too good for you. Then, why not take advantage of the fact of your being rich? Wealth adds to happiness."

Cosette made no reply. Jean Valjean's visits did not grow shorter; on the contrary, for when it is the heart that is slipping, a man does not stop on the incline. When Jean Valjean wished to prolong his visit and make the hour be forgotten, he sang the praises of Marius; he found him handsome, noble, brave, witty, eloquent, and good. Cosette added to the praise, and Jean Valjean began again. It was an inexhaustible subject, and there were volumes in the six letters composing Marius's name. In this way Jean Valjean managed to stop for a long time, for it was so sweet to see Cosette and forget by her side. It was a dressing for his wound. It frequently happened that Basque would come and say twice, "M. Gillenormand has sent me to remind Madame la Baronne that dinner is waiting." On those days Jean Valjean would return home very thoughtful. Was there any truth in that comparison of the chrysalis which had occurred to Marius's mind? Was Jean Valjean really an obstinate chrysalis, constantly paying visits to his butterfly? One day he remained longer than usual, and the next noticed there was no fire in the grate. "Stay," he thought, "no fire"; and he gave himself this explanation, "It is very simple; we are in April, and the cold weather has passed."

"Good gracious! how cold it is here!" Cosette exclaimed as she came in.

"Oh, no," said Jean Valjean.

"Then it was you who told Basque not to light a fire?"

"Yes, we shall have May here directly."

"But fires keep on till June; in this cellar there ought to be one all the year round."

"I thought it was unnecessary."

"That is just like one of your ideas," Cosette remarked.

The next day there was a fire, but the two chairs were placed at the other end of the room, near the door. "What is the meaning of that?" Jean Valjean thought; he fetched the chairs and placed them in their usual place near the chimney. This rekindled fire, however, encouraged him, and he made the conversation last even longer than usual. As he rose to leave, Cosette remarked to him:

"My husband said a funny thing to me yesterday."

"What was it?"

"He said to me, 'Cosette, we have thirty thousand francs a year,—twenty-seven of yours, and three that my grandfather allows me.' I replied, 'That makes thirty'; and he continued, 'Would you have the courage to live on the three thousand?' I answered, 'Yes, on nothing, provided that it be with you'; and then I asked him, 'Why did you say that to me?' He replied, 'I merely wished to know'."

Jean Valjean had not a word to say. Cosette probably expected some explanation from him, but he listened to her in a sullen silence. He went back to the Rue de l'Homme Armé, and was so profoundly abstracted that, instead of entering his own house, he went into the next one. It was not till he had gone up nearly two flights of stairs that he noticed his mistake, and came down again. His mind was filled full with conjectures; it was evident that Marius entertained doubts as to the origin of the six hundred thousand francs, that he feared some impure source; he might even—who knew?—have discovered that this money came from him, Jean Valjean; that he hesitated to touch this suspicious fortune, and was repugnant to use it as his own, preferring that Cosette and he should remain poor than be rich with dubious wealth. Moreover, Jean Valjean was beginning to feel himself shown to the door.

On the following day he had a species of shock on entering the basement-room; the fauteuils had disappeared, and there was not even a seat of any sort.

"Dear me, no chairs," Cosette exclaimed on entering; "where are they?"

"They are no longer here," Jean Valjean replied.

"That is rather too much."

Jean Valjean stammered: "I told Basque to remove them."

"For what reason?"

"I shall only remain a few minutes to-day."

"Few or many, that is no reason for standing."

"I believe that Basque required the chairs for the drawing-room."

"Why?"

"You have probably company this evening."

"Not a soul."

Jean Valjean had not another word to say, and Cosette shrugged her shoulders.

"Have the chairs removed! The other day you ordered the fire to be left off! How singular you are!"

"Good-bye," Jean Valjean murmured.

He did not say "Good-bye, Cosette," but he had not the strength to say "Good-bye, madame."

He went away, crushed, for this time he had comprehended. The next day he did not come, and Cosette did not remark this till the evening.

"Dear me," she said, "Monsieur Jean did not come to-day."

She felt a slight pang at the heart, but she scarce noticed it, as her attention was at once diverted by a kiss from Marius. The next day he did not come either. Cosette paid no attention to this, spent the evening, and slept at night as usual, and only thought of it when she woke; she was so happy! She very soon sent Nicolette to Monsieur Jean's to see whether he were ill, and why he did not come to see her on the previous day, and Nicolette brought back Monsieur Jean's answer. "He was not ill, but was busy, and would come soon, so soon as he could. But he was going to make a little journey, and madame would remember that he was accustomed to do so every now and then. She need not feel at all alarmed or trouble herself about him."

Nicolette, on entering Monsieur Jean's room, had repeated to him her mistress's exact words, "That madame sent to know 'why Monsieur Jean had not called on the previous day?'" "I have not called for two days," Jean Valjean said quietly, but the observation escaped Nicolette's notice, and she did not repeat it to Cosette.

4. *ATTRACTION AND EXTINCTION*

DURING the last months of spring and the early months of summer, 1833, the scanty passers-by in the Marais, the shopkeepers, and the idlers in the door-ways noticed an old gentleman, decently dressed in black, who every day, at nearly the same hour in the evening, left the Rue de l'Homme Armé, in the direction of the Rue Saint Croix de la Bretonnerie, passed in front of the Blancs Manteaux, reached the Rue Culture Sainte Catherine, and on coming to the Rue de l'Echarpe turned to his left and entered the Rue Saint Louis.

There he walked slowly, with head stretched forward, seeing nothing, hearing nothing, with his eye incessantly fixed on a spot which always seemed his magnet, and which was naught else than the corner of the Rue des Filles du Calvaire. The nearer he came to this corner, the more brightly his eye flashed, a sort of joy illumined his eyeballs like an internal dawn; he had a fascinated and affectionate air, his lips made obscure movements as if speaking to some one whom he could not see, he smiled vaguely, and he advanced as slowly as he could. It seemed as if, while wishing to arrive, he was afraid of the moment when he would be quite close. When he had only a few houses between himself and the street which appeared to attract him, his steps became so slow that at moments he seemed not to be moving at all. The vacillation of his head and the fixedness of his eye suggested the needle seeking the pole. However long he might protract the time of his arrival, he must arrive in the end; when he reached the corner of the Rue des Filles du Calvaire, he trembled, thrust his head with a species of gloomy timidity beyond the corner of the last house, and looked into this street, and there was in this glance something that resembled the be-dazzlement of the impossible and the reflection of a closed paradise. Then a tear, which had been gradually collecting in the corner of his eyelashes, having grown large enough to fall, glided down his cheeks, and sometimes stopped at his mouth. The old man tasted its bitter flavor. He stood thus for some minutes as if he were of stone; then returned by the same road, at the same pace, and the further he got away the more lusterless his eye became.

By degrees this old man ceased going as far as the corner of the Rue des Filles du Calvaire; he stopped half-way in the Rue St. Louis—at times a little further off, at times a little nearer. One day he stopped at the corner of the Rue Culture Sainte Catherine, and gazed at the Rue des Filles du Calvaire from a distance; then he silently shook his head from right to left, as if refusing himself something, and turned back. Ere long he did not reach even the Rue St. Louis; he arrived at the Rue Pavée, shook his head, and turned back; then he did not go beyond the Rue des Trois Pavillons; and then he did not pass the Blancs Manteaux. He seemed like a clock which was not wound up, and whose oscillations grow shorter and shorter till they stop.

Every day he left his house at the same hour, undertook the same walk, but did not finish it, and incessantly shortened it, though probably unconscious of the fact. His whole countenance expressed this sole idea, Of what good is it? His eyes were lusterless, and there was no radiance in them. The tears were also dried up; they no longer collected in the corner of his eyelashes, and this pensive eye was dry. The old man's head was still thrust forward; the chin moved at times, and the creases in his thin neck were painful to look on. At times, when the weather was bad, he had an umbrella under his arm, which he never opened.

The good women of the district said, "He is an innocent," and the children followed him with shouts of laughter.

BOOK IX

SUPREME DARKNESS, SUPREME DAWN

1. PITY THE UNHAPPY, BUT BE INDULGENT TO THE HAPPY

IT is a terrible thing to be happy! How satisfied people are! how sufficient they find it! how, when possessed of the false object of life, happiness, they forget the true one, duty! We are bound to say, however, that it would be unjust to accuse Marius. Marius, as we have explained, before his marriage asked no questions of M. Fauchelevent, and since had been afraid to ask any of Jean Valjean. He had regretted the promise which he had allowed to be drawn from him, and had repeatedly said to himself that he had done wrong in making this concession to despair. He had restricted himself to gradually turning Jean Valjean out of his house, and effacing him as far as possible in Cosette's mind. He had to some extent constantly stationed himself between Cosette and Jean Valjean, feeling certain that in this way she would not perceive it or think of it. It was more than an effacement, it was an eclipse.

Marius did what he considered necessary and just; he believed that he had serious reasons, some of which we have seen, and some we have yet to see, for getting rid of Jean Valjean, without harshness, but without weakness. Chance having made him acquainted, in a trial in which he was retained, with an ex-clerk of Lafitte's bank, he had obtained, without seeking it, mysterious information, which, in truth, he had not been able to examine, through respect for the secret he had promised to keep, and through regard for Jean Valjean's perilous situation. He believed, at this very moment, that he had a serious duty to perform, the restitution of the six hundred thousand francs to some one whom he was seeking as discreetly as he could. In the meanwhile he abstained from touching that money.

As for Cosette, she was not acquainted with any of these secrets; but it would be harsh to condemn her either. Between Marius and her was an omnipotent magnetism, which made her do, instinctively and almost mechanically, whatever Marius wished. She felt a wish of Marius in the matter of Monsieur Jean, and she conformed to it. Her husband had said nothing to her, but she was subject to the vague but clear presence of his tacit intentions, and blindly obeyed. Her obedience in this case consisted in not remembering what Marius forgot; and she had no effort to make in doing so. Without her knowing why, and without any ground for accusing her, her mind had so thoroughly become that of her husband, that whatever covered itself with a shadow in Marius's thoughts was obscured in hers. Let us not go too far, however; as regards Jean Valjean, this effacement and this forgetfulness were only superficial, and she was thoughtless rather than forgetful. In her heart she truly loved the man whom she had so long called father, but she loved her husband more, and this had slightly falsified the balance of this heart, which weighed down on one side only.

It happened at times that Cosette would speak of Jean Valjean and express her surprise, and then Marius would calm her. "He is away, I believe; did he not say that he was going on a journey?"—"That is true," Cosette thought; "he used to disappear like that, but not for so long a time." Twice or thrice she sent Nicolette to inquire in the Rue de l'Homme Armé whether Monsieur Jean had returned from his tour, and Jean Valjean sent answer in the negative. Cosette asked no more, as she had on earth but one want—Marius.

Let us also say that Marius and Cosette had been absent too. They went to Vernon, and Marius took Cosette to his father's tomb. Marius had gradually abstracted Cosette from Jean Valjean, and Cosette had allowed it.

However, what is called, much too harshly in certain cases, the ingratitude of children is not always so reprehensible a thing as may be believed. It is the ingratitude of nature, for nature, as we have said elsewhere, "looks before her," and divides living beings into arrivals and departures. The departures are turned to the darkness, and the arrivals toward light. Hence a divergence which on the part of the old is fatal, on the part of the young is involuntary, and this divergence, at first insensible, increases slowly, like every separation of branches, and the twigs separate without detaching themselves from the parent stem. It is not their fault, for youth goes where there is joy, to festivals, to bright light, and to love, while old age proceeds toward the end. They do not lose each other out of sight, but there is no longer a connecting link; the young people feel the chill of life, and the old that of the tomb. Let us not accuse these poor children.

2. *THE LAST FLICKERINGS OF THE LAMP WITHOUT OIL*

ONE day Jean Valjean went down his staircase, took three steps in the street, sat down upon a post, the same one on which Gavroche had found him sitting in thought on the night of June 5; he stayed there a few minutes and then went up again. This was the last oscillation of the pendulum; the next day he did not leave his room; the next to that he did not leave his bed. The porter's wife, who prepared his poor meals for him, some cabbage or a few potatoes and a little bacon, looked at the brown earthenware plate and exclaimed:

"Why, poor dear man, you ate nothing yesterday."

"Yes I did," Jean Valjean answered.

"The plate is quite full."

"Look at the water-jug; it is empty."

"That proves you have drunk, but does not prove that you have eaten."

"Well," said Jean Valjean, "suppose that I only felt hungry for water?"

"That is called thirst, and if a man does not eat at the same time it is called fever."

"I will eat to-morrow."

"Or on Trinity Sunday. Why not to-day? whoever thought of saying, 'I will eat to-morrow?' To leave my dish without touching it; my rashers were so good."

Jean Valjean took the old woman's hand.

"I promise you to eat them," he said, in his gentle voice.

"I am not pleased with you," the woman replied.

Jean Valjean never saw any other human creature but this good woman; there are in Paris streets through which people never pass, and houses which people never enter, and he lived in one of those streets and one of those houses.

During the time when he still went out, he had bought at a brazier's for a few sous a small copper crucifix, which he suspended from a nail opposite his bed; that gibbet is ever good to look on.

A week passed thus, and Jean Valjean still remained in bed. The porter's wife said to her husband, "The old gentleman upstairs does not get up, he does not eat, and he will not last long. He has a sorrow, and no one will get it out of my head but that his daughter has made a bad match."

The porter replied, with the accent of marital sovereignty:

"If he is rich, he can have a doctor; if he is not rich, he can't. If he has no doctor, he will die."

"And if he has one?"

"He will die," said the porter.

The porter's wife began digging up with an old knife the grass between what she called her pavement, and while doing so grumbled:

"It's a pity. An old man who is so nice. He is as white as a pullet."

She saw a doctor belonging to the quarter passing along the bottom of the street, and took upon herself to ask him to go up.

"It's on the second floor," she said; "you will have only to go in, for, as the old gentleman no longer leaves his bed, the key is always in the door."

The physician saw Jean Valjean and spoke to him; when he came down again, the porter's wife was waiting for him.

"Well, doctor?"

"He is very ill."

"What is the matter with him?"

"Everything and nothing. He is a man who, from all appearances, has lost some one he loved. People die of that."

"What did he say to you?"

"He told me that he was quite well."

"Will you call again, doctor?"

"Yes," the physician replied, "but some one besides me ought to come too."

3. *A FEATHER IS TOO HEAVY FOR HIM WHO LIFTED FAUCHELEVENT'S CART*

ONE evening Jean Valjean had a difficulty in rising on his elbow; he took hold of his wrist and could not find his pulse; his breathing was short, and stopped every now and then, and he perceived that he was weaker than he had ever yet been. Then, doubtless under the pressure of some supreme preoccupation, he made an effort, sat up, and dressed himself. He put on his old workman's clothes; for, as he no longer went out, he had returned to them and preferred them. He was compelled to pause several times while dressing himself, and the perspiration poured off his forehead merely through the effort of putting on his jacket.

Ever since he had been alone he had placed his bed in the anteroom, so as to occupy as little as possible of the deserted apartments. He opened the valise and took out Cosette's clothing, which he spread on his bed.

The bishop's candlesticks were at their place on the mantel-piece; he took two wax candles out of a drawer and put them up, and then, though it was broad summer daylight, he lit them. We sometimes see candles lighted thus in open day in rooms where dead men are lying.

Each step he took in going from one article of furniture to another exhausted him, and he was obliged to sit down. It was not ordinary fatigue, which expends the strength in order to renew it; it was the remnant of possible motion; it was exhausted life falling drop by drop in crushing efforts which will not be made again.

One of the chairs on which he sank was placed near the mirror, so fatal for him, so providential for Marius, in which he had read Cosette's reversed writing on the blotting-book.

He saw himself in this mirror, and could not recognize himself. He was eighty years of age; before Marius's marriage he had looked scarce fifty, but the last year had reckoned as thirty. What he had on his forehead was no longer the wrinkle of age, but the mysterious mark of death, and the laceration of the pitiless nail could be traced on it. His cheeks were flaccid, the skin of his face had that color which leads to the belief that there is already earth upon it; the two corners of his mouth drooped as in that mask which the ancients sculptured on the tomb; he looked into space reproachfully, and he resembled one of those tragic beings who have cause to complain of some one.

He had reached that stage, the last phase of dejection, in which grief no longer flows; it is, so to speak, coagulated, and there is on the soul something like a clot of despair. Night had set in, and he, with difficulty, dragged a table and the old easy-chair to the chimney, and laid on the table pen, ink, and paper. This done he fainted away, and when he regained his senses he was thirsty; as he could not lift the water-jar, he bent down with an effort and drank a mouthful.

Then he turned to the bed, and still seated, for he was unable to stand, he gazed at the little black dress and all those dear objects. Such contemplations last for hours, which appear minutes. All at once he shuddered, and felt that the cold had struck him. He leaned his elbows on the table which the bishop's candlesticks illumined, and took up the pen. As neither the pen nor the ink had been used for a long time, the nibs of the pen were bent, the ink was dried up, and he was, therefore, obliged to put a few drops of water in the ink, which he could not do without stopping and sitting down twice or thrice, and was forced to write with the back of the pen. He wiped his forehead from time to time, and his hand trembled as he wrote the few following lines:

Cosette, I bless you. I am about to explain to you. Your husband did right in making me understand that I ought to go away: still, he was slightly in error as to what he believed, but he acted rightly. He is a worthy man. Love him dearly when I am gone from you. Monsieur Pontmercy, always love my beloved child. Cosette, this paper will be found; this is what I wish to say to you; you shall see the figures if I have the strength to remember them; but listen to me, the money is really yours. This is the whole affair: white jet comes from Norway, black jet comes from England, and black beads come from Germany. Jet is lighter, more valuable, and dearer, but imitations can be made in France as well as in Germany. You must have a small anvil, two inches square, and a spirit-

lamp to soften the wax. The wax used to be made with resin and lamp-black, and costs four francs the pound, but I hit on the idea of making it of shellac and turpentine. It only costs thirty sous, and is much better. The rings are made of violet glass fastened by means of this wax on a small black iron wire. The glass must be violet for iron ornaments and black for gilt ornaments. Spain buys large quantities; it is the country of jet—

Here he stopped, the pen slipped from his fingers, he burst into one of those despairing sobs which rose at times from the depths of his being; the poor man took his head between his hands and thought.

"Oh!" he exclaimed internally (lamentable cries heard by God alone), "it is all over. I shall never see her again; it is a smile which flashed across me, and I am going to enter night without even seeing her; oh! for one moment, for one instant to hear her voice, to touch her, to look at her, her, the angel, and then die! death is nothing, but the frightful thing is to die without seeing her. She would smile on me, say a word to me, and would that do anyone harm? No, it is all over, forever. I am all alone, my God! my God! I shall see her no more."

At this moment there was a knock at his door.

4. *A BOTTLE OF INK WHICH ONLY WHITENS*

THAT same day, or, to speak more correctly, that same evening, as Marius was leaving the dinner-table to withdraw to his study, as he had a brief to get up, Basque handed him a letter, saying, "The person who wrote the letter is in the anteroom."

Cosette had seized her grandfather's arm, and was taking a turn round the garden.

A letter may have an ugly appearance, like a man, and the mere sight of coarse paper and clumsy folding is displeasing. The letter which Basque brought was of that description. Marius took it, and it smelled of tobacco. Nothing arouses a recollection so much as a smell, and Marius recognized the tobacco. He looked at the address, *To Monsieur le Baron Pommerci. At his house.* The recognition of the tobacco made him recognize the handwriting. It might be said that astonishment has its flashes of lightning, and Marius was, as it were, illumined by one of these flashes. The odor, that mysterious aid to memory, had recalled to him a whole world; it was really the paper, the mode of folding, the pale ink, it was really the well-known hand-writing, and, above all, it was the tobacco. The Jondrette garret rose again before him. Hence—strange blow of accident!—one of the two trails which he had so long sought, the one for which he had latterly made so many efforts and believed lost forever, came to offer itself voluntarily to him. He eagerly opened the letter and read:

Monsieur le Baron,
If the Supreme Being had endowed me with talents, I might have been Baron Thénard, member of the Institute (academy of cienses), but I am not so, I merely bear the same name with him, and shall be happy if this reminisence recommends me to the excellense of your kindness. The benefits with which you may honor me will be reciprocal, for I am in possession of a secret conserning an individual. This individual conserns you. I hold the secret at your disposal, as I desire to have the honor of being huseful to you. I will give you the simple means for expeling from your honorable family this individual who has no right in it, Madam la Barronne being of high birth. The sanctuary of virtue could no longer coabit with crime without abdicating.
I await in the anteroom the order of Monsieur le Baron.
                                        Respectfully.

The letter was signed "THÉNARD." This signature was not false, but only slightly abridged. However, the bombast and the orthography completed the revelation; the certificate of origin was perfect, and no doubt was possible. Marius's emotion was profound; and after the movement of surprise he had a movement of happiness. Let him now find the other man he sought, the man who had saved him, Marius, and he would have nothing more to desire. He opened a drawer in his bureau, took out several bank-notes, which he put in his pocket, closed the bureau again, and rang. Basque opened the door partly.

"Show the man in," said Marius.

Basque announced:

"M. Thénard."

A man came in, and it was a fresh surprise for Marius, as the man he now saw was a perfect stranger to him. This man, who was old, by the way, had a large nose, his chin in his cravat, green spectacles, with a double shade of green silk over his eyes, and his hair smoothed down and flattened on his forehead over his eyebrows, like the wig of English coachmen of high life. His hair was gray. He was dressed in black from head to foot, a very seedy but clean black, and a bunch of seals, emerging from his fob, led to the supposition that he had a watch. He held an old hat in his hand, and walked bent, and the curve in his back augmented the depth of his bow. The thing which struck most at the first glance was that this person's coat, too large, though carefully buttoned, had not been made for him.

A short digression is necessary here.

There was at that period in Paris, in an old house situated in the Rue Beautreillis near the Arsenal, an old Jew whose trade it was to convert a rogue into an honest man, though not for too long a period, as it might have been troublesome to the rogue. The change was effected at sight, for one day or two, at the rate of thirty sous a day, by means of a costume resembling as closely as possible every-day honesty. This letter-out of suits was called the *Changer*. Parisian thieves had given him that name, and knew him by no other. He had a very complete wardrobe, and the clothes in which he invested people were almost respectable. He had specialties and categories; from each nail of his store hung a rank in society, worn and threadbare; here the magistrate's coat, there the curé's coat and the banker's coat; in one corner the coat of an officer on half-pay, elsewhere the coat of a man of letters, and further on the statesman's coat. This creature was the costumer of the immense drama which roguery plays in Paris, and his den was the side-scene from which robbery emerged and whither swindling returned. A ragged rogue arrived at this wardrobe, deposited thirty sous, and selected, according to the part which he wished to play on that day, the clothes which suited him; and, on going down stairs again, the rogue was somebody. The next day the clothes were faithfully brought back, and the Changer, who entirely trusted to the thieves, was never robbed. These garments had one inconvenience,—they did not fit; not being made for the man who wore them, they were tight on one, loose on another, and fitted nobody. Any swindler who exceeded the average mean in height or shortness was uncomfortable in the Changer's suits. A man must be neither too stout nor too thin, for the Changer had only provided for ordinary mortals, and had taken the measure of the species in the person of the first thief who turned up, and who is neither stout nor thin, not tall nor short. Hence arose at times difficult adaptations, which the Changer's customers got over as best they could. All the worse for the exceptions! The statesman's garments, for instance, black from head to foot, would have been too loose for Pitt and too tight for Castelcicala. The statesman's suit was thus described in the Changer's catalogue, from which we copied it: "A black cloth coat, black moleskin trousers, a silk waistcoat, boots, and white shirt." There was on the margin *Ex-Ambassador,* and a note which we will also transcribe: "In a separate box a carefully dressed peruke, green spectacles, bunch of seals, and two little quills an inch in length, wrapped in cotton." All this belonged to the statesman or ex-ambassador. The whole of this costume was, if we may say so, extenuated. The seams were white, and a small button-hole gaped at one of the elbows; moreover, a button was missing off the front,—but that is only a detail, for, as the hand of the statesman must always be thrust into the coat and upon the heart, it had the duty of hiding the absence of the button.

Had Marius been familiar with the occult institutions of Paris, he would at once have recognized in the back of the visitor whom Basque had just shown in, the coat of the statesman borrowed from the "Unhook-me-that" of the Changer. Marius's disappointment, on seeing a different man from the one whom he expected to enter, turned into disgust with the new-comer. He examined him from head to foot, while the personage was giving him an exaggerated bow, and asked him curtly, "What do you want?"

The man replied with an amiable *rictus,* of which the caressing smile of a crocodile would supply some idea:

"It appears to me impossible that I have not already had the honor of seeing Monsieur le Baron in society. I have a peculiar impression of having met you, a few years back, at the Princess Bagration's, and in the salons of his Excellency Viscomte Dambray, Peer of France."

It is always good tactics in swindling to pretend to recognize a person whom the swindler does not know. Marius paid attention to the man's words, he watched the accent and gestures, but his disappointment increased; it was a nasal pronunciation, absolutely different from the sharp, dry voice he expected. He was utterly thrown off the track.

"I do not know," he said, "either Madame Bagration or Monsieur Dambray. I never set foot in the house of either of them."

The answer was rough, but the personage continued with undiminished affability:

"Then it must have been at Chateaubriand's that I saw you! I know Chateaubriand intimately, and he is a most affable man. He says to me sometimes, 'Thénard, my good friend, will you not drink a glass with me?'"

Marius's brow became sterner and sterner. "I never had the honor of being introduced to M. de Chateaubriand. Come to the point; what do you want with me?"

The man bowed lower still before this harsh voice.

"Monsieur le Baron, deign to listen to me. There is in America, in a country near Panama, a village called La Joya, and this village is composed of a single house—a large square house, three stories high, built of bricks dried in the sun, each side of the square being five hundred feet long, and each story retiring from the one under it for a distance of twelve feet, so as to leave in front of it a terrace which runs all round the house. In the center is an inner court, in which provisions and ammunition are stored; there are no windows, only loop-holes; no door, only ladders—ladders to mount from the ground to the first terrace, and from the first to the second, and from the second to the third, ladders to descend into the inner court; no doors to the rooms, only traps; no staircases to the apartments, only ladders. At night the trap-doors are closed, the ladders are drawn up, and blunderbusses and carbines are placed in the loop-holes; there is no way of entering; it is a house by day, a citadel by night. Eight hundred inhabitants. Such is this village. Why such precautions? Because the country is dangerous, and full of cannibals. Then why do people go there? Because it is a marvelous country, and gold is found there."

"What are you driving at?" Marius, who had passed from disappointment to impatience, interrupted.

"To this, M. le Baron. I am an ex-worn-out diplomatist. I am sick of our old civilization, and wish to try the savages."

"What next?"

"Monsieur le Baron, egotism is the law of the world. The proletarian peasant wench who works by the day turns round when the diligence passes, but the peasant woman who is laboring on her own field does not turn. The poor man's dog barks after the rich; the rich man's dog barks after the poor; each for himself, and self-interest is the object of mankind. Gold is the magnet."

"What next? conclude."

"I should like to go and settle at La Joya. There are three of us. I have my wife and my daughter, a very lovely girl. The voyage is long and expensive, and I am short of funds."

"How does that concern me?" Marius asked.

The stranger thrust his neck out of his cravat, with a gesture peculiar to the vulture, and said, with a more affable smile than before:

"Monsieur le Baron cannot have read my letter!"

That was almost true, and the fact is that the contents of the epistle had escaped Marius; he had seen the writing rather than read the letter, and he scarce remembered it. A new hint had just been given him, and he noticed the detail, "My wife and daughter." He fixed a penetrating glance on the stranger, a magistrate could not have done it better, but he confined himself to saying:

"Be more precise."

The stranger thrust his hands into his trousers-pockets, raised his head without straightening his backbone, but on his side scrutinizing Marius through his green spectacles.

"Very good, M. le Baron. I will be precise. I have a secret to sell you."

"Does it concern me?"

"Slightly."

"What is it?"

Marius more and more examined the man while listening.

"I will begin gratis," the stranger said; "you will soon see that it is interesting."

"Speak."

"Monsieur le Baron, you have in your house a robber and assassin."

Marius gave a start.

"In my house? no," he said.

The stranger imperturbably brushed his hat with his arm, and went on:

"An assassin and robber. Remark, M. le Baron, that I am not speaking here of old, forgotten facts, which might be effaced by prescription before the law, and by repentance before God. I am speaking of recent facts, present facts, of facts still unknown to justice. I continue. This man has crept into your confidence, and almost into your family, under a false name. I am going to tell you his real name, and tell you it for nothing."

"I am listening."

"His name is Jean Valjean."

"I know it."

"I will tell, equally for nothing, who he is."

"Speak."

"He is an ex-convict."

"I know it."

"You have known it since I had the honor of telling you."

"No, I was aware of it before."

Marius's cold tone, this double reply, *I know it,* and his laconic replies so inimical to dialogue, aroused some latent anger in the stranger, and he gave Marius a furious side-glance, which was immediately extinguished. Rapid though it was, the glance was one of those which are recognized if they have once been seen, and it did not escape Marius. Certain flashes can only come from certain souls; the eyeball, that cellar-door of the soul, is lit up by them, and green spectacles conceal nothing; you might as well put up a glass window to hell.

The stranger continued, smiling:

"I will not venture to contradict M. le Baron, but in any case you will see that I am well informed. Now, what I have to tell you is known to myself alone, and it affects the fortune of Madame la Baronne. It is an extraordinary secret, and is for sale. I offer it you first. Cheap. Twenty thousand francs."

"I know that secret as I know the other," said Marius.

The personage felt the necessity of lowering his price a little.

"Monsieur le Baron, let us say ten thousand francs, and I will speak."

"I repeat to you that you have nothing to tell me. I know what you want to say to me."

There was a fresh flash in the man's eye as he continued:

"Still I must dine to-day. It is an extraordinary secret, I tell you. Monsieur, I am going to speak, I am speaking. Give me twenty francs."

Marius looked at him fixedly. "I know your extraordinary secret just as I knew Jean Valjean's name, and as I know yours."

"My name?"

"Yes."

"That is not difficult, M. le Baron, for I had the honor of writing it and mentioning it to you. Thénard—"

"—dier."

"What?"

"Thénardier."

"What does that mean?"

In danger the porcupine bristles, the beetle feigns death, the old guard forms a square. This man began laughing. Then he flipped a grain of dust off his coat-sleeve. Marius continued:

"You are also the workman Jondrette, the actor Fabantou, the poet Genflot, the Spanish Don Alvares, and Madame Balizard."

"Madame who?"

"And you once kept a pot-house at Montfermeil."

"A pot-house! never!"

"And I tell you that you are Thénardier."

"I deny it."

"And that you are a scoundrel. Take that."

And Marius, taking a bank-note from his pocket, threw it in his face.

"Five hundred francs! Monsieur le Baron!"

And the man, overwhelmed and bowing, clutched the note and examined it.

"Five hundred francs," he continued, quite dazzled.

And he stammered half aloud, "No counterfeit."

Then suddenly exclaimed:

"Well, be it so; let us be at our ease."

And with monkey-like dexterity, throwing back his hair, tearing off his spectacles, and removing the two quills to which we alluded just now, and which we have seen before in another part of this book, he took off his face as you or I take off our hat. His eye grew bright; the forehead, uneven, scarred, lumpy, hideously wrinkled at top, became visible, the nose sharp as a beak, and the ferocious and cunning profile of the man of prey re-appeared.

"Monsieur le Baron is infallible," he said in a sharp voice, from which the nasal twang had entirely disappeared; "I am Thénardier."

And he drew up his curved back.

Thénardier, for it was really he, was strangely surprised, and would have been troubled could he have been so. He had come to bring astonishment, and it was himself who experienced it. This humiliation was paid for with five hundred francs, and he accepted it; but he was not the less stunned. He saw for the first time this Baron Pontmercy, and in spite of his disguise this Baron Pontmercy recognized him, and recognized him thoroughly; and not alone was this Baron acquainted with Thénardier, but he also seemed acquainted with Jean Valjean. Who was this almost beardless young man, so cold and so generous; who knew people's names, knew all their names, and opened his purse to them; who bullied rogues like a judge, and paid them like a duke?

Thénardier, it will be remembered, though he had been Marius's neighbor, had never seen him, which is frequently the case in Paris; he had formerly vaguely heard his daughter speak of a very poor young man of the name of Marius, who lived in the house, and he had written him, without knowing him, the letter we formerly read. No approximation between this Marius and M. le Baron Pontmercy was possible in his mind.

As to the name Pontmercy, it must be remembered that on the field of Waterloo he had heard only the last two syllables, for which he had always entertained the legitimate disdain due to a mere expression of thanks.

However, he had managed, through his daughter Azelma, whom he had put on the track of the married couple on February 16, and by his own researches, to learn a good many things, and in his dark den had succeeded in seizing more than one mysterious thread. He had by sheer industry discovered, or at least by the inductive process had divined, who the man was whom he had met on a certain day in the great sewer. From the man he had easily arrived at the name, and he knew that Madame la Baronne Pontmercy was Cosette. But on that point he intended to be discreet; who Cosette was he did not know exactly himself. He certainly got a glimpse of some bastardism, and Fantine's story had always appeared to him doubtful. But what was the good of speaking? To have his silence paid? He had, or fancied he had, something better to sell than that, and, according to all expectation, to go and make Baron Pontmercy, without further proof, the revelation, *Your wife is only a bastard,* would only have succeeded in attracting the husband's boot to the broadest part of his person.

In Thénardier's thoughts the conversation with Marius had not yet begun; he had been obliged to fall back, modify his strategy, leave a position and make a change of front; but nothing essential was as yet compromised, and he had five hundred francs in his pocket. Moreover, he had something decisive to tell, and he felt himself strong even against this Baron Pontmercy, who was so well informed and so was armed. For men of Thénardier's nature every dialogue is a combat, and what was his situation in the one which was about to begin? He did not know to whom he was speaking, but he knew of what he was speaking. He rapidly made this mental review of his forces, and after saying, *I am Thénardier,* waited.

Marius was in deep thought; he at length had Thénardier before him, and the man whom he had so eagerly desired to find again was here. He would be able at last to honor Colonel Pontmercy's recommendation. It humiliated him that this hero owed anything to this bandit, and that the bill of exchange drawn by his father from the tomb upon him, Marius, had remained up to this day protested. It seemed to him, too, in the complex state of his mind as regarded Thénardier, that he was bound to avenge the colonel for the misfortune of having been saved by such a villain. But, however this might be, he was satisfied; he was at length going to free the colonel's shadow from this unworthy creditor, and felt as if he were releasing his father's memory from a debtor's prison. By the side of this duty he had another—clearing up, if possible, the source of Cosette's fortune. The opportunity appeared to present itself, for Thénardier probably knew something, and it might be useful to see to the bottom of this man; so he began with that.

Thénardier put away the "no counterfeit" carefully in his pocket, and looked at Marius with almost tender gentleness. Marius was the first to break the silence.

"Thénardier, I have told you your name, and now do you wish me to tell you the secret which you have come to impart to me? I have my information also, and you shall see that I know more than you do. Jean Valjean, as you said, is an assassin and a robber. A robber, because he plundered a rich manufacturer, M. Madeleine, whose ruin he caused; an assassin, because he murdered Inspector Javert."

"I do not understand you, M. le Baron," said Thénardier.

"I will make you understand; listen. There was in a district of the Pas de Calais, about the year 1822, a man who had been in some trouble with the authorities, and who had rehabilitated and restored himself under the name of Monsieur Madeleine. This man had become, in the fullest extent of the term, a just man, and he made the fortune of an entire town by a trade, the manufacture of black beads. As for his private fortune, he had made that too, but secondarily, and to some extent as occasion offered. He was the foster-father of the poor, he founded hospitals, opened schools, visited the sick, dowered girls, supported widows, adopted orphans, and was, as it were, guardian of the town. He had refused the cross of the Legion of Honor, and was appointed mayor. A liberated convict knew the secret of a penalty formerly incurred by this man; he denounced and had him arrested, and took advantage of the arrest to come to Paris and draw out of Lafitte's,—I have the facts from the cashier himself,—by means of a false signature, a sum of half a million and more, which belonged to M. Madeleine. The convict who robbed M. Madeleine was Jean Valjean; as for the other fact, you can tell me no more than I know either. Jean Valjean killed Inspector Javert with a pistol-shot, and I, who am speaking to you, was present."

Thénardier gave Marius the sovereign glance of a beaten man who recovers his grasp on victory, and has regained in a minute all the ground he had lost. But the smile at once returned, for the inferior, when in presence of his superior, must keep his triumph to himself, and Thénardier confined himself to saying to Marius:

"Monsieur le Baron, we are on the wrong track." And he underlined this sentence by giving his bunch of seals an expressive twirl.

"What!" Marius replied, "do you dispute it? They are facts."

"They are chimeras. The confidence with which Monsieur le Baron honors me makes it my duty to tell him so. Before all, truth and justice, and I do not like to see people accused wrongfully. Monsieur le Baron, Jean Valjean did not rob M. Madeleine, and Jean Valjean did not kill Javert."

"That is rather strong. Why so?"

"For two reasons."

"What are they? speak."

"The first is this: he did not rob M. Madeleine, because Jean Valjean himself is M. Madeleine."

"What nonsense are you talking?"

"And this is the second: he did not assassinate Javert, because the man who killed Javert was Javert."

"What do you mean?"

"That Javert committed suicide."

"Prove it, prove it," Marius cried wildly.

Thénardier repeated slowly, scanning his sentence after the fashion of an ancient Alexandrian: "Police-Agent-Javert-was-found-drowned-under-a-boat-at-Pont-au-Change."

"But prove it, then."

Thénardier drew from his side-pocket a large gray-paper parcel, which seemed to contain folded papers of various sizes.

"I have my proofs," he said calmly, and he added:

"Monsieur le Baron, I wished to know Jean Valjean thoroughly on your behalf. I say that Jean Valjean and Madeleine are the same, and I say that Javert had no other assassin but Javert, and when I say this, I have the proofs, not manuscript proofs, for writing is suspicious and complaisant, but printed proofs."

While speaking, Thénardier extracted from the parcel two newspapers, yellow, faded and strongly saturated with tobacco. One of these papers, broken in all the folds, and falling in square rags, seemed much older than the other.

"Two facts, two proofs," said Thénardier, as he handed Marius the two open newspapers.

These two papers the reader knows: one, the older, a number of the *Drapeau Blanc* for July 25, 1823, of which the exact text was given at page 61, Vol. II, established the identity of M. Madeleine and Jean Valjean; the other, a *Moniteur,* of June 15, 1832, announced the suicide of Javert, adding that it was found, from a verbal report made by Javert to the préfet, that he had been made prisoner at the barricade of the Rue de la Chanvrerie, and owed his life to the magnanimity of an insurgent, who, when holding him under his pistol, instead of blowing out his brains fired in the air. Marius read. Here was evidence, a certain date, irrefragable proof, for these two papers had not been printed expressly to support Thénardier's statement, and the note published in the *Moniteur* was officially communicated by the prefecture of police. Marius could no longer doubt, the cashier's information was false, and he was himself mistaken. Jean Valjean, suddenly growing grand, issued from the cloud, and Marius could not restrain a cry of joy.

"What, then, this poor fellow is an admirable man! all this fortune is really his! He is Madeleine, the providence of an entire town! he is Jean Valjean, the saviour of Javert! he is a hero! he is a saint!"

"He is not a saint, and he is not a hero," said Thénardier; "he is an assassin and a robber."

And he added with the accent of a man beginning to feel himself possessed of some authority, "Let us calm ourselves."

Robber, assassin; these words, which Marius believed had disappeared, and which had returned, fell upon him like an icy douche.

"Still," he said—

"Still," said Thénardier, "Jean Valjean did not rob M. Madeleine, but he is a robber; he did not assassinate Javert, but he is an assassin."

"Are you alluding," Marius continued, "to that wretched theft committed forty years back, and expiated, as is proved from those very papers, by a whole life of repentance, self denial, and virtue?"

"I say assassination and robbery, M. le Baron, and repeat that I am alluding to recent facts. What I have to reveal to you is perfectly unknown and unpublished, and you may perhaps find in it the source of the fortune cleverly offered by Jean Valjean to Madame la Baronne. I say skillfully, for it would not be a stupid act, by a donation of that nature, to step into an honorable house, whose comforts he would share, and at the same time hide the crime, enjoy his robbery, bury his name, and create a family."

"I could interrupt you here," Marius observed, "but go on."

"Monsieur le Baron, I will tell you all, leaving the reward to your generosity, for the secret is worth its weight in gold. You will say to me, 'Why not apply to Jean Valjean?' For a very simple reason. I know that he has given up all his property in your favor, and I consider the combination ingenious; but he has not a half-penny left. He would show me his empty hands, and as I want money for my voyage to La Joya, I prefer you, who have everything, to him who has nothing. As I am rather fatigued, permit me to take a chair."

Marius sat down, and made him a sign to do the same. Thénardier installed himself in an easy-chair, took up the newspapers, put them back in the parcel, and muttered, as he dug his nail into the *Drapeau Blanc,* "It cost me a deal of trouble to procure this." This done, he crossed his legs, threw himself in the chair in the attitude of men who are certain of what they are stating, and then began his narrative gravely, and laying a stress on his words:

"Monsieur le Baron, on June 6, 1832, about a year ago, and on the day of the riots, a man was in the great sewer of Paris, at the point where the sewer falls into the Seine, between the Pont des Invalides and the Pont de Jena."

Marius hurriedly drew his chair closer to Thénardier's. Thénardier noticed this movement, and continued with the slowness of an orator who holds his hearer and feels his adversary quivering under his words:

"This man, forced to hide himself, for reasons, however, unconnected with politics, had selected the sewer as his domicile, and had the key of it. It was, I repeat, June 6, and about eight in the evening the man heard a noise in the sewer; feeling greatly surprised, he concealed himself and watched. It was a sound of footsteps; some one was walking in the darkness and coming in his direction; strange to say, there was another man beside himself in the sewer. As the outlet of the sewer was no great distance off, a little light which passed through enabled him to see the new-comer, and that he was carrying something on his back. He walked in a stooping posture; he was an ex-convict, and what he had on his shoulders was a corpse. A flagrant case of assassination, if ever there was one; as for the robbery, that is a matter of course, for no one kills a man gratis. This convict was going to throw the body into the river, and a fact worth notice is, that before reaching the outlet the convict, who had come a long way through the sewer, was obliged to pass a frightful hole, in which it seems that he might have left the corpse; but the sewer-men who came to effect the repairs next day would have found the murdered man there, and that did not suit the assassin. Hence he preferred carrying the corpse across the slough, and his efforts must have been frightful; it was impossible to risk one's life more completely, and I do not understand how he got out of it alive."

Marius's chair came nearer, and Thénardier took advantage of it to draw a long breath; then he continued:

"Monsieur le Baron, a sewer is not the Champ de Mars; everything is wanting there, even space, and when two men are in it together, they must meet. This happened, and the man who was domiciled there and the passer-by were compelled to bid each other good-evening, to their mutual regret. The passer-by said to the domiciled man, *You see what I have on my back. I must go out; you have the key, so give it to me.* This convict was a man of terrible strength, and there was no chance of refusing him; still, the man who held the key parleyed, solely to gain time. He examined the dead man, but he could see nothing, except that he was young, well dressed, had a rich look, and was quite disfigured with blood. While talking, he managed to tear off, without the murderer perceiving it, a piece of the skirt of the victim's coat, as a convincing proof, you understand, a means of getting on the track of the affair, and bringing the crime home to the criminal. He placed the piece of cloth in his pocket; after which he opened the grating, allowed the man with the load on his back to go out, locked the grating again, and ran away, not feeling at all desirous to be mixed up any further in the adventure, or to be present when the assassin threw the corpse into the river. You now understand; the man who carried the corpse was Jean Valjean, the one who had the key is speaking to you at this moment, and the piece of the coat-skirt—"

Thénardier completed the sentence by drawing from his pocket and holding level with his eyes a ragged piece of black cloth, all covered with dark spots. Marius had risen, pale, scarce breathing, with his eyes fixed on the black patch, and, without uttering a syllable, or without taking his eyes off the rag, he fell back, and, with his right hand extended behind him, felt for the key of a wall-cupboard near the mantelpiece. He found this key, opened the cupboard, and thrust in his hand without looking or once taking his eyes off the rag which Thénardier displayed. In the meanwhile Thénardier continued:

"Monsieur le Baron, I have the strongest grounds for believing that the assassinated young man was a wealthy foreigner, drawn by Jean Valjean into a trap, and carrying an enormous sum about him."

"I was the young man, and here is the coat!" cried Marius as he threw on the floor an old blood-stained coat. Then, taking the patch from Thénardier's hand, he bent over the coat and put it in its place in the skirt; the rent fitted exactly, and the fragment completed the coat. Thénardier was petrified, and thought, "I'm sold."

Marius drew himself up, shuddering, desperate, and radiant; he felt in his pocket, and walking furiously toward Thénardier; thrusting almost into his face his hand full of five hundred and thousand francs notes:

"You are an infamous wretch! you are a liar, a calumniator, and a villain! You came to accuse that man, and you have justified him; you came to ruin him, and have only succeeded in glorifying him. And it is you who are a robber! it is you who are an assassin! I saw you, Thénardier Jondrette, at that den on the Boulevard de l'Hôpital. I know enough about you to send you to the galleys, and even further if I liked. There are a thousand francs, ruffian that you are."

And he threw a thousand-franc note at Thénardier.

"Ah, Jondrette—Thénardier, vile scoundrel, let this serve you as a lesson, you hawker of secrets, you dealer in mysteries, you searcher in the darkness, you villain, take these five hundred francs, and be off. Waterloo protects you."

"Waterloo!" Thénardier growled, as he pocketed the five hundred francs.

"Yes, assassin! you saved there the life of a colonel."

"A general!" Thénardier said, raising his head.

"A colonel," Marius repeated furiously, "I would not give a farthing for a general. And you come here to commit an infamy! I tell you that you have committed every crime! Begone! Be off! Be happy, that is all I desire! Ah, monster! here are three thousand francs more; take them. You will start to-morrow for America with your daughter, for your wife is dead, you abominable liar! I will watch over your departure, bandit, and at the moment when you set sail, pay you twenty thousand francs. Go and get hanged elsewhere."

"Monsieur le Baron," Thénardier answered, bowing to the ground, "accept my eternal gratitude."

And Thénardier left the room, understanding nothing of all this, but stupefied and ravished by this sweet crushing under bags of gold, and this lightning flashing over his head in the shape of bank-notes.

Let us finish at once with this man: two days after the events we have just recorded he started for America, under a false name, with his daughter Azelma, and provided with an order on a New-York banker for twenty thousand francs. The moral corruption of Thénardier, the spoiled bourgeois, was irremediable, and he was in America what he had been in Europe. The contact with a wicked man is sometimes sufficient to rot a good action, and to make something bad issue from it; with this money of Marius, Thénardier turned slave-dealer.

So soon as Thénardier had departed, Marius ran into the garden where Cosette was still walking.

"Cosette, Cosette," he cried, "come, come quickly, let us be off. Basque, a hackney-coach. Cosette, come! oh heavens! it was he who saved my life! let us not lose a minute! Put on your shawl."

Cosette thought him mad and obeyed. He could not breathe, and laid his hand on his heart to check its beating. He walked up and down with long strides, and embraced Cosette. "O Cosette," he said, "I am wretched." Marius was amazed, for he was beginning to catch a glimpse of some strange, lofty, and somber figure in this Jean Valjean. An extraordinary virtue appeared before him, supreme and gentle, and humble in its immensity, and the convict was transfigured into Christ. Marius was dazzled by this prodigy, and though he knew not exactly what he saw, it was grand. In an instant the hackney-coach was at the gate. Marius helped Cosette in and followed her.

"Driver," he cried, "No. 7, Rue de l'Homme Armé."

"Oh, how glad I am," said Cosette, "Rue de l'Homme Armé; I did not dare speak to you about Monsieur Jean, but we are going to see him."

"Your father, Cosette! your father more than ever. Cosette, I see it all. You told me you never received the letter I sent you by Gavroche. It must have fallen into his hands, Cosette, and he came to the barricade to save me. As it is his sole duty to be an angel, in passing he saved others: he saved Javert. He drew me out of that gulf to give me to you; he carried me on his back through that frightful sewer. Ah! I am a monstrous ingrate! Cosette, after having been your providence, he was mine. Just imagine that there was a horrible pit, in which a man could be drowned a hundred times, drowned in mud, Cosette; and, he carried me through it. I had fainted; I saw nothing, I heard nothing, I could not know anything about my own adventures. We are going to bring him back with us, and, whether he is willing or not, he shall never leave us again. I only hope he is at home! I only hope we shall find him! I will spend the rest of my life in revering him. Yes, it must have been so, Cosette, and Gavroche must have given him my letter. That explains everything. You understand."

Cosette did not understand a word.

"You are right," she said to him.

In the meanwhile the hackney-coach rolled along.

5. *A NIGHT BEHIND WHICH IS DAY*

AT the knock he heard at his door, Jean Valjean turned round.

"Come in," he said feebly.

The door opened, and Cosette and Marius appeared. Cosette rushed into the room. Marius remained on the threshold, leaning against the door-post.

"Cosette," said Jean Valjean; and he sat up in his chair, with his arms outstretched and open, haggard, livid, and sinister, but with an immense joy in his eyes. Cosette, suffocated with emotion, fell on Jean Valjean's breast.

"Father," she said.

Jean Valjean, utterly overcome, stammered, "Cosette! she—you—madame! it is you! oh, my God!"

And clasped in Cosette's arms, he exclaimed:

"It is you! you are here; you forgive me, then!"

Marius, drooping his eyelids to keep his tears from flowing, advanced a step, and muttered between his lips, which were convulsively clenched to stop his sobs:

"Father!"

"And you, too, you forgive me," said Jean Valjean.

Marius could not find a word to say, and Jean Valjean added, "Thank you." Cosette took off her shawl and threw her bonnet on the bed.

"It is in my way," she said.

And, sitting down on the old man's knees, she parted his gray hair with an adorable movement, and kissed his forehead. Jean Valjean, who was wandering, let her do so. Cosette, who only comprehended very vaguely, redoubled her caresses, as if she wished to pay the debt of Marius, and Jean Valjean stammered:

"How foolish a man can be! I fancied that I should not see her again. Just imagine, Monsieur Pontmercy, that at the very moment when you came in I was saying, 'It is all over. There is her little dress. I am a wretched man. I shall not see Cosette again,' I was saying at the very moment when you were coming up the stairs. What an idiot I was! a man can be as idiotic as that! but people count without God. God says, 'You imagine that you are going to be abandoned; no; things will not happen like that. Down below, there is a poor old fellow who wants an angel.' And the angel comes, and he sees Cosette again, and he sees his little Cosette again. Oh! I was very unhappy."

For a moment he was unable to speak; then he went on:

"I really wanted to see Cosette for a little while every now and then, for a heart requires a bone to gnaw. Still, I felt that I was in the way. I said to myself, 'They do not want you, so stop in your corner; a man has no right to pay everlasting visits.' Ah! blessed be God! I see her again. Do you know, Cosette, that your husband is very handsome? What a pretty embroidered collar you are wearing, I like that pattern; your husband chose it, did he not? And, then, you will need cashmere shawls. Monsieur Pontmercy, let me call her Cosette; it will not be for long."

And Cosette replied:

"How unkind to have left us like that! where have you been to? why were you away so long? Formerly, your absence did not last over three or four days. I sent Nicolette, and the answer always was, 'He has not returned.' When did you get back? why did you not let us know? are you aware that you are greatly changed? Oh, naughty papa, he has been ill, and we did not know it. Here, Marius, feel how cold his hand is!"

"So you are here! so you forgive me, Monsieur Pontmercy!" Jean Valjean repeated.

At this remark, all that was swelling in Marius's heart found vent, and he burst forth:

"Do you hear, Cosette? he asks my pardon. And do you know what he did for me, Cosette? He saved my life; he did more,—he gave you to me; and, after saving me and giving you to me, Cosette, what did he do for himself? He sacrificed himself. That is the man he is! And to me, who am so ungrateful, so pitiless, so forgetful, and so guilty, he says, 'Thank you!' Cosette, my whole life spent at this man's feet would be too little. That barricade, that sewer, that furnace, that pit, he went through them all for me and for you, Cosette! He carried me through every form of death, which he held at bay from me and accepted for himself. This man possesses every courage, every virtue, every heroism, and every holiness. He is an angel, Cosette."

"Stop, stop!" Jean Valjean said in a whisper; "why talk in that way?"

"But why did you not tell me of it?" exclaimed Marius, with a passion in which was veneration; "it is your fault, also. You save people's lives, and conceal the fact from them! You do more; under the pretext of unmasking yourself, you calumniate yourself. It is frightful."

"I told the truth," Jean Valjean replied.

"No," Marius retorted, "the truth is the whole truth, and you did not tell that. You were Monsieur Madeleine, why not tell me so? You saved Javert, why not tell me so? I owed you life, why not tell me so?"

"Because I thought like you, and found that you were right. It was necessary that I should leave you. Had you known of the sewer, you would have compelled me to remain with you, and hence I held my tongue. Had I spoken, I should have been in the way."

"Been in the way of whom? of what?" Marius broke out. "Do you fancy that you are going to remain here? We mean to take you back with us. Oh! good heaven! when I think that I only learned all this by accident! We shall take you away with us, for you form a part of ourselves; you are her father and mine. You shall not spend another day in this frightful house, so do not fancy you will be here to-morrow."

"To-morrow," said Jean Valjean, "I shall be no longer here, but I shall not be at your house."

"What do you mean?" Marius asked. "Oh! no, we shall not let you travel any more; you shall not leave us again, for you belong to us, and we will not let you go."

"This time it is for good," Cosette added; "we have a carriage below, and I mean to carry you off; if necessary, I shall employ force."

And, laughing, she feigned to raise the old man in her arms.

"Your room is still all ready in our house," she went on. "If you only knew how pretty the garden is just at present! the azaleas are getting on splendidly; the walks are covered with river sand, and there are little violet shells. You shall eat my strawberries, for it is I who water them. And no more madame and no more Monsieur Jean, for we live in a republic, do we not, Marius? The programme is changed. If you only knew, father, what a sorrow I had; a redbreast had made its nest in a hole in the wall, and a horrible cat killed it for me. My poor, pretty little redbreast, that used to thrust its head out of its window and look at me! I cried about it, and could have killed the cat! But now, nobody weeps, everybody laughs, everybody is happy. You will come with us; how pleased grandfather will be! You will have your bed in the garden, you will cultivate it, and we will see whether your strawberries are as fine as mine. And then, I will do all you wish, and you will obey me."

Jean Valjean listened without hearing; he heard the music of her voice rather than the meaning of her words, and one of those heavy tears, which are the black pearls of the soul, slowly collected in his eye. He murmured:

"The proof that God is good is that she is here."

"My father!" Cosette said.

Jean Valjean continued:

"It is true it would be charming to live together. They have their trees full of birds, and I should walk about with Cosette. It is sweet to be with persons who live, who say to each other good-morning, and call each other in the garden. We should each cultivate a little bed, she would give me her strawberries to eat, and I would let her pick my roses. It would be delicious, but—"

He broke off, and said gently, "It is a pity."

The tear did not fall; it was recalled, and Jean Valjean substituted a smile for it. Cosette took both the old man's hands in hers.

"Good Heaven!" she said, "your hands have grown colder. Can you be ill? are you suffering?"

"I—no," Jean Valjean replied; "I am quite well. It is only—" He stopped.

"Only what?"

"I am going to die directly."

Marius and Cosette shuddered.

"Die!" Marius exclaimed.

"Yes, but that is nothing," said Jean Valjean.

He breathed, smiled, and added:

"Cosette, you were talking to me; go on, speak again; your redbreast is dead, then? speak, that I may hear your voice."

Marius, who was petrified, looked at the old man, and Cosette uttered a piercing shriek.

"Father, father, you will live! you are going to live. I insist on your living; do you hear?"

Jean Valjean raised his head to her, with adoration.

"Oh, yes, forbid me dying. Who knows? Perhaps I shall obey. I was on the road to death when you arrived, but that stopped me. I fancied I was being born again."

"You are full of strength and life," Marius exclaimed; "can you suppose that a man dies like that? You have known grief, but you shall know it no more. It is I who ask pardon of you on my knees! You are going to live and live with us, and live a long time. We will take you with us, and shall have henceforth but one thought—your happiness!"

"You hear," said Cosette, who was all in tears, "Marius says that you will not die."

Jean Valjean continued to smile.

"Even if you were to take me home with you, Monsieur Pontmercy, would that prevent me being what I am? No. God has thought, the same as you and I, and He does not alter his opinion. It is better for me to be gone. Death is an excellent arrangement, and God knows better than we do what we want. I am certain that it is right, that you should be happy, that Monsieur Pontmercy should have Cosette, that youth should espouse the dawn, that there should be around you, my children, lilacs and nightingales, that your life should be a smooth lawn bathed in sunlight, that all the enchantments of heaven should fill your souls, and that I who am good for nothing should now die. Come, be reasonable, nothing is possible now, and I fully feel that all is over. An hour ago I had a fainting-fit, and last night I drank the whole of that jug of water. How kind your husband is, Cosette! You are much better with him than with me!"

There was a noise at the door; it was the physician come to pay his visit.

"Good-day, and good-bye, doctor," said Jean Valjean, "here are my poor children."

Marius went up to the physician, and addressed but one word to him, "Sir?"—but in the manner of pronouncing it there was a whole question. The physician answered the question by an expressive glance.

"Because things are unpleasant," said Jean Valjean, "that is no reason to be unjust to God."

There was a silence, and every chest was oppressed. Jean Valjean turned to Cosette, and began contemplating her, as if he wished to take that last look with him into eternity. In the deep shadow into which he had already sunk ecstasy was still possible for him in gazing on Cosette. The reflection of her sweet countenance illumined his pale face, for the sepulcher may have its brilliancy.

The physician felt his pulse.

"Ah, it was you that he wanted," he said, looking at Marius and Cosette.

And, bending down to Marius's ear, he whispered:

"Too late."

Jean Valjean, almost without ceasing to regard Cosette, looked at Marius and the physician with serenity, and the scarcely articulated words could be heard pass his lips:

"It is nothing to die, but it is frightful not to live."

All at once he rose—such return of strength is at times a sign of the death-agony. He walked with a firm step to the wall, thrust aside Marius and the doctor, who wished to help him, detached from the wall the small copper crucifix hanging on it, returned to his seat with all the vigor of full health, and said, as he laid the crucifix on the table:

"There is the great martyr."

Then his chest sank in, his head vacillated, as if the intoxication of the tomb were seizing on him, and his hands, lying on his knees, began pulling at the cloth of his trousers. Cosette supported his shoulders and sobbed, and tried to speak to him, but was unable to do so. Through her words mingled with that lugubrious saliva which accompanies tears, such sentences as this could be distinguished: "Father, do not leave us. Is it possible that we have only found you again to lose you?" It might be said that the death-agony moves like a serpent; it comes, goes, advances toward the grave, and then turns back toward life; there is a species of groping in the action of death. Jean Valjean, after this partial syncope, rallied, shook his forehead as if to make the darkness fall off it, and became again almost quite lucid. He caught hold of Cosette's sleeve and kissed it.

"He is recovering, doctor, he is recovering," Marius cried.

"You are both good," said Jean Valjean, " and I am going to tell you what causes me sorrow. It causes me sorrow, Monsieur Pontmercy, that you have refused to touch that money, but it is really your wife's. I will explain to you, my children, and that is why I am so glad to see you. Black jet comes from England, and white jet from Norway; it is all in that paper there which you will read. I invented the substitution of soldered snaps for welded snaps in bracelets; they are prettier, better, and not so dear. You can understand what money can be earned by it; so Cosette's fortune is really hers. I give you these details that your mind may be at rest!"

The porter's wife had come up, and was peeping through the open door; the physician sent her off, but could not prevent the zealous old woman crying to the dying man before she went:

"Will you have a priest?"

"I have one," Jean Valjean answered.

And he seemed to point with his finger to a spot over his head, where, one might say, he saw some one; it is probable, in truth, that the bishop was present at this death scene.

Cosette gently placed a pillow behind Jean Valjean's back, and he continued:

"Monsieur Pontmercy, have no fears, I conjure you. The six hundred thousand francs are really Cosette's! I should have thrown away my life if you do not employ them! We had succeeded in making those beads famously, and we competed with what is called Berlin jewelry. For instance, the black beads of Germany cannot be equalled, for a gross, which contains twelve hundred well-cut beads, only costs three francs."

When a being who is dear to us is about to die, we regard him with a look which grapples him, and would like to retain him. Cosette and Marius stood before him, hand in hand, dumb through agony, not knowing what to say to death, despairing and trembling. With each moment Jean Valjean declined, sank, and approached nearer to the dark horizon. His breathing had become intermittent, and a slight rattle impeded it. He had a difficulty in moving his fore-arm, his feet had lost all movement, and at the same time, as the helplessness of the limbs and the exhaustion of the body increased, all the majesty of the soul ascended and was displayed on his forehead. The light of the unknown world was already visible in his eyeballs.

His face grew pale, and at the same time smiling; life was no longer there, but there was something else. His breath stopped, but his glance expanded; he was a corpse on whom wings could be seen. He made Cosette a sign to approach, and then Marius; it was evidently the last minute of the last hour, and he began speaking to them in so faint a voice that it seemed to come from a distance, and it was as if there were henceforth a wall between them and him.

"Come hither, both of you; I love you dearly. Oh! how pleasant it is to die like this! You, too, love me, my Cosette; I felt certain that you had always a fondness for the poor old man. How kind it was of you to place that pillow at my back! You will weep for me a little, will you not? but not too much, for I do not wish you to feel real sorrow. You must amuse yourselves, my children. I forgot to tell you that more profit was made on the buckles without tongues than on all the rest; the gross cost two francs to produce, and sold for sixty. It was really a good trade, so you must not feel surprised at the six hundred thousand francs, Monsieur Pontmercy. It is honest money. You can be rich without any fear. You must have a carriage, now and then a box at the opera, handsome ball-dresses, my Cosette, and give good dinners to your friends, and be very happy. I was writing just now to Cosette. She will find my letter. To her I leave the two candlesticks on the mantel-piece. They are silver, but to me they are made of gold, of diamonds; they change the candles placed in them into consecrated tapers. I know not whether the man who gave them to me is satisfied with me above, but I have done what I could. My children, you will not forget that I am a poor man; you will have me buried in some corner, with a stone to mark the spot. That is my wish; no name on the stone. If Cosette comes to see it now and then, it will cause me pleasure. And you, too, Monsieur Pontmercy. I must confess to you that I did not always like you, and I ask your forgiveness. Now, she and you are only one for me. I am very grateful to you, for I feel that you render Cosette happy. If you only knew, Monsieur Pontmercy, her pretty pink cheeks were my joy, and when I saw her at all pale I was miserable. There is in the chest of drawers a five-hundred-franc note; I have not touched it, for it is for the poor, Cosette. Do you see your little dress there on the bed? do you recognize it? and yet it was only ten years ago! How time passes! We have been very happy, and it is all over. Do not weep, my children; I am not going very far, and I shall see you from there; you will only have to look when it is dark, and you will see me smile. Cosette, do you remember Montfermeil? You were in the wood, and very frightened; do you remember when I took the bucket-handle? It was the first time I touched your pretty little hand. It was so cold. Ah, you had red hands in those days, miss, but now they are very white. And the large doll? do you remember? you christened it Catherine, and were sorry that you did not take it with you to the convent. How many times you have made me laugh, my sweet angel! When it had rained, you used to set straws floating in the gutter, and watched them go. One day I gave you a wicker battledore and a shuttlecock with yellow, blue, and green feathers. You have forgotten it. You were so merry when a little girl. You used to play. You would put cherries on your ears. All these are things of the past. The forests through which one has passed with one's child, the trees under which we have walked, the convent in which we hid, the sports, the hearty laughter of childhood, are shadows. I imagined that all this belonged to me, and that was my stupidity. Those Thénardiers were very wicked, but we must forgive them. Cosette, the moment has arrived to tell you your mother's name. It was Fantine. Remember this name—Fantine. Fall on your knees every time that you pronounce it. She suffered terribly. She loved you dearly. She knew as much misery as you have known happiness. Such are the distributions of God. He is above. He sees us all, and He knows all that He does amid his great stars. I am going away, my children. Love each other dearly and always. There is no other thing in the world but that; love one another. You will sometimes think of the poor old man who died here. Ah, my Cosette, it is not my fault that I did not see you every day, for it broke my heart. I went as far as the corner of the street, and must have produced a strange effect on the people who saw me pass, for I was like a madman, and even went out without my hat. My children, I can no longer see very clearly. I had several things to say to you, but no matter. Think of me a little. You are blessed beings. I know not what is the matter with me, but I see light. Come hither. I die happy. Let me lay my hands on your beloved heads."

Cosette and Marius fell on their knees, heart-broken and choked with sobs, each under one of Jean Valjean's hands. These august hands did not move again.

He had fallen back, and the light from the two candles illumined him; his white face looked up to heaven, and he let Cosette and Marius cover his hands with kisses.

He was dead.

The night was starless and intensely dark; doubtless some immense angel was standing in the gloom, with outstretched wings, waiting for the soul.

6. *THE GRASS HIDES, AND THE RAIN EFFACES*

THERE is at the cemetery of Père-Lachaise, in the vicinity of the poor side, far from the elegant quarter of that city of sepulchers, far from those fantastic tombs which display in the presence of eternity the hideous fashions of death, in a deserted corner near an old wall, under a yew up which bind-weed climbs, and amid couch-grass and moss,—a tombstone. This stone is no more exempt than the others from the results of time, from mildew, lichen, and the deposits of birds. Water turns it green and the atmosphere blackens it. It is not in the vicinity of any path, and people do not care to visit that part, because the grass is tall and they get their feet wet. When there is a little sunshine the lizards disport on it; there is all around a rustling of wild oats, and in spring linnets sing on the trees.

This tombstone is quite bare. In cutting it, only the necessities of the tomb were taken into consideration; no further care was taken than to make the stone long enough and narrow enough to cover a man.

No name can be read on it.

Many, many years ago, however, a hand wrote on it in pencil these lines, which became almost illegible through rain and dust; and which are probably effaced at the present day:

> *Il dort. Quoique le sort fût pour lui bien étrange,*
> *Il vivait. Il mourut quand il n'eut pas son ange;*
> *La chose simplement d'elle-même arriva,*
> *Comme la nuit se fait lorsque le jour s'en va.*